I0748366

The Novels of Sheridan Le Fanu, Volume Two

By

Sheridan Le Fanu

Cover Photograph: Elliott Brown

ISBN: 978-1-78139-494-6

Contents

CHECKMATE

WILLING TO DIE.

UNCLE SILAS

CHECKMATE

CHAPTER I.

MORTLAKE HALL.

There stands about a mile and a half beyond Islington, unless it has come down within the last two years, a singular and grand old house. It belonged to the family of Arden, once distinguished in the Northumbrian counties. About fifty acres of ground, rich with noble clumps and masses of old timber, surround it; old-world fish-ponds, with swans sailing upon them, tall yew hedges, quincunxes, leaden fauns and goddesses, and other obsolete splendours surround it. It rises, tall, florid, built of Caen stone, with a palatial flight of steps, and something of the grace and dignity of the genius of Inigo Jones, to whom it is ascribed, with the shadows of ancestral trees and the stains of two centuries upon it, and a vague character of gloom and melancholy, not improved by some indications not actually of decay, but of something too like neglect.

It is now evening, and a dusky glow envelopes the scene. The setting sun throws its level beams, through tall drawing-room windows, ruddily upon the Dutch tapestry on the opposite walls, and not unbecomingly lights up the little party assembled there.

Good-natured, fat Lady May Penrose, in her bonnet, sips her tea and chats agreeably. Her carriage waits outside. You will ask who is that extremely beautiful girl who sits opposite, her large soft grey eyes gazing towards the western sky with a look of abstraction, too forgetful for a time of her company, leaning upon the slender hand she has placed under her cheek. How silken and golden-tinted the dark brown hair that grows so near her brows, making her forehead low, and marking with its broad line the beautiful oval of her face! Is there carmine anywhere to match her brilliant lips? And when, recollecting something to tell Lady May, she turns on a sudden, smiling, how soft and pretty the dimples, and how even the little row of pearls she discloses!

This is Alice Arden, whose singularly handsome brother Richard, with some of her tints and outlines translated into masculine beauty, stands leaning on the back of a prie-dieu chair, and chatting gaily.

But who is the thin, tall man—the only sinister figure in the group—with one hand in his breast, the other on a cabinet, as he leans against the wall? Who is that pale, thin-lipped man, "with cadaverous aspect and broken beak," whose eyes never seem to light up, but maintain their dismal darkness while his pale lips smile? Those eyes are fixed on the pretty face of Alice Arden, as she talks to Lady May, with a strangely intense gaze. His eyebrows rise a little, like those of Mephistopheles, towards his temples, with an expression that is inflexibly sarcastic, and sometimes menacing. His jaw is slightly underhung, a formation which heightens the satirical effect of his smile, and, by contrast, marks the depression of his nose.

There was at this time in London a Mr. Longcluse, an agreeable man, a convenient man, who had got a sort of footing in many houses, nobody exactly knew how. He had a knack of obliging people when they really wanted a trifling kindness, and another of holding fast his advantage, and, without seeming to push, or ever appearing to flatter, of maintaining the acquaintance he had once founded. He looked about eight-and-thirty: he was really older. He was gentlemanlike, clever, and rich; but not a soul of all the men who knew him had ever heard of him at school or college. About his birth, parentage, and education, about his "life and adventures," he was dark.

How were his smart acquaintance made? Oddly, as we shall learn when we know him a little better. It was a great pity that there were some odd things said about this very agreeable, obliging, and gentlemanlike person. It was a pity that more was not known about him. The man had enemies, no doubt, and from the sort of reserve that enveloped him their opportunity arose. But were there not about town hundreds of men, well enough accepted, about whose early days no one cared a pin, and everything was just as dark?

Now Mr. Longcluse, with his pallid face, his flat nose, his sarcastic eyebrows, and thin-lipped smile, was overlooking this little company, his shoulder leaning against the frame that separated two pieces of the pretty Dutch tapestry which covered the walls.

"By-the-bye, Mr. Longcluse—you can tell me, for you always know everything," said Lady May—"is there still any hope of that poor child's recovering—I mean the one in that dreadful murder in Thames Street, where the six poor little children were stabbed?"

Mr. Longcluse smiled.

"I'm so glad, Lady May, I can answer you upon good authority! I stopped today to ask Sir Edwin Dudley that very question through his carriage window, and he said that he had just been to the hospital to see the poor little thing, and that it was likely to do well."

"I'm so glad! And what do they say can have been the motive of the murder?"

"Jealousy, they say; or else the man is mad."

"I should not wonder. I'm sure I hope he is. But they should take care to put him under lock and key."

"So they will, rely on it; that's a matter of course."

"I don't know how it is," continued Lady May, who was garrulous, "that murders interest people so much, who ought to be simply shocked at them."

"We have a murder in our family, you know," said Richard Arden.

"That was poor Henry Arden—I know," she answered, lowering her voice and dropping her eyes, with a side glance at Alice, for she did not know how she might like to hear it talked of.

"Oh, that happened when Alice was only five months old, I think," said Richard; and slipping into the chair beside Lady May, he laid his hand upon hers with a smile, and whispered, leaning towards her—

"You are always so thoughtful; it is so nice of you!"

And this short speech ended, his eyes remained fixed for some seconds, with a glow of tender admiration, on those of fat Lady May, who simpered with effusion, and did not draw her hand away until she thought she saw Mr. Longcluse glance their way.

It was quite true, all he said of Lady May. It would not be easy to find a simpler or more good-natured person. She was very rich also, and, it was said by people who love news and satire, had long been willing to share her gold and other chattels with handsome Richard Arden, who being but five-and-twenty, might very nearly have been her son.

"I remember that horrible affair," said Mr. Longcluse, with a little shrug and a shake of his head. "Where was I then—Paris or Vienna? Paris it was. I recollect it all now, for my purse was stolen by the very man who made his escape—Mace was his name; he was a sort of low man on the turf, I believe. I was very young then—somewhere about seventeen, I think."

"You can't have been more, of course," said good-natured Lady May.

"I should like very much some time to hear all about it," continued Mr. Longcluse.

"So you shall," said Richard, "whenever you like."

"Every old family has a murder, and a ghost, and a beauty also, though she does not always live and breathe, except in the canvas of Lely, or Kneller, or Reynolds: and they, you know, had roses and lilies to give away at discretion, in their paint-boxes, and were courtiers," remarked Mr. Longcluse, "who dealt sometimes in the old-fashioned business of making compliments. I say happy the man who lives in those summers when the loveliness of some beautiful family culminates, and who may, at ever such a distance, gaze and worship."

This ugly man spoke in a low tone, and his voice was rather sweet. He looked as he spoke at Miss Arden, from whom, indeed, his eyes did not often wander.

"Very prettily said!" applauded Lady May affably.

"I forgot to ask you, Lady May," inquired Alice, cruelly, at this moment, "how the pretty little Italian greyhound is that was so ill—better, I hope."

"Ever so much—quite well almost. I'd have taken him out for a drive to-day, poor dear little Pepsie! but that I thought the sun just a little overpowering. Didn't you?"

"Perhaps a little."

Mr. Longcluse lowered his eyes as he leaned against the wall and sighed, with a pained smile, that even upon his plain, pallid face, was pathetic.

Did proud Richard Arden perceive the devotion of the dubious Longcluse—undefined in position, in history, in origin, in character, in all things but in wealth? Of course he did, perfectly. But that wealth was said to be enormous. There were Jews, who ought to know, who said he was worth one million eight hundred thousand pounds, and that his annual income was considerably more than a hundred thousand pounds a year.

Was a man like that to be dismissed without inquiry? Had he not found him good-natured and gentlemanlike? What about those stories circulated among Jews and croupiers? Enemies might affect to believe them, and quote the old saw, "There is never smoke without fire;" but dare one of them utter a word of the kind aloud? Did they stand the test of five minutes' inquiry, such even as he had given them? Had he found a particle of proof, of evidence, of suspicion? Not a spark. What man had ever escaped stories who was worth forging a lie about?

Here was a man worth more than a million. Why, if he let him slip through his fingers, some duchess would pounce on him for her daughter.

It was well that Longcluse was really in love—well, perhaps, that he did not appreciate the social omnipotence of money.

"Where is Sir Reginald at present?" asked Lady May.

"Not here, you may be sure," answered Richard. "My father does not admit my visits, you know."

"Really! And is that miserable quarrel kept up still?"

"Only too true. He is in France at present; at Vichy—ain't it Vichy?" he said to Alice.

But she, not choosing to talk, said simply, "Yes—Vichy."

"I'm going to take Alice into town again; she has promised to stay with me a little longer. And I think you neglect her a little, don't you? You ought to come and see her a little oftener," pleaded Lady May, in an undertone.

"I only feared I was boring you all. Nothing, you know, would give me half so much pleasure," he answered.

"Well, then, she'll expect your visits, mind."

A little silence followed. Richard was vexed with his sister; she was, he thought, snubbing his friend Longcluse.

Well, when once he had spoken his mind and disclosed his treasures, Richard flattered himself he had some influence; and did not Lady May swear by Mr. Longcluse? And was his father, the most despotic and violent of baronets, and very much dipt, likely to listen to sentimental twaddle pleading against a hundred thousand a year? So, Miss Alice, if you were disposed to talk nonsense, it was not very likely to be listened to, and sharp and short logic might ensue.

How utterly unconscious of all this she sits there, thinking, I daresay, of quite another person!

Mr. Longcluse was also for a moment in profound reverie; so was Richard Arden. The secrecy of thought is a pleasant privilege to the thinker—perhaps hardly less a boon to the person pondered upon.

If each man's forehead could project its shadows and the light of his spirit shine through, and the confluence of figures and phantoms that cross and march behind it become visible, how that magic-lantern might appal good easy people!

And now the ladies fell to talking and comparing notes about their guipure lacework.

“How charming yours looks, my dear, round that little table!” exclaimed Lady May in a rapture. “I'm sure I hope mine may turn out half as pretty. I wanted to compare; I'm not quite sure whether it is exactly the same pattern.”

And so on, until it was time for them to order their wings for town.

The gentlemen have business of their own to transact, or pleasures to pursue. Mr. Longcluse has his trap there, to carry them into town when their hour comes. They can only put the ladies into their places, and bid them good-bye, and exchange parting reminders and good-natured speeches.

Pale Mr. Longcluse, as he stands on the steps, looks with his dark eyes after the disappearing carriage, and sighs deeply. He has forgotten all for the moment but one dream. Richard Arden wakens him, by laying his hand on his shoulder.

“Come, Longcluse, let us have a cigar in the billiard-room, and a talk. I have a box of Manillas that I think you will say are delicious—that is, if you like them full-flavoured.”

CHAPTER II.

MARTHA TANSEY.

"By-the-bye, Longcluse," said Richard, as they entered together the long tiled passage that leads to the billiard-room, "you like pictures. There is one here, banished to the housekeeper's room, that they say is a Vandyck; we must have it cleaned and backed, and restored to its old place—but would you care to look at it?"

"Certainly, I should like extremely," said Mr. Longcluse.

They were now at the door of the housekeeper's room, and Richard Arden knocked.

"Come in," said the quavering voice of the old woman from within.

Richard Arden opened the door wide. The misty rose-coloured light of the setting sun filled the room. From the wall right opposite, the pale portrait of Sir Thomas Arden, who fought for the king during the great Civil War, looked forth from his deep dingy frame full upon them, stern and melancholy; the misty beams touching the softer lights of his long hair and the gleam of his armour so happily, that the figure came out from its dark background, and seemed ready to step forth to meet them. As it happened, there was no one in the room but old Mrs. Tansey, the housekeeper, who received Richard Arden standing.

From the threshold, Mr. Longcluse, lost in wonder at the noble picture, gazed on it, with the exclamation, almost a cry, "Good heaven! what a noble work! I had no idea there could be such a thing in existence and so little known." And he stood for awhile in a rapture, gazing from the threshold on the portrait.

At sound of that voice, with a vague and terrible recognition, the housekeeper turned with a start towards the door, expecting, you'd have fancied from her face, the entrance of a ghost. There was a tremble in the voice with which she cried, "Lord! what's that?" a tremble in the hand extended towards the door, and a shake also in the pale frowning face, from which shone her glassy eyes.

Mr. Longcluse stepped in, and the old woman's gaze became, as he did so, more shrinking and intense. When he saw her he recoiled, as a man might who had all but trod upon a snake; and these two people gazed at one another with a strange, uncertain scowl.

In Mr. Longcluse's case, this dismal caprice of countenance did not last beyond a second or two. Richard Arden, as he turned his eyes from the picture to say a word to his companion, saw it for a moment, and it faded from his features—saw it, and the darkened countenance of the old housekeeper, with a momentary shock. He glanced from one to the other quickly, with a look of unconscious surprise. That look instantly recalled Mr. Longcluse, who, laying his hand on Richard Arden's arm, said, with a laugh—"I do believe I'm the most nervous man in the world."

"You don't find the room too hot?" said Richard, inwardly ruminating upon the strange looks he had just seen exchanged. "Mrs. Tansey keeps a fire all the year round—don't you, Martha?"

Martha did not answer, nor seem to hear; she pressed her lean hand, instead, to her heart, and drew back to a sofa and sat down, muttering, "My God, lighten our darkness, we beseech thee!" and she looked as if she were on the point of fainting.

"That is a true Vandyck," said Mr. Longcluse, who was now again looking stedfastly at the picture. "It deserves to rank among his finest portraits. I have never seen anything of his more forcible. You really ought not to leave it here, and in this state." He walked over and raised the lower end of the frame gently from the wall. "Yes, just as you said, it wants to be backed. That portrait would not stand a shake, I can tell you. The canvas is perfectly rotten, and the paint—if you stand here you'll see—is ready to flake off. It is an awful pity. You shouldn't leave it in such danger."

"No," said Richard, who was looking at the old woman. "I don't think Martha's well—will you excuse me for a moment?" And he was at the housekeeper's side. "What's the matter, Martha?" he said kindly. "Are you ill?"

"Very bad, Sir. I beg your pardon for sitting, but I could not help; and the gentleman will excuse me."

"Of course—but what's the matter?" said Richard.

"A sudden fright like, Sir. I'm all over on a tremble," she quavered.

"See how exquisitely that hand is painted," continued Mr. Longcluse, pursuing his criticism, "and the art with which the lights are managed. It is a wonderful picture. It makes one positively angry to see it in that state, and anywhere but in the most conspicuous and honourable place. If I owned that picture, I should never be tired showing it. I should have it where everyone who came into my house should see it; and I should watch every crack and blur on its surface, as I should the symptoms of a dying child, or the looks of the mistress of my heart. Now just look at this. Where is he? Oh!"

"I beg your pardon, a thousand times, but I find my old friend Martha feels a little faint and ill," said Richard.

"Dear me! I hope she's better," said Mr. Longcluse, approaching with solicitude. "Can I be of any use? Shall I touch the bell?"

"I'm better, Sir, I thank you; I'm much better," said the old woman. "It won't signify nothing, only—" She was looking hard again at Mr. Longcluse, who now seemed perfectly at his ease, and showed in his countenance nothing but the commiseration befitting the occasion. “A sort of a weakness—a fright like—and I can't think, quite, what came over me.”

“Don't you think a glass of wine might do her good?” asked Mr. Longcluse.

“Thanks, Sir, I don't drink it. Oh, lighten our darkness, we beseech thee! Good Lord, a' mercy on us! I take them drops, hartshorn and valerian, on a little water, when I feel nervous like. I don't know when I was took wi' t' creepins before.”

“You look better,” said Richard.

“I'm quite right again, Sir,” she said, with a sigh. She had taken her “drops,” and seemed restored.

“Hadn't you better have one of the maids with you? I'm going now; I'll send some one,” he said. “You must get all right, Martha. It pains me to see you ill. You're a very old friend, remember. You must be all right again; and, if you like, we'll have the doctor out, from town.”

He said this, holding her thin old hand very kindly, for he was by no means without good-nature. So sending the promised attendant, he and Longcluse proceeded to the billiard-room, where, having got the lamps lighted, they began to enjoy their smoke. Each, I fancy, was thinking of the little incident in the housekeeper's room. There was a long silence.

“Poor old Tansey! She looked awfully ill,” said Richard Arden at last.

“By Jove! she did. Is that her name? She rather frightened me,” said Mr. Longcluse. “I thought we had stumbled on a mad woman—she stared so. Has she ever had any kind of fit, poor thing?”

“No. She grumbles a good deal, but I really think she's a healthy old woman enough. She says she was frightened.”

“We came in too suddenly, perhaps?”

“No, that wasn't it, for I knocked first,” said Arden.

“Ah, yes, so you did. I only know she frightened me. I really thought she was out of her mind, and that she was going to stick me with a knife, perhaps,” said Mr. Longcluse, with a little laugh and a shrug.

Arden laughed, and puffed away at his cigar till he had it in a glow again. Was this explanation of what he had seen in Longcluse's countenance—a picture presented but for a fraction of a second, but thenceforward ineffaceable—quite satisfactory?

In a short time Mr. Longcluse asked whether he could have a little brandy and water, which accordingly was furnished. In his first glass there was a great deal of brandy, and very little water indeed; and his second, sipped more at his leisure, was but little more diluted. A very faint flush tinged his pallid cheeks.

Richard Arden was, by this time, thinking of his own debts and ill-luck, and at last he said, “I wonder what the art of getting on in the world is. Is it communicable? or is it no art at all, but a simple run of luck?”

Mr. Longcluse smiled scornfully. “There are men who have immense faith in themselves,” said he, “who have indomitable will, and who are provided with craft and pliancy for any situation. Those men are giants from the first to the last hour of action, unless, as happened to Napoleon, success enervates them. In the cradle, they strangle serpents; blind, they pull down palaces; old as Dandolo, they burn fleets and capture cities. It is only when they have taken to bragging that the lues Napoleonica has set in. Now I have been, in a sense, a successful man—I am worth some money. If I were the sort of man I describe, I should be worth, if I cared for it, ten times what I have in as many years. But I don't care to confess I made my money by flukes. If, having no tenderness, you have two attributes—profound cunning and perfect audacity—nothing can keep you back. I'm a common-place man, I say; but I know what constitutes power. Life is a battle, and the general's qualities win."

"I have not got the general's qualities, I think; and I know I haven't luck," said Arden; "so for my part I may as well drift, with as little trouble as may be, wherever the current drives. Happiness is not for all men."

"Happiness is for no man," said Mr. Longcluse. And a little silence followed. "Now suppose a fellow has got more money than ever he dreamed of," he resumed, "and finds money, after all, not quite what he fancied, and that he has come to long for a prize quite distinct and infinitely more precious; so that he finds, at last, that he never can be happy for an hour without it, and yet, for all his longing and his pains, sees it is unattainable as that star." (He pointed to a planet that shone down through the skylight.) "Is that man happy? He carries with him, go where he may, an aching heart, the pangs of jealousy and despair, and the longing of the damned for Paradise. That is my miserable case."

Richard Arden laughed, as he lighted his second cigar.

"Well, if that's your case, you can't be one of those giants you described just now. Women are not the obdurate and cruel creatures you fancy. They are proud, and vain, and unforgiving; but the misery and the perseverance of a lover constitute a worship that first flatters and then wins them. Remember this, a woman finds it very hard to give up a worshipper, except for another. Now why should you despair? You are a gentleman, you are a clever fellow, an agreeable fellow; you are what is accounted a young man still, and you can make your wife rich. They all like that. It is not avarice, but pride. I don't know the young lady, but I see no good reason why you should fail."

"I wish, Arden, I dare tell you all; but some day I'll tell you more."

"The only thing is —— You'll not mind my telling you, as you have been so frank with me?"

"Pray say whatever you think. I shall be ever so much obliged. I forget so many things about English manners and ways of thinking—I have lived so very much abroad. Should I be put up for a club?"

"Well, I should not mind a club just yet, till you know more people—quite time enough. But you must manage better. Why should those Jew fellows, and other people, who don't hold, and never can, a position the least like yours, be among your acquaintance? You must make it a rule to drop all objectionable persons, and know none but good people. Of course, when you are strong enough it doesn't so much matter, provided you keep them at arm's length. But you passed your younger days abroad, as you say, and not being yet so well known here, you will have to be particular—don't you see? A man is so much judged by his acquaintance; and, in fact, it is essential."

"A thousand thanks for any hints that strike you," said Longcluse good-humouredly.

"They sound frivolous; but these trifles have immense weight with women," said Arden. "By Jove!" he added, glancing at his watch, "we shall be late. Your trap is at the door—suppose we go?"

CHAPTER III.

MR. LONGCLUSE OPENS HIS HEART.

The old housekeeper had drawn near her window, and stood close to the pane, through which she looked out upon the star-lit night. The stars shine down over the foliage of huge old trees. Dim as shadows stand the horse and tax-cart that await Mr. Longcluse and Richard Arden, who now at length appear. The groom fixes the lamps, one of which shines full on Mr. Longcluse's peculiar face.

"Ay—the voice; I could a' sworn to that," she muttered. "It went through me like a scythe. But that's a strange face; and yet there's summat in it, just a hint like, to call my thoughts out a-seeking up and down, and to and fro; and 'twill not let me rest until I come to find the truth. Mace? No, no. Langly? Not he. Yet 'twas summat that night, I think—summat awful. And who was there? No one. Lighten our darkness, we beseech thee, O Lord! for my heart is sore troubled."

Up jumped the groom. Mr. Longcluse had the reins in his hand, and he and his companion passed swiftly by the window, and the flash of the lamps crossed the panelled walls of the housekeeper's room. The light danced wildly from corner to corner of the wainscot, accompanied by the shadows of two geraniums in bow-pots on the window-stool. The lamps flew by, and she still stood there, with the palsied shake of her head and hand, looking out into the darkness, in rumination.

Arden and Longcluse glided through the night air in silence, under the mighty old trees that had witnessed generations of Ardens, down the darker, narrow road, and by the faded old inn, once famous in those regions as the "Guy of Warwick," representing still on its board, in tarnished gold and colours, that redoubted champion, with a boar's head on the point of his sword, and a grotesque lion winding itself fawningly about his horse's legs.

As they passed swiftly along this smooth and deserted road, Longcluse spoke. Aperit præcordia vinum. In his brandy and water he had not spared alcohol, and the quantity was considerable.

"I have lots of money, Arden, and I can talk to people, as you say," he suddenly said, as if Richard Arden had spoken but a moment before; "but, on the whole, is there on earth a more miserable dog than I? There are things that trouble me that would make you laugh; there are others that would, if I dare tell them, make you sigh. Soon I shall be able; soon you shall know all. I'm not a bad fellow. I know how to give away money, and, what is harder to bestow on others, my time and labour. But who to look at me would believe it? I'm not a worse fellow than Penruddock. I can cry for pity and do a kind act like him; but I look in my glass, and I also feel like him, 'the mark of Cain' is on me—cruelty in my face. Why should Nature write on some men's faces such libels on their characters? Then here's another thing to make you laugh—you, a handsome fellow, to whom beauty belongs, I say, by right of birth—it would make me laugh also if I were not, as I am, forced every hour I live to count up, in agonies of hope and terror, my chances in that enterprise in which all my happiness for life is staked so wildly. Common ugliness does not matter, it is got over. But such a face as mine! Come, come! you are too good-natured to say. I'm not asking for consolation; I am only summing up my curses."

"You make too much of these. Lady May thinks your face, she says, very interesting—upon my honour, she does."

"Oh, heaven!" exclaimed Mr. Longcluse, with a shrug and a laugh.

"And what is more to the purpose (will you forgive my reporting all this—you won't mind?), some young lady friends of hers who were by said, I assure you, that you had so much expression, and that your features were extremely refined."

"It won't do, Arden; you are too good-natured," said he, laughing more bitterly.

"I should much rather be as I am, if I were you, than be gifted with vulgar beauty—plump, pink and white, with black beady eyes, and all that," said Arden.

"But the heaviest curse upon me is that which, perhaps, you do not suspect—the curse of—secrecy."

"Oh, really!" said Arden, laughing, as if he had thought up to then that Mr. Longcluse's history was as well known as that of the ex-Emperor Napoleon.

"I don't say that I shall come out like the enchanted hero in a fairy tale, and change in a moment from a beast into a prince; but I am something better than I seem. In a short time, if you cared to be bored with it, I shall have a great deal to tell you."

There followed here a silence of two or three minutes, and then, on a sudden, pathetically, Mr. Longcluse broke forth—

"What has a fellow like me to do with love? and less than beloved, can I ever be happy? I know something of the world—not of this London world, where I live less than I seem to do, and into which I came too late ever to understand it thoroughly—I know something of a greater world, and human nature is the same everywhere. You talk of a girl's pride inducing her to marry a man for the sake of his riches. Could I possess my beloved on those terms? I would rather place a pistol in my mouth, and blow my skull off. Arden, I'm unhappy; I'm the most miserable dog alive."

"Come, Longcluse, that's all nonsense. Beauty is no advantage to a man. The being agreeable is an immense one. But success is what women worship, and if, in addition to that, you possess wealth—not, as I said, that they are sordid, but only vain-glorious—you become very nearly irresistible. Now you are agreeable, successful and wealthy—you must see what follows."

"I'm out of spirits," said Longcluse, and relapsed into silence, with a great sigh.

By this time they had got within the lamps, and were threading streets, and rapidly approaching their destination. Five minutes more, and these gentlemen had entered a vast room, in the centre of which stood a billiard-table, with benches rising tier above tier to the walls, and a gallery running round the building above them, brilliantly lighted, as such places are, and already crowded with all kinds of people. There is going to be a great match of a "thousand up" played between Bill Hood and Bob Markham. The betting has been unusually high; it is still going on. The play won't begin for nearly half an hour. The "admirers of the game" have mustered in great force and variety. There are young peers, with sixty thousand a year, and there are gentlemen who live by their billiards. There are, for once in a way, grave persons, bankers, and counsel learned in the law; there are Jews and a sprinkling of foreigners; and there are members of Parliament and members of the swell mob.

Mr. Longcluse has a good deal to think about this night. He is out of spirits. Richard Arden is no longer with him, having picked up a friend or two in the room. Longcluse, with folded arms, and his shoulders against the wall, is in a profound reverie, his dark eyes for the time lowered to the floor, beside the point of his French boot. There unfold themselves beneath him picture after picture, the scenes of many a year ago. Looking down, there creeps over him an old horror, a supernatural disgust, and he sees in the dark a pair of wide, white eyes, staring up at him in an agony of terror, and a shrill yell, piercing a distance of many years, makes him shake his ears with a sudden chill. Is this the witches' Sabbath of our pale Mephistopheles—his night of goblins? He raised his eyes, and they met those of a person whom he had not seen for a very long time—a third part of his whole life. The two pairs of eyes, at nearly half across the room, have met, and for a moment fixed. The stranger smiles and nods. Mr. Longcluse does neither. He affects now to be looking over the stranger's shoulder at some more distant object. There is a strange chill and commotion at his heart.

CHAPTER IV.

MONSIEUR LEBAS.

Mr. Longcluse leaned still with folded arms, and his shoulder to the wall. The stranger, smiling and fussy, was making his way to him. There is nothing in this man's appearance to associate him with tragic incident or emotion of any kind. He is plainly a foreigner. He is short, fat, middle-aged, with a round fat face, radiant with good humour and good-natured enjoyment. His dress is cut in the somewhat grotesque style of a low French tailor. It is not very new, and has some spots of grease upon it. Mr. Longcluse perceives that he is now making his way towards him. Longcluse for a moment thought of making his escape by the door, which was close to him; but he reflected, "He is about the most innocent and good-natured soul on earth, and why should I seem to avoid him? Better, if he's looking for me, to let him find me, and say his say." So Longcluse looked another way, his arms still folded, and his shoulders against the wall as before.

"Ah, ha! Monsieur is thinking profoundly," said a gay voice in French. "Ah, ha, ha, ha! you are surprised, Sir, to see me here. So am I, my faith! I saw you. I never forget a face."

"Nor a friend, Lebas. Who could have imagined anything to bring you to London?" answered Longcluse, in the same language, shaking him warmly by the hand, and smiling down on the little man. "I shall never forget your kindness. I think I should have died in that illness but for you. How can I ever thank you half enough?"

"And the grand secret—the political difficulty—Monsieur found it well evaded," he said, mysteriously touching his upper lip with two fingers.

"Not all quiet yet. I suppose you thought I was in Vienna?"

"Eh? well, yes—so I did," answered Lebas, with a shrug. "But perhaps you think this place safer."

"Hush! You'll come to me to-morrow. I'll tell you where to find me before we part, and you'll bring your portmanteau and stay with me while you remain in London, and the longer the better."

"Monsieur is too kind, a great deal; but I am staying for my visit to London with my brother-in-law, Gabriel Laroque, the watchmaker. He lives on the Hill of

Ludgate, and he would be offended if I were to reside anywhere but in his house while I stay. But if Monsieur would be so good as to permit me to call ——"

"You must come and dine with me to-morrow; I have a box for the opera. You love music, or you are not the Pierre Lebas whom I remember sitting with his violin at an open window. So come early, come before six; I have ever so much to ask you. And what has brought you to London?"

"A very little business and a great deal of pleasure; but all in a week," said the little man, with a shrug and a hearty laugh. "I have come over here about some little things like that." He smiled archly as he produced from his waistcoat pocket a little flat box with a glass top, and shook something in it. "Commerce, you see. I have to see two or three more of the London people, and then my business will have terminated, and nothing remain for the rest of the week but pleasure—ha, ha!"

"You left all at home well, I hope—children?" He was going to say "Madame," but a good many years had passed.

"I have seven children. Monsieur will remember two. Three are by my first marriage, four by my second, and all enjoy the very best health. Three are very young—three, two, one year old; and they say a fourth is not impossible very soon," he added archly.

Longcluse laughed kindly, and laid his hand upon his shoulder.

"You must take charge of a little present for each from me, and one for Madame. And the old business still flourishes?"

"A thousand thanks! yes, the business is the same—the file, the chisel, and knife." And he made a corresponding movement of his hand as he mentioned each instrument.

"Hush!" said Longcluse, smiling, so that no one who did not hear him would have supposed there was so much cautious emphasis in the word. "My good friend, remember there are details we talk of, you and I together, that are not to be mentioned so suitably in a place like this," and he pressed his hand on his wrist, and shook it gently.

"A thousand pardons! I am, I know, too careless, and let my tongue too often run before my caution. My wife, she says, 'You can't wash your shirt but you must tell the world.' It is my weakness truly. She is a woman of extraordinary penetration."

Mr. Longcluse glanced from the corners of his eyes about the room. Perhaps he wished to ascertain whether his talk with this man, whom you would have taken to be little above the level of a French mechanic, had excited anyone's attention. But there was nothing to make him think so.

"Now, Pierre, my friend, you must win some money upon this match—do you see? And you won't deny me the pleasure of putting down your stake for you; and, if you win, you shall buy something pretty for Madame—and, win or lose, I shall think it friendly of you after so many years, and like you the better."

"Monsieur is too good," he said with effusion.

"Now look. Do you see that fat Jew over there on the front bench—you can't mistake him—with the velvet waistcoat all in wrinkles, and the enormous lips, who talks to every second person who passes?"

"I see perfectly, Monsieur."

"He is betting three to one upon Markham. You must take his offer, and back Hood. I'm told he'll win. Here are ten pounds, you may as well make them thirty. Don't say a word. Our English custom is to tip, as we say, our friend's sons at school, and to make presents to everybody, as often as we like. Now there—not a word." He quietly slipped into his hand a little rouleau of ten pounds in gold. "If you say one word you wound me," he continued. "But, good Heaven! my dear friend, haven't you a breast-pocket?"

"No, Monsieur; but this is quite safe. I was paid, only five minutes before I came here, fifteen pounds in gold, a cheque of forty-four pounds, and ——"

"Be silent. You may be overheard. Speak here in a very low tone, as I do. And do you mean to tell me that you carry all that money in your coat pocket?"

"But in a pocket-book, Monsieur."

"All the more convenient for the chevalier d'industrie," said Longcluse. "Stop. Pray don't produce it; your fate is, perhaps, sealed if you do. There are gentlemen in this room who would hustle and rob you in the crowd as you get out; or, failing that, who, seeing that you are a stranger, would follow and murder you in the streets, for the sake of a twentieth part of that sum."

"Gabriel thought there would be none here but men distinguished," said Lebas, in some consternation.

"Distinguished by the special attention of the police, some of them," said Longcluse.

"Hé! that is very true," said Monsieur Lebas—"very true, I am sure of it. See you that man there, Monsieur? Regard him for a moment. The tall man, who leans with his shoulder to the metal pillar of the gallery. My faith! he has observed my steps and followed me. I thought he was a spy. But my friend he says 'No, that is a man of bad character, dismissed for bad practices from the police.' Aha! he has watched me sideways, with the corner of his eye. I will watch him with the corner of mine—ha, ha!"

"It proves, at all events, Lebas, that there are people here other than gentlemen and men of honest lives," said Longcluse.

"But," said Lebas, brightening a little, "I have this weapon," producing a dagger from the same pocket.

"Put it back this instant. Worse and worse, my good friend. Don't you know that just now there is a police activity respecting foreigners, and that two have been arrested only yesterday on no charge but that of having weapons about their persons? I don't know what the devil you had best do."

"I can return to the Hill of Ludgate—eh?"

"Pity to lose the game; they won't let you back again," said Longcluse.

"What shall I do?" said Lebas, keeping his hand now in his pocket on his treasure.

Longcluse rubbed the tip of his finger a little over his eyebrow, thinking.

"Listen to me," said Longcluse, suddenly. "Is your brother-in-law here?"

"No, Monsieur."

"Well, you have some London friend in the room, haven't you?"

"One—yes."

"Only be sure he is one whom you can trust, and who has a safe pocket."

"Oh, yes, Monsieur, entirely! and I saw him place his purse so," he said, touching his coat, over his heart, with his fingers.

"Well, now, you can't manage it here, under the gaze of the people; but—where is best? Yes—you see those two doors at opposite sides in the wall, at the far end of the room? They open into two parallel corridors leading to the hall, and a little way down there is a cross passage, in the middle of which is a door opening into a smoking-room. That room will be deserted now, and there, unseen, you can place your money and dagger in his charge."

"Ah, thank you a hundred thousand times, Monsieur!" answered Lebas. "I shall be writing to the Baron van Boeren to-morrow, and I will tell him I have met Monsieur."

"Don't mind; how is the baron?" asked Longcluse.

"Very well. Beginning to be not so young, you know, and thinking of retiring. I will tell him his work has succeeded. If he demolishes, he also secures. If he sometimes sheds blood ——"

"Hush!" whispered Longcluse, sternly.

"There is no one," murmured little Lebas, looking round, but dropping his voice to a whisper. "He also saves a neck sometimes from the blade of the guillotine."

Longcluse frowned, a little embarrassed. Lebas smiled archly. In a moment Longcluse's impatient frown broke into a mysterious smile that responded.

"May I say one word more, and make one request of Monsieur, which I hope he will not think very impertinent?" asked Monsieur Lebas, who had just been on the point of taking his leave.

"It mayn't be in my power to grant it; but you can't be what you say—I am too much obliged to you—so speak quite freely," said Longcluse.

So they talked a little more and parted, and Monsieur Lebas went on his way.

CHAPTER V.

A CATASTROPHE.

The play has commenced. Longcluse, who likes and understands the game, sitting beside Richard Arden, is all eye. He is intensely eager and delighted. He joins modestly in the clapping that now and then follows a stroke of extraordinary brilliancy. Now and then he whispers a criticism in Arden's ear. There are many vicissitudes in the game. The players have entered on the third hundred, and still "doubtful it stood." The excitement is extraordinary. The assembly is as hushed as if it were listening to a sermon, and, I am afraid, more attentive. Now, on a sudden, Hood scores a hundred and sixty-eight points in a single break. A burst of prolonged applause follows, and, during the clapping, in which he had at first joined, Longcluse says to Arden,—

"I can't tell you how that run of Hood's delights me. I saw a poor little friend of mine here before the play began—I had not seen him since I was little more than a boy—a Frenchman, a good-natured little soul, and I advised him to back Hood, and I have been trembling up to this moment. But I think he's safe now to win. Markham can't score this time. If he's in 'Queer Street,' as they whisper round the room, you'll find he'll either give a simple miss, or put himself into the pocket."

"Well, I'm sure I hope your friend will win, because it will put three hundred and eighty pounds into my pocket," said Richard Arden.

And now silence was called, and the building became, in a moment, hushed as a cathedral before the anthem; and Markham knocked his own ball into the pocket as Longcluse had predicted.

On sped the game, and at last Hood scored a thousand, and won the match, greeted by an uproar of applause that, now being no longer restrained, lasted for nearly five minutes. The assemblage had, by this time, descended from the benches, and crowded the floor in clusters, discussing the play or settling bets. The people in the gallery were pouring down by the four staircases, and adding to the crowd and buzz.

Suddenly there is a sort of excitement perceptible of a new kind—a gathering and pressure of men about one of the doors at the far corner of the room. Men are looking back and beckoning to their companions; others are shouldering forward as strenuously as they can. What is it—any dispute about the score?—a pair of men boxing in the passage?

"No suspicion of fire?" the men at this near end exclaim, and sniff over their shoulders, and look about them, and move toward the point where the crowd is thickening, not knowing what to make of the matter. But soon there runs a rumour about the room—"a man has just been found murdered in a room outside," and the crowd now press forward more energetically to the point of attraction.

In the cross-passage which connects the two corridors, as Mr. Longcluse described, there is an awful crush, and next to no light. A single jet of gas burns in the smoking room, where the pressure of the crowd is not quite so much felt. There are two policemen in that chamber, in the ordinary uniform of the force, and three detectives in plain clothes, one supporting a corpse already stiffening, in a sitting posture, as it was found, in a far angle of the room, on the bench to your left as you look in. All the people are looking up the room. You can see nothing but hats, and backs of heads, and shoulders. There is a ceaseless buzz and clack of talk and conjecture. Even the policemen are looking, as the rest do, at the body. The man who has mounted on the chair near the door, with the other beside him, who has one foot on the rung and another on the seat, and an arm round the first gentleman's neck, although he has not the honour of his acquaintance, to support himself, can see, over the others' heads, the one silent face which looks back towards the door, upon so many gaping, and staring, and gabbling ones. The light is faint. It has occurred to no one to light the gas lamps in the centre. But that forlorn face is distinct enough. Fixed and leaden it is, with the chin a little raised. The eyes are wide open, with a deep and awful gaze; the mouth slightly distorted with what the doctors call "a convulsive smile," which shows the teeth a little, and has an odd, wincing look.

As I live, it is the little Frenchman, Pierre Lebas, who was talking so gaily tonight with Mr. Longcluse!

The ebony haft of a dagger, sticking straight out, shows where the hand of the assassin planted the last stab of four, through his black satin waistcoat, embroidered with green leaves, red strawberries, and yellow flowers, which, I suppose, was one of the finest articles in the little wardrobe that Madame Lebas packed up for his holiday. It is not worth much now. It has four distinct cuts, as I have said, on the left side, right through it, and is soaked in blood.

His pockets have been rifled. The police have found nothing in them but a red pocket-handkerchief and a papier-maché snuff-box. If that dumb mouth could speak but fifty words, what a world of conjecture it would end, and poor Lebas's story would be listened to as never was story of his before!

A policeman now takes his place at the door to prevent further pressure. No new-comers will be admitted, except as others go out. Those outside are asking questions of those within, and transmitting, over their shoulders, particulars, eagerly repeated. On a sudden there is a subsidence of the buzz and gabble within, and one voice, speaking almost at the pitch of a shriek, is heard declaiming. White as a sheet, Mr. Longcluse, in high excitement, is haranguing in the smoking-room, mounted on a table.

"I say," he cried, "gentlemen, excuse me. There are so many together here, so many known to be wealthy, it is an opportunity for a word. Things are coming to a pretty pass—garotters in our streets and assassins in our houses of entertainment! Here is a poor little fellow—look at him—here to-night to see the game, perfectly well and happy, murdered by some miscreant for the sake of the money he had about him. It might have been the fate of anyone of us. I spoke to him to-night. I had not seen him since I was a boy almost. Seven children and a wife, he told me, dependent on him. I say there are two things wanted—first, a reward of such magnitude as will induce exertion. I promise, for my own share, to put down double the amount promised by the highest subscriber. Secondly, something should be done for the family he has left, in proportion to the loss they have sustained. Upon this point I shall make inquiry myself. But this is plain, the danger and scandal have attained a pitch at which none of us who cares to walk the streets at night, or at any time to look in upon amusements like that we attended this evening, can permit them longer to stand. There is a fatal defect somewhere. Are our police awake and active? Very possibly; but if so the force is not adequate. I say this frightful scandal must be abated if, as citizens of London, we desire to maintain our reputation for common sense and energy."

There was a tall thin fellow, shabbily dressed, standing nearly behind the door, with a long neck, and a flat mean face, slightly pitted with small-pox, rather pallid, who was smiling lazily, with half-closed eyes, as Mr. Longcluse declaimed; and when he alluded pointedly to the inadequacy of the police, this man's amusement improved, and he winked pleasantly at the clock which he was consulting at the moment with the corner of his eye.

And now a doctor arrived, and Gabriel Laroque the watchmaker, and more police, with an inspector. Laroque faints when he sees his murdered friend. Recovered after a time, he identifies the body, identifies the dagger also as the property of poor Lebas.

The police take the matter now quite into their hands, and clear the room.

CHAPTER VI.

TO BED.

Mr. Longcluse jumped into a cab, and told the man to drive to his house in Bolton Street, Piccadilly. He rolled his coat about him with a kind of violence, and threw himself into a corner. Then, as it were, in furore, and with a stamp on the floor, he pitched himself into the other corner.

"I've seen to-night what I never thought I should see. What devil possessed me to tell him to go into that black little smoking-room?" he muttered. "What a room it is! It has seized my brain somehow. Am I in a fever, or going mad, or what? That cursed smoking-room! I can't get out of it. It is in the centre of the earth. I'm built round and round in it. The moment I begin to think, I'm in it. The moment I close my eyes, its four stifling walls are round me. There is no way out. It is like hell."

The wind had come round to the south, and a soft rain was pattering on the windows. He stopped the cab somewhere near St. James's Street, and got out. It was late—it was just past two o'clock, and the streets were quiet. Wonderfully still was the great city at this hour, and the descent of the rain went on with a sound like a prolonged "hush" all round. He paid the man, and stood for a while on the kerbstone, looking up and down the street, under the downpour of the rain. You might have taken this millionaire for a man who knew not where to lay his head that night. He took off his hat, and let the refreshing rain saturate his hair, and stream down his forehead and temples.

"Your cab's stuffy and hot, ain't it? Standing half the day with the glass in the sun, I daresay," said he to the man, who was fumbling in his pockets, and pretending a difficulty about finding change.

"See, never mind, if you haven't got change; I'll go on. Heavier rain than I fancied; very pleasant though. When did the rain begin?" asked Mr. Longcluse, who seemed in no hurry to get back again.

"A trifle past ten, Sir."

"I say, your horse's knees are a bit broken, ain't they? Never mind, I don't care. He can pull you and me to Bolton Street, I daresay."

"Will you please to get in, Sir?" inquired the cabman.

Mr. Longcluse nodded, frowning and thinking of something else; the rain still descending on his bare head, his hat in his hand.

The cabman thought this "cove" had been drinking and must be a trifle "tight." He would not mind if he stood so for a couple of hours; it would run his fare up to something pretty. So cabby had thoughts of clapping a nosebag to his horse's jaws, and was making up his mind to a bivouac. But Mr. Longcluse on a sudden got in, repeating his direction to the driver in a gay and brisk tone, that did not represent his real sensations.

"Why should I be so disturbed at that little French fellow? Have I been ill, that my nerve is gone and I such a fool? One would think I had never seen a dead fellow till now. Better for him to be quiet than at his wit's ends, devising ways and means to keep his seven cubs in bread and butter. I should have gone away when the game was over. What earthly reason led me into that d——d room, when I heard the fuss there? I've a mind to go and play hazard, or see a doctor. Arden said he'd look in, in the morning. I should like that; I'll talk to Arden. I sha'n't sleep, I know; I can't, all night; I've got imprisoned in that suffocating room. Shall I ever close my eyes again?"

They had now reached the door of the small, unpretending house of this wealthy man. The servant who opened the door, though he knew his business, stared a little, for he had never seen his master return in such a plight before, and looking so haggard.

"Where's Franklin?"

"Arranging things in your room, Sir."

"Give me a candle. The cab is paid. Mr. Arden, mind, may call in the morning; if I should not be down, show him to my room. You are not to let him go without seeing me."

Up-stairs went the pale master of the house. "Franklin!" he called, as he mounted the last flight of stairs, next his bed-room.

"Yes, Sir."

"I sha'n't want you to-night, I think—that is, I shall manage what I want for myself; but I mean to ring for you by-and-by." He was in his dressing-room by this time, and looked round to see that his comforts were provided for as usual—his foot-bath and hot water.

"Shall I fetch your tea, Sir?"

"I'll drink no tea to-night; I've been disgusted. I've seen a dead man, quite unexpectedly; and I sha'n't get over it for some hours, I daresay. I feel ill. And what you must do is this: when I ring my bell, you come back, and you must sit up here till eight in the morning. I shall leave the door between this and the next room open; and should you hear me sleeping uneasily, moaning, or anything like nightmare, you must come in and waken me. And you are not to go to sleep, mind; the moment I call, I expect you in my room. Keep yourself awake how you can; you may sleep all to-morrow, if you like."

With this charge Franklin departed.

But Mr. Longcluse's preparations for bed occupied a longer time than he had anticipated. When nearly an hour had passed, Mr. Franklin ventured up-stairs, and quietly approached the dressing-room door; but there he heard his master still busy with his preparations, and withdrew. It was not until nearly half-an-hour more had passed that his bell gave the promised signal, and Mr. Franklin established himself for the night, in the easy-chair in the dressing-room, with the connecting door between the two rooms open.

Mr. Longcluse was right. The shock which his nerves had received did not permit him to sleep very soon. Two hours later he called for the Eau-de-Cologne that stood on his dressing-table; and although he made belief to wet his temples with it, and kept it at his bedside with that professed design, it was Mr. Franklin's belief that he drank the greater part of what remained in the capacious cut-glass bottle. It was not until people were beginning to "turn out" for their daily labour that sleep at length visited the wearied eye-balls of the Crœsus.

Three hours of death-like sleep, and Mr. Longcluse, with a little start, was wide awake.

"Franklin!"

"Yes, Sir." And Mr. Franklin stood at his bedside.

"What o'clock is it?"

"Just struck ten, Sir."

"Hand me the Times." This was done.

"Tell them to get breakfast as usual. I'm coming down. Open the shutters, and draw the curtains, quite."

When Franklin had done this and gone down, Mr. Longcluse read the Times with a stern eagerness, still in bed. The great billiard match between Hood and Markham was given in spirited detail; but he was looking for something else. Just under this piece of news, he found it—"Murder and Robbery, in the Saloon Tavern." He read this twice over, and then searched the paper in vain for any further news respecting it. After this search, he again read the short account he had seen before, very carefully, and more than once. Then he jumped out of bed, and looked at himself in the glass in his dressing-room.

"How awfully seedy I am looking!" he muttered, after a careful inspection. "Better by-and-by."

His hand was shaking like that of a man who had made a debauch, or was worn out with ague. He looked ten years older.

"I should hardly know myself," muttered he. "What a confounded, sinful old fogey I look, and I so young and innocent!"

The sneer was for himself and at himself. The delivery of such is an odd luxury which, at one time or other, most men indulge in. Perhaps it should teach us to take them more kindly when other people crack such cynical jokes on our heads, or, at least, to perceive that they don't always argue personal antipathy.

The sour smile which had, for a moment, flickered with a wintry light on his face, gave place suddenly to a dark fatigue; his features sank, and he heaved a long, deep, and almost shuddering sigh.

There are moments, happily very rare, when the idea of suicide is distinct enough to be dangerous, and having passed which, a man feels that Death has looked him very nearly in the face. Nothing more trite and true than the omnipresence of suffering. The possession of wealth exempts the unfortunate owner from, say, two-thirds of the curse that lies heavy on the human race. Two thirds is a great deal; but so is the other third, and it may have in it, at times, something as terrible as human nature can support.

Mr. Longcluse, the millionaire, had, of course, many poor enviers. Had any one of all these uttered such a sigh that morning? Or did any one among them feel wearier of life?

"When I have had my tub, I shall be quite another man," said he.

But it did not give him the usual fillip; on the contrary, he felt rather chilled.

"What can the matter be? I'm a changed man," said he, wondering, as people do at the days growing shorter in autumn, that time had produced some changes. "I remember when a scene or an excitement produced no more effect upon me, after the moment, than a glass of champagne; and now I feel as if I had swallowed poison, or drunk the cup of madness. Shaking!—hand, heart, every joint. I have grown such a muff!"

Mr. Longcluse had at length completed his very careless toilet, and looking ill, went down-stairs in his dressing-gown and slippers.

CHAPTER VII.

FAST FRIENDS.

In little more than half-an-hour, as Mr. Longcluse was sitting at his breakfast in his dining-room, Richard Arden was shown in.

"Dressing-gown and slippers—what a lazy dog I am compared with you!" said Longcluse gaily as he entered.

"Don't say another word on that subject, I beg. I should have been later myself, had I dared; but my Uncle David had appointed to meet me at ten."

"Won't you take something?"

"Well, as I have had no breakfast, I don't mind if I do," said Arden, laughing.

Longcluse rang the bell.

"When did you leave that place last night?" asked Longcluse.

"I fancy about the same time that you went—about five or ten minutes after the match ended. You heard there was a man murdered in a passage there? I tried to get down and see it but the crowd was awful."

"I was more lucky—I came earlier," said Longcluse. "It was perfectly sickening, and I have been seedy ever since. You may guess what a shock it was to me. The murdered man was that poor little Frenchman I told you of, who had been talking to me, in high spirits, just before the play began—and there he was, poor fellow! You'll see it all there; it makes me sick."

He handed him the Times.

"Yes, I see. I daresay the police will make him out," said Arden, as he glanced hastily over it. "Did you remark some awfully ill-looking fellows there?"

"I never saw so many together in a place of the kind before," said Longcluse.

"That's a capital account of the match," said Arden, whom it interested more than the tragedy of poor little Lebas did. He read snatches of it aloud as he ate his breakfast: and then, laying the paper down, he said, "By-the-bye, I need not bother you by asking your advice, as I intended. My uncle David has been blowing me up, and I think he'll make everything straight. When he sends for me and gives me an awful lecture, he always makes it up to me afterwards."

"I wish, Arden, I stood as little in need of your advice as you do, it seems, of mine," said Longcluse suddenly, after a short silence. His dark eyes were fixed on

Richard Arden's. "I have been fifty times on the point of making a confession to you, and my heart has failed me. The hour is coming. These things won't wait. I must speak, Arden, soon or never—very soon, or never. Never, perhaps, would be wisest."

"Speak now, on the contrary," said Arden, laying down his knife and fork, and leaning back. "Now is the best time always. If it's a bad thing, why, it's over; and if it's a good one, the sooner we have it the better."

Longcluse rose, looking down in meditation, and in silence walked slowly to the window, where, for a time, without speaking he stood in a reverie. Then, looking up, he said, "No man likes a crisis. 'No good general ever fights a pitched bat-battle if he can help it.' Wasn't that Napoleon's saying? No man who has not lost his head likes to get together all he has on earth, and make one stake of it. I have been on the point of speaking to you often. I have always recoiled."

"Here I am, my dear Longcluse," said Richard Arden, rising and following him to the window, "ready to hear you. I ought to say, only too happy if I can be of the least use."

"Immense! everything?" said Longcluse vehemently. "And yet I don't know how to ask you—how to begin—so much depends. Don't you conjecture the subject?"

"Well, perhaps I do—perhaps I don't. Give me some clue."

"Have you formed no conjecture?" asked Longcluse.

"Perhaps."

"Is it anything in any way connected with your sister, Miss Arden?"

"It may be, possibly."

"Say what you think, Arden, I beseech you."

"Well, I think, perhaps, you admire her."

"Do I? Do I? Is that all? Would to God I could say that is all! Admiration, what is it?—Nothing. Love?—Nothing. Mine is adoration and utter madness. I have told my secret. What do you say? Do you hate me for it?"

"Hate you, my dear fellow! Why on earth should I hate you? On the contrary, I ought, I think, to like you better. I'm only a little surprised that your feelings should so much exceed anything I could have supposed."

"Yesterday, Arden, you spoke as if you liked me. As we drove into that place, I fancied you half understood me; and cheered by what you then said, I have spoken that which might have died with me, but for that."

"Well, what's the matter? My dear Longcluse, you talk as if I had shown signs of wavering friendship. Have I? Quite the contrary."

"Quite the contrary, that is true," said Longcluse eagerly. "Yes, you should like me better for it—that is true also. Yours is no wavering friendship, I'm sure of it. Let us shake hands upon it. A treaty, Arden, a treaty!"

With a fierce smile upon his pale face, and a sudden fire in his eyes, he extended his hand energetically, and took that of Arden, who answered the invitation with a look in which gleamed faintly something of amusement.

"Now, Richard Arden," he continued excitedly, "you have more influence with Miss Arden than falls commonly to the lot of a brother. I have observed it. It results from her having had during her earlier years little society but yours, and from your being some years her senior. It results from her strong affection for you, from her admiration of your talents, and from her having neither brother nor sister to divide those feelings. I never yet saw brother possessed of so evident and powerful an influence with a sister. You must use it all for me."

He continued to hold Arden's hand in his as he spoke.

"You can withdraw your hand if you decline," said he. "I sha'n't complain. But your hand remains—you don't. It is a treaty, then. Henceforward we live fædere icto. I'm an exacting friend, but a good one."

"My dear fellow, you do me but justice. I am your friend, altogether. But you must not mistake me for a guardian or a father in the matter. I wish I could make my sister think exactly as I do upon every subject, and that above all others. All I can say is, in me you have a fast friend."

Longcluse pressed his hand, which he had not relinquished, at these words, with a firm grasp and a quick shake.

"Now listen. I must speak on this point, the one that is in my mind, my chief difficulty. Personally, there is not, I think, a living being in England who knows my history. I am glad of it, for reasons which you will approve by-and-by. But this is an enormous disadvantage, though only temporary, and the friends of the young lady must weigh my wealth against it for the present. But when the time comes, which can't now be distant, upon my honour! upon my soul!—by Heaven, I'll show you I'm of as good and old a family as any in England! We have been gentlemen up to the time of the Conqueror, here in England, and as far before him as record can be traced in Normandy. If I fail to show you this when the hour comes, stigmatise me as you will."

"I have not a doubt, dear Longcluse. But you are urging a point that really has no weight with us people in England. We have taken off our hats to the gentlemen in casques and tabards, and feudal glories are at a discount everywhere but in Debrett, where they are taken with allowance. Your ideas upon these matters are more Austrian than ours. We expect, perhaps, a little more from the man, but certainly less from his ancestors than our forefathers did. So till a title turns up, and the heralds want them, make your mind easy on matters of pedigree, and then you can furnish them with effect. All I can tell you is this—there are hardly fifty men in England who dare tell all the truth about their families."

"We are friends, then; and in that relation, Arden, if there are privileges, there are also liabilities, remember, and both extend into a possibly distant future."

Longcluse spoke with a gloomy excitement that his companion did not quite understand.

"That is quite true, of course," said Arden.

Each was looking in the other's face for a moment, and each face grew suddenly dark, darker—and the whole room darkened as the air was overshadowed by a mass of cloud that eclipsed the sun, threatening thunder.

"By Jove! How awfully dark in a moment!" said Arden, looking from the face thus suddenly overcast through the window towards the sky.

"Dark as the future we were speaking of," said Longcluse, with a sad smile.

"Dark in one sense, I mean unseen, but not darkened in the ill-omened sense," said Richard Arden. "I have great confidence in the future. I suppose I am sanguine."

"I ought to be sanguine, if having been lucky hitherto should make one so, and yet I'm not. My happiness depends on that which I cannot, in the least, control. Thought, action, energy, contribute nothing, and so I but drift, and—my heart fails me. Tell me, Arden, for Heaven's sake, truth—spare me nothing, conceal nothing. Let me but know it, however bitter. First tell me, does Miss Arden dislike me—has she an antipathy to me?"

"Dislike you! Nonsense. How could that be? She evidently enjoys your society, when you are in spirits and choose to be amusing. Dislike you? Oh, my dear Longcluse, you can't have fancied such a thing!" said Arden.

"A man placed as I am may fancy anything—things infinitely more unlikely. I sometimes hope she has never perceived my admiration. It seems strange and cruel, but I believe where a man cannot be beloved, nothing is so likely to make him hated as his presuming to love. There is the secret of half the tragedies we read of. The man cannot cease to love, and the idol of his passion not only disregards but insults it. It is their cruel nature; and thus the pangs of jealousy and the agitations of despair are heightened by a peculiar torture, the hardest of all hell's torture to endure."

"Well, I have seen you pretty often together, and you must see there is nothing of that kind," said Arden.

"You speak quite frankly, do you? For Heaven's sake don't spare me!" urged Longcluse.

"I say exactly what I think. There can't be any such feeling," said Arden.

Longcluse sighed, looked down thoughtfully, and then, raising his eyes again, he said—

"You must answer me another question, dear Arden, and I shall, for the present, task your kindness no more. If you think it a fair question, will you promise to answer me with unsparing frankness? Let me hear the worst."

"Certainly," answered his companion.

"Does your sister like anyone in particular—is she attached to anyone—are her affections quite disengaged?"

"So far as I am aware, certainly. She never cared for any one among all the people who admired her, and I am quite certain such a thing could not be without my observing it," answered Richard Arden.

"I don't know; perhaps not," said Longcluse. "But there is a young friend of yours, who I thought was an admirer of Miss Arden's, and possibly a favoured one. You guess, I daresay, who it is I mean?"

"I give you my honour I have not the least idea."

"I mean an early friend of yours—a man about your own age—who has often been staying in Yorkshire and at Mortlake with you, and who was almost like a brother in your house—very intimate."

"Surely you can't mean Vivian Darnley?" exclaimed Richard Arden.

"I do. I mean no other."

"Vivian Darnley? Why, he has hardly enough to live on, much less to marry on. He has not an idea of any such thing. If my father fancied such an absurdity possible, he would take measures to prevent his ever seeing her more. You could not have hit upon a more impossible man," he resumed, after a moment's examination of a theory which, notwithstanding, made him a little more uneasy than he would have cared to confess. "Darnley is no fool either, and I think he is a honourable fellow; and altogether, knowing him as I do, the thing is utterly incredible. And as for Alice, the idea of his imagining any such folly, I can undertake to say, positively never entered her mind."

Here was another pause. Longcluse was again thoughtful.

"May I ask one other question, which I think you will have no difficulty in answering?" said he.

"What you please, dear Longcluse; you may command me."

"Only this, how do you think Sir Reginald would receive me?"

"A great deal better than he will ever receive me; with his best bow—no, not that, but with open arms and his brightest smile. I tell you, and you'll find it true, my father is a man of the world. Money won't, of course, do everything; but it can do a great deal. It can't make a vulgar man a gentleman, but it may make a gentleman anything. I really think you would find him a very fast friend. And now I must leave you, dear Longcluse. I have just time, and no more, to keep my appointment with old Mr. Blount, to whom my uncle commands me to go at twelve."

"Heaven keep us both, dear Arden, in this cheating world! Heaven keep us true in this false London world! And God punish the first who breaks faith with the other!"

So spoke Longcluse, taking his hand again, and holding it hard for a moment, with his unfathomable dark eyes on Arden. Was there a faint and unconscious menace in his pale face, as he uttered these words, which a little stirred Arden's pride?

"That's a comfortable litany to part with—a form of blessing elevated so neatly, at the close, into a malediction. However, I don't object. Amen, by all means," laughed Arden.

Longcluse smiled.

"A malediction? I really believe it was. Something very like it, and one that includes myself, doesn't it? But we are not likely to earn it. An arrow shot into the sea, it can hurt no one. But oh, dear Arden, what does such language mean but suffering? What is all bitterness but pain? Is any mind that deserves the name ever cruel, except from misery? We are good friends, Arden: and if ever I seem to you for a moment other than friendly, just say, 'It is his heart-ache and not he that speaks.' Good-bye! God bless you!"

At the door there was another parting.

"There's a long dull day before me—say, rather, night; weary eyes, sleepless brain," murmured Longcluse, in a rather dismal soliloquy, standing in his slippers and dressing-gown again at the window. "Suspense! What a hell is in that word! Chain a man across a rail, in a tunnel—pleasant situation! let him listen for the faint fifing and drumming of the engine, miles away, not knowing whether deliverance or death may come first. Bad enough, that suspense. What is it to mine! I shall see her to-night. I shall see her, and how will it all be? Richard Arden wishes it—yes, he does. 'Away, slight man!' It is Brutus who says that, I think. Good Heaven! Think of my life—the giddy steps I go by. That dizzy walk by moonlight, when I lost my way in Switzerland—beautiful nightmare!—the two mile ledge of rock before me, narrow as a plank; up from my left, the sheer wall of rock; at my right so close that my glove might have dropped over it, the precipice; and curling vapour on the cliffs above, that seem about to break, and envelope all below in blinding mist. There is my life translated into landscape. It has been one long adventure—danger—fatigue. Nature is full of beauty—many a quiet nook in life, where peace resides; many a man whose path is broad and smooth. Woe to the man who loses his way on Alpine tracks, and is benighted!"

Now Mr. Longcluse recollected himself. He had letters to read and note. He did this rapidly. He had business in town. He had fifty things on his hands; and, the day over, he would see Alice Arden again.

CHAPTER VIII.

CONCERNING A BOOT.

Several pairs of boots were placed in Mr. Longcluse's dressing-room.

"Where are the boots that I wore yesterday?" asked he.

"If you please, Sir," said Mr. Franklin, "the man called this morning for the right boot of that pair."

"What man?" asked Mr. Longcluse, rather grimly.

"Mr. Armagnac's man, Sir."

"Did you desire him to call for it?" asked Mr. Longcluse.

"No, Sir. I thought you must have told some one else to order him to send for it," said Franklin.

"I? You ought to know I leave those things to you," said Mr. Longcluse, staring at him more aghast and fierce than the possible mislaying of a boot would seem to warrant. "Did you see Armagnac's man?"

"No, Sir. It was Charles who came up, at eight o'clock, when you were still asleep, and said the shoemaker had called for the right boot of the pair you wore yesterday. I had placed them outside the door, and I gave it him, Sir, supposing it all right."

"Perhaps it was all right; but you know Charles has not been a week here. Call him up. I'll come to the bottom of this."

Franklin disappeared, and Mr. Longcluse, with a stern frown, was staring vaguely at the varnished boot, as if it could tell something about its missing companion. His brain was already at work. What the plague was the meaning of this manœuvre about his boot? And why on earth, think I, should he make such a fuss and a tragedy about it? Charles followed Mr. Franklin up the stairs.

"What's all this about my boot?" demanded Mr. Longcluse, peremptorily. "Who has got it?"

"A man called for it this morning, Sir."

"What man?"

"I think he said he came from Mr. Armagnac's, Sir."

"You think. Say what you know, Sir. What did he say?" said Mr. Longcluse, looking dangerous.

"Well, Sir," said the man, mending his case, "he did say, Sir, he came from Mr. Armagnac's, and wanted the right boot."

"What right boot?—any right boot?"

"No, Sir, please; the right boot of the pair you wore last night," answered the servant.

"And you gave it to him?"

"Yes, Sir, 'twas me," answered Charles.

"Well, you mayn't be quite such a fool as you look. I'll sift all this to the bottom. You go, if you please, this moment, to Monsieur Armagnac, and say I should be obliged to him for a line to say whether he this morning sent for my boot, and got it—and I must have it back, mind; you shall bring it back, you understand? And you had better make haste."

"I made bold, Sir," said Mr. Franklin, "to send for it myself, when you sent me down for Charles; and the boy will be back, Sir, in two or three minutes."

"Well, come you and Charles here again when the boy comes back, and bring him here also. I'll make out who has been playing tricks."

Mr. Longcluse shut his dressing-room door sharply; he walked to the window, and looked out with a vicious scowl; he turned about, and lifted up his clenched hand, and stamped on the floor. A sudden thought now struck him.

"The right foot? By Jove! it may not be the one."

The boot that was left was already in his hand. He was examining it curiously.

"Ay, by heaven! The right was the boot! What's the meaning of this? Conspiracy? I should not wonder."

He examined it carefully again, and flung it into its corner with violence.

"If it's an accident, it is a very odd one. It is a suspicious accident. It may be, of course, all right. I daresay it is all right. The odds are ten, twenty, a thousand to one that Armagnac has got it. I should have had a warm bath last night, and taken a ten miles' ride into the country this morning. It must be all right, and I am plaguing myself without a cause."

Yet he took up the boot, and examined it once more; then, dropping it, went to the window and looked into the street—came back, opened his door, and listened for the messenger's return.

It was not long deferred. As he heard them approach, Mr. Longcluse flung open his door and confronted them, in white waistcoat and shirt-sleeves, and with a very white and stern face—face and figure all white.

"Well, what about it? Where's the boot?" he demanded, sharply.

"The boy inquired, Sir," said Mr. Franklin, indicating the messenger with his open hand, and undertaking the office of spokesman; "and Mr. Armagnac did not send for the boot, Sir, and has not got it."

"Oh, oh! very good. And now, Sir," he said, in rising fury, turning upon Charles, "what have you got to say for yourself?"

"The man said he came from Mr. Armagnac, please, Sir," said Charles, "and wanted the boot, which Mr. Franklin should have back as early as he could return it."

"Then you gave it to a common thief with that cock-and-a-bull story, and you wish me to believe that you took it all for gospel. There are men who would pitch you over the bannisters for a less thing. If I could be certain of it, I'd put you beside him in the dock. But, by heavens! I'll come to the bottom of the whole thing yet."

He shut the door with a crash, in the faces of the three men, who stood on the lobby.

Mr. Franklin was a little puzzled at these transports, all about a boot. The servants looked at one another without a word. But just as they were going down, the dressing-room door opened, and the following dialogue ensued:—

"See, Charles, it was you who saw and spoke with that man?" said Longcluse.

"Yes, Sir."

"Should you know him again?"

"Yes, Sir, I think I should."

"What kind of man was he?"

"A very common person, Sir."

"Was he tall or short? What sort of figure?"

"Tall, Sir."

"Go on; what more? Describe him."

"Tall, Sir, with a long neck, and held himself straight; very flat feet, I noticed; a thin man, broad in the shoulders—pretty well that."

"Describe his face," said Longcluse.

"Nothing very particular, Sir; a shabby sort of face—a bad colour."

"How?"

"A bad white, Sir, and pock-marked something; a broad face and flat, and a very little bit of a nose; his eyes almost shut, and a sort of smile about his mouth, and stingy bits of red whiskers, in a curl, down each cheek."

"How old?"

"He might be nigh fifty, Sir."

"Ha, ha! very good. How was he dressed?"

"Black frock coat, Sir, a good deal worn; an old flowered satin waistcoat, worn and dirty, Sir; and a pair of raither dirty tweed trousers. Nothing fitted him, and his hat was brown and greasy, begging your parding, Sir; and he had a stick in his hand, and cotton gloves—a-trying to look genteel."

"And he asked for the right boot?" asked Mr. Longcluse.

"Yes, Sir."

"You are quite sure of that? Did he take the boot without looking at it, or did he examine it before he took it away?"

"He looked at it sharp enough, Sir, and turned up the sole, and he said 'It's all right,' and he went away, taking it along with him."

"He asked for the boot I wore yesterday, or last night—which did he say?" asked Mr. Longcluse.

"I think it was last night he said, Sir," answered Charles.

"Try to recollect yourself. Can't you be certain? Which was it?"

"I think it was last night, Sir, he said."

"It doesn't signify," said Mr. Longcluse; "I wanted to see that your memory was pretty clear on the subject. You seem to remember all that passed pretty accurately."

"I recollect it perfectly well, Sir."

"H'm! That will do. Franklin, you'll remember that description—let every one of you remember it. It is the description of a thief; and when you see that fellow again, hold him fast till you put him in the hands of a policeman. And, Charles, you must be prepared, d'ye see, to swear to that description; for I am going to the detective office, and I shall give it to the police."

"Yes, Sir," answered Charles.

"I sha'n't want you, Franklin; let some one call a cab."

So he returned to his dressing-room, and shut the door, and thought—"That's the fellow whom that miserable little fool, Lebas, pointed out to me at the saloon last night. He watched him, he said, wherever he went. I saw him. There may be other circumstances. That is the fellow—that is the very man. Here's matter to think over! By heaven! that fellow must be denounced, and discovered, and brought to justice. It is a strong case—a pretty hanging case against him. We shall see."

Full of surmises about his lost boot, Atra Cura walking unheard behind him, with her cold hand on his shoulder, and with the image of the ex-detective always gliding before or beside him, and peering with an odious familiarity over his shoulder into his face, Mr. Longcluse marched eastward with a firm tread and a cheerful countenance. Friends who nodded to him, as he walked along Piccadilly, down Saint James's Street, and by Pall Mall, citywards, thought he had just been listening to an amusing story. Others, who, more deferentially, saluted the great man as he walked lightly by Temple Bar, towards Ludgate Hill, for a moment perplexed themselves with the thought, "What stock is up, and what down, on a sudden, to-day, that Longcluse looks so radiant?"

CHAPTER IX.

THE MAN WITHOUT A NAME.

Mr. Longcluse had made up his mind to a certain course—a sharp and bold one. At the police office he made inquiry. "He understood a man had been lately dismissed from the force, answering to a certain description, which he gave them; and he wished to know whether he was rightly informed, because a theft had been that morning committed at his house by a man whose appearance corresponded, and against whom he hoped to have sufficient evidence."

"Yes, a man like that had been dismissed from the detective department within the last fortnight."

"What was his name?" Mr. Longcluse asked.

"Paul Davies, Sir."

"If it should turn out to be the same, I may have a more serious charge to bring against him," said Mr. Longcluse.

"Do you wish to go before his worship, and give an information, Sir?" urged the officer, invitingly.

"Not quite ripe for that yet," said Mr. Longcluse, "but it is likely very soon."

"And what might be the nature of the more serious charge, Sir?" inquired the officer, insinuatingly.

"I mean to give my evidence at the coroner's inquest that will be held to-day, on the Frenchman who was murdered last night at the Saloon Tavern. It is not conclusive—it does not fix anything upon him; it is merely inferential."

"Connecting him with the murder?" whispered the man, something like reverence mingling with his curiosity, as he discovered the interesting character of his interrogator.

"I can only say possibly connecting him in some way with it. Where does the man live?"

"He did live in Rosemary Court, but he left that, I think. I'll ask, if you please, Sir. Tompkins—hi! You know where Paul Davies puts up. Left Rosemary Court?"

"Yes, five weeks. He went to Gold Ring Alley, but he's left that a week ago, and I don't know where he is now, but will easy find him. Will it answer at eight this evening, Sir?"

"Quite. I want a servant of mine to have a sight of him," said Longcluse.

"If you like, Sir, to leave your address and a stamp, we'll send you the information by post, and save you calling here."

"Thanks, yes, I'll do that."

So Mr. Longcluse took his leave, and proceeded to the place where the coroner was sitting. Mr. Longcluse was received in that place with distinction. The moneyed man was honoured—eyes were gravely fixed on him, and respectful whispers went about. A seat was procured for him; and his evidence, when he came to give it, was heard with marked attention, and a general hush of expectation.

The reader, with his permission, must now pass away, seaward, from this smoky London, for a few minutes, into a clear air, among the rustling foliage of ancient trees, and the fragrance of hay-fields, and the song of small birds.

On the London and Dover road stands, as you know, the "Royal Oak," still displaying its ancient signboard, where you behold King Charles II sitting with laudable composure, and a crown of Dutch gold on his head, and displaying his finery through an embrasure in the foliage, with an ostentation somewhat inconsiderate, considering the proximity of the halberts of the military emissaries in search of him to the royal features. As you drive towards London, it shows at the left side of the road, a good old substantial inn and posting-house. Its business has dwindled to something very small indeed, for the traffic prefers the rail, and the once bustling line of road is now quiet. The sun had set, but a reflected glow from the sky was still over everything; and by this somewhat lurid light Mr. Truelock, the innkeeper, was observing from the steps the progress of a chaise, with four horses and two postilions, which was driving at a furious pace down the gentle declivity about a quarter of a mile away, from the Dover direction towards the "Royal Oak" and London.

"It's a runaway. Them horses has took head. What do you think, Thomas?" he asked of the old waiter who stood beside him.

"No. See, the post-boys is whipping the hosses. No, Sir, it's a gallop, but no runaway."

"There's luggage a' top?" said the innkeeper.

"Yes, Sir, there's something," answered Tom.

"I don't see nothing a-followin' them," said Mr. Truelock, shading his eyes with his hand as he gazed.

"No—there is nothing," said Tom.

"They're in fear o' summat, or they'd never go at that lick," observed Mr. Truelock, who was inwardly conjecturing the likelihood of their pulling up at his door.

"Lawk! there was a jerk. They was nigh over at the finger-post turn," said Tom, with a grin.

And now the vehicle and the reeking horses were near. The post-boys held up their whips by way of signal to the "Royal Oak" people on the steps, and pulled up the horses with all their force before the door. Trembling, snorting, rolling up wreaths of steam, the exhausted horses stood.

"See to the gentleman, will ye?" cried one of the postilions.

Mr. Truelock, with the old-fashioned politeness of the English innkeeper, had run down in person to the carriage door, which Tom had opened. Master and man were a little shocked to behold inside an old gentleman, with a very brown, or rather a very bilious visage, thin, and with a high nose, who looked, as he lay stiffly back in the corner of the carriage, enveloped in shawls, with a velvet cap on, as if he were either dead or in a fit. His eyes were half open, and nothing but the white balls partly visible. There was a little froth at his lips. His mouth and delicately-formed hands were clenched, and all the furrows and lines of a selfish face fixed, as it seemed, in the lock of death. John Truelock said not a word, but peered at this visitor with a horrible curiosity.

"If he's dead," whispered Tom in his ear, "we don't take in no dead men here. Ye'll have the coroner and his jury in the house, and the place knocked up-side down; and if ye make five pounds one way ye'll lose ten the tother."

"Ye'll have to take him on, I'm thinkin'," said Mr. Truelock, rousing himself, stepping back a little, and addressing the post-boys sturdily. "You've no business bringin' a deceased party to my house. You must go somewhere else, if so be he is deceased."

"He's not gone dead so quick as that," said the postilion, dismounting from the near leader, and throwing the bridle to a boy who stood by, as he strutted round bandily to have a peep into the chaise. The postilion on the "wheeler" had turned himself about in the saddle in order to have a peep through the front window of the carriage. The innkeeper returned to the door.

If the old London and Dover road had been what it once was, there would have been a crowd about the carriage by this time. Except, however, two or three servants of the "Royal Oak," who had come out to see, no one had yet joined the little group but the boy who was detained, bridle in hand, at the horse's head.

"He'll not be dead yet," repeated the postilion dogmatically.

"What happened him?" asked Mr. Truelock.

"I don't know," answered the post-boy.

"Then how can you say whether he be dead or no?" demanded the innkeeper.

"Fetch me a pint of half-and-half," said the dismounted post-boy, aside, to one of the "Royal Oak" people at his elbow.

"We was just at this side of High Hixton," said his brother in the saddle, "when he knocked at the window with his stick, and I got a cove to hold the bridle, and I came round to the window to him. He had scarce any voice in him, and looked awful bad, and he said he thought he was a-dying. 'And how far on is the next inn?' he asked; and I told him the 'Royal Oak' was two miles; and he said, 'Drive like lightning, and I'll give you half a guinea a-piece'—I hope he's not gone dead—'if you get there in time.'"

By this time their heads were in the carriage again.

"Do you notice a sort of a little jerk in his foot, just the least thing in the world?" inquired the landlord, who had sent for the doctor. "It will be a fit, after all. If he's living, we'll fetch him into the 'ouse."

The doctor's house was just round the corner of the road, where the clump of elms stands, little more than a hundred yards from the sign of the "Royal Oak."

"Who is he?" inquired Mr. Truelock.

"I don't know," answered the postilion.

"What's his name?"

"Don't know that, neither."

"Why, it'll be on that box, won't it?" urged the innkeeper, pointing to the roof, where a portmanteau with a glazed cover was secured.

"Nothing on that but 'R. A.,'" answered the man, who had examined it half an hour before, with the same object.

"Royal Artillery, eh?"

While they were thus conjecturing, the doctor arrived. He stepped into the chaise, felt the old man's hand, tried his pulse, and finally applied the stethoscope.

"It is a nervous seizure. He is in a very exhausted state," said the doctor, stepping out again, and addressing Truelock. "You must get him into bed, and don't let his head down; take off his handkerchief, and open his shirt-collar—do you mind? I had best arrange him myself."

So the forlorn old man, without a servant, without a name, is carried from the chaise, possibly to die in an inn.

The Rev. Peter Sprott, the rector, passing that way a few minutes later, and hearing what had befallen, went up to the bed-room, where the old gentleman lay in a four-poster, still unconscious.

"Here's a case," said the doctor to his clerical friend. "A nervous attack. He'd be all right in no time, but he's so low. I daresay he crossed the herring-pond to-day, and was ill; he's in such an exhausted state. I should not wonder if he sank; and here we are, without a clue to his name or people. No servant, no name on his trunk; and, certainly, it would be awkward if he died unrecognised, and without a word to apprise his relations."

"Is there no letter in his pockets?"

"Not one," Truelock says.

The rector happened to take up the great-coat of the old gentleman, in which he found a small breast pocket, that had been undiscovered till now, and in this a letter. The envelope was gone, but the letter, in a lady's hand began: "My dearest papa."

"We are all right, by Jove, we're in luck!"

"How does she sign herself?" said the doctor.

"'Alice Arden,' and she dates from 8, Chester Terrace," answered the clergyman.

"We'll telegraph forthwith," said the doctor. "It had best be in your name—the clergyman, you know—to a young lady."

So together they composed the telegram.

“Shall it be ill simply, or dangerously ill?” inquired the clergyman.

“Dangerously,” said the doctor.

“But dangerously may terrify her.”

“And if we say only ill, she mayn't come at all,” said the doctor.

So the telegram was placed in Truelock's hands, who went himself with it to the office; and we shall follow it to its destination.

CHAPTER X.

THE ROYAL OAK.

Three people were sitting in Lady May Penrose's drawing-room, in Chester Terrace, the windows of which, as all her ladyship's friends are aware, command one of the parks. They were looking westward, where the sky was all a-glow with the fantastic gold and crimson of sunset. It is quite a mistake to fancy that sunset, even in the heart of London—which this hardly could be termed—has no rural melancholy and poetic fascination in it. Should that hour by any accident overtake you, in the very centre of the city, looking, say, from an upper window, or any other elevation toward the western sky beyond stacks of chimneys, roofs, and steeples, even through the smoke of London, you will feel the melancholy and poetry of sunset, in spite of your surroundings.

A little silence had stolen over the party; and young Vivian Darnley, who stole a glance now and then at beautiful Alice Arden, whose large, dark, grey eyes were gazing listlessly towards the splendid mists, that were piled in the west, broke the silence by a remark that, without being very wise, or very new, was yet, he hoped, quite in accord with the looks of the girl, who seemed for a moment saddened.

"I wonder why it is that sunset, which is so beautiful, makes us all sad!"

"It never made me sad," said good Lady May Penrose, comfortably. "There is, I think, something very pleasant in a good sunset; there must be, for all the little birds begin to sing in it—it must be cheerful. Don't you think so, Alice?"

Alice was, perhaps, thinking of something quite different, for rather listlessly, and without a change of features, she said, "Oh, yes, very."

"So, Mr. Darnley, you may sing, 'Oh, leave me to my sorrow!' for we won't mope with you about the sky. It is a very odd taste, that for being dolorous and miserable. I don't understand it—I never could."

Thus rebuked by Lady Penrose, and deserted by Alice, Darnley laughed and said—

"Well, I do seem rather to have put my foot in it—but I did not mean miserable, you know; I meant only that kind of thing that one feels when reading a bit of really good poetry—and most people do not think it a rather pleasant feeling."

"Don't mind that moping creature, Alice; let us talk about something we can all understand. I heard a bit of news to-day—perhaps, Mr. Darnley, you can throw a light upon it. You are a distant relation, I think, of Mr. David Arden."

"Some very remote cousinship, of which I am very proud," answered the young man gaily, with a glance at Alice.

"And what is that—what about uncle David?" inquired the young lady, with animation.

"I heard it from my banker to-day. Your uncle, you know, dear, despises us and our doings, and lives, I understand, very quietly; I mean, he has chosen to live quite out of the world, so we have no chance of hearing anything except by accident, from people we are likely to know. Do you see much of your uncle, my dear?"

"Not a great deal; but I am very fond of him—he is such a good man, or at least, what is better," she laughed, "he has always been so very kind to me."

"You know him, Mr. Darnley?" inquired Lady May.

"By Jove, I do!"

"And like him?"

"No one on earth has better reason to like him," answered the young man warmly—"he has been my best friend on earth."

"It is pleasant to know two people who are not ashamed to be grateful," said fat Lady May, with a smile.

The young lady returned her smile very kindly. I don't think you ever beheld a prettier creature than Alice Arden. Vivian Darnley had wasted many a secret hour in sketching that oval face. Those large, soft, grey eyes, and long dark lashes, how difficult they are to express! And the brilliant lips! Could art itself paint anything quite like her? Who could paint those beautiful dimples that made her smiles so soft, or express the little circlet of pearly teeth whose tips were just disclosed? Stealthily he was now, for the thousandth time, studying that bewitching smile again.

"And what is the story about Uncle David?" asked Alice again.

"Well, what will you say—and you, Mr. Darnley, if it should be a story about a young lady?"

"Do you mean that Uncle David is going to marry? I think it would be an awful pity!" exclaimed Alice.

"Well, dear, to put you out of pain, I'll tell you at once; I only know this—that he is going to provide for her somehow, but whether by adopting her as a child, or taking her for a wife, I can't tell. Only I never saw any one looking archer than Mr. Brounker did to-day when he told me; and I fancied from that it could not be so dull a business as merely making her his daughter."

"And who is the young lady?" asked Alice.

"Did you ever happen to meet anywhere a Miss Grace Maubray?"

"Oh, yes," answered Alice quickly. "She was staying, and her father, Colonel Maubray, at the Wymerings' last autumn. She's quite lovely, I think, and very clever—but I don't know—I think she's a little ill-natured, but very amusing. She seems to have a talent for cutting people up—and a little of that kind of thing, you know, is very well, but one does not care for it always. And is she really the young lady?"

"Yes, and —— Dear me! Mr. Darnley, I'm afraid my story has alarmed you."

"Why should it?" laughed Vivian Darnley, partly to cover, perhaps, a little confusion.

"I can't tell, I'm sure, but you blushed as much as a man can; and you know you did. I wonder, Alice, what this under-plot can be, where all is so romantic. Perhaps, after all, Mr. David Arden is to adopt the young lady, and some one else, to whom he is also kind, is to marry her. Don't you think that would be a very natural arrangement?"

Alice laughed, and Darnley laughed; but he was embarrassed.

"And Colonel Maubray, is he still living?" asked Alice.

"Oh, no, dear; he died ten or eleven months ago. A very foolish man, you know; he wasted a very good property. He was some distant relation, also; Mr. Brounker said your uncle, Mr. David Arden, was very much attached to him—they were schoolfellows, and great friends all their lives."

"I should not wonder," said Alice smiling—and then became silent.

"Do you know the young lady, this fortunate Miss Maubray?" said Lady May, turning to Vivian Darnley again.

"I? Yes—that is, I can't say more than a mere acquaintance—and not an old one. I made her acquaintance at Mr. Arden's house. He is her guardian. I don't know about any other arrangements. I daresay there may be."

"Well, I know her a little, also," said Lady May. "I thought her pretty—and she sings a little, and she's clever."

"She's all that," said Alice. "Oh, here comes Dick! What do you say, Richard—is not Miss Maubray very pretty? We are making a plot to marry her to Vivian Darnley, and get Uncle David to contribute her dot."

"What benevolent people! You don't object, I dare say, Vivian."

"I have not been consulted," said he; "and, of course, Uncle David need not be consulted, as he has simply to transfer the proper quantity of stock."

Richard Arden had drawn near Lady May, and said a few words in a low tone, which seemed not unwelcome to her.

"I saw Longcluse this morning. He has not been here, has he?" he added, as a little silence threatened the conversation.

"No, he has not turned up. And what a charming person he is!" exclaimed Lady May.

"I quite agree with you, Lady May," said Arden. "He is, take him on every subject, I think, about the cleverest fellow I ever met—art, literature, games, chess, which I take to be a subject by itself. He is very great at chess—for an amateur, I mean—and when I was chess-mad, nearly a year ago and beginning to grow conceited, he opened my eyes, I can tell you; and Airly says he is the best musical critic in England, and can tell you at any hour who is who in the opera, all over Europe; and he really understands, what so few of us here know anything about, foreign politics, and all the people and their stories and scandals he has at his fingers' ends. And he is such good company, when he chooses, and such a gentleman always!"

"He is very agreeable and amusing when he takes the trouble; I always like to listen when Mr. Longcluse talks," said Alice Arden, to the secret satisfaction of her brother, whose enthusiasm was, I think, directed a good deal to her—and to, perhaps, the vexation of other people, whom she did not care at that moment to please.

"An Admirable Crichton!" murmured Vivian Darnley, with a rather hackneyed sneer. "Do you like his style of—beauty, I suppose I should call it? It has the merit of being very uncommon, at least, don't you think?"

"Beauty, I think, matters very little. He has no beauty, but his face has what, in a man, I think a great deal better—I mean refinement, and cleverness, and a kind of satire that rather interests one," said Miss Arden, with animation.

Sir Walter Scott, in his "Rob Roy"—thinking, no doubt, of the Diana Vernon of his early days, the then beautiful lady, long afterwards celebrated by Basil Hall as the old Countess Purgstorf (if I rightly remember the title), and recurring to some cherished incident, and the thrill of a pride that had ceased to agitate, but was at once pleasant and melancholy to remember—wrote these words: "She proceeded to read the first stanza, which was nearly to the following purpose. [Then follow the verses.] 'There is a great deal of it,' said she, glancing along the paper, and interrupting the sweetest sounds that mortal ears can drink in—those of a youthful poet's verses, namely, read by the lips which are dearest to them." So writes Walter Scott. On the other hand, in certain states, is there a pain intenser than that of listening to the praises of another man from the lips we love?

"Well," said Darnley, "as you say so, I suppose there is all that, though I can't see it. Of course, if he tries to make himself agreeable (which he never does to me), it makes a difference, it affects everything—it affects even his looks. But I should not have thought him good-looking. On the contrary, he appears to me about as ugly a fellow as one could see in a day."

"He's not that," said Alice. "No one could be ugly with so much animation and so much expression."

"You take up the cudgels very prettily, my dear, for Mr. Longcluse," said Lady May. "I'm sure he ought to be extremely obliged to you."

"So he would be," said Richard Arden. "It would upset him for a week, I have no doubt."

There are few things harder to interpret than a blush. At these words the beautiful face of Alice Arden flushed, first with a faint, and then, as will happen, with a brighter crimson. If Lady May had seen it, she would have laughed, probably, and told her how much it became her. But she was, at that moment, going to her chair in the window, and Richard Arden would, of course, accompany her. He did see it, as distinctly as he saw the glow in the sky over the park trees. But, knowing what a slight matter will sometimes make a recoil, and even found an antipathy, he wisely chose to see it not—and chatting gaily, followed Lady May to the window.

But Vivian Darnley, though he said nothing, saw that blush, of which Alice, with a sort of haughty defiance, was conscious. It did not make him like or admire Mr. Longcluse more.

"Well, I suppose he is very charming—I don't know him well enough myself to give an opinion. But he makes his acquaintances rather oddly, doesn't he? I don't think any one will dispute that."

"I don't know really. Lady May introduced him to me, and she seems to like him very much. So far as I can see, people are very well pleased at knowing him, and don't trouble their heads as to how it came about," said Miss Arden.

"No, of course; but people not fortunate enough to come within the influence of his fascination, can't help observing. How did he come to know your brother, for instance? Did any one introduce him? Nothing of the kind. Richard's horse was hurt or lame at one of the hunts in Warwickshire, and he lent him a horse, and introduced himself, and they dined together that evening on the way back, and so the thing was done."

"Can there be a better introduction than a kindness?" asked Alice.

"Yes, where it is a kindness, I agree; but no one has a right to push his services upon a stranger who does not ask for them."

"I really can't see. Richard need not have taken his horse if he had not liked," she answered.

"And Lady May, who thinks him such a paragon, knows no more about him than any one else. She had her footman behind her—didn't she tell you all about it?"

"I really don't recollect; but does it very much matter?"

"I think it does—that is, it has been a sort of system. He just gave her his arm over a crossing, where she had taken fright, and then pretended to think her a great deal more frightened than she really can have been, and made her sit down to recover in a confectioner's shop, and so saw her home, and that affair was concluded. I don't say, of course, that he is never introduced in the regular way; but a year or two ago, when he was beginning, he always made his approaches by means of that kind of stratagem; and the fact is, no one knows anything on earth about him; he has emerged, like a figure in a phantasmagoria, from total darkness, and may lose himself in darkness again at any moment."

"I am interested in that man, whoever he is; his entrance, and his probable exit, so nearly resemble mine," said a clear, deep-toned voice close to them; and looking up, Miss Arden saw the pale face and peculiar smile of Mr. Longcluse in the fading twilight.

Mr. Longcluse was greeted by Lady May and by Richard Arden, and then again he drew near Alice, and said, "Do you recollect, Miss Arden, about ten days ago I told you a story that seemed to interest you—the story of a young and eloquent friar, who died of love in his cell in an abbey in the Tyrol, and whose ghost used to be seen pensively leaning on the pulpit from which he used to preach, too much thinking of the one beautiful face among his audience, which had enthralled him. I had left the enamel portrait I told you of at an artist's in Paris, and I wrote for it, thinking you might wish to see it—hoping you might care to see it," he added, in a lower tone, observing that Vivian Darnley, who was not in a happy temper, had, with a sudden impulse of disdain, removed himself to another window, there to contemplate the muster of the stars in the darkening sky, at his leisure.

"That was so kind of you, Mr. Longcluse! You have had a great deal of trouble. It is such an interesting story!" said Alice.

In his reception, Mr. Longcluse found something that pleased, almost elated him. Had Richard Arden been speaking to her on the subject of their morning's conversation? He thought not, Lady May had mentioned that he had not been with them till just twenty minutes ago, and Arden had told him that he had dined with his uncle David and Mr. Blount, upon the same business on which he had been occupied with both nearly all day. No, he could not have spoken to her. The slight change which made him so tumultuously proud and happy, was entirely spontaneous.

"So it seemed to me—an eccentric and interesting story—but pray do not wound me by speaking of trouble. I only wish you knew half the pleasure it has been to me to get it to show you. May I hold the lamp near for a moment while you look at it?" he said, indicating a tiny lamp which stood on a pier-table, showing a solitary gleam, like a lighthouse, through the gloom; "you could not possibly see it in this faint twilight."

The lady assented. Had Mr. Longcluse ever felt happier?

CHAPTER XI.

THE TELEGRAM ARRIVES.

Mr. Longcluse placed the little oval enamel, set in gold, in Miss Arden's fingers, and held the lamp beside her while she looked.

"How beautiful!—how very interesting!" she exclaimed. "What suffering in those thin, handsome features! What a strange enthusiasm in those large hazel eyes! I could fancy that monk the maddest of lovers, the most chivalric of saints. And did he really suffer that incredible fate? Did he really die of love?"

"So they say. But why incredible? I can quite imagine that wild shipwreck, seeing what a raging sea love is, and how frail even the strongest life."

"Well, I can't say, I am sure. But your own novelists laugh at the idea of any but women—whose business it is, of course, to pay that tribute to their superiors—dying of love. But if any man could die such a death, he must be such as this picture represents. What a wild, agonised picture of passion and asceticism! What suicidal devotion and melancholy rapture! I confess I could almost fall in love with that picture myself."

"And I think, were I he, I could altogether die to earn one such sentence, so spoken," said Mr. Longcluse.

"Could you lend it to me for a very few days?" asked the young lady.

"As many—as long as you please. I am only too happy."

"I should so like to make a large drawing of this in chalks!" said Alice, still gazing on the miniature.

"You draw so beautifully in chalks! Your style is not often found here—your colouring is so fine."

"Do you really think so?"

"You must know it, Miss Arden. You are too good an artist not to suspect what everyone else must see, the real excellence of your drawings. Your colouring is better understood in France. Your master, I fancy, was a Frenchman?" said Mr. Longcluse.

"Yes, he was, and we got on very well together. Some of his young lady pupils were very much afraid of him."

"Your poetry is fired by that picture, Miss Arden. Your copy will be a finer thing than the original," said he.

"I shall aim only at making it a faithful copy; and if I can accomplish anything like that, I shall be only too glad."

"I hope you will allow me to see it?" pleaded Longcluse.

"Oh, certainly," she laughed. "Only I'm a little afraid of you, Mr. Longcluse."

"What can you mean, Miss Arden?"

"I mean, you are so good a critic in art, every one says, that I really am afraid of you," answered the young lady, laughing.

"I should be very glad to forfeit any little knowledge I have, if it were attended with such a misfortune," said Longcluse. "But I don't flatter; I tell you truly, a critic has only to admire, when he looks at your drawings; they are quite above the level of an amateur's work."

"Well, whether you mean it or not, I am very much flattered," she laughed. "And though wise people say that flattery spoils one, I can't help thinking it very agreeable to be flattered."

At this point of the dialogue Mr. Vivian Darnley—who wished that it should be plain to all, and to one in particular, that he did not care the least what was going on in other parts of the room—began to stumble through the treble of a tune at the piano with his right hand. And whatever other people may have thought of his performance, to Miss Alice Arden it seemed very good music indeed, and inspired her with fresh animation. Such as it was, Mr. Darnley's solo also turned the course of Miss Arden's thoughts from drawing to another art, and she said—

"You, Mr. Longcluse, who know everything about the opera, can you tell me—of course you can—anything about the great basso who is coming?"

"Stentoroni?"

"Yes; the newspapers and critics promise wonders."

"It is nearly two years since I heard him. He was very great, and deserves all they say in 'Robert le Diable.' But there his greatness began and ended. The voice, of course, you had, but everything else was defective. It is plain, however, that the man who could make so fine a study of one opera, could with cqual labour make as great a success in others. He has not sung in any opera for more than a year and a half, and has been working diligently; and so everyone is in the dark very much, and I am curious to hear the result—and nobody knows more than I have told you. You are sure of a good 'Robert le Diable,' but all the rest is speculation."

"And now, Mr. Longcluse, I shall try your good-nature."

"How?"

"I am going to make Lady May ask you to sing a song."

"Pray don't."

"Why not?"

"I should so much rather you asked me yourself."

"That's very good of you; then I certainly shall. I do ask you."

"And I instantly obey. And what shall the song be?" asked he, approaching the piano, to which she also walked.

"Oh, that ghostly one that I liked so much when you sang it here about a week ago," she answered.

"I know it—yes, with pleasure." And he sat down at the piano, and in a clear, rich baritone, sang the following odd song:—

"The autumn leaf was falling
At midnight from the tree,
When at her casement calling,
'I'm here, my love,' says he.
'Come down and mount behind me,
And rest your little head,
And in your white arms wind me,
Before that I be dead.

"'You've stolen my heart by magic,
I've kissed your lips in dreams:
Our wooing wild and tragic
Has been in ghostly scenes.
The wondrous love I bear you
Has made one life of twain,
And it will bless or scare you,
In deathless peace or pain.

"'Our dreamland shall be glowing,
If you my bride will be;
To darkness both are going,
Unless you come with me.
Come now, and mount behind me,
And rest your little head,
And in your white arms wind me,
Before that I be dead.'"

"Why, dear Alice, will you choose that dismal song, when you know that Mr. Longcluse has so many others that are not only charming, but cheery and natural?"

"It is because it is unnatural that I like that song so much; the air is so ominous and spectral, and yet so passionate. I think the idea is Icelandic—those ghostly lovers that came in the dark to win their beloved maidens, who as yet knew nothing of their having died, to ride with them over the snowy fields and frozen rivers, to join their friends at a merry-making which they were never to see; but there is something more mysterious even in this lover, for his passion has unearthly beginnings that lose themselves in utter darkness. Thank you very much, Mr.

Longcluse. It is so very kind of you! And now, Lady May, isn't it your turn to choose? May she choose, Mr. Longcluse?"

"Any one, if you desire it, may choose anything I possess, and have it," said he, in a low impassioned murmur.

How the young lady would have taken this, I know not, but all were suddenly interrupted. For at this moment a servant entered with a note, which he presented, upon a salver, to Mr. Longcluse.

"Your servant is waiting, Sir, please, for orders in the awl," murmured the man.

"Oh, yes—thanks," said Mr. Longcluse, who saw a shabby letter, with the words "Private" and "Immediate" written in a round, vulgar hand over the address.

"Pray read your note, Mr. Longcluse, and don't mind us," said Lady May.

"Thank you very much. I think I know what this is. I gave some evidence today at an inquest," began Mr. Longcluse.

"That wretched Frenchman," interposed Lady May, "Monsieur Lebrun or ——"

"Lebas," said Vivian Darnley.

"Yes, so it was, Lebas; what a frightful thing that was!" continued Lady May, who was always well up in the day's horrors.

"Very melancholy, and very alarming also. It is a selfish way of looking at it, but one can't help thinking it might just as well have happened to any one else who was there. It brings it home to one a little uncomfortably," said Mr. Longcluse, with an uneasy smile and a shrug.

"And you actually gave evidence, Mr. Longcluse?" said Lady May.

"Yes, a little," he answered. "It may lead to something. I hope so. As yet it only indicates a line of inquiry. It will be in the papers, I suppose, in the morning. There will be, I daresay, a pretty full report of that inquest."

"Then you saw something occur that excited your suspicions?" said Lady May.

Mr. Longcluse recounted all he had to tell, and mentioned having made inquiries as to the present abode of the man, Paul Davies, at the police office.

"And this note, I daresay, is the one they promised to send me, telling the result of their inquiries," he added.

"Pray open it and see," said Lady May.

He did so. He read it in silence. From his foot to the crown of his head there crept a cold influence as he read. Stream after stream, this aura of fear spread upwards to his brain. Pale Mr. Longcluse shrugged and smiled, and smiled and shrugged, as his dark eye ran down the lines, and with a careless finger he turned the page over. He smiled, as prizefighters smile for the spectators, while every nerve quivered with pain. He looked up, smiling still, and thrust the note into his breast-pocket.

"Well, Mr. Longcluse, a long note it seems to have been," said Lady May, curiously.

"Not very long, but what is as bad, very illegible," said Mr. Longcluse gaily.

"And what about the man—the person the police were to have inquired after?" she persisted.

"I find it is no police information, nothing of the kind," answered Longcluse with the same smile. "It comes by no means from one of that long-headed race of men; on the contrary, poor fellow, I believe he is literally a little mad. I make him a trifling present every Christmas, and that is a very good excuse for his plaguing me all the year round. I was in hopes this letter might turn out an amusing one, but it is not; it is a failure. It is rather sensible, and disgusting."

"Well, then, I must have my song, Mr. Longcluse," said Lady May, who, under cover of music, sometimes talked a little, in gentle murmurs, to that person with whom talk was particularly interesting.

But that song was not to be heard in Lady May's drawing-room that night, for a kindred interruption, though much more serious in its effects upon Mr. Longcluse's companions, occurred. A footman entered, and presented on a salver a large brown envelope to Miss Alice Arden.

"Oh, dear! It is a telegram," exclaimed Miss Arden, who had taken it to the window. Lady May Penrose was beside her by this time. Alice looked on the point of fainting.

"I'm afraid papa is very ill," she whispered, handing the paper, which trembled very much in her hand, to Lady May.

"H'm! Yes—but you may be sure it's exaggerated. Bring some sherry and water, please. You look a little frightened, my dear. Sit down, darling. There now! These messages are always written in a panic. What do you mean to do?"

"I'll go, of course," said Alice.

"Well, yes—I think you must go. What is the place? Twyford, the 'Royal Oak?' Look out Twyford, please Mr. Darnley—there's a book there. It must be a post-town. It was thoughtful saying it is on the Dover coach road."

Vivian Darnley was gazing in deep concern at Alice. Instantly he began turning over the book, and announced in a few moments more—"It is a post-town—only thirty-six miles from London," said Mr. Darnley.

"Thanks," said Lady May. "Oh, here's the wine—I'm so glad! You must have a little, dear; and you'll take Louisa Diaper with you, of course; and you shall have one of my carriages, and I'll send a servant with you, and he'll arrange everything; and how soon do you wish to go?"

"Immediately, instantly—thanks, darling. I'm so much obliged!"

"Will your brother go with you?"

"No, dear. Papa, you know, has not forgiven him, and it is, I think, two years since they met. It would only agitate him."

And with these words she hurried to her room, and in another moment, with the aid of her maid, was completing her hasty preparations.

In wonderfully little time the carriage was at the door. Mr. Longcluse had taken his leave. So had Richard Arden, with the one direction to the servant, "If anything should go very wrong, be sure to telegraph for me. Here is my address."

"Put this in your purse, dear," said Lady May. "Your father is so thoughtless, he may not have brought money enough with him; and you will find it is as I say—he'll be a great deal better by the time you get there; and God bless you, my dear."

And she kissed her as heartily as she dared, without communicating the rouge and white powder which aided her complexion.

As Alice ran down, Vivian Darnley awaited her outside the drawing-room door, and ran down with her, and put her into the carriage. He leaned for a moment on the window, and said—

"I hope you didn't mind that nonsense Lady May was talking just now about Miss Grace Maubray. I assure you it is utter folly. I was awfully vexed; but you didn't believe it?"

"I didn't hear her say anything, at least seriously. Wasn't she laughing? I'm in such trouble about that message! I am so longing to be at my journey's end!"

He took her hand and pressed it, and the carriage drove away. And standing on the steps, and quite forgetting the footman close behind him, he watched it as it drove rapidly southward, until it was quite out of sight, and then with a great sigh and "God for ever bless you!"—uttered not above his breath—he turned about, and saw those powdered and liveried effigies, and walked up with his head rather high to the drawing-room, where he found Lady May.

"I sha'n't go to the opera to-night; it is out of the question," said she. "But you shall. You go to my box, you know; Jephson will put you in there."

It was plain that the good-natured soul was unhappy about Alice, and, Richard Arden having departed, wished to be alone. So Vivian took his leave, and went away—but not to the opera—and sauntered for an hour, instead, in a melancholy romance up and down the terrace, till the moon rose and silvered the trees in the park.

CHAPTER XII.

SIR REGINALD ARDEN.

The human mind being, in this respect, of the nature of a kaleidoscope, that the slightest hitch, or jolt, or tremor is enough to change the entire picture that occupies it, it is not to be supposed that the illness of her father, alarming as it was, could occupy Alice Arden's thoughts to the exclusion of every other subject, during every moment of her journey. One picture, a very pretty one, frequently presented itself, and always her heart felt a strange little pain as this pretty phantom appeared. It was the portrait of a young girl, with fair golden hair, a brilliant complexion, and large blue eyes, with something riant, triumphant, and arch to the verge of mischief, in her animated and handsome face.

The careless words of good Lady May, this evening, and the very obvious confusion of Vivian Darnley at mention of the name of Grace Maubray, troubled her. What was more likely than that Uncle David, interested in both, should have seriously projected the union which Lady May had gaily suggested? If she—Alice Arden—liked Vivian Darnley, it was not very much, her pride insisted. In her childhood they had been thrown together. He had seemed to like her; but had he ever spoken? Why was he silent? Was she fool enough to like him?—that cautious, selfish young man, who was thinking, she was quite certain now, of a marriage of prudence or ambition with Grace Maubray? It was a cold, cruel, sordid world!

But, after all, why should he have spoken? or why should he have hoped to be heard with favour? She had been to him, thank Heaven, just as any other pleasant, early friend. There was nothing to regret—nothing fairly to blame. It was just that a person whom she had come to regard as a property was about to go, and belong quite, to another. It was the foolish little jealousy that everyone feels, and that means nothing. So she told herself; but constantly recurred the same pretty image, and with it the same sudden little pain at her heart.

But now came the other care. As time and space shorten, and the moment of decision draws near, the pain of suspense increases. They were within six miles of Twyford. Her heart was in a wild flutter—now throbbing madly, now it seemed standing still. The carriage window was down. She was looking out on the scenery—strange to her—all bright and serene under a brilliant moon. What message awaited her at the inn to which they were travelling at this swift pace? How frightful it might be!

"Oh, Louisa!" she every now and then imploringly cried to her maid, "how do you think it will be? Oh! how will it be? Do you think he'll be better? Oh! do you think he'll be better? Tell me again about his other illness, and how he recovered? Don't you think he will this time? Oh, Louisa, darling! don't you think so? Tell me—tell me you do!"

Thus, in her panic, the poor girl wildly called for help and comfort, until at last the carriage turned a curve in the road at which stood a shadowy clump of elms, and in another moment the driver pulled up under the sign of the "Royal Oak."

"Oh, Louisa! Here it is," cried the young lady, holding her maid's wrist with a trembling grasp.

The inn-door was shut, but there was light in the hall, and light in an upper room.

"Don't knock—only ring the bell. He may be asleep, God grant!" said the young lady.

The door was quickly opened, and a waiter ran down to the carriage window, where he saw a pair of large wild eyes, and a very pale face, and heard the question—"An old gentlemen has been ill here, and a telegram was sent; is he—how is he?"

"He's better, Ma'am," said the man.

With a low, long "O—Oh!" and clasped hands and upturned eyes, she leaned back in the carriage, and a sudden flood of tears relieved her. Yes; he was a great deal better. The attack was quite over; but he had not spoken. He seemed much exhausted; and having swallowed some claret, which the doctor prescribed, he had sunk into a sound and healthy sleep, in which he still lay. A message by telegraph had been sent to announce the good news, but Alice was some way on her journey before it had reached.

Now the young lady got down, and entered the homely old inn, followed by her maid. She could have dropped on her knees in gratitude to her Maker; but true religion, like true affection, is shy of demonstrating its fervours where sympathy is doubtful.

Gently, hardly breathing, guided by the "chambermaid," she entered her father's room, and stood at his bedside. There he lay, yellow, lean, the lines of his face in repose still forbidding, the thin lips and thin nose looking almost transparent, and breathing deeply and regularly, as a child in his slumbers. In that face Alice could not discover what any stranger would have seen. She only saw the face of her father. Selfish and capricious as he was, and violent too—a wicked old man, if one could see him justly—he was yet proud of her, and had many schemes and projects afloat in his jaded old brain, of which her beauty was the talisman, of which she suspected nothing, and with which his head was never more busy than at the very moment when he was surprised by the aura of his coming fit.

The doctor's conjecture was right. He had crossed the Channel that morning. In his French coupée, he had for companion the very man he had most wished and contrived to travel homeward with. This was Lord Wynderbroke.

Lord Wynderbroke was fifty years old and upwards. He was very much taken with Alice, whom he had met pretty often. He was a man who was thought likely to marry. His estate was in the nattiest order. He had always been prudent, and cultivated a character. He had, moreover, mortgages over Sir Reginald Arden's estate, the interest of which the baronet was beginning to find it next to impossible to pay. They had been making a little gouty visit to Vichy, and Sir Reginald had taken good care to make the journey homeward with Lord Wynderbroke, who knew that when he pleased he could be an amusing companion, and who also felt that kind of interest in him which everyone experiences in the kindred of the young lady of whom he is enamoured.

The baronet, who tore up or burnt his letters for the most part, had kept this particular one by which his daughter had been traced and summoned to the "Royal Oak." It was, he thought, clever. It was amusing, and had some London gossip. He had read bits of it to Lord Wynderbroke in the coupée. Lord Wynderbroke was delighted. When they parted, he had asked leave to pay him a visit at Mortlake.

"Only too happy, if you are not afraid of the old house falling in upon us. Everything there, you know, is very much as my grandfather left it. I only use it as a caravanserai, and alight there for a little, on a journey. Everything there is tumbling to pieces. But you won't mind—no more than I do."

So the little visit was settled. The passage was rough. Peer and baronet were ill. They did not care to reunite their fortunes after they touched English ground. As the baronet drew near London, for certain reasons he grew timid. He got out with a portmanteau and dressing-case, and an umbrella, at Drowark station, sent his servant on with the rest of the luggage by rail, and himself took a chaise; and, after one change of horses, had reached the "Royal Oak" in the state in which we first saw him.

The doctor had told the people at that inn that he would look in, in the course of the night, some time after one o'clock, being a little uneasy about a possible return of the old man's malady. There was that in the aristocratic looks and belongings of his patient, and in the very fashionable address to which the message to his daughter was transmitted, which induced in the mind of the learned man a suspicion that a "swell" might have accidentally fallen into his hands.

By this time, thanks to the diligence of Louisa Diaper, every one in the house had been made acquainted with the fact that the sick man was no other than Sir Reginald Arden, Bart., and with many other circumstances of splendour, which would not, perhaps, have so well stood the test of inquiry. The doctor and his crony, the rector—simplest of parsons—who had agreed to accompany him in this nocturnal call, being a curious man, as gentlemen inhabiting quiet villages will be—these two gentlemen now heard all this lore in the hall at a quarter past one, and entered the patient's chamber (where they found Miss Arden and her maid) accordingly. In whispers, the doctor made to Miss Arden a most satisfactory report. He made his cautious inspection of the patient, and again had nothing but what was cheery to say.

If the rector had not prided himself upon his manners, and had been content with one bow on withdrawing from the lady's presence, they would not that night have heard the patient's voice—and perhaps, all things considered, so much the better.

"I trust, Madam, in the morning Sir Reginald may be quite himself again. It is pleasant, Madam, to witness slumber so quiet," murmured the clergyman kindly, and in perfect good faith. "It is the slumber of a tranquil mind—a spirit at peace with itself."

Smiling kindly in making the last stiff bow which accompanied these happy words, the good man tilted over a little table behind him, on which stood a decanter of claret, a water caraffe, and two glasses, all of which came to the ground with a crash that wakened the baronet. He sat up straight in his bed and stared round, while the clergyman, in consternation, exclaimed—"Good gracious!"

"Hollo! what is it?" cried the fierce, thin voice of the baronet. "What the devil's all this? Where's Crozier? Where's my servant? Will you, will you, some of you, say where the devil I am?" He was screaming all this, and groping and clutching at either side of the bed's head for a bell-rope, intending to rouse the house. "Where's Crozier, I say? Where the devil's my servant? eh? He's gone by rail, ain't he? No one came with me. And where's this? What is it? Are you all tongue-tied?—haven't you a word among you?"

The clergyman had lifted his hands in terror at the harangue of the old man of the "tranquil mind." Alice had taken his thin hand, standing beside him, and was speaking softly in his ear. But his prominent brown eyes were fiercely scanning the strangers, and the hand which clutched hers was trembling with eager fury. "Will some of you say what you mean, or what you are doing, or where I am?" and he screeched another sentence or two, that made the old clergyman very uncomfortable.

"You arrived here, Sir Reginald, about six hours ago—extremely ill, Sir," said the doctor, who had placed himself close to his patient, and spoke with official authority; "but we have got you all right again, we hope; and this is the 'Royal Oak,' the principal hotel of Twyford, on the Dover and London road; and my name is Proby."

"And what's all this?" cried the baronet, snatching up one of the medicine-bottles from the little table by his bed, and plucking out the cork and smelling at the fluid. "By heaven?" he screamed, "this is the very thing. I could not tell what d——d taste was in my mouth, and here it is. Why, my doctor tells me—and he knows his business—it is as much as my life's worth to give me anything like—like that, pah! assafœtida! If my stomach is upset with this filthy stuff, I give myself up! I'm gone. I shall sink, Sir. Was there no one here, in the name of Heaven, with a grain of sense or a particle of pity, to prevent that beast from literally poisoning me? Egad! I'll make my son punish him! I'll make my family hang him if I die!" There was a quaver of misery in his shriek of fury, as if he was on the point of bursting into tears. "Doctor, indeed! who sent for him? I didn't. Who gave him leave to drug me? Upon my soul, I've been poisoned. To think of a creature in my state, dependent on nourishment every hour, having his digestion destroyed! Doctor, indeed! Pay him? Not I, begad," and he clenched his sentence with an ugly expletive.

But all this concluding eloquence was lost upon the doctor, who had mentioned, in a lofty "aside" to Miss Arden, that "unless sent for he should not call again;" and with a marked politeness to her, and no recognition whatever of the baronet, he had taken his departure.

"I'm not the doctor, Sir Reginald; I'm the clergyman," said the Reverend Peter Sprott, gravely and timidly, for the prominent brown eyes were threatening him.

"Oh, the clergyman! Oh, I see. Will you be so good as to ring the bell, please, and excuse a sick man giving you that trouble. And is there a post-office near this?"

"Yes, Sir—close by."

"This is you, Alice? I'm glad you're here. You must write a letter this moment—a note to your brother. Don't be afraid—I'm better, a good deal—and tell the people, when they come, to get me some strong soup this moment, and—good evening, Sir, or good-night, or morning, or whatever it is," he added, to the clergyman, who was taking his leave. "What o'clock is it?" he asked Alice. "Well, you'll write to your brother to meet me at Mortlake. I have not seen him, now, for how many years? I forget. He's in town, is he? Very good. And tell him it is perhaps the last time, and I expect him. I suppose he'll come. Say at a quarter past nine in the evening. The sooner it's over the better. I expect no good of it; it is only just to try. And I shall leave this early—immediately after breakfast—as quickly as we can. I hate it!"

CHAPTER XIII.

ON THE ROAD.

Next morning the baronet was in high good-humour. He has written a little reminder to Lord Wynderbroke. He will expect him at Mortlake the day he named, to dinner. He remembers he promised to stay the night. He can offer him, still, as good a game of piquet as he is likely to find in his club; and he almost feels that he has no excuse but a selfish one, for exacting the performance of a promise which gave him a great deal of pleasure. His daughter, who takes care of her old father, will make their tea and—voilà tout!

Sir Reginald was in particularly good spirits as he sent the waiter to the post-office with this little note. He thinks within himself that he never saw Alice in such good looks. His selfish elation waxes quite affectionate, and Alice never remembered him so good-natured. She doesn't know what to make of it exactly; but it pleases her, and she looks all the more brilliant.

And now these foreign birds, whom a chance storm has thrown upon the hospitality of the "Royal Oak," are up and away again. The old baronet and his pretty daughter, Louisa Diaper sitting behind, in cloaks and rugs, and the footman in front, to watch the old man's signals, are whirling dustily along with a team of four horses; for Sir Reginald's arrangements are never economical, and a pair would have brought them over these short stages and home very nearly as fast. Lady May's carriage pleases the old man, and helps his transitory good-humour: it is so much more luxurious than the jolty hired vehicle in which he had arrived.

Alice is permitted her thoughts to herself. The baronet has taken his into companionship, and is leaning back in his corner, with his eyes closed; and his pursed mouth, with its wonderful involution of wrinkles round it, is working unconsciously; and his still dark eyebrows, now elevating, now knitting themselves, indicate the same activity of brain.

With a silent look now and then at his face—for she need not ask whether Sir Reginald wants anything, or would like anything changed, for the baronet needs no inquiries of this kind, and makes people speedily acquainted with his wants and fancies—she occupies her place beside him, for the most part looking out listlessly from the window, and thinks of many things. The baronet opens his eyes at last, and says abruptly,

"Charming prospect! Charming day! You'll be glad to hear, Alice, I'm not tired; I'm making my journey wonderfully! It is so pretty, and the sun so cheery. You are looking so well, it is quite a pleasure to look at you—charming! You'll come to me at Mortlake for a few days, to take care of me, you know. I shall go on to Buxton in a week or so, and you can return to Lady May to-night, and come to Mortlake shortly; and your brother, graceless creature! I suppose, will come to-night. I expect nothing from his visit, absolutely. He has been nothing to me but a curse all his life. I suppose, if there's justice anywhere, he'll have his deserts some day. But for the present I put him aside—I sha'n't speak of him. He disturbs me."

They drove through London over Westminster Bridge, the servant thinking that they were to go to Lady May Penrose's in Chester Terrace. It was the first time that day, since he had talked of his son, that a black shadow crossed Sir Reginald's face. He shrunk back. He drew up his Chinese silk muffler over his chin. He was fearful lest some prowling beak or eagle-eyed Jew should see his face, for Sir Reginald was just then in danger. Glancing askance under the peak of his travelling cap, he saw Talkington, with Wynderbroke on his arm, walking to their club. How free and fearless those happy mortals looked! How the old man yearned for his chat and his glass of wine at B ——'s, and his afternoon whist at W ——'s! How he chafed and blasphemed inwardly at the invisible obstacle that insurmountably interposed, and with what a fiery sting of malice he connected the idea of his son with the fetters that bound him!

"You know that man?" said Sir Reginald sharply, as he saw Mr. Longcluse raise his hat to her as they passed.

"Yes, I've met him pretty often at Lady May's."

"H'm! I had not an idea that anyone knew him. He's a man who might be of use to one."

Here followed a silence.

"I thought, papa, you wished to go direct to Mortlake, and I don't think this is the way," suggested Alice.

"Eh? heigho! You're right, child; upon my life, I was not thinking," said Sir Reginald, at the same time signalling vehemently to the servant, who, having brought the carriage to a stand-still, came round to the window.

"We don't stop anywhere in town, we go straight to Mortlake Hall. It is beyond Islington. Have you ever been there? Well, you can tell them how to reach it."

And Sir Reginald placed himself again in his corner. They had not started early, and he had frequently interrupted their journey on various whimsical pretexts. He remembered one house, for instance, where there was a stock of the very best port he had ever tasted, and then he stopped and went in, and after a personal interview with the proprietor, had a bottle opened, and took two glasses, and so paid at the rate of half a guinea each for them. It had been an interrupted journey, late begun, and the sun was near its setting by the time they had got a mile beyond the outskirts of Islington, and were drawing near the singular old house where their journey was to end.

Always with a melancholy presentiment, Alice approached Mortlake Hall. But never had she felt it more painfully than now. If there be in such misgivings a prophetic force, was it to be justified by the coming events of Miss Arden's life, which were awfully connected with that scene?

They passed a quaint little village of tall stone houses, among great old trees, with a rural and old-world air, and an ancient inn, with the sign of "Guy of Warwick"—an inn of which we shall see more by-and-by—faded, and like the rest of this little town, standing under the shadow of old trees. They entered the road, dark with double hedge-rows, and with a moss-grown park-wall on the right, in which, in a little time, they reached a great iron gate with fluted pillars. They drove up a broad avenue, flanked with files of gigantic trees, and showing grand old timber also upon the park-like grounds beyond. The dusky light of evening fell upon these objects, and the many windows, the cornices, and the smokeless chimneys of a great old house. You might have fancied yourself two hundred miles away from London.

"You don't stay here to-night, Alice. I wish you to return to Lady May, and give her the note I am going to write. You and she come out to dine here on Friday. If she makes a difficulty, I rely on you to persuade her. I must have someone to meet Mr. Longcluse. I have reasons. Also, I shall ask my brother David, and his ward Miss Maubray. I knew her father: he was a fool, with his head full of romance, and he married a very pretty woman who was a devil, without a shilling on earth. The girl is an orphan, and David is her guardian, and he would like any little attention we can show her. And we shall ask Vivian Darnley also. And that will make a very suitable party."

Sir Reginald wrote his note, talking at intervals.

"You see, I want Lady May to come here again in a day or two, to stay only for two or three days. She can go into town and remain there all day, if she likes it. But Wynderbroke will be coming, and I should not like him to find us quite deserted; and she said she'd come, and she may as well do it now as another time. David lives so quietly, we are sure of him; and I commit May Penrose to you. You must persuade her to come. It will be cruel to disappoint. Here is her note—I will send the others myself. And now, God bless you, dear Alice!"

"I am so uncomfortable at the idea of leaving you, papa." Her hand was on his arm, and she was looking anxiously into his face.

"So of course you should be; only that I am so perfectly recovered, that I must have a quiet evening with Richard; and I prefer your being in town to-night, and you and May Penrose can come out to-morrow. Good-bye, child, God bless you!"

CHAPTER XIV.

MR. LONGCLUSE'S BOOT FINDS A TEMPORARY ASYLUM.

In the papers of that morning had appeared a voluminous report of the proceedings of the coroner's inquest which sat upon the body of the deceased Pierre Lebas. I shall notice but one passage referring to the evidence which, it seems, Mr. Longcluse volunteered. It was given in these terms:—

"At this point of the proceedings, Mr. R. D. Longcluse, who had arrived about half an hour before, expressed a wish to be examined. Mr. Longcluse was accordingly sworn, and deposed that he had known the deceased, Pierre Lebas, when he (Mr. Longcluse) was little more than a boy, in Paris. Lebas at that time let lodgings, which were neat and comfortable, in the Rue Victoire. He was a respectable and obliging man. He had some other occupation besides that of letting lodgings, but he (Mr. Longcluse) could not say what it might be." Then followed particulars with which we are already acquainted; and the report went on to say: "He seemed surprised when witness told him that there might be in the room persons of the worst character; and he then, in considerable alarm, pointed out to him (witness) a man who was and had been following him from place to place, he fancied with a purpose. Witness observed the man and saw him watch deceased, turning his eyes repeatedly upon him. The man had no companions, so far as he could see, and affected to be looking in a different direction. It was sideways and stealthily that he was watching deceased, who had incautiously taken out and counted some of his money in the room. Deceased did not conceal from the witness his apprehensions from this man, and witness advised him again to place his money in the hands of some friend who had a secure pocket, and recommended, in case his friend should object to take so much money into his care—Lebas having said he had a large sum about him—under the gaze of the public, that he should make the transfer in the smoking-room, the situation of which he described to him. Mr. Longcluse then proceeded to give an exact description of the man who had been dogging the deceased; the particulars were as follows:—"

Here I arrest my quotation, for I need not recapitulate the details of the tall man's features, dress, and figure, which are already familiar to the reader.

MR. LONGCLUSE'S BOOT FINDS A TEMPORARY ASYLUM.

In a court off High Holborn there was, and perhaps is, a sort of coffee-shop, in the small drawing-rooms of which, thrown into one room, are many small and homely tables, with penny and halfpenny papers, and literature with startling woodcuts. Here working mechanics and others snatch a very early breakfast, and take their dinners, and such as can afford time loiter their half-hour or so over this agreeable literature. One penny morning paper visited that place of refection, for three hours daily, and then flitted away to keep an appointment elsewhere. It was this dull time in that peculiar establishment—namely, about nine o'clock in the morning—and there was but one listless guest in the room. It was the identical tall man in question. His flat feet were planted on the bare floor, and he leaned a shoulder against the window-case, with a plug of tobacco in his jaw, as, at his leisure, he was getting through the coroner's inquest on Pierre Lebas. He was smiling with half-closed eyes and considerable enjoyment, up to the point where Mr. Longcluse's evidence was suddenly directed upon him. There was a twitching scowl, as if from a sudden pain; but his smile continued from habit, although his face grew paler. This man, whose name was Paul Davies, winked hard with his left eye, as he got on, and read fiercely with his right. His face was whiter now, and his smile less easy. It was a queerish situation, he thought, and might lead to consequences.

There was a little bit of a looking-glass, picked up at some rubbishy auction, as old as the hills, with some tarnished gilding about it, in the narrow bit of wall between the windows. Paul Davies could look at nothing quite straight. He looked now at himself in this glass, but it was from the corners of his eyes, askance, and with his sly, sleepy depression of the eye-lids, as if he had not overmuch confidence even in his own shadow. He folded the morning paper, and laid it, with formal precision, on the table, as if no one had disturbed it; and taking up the Halfpenny Illustrated Broadsheet of Fiction, and with it flourishing in his hand by the corner, he called the waiter over the bannister, and paid his reckoning, and went off swiftly to his garret in another court, a quarter of a mile nearer to Saint Paul's—taking an obscure and devious course through back-lanes and sequestered courts.

When he got up to his garret, Mr. Davies locked his door and sat down on the side of his creaking settle-bed, and, in his playful phrase, "put on his considering cap."

"That's a dangerous cove, that Mr. Longcluse. He's done a bold stroke. And now it's him or me, I do suppose—him or me; me or him. Come, Paul, shake up your knowledge-box; I'll not lose this cast simple. He's gave a description of me. The force will know it. And them feet o' mine, they are a bit flat: but any chap can make a pair of insteps with a penn'orth o' rags. I wouldn't care tuppence if it wasn't for them pock-marks. There's no managing them. A scar or a wart you may touch over with paint and sollible gutta-percha, or pink wafers and gelatine, but pock-marks is too many for any man."

He was looking with some anxiety in the triangular fragment of looking-glass—balanced on a nail in the window-case—at his features.

"I can take off them whiskers; and the long neck he makes so much of, if it was as long as an oystrich, with fourpenn'orth of cotton waste and a cabbage-net, I'd make a bull of it, and run my shoulders up to my ears. I'll take the whiskers off, anyhow. That's no treason; and he mayn't identify me. If I'm not had up for a fortnight my hair would be grew a bit, and that would be a lift. But a fellow must think twice before he begins disguisin'. Juries smells a rat. Howsomever, a cove may shave, and no harm done; or his hair may grow a bit, and how can he help it? Longcluse knows what he's about. He's a sharp lad, but for all that Paul Davies 'ill sweat him yet."

Mr. Davies turned the button of his old-fashioned window, and let it down. He shut out his two scarlet geraniums, which accompanied him in all his changes from one lodging to another.

"Suppose he tries the larceny—that's another thing he may do, seeing what my lay is. It wouldn't do to lose that thing; no more would it answer to let them find it."

This last idea seemed to cause Paul Davies a good deal of serious uneasiness. He began looking about at the walls, low down near the skirting, and up near the ceiling, tapping now and then with his knuckles, and sounding the plaster as a doctor would the chest of a wheezy patient. He was not satisfied. He scratched his head, and fiddled with his ear, and plucked his short nose dubiously, and winked hard at his geraniums through the window.

Paul Davies knew that the front garret was not let. He opened his door and listened. Then he entered that room. I think he had a notion of changing his lodgings, if only he could find what he wanted. That was such a hiding-place as professional seekers were not likely to discover. But he could not satisfy himself.

A thought struck him, however, and he went into the lobby again; he got on a chair and pushed open the skylight, and out went Mr. Davies on the roof. He looked and poked about here. He looked to the neighbouring roofs, lest any eye should be upon him; but there was no one. A maid hanging clothes upon a line, on a sort of balcony, midway down the next house, was singing, "The Ratcatcher's Daughter," he thought rather sweetly—so well, indeed, that he listened for two whole verses—but that did not signify.

Paul Davies kneeled down, and loosed and removed, one after the other, several slates near the lead gutter, between the gables; and, having made a sufficient opening in the roof for his purpose, he returned, let himself down lightly through the skylight, entered his room, and locked himself up. He then unlocked his trunk and took from under his clothes, where it lay, a French boot—the veritable boot of Mr. Longcluse—which, for greater security, he popped under the coarse coverlet of his bed. He next took from his trunk a large piece of paper which, being unfolded at the window, disclosed a rude drawing with a sentence or two underneath, and three signatures, with a date preceding.

Having read this document over twice or thrice, with a rather menacing smile, he rolled it up in brown paper and thrust it into the foot of the boot, which he popped under the coverlet and bolster. He then opened his door wide. Too long a silence might possibly have seemed mysterious, and called up prying eyes, so, while he filled his pipe with tobacco, he whistled, "Villikins and his Dinah" lustily. He was very cautious about this boot and paper. He got on his great-coat and felt hat, and took his pipe and some matches—the enjoying a quiet smoke without troubling others with the perfume was a natural way of accounting for his visit to the roof. He listened. He slipped his boot and its contents into his capacious great-coat pocket, with a rag of old carpet tied round it; and then, whistling still cheerily, he mounted the roof again, and placed the precious parcel within the roof, which he, having some skill as a slater, proceeded carefully and quickly to restore.

Down came Mr. Davies now, and shaved off his whiskers. Then he walked out, with a bundle consisting of the coat, waistcoat, and blue necktie he had worn on the evening of Lebas's murder. He was going to pay a visit to his mother, a venerable greengrocer, who lived near the Tower of London; and on his way he pledged these articles at two distinct and very remote pawnbrokers', intending on his return to release, with the proceeds, certain corresponding articles of his wardrobe, now in ward in another establishment. These measures of obliteration he was taking quietly. His visit to his mother, a very honest old woman, who believed him to be the most virtuous, agreeable, and beautiful young man extant, was made with a very particular purpose.

"Well, Ma'am," he said, in reply to the old lady's hospitable greeting, "I won't refuse a pot of half-and-half and a couple of eggs, and I'll go so far as a cut or two of bacon, bein' 'ungry; and I'm a-goin' to write a paper of some consequence, if you'll obleege me with a sheet of foolscap and a pen and ink; and I may as well write it while the things is a-gettin' ready, accordin' to your kind intentions."

And accordingly Mr. Paul Davies sat in silence, looking very important—as he always did when stationery was before him—at a small table, in a dark back room, and slowly penned a couple of pages of foolscap.

"And now," said he, producing the document after his repast, "will you be so good, Ma'am, as to ask Mr. Sildyke and Mrs. Rumble to come down and witness my signing of this, which I mean to leave it in your hands and safe keepin', under lock and key, until I take it away, or otherwise tells you what you must do with it. It is a police paper, Ma'am, and may be wanted any time. But you keep it dark till I tells you."

This settled, Mr. Sildyke and Mrs. Rumble arrived obligingly; and Paul Davies, with an adroit wink at his mother—who was a little shocked and much embarrassed by the ruse, being a truth-loving woman—told them that here was his last will and testament, and he wanted only that they should witness his signature; which, with the date, was duly accomplished. Paul Davies was, indeed, a man of that genius which requires to proceed by stratagem, cherishing an abhorrence of straight lines, and a picturesque love of the curved and angular. So, if Mr. Longcluse was doing his duty at one end of the town, Mr. Davies, at the other, was by no means wanting in activity, or, according to the level of his intellect and experience, in wisdom.

We have recurred to these scenes in which Mr. Paul Davies figures, because it was indispensable to the reader's right understanding of some events that follow. Be so good, then, as to find Sir Reginald exactly where I left him, standing on the steps of Mortlake Hall. His daughter would have stayed, but he would not hear of it. He stood on the steps, and smirked a yellow and hollow farewell, waving his hand as the carriage drove away. Then he turned and entered the lofty hall, in which the light was already failing.

Sir Reginald did not like the trouble of mounting the stairs. His bed-room and sitting-room were on a level with the hall. As soon as he came in, the gloom of his old prison-house began to overshadow him, and his momentary cheer and good-humour disappeared.

"Where is Tansey? I suppose she's in her bed, or grumbling in toothache," he snarled to the footman. "And where the devil's Crozier? I have the fewest and the worst servants, I believe, of any man in England."

He poked open the door of his sitting-room with the point of his walking-stick.

"Nothing ready, I dare swear," he quavered, and shot a peevish and fiery glance round it.

Things were not looking quite so badly as he expected. There was just the little bit of expiring fire in the grate which he liked, even in summer. His sealskin slippers were on the hearth-rug, and his easy-chair was pushed into its proper place.

"Ha! Crozier, at last! Here, get off this coat, and these mufflers, and —— I was d——d near dying in that vile chaise. I don't remember how they got me into the inn. There, don't mind condoling. You're privileged, but don't do that. As near dying as possible—rather an awkward business for useless old servants here, if I had. I'll dress in the next room. My son's coming this evening. Admit him, mind. I'll see him. How long is it since we met last? Two years, egad! And Lord Wynderbroke has his dinner here—I don't know what day, but some day very soon—Friday, I think; and don't let the people here go to sleep. Remember!"

And so on, with his old servant, he talked, and sneered, and snarled, and established himself in his sitting-room, with his reviews, and his wine, and his newspapers.

Night fell over dark Mortlake Hall, and over the blazing city of London. Sir Reginald listened, every now and then, for the approach of his son. Talk as he might, he did expect something—and a great deal—from the coming interview. Two years without a home, without an allowance, with no provision except a hundred and fifty pounds a year, might well have tamed that wilful beast!

With the tremor of acute suspense, the old man watched and listened. Was it a good or an ill sign, his being so late?

The city of London, with its still roaring traffic and blaze of gas-lamps, did not contrast more powerfully with the silent shadows of the forest-grounds of Mortlake, than did the drawing-room of Lady May Penrose, brilliant with a profusion of light, and resonant with the gay conversation of inmates, all disposed to enjoy themselves, with the dim and vast room in which Sir Reginald sat silently communing with his own dismal thoughts.

Nothing so contagious as gaiety. Alice Arden, laughingly, was "making her book" rather prematurely in dozens of pairs of gloves, for the Derby. Lord Wynderbroke was deep in it. So was Vivian Darnley.

"Your brother and I are to take the reins, turn about, Lady May says. He's a crack whip. He's better than I, I think," said Vivian to Alice Arden.

"You mustn't upset us, though. I am so afraid of you crack whips!" said Alice. "Nor let your horses run away with us; I've been twice run away with already."

"I don't the least wonder at Miss Arden's being run away with very often," said Lord Wynderbroke, with all the archness of a polite man of fifty.

"Very prettily said, Wynderbroke," smiled Lady May. "And where is your brother? I thought he'd have turned up to-night," asked she of Alice.

"I quite forgot. He was to see papa this evening. They wanted to talk over something together."

"Oh, I see!" said Lady May, and she became thoughtful.

What was the exact nature of the interest which good Lady May undoubtedly took in Richard Arden? Was it quite so motherly as years might warrant? At that time people laughed over it, and were curious to see the progress of the comedy. Here was light and gaiety—light within, lamps without; spirited talk in young anticipation of coming days of pleasure; and outside the roll of carriage-wheels making a humming bass to this merry treble.

Over the melancholy precincts of Mortlake the voiceless darkness of night descends with unmitigated gloom. The centre—the brain of this dark place—is the house: and in a large dim room, near the smouldering fire, sits the image that haunts rather than inhabits it.

CHAPTER XV.

FATHER AND SON.

Sir Reginald Arden had fallen into a doze, as he sat by the fire with his Revue des Deux Mondes, slipping between his finger and thumb, on his knees. He was recalled by Crozier's voice, and looking up, he saw, standing near the door, as if in some slight hesitation, a figure not seen for two years before.

For a moment Sir Reginald doubted his only half-awakened senses. Was that handsome oval face, with large, soft eyes, with such brilliant lips, and the dark-brown moustache, so fine, and silken, that had never known a razor, an unsubstantial portrait hung in the dim air, or his living son? There were perplexity and surprise in the old man's stare.

"I should have been here before, Sir, but your letter did not reach me until an hour ago," said Richard Arden.

"By heaven! Dick? And so you came! I believe I was asleep. Give me your hand. I hope, Dick, we may yet end this miserable quarrel happily. Father and son can have no real interests apart."

Sir Reginald Arden extended his thin hand, and smiled invitingly but rather darkly on his son. Graceful and easy this young man was, and yet embarrassed, as he placed his hand within his father's.

"You will take something, Dick, won't you?"

"Nothing, Sir, thanks."

Sir Reginald was stealthily reading his face. At last he began circuitously—

"I've a little bit of news to tell you about Alice. How long shall I allow you to guess what it is?"

"I'm the worst guesser in the world—pray don't wait for me, Sir."

"Well, I have in my desk there—would you mind putting it on the table here?—a letter from Wynderbroke. You know him?"

"Yes, a little."

"Well, Wynderbroke writes—the letter arrived only an hour ago—to ask my leave to marry your sister, if she will consent; and he says all he will do, which is very handsome—very generous indeed. Wait a moment. Yes, here it is. Read that."

Richard Arden did read the letter, with open eyes and breathless interest. The old man's eyes were upon him as he did so.

"Well, Richard, what do you think?"

"There can be but one opinion about it. Nothing can be more handsome. Everything suitable. I only hope that Alice will not be foolish."

"She sha'n't be that, I'll take care," said the old man, locking down his desk again upon the letter.

"It might possibly be as well, Sir, to prepare her a little at first. I may possibly be of some little use, and so may Lady May. I only mean that it might hardly be expedient to make it from the first a matter of authority, because she has romantic ideas, and she is spirited."

"I'll sleep upon it. I sha'n't see her again till to-morrow evening. She does not care about anyone in particular, I suppose?"

"Not that I know of," said Richard.

"You'll find it will all be right—it will—all right. It shall be right," said Sir Reginald. And then there was a silence. He was meditating the other business he had in hand, and again circuitously he proceeded.

"What's going on at the opera? Who is your great danseuse at present?" inquired the baronet, with a glimmer of a leer. "I haven't seen a ballet for more than six years. And why? I needn't tell you. You know the miserable life I lead. Egad! there are fellows placed everywhere to watch me. There would be an execution in this house this night, if the miserable tables and chairs were not my brother David's property. Upon my life, Craven, my attorney, had to serve two notices on the sheriff in one term, to caution him not to sell your uncle's furniture for my debts. I shouldn't have had a joint-stool to sit down on, if it hadn't been for that. And I had to get out of the railway-carriage, by heaven! for fear of arrest, and come home—if home I can call this ruin—by posting all the way, except a few miles. I did not dare to tell Craven I was coming back. I wrote from Twyford, where I—I—took a fancy to sleep last night, to no human being but yourself. My comfort is that they and all the world believe that I'm still in France. It is a pleasant state of things!"

"I am grieved, Sir, to think you suffer so much."

"I know it. I knew it. I know you are, Dick," said the old man eagerly. "And my life is a perfect hell. I can nowhere in England find rest for the sole of my foot. I am suffering perpetually the most miserable mortifications, and the tortures of the damned. I know you are sorry. It can't be pleasant to you to see your father the miserable outcast, and fugitive, and victim he so often is. And I'll say distinctly—I'll say at once—for it was with this one purpose I sent for you—that no son with a particle of human feeling, with a grain of conscience, or an atom of principle, could endure to see it, when he knew that by a stroke of his pen he could undo it all, and restore a miserable parent to life and liberty! Now, Richard, you have my mind. I have concealed nothing, and I'm sure, Dick, I know, I know you won't see your father perish by inches, rather than sign the warrant for his liberation. For God's sake, Dick, my boy speak out! Have you the heart to reject your miserable father's petition? Do you wish me to kneel to you? I love you, Dick, although you don't admit it. I'll kneel to you, Dick—I'll kneel to you. I'll go on my knees to you."

His hands were clasped; he made a movement. His great prominent eyes were fixed on Richard Arden's face, which he was reading with a great deal of eagerness, it is true, but also with a dark and narrow shrewdness.

"Good heaven, Sir, don't stir, I implore! If you do, I must leave the room," said Richard, embarrassed to a degree that amounted to agitation. "And I must tell you, Sir—it is very painful, but, I could not help it, necessity drove me to it—if I were ever so desirous, it is out of my power now. I have dealt with my reversion. I have executed a deed."

"You have been with the Jews!" cried the old man, jumping to his feet. "You have been dealing, by way of post obit, with my estate!"

Richard Arden looked down. Sir Reginald was as nearly white as his yellow tint would allow; his large eyes were gleaming fire—he looked as if he would have snatched the poker, and brained his son.

"But what could I do, Sir? I had no other resource. I was forbidden your house; I had no money."

"You lie, Sir!" yelled the old man, with a sudden flash, and a hammer of his thin trembling fist on the table. "You had a hundred and fifty pounds a year of your mother's."

"But that, Sir, could not possibly support any one. I was compelled to act as I did. You really, Sir, left me no choice."

"Now, now, now, now, now! you're not to run away with the thing, you're not to run away with it; you sha'n't run away with it, Sir. You could have made a submission, you know you could. I was open to be reconciled at any time—always too ready. You had only to do as you ought to have done, and I'd have received you with open arms; you know I would—I would—you had only to unite our interests in the estates, and I'd have done everything to make you happy, and you know it. But you have taken the step—you have done it, and it is irrevocable. You have done it, and you've ruined me; and I pray to God you have ruined yourself!"

With every sinew quivering, the old man was pulling the bell-rope violently with his left hand. Over his shoulder, on his son, he glanced almost maniacally. "Turn him out!" he screamed to Crozier, stamping; "put him out by the collar. Shut the door upon him, and lock it; and if he ever dares to call here again, slam it in his face. I have done with him for ever!"

Richard Arden had already left the room, and this closing passage was lost on him. But he heard the old man's voice as he walked along the corridor, and it was still in his ears as he passed the hall-door; and, running down the steps, he jumped into his cab. Crozier held the cab-door open, and wished Mr. Richard a kind good-night. He stood on the steps to see the last of the cab as it drove down the shadowy avenue and was lost in gloom. He sighed heavily. What a broken family it was! He was an old servant, born on their northern estate—loyal, and somewhat rustic—and, certainly, had the baronet been less in want of money, not exactly the servant he would have chosen.

"The old gentleman cannot last long," he said, as he followed the sound of the retreating wheels with his gaze, "and then Master Richard will take his turn, and what one began the other will finish. It is all up with the Ardens. Sir Reginald ruined, Master Harry murdered, and Master David turned tradesman! There's a curse on the old house."

He heard the baronet's tread faintly, pacing the floor in agitation, as he passed his door; and when he reached the housekeeper's room, that old lady, Mrs. Tansey, was alone and all of a tremble, standing at the door. Before her dim staring eyes had risen an oft-remembered scene: the ivy-covered gatehouse at Mortlake Hall; the cold moon glittering down through the leafless branches; the grey horse on its side across the gig-shaft, and the two villains—one rifling and the other murdering poor Henry Arden, the baronet's gay and reckless brother.

"Lord, Mr. Crozier! what's crossed Sir Reginald?" she said huskily, grasping the servant's wrist with her lean hand. "Master Dick, I do suppose. I thought he was to come no more. They quarrel always. I'm like to faint, Mr. Crozier."

"Sit ye down, Mrs. Tansey, Ma'am; you should take just a thimbleful of something. What has frightened you?"

"There's a scritch in Sir Reginald's voice—mercy on us!—when he raises it so; it is the very cry of poor Master Harry—his last cry, when the knife pierced him. I'll never forget it!"

The old woman clasped her fingers over her eyes, and shook her head slowly.

"Well, that's over and ended this many a day, and past cure. We need not fret ourselves no more about it—'tis thirty years since."

"Two-and-twenty the day o' the Longden steeple-chase. I've a right to remember it." She closed her eyes again. "Why can't they keep apart?" she resumed. "If father and son can't look one another in the face without quarrelling, better they should turn their backs on one another for life. Why need they come under one roof? The world's wide enough."

"So it is—and no good meeting and argufying; for Mr. Dick will never open the estate," remarked Mr. Crozier.

"And more shame for him!" said Mrs. Tansey. "He's breaking his father's heart. It troubles him more," she added in a changed tone, "I'm thinking, than ever poor Master Harry's death did. There's none living of his kith or kin cares about it now but Master David. He'll never let it rest while he lives."

"He may let it rest, for he'll never make no hand of it," said Crozier. "Would you object, Ma'am, to my making a glass of something hot?—you're gone very pale."

Mrs. Tansey assented, and the conversation grew more comfortable. And so the night closed over the passions and the melancholy of Mortlake Hall.

CHAPTER XVI.

A MIDNIGHT MEETING.

A couple of days passed; and now I must ask you to suppose yourself placed, at night, in the centre of a vast heath, undulating here and there like a sea arrested in a ground-swell, lost in a horizon of monotonous darkness all round. Here and there rises a scrubby hillock of furze, black and rough as the head of a monster. The eye aches as it strains to discover objects or measure distances over the blurred and black expanse. Here stand two trees pretty close together—one in thick foliage, a black elm, with a funereal and plume-like stillness, and blotting out many stars with its gigantic canopy; the other, about fifty paces off, a withered and half barkless fir, with one white branch left, stretching forth like the arm of a gibbet. Nearly under this is a flat rock, with one end slanting downwards, and half buried in the ferns and the grass that grow about that spot. One other fir stands a little way off, smaller than these two trees, which in daylight are conspicuous far away as landmarks on a trackless waste. Overhead the stars are blinking, but the desolate landscape lies beneath in shapeless obscurity, like drifts of black mist melting together into one wide vague sea of darkness that forms the horizon. Over this comes, in fitful moanings, a melancholy wind. The eye stretches vainly to define the objects that fancy sometimes suggests, and the ear is strained to discriminate the sounds, real or unreal, that seem to mingle in the uncertain distance.

If you can conjure up all this, and the superstitious freaks that in such a situation imagination will play in even the hardest and coarsest natures, you have a pretty distinct idea of the feelings and surroundings of a tall man who lay that night his length under the blighted tree I have mentioned, stretched on its roots, with his chin supported on his hands, and looking vaguely into the darkness. He had been smoking, but his pipe was out now, and he had no occupation but that of forming pictures on the dark back-ground, and listening to the moan and rush of the distant wind, and imagining sometimes a voice shouting, sometimes the drumming of a horse's hoofs approaching over the plain. There was a chill in the air that made this man now and then shiver a little, and get up and take a turn back and forward, and stamp sharply as he did so, to keep the blood stirring in his legs and feet. Then down he would lay again, with his elbows on the ground, and his hands propping his chin. Perhaps he brought his head near the ground, thinking that thus he could hear distant sounds more sharply. He was growing impatient, and well he might.

The moon now began to break through the mist in fierce red over the far horizon. A streak of crimson, that glowed without illuminating anything, showed through the distant cloud close along the level of the heath. Even this was a cheer, like a red ember or two in a pitch-dark room. Very far away he thought now he heard the tread of a horse. One can hear miles away over that level expanse of death-like silence. He pricked his ears, he raised himself on his hands, and listened with open mouth. He lost the sound, but on leaning his head again to the ground, that vast sounding-board carried its vibration once more to his ear. It was the canter of a horse upon the heath. He was doubtful whether it was approaching, for the sound subsided sometimes; but afterwards it was renewed, and gradually he became certain that it was coming nearer. And now, like a huge, red-hot dome of copper, the moon rose above the level strips of cloud that lay upon the horizon of the heath, and objects began to reveal themselves. The stunted fir, that had looked to the fancy of the solitary watcher like a ghostly policeman, with arm and truncheon raised, just starting in pursuit, now showed some lesser branches, and was more satisfactorily a tree; distances became measurable, though not yet accurately, by the eye; and ridges and hillocks caught faintly the dusky light, and threw blurred but deep shadows backward.

The tread of the horse approaching had become a gallop as the light improved, and horse and horseman were soon visible. Paul Davies stood erect, and took up a position a few steps in advance of the blighted tree at whose foot he had been stretched. The figure, seen against the dusky glare of the moon, would have answered well enough for one of those highwaymen who in old times made the heath famous. His low-crowned felt hat, his short coat with a cape to it, and the leather casings, which looked like jack-boots, gave this horseman, seen in dark outline against the glow, a character not unpicturesque. With a sudden strain of the bridle, the gaunt rider pulled up before the man who awaited him.

"What are you doing there?" said the horseman roughly.

"Counting the stars," answered he.

Thus the signs and countersigns were exchanged, and the stranger said—

"You're alone, Paul Davies, I take it."

"No company but ourselves, mate," answered Davies.

"You're up to half a dozen dodges, Paul, and knows how to lime a twig; that's your little game, you know. This here tree is clean enough, but that 'ere has a hatful o' leaves on it."

"I didn't put them there," said Paul, a little sulkily.

"Well, no. I do suppose a sight o' you wouldn't exactly put a tree in leaf, or a rose-bush in blossom; nor even make wegitables grow. More like to blast 'em, like that rum un over your head."

"What's up?" asked the ex-detective.

"Jest this—there's leaves enough for a bird to roost there, so this won't do. Now, then, move on you with me."

As the gaunt rider thus spoke, his long red beard was blowing this way and that in the breeze; and he turned his horse, and walked him towards that lonely tree in which, as he lay gazing on its black outline, Paul had fancied the shape of a phantom policeman.

"I don't care a cuss," said Davies. "I'm half sorry I came a leg to meet yer."

"Growlin', eh?" said the horseman.

"I wish you was as cold as me, and you'd growl a bit, maybe, yourself," said Paul. "I'm jolly cold."

"Cold, are ye?"

"Cold as a lock-up."

"Why didn't ye fetch a line o' the old author with you?" asked the rider—meaning brandy.

"I had a pipe or two."

"Who'd a-guessed we was to have a night like this in summer-time?"

"I do believe it freezes all the year round in this queer place."

"Would ye like a drop of the South-Sea mountain (gin)?" said the stranger, producing a flask from his pocket, which Paul Davies took with a great deal of good-will, much to the donor's content, for he wished to find that gentleman in good-humour in the conversation that was to follow.

"Drink what's there, mate. D'ye like it?"

"It ain't to be by no means sneezed at," said Paul Davies.

The horseman looked back over his shoulder. Paul Davies remarked that his shoulders were round enough to amount almost to a deformity. He and his companion were now a long way from the tree whose foliage he feared might afford cover to some eavesdropper.

"This tree will answer. I suppose you like a post to clap your back to while we are palaverin'," said the rider. "Make a finish of it, Mr. Davies," he continued, as that person presented the half-emptied flask to his hand. "I'm as hot as steam, myself, and I'd rather have a smoke by-and-by."

He touched the bridle here, and the horse stood still, and the rider patted his reeking neck, as he stooped with a shake of his ears and a snort, and began to sniff the scant herbage at his feet.

"I don't mind if I have another pull," said Paul, replenishing the goblet that fitted over the bottom of the flask.

"Fill it again, and no heel-taps," said his companion.

Mr. Davies sat down, with his mug in his hand, on the ground, and his back against the tree. Had there been a donkey near, to personate the immortal Dapple, you might have fancied, in that uncertain gloom, the Knight and Squire of La Mancha overtaken by darkness, and making one of their adventurous bivouacs under the boughs of the tree.

"What you saw in the papers three days ago did give you a twist, I take it?" observed the gentleman on horseback, with a grin that made the red bristles on his upper lip curl upwards and twist like worms.

"I can't tumble to a right guess what you means," said Mr. Davies.

"Come, Paul, that won't never do. You read every line of that there inquest on the French cove at the Saloon, and you have by rote every word Mr. Longcluse said. It must be a queer turning of the tables, for a clever chap like you to have to look slippy, for fear other dogs should lag you."

"'Tain't me that 'ill be looking slippy, as you and me well knows; and it's jest because you knows it well you're here. I suppose it ain't for love of me quite?" sneered Paul Davies.

"I don't care a rush for Mr. Longcluse, no more nor I care for you; and I see he's goin' where he pleases. He made a speech in yesterday's paper, at the meetin' at the Surrey Gardens. He was canvassin' for Parliament down in Derbyshire a week ago; and he printed a letter to the electors only yesterday. He don't care two pins for you."

"A good many rows o' pins, I'm thinkin'," sneered Mr. Davies.

"Thinkin' won't make a loaf, Mr. Davies. Many a man has bin too clever, and thought himself into the block-house. You're making too fine a game, Mr. Davies; a playin' a bit too much with edged tools, and fiddlin' a bit too freely with fire. You'll burn your fingers, and cut 'em too, do ye mind? unless you be advised, and close the game where you stand to win, as I rather think you do now."

"So do I, mate," said Paul Davies, who could play at brag as well as his neighbour.

"I'm on another lay, a safer one by a long sight. My maxim is the same as yours, 'Grab all you can;' but I do it safe, d'ye see? You are in a fair way to end your days on the twister."

"Not if I knows it," said Paul Davies. "I'm afeared o' no man livin'. Who can say black's the white o' my eye? Do ye take me for a child? What do ye take me for?"

"I take you for the man that robbed and done for the French cove in the Saloon. That's the child I take ye for," answered the horseman cynically.

"You lie! You don't! You know I han't a pig of his money, and never hurt a hair of his head. You say that to rile me, jest."

"Why should I care a cuss whether you're riled or no? Do you think I want to get anything out o' yer? I knows everything as well as you do yourself. You take me for a queer gill, I'm thinking; that's not my lay. I wouldn't wait here while you'd walk round my hoss to have every secret you ever know'd."

"A queer gill, mayhap. I think I know you," said Mr. Davies, archly.

"You do, do ye? Well, come, who do you take me for?" said the stranger, turning towards him, and sitting erect in the saddle, with his hand on his thigh, to afford him the amplest view of his face and figure.

"Then I take you for Mr. Longcluse," said Paul Davies, with a wag of his head.

"For Mr. Longcluse!" echoed the horseman, with a boisterous laugh. "Well, there's a guess to tumble to! The worst guess I ever heer'd made. Did you ever see him? Why, there's not two bones in our two bodies the same length, and not two inches of our two faces alike. There's a guess for a detective! Be my soul, it's well for you it ain't him, for I think he'd a shot ye!"

The rider lifted his hand from his coat-pocket as he said this, but there was no weapon in it. Mistaking his intention, however, Paul Davies skipped behind the tree, and levelled a revolver at him.

"Down with that, you fool!" cried the horseman. "There's nothing here." And he gave his horse the spur, and made him plunge to a little distance, as he held up his right hand. "But I'm not such a fool as to meet a cove like you without the lead towels, too, in case you should try that dodge." And dipping his hand swiftly into his pocket again, he also showed in the air the glimmering barrels of a pistol. "If you must be pullin' out your barkers every minute, and can't talk like a man, where's the good of coming all this way to palaver with a cove. It ain't not tuppence to me. Crack away if you likes it, and see who shoots best; or, if you likes it better, I don't mind if I get down and try who can hit hardest t'other way, and you'll find my fist tastes very strong of the hammer."

"I thought you were up for mischief," said Davies, "and I won't be polished off simple, that's all. It's best to keep as we are, and no nearer; we can hear one another well enough where we stand."

"It's a bargain," said the stranger, "and I don't care a cuss who you take me for. I'm not Mr. Longcluse; but you're welcome, if it pleases you, to give me his name, and I wish I could have the old bloke's tin as easy. Now here's my little game, and I don't find it a bad one. When two gentlemen—we'll say, for instance, you and Mr. Longcluse—differs in opinion (you says he did a certain thing, and he says he didn't, or goes the whole hog and says you did it, and not him), it's plain, if the matter is to be settled amigable, it's best to have a man as knows what he's about, and can find out the cove as threatens the rich fellow, and deal with him handsome, according to circumstances. My terms is moderate. I takes five shillins in the pound, and not a pig under; and that puts you and I in the same boat, d'ye see? Well, I gets all I can out of him, and no harm can happen me, for I'm but a cove a-carryin' of messages betwixt you, and the more I gets for you the better for me. I settled many a business amigable the last five years that would never have bin settled without me. I'm well knowing to some of the swellest lawyers in town, and whenevbr they has a dilikite case, like a gentleman threatened with informations or the like, they sends for me, and I arranges it amigable, to the satisfacshing of both parties. It's the only way to settle sich affairs with good profit and no risk. I have spoke to Mr. Longcluse. He was all for having your four bones in the blockhouse, and yourself on the twister; and he's not a cove to be bilked out of his tin. But he would not like the bother of your cross-charge, either, and I think I could make all square between ye. What do you say?"

"How can I tell that you ever set eyes on Mr. Longcluse?" said Davies, more satisfied as the conference proceeded that he had misdirected his first guess at the identity of the horseman. "How can I tell you're not just a-gettin' all you can out o' me, to make what you can of it on your own account in that market?"

"That's true, you can't tell, mate."

"And what do I know about you? What's your name?" pursued Paul Davies.

"I forgot my name, I left it at home in the cupboard; and you know nothing about me, that's true, excepting what I told you, and you'll hear no more."

"I'm too old a bird for that; you're a born genius, only spoilt in the baking. I'm thinking, mate, I may as well paddle my own canoe, and sell my own secret on my own account. What can you do for me that I can't do as well for myself?"

"You don't think that, Paul. You dare not show to Mr. Longcluse, and you know he's in a wax; and who can you send to him? You'll make nothing o' that brag. Where's the good of talking like a blast to a chap like me? Don't you suppose I take all that at its vally? I tell you what, if it ain't settled now, you'll see me no more, for I'll not undertake it." He pulled up his horse's head, preparatory to starting.

"Well, what's up now?—what's the hurry?" demanded Mr. Davies.

"Why, if this here meetin' won't lead to business, the sooner we two parts and gets home again, the less time wasted," answered the cavalier, with his hand on the crupper of the saddle, as he turned to speak.

Each seemed to wait for the other to add something.

CHAPTER XVII.

MR. LONGCLUSE AT MORTLAKE HALL.

"If you let me go this time, Mr. Wheeler, you'll not catch me a-walking out here again," said Mr. Davies sourly. "If there's business to be done, now's the time."

"Well, I can't make it no plainer—'tis as clear as mud in a wine-glass," said the mounted man gaily, and again he shook the bridle and hitched himself in the saddle, and the horse stirred uneasily, as he added, "Have you any more to say?"

"Well, supposin' I say ay, how soon will it be settled?" said Paul Davies, beginning to think better of it.

"These things doesn't take long with a rich cove like Mr. Longcluse. It's where they has to scrape it up, by beggin' here and borrowin' there, and sellin' this and spoutin' that—there's a wait always. But a chap with no end o' tin—that has only to wish and have—that's your sort. He swears a bit, and threatens, and stamps, and loses his temper summat, ye see; and if I was the prencipal, like you are in this 'ere case, and the police convenient, or a poker in his fist, he might make a row. But seein' I'm only a messenger like, it don't come to nothin'. He claps his hand in his pocket, and outs with the rino, and there's all; and jest a bit of paper to sign. But I won't stay here no longer. I'm getting a bit cold myself; so it's on or off now. Go yourself to Longcluse, if you like, and see if you don't catch it. The least you get will be seven-penn'orth, for extortin' money by threatenin' a prosecution, if he don't hang you for the murder of the Saloon cove. How would you like that?"

"It ain't the physic that suits my complaint, guvnor. But I have him there. I have the statement wrote, in sure hands, and other hevidence, as he may suppose, and dated, and signed by respectable people; and I know his dodge. He thinks he came out first with his charge against me, but he's out there; and if he will have it, and I split, he'd best look slippy."

"And how much do you want? Mind, I'll funk him all I can, though he's a wideawake chap; for it's my game to get every pig I can out of him."

"I'll take two thousand pounds, and go to Canada or to New York, my passage and expenses being paid, and sign anything in reason he wants; and that's the shortest chalk I'll offer."

"Don't you wish you may get it? I do, I know, but I'm thinking you might jest as well look for the naytional debt."

"What's your name?" again asked Davies, a little abruptly.

"My name fell out o' window and was broke, last Tuesday mornin'. But call me Tom Wheeler, if you can't talk without calling me something."

"Well, Tom, that's the figure," said Davies.

"If you want to deal, speak now," said Wheeler. "If I'm to stand between you, I must have a power to close on the best offer I'm like to get. I won't do nothing in the matter else-ways."

With this fresh exhortation, the conference on details proceeded; and when at last it closed, with something like a definite understanding, Tom Wheeler said,—"Mind, Paul Davies, I comes from no one, and I goes to no one; and I never seed you in all my days."

"And where are you going?"

"A bit nearer the moon," said the mysterious Mr. Wheeler, lifting his hand and pointing towards the red disk, with one of his bearded grins. And wheeling his horse suddenly, away he rode at a canter, right toward the red moon, against which for a few moments the figure of the retreating horse and man showed black and sharp, as if cut out of cardboard.

Paul Davies looked after him with his left eye screwed close, as was his custom, in shrewd rumination. Before the horseman had got very far, the moon passed under the edge of a thick cloud, and the waste was once more enveloped in total darkness. In this absolute obscurity the retreating figure was instantaneously swallowed, so that the shrewd ex-detective, who had learned by rote every article of his dress, and every button on it, and could have sworn to every mark on his horse at York Fair, had no chance of discovering in the ultimate line of his retreat, any clue to his destination. He had simply emerged from darkness, and darkness had swallowed him again.

We must now see how Sir Reginald's little dinner-party, not a score of miles away, went off only two days later. He was fortunate, seeing he had bidden his guests upon very short notice, not one disappointed.

I daresay that Lady May—whose toilet, considering how quiet everything was, had been made elaborately—missed a face that would have brightened all the rooms for her. But the interview between Richard Arden and his father had not, as we know, ended in reconciliation, and Lady May's hopes were disappointed, and her toilet labour in vain.

When Lady May entered the room with Alice, she saw standing on the hearth-rug, at the far end of the handsome room, a tall and very good-looking man of sixty or upwards, chatting with Sir Reginald, one of whose feet was in a slipper, and who was sitting in an easy-chair. A little bit of fire burned in the grate, for the day had been chill and showery. This tall man, with white silken hair, and a countenance kind, frank, and thoughtful, with a little sadness in it, was, she had no doubt, David Arden, whom she had last seen with silken brown locks, and the cheerful aspect of early manhood.

Sir Reginald stood up, with an uncomfortable effort, and, smiling, pointed to his slippers in excuse for his limping gait, as he shuffled forth across the carpet to meet her, with a good-humoured shrug.

"Wasn't it good of her to come?" said Alice.

"She's better than good," said Sir Reginald, with his thin, yellow smile, extending his hand, and leading her to a chair; "it is visiting the sick and the halt, and doing real good, for it is a pleasure to see her—a pleasure bestowed on a miserable soul who has very few pleasures left;" and with his other thin hand he patted gently the fingers of her fat hand. "Here is my brother David," continued the baronet. "He says you will hardly know him."

"She'll hardly believe it. She was very young when she last saw me, and the last ten years have made some changes," said Uncle David, laughing gently.

At the baronet's allusion to that most difficult subject, the lapse of time, Lady May winced and simpered uneasily; but she expanded gratefully as David Arden disposed of it so adroitly.

"We'll not speak of years of change. I knew you instantly," said Lady May happily. "And you have been to Vichy, Reginald. What stay do you make here?"

"None, almost; my crippled foot keeps me always on a journey. It seems a paradox, but so it is. I'm ordered to visit Buxton for a week or so, and then I go, for change of air, to Yorkshire."

As Alice entered, she saw the pretty face, the original of the brilliant portrait which had haunted her on her night journey to Twyford, and she heard a very silvery voice chatting gaily. Mr. Longcluse was leaning on the end of the sofa on which Grace Maubray sat; and Vivian Darnley, it seemed in high spirits, was standing and laughing nearly before her. Alice Arden walked quickly over to welcome her handsome guest. With a misgiving and a strange pain at her heart, she saw how much more beautiful this young lady had grown. Smiling radiantly, with her hand extended, she greeted and kissed her fair kinswoman; and, after a few words, sat down for a little beside her; and asked Mr. Longcluse how he did; and finally spoke to Vivian Darnley, and then returned to her conventional dialogue of welcome and politeness with her cousin—how cousin, she could not easily have explained.

The young ladies seemed so completely taken up with one another that, after a little waiting, the gentlemen fell into a desultory talk, and grew gradually nearer to the window. They were talking now of dogs and horses, and Mr. Longcluse was stealing rapidly into the good graces of the young man.

"When we come up after dinner, you must tell me who these people are," said Grace Maubray, who did not care very much what she said. "That young man is a Mr. Vivian, ain't he?"

"No—Darnley," whispered Alice; "Vivian is his Christian name."

"Very romantic names; and, if he really means half he says, he is a very romantic person." She laughed.

"What has he been saying?" Alice wondered. But, after all, it was possible to be romantic on almost any subject.

"And the other?"

"He's a Mr. Longcluse," answered Alice.

"He's rather clever," said the young lady, with a grave decision that amused Alice.

"Do you think so? Well, so do I; that is, I know he can interest one. He has been almost everywhere, and he tells things rather pleasantly."

Before they could go any further, Vivian Darnley, turning from the window toward the two young ladies, said—"I've just been saying that we must try to persuade Lady May to get up that party to the Derby."

"I can place a drag at her disposal," said Mr. Longcluse.

"And a splendid team—I saw them," threw in Darnley.

"There's nothing I should like so much," said Alice. "I've never been to the Derby. What do you say, Grace? Can you manage Uncle David?"

"I'll try," said the young lady gaily.

"We must all set upon Lady May," said Alice. "She is so good-natured, she can't resist us."

"Suppose we begin now?" suggested Darnley.

"Hadn't we better wait till we have her quite to ourselves? Who knows what your papa and your uncle might say?" said Grace Maubray, turning to Alice. "I vote for saying nothing to them until Lady May has settled, and then they must only submit."

"I agree with you quite," said Alice laughing.

"Sage advice!" said Mr. Longcluse, with a smile; "and there's time enough to choose a favourable moment. It comes off exactly ten days from this."

"Oh, anything might be done in ten days," said Grace. "I'm sorry it is so far away."

"Yes, a great deal might be done in ten days; and a great deal might happen in ten days," said Longcluse, listlessly looking down at the floor—"a great deal might happen."

He thought he saw Miss Arden's eye turned upon him, curiously and quickly, as he uttered this common-place speech, which was yet a little odd.

"In this busy world, Miss Arden, there is no such thing as quiet, and no one acts without imposing on other people the necessity for action," said Mr. Longcluse; "and I believe that often the greatest changes in life are the least anticipated by those who seem to bring them about spontaneously."

At this moment, dinner being announced, the little party transferred itself to the dining-room, and Miss Arden found herself between Mr. Longcluse and Uncle David.

CHAPTER XVIII.

THE PARTY IN THE DINING-ROOM.

And now, all being seated, began the talk and business of dinner.

"I believe," said Mr. Longcluse, with a laugh, "I am growing metaphysical."

"Well, shall I confess, Mr. Longcluse, you do sometimes say things that are, I fear, a little too wise for my poor comprehension?"

"I don't express them; it is my fault," he answered, in a very low tone. "You have mind, Miss Arden, for anything. There is no one it is so delightful to converse with, owing in part to that very faculty—I mean quick apprehension. But I know my own defects. I know how imperfectly I often express myself. By-the-way, you seemed to wish to have that curious little wild Bohemian air I sang the other night, 'The Wanderer's Bride'—the song about the white lily, you know. I ventured to get a friend, who really is a very good musician, to make a setting of it, which I so very much hope you will like. I brought it with me. You will think me very presumptuous, but I hoped so much you might be tempted to try it."

When Mr. Longcluse spoke to Alice, it was always in a tone so very deferential, that it was next to impossible that a very young girl should not be flattered by it—considering, especially, that the man was reputed clever, had seen the world, and had met with a certain success, and that by no means of a kind often obtained, or ever quite despised. There was also a directness in his eulogy which was unusual, and which spoken with a different manner would have been embarrassing, if not offensive. But in Mr. Longcluse's manner, when he spoke such phrases, there appeared a real humility, and even sadness, that the boldness of the sentiment was lost in the sincerity and dejection of the speaker, which seemed to place him on a sudden at the immeasurable distance of a melancholy worship.

"I am so much obliged!" said Alice. "I did wish so much to have it when you sang it. It may not do for my voice at all, but I longed to try it. When a song is sung so as to move one, it is sure to be looked out and learned, without any thought wasted on voice, or skill, or natural fitness. It is, I suppose, like the vanity that makes one person dress after another. Still, I do wish to sing that song, and I am so much obliged!"

From the other side her uncle said very softly—"What do you think of my ward, Grace Maubray?"

"Oughtn't I to ask, rather, what you think of her?" she laughed archly.

"Oh! I see," he answered, with a pleasant and honest smile; "you have the gift of seeing as far as other clever people into a millstone. But, no—though perhaps I ought to thank you for giving me credit for so much romance and good taste—I don't think I shall ever introduce you to an aunt. You must guess again, if you will have a matrimonial explanation; though I don't say there is any such design. And perhaps, if there were, the best way to promote it would be to leave the intended hero and heroine very much to themselves. They are both very good-looking."

"Who?" asked Alice, although she knew very well whom he meant.

"I mean that pretty creature over there, Grace Maubray, and Vivian Darnley," said he quietly.

She smiled, looking very much pleased and very arch.

With how Spartan a completeness women can hide the shootings and quiverings of mental pain, and of bodily pain too, when the motive is sufficient! Under this latter they are often clamorous, to be sure; but the demonstration expresses not want of patience, but the feminine yearning for compassion.

"I fancy nothing would please the young rogue Vivian better. I wish I were half so sure of her. You girls are so unaccountable, so fanciful, and—don't be angry—so uncertain."

"Well, I suppose, as you say, we must only have patience, and leave the matter in the hands of Time, who settles most things pretty well."

She raised her eyes, and fancied she saw Grace Maubray at the same moment withdraw hers from her face. Lady May was talking from the end of the table with Mr. Longcluse.

"Your neighbour who is talking to Lady May is a Mr. Longcluse?"

"Yes."

"He is a City notability; but oddly, I never happened to see him till this evening. Do you think there is something curious in his appearance?"

"Yes, a little, perhaps. Don't you?"

"So odd that he makes my blood run cold," said Uncle David, with a shrug and a little laugh. "Seriously, I mean unpleasantly odd. What is Lady May talking about? Yes—I thought so—that horrid murder at the 'Saloon Tavern.' For so good-natured a person, she has the most bloodthirsty tastes I know of; she's always deep in some horror."

"My brother Dick told me that Mr. Longcluse made a speech there."

"Yes, so I heard; and I think he said what is true enough. London is growing more and more insecure; and that certainly was a most audacious murder. People make money a little faster, that is true; but what is the good of money, if their lives are not their own? It is quite true that there are streets in London, which I remember as safe as this room, through which no one suspected of having five pounds in his pocket could now walk without a likelihood of being garotted."

"How dreadful!" said Alice, and Uncle David laughed a little at her horror.

"It is too true, my dear. But, to pass to pleasanter subjects, when do you mean to choose among the young fellows, and present me to a new nephew?" said Uncle David.

"Do you fancy I would tell anyone if I knew?" she answered, laughing. "How is it that you men, who are always accusing us weak women of thinking of nothing else, can never get the subject of matrimony out of your heads? Now, uncle, as you and I may talk confidentially, and at our ease, I'll tell you two things. I like my present spinster life very well—I should like it better, I think, if it were in the country; but town or country, I don't think I should ever like a married life. I don't think I'm fit for command."

"Command! I thought the prayer-book said something about obeying, on the contrary," said Uncle David.

"You know what I mean. I'm not fit to rule a household; and I am afraid I am a little idle, and I should not like to have it to do—and so I could never do it well."

"Nevertheless, when the right man comes, he need but beckon with his finger, and away you go, Miss Alice, and undertake it all."

"So we are whistled away, like poodles for a walk, and that kind of thing! Well, I suppose, uncle, you are right, though I can't see that I'm quite so docile a creature. But if my poor sex is so willing to be won, I don't know how you are to excuse your solitary state, considering how very little trouble it would have taken to make some poor creature happy."

"A very fair retort!" laughed Uncle David. And he added, in a changed tone, for a sudden recollection of his own early fortunes crossed him—"But even when the right man does come, it does not always follow, Miss Alice, that he dares make the sign; fate often interposes years, and in them death may come, and so the whole card-castle falls."

"I've had a long talk," he resumed, "with Richard; he has made me promises, and I hope he will be a better boy for the future. He has been getting himself into money troubles, and acquiring—I'm afraid I should say cultivating—a taste for play. I know you have heard something of this before; I told you myself. But he has made me promises, and I hope, for your sake, he'll keep them; because, you know, I and your father can't last for ever, and he ought to take care of you; and how can he do that, if he's not fit to take care of himself? But I believe there is no use in thinking too much about what is to come. One has enough to do in the present. I think poor Lady May has been disappointed," he said, with a very cautious smile, his eye having glanced for a moment on her; "she looks a little forlorn, I think."

"Does she? And why?"

"Well, they say she would not object to be a little more nearly related to you than she is."

"You can't mean papa—or yourself!"

"Oh, dear, no!" he answered, laughing. "I mean that she misses Dick a good deal."

"Oh, dear! uncle, you can't be serious!"

"It might be a very serious affair for her; but I don't know that he could do a wiser thing. The old quarrel is still raging, he tells me, and that he can't appear in this house."

"It is a great pity," said she.

"Pity! Not at all. They never could agree; and it is much better for Dick they should not—on the terms Reginald proposes, at least. I see Lady May trying to induce you to make her the sign at which ladies rise, and leave us poor fellows to shift for ourselves."

"Ungallant old man! I really believe she is."

And in a moment more the ladies were floating from the room, Vivian Darnley standing at the door. Somehow he could not catch Alice's eye as they passed; she was smiling an answer to some gabble of Lady May's. Grace gave him a very kind look with her fine eyes as she went by; and so the young man, who had followed them up the massive stairs with his gaze, closed the door and sat down again, before his claret glass, and his little broken cluster of grapes, and half-dozen distracted bits of candied fruit, and sighed deeply.

"That murder in the City that you were speaking of just now to Lady May is a serious business for men who walk the streets, as I do sometimes, with money in their pockets," said David Arden, addressing Mr. Longcluse.

"So it struck me—one feels that instinctively. When I saw that poor little good-natured fellow dead, and thought how easily I might have walked in there myself, with the assassin behind me, it seemed to me simply the turn of a die that the lot had not fallen upon me," said Longcluse.

"He was robbed, too, wasn't he?" croaked Sir Reginald, who was growing tired; and with his fatigue came evidences of his temper.

"Oh, yes," said David; "nothing left in his pockets."

"And Laroque, a watchmaker, a relation of his, said he had cheques about him, and foreign money," said Longcluse; "but, of course, the cheques were not presented, and foreign money is not easily traced in a big town like London. I made him a present of ten pounds to stake on the game; I could not learn that he did stake it, and I suppose the poor fellow intended applying it in some more prudent way. But my present was in gold, and that, of course, the robber applied without apprehension."

"Now, you fellows who have a stake in the City, it is a scandal your permitting such a state of things to continue," said Sir Reginald; "because, though your philanthropy may not be very diffuse, each of you cares most tenderly for one individual at least in the human race—I mean self—and whatever you may think of personal morality, and even life—for you don't seem to me to think a great deal of grinding operatives in the cranks of your mills, or blowing them up by bursting steam-boilers, to say nothing of all the people you poison with adulterated food, or with strychnine in beer, or with arsenic in candles, or pretty green papers for bed-rooms—or smash or burn alive on railways—yet you should, on selfish grounds, set your faces against a system of assassination for pocket-books and purses, the sort of things precisely you have always about you. Don't you see?

And it's inconsistent besides, because, as I said, although you care little for life—other people's, I mean—in the abstract, yet you care a great deal for property. I think it's your idol, by Jove! and worshipping money—positively worshipping it, as you do, it seems a scandalous inconsistency that you should—of course, I don't mean you two individually," he said, perhaps recollecting that he might be going a little too fast; "you never, of course, fancied that. I mean, of course, the class of men we have all heard of, or seen—but I do say, with that sort of adoration for money and property, I can't understand their allowing their pockets to be profaned and their purses made away with."

Sir Reginald, having thus delivered himself with considerable asperity, poured some claret into his glass, and pushed the jugs on to his brother, and then, closing his eyes, composed himself either to listen or to sleep.

"City or country, East End or West End, I fancy we are all equally anxious to keep other people's hands out of our pockets," said David Arden; "and I quite agree with Mr. Longcluse in all he is reported to have said with respect to our police system."

"But is it so certain that the man was robbed?" said Vivian Darnley.

"Everything he had about him was taken," said Mr. Longcluse.

"But they pretend to rob men sometimes, when they murder them, only to conceal the real motive," persisted Vivian Darnley.

"Yes, that's quite true; but then there must be some motive," said Mr. Longcluse, with something a little supercilious in his smile: "and it isn't easy to conceive a motive for murdering a poor little good-natured letter of lodgings, a person past the time of life when jealousy could have anything to do with it, and a most inoffensive and civil creature. I confess, if I were obliged to seek a motive other than the obvious one, for the crime, I should be utterly puzzled."

"When I was travelling in Prussia," said Vivian Darnley, "I saw two people in different prisons—one a woman, the other a middle-aged man—both for murder. They had been found guilty, and had been kept there only to get a confession from them before execution. They won't put culprits to death there, you know, unless they have first admitted their guilt; and one of these had actually confessed. Well, each had borne an unexceptionable character up to the time when suspicion was accidentally aroused, and then it turned out that they had been poisoning and otherwise making away with people, at the rate of two or three a year, for half their lives. Now, don't you see, these masked assassins, having, as it appeared, absolutely no intelligible motive, either of passion or of interest, to commit these murders, could have had no inducement, as the woman had actually confessed, except a sort of lust of murder. I suppose it is a sort of madness, but these people were not otherwise mad; and it is quite possible that the same sort of thing may be going on in other places. People say that the police would have got a clue to the mystery by means of the foreign coin and the bank-notes, if they had not been destroyed."

"But there are traces of organisation," said Mr. Longcluse. "In a crowded place like that, such things could hardly be managed without it, and insanity such as you describe is very rare; and you'll hardly get people to believe in a swell-mob of madmen, committing murder in concert simply for the pleasure of homicide. They will all lean to a belief in the coarse but intelligible motive of the highwayman."

"I saw in the newspapers," said David Arden, "some evidence of yours, Mr. Longcluse, which seemed rather to indicate a particular man as the murderer."

"I have my eye upon him," said Longcluse. "There are suspicious circumstances. The case in a little time may begin to clear; at present the police are only groping."

"That's satisfactory; and those fellows are paid so handsomely for groping," said Sir Reginald, opening his eyes suddenly. "I believe that we are the worst-governed and the worst-managed people on earth, and that our merchants and tradespeople are rich simply by flukes—simply by a concurrence of lucky circumstances, with which they have no more to do than Prester John or the Man in the Moon. Take a little claret, Mr. Longcluse, and send it on."

"No more, thanks."

And all the guests being of the same mind, they marched up the broad stairs to the ladies.

CHAPTER XIX.

IN MRS. TANSEY'S ROOM.

There were sounds of music and laughter faintly audible through the drawing-room door. The music ceased as the door opened, and the gentlemen entered an atmosphere of brilliant light, and fragrant with the pleasant aroma of tea.

"Pray, Miss Arden, don't let us interrupt you," said Mr. Longcluse. "I thought I heard singing as we came up the stairs." He had come to the piano, and was now at her side.

She did not sing or play, but Vivian Darnley thought that her conversation with Longcluse, as, with one knee on his chair, he leaned over the back of it and talked, seemed more interesting than usual.

"I say, Reginald," said David Arden softly to his brother, "I must run down and pay Martha Tansey my usual visit. She's in her room, I suppose. I'll steal away and return quietly."

And so he was gone. He closed the door softly behind him, and slowly descended the wide staircase, with many vague conjectures and images revolving in his mind. He paused at the great window on the landing, and looked out upon the solemn and familiar landscape. A brilliant moon was high in the sky, and the stars glimmered brightly. His hand was on the window as he looked out, thinking.

Uncle David was a man impulsive, prompt, sanguine—a temperament, in short, which, directed by an able intellect, would have made a good general. When an idea had got into his head, he could not rest until he had worked it out. On the whole, throughout his life these fits of sudden and feverish concentration had been effective, and aided his fortunes. It is, perhaps, an unbusiness-like temperament; but commercial habits and example had failed to control that natural ardour, and, when once inflamed, it governed his actions implicitly.

An idea, very vague, very little the product of reason, had now taken possession of his brain, and he relied upon it as an intuition. He had been thinking over it. It first warmed, then simmered, then, as it were, boiled. The process had been one of an hour and more, as he sat at his brother's table and took his share in the conversation. When the steam got up and the pressure rose to the point of action, forth went Uncle David to have his talk with his early friend Tansey. He stopped, as I have said, at the great window on the staircase, and looked out and up. The moon was splendid; the stars were glimmering brightly; they looked down like a thousand eyes set upon him, to watch the prowess and perseverance of the man on whom fate had imposed a mission.

Some idea like this seized him, for, like many men of a similar temperament, he had an odd and unconfessed vein of poetry in his nature. He had looked out and up in a listless abstraction, and the dark heaven above him, brilliant with its eternal lights, had for a moment withdrawn and elevated his thoughts as if he had entered a cathedral.

"What specks and shadows we are, and how eternal is duty! And if we are in another place to last like those unfailing lights—to become happy or wretched, and, in either state, indestructible for ever—what signify the labour and troubles of life, compared with that by which our everlasting fate is fixed? God help us! Am I consulting revenge or conscience in pursuing this barren inquiry? Do I mistake for the sublime impulse of conscience a vulgar thirst for blood? I think not. I never harboured malice; I hate punishing people. But murder is a crime against God himself, respecting which he imposes duties upon man, and seconds them by all the instincts of affection. Dare I neglect them, then, in the case of poor loving Harry, my brother?"

The drawing-room door had been opened a little, the night being sultry, and through it now came the clear tones of a well-taught baritone. It was singing a slow and impassioned air, and its tones, though sweet, chilled him with a strange pain. It seemed like instinct that told him it was the stranger's voice. One moment's thought would have proved it equally. There was no one else present to suspect but Vivian Darnley, and he was no musician; but to David Arden it seemed that if a hundred people were there he should have felt it all the same, and intuitively recognised it as Longcluse's voice.

"What is it in that voice which is so hateful? What is it in that passion which sounds insincere? What gives to those sweet tones a latent discord, that creeps so coldly through my nerves?"

So thought David Arden, as, with one hand still upon the window-sash, he listened and turned toward the open door, with a frown akin to one of pain.

Spell-bound, he listened till the song was over, and sighed and shook his ears with a sort of shudder when the music ceased.

"I don't know why I stayed to listen. Face—voice—what is the agency about that fellow? I daresay I'm a fool, but I can't help it, and I must bring the idea to the test."

He descended the stairs slowly, crossed the hall, and walked thoughtfully down the passage leading to the housekeeper's room. At this hour the old woman had it usually to herself. He knocked at the housekeeper's door, and recognised the familiar voice that answered.

"How do you do, Martha?" said he, striding cheerily into the room.

"Ah! Master David? So it is, sure!"

"Ay, sure and sure, Martha," said he, taking the old woman's hand, with his kind smile. "And how are you, Martha? Tell me how you are."

"I won't say much. I'm not so canty as you'll mind me. I'm an old wife now, Master David, and not much for this world, I'm thinking," she answered dolorously.

"You may outlive much younger people, Martha; we are all in the hands of God," said David, smiling. "It seems to me but yesterday that I and poor Harry used to run in here to you from our play in the grounds, and you had always a bit of something for us hungry fellows to eat, come when we might."

"Ah, ha! Yes, ye were hungry fellows then—spirin' up, fine tall lads. Reginald was never like ye; he was seven years older than you. And hungry? Yes! The cold turkey and ham, ye mind—by Jen! I have seen ye eat hearty; and pancakes—ye liked them best of all. And it went a' into a good skin. I will say—you and Master Harry (God be wi' him!) a fine, handsome pair o' lads ye were. And you're a handsome fellow still, Master David, and might have married well, no doubt; but man proposes and God disposes, and time and tide 'll wait for no man, and what's one man's meat's another man's poison. Who knows and all may be for the best? And that Mr. Longcluse is dining here to-day?" she added, not very coherently, and with a sudden gloom.

"Yes, Martha, that Mr. Longcluse is dining here to-day; and Master Dick tells me you did not fall in love with him at first sight, when they paid you a visit here. Is that true?"

"I don't know. I don't know what. The sight of him—or the sound of his voice, I don't know which—gave me a turn," said the old woman.

"Well, Martha, I don't like his face, either. He gave me, also, what you call a turn. He's very pale, and I felt as if I had been frightened by him when I was a child; and yet he must be some five and twenty years younger than I am, and I'm almost certain I never saw him before. So I say it must be something that's no' canny as you used to say. What do you think, Martha?"

"Ye may be funnin', Master David. Ye were always a canty lad. But it's o'er true. I can't bring to mind what it is—I can't tell—but something in that man's face gev me a sten. I conceited I was just goin' to swound; and he looked sa straight at me, like a ghost."

"Master Richard says you looked very hard at Mr. Longcluse; you had both a good stare at each other," said Uncle David. "He thought there was going to be a recognition."

"Did I? Well, no: I don't know him, I think. 'Tis all a jummlement, like. I couldn't bring nout to mind."

"I know, Martha, you liked poor Harry well," said David Arden, not with a smile, but with a very sad countenance.

"That I did," said Mrs. Tansey.

"And I think you like me, Martha?"

"Ye're not far wrong there, Master David."

"And for both our sakes—for mine and his, for the dead no less than the living—I am sure you won't allow any thought of trouble, or nervousness, or fear of lawyers' browbeating, or that sort of thing, to deter you from saying, wherever and whenever justice may require it, everything you know or suspect respecting that dreadful occurrence."

"The death o' Master Harry, ye mean!" exclaimed Mrs. Tansey sternly, drawing herself up on a sudden, with a pale frown, and looking full at him. "Me to hide or hold back aught that could bring the truth to light! Oh! Master David, do you know what ye're sayin'?"

"Perfectly," said he, with a melancholy smile; "and I am glad it vexes you, Martha, because I need no answer on that point more than your honest voice and face."

"Keep back aught, man!" she repeated, striking her hand on the table. "Why, lad, I'd lose that old hand under the chopper for one gliff o' the truth into that damned story. Why, lawk! where's yer head, boy? Wasn't I maist killed myself, for sake o' him that night?"

"Ay, Martha, brave girl, I'm satisfied; and I ask your pardon for the question. But years bring alteration, you know; and I'm changed in mind myself in many ways I never could have believed. And everyone doesn't see with me that it is our duty to explore a crime like that, to track the villain, if we can, and bring him to justice. You do, Martha; but there are many in whose veins poor Harry's blood is running, who don't feel like you. Master Richard said that the gentleman looked as if he did not know what to make of you; 'and, by Jove!' said he, 'I didn't either—Martha stared so.'"

"I couldn't help. 'Twas scarce civil; but truly I couldn't, Sir," said Martha Tansey, who had by this time recovered her equanimity. "He did remind me of summat."

"We will talk of that by-and-by, Martha; we will try to recall it. What I want you first to tell me is exactly your recollection of the lamentable occurrence of that night. I have a full note of it at home; but I have not looked at it for years, and I want my recollection confirmed to-night, that you and I may talk over some possibilities which I should like to examine with your help."

"I can talk of it now," said the old woman; "but for many a year after it happened I dare not. I could not sleep for many a night after I told it to anyone. But now I can bear it. So, Master David, you may ask what you please."

"First let me hear your recollection of what happened," said David Arden.

"Ay, Master David, that I will. Sit ye down, for my old bones won't carry me standing no time now, and sit I must. Right well ye're lookin', and right glad am I to see it, Master David; and ye were always a handsome laddie. God bless ye, and God be wi' the old times! And poor Master Harry—poor laddie!—I liked him well. You two looked beautiful, walkin' up to t' house together—two conny, handsome boys ye were."

CHAPTER XX.

MRS. TANSEY'S STORY.

"The sun don't touch these windows till nigh nightfall. In the short days o' winter, the last sunbeam at the settin' just glints along the wall, and touches a sprig or two o' them scarlet geraniums on the windastone. 'Tis a cold room, Master David. In summer evenins, like this, ye have just a chilly flush o' the sun settin', and, before it's well on the windas, the bats and beetles is abroad, and the moth is flittin', and the gloamin' fa's," said the old woman. "The windas looks to the west, but also a bit to the north, ye'll mind, and that's the cause o't. I don't complain. I ha' suffered it these thirty years and more, and 'tain't worth while, for the few years that's left, makin' a blub and a blither about it. I'm an old wife now, Master David, and there can't be many more years for me left aboon the grass, sa I e'en let be and taks the world easy, ye see; and that's the reason I aye keep a bit o' wood burnin' on the hearth—it keeps the life in my old bones—and I hope it ain't too warm for you, Master David?"

"Not a bit, Martha. This side of the house is cool. I remember that our room, when we were boys, looked out from it, high up, you recollect, and it never was hot."

"That's it, ye were in the top o' the house; and poor Harry, wi' his picturs o' horses and dogs hangin' up on the wa's. Lawk! it seems but last week. How the years flits! I often thinks of him. See what a moon there is to-night. 'Twas just such a moon that night, only frostier, ye see—the same clear sky and bright moon; 'twould make ye wink to look at. Ye're not too hot wi' that bit o' wood lightin' in the grate?"

"I like the fire, Martha, and I like the moon, and I like your company best of all."

The truth was, he did like the flicker of the wood fire. The flame was cheery, and took off something of the dismal shadow that stole over everything whenever he applied his affectionate mind to the horrors of the dreadful night on which he was now ruminating. One of the window-shutters was open, and the chill brilliancy of the moon, and the deep blue sky, were serenely visible over the black foreground of trees. The wavering of the redder light of the fire, as its reflection spread and faded upon the wainscot, was warm and pleasant; and, had their talk been of less ghastly things, would have brightened their thoughts with a sense of comfort.

"I have not very long to stay, Martha," said David Arden, looking at his watch, "so tell me your recollection as accurately as you can. Let me hear that first; and then I want to ask you for some particular information, which I am sure you can give me."

"Why not? Who should I give it sooner to? Will ye take a cup o' coffee? No. Well, a glass o' curaçoa? No. And what will ye take?"

"You forget that I have taken everything, and come to you with all my wants supplied. So now, dear Martha, let me hear it all."

"I'll tell ye all about it. I was younger and stronger, mind, than I am now, by twenty years and more. 'Tis a short time to look back on, but a good while passing, and leaves many a gap and change, and many a scar and wrinkle."

There was a palpable tremble always in Mrs. Tansey's voice, in the thin hand she extended towards him, and in the head from which her old eyes glittered glassily on him.

"The road is very lonely by night—the loneliest road in all England. When it passes ten o'clock, you might listen till cock-crow for a footfall. Well, I, and Thomas Ridley, and Anne Haslett, was all the people at Mortlake just then, the family being in the North, except Master Harry. He went to a race across country, that was run that day; and he told me, laughing, he would not ask me to throw an old shoe after him, as he stood sure to win two thousand pounds. And away he went, little thinking, him and me, how our next meetin' would be. At that time old Tom Clinton—ye'll mind Clinton?"

"To be sure I do," acquiesced David Arden.

"Well, Tom was in the gatehouse then; after he died, his daughter's husband got it, ye know. And when he had outstayed his time by two hours—for he was going northwards in the morning, and told me he'd be surely back before ten—I began to grow frightened, and I put on my bonnet and cloak, and down I runs to the gatehouse, and knocks up Tom Clinton. It was nigh twelve o'clock then. When Tom came to the door, having dressed in haste, I said, 'Tom, which way will Master Harry return? he's not been since.' And says Tom, 'If he's comin' straight from the course, he'll come down from the country; but if he's dinin' instead in London, he'll come up the Islington way.' 'Well,' said I, 'go you, Tom, to the turn o' the road, and look and listen for sight or sound, and bring me word.' I don't know what was frightenin' me. He was often later, and I never minded; but something that night was on my mind, like a warning, for I couldn't get the fear out o' my heart. Well, who comes ridin' back but Dick Wallock, the groom, that had drove away with him in the gig in the mornin'; and glad I was to see his face at the gate. It was bright moonlight, and says I, 'Dick, how is Master Harry? Is all well with him?' So he tells me, ay, all was well, and he goin' to drive the gig out himself from town. He was at a place—you'll mind the name of it—where it turned out they played cards and dice, and won and lost like—like fools, or worse, as some o' them no doubt was. 'Well,' says I, 'go you up, as he told you, with the horse, and I'll stay here till he comes back, if it wasn't till daybreak.' For all the time, ye see, my heart misgave me that there was summat bad to happen; and when Tom Clinton came back, says I, 'Tom, you go in, and get to your room, and let me sit down in your kitchen; and I'll let him in when he comes, for I can't go up to the house, nor close an eye, till he comes.' Well, it was a full hour after, and I was sittin' in the kitchen window that looks out on the road, starin' wide awake, and lookin', now one way and now another, up and down, when I hears the clink of a footfall on the stones, and a tall, ill-favoured man walks slowly by, and turns his face toward the window as he passed."

"You saw him distinctly, then?" said David.

"As plain as ever I saw you. An ill-favoured fellow in a light drab great coat wi' a cape to it. He looked white wi' fear, and wild big eyes, and a high hooked nose—a tall chap wi' his hands in his pockets, and a low-crowned hat on. He went on slow, till a whistle sounded, and then he ran down the road a bit toward the signal."

"That was toward the Islington side?"

"Ay, Sir, and I grew more uneasy. I was scared wi' the sight o' such a man at that time o' night, in that lonesome place, and the whistlin' and runnin'."

"Did you see the same man again that night?" asked David.

"Yes, 'twas the same I saw afterwards—Lord ha' mercy on us! I saw him again, at his murderin' work. Oh, Master David! it makes my brain wild, and my skin creep, to think o' that sight."

"I did wrong to interrupt you; tell it your own way, Martha, and I can afterwards ask you the questions that lie near my heart," said Mr. Arden.

"'Tis easy told, Sir; the candle was burnt down almost in the socket, and I went to look out another—but before I could find one, it went out. 'Twas but a stump I found and lighted, after I saw that fellow in the light drab surtout go by. I wished to let them know, if they had any ill design, there was folks awake in the lodge. But he was gone by before I found the matches, and now that he was comin' again, the candle went out—things goes so cross. It was to be, ye see. Well, while I was rummagin' about, looking for a candle, I heard the sound of a horse trotting hard, and wheels rollin' along; so says I, 'Thank God!' for then I was sure it must be Harry, poor lad. So I claps on my bonnet, and out wi' me, wi' t' key. I thought I heard voices, as the hoofs and wheels came clinkin' up to the gate; but I could not be quite sure. I was huffed wi' Master Harry for the long wait he gev me, and the fright, and I took my time comin' round the corner of the gatehouse. And thinks I to myself, he'll be offerin' me a seat in the gig up to the house, but I won't take it. God forgi'e me for them angry thoughts to the poor laddie that I was never to have a word wi' more! When I came to the gate there was never a call, and nothing but voices talking and gaspin' like, under their breath a'most, and a queer scufflin' sound, that I could not make head nor tail on. So I unlocked the wicket, and out wi' me, and, Lord ha' mercy on us, what a sight for me! The gig was there, with its shafts on the ground, and its back cocked up, and the iron-grey flat on his side, lashin' and scramblin', poor brute, and two villains in the gig, both pullin' at poor Master Harry, one robbin', and t'other murderin' him. I took one o' them—a short, thick fellow—by the skirt o' his coat, to drag him out, and I screamed for Tom Clinton to come out. The short fellow turned, and struck at me wi' somethin'; but, lucky for me, 'appen, the lashin' horse that minute took me on the foot, and brought me down. But up I scrambles wi' a stone in my hand, and I shied it, the best I could, at the head o' the villain that was killin' Master Harry. But what can a woman do? It did not go nigh him, I'm thinkin'. I was, all the time, calling on Tom to come, and cryin' 'Murder!' that you'd think my throat'd split. That bloody wretch in the gig had got poor Master Harry's head back over the edge of it, and his knee to his chest, a-strivin' to break his neck across the back-rails; and poor dear lad, Master Harry, he just scritched, 'Yelland Mace! for God's sake!' They were the last words I ever heard from him, and I'll never forget that horrid scritch, nor the face of the villain that was over him, like a beast over its prey. He was tuggin' at his throat, like you'd be tryin' to tear up a tree by the roots—you never see such a face. His teeth was set, and the froth comin' through, and his black eyebrows screwed together, you'd think they'd crack the thin hooked nose of him between them, and he pantin' like a wild beast. He looked like a madman, I tell you; 'twas bright moonlight, and the trees bare, and the shadows of the branches was switchin' across his face."

"You saw that face distinctly?" asked David Arden.

"As clear as yours this minute."

"Now tell me—and think first—was he a bit like that Mr. Longcluse whose appearance startled you the other evening?" asked Mr. Arden, in a very low tone, with his eyes fixed on her intensely.

"No, no, no! not a bit. He had a small mouth and white teeth, and a great beak of a nose. No, no, no! not he. I saw him strike somethin' that shone—a knife or a dagger—into the poor lad's throat, and he struck it down at my head, as you know, and I mind nothin' after that. I'll carry the scar o' that murderer's blow to my grave. There's the whole story, and God forgi'e ye for asking me, for it gi'es me t' creepins for a week after; and I didn't conceit 'twould 'a' made me sa excited, Sir, or I would not 'a' bargained to tell it to-night—not that I blame ye, Master David, for I thought, myself, that I could bear it better—and I do believe, as I have gone so far in it, 'tis better to make one job of it, and a finish. So ye'll ask me any question ye like, and I'll make the best answer I can; only, Master David, ye'll not be o'er long about it?"

"You are a good creature, Martha. I am sorry to pain you, but I pain myself, and you know why I ask these questions."

"Ay, Sir, and I'd rather hear ye ask them than see you sit as easy under all that as some does, that owed the poor fellow as much love as ever you did, and were as near akin."

"I am puzzled, Martha, and hitherto I have been baffled, but I won't give it up yet. You say that the wretch who struck you was a singular-looking man, at least as you describe him. I know, Martha, I can rely upon your caution—you will not repeat to any one what passes in our interview." He lowered his voice. "You do not think that this Mr. Longcluse—a rich gentleman, you know and a person who thinks he's of some consequence, a person whom we must not look at, you know, as if he had two heads—you really don't think that this Mr. Longcluse has any resemblance to the villain whom you saw stab my brother, and who struck you?"

"Not he—no more than I have. No, no, Mr. Longcluse is quite another sort of face; but for all that, when he came in here, and I saw him before me, his face and his speech reminded me of that night."

"How was that, Martha? Did he resemble the other man—the man who was aiding?"

"That fellow was hanged, ye'll mind, Master David."

"Yes, but a likeness might have struck and startled you."

"No, Sir—no, Master David, not him; surely not him. I can't bring it to mind, but it frightens me. It is queer, Sir. All I can say for certain is this, Master David. The minute I heard his voice, and got sight of his face, like that," and she dropped her hand on the table, "the thought of that awful night came back, bright and cold, Sir, and them black shadows—'twas all about me, I can't tell how, and I hope I may never see him again."

"Do you think there was another man by, besides the two villains in the gig?" suggested David Arden.

"Not a living soul except them and myself. Poor Master Harry said to Tom Clinton, ye'll mind, for he lived half-an-hour after, and spoke a little, though faint and with great labour, and says he, 'There were two: Yelland Mace killed me, and Tom Todry took the money.' Tom Clinton heard him say that, and swore to it before the justice o' peace, and after, on the trial. No, no, there wasn't a soul there but they two villains, and the poor dear lad they murdered, and me and Tom Clinton, that might as well 'a' bin in York for any good we did. Oh, no, Heaven forbid I should be so unmannerly as to compare a gentleman like Mr. Longcluse to such folk as that! Oh, lawk, no, Sir! But there's something, there's a look—or a sound in his voice—I can't get round it quite—but it reminds me of something about that night, with a start like, I can't tell how—something unlucky and awful—and I would not see him again for a deal."

"Well, Martha, a thousand thanks. I'm puzzled, as I said. Perhaps it is only something strange in his face that caused that odd misgiving. For I who saw but one of the wretches engaged in the crime, the man who was convicted, who certainly did not in the slightest degree resemble Mr. Longcluse, experienced the same unpleasant sensation on first seeing him. I don't know how it is, Martha, but the idea clings to me, as it does to you. Some light may come. Something may turn up. I can't get it out of my mind that somehow—it may be circuitously—he has, at least, got the thread in his fingers that may lead us right. Good-night, Martha. I have got the Bible with large print you wished for; I hope you will like the binding. And now, God bless you! It is time I should bid them good-night upstairs. Farewell, my good old friend." And, so saying, he shook her hard and shrivelled hand.

His steps echoed along the long tiled passage, with its one dim light, and his mind was still haunted by its one obscure idea.

"It is strange," he thought, "that Martha and I—the only two living persons, I believe, who care still for poor Harry, and feel alike respecting the expiation that is due to his memory—should both have been struck with the same odd feeling on seeing Longcluse. From that white sinister face, it seems to me, I know not why, will shine the light that will yet clear all up."

CHAPTER XXI.

A WALK BY MOONLIGHT.

While Martha Tansey was telling her grisly story in the housekeeper's room, and David Arden listening to the oft-told tale, for the sake of the possible new lights which the narration might throw upon his present theory, the little party in the drawing-room had their music and their talk. Mr. Longcluse sang the song which, standing beside Uncle David on the landing, near the great window on the staircase, we have faintly heard; and then he sang that other song, of the goblin wooer, at Alice's desire.

"Was the poor girl fool enough to accept his invitation?" inquired Miss Maubray.

"That I really can't say," laughed Mr. Longcluse.

"Yes, indeed, poor thing! I so hope she didn't," said Lady May.

"It's very likely she did," interposed Sir Reginald, opening his eyes—every one thought he was dozing—"nothing more foolish, and therefore, nothing more likely. Besides, if she didn't, she probably did worse. Better to go straight to the ——"

"Oh, dear Reginald!" exclaimed Lady May.

"Than by a tedious circumbendibus. I suppose her parents highly disapproved of the goblin; wasn't that alone an excellent reason for going away with him?"

And Sir Reginald closed his eyes again.

"Perhaps," said Miss Maubray aside to Vivian Darnley, "that romantic young lady may have had a cross papa, and thought that she could not change very much for the worse."

"Shall I tell that to Sir Reginald?—it would amuse him," inquired Darnley.

"Not as my remark; but I make you a present of it."

"Thanks; but that, even with your permission, would be a plagiarism, and robbing you of his applause."

Vivian Darnley was very inattentive to his own nonsense. He was talking very much at random, for his mind, and occasionally his eyes, were otherwise occupied.

Alice Arden was sitting near the piano, and talking to Mr. Longcluse.

"Is that meant to be a ghost, I wonder, in our sense, like the ghost of Wilhelm in the ballad of Leonora? or is the lover a demon?"

"A demon, surely," answered Longcluse, "a spirit appointed to her destruction. In an old ghostly writer there is a Latin sentence, Unicuique nascenti, adest dæmon vitæ mystagogus, which I will translate, 'There is present at the birth of every human being a demon, who is the conductor of his life.' Be it fortunate, or be it direful, to this supernatural influence he owes it all. So they thought; and to families such a demon is allotted also, and they prosper or wane as his function is ordained. I wonder whether such demons ever enter into human beings, and, in the shape of living men, haunt, plague, and ruin their predestinated victims."

This sort of mysticism for a time they talked, and then wandered away to other themes, and the talk grew general; and Mr. Longcluse, with a pang, discovered that it was late. He had something on his mind that night. He had an undivulged use, also, to which to apply David Arden. As the hour drew near it weighed more and more heavily at his heart. That hour must be observed; he wished to be away before it arrived. There was still ample time; but Lady May was now talking of going, and he made up his mind to say farewell.

Lingeringly Mr. Longcluse took his leave. But go he must; and so, a last touch of the hand, a last look, and the parting is over. Down-stairs he runs; his groom and his brougham are at the door. What a glorious moon! The white light upon all things around is absolutely dazzling. How sharp and black the shadows! How light and filmy rises the old house! How black the nooks of the thick ivy! Every drop of dew that hangs upon its leaves, or on the drooping stalks of the neglected grass, is transmuted into a diamond. As he stands for an instant upon the broad platform of the steps, he looks round him with a deep sigh, and with a strange smile of rapture. The man standing with the open door of the brougham in his hand caught his eye.

"Go you down as far as the little church, before you reach the 'Guy of Warwick,' in the village, quite close to this—you know it—and wait there for me. I shall walk."

The man touched his hat, shut the door, and mounted the box beside the driver, and away went the brougham. Mr. Longcluse lit a cigarette, and slowly walked down the broad avenue after the vehicle. By the time he had got about half-way, he heard the iron gates swing together, the sound of the wheels was lost in distance, and the feeling of seclusion returned. In the same vague intoxication of poetry and romance, he paused and looked round again, and sighed. The trunk of a great tree overthrown in the last year's autumnal gales, with some of its boughs lopped off, lay on the grass at the edge of the avenue. There remained a little of his cigarette to smoke, and the temptation of this natural seat was irresistible; so he took it, and smoked, and gazed, and dreamed, and sometimes, as he took the cigarette from his lips, he sighed—never was man in a more romantic vein. He looked back on the noble front of the picturesque old house. The cold moonlight gleamed on most of the window-panes: but from a few tall windows glowed faintly the warmer light of candles. If anyone had ever felt the piercing storms of life, the treachery of his species, and the mendacity of the illusions that surround us, Longcluse was that man. He had accepted the conditions of life, and was a man of the world; but no boy of eighteen was ever more in love than he at this moment.

Gazing back at the dim glow that flushed through the tall window-blinds of the distant drawing-room, his fancy weaving all those airy dreams that passion lives in, this pale, solitary man—whom no one quite knew, who trusted no one, who had his peculiar passions, his sorrows, his fears, and strange remembrances; everything connected with his origin, vicissitudes, and character, except this one wild hope, locked up, as it were, in an iron casket, and buried in a grave fathoms deep—was now floated back, he knew not how, to that time of sweet perturbation and agonising hope at which the youth of Shakespeare's time were wont to sigh like a furnace, and indite woeful ballads to their mistress's eyebrows. Now he saw lights in an upper room. Imagination and conjecture were in a moment at work. No servant's apartment, its dimensions were too handsome; and had not Sir Reginald mentioned that his room was upon a level with the hall? Just at this moment Lady May's carriage drove down the avenue and past him. Yes, she had run up direct to her room on bidding Lady May good-night. How he drank in these rosy lights through his dark eyes! and how their tremble seemed to quicken the pulsations of his heart! Gradually his thoughts saddened, and his face grew dark.

"Two doors in life—only in this life, if all bishops and curates speak truth—one or other shut for ever in the next. The gate to heaven, the gate to hell. Heaven! Facilis decensus. Life is such a sophism. Yet even those canting dogs in the pulpit can't bark away the truth. God sees not with our eyes! Revealed religion—Mahomet, Moses, Mormon, Borgia! What is the first lesson inscribed by his Maker on every man's heart, instinct, intellect? I read the mandate thus: 'Take the best care you can of number one.' Bah! 'It is he that hath made us, and not we ourselves.'"

Uncle David's carriage now drove by.

"There goes that sharp girl—pretty, vain—and they're all vain; they ought to be vain; they could not please if they were not. Vain she is—devoured, mind, soul, passion, by vanity. Yes, and power—the lust of power, conquest, acquisition. She's greedy and crafty, I daresay. Oh! Alice, who was ever quite like you? The most beautiful, the best, my darling! Oh! enchantress, work the miracle, and make this forlorn man what he might be!"

It passed like a magic-lantern picture, and was gone. The distant clang of the iron gate was heard again, the avenue was deserted and silent, and Longcluse once more alone in his dream. He was looking towards the house, sometimes breaking into a few murmured words, sometimes smoking, and just as his cigarette was out he saw a figure approaching. It was Uncle David, who was walking down the avenue. It so happened that his mind was at that moment busy with Mr. Longcluse, and it was with an odd little shock, therefore, that he saw the very man—whom he fancied by that time to be at least two miles away—rise up in his path, and stand before him, smiling, in the moonlight.

"Oh!—Mr. Longcluse?" exclaimed David Arden, coming suddenly to a halt.

"So it is," said Longcluse, with a little laugh. "You are surprised to find me here, and I fancied I had seen your carriage go on."

"So you did; it is waiting near the gate for me. Can I give you a seat into town?"

"Thanks," said Longcluse, smiling; "mine is waiting for me a little further on."

Longcluse walked slowly on toward the gate, with David Arden at his side.

"My ward, Miss Maubray, has gone on with Lady May, and Darnley went with them. So I'm not such a brute as I should be if I were making a young lady wait while I was enjoying the moonlight."

"It was this wonderful moon that led me, also, into this night-ramble on foot," said Mr. Longcluse; "I found the temptation absolutely irresistible."

As they thus talked, Mr. Longcluse had formed the resolution of choosing that moment for a confidence which, considering how slender was his acquaintance with Mr. David Arden, was, to say the least, a little bold and odd. They had not very far to walk before reaching the gate, so, a little abruptly turning the course of their talk, Mr. Longcluse said, with a chilly little laugh, and a smile more pallid than ever in the moonlight—

"By-the-bye, we were talking of that shocking occurrence in the Saloon Tavern; and connected with it, I have had two threatening letters."

"Indeed!" said David Arden.

"Fact, I assure you," said Mr. Longcluse, with a shrug and another cold little laugh.

CHAPTER XXII.

MR. LONGCLUSE MAKES AN ODD CONFIDENCE.

David Arden looked at Mr. Longcluse with a sudden glance, that was, for a moment, shrinking and sharp. This confidence connected with such a scene chimed in, with a harmony that was full of pain, with the utterly vague suspicions that had somehow got into his imagination.

"Yes, and I have been a little puzzled," continued Longcluse. "They say the man who is his own lawyer has a fool for his client; but there are other things besides law to which the spirit of the canon more strongly still applies. I think you could give me just the kind of advice I need, if you were not to think my asking it too great a liberty. I should not dream of doing so if the matter were simply a private one, and began and ended in myself; but you will see in a moment that public interests of some value are involved, and I am a little doubtful whether the course I am taking is in all respects the right one. I have had two threatening letters; would you mind glancing at them? The moon is so brilliant, one has no difficulty in reading. This is the first. And may I ask you, kindly, until I shall have determined, I hope, with your aid, upon a course, to treat the matter as quite between ourselves? I have mentioned it to but one other person."

"Certainly," said David, "you have a right to your own terms."

He took the letter and stopped short where he was, unfolding it. The light was quite sufficient, and he read the odd and menacing letter which Mr. Longcluse had received a few evenings before, as we know, at Lady May's. It was to the following effect:

> "SIR,—The unfortunate situation in which you stand, the proof being so, as you must suppose, makes it necessary for you to act considerately, and no nonsense can be permitted by your well wishers. The poor man has his conscience all one as as the rich, and must be cautious as well as him. I can not put myself in no dainger for you, Sir, nor won't hold back the truth, so welp me. I have heerd tell of your boote bin took away. I would be happy to lend an and, Sir, to recover that property. How all will end otherwise I regrett. Knowing well who it will be that takes so mutch consern for your safety, you

cannot doubt who I am, and if you wishes to meat me quiet to consult, you need only to name the place and time in the times newspaper, which I sees it every day. It must be put part in one days times, for the daite, saying a friend will show on sich a night, and in next days times for the place, saying the dogs will meet at sich and sich a place, and it shall hev the attenshen of your

Fast Frend."

"That's a cool letter, upon my word," said David Arden. "Have you an idea who wrote it?"

"Yes, a very good guess. I'll tell you all that if you allow me, just now. I should say, indeed, an absolute certainty, for I have had another this afternoon with the name of the writer signed, and he turns out to be the very man whom I suspected. Here it is."

David Arden's curiosity was piqued. He took the last note and read as follows:—

"SIR,—My last Letter must have came to Hand, and you been in reseet of it since the 11th instant, has took no Notice thereoff, I have No wish for justice, as you may Suppose, and has no Fealing against you Mr. Longcluse Persanelly and to shew you plainly that Such is the case, I will meet you for an intervue if such is your Wishes in your Own house, if you should Raything than name another place. I do not objeck To one frend been Present providing such Be not a lawyer. The subjek been Dellicat, I will Attend any hour and Place you appoint. If you should faile I must put my Proofs in the hands of the police, for I will take it for a sure sine of guilt if you fail after this to appoint for a meating.

"I remain, Sir, Your obedient servent,
"PAUL DAVIES.

"No. 2 Rosemary Court."

"Well, that's pretty frank," said Longcluse, observing that he had read to the end.

"Extremely. What do you suppose his object to be—to extort money?"

"Possibly; but he may have another object. In any case, he wants to make money by this move."

"Very audacious, then. He must know, if he is fit for his trade, how much risk there is in it; and his signing his name and address to his letter, and seeking an interview with a witness by seems to me utterly infatuated," said David Arden, with his eye upon Mr. Longcluse.

"So it does, except upon one supposition; I mean that the man believes his story," said Mr. Longcluse, walking beside him, for they had resumed their march towards the gate.

"Really! believes that you committed the murder?" said Uncle David, again coming to a halt and looking full at him.

"I can't quite account for it otherwise," said Longcluse; "and I think the right course is for me to meet him. But I have no intimacies in London, and that is my difficulty."

"How? Why don't you arrest him?" said David Arden.

David Arden had seldom felt so oddly. A quarter-of-an-hour since, he expected to have been seated in his carriage with his ward and Vivian Darnley, driving into town in quiet humdrum fashion, by this time. How like a dream was the actual scene! Here he was, standing on the grass among the noble timber, under the moonlight, with the pale face beside him which had begun to haunt him so oddly. The strange smile of his mysterious companion, the cold tone that jarred sweetly, somehow, on his ear, lending a sinister eccentricity to the extraordinary confession he was making.

In this situation, which had come about almost unaccountably, there was a strange feeling of unreality. Was this man, from whom he had felt an indescribable repulsion, now by his side, and drawing him, in this solitude, into a mysterious confidence? and had not this confidence an unaccountable though distant relation to the vague suspicions that had touched his mind? With a little effort he resumed,—

"I beg pardon, but if the case were mine I should put the letters at once into the hands of the police and prosecute him."

"Precisely my own first impulse. But the letters are more cautiously framed than you might at first sight suppose. I should be placed in an awkward position were my prosecution to fail. I am obliged to think of this because, although I am nothing to the public, I am a good deal to myself. But I've resolved to take a course not less bold, though less public. I am determined to meet him face to face with an unexceptionable witness present, and to discover distinctly whether he acts from fraud or delusion, and then to proceed accordingly. I have communicated with him."

"Oh, really!"

"Yes, I was clear I ought to meet him, but I would consent to nothing with an air of concealment."

"I think you were right, Sir."

"He wanted our meeting by night on board a Thames boat; then in a dilapidated house in Southwark; then in a deserted house that is to be let in Thames Street; but I named my own house, in Bolton Street, at half-past twelve to-night."

"Then you really wish to see him. I suppose you have thought it well over; but I am always for taking such miscreants promptly by the throat. However, as you say, cases differ, and I daresay you are well advised."

"And now may I venture a request, which, were it not for two facts within my knowledge, I should not presume to make? But I venture it to you, who take so special an interest in this case, because you have already taken trouble and, like myself, contributed money to aid the chances of discovery; and because only this evening you said you would bestow more labour, more time, and more money with pleasure to procure the least chance of an additional light upon it: now it strikes me as just possible that the writer of those letters may be, to some extent, honest. Though utterly mistaken about me, still he may have evidence to give, be it worth much or little; and so, Mr. Arden, having the pleasure of being known to some members of your family, although till to-night by name only to you, I beg as a great kindness to a man in a difficulty, and possibly in the interests of the public, that you will be so good as to accompany me, and be present at the interview, that cannot be so well conducted before any other witness whom I can take with me."

David Arden paused for a moment, but independently quite of his interest in this case: he felt a strange curiosity about this pale man, whose eyes from under their oblique brows gleamed back the cold moonlight; while a smile, the character of which a little puzzled him, curled his nostril and his thin lip, and showed the glittering edge of his teeth. Did it look like treachery? or was it defiance, or derision? It was a face, thus seen, so cadaverous and Mephistophelian, that an artist would have given something for a minute to fix a note of it in white and black.

David Arden was not to be disturbed in a practical matter by a pictorial effect, however, and in another moment he said—

"Yes, Mr. Longcluse, as you desire it I will accompany you, and see this fellow, and hear what he has to say. Certainly."

"That's very kind—only what I should have expected, also, from your public spirit. I'm extremely obliged."

They resumed their walk towards the gate.

"I shall get into my brougham and call at home, to tell them not to expect me for an hour or so. And what is the number of your house?"

He told him; and David Arden having offered to take him, in his carriage, to the place where his own awaited him, which however he declined, they parted for a little time, and Mr. Arden's brougham quickly disappeared under the shadow of the tall trees that lined the curving road.

CHAPTER XXIII.

THE MEETING.

As David Arden drove towards town, his confusion rather increased. Why should Mr. Longcluse select him for this confidence? There were men in the City whom he must know, if not intimately, at least much better than he knew him. It was a very strange occurrence; and was not Mr. Longcluse's manner, also, strange? Was he not, somehow, very oddly cool under a charge of murder? There was something, it seemed, indefinably incongruous in the nature of his story, his request, and his manner.

It was five or ten minutes before the appointed time when David Arden and Longcluse met in the latter gentleman's "study" in Bolton Street. There was a slight, odd flutter at Longcluse's heart, although his pale face betrayed no sign of agitation, as the shuffling tread of a heavy foot was heard on the doorsteps, followed by a faint knock, like that of a tremulous postman. It was the preconcerted summons of Mr. Paul Davies.

Longcluse smiled at David Arden and raised his finger, as he lightly drew near the room door, with an air of warning. He wished to remind his companion that he was to receive their visitor alone. Mr. Arden nodded, and Mr. Longcluse withdrew. In a minute more the servant opened the study-door, and said—"Mr. Davies, Sir."

And the tall ex-detective entered, and looked with a silky simper stealthily to the right and to the left from the corners of his eyes, and glided in, shutting the door behind him.

Uncle David received this man without even a nod. He eyed him sternly, from his chair at the end of the table.

"Sit in that chair, please," said he, pointing to a seat at the other end.

The ex-policeman made his best bow, and turning out his toes very much, he shuffled with his habitual sly smirk on, to the chair, in which he seated himself, and with his big red hands on the table began turning, and twisting, and twiddling a short pencil, which was a good deal bitten at the uncut end, between his fingers and thumbs.

"You came here to see Mr. Longcluse?" asked David Arden.

"A few words of business at his desire. Sir, I ask your parding, I came, Sir, by his wishes, not mine, which has brought me here at his request."

"And who am I, do you suppose?"

The man, still smiling, looked at him shrewdly. "Well, I don't know, I'm sure; I may 'a' seen you."

"Did you ever see that gentleman?" said David Arden, as Mr. Longcluse entered the room.

The ex-detective looked also shrewdly at Longcluse, but without any light of recognition. "I may have seen him, Sir. Yes, I saw him in Saint George's, Hanover Square, the day Lord Charles Dillingsworth married Miss Wygram, the hairess. I saw him at Sydenham the second week in February last when the Freemasons' dinner was there; and I saw him on the night of the match between Hood and Markham, at the Saloon Tavern."

"Do you know my name?" said David Arden.

"Well, no, I don't at present remember."

"Do you know that gentleman's name?"

"His name?"

"Ay, his name."

"Well, no; I may have heard it, and I may bring it to mind, by-and-by."

Longcluse smiled and shrugged, looking at Mr. Arden, and he said to the man—

"So you don't know that gentleman's name, nor mine?"

The man looked at each, hard and a little anxiously, like a person who feels that he may be making a very serious mistake; but after a pause he said decisively—"No, I don't at present. I say I don't know your names, either of you gentlemen, and I don't."

The two gentlemen exchanged glances.

"Is either of us as tall as Mr. Longcluse?" asked David Arden, standing up.

The man stood up also, to make his inspection.

"You're both," he said, after a pause, "much about his height."

"Is either of us like him?"

"No," answered Davies, after a pause.

"Did you write these letters?" asked Mr. Longcluse laughing.

"Well, I did, or I didn't, and what's that to you?"

"Something, as you shall know presently."

"I think you're trying it on. I reckon this is a bit of a plant. I don't care a scratch o' that pencil if it be. I wrote them letters, and I said nothin' but what's true, and I'll go with you now to the station if you like, and tell all I knows."

The fellow seemed nettled, and laughed viciously a little, and swaggered at the close of his speech. The faintest flush imaginable tinged Longcluse's forehead, as he shot a searching glance at him.

"No, we don't want that," said he; "but you may be of more use in another way, although just now you are in the wrong box, and have mistaken your man, for I am Mr. Longcluse. You have been misinformed, you see, as to the identity of the person you suspect; but some person you have, no doubt, in your mind, and possibly a case worth sifting, although you have been deceived as to his name. Describe the appearance of the man you supposed to be Mr. Longcluse. You may be frank with me; I mean you no harm."

"I defy any man to harm me, Sir, if you please, so long as I do my dooty," said Paul Davies. "Mr. Longcluse, if that be his name, the man I mean, he's about your height, with round shoulders and red hair, and talks with a north-country twang on his tongue; he's a bit rougher, and a swaggerin' cove, and a yard o' red beard over his waistcoat, and bigger hands a deal than you, and broader feet."

"And have you a case against him?"

"Partly, but it ain't, Sir, if you please, by no means so complete as would answer as yet. If I was sure you were really Mr. Longcluse, I could say more, for I partly guess who this other gent is—a most respectable party. I think I do know you, Sir, by appearance; if you had your 'at on, Sir, I could say to a certainty. But I think, Sir, if you please, I'm not very far wrong when I say that I would identify you for Mr. David Arden."

"So I am; that is quite true."

"Thank you, Sir, I am obleeged; that's very quietin' to my mind, Sir, having full confidence in your character; and if you, Sir, please to tell me that gentleman is undoubtingly Mr. Longcluse, the propperieter of this house, I must 'a' been let into a mistake; I don't think they was agreenin' of me, but it was a mistake, if you please, Sir, if you say so."

"This is Mr. Longcluse—I know of no other—and he resides in this house," said David Arden. "But if you have information to give respecting that red-bearded fellow, there is no reason why you should not give it forthwith to the police."

"Parding me, Sir, if you please, Mr. Arden. There is, I would say, strong reasons for a poor man in rayther anxious circumstances, like myself, Sir, 'aving an affectionate mother to, in a measure, support, and been himself unfortunately rayther hard up, he can't answer it nohow to his conscience if he lets a hoppertunity like the present pass him and his aged mother by unimproved. There been a reward offered, Sir, I naturally wish, Sir, if you please, to earn it myself by valuable evidence leading to the conviction of the guilty cove; and if I was to tell all I knows and 'av' made out by my own hindustry to the force, Sir, other persons would, don't you conceive, Sir, draw the reward, and me and my mother should go without. If I could get a hinterview with the man I 'av' bin a-gettin' things together for, I'd lead him, I 'av' no doubt, to make such hadmissions as would clench the prosecution, and vendicate justice."

"I see what you mean," said David Arden.

"And fair enough, I think," added Longcluse.

CHAPTER XXIV.

MR. LONGCLUSE FOLLOWS A SHADOW.

The ex-detective cleared his voice, shook his head, and smirked.

"A hinterview, gentlemen," said he, "is worth much in the hands of a persuasive party. I have hanged several obnoxious characters, and let others in for penal for life, by means of a hinterview. You remember Spikes, gentlemen, as got into difficulties for breaking Mr. Winterbotham's desk? Spikes would have frusterated justice, if it wasn't for me. It was done in one hinterview. Says I, 'Mr. Spikes, you have a wife and five children.'"

The recollection of Mr. Paul Davies' diplomacy was so gratifying to that smiling gentleman, that he could not forbear winking at his auditors as he proceeded.

"'And my belief is, Mr. Spikes, Sir,'" he continued, "'that it was all the hinfluence of Tom Sprowles. It was Sprowles persuaded yer—it was him as got the whole thing up. That's my belief; and you did not want to do it, no-wise, and only consented to force the henges in the belief that Sprowles wanted to read the papers, and no more. I have a bad opinion of Sprowles,' says I, 'for deceiving you, I may say innocently;' and talking this way, you conceive, I got it all out of him, and he's under penal for life. Whenever you want to get round a man, and to turn him inside out, your way is to sympathise with him. If I had but an hinterview with that man, I know enough to draw it out of him, every bit. It's all done by sympathising."

"But do you think you can discover the man?" asked Mr. Arden.

"I'm sure to make him out, if you please, Sir; I'll find out all about him. I'd a found out the facks long ago, but for the mistake, which it occurred most unlucky. I saw him twice sence, and I know well where to look for him; and I'll have it all right before long, I'm thinkin'."

"That will do, then, for the present," said Mr. Longcluse. "You have said all you have to say, and you see into what a serious mistake you have blundered; but I sha'n't give you any trouble about it—it is too ridiculous. Good-night, Mr. Davies."

"No mistake of mine, Sir, please. Misinformed, Sir, you will kindly remark—misinformed, if you please—misinformed, as may occur to the sharpest party going. Good-night, gentlemen; I takes my leave without no unpleasant feelin', and good wishes for your 'ealth and 'appiness, both, gentlemen." And blandly, and with a sly sleepy smile, this insinuating person withdrew.

"It is the reward he is thinking of," said Longcluse.

"Yes, he won't spare himself; you mentioned that your own suspicions respecting him were but vague," said David Arden.

"I merely stated what I saw to the coroner, and it was answered that he was watching the Frenchman Lebas, because the detective police, before Paul Davies' dismissal, had received orders to keep an eye on all foreigners; and he hoped to conciliate the authorities, and get a pension, by collecting and furnishing information. The police did not seem to think his dogging and watching the unfortunate little fellow really meant more than this."

"Very likely. It is a very odd affair. I wonder who that fellow is whom he described. He did not give a hint as to the circumstances which excited his suspicions."

"It is strange. But that man, Paul Davies, kept his eye upon Lebas from the motive I mentioned, and this circumstance may have led to his seeing more of the matter than, with the reward in his mind, he cares to make known at present. I think I did right in meeting him face to face."

"Quite right, Sir."

"It has been always a rule with me to go straight at everything. I think the best diplomacy is directness, and that the truest caution lies in courage."

"Precisely my opinion, Mr. Longcluse," said Uncle David, looking on him with eyes of approbation. He was near adding something hearty in the spirit of our ancestors' saying, "I hope you and I, Sir, may be better acquainted;" but something in the look and peculiar face of this unknown Mr. Longcluse chilled him, and he only said—

"As you say, Mr. Longcluse, courage is safety, and honesty the best policy. Good-night, Sir."

"A thousand thanks, Mr. Arden. Might I ask one more favour, that you will endorse on each of these threatening letters a memorandum of the facts of this strange interview?—I mean a sentence or two, which may at any time confound this fellow, should he turn out to be a villain."

"Certainly," said Mr. Arden thoughtfully, and he sat down again, and wrote a few lines on the back of each, which, having signed, he handed them to Mr. Longcluse, with the question, "Will that answer?"

"Perfectly, thank you very much; it is indeed impossible for me to thank you as I ought and wish to," said Mr. Longcluse with effusion, extending his hand at the same time; but Mr. Arden took it without much warmth, and said, in comparison a little drily—

"No need to thank me, Mr. Longcluse; as you said at first, there are motives quite sufficient, of a kind for which you can owe me, personally, no thanks whatever, to induce the very slight trouble of coming here."

"Well, Mr. Arden, I am very much obliged to you, notwithstanding;" and so he gratefully saw him to the door, and smiled and bowed him off, and stood for a moment as his carriage whirled down the short street.

"He does not like me—nor I, perhaps, him. Ha! ha! ha!" he laughed, very softly and reservedly, looking down on the flags. "What an odd thing it is! Those instincts and antipathies, they are very odd." All this, except the faint laughter, was in thought.

Mr. Longcluse stepped back. He was negatively happy—he was rid of an anxiety. He was positively happy—he had been better received by Miss Arden, this evening, than he had ever been before. So he went to his bed with a light heart, and a head full of dreams.

All the next day, one beautiful image haunted Longcluse's imagination. He was delayed in town; he had to consult about operations in foreign stocks; he had many words to say, directions to modify, and calls to make on this man and that. He had hoped to be at Mortlake Hall at three o'clock. But it was past six before he could disentangle himself from the tenacious meshes of his business. Never had he thought it so irksome. Was he not rich enough—too rich? Why should he longer submit to a servitude so wearisome? It was high time he should begin to enjoy his days in the sunshine of his gold and the companionship of his beautiful idol. But "man proposes," says the ancient saw, "and God disposes."

It was just seven o'clock when Mr. Longcluse descended at the steps of old Mortlake Hall.

Sir Reginald, who is writhing under a letter from the attorney of the millionaire mortgagee of his Yorkshire estate, making an alternative offer, either to call in the principal sum or to allow it to stand out on larger interest, had begged of Mr. Longcluse, last night, to give him a few words of counsel some day. He had, in a quiet talk the evening before, taken the man of huge investments rather into his confidence.

"I don't know, Mr.—a—Mr. Longcluse, whether you are aware how cruelly my property is tied up," he said, as he talked in a low tone with him, in a corner of the drawing-room. "A life estate, and my son, who declines bearing any part of the burden of his own extravagance, will do nothing to facilitate my efforts to pay his debts for him; and I declare solemnly, if they raise the interest on this very oppressive mortgage, I don't know how on earth I can pay my insurances. I don't see how I am to do it. I should be so extremely obliged to you, Mr. Longcluse, if you would, with your vast experience and knowledge in all—all financial matters, give me any advice that strikes you—if you could, with perfect convenience, afford so much time. I don't really know what rate of interest is usual. I only know this, that interest, as a rule, has been steadily declining ever since I can remember—perpetually declining; I mean, of course, upon perfect security like this; and now this confounded harpy wants, after ten years, to raise it! I believe they want to drive me out of the world, among them! and they well know the cruelty of it, for I have never been able to pay them a single half-year punctually. Will you take some tea?"

So Longcluse had promised his advice very gladly next day; and now he asked for Sir Reginald. Sir Reginald was very particularly engaged at this moment on business; Mr. Arden was with him at present; but if Mr. Longcluse would wait for a few minutes, Sir Reginald would be most happy to see him. So there was to be a little wait. How could he better pass the interval than in Miss Arden's company?

CHAPTER XXV.

A TETE-A-TETE.

Up to the drawing-room went Mr. Longcluse, and there he found Miss Arden finishing a drawing. He fancied a very slight flush on her cheek as he entered. Was there really a heightening of that beautiful tint as she smiled? How lovely her long lashes, and her even little teeth, and the lustrous darkness of her eyes, in that subdued light!

"I so wanted advice, Mr. Longcluse, and you have come in so fortunately! I am not satisfied with my sky and mountains, and the foreground where the light touches that withered branch is a horrible failure. In nature, it looked quite beautiful. I remember it so well. It looked on fire, almost. This is Saxteen Castle, near Golden Friars, and that is a bit of the lake and those are the fells. I sketched it in pencil, and trusted to memory for colouring. It was just at the most picturesque moment, when the sun was going down between the two mountains that overhang the little town on the west."

"Sunset is very well expressed. You indicated all those long shadows, Miss Arden, in pencil, and I envy your perspective, and I think your colouring so extremely good! The distances are admirably marked. Try a little cadmium, burnt sienna, and lake for the intense touches of light in the foreground, on that barkless branch. Your own eye will best regulate the proportions. I am one of those vandals who prefer colour a little too bold and overdone to any timidity in that respect. Exuberance in a beginner is always, in my mind, an augury of excellence. It is so easy to moderate afterwards."

"Yes, I daresay; I'm very glad you advise that, because I always thought so myself; but I was half afraid to act on it. I think that is about the tint—a little more yellow, perhaps. Yes; how does it look now?—what do you think?"

"Now judge yourself, Miss Arden. Do not those three sharp little touches of reflected fire light up the whole drawing? I say it is admirable. It is really quite a beautiful little drawing."

"I'm growing so vain! you will quite spoil me, Mr. Longcluse."

"Truth will never spoil any one. Praise is very delightful. I have not had much of it in my day, but I think it makes one better as well as happier; and to speak simple truth of you, Miss Arden, is inevitably to praise you."

"Those are compliments, Mr. Longcluse, and they bewilder me—anything one does not know how to answer; so I would rather you pointed me out four or five faults in my drawing, and I should be very well content if you said no more. I believe you know the scenery of Golden Friars."

"I do. Beautiful, and so romantic, and full of legends! the whole place with its belongings is a poem."

"So I think. And the hotel—the inn I prefer calling it—the 'George and Dragon,' is so picturesque and delightfully old, and so comfortable! Our head-quarters were there for two or three weeks. And did you see Childe Waylin's Leap?"

"Yes, an awful scene; what a terrible precipice! I saw it to great advantage from a boat, while a thunderstorm was glaring and pealing over its summit. You know the legend, of course?"

"No, I did not hear it."

"Oh, it is a very striking one, and won't take many words to tell. Shall I tell it?"

"Pray do," said Alice, with her bright look of expectation.

He smiled sadly. Perhaps the story returned with an allegoric melancholy to his mind. With a sigh and a smile he continued—

"Childe Waylin fell in love with a phantom lady, and walked day and night along the fells—people thought in solitude, really lured on by the beautiful apparition, which, as his love increased, grew less frequent, more distant and fainter, until at last, in the despair of his wild pursuit, he threw himself over that terrible precipice, and so perished. I have faith in instinct—faith in passion, which is but a form of instinct. I am sure he did wisely."

"I sha'n't dispute it; it is not a case likely to happen often. These phantom ladies seem to have given up practice of late years, or else people have become proof against their wiles, and neither follow, nor adore, nor lament them."

"I don't think these phantom ladies are at all out of date," said Mr. Longcluse.

"Well, men have grown wiser, at all events."

"No wiser, no happier; in such a case there is no room for what the world calls wisdom. Passion is absolute, and as for happiness, that or despair hangs on the turn of a die."

"I have made that shadow a little more purple—do you think it an improvement?"

"Yes, certainly. How well it throws out that bit of the ruin that catches the sunlight! You have made a very poetical sketch; you have given not merely the outlines, but the character of that singular place—the genus loci is there."

Just as Mr. Longcluse had finished this complimentary criticism, the door opened, and rather unexpectedly Richard Arden entered the room. Very decidedly de trop at that moment, his friend thought Mr. Arden. Longcluse meant again to have turned the current of their talk into the channel he liked best, and here was interruption. But was not Richard Arden his sworn brother, and was he not sure to make an excuse of some sort, and take his leave, and thus restore him to his tête-à-tête.

But was there—or was it fancy—a change scarcely perceptible, but unpleasant, in the manner of this sworn brother? Was it not very provoking, and a little odd, that he did not go away, but stayed on and on, till at length a servant came in with a message from Sir Reginald to Mr. Longcluse, to say that he would be very happy to see him whenever he chose to come to his room? Mr. Longcluse was profoundly vexed. Richard Arden, however, had resumed his old manner pretty nearly. Was the interruption he had persisted in designed, or only accidental? Could he suppose Richard Arden so stupid? He took his leave smiling, but with an uncomfortable misgiving at his heart.

Richard Arden now proceeded in his own way, with some colouring and enormous suppression at discretion, to give his sister such an account as he thought would best answer of the interview he had just had with his father. Honestly related, what occurred between them was as follows:—

Richard Arden had come on summons from his father. Without a special call, he never appeared at Mortlake while his father was there, and never in his absence but with an understanding that Sir Reginald was to hear nothing of it. He sat for a considerable time in the apartment that opened from his father's dressing-room. He heard the baronet's peevish voice ordering Crozier about. Something was dropped and broken, and the same voice was heard in angrier alto. Richard Arden looked out of the window and waited uncomfortably. He hated his father's pleadings with him, and he did not know for what purpose he had appointed this interview.

The door opened, and Sir Reginald entered, limping a little, for his gout had returned slightly. He was leaning on a stick. His thin, dark face and prominent eyes looked angry, and he turned about and poked his dressing-room door shut with the point of his stick, before taking any noticc of his son.

"Sit down, if you please, in that chair," he said, pointing to the particular seat he meant him to occupy with two vicious little pokes, as if he were running a small-sword through it. "I wrote to ask you to come, Sir, merely to say a word respecting your sister, for whom, if not for other members of your family, you still retain, I suppose, some consideration and natural affection."

Here was a pause which Richard Arden did not very well know what to do with. However, as his father's fierce eyes were interrogating him, he murmured—

"Certainly, Sir."

"Yes, and under that impression I showed you Lord Wynderbroke's letter. He is to dine here to-morrow at a quarter to eight—please to recollect—precisely. Do you hear?"

"I do, Sir, everything."

"You must meet him. Let us not appear more divided than we are. You know Wynderbroke—he's peculiar. Why the devil shouldn't we appear united? I don't say be united, for you won't. But there is something owed to decency. I suppose you admit that? And before people, confound you, Sir, can't we appear affectionate? He's a quiet man, Wynderbroke, and makes a great deal of these domestic sentiments. So you'll please to show some respect and affection while he's present, and I mean to show some affection for you; and after that, Sir, you may go to the devil for me! I hope you understand?"

"Perfectly, Sir."

"As to Wynderbroke, the thing is settled—it is there." He pointed to his desk. "What I told you before, I tell you now—you must see that your sister doesn't make a fool of herself. I have nothing more to say to you at present—unless you have something to say to me?"

This latter part of the sentence had something sharp and interrogative in it. There was just a chance, it seemed to imply, that his son might have something to say upon the one point that lay near the old man's heart.

"Nothing, Sir," said Richard, rising.

"No, no; so I supposed. You may go, Sir—nothing."

Of this interview, one word of the real purport of which he could not tell to his sister, he gave her an account very slight indeed, but rather pleasant.

CHAPTER XXVI.

THE GARDEN AT MORTLAKE.

Alice leaned back in her chair, smiling, and very much pleased.

"So my father seems disposed to relent ever so little—and ever so little, you know, is better than nothing," said Richard Arden.

"I'm so glad, Dick, that he wishes you to take your dinner with us to-morrow; it is a very good sign. It would be so delightful if you could be at home with us, as you used to be."

"You are a good little soul, Alice—a dear little thing! This is very pretty," he said, looking at her drawing. "What is it?"

"The ruined castle near the northern end of the lake at Golden Friars. Mr. Longcluse says it is pretty good. Is he to dine here, do you know?"

"No—I don't know—I hope not," said Richard shortly.

"Hope not! why?" said she. "I thought you liked him extremely."

"I thought he was very well for a sort of outdoor acquaintance for men; but I don't even know that, now. There's no use in speaking to Lady May, but I warn you—you had better drop him. There is very little known about him, but there is a great deal that is not pleasant said."

"Really?"

"Yes, really."

"But you used to speak so highly of him. I'm so surprised!"

"I did not know half what people said of him. I've heard a great deal since."

"But is it true?" asked Alice.

"It is nothing to me whether it is true or not. It is enough if a man is talked about uncomfortably, to make it unpleasant to know him. We owe nothing to Mr. Longcluse; there is no reason why you should have an acquaintance that is not desirable. I mean to drop him quietly, and you can't know him, really you mustn't, Alice."

"I don't know. It seems to me very hard," said Miss Alice spiritedly. "It is not many days since you spoke of him so highly; and I was quite pained when you came in just now. I don't know whether he perceived it, but I think he must. I only know that I thought you were so cold and strange to him, your manner so unlike what it always was before. I thought you had been quarrelling. I fancied he was vexed, and I felt quite sorry; and I don't think what you say, Richard, is manly, or like yourself. You used to praise him so, and fight his battles; and he is, though very distinguished in some ways, rather a stranger in London; and people, you told me, envy him, and try in a cowardly way to injure him; and what more easy than to hint discreditable things of people? and you did not believe a word of those reports when last you spoke of him; and considering that he had no people to stand by him in London, or to take his part, and that he may never even hear the things that are said by low people about him, don't you think it would be cowardly of us, and positively base to treat him so?"

"Upon my word, Miss Alice, that is very good oratory indeed! I don't think I ever heard you so eloquent before, at least upon the wrongs of one of my sex."

"Now, Dick, that sneer won't do. There may possibly be reasons why it would have been wiser never to have made Mr. Longcluse's acquaintance; I can't say. Those reasons, however, you treated very lightly indeed a little time ago—you know you did—and now, upon no better, you say you are going to cut him. I can't bring myself to do any such thing. He is always looking in at Lady May's, and I can't help meeting him unless I am to cut her also. Now don't you see how odious I should appear, and how impossible it is?"

"I won't argue it now, dear Alice; there is quite time enough. I shall come an hour before dinner, to-morrow, and we can have a quiet talk; and I am quite sure I shall convince you. Mind, I don't say we should insult him," he laughed. "I only say this, and I'll maintain it—and I'll show you why—that he is not a desirable acquaintance. We have taken him up very foolishly, and we must drop him. And now, darling, good-bye."

He kissed her—she kissed him. She looked grave for a moment after, after he had run down the stairs. He has quarrelled with Mr. Longcluse about something, she thought, as she stood at the window with the tip of her finger to her lip, looking at her brother as he mounted the showy horse which had cantered with him up and down Rotten Row for two hours or more, before he had ridden out to Mortlake. She saw him now ride away.

It was near eight o'clock, and all this time Mr. Longcluse had been in confidence with Sir Reginald about his miserable mortgage. Mr. Longcluse was cautious; but there floated in his mind certain possible contingencies, under which he might perhaps make the financial adjustment, which Sir Reginald desired, very easy indeed to the worthy baronet.

It was the tempting hour of evening when the birds begin to sing, and the level beams from the west glorify all objects. Alice put on her hat and ran out to the old gardens of Mortlake. They are enclosed in a grey wall, and lie one above the other in three terraces, with tall standard fruit trees, so old that their fruit was now dwarfed in size to half its earlier bearings, standing high with a dark and sylvan luxuriance, and at this moment, sheltering among their sunlit leaves, nestle and flutter the small birds whose whistlings cheer and sadden the evening air. Every tree and bush that bore fruit, in this old garden, had grown quite beyond the common stature of its kind, and a good gardener would have cut them all down fifty years ago. But there was a kind of sylvan and stately beauty in those wonderful lofty pear-trees, with their dense dark foliage, and in the standard cherries so tall and prim, and something homely and comfortable in the great straggling apples and plums, dappled with grey lichens and tufted with moss. There were flowers as well as fruits, of all sorts, in this garden. All its arrangements were out of date. There was an air, not actually of neglect—for it was weeded, and the walks were trim and gravelled—but of carelessness and rusticity, not unpleasant, in the place. Trees were allowed to straggle and spread, and rise aloft in the air, just as they pleased. Tall roses climbed the walls about the door, and clustered in nodding masses overhead; and no end of pretty annuals and other flowers, quite out of fashion, crowded the dishevelled currant bushes, and the forest of raspberries. Here and there were very tall myrtles, and the quince, and obsolete medlars, were discoverable among the other fruit-trees. The summits of the walls were in some places crowned, to the scandal of all decent gardening, with ivy, and a carved shaft in the centre of each garden supported a sun-dial as old as the Hall itself.

There are fancies, as well as likings and lovings. Where there is a real worship, however cautiously masked—and Mr. Longcluse was by no means so—it is never a mystery to a clever girl. And such adoration, although it be not at all reciprocated, is sometimes hard to part with. There is something of the nature of compassion, with a little gratitude, perhaps, mingling in the pang which a gentle lady feels at having to discharge for ever an honest love and a true servant, and send him away to solitary suffering for her sake. Some little pang of reproach of this sensitive kind had, perhaps, armed her against her brother's sudden sentence of exclusion pronounced against Mr. Longcluse.

The evening sunlight travelled over the ivy on the discoloured wall, and glittered on the leaves of the tall fruit-trees, in whose thick foliage the birds were still singing their vespers. Walking down the broad walk towards the garden-door, she felt the saddening influence of the hour returning; and as she reached the door, overclustered with roses, it opened, and Mr. Longcluse stood in the shadow before her.

Miss Arden, thus surprised in the midst of thoughts which at that moment happened to be employed about him, showed for a second, as she suddenly stopped, something in her beautiful face almost amounting to embarrassment.

“I was called away so suddenly to see Sir Reginald, that I went without saying good-bye; so I ran up to the drawing-room, and the servant told me I should probably find you here; and, really without reflecting—I act, I'm afraid, so much from impulse that I might appear very impertinent—I ventured to follow. What a beautiful evening! How charming the light! You, who are such an artist, and understand the poetry of colour so, must admire this cloister-like garden, so beautifully illuminated.”

Was Mr. Longcluse also a very little embarrassed as he descanted thus on light and colour?

"It is a very old garden and does very little credit, I'm afraid, to our care; but I greatly prefer it to our formal gardens and all their finery, in Yorkshire."

She moved her hand as if she expected Mr. Longcluse to take it and his leave, for it was high time her visitor should "order his wings and be off the west," in which quarter, as we know, lay Mr. Longcluse's habitation. He had stepped in, however, and the door closed softly before the light evening breeze that swung it gently. She was standing under the wild canopy of roses, and he under the sterner arch of grooved and fluted stone that overhung the doorway.

CHAPTER XXVII.

WINGED WORDS.

"I was afraid I had vexed your brother somehow," said Mr. Longcluse—"I thought he seemed to meet me a little formally. I should be so sorry if I had annoyed him by any accident!"

He paused, and Miss Arden said, half laughing—"Oh, don't you know, Mr. Longcluse, that people are out of spirits sometimes, and now and then a little offended with all the world? It is nothing, of course."

"What a fib!" whispered conscience in the young lady's pretty ear, while she smiled and blushed.

Again she raised her hand a little, expecting Mr. Longcluse's farewell. But she looked a great deal too beautiful for a farewell. Mr. Longcluse could not deny himself a minute more, and he said, "It is a year, Miss Arden, since I first saw you."

"Is it really? I daresay."

"Yes, at Lady May Penrose's. Yes, I remember it distinctly—so distinctly that I shall never forget any circumstance connected with it. It is exactly a year and four days. You smile, Miss Arden, because for you the event can have had no interest; for me it is different—how different I will not say."

Miss Arden coloured and then grew pale. She was very much embarrassed. She was about to say a word to end the interview, and go. Perhaps Mr. Longcluse was, as he said, impulsive—too precipitate and impetuous. He raised his hand entreatingly,—

"Oh, Miss Arden, pray, only a word!—I must speak it. Ever since then—ever since that hour—I have been the slave of a single thought; I have worshipped before one beautiful image, with an impious adoration, for there is nothing—no sacrifice, no crime—I would shrink from for your sake. You can make of me what you will; all I possess, all my future, every thought and feeling and dream—all are yours. No, no; don't interrupt the few half desperate words I have to speak, they may move you to pity. Never before, in a life of terrible vicissitude, of much suffering, of many dangers, have I seen the human being who could move me as you have done. I did not believe my seared heart capable of passion.

And I stand now aghast at what I have spoken. I stand at the brink of a worse death, by the word that trembles on your lips, than the cannon's mouth could give me. I see I have spoken rashly—I see it in your face—oh, Heaven! I see what you would say."

His hands were clasped in desperate supplication, as he continued; and the fitful breeze shook the roses above them, and the fading leaves fell softly in a shower about his feet.

"No, don't speak—your silence is sacred. I sha'n't misinterpret—I conjure you, don't answer! Forget that I have spoken. Oh! let it, in mercy, be all forgotten, and let us meet again as if there never had been this moment of madness, and in pity—as you look for mercy—forget it and forgive it!"

He waited for no answer: he was gone: the door closed as it was before. Another breath of wind ruffled the roses, and a few more sere leaves fell where he had just been standing. She drew a long breath, like one awaking from a vision. She was trembling slightly. Never before had she seen such agony in a human face! All had happened so suddenly. It was an effort to believe it real. It seemed as if she could see nothing while he spoke, but that intense, pale face. She heard nothing but his deep and thrilling words. Now it seemed as if flowers, and trees, and wall, and roses, all emerged suddenly again from mist, and as if all the birds had resumed their singing after a silence.

"Forget it—forgive it! Let it, as you look for mercy, be all forgotten. Let us meet again as if it never was." This strange petition still rang in the ears of the astonished girl.

She was still too much flurried by the shock of this wild and sudden outbreak of passion, and appeal to mercy, quite to see her true course in the odd combination that had arisen. She was a little angry, and a little flattered. There was a confusion of resentment and compassion. What business had this Mr. Longcluse to treat her to those heroics! What right had he to presume that he would be listened to? How dared he ask her to treat all that had happened as if it had never been? How dared he seek to found on this unwarrantable liberty relations of mystery between them? How dared he fancy that she would consent to play at this game of deception with him?

Mingled with these angry thoughts, however, were the recollections of his homage, his tone of melancholy deference ever since she had known him, and his admiration.

Underlying all his trifling talk, there had always been toward her a respect which flattered her, which could not have been exceeded had she been an empress in her own right. No, if he had said more than he had any right to suppose would be listened to, the extravagance was due to no want of respect for her, but to the vehemence of passion.

He was driving now into town, at a great pace. His cogitations were still more perturbed. Had he, by one frantic precipitation, murdered his best hopes?

One consolation at least he had. Being a man, not without reason, prone to suspicion, he had a deep conviction that, for some reason, Richard Arden was opposed to his suit, and had already begun to work upon Miss Arden's mind to his prejudice. His best chance, then, he still thought, was to anticipate that danger by a declaration. If that declaration could only be forgiven, and the little scene at old Mortlake garden door sponged out, might not his chances stand better far than before? Would not the past, though never spoken of, give meaning, fire, and melancholy to things else insignificant, and keep him always before her, and her alone, be his demeanour and language ever so reserved and cold, as an impassioned lover? Did not his knowledge of human nature assure him that these relations of mystery would, more than any other, favour his fortunes?

"That she should consign what has passed, in a few impetuous moments, to oblivion and silence, is no unreasonable prayer, and one as easy to grant as to will it. She will think it over, and, for my part, I will meet her as if nothing had ever happened to change our trifling but friendly relations. I wish I knew what Richard Arden was about. I soon shall. Yes, I shall—I soon shall."

An opportunity seemed to offer sooner even than he had hoped; for as he drove towards St. James's Street, passing one of Richard Arden's clubs, he saw that young gentleman ascending the steps with Lord Wynderbroke.

Longcluse stopped his brougham, jumped out, and overtook Richard Arden in the hall, where he stood, taking his letters from the hall-porter.

"How d'ye do, again? I sha'n't detain you a minute. I have had a long talk with your father about business," said Longcluse, seizing the topic most likely to secure a few minutes, and speaking very low. "You can bring me into a room here, and I'll tell you all that is necessary in two minutes."

"Certainly," said Richard, yielding to his curiosity. "I have only two or three minutes. I dine here with a friend, who is at this moment ordering dinner; so, you see, I am rather hurried."

He opened a door, and looking in said—

"Yes, we shall be quite to ourselves here."

Longcluse shut the door. There was no one to overhear them.

Richard Arden sat down on a sofa, and Mr. Longcluse threw himself into a chair.

"And what did he say?" asked Richard.

"They want to raise his interest on the Yorkshire estate; and he says you won't help him; but that of course is your affair, and I declined, point-blank, to intervene in it. And before I go further, it strikes me, as it did to-day at Mortlake, that your manner to me has undergone a slight change."

"Has it? I did not mean it, I assure you," said Richard Arden, with a little laugh.

"Oh! yes, Arden, it has, and you must know it, and—pardon me—you must intend it also; and now I want to know what I have done, or how I have hurt you, or who has been telling lies of me?"

"Nothing of all these, that I know of," said Richard, with a cold little laugh.

"Well, of course, if you prefer it, you may decline an explanation. I must however, remind you, because it concerns my happiness, and possibly other interests dearer to me than my life, too nearly to be trifled with, that you heard all I said respecting your sister with the friendliest approbation and encouragement. You knew as much and as little about me then as you do now. I am not conscious of having said or done anything to warrant the slightest change in your feelings or opinion; and in your manner there is a change, and a very decided change, and I tell you frankly I can't understand it."

Thus directly challenged, Richard Arden looked at him hard for a moment. He was balancing in his mind whether he should evade or accept the crisis. He preferred the latter.

"Well, I can only say I did not intend to convey anything by my manner; but, as you know, when there is anything in one's mind it is not always easy to prevent its affecting, as you say, one's manner. I am not sorry you have asked me, because I spoke without reflection the other day. No one should answer, I really think, for any one else, in ever so small a matter, in this world."

"But you didn't—you spoke only for yourself. You simply promised me your friendship, your kind offices—you said, in fact, all I could have hoped for."

"Yes, perhaps—yes, I may, I suppose I did. But don't you see, dear Longcluse, things may come to mind, on thinking over."

"What things?" demanded Longcluse quickly, with a sudden energy that called a flush to his temples; and fire gleamed for a moment from his deep-set, gloomy eyes.

"What things? Why, young ladies are not always the most intelligible problems on earth. I think you ought to know that; and really I do think, in such matters, it is far better that they should be left to themselves as much as possible; and I think, besides, that there are some difficulties that did not strike us. I mean, that I now see that there really are great difficulties—insuperable difficulties."

"Can you define them?" said Longcluse coldly.

"I don't want to vex you, Longcluse, and I don't want to quarrel."

"That's extremely kind of you."

"I don't know whether you are serious, but it is quite true. I don't wish any unpleasantness between us. I don't think I need say more than that; having thought it over, I don't see how it could ever be."

"Will you give me your reasons?"

"I really don't see that I can add anything in particular to what I have said."

"I think, Mr. Arden, considering all that has passed between us on this subject, that you are bound to let me know your reasons for so marked a change of opinion."

"I can't agree with you, Mr. Longcluse. I don't see in the least why I need tell you my particular reasons for the opinion I have expressed. My sister can act for herself, and I certainly shall not account to you for my reasons or opinions in the matter."

Mr. Longcluse's pale face grew whiter, and his brows knit, as he fixed a momentary stare on the young man; but he mastered his anger, and said in a cold tone—

"We disagree totally upon that point, and I rather think the time will come when you must explain."

"I have no more to say upon the subject, Sir, except this," said Arden, very tartly, "that it is certain your hopes can never lead to anything, and that I object to your continuing your visits at Mortlake."

"Why, the house does not belong to you—it belongs to Sir Reginald Arden, who objects to your visits and receives mine. Your ideas seem a little confused," and he laughed gently and coldly.

"Very much the reverse, Sir. I object to my sister being exposed to the least chance of annoyance from your visits. I protest against it, and you will be so good as to understand that I distinctly forbid them."

"The young lady's father, I presume, will hardly ask your advice in the matter, and I certainly shall not ask your leave. I shall call when I please, so long as I am received at Mortlake, and shall direct my own conduct, without troubling you for counsel in my affairs." Mr. Longcluse laughed again icily.

"And so shall I, mine," said Arden sharply.

"You have no right to treat anyone so," said Longcluse angrily—"as if one had broken his honour, or committed a crime."

"A crime!" repeated Richard Arden. "Oh! That, indeed, would pretty well end all relations."

"Yes, as, perhaps, you shall find," answered Longcluse, with sudden and oracular ferocity.

Each gentleman had gone a little farther than he had at first intended. Richard Arden had a proud and fierce temper when it was roused. He was near saying what would have amounted to insult. It was a chance opening of the door that prevented it. Both gentlemen had stood up.

"Please, Sir, have you done with the room, Sir?" asked the man.

"Yes," said Longcluse, and laughed again as he turned on his heel.

"Because three gentlemen want the room, if it's not engaged, Sir. And Lord Wynderbroke is waiting for you, please, Mr. Arden."

So with a little toss of his head, which he held unusually high, and a flushed and "glooming" countenance, Richard Arden marched a little swaggeringly forth, to his dinner tête-à-tête with Lord Wynderbroke.

CHAPTER XXVIII.

STORIES ABOUT MR. LONGCLUSE.

The irritation of this unpleasant interview soon subsided, but Mr. Longcluse's anxiety rather increased.

Next day early in the afternoon he drove to Lady May's and she received him just as usual. He learned from her, without appearing to seek the information, that Alice Arden was still at Mortlake. His visit was one of but two or three minutes. He jumped into a hansom and drove out to Mortlake. He knocked. Man of the world as he was, his heart beat faster.

"Is Miss Arden at home?"

"No, Sir."

"Not at home?"

"Miss Arden is gone out, Sir."

"Oh! perhaps in the garden?"

"No, Sir; she has gone out, and won't be back for some time."

The man spoke with the promptitude and decision of a servant instructed to deny his mistress to the visitor. He had not a card; he would call again another day.

He heard the piano faintly, and, he thought, Alice's voice also; and certainly he saw Vivian Darnley in the drawing-room window, as his cab turned away from the door. With a swelling heart he drove into town. The portcullis, then, had fallen; access was denied him; and he should see her no more!

Good Heaven! what had he done? He walked distractedly, for a while, up and down his study. Should he employ Lady May's intervention, and tell her the whole story? Good-natured Lady May! Perhaps she would undertake his cause, and plead for his re-admission. But was even that so certain? How could he tell what view she might take of the matter? And were she to intercede for him ever so vehemently, how could he tell that she had any chance of prevailing?

No; on the whole it was better to be his own advocate. He would sit down then and there, and write to the offended or alarmed lady, and lay his piteous case before her in his own words and rely on her compassion, without an intervenient.

How many letters he began, how many he even finished, and rejected, I need not tire you by telling. Some were composed in the first, others in the third person. Not one satisfied him. Here was the man of a million and more, who would dash off a note to his stock-broker, to buy or sell a hundred thousand pounds' worth of stock—who would draft a resolution of the bank of which he was the chairman, directing an operation which would make men open their eyes, without the tremor of a nerve or the hesitation of a moment—unmanned, helpless, distracted in the endeavour to write a note to a young and inexperienced girl!

O beautiful sex! what a triumph is here! O Love! what fools will you not make of us poor masculine wiseacres! The letter he dispatched was in these terms. I daresay he had torn better ones to pieces:—

> "DEAR MISS ARDEN,—I had hoped that my profound contrition might have atoned for a momentary indiscretion—the declaration, though in terms the most respectful, of feelings which I had not self-command sufficient to suppress, and which had for nearly a year remained concealed in my own breast. I am sure, Miss Arden, that you are incapable of a gratuitous cruelty. Have I not sworn that one word to recall the remembrance of that, to me, all but fatal madness shall never escape my lips, in your presence? May I not entreat that you will forget it, that you will forbear to pass upon me the agonising sentence of exclusion? You shall never again have to complain of my uttering one word that the merest acquaintance, who is permitted the happiness of conversing with you, might not employ. You shall never regret your forbearance. I shall never cease to bless you for it; and whatever decision you arrive at, it shall be respected by me as sacred law. I shall never cease to reverence and bless the hand that spares or—afflicts me. May I be permitted this one melancholy hope, may I be allowed to interpret your omitting to answer this miserable letter as a concession of its prayer? Unless forbidden, I will endeavour to construe your silence as oblivion.
>
> "I have the honour to remain, dear Miss Arden, with deep compunction and respect, but not altogether without hope in your mercy,
>
> "Yours the most unhappy and distracted man in England,
>
> "Walter Longcluse."

Mr. Longcluse sealed this letter in its envelope, and addressed it. He would have liked to send it that moment, by his servant, but an odd shyness prevented. He did not wish his servants to conjure and put their heads together over it; he could not endure the idea; so with his own hand he dropped it in the post. Somewhat in the style of the old novel was this composition of Mr. Longcluse's—a little theatrical, and, one would have fancied, even affected; yet never was man more desperately sincere.

Night came, and brought no reply. Was no news good news, or would the morning bring, perhaps from Richard Arden, a withering answer? Morning came, and no answer: what was he to conjecture?

That day, in Grosvenor Square, he passed Richard Arden, who looked steadily and sternly a little to his right, and cut him.

It was a marked and decided cut. His ears tingled as if he had received a slap in the face. So things had assumed a very decided attitude indeed! Longcluse felt very oddly enraged, at first; then anxious. It was insulting that Richard Arden should have taken the initiative in dissolving relations. But had he not been himself studiously impertinent to Arden, in that brief colloquy of yesterday? He ought to have been prepared for this. Without explanation, and the shaking of hands, it was impossible that relations of amity should have been resumed between them. But Longcluse had been entirely absorbed by a threatened alienation that affected him much more nearly. There was a thesis for conjecture in the situation, which made him still more anxious. A very little time would probably clear all up.

He was walking homeward, saying to himself as he went, "No, I shall find no answer; I should be a fool to fancy anything else;" and yet walking all the more quickly, as he approached his house, in the hope of the very letter which he affected, to himself, to have quite rejected as an impossibility. Some letters had come, but none from Mortlake. His letter to Alice was still unanswered. He was now in the agony of suspense and distraction.

The same evening Richard Arden was talking about him, as he leaned with his elbow on the mantelpiece at Mortlake. He and Alice were alone in the drawing-room, awaiting the arrival of the little dinner-party. This, as you know, was to include Lord Wynderbroke, before whose advances, in Richard Arden's vision, Mr. Longcluse had waned, and even become an embarrassment and a nuisance.

"It is easier to cut him than to explain," thought Richard Arden. "It bores one so inexpressibly, giving reasons for what one does, and I'm so glad he has saved me the trouble by his vulgar impertinence."

They had talked for some time, Alice chiefly a listener. How was she affected toward Mr. Longcluse? He was agreeable; he flattered her; he was passionately in love with her. All but this latter condition she liked very well; but this was embarrassing, and quite impracticable. Who knows what that tiny spark we term a fancy, a whim, a penchant might have grown to, had it not been blown away by this untimely gust? But, for my part, I don't think it ever would have grown to a matter of the heart. There was something in the way. A fancy is one thing, and passion quite another. Pique is a common state of mind, and comes and goes, and comes again, in many a courtship. But a liking that has once entered the heart cannot be torn out in a hasty moment, and takes a long time, and many a struggle, to kill.

She was a little sorry, just then, to lose him so inevitably. Perhaps his letter, to which he had trusted to move her, had rendered the return of old relations impossible. In this letter she felt herself the owner of a secret—a secret which she could not keep without a sort of understanding growing up between them—which therefore she had no idea of keeping.

She was resolved to tell it. The letter she had locked, in marked isolation, as if no property of hers, but simply a document that was in her keeping, in the pretty ormolu casket that stood on the drawing-room chimney-piece. She had intended showing it, and telling the story of the scene in the garden, to Richard. But he was speaking with a mysterious asperity of Mr. Longcluse, which made her hesitate. A very little thing, it seemed to her, might suffice to make a very violent quarrel out of a coldness. Instinctively, therefore, she refrained, and listened to Richard while, with his arm touching the casket on the chimney-piece, he descanted on the writer of the unknown letter.

She experienced an odd feeling of insecurity as, in the course of his talk, his fingers began to trifle with the pretty fingers that stood out in relief upon the casket; for she knew that the ordeal of the pistol, discountenanced in England, was still in force on the Continent, and Mr. Longcluse's ideas were all Continental; and how near were those fingers to the letter which might suffice to explode the dangerous element that had already accumulated!

"He has talked of us to his low companions; he chooses to associate with usurers and worse people; and he has been speaking of us in the most insolent terms."

"Really!" said Alice. Her large eyes looked larger as they fixed on him.

"Yes, and I'll tell you how I heard it. You must know, dear Alice, that I happened to want a little money; and when one does, the usual course is to borrow it. So I paid a visit to my harpy—and a harpy in need is a harpy indeed. Being hard up, he fleeced me; and the gentleman, I suppose, thinking he might be familiar, told me he was on confidential terms with Mr. Longcluse and wished me a good deal of joy. 'Of what?' I ventured to ask, for he had just hit me rather hard. 'Of your chance,' or, as he called it chanshe, he said, with a delightfully arch leer. I thought he meant I had backed the right horse for the Derby, but it turned out he meant our chance of inducing Mr. Longcluse to make up his mind to marry you. I was very near knocking him down; but a man who has one's bill for three hundred pounds must be respected. So I merely ventured to ask on whose authority he congratulated me, when it appeared it was on Mr. Longcluse's own, who, it seems, had said a great deal more, equally intolerable. In plain, coarse terms, he says that, being poor, we have conspired with you to secure him, Mr. Longcluse, for your husband. As to the fact of his having actually conveyed that, and to more people than one, there is and can be no doubt whatever. I can imagine, considering all things, nothing more vulgar, audacious, and cowardly."

A blush of anger glowed in Alice's face. Richard Arden liked the proud fire that gleamed from her dark grey eyes. It satisfied him that his words were not lost.

"I lighted on a man who knew more about him than I had learned before," resumed Richard Arden. "He was suspected at Berlin of having been engaged in a conspiracy to pigeon Dacre and Wilmot, who were travelling. He did not appear, but he is said to have supplied the money, and had a lion's share of the spoil. There is no good in repeating these things generally, you know, because they are so hard to prove; and a fellow like that is dangerous. They say he is very litigious."

"Upon my word, if your information is at all to be relied on, it is plain we have made a great mistake. It is a disappointing world, but I could not have fancied him doing anything so low; and I must say for him that he was gentlemanlike and quiet, and very unlike the person he appears to be. I think I never heard of anything so outrageous! Vivian Darnley told me that he was a great duellist, and thought to be a very quarrelsome, dangerous companion abroad. But he had only heard this, and what you tell me is so much worse, so mean, so utterly intolerable!"

"Oh! There's worse than that," said Richard, with a faint sinister smile.

"What?" said she, returning it with an almost frightened gaze.

"There was a very beautiful girl at the opera in Vienna; her name was Piccardi, a daughter of a good old Roman family. You can't imagine how admired she was! And she was thought to be on the point of marrying Count Baddenoff; Mr. Longcluse, it seems, chose to be in love with her; he was not then anything like so rich as he became afterwards—and this poor girl was killed."

"Good heavens! Richard—what can you mean?"

"I mean that she was assassinated, and that from that day Mr. Longcluse was never received in society in Vienna, and had to leave it."

"You ought to tell May Penrose," said she, after a silence of dismay.

"Not for the world," said Richard; "she talks enough for six—and where's the good? She'll only take up the cudgels for him, and we shall be in the centre of a pretty row."

"Well, if you think it best ——" she began.

"Certainly," said he. And a silence followed.

"Here is a carriage at the door," said Richard Arden. "Let us dismiss Longcluse, and look a little more like ourselves."

That evening there came letters as usual to Mr. Longcluse, and among others a note from Lady May Penrose, reminding him of her little garden-party at Richmond next day.

"By Jove!" he exclaimed, starting up and reading the cards on his chimney, "I thought it was the day after. It was very good-natured, poor old thing, her reminding me. I shall see Alice Arden there. Not one line does she vouchsafe. But is not she right? I think the more highly of her for not writing. I don't think she ought to write. Oh, Heaven grant she may meet me as usual? Does she mean it? If she did not, would she not have got her brother to write, or have written herself a cold line, to end our acquaintance?"

So he tried to comfort himself, and to keep alive his dying hope by these artificial stimulants.

CHAPTER XXIX.

THE GARDEN PARTY.

Next morning Mr. Longcluse rose with a sense of something before him.

"So I shall see her to-day! If she's the girl I've thought her, she will meet me as usual. That frantic scene, in which I risked all on the turn of a die, will be forgotten. Hasty words, or precipitate letters, are passed over every day; the man who commits such follies, under a transitory insanity, is allowed the privilege of recalling them. There were no witnesses present to make forgiveness difficult. It all lies with her own good sense, and a heart proud but gentle. Let but those mad words be sponged out, and I am happy. Alice, if you forgive me, I forgive your brother, and take his name from where it is, and write it in my heart. Oh, beautiful Alice! will you belie your looks? Oh, clear bright mind! will you be clouded and perverted? Oh, gentle heart! can you be merciless?"

Mr. Longcluse made his simple morning toilet very carefully. A very plain man, extremely ugly some pronounce him; yet his figure is good, his get-up unexceptionable, and altogether he is a most gentlemanlike man to look upon, and in his movements and attitudes, quite unstudied, there is an undefinable grace. His accent is a little foreign—the slightest thing in the world, and Lady May Penrose declares it is so very pretty. Then he is so agreeable, when he pleases; and he is so very rich!

Some people wonder why he does not withdraw from all speculations, retire upon his enormous wealth, and with his elegant tastes, and the art of being magnificent without glare, even gorgeous without vulgarity—for has he not shown this refined talent in the service of others, who have taken him into council?—he could eclipse all the world in splendid elegance, and make his way, force d'argent, to the pinnacle of half the world's ambition. Were those stories true that Richard Arden told his sister on the night before?

I don't think that Richard Arden stuck at trifles, where he had an object to gain, and I don't believe a word of his story of Mr. Longcluse's insulting talk. It was not his way to boast and vapour; and he had a secret contempt for many of the Jewish and other agents whom he chose to employ. But undoubtedly Mr. Longcluse had the reputation among his discounting admirers of being a dangerous man to quarrel with; and also it was true that he had fought three or four savage duels in the course of his Continental life. There were other stories, unauthenticated, unpleasant. These were whispered with sneers by Mr. Longcluse's enemies. But there's a divinity doth hedge a King Crœsus, and his character bore a charmed life, among the missiles that would have laid that of many a punier man in the dust.

With an agitated heart, Mr. Longcluse approached the pretty little place known as Raleigh Court, to which he had been invited. Through the quaint, old-fashioned gate-way, under the embowering branches of tall trees, he drove up a short, broad avenue, clumped at each side with old timber, to the open hall-door of the pretty Elizabethan house. Carriages of all sorts were discernible under the branches, assembled at the further side to the right of the hall-door, over the wide steps of which was spread a scarlet cloth. Croquet parties were already visible on the shorn grass, under boughs that spread high in the air, and cast a pleasant shadow on the sward. Groups were strolling among the flower-beds—some walking in, some emerging from the open door—and the scene presented the usual variety of dress, and somewhat listless to-ing and fro-ing.

Did anyone, of all the guests of Lady May, mask so profound an agitation, under the conventional smile, as that which beat at Walter Longcluse's heart? Two or three people whom he knew, he met and talked to—some for a minute, others for a longer time—as he drew near the steps. His eye all the time was busy in the search after one pretty figure, the least glimpse of which he would have recognised with the thrill of a sure intuition, far or near. He would have liked to ask the friends he met whether the Ardens were here. But what would have been easy to him a week before, was now an effort for which he could not find courage.

He entered the hall, quaint and lofty, rising to the entire height of the house, with two galleries, one above the other, surrounding it on three sides. Ancestors of the late Mr. Penrose, who had left all this and a great deal more to his sorrowing relict, stood on the panelled walls at full length—some in ruffs and trunk-hose, others in perukes and cut-velvet, one with a bâton in his hand, and three with falcon on fist—all stately and gentlemanlike, according to their several periods; with corresponding ladies, some stiff and pallid, who figured in the days of the virgin queen, and others in the graceful déshabille of Sir Peter Lely. This quaint oak hall was now resonant with the buzz and clack of modern gossip, prose, and flirtation, and a great deal crowded, notwithstanding its commodious proportions. Lady May was still receiving her company near the doorway of the first drawing-room, and her kindly voice was audible from within as the visitor approached. Mr. Longcluse was very graciously received.

"I want you so particularly, to introduce you to Lady Hummington. She is such a charming person. She is so thoroughly up in German literature. She's a great deal too learned for me, but you and she will understand one another so perfectly, and you will be quite charmed with her. Mr. Addlings, did you happen to see Lady Hummington, or have you any idea where she's gone?"

"I shall go and look for her, with pleasure. Is not she the tall lady with grey hair? Shall I tell her you want to say a word to her?"

"You're very kind, but I'll not mind, thank you very much. It is so provoking, Mr. Longcluse! you would have been perfectly charmed with her."

"I shall be more fortunate, by-and-by, perhaps," said Mr. Longcluse. "Are any of our friends from Mortlake here?" he added, looking a little fixedly in her eyes, for he was thinking whether Alice had betrayed his secret, and was trying to read an answer there.

Lady May answered quite promptly—

"Oh, yes, Alice is here, and her brother. He went out that way with some friends," she said, indicating with a little nod a door which, from a second hall, opened on a terrace. "I asked him to show them the three fountains. You must see them also; they are in the Dutch garden; they were put up in the reign of George the First.—How d'ye do, Mrs. Frumply? How d'ye do, Miss Frumply?"

"What a charming house!" exclaims Mrs. Frumply, "and what a day! We were saying, Arabella and I, as we drove out, that you must really have an influence with the clerk of the weather, ha, ha, ha! didn't we, Arabella? So charming!"

Lady May laughed affably, and said—"Won't you and your daughter go in and take some tea? Mr. (she was going to call on Longcluse, but he had glided away)—Oh, Mr. Darnley!"

And the introduction was made, and Vivian Darnley, with Mrs. Frumply on his arm, attended by her daughter Arabella, did as he was commanded and got tea for that simpering lady, and fruit and Naples biscuits, and plum-cake, and was rewarded with the original joke about the clerk of the weather.

Mr. Longcluse, in the meantime, had passed the door indicated by Lady May, and stood upon the short terrace that overlooked the pretty flower-garden cut out in grotesque patterns, so that looking down upon its masses of crimson, blue, and yellow, as he leaned on the balustrade, it showed beneath his eye like a wide deep-piled carpet, on the green ground of which were walking groups of people, the brilliant hues of the ladies' dresses rivalling the splendour of the verbenas, and making altogether a very gay picture.

The usual paucity of male attendance made Mr. Longcluse's task of observation easy. He was looking for Richard Arden's well-known figure among the groups, thinking that probably Alice was not far off. But he was not there, nor was Alice; and Walter Longcluse, gloomy and lonely in this gay crowd, descended the steps at the end of this terrace, and sauntered round again to the front of the house, now and then passing some one he knew, with an exchange of a smile or a bow, and then lost again in the Vanity Fair of strange faces and voices.

Now he is at the hall door—he mounts the steps. Suddenly, as he stands upon the level platform at top, he finds himself within four feet of Richard Arden. He looks on him as he might on the carved pilaster, at the side of the hall door; no one could have guessed, by his inflexible but unaffected glance, that he and Mr. Arden had ever been acquainted. The younger man showed something in his countenance, a sudden hauteur, a little elevation of the chin, a certain sternness, more melodramatic, though less effective, than the simple blank of Mr. Longcluse's glance.

That gentleman looked about coolly. He was in search of Miss Arden, but he did not see her. He entered the hall again, and Richard Arden a little awkwardly resumed his conversation, which had suddenly subsided into silence on Longcluse's appearance.

By this time Lady May was more at ease, having received all her company that were reasonably punctual, and in the hall Longcluse now encountered her.

"Have you seen Mr. Arden?" she inquired of him.

"Yes, he's at the door, at the steps."

"Would you mind telling him kindly that I want to say a word to him?"

"Certainly, most happy," said Longcluse, without any distinct plan as to how he was to execute her awkward commission.

"Thank you very much. But, oh! dear, here is Lady Hummington, and she wishes so much to know you; I'll send some one else. I must introduce you, come with me—Lady Hummington, I want to introduce my friend, Mr. Longcluse." So Mr. Longcluse was presented to Lady Hummington, who was very lean, and a "blue," and most fatiguingly well up in archæology, and all new books on dry and difficult subjects. So that Mr. Longcluse felt that he was, in Joe Willett's phrase, "tackled" by a giant, and was driven to hideous exertions of attention and memory to hold his own. When Lady Hummington, to whom it was plain kind Lady May, with an unconscious cruelty, had been describing Mr. Longcluse's accomplishments and acquirements, had taken some tea and other refection, and when Mr. Longcluse's kindness "had her wants supplied," and she, like Scott's "old man" in the "Lay of the Last Minstrel," "was gratified," she proposed visiting the music-room, where she had heard a clever organist play, on a harmonium, three distinct tunes at the same time, which being composed on certain principles, that she explained with much animation and precision, harmonised very prettily.

So this clever woman directed, and Mr. Longcluse led, the way to the music-room.

CHAPTER XXX.

HE SEES HER.

Mr. Longcluse's attention was beginning to wander a little, and his eyes were now busy in search of some one whom he had not found; and knowing that the duration of people's stay at a garden-party is always uncertain, and that some of those gaily-plumed birds who make the flutter, and chirping, and brilliancy of the scene, hardly alight before they take wing again, he began to fear that Alice Arden had gone.

"Just like my luck!" he thought bitterly; "and if she is gone, when shall I have an opportunity of seeing her again?"

Lady Hummington's well-informed conversation had been, unheeded, accompanying the ruminations and distractions of this "passionate pilgrim;" and as they approached the door of the music-room, the little crush there brought the learned lady's lips so near to his ear, that with a little start he heard the words—"All strictly arithmetical, you know, and adjusted by the relative frequency of vibrations. That theory, I am sure, you approve, Mr. Longcluse."

To which the distracted lover made answer, "I quite agree with you, Lady Hummington."

The music-room at Raleigh Court is an apartment of no great size, and therefore when, with Lady Hummington on his arm, he entered, it was at no great distance that he saw Miss Arden standing near the window, and talking with an elderly gentleman, whose appearance he did not know, but who seemed to be extremely interested in her conversation. She saw him, he had not a doubt, for she turned a little quickly, and looked ever so little more directly out at the window, and a very slight tinge flushed her cheek. It was quite plain, he thought, and a dreadful pang stole through his breast, that she did not choose to see him—quite plain that she did see him—and he thought, from a subtle scrutiny of her beautiful features, quite plain also that it gave her pain to meet without acknowledging him.

Lady Hummington was conversing with volubility; but the air felt icy, and there was a strange trembling at his heart, and this, in many respects, hard man of the world, felt that the tears were on the point of welling from his eyes. The struggle was but for a few moments, and he seemed quite himself again. Lady

Hummington wished to go to the end of the room where the piano was, and the harmonium on which the organist had performed his feat of the three tunes. That artist was taking his departure, having a musical assignation of some kind to keep. But to oblige Lady Hummington, who had heard of Thalberg's doing something of the kind, he sat down and played an elaborate piece of music on the piano with his thumbs only. This charming effort over, and applauded, the performer took his departure. And Lady Hummington said—

"I am told, Mr. Longcluse, that you are a very good musician."

"A very indifferent performer, Lady Hummington."

"Lady May Penrose tells a very different tale."

"Lady May Penrose is too kind to be critical," said Longcluse; and as he maintained this dialogue, his eye was observing every movement of Alice Arden. She seemed, however, to have quite made up her mind to stand her ground. There was a strange interest, to him, even in being in the same room with her. Perhaps Miss Arden saw that Mr. Longcluse's movements were dependent upon those of the lady whom he accompanied, and might have thought that, the musician having departed, their stay in that room would not be very long.

"I should be so glad to hear you sing, Mr. Longcluse," pursued Lady Hummington. "You have been in the East, I think; have you any of the Hindostanee songs? There are some, I have read, that embody the theories of the Brahmin philosophy."

"Long-winded songs, I fancy," said Mr. Longcluse, laughing; "it is a very voluminous philosophy, but the truth is, I've got a little cold, and I should not like to make a bad impression so early."

"But surely there are some simple little things, without very much compass, that would not distress you. How pretty those old English songs are that they are collecting and publishing now! I mean songs of Shakespeare's time—Ben Jonson's, Beaumont and Fletcher's, and Massinger's, you know. Some of them are so extremely pretty!"

"Oh! yes, I'll sing you one of those with pleasure," said he with a strange alacrity, quite forgetting his cold, sitting down at the instrument, and striking two or three fierce chords.

I am sure that most of my readers are acquainted with that pretty old English song, of the time of James the First, entitled, "Once I Loved a Maiden Fair." That was the song he chose.

Never, perhaps, did he sing so well before, with a fluctuation of pathos and scorn, tenderness and hatred, expressed with real dramatic fire, and with more power of voice than at moments of less excitement he possessed. He sang it with real passion, and produced, exactly where he wished, a strange but unavowed sensation. He omitted one verse, and the song as he delivered it was thus:—

"Once I loved a maiden fair,
But she did deceive me:
She with Venus could compare,
In my mind, believe me.
She was young, and among
All our maids the sweetest:
Now I say, Ah, well-a-day!
Brightest hopes are fleetest.

Maidens wavering and untrue
Many a heart have broken;
Sweetest lips the world e'er knew
Falsest words have spoken.
Fare thee well, faithless girl,
I'll not sorrow for thee:
Once I held thee dear as pearl,
Now I do abhor thee."

When he had finished the song, he said coldly, but very distinctly, as he rose—

"I like that song, there is a melancholy psychology in it. It is a song worthy of Shakespeare himself."

Lady Hummington urged him with an encore, but he was proof against her entreaties. And so, after a little, she took Mr. Longcluse's arm; and Alice felt relieved when the room was rid of them.

CHAPTER XXXI.

ABOUT THE GROUNDS.

Lady Hummington, well pleased at having found in Mr. Longcluse what she termed a kindred mind, was warned by the hour that she must depart. She took her leave of Mr. Longcluse with regret, and made him promise to come to luncheon with her on the Thursday following. Mr. Longcluse called her carriage for her, and put in, besides herself, her maiden sister and two daughters, who all exhibited the family leanness, with noses more or less red and aquiline, and small black eyes, set rather close together.

As he ascended the steps he was accosted by a damsel in distress.

"Mr. Longcluse, I'm so glad to see you! You must do a very good-natured thing," said handsome Miss Maubray, smiling on him. "I came here with old Sir Arthur and Lady Tramway, and I've lost them; and I've been bored to death by a Mr. Bagshot, and I've sent him to look for my pocket-handkerchief in the tea-room; and I want you, as you hope for mercy, to show it now, and rescue me from my troubles."

"I'm too much honoured. I'm only too happy, Miss Maubray. I shall put Mr. Bagshot to death, if you wish it, and Sir Arthur and Lady Tramway shall appear the moment you command."

Mr. Longcluse was talking his nonsense with the high spirits which sometimes attend a painful excitement.

"I told them I should get to that tree if I were lost in the crowd, and that they would be sure to find me under it after six o'clock. Do take me there; I am so afraid of Mr. Bagshot's returning!"

So over the short grass that handsome girl walked, with Mr. Longcluse at her side.

"I'll sit at this side, thank you; I don't want to be seen by Mr. Bagshot."

So she sat down, placing herself at the further side of the great trunk of the old chestnut-tree. Mr. Longcluse stood nearly opposite, but so placed as to command a view of the hall-door steps. He was still watching the groups that emerged, with as much interest as if his life depended on the order of their to-ing and fro-ing. But, in spite of this, very soon Miss Maubray's talk began to interest him.

"Whom did Alice Arden come with?" asked Miss Maubray. "I should like to know; because, if I should lose my people, I must find some one to take me home."

"With her brother, I fancy."

"Oh! yes, to be sure—I saw him here. I forgot. But Alice is very independent, just now, of his protection," and she laughed.

"How do you mean?"

"Oh! Lord Wynderbroke, of course, takes care of her while she's here. I saw them walking about together, so happy! I suppose it is all settled."

"About Lord Wynderbroke?" suggested Longcluse, with a gentle carelessness, as if he did not care a farthing—as if a dreadful pain had not at that moment pierced his heart.

"Yes, Lord Wynderbroke. Why, haven't you heard of that?"

"Yes, I believe—I think so. I am sure I have heard something of it; but one hears so many things, one forgets, and I don't know him. What kind of man is he?"

"He's hard to describe; he's not disagreeable, and he's not dull; he has a great deal to say for himself about pictures, and the East, and the Crimea, and the opera, and all the people at all the courts in Europe, and he ought to be amusing; but I think he is the driest person I ever talked to. And he is really good-natured; but I think him much more teasing than the most ill-natured man alive, he's so insufferably punctual and precise."

"You know him very well, then?" said Longcluse, with an effort to contribute his share to the talk.

"Pretty well," said the young lady, with just a slight tinge flushing her haughty cheek. "But no one, who has been a week in the same house with him, could fail to see all that."

Miss Maubray herself, I am told, had hopes of Lord Wynderbroke about a year before, and was not amiably disposed towards him now, and looked on the triumph of Alice a little sourly; although something like the beginning of a real love had since stolen into her heart—not, perhaps, destined to be much more happy.

"Lord Wynderbroke—I don't know him. Is that gentleman he whom I saw talking to Miss Arden in the music-room, I wonder? He's not actually thin, and he is not at all stout; he's a little above the middle height, and he stoops just a little. He appears past fifty, and his hair looks like an old-fashioned brown wig, brushed up into a sort of cone over his forehead. He seems a little formal, and very polite and smiling, with a flower in his button-hole; a blue coat; and he has a pair of those little gold Paris glasses, and was looking out through the window with them."

"Had he a high nose?"

"Yes, rather a thin, high nose, and his face is very brown."

"Well, if he was all that, and had a brown face and a high nose, and was pretty near fifty-three, and very near Alice Arden, he was positively Lord Wynderbroke."

"And has this been going on for some time, or is it a sudden thing?"

"Both, I believe. It has been going on a long time, I believe, in old Sir Reginald's head; but it has come about, after all, rather suddenly; and my guardian says—Mr. David Arden, you know—that he has written a proposal in a letter to Sir Reginald, and you see how happy the young lady looks. So I think we may assume that the course of true love, for once, runs smooth—don't you?"

"And I suppose there is no objection anywhere?" said Longcluse, smiling. "It is a pity he is not a little younger, perhaps."

"I don't hear any complaints; let us rather rejoice he is not ten or twenty years older. I am sure it would not prevent his happiness, but it would heighten the ridicule. Are you one of Lady May Penrose's party to the Derby to-morrow?" inquired the young lady.

"No; I haven't been asked."

"Lord Wynderbroke is going."

"Oh! of course he is."

"I don't think Mr. David Arden likes it; but, of course, it is no business of his if other people are pleased. I wonder you did not hear all this from Richard Arden, you and he are so intimate."

So said the young lady, looking very innocent. But I think she suspected more than she said.

"No, I did not hear it," he said carelessly; "or, if I did, I forgot it. But do you blame the young lady?"

"Blame her! not at all. Besides, I am not so sure that she knows."

"How can you think so?"

"Because I think she likes quite another person."

"Really! And who is he?"

"Can't you guess?"

"Upon my honour, I can't."

There was something so earnest, and even vehement, in this sudden asseveration, that Miss Maubray looked for a moment in his face; and seeing her curious expression, he said more quietly, "I assure you I don't think I ever heard; I'm rather curious to know."

"I mean Mr. Vivian Darnley."

"Oh! Well, I've suspected that a long time. I told Richard Arden, one day—I forget how it came about—but he said no."

"Well, I say yes," laughed the young lady, "and we shall see who's right."

"Oh! Recollect I'm only giving you his opinion. I rather lean to yours, but he said there was positively nothing in it, and that Mr. Darnley is too poor to marry."

"If Alice Arden resembles me," said the young lady, "she thinks there are just two things to marry for—either love or ambition."

"You place love first, I'm glad to hear," said Mr. Longcluse, with a smile.

"So I do, because it is most likely to prevail with a pig-headed girl; but what I mean is this: that social pre-eminence—I mean rank, and not trumpery rank; but such as, being accompanied with wealth and precedence, is also attended with power—is worth an immense sacrifice of all other objects; my reason tells me, worth the sacrifice of love. But that is a sacrifice which impatient, impetuous people can't always so easily make—which I daresay I could not make if I were tried; but I don't think I shall ever be fool enough to become so insane, for the state of a person in love is a state of simple idiotism. It is pitiable, I allow, but also contemptible; but, judging by what I see, it appears to me a more irresistible delusion than ambition. But I don't understand Alice well. I think, if I knew a little more of her brother—certain qualities so run in families—I should be able to make a better guess. What do you think of him?"

"He's very agreeable, isn't he? and, for the rest, really, until men are tried as events only can try them, it is neither wise nor safe to pronounce."

"Is he affectionate?"

"His sister seems to worship him," he answered; "but young ladies are so angelic, that where they like they resent nothing, and respect selfishness itself as a manly virtue."

"But you know him intimately; surely you must know something of him."

Under different circumstances, this audacious young lady's cross-examination would have amused Mr. Longcluse; but in his present relations, and spirits, it was otherwise.

"I should but mislead you if I were to answer more distinctly. I answer for no man, hardly for myself. Besides, I question your theory. I don't think, except by accident, that a brother's character throws any light upon a sister's; and I hope—I think, I mean—that Miss Arden has qualities illimitably superior to those of her brother. Are these your friends, Miss Maubray?" he continued.

"So they are," she answered. "I'm so much obliged to you, Mr. Longcluse! I think they are leaving."

Mr. Longcluse, having delivered her into the hands of her chaperon, took his leave, and walked into the broad alleys among the trees, and in solitude under their shade, sat himself down by a pond, on which two swans were sailing majestically. Looking down upon the water with a pallid frown, he struck the bank beneath him viciously with his heel, peeling off little bits of the sward, which dropped into the water.

"It is all plain enough now. Richard Arden has been playing me false. It ought not to surprise me, perhaps. The girl, I still believe, has neither act nor part in the conspiracy. She has been duped by her brother. I have thrown myself upon her mercy; I will now appeal to her justice. As for him—what vermin mankind are! He must return to his allegiance; he will. After all, he may not like to lose me. He will act in the way that most interests his selfishness. Come, come! it is no impracticable problem. I'm not cruel? Not I! No, I'm not cruel; but I am utterly just. I would not hang a mouse up by the tail to die, as they do in France, head downwards, of hunger, for eating my cheese; but should the vermin nibble at my heart, in that case, what says justice? Alice, beautiful Alice, you shall have every chance before I tear you from my heart—oh, for ever! Ambition! That coarse girl, Miss Maubray, can't understand you. Ambition, in her sense, you have none; there is nothing venal in your nature. Vivian Darnley, is there anything in that either? I think nothing. I observed them closely, that night, at Mortlake. No, there was nothing. My conversation and music interested her, and when I was by, he was nothing.

"They are going to the Derby to-morrow. I think Lady May has treated me rather oddly, considering that she had all but borrowed my drag. She might have put me off civilly; but I don't blame her. She is good-natured, and if she has any idea that I and the Ardens are not quite on pleasant terms, it quite excuses it. Her asking me here, and her little note to remind, were meant to show that she did not take up the quarrel against me. Never mind; I shall know all about it, time enough. They are going to the Derby to-morrow. Very well, I shall go also. It will all be right yet. When did I fail? When did I renounce an object? By Heaven, one way or other, I'll accomplish this!"

Tall Mr. Longcluse rose, and looked round him, and in deep thought, marched with a resolute step towards the house.

CHAPTER XXXII.

UNDER THE LIME-TREES.

At this garden-party, marvellous as it may appear, Lord Wynderbroke has an aunt. How old she is I know not, nor yet with what conscience her respectable relations can permit her to haunt such places, and run a risk of being suffocated in doorways, or knocked down the steps by an enamoured couple hurrying off to more romantic quarters, or of having her maundering old head knocked with a croquet mallet, as she totters drearily among the hoops.

This old lady is worth conciliating, for she has plate and jewels, and three thousand a-year to leave; and Lord Wynderbroke is a prudent man. He can bear a great deal of money, and has no objection to jewels, and thinks that the plate of his bachelor and old-maid kindred should gravitate to the centre and head of the house. Lord Wynderbroke was indulgent, and did not object to her living a little longer, for this aunt conduced to his air of juvenility more than the flower in his button-hole. However, she was occasionally troublesome, and on this occasion made an unwise mixture of fruit and other things; and a servant glided into the music-room, and with a proper inclination of his person, in a very soft tone said,—

"My lord, Lady Witherspoons is in her carriage at the door, my lord, and says her ladyship is indisposed, and begs, my lord, that your lordship will be so good as to hacompany her 'ome in her carriage, my lord."

"Oh! tell her ladyship I am so very sorry, and will be with her in a moment." And he turned with a very serious countenance to Alice. "How extremely unfortunate! When I saw those miserable cherries, I knew how it would be; and now I am torn away from this charming place; and I'm sure I hope she may be better soon, it is so (disgusting, he thought, but he said) melancholy! With whom shall I leave you, Miss Arden?"

"Thanks, I came with my brother, and here is my cousin, Mr. Darnley, who can tell me where he is."

"With a croquet party, near the little bridge. I'll be your guide, if you'll allow me," said Vivian Darnley eagerly.

"Pray, Lord Wynderbroke, don't let me delay you longer. I shall find my brother quite easily now. I so hope Lady Witherspoons may soon be better!"

"Oh, yes, she always is better soon; but in the meantime one is carried away, you see, and everything upset; and all because, poor woman, she won't exercise the smallest restraint. And she has, of course, a right to command me, being my aunt, you know, and—and—the whole thing is ineffably provoking."

And thus he took his reluctant departure, not without a brief but grave scrutiny of Mr. Vivian Darnley. When he was gone, Vivian Darnley proffered his arm, and that little hand was placed on it, the touch of which made his heart beat faster. Though people were beginning to go, there was still a crush about the steps. This little resistance and mimic difficulty were pleasant to him for her sake. Down the steps they went together, and now he had her all to himself; and silently for a while he led her over the closely-shorn grass, and into the green walk between the lime-trees, that leads down to the little bridge.

"Alice," at last he said—"Miss Arden, what have I done that you are so changed?"

"Changed! I don't think I am changed. What is there to change me?" she said carelessly, but in a low tone, as she looked along towards the flowers.

"It won't do, Alice, repeating my question, for that is all you have done. I like you too well to be put off with mere words. You are changed, and without a cause—no, I could not say that—not without a cause. Circumstances are altered; you are in the great world now, and admired; you have wealth and titles at your feet—Mr. Longcluse with his millions, Lord Wynderbroke with his coronet."

"And who told you that these gentlemen were at my feet?" she exclaimed, with a flash from her fine eyes, that reminded him of moments of pretty childish anger, long ago. "If I am changed—and perhaps I am—such speeches as that would quite account for it. You accuse me of caprice—has any one ever accused you of impertinence?"

"It is quite true, I deserve your rebuke. I have been speaking as freely as if we were back again at Arden Court, or Ryndelmere, and ten years of our lives were as a mist that rolls away."

"That's a quotation from a song of Tennyson's."

"I don't know what it is from. Being melancholy myself, I say the words because they are melancholy."

"Surely you can find some friend to console you in your affliction."

"It is not easy to find a friend at any time, much less when things go wrong with us."

"It is very hard if there is really no one to comfort you. Certainly I sha'n't try anything so hopeless as comforting a person who is resolved to be miserable. 'There's such a charm in melancholy, I would not if I could, be gay.' There's a quotation for you, as you like verses—particularly what I call moping verses."

"Come, Alice! this is not like you; you are not so unkind as your words would seem; you are not cruel, Alice—you are cruel to no one else, only to me, your old friend."

"I have said nothing cruel," said Miss Alice, looking on the grass before her; "cruelty is too sublime a phrase. I don't think I have ever experienced cruelty in my life; and I don't think it likely that you have; I certainly have never been cruel to any one. I'm a very good-natured person, as my birds and squirrel would testify if they could."

She laughed.

"I suppose people call that cruel which makes them suffer very much; it may be but a light look, or a cold word, but still it may be more than years of suffering to another. But I don't think, Alice, you ought to be so with me. I think you might remember old times a little more kindly."

"I remember them very kindly—as kindly as you do. We were always very good friends, and always, I daresay, shall be. I sha'n't quarrel. But I don't like heroics, I think they are so unmeaning. There may be people who like them very well and —— There is Richard, I think, and he has thrown away his mallet. If his game is over, he will come now, and Lady May doesn't want the people to stay late; she is going into town, and I stay with her to-night. We are going to the Derby to-morrow."

"I am going also—it was so kind of her!—she asked me to be of her party," said Vivian Darnley.

"Richard is coming also; I have never been to the Derby, and I daresay we shall be a very pleasant party; I know I like it of all things. Here comes Richard—he sees me. Was my uncle David here?"

"No."

"I hardly thought he was, but I saw Grace Maubray, and I fancied he might have come with her," she said carelessly.

"Yes, she was here; she came with Lady Tramway. They went away about half-an-hour ago."

So Richard joined her, and they walked to the house together, Vivian Darnley accompanying them.

"I think I saw you a little spooney to-day, Vivian, didn't I?" said Richard Arden, laughing. He remembered what Longcluse once said to him, about Vivian's tendre for his sister, and did not choose that Alice should suspect it. "Grace Maubray is a very pretty girl."

"She may be that, though it doesn't strike me," began Darnley.

"Oh! come, I'm too old for that sort of disclaimer; and I don't see why you should be so modest about it. She is clever and pretty."

"Yes, she is very pretty," said Alice.

"I suppose she is, but you're quite mistaken if you really fancy I admire Miss Maubray. I don't, I give you my honour, I don't," said Vivian vehemently.

Richard Arden laughed again, but prudently urged the point no more, intending to tell the story that evening as he and Alice drove together into town, in the way that best answered his purpose.

CHAPTER XXXIII.

THE DERBY.

The morning of the Derby day dawned auspiciously. The weather-cocks, the sky, and every other prognostic portended a fine cloudless day, and many an eye peeped early from bed-room window to read these signs, rejoicing.

"Ascot would have been more in our way," said Lady May, glancing at Alice, when the time arrived for taking their places in the carriage. "But the time answered, and we shall see a great many people we know there. So you must not think I have led you into a very fast expedition."

Richard Arden took the reins. The footmen were behind, in charge of hampers from Fortnum and Mason's, and inside, opposite to Alice, sat Lord Wynderbroke; and Lady May's vis-à-vis was Vivian Darnley. Soon they had got into the double stream of carriages of all sorts. There are closed carriages with pairs or fours, gigs, hansom cabs fitted with gauze curtains, dog-carts, open carriages with hampers lashed to the foot-boards, dandy drags, bright and polished, with crests; vans, cabs, and indescribable contrivances. There are horses worth a hundred and fifty guineas a-piece, and there are others that look as if the knacker should have them. There are all sorts of raws, and sand-cracks, and broken knees. There are kickers and roarers, and bolters and jibbers, such a crush and medley in that densely packed double line, that jogs and crushes along you can hardly tell how.

Sometimes one line passes the other, and then sustains a momentary check, while the other darts forward; and now and then a panel is smashed, with the usual altercation, and dust unspeakable eddying and floating everywhere in the sun; all sorts of chaff exchanged, mail-coach horns blowing, and general impudence and hilarity; gentlemen with veils on, and ladies with light hoods over their bonnets, and all sorts of gauzy defences against the dust. The utter novelty of all these sights and sounds highly amuses Alice, to whom they are absolutely strange.

"I am so amused," she said, "at the gravity you all seem to take these wonderful doings with. I could not have fancied anything like it. Isn't that Borrowdale?"

"So it is," said Lady May. "I thought he was in France. He doesn't see us, I think."

He did see them, but it was just as he was cracking a personal joke with a busman, in which the latter had decidedly the best of it, and he did not care to recognise his lady acquaintances at disadvantage.

"What a fright that man is!" said Lord Wynderbroke.

"But his team is the prettiest in England, except Longcluse's," said Darnley; "and, by Jove, there's Longcluse's drag!"

"Those are very nice horses," said Lord Wynderbroke looking at Longcluse's team, as if he had not heard Darnley's observation. "They are worth looking at, Miss Arden."

Longcluse was seated on the box, with a veil on, through which his white smile was indistinctly visible.

"And what a fright he is, also! He looks like a picture of Death I once saw, with a cloth half over his face; or the Veiled Prophet. By Jove, a curious thing that the two most hideous men in England should have between them the two prettiest teams on earth!"

Lord Wynderbroke looks at Darnley with raised brows, vaguely. He has been talking more than his lordship perhaps thinks he has any business to talk, especially to Alice.

"You will be more diverted still when we have got upon the course," interposes Lord Wynderbroke. "The variety of strange people there—gipsies, you know, and all that—mountebanks, and thimble-riggers, and beggars, and musicians—you'll wonder how such hordes could be collected in all England, or where they come from."

"And although they make something of a day like this, how on earth they contrive to exist all the other days of the year, when people are sober, and minding their own business," added Darnley.

"To me the pleasantest thing about the drive is our finding ourselves in the open country. Look out of the window there—trees and farm-steads—it is so rural, and such an odd change!" said Lady May.

"And the young corn, I'm glad to see, is looking very well," said Lord Wynderbroke, who claimed to be something of an agriculturist.

"And the oddest thing about it is our being surrounded, in the midst of all this rural simplicity, with the population of London," threw in Vivian Darnley.

"Remember, Miss Arden, our wager," said Lord Wynderbroke; "you have backed May Queen."

"May! she should be a cousin of mine," said good Lady May, firing off her little pun, which was received very kindly by her audience.

"Ha, ha! I did not think of that; she should certainly be the most popular name on the card," said Lord Wynderbroke. "I hope I have not made a great mistake, Miss Arden, in betting against so—so auspicious a name."

"I sha'n't let you off, though. I'm told I'm very likely to win—isn't it so?" she asked Vivian.

"Yes, the odds are in favour of May Queen now; you might make a capital hedge."

"You don't know what a hedge is, I daresay, Miss Arden; ladies don't always quite understand our turf language," said Lord Wynderbroke, with a consideration which he hoped that very forward young man, on whom he fancied Miss Arden looked good-naturedly, felt as he ought. "It is called a hedge, by betting men, when ——" and he expounded the meaning of the term.

The road had now become more free, as they approached the course, and Dick Arden took advantage of the circumstance to pass the omnibuses, and other lumbering vehicles, which he soon left far behind. The grand stand now rose in view—and now they were on the course. The first race had not yet come off, and young Arden found a good place among the triple line of carriages. Off go the horses! Miss Arden is assisted to a cushion on the roof; Lord Wynderbroke and Vivian take places beside her. The sun is growing rather hot, and the parasol is up. Good-natured Lady May is a little too stout for climbing, but won't hear of anyone's staying to keep her company. Perhaps when Richard Arden, who is taking a walk by the ropes, and wants to see the horses which are showing, returns, she may have a little talk with him at the window. In the meantime, all the curious groups of figures, and a hundred more, which Lord Wynderbroke promised—the monotonous challenges of the fellows with games of all sorts, the whine of the beggar for a little penny, the guitarring, singing, barrel-organing, and the gipsy inviting Miss Arden to try her lucky sixpence—all make a curious and merry Babel about her.

CHAPTER XXXIV.

A SHARP COLLOQUY.

On foot, near the weighing stand, is a tall, powerful, and clumsy fellow, got up gaudily—a fellow with a lowering red face, in loud good-humour, very ill-looking. He is now grinning and chuckling with his hands in his pockets, and talking with a little Hebrew, young, sable-haired, with the sallow tint, great black eyes, and fleshy nose that characterise his race. A singularly sullen mouth aids the effect of his vivid eyes, in making this young Jew's face ominous.

"Young Dick Harden's 'ere," said Mr. Levi.

"Eh? is he?" said the big man with the red face and pimples, the green cut-away coat, gilt buttons, purple neck-tie, yellow waistcoat, white cord tights, and top boots.

"Walking down there," said Levi, pointing with his thumb over his shoulder. "I shaw him shpeak to a fellow in chocolate and gold livery."

"And an eagle on the button, I know. That's Lady May Penrose's livery," said his companion. "He came down with her, I lay you fifty. And he has a nice sister as ever you set eyes on—pretty gal, Mr. Levi—a reg'lar little angel," and he giggled after his wont. "If there's a dragful of hangels anyvere, she's one of them. I saw her yesterday in one of Lady May Penrose's carriages in St. James' Street. Mr. Longcluse is engaged to get married to her; you may see them linked arm-in-arm, any day you please, walkin' hup and down Hoxford Street. And her brother, Richard Harden, is to marry Lady May Penrose. That will be a warm family yet, them Hardens, arter all."

"A family with a title, Mr. Ballard, be it never so humble, Sir, like 'ome shweet 'ome, hash nine livesh in it; they'll be down to the last pig, and not the thickness of an old tizzy between them and the glue-pot; and while you'd write your name across the back of a cheque, all's right again. The title doesh it. You never shaw a title in the workus yet, Mr. Ballard, and you'll wait awhile before you 'av a hop-pertunity of shayin', 'My lord Dooke, I hope your grashe's water-gruel is salted to your noble tasht thish morning,' or, 'My noble marquishe, I humbly hope you are pleashed with the fit of them pepper-and-salts;' and, 'My lord earl, I'm glad to see by the register you took a right honourable twisht at the crank thish morning.' No, Mishter Ballard, you nor me won't shee that, Shir."

While these gentlemen enjoyed their agreeable banter, and settled the fortunes of Richard Arden and Mr. Longcluse, the latter person was walking down the course in the direction in which Mr. Levi had seen Arden go, in the hope of discovering Lady May's carriage. Longcluse was in an odd state of excitement. He had entered into the spirit of the carnival. Voices all around were shouting, "Twenty to five on Dotheboys;" or, "A hundred to five against Parachute."

"In what?" called Mr. Longcluse to the latter challenge.

"In assassins!" cried a voice from the crowd.

Mr. Longcluse hustled his way into the thick of it.

"Who said that?" he thundered.

No one could say. No one else had heard it. Who cared? He recovered his coolness quickly, and made no further fuss about it. People were too busy with other things to bother themselves about his questions, or his temper. He hurried forward after young Arden, whom he saw at the turn of the course a little way on.

"The first race no one cares much about; compared with the great event of the day, it is as the farce before the pantomime, or the oyster before the feast."

The bells had not yet rung out their warning, and Alice said to Vivian,—

"How beautifully that girl with the tambourine danced and sang! I do so hope she'll come again; and she is, I think, so perfectly lovely. She is so like the picture of La Esmeralda; didn't you think so?"

"Do you really wish to see her again?" said Vivian. "Then if she's to be found on earth you shall see her."

He was smiling, but he spoke in the low tone that love is said to employ and understand, and his eyes looked softly on her. He was pleased that she enjoyed everything so. In a moment he had jumped to the ground, and with one smile back at the eager girl he disappeared.

And now the bells were ringing, and the police clearing the course. And now the cry, "They're off, they're off!" came rolling down the crowd like a hedge-fire. Lord Wynderbroke offered Alice his race-glass, but ladies are not good at optical aids, and she prefers her eyes; and the Earl constitutes himself her sentinel, and will report all he sees, and stands on the roof beside her place, with the glasses to his eyes. And now the excitement grows. Beggar-boys, butcher-boys, stable-helps, jump up on carriage-wheels unnoticed, and cling to the roof with filthy fingers. And now they are in sight, and a wild clamour arises. "Red's first!" "No, Blue!" "White leads!" "Pink's first!"

And here they are! White, crimson, pink, black, yellow—the silk jackets quivering like pennons in a storm—the jockeys tossing their arms madly about, the horses seeming actually to fly; swaying, reeling, whirring, the whole thing passes in a beautiful drift of a moment, and is gone!

Lord Wynderbroke is standing on tip-toe, trying to catch a glimpse of the caps as they show at the opening nearer the winning-post. Vivian Darnley is away in search of La Esmeralda. Miss Arden has seen the first race of the day, the first she has ever seen, and is amazed and delighted. The intruders who had been clinging to the carriage now jump down, and join the crowd that crush on towards the winning-post, or break in on the course. But there rises at the point next her a figure she little expected to see so near that day. Mr. Longcluse has swung himself up, and stands upon the wheel. He is bare-headed, his hat is in the hand he clings by. In the other hand he holds up a small glove—a lady's glove. His face is very pale. He is not smiling; he looks with an expression of pain, on the contrary, and very great respect.

"Miss Arden, will you forgive my venturing to restore this glove, which I happened to see you drop as the horses passed?"

She looked at him with something of surprise and fear, and drew back a little instead of taking the proffered glove.

"I find I have been too presumptuous," he said gently. "I place it there. I see, Miss Arden, I have been maligned. Some one has wronged me cruelly. I plead only for a fair chance—for God's sake, give me a chance. I don't say hear me now, only say you won't condemn me utterly unheard."

He spoke vehemently, but so low that, amid the hubbub of other voices, no one but Miss Arden, on whom his eyes were fixed, could hear him.

"I take my leave, Miss Arden, and may God bless you. But I rest in the hope that your noble nature will refuse to treat any creature as my enemies would have you treat me."

His looks were so sad and even reverential, and his voice, though low, so full of agony, that no one could suppose the speaker had the least idea of forcing his presence upon the lady a moment longer than sufficed to ascertain that it was not welcome. He was about to step to the ground, when he saw Richard Arden striding rapidly up with a very angry countenance. Then and there seemed likely to occur what the newspapers term an ungentlemanlike fracas. Richard Arden caught him, and pulled him roughly to the ground. Mr. Longcluse staggered back a step or two, and recovered himself. His pale face glared wickedly, for a moment or two, on the flushed and haughty young man; his arm was a little raised, and his fist clenched. I daresay it was just the turn of a die, at that moment, whether he struck him or not.

These two bosom friends, and sworn brothers, of a week or two ago, were confronted now with strange looks, and in threatening attitude. How frail a thing is the worldly man's friendship, hanging on flatteries and community of interest! A word or two of truth, and a conflict or even a divergence of interest, and where is the liking, the friendship, the intimacy?

A sudden change marked the face of Mr. Longcluse. The vivid fires that gleamed for a moment from his eyes sunk in their dark sockets, the intense look changed to one of sullen gloom. He beckoned, and said coldly, "Please follow me;" and then turned and walked, at a leisurely pace, a little way inward from the course.

Richard Arden, perhaps, felt that had he hesitated it would have reflected on his courage. He therefore disregarded the pride that would have scorned even a seeming compliance with that rather haughty summons, and he followed him with something of the odd dreamy feeling which men experience when they are stepping, consciously, into a risk of life. He thought that Mr. Longcluse was inviting the interview for the purpose of arranging the preliminaries of who were to act as their "friends," and where each gentleman was to be heard of that evening. He followed, with oddly conflicting feelings, to a place in the rear of some tents. Here was a sort of booth. Two doors admitted to it—one to the longer room, where was whirling that roulette round which men who, like Richard Arden, could not deny themselves, even on the meanest scale, the excitement of chance gain and loss, were betting and bawling. Into the smaller room of plank, which was now empty, they stepped.

"Now, Sir, you'll be so good as to observe that you have taken upon you a rather serious responsibility in laying your hand on me," said Longcluse, in a very low tone, coldly and gently. "In France, such a profanation would be followed by an exchange of shots, and here, under other circumstances, I should exact the same chance of retaliation. I mean to deal differently—quite differently. I have fought too many duels, as you know, to be the least apprehensive of being misunderstood or my courage questioned. For your sister's sake, not yours, I take a peculiar course with you. I offer you an alternative; you may have reconciliation—here is my hand" (he extended it)—"or you may abide the other consequence, at which I sha'n't hint, in pretty near futurity. You don't accept my hand?"

"No, Sir," said Arden haughtily—more than haughtily, insolently. "I can have no desire to renew an acquaintance with you. I sha'n't do that. I'll fight you, if you like it. I'll go to Boulogne, or wherever you like, and we can have our shot, Sir, whenever you please."

"No, if you please—not so fast. You decline my friendship—that offer is over," said Longcluse, lowering his hand resolutely. "I am not going to shoot you—I have not the least notion of that. I shall take, let me see, a different course with you, and I shall obtain on reflection your entire concurrence with the hopes I have no idea of relinquishing. You will probably understand me pretty clearly by-and-by."

Richard Arden was angry; he was puzzled; he wished to speak, but could not light quickly on a suitable answer. Longcluse stood for some seconds, smiling his pale sinister smile upon him, and then turned on his heel, and walked quietly out upon the grass, and disappeared in the crowd.

Richard Arden was irresolute. He threw open the door, and entered the roulette-room—looked round on all the strange faces, that did not mind him, or seem to see that he was there—then, with a sudden change of mind, he retraced his steps more quickly, and followed Longcluse through the other door. But there he could not trace him. He had quite vanished. Perhaps, next morning, he was glad that he had missed him, and had been compelled to "sleep upon it."

Now and then, with a sense of disagreeable uncertainty, recurred to his mind the mysterious intimation, or rather menace, with which he had taken his departure. It was not, however, his business to look up Longcluse. He had himself seemed to intimate that the balance of insult was the other way. If "satisfaction," in the slang of the duellist, was to be looked for, the initiative devolved undoubtedly upon Longcluse.

Alice was so placed on the carriage, that she did not see what passed immediately beside it, between Longcluse and her brother. Still, the appearance of this man, and his having accosted her, had agitated her a good deal, and for some hours the unpleasant effect of the little scene spoiled her enjoyment of this day of wonders.

Very gaily, notwithstanding, the party returned—except, perhaps, one person who had reason to remember that day.

CHAPTER XXXV.

DINNER AT MORTLAKE.

Lady May's party from the Derby dined together late, that evening, at Mortlake. Lord Wynderbroke, of course, was included. He was very happy, and extremely agreeable. When Alice, and Lady May, who was to stay that night at Mortlake, and Miss Maubray, who had come with Uncle David, took their departure for the drawing-room, the four gentlemen who remained over their claret drew more together, and chatted at their ease.

Lord Wynderbroke was in high spirits. He admired Alice more than ever. He admired everything. A faint rumour had got about that something was not very unlikely to be. It did not displease him. He had been looking at diamonds the day before; he was not vexed when that amusing wag, Pokely, who had surprised him in the act, asked him that day, on the Downs, some sly questions on the subject, with an arch glance at beautiful Miss Arden. Lord Wynderbroke pooh-pooh'd this impertinence very radiantly. And now this happy peer, pleased with himself, pleased with everybody, with the flush of a complacent elation on his thin cheeks, was simpering and chatting most agreeably, and commending everything to which his attention was drawn.

In very marked contrast with this happy man was Richard Arden, who talked but little, was absent, utterly out of spirits, and smiled with a palpable effort when he did smile. His conversation with Lady May showed the same uncomfortable peculiarities. It was intermittent and bewildered. It saddened the good lady. Was he ill? or in some difficulty?

Now that she had withdrawn, Richard Arden seemed less attentive to Lord Wynderbroke than to his uncle. In so far as a wight in his melancholy mood could do so, he seemed to have laid himself out to please his uncle in those small ways where, in such situations, an anxiety to please can show itself. Once his father's voice had roused him with the intimation, "Richard, Lord Wynderbroke is speaking to you;" and he saw a very urbane smile on his thin lips, and encountered a very formidable glare from his dark eyes. The only subject on which Richard Arden at all brightened up was the defeat of the favourite. Lord Wynderbroke remarked,—

"It seems to have caused a good deal of observation. I saw Hounsley and Crackham, and they shake their heads at it a good deal, and ——"

He paused, thinking that Richard Arden was going to interpose something, but nothing followed, and he continued,—

"And Lord Shillingsworth, he's very well up in all these things, and he seems to think it is a very suspicious affair; and old Sir Thomas Fetlock, who should have known better, has been hit very hard, and says he'll have it before the Jockey Club."

"I don't mind Sir Thomas, he blusters and makes a noise about everything," said Richard Arden; "but it was quite palpable, when the horse showed, he wasn't fit to run. I don't suppose Sir Thomas will do it, but it certainly will be done. I know a dozen men who will sell their horses, if it isn't done. I don't see how any man can take payment of the odds on Dotheboys—I don't, I assure you—till the affair is cleared up: gentlemen, of course, I mean; the other people would like the money all the better if it came to them by a swindle. But it certainly can't rest where it is."

No one disputing this, and none of the other gentlemen being authorities of any value upon turf matters, the subject dropped, and others came on, and Richard Arden was silent again. Lord Wynderbroke, who was to pass two or three days at Mortlake, and who had made up his mind that he was to leave that interesting place a promesso sposo, was restless, and longed to escape to the drawing-room. So the sitting over the wine was not very long.

Richard Arden made an effort, in the drawing-room, to retrieve his character with Lady May and Miss Maubray, who had been rather puzzled by his hang-dog looks and flagging conversation.

"There are times, Lady May," said he, placing himself on the sofa beside her, "when one loses all faith in the future—when everything goes wrong, and happiness becomes incredible. Then one's wisest course seems to be, to take off one's hat to the good people in this planet, and go off to another."

"Only that I know you so well," said Lady May, "I should tell Reginald—I mean your father—what you say; and I think your uncle, there, is a magistrate for the county of Middlesex, and could commit you, couldn't he? for any such foolish speech. Did you observe to-day—you saw him, of course—how miserably ill poor Pindledykes is looking? I don't think, really, he'll be alive in six months."

"Don't throw away your compassion, dear Lady May. Pindledykes has always looked dying as long as I can remember, and on his last legs; but those last legs carry some fellows a long way, and I'm very sure he'll outlive me."

"And what pleasure can a person so very ill as he looks take in going to places like that?"

"The pleasure of winning other people's money," laughed Arden sourly. "Pindledykes knows very well what he's about. He turns his time to very good account, and wastes very little of it, I assure you, in pitying other people's misfortunes."

"I'm glad to see that you and Richard are on pleasanter terms," said David Arden to his brother, as he sipped his tea beside him.

"Egad! we are not, though. I hate him worse than ever. Would you oblige me by putting a bit of wood on the fire? I told you how he has treated me. I wonder, David, how the devil you could suppose we were on pleasanter terms!"

Sir Reginald was seated with his crutch-handled stick beside him, and an easy fur slipper on his gouty foot, which rested on a stool, and was a great deal better. He leaned back in a cushioned arm-chair, and his fierce prominent eyes glanced across the room, in the direction of his son, with a flash like a scimitar's.

"There's no good, you know, David, in exposing one's ulcers to strangers—there's no use in plaguing one's guests with family quarrels."

"Upon my word, you disguised this one admirably, for I mistook you for two people on tolerably friendly terms."

"I don't want to plague Wynderbroke about the puppy; there is no need to mention that he has made so much unhappiness. You won't, neither will I."

David nodded.

"Something has gone wrong with him," said David Arden, "and I thought you might possibly know."

"Not I."

"I think he has lost money on the races to-day," said David.

"I hope to Heaven he has! I'm glad of it. It will do me good; let him settle it out of his blackguard post-obit," snarled Sir Reginald, and ground his teeth.

"If he has been gambling, he has disappointed me. He can, however, disappoint me but once. I had better thoughts of him."

So said David Arden, with displeasure in his frank and manly face.

"Playing? Of course he plays, and of course he's been making a blundering book for the Derby. He likes the hazard-table and the turf, he likes play, and he likes making books; and what he likes he does. He always did. I'm rather pleased you have been trying to manage him. You'll find him a charming person, and you'll understand what I have had to combat with. He'll never do any good; he is so utterly graceless."

"I see my father looking at me, and I know what he means," said Richard Arden, with a smile, to Lady May; "I'm to go and talk to Miss Maubray. He wishes to please Uncle David, and Miss Maubray must be talked to; and I see that Uncle David envies me my little momentary happiness, and meditates taking that empty chair beside you. You'll see whether I am right. By Jove! here he comes; I sha'n't be turned away so ——"

"Oh, but, really, Miss Maubray has been quite alone," urged poor Lady May, very much pleased; "and you must, to please me; I'm sure you will."

Instantly he arose.

"I don't know whether that speech is most kind or un-kind; you banish me, but in language so flattering to my loyalty, that I don't know whether to be pleased or pained. Of course I obey." He said these parting words in a very low tone, and had hardly ended them, when David Arden took the vacant chair beside the good lady, and began to talk with her.

Once or twice his eyes wandered to Richard Arden, who was by this time talking with returning animation to Grace Maubray, and the look was not cheerful. The young lady, however, was soon interested, and her good-humour was clever and exhilarating. I think that she a little admired this handsome and rather clever young man, and who can tell what such a fancy may grow to?

That night, as Richard Arden bid him good-bye, his uncle said, coldly enough,—

"By-the-bye, Richard, would you mind looking in upon me to-morrow, at five in the afternoon? I shall have a word to say to you."

So the appointment was made, and Richard entered his cab, and drove into town dismally.

CHAPTER XXXVI.

MR. LONGCLUSE SEES A LADY'S NOTE.

Next day Mr. Longcluse paid an early visit at Uncle David's house, and saw Miss Maubray in the drawing-room. The transition from that young lady's former, to her new life, was not less dazzling than that of the heroine of an Arabian tale, who is transported by friendly genii, while she sleeps, from a prison to the palace of a sultan. Uncle David did not care for finery; no man's tastes could be simpler and more camp-like. But these drawing-rooms were so splendid, so elegant and refined, and yet so gorgeous in effect, that you would have fancied that he had thought of nothing else all his life but china, marqueterie, buhl, Louis Quatorze clocks, mirrors, pale-green and gold cabriole chairs, bronzes, pictures, and all the textile splendours, the names of which I know not, that make floors and windows magnificent.

The feminine nature, facile and self-adapting, had at once accommodated itself to the dominion over all this, and all that attended it. And Miss Maubray being a lady, a girl who had, in her troubled life, been much among high-bred people—her father a gentle, fashionable, broken-down man, and her mother a very elegant and charming woman—there was no contrast, in look, air, or conversation, to mark that all this was new to her: on the contrary, she became it extremely.

The young lady was sitting at the piano when Longcluse came in, and to the expiring vibration of the chord at which she was interrupted she rose, with that light, floating ascent which is so pretty, and gave him her hand, and welcomed him with a very bright smile. She thought he was a likely person to be able to throw some light upon two rumours which interested her.

"How do you contrive to keep your rooms so deliciously cool? The blinds are down and the windows open, but that alone won't do, for I have just left a drawing-room that is very nearly insupportable; yours must be the work of some of those pretty sylphs that poets place in attendance upon their heroines. How fearfully hot yesterday was! You did not go to the Derby with Lady May's party, I believe."

He watched her clever face, to discover whether she had heard of the scene between him and Richard Arden—"I don't think she has."

"No," she said, "my guardian, Mr. Arden, took me there instead. On second thoughts, I feared I should very likely be in the way. One is always de trop where there is so much love-making; and I am a very bad gooseberry."

"A very dangerous one, I should fancy. And who are all these lovers?"

"Oh, really, they are so many, it is not easy to reckon them up. Alice Arden, for instance, had two lovers—Lord Wynderbroke and Vivian Darnley."

"What, two lovers charged upon one lady? Is not that false heraldry? And does she really care for that young fellow, Darnley?"

"I'm told she really is deeply attached to him. But that does not prevent her accepting Lord Wynderbroke. He has spoken, and been accepted. Old Sir Reginald told my guardian his brother, last night, and he told me in the carriage, as we drove home. I wonder how soon it will be. I should rather like to be one of her bridesmaids. Perhaps she will ask me."

Mr. Longcluse felt giddy and stunned; but he said, quite gaily—

"If she wishes to be suitably attended, she certainly will. But young ladies generally prefer a foil to a rival, even when so very beautiful as she is."

"And there was Vivian Darnley at one side, I'm told, whispering all kinds of sweet things, and poor old Wynderbroke at the other, with his glasses to his eyes, reporting all he saw. Only think! What a goose the old creature must have looked!" And the young lady laughed merrily. "But can you tell me about the other affair?" she asked.

"What is it?"

"Oh! you know, of course—Lady May and Richard Arden; is it true that it was all settled the day before yesterday, at that kettle-drum?"

"There again my information is quite behind yours. I did not hear a word of it."

"But you must have seen how very much in love they both are. Poor young man! I really think it would have broken his heart if she had been cruel, particularly if it is true that he lost so much as they say at the Derby yesterday. I suppose he did. Do you know?"

"I'm sorry to say," said Mr. Longcluse, "I'm afraid it's only too true. I don't know exactly how much it is, but I believe it is more than he can, at present, very well bear. A mad thing for him to do. I'm really sorry, although he has chosen to quarrel with me most unreasonably."

"Oh? I wasn't aware. I fancied you would have heard all from him."

"No, not a word—no."

"Lady May was talking to me at Raleigh Court, the day we were there—she can talk of no one else, poor old thing!—and she said something had happened to make him and his sister very angry. She would not say what. She only said, 'You know how very proud they are, and I really think,' she said, 'they ought to have been very much pleased, for everything, I think, was most advantageous.' And from this I conclude there must have been a proposal for Alice; I shall ask her when I see her."

"Yes, I daresay they are proud. Richard Arden told me so. He said that his family were always considered proud. He was laughing, of course, but he meant it."

"He's proud of being proud, I daresay. I thought you would be likely to know whether all they say is true. It would be a great pity he should be ruined; but, you know, if all the rest is true, there are resources."

Longcluse laughed.

"He has always been very particular and a little tender in that quarter; very sweet upon Lady May, I thought," said he.

"Oh, very much gone, poor thing!" said Grace Maubray. "I think my guardian will have heard all about it. He was very angry, once or twice, with Richard Arden about his losing so much money at play. I believe he has lost a great deal at different times."

"A great many people do lose money so. For the sake of excitement, they incur losses, and risk even their utter ruin."

"How foolish!" exclaimed Miss Maubray. "Have you heard anything more about that affair of Lady Mary Playfair and Captain Mayfair? He is now, by the death of his cousin, quite sure of the title, they say."

"Yes it must come to him. His uncle has got something wrong with his leg, a fracture that never united quite; it is an old hurt, and I'm told he is quite breaking up now. He is at Buxton, and going on to Vichy, if he lives, poor man."

"Oh, then, there can be no difficulty now."

"No, I heard yesterday it is all settled."

"And what does Caroline Chambray say to that?"

And so on they chatted, till his call was ended, and Mr. Longcluse walked down the steps with his head pretty busy.

At the corner of a street he took a cab; and as he drove to Lady May's, those fragments of his short talk with Grace Maubray that most interested him were tumbling over and over in his mind. "So they are angry, very angry; and very proud and haughty people. I had no business dreaming of an alliance with Mr. Richard Arden. Angry, he may be—he may affect to be—but I don't believe she is. And proud, is he? Proud of her he might be, but what else has he to boast of? Proud and angry—ha, ha! Angry and proud. We shall see. Such people sometimes grow suddenly mild and meek. And she has accepted Lord Wynderbroke. I doubt it. Miss Maubray, you are such a good-natured girl that, if you suspected the torture your story inflicted, you would invent it, rather than spare a fellow-mortal that pang."

In this we know he was a little unjust.

"Well, Miss Arden, I understand your brother; I shall soon understand you. At present I hesitate. Alas! must I place you, too, in the schedule of my lost friends? Is it come to this?—

> 'Once I held thee dear as pearl,
> Now I do abhor thee.'"

Mr. Longcluse's chin rests on his breast as, with a faint smile, he thus ruminates.

The cab stops. The light frown that had contracted his eyebrows disappears, he glances quickly up at the drawing-room windows, mounts the steps, and knocks at the hall door.

"Is Lady May Penrose at home?" he asked.

"I'll inquire, Sir."

Was it fancy, or was there in his reception something a little unusual, and ominous of exclusion?

He was, notwithstanding, shown up-stairs. Mr. Longcluse enters the drawing-room: Lady May will see him in a few minutes. He is alone. At the further end of this room is a smaller one, furnished like the drawing-room, the same curtains, carpet, and style, but much more minute and elaborate in ornamentation—an extremely pretty boudoir. He just peeps in. No, no one there. Then slowly he saunters into the other drawing-room, picks up a book, lays it down, and looks round. Quite solitary is this room also. His countenance changes a little. With a swift, noiseless step, he returns to the room he first entered. There is a little marqueterie table, to which he directs his steps, just behind the door from the staircase, under the pretty old buhl clock that ticks so merrily with its old wheels and lever, exciting the reverential curiosity of Monsieur Racine, who keeps it in order, and comments on its antique works with a mysterious smile every time he comes, to any one who will listen to him. The door is a little bit open. All the better, Mr. Longcluse will hear any step that approaches. On this little table lies an open note, hastily thrown there, and the pretty handwriting he has recognised. He knows it is Alice Arden's. Without the slightest scruple, this odd gentleman takes it up and reads a bit, and looks toward the door; reads a little more, and looks again, and so on to the end.

On the principle that listeners seldom hear good of themselves, Mr. Longcluse's cautious perusal of another person's letter did not tell him a pleasant tale.

CHAPTER XXXVII.

WHAT ALICE COULD SAY.

The letter which Mr. Longcluse held before his eyes was destined to throw a strong light upon the character of Alice Arden's feelings respecting himself. After a few lines, it went on to say:—"And, darling, about going to you this evening, I hardly know what to say, or, I mean, I hardly know how to say it. Mr. Longcluse, you know, may come in at any moment, and I have quite made up my mind that I cannot know him. I told you all about the incredible scene in the garden at Mortlake, and I showed you the very cool letter with which he saw fit to follow it—and yesterday the scene at the races, by which he contrived to make everything so uncomfortable—so, my dear creature, I mean to be cruel, and cut him. I am quite serious. He has not an idea how to behave himself; and the only way to repair the folly of having made the acquaintance of such an ill-bred person is, as I said, to cut him—you must not be angry—and Richard thinks exactly as I do. So, as I long to see you, and, in fact, can't live away from you very long, we must contrive some way of meeting now and then, without the risk of being disturbed by him. In the meantime, you must come more to Mortlake. It is too bad that an impertinent, conceited man should have caused me all this very real vexation."

There was but little more, and it did not refer to the only subject that interested Longcluse just then. He would have liked to read it through once more, but he thought he heard a step. He let it fall where he had found it, and walked to the window. Perhaps, if he had read it again, it would have lost some of the force which a first impression gives to sentences so terrible; as it was, they glared upon his retina, through the same exaggerating medium through which his excited imagination and feelings had scanned them at first.

Lady May entered, and Mr. Longcluse paid his respects, just as usual. You would not have supposed that anything had occurred to ruffle him. Lady May was just as affable as usual, but very much graver. She seemed to have something on her mind, and not to know how to begin.

At length, after some little conversation, which flagged once or twice—

"I have been thinking, Mr. Longcluse, I must have appeared very stupid," says Lady May. "I did not ask you to be one of our party to the Derby: and I think it is always best to be quite frank, and I know you like it best. I'm afraid there has been some little misunderstanding. I hope in a short time it will be all got over, and everything quite pleasant again. But some of our friends—you, no doubt, know more about it than I do, for I must confess, I don't very well understand it—are vexed at something that has occurred, and ——"

Poor Lady May was obviously struggling with the difficulties of her explanation, and Mr. Longcluse relieved her.

"Pray, dear Lady May, not a word more; you have always been so kind to me. Miss Arden and her brother choose to visit me with displeasure. I have nothing to reproach myself with, except with having misapprehended the terms on which Miss Arden is pleased to place me. She may however, be very sure that I sha'n't disturb her happy evenings here, or anywhere assume my former friendly privileges."

"But Mr. Longcluse, I'm not to lose your acquaintance," said kindly Lady May, who was disposed to take an indulgent and even a romantic view of Mr. Longcluse's extravagances. "Perhaps it may be better to avoid a risk of meeting, under present circumstances; and, therefore, when I'm quite sure that no such awkwardness can occur, I can easily send you a line, and you will come if you can. You will do just as it happens to answer you best at the time."

"It is extremely kind of you, Lady May. My evenings here have been so very happy that the idea of losing them altogether would make me more melancholy than I can tell."

"Oh, no, I could not consent to lose you, Mr. Longcluse, and I'm sure this little quarrel can't last very long. Where people are amiable and friendly, there may be a misunderstanding, but there can't be a real quarrel, I maintain."

With this little speech the interview closed, and the gentleman took a very friendly leave.

Mr. Longcluse was in trouble. Blows had fallen rapidly upon him of late. But, as light is polarised by encountering certain incidents of reflection and refraction, grief entering his mind changed its character.

The only articles of expense in which Mr. Longcluse indulged and even in those his indulgence was very moderate—were horses. He was something of a judge of horses, and had that tendency to form friendships and intimacies with them which is proper to some minds. One of these he mounted, and rode away into the country, unattended. He took a long ride, at first at a tolerably hard pace. He chose the loneliest roads he could find. His exercise brought him no appetite; the interesting hour of dinner passed unimproved. The horse was tired now. Longcluse was slowly returning, and looking listlessly to his right, he thus soliloquised:—

"Alone again. Not a soul in human shape to disclose my wounds to, not a soul. This is the way men go mad. He knows too well the torture he consigns me to. How often has my hand helped him out of the penalties of the dice-box and betting-book! How wildly have I committed myself to him!—how madly have I trusted him! How plausibly has he promised. The confounded miscreant! Has he good-nature, gratitude, justice, honour? Not a particle. He has betrayed me, slandered me fatally, where only on earth I dreaded slander, and he knew it; and he has ruined the only good hope I had on earth. He has launched it: sharp and heavy is the curse. Wait: it shall find him out. And she! I did not think Alice Arden could have written that letter. My eyes are opened. Well, she has refused to hear my good angel; the other may speak differently."

He was riding along a narrow old road, with palings, and quaint old hedgerows, and now and then an old-fashioned brick house, staid and comfortable, with a cluster of lofty timber embowering it, and chimney smoke curling cosily over the foliage; and as he rode along, sometimes a window, with very thick white sashes, and a multitude of very small panes, sometimes the summit of a gable appeared. The lowing of unseen cows was heard over the fields, and the whistle of the birds in the hedges; and behind spread the cloudy sky of sunset, showing a peaceful old-world scene, in which Izaak Walton's milkmaid might have set down her pail, and sung her pretty song.

Not another footfall was heard but the clink of his own horse's hoofs along the narrow road; and, as he looked westward, the flush of the sky threw an odd sort of fire-light over his death-pale features.

"Time will unroll his book," said Longcluse, dreamily, as he rode onward, with a loose bridle on his horse's neck, "and my fingers will trace a name or two on the pages that are passing. That sunset, that sky—how grand, and glorious, and serene—the same always. Charlemagne saw it, and the Cæsars saw it, and the Pharaohs saw it, and we see it to-day. Is it worth while troubling ourselves here? How grand and quiet nature is, and how beautifully imperturbable! Why not we, who last so short a time—why not drift on with it, and take the blows that come, and suffer and enjoy the facts of life, and leave its dreadful dreams untried? Of all the follies we engage in, what more hollow than revenge—vainer than wealth?"

Mr. Longcluse was preaching to himself, with the usual success of preachers. He knew himself what his harangue was driving at, although it borrowed the vagueness of the sky he was looking on. He fancied that he was discussing something with himself, which, nevertheless, was settled—so fixed, indeed, that nothing had power to alter it.

CHAPTER XXXVIII.

GENTLEMEN IN TROUBLE.

Mr. Longcluse had now reached a turn in the road, at which stands an old house that recedes a little way and has four poplars growing in front of it, two at each side of the door. There are mouldy walls, and gardens, fruit and vegetables, in the rear, and in one wing of the house the proprietor is licenced to sell beer and other refreshing drinks. This quaint greengrocery and pot-house was not flourishing, I conjecture, for a cab was at the door, and Mr. Goldshed, the eminent Hebrew, on the steps, apparently on the point of leaving.

He is a short, square man, a little round shouldered. He is very bald, with coarse, black hair, that might not unsuitably stuff a chair. His nose is big and drooping, his lips large and moist. He wears a black satin waistcoat, thrust up into wrinkles by his habit of stuffing his short hands, bedizened with rings, into his trousers pockets. He has on a peculiar low-crowned hat. He is smoking a cigar, and talking over his shoulder, at intervals, in brief sentences that have a harsh, brazen ring, and are charged with scoff and menace. No game is too small for Mr. Goldshed's pursuit. He ought to have made two hundred pounds of this little venture. He has not lost, it is true; but, when all is squared, he'll not have made a shilling, and that for a Jew, you know, is very hard to bear.

In the midst of this intermittent snarl, the large, dark eyes of this man lighted on Mr. Longcluse, and he arrested the sentence that was about to fly over his shoulder, in the disconsolate faces of the broken little family in the passage. A smile suddenly beamed all over his dusky features, his airs of lordship quite forsook him, and he lifted his hat to the great man with a cringing salutation. The weaker spirit was overawed by the more potent. It was the catape doing homage to Mephistopheles, in the witch's chamber.

He shuffled out upon the road, with a lazy smile, lifting his hat again, and very deferentially greeted “Mishter Longclooshe.” He had thrown away his exhausted cigar, and the red sun glittered in sparkles on the chains and jewelry that were looped across his wrinkled black satin waistcoat.

“How d'ye do, Mr. Goldshed? Anything particular to say to me?”

"Nothing, no, Mr. Longclooshe. I sposhe you heard of that dip in the Honduras?"

"They'll get over it, but we sha'n't see them so high again soon. Have you that cab all to yourself, Mr. Goldshed?"

"No, Shir, my partner'sh with me. He'll be out in a minute; he'sh only puttin' a chap on to make out an inventory."

"Well, I don't want him. Would you mind walking down the road here, a couple of hundred steps or so? I have a word for you. Your partner can overtake you in the cab."

"Shertainly, Mr. Longclooshe, shertainly, Shir."

And he halloed to the cabman to tell the "zhentleman" who was coming out to overtake him in the cab on the road to town.

This settled, Mr. Longcluse, walking his horse along the road, and his City acquaintance by his side, slowly made their way towards the City, casting long shadows over the low fence into the field at their left; and Mr. Goldshed's stumpy legs were projected across the road in such slender proportions that he felt for a moment rather slight and elegant, and was unusually disgusted, when he glanced down upon the substance of those shadows, at the unnecessarily clumsy style in which Messrs. Shears and Goslin had cut out his brown trousers.

Mr. Longcluse had a good deal to say when they got on a little. Being earnest, he stopped his horse; and Mr. Goldshed, forgetting his reverence in his absorption, placed his broad hand on the horse's shoulder, as he looked up into Mr. Longcluse's face, and now and then nodded, or grunted a "Surely." It was not until the shadows had grown perceptibly longer, until Mr. Longcluse's hat had stolen away to the gilded stem of the old ash-tree that was in perspective to their left, and until Mr. Goldshed's legs had grown so taper and elegant as to amount to the spindle, that the talk ended, and Mr. Longcluse, who was a little shy of being seen in such company, bid him good evening, and rode away townward at a brisk trot.

That morning Richard Arden looked as if he had got up after a month's fever. His dinner had been a pretence, and his breakfast was a sham. His luck, as he termed it, had got him at last pretty well into a corner. The placing of the horses was a dreadful record of moral impossibilities accomplished against him. Five minutes before the start he could have sold his book for three thousand pounds; five minutes after it no one would have accepted fifteen thousand to take it off his hands. The shock, at first a confusion, had grown in the night into ghastly order. It was all, in the terms of the good old simile, "as plain as a pike-staff." He simply could not pay. He might sell everything he possessed, and pay about ten shillings in the pound, and then work his passage to another country, and become an Australian drayman, or a New Orleans billiard-marker.

But not pay his bets! And how could he? Ten shillings in the pound? Not five. He forgot how far he was already involved. What was to become of him. Breakfast he could eat none. He drank a cup of tea, but his tremors grew worse. He tried claret, but that, too, was chilly comfort. He was driven to an experiment he had never ventured before. He had a "nip," and another, and with this Dutch courage rallied a little, and was able to talk to his friend and admirer, Vandeleur, who had made a miniature book after the pattern of Dick Arden's and had lost some hundreds, which he did not know how to pay; and who was, in his degree, as misera-miserable as his chief; for is it not established that—

> "The poor beetle, that we tread upon,
> In corporal sufferance feels a pang as great
> As when a giant dies"?

Young Vandeleur, with light silken hair, and innocent blue eyes, found his paragon the picture of "grim-visaged, comfortless despair," drumming a tattoo on the window, in slippers and dressing-gown, without a collar to his shirt.

"You lost, of course," said Richard savagely; "you followed my lead. Any fellow that does is sure to lose."

"Yes," answered Vandeleur, "I did, heavily; and, I give you my honour, I believe I'm ruined."

"How much?"

"Two hundred and forty pounds!"

"Ruined! What nonsense! Who are you? or what the devil are you making such a row about? Two hundred and forty! How can you be such an ass? Don't you know it's nothing?"

"Nothing! By Jove! I wish I could see it," said poor Van; "everything's something to any one, when there's nothing to pay it with. I'm not like you, you know; I'm awfully poor. I have just a hundred and twenty pounds from my office, and forty my aunt gives me, and ninety I get from home, and, upon my honour, that's all; and I owed just a hundred pounds to some fellows that were growing impertinent. My tailor is sixty-four, and the rest are trifling, but they were the most impertinent, and I was so sure of this unfortunate thing that I told them I—really did—to call next week; and now I suppose it's all up with me, I may as well make a bolt of it. Instead of having any money to pay them, I'm two hundred and forty pounds worse than ever. I don't know what on earth to do. Upon my honour, I haven't an idea."

"I wish we could exchange our accounts," said Richard grimly: "I wish you owed my sixteen thousand. I think you'd sink through the earth. I think you'd call for a pistol, and blow"—(he was going to say, "your brains out," but he would not pay him that compliment)—"blow your head off."

So it was the old case—"Enter Tilburina, mad, in white satin; enter her maid, mad, in white linen."

And Richard Arden continued—

"What's your aunt good for? You know she will pay that; don't let me hear a word more about it."

"And your uncle will pay yours, won't he?" said Van, with an innocent gaze of his azure eyes.

"My uncle has paid some trifles before, but this is too big a thing. He's tired of me and my cursed misfortunes, and he's not likely to apply any of his overgrown wealth in relieving a poor tortured beggar like me. I'm simply ruined."

CHAPTER XXXIX.

BETWEEN FRIENDS.

Van was looking ruefully out of the window, down upon the deserted pavement opposite. At length he said,—

"And why don't you give your luck a chance?"

"Whenever I give it a chance it hits me so devilish hard," replied Richard Arden.

"But I mean at play to retrieve," said Van.

"So do I. So I did, last night, and lost another thousand. It is utterly monstrous."

"By Jove! that is really very extraordinary," exclaimed little Van. "I tried it, too, last night. Tom Franklyn had some fellows to sup with him, and I went in, and they were playing loo; and I lost thirty-seven pounds more!"

"Thirty-seven confounded flea-bites! Why, don't you see how you torture me with your nonsense? If you can't talk like a man of sense, for Heaven's sake, shut up, and don't distract me in my misery."

He emphasised the word with a Lilliputian thump with the side of his fist—that which presents the edge of the doubled-up little finger and palm—a sort of buffer, which I suppose he thought he might safely apply to the pane of glass on which he had been drumming. But he hit a little too hard, or there was a flaw in the glass, for the pane flew out, touching the window-sill, and alighted in the area with a musical jingle.

"There! see what you made me do. My luck! Now we can't talk without those brutes at that open window, over the way, hearing every word we say. By Jove, it is later than I thought! I did not sleep last night."

"Nor I, a moment," said Van.

"It seems like a week since that accursed race, and I don't know whether it is morning or evening, or day or night. It is past four, and I must dress and go to my uncle—he said five. Don't leave me, Van, old fellow! I think I should cut my throat if I were alone."

"Oh, no, I'll stay with pleasure, although I don't see what comfort there is in me, for I am about the most miserable dog in London."

"Now don't make a fool of yourself any more," said Richard Arden. "You have only to tell your aunt, and say that you are a prodigal son, and that sort of thing, and it will be paid in a week. I look as if I was going to be hanged—or is it the colour of that glass? I hate it. I'll leave these cursed lodgings. Did you ever see such a ghost?"

"Well, you do look a trifle seedy: you'll look better when you're dressed. It's an awful world to live in," said poor Van.

"I'll not be five minutes; you must walk with me a bit of the way. I wish I had some fellow at my other side who had lost a hundred thousand. I daresay he'd think me a fool. They say Chiffington lost a hundred and forty thousand. Perhaps he'd think me as great an ass as I think you—who knows? I may be making too much of it—and my uncle is so very rich, and neither wife nor child; and, I give you my honour, I am sick of the whole thing. I'd never take a card or a dice-box in my hand, or back a horse, while I live, if I was once fairly out of it. He might try me, don't you think? I'm the only near relation he has on earth—I don't count my father, for he's—it's a different thing, you know—I and my sister, just. And, really, it would be nothing to him. And I think he suspected something about it last night; perhaps he heard a little of it. And he's rather hot, but he's a good-natured fellow, and he has commercial ideas about a man's going into the insolvent court; and, by Jove, you know, I'm ruined, and I don't think he'd like to see our name disgraced—eh, do you?"

"No, I'm quite sure," said Van. "I thought so all along."

"Peers and peeresses are very fine in their way, and people, whenever the peers do anything foolish, and throw out a bill, exclaim 'Thank Heaven we have still a House of Lords!' but you and I, Van, may thank Heaven for a better estate, the order of aunts and uncles. Do you remember the man you and I saw in the vaudeville, who exclaims every now and then, 'Vive mon oncle! Vive ma tante!'?"

So, in better spirits, Arden prepared to visit his uncle.

"Let us get into a cab; people are staring at you," said Richard Arden, when they had walked a little way towards his uncle's house. "You look so utterly ruined, one would think you had swallowed poison, and were dying by inches, and expected to be in the other world before you reached your doctor's door. Here's a cab."

They got in, and sitting side by side, said Vandeleur to him, after a minute's silence,—

"I've been thinking of a thing—why did not you take Mr. Longcluse into council? He gave you a lift before, don't you remember? and he lost nothing by it, and made everything smooth. Why don't you look him up?"

"I've been an awful fool, Van."

"How so?"

"I've had a sort of row with Longcluse, and there are reasons—I could not, at all events, have asked him. It would have been next to impossible, and now it is quite impossible."

"Why should it be? He seemed to like you; and I venture to say he'd be very glad to shake hands."

"So he might, but I shouldn't," said Richard imperiously. "No, no, there's nothing in that. It would take too long to tell; but I should rather go over the precipice than hold by that stay. I don't know how long my uncle may keep me. Would you mind waiting for me at my lodgings? Thompson will give you cigars and brandy and water; and I'll come back and tell you what my uncle intends."

This appointment made, they parted, and he knocked at his uncle's door. The sound seemed to echo threateningly at his heart, which sank with a sudden misgiving.

CHAPTER XL.

AN INTERVIEW IN THE STUDY.

"Is my uncle at home?"

"No, Sir; I expect him at five. It wants about five minutes; but he desired me to show you, Sir, into the study."

He was now alone in that large square room. The books, each in its place, in a vellum uniform, with a military precision and nattiness—seldom disturbed, I fancy, for Uncle David was not much of a book-worm—chilled him with an aspect of inflexible formality; and the busts, in cold white marble, standing at intervals on their pedestals, seemed to have called up looks, like Mrs. Pentweezle, for the occasion. Demosthenes, with his wrenched neck and square brow, had evidently heard of his dealings with Lord Pindledykes, and made up his mind, when the proper time came, to denounce him with a tempest of appropriate eloquence. There was in Cicero's face, he thought, something satirical and conceited which was new and odious; and under Plato's external solemnity he detected a pleasurable and roguish anticipation of the coming scene.

His uncle was very punctual. A few minutes would see him in the room, and then two or three sentences would disclose the purpose he meditated. In the midst of the trepidation which had thus returned, he heard his uncle's knock at the hall-door, and in another moment he entered the study.

"How d'ye do, Richard? You're punctual. I wish our meeting was a pleasanter one. Sit down. You haven't kept faith with me. It is scarcely a year since, with a large sum of money, such as at your age I should have thought a fortune, I rescued you from bad hands and a great danger. Now, Sir, do you remember a promise you then made me? and have you kept your word?"

"I confess, uncle, I know I can't excuse myself; but I was tempted, and I am weak—I am a fool, worse than a fool—whatever you please to call me, and I'm sorry. Can I say more?" pleaded the young man.

"That is saying nothing. It simply means that you do the thing that pleases you, and break your word where your inclination prompts; and you are sorry because it has turned out unluckily. I have heard that you are again in danger. I am not going to help you." His blue eyes looked cold and hard, and the oblique light showed severe lines at his brows and mouth. It was a face which, generally kindly, could yet look, on occasion, stern enough. "Now, observe, I'm not going to help you; I'm not even going to reason with you—you can do that for yourself, if you please—I will simply help you with light. Thus forewarned, you need not, of course, answer any one of the questions I am about to put, and to ask which, I have no other claim than that which rests upon having put you on your feet, and paid five thousand pounds for you, only a year ago."

"But I entreat that you do put them. I'm ashamed of myself, dear Uncle David; I implore of you to ask me whatever you please: I'll answer everything."

"Well, I think I know everything; Lord Pindledykes makes no secret of it. He's the man, isn't he?"

"Yes, Sir."

"That's the sallow, dissipated-looking fellow, with the eye that squints outward. I know his appearance very well; I knew his good-for-nothing father. No one likes to have transactions with that fellow—he's shunned—and you chose him, of all people; and he has pigeoned you. I've heard all about it. Everybody knows by this time. And you have really lost fifteen thousand pounds to him?"

"I am afraid, uncle, it is very near that."

"This, you know," resumed Uncle David, "is not debt: it is ruin. You chose to mortgage your reversion to some Jews, for fifteen hundred a year, during your father's lifetime. Three hundred would have been ample, with the hundred a year you had before—ample; but you chose to do it, and the estates, whenever you succeed to them, will come to you with a very heavy debt charged, for those Jews, upon them. I don't suppose the estates are destined to continue long in our family; but this is a vexation which don't touch you, nephew. I am, I confess, sorry. They were in our family, some of them, before the Conquest. No matter. What you have to consider is your present position. They will come to you, if ever, saddled with a heavy debt; and, in the meantime, you have fifteen hundred a year for your father's life; and I don't think it will sell for anything like the fifteen thousand pounds you have just lost. You are therefore insolvent; there is the story told. I see nothing for it but your becoming formally an insolvent. It is the bourgeoisie who shrink from that sort of thing; titled men, and men of pleasure and fashion, don't seem to mind it. There are Lord Harry Newgate, and the Honourable Alfred Pentonville, and Sir Aymerick Pigeon, one of the oldest baronets in England, have been in the Gazette within the last twelve months. The money I paid, on the faith of your promise, is worse than wasted. I'll pay no more into the pockets of rooks and scoundrels; I'll divide no more of my money among blackguard jockeys and villanous peers, simply to defer for a few months the consequences of a fool's incorrigible folly."

"But, you know, uncle, I was not quite so mad. The thing was a swindle; it can't stand. The horse was not fairly treated."

"I daresay: I suppose it was doctored. I don't care; I only think that unless you meant to go in for drugging horses and bribing jockeys, you had no business among such people, and at that sort of game. All I want is that you clearly understand that in this matter—though I would gladly see you safely out of it—I'll waste no more money in paying gambling debts."

"This might have happened to anyone, Sir; it might indeed, uncle. Every second man you meet is more or less on the turf, and they never come to grief by it. No one, of course, can stand against a barefaced swindle, like this thing."

"I don't care a farthing about other people; I've seen how it tells upon you. I don't affect to value your promises, Dick; I don't think that they are worth a shilling. How many have you made me, and broken? To me it seems the vice is incurable, like drunkenness. Tattersall's, or whatever is your place of business, is no better than the gin-palace; and when once a fellow is fairly on the turf, the sooner he is under it, the better for himself and all who like him. And you have lost money at play besides. I heard that quite accidentally; and I daresay that is a ruinous item in what I may call your schedule."

"I know what people are saying; but it isn't so immense a sum, by any means."

"I'm sorry to hear it. I wish it was enormous; I wish it was a million. I wish your failure could ruin every blackguard in England: the more heavily you have hit them all round, the better I am pleased. They hit you and me, Dick, pretty hard last time; it is our turn now. It is not my fault now, Dick, if you don't understand me perfectly. If at any future time I should do anything for you—by my will, mind—I shall take care so to tie it up that you can't make away with a guinea. My advice is not worth much to you, but I venture to give it, and I think the best thing you can do is to submit to your misfortune, and file your schedule; and when you are your own master again, I shall see if I can manage some small thing for you. You will have to work for your bread, you know, and you can't expect very much at first; but there are things—of course, I mean in commercial establishments, and railways, and that kind of thing—where I have an influence, of from a hundred and twenty to two hundred pounds a year, and for some of them you would answer pretty well, and you can tide over the time till you succeed to the title: and after a little while I may be able to get you raised a step; and when once you get accustomed to work, you can't think how you will come to like it. So that, on the whole, the knock you have got may do you some good, and make you prize your position more when you come to it. Will you go up-stairs, and take a cup of tea with Miss Maubray?"

He used to call her Grace, when speaking to Richard. Perhaps, in the concussion of this earthquake, the fabric of a matrimonial scheme may have fallen to the ground.

Richard Arden was too dejected and too agitated to accept this invitation, I need hardly tell you. He took his leave, chapfallen.

CHAPTER XLI.

VAN APPOINTS HIMSELF TO A DIPLOMATIC POST.

Mr. Vandeleur had availed himself very freely of Richard Arden's invitation, to amuse himself during his absence with his cheroots and manillas, as the clouded state of the atmosphere of his drawing-room testified to that luckless gentleman—if indeed he was in a condition to observe anything, on returning from his dreadful interview with his uncle.

Richard's countenance was full of thunder and disaster. Vandeleur looked in his face, with his cigar in his fingers, and said in a faint and hollow tone—

"Well?"

To which inappropriate form of inquiry, Richard Arden deigned no reply; but in silence stalked to the box of cigars on the table, threw himself into a chair, and smoked violently for awhile.

Some minutes passed. Vandeleur's eyes were fixed, through the smoke, on Richard's, who had fixed his on the chimney-piece. Van respected his ruminations. With a delicate and noiseless attention, indeed, he ventured to slide gently to his side the water carafe, and the brandy, and a tumbler.

Still silence prevailed. After a time, Richard Arden poured brandy and water suddenly into his glass.

"Think of that fellow, that uncle of mine—pretty uncle! Kind relation—rolling in money! He sends for me simply to tell me that he won't give me a guinea. He might have waited till he was asked. If he had nothing better to say, he need not have given me the trouble of going to his odious, bleak study, to hear all his vulgar advice and arithmetic, ending in—what do you think? He says that I'm to be had up in the bankrupt court, and when all that is over he'll get me appointed a ticket-taker on a railway, or a clerk in a pawn-office, or something. By Heaven! when I think of it, I wonder how I kept my temper. I'm not quite driven to those curious expedients, that he seems to think so natural. I've some cards still left in my hand, and I'll play them first, if it is the same to him; and, hang it! my luck can't always run the same way. I'll give it another chance before I give up, and to-morrow morning things may be very different with me."

"It's an awful pity you quarrelled with Longcluse!" exclaimed Vandeleur.

"That's done, and can't be undone," said Richard Arden, resuming his cigar.

"I wonder why you quarrelled with him. Why, good heavens! that man is made of money, and he got you safe out of that fellow's clutches—I forget his name—about that bet with Mr. Slanter, don't you remember—and he was so very kind about it; and I'm sure he'd shake hands if you'd only ask him, and one way or another he'd pull you through."

"I can't ask him, and I won't; he may ask me if he likes. I'm very sure there is nothing he would like better, for fifty reasons, than to be on good terms with me again, and I have no wish to quarrel any more than he has. But if there is to be a reconciliation, I can't begin it. He must make the overtures, and that's all."

"He seemed such an awfully jolly fellow that time. And it is such a frightful state we are both in. I never came such a mucker before in my life. I know him pretty well. I met him at Lady May Penrose's, and at the Playfairs', and one night I walked home with him from the opera. It is an awful pity you are not on terms with him, and—by Jove! I must go and have something to eat; it is near eight o'clock."

Away went Van, and out of the wreck of his fortune contrived a modest dinner at Verey's; and pondering, after dinner, upon the awful plight of himself and his comrade, he came at last to the heroic resolution of braving the dangers of a visit to Mr. Longcluse, on behalf of his friend; and as it was now past nine, he hastily paid the waiter, took his hat, and set out upon his adventure. It was a mere chance, he knew, and a very unlikely one, his finding Mr. Longcluse at home at that hour. He knew that he was doing a very odd thing in calling at past nine o'clock; but the occasion was anomalous, and Mr. Longcluse would understand. He knocked at the door, and learned from the servant that his master was engaged with a gentleman in the study, on business. From this room he heard a voice, faintly discoursing in a deep metallic drawl.

"Who shall I say, Sir?" asked the servant.

If his mission had been less monotonous, and he less excited and sanguine as to his diplomatic success, he would have, as he said, "funked it altogether," and gone away. He hesitated for a moment, and determined upon the form most likely to procure an interview.

"Say Mr. Vandeleur—a friend of Mr. Richard Arden's; you'll remember, please—a friend of Mr. Richard Arden's."

In a moment the man returned.

"Will you please to walk up-stairs?" and he showed him into the drawing-room.

In little more than a minute, Mr. Longcluse himself entered. His eyes were fixed on the visitor with a rather stern curiosity. Perhaps he had interpreted the term "friend" a little too technically. He made him a ceremonious bow, in French fashion, and placed a chair for him.

"I had the pleasure of being introduced to you, Mr. Longcluse, at Lady May Penrose's. My name is Vandeleur."

"I have had that honour, Mr. Vandeleur, I remember perfectly. The servant mentioned that you announced yourself as Mr. Arden's friend, if I don't mistake."

CHAPTER XLII.

DIPLOMACY.

Mr. Vandeleur and Mr. Longcluse were now seated, and the former gentleman said—

"Yes, I am a friend of Mr. Arden's—so much so, that I have ventured what I hope you won't think a very impertinent liberty. I was so very sorry to hear that a misunderstanding had occurred—I did not ask him about what—and he has been so unlucky about the Derby, you know—I ought to say that I am, upon my honour, a mere volunteer, so perhaps you will think I have no right to ask you to listen to me."

"I shall be happy to continue this conversation, Mr. Vandeleur, upon one condition."

"Pray name it."

"That you report it fully to the gentleman for whom you are so kind as to interest yourself."

"Yes, I'll certainly do that."

Mr. Longcluse looked by no means so jolly as Van remembered him, and he thought he detected, at mention of Richard Arden's name, for a moment, a look of positive malevolence—I can't say absolutely, it may have been fancy—as he turned quickly, and the light played suddenly on his face.

Mr. Longcluse could, perhaps, dissemble as well as other men; but there were cases in which he would not be at the trouble to dissemble. And here his expression was so unpleasant, upon features so strangely marked and so white, that Van thought the effect ugly, and even ghastly.

"I shall be happy, then, to hear anything you have to say," said Longcluse gently.

"You are very kind. I was just going to say that he has been so unlucky—he has lost so much money ——"

"I had better say, I think, at once, Mr. Vandeleur, that nothing shall tempt me to take any part in Mr. Arden's affairs."

Van's mild blue eyes looked on him wonderingly.

"You could be of so much use, Mr. Longcluse!"

"I don't desire to be of any."

"But—but that may be, I think it must, in consequence of the unhappy estrangement."

He had been conning over phrases on his way, and thought that a pretty one.

"A very happy estrangement, on the contrary, for the man who is straight and true, and who is by it relieved of a great—mistake."

"I should be so extremely happy," said Van lingeringly, "if I were instrumental in inducing both parties to shake hands."

"I don't desire it."

"But, surely, if Richard Arden were the first to offer ——"

"I should decline."

Van rose; he fiddled with his hat a little; he hesitated. He had staked too much on this—for had he not promised to report the whole thing to Richard Arden, who was not likely to be pleased?—to give up without one last effort.

"I hope I am not very impertinent," he said, "but I can hardly think, Mr. Longcluse, that you are quite indifferent to a reconciliation."

"I'm not indifferent—I'm averse to it."

"I don't understand."

"Will you take some tea?"

"No, thanks; I do so hope that I don't quite understand."

"That's hardly my fault; I have spoken very distinctly."

"Then what you wish to convey is ——" said Van, with his hand now at the door.

"Is this," said Longcluse, "that I decline Mr. Arden's acquaintance, that I won't consider his affairs, and that I peremptorily refuse to be of the slightest use to him in his difficulties. I hope I am now sufficiently distinct."

"Oh, perfectly—I ——"

"Pray take some tea."

"And my visit is a failure. I'm awfully sorry I can't be of any use!"

"None here, Sir, to Mr. Arden—none, no more than I."

"Then I have only to beg of you to accept my apologies for having given you a great deal of trouble, and to beg pardon for having disturbed you, and to say good-night."

"No trouble—none. I am glad everything is clear now. Good-night."

And Mr. Longcluse saw him politely to the door, and said again, in a clear, stern tone, but with a smile and another bow, "Good-night," as he parted at the door.

About an hour later a servant arrived with a letter for Mr. Longcluse. That gentleman recognised the hand, and suspended his business to read it. He did so with a smile. It was thus expressed:—

"Sir,

> "I beg to inform you, in the distinctest terms, that neither Mr. Vandeleur, nor any other gentleman, had any authority from me to enter into any discussion with you, or to make the slightest allusion

to subjects upon which Mr. Vandeleur, at your desire, tells me he, this evening, thought fit to converse with you. And I beg, in the most pointed manner, to disavow all connection with, or previous knowledge of, that gentleman's visit and conversation. And I do so lest Mr. Vandeleur's assertion to the same effect should appear imperfect without mine.—I remain, Sir, your obedient servant,

"Richard Arden.

"To Walter Longcluse, Esq."

"Does any one wait for an answer?" he asked, still smiling.

"Yes, Sir: Mr. Thompson, please, Sir."

"Very well; ask him to wait a moment," said he, and he wrote as follows:—

"Mr. Longcluse takes the liberty of returning Mr. Arden's letter, and begs to decline any correspondence with him."

And this note, with Richard Arden's letter, he enclosed in an envelope, and addressed to that gentleman.

While this correspondence, by no means friendly, was proceeding, other letters were interesting, very profoundly, other persons in this drama.

Old David Arden had returned early from a ponderous dinner of the magnates of that world which interested him more than the world of fashion, or even of politics, and he was sitting in his study at half-past ten, about a quarter of a mile westward of Mr. Longcluse's house in Bolton Street.

Not many letters had come for him by the late post. There were two which he chose to read forthwith. The rest would, in Swift's phrase, keep cool, and he could read them before his breakfast in the morning. The first was a note posted at Islington. He knew his niece's pretty hand. This was an "advice" from Mortlake. The second which he picked up from the little pack was a foreign letter, of more than usual bulk.

CHAPTER XLIII.

A LETTER AND A SUMMONS.

Paris? Yes, he knew the hand well. His face darkened a little with a peculiar anxiety. This he will read first. He draws the candles all together, near the corner of the table at which he sits. He can't have too much light on these formal lines, legible and tall as the letters are. He opens the thin envelope, and reads what follows:—

"DEAR AND HONOURED SIR,

"I am in receipt of yours of the 13th instant. You judge me rightly in supposing that I have entered on my mission with a willing mind, and no thought of sparing myself. On the 11th instant I presented the letter you were so good as to provide me with to M. de la Perriere. He received me with much consideration in consequence. You have not been misinformed with regard to his position. His influence is, and so long as the present Cabinet remain in power will continue to be, more than sufficient to procure for me the information and opportunities you so much desire. He explained to me very fully the limits of that assistance which official people here have it in their power to afford. Their prerogative is more extensive than with us, but at the same time it has its points of circumscription. Every private citizen has his well-defined rights, which they can in no case invade. He says that had I come armed with affidavits criminating any individual, or even justifying a strong and distinct suspicion, their powers would be much larger. As it is, he cautions me against taking any steps that might alarm Vanboeren. The baron is a suspicious man, it seems, and has, moreover, once or twice been under official surveillance, which has made him crafty. He is not likely to be caught napping. He ostensibly practises the professions of a surgeon and dentist. In the latter capacity he has a very considerable business. But his principal income is derived, I am informed, from sources of a different kind."

"H'm! what can he mean? I suppose he explains a little further on," mused Mr. Arden.

> "He is, in short, a practitioner about whom suspicions of an infamous kind have prevailed. One branch of his business, a rather strange one, has connected him with persons, more considerable in number than you would readily believe, who were, or are, political refugees."

"Can this noble baron be a distiller of poisons?" David Arden ruminated.

> "In all his other equivocal doings, he found, on the few occasions that seemed to threaten danger, mysterious protectors, sufficiently powerful to bring him off scot-free. His relations of a political character were those which chiefly brought him under the secret notice of the police. It is believed that he has amassed a fortune, and it is certain that he is about to retire from business. I can much better explain to you, when I see you, the remarkable circumstances to which I have but alluded. I hope to be in town again, and to have the honour of waiting upon you, on Thursday, the 29th instant."

"Ay, that's the day he named at parting. What a punctual fellow that is!"

> "They appear to me to have a very distinct bearing upon some possible views of the case in which you are so justly interested. The Baron Vanboeren is reputed very wealthy, but he is by no means liberal in his dealings, and is said to be insatiably avaricious. This last quality may make him practicable ——"

"Yes, so it may," acquiesced Uncle David.

> "so that disclosures of importance may be obtained, if he be approached in the proper manner. Lebas was connected, as a mechanic, with the dentistry department of his business. Mr. L —— has been extremely kind to Lebas' widow and children, and has settled a small annuity upon her, and fifteen hundred francs each upon his children."

"Eh? Upon my life, that is very handsome—extremely handsome. It gives me rather new ideas of this man—that is, if there's nothing odd in it," said Mr. Arden.

> "The deed by which he has done all this is, in its reciting part, an eccentric one. I waited, as I advised you in mine of the 12th, upon M. Arnaud, who is the legal man employed by Madame Lebas, for the purpose of handing him the ten napoleons which you were so good as to transmit for the use of his family; which sum he has, with many thanks on the part of Madame Lebas, declined, and which, therefore, I hold still to your credit. When explaining to me that lady's reasons for declining your remittance, he requested me to read a deed of gift from Mr. Longcluse, making the provisions I have before referred

> to, and reciting, as nearly in these words as I can remember:—'Whereas I entertained for the deceased Pierre Lebas, in whose house in Paris I lodged when very young, for more than a year and a half, a very great respect and regard: and whereas I hold myself to have been the innocent cause of his having gone to the room, as appears from my evidence, in which, unhappily, he lost his life: and whereas I look upon it as a disgrace to our City of London that such a crime could have been committed in a place of public resort, frequented as that was at the time, without either interruption or detection; and whereas, so regarding it, I think that such citizens as could well afford to subscribe money, adequately to compensate the family of the deceased for the pecuniary loss which both his widow and children have sustained by reason of his death, were bound to do so; his visit to London having been strictly a commercial one; and all persons connected with the trade of London being more or less interested in the safety of the commercial intercourse between the two countries: and whereas the citizens of London have failed, although applied to for the purpose, to make any such compensation; now this deed witnesseth,' etc."

"Well, in all that, I certainly go with him. We Londoners ought to be ashamed of ourselves."

> "The widow has taken her children to Avranches, her native place, where she means to live. Please direct me whether I shall proceed thither, and also upon what particular points you would wish me to interrogate her. I have learned, this moment, that the Baron Vanboeren retires in October next. It is thought that he will fix his residence after that at Berlin. My informant undertakes to advise me of his address, whenever it is absolutely settled. In approaching this baron, it is thought you will have to exercise caution and dexterity, as he has the reputation of being cunning and unscrupulous."

"I'm not good at dealing with such people—I never was. I must engage some long-headed fellow who understands them," said he.

> "I debit myself with two thousand five hundred francs, the amount of your remittance on the 15th inst., for which I will account at sight.—I remain, dear and honoured Sir, your attached and most obedient servant,

"Christopher Blount."

"I shall learn all he knows in a few days. What is it that deprives me of quiet till a clue be found to the discovery of Yelland Mace? And why is it that the fancy has seized me that Mr. Longcluse knows where that villain may be found? He admitted, in talking to Alice, she says, that he had seen him in his young days. I will pick up all the facts, and then consider well all that they may point to. Let us but get the letters together, and in time we may find out what they spell. Here am I, a rich but sad old bachelor, having missed for ever the best hope of my life. Poor Harry long dead, and but one branch of the old tree with fruit upon it—Reginald, with his two children: Richard, my nephew—Richard Arden, in a few years the sole representative of the whole family of Arden, and he such a scamp and fool! If a childless old fellow could care for such things, it would be enough to break my heart. And poor little Alice! So affectionate and so beautiful, left, as she will be, alone, with such a protector as that fellow! I pity her."

At that moment her unopened note caught his eye, as it lay on the table. He opened it, and read these words:—

"MY DEAREST UNCLE DAVID,

> "I am so miserable and perplexed, and so utterly without any one to befriend or advise me in my present unexpected trouble, that I must implore of you to come to Mortlake, if you can, the moment this note reaches you. I know how unreasonable and selfish this urgent request will appear. But when I shall have told you all that has happened, you will say, I know, that I could not have avoided imploring your aid. Therefore, I entreat, distracted creature as I am, that you, my beloved uncle, will come to aid and counsel me; and believe me when I assure you that I am in extreme distress, and without, at this moment, any other friend to help me.—Your very unhappy niece,
>
> "Alice."

He read this short note over again.

"No; it is not a sick lap-dog, or a saucy maid: there is some real trouble. Alice has, I think, more sense—I'll go at once. Reginald is always late, and I shall find them" (he looked at his watch)—"yes, I shall find them still up at Mortlake."

So instantly he sent for a cab, and pulled on again a pair of boots, instead of the slippers he had donned, and before five minutes was driving at a rapid pace towards Mortlake.

CHAPTER XLIV.

THE REASON OF ALICE'S NOTE.

The long drive to Mortlake was expedited by promises to the cabman; for, in this acquisitive world, nothing for nothing is the ruling law of reciprocity. It was about half-past eleven o'clock when they reached the gate of the avenue; it was a still night, and a segment of the moon was high in the sky, faintly silvering the old fluted piers and urns, and the edges of the gigantic trees that overhung them. They were now driving up the avenue. How odd was the transition from the glare and hurly-burly of the town to the shadowy and silent woodlands on which this imperfect light fell so picturesquely.

There were associations enough to induce melancholy as he drove through those neglected scenes, his playground in boyish days, where he, and Harry whom he loved, had passed so many of the happy days that precede school. He could hear his laugh floating still among the boughs of the familiar trees, he could see his handsome face smiling down through the leaves of the lordly chestnut that stood, at that moment, by the point of the avenue they were passing, like a forsaken old friend overlooking the way without a stir.

"I'll follow this clue to the end," said David Arden. "I sha'n't make much of it, I fear; but if it ends, as others in the same inquiry have, in smoke, I shall, at least, have done my utmost, and may abandon the task with a good grace, and conclude that Heaven declines to favour the pursuit. Taken for all-in-all, he was the best of his generation, and the fittest to head the house. Something, I thought, was due, in mere respect to his memory. The coldness of Reginald insulted me. If a favourite dog had been poisoned, he would have made more exertion to commit the culprit. And once in pursuit of this dark shadow, how intense and direful grew the interest of the chase, and —— Here we are at the hall-door. Don't mind knocking, ring the bell," he said to the driver.

He was himself at the threshold before the door was opened.

"Can I see my brother?" he asked.

"Sir Reginald is in the drawing-room—a small dinner-party to-day, Sir—Lady May Penrose, and Lady Mary Maypol, they returned to town in Lady May Penrose's carriage, Lord Wynderbroke remains, Sir, and two gentlemen; they are at present with Sir Reginald in the smoking-room."

He learned that Miss Arden was alone in the small sitting-room, called the card-room. David Arden had walked through the vestibule, and into the capacious hall. The lights were all out, but one.

"Well, I sha'n't disturb him. Is Miss Alice ——"

"Yes, Alice is here. It is so kind of you to come!" said a voice he well knew. "Here I am! Won't you come up to the drawing-room, Uncle David?"

"So you want to consult Uncle David," he said, entering the room, and looking round. "In my father's time the other drawing-rooms used to be open; it is a handsome suite—very pretty rooms. But I think you have been crying, my poor little Alice. What on earth is all this about, my dear! Here I am, and it is past eleven; so we must come to the point, if I am to hear it to-night. What is the matter?"

"My dear uncle, I have been so miserable!"

"Well, what is it?" he said, taking a chair; "you have refused some fellow you like, or accepted some fellow you don't like. I am sure you are at the bottom of your own misery, foolish little creature! Girls generally are, I think, the architects of their own penitentiaries. Sit there, my dear, and if it is anything I can be of the least use in, you may count on my doing my utmost. Only you must tell me the whole case, and you mustn't colour it a bit."

So they sat down on a sofa, and Miss Alice told him in her own way that, to her amazement, that day Lord Wynderbroke had made something very like a confession of his passion, and an offer of his hand, which this unsophisticated young lady was on the point of repelling, when Lady May entered the room, accompanied by her friend, Lady Mary Maypol; and, of course, the interesting situation, for that time, dissolved. About an hour after, Alice, who was shocked at the sudden distinction of which she had become the object, and extremely vexed at the interruption which had compelled her to suspend her reply, and very anxious for an opportunity to answer with decision, found that opportunity in a little saunter which she and the two ladies took in the grounds, accompanied by Lord Wynderbroke and Sir Reginald.

When the opportunity came, with a common inconsistency, she rather shrank from the crisis; and a slight uncertainty as to the actual meaning of the noble lord, rendered her perplexity still more disagreeable. It occurred thus: the party had walked some little distance, and when Alice was addressed by her father—

"Here is Wynderbroke, who says he has never seen my Roman inscription! You, Alice, must do the honours, for I daren't yet venture on the grass,"—he shrugged and shook his head over his foot—"and I will take charge of Lady Mary and Lady May, who want to see the Derbyshire thistles—they have grown so enormous under my gardener's care. You said, May, the other evening, that you would like to see them."

Lady May acquiesced with true feminine sympathy with the baronet's stratagem, notwithstanding an imploring glance from Alice! and Lady Mary Maypol, exchanging a glance with Lady May, expressed equal interest in the Derbyshire thistles.

"You will find the inscription at the door of the grotto, only twenty steps from this; it was dug up when my grandfather made the round pond, with the fountain in it. You'll find us in the garden."

Lord Wynderbroke beamed an insufferable smile on Alice, and said something pretty that she did not hear. She knew perfectly what was coming, and although resolved, she was yet in a state of extreme confusion.

Lord Wynderbroke was talking all the way as they approached the grotto; but not one word of his harmonious periods did she clearly hear. By the time they reached the little rocky arch under the evergreens, through the leaves of which the marble tablet and Roman inscription were visible, they had each totally forgotten the antiquarian object with which they had set out.

Lord Wynderbroke came to a standstill, and then with a smiling precision and distinctness, and in accents that seemed, somehow, to ring through her head, he made a very explicit declaration and proposal; and during the entire delivery of this performance, which was neat and lucid rather than impassioned, she remained tongue-tied, listening as if to a tale told in a dream.

She withdrew her hand hastily from Lord Wynderbroke's tender pressure, and the young lady with a sudden effort, replied collectedly enough, in a way greatly to amaze Lord Wynderbroke.

When she had done, that nobleman was silent for some time, and stood in the same attitude of attention with which he had heard her. With a heightened colour he cleared his voice, and his answer, when it came, was dry and pettish. He thought with great deference, that he was, perhaps entitled to a little consideration, and it appeared to him that he had quite unaccountably misunderstood what had seemed the very distinct language of Sir Reginald. For the present he had no more to say. He hoped to explain more satisfactorily to Miss Arden, after he had himself had a few words of explanation, to which he thought he had a claim, from Sir Reginald; and he must confess that, after the lengths to which he had been induced to proceed, he was quite taken by surprise, and inexpressibly wounded by the tone which Miss Arden had adopted.

Side by side, at a somewhat quick pace, Miss Arden with a heightened colour, and Lord Wynderbroke with his ears tingling, rejoined their friends.

"Well, my dear child," said Uncle David, with a laugh, "if you have nothing worse to complain of, though I am very glad to see you, I think we might have put off our meeting till daylight."

"Oh! but you have not heard half what has happened. He has behaved in the most cowardly, treacherous, ungentlemanlike way," she continued vehemently. "Papa sent for me, and I never saw him so angry in my life. Lord Wynderbroke has been making his unmanly complaints to him, and papa spoke so violently. And he, instead of going away, having had from me the answer which nothing on earth shall ever induce me to change, he remains here; and actually had the audacity to tell me, very nearly in so many words, that my decision went for nothing. I spoke to him quite frankly, but said nothing that was at all rude—nothing that could have made him the least angry. I implored of him to believe me that I never could change my mind; and I could not help crying, I was so agitated and wretched. But he seemed very much vexed, and simply said that he placed himself entirely in papa's hands. In fact, I've been utterly miserable and terrified, and I do not know how I can endure those terrible scenes with papa. The whole thing has come upon me so suddenly. Could you have imagined any gentleman capable of acting like Lord Wynderbroke—so selfish, cruel, and dastardly?" and with these words she burst into tears.

"Do you mean to say that he won't take your refusal?" said her uncle, looking very angry.

"That is what he says," she sobbed. "He had an opportunity only for a few words, and that was the purport of them; and I was so astounded, I could not reply; and, instead of going away, he remains here. Papa and he have arranged to prolong his visit; so I shall be teased and frightened, and I am so nervous and agitated; and it is such an outrage!"

"Now, we must not lose our heads, my dear child; we must consult calmly. It seems you don't think it possible that you may come to like Lord Wynderbroke sufficiently to marry him."

"I would rather die! If this goes on, I sha'n't stay here. I'd go and be a governess rather."

"I think you might give my house a trial first," said Uncle David merrily; "but it is time to talk about that by-and-by. What does May Penrose think of it? She sometimes, I believe, on an emergency, lights on a sensible suggestion."

"She had to return to town with Lady Mary, who dined here also; I did not know she was going until a few minutes before they left. I've been so miserably unlucky! and I could not make an opportunity without its seeming so rude to Lady Mary, and I don't know her well enough to tell her; and, you have no idea, papa is so incensed, and so peremptory; and what am I to do? Oh! dear uncle, think of something. I know you'll help me."

"That I will," said the old gentleman. "But allowances are to be made for a poor old devil so much in love as Lord Wynderbroke."

"I don't think he likes me now—he can't like me," said Alice. "But he is angry. It is simply pride and vanity. From something papa said, I am sure of it, Lord Wynderbroke has been telling his friends, and speaking, I fancy, as if everything was arranged, and he never anticipated that I could have any mind of my own; and I suppose he thinks he would be laughed at, and so I am to undergo a persecution, and he won't hear of anything but what he pleases; and papa is determined to accomplish it. And, oh! what am I to do?"

"I'll tell you, but you must do exactly as I bid you. Who's there?" he said suddenly, as Alice's maid opened the door.

"Oh! I beg pardon—Miss Alice, please," she said, dropping a curtsey and drawing back.

"Don't go," said Uncle David, "we shall want you. What's the matter?"

"Sir Reginald has been took bad with his foot again, please, Miss."

"Nothing serious?" said Uncle David.

"Only pain, please, Sir, in the same place."

"All the better it should fix itself well in his foot. You need not be uneasy about it, Alice. You and your maid must be in my cab, which is at the hall door, in five minutes. Take leave of no one, and don't waste time over finery; just put a few things up, and take your dressing-case; and you and your maid are coming to town with me. Is my brother in the drawing-room?"

"No, Sir, please; he is in his own room."

"Are the gentlemen who dined still here?"

"Two left, Sir, when Sir Reginald took ill; but Lord Wynderbroke remains."

"Oh! and where is he?"

"Sir Reginald sent for him, please, Sir—just as I came up—to his room."

"Very good, then I shall find them both together. Now, Alice, I must find you and your maid in the cab in five minutes. I shall get your leave from Reginald, and you order the fellow to drive down to the little church gate in the village close by, and I'll walk after and join you there in a few minutes. Lose no time."

With this parting charge, Uncle David ran down the stairs, and met Lord Wynderbroke at the foot of them, returning from his visit of charity to Sir Reginald's room.

CHAPTER XLV.

COLLISION.

"Lord Wynderbroke!" said Uncle David, and bowed rather ceremoniously.

Lord Wynderbroke, a little surprised, extended two fingers and said, "How d'ye do, Mr. Arden?" and smiled drily, and then seemed disposed to pass on.

"I beg your pardon, Lord Wynderbroke," said David Arden, "but would you mind giving me a few minutes? I have something you may think a little important to say, and if you will allow me, I'll say it in this room"—he indicated the half-open door of the dining-room, in which there was still some light—"I shall not detain you long."

The urbane and smiling peer looked on him for a moment—rather darkly—with a shrewd eye; and he said, still smiling,—

"Certainly, Mr. Arden; but at this hour, and being about to write a note, you will see that I have very little time indeed—I'm very sorry."

He was speaking stiffly, and any one might have seen that he suspected nothing very agreeable as the result of Mr. Arden's communication.

When they had got into the dining-room, and the door was closed, Lord Wynderbroke, with his head a little high, invited Mr. Arden to proceed.

"Then, as you are in a hurry, you'll excuse my going direct to the point. I've come here in consequence of a note that reached me about an hour ago, informing me that my niece, Alice Arden, has suffered a great deal of annoyance. You know, of course, to what I refer?"

"I should extremely regret that the young lady, your niece, should suffer the least vexation, from any cause; but I should have fancied that her happiness might be more naturally confided to the keeping of her father, than of a relation residing in a different house, and by no means so nearly interested in consulting it."

"I see, Lord Wynderbroke, that I must address you very plainly, and even coarsely. My brother Reginald does not consult her happiness in this matter, but merely his own ideas of a desirable family connection. She is really quite miserable; she has unalterably made up her mind. You'll not induce her to change it.

There is no chance of that. But by permitting my brother to exercise a pressure in favour of your suit ——"

"You'll excuse my interrupting for a moment, to say that there is, and can be, nothing but the perfectly legitimate influence of a parent. Pressure, there is none—none in the world, Sir; although I am not, like you, Mr. Arden, a relation—and a very near one—of Sir Reginald Arden's, I think I can undertake to say that he is quite incapable of exercising what you call a pressure upon the young lady his daughter; and I have to beg that you will be so good as to spare me the pain of hearing that term employed, as you have just now employed it—or at all, Sir, in connection with me. I take the liberty of insisting upon that, peremptorily."

Mr. Arden bowed, and went on:

"And when the young lady distinctly declines the honour you propose, you persist in paying your addresses, as though her answer meant just nothing."

"I don't quite know, Sir, why I've listened so long to this kind of thing from you; you have no right on earth, Sir, to address that sort of thing to me. How dare you talk to me, Sir, in that—a—a—audacious tone upon my private affairs and conduct?"

Uncle David was a little fiery, and answered, holding his head high,—

"What I have to say is short and clear. I don't care twopence about your affairs, or your conduct, but I do very much care about my niece's happiness; and if you any longer decline to take the answer she has given you, and continue to cause her the slightest trouble, I'll make it a personal matter with you. Good-night!" he added, with an inflamed visage, and a stamp on the floor, thundering his valediction. And forth he went to pay his brief visit to his brother—not caring twopence, as he said, what Lord Wynderbroke thought of him.

Sir Reginald had got into his dressing-gown. He was not now in any pain to speak of, and expressed great surprise at the sudden appearance of his brother.

"You'll take something, won't you?"

"Nothing, thanks," answered David. "I came to beg a favour."

"Oh! did you? You find me very poorly," said the baronet, in a tone that seemed to imply, "You might easily kill me, by imposing the least trouble just now."

"You'll be all the better, Reginald, for this little attack; it is so comfortably established in your foot."

"Comfortably! I wish you felt it," said Sir Reginald, sharply; "and it's confoundedly late. Why didn't you come to dinner?"

David laughed good-humouredly.

"You forgot, I think, to ask me," said he.

"Well, well, you know there is always a chair and a glass for you; but won't it do to talk about any cursed thing you wish to-morrow? I—I never, by any chance, hear anything agreeable. I have been tortured out of my wits and senses all day long by a tissue of pig-headed, indescribable frenzy. I vow to Heaven there's a conspiracy to drive me into a mad-house, or into my grave; and I declare to my

Maker, I wish the first time I'm asleep, some fellow would come in and blow my brains out on the pillow."

"I don't know an easier death," said David; and his brother, who meant it to be terrific, did not pretend to hear him. "I have only a word to say," he continued, "a request you have never refused to other friends, and, in fact, dear Reginald, I ventured to take it for granted you would not refuse me; so I have taken Alice into town, to make me a little visit of a day or two."

"You haven't taken Alice—you don't mean—she's not gone?" exclaimed the baronet, sitting up with a sudden perpendicularity, and staring at his brother as if his eyes were about to leap from their sockets.

"I'll take the best care of her. Yes, she is gone," said David.

"But my dear, excellent, worthy—why, curse you, David, you can't possibly have done anything so clumsy! Why, you forgot that Wynderbroke is here; how on earth am I to entertain Wynderbroke without her?"

"Why, it is exactly because Lord Wynderbroke is here, that I thought it the best time for her to make me a visit."

"I protest to Heaven, David, I believe you're deranged! Do you the least know what you are saying?"

"Perfectly. Now, my dear Reginald, let us look at the matter quietly. The girl does not like him; she would not marry him, and never will; she has grown to hate him; his own conduct has made her despise and detest him; and she's not the kind of girl who would marry for a mere title. She has unalterably made up her mind; and these are not times when you can lock a young lady into her room, and starve her into compliance; and Alice is a spirited girl—all the women of our family were. You're no goose like Wynderbroke—you only need to know that the girl has quite made up her mind, or her heart, or her hatred, or whatever it is, and she won't marry him. It is as well he should know it at first, as at last; and I don't think, if he were a gentleman, peer though he be, he would have been in this house to-night. He counted on his title: he was too sure. I am very proud of Alice. And now he can't bear the mortification—having, like a fool, disclosed his suit to others before it had succeeded—of letting the world know he has been refused; and to this petty vanity he would sacrifice Alice, and prevail on you, if he could, to bully her into accepting him, a plan in which, if he perseveres, I have told him he shall, besides failing ridiculously, give me a meeting; for I will make it a personal quarrel with him."

Sir Reginald sat in his chair, looking very white and wicked, with his eyes gleaming fire on his brother. He opened his mouth once or twice, to speak, but only drew a short breath at each attempt.

David Arden rather wondered that his brother took all this so quietly. If he had observed him a little more closely, he would have seen that his hands were trembling, and perceived also that he had tried repeatedly to speak, and that either voice or articulation failed him. On a sudden he recovered, and regardless of his gout started to his feet, and limped along the floor, exclaiming,—

"Help us—help us—God help us! What's this? My—my—oh, my God! It's very bad!" He was stumping round and round the table, near which he had sat, and restlessly shoving the pamphlets and books hither and thither as he went. "What have I done to earn this curse?—was ever mortal so pursued? The last thing, this was; now all's gone—quite gone—it's over, quite. They've done it—they've done it. Bravo! bravi tutti! brava! All—all, and everything gone! To think of her—only to think of her! She was my pet." (And in his bleak, trembling voice, he cried a horrid curse at her.) "I tell you," he screamed, dashing his hand on the table, at the other end of which he had arrested his monotonous shuffle round it, when his brother caught suddenly his vacant eye, "you think, because I'm down in the world, and you are prosperous, that you can do as you like. If I was where I should be, you daren't. I'll have her back, Sir. I'll have the police with you. I'll—I'll indict you—it's a police-office affair. They'll take her through the streets. Where's the wretch like her? I charge her—let them take her by the shoulder. And my son, Richard—to think of him!—the cursed puppy!—his post obit! One foot in the grave, have I? No, I'm not so near smoked out as you take me—I've a long time for it—I've a long life. I'll live to see him broken—without a coat to his back—you villanous, swindling dandy, and I'll ——"

His voice got husky, and he struck his thin fist on the table, and clung to it, and the room was suddenly silent.

David Arden rang the bell violently, and got his arm round his brother, who shook himself feebly, and shrugged, as if he disdained and hated that support.

In came Crozier, who looked aghast, but wheeled his easy-chair close to where he stood, and between them they got him into it, trembling from head to foot.

Martha Tansey came in and lent her aid, and beckoning her to the door, David Arden asked her if she thought him very ill.

"I 'a' seen him just so a dozen times over. He'll be well enough, soon, and if ye knew him as weel in they takins, ye'd ho'd wi' me, there's nothing more than common in't; he's a bit teathy and short-waisted, and always was, and that's how he works himself into them fits."

So spoke Tansey, into whose talk, in moments of excitement, returned something of her old north-country dialect.

"Well, so he was, vexed with me, as with other people, and he has over-excited himself; but as he has this little gout about him, I may as well send out his doctor as I return."

This little conversation took place outside Sir Reginald's room-door, which David did not care to re-enter, as his brother might have again become furious on seeing him. So he took his leave of Martha Tansey, and their whispered dialogue ended. One or two sighs and groans showed that Sir Reginald's energies were returning. David Arden walked quickly across the vast hall, in which now burned duskily but a single candle, and let himself out into the clear, cold night; and as he walked down the broad avenue he congratulated himself on having cut the Gordian knot, and liberated his niece.

It was a pleasant walk by the narrow road, with its lofty groining of foliage, down to the village outpost of Islington, where, under the shadow of the old church-spire, he found his cab waiting, with Alice and her maid in it.

CHAPTER XLVI.

AN UNKNOWN FRIEND.

As they drove into town, Uncle David was thinking how awkward it would be if Sir Reginald should have recovered his activity, and dispatched a messenger to recall Alice, and await their arrival at his door. Well, he did not want a quarrel; he hated a fracas; but he would not send Alice back till next morning, come what might; and then he would return with her, and see Lord Wynderbroke again, and take measures to compel an immediate renunciation of his suit. As for Reginald, he would find arguments to reconcile him to the disappointment. At all events, Alice had thrown herself upon his protection, and he would not surrender her except on terms.

Uncle David was silent, having all this matter to ruminate upon. He left a pencilled line for Sir Henry Margate, his brother's physician, and then drove on towards home.

Turning into Saint James's Street, Alice saw her brother standing at the side of a crossing, with a great-coat and a white muffler on, the air being sharp. A couple of carriages drawn up near the pavement, and the passing of two or three others on the outside, for a moment checked their progress, and Alice, had not the window been up, could have spoken to him as they passed. He did not see them, but the light of a lamp was on his face, and she was shocked to see how ill he looked.

"There is Dick," she said, touching her uncle's arm, "looking so miserable! Shall we speak to him!"

"No, dear, never mind him—he's well enough." David Arden peeped at his nephew as they passed. "He is beginning to take an interest in what really concerns him."

She looked at her uncle, not understanding his meaning.

"We can talk of it another time, dear," he added with a cautionary glance at the maid, who sat in the corner at the other side.

Richard Arden was on his way to the place where he meant to recover his losses. He had been playing deep at Colonel Marston's lodgings, but not yet luckily. He thought he had used his credit there as far as he could successfully press it.

The polite young men who had their supper there that night, and played after he left till nearly five o'clock in the morning, knew perfectly what he had lost at the Derby; but they did not know how perilously, on the whole, he was already involved. Was Richard Arden, who had lost nearly seven hundred pounds at Colonel Marston's little gathering, though he had not paid them yet, now quite desperate? By no means. It is true he had, while Vandeleur was out, made an excursion to the City, and, on rather hard terms, secured a loan of three hundred pounds—a trifle which, if luck favoured, might grow to a fortune; but which, if it proved contrary, half an hour would see out.

He had locked this up in his desk, as a reserve for a theatre quite different from Marston's little party; and on his way to that more public and also more secret haunt, he had called at his lodgings for it. It was not that small deposit that cheered him, but a curious and unexpected little note which he found there. It presented by no means a gentlemanlike exterior. The hand was a round clerk's-hand, with flourishing capitals, on an oblong blue envelope, with a vulgar little device. A dun, he took it to be; and he was not immediately relieved when he read at the foot of it, "Levi." Then he glanced to the top, and read, "DEAR SIR."

This easy form of address he read with proper disdain.

> "I am instructed by a most respectable party who is desirous to assist you, to the figure of £1,000 or upwards, at nominal discounts, to meet you and ascertain your wishes thereupon, if possible to-night, lest you should suffer inconvenience.
>
> "Yours truly,
> "ISRAEL LEVI.
>
> "P.S.—In furtherance of the above, I shall be at Dignum's Divan, Strand, from 11 P.M. to-night to 1 A.M."

Here then, at last, was a sail in sight!

With this note in his pocket, he walked direct to the place of rendezvous, in the Strand. It was on his way that, unseen by him, his sister and his uncle had observed him, on their drive to David Arden's house.

There were two friends only whom he strongly suspected of this very well-timed interposition—there was Lady May Penrose, and there was Uncle David. Lady May was rich, and quite capable of a generous sacrifice for him. Uncle David, also rich, would like to show an intimidating front, as he had done, but would hardly like to see him go to the wall. There was, I must confess, a trifling bill due to Mr. Longcluse, who had kindly got or given him cash for it. It was something less than a hundred pounds—a mere nothing; but in their altered relations, it would not do to permit any miscarriage of this particular bill. He might have risked it in the frenzy of play. But to stoop to ask quarter from Longcluse was more than his pride could endure. No; nor would the humiliation avail to arrest the consequences of his neglect. In the general uneasiness and horror of his situation, this little point was itself a centre of torture, and now his unknown friend had come to the rescue, and in the golden sunshine of his promise it, like a hundred minor troubles, was dissolving.

In Pall Mall he jumped into a cab, feeling strangely like himself again. The lights, the clubs, the well-known perspectives, the stars above him, and the gliding vehicles and figures that still peopled the streets, had recovered their old cheery look; he was again in the upper world, and his dream of misery had broken up and melted. Under the great coloured lamp, yellow, crimson, and blue, that overhung the pavement, emblazoned on every side with transparent arabesques, and in gorgeous capitals proclaiming to all whom it might concern "DIGNUM'S DIVAN," he dismissed his cab, took his counter in the cigar shop, and entered the great rooms beyond. The first of these, as many of my readers remember, was as large as a good-sized Methodist Chapel; and five billiard-tables, under a blaze of gas, kept the many-coloured balls rolling, and the marker busy, calling "Blue on brown, and pink your player," and so forth; and gentlemen young and old, Christians and Hebrews, in their shirt-sleeves, picked up shillings when they took "lives," or knocked the butts of their cues fiercely on the floor when they unexpectedly lost them.

Among a very motley crowd, Richard Arden slowly sauntering through the room found Mr. Levi, whose appearance he already knew, having once or twice had occasion to consult him financially. His play was over for the night. The slim little Jew, with black curly head, large fierce black eyes, and sullen mouth, stood with his hands in his pockets, gaping luridly over the table where he had just, he observed to his friend Isaac Blumer, who did not care if he was hanged, "losht sheven pound sheventeen, ash I'm a shinner!"

Mr. Levi saw Richard Arden approaching, and smiled on him with his wide show of white fangs. Richard Arden approached Mr. Levi with a grave and haughty face. Here, to be sure, was nothing but what Horace Walpole used to call "the mob." Not a human being whom he knew was in the room; still he would have preferred seeing Mr. Levi at his office; and the audacity of his presuming to grin in that familiar fashion! He would have liked to fling one of the billiard-balls in his teeth. In a freezing tone, and with his head high, he said,—

"I think you are Mr. Levi."

"The shame," responded Levi, still smiling; "and 'ow ish Mr. Harden thish evening?"

"I had a note from you," said Arden, passing by Mr. Levi's polite inquiry, "and I should like to know if any of that money you spoke of may be made available to-night."

"Every shtiver," replied the Jew cheerfully.

"I can have it all? Well, this is rather a noisy place," hesitated Richard Arden, looking around him.

"I can get into Mishter Dignum's book-offish here, Mr. Harden, and it won't take a moment. I haven't notes, but I'll give you our cheques, and there'sh no place in town they won't go down as slick as gold. I'll fetch you to where there's pen and ink."

"Do so," said he.

In a very small room, where burned a single jet of gas, Mr. Arden signed a promissory note for, £1,012 10s., for which Mr. Levi handed him cheques of his firm for £1,000.

Having exchanged these securities, Richard Arden said—

"I wish to put one or two questions to you, Mr. Levi." He glanced at a clerk who was making "tots" from a huge folio before him, on a slip of paper, and transferring them to a small book, with great industry.

Levi understood him and beckoned in silence, and when they both stood in the passage he said—

"If you want a word private with me, Mr. Harden, where there'sh no one can shee us, you'll be as private as the deshert of Harabia if you walk round the corner of the shtreet."

Arden nodded, and walked out into the Strand, accompanied by Mr. Levi. They turned to the left, and a few steps brought them to the corner of Cecil Street. The street widens a little after you pass its narrow entrance. It was still enough to justify Mr. Levi's sublime comparison. The moon shone mistily on the river, which was dotted and streaked, at its further edge with occasional red lights from windows, relieved by the black reflected outline of the building which made their back-ground. At the foot of the street, at that time, stood a clumsy rail, and Richard Arden leaned his arm on this, as he talked to the Jew, who had pulled his short cloak about him; and in the faint light he could not discern his features, near as he stood, except, now and then, his white eye-balls, faintly, as he turned, or his teeth when he smiled.

CHAPTER XLVII.

BY THE RIVER.

"You mentioned, Mr. Levi, in your note, that you were instructed, by some person who takes an interest in me, to open this business," said Richard Arden, in a more conciliatory tone. "Will your instructions permit you to tell me who that person is?"

"No, no," drawled Mr. Levi, with a slow shake of his head; "I declare to you sholemnly, Mr. Harden, I couldn't. I'm employed by a third party, and though I may make a tolerable near guess who's firsht fiddle in the bishness, I can't shay nothin'."

"Surely you can say this—it is hardly a question, I am so sure of it—is the friend who lends this money a gentleman?"

"I think the pershon as makesh the advanshe is a bit of a shwell. There, now, that'sh enough."

"But I said a gentleman," persisted Arden.

"You mean to ask, hashn't a lady got nothing to do with it?"

"Well, suppose I do?"

Mr. Levi shook his head slowly, and all his white teeth showed dimly, as he answered with an unctuous significance that tempted Arden strongly to pitch him into the river.

"We puts the ladiesh first; ladiesh and shentlemen, that's the way it goes at the theaytre; if a good-looking chap's a bit in a fix, there'sh no one like a lady to pull him through."

"I really want to know," said Richard Arden, with difficulty restraining his fury. "I have some relations who are likely enough to give me a lift of this kind; some are ladies, and some gentlemen, and I have a right to know to whom I owe this money."

"To our firm; who elshe? We have took your paper, and you have our cheques on Childs'."

"Your firm lend money at five per cent.!" said Arden with contempt. "You forget, Mr. Levi, you mentioned in your note, distinctly, that you act for another person. Who is that principal for whom you act?"

"I don't know."

"Come, Mr. Levi! you are no simpleton; you may as well tell me—no one shall be a bit the wiser—for I will know."

"Azh I'm a shinner—as I hope to be shaved ——" began Mr. Levi.

"It won't do—you may just as well tell me—out with it!"

"Well, here now; I don't know, but if I did, upon my shoul, I wouldn't tell you."

"It is pleasant to meet with so much sensitive honour, Mr. Levi," said Richard Arden very scornfully. "I have nothing particular to say, only that your firm were mistaken, a little time ago, when they thought that I was without resources; I've friends, you now perceive, who only need to learn that I want money, to volunteer assistance. Have you anything more to say?"

Richard Arden saw the little Jew's fine fangs again displayed in the faint light, as he thus spoke; but it was only prudent to keep his temper with this lucky intervenient.

"I have nothing to shay, Mr. Harden, only there'sh more where that came from, and I may tell you sho, for that'sh no shecret. But don't you go too fasht, young gentleman—not that you won't get it—but don't you go too fasht."

"If I should ever ask your advice, it will be upon other things. I'm giving the lender as good security as I have given to any one else. I don't see any great wonder in the matter. Good-night," he said haughtily, not taking the trouble to look over his shoulder as he walked away.

"Good-night," responded Mr. Levi, taking one of Dignum's cigars from his waistcoat-pocket, and preparing to light it with a lazy grin, as he watched the retreating figure lessening in the perspective of the street, "and take care of yourshelf for my shake, do, and don't you be lettin' all them fine women be throwin' their fortunes like that into your 'at, and bringin' themshelves to the workus, for love of your pretty fashe—poor, dear, love-sick little fools! There you go, right off to Mallet and Turner's, I dareshay, and good luck attend you, for a reglar lady-killin', 'ansome, sweet-spoken, broken-down jackass!"

At this period of his valediction the vesuvian was applied to his cigar, and Richard Arden, turning the far corner of the street, escaped the remainder of his irony, as the Jew, with his hands in his pockets, sauntered up its quiet pavement, in the direction in which Richard Arden had just disappeared. It seemed to that young gentleman that his supplies, no less than thirteen hundred pounds, would all but command the luck of which, as his spirits rose, he began to feel confident. "Fellows," he thought, "who have gone in with less than fifty, have come out, to my knowledge, with thousands; and if less than fifty could do that, what might not be expected from thirteen hundred?"

He picked up a cab. Never did lover fly more impatiently to the feet of his mistress than Richard Arden did, that night, to the shrine of the goddess whom he worshipped.

The muttered scoffs, the dark fiery gaze, the glimmering teeth of this mocking, malicious little Jew, represented an influence that followed Richard Arden that night.

CHAPTER XLVIII.

SUDDEN NEWS.

What is luck? Is there such an influence? What type of mind rejects altogether, and consistently, this law or power? Call it by what name you will, fate or fortune, did not Napoleon, the man of death and of action, and did not Swedenborg, the man of quietude and visions, acknowledge it? Where is the successful gamester who does not "back his luck," when once it has declared itself, and bow before the storms of fortune when they in turn have set in? I take Napoleon and Swedenborg—the man of this visible world, and the man of the invisible world—as the representatives of extreme types of mind. People who have looked into Swedenborg's works will remember curious passages on the subject, and find more dogmatical, and less metaphysical admissions in Napoleon's conversations everywhere.

In corroboration of this theory, that luck is an element, with its floods and ebbs, against which it is fatuity to contend, was the result of Richard Arden's play.

Before half-past two, he had lost every guinea of his treasure. He had been drinking champagne. He was flushed, dismal, profoundly angry. Hot and headachy, he was ready to choke with gall. There was a big, red-headed, vulgar fellow beside him, with a broad-brimmed white hat, who was stuffing his pockets and piling the table before him, as though he had found the secret of an "open sesame," and was helping himself from the sacks of the Forty Thieves.

When Richard had lost his last pound, he would have liked to smash the gas-lamps and windows, and the white hat and the red head in it, and roar the blasphemy that rose to his lips. But men can't afford to make themselves ridiculous, and as he turned about to make his unnoticed exit, he saw the little Jew, munching a sandwich, with a glass of champagne beside him.

"I say," said Richard Arden, walking up to the little man, whose big mouth was full of sandwich, and whose fierce black eyes encountered his instantaneously, "you don't happen to have a little more, on the same terms, about you?"

Mr. Levi waited to bolt his sandwich, and then swallow down his champagne.

"Shave me!" exclaimed he, when this was done. "The thoushand gone! every rag! and" (glancing at his watch) "only two twenty-five! Won't it be rayther young, though, backin' such a run o' bad luck, and throwin' good money after bad, Mr. Harden?"

"That's my affair, I fancy; what I want to know is whether you have got a few hundreds more, on the same terms—I mean, from the same lender. Hang it, say yes or no—can't you?"

"Well, Mr. Harden, there's five hundred more—but 'twasn't expected you'd a' drew it so soon. How much do you say, Mr. Harden?"

"I'll take it all," said Richard Arden. "I wish I could have it without these blackguards seeing."

"They don't care, blesh ye! if you got it from the old boy himself. That is a rum un!" There were pen and ink on a small table beside the wall, at which Mr. Levi began rapidly to fill in the blanks of a bill of exchange. "Why, there's not one o' them, almost, but takes a hundred now and then from me, when they runs out a bit too fast. You'd better shay one month."

"Say two, like the other, and don't keep me waiting."

"You'd better shay one—your friend will think you're going a bit too quick to the devil. Remember, as your proverb shays, 'taint the thing to kill the gooshe that laysh the golden eggs—shay one month."

Levi's large black eye was fixed on him, and he added, "If you want it pushed on a bit when it comes due, there won't be no great trouble about it, I calculate."

Richard Arden looked at the large fierce eyes that were silently fixed on him: one of those eyes winked solemnly and significantly.

"Well, what way you like, only be quick," said Richard Arden.

His new sheaf of cheques were quickly turned into counters; and, after various fluctuations, these counters followed the rest, and in the grey morning he left that haunt jaded and savage, with just fifteen pounds in his pocket, the wreck of the large sum which he had borrowed to restore his fortunes.

It needs some little time to enable a man, who has sustained such a shock as Richard Arden had, to collect his thoughts and define the magnitude of his calamity. He let himself in by a latch-key: the grey light was streaming through the shutters, and turning the chintz pattern of his window-curtains here and there, in streaks, into transparencies. He went into his room and swallowed nearly a tumbler of brandy, then threw off his clothes, drank some more, and fell into a flushed stupor, rather than a sleep, and lay for hours as still as any dead man on the field of battle.

Some four hours of this lethargy, and he became conscious, at intervals, of a sound of footsteps in his room. The shutters were still closed. He thought he heard a voice say, "Master Richard!" but he was too drowsy, still, to rouse himself.

At length a hand was laid upon him, and a voice that was familiar to his ear repeated twice over, more urgently, "Master Richard! Master Richard!" He was now awake: very dimly, by his bedside, he saw a figure standing. Again he heard the same words, and wondered, for a few seconds, where he was.

"That's Crozier talking," said Richard.

"Yes, Sir," said Crozier, in a low tone; "I'm here half-an-hour, Sir, waiting till you should wake."

"Let in some light; I can't see you."

Crozier opened half the window-shutter, and drew the curtain.

"Are ye ailin', Master Richard—are ye bad, Sir?"

"Ailing—yes, I'm bad enough, as you say—I'm miserable. I don't know where to turn or what to do. Hold my coat while I count what's in the pocket. If my father, the old scoundrel ——"

"Master Richard, don't ye say the like o' that no more; all's over, this morning, wi' the old master—Sir Reginald's dead, Sir," said the old follower, sternly.

"Good God!" cried Richard, starting up in his bed and staring at old Crozier with a frightened look.

"Ay, Sir," said the old servant, in a low stern tone, "he's gone at last: he was took just a quarter past five this mornin', by the clock at Mortlake, about four minutes before St. Paul's chimed the quarter. The wind being southerly, we heard the chimes. We thought he was all right, and I did not leave him until half-past twelve o'clock, having given him his drops, and waited till he went asleep. It was about three he rang his bell, and in I goes that minute, and finds him sitting up in his bed, talking quite silly-like about old Wainbridge, the groom, that's dead and buried, away in Skarkwynd Churchyard, these thirty year."

Crozier paused here. He had been crying hours ago, and his eyes and nose still showed evidences of that unbecoming weakness. Perhaps he expected Richard, now Sir Richard Arden, to say something, but nothing came.

"'Tis a change, Sir, and I feel a bit queer; and as I was sayin', when I went in, 'twas in his head he saw Tom Wainbridge leadin' a horse saddled and all into the room, and standin' by the side of his bed, with the bridle in his hand, and holdin' the stirrup for him to mount. 'And what the devil brings Wainbridge here, when he has his business to mind in Yorkshire? and where could he find a horse like that beast? He's waiting for me; I can hear the roarin' brute, and I see Tom's parchment face at the door—there,' he'd say, 'and there—where are your eyes, Crozier, can't you see, man? Don't be afraid—can't you look—and don't you hear him? Wainbridge's old nonsense.' And he'd laugh a bit to himself every now and again, and then he'd whimper to me, looking a bit frightened, 'Get him away, Crozier, will you? He's annoying me, he'll have me out,' and this sort o' talk he went on wi' for full twenty minutes. I rang the bell to Mrs. Tansey's room, and when she was come we agreed to send in the brougham for the doctor. I think he was a bit wrong i' the garrets, and we were both afraid to let it be no longer."

Crozier paused for a moment, and shook his head.

"We thought he was goin' asleep, but he wasn't. His eyes was half shut, and his shoulders against the pillows, and Mrs. Tansey was drawin' the eider-down coverlet over his feet, softly, when all on a sudden—I thought he was laughin'—a noise like a little flyrin' laugh, and then a long, frightful yellock, that would make your heart tremble, and awa' wi' him into one o' them fits, and so from one into another, until when the doctor came he said he was in an apoplexy; and so, at just a quarter past five the auld master departed. And I came in to tell you, Sir; and have you any orders to give me, Master Richard? and I'm going on, I take it you'd wish me, to your uncle, Mr. David, and little Miss Alice, that han't heard nout o' the matter yet."

"Yes, Crozier—go," said Richard Arden, staring on him as if his soul was in his eyes; and, after a pause, with an effort, he added—"I'll call there as I go on to Mortlake; tell them I'll see them on my way."

When Crozier was gone, Richard Arden got up, threw his dressing-gown about him, and sat on the side of his bed, feeling very faint. A sudden gush of tears relieved the strange paroxysm. Then come other emotions less unselfish. He dressed hastily. He was too much excited to make a breakfast. He drank a cup of coffee, and drove to Uncle David's house.

CHAPTER XLIX.

VOWS FOR THE FUTURE.

As he drove to his uncle's house, he was tumbling over facts and figures, in the endeavour to arrive at some conclusion as to how he stood in the balance-sheet that must now be worked out. What a thing that post-obit had turned out! Those cursed Jews who had dealt with him must have known ever so much more about his poor father's health than he did. They are such fellows to worm out the secrets of a family—all through one's own servants, and doctors, and apothecaries. The spies! They stick at nothing—such liars! How they pretended to wish to be off! What torture they kept him in! How they talked of the old man's nervous fibre, and pretended to think he would live for twenty years to come!

"And the deed was not six weeks signed when I found out he had those epileptic fits, and they knew it, the wretches!—and so I've been hit for that huge sum of money. And there is interest, two years' nearly, on that other charge, and that swindle that half ruined me on the Derby. And there are those bills that Levi has got, but that is only fifteen hundred, and I can manage that any time, and a few other trifles."

And he thought what yeoman's service Longcluse might and would have rendered him in this situation. How translucent the whole opaque complexity would have become in a hour or two, and at what easy interest he would have procured him funds to adjust these complications! But here, too, fortune had dealt maliciously. What a piece of cross-grained luck that Longcluse should have chosen to fall in love with Alice! And now they two had exchanged, not shots, but insults, harder to forgive. And that officious fool, Vandeleur, had laid him open to a more direct and humiliating affront than had before befallen him. Henceforward, between him and Longcluse no reconciliation was possible. Fiery and proud by nature was this Richard Arden, and resentful. In Yorkshire the family had been accounted a vindictive race. I don't know. I have only to do with those inheritors of the name who figure in this story.

There remained an able accountant and influential man on 'Change, on whose services he might implicitly reckon—his uncle, David Arden. But he was separated from him by the undefinable chasm of years—the want of sympathy, the sense of authority. He would take not only the management of this financial adjustment, but the carriage of the future of this young, handsome, full-blooded fellow, who had certainly no wish to take unto himself a Mentor.

Here have been projected on this page, as in the disk of an oxy-hydrogen microscope, some of the small and active thoughts that swarmed almost unsuspected in Richard Arden's mind. But it would be injustice to Sir Richard Arden (we may as well let him enjoy at once the title which stately Death has just presented him with—it seems to me a mocking obeisance) to pretend that higher and kinder feelings had no place in his heart.

Suddenly redeemed from ruin, suddenly shocked by an awful spectacle, a disturbance of old associations where there had once been kindness, where estrangements and enmity had succeeded: there was in all this something moving and agitating, that stirred his affections strangely when he saw his sister.

David Arden had left his house an hour before the news reached its inmates. Sir Richard was shown to the drawing-room, where there was no one to receive him; and in a minute Alice, looking very pale and miserable, entered, and running up to him, without saying a word threw her arms about his neck, and sobbed piteously.

Her brother was moved. He folded her to his heart. Broken and hurried words of tenderness and affection he spoke, as he kissed her again and again. Henceforward he would live a better and wiser life. He had tasted the dangers and miseries that attend on play. He swore he would give it up. He had done with the follies of his youth. But for years he had not had a home. He was thrown into the thick of temptation. A fellow who had no home was so likely to amuse himself with play; and he had suffered enough to make him hate it, and she should see what a brother he would be, henceforward, to her.

Alice's heart was bursting with self-reproach; she told Richard the whole story of her trouble of the day before, and the circumstances of her departure from Mortlake, all in an agony of tears; and declared, as young ladies often have done before, that she never could be happy again.

He was disappointed, but generous and gentle feelings had been stirred within him.

"Don't reproach yourself, darling; that is mere folly. The entire responsibility of your leaving Mortlake belongs to my uncle; and about Wynderbroke, you must not torment yourself; you had a right to a voice in the matter, surely, and I daresay you would not be happier now if you had been less decided, and found yourself at this moment committed to marry him. I have more reason to upbraid myself, but I'm sure I was right, though I sometimes lost my temper; I know my Uncle David thinks I was right; but there is no use now in thinking more about it; right or wrong, it is all over, and I won't distract myself uselessly. I'll try to be a better brother to you than I ever have been; and I'll make Mortlake our head-quarters: or we'll live, if you like it better, at Arden Manor, or I'll go abroad with you. I'll lay myself out to make you happy. One thing I'm resolved on, and that is to give up play, and find some manly and useful pursuit; and you'll see I'll do you some credit yet, or at least, as a country squire, do some little good, and be not quite useless in my generation; and I'll do my best, dear Alice, to make you a happy home, and to be all that I ought to be to you, my darling."

Very affectionately he both spoke and felt, and left Alice with some of her anxieties lightened, and already more interest in the future than she had thought possible an hour before.

Richard Arden had a good deal upon his hands that morning. He had money liabilities that were urgent. He had to catch his friend Mardykes at his lodgings, and get him to see the people in whose betting-books he stood for large figures, to represent to them what had happened, and assure them that a few days should see all settled. Then he had to go to the office of his father's attorney, and learn whether a will was forthcoming; then to consult with his own attorney, and finally to follow his uncle, David Arden, from place to place, and find him at last at home, and talk over details, and advise with him generally about many things, but particularly about the further dispositions respecting the funeral; for a little note from his Uncle David had offered to relieve him of the direction of those hateful details transacted with the undertaker, which every one is glad to depute.

CHAPTER L.

UNCLE DAVID'S SUSPICIONS.

Mr. David Arden, therefore, had made a call at the office of Paller, Crapely, Plumes, and Co., eminent undertakers in the most gentleman-like, and, indeed, aristocratic line of business, with immense resources at command, and who would undertake to bury a duke, with all the necessary draperies, properties, and dramatis personæ, if required, before his grace was cold in his bed.

A little dialogue occurred here, which highly interested Uncle David. A stout gentleman, with a muddy and melancholy countenance, and a sad suavity of manner, and in the perennial mourning that belongs to gentlemen of his doleful profession, presents himself to David Arden, to receive his instructions respecting the deceased baronet's obsequies. The top of his head is bald, his face is furrowed and baggy; he looks fully sixty-five, and he announces himself as the junior partner, Plumes by name.

Having made his suggestions and his notes, and taken his order for a strictly private funeral in the neighbourhood of London, Mr. Plumes thoughtfully observes that he remembers the name well, having been similarly employed for another member of the same family.

"Ah! How was that? How long ago?" asked Mr. Arden.

"About twenty years, Sir."

"And where was that funeral?"

"The same place, Sir, Mortlake."

"Yes, I know that was ——?"

"It was Mr. 'Enry, or rayther 'Arry Harden. We 'ad to take back the plate, Sir, and change 'Enry to 'Arry—'Arry being the name he was baptised by. There was a hinquest connected with that horder."

"So there was, Mr. Plumes," said Uncle David with awakened interest, for that gentleman spoke as if he had something more to say on the subject.

"There was, Sir,—and it affected me very sensibly. My niece, Sir, had a wery narrow escape."

"Your niece! Really? How could that be?"

"There was a Mister Yelland Mace, Sir, who paid his haddresses to her, and I do believe, Sir, she rayther liked him. I don't know, I'm sure, whether he was serious in 'is haddresses, but it looked very like as if he meant to speak; though I do suppose he was looking 'igher for a wife. Well, he was believed to 'ave 'ad an 'and in that 'orrible business."

"I know—so he undoubtably had—and the poor young lady, I suppose, was greatly shocked and distressed."

"Yes, Sir, and she died about a year after."

David Arden expressed his regret, and then he asked—

"You have often seen that man, Yelland Mace?"

"Not often, Sir."

"You remember his face pretty well, I daresay?"

"Well, no, Sir, not very well. It is a long time."

"Do you recollect whether there was anything noticeable in his features?—had he, for instance, a remarkably prominent nose?"

"I don't remember that he 'ad, Sir. I rather think not, but I can't by no means say for certain. It is a long time, and I 'aven't much of a memory for faces. There is a likeness of him among my poor niece's letters."

"Really? I should be so much obliged if you would allow me to see it."

"It is at 'ome, Sir, but I shall be 'ome to dinner before I go out to Mortlake; and, if you please, I shall borrow it of my sister, and take it with me."

This offer David Arden gladly accepted.

When the events were recent, he could have no difficulty in identifying Yelland Mace, by the evidence of fifty witnesses, if necessary. But it was another thing now. The lapse of time had made matters very different. It was recent impressions of a vague kind about Mr. Longcluse that had revived the idea, and prompted a renewal of the search. Martha Tansey was aged now, and he had misgivings about the accuracy of her recollection. Was it possible, after all, that he was about to see that which would corroborate his first vague suspicions?

Sir Richard had a busy and rather harassing day, the first of his succession to an old title and a new authority, and he was not sorry when it closed. He had stolen about from place to place in a hired cab, and leaned back to avoid a chance recognition, like an absconding debtor; and had talked with the people whom he was obliged to call on and see, in low and hurried colloquy, through the window of the cab. And now night had fallen, the lamps were glaring, and tired enough he returned to his lodgings, sent for his tailor, and arranged promptly about the

> " ——inky cloak, good mother,
> And customary suits of solemn black;"

and that done, he wrote two or three notes to kindred in Yorkshire, with whom it behoved him to stand on good terms; and then he determined to drive out to Mortlake Hall. An unpleasant mixture of feelings was in his mind as he thought of that visit, and the cold tenant of the ancestral house, whom in the grim dignity of death, it would not have been seemly to leave for a whole day and night unvisited. It was to him a repulsive visit, but how could he postpone it?

Behold him, then, leaning back in his cab, and driving through glaring lamps, and dingy shops, and narrow ill-thriven streets, eastward and northward; and now, through the little antique village, with trembling lights, and by the faded splendours of the "Guy of Warwick." And he sat up and looked out of the windows, as they entered the narrow road that is darkened by the tall overhanging timber of Mortlake grounds.

Now they are driving up the broad avenue, with its noble old trees clumped at either side; and with a shudder Sir Richard Arden leans back and moves no more until the cab pulls up at the door-steps, and the knock sounds through hall and passages, which he dared not so have disturbed, uninvited, a day or two before. Crozier ran down the steps to greet Master Richard.

"How are you, old Crozier?" he said, shaking hands from the cab-window, for somehow he liked to postpone entering the house as long as he could. "I could not come earlier. I have been detained in town all day by business, of various kinds, connected with this." And he moved his hand toward the open hall-door, with a gloomy nod or two. "How is Martha?"

"Tolerable, Sir, thankye, considerin'. It's a great upset to her."

"Yes, poor thing, of course. And has Mr. Paller been here—the person who is to—to ——"

"The undertaker? Yes, Sir, he was here at two o'clock, and some of the people has been busy in the room, and his men has come out again with the coffin, Sir. I think they'll soon be leaving; they've been here a quarter of an hour, and—if I may make bold to ask, Sir,—what day will the funeral be?"

"I don't know myself, Crozier; I must settle that with my uncle. He said he thought he would come here himself this evening, at about nine, and it must be very near that now. Where is Martha?"

"In her room, Sir, I think."

"I won't see her there. Ask her to come to the oak-room."

Richard got out and entered the house of which he was now the master, with an oppressive misgiving.

The oak-parlour was a fine old room, and into the panels were set four full-length portraits. Two of these were a lady and gentleman, in the costume of the beginning of Charles the Second's reign. The lady held an Italian greyhound by a blue ribbon, and the gentleman stood booted for the field, and falcon on fist. It struck Richard, for the first time, how wonderfully like Alice that portrait of the beautiful lady was. He raised the candle to examine it. There was a story about this lady. She had been compelled to marry the companion portrait, with the hawk on his hand, and those beautiful lips had dropped a curse, in her despair, when she was dying, childless, and wild with grief. She prayed that no daughter of the house of Arden might ever wed the man of her love, and it was said that a fatality had pursued the ladies of that family, which looked like the accomplishment of the malediction; and a great deal of curious family lore was connected with this legend and portrait.

As he held the candle up to this picture, still scanning its features, the door slowly opened, and Martha Tansey, arrayed in a black silk dress of a fashion some twenty years out of date, came in. He set down the candle, and took the old woman's hand, and greeted her very kindly.

"How's a' wi' you, Master Richard? A dowly house ye've come too. Ye didna look to see this sa soon?"

"Very sudden, Martha—awfully sudden. I could not let the day pass without coming out to see you."

"Not me, Master Richard, but to ha'e a last look at the face of the father that begot ye. He'll be shrouded and coffined by this time—the light 'ill not be lang on that face. The lid will be aboon it and screwed down to-morrow, I dar' say. Ay, there goes the undertaker's men; and there's a man from Mr. Paller—Mr. Plumes is his name—that says he'll stay till your Uncle David comes, for he told him he had something very particular to say to him; and I desired him to wait in my room after his business about the poor master was over; and the a'ad things is passin' awa' and it's time auld Martha was fittin' herself."

"Don't say that, Martha, unless you would have me think you expect to find me less kind than my father was."

"There's good and there's bad in every one, Master Richard. Ye can't take it in meal and take it in malt. A bit short-waisted he was, there's no denyin', and a sharp word now and again; but none so hard to live wi' as many a one that was cooler-tempered, and more mealy-mouthed; and I think ye were o'er hard wi' him, Master Richard. Ye should have opened the estate. It was that killed him," she continued considerately. "Ye broke his heart, Master Richard; he was never the same man after he fell out wi' you."

"Some day, Martha, you'll learn all about it," said he gently. "It was no fault of mine—ask my Uncle David. I'm not the person to persuade you; and, beside, I have not courage to talk over that cruel quarrel now."

"Come and see him," said the old woman grimly, taking up the candle.

"No, Martha, no; set it down again—I'll not go."

"And when will you see him?"

"Another time—not now—I can't."

"He's laid in his coffin now; they'll be out again in the mornin'. If you don't see him now, ye'll never see him; and what will the folk down in Yorkshire say, when it's told at Arden Court that Master Richard never looked on his dead father's face, nor saw more of him after his flittin' than the plate on his coffin. By Jen! 'twill stir the blood o' the old tenants and gar them clench their fists and swear, I warrant, at the very sound o' yer name; for there never was an Arden died yet, at Arden Court, but he was waked, and treated wi' every respect, and visited by every living soul of his kindred, for ten mile round."

"If you think so, Martha, say no more. I'll—go as well now as another time—and, as you say, sooner or later it must be done."

CHAPTER LI.

THE SILHOUETTE.

"He's lookin' very nice and like himself," mumbled the old woman, as she led the way.

At the open door of Sir Reginald's room stood Mr. Plumes, in professional black with a pensive and solemn countenance, intending politely to do the honours.

"Thank you, Sir," said the old woman graciously, taking the lead in the proceedings. "This is the young master, and he won't mind troublin' you, Mr. Plumes. If you please to go to my room, Sir, the third door on the right, you'll find tea made, Sir; and Mr. Crozier, I think, will be there."

And having thus disposed of the stranger, they entered the room, in which candles were burning.

Sir Reginald had, as it were, already made dispositions for his final journey. He had left his bed, and lay instead, in the handsomely upholstered coffin which stood on tressels beside it. Thin and fixed were the cold, earthly features that looked upward from their white trimmings. Sir Richard Arden checked his step and held his breath as he came in sight of these stern lineaments. The pale light that surrounds the dead face of the martyr was wanting here: in its stead, upon selfish lines and contracted features, a shadow stood.

Mrs. Tansey, with a feather-brush placed near, drove away a fly that was trying to alight on the still face.

"I mind him when he was a boy," she said, with a groan and a shake of the head. "There was but six years between us, and the life that's ended is but a dream, all like yesterday—nothing to look back on; and, I'm sure, if there's rest for them that has been troubled on earth, he's happy now: a blessed change 'twill be."

"Yes, Martha, we all have our troubles."

"Ay, it's well to know that in time: the young seldom does," she answered sardonically.

"I'll go, Martha. I'll return to the oak-room. I wish my uncle were come."

"Well, you have took your last look, and that's but decent, and —— Dear me, Master Richard, you do look bad!"

"I feel a little faint, Martha. I'll go there; and will you give me a glass of sherry?"

He waited at the room door, while Martha nimbly ran to her room, and returned with some sherry and a wine-glass. He had hardly taken a glass, and begun to feel himself better, when David Arden's step was heard approaching from the hall. He greeted his nephew and Martha in a hushed undertone, as he might in church; and then, as people will enter such rooms, he passed in and crossed with a very soft tread, and said a word or two in whispers. You would have thought that Sir Reginald was tasting the sweet slumber of precarious convalescence, so tremendously does death simulate sleep.

When Uncle David followed his nephew to the oak-room, where the servants had now placed candles, he appeared a little paler, as a man might who had just witnessed an operation. He looked through the unclosed shutters on the dark scene; then he turned, and placed his hand kindly on his nephew's arm, and said he, with a sigh—

"Well, Dick, you're the head of the house now; don't run the old ship on the rocks. Remember, it is an old name, and, above all, remember, that Alice is thrown upon your protection. Be a good brother, Dick. She is a true-hearted, affectionate creature: be you the same to her. You can't do your duty by her unless you do it also by yourself. For the first time in your life, a momentous responsibility devolves upon you. In God's name, Dick, give up play and do your duty!"

"I have learned a lesson, uncle; I have not suffered in vain. I'll never take a dice-box in my hand again; I'd as soon take a burning coal. I shall never back a horse again while I live. I am quite cured, thank God, of that madness. I sha'n't talk about it; let time declare how I am changed."

"I am glad to hear you speak so. You are right, that is the true test. Spoken like a man!" said Uncle David, and he took his hand very kindly.

The entrance of Martha Tansey at this moment gave the talk a new turn.

"By-the-bye, Martha," said he, "has Mr. Plumes come? He said he would be here at eight o'clock."

"He's waitin', Sir; and 'twas to tell you so I came in. Shall I tell him to come here?"

"I asked him to come, Dick; I knew you would allow me. He has some information to give me respecting the wretch who murdered your poor Uncle Harry."

"May I remain?" asked Richard.

"Do; certainly."

"Then, Martha, will you tell him to come here?" said Richard, and in another minute the sable garments and melancholy visage of Mr. Plumes entered the room slowly.

When Mr. Plumes was seated, he said, with much deliberation, in reply to Uncle David's question—

"Yes, Sir, I have brought it with me. You said, I think, you wished me to fetch it, and as my sister was at home, she hobleeged me with a loan of it. It belonged, you may remember, to her deceased daughter—my niece. I have got it in my breast-pocket; perhaps you would wish me now to take it hout?"

"I'm most anxious to look at it," said Uncle David, approaching with extended hand. "You said you had seen him; was this a good likeness?"

These questions and the answers to them occupied the time during which Mr. Plumes, whose proceedings were slow as a funeral, disengaged the square parcel in question from his pocket, and then went on to loosen the knots in the tape which tied it up, and afterwards to unfold the wrappings of paper which enveloped it.

"I don't remember him well enough, only that he was good-looking. And this was took by machinery, and it must be like. The ball and socket they called it. It must be hexact, Sir."

So saying, he produced a square black leather case, which being opened displayed a black profile, the hair and whiskers being indicated by a sort of gilding which, laid upon sable, reminded one of the decorations of a coffin, and harmonised cheerfully with Mr. Plumes' profession.

"Oh!" exclaimed Uncle David with considerable disappointment, "I thought it was a miniature; this is only a silhouette; but you are sure it is the profile of Yelland Mace?"

"That is certain, Sir. His name is on the back of it, and she kept it, poor young woman! with a lock of his 'air and some hother relics in her work-box."

By this time Uncle David was examining it with deep interest. The outline demolished all his fancies about Mr. Longcluse. The nose, though delicately formed, was decidedly the ruling feature of the face. It was rather a parrot face, but with a good forehead. David Arden was disappointed. He handed it to his nephew.

"That is a kind of face one would easily remember," he observed to Richard as he looked. "It is not like any one that I know, or ever knew."

"No," said Richard; "I don't recollect any one the least like it." And he replaced it in his uncle's hand.

"We are very much obliged to you, Mr. Plumes; it was your mention of it this morning, and my great anxiety to discover all I can respecting that man, Yelland Mace, that induced me to make the request. Thank you very much," said old Mr. Arden, placing the profile in the fat fingers of Mr. Plumes. "You must take a glass of sherry before you leave. And have you got a cab to return in?"

"The men are waiting for me, I thank you, and I have just 'ad my tea, Sir, much obleeged, and I think I had best return to town, gentlemen, as I have some few words to say to-night to our Mr. Trimmer; so, with your leave, gentlemen, I'll wish you good-night."

And with a solemn bow, first to Mr. Arden, then to the young scion of the house, and lastly a general bow to both, that grave gentleman withdrew.

“I could see no likeness in that thing to any one,” repeated old Mr. Arden. “Mr. Longcluse is a friend of yours?” he added a little abruptly.

“I can't say he was a friend; he was an acquaintance, but even that is quite ended.”

“What! you don't know him any longer?”

“No.”

“You're quite sure!”

“Perfectly.”

“Then I may say I'm very glad. I don't like him, and I can't say why; but I can't help connecting him with your poor uncle's death. I must have dreamed about him and forgot the dream, while the impression continues; for I cannot discover in any fact within my knowledge the slightest justification for the unpleasant persuasion that constantly returns to my mind. I could not trace a likeness to him in that silhouette.”

He looked at his nephew, who returned his steady look with one of utter surprise.

“Oh, dear! no. There is not a vestige of a resemblance,” said Richard. “I know his features very well.”

“No,” said Uncle David, lowering his eyes to the table, on which he was tapping gently with his fingers; “no, there certainly is not—not any. But I can't dismiss the suspicion. I can't get it out of my head, Richard, and yet I can't account for it,” he said, raising his eyes to his nephew's. “There is something in it; I could not else be so haunted.”

CHAPTER LII.

MR. LONGCLUSE EMPLOYED.

The funeral was not to be for some days, and then to be conducted in the quietest manner possible. Sir Reginald was to be buried in a small vault under the little church, whose steeple cast its shadow every sunny evening across the garden-hedges of the "Guy of Warwick," and could be seen to the left from the door of Mortlake Hall, among distant trees. Further it was settled by Richard Arden and his uncle, on putting their heads together, that the funeral was to take place after dark in the evening; and even the undertaker's people were kept in ignorance of the exact day and hour.

In the meantime, Mr. Longcluse did not trouble any member of the family with his condolences or inquiries. As a raven perched on a solitary bough surveys the country round, and observes many things—very little noticed himself—so Mr. Longcluse made his observations from his own perch and in his own way. Perhaps he was a little surprised on receiving from Lady May Penrose a note, in the following terms:—

> "DEAR MR. LONGCLUSE,
>
> "I have just heard something that troubles me; and as I know of no one who would more readily do me a kindness, I hope you won't think me very troublesome if I beg of you to make me a call to-morrow morning, at any time before twelve.
>
> "Ever yours sincerely,
> "MAY PENROSE."

Mr. Longcluse smiled darkly, as he read this note again. "It is better to be sought after than to offer one's self."

Accordingly, next morning, Mr. Longcluse presented himself in Lady May's drawing-room; and after a little waiting, that good-natured lady entered the room. She liked to make herself miserable about the troubles of her friends, and on this occasion, on entering the door, she lifted her hands and eyes, and quickened her step towards Mr. Longcluse, who advanced a step or two to meet her.

"Oh! Mr. Longcluse, it is so kind of you to come," she exclaimed; "I am in such a sea of troubles! and you are such a friend, I know I may tell you. You have heard, of course, of poor Reginald's death. How horribly sudden!—shocking! and dear Alice is so broken by it! He had been, the day before, so cross—poor Reginald, everybody knows he had a temper, poor old soul!—and had made himself so disagreeable to her, and now she is quite miserable, as if it had been her fault. But no matter; it's not about that. Only do you happen to know of people—bankers or something—called Childers and Ballard?"

"Oh! dear, yes; Childers and Ballard; they are City people, on 'Change—stockbrokers. They are people you can quite rely on, so far as their solvency is concerned."

"Oh! it isn't that. They have not been doing any business for me. It is a very unpleasant thing to speak about, even to a kind friend like you; but I want you to advise what is best to be done; and to ask you, if it is not very unreasonable, to use any influence you can—without trouble, of course, I mean—to prevent anything so distressing as may possibly happen."

"You have only to say, dear Lady May, what I can do. I am too happy to place my poor services at your disposal."

"I knew you would say so," said Lady May, again shaking hands in a very friendly way; "and I know what I say won't go any further. I mean, of course, that you will receive it entirely as a confidence."

Mr. Longcluse was earnest in his assurances of secresy and good faith.

"Well," said Lady May, lowering her voice, "poor Reginald, he was my cousin, you know, so it pains me to say it; but he was a good deal embarrassed; his estates were very much in debt. He owed money to a great many people, I believe."

"Oh! Really?" Mr. Longcluse expressed his well-bred surprise very creditably.

"Yes, indeed; and these people, Childers and Ballard, have something they call a judgment, I think. It is a kind of debt, for about twelve hundred pounds, which they say must be paid at once; and they vow that if it is not they will seize the coffin, and—and—all that, at the funeral. And David Arden is so angry, you can't think! and he says that the money is not owed to them, and that they have no right by law to do any such thing; and that from beginning to end it is a mere piece of extortion. And he won't hear of Richard's paying a farthing of it; and he says that Richard must bring a law-suit against them, for ever so much money, if they attempt anything of the kind, and that he's sure to win. But that is not what I am thinking of—it is about poor Alice, she is so miserable about the mere chance of its happening. The profanation—the fracas—all so shocking and so public—the funeral, you know."

"You are quite sure of that, Lady May?" said Longcluse.

"I heard it all as I tell you. My man of business told me; and I saw David Arden," she answered.

"Oh! yes; but I mean, with respect to Miss Arden. Does she, in particular, so very earnestly desire intervention in this awkward business?"

"Certainly; only she—only Miss Arden—only Alice."

He looked down in thought, and then again in her face, paler than usual. He had made up his mind.

"I shall take measures," he said quietly. "I shall do everything—anything in my power. I shall even expose myself to the risk of insult, for her sake; only let it soften her. After I have done it, ask her, not before, to think mercifully of me."

He was going.

"Stay, Mr. Longcluse, just a moment. I don't know what I am to say to you; I am so much obliged. And yet how can I undertake that anything you do may affect other people as you wish?"

"Yes, of course you are right; I am willing to take my chance of that. Only, dear Lady May, will you write to her? All I plead for—and it is the last time I shall sue to her for anything—is that my folly may be forgotten, and I restored to the humble privileges of an acquaintance."

"But do you really wish me to write? I'll take an opportunity of speaking to her. Would not that be less formal?"

"Perhaps so; but, forgive me, it would not answer. I beg of you to write."

"But why do you prefer my writing?"

"Because I shall then read her answer."

"Then I must tell her that you are to read her reply."

"Certainly, dear Lady May; I meant nothing else."

"Well, Mr. Longcluse, there is no great difficulty."

"I only make it a request, not a condition. I shall do my utmost in any case. Pray tell her that."

"Yes, I'll write to her, as you wish it; or, at least, I'll ask her to put on paper what she desires me to say, and I'll read it to you."

"That will answer as well. How can I thank you?"

"There is no need of thanks. It is I who should thank you for taking, I am afraid, a great deal of trouble so promptly and kindly."

"I know those people; they are cunning and violent, difficult to deal with, harder to trust," said Longcluse, looking down in thought. "I should be most happy to settle with them, and afterwards the executor might settle with me at his convenience; but, from what you say, Mr. David Arden and his nephew won't admit their claim. I don't believe such a seizure would be legal; but they are people who frequently venture illegal measures, upon the calculation that it would embarrass those against whom they adopt them more than themselves to bring them into court. It is not an easy card to play, you see, and they are people I hate; but I'll try."

In another minute Mr. Longcluse had taken his leave, and was gone.

CHAPTER LIII.

THE NIGHT OF THE FUNERAL.

Mr. Longcluse smiled as he sat in his cab, driving City-ward to the office of Messrs. Childers and Ballard.

"How easily, now, one might get up a scene! Let Ballard, the monster—he would look the part well—with his bailiffs, seize the coffin and its precious burden in the church; and I, like Sir Edward Maulay, step forth from behind a pillar to stay the catastrophe. We could make a very fine situation, and I the hero; but the girl is too clever for that, and Richard as sharp—that is, as base—as I; knowing my objects, he would at once see a plant, and all would be spoiled. I shall do it in the least picturesque and most probable way. I should like to know the old housekeeper, Mrs. Tansey, better; I should like to be on good terms with her. An awkward meeting with Arden. What the devil do I care? besides, it is but one chance in a hundred. Yes, that is the best way. Can I see Mr. Ballard in his private room for a minute?" he added aloud, to the clerk, Mr. Blotter, behind the mahogany counter, who turned from his desk deferentially, let himself down from his stool, and stood attentive before the great man, with his pen behind his ear.

"Certainly, Mr. Longcluse—certainly, Sir. Will you allow me, Sir, to conduct you?"

Most men would have been peremptorily denied; the more fortunate would have had to await the result of an application to Mr. Ballard; but to Mr. Longcluse all doors flew open, and wherever he went, like Mephistopheles, the witches received him gaily, and the cat-apes did him homage.

Without waiting for the assistance of Mr. Blotter, he ran up the back-stairs familiarly to see Mr. Ballard; and when Mr. Longcluse came down, looking very grave, Mr. Ballard, with the red face and lowering countenance which he could not put off, accompanied him down-stairs deferentially, and held open the office-door for him; and could not suppress his grins for some time in the consciousness of the honour he had received. Mr. Ballard hoped that the people over the way had seen Mr. Longcluse step from his door; and mentioned to everyone he talked to for a week, that he had Mr. Longcluse in his private office in consultation—first it was "for a quarter of an hour by the clock over the chimney," speedily it grew to "half-an-hour," and finally to "upwards of an hour, by ——," with a stare in the face of the wondering, or curious, listener. And when clients looked in, in the course of the day, to consult him, he would say, with a wag of his head and a little looseness about minutes, "There was a man sitting here a minute ago, Mr. Longcluse—you may have met him as you came up the stairs—that could have given us a wrinkle about that;" or, "Longcluse, who was here consulting with me this morning, is clearly of opinion that Italian bonds will be down a quarter by settling day;" or, "Take my advice, and don't burn your fingers with those things, for it is possible something queer may happen any day after Wednesday. I had Longcluse—I daresay you may have heard of him," he parenthesised jocularly—"sitting in that chair to-day for very nearly an hour and a half, and that's a fellow one doesn't sit long with without hearing something worth remembering."

From the attorney of Sir Richard Arden was served upon Messrs. Childers and Ballard, that day, a cautionary notice in very stern terms respecting their threatened attack upon Sir Reginald's funeral appointments and body; to which they replied in terms as sharp, and fixed three o'clock for payment of the bond.

It was a very short mile from Mortlake to that small old church near the "Guy of Warwick," the bit of whose grey spire and the pinnacle of whose weather-cock you could see between the two great clumps of elms to the left. Sir Reginald, feet foremost, was to make this little journey that evening under a grove of black plumes, to the small, quiet room, which he was henceforward to share with his ancestor Sir Hugh Arden, of Mortlake Hall, Baronet, whose pillard monument decorated the little church.

He lies now, soldered up and screwed down, in his strait bed, triply secured in lead, mahogany, and oak, and as safe as "the old woman of Berkeley" hoped to be from the grip of marauders. Once there, and the stone door replaced and mortared in, the irritable old gentleman might sleep the quietest sleep his body had ever enjoyed, to the crack of doom. The space was short, too, which separated that from the bed-room he was leaving; but the interval was "Jew's ground," trespassing on which, it was thought, he ran a great risk of being clutched by frantic creditors. A whisper of the danger had got into the housekeeper's room; and Crozier, whose north-country blood was hot, and temper warlike, had loaded the horse-pistols, and swore that he would shoot the first man who laid a hand unfriendly on the old master's coffin.

There was an agitation simmering under the grim formalities and tip-toe treadings of the house of death. Martha Tansey grew frightened, angry as she was, and told Richard Arden that Crozier was "neither to hold nor to bind, and meant to walk by the hearse, and stand by the coffin till it was shut into the vault, with loaded pistols in his coat-pockets, and would make food for worms so sure as they villains dar'd to interrupt the funeral."

Whereupon Richard saw Crozier, took the pistols from him, shook him very hard by the hand, for he liked him all the more, and told him that he would desire nothing better than their attempting to accomplish their threats, as he was well advised the law would make examples of them. Then he went up-stairs, and saw

Alice, and he could not help thinking how her black crapes became her. He kissed her, and, sitting down beside her, said,—

"Martha Tansey says, darling, that you are unhappy about something she has been telling you concerning this miserable funeral. She ought not to have alarmed you about it. If I had known that you were frightened, or, in fact, knew anything about it, I should have made a point of coming out here yesterday, although I had fifty things to do."

"I had a very good-natured note to-day, Dick, from Lady May," she said—"only a word, but very kindly intended." And she placed the open note in his fingers. When he had read it, Richard dropped the note on the table with a sneer.

"That man, I suspect, is himself the secret promoter of this outrage—a very inexpensive way, this, of making character with Lady May, and placing you under an obligation—the scoundrel!"

Looks and language of hatred are not very pretty at any time, but in the atmosphere of death they acquire a character of horror. Some momentary disturbance of this kind Richard may have seen in his sister's pale face, for he said,—

"Don't mind what I say about that fellow, for I have no patience with myself for having ever known him."

"I am so glad, Dick, you have dropped that acquaintance!" said the young lady.

"You have come at last to think as I do," said Richard.

"It is not so much thinking as something different; the uncertainty about him—the appalling stories you have heard—and, oh! Richard, I had such a dream last night! I dreamt that Mr. Longcluse murdered you. You smile, but I could not have imagined anything that was not real, so vivid, and it was in this room, and—I don't know how, for I forget the beginning of it—the candles went out, and you were standing near the door talking to me, and bright moonlight was at the window, and showed you quite distinctly, and the open door; and Mr. Longcluse came from behind it with a pistol, and I tried to scream, but I couldn't. But you turned about and stabbed at him with a knife or something; it shone in the moonlight, and instantly there was a line of blood across his face; he fired, and I saw you fall back on the floor; I knew you were dead, and I awoke in terror. I thought I still saw his wicked face in the dark, quite white as it was in my dream. I screamed, and thought I was going mad."

"It is only, darling, that all that has happened has made you nervous, and no wonder. Don't mind your dreams. Longcluse and I will never exchange a word more. We have turned our backs on one another, and our paths lie in very different directions."

This was a melancholy and grizzly evening at Mortlake Hall. The undertakers were making some final and mysterious arrangements about the coffin, and stole in and out of the dead baronet's room, of which they had taken possession.

Martha Tansey was alone in her room. It was a lurid sunset. Immense masses of black cloud were piled in the west, and from a long opening in that sombre screen, near the horizon, the expiring light glared like the red fire at night, through the clink of a smithy. Mrs. Tansey, dressed in deepest mourning, awaited the hour when she was to accompany the funeral of her old master.

Without succumbing to the threat of Messrs. Childers and Ballard, David Arden and his nephew would have been glad to evade the risk of the fracas, which would no doubt have been a dismal scandal. Martha Tansey herself was not quite sure at what hour the funeral was to leave Mortlake. Opposite the window from which she looked, stand groups of gigantic elms that darken that side of the house, and underwood forms a thick screen among their trunks. Upon the edges of this foliage glinted that fierce farewell gleam, and among the glimmering leaves behind she thought she saw the sinister face of Mr. Longcluse looking toward her. Her fear and horror of Longcluse had increased, and if the very remembrance of him visited her with a sudden qualm, you may be sure that the sight of him, on this melancholy evening, was a shock. Alice's wild dream, which she had recounted to her, did not serve to dissociate him from the vague misgivings that his image called up. She stared aghast at the apparition—itself uncertain—while in the deep shadow, with a foreground of fiercely flashing leaves, had on a sudden looked at her, and before she could utter an exclamation it was gone.

"I think it is my old eyes that plays me tricks, and my weary head that's 'wildered wi' all this dowly jummlement! What sud bring him there? It was never him I sid, only a fancy, and it's past and gone; and so, in the name of God, be it now, and ever, amen! For an evil sight it is, and bodes us no good. Who's there?"

"It's me, Mrs. Tansey," said Crozier, who had just come in. "Master Richard desired me to tell you it is to be at ten o'clock to-night. He and Mr. David thinks that best, and you're to please not to mention it to no one."

"Ten o'clock! That's very late, ain't it? No, surely, I'll not blab to no one; let him tell them when he sees fit. Martha Tansey's na that sort; she has had mony a secret to keep, and always the confidence o' the family, and 'twould be queer if she did not know to ho'd her tongue by this time. Sit ye down, Mr. Crozier—ye're wore off yer feet, man, like myself, ever since this happened—and rest a bit; the kettle's boilin', and ye'll tak' a cup o' tea. It's hours yet to ten o'clock."

So Mr. Crozier, who was in truth a tired man, complied, and took his seat by the fire, and talked over Sir Reginald's money matters, his fits, and his death; and, finally, he fell asleep in his chair, having taken three cups of tea.

The twilight had melted into darkness by this time, and the clear, cold moonlight was frosting all the landscape, and falling white and bright on the carriage-way outside, and casting on the floor the sharp shadows of the window-sashes, and giving the brilliant representations of the windows and the very veining of the panes of glass upon the white boards.

As Martha sat by the table, with her eyes fixed, in a reverie, on one of these reflections upon the floor, the shadow of a man was suddenly presented upon it, and raising her eyes she saw a figure, black against the moonlight, beckoning gently to her to approach.

Martha Tansey was an old lass of the Northumbrian counties, and had in her veins the fiery blood of the Border. The man wore a great-coat, and she could not discern his features; but he was tall and slight, and she was sure he was Mr. Longcluse. But "what dar' Longcluse say or do that she need fear?" And was not Crozier dozing there in the chair, "ready at call?"

Up she got, and stalked boldly to the window, and, drawing near, she plainly saw, as the stranger drew himself up from the window-pane through which he had been looking, and the moonlight glanced on his features, that the face was indeed that of Mr. Longcluse. He looked very pale, and was smiling. He nodded to her in a friendly way once or twice as she approached. She stood stock-still about two yards away, and though she knew him well, she deigned no sign of recognition, for she had learned vaguely something of the feud that had sprung up between him and the young head of the family, and no daughter of the marches was ever a fiercer partisan than lean old Martha. He tapped at the window, still smiling, and beckoned her nearer. She did come a step nearer, and asked sternly—

"What's your will wi' me?"

"I'm Mr. Longcluse," he said, in a low tone, but with sharp and measured articulation. "I have something important to say. Open the window a little; I must not raise my voice, and I have this to give you." He held a note by the corner, and tapped it on the glass.

Martha Tansey thought for a moment. It could not be a law-writ he had to serve; a rich man like him would never do that. Why should she not take his note, and hear what he had to say? She removed the bolt from the sash, and raised the window. There was not a breath stirring.

CHAPTER LIV.

AMONG THE TREES.

When the old woman had raised the window, "Thanks," said Mr. Longcluse, almost in a whisper. "There are people, Lady May Penrose told me this morning, threatening to interrupt the funeral to-night. Of course you know—you must know."

"I have heard o' some such matter, but 'tis nout to no one here. We don't care a snap for them, and if they try any sich lids, by my sang, we'll fit them. And I think, Sir, if ye've any thing o' consequence to tell to the family, ye'll not mind my saying 'twould be better ye sud go, like ither folk, to the hall-door, and leave your message there."

"Your reproof would be better deserved, Mrs. Tansey," he answers good-humouredly, "if there had not been a difficulty. Mr. Richard Arden is not on pleasant terms with me, and my business will not afford to wait. I understand that Miss Arden has suffered much anxiety. It is entirely on her account that I have interested myself so much in it; and I don't see, Mrs. Tansey, why you and I should not be better friends," he adds, extending his long slender hand gently towards her.

She does not take it, but makes a stiff little curtsey instead, and draws back about six inches.

Perhaps Mr. Longcluse had meditated making her a present, but her severe looks daunted him, and he thought that he might as well be a little better acquainted before he made that venture. He went on—

"You have spoken very wisely, Mrs. Tansey; I am sure if these people do as they threaten, it will be contrary to law, and so, as you say, you may snap your fingers at them at last. But in the meantime they may enter the house and seize the coffin, or possibly cause some disgraceful interruption on the way. Lady May tells me that Miss Alice has suffered a great deal in consequence. Will you tell her to set her mind at ease? Pray assure her that I have seen the people, that I have threatened them into submission, that I am confident no such attempt will be made, and that should the slightest annoyance be attempted, Crozier has only to present the notice enclosed in this to the person offering it, and it will instantly be discontinued. I have done all this entirely on her account, and pray lose no time in quieting her alarms. I am sure, Mrs. Tansey, you and I shall be better friends some day."

Mrs. Tansey curtseyed again.

"Pray take this note."

She took it.

"Give it to Crozier; and pray tell Miss Alice Arden, immediately, that she need have no fears. Good-night."

And pale Mr. Longcluse, with his smile and his dismally dark gaze, and the strange suggestion of something undefined in look or tone, or air, that gradually overcame her more and more till she almost felt faint, as he smiled and murmured at the open window, in the moonlight, was gone. Then she stood with the note in her thin fingers, without moving, and called to Crozier with a shrill and earnest summons as one who has just had a frightful dream will call up a sleeper in the same room.

Mr. Longcluse walks boldly and listlessly through this forbidden ground. He does not care who may meet him. Near the house, indeed, he would not like an encounter with Sir Richard Arden, because he knows that his being involved in a quarrel at such a moment, so near, especially with her brother, would not subserve his interests with Alice Arden.

For hours he strode or loitered alone through the solitary woodlands. The moonlight was beautiful; the old trees stand mournful and black against the luminous sky; there is for him a fascination in the solitude, as his noiseless steps lead him alternately into the black shadow cast on the sward by the towering foliage, and into the clear moonlight, on dewy grass that shows grey in that cold brightness. He was in the excitement of hope and suspense. Things had looked very black, but a door had opened and light came out. Was it a dream?

He leans with folded arms against the trunk of one of the trees that stand there, and from the slight elevation of the ground he can see the avenue under the boughs of the trees that flank it, and the chimneys of Mortlake Hall through the summits of the opening clumps. How melancholy and still the whole scene looks under that light!

"When I succeed to all this, who will be mistress of it?" he says, with his strange smile, looking toward the summits of the chimneys, that indicate the site of the Hall. "No one knows who I am; who can tell my history? What about that opera-girl? What about my money?—money is alway exaggerated. How many humbugs! how many collapses! stealing into society by evasions, on false pretences, in disguise! The man in the mask, ha! ha! Really perhaps two masks; not a bad fluke, that. The villain! You would not take a thousand pounds and know me—that is speaking boldly. A thousand pounds is still something in your book. You would not take it. The time will come, perhaps, when you'd give a thousand—ten thousand, if you had them—that I were your friend. Slanderous villain! To think of his talking so of me! The man in the mask trying to excite suspicion. My two masks are broken, and I all the better. By—! you shall meet me yet without a mask. Alice! will you be my idol? There is no neutrality with one like me in such a case. If I don't worship, I must break the image. What a speck we stand on between the illimitable—the eternal past and the eternal future—always looking for a present that shall be something tangible; always finding it a mathematical point, cujus nulla est pars—the mere stand-point of a retrospect and a conjecture. Ha! There are the wheels: there goes the funeral!"

He holds his breath, and watches. How interesting is everything connected with Alice! Slowly it passes along. Through one opening made by the havoc of a storm in the line of trees that form the avenue, he sees it plainly enough. A very scanty procession—the plumed hearse and three carriages, and a few persons walking beside. It passes. The great iron gate shrieks its long and dolorous note as it opened, and Longcluse heard it clang after the last carriage had passed, and with this farewell the old gate sent forth the dead master of Mortlake.

"Farewell to Mortlake," murmured Longcluse, as he heard these sounds, with a shrug and his peculiar smile; "farewell, the lights, the claret-jug, the whist, and all the rest. You 'fear neither justices nor bailiffs,' as the song says, any longer. Very easy about your interest and your premiums; very careless who arrests you in your leaden vesture; and having paid, if nothing else, at least your beloved son's post obit. Courage, Sir Reginald! your earthly troubles are over. Here am I, erect as this tree, and as like to live my term out, with all that money, and no will made, and yet as tired as ever you were, and very willing, if the transaction were feasible, to die, and be bothered no more, instead of you."

He sighs, and looks toward the house, and sighs again.

"Does she relent? Was it not she who told Lady May to ask this service of me? If I could only be sure of that, I should stand here, this moment, the proudest man in England. I think I know myself—a very simple character; just two principles—love and malice; for the rest, unscrupulous. Mere cruelty gives me no pleasure: well for some people it don't. Revenge does make me happy: well for some people if it didn't. Except for those I love or those I hate, I live for none. The rest live for me. I owe them no more than I do this rotten stick. Let them rot and fatten my land; let them burn and bake my bread."

With these words he kicked the fragments of a decayed branch that lay at his foot, and glided over the short grass, like a ghost, toward the gate.

CHAPTER LV.

MR. LONGCLUSE SEES A FRIEND.

Sir Reginald Arden, then, is actually dead and buried, and is quite done with the pomps and vanities, the business and the miseries of life—dead as King Duncan, and cannot come out of his grave to trouble any one with protest or interference; and his son, Sir Richard, is in possession of the title, and seized of the acres, and uses them, without caring to trouble himself with conjectures as to what his father would have liked or abhorred.

A week has passed since the funeral. Lady May has spent two days at Mortlake, and then gone down to Brighton. Alice does not leave Mortlake; her spirits do not rise. Kind Lady May has done her best to persuade her to come down with her to Brighton, but the perversity or the indolence of grief has prevailed, and Alice has grown more melancholy and self-upbraiding about her quarrel ,with her father, and will not be persuaded to leave Mortlake, the very worst place she could have chosen, as Lady May protests, for a residence during her mourning. Perhaps in a little while she may feel equal to the effort, but now she can't. She has quite lost her energy, and the idea of a place like Brighton, or even the chance of meeting people, is odious to her.

"So, my dear, do what I may, there she will remain, in that triste place," says Lady May Penrose; "and her brother, Sir Richard, has so much business just now on his hands, that he is often away two or three days at a time, and then she stays moping there quite alone; and only that she likes gardening and flowers, and that kind of thing, I really think she would go melancholy mad. But you know that kind of folly can't go on always, and I am determined to take her away in a month or so. People at first are so morbid, and make recluses of themselves."

Lady May stayed away at Brighton for about a week. On her return, Mr. Longcluse called to see her.

"It was so kind of you, Mr. Longcluse, to take all the trouble you did about that terrible business! and it was perfectly successful. There was not the slightest unpleasantness."

"Yes, I knew I had made anything of that kind all but impossible, but you are not to thank me. It made me only too happy to have an opportunity of being of any use—of relieving any anxiety."

Longcluse sighed.

"You have placed me, I know, under a great obligation, and if every one felt it as I do, you would have been thanked as you deserved before now."

A little silence followed.

"How is Miss Arden?" asked he in a low tone, and hardly raising his eyes.

"Pretty well," she answered, a little dryly. "She's not very wise, I think, in planning to shut herself up so entirely in that melancholy place, Mortlake. You have seen it?"

"Yes, more than once," he answered.

Lady May appeared more embarrassed as Mr. Longcluse grew less so. They became silent again. Mr. Longcluse was the first to speak, which he did a little hesitatingly.

"I was going to say that I hoped Miss Arden was not vexed at my having ventured to interfere as I did."

"Oh! about that, of course there ought to be, as I said, but one opinion; but you know she is not herself just now, and I shall have, perhaps, something to tell by-and-by; and, to say truth—you won't be vexed, but I'm sorry I undertook to speak to her, for on that point I really don't quite understand her; and I am a little vexed—and—I'll talk to you more another time. I'm obliged to keep an appointment just now, and the carriage," she added, glancing at the pendule on the bracket close by, "will be at the door in two or three minutes; so I must do a very ungracious thing, and say good-bye; and you must come again very soon—come to luncheon to-morrow—you must, really; I won't let you off, I assure you; there are two or three people coming to see me, whom I think you would like to meet."

And, looking very good-natured, and a little flushed, and rather avoiding Mr. Longcluse's dark eyes, she departed.

He had been thinking of paying Miss Maubray a visit, but he had not avowed, even to himself, how high his hopes had mounted; and here was, in Lady May's ominous manner and determined evasion, matter to disturb and even shock him. Instead, therefore, of pursuing the route he had originally designed, he strolled into the park, and under the shade of green boughs he walked, amid the twitter of birds and the prattle of children and nursery-maids, with despair at his heart, and a brain in chaos.

As he sauntered, with downcast looks, under the trees, he came upon a humble Hebrew friend, Mr. Goldshed, a magnate in his own circle, but dwarfed into nothing beside the paragon of Mammon who walked on the grass, so unpretentiously, and with a face as anxious as that of the greengrocer who had just been supplicating the Jew for a renewal of his twenty-five pound bill.

Mr. Goldshed came to a full stop a little way in advance of Mr. Longcluse, anxious to attract his attention. Mr. Longcluse did see him, as he sauntered on; and the fat old Jew, with the seedy velvet waistcoat, crossed with gold chains, and with an old-fashioned gold eye-glass dangling at his breast, first smiled engagingly, then looked reverential and solemn, and then smiled again with his great moist lips, and raised his hat. Longcluse gave him a sharp, short nod, and intended to pass him.

"Will you shpare me one word, Mr. Lonclushe?"

"Not to-day, Sir."

"But I've been to your chambers, Sir, and to your houshe, Mr. Lonclushe."

"You've wasted time—waste no more."

"I do assure you, Shir, it'sh very urgent."

"I don't care."

"It'sh about that East Indian thing," and he lowered his voice as he concluded the sentence.

"I don't care a pin, Sir."

The amiable Mr. Goldshed hesitated; Mr. Longcluse passed him as if he had been a post. He turned, however, and walked a few steps by Mr. Longcluse's side.

"And everything elshe is going sho vell; and it would look fishy, don't you think, to let thish thing go that way?"

"Let them go—and go you with them. I wish the earth would swallow you all—scrip, bonds, children, and beldames." And if a stamp could have made the earth open at his bidding, it would have yawned wide enough at that instant. "If you follow me another step, by Heaven, I'll make it unpleasant to you."

Mr. Longcluse looked so angry, that the Jew made him an unctuous bow, and remained fixed for a while to the earth, gazing after his patron with his hands in his pockets; and, with a gloomy countenance, he took forth a big cigar from his case, lighted a vesuvian, and began to smoke, still looking after Mr. Longcluse.

That gentleman sauntered on, striking his stick now and then to the ground, or waving it over the grass in as many odd flourishes as a magician in a pantomime traces with his wand.

If men are prone to teaze themselves with imaginations, they are equally disposed to comfort themselves with the same shadowy influences.

"I'm so nervous about this thing, and so anxious, that I exaggerate everything that seems to tell against me. How did I ever come to love her so? And yet, would I kill that love if I could? Should I not kill myself first? I'll go and see Miss Maubray—I may hear something from her. Lady May was embarrassed: what then? Were I a simple observer of such a scene in the case of another, I should say there was nothing in it more than this—that she had quite forgotten all about her promise. She never mentioned my name, and when the moment came, and I had come to ask for an account, she did not know what to say. It was well done, to see old Mrs. Tansey as I did. Lady May is so good-natured, and would feel her little neglect so much, and she will be sure to make it up. Fifty things may have prevented her. Yes, I'll go and hear what Miss Maubray has to say, and I'll lunch with Lady May to-morrow. I suspect that her visit to-day was to Mortlake."

With these reflections, Mr. Longcluse's pace became brisker, and his countenance brightened.

CHAPTER LVI.

A HOPE EXPIRES.

Mr. Longcluse knocked at Mr. David Arden's door. Yes, Miss Maubray was at home. He mounted the stairs, and was duly announced at the drawing-room door, and saw the brilliant young lady, who received him very graciously. She was alone.

Mr. Longcluse began by saying that the weather was cooler, and the sun much less intolerable.

"I wish we could say as much for the people, though, indeed, they are cool enough. There are some people called Tramways: he's a baronet—a very new one. Do you know anything of them? Are they people one can know?"

"I only know that Lady Tramway chaperoned a very charming young lady, whom everybody is very glad to know, to Lady May's garden-party the other day, at Richmond."

"Yes, very true; I'm that young lady, and that is the very reason I want to know. My uncle placed me in their hands."

"Oh, he knows everybody."

"Yes, and every one, which is quite another thing; and the woman has never given me an hour's quiet since. She presents me with bouquets, and fruit, and every imaginable thing I don't want, herself included, at least once a day; and I assure you I live in hourly terror of her getting into the drawing-room. You don't know anything about them?"

"I only know that her husband made a great deal of money by a contract."

"That sounds very badly, and she is such a vulgar woman?"

"I know no more of them; but Lady May had her to Raleigh Hall, and surely she can satisfy your scruples."

"No, it was my guardian who asked for their card, so that goes for nothing. It is really too bad."

"My heart bleeds for you."

"By-the-bye, talking of Lady May, I had a visit from her not a quarter-of-an-hour ago. What a fuss our friends at Mortlake do make about the death of that disagreeable old man!—Alice, I mean. Richard Arden bears it wonderfully. When did you see either?" she asked, innocently.

"You forget he has not been dead three weeks, and Alice Arden is not likely to see any one but very intimate friends for a long time; and—and I daresay you have heard that Sir Richard Arden and I are not on very pleasant terms."

"'Oh! Pity such difference should be ——.'"

"Thanks, and Tweedledum and Tweedledee are not likely to make it up. I'm afraid people aren't always reasonable, you know, and expect, often, things that are not quite fair."

"He ought to marry some one with money, and give up play."

"What! give up play, and commence husband? I'm afraid he'd think that a rather dull life."

"Well, I'm sure I'm no judge of that, although I give an opinion. Whatever he may be, you have a very staunch friend in Lady May."

"I'm glad of that; she's always so kind." And he looked rather oddly at the young lady.

Perhaps she seemed conscious of a knowledge more than she had yet divulged.

This young lady was, I need not tell you, a little coarse. She had, when she liked, the frankness that can come pretty boldly to the point; but I think she could be sly enough when she pleased; and was she just a little mischievous?

"Lady May has been talking to me a great deal about Alice Arden. She has been to see her very often since that poor old man died, and she says—she says, Mr. Longcluse—will you be upon honour not to repeat this?"

"Certainly, upon my honour."

"Well, she says ——"

Miss Maubray gets up quickly, and settles some flowers over the chimney-piece.

"She says that there is a coolness in that quarter also."

"I don't quite see," says Mr. Longcluse.

"Well, I must tell you she has taken me into council, and told me a great deal; and she spoke to Alice, and wrote to her. Did she say she would show you the answer? I have got it; she left it with me, and asked me—she's so good-natured—to use my influence—she said my influence! She ought to know I've no influence."

Longcluse felt very oddly indeed during this speech; he had still presence of mind not to add anything to the knowledge the young lady might actually possess.

"You have not said a great deal, you know; but Lady May certainly did promise to show me an answer which she expected to a note she wrote about three weeks ago, or less, to Miss Arden."

"I really don't know of what use I can be in the matter. I have no excuse for speaking to Alice on the subject of her note—none in the world. I think I may as well let you see it; but you will promise—you have promised—not to tell any one?"

"I have—I do—I promise. Lady May herself said she would show me that letter."

"Well, I can't, I suppose, be very wrong. It is only a note: it does not say much, but quite enough, I'm afraid, to make it useless, and almost impertinent, for me, or any one else, to say a word more on the subject to Alice Arden."

All this time she is opening a very pretty marqueterie writing-desk, on spiral legs, which Longcluse has been listlessly admiring, little thinking what it contains. She now produced a little note, which, disengaging from its envelope, she places in the hand that Mr. Longcluse extended to receive it.

"I do so hope," she said, as she gave it to him, "that I am doing what Lady May would wish. I think she shrank a little from showing it to you herself, but I am certain she wished you to know what is in it."

He opened it quickly. It ran thus ("Merry," I must remark, was a pet name, originating, perhaps, in Shakespeare's song that speaks of "the merry month of May"):—

"DEAREST MERRY,

> "I hope you will come to see me to-morrow. I cannot yet bear the idea of going into town. I feel as if I never should, and I think I grow more and more miserable every day. You are one of the very few friends whom I can see. You can't think what a pleasure a call from you is—if, indeed, in my miserable state, I can call anything a pleasure. I have read your letter about Mr. Longcluse, and parts of it a little puzzle me. I can't say that I have anything to forgive, and I am sure he has acted just as kindly as you say. But our acquaintance has ended, and nothing shall ever induce me to renew it. I can give you fifty reasons, when I see you, for my not choosing to know him. Darling Merry, I have quite made up my mind upon this point. I don't know Mr. Longcluse, and I won't know Mr. Longcluse; and I'll tell you all my reasons, if you wish to hear them, when we meet. Some of them, which seem to me more than sufficient, you do know. The only condition I make is that you don't discuss them with me. I have grown so stupid that I really cannot. I only know that I am right, and that nothing can change me. Come, darling, and see me very soon. You have no idea how very wretched I am. But I do not complain: it has drawn me, I hope, to higher and better thoughts. The world is not what it was to me, and I pray it never may be. Come and see me soon, darling; you cannot think how I long to see you.—Your affectionate,

"Alice Arden."

"What mountains of molehills!" said Mr. Longcluse, very gently, smiling with a little shrug, as he placed the letter again in Miss Maubray's hand.

"Making such a fuss about that poor old man's death! It certainly does look a little like a pretty affectation. Isn't that what you mean? He was so insupportable!"

"No, I know nothing about that. I mean such a ridiculous fuss about nothing. Why, people cease to be acquainted every day for much less reason. Sir Reginald chose to talk over his money matters with me, and I think he expected me to do things which no stranger could be reasonably invited to do. And I suppose, now that he is gone, Miss Arden resents my insensibility to his hints; and I daresay Sir Richard, who, I may say, on precisely similar grounds, chooses to quarrel with me, does not spare invective, and has, of course, a friendly listener in his sister. But how absurdly provoking that Lady May should have made such a diplomacy, and given herself so much trouble! And—I'm afraid I appear so foolish—I merely assented to Lady May's kind proposal to mediate, and I could not, of course, appear to think it a less important mission than she did; and—where are you going—Scotland? Italy?"

"My guardian, Mr. Arden, has not yet settled anything," she answered; and upon this, Mr. Longcluse begins to recommend, and with much animation to describe, several Continental routes, and then he tells her all his gossip, and takes his leave, apparently in very happy spirits.

I doubt very much whether the face can ever be taught to lie as impudently as the tongue. Its muscles, of course, can be trained; but the young lady thought that Mr. Longcluse's pallor, as he smiled and returned the note, was more intense, and his dark eyes strangely fierce.

"He was more vexed than he cared to say," thought the young lady. "Lady May has not told me the whole story yet. There has been a great deal of fibbing, but I shall know it all."

Mr. Longcluse had to dine out. He drove home to dress. On arriving, he first sat down and wrote a note to Lady May.

"DEAR LADY MAY,

> "I am so grateful. Miss Maubray told me to-day all the trouble you have been taking for me. Pray think no more of that little vexation. I never took so serious a view of so commonplace an unpleasantness, as to dream of tasking your kindness so severely. I am quite ashamed of having given you so much trouble.—Yours, dear Lady May, sincerely,

"Walter Longcluse."

"P.S.—I don't forget your kind invitation to lunch to-morrow."

Longcluse dispatched this note, and then wrote a few words of apology to the giver of the City dinner, to which he had intended to go. He could not go. He was very much agitated: he knew that he could not endure the long constraint of that banquet. He was unfit, for the present, to bear the company of any one. Gloomy and melancholy was the pale face of this man, as if he were going to the funeral of his beloved, when he stepped from his door in the dark. Was he going to walk out to Mortlake, and shoot himself on the steps?

As Mr. Longcluse walked into town, he caught a passing sight of a handsome young face that jarred upon him. It was that of Richard Arden, who was walking, also alone, not under any wild impulse, but to keep an appointment. This handsome face appeared for a moment gliding by, and was lost. Melancholy and thoughtful he looked, and quite unconscious of the near vicinity of his pale adversary. We shall follow him to his place of rendezvous.

He walked quickly by Pall Mall, and down Parliament Street, into the ancient quarter of Westminster, turned into a street near the Abbey, and from it into another that ran toward the river. Here were tall and dingy mansions, some of which were let out as chambers. In one of these, in a room over the front drawing-room, Mr. Levi received his West-end clients; and here, by appointment, he awaited Sir Richard Arden.

The young baronet, a little paler, and with the tired look of a man who was made acquainted with care, enters this room, hot with the dry atmosphere of gaslight. With his back towards the door, and his feet on the fender, smoking, sits Mr. Levi. Sir Richard does not remove his hat, and he stands by the table, which he slaps once or twice sharply with his stick. Mr. Levi turns about, looking, in his own phrase, unusually "down in the mouth," and his big black eyes are glowing angrily.

"Ho! Shir Richard Harden," he says, rising, "I did not think we was sho near the time. Izh it a bit too soon?"

"A little later than the time I named."

"Crikey! sho it izh."

CHAPTER LVII.

LEVI'S APOLOGUE.

The room had once been a stately one. Three tall windows looked toward the street. Its cornices and door-cases were ponderous, and its furniture was heterogeneous, and presented the contrasts that might be expected in a broker's store. A second-hand Turkey carpet, in a very dusty state, covered part of the floor; and a dirty canvas sack lay by the door for people coming in to rub their feet on. The table was a round one, that turned on a pivot; it was oak, massive and carved, with drawers; there were two huge gilt arm-chairs covered with Utrecht velvet, a battered office-stool, and two or three bed-room chairs that did not match. There were two great iron safes on tressels. On the top of one was some valuable old china, and on the other an electrifying machine; a French harp with only half-a-dozen strings stood in the corner near the fire-place, and several dusty pictures of various sizes leaned with their faces against the wall. A jet of gas burned right over the table, and had blackened the ceiling by long use, and a dip candle, from which Mr. Levi lighted his cigars, burned in a brass candlestick on the hob of the empty grate. Over everything lay a dark grey drift of dust. And the two figures, the elegant young man in deep mourning, and the fierce vulgar little Jew, shimmering all over with chains, rings, pins, and trinkets, stood in a narrow circle of light, in strong relief against the dim walls of the large room.

"So you will want that bit o' money in hand?" said Mr. Levi.

"I told you so."

"Don't you think they'll ever get tired helpin' you, if you keep pulling alwaysh the wrong way?"

"You said, this morning, I might reckon upon the help of that friend to any extent within reason," said Sir Richard, a little sourly.

"Ye're goin' fashter than yer friendsh li-likesh; ye're goin' al-ash—ye're goin' a terrible lick, you are!" said Mr. Levi, solemnly.

His usually pale face was a little flushed; he was speaking rather thickly, and there came at intervals a small hiccough, which indicated that he had been making merry.

"That's my own affair, I fancy," replied Sir Richard, as haughtily as prudence would permit. "You are simply an agent."

"Wish shome muff would take it off my hands; 'shan agenshy tha'll bring whoever takesh it more tr-tr-ouble than tin. By my shoul I'll not keepsh long! I'm blowsh if I'll be fool any longer!"

"I'm to suppose, then, that you have made up your mind to act no longer for my friend, whoever that friend may be?" said Sir Richard, who boded no good to himself from that step.

Mr. Levi nodded surlily.

"Have you drawn those bills?"

Mr. Levi gave the table a spin, unlocked a drawer, and threw two bills across to Sir Richard, who glancing at them said,—

"The date is ridiculously short!"

"How can I 'elp 't? and the interesht shlesh than nothin': sh-shunder the bank termsh f-or the besht paper going—I'm blesht if it ain't—it ain't f-fair interesh—the timesh short becaushe the partiesh, theysh—they shay they're 'ard hup, Shir, 'eavy sharge to pay hoff, and a big purchashe in Austriansh!"

"My uncle, David Arden, I happen to know, is buying Austrian stock this week; and Lady May Penrose is to pay off a charge on her property next month."

The Jew smiled mysteriously.

"You may as well be frank with me," added Sir Richard Arden, pleased at having detected the coincidence, which was strengthened by his having, the day before, surprised his uncle in conference with Lady May.

"If you don't like the time, why don't you try shomwhere else? why don't you try Lonclushe? There'sh a shwell! Two millionsh, if he's worth a pig! A year, or a month, 'twouldn't matter a tizhy to him, and you and him'sh ash thick ash two pickpockets!"

"You're mistaken; I don't choose to have any transactions with Mr. Longcluse."

There was a little pause.

"By-the-bye, I saw in some morning paper—I forget which—a day or two ago, a letter attacking Mr. Longcluse for an alleged share in the bank-breaking combination; and there was a short reply from him."

"I know, in the Timesh," interposed Levi.

"Yes," said Arden, who, in spite of himself, was always drawn into talk with this fellow more than he intended; such was the force of the ambiguously confidential relations in which he found himself. "What is thought of that in the City?"

"There'sh lotsh of opinionsh about it; not a shafe chap to quar'l with. If you rub Lonclushe this year, he'll tear you for itsh the next. He'sh a bish—a bish—a bit—bit of a bully, is Lonclushe, and don't alwaysh treat 'ish people fair. If you've quar'led with him, look oush—I shay, look oush!"

"Give me the cheque," said Sir Richard, extending his fingers.

"Pleashe, Shir Richard, accept them billsh," replied Levi, pushing an ink-stand toward him, "and I'll get our cheque for you."

So Mr. Levi took the dip candle and opened one of the safes, displaying for a moment cases of old-fashioned jewellery, and a number of watches. I daresay Mr. Levi and his partner made advances on deposits.

"Why don't you cut them confounded rasesh, Shir Richard? I'm bleshed if I didn't lose five pounds on the Derby myself! There'sh lotsh of field sportsh," he continued, approaching the table with his cheque-book. "Didn't you never shee a ferret kill a rabbit? It'sh a beautiful thing; it takesh it shomeway down the back, and bit by bit it mendsh itsh grip, moving up to-wards the head. It is really beautiful, and not a shound from either, only you'll see the rabbitsh big eyes lookin' sho wonderful! and the ferret hangsh on, swinging this way and that like a shna-ake—'tish wery pretty!—till he worksh hish grip up to where the backbone joinish in with the brain; and then in with itsh teeth, through the shkull! and the rabbit givesh a screetch like a child in a fit. Ha, ha, ha! I'm blesht if it ain't done ash clever ash a doctor could do it. 'Twould make you laugh. That will do."

And he took the bills from Sir Richard, and handed him two cheques, and as he placed the bills in the safe, and locked them up, he continued,—

"It ish uncommon pretty! I'd rayther shee it than a terrier on fifty rats. The rabbit's sho shimple—there'sh the fun of it—and looksh sho foolish; and every rabbit had besht look sharp," he continued, turning about as he put the keys in his pocket, and looking with his burning black eyes full on Sir Richard, "and not let a ferret get a grip anywhere; for if he getsh a good purchase, he'll never let go till he hash his teeth in his brain, and then he'sh off with a shqueak, and there's an end of him."

"I can get notes for one of these cheques to-night?" said Sir Richard.

"The shmall one, yesh, eashy," answered Mr. Levi. "I'm a bachelor," he added jollily, in something like a soliloquy, "and whenever I marry I'll be the better of it; and I'm no muff, and no cove can shay that I ever shplit on no one. And what do I care for Lonclushe? Not the snuff of this can'le!" And he snuffed the dip scornfully with his fingers, and flung the sparkling wick over the bannister, as he stood at the door, to light Sir Richard down the stairs.

CHAPTER LVIII.

THE BARON COMES TO TOWN.

Weeks flew by. The season was in its last throes: the session was within a day or two of its death. Lady May drove out to Mortlake with a project in her head.

Alice Arden was glad to see her.

"I've travelled all this way," she said, "to make you come with me on Friday to the Abbey."

"On Friday? Why Friday, dear?" answered Alice.

"Because there is to be a grand oratorio of Handel's. It is for the benefit of the clergy's sons' school, and it is one that has not been performed in England for I forget how many years. It is Saul. You have heard the Dead March in Saul, of course; everyone has; but no one has ever heard the oratorio, and come you must. There shall be no one but ourselves—you and I, and your uncle and your brother to take care of us. They have promised to come; and Stentoroni is to take Saul, and they have the finest voices in Europe; and they say that Herr Von Waasen, the conductor, is the greatest musician in the world. There have been eight performances in that great room—oh! what do you call it?—while I was away; and now there is only to be this one, and I'm longing to hear it; but I won't go unless you come with me—and you need not dress. It begins at three o'clock, and ends at six, and you can come just as you are now; and an oratorio is really exactly the same as going to church, so you have no earthly excuse; and I'll send out my carriage at one for you; and you'll see, it will do you all the good in the world."

Alice had her difficulties, but Lady May's vigorous onset overpowered them, and at length she consented.

"Does your uncle come out here to see you?" asks Lady May.

"Often; he's very kind," she replies.

"And Grace Maubray?"

"Oh, yes; I see her pretty often—that is, she has been here twice, I think—quite often enough."

"Well, do you know, I never could admire Grace Maubray as I have heard other people do," says Lady May. "There is something harsh and bold, don't you think?—something a little cruel. She is a girl that I don't think could ever be in love."

"I don't know that," says Alice.

"Oh! really?" says Lady May, "and who is it?"

"It is merely a suspicion," says Alice.

"Yes—but you think she likes some one—do, like a darling, tell me who it is," urges Lady May, a little uneasily.

"You must not tell anyone, because they would say it was sisterly vanity, but I think she likes Dick."

"Sir Richard?" says Lady May, with as much indifference as she could.

"Yes, I think she likes my brother."

Lady May smiles painfully.

"I always thought so," she says; "and he admires her, of course?"

"No, I don't think he admires her at all. I'm certain he doesn't," said Alice.

"Well, certainly he always does speak of her as if she belonged to Vivian Darnley," remarks Lady May, more happily.

"So she does, and he to her, I hope," said Alice.

"Hope?" repeated Lady May, interrogatively.

"Yes—I think nothing could be more suitable."

"Perhaps so; you know them better than I do."

"Yes, and I still think Uncle David intends them for one another."

"I would have asked Mr. Longcluse," Lady May begins, after a little interval, "to use his influence to get us good hearing-places, but he is in such disgrace—is he still, or is there any chance of his being forgiven?"

"I told you, darling, I have really nothing to forgive—but I have a kind of fear of Mr. Longcluse—a fear I can't account for. It began, I think, with that affair that seemed to me like a piece of insanity, and made me angry and bewildered; and then there was a dream, in which I saw such a horrible scene, and fancied he had murdered Richard, and I could not get it out of my head. I suppose I am in a nervous state—and there were other things; and, altogether, I think of him with a kind of horror—and I find that Martha Tansey has an unaccountable dread of him exactly as I have; and even Uncle David says that he has a misgiving about him that he can't get rid of, or explain."

"I can't think, however, that he is a ghost or even a malefactor," said Lady May, "or anything worse than a very agreeable, good-natured person. I never knew anything more zealous than his good-nature on the occasion I told you of; and he has always approached you with so much devotion and respect—he seemed to me so sensitive, and to watch your very looks; I really think that a frown from you would have almost killed him."

Alice sighs, and looked wearily through the window, as if the subject bored her; and she said listlessly,—

"Oh, yes, he was kind, and gentlemanlike, and sang nicely, I grant you everything; but—there is something ominous about him, and I hate to hear him mentioned, and with my consent I'll never meet him more."

THE BARON COMES TO TOWN.

Connected with the musical venture which the ladies were discussing, a remarkable person visited London. He had a considerable stake in its success. He was a penurious German, reputed wealthy, who ran over from Paris to complete arrangements about ticket-takers and treasurer, so as to ensure a system of check, such as would make it next to impossible for the gentlemen his partners to rob him. This person was the Baron Vanboeren.

Mr. Blount had an intimation of this visit from Paris, and Mr. David Arden invited him to dine, of which invitation he took absolutely no notice; and then Mr. Arden called upon him in his lodging in St. Martin's Lane. There he saw him, this man, possibly the keeper of the secret which he had for twenty years of his life been seeking for. If he had a feudal ideal of this baron, he was disappointed. He beheld a short, thick man, with an enormous head and grizzled hair, coarse pug features, very grimy skin, and a pair of fierce black eyes, that never rested for a moment, and swept the room from corner to corner with a rapid and unsettled glance that was full of fierce energy.

"The Baron Vanboeren?" inquires Uncle David courteously.

The baron, who is smoking, nods gruffly.

"My name is Arden—David Arden. I left my card two days ago, and having heard that your stay was but for a few days, I ventured to send you a very hurried invitation."

The baron grunts and nods again.

"I wrote a note to beg the pleasure of a very short interview, and you have been so good as to admit me."

The baron smokes on.

"I am told that you possibly are possessed of information which I have long been seeking in vain."

Another nod.

"Monsieur Lebas, the unfortunate little Frenchman who was murdered here in London, was, I believe, in your employment?"

The baron here had a little fit of coughing.

Uncle David accepted this as an admission.

"He was acquainted with Mr. Longcluse?"

"Was he?" says the baron, removing and replacing his pipe quickly.

"Will you, Baron Vanboeren, be so good as to give me any information you possess respecting Mr. Longcluse? It is not, I assure you, from mere curiosity I ask these questions, and I hope you will excuse the trouble I give you."

The baron took his pipe from his mouth, and blew out a thin stream of smoke.

"I have heard," said he, in short, harsh tones, "since I came to London, nosing but good of Mr. Longcluse. I have ze greadest respect for zat excellent gendleman. I will say nosing bud zat—ze greadest respect."

"You knew him in Paris, I believe?" urges Uncle David.

"Nosing but zat—ze greadest respect," repeats the baron. "I sink him a very worzy gendleman."

"No doubt, but I venture to ask whether you were acquainted with Mr. Longcluse in Paris?"

"Zere are a gread many beoble in Paris. I have nosing to say of Mr. Longcluse, nosing ad all, only he is a man of high rebudation."

And on completing this sentence the baron replaced his pipe, and delivered several rapid puffs.

"I took the liberty of enclosing a letter from a friend explaining who I am, and that the questions I should entreat you to answer are not prompted by any idle or impertinent curiosity; perhaps, then, you would be so good as to say whether you know anything of a person named Yelland Mace, who visited Paris some twenty years since?"

"I am in London, Sir, ubon my business, and no one else's. I am sinking of myself, and not about Mace or Longcluse, and I will not speak about eizer of zem. I am well baid for my dime. I will nod waste my dime on dalking—I will nod," he continues, warming as he proceeds; "nosing shall induce me do say one word aboud zoze gendlemen. I dake my oas I'll not, mein Gott! What do you mean by asking me aboud zem?"

He looks positively ferocious as he delivers this expostulation.

"My request must be more unreasonable than it appeared to me."

"Nosing can be more unreasonable!"

"And I am to understand that you positively object to giving me any information respecting the persons I have named?"

The baron appeared extremely uneasy. He trotted to the door on his short legs, and looked out. Returning, he shut the door carefully. His grimy countenance, under the action of fear, assumes an expression peculiarly forbidding; and he said, with angry volubility—

"Zis visit must end, Sir, zis moment. Donnerwesser! I will nod be combromised by you. But if you bromise as a Christian, ubon your honour, never to mention what I say ——"

"Never, upon my honour."

"Nor to say you have talked with me here in London ——"

"Never."

"I will tell you that I have no objection to sbeak wis you, privately in Paris, whenever you are zere—now, now! zat is all. I will not have one ozer word—you shall not stay one ozer minude."

He opens the door and wags his head peremptorily, and points with his pipe to the lobby.

"You'll not forget your promise, Baron, when I call? for visit you I will."

"I never forget nosing. Monsieur Arden, will you go or nod?"

"Farewell, Sir," says his visitor, too much excited by the promise opened to him, for the moment to apprehend what was ridiculous in the scene or in the brutality of the baron.

CHAPTER LIX.

TWO OLD FRIENDS MEET AND PART.

When he was gone the Baron Vanboeren sat down and panted; his pipe had gone out, and he clutched it in his hand like a weapon and continued for some minutes, in the good old phrase, very much disordered.

"That old fool," he mutters, in his native German, "won't come near me again while I remain in London."

This assurance was, I suppose, consolatory, for the baron repeated it several times; and then bounced to his feet, and made a few hurried preparations for an appearance in the streets. He put on a short cloak which had served him for the last thirty years, and a preposterous hat; and with a thick stick in his hand, and a cigar lighted, sallied forth, square and short, to make Mr. Longcluse a visit by appointment.

By this time the lamps were lighted. There had been a performance of Saul, a very brilliant success, although it pleased the baron to grumble over it that day. He had not returned from the great room where it had taken place more than an hour, when David Arden had paid his brief visit. He was now hastening to an interview which he thought much more momentous. Few persons who looked at that vulgar seedy figure, strutting through the mud, would have thought that the thread-bare black cloak, over which a brown autumnal tint had spread, and the monstrous battered felt hat, in which a costermonger would scarcely have gone abroad, covered a man worth a hundred and fifty thousand pounds.

Man is mysteriously so constructed that he cannot abandon himself to selfishness, which is the very reverse of heavenly love, without in the end contracting some incurable insanity; and that insanity of the higher man constitutes, to a great extent, his mental death. The Baron Vanboeren's insanity was avarice; and his solitary expenses caused him all the sordid anxieties which haunt the unfortunate gentleman who must make both ends meet on five-and-thirty pounds a year.

Though not sui profusus, he was alieni appetens in a very high degree; and his visit to Mr. Longcluse was not one of mere affection.

Mr. Longcluse was at home in his study. The baron was instantly shown in. Mr. Longcluse, smiling, with both hands extended to grasp his, advances to meet him.

"My dear Baron, what an unexpected pleasure! I could scarcely believe my eyes when I read your note. So you have a stake in this musical speculation, and though it is very late, and, of course, everything at a disadvantage, I have to congratulate you on an immense success."

The baron shrugs, shakes his head, and rolls his eyes dismally.

"Ah, my friend, ze exbenses are enormous."

"And the receipts still more so," says Longcluse cheerfully; "you must be making, among you, a mint of money."

"Ah! Monsieur Longcluse, id is nod what it should be! zay are all such sieves and robbers! I will never escape under a loss of a sousand bounds."

"You must be cheerful, my dear Baron. You shall dine with me to-day. I'll take you with me to half a dozen places of amusement worth seeing after dinner. To-morrow morning you shall run down with me to Brighton—my yacht is there—and when you have had enough of that, we shall run up again and have a white-bait dinner at Greenwich; and come into town and see those fellows, Markham and the other, that poor little Lebas saw play, the night he was murdered. You must see them play the return match, so long postponed. Next day we shall ——"

"Bardon, Monsieur, bardon! I am doo old. I have no spirits."

"What, not enough to see a game of billiards between Markham and Hood! Why, Lebas was charmed so far as he saw it, poor fellow, with their play."

"No, no, no, no, Monsieur; a sousand sanks, no, bardon, I cannod," says the baron. "I do not like billiards, and your friends have not found it a lucky game."

"Well, if you don't care for billiards, we'll find something else," replies hospitable Mr. Longcluse.

"Nosing else, nosing else," answers the baron hastily. "I hade all zese sings, ze seatres, ze bubbedshows, and all ze ozer amusements, I give you my oas. Did you read my liddle node?"

"I did indeed, and it amused me beyond measure," says Longcluse joyously.

"Amuse!" repeats the baron, "how so?"

"Because it is so diverting; one might almost fancy it was meant to ask me for fifteen hundred pounds."

"I have lost, by zis sing, a vast deal more zan zat."

"And, my dear Baron, what on earth have I to do with that?"

"I am an old friend, a good friend, a true friend," says the baron, while his fierce little eyes sweep the walls, from corner to corner, with quivering rapidity. "You would not like to see me quide in a corner. You're the richest man in England, almost; what's one sousand five hundred to you? I have not wridden to you, or come to England, dill now. You have done nosing for your old friend yet: what are you going to give him?"

"Not as much as I gave Lebas," said Longcluse, eyeing him askance, with a smile.

"I don't know what you mean."

"Not a napoleon, not a franc, not a sou."

"You are jesding; sink, sink, sink, Monsieur, what a friend I have been and am to you."

"So I do, my dear Baron, and consider how I show my gratitude. Have I ever given a hint to the French police about the identity of the clever gentleman who managed the little tunnel through which a river of champagne flowed into Paris, under the barrier, duty free? Have I ever said a word about the confiscated jewels of the Marchioness de la Sarnierre? Have I ever asked how the Comte de Loubourg's little boy is, or directed an unfriendly eye upon the conscientious physician who extricates ladies and gentlemen from the consequences of late hours, nervous depression, and fifty other things that war against good digestion and sound sleep? Come, come, my good Baron, whenever we come to square accounts, the balance will stand very heavily in my favour. I don't want to press for a settlement, but if you urge it, by Heaven, I'll make you pay the uttermost farthing!"

Longcluse laughs cynically. The baron looks very angry. His face darkens to a leaden hue. The fingers which he plunged into his snuff-box are trembling. He takes two or three great pinches of snuff before speaking.

Mr. Longcluse watches all these symptoms of his state of mind with a sardonic enjoyment, beneath which, perhaps, is the sort of suspense with which a beast-tamer watches the eye of the animal whose fury he excites only to exhibit the coercion which he exercises through its fears, and who is for a moment doubtful whether its terrors or its fury may prevail.

The baron's restless eyes roll wickedly. He puts his hand into his pocket irresolutely, and crumbles some papers there. There was no knowing, for some seconds, what turn things might take. But if he had for a moment meditated a crisis, he thought better of it. He breaks into a fierce laugh, and extends his hand to Mr. Longcluse, who as frankly places his own in it, and the baron shakes it vehemently. And Mr. Longcluse and he laugh boisterously and oddly together. The baron takes another great pinch of snuff, and then he says, sponging out as it were, as an ignored parenthesis, the critical part of their conversation—

"No, no, I sink not; no, no, surely not. I am not fit for all zose amusements. I cannot knog aboud as I used; an old fellow, you know: beace and tranquilidy. No, I cannot dine with you. I dine with Stentoroni to-morrow; to-day I have dined with our tenore. How well you look! What nose, what tees, what chin! I am proud of you. We bart good friends, bon soir, Monsieur Longcluse, farewell. I am already a liddle lade."

"Farewell, dear Baron. How can I thank you enough for this kind meeting? Try one of my cigars as you go home."

The baron, not being a proud man, took half-a-dozen, and with a final shaking of hands these merry gentlemen parted, and Longcluse's door closed for ever on the Baron Vanboeren.

"That bloated spider?" mused Mr. Longcluse. "How many flies has he sucked! It is another matter when spiders take to catching wasps."

Every man of energetic passions has within him a principle of self-destruction. Longcluse had his. It had expressed itself in his passion for Alice Arden. That passion had undergone a wondrous change, but it was imperishable in its new as in its pristine state.

This gentleman was in the dumps so soon as he was left alone. Always uncertainty; always the sword of Damocles; always the little reminders of perdition, each one contemptible, but each one in succession touching the same set of nerves, and like the fall of the drop of water in the inquisition, non vi, sed sæpe cadendo, gradually heightening monotony into excitement, and excitement into frenzy. Living always with a sense of the unreality of life and the vicinity of death, with a certain stern tremor of the heart, like that of a man going into action, no wonder if he sometimes sickened of his bargain with Fate, and thought life purchased too dear on the terms of such a lease.

Longcluse bolted his door, unlocked his desk, and there what do we see? Six or seven miniatures—two enamels, the rest on ivory—all by different hands; some English, some Parisian; very exquisite, some of them. Every one was Alice Arden. Little did she dream that such a gallery existed. How were they taken? Photographs are the colourless phantoms from which these glowing life-like beauties start. Tender-hearted Lady May has in confidence given him, from time to time, several of these from her album; he has induced foreign artists to visit London, and managed opportunities by which, at parties, in theatres, and I am sorry to say even in church, these clever persons succeeded in studying from the life, and learning all the tints which now glow before him. If I had mentioned what this little collection cost him, you would have opened your eyes. The Baron Vanboeren would have laughed and cursed him with hilarious derision, and a money-getting Christian would have been quite horror-struck, on reading the scandalous row of figures.

Each miniature he takes in turn, and looks at for a long time, holding it in both hands, his hands resting on the desk, his face inclined and sad, as if looking down into the coffin of his darling. One after the other he puts them by, and returns to his favourite one; and at last he shuts it up also, with a snap, and places it with the rest in the dark, under lock and key.

He leaned back and laid his thin hand across his eyes. Was he looking at an image that came out in the dark on the retina of memory? Or was he shedding tears?

CHAPTER LX.

"SAUL."

The day arrived on which Alice Arden had agreed to go with Lady May to Westminster Abbey, to hear the masterly performance of Saul. When it came to the point, she would have preferred staying at home; but that was out of the question. Every one has experienced that ominous forboding which overcomes us sometimes with a shapeless forecasting of evil. It was with that vague misgiving that she had all the morning looked forward to her drive to town, and the long-promised oratorio. It was a dark day, and there was a thunderous weight in the air, and the melancholy atmosphere deepened her gloom.

Her Uncle David arrived in Lady May's carriage, to take care of her. They were to call at Lady May's house, where its mistress and Sir Richard Arden awaited them.

A few kind words followed Uncle David's affectionate greeting, as they drove into town. He did not observe that Alice was unusually low. He seemed to have something not very pleasant himself to think upon, and he became silent for some time.

"I want," said he at last, looking up suddenly, "to give you a little advice, and now mind what I say. Don't sign any legal paper without consulting me, and don't make any promise to Richard. It is just possible—I hope he may not, but it is just possible—that he may ask you to deal in his favour with your charge on the Yorkshire estate. Do you tell him if he should, that you have promised me faithfully not to do anything in the matter, except as I shall advise. He may, as I said, never say a word on the subject, but in any case my advice will do you no harm. I have had bitter experience, my dear, of which I begin to grow rather ashamed, of the futility of trying to assist Richard. I have thrown away a great deal of money upon him, utterly thrown it away. I can afford it, but you cannot, and you shall not lose your little provision." And here he changed the subject of his talk, I suppose to avoid the possibility of discussion. "How very early the autumn has set in this year! It is the extraordinary heat of the summer. The elms in Mortlake are quite yellow already."

And so they talked on, and returned no more to the subject at which he had glanced. But the few words her uncle had spoken gave Alice ample matter to think on, and she concluded that Richard was in trouble again.

Lady May did not delay them a moment, and Sir Richard got into the carriage after her, with the tickets in his charge. Very devoted, Alice thought him, to Lady May, who appeared more than usually excited and happy.

We follow our party without comment into the choir, where they take possession of their seats. The chorus glide into their places like shadows, and the vast array of instrumental musicians as noiselessly occupy the seats before their desks. The great assembly is marshalled in a silence almost oppressive, but which is perhaps the finest preparation for the wondrous harmonies to come.

And now the grand and unearthly oratorio has commenced. Each person in our little group hears it with different ears. I wonder whether any two persons in that vast assembly heard it precisely alike. Sir Richard Arden, having many things to think about, hears it intermittently as he would have listened to a bore, and with a secret impatience. Lady May hears it not much better, but felt as if she could have sat there for ever. Old David Arden enjoyed music, and is profoundly delighted with this. But his thoughts also begin to wander, for as the mighty basso singing the part of Saul delivers the words,

> "I would that, by thy art, thou bring me up
> The man whom I shall name,"

David Arden's eye lighted, with a little shock, upon the enormous head and repulsive features of the Baron Vanboeren. What a mask for a witch! The travesti lost its touch of the ludicrous, in Uncle David's eye, by virtue of the awful interest he felt in the possible revelations of that ugly magician, who could, he fancied, by a word, call up the image of Yelland Mace. The baron is sitting about the steps in front of him, face to face. He wonders he has not seen him till now. His head is a little thrown back, displaying his short bull neck. His restless eyes are fixed now in a sullen reverie. His calculation as to the exact money value of the audience is over; he is polling them no longer, and his unresting brain is projecting pictures into the darkness of the future.

His face in a state of apathy was ill-favoured and wicked, and now lighted with a cadaverous effect, by the dull purplish halo which marks the blending of the feeble daylight, with the glow of the lamp that is above him.

The baron had seen and recognised David Arden, and a train of thoughts horribly incongruous with the sacred place was moving through his brain. As he looks on, impassive, the great basso rings out—

> "If heaven denies thee aid, seek it from hell."

And the soprano sends forth the answering incantation, wild and piercing—

"Infernal spirits, by whose power
  Departed ghosts in living forms appear,
 Add horror to the midnight hour,
  And chill the boldest hearts with fear;
 To this stranger's wondering eyes
  Let the man he calls for rise."

If Mr. Longcluse had been near, he might have made his own sad application of the air so powerfully sung by the alto to whom was committed the part of David—

"Such haughty beauties rather move
 Aversion, than engage our love."

He might with an undivulged anguish have heard the adoring strain—

"O lovely maid! thy form beheld
  Above all beauty charms our eyes,
 Yet still within that form concealed,
  Thy mind a greater beauty lies."

In a rapture Alice listened on. The famous "Dead March" followed, interposing its melancholy instrumentation, and arresting the vocal action of the drama by the pomp of that magnificent dirge.

To her the whole thing seemed stupendous, unearthly, glorious beyond expression. She almost trembled with excitement. She was glad she had come. Tears of ecstasy were in her eyes.

And now, at length, the three parts are over, and the crowd begin to move outward. The organ peals as they shuffle slowly along, checked every minute, and then again resuming their slow progress, pushing on in those little shuffling steps of two or three inches by which well-packed crowds get along, every one wondering why they can't all step out together, and what the people in front can be about.

In two several channels, through two distinct doors, this great human reservoir floods out. Sir Richard has undertaken the task of finding Lady May's carriage, and bringing it to a point where they might escape the tedious waiting at the door; and David Arden, with Lady May on one arm and Alice on the other, is getting on slowly in the thick of this well-dressed and aristocratic mob.

"I think, Alice," said Uncle David, "you would be more out of the crush, and less likely to lose me, if you were to get quite close behind us—do you see?—between Lady May and me, and hold me fast."

The pressure of the stream was so unequal, and a front of three so wide, that Alice gladly adopted the new arrangement, and with her hand on her uncle's arm, felt safer and more comfortable than before.

This slow march, inch by inch, is strangely interrupted. A well-known voice, close to her ear, says—

"Miss Arden, a word with you."

A pale face, with flat nose and Mephistophelian eyebrows, was stooping near her. Mr. Longcluse's thin lips were close to her ear. She started a little aside, and tried to stop. Recovering, she stretched her hand to reach her uncle, and found that there were strangers between them.

CHAPTER LXI.

A WAKING DREAM.

There is something in that pale face and spectral smile that fascinates the terrified girl; she cannot take her eyes off him. His dark eyes are near hers; his lips are still close to her; his arm is touching her dress; he leans his face to her, and talks on, in an icy tone little above a whisper, and an articulation so sharply distinct that it seems to pain her ear.

"The oratorio!" he continued: "the music! The words, here and there are queer—a little sinister—eh? There are better words and wilder music—you shall hear them some day! Saul had his evil spirit, and a bad family have theirs—ay, they have a demon who is always near, and shapes their lives for them; they don't know it, but, sooner or later justice catches them. Suppose I am the demon of your family—it is very funny, isn't it? I tried to serve you both, but it wouldn't do. I'll set about the other thing now: the evil genius of a bad family; I'm appointed to that. It almost makes me laugh—such cross-purposes! You're frightened? That's a pity; you should have thought of that before. It requires some nerve to fight a man like me. I don't threaten you, mind, but you are frightened. There is such a thing as getting a dangerous fellow bound over to keep the peace. Try that. I should like to have a talk with you before his worship in the police-court, across the table, with a corps of clever newspaper reporters sitting there. What fun in the Times and all the rest next morning."

It is plain to Miss Arden that Mr. Longcluse is speaking all this time with suppressed fury, and his countenance expresses a sort of smiling hatred that horrifies her.

"I'm not bad at speaking my mind," he continues. "It is unfortunate that I am so well thought of and listened to in London. Yes, people mind what I say a good deal. I rather think they'll choose to believe my story. But there's another way, if you don't like that. Your brother's not afraid—he'll protect you. Tell your brother what a miscreant I am, and send him to me—do, pray! Nothing on earth I should like better than to have a talk with that young gentleman. Do pray, send him, I entreat. He'd like satisfaction—ha! ha!—and, by Heaven, I'll give it him! Tell him to get his pistols ready; he shall have his shop! Let him come to Boulogne, or where he likes—I'll stand it—and I don't think he'll need to pay his way back again. He'll stay in France; he'll not walk in at your hall-door, and call for luncheon, I promise you. Ha! ha! ha!"

This pale man enjoys her terror cruelly.

"I'm not worthy to speak to you, I believe—eh? That's odd, for the time isn't far off when you'll pray to God I may have mercy on you. You had no business to encourage me. I'm afraid the crowd is getting on very slowly, but I'll try to entertain you: you are such a good listener!"

Miss Arden often wondered afterwards at her own passiveness through all this. There were, no doubt, close by, many worthy citizens, fathers of families, who would have taken her for a few minutes under their protection with honest alacrity. But it was a fascination; her state was cataleptic: and she could no more escape than the bird that is throbbing in the gaze of a snake. The cold murmur went distinctly on and on:

"Your brother will probably think I should treat you more ceremoniously. Don't you agree with him? Pray, do complain to him. Pray, send him to me, and I'll thank him for his share in this matter. He wanted to make it a match between us—I'm speaking coarsely, for the sake of distinctness—till a title turned up. What has become of the title, by-the-bye?—I don't see him here. The peer wasn't in the running, after all: didn't even start! Ha! ha! ha! Remember me to your brother, pray, and tell him the day will come when he'll not need to be reminded of me: I'll take care of that. And so Sir Richard is doomed to disappointment! It is a world of disappointment. The earl is nowhere! And the proudest family on earth—what is left of it—looks a little foolish. And well it may: it has many follies to expiate. You had no business encouraging me, and you are foolish enough to be terribly afraid now—ha! ha! ha! Too late, eh? I daresay you think I'll punish you! Not I! Nothing of the sort! I'll never punish anyone. Why should I take that trouble about you. Not I: not even your brother. Fate does that. Fate has always been kind to me, and hit my enemies pretty hard. You had no business encouraging me. Remember this: the day is not far off when you will both rue the hour you threw me over!"

She is gazing helplessly into that dreadful face. There is a cruel elation in it. He looks on her, I think, with admiration. Mixed with his hatred, did there remain a fraction of love?

On a sudden the voice, which was the only sound she heard, was in her ear no longer. The face which had transfixed her gaze was gone. Longcluse had apparently pushed a way for her to her friends, for she found herself again next her Uncle David. Holding his arm fast, she looked round quickly for a moment: she saw Mr. Longcluse nowhere. She felt on the point of fainting. The scene must have lasted a shorter time than she supposed, for her uncle had not missed her.

"My dear, how pale you look! Are you tired?" exclaims Lady May, when they have come to a halt at the door.

"Yes, indeed, so she does. Are you ill, dear?" added her uncle.

"No, nothing, thanks, only the crowd. I shall be better immediately." And so waiting in the air, near the door, they were soon joined by Sir Richard, and in his carriage he and she drove home to Mortlake. Lady May, taking hers, went to a tea at old Lady Elverstone's; and David Arden, bidding them good-bye, walked homeward across the park.

Richard had promised to spend the evening at Mortlake with her, and side by side they were driving out to that sad and sombre scene. As they entered the shaded road upon which the great gate of Mortlake opens, the setting sun streamed through the huge trunks of the trees, and tinted the landscape with a subdued splendour.

"I can't imagine, dear Alice, why you will stay here. It is enough to kill you," says Sir Richard, looking out peevishly on the picturesque woodlands of Mortlake, and interrupting a long silence. "You never can recover your spirits while you stay here. There is Lady May going all over the world—I forget where, but she will be at Naples—and she absolutely longs to take you with her; and you won't go! I really sometimes think you want to make yourself melancholy mad."

"I don't know," said she, waking herself from a reverie in which, against the dark background of the empty arches she had left, she still saw the white, wicked face that had leaned over her, and heard the low murmured stream of insult and menace. "I'm not sure that I shall not be worse anywhere else. I don't feel energy to make a change. I can't bear the idea of meeting people. By-and-by, in a little time, it will be different. For the present, quiet is what I like best. But you, Dick, are not looking well, you seem so over-worked and anxious. You really do want a little holiday. Why don't you go to Scotland to shoot, or take a few weeks' yachting? All your business must be pretty well settled now."

"It will never be settled," he said, a little sourly. "I assure you there never was property in such a mess—I mean leases and everything. Such drudgery, you have no idea; and I owe a good deal. It has not done me any good. I'd rather be as I was before that miserable Derby. I'd gladly exchange it all for a clear annuity of a thousand a year."

"Oh! my dear Dick, you can't mean that! All the northern property, and this, and Morley?"

"I hate to talk about it. I'm tired of it already. I have been so unlucky, so foolish, and if I had not found a very good friend, I should have been utterly ruined by that cursed race; and he has been aiding me very generously, on rather easy terms, in some difficulties that have followed; and you know I had to raise money on the estate before all this happened, and have had to make a very heavy mortgage, and I am getting into such a mess—a confusion, I mean—and really I should have sold the estates, if it had not been for my unknown friend, for I don't know his name."

"What friend?"

"The friend who has aided me through my troubles—the best friend I ever met, unless it be as I half suspect. Has anyone spoken to you lately, in a way to lead you to suppose that he, or anyone else among our friends, has been lending me a helping hand?"

"Yes, as we were driving into town to-day, Uncle David told me so distinctly; but I am not sure that I ought to have mentioned it. I fancy, indeed," she added, as she remembered the reflection with which it was accompanied, "that he meant it as a secret, so you must not get me into disgrace with him by appearing to know more than he has told you himself."

"No, certainly," said Richard; "and he said it was he who lent it?"

"Yes, distinctly."

"Well, I all but knew it before. Of course it is very kind of him. But then, you know he is very wealthy; he does not feel it; and he would not for the world that our house should lose its position. I think he would rather sell the coat off his back, than that our name should be slurred."

Sir Richard was pleased that he had received this light in corroboration of his suspicions. He was glad to have ascertained that the powerful motives which he had conjectured were actually governing the conduct of David Arden, although for obvious reasons he did not choose that his nephew should be aware of his weakness.

The carriage drew up at the hall-door. The old house in the evening beams, looked warm and cheery, and from every window in its broad front flamed the reflection which showed like so many hospitable winter fires.

CHAPTER LXII.

LOVE AND PLAY.

"Here we are, Alice," says Sir Richard, as they entered the hall. "We'll have a good talk this evening. We'll make the best of everything; and I don't see if Uncle David chooses to prevent it, why the old ship should founder after all."

They are now in the house. It is hard to get rid of the sense of constraint that, in his father's time, he always experienced within those walls; to feel that the old influence is exorcised and utterly gone, and that he is himself absolute master where so lately he hardly ventured to move on tip-toe.

They did not talk so much as Sir Richard had anticipated. There were upon his mind some things that weighed heavily. He had got from Levi a list of the advances made by his luckily found friend, and the total was much heavier than he had expected. He began to fear that he might possibly exceed the limits which his uncle must certainly have placed somewhere. He might not, indeed, allow him to suffer the indignity of a bankruptcy; but he would take a very short and unpleasant course with him. He would seize his rents, and, with a friendly roughness, put his estates to nurse, and send the prodigal on a Childe Harold's pilgrimage of five or six years, with an allowance, perhaps, of some three hundred a year, which in his frugal estimate of a young man's expenditure, would be handsome.

While he was occupied in these ruminations, Alice cared not to break the silence. It was a very unsociable tête-à-tête. Alice had a secret of her own to brood over. If anything could have made Longcluse now more terrible to her imagination, it would have been a risk of her brother's knowing anything of the language he had dared to hold to her. She knew from her brother's own lips, that he was a duellist; and she was also persuaded that Mr. Longcluse was, in his own playful and sinister phrase, very literally a "miscreant." His face, ever since that interview, was always at her right side, with its cruel pallor, and the vindictive sarcasm of lip and tone. How she wished that she had never met that mysterious man! What she would have given to be exempted from his hatred, and blotted from his remembrance!

One object only was in her mind, distinctly, with respect to that person. She was, thank God, quite beyond his power. But men, she knew, live necessarily a life so public, and have so many points of contact, that better opportunities present themselves for the indulgence of a masculine grudge; and she trembled at the thought of a collision. Why, then, should not Dick seek a reconciliation with him, and, by any honourable means, abate that terrible enmity.

"I have been thinking, Dick, that, as Uncle David makes the interest he takes in your affairs a secret, and you can't consult him, it would be very well indeed if you could find some one else able to advise, who would consult with you when you wished."

"Of course, I should be only too glad," says Sir Richard, yawning and smiling as well as he could at the same time; "but an adviser one can depend on in such matters, my dear child, is not to be picked up every day."

"Poor papa, I think, was very wise in choosing people of that kind. Uncle David, I know, said that he made wonderfully good bargains about his mortgages, or whatever they are called."

"I daresay—I don't know—he was always complaining, and always changing them," says Sir Richard. "But if you can introduce me to a person who can disentangle all my complications, and take half my cares off my shoulders, I'll say you are a very wise little woman indeed."

"I only know this—that poor papa had the highest opinion of Mr. Longcluse, and thought he was the cleverest person, and the most able to assist, of any one he knew."

Sir Richard Arden hears this with a stare of surprise.

"My dear Alice, you seem to forget everything. Why, Longcluse and I are at deadly feud. He hates me implacably. There never could be anything but enmity between us. Not that I care enough about him to hate him, but I have the worst opinion of him. I have heard the most shocking stories about him lately. They insinuate that he committed a murder! I told you of that jealousy and disappointment, about a girl he was in love with and wanted to marry, and it ended in murder! I'm told he had the reputation of being a most unscrupulous villain. They say he was engaged in several conspiracies to pigeon young fellows. He was the utter ruin, they say, of young Thornley, the poor muff who shot himself some years ago; and he was thought to be a principal proprietor of that gaming-house in Vienna, where they found all the apparatus for cheating so cleverly contrived."

"But are any of these things proved?" urges Miss Arden.

"I don't suppose he would be at large if they were," says Sir Richard, with a smile. "I only know that I believe them."

"Well, Dick, you know I reminded you before—you used not to believe those stories till you quarrelled with him."

"Why, what do you want, Alice?" he exclaims, looking hard at her. "What on earth can you mean? And what can possibly make you take an interest in the character of such a ruffian?"

Alice's face grew pale under his gaze. She cleared her voice and looked down; and then she looked full at him, with burning eyes, and said—

"It is because I am afraid of him, and think he may do you some dreadful injury, unless you are again on terms with him. I can't get it out of my head; and I daresay I am wrong, but I am sure I am miserable."

She burst into tears.

"Why, you darling little fool, what harm can he do me?" said Richard fondly, throwing his arms about her neck and kissing her, as he laughed tenderly. "He exhausted his utmost malice when he angrily refused to lend me a shilling in my extremity, or to be of the smallest use to me, at a moment when he might have saved me, without risk to himself, by simply willing it. I didn't ask him, you may be sure. An officious, foolish little friend, doing all, of course, for the best, did, without once consulting me, or giving me a voice in the matter, until he had effectually put his foot in it, as I told you. I would not for anything on earth have applied to him, I need not tell you; but it was done, and it only shows with what delight he would have seen me ruined, as, in fact, I should have been, had not my own relations taken the matter up. I do believe, Alice, the best thing I could do for myself and for you would be to marry," he says, a little suddenly, after a considerable silence.

Alice looks at him, doubtful whether he is serious.

"I really mean it. It is the only honest way of making or mending a fortune now-a-days."

"Well, Dick, it is time enough to think of that by-and-by, don't you think?"

"Perhaps so; I hope so. At present it seems to me that, as far as I am concerned, it is just a race between the bishop and the bailiff which shall have me first. If any lady is good enough to hold out a hand to a poor drowning fellow, she had better ——"

"Take care, Dick, that the poor drowning fellow does not pull her in. Don't you think it would be well to consider first what you have got to live on?"

"I have plenty to live on; I know that exactly," said Dick.

"What is it?"

"My wife's fortune."

"You are never serious for a minute, Dick! Don't you think it would be better first to get matters a little into order, so as to know distinctly what you are worth?"

"Quite the contrary; she'd rather not know. She'd rather exercise her imagination than learn distinctly what I am worth. Any woman of sense would prefer marrying me so."

"I don't understand you."

"Why, if I succeed in making matters quite lucid, I don't think she would marry me at all. Isn't it better to say, 'My Angelina,' or whatever else it may be, 'you see before you Sir Richard Arden, who has estates in Yorkshire, in Middlesex, and in Devonshire, thus spanning all England from north to south. We had these estates at the Conquest. There is nothing modern about them but the mortgages. I have never been able to ascertain exactly what they bring in by way of rents, or pay out by way of interest. That I stand here, with flesh upon my bones, and pretty well-made clothes, I hope, upon both, is evidence in a confused way that an English gentleman—a baronet—can subsist upon them; and this magnificent muddle I lay at your feet with the devotion of a passionate admirer of your personal—property!' That, I say, is better than appearing with a balance-sheet in your hand, and saying, 'Madam, I propose marrying you, and I beg to present you with a balance-sheet of the incomings and outgoings of my estates, the intense clearness of which will, I hope, compensate for the nature of its disclosures. I am there shown in the most satisfactory detail to be worth exactly fifteen shillings per annum, and how unlimited is my credit will appear from the immense amount and variety of my debts. In pressing my suit I rely entirely upon your love of perspicuity and your passion for arithmetic, which will find in the ledgers of my steward an almost inexhaustible gratification and indulgence.' However, as you say, Alice, I have time to look about me, and I see you are tired. We'll talk it over tomorrow morning at breakfast. Don't think I have made up my mind; I'll do exactly whatever you like best. But get to your bed, you poor little soul; you do look so tired!"

With great affection they parted for the night. But Sir Richard did not meet her at breakfast.

After she had left the room some time, he changed his mind, left a message for his sister with old Crozier, ordered his servant and trap to the door, and drove into town. It was not his good angel who prompted him. He drove to a place where he was sure to find high play going on, and there luck did not favour him.

What had become of Sir Richard Arden's resolutions? The fascinations of his old vice were irresistible. The ring of the dice, the whirl of the roulette, the plodding pillage of whist—any rite acknowledged by Fortune, the goddess of his soul, was welcome to that keen worshipper. Luck was not always adverse; once or twice he might have retreated in comparative safety; but the temptation to "back his luck" and go on prevailed, and left him where he was.

About a week after the evening passed at Mortlake, a black and awful night of disaster befel him.

Every other extravagance and vice draws its victim on at a regulated pace, but this of gaming is an hourly trifling with life, and one infatuated moment may end him. How short had been the reign of the new baronet, and where were prince and princedom now?

Before five o'clock in the morning, he had twice spent a quarter of an hour tugging at Mr. Levi's office-bell, in the dismal old street in Westminster. Then he drove off toward his lodgings. The roulette was whirling under his eyes whenever for a moment he closed them. He thought he was going mad.

The cabman knew a place where, even at that unseasonable hour, he might have a warm bath; and thither Sir Richard ordered him to drive. After this, he again essayed the Jew's office. The cool early morning was over still quiet London—hardly a soul was stirring. On the steps he waited, pulling the office-bell at intervals. In the stillness of the morning, he could hear it distinctly in the remote room, ringing unheeded in that capacious house.

CHAPTER LXIII.

PLANS.

It was, of course, in vain looking for Mr. Levi there at such an hour. Sir Richard Arden fancied that he had, perhaps, a sleeping-room in the house, and on that chance tried what his protracted alarm might do.

Then he drove to his own house. He had a latch-key, and let himself in. Just as he is, he throws himself into a chair in his dressing-room. He knows there is no use in getting into his bed. In his fatigued state, sleep was quite out of the question. That proud young man was longing to open his heart to the mean, cruel little Jew.

Oh, madness! why had he broken with his masterly and powerful friend, Longcluse? Quite unavailing now, his repentance. They had spoken and passed like ships at sea, in this wide life, and now who could count the miles and billows between them! Never to cross or come in sight again!

Uncle David! Yes, he might go to him; he might spread out the broad evidences of his ruin before him, and adjure him, by the God of mercy, to save him from the great public disgrace that was now imminent; implore of him to give him any pittance he pleased, to subsist on in exile, and to deal with the estates as he himself thought best. But Uncle David was away, quite out of reach. After his whimsical and inflexible custom, lest business should track him in his holiday, he had left no address with his man of business, who only knew that his first destination was Scotland; none with Grace Maubray, who only knew that, attended by Vivian Darnley, she and Lady May were to meet him in about a fortnight on the Continent, where they were to plan together a little excursion in Switzerland or Italy.

Sir Richard quite forgot there was such a meal as breakfast. He ordered his horse to the door, took a furious two hours' ride beyond Brompton, and returned and saw Levi at his office, at his usual hour, eleven o'clock. The Jew was alone. His large lowering eyes were cast on Sir Richard as he entered and approached.

"Look, now; listen," says Sir Richard, who looks wofully wild and pale, and as he seats himself never takes his eyes off Mr. Levi. "I don't care very much who knows it—I think I'm totally ruined."

The Jew knows pretty well all about it, but he stares and gapes hypocritically in the face of his visitor as if he were thunderstruck, and he speaks never a word. I suppose he thought it as well, for the sake of brevity and clearness, to allow his client "to let off the shteam" first, a process which Sir Richard forthwith commenced, with both hands on the table—sometimes clenched, sometimes expanded, sometimes with a thump, by blowing off a cloud of oaths and curses, and incoherent expositions of the wrongs and perversities of fortune.

"I don't think I can tell you how much it is. I don't know," says Sir Richard bleakly, in reply to a pertinent question of the Jew's. "There was that rich fellow, what's his name, that makes candles—he's always winning. By Jove, what a thing luck is! He won—I know it is more than two thousand. I gave him I O U's for it. He'd be very glad, of course, to know me, curse him! I don't care, now, who does. And he'd let me owe him twice as much, for as long as I like. I daresay, only too glad—as smooth as one of his own filthy candles. And there were three fellows lending money there. I don't know how much I got—I was stupid. I signed whatever they put before me. Those things can't stand, by heavens; the Chancellor will set them all aside. The confounded villains! What's the Government doing? What's the Government about, I say? Why don't Parliament interfere, to smash those cursed nests of robbers and swindlers? Here I am, utterly robbed—I know I'm robbed—and all by that cursed temptation; and—and—and I don't know what cash I got, nor what I have put my name to!"

"I'll make out that in an hour's time. They'll tell me at the houshe who the shentleman wazh."

"And—upon my soul that's true—I owe the people there something too; it can't be much—it isn't much. And, Levi, like a good fellow—by Heaven, I'll never forget it to you, if you'll think of something. You've pulled me through so often; I am sure there's good-nature in you; you wouldn't see a fellow you've known so long driven to the wall and made a beggar of, without—without thinking of something."

Levi looked down, with his hands in his pockets, and whistled to himself, and Sir Richard gazed on his vulgar features as if his life or death depended upon every variation of their expression.

"You know," says Levi, looking up and swaying his shoulders a little, "the old chap can't do no more. He's taken a share in that Austrian contract, and he'll want his capital, every pig. I told you lasht time. Wouldn't Lonclushe give you a lift?"

"Not he. He'd rather give me a shove under."

"Well, they tell me you and him wazh very thick; and your uncle'sh man, Blount, knowshe him, and can just ashk him, from himself, mind, not from you."

"For money?" exclaimed Richard.

"Not at a—all," drawled the Jew impatiently. "Lishen—mind. The old fellow, your friend ——"

"He's out of town," interrupted Richard.

"No, he'sh not. I shaw him lasht night. You're a—all wrong. He'sh not Mr. David Harden, if that'sh what you mean. He'sh a better friend, and he'll leave you a lot of tin when he diesh—an old friend of the family—and if all goeshe shmooth he'll come and have a talk with you fashe to fashe, and tell you all his plansh about you, before a week'sh over. But he'll be at hish lasht pound for five or six weeksh to come, till the firsht half-million of the new shtock is in the market; and he shaid, 'I can't draw out a pound of my balanshe, but if he can get Lonclushe's na—me, I'll get him any shum he wantsh, and bear Lonclushe harmlesh.'"

"I don't think I can," said Sir Richard; "I can't be quite sure, though. It is just possible he might."

"Well, let Blount try," said he.

There was another idea also in Mr. Levi's head. He had been thinking whether the situation might not be turned to some more profitable account, for him, than the barren agency for the "friend of the family," who "lent out money gratis," like Antonio; and if he did not "bring down the rate of usance," at all events, deprived the Shylocks of London, in one instance at least, of their fair game.

"If he won't do that, there'sh but one chansh left."

"What is that?" asked Sir Richard, with a secret flutter at his heart. It was awful to think of himself reduced to his last chance, with his recent experience of what a chance is.

"Well," says Mr. Levi, scrawling florid capitals on the table with his office pen, and speaking with much deliberation, "I heard you were going to make a very rich match; and if the shettlementsh was agreed on, I don't know but we might shee our way to advancing all you want."

Sir Richard gets up, and walks slowly two or three times up and down the room.

"I'll see about Blount," said he; "I'll talk to him. I think those things are payable in six or eight days; and that tallow-chandler won't bother me to-morrow, I daresay. I'll go to-day and talk to Blount, and suppose you come to me to-morrow evening at Mortlake. Will nine o'clock do for you? I sha'n't keep you half-an-hour."

"A—all right, Shir—nine, at Mortlake. If you want any diamondsh, I have a beoo—ootiful collar and pendantsh, in that shaafe—brilliantsh. I can give you the lot three thoushand under cosht prishe. You'll wa—ant a preshent for the young la—ady."

"Yes, I suppose so," said Sir Richard, abstractedly. "To-morrow night—to-morrow evening at nine o'clock."

He stopped at the door, looking silently down the stairs, and then without leave-taking or looking behind him, he ran down, and drove to Mr. Blount's house, close by, in Manchester Buildings.

For more than a year the young gentleman whom we are following this morning had cherished vague aspirations, of which good Lady May had been the object. There was nothing to prevent their union, for the lady was very well disposed to listen. But Richard Arden did not like ridicule, and there was no need to hurry; and besides, within the last half-year had arisen another flame, less mercenary; also, perhaps, reciprocated.

Grace Maubray was handsome, animated; she had that combination of air, tact, cleverness, which enter into the idea of chic. With him it had been a financial, but notwithstanding rather agreeable, speculation. Hitherto there seemed ample time before him, and there was no need to define or decide.

Now, you will understand, the crisis had arrived, which admitted of neither hesitation nor delay. He was now at Blount's hall-door. He was certain that he could trust Blount with anything, and he meant to learn from him what dot his Uncle David intended bestowing on the young lady.

Mr. Blount was at home. He smiled kindly, and took the young gentleman's hand, and placed a chair for him.

CHAPTER LXIV.

FROM FLOWER TO FLOWER.

Mr. Blount was intelligent: he was an effective though not an artful diplomatist. He promptly undertook to sound Mr. Longcluse without betraying Sir Richard.

Richard Arden did not allude to his losses. He took good care to appear pretty nearly as usual. When he confessed his tendresse for Miss Maubray, the grave gentleman smiled brightly, and took him by the hand.

"If you should marry the young lady, mark you, she will have sixty thousand pounds down, and sixty thousand more after Mr. David Arden's death. That is splendid, Sir, and I think it will please him very much."

"I have suffered a great deal, Mr. Blount, by neglecting his advice hitherto. It shall be my chief object, henceforward, to reform, and to live as he wishes. I believe people can't learn wisdom without suffering."

"Will you take a biscuit and a glass of sherry, Sir Richard?" asked Mr. Blount.

"Nothing, thanks," said Sir Richard. "You know, I'm not as rich as I might have been, and marriage is a very serious step; and you are one of the oldest and most sensible friends I have, and you'll understand that it is only right I should be very sure before taking such a step, involving not myself only, but another who ought to be dearer still, that there should be no mistake about the means on which we may reckon. Are you quite sure that my uncle's intentions are still exactly what you mentioned?"

"Perfectly; he authorised me to say so two months ago, and on the eve of his departure on Friday last he repeated his instructions."

Sir Richard, in silence, shook the old man very cordially by the hand, and was gone.

As he drove to his house in May Fair, Sir Richard's thoughts, among other things, turned again upon the question, "Who could his mysterious benefactor be?"

Once or twice had dimly visited his mind a theory which, ever since his recent conversation with Mr. Levi, had been growing more solid and vivid. An illegitimate brother of his father's, Edwin Raikes, had gone out to Australia early in life, with a purse to which three brothers, the late Sir Reginald, Harry, and David, had contributed. He had not maintained any correspondence with English friends and kindred; but rumours from time to time reached home that he had amassed a fortune. His feelings to the family of Arden had always been kindly. He was older than Uncle David, and had well earned a retirement from the life of exertion and exile which had consumed all the vigorous years of his manhood. Was this the "old party" for whom Mr. Levi was acting?

With this thought opened a new and splendid hope upon the mind of Sir Richard. Here was a fortune, if rumour spoke truly, which, combined with David Arden's, would be amply sufficient to establish the old baronetage upon a basis of solid magnificence such as it had never rested on before.

It would not do, however, to wait for this. The urgency of the situation demanded immediate action. Sir Richard made an elaborate toilet, after which, in a hansom, he drove to Lady May Penrose's.

If our hero had had fewer things to think about he would have gone first, I fancy, to Miss Grace Maubray. It could do no great harm, however, to feel his way a little with Lady May, he thought, as he chatted with that plump alternative of his tender dilemma. But in this wooing there was a difficulty of a whimsical kind. Poor Lady May was so easily won, and made so many openings for his advances, that he was at his wits' end to find evasions by which to postpone the happy crisis which she palpably expected. He did succeed, however; and with a promise of calling again, with the lady's permission, that evening, he took his leave.

Before making his call at his uncle's house, in the hope of seeing Grace Maubray, he had to return to Mr. Blount, in Manchester Buildings, where he hoped to receive from that gentleman a report of his interview with Mr. Longcluse.

I shall tell you here what that report related. Mr. Longcluse was fortunately still at his house when Mr. Blount called, and immediately admitted him. Mr. Longcluse's horse and groom were at the door; he was on the point of taking his ride. His gloves and whip were beside him on the table as Mr. Blount entered.

Mr. Blount made his apologies, and was graciously received. His visit was, in truth, by no means unwelcome.

"Mr. David Arden very well, I hope?"

"Quite well, thanks. He has left town."

"Indeed! And where has he gone—the moors?"

"To Scotland, but not to shoot, I think. And he's going abroad then—going to travel."

"On the Continent? How nice that is! What part?"

"Switzerland and Italy, I think," said Mr. Blount, omitting all mention of Paris, where Mr. Arden was going first to make a visit to the Baron Vanboeren.

"He's going over ground that I know very well," said Mr. Longcluse. "Happy man! He can't quite break away from his business, though, I daresay."

"He never tells us where a letter will find him, and the consequence is his holidays are never spoiled."

"Not a bad plan, Mr. Blount. Won't he visit the Paris Exhibition?"

"I rather think not."

"Can I do anything for you, Mr. Blount?"

"Well, Mr. Longcluse, I just called to ask you a question. I have been invited to take part in arranging a little matter which I take an interest in, because it affects the Arden estates."

"Is Sir Richard Arden interested in it?" inquired Mr. Longcluse, gently and coldly.

"Yes, I rather fancy he would be benefited."

"I have had a good deal of unpleasantness, and, I might add, a great deal of ingratitude from that quarter, and I have made up my mind never again to have anything to do with him or his affairs. I have no unpleasant feeling, you understand; no resentment; there is nothing, of course, he could say or do that could in the least affect me. It is simply that, having coolly reviewed his conduct, I have quite made up my mind to aid in nothing in which he has act, part, or interest."

"It was not directly, but simply as a surety ——"

"All the same, so far as I'm concerned," said Mr. Longcluse sharply.

"And only, I fancied, it might be, as Mr. David Arden is absent, and you should be protected by satisfactory joint security ——"

"I won't do it," said Mr. Longcluse, a little brusquely; and he took out his watch and glanced at it impatiently.

"Sir Richard, I think, will be in funds immediately," said Mr. Blount.

"How so?" asked Mr. Longcluse. "You'll excuse me, as you press the subject, for saying that will be something new."

"Well," said Mr. Blount, who saw that his last words had made an impression, "Sir Richard is likely to be married, very advantageously, immediately."

"Are settlements agreed on?" inquired Mr. Longcluse, with real interest.

"No, not yet; but I know all about them."

"He is accepted then?"

"He has not proposed yet; but there can be, I fancy, no doubt that the lady likes him, and all will go right."

"Oh! and who is the lady?"

"I'm not at liberty to tell."

"Quite right; I ought not to have asked," says Mr. Longcluse; and looks down, slapping at intervals the side of his trousers lightly with his whip. He raises his eyes to Mr. Blount's face, and looks on the point of asking another question, but he does not.

"It is my opinion," said Mr. Blount, "the kindness would involve absolutely no risk whatever."

There was a little pause. Mr. Longcluse looks rather dark and anxious; perhaps his mind has wandered quite from the business before them. But it returns, and he says,—

"Risk or no risk, Mr. Blount, I don't mean to do him that kindness; and for how long will Mr. David Arden be absent?"

"Unless he should take a sudden thought to return, he'll be away at least two months."

"Where is he?—in Scotland?"

"I really don't know."

"Couldn't one see him for a few minutes before he starts? Where does he take the steamer?"

"Southampton."

"And on what day?"

"You really want a word with him?" asked Blount, whose hopes revived.

"I may."

"Well, the only person who will know that is Mr. Humphries, of Pendle Castle, near that town; for he has to transact some trust-business with that gentleman as he passes through."

"Humphries, of Pendle Castle. Very good; thanks."

Mr. Longcluse looks again at his watch.

"And perhaps you will reconsider the matter I spoke of?"

"No use, Mr. Blount—not the least. I have quite made up my mind. Anything more? I am afraid I must be off."

"Nothing, thanks," said Mr. Blount.

And so the interview ended.

When he was gone, Mr. Longcluse thought darkly for a minute.

"That's a straightforward fellow, they say. I suppose the facts are so. It can't be, though, that Miss Maubray, that handsome creature with so much money, is thinking of marrying that insolent coxcomb. It may be Lady May, but the other is more likely. We must not allow that, Sir Richard. That would never do."

There was a fixed frown on his face, and he was smiling in his dream. Out he went. His pale face looked as if he meditated a wicked joke, and, frowning still in utter abstraction, he took the bridle from his groom, mounted, looked about him as if just wakened, and set off at a canter, followed by his servant, for David Arden's house.

Smiling, gay, as if no care had ever crossed him, Longcluse enters the drawing-room, where he finds the handsome young lady writing a note at that moment.

"Mr. Longcluse, I'm so glad you've come!" she says, with a brilliant smile. "I was writing to poor Lady Ethel, who is mourning, you know, in the country. The death of her father in the house was so awfully sudden, and I'm telling her all the news I can think of to amuse her. And is it really true that old Sir Thomas Giggles has grown so cross with his pretty young wife, and objects to her allowing Lord Knocknea to make love to her?"

"Quite true. It is a very bad quarrel, and I'm afraid it can't be made up," said Mr. Longcluse.

"It must be very bad, indeed, if Sir Thomas can't make it up; for he allowed his first wife, I am told, to do anything she pleased. Is it to be a separation?"

"At least. And you heard, I suppose, of poor old Lady Glare?"

"No!"

"She has been rolling ever so long, you know, in a sea of troubles, and now, at last, she has fairly foundered."

"How do you mean?"

"They have sold her diamonds," said Mr. Longcluse. "Didn't you hear?"

"No! Really? Sold her diamonds? Good Heaven! Then there's nothing left of her but her teeth. I hope they won't sell them."

"It is an awful misfortune," said Mr. Longcluse.

"Misfortune! She's utterly ruined. It was her diamonds that people asked. I am really sorry. She was such fun; she was so fat, and such a fool, and said such delicious things, and dressed herself so like a macaw. Alas! I shall never see her more; and people thought her only use on earth was to carry about her diamonds. No one seemed to perceive what a delightful creature she was. What about Lady May Penrose? I have not seen her since I came back from Cowes, the day before yesterday, and we leave London together on Tuesday."

"Lady May! Oh! she is to receive a very interesting communication, I believe. She is one name on a pretty long and very distinguished list, which Sir Richard Arden, I am told, has made out, and carries about with him in his pocket-book."

"You're talking riddles; pray speak plainly."

"Well, Lady May is one of several ladies who are to be honoured with a proposal."

"And would you have me believe that Sir Richard Arden has really made such a fool of himself as to make out a list of eligible ladies whom he is about to ask to marry him, and that he has had the excellent good sense and taste to read this list to his acquaintance?"

"I mean to say this—I'll tell the whole story—Sir Richard has ruined himself at play; take that as a fact to start with. He is literally ruined. His uncle is away; but I don't think any man in his senses would think of paying his losses for him. He turns, therefore, naturally, to the more amiable and less arithmetical sex, and means to invite, in turn, a series of fair and affluent admirers to undertake, by means of suitable settlements, that interesting office for him."

"I don't think you like him, Mr. Longcluse; is not that a story a little too like 'The Merry Wives of Windsor?'"

"It is quite certain I don't like him, and it is quite certain," added Mr. Longcluse, with one of his cold little laughs, "that if I did like him, I should not tell the story; but it is also certain that the story is, in all its parts, strictly fact. If you permit me the pleasure of a call in two or three days, you will tell me you no longer doubt it."

Mr. Longcluse was looking down as he said that with a gentle and smiling significance. The young lady blushed a little, and then more intensely, as he spoke, and looking through the window, asked with a laugh,—

"But how shall we know whether he really speaks to Lady May?"

"Possibly by his marrying her," laughed Mr. Longcluse. "He certainly will if he can, unless he is caught and married on the way to her house."

"He was a little unfortunate in showing you his list, wasn't he?" said Grace Maubray.

"I did not say that. If there had been any, the least, confidence, nothing on earth could have induced me to divulge it. We are not even, at present, on speaking terms. He had the coolness to send a Mr. Blount, who transacts all Mr. David Arden's affairs, to ask me to become his security, Mr. Arden being away; and by way of inducing me to do so, he disclosed, with the coarseness which is the essence of business, the matrimonial schemes which are to recoup, within a few days, the losses of the roulette, the whist-table, or the dice-box."

"Oh! Mr. Blount, I'm told, is a very honest man."

"Quite so; particularly accurate, and I don't think anything on earth would induce him to tell an untruth," testifies Mr. Longcluse.

After a little pause, Miss Maubray laughs.

"One certainly does learn," she said, "something new every day. Could any one have fancied a gentleman descending to so gross a meanness?"

"Everybody is a gentleman now-a-days," remarked Mr. Longcluse with a smile; "but every one is not a hero—they give way, more or less, under temptation. Those who stand the test of the crucible and the furnace are seldom met with."

At this moment the door opened, and Lord Wynderbroke was announced. A little start, a lighting of the eyes, as Grace rose, and a fluttered advance, with a very pretty little hand extended, to meet him, testified, perhaps, rather more surprise than one would have quite expected. For Mr. Longcluse, who did not know him so well as Miss Maubray, recognised his voice, which was peculiar, and resembling the caw of a jay, as he put a question to the servant on his way up.

Mr. Longcluse took his leave. He was not sorry that Lord Wynderbroke had called. He wished no success to Sir Richard's wooing. He thought he had pretty well settled the question in Miss Maubray's mind, and smiling, he rode at a pleasant canter to Lady May's. It was as well, perhaps, that she should hear the same story. Lady May, however, unfortunately, had just gone out for a drive.

CHAPTER LXV.

BEHIND THE ARRAS.

It was quite true that Lady May was not at home. She was actually, with a little charming palpitation, driving to pay a very interesting visit to Grace Maubray. In affairs of the kind that now occupied her mind, she had no confidants but very young people.

Miss Maubray was at home—and instantly Lady May's plump instep was seen on the carriage step. She disdained assistance, and descended with a heavy skip upon the flags, where she executed an involuntary frisk that carried her a little out of the line of advance.

As she ascended the stairs, she met her friend Lord Wynderbroke coming down. They stopped for a moment on the landing, under a picture of Cupid and Venus; Lady May, smiling, remarked, a little out of breath, what a charming day it was, and expressed her amazement at seeing him in town—a surprise which he agreeably reciprocated. He had been at Glenkiltie in the Highlands, where he had accidentally met Mr. David Arden. "Miss Maubray is in the drawing-room," he said, observing that the eyes of the good lady glanced unconsciously upward at the door of that room. And then they parted affectionately, and turned their backs on each other with a sense of relief.

"Well, my dear," she said to Grace Maubray as soon as they had kissed, "longing to have a few minutes with you, with ever so much to say. You have no idea what it is to be stopped on the stairs by that tiresome man—I'll never quarrel with you again for calling him a bore. No matter, here I am; and really, my dear, it is such an odd affair—not quite that; such an odd scene, I don't know where or how to begin."

"I wish I could help you," said Miss Maubray laughing.

"Oh, my dear, you'd never guess in a hundred years."

"How do you know? Hasn't a certain baronet something to do with it?"

"Well, well—dear me! That is very extraordinary. Did he tell you he was going to—to—Good gracious! My dear, it is the most extraordinary thing. I believe you hear everything; but—a—but listen. Not an hour ago he came—Richard Arden, of course, we mean—and, my dear Grace, he spoke so very nicely of his troubles, poor fellow, you know—debts I mean, of course—not the least his fault, and all that kind of thing, and—he went on—I really don't know how to tell you. But he said—he said—he said he liked me, and no one else on earth; and he was on the very point of saying everything, when, just at that moment, who should come in but that gossiping old woman, Lady Botherton—and he whispered, as he was going, that he would return, after I had had my drive. The carriage was at the door, so, when I got rid of the old woman, I got into it, and came straight here to have a talk with you; and what do you think I ought to say? Do tell me, like a darling, do!"

"I wish you would tell me what one ought to say to that question," said Grace Maubray with a slight disdain (that young lady was in the most unreasonable way piqued), "for I'm told he's going to ask me precisely the same question."

"You, my dear?" said Lady May after a pause, during which she was staring at the smiling face of the young lady; "you can't be serious!"

"He can't be serious, you mean," answered the young lady, "and—who's this?" she broke off, as she saw a cab drive up to the hall-door. "Dear me! is it? No. Yes, indeed, it is Sir Richard Arden. We must not be seen together. He'll know you have been talking to me. Just go in here."

She opened the door of the boudoir adjoining the room.

"I'll send him away in a moment. You may hear every word I have to say. I should like it. I shall give him a lecture."

As she thus spoke she heard his step on the stair, and motioned Lady May into the inner room, into which she hurried and closed the door, leaving it only a little way open.

These arrangements are hardly completed when Sir Richard is announced. Grace is positively angry. But never had she looked so beautiful; her eyes so tenderly lustrous under their long lashes; her colour so brilliant—an expression so maidenly and sad. If it was acting, it was very well done. You would have sworn that the melancholy and agitation of her looks, and the slightly quickened movement of her breathing, were those of a person who felt that the hour of her fate had come.

With what elation Richard Arden saw these beautiful signs!

CHAPTER LXVI.

A BUBBLE BROKEN.

After a few words had been exchanged, Grace said in reply to a question of Sir Richard's,—

"Lady May and I are going together, you know: in a day or two we shall be at Brighton. I mean to bid Alice good-bye to-day. There—I mean at Brighton—we are to meet Vivian Darnley, and possibly another friend; and we go to meet your uncle at that pretty little town in Switzerland, where Lady May ——I wonder, by-the-bye, you did not arrange to come with us; Lady May travels with us the entire time. She says there are some very interesting ruins there."

"Why, dear old soul!" said Sir Richard, who felt called upon to say something to set himself right with respect to Lady May, "she's thinking of quite another place. She will be herself the only interesting ruin there."

"I think you wish to vex me," said pretty Grace, turning away with a smile, which showed, nevertheless, that this kind of joke was not an unmixed vexation to her. "I don't care for ruins myself."

"Nor do I," he said, archly.

"But you don't think so of Lady May. I know you don't. You are franker with her than with me, and you tell her a very different tale."

"I must be very frank, then, if I tell her more than I know myself. I never said a civil thing of Lady May, except once or twice, to the poor old thing herself, when I wanted her to do one or two little things, to please you."

"Oh! come, you can't deceive me; I've seen you place your hand to your heart, like a theatrical hero, when you little fancied any one but she saw it."

"Now, really, that is too bad. I may have put my hand to my side, when it ached from laughing."

"How can you talk so? You know very well I have heard you tell her how you admire her music and her landscapes."

"No, no—not landscapes—she paints faces. But her colouring is, as artists say, too chalky—and nothing but red and white, like—what is it like?—like a clown. Why did not she get the late Mr. Etty—she's always talking of him—to teach her something of his tints?"

"You are not to speak so of Lady May. You forget she is my particular friend," says the young lady; but her pretty face does not express so much severity as her words. "I do think you like her. You merely talk so to throw dust in people's eyes. Why should not you be frank with me?"

"I wish I dare be frank with you," said Sir Richard.

"And why not?"

"How can I tell how my disclosures might be punished? My frankness might extinguish the best hope I live for; a few rash words might make me a very unhappy man for life."

"Really? Then I can quite understand that reflection alarming you in the midst of a tête-à-tête with Lady May; and even interrupting an interesting conversation."

Sir Richard looked at her quickly, but her looks were perfectly artless.

"I really do wish you would spare me all further allusion to that good woman. I can bear that kind of fun from any one but you. Why will you? she is old enough to be my mother. She is fat, and painted, and ridiculous. You think me totally without romance? I wish to heaven I were. There is a reason, that makes your saying all that particularly cruel. I am not the sordid creature you take me for. I'm not insensible. I'm not a mere stock of stone. Never was human being more capable of the wildest passion. Oh, if I dare tell you all!"

Was all this acting? Certainly not. Never was shallow man, for the moment, more in earnest. Cool enough he was, although he had always admired this young lady, when he entered the room. He had made that entrance, nevertheless, in a spirit quite dramatic. But Miss Maubray never looked so brilliant, never half so tender. He took fire—the situation aiding quite unexpectedly—and the flame was real. It might have been over as quickly as a balloon on fire; but for the moment the conflagration was intense.

How was Miss Maubray affected? An immensely abler performer than the young gentleman who had entered the room with his part at his fingers' ends, and all his looks and emphasis arranged—only to break through all this, and begin extemporising wildly—she, on the contrary, maintained her rôle with admirable coolness. It was not, perhaps, so easy; for notwithstanding appearances, her histrionic powers were severely tasked; for never was she more angry. Her self-esteem was wounded; the fancy (it was no more), she had cherished for him was gone, and a great disgust was there instead.

"You shall ask me no questions till I have done asking mine," said the young lady, with decision; "and I will speak as much as I please of Lady May!"

This jealousy flattered Sir Richard.

"And I will say this," continued Grace Maubray, "you never address her except as a lover, in what you romantic people would call the language of love."

"Now, now, now! How can you say that? Is that fair?"

"You do."

"No, really, I swear—that's too bad!"

"Yes, the other day, when you spoke to her at the carriage window—you did not think I heard—you accused her so tenderly of having failed to go to Lady Harbroke's garden-party, and you couldn't say what you meant in plain terms, but you said, 'Why were you false?'"

"I didn't, I swear."

"Oh! you did; I heard every syllable; 'false' was the word."

"Well, if I said 'false,' I must have been thinking of her hair; for she is really a very honest old woman."

At this moment a female voice in distress is heard, and poor Lady May comes pushing out of the pretty little room, in which Grace Maubray had placed her, sobbing and shedding floods of tears.

"I can't stay there any longer, for I hear everything; I can't help hearing every word—honest old woman, and all—opprobrious. Oh! how can people be so? how can they? Oh! I'm very angry—I'm very angry—I'm very angry!"

If Miss Maubray were easily moved to pity she might have been at sight of the big innocent eyes turned up at her, from which rolled great tears, making visible channels through the paint down her cheeks. She sobbed and wept like a fat, good-natured child, and pitifully she continued sobbing, "Oh, I'm a-a-ho—very angry; wha-at shall I do-o-o, my dear? I-I'm very angry—oh, oh—I'm very a-a-angry!"

"So am I," said Grace Maubray, with a fiery glance at the young baronet, who stood fixed where he was, like an image of death; "and I had intended, dear Lady May, telling you a thing which Sir Richard Arden may as well hear, as I mean to write to tell Alice to-day; it is that I am to be married—I have accepted Lord Wynderbroke—and—and that's all."

Sir Richard, I believe, said "Good-bye." Nobody heard him. I don't think he remembers how he got on his horse. I don't think the ladies saw him leave the room—only, he was gone.

Poor Lady May takes her incoherent leave. She has got her veil over her face, to baffle curiosity. Miss Maubray stands at the window, the tip of her finger to her brilliant lip, contemplating Lady May as she gets in with a great jerk and swing of the carriage, and she hears the footman say "Home," and sees a fat hand, in a lilac glove, pull up the window hurriedly. Then she sits down on a sofa, and laughs till she quivers again, and tears overflow her eyes; and she says in the intervals, almost breathlessly,—

"Oh, poor old thing! I really am sorry. Who could have thought she cared so much? Poor old soul! what a ridiculous old thing!"

Such broken sentences of a rather contemptuous pity rolled and floated along the even current of her laughter.

CHAPTER LXVII.

BOND AND DEED.

The summer span of days was gone; it was quite dark, and long troops of withered leaves drifted in rustling trains over the avenue, as Mr. Levi, observant of his appointment, drove up to the grand old front of Mortlake, which in the dark spread before him like a house of white mist.

"I shay," exclaimed Mr. Levi, softly, arresting the progress of the cabman, who was about running up the steps, "I'll knock myshelf—wait you there."

Mr. Levi was smoking. Standing at the base of the steps, he looked up, and right and left with some curiosity. It was too dark; he could hardly see the cold glimmer of the windows that reflected the grey horizon. Vaguely, however, he could see that it was a grander place than he had supposed. He looked down the avenue, and between the great trees over the gate he saw the distant lights, and heard through the dim air the chimes, far off, from London steeples, succeeding one another, or mingling faintly, and telling all whom it might concern the solemn lesson of the flight of time.

Mr. Levi thought it might be worth while coming down in the day-time, and looking over the house and place to see what could be made of them; the thing was sure to go a dead bargain. At present he could see nothing but the wide, vague, grey front, and the faint glow through the hall windows, which showed their black outlines sharply enough.

"Well, he'sh come a mucker, anyhow," murmured Mr. Levi, with one of his smiles that showed so wide his white sharp teeth.

He knocked at the door and rang the bell. It was not a footman, but Crozier who opened it. The old servant of the family did not like the greasy black curls, the fierce jet eyes, the sallow face and the large, moist, sullen mouth, that presented themselves under the brim of Mr. Levi's hat, nor the tawdry glimmer of chains on his waistcoat, nor the cigar still burning in his fingers. Sir Richard had told Crozier, however, that a Mr. Levi, whom he described, was to call at a certain hour, on very particular business, and was to be instantly admitted.

Mr. Levi looks round him, and extinguishes his cigar before following Crozier, whose countenance betrays no small contempt and dislike, as he eyes the little man askance, as if he would like well to be uncivil to him.

Crozier leads him to the right, through a small apartment, to a vast square room, long disused, still called the library, though but few books remain on the shelves, and those in disorder. It is a chilly night, and a little fire burns in the grate, over which Sir Richard is cowering. Very haggard, the baronet starts up as the name of his visitor is announced.

"Come in," cries Sir Richard, walking to meet him. "Here—here I am, Levi, utterly ruined. There isn't a soul I dare tell how I am beset, or anything to, but you. Do, for God's sake take pity on me, and think of something! my brain's quite gone—you're such a clever fellow" (he is dragging Levi by the arm all this time towards the candles): "do now, you're sure to see some way out. It is a matter of honour; I only want time. If I could only find my Uncle David: think of his selfishness—good heaven! was there ever man so treated? and there's the bank letter—there—on the table; you see it—dunning me, the ungrateful harpies, for the trifle—what is it?—three hundred and something, I overdrew; and that blackguard tallow-chandler has been three times to my house in town, for payment to-day, and it's more than I thought—near four thousand, he says—the scoundrel! It's just the same to him two months hence; he's full of money, the beast—a fellow like that—it's delight to him to get hold of a gentleman, and he won't take a bill—the lying rascal! He is pressed for cash just now—a pug-faced villain with three hundred thousand pounds! Those scoundrels! I mean the people, whatever they are, that lent me the money; it turns out it was all but at sight, and they were with my attorney to-day, and they won't wait. I wish I was shot; I envy the dead dogs rolling in the Thames! By heaven; Levi, I'll say you're the best friend man ever had on earth, I will, if you manage something! I'll never forget it to you; I'll have it in my power, yet! no one ever said I was ungrateful; I swear I'll be the making of you! Do, Levi, think; you're accustomed to—to emergency, and unless you will, I'm utterly ruined—ruined, by heaven, before I have time to think!"

The Jew listened to all this with his hands in his pockets, leaning back in his chair, with his big eyes staring on the wild face of the baronet, and his heavy mouth hanging. He was trying to reduce his countenance to vacancy.

"What about them shettlements, Sir Richard—a nishe young lady with a ha-a-tful o' money?" insinuated Levi.

"I've been thinking over that, but it wouldn't do, with my affairs in this state, it would not be honourable or straight. Put that quite aside."

Mr. Levi gaped at him for a moment solemnly, and turned suddenly, and, brute as he was, spit on the Turkey carpet. He was not, as you perceive, ceremonious; but he could not allow the baronet to see the laughter that without notice caught him for a moment, and could think of no better way to account for his turning away his head.

"That'sh wery honourable indeed," said the Jew, more solemn than ever; "and if you can't play in that direction, I'm afraid you're in queer shtreet."

The baronet was standing before Levi, and at these words from that dirty little oracle, a terrible chill stole up from his feet to the crown of his head. Like a frozen man he stood there, and the Jew saw that his very lips were white. Sir Richard feels, for the first time, actually, that he is ruined.

The young man tries to speak, twice. The big eyes of the Jew are staring up at the contortion. Sir Richard can see nothing but those two big fiery eyes; he turns quickly away and walks to the end of the room.

"There's just one fiddle-string left to play on," muses the Jew.

"For God's sake!" exclaims Sir Richard, turning about, in a voice you would not have known, and for fully a minute the room was so silent you could scarcely have believed that two men were breathing in it.

"Shir Richard, will you be so good as to come nearer a bit? There, that'sh the cheeshe. I brought thish 'ere thing."

It is a square parchment with a good deal of printed matter, and blanks, written in, and a law stamp fixed with an awful regularity, at the corner.

"Casht your eye over it," says Levi, coaxingly, as he pushes it over the table to the young gentleman, who is sitting now at the other side.

The young man looks at it, reads it, but just then, if it had been a page of "Robinson Crusoe," he could not have understood it.

"I'm not quite myself, I can't follow it; too much to think of. What is it?"

"A bond and warrant to confess judgment."

"What is it for?"

"Ten thoushand poundsh."

"Sign it, shall I? Can you do anything with it?"

"Don't raishe your voishe, but lishten. Your friend"—and at the phrase Mr. Levi winked mysteriously—"has enough to do it twishe over; and upon my shoul, I'll shwear on the book, azh I hope to be shaved, it will never shee the light; he'll never raishe a pig on it, sho' 'elp me, nor let it out of hish 'ands, till he givesh it back to you. He can't ma-ake no ushe of it; I knowshe him well, and he'll pay you the ten thoushand to-morrow morning, and he wantsh to shake handsh with you, and make himself known to you, and talk a bit."

"But—but my signature wouldn't satisfy him," began Sir Richard bewildered.

"Oh! no—no, no?" murmured Mr. Levi, fiddling with the corner of the bank's reminder which lay on the table.

"Mr. Longcluse won't sign it," said Sir Richard.

Mr. Levi threw himself back in his chair, and looked with a roguish expression still upon the table, and gave the corner of the note a little fillip.

"Well," said Levi, after both had been some time silent, "it ain't much, only to write his name on the penshil line, there, you see, and there—he shouldn't make no bonesh about it. Why, it's done every day. Do you think I'd help in a thing of the short if there was any danger? The Sheneral's come to town, is he? What are you afraid of? Don't you be a shild—ba-ah!"

All this Mr. Levi said so low that it was as if he were whispering to the table, and he kept looking down as he put the parchment over to Sir Richard, who took it in his hand, and the bond trembled so much that he set it down again.

"Leave it with me," he said faintly.

Levi got up with an unusual hectic in each cheek, and his eyes very brilliant.

"I'll meet you what time you shay to-night; you had besht take a little time. It'sh ten now. Three hoursh will do it. I'll go on to my offish by one o'clock, and you come any time from one to two."

Sir Richard was trembling.

"Between one and two, mind. Hang it! Shir Richard, don't you be a fool about nothing," whispers the Jew, as black as thunder.

He is fumbling in his breast-pocket, and pulling out a sheaf of letters; he selects one, which he throws upon the parchment that lies open on the table.

"That'sh the note you forgot in my offish yeshterday, with hish name shined to it. There, now you have everything."

Without any form of valediction, the Jew had left the room. Sir Richard sits with his teeth set, and a strange frown upon his face, scarcely breathing. He hears the cab drive away. Before him on the table lie the papers.

CHAPTER LXVIII.

SIR RICHARD'S RESOLUTION.

Two hours had passed, and more, of solitude. With a candle in his hand, and his hat and great-coat on, Sir Richard Arden came out into the hall. His trap awaited him at the door.

In the interval of his solitude, something incredible has happened to him. It is over. A spectral secret accompanies him henceforward. A devil sits in his pocket, in that parchment. He dares not think of himself. Something sufficient to shake the world of London, and set all English Christian tongues throughout the earth wagging on one theme, has happened.

Does he repent? One thing is certain: he dares not falter. Something within him once or twice commanded him to throw his crime into the fire, while yet it is obliterable. But what then? what of to-morrow? Into that sheer black sea of ruin, that reels and yawns as deep as eye can fathom beneath him, he must dive and see the light no more. Better his chance.

He won't think of what he has done, of what he is going to do. He suspects his courage: he dares not tempt his cowardice. Braver, perhaps, it would have been to meet the worst at once. But surely, according to the theory of chances, we have played the true game. Is not a little time gained, everything? Are we not in friendly hands? Has not that little scoundrel committed himself, by an all but actual participation in the affair? It can never come to that. "I have only to confess, and throw myself at Uncle David's feet, and the one dangerous debt would instantly be brought up and cancelled."

These thoughts came vaguely, and on his heart lay an all but insupportable load. The sight of the staircase reminded him that Alice must long since have gone to her room. He yearned to see her and say good-night. It was the last farewell that the brother she had known from her childhood till now should ever speak or look. That brother was to die to-night, and a spirit of guilt to come in his stead.

He taps lightly at her door. She is asleep. He opens it, and dimly sees her innocent head upon the pillow. If his shadow were cast upon her dream, what an image would she have seen looking in at the door! A sudden horror seizes him—

he draws back and closes the door; on the lobby he pauses. It was a last moment of grace. He stole down the stairs, mounted his tax-cart, took the reins from his servant in silence, and drove swiftly into town. In Parliament Street, near the corner of the street leading to Levi's office, they passed a policeman, lounging on the flagway. Richard Arden is in a strangely nervous state; he fancies he will stop and question him, and he touches the horse with the whip to get quickly by.

In his breast-pocket he carried his ghastly secret. A pretty business if he happened to be thrown out, and a policeman should make an inventory of his papers, as he lay insensible in an hospital—a pleasant thing if he were robbed in these villanous streets, and the bond advertised, for a reward, by a pretended finder. A nice thing, good heaven! if it should wriggle and slip its way out of his pocket, in the jolting and tremble of the drive, and fall into London hands, either rascally or severe. He pulled up, and gave the reins to the servant, and felt, however gratefully, with his fingers, the crisp crumple of the parchment under the cloth! Did his servant look at him oddly as he gave him the reins? Not he; but Sir Richard began to suspect him and everything. He made him stop near the angle of the street, and there he got down, telling him rather savagely—for his fancied look was still in the baronet's brain—not to move an inch from that spot.

It was half-past one as his steps echoed down the street in which Mr. Levi had his office. There was a figure leaning with its back in the recess of Levi's door, smoking. Sir Richard's temper was growing exasperated.

It was Levi himself. Upstairs they stumble in the dark. Mr. Levi has not said a word. He is not treating his visitor with much ceremony. He lets himself into his office, secured with a heavy iron bar, and a lock that makes a great clang, and proceeds to light a candle. The flame expands and the light shows well-barred shutters, and the familiar objects.

When Mr. Levi had lighted a second candle, he fixed his great black eyes on the young baronet, who glances over his shoulder at the door, but the Jew has secured it. Their eyes meet for a moment, and Sir Richard places his hand nervously in his breast-pocket and takes out the parchment. Levi nods and extends his hand. Each now holds it by a corner, and as Sir Richard lets it go hesitatingly, he says faintly—

"Levi, you wouldn't—you could not run any risk with that?"

Levi stands by his great iron safe, with the big key in his hand. He nods in reply, and locking up the document, he knocks his knuckles on the iron door, with a long and solemn wink.

"Sha-afe!—that'sh the word," says he, and then he drops the keys into his pocket again.

There was a silence of a minute or more. A spell was stealing over them; an influence was in the room. Each eyed the other, shrinkingly, as a man might eye an assassin. The Jew knew that there was danger in that silence; and yet he could not break it. He could not disturb the influence acting on Richard Arden's mind. It was his good angel's last pleading, before the long farewell.

In a dreadful whisper Richard Arden speaks:—

"Give me that parchment back," says he.

Satan finds his tongue again.

"Give it back?" repeats Levi, and a pause ensues. "Of course I'll give it back; and I wash my hands of it and you, and you're throwing away ten thoushand poundsh for nothing."

Levi was taking out his keys as he spoke, and as he fumbled them over one by one, he said—

"You'll want a lawyer in the Insholwent Court, and you'd find Mishter Sholomonsh azh shatisfactory a shengleman azh any in London. He'sh an auctioneer, too; and there'sh no good in your meetin' that friendly cove here to-morrow, for he'sh one o' them honourable chaps, and he'll never look at you after your schedule's lodged, and the shooner that'sh done the better; and them women we was courting, won't they laugh!"

Hereupon, with great alacrity, Mr. Levi began to apply the key to the lock.

"Don't mind. Keep it; and mind, you d——d little swindler, so sure as you stand there, if you play me a trick, I'll blow your brains out, if it were in the police-office!"

Mr. Levi looked hard at him, and nodded. He was accustomed to excited language in certain situations.

"Well," said he coolly, a second time returning the keys to his pocket, "your friend will be here at twelve to-morrow, and if you please him as well as he expects, who knows wha-at may be? If he leavesh you half hish money, you'll not 'ave many bill transhactionsh on your handsh."

"May God Almighty have mercy on me!" groans Sir Richard, hardly above his breath.

"You shall have the cheques then. He'll be here all right."

"I—I forget; did you say an hour?"

Levi repeats the hour. Sir Richard walks slowly to the stairs, down which Levi lights him. Neither speaks.

In a few minutes more the young gentleman is driving rapidly to his town house, where he means to end that long-remembered night.

When he had got to his room, and dismissed his valet, he sat down. He looked round, and wondered how collected he now was. The situation seemed like a dream, or his sense of danger had grown torpid. He could not account for the strange indifference that had come over him. He got quickly into bed. It was late, and he exhausted, and aided, I know not by what narcotic, he slept a constrained, odd sleep—black as Erebus—the thread of which snaps suddenly, and he is awake with a heart beating fast, as if from a sudden start. A hard bitter voice has said close by the pillow, "You are the first Arden that ever did that!" and with these words grating in his ears, he awoke, and had a confused remembrance of having been dreaming of his father.

Another dream, later on, startled him still more. He was in Levi's office, and while they were talking over the horrid document, in a moment it blew out of the window; and a lean, ill-looking man, in a black coat, like the famous person who, in old woodcuts, picked up the shadow of Peter Schlemel, caught the parchment from the pavement, and with his eyes fixed corner-wise upon him, and a dreadful smile, tapped his long finger on the bond, and with wide paces stepped swiftly away with it in his hand.

Richard Arden started up in his bed; the cold moisture of terror was upon his forehead, and for a moment he did not know where he was, or how much of his vision was real. The grey twilight of early morning was over the town. He welcomed the light; he opened the window-shutters wide. He looked from the window down upon the street. A lean man with tattered black, with a hammer in his hand, just as the man in his dream had held the roll of parchment, was slowly stepping with long strides away from his house, along the street.

As his thoughts cleared, his panic increased. Nothing had happened between the time of his lying down and his up-rising to alter his situation, and the same room sees him now half mad.

CHAPTER LXIX.

THE MEETING.

Near the appointed hour, he walked across the park, and through the Horse Guards, and in a few minutes more was between the tall old-fashioned houses of the street in which Mr. Levi's office is to be found. He passes by a dingy hired coach, with a tarnished crest on the door, and sees two Jewish-looking men inside, both smiling over some sly joke. Whose door are they waiting at? He supposes another Jewish office seeks the shade of that pensive street.

Mr. Levi opened his office door for his handsome client. They were quite to themselves. Mr. Levi did not look well. He received him with a nod. He shut the door when Sir Richard was in the room.

"He'sh not come yet. We'll talk to him inshide." He indicates the door of the inner room, with a little side jerk of his head. "That'sh private. He hazh that—thing all right."

Sir Richard says nothing. He follows Levi into a small inner room, which had, perhaps, originally been a lady's boudoir, and had afterwards, one might have conjectured, served as the treasury of cash and jewels of a pawn-office; for its door was secured with iron bars, and two great locks, and the windows were well barred with iron. There were two huge iron safes in the room, built into the wall.

"I'll show you a beauty of a dresshing-ca-ashe," said Levi, rousing himself; "I'll shell it a dead bargain, and give time for half, if you knowsh any young shwell as wantsh such a harticle. Look here; it was made for the Duchess of Horleans—all in gold, hemerald, and brilliantsh."

And thus haranguing, he displayed its contents, and turned them over, staring on them with a livid admiration. Sir Richard is not thinking of the duchess's dressing-case, nor is he much more interested when Mr. Levi goes on to tell him, "There'sh three executions against peersh out thish week—two gone down to the country. Sholomonsh nobbled Lord Bylkington's carriage outshide Shyner's at two o'clock in the morning, and his lordship had to walk home in the rain;" and Levi laughs and wriggles pleasantly over the picture. "I think he'sh coming," says Levi suddenly, inclining his ear toward the door. He looked back over his shoulder with an odd look, a little stern, at the young gentleman.

"Who?" asked the young man, a little uncertain, in consequence of the character of that look.

"Your—that—your friend, of course," said Levi, with his eyes again averted, and his ear near the door.

It was a moment of trepidation and of hope to Richard Arden. He hears the steps of several persons in the next room. Levi opens a little bit of the door, and peeps through, and with a quick glance towards the baronet, he whispers, "Ay, it's him."

Oh, blessed hope! here comes, at last, a powerful friend to take him by the hand, and draw him, in his last struggle, from the whirlpool.

Sir Richard glances towards the door through which the Jew is still looking, and signing with his hand as, little by little, he opens it wider and wider; and a voice in the next room, at sound of which Sir Richard starts to his feet, says sharply, "Is all right?"

"All right," replies Levi, getting aside; and Mr. Longcluse entered the room and shut the door.

His pale face looked paler than usual, his thin cruel lips were closed, his nostrils dilated with a terrible triumph, and his eyes were fixed upon Arden, as he held the fatal parchment in his hand.

Levi saw a scowl so dreadful contract Sir Richard Arden's face—was it pain, or was it fury?—that, drawing back as far as the wall would let him, he almost screamed, "It ain't me!—it ain't my fault!—I can't help it!—I couldn't!—I can't!" His right hand was in his pocket, and his left, trembling violently, extended toward him, as if to catch his arm.

But Richard Arden was not thinking of him—did not hear him. He was overpowered. He sat down in his chair. He leaned back with a gasp and a faint laugh, like a man just overtaken by a wave, and lifted half-drowned from the sea. Then, with a sudden cry, he threw his hands and head on the table.

There was no token of relenting in Longcluse's cruel face. There was a contemptuous pleasure in it. He did not remove his eyes from that spectacle of abasement as he replaced the parchment in his pocket. There is a silence of about a minute, and Sir Richard sits up and says vaguely,—

"Thank God, it's over! Take me away; I'm ready to go."

"You shall go, time enough; I have a word to say first," said Longcluse, and he signs to the Jew to leave them.

On being left to themselves, the first idea that struck Sir Richard was the wild one of escape. He glanced quickly at the window. It was barred with iron. There were men in the next room—he could not tell how many—and he was without arms. The hope lighted up, and almost at the same moment expired.

CHAPTER LXX.

MR. LONGCLUSE PROPOSES.

"Clear your head," says Mr. Longcluse, sternly, seating himself before Sir Richard, with the table between; "you must conceive a distinct idea of your situation, Sir, and I shall then tell you something that remains. You have committed a forgery under aggravated circumstances, for which I shall have you convicted and sentenced to penal servitude at the next sessions. I have been a good friend to you on many occasions; you have been a false one to me—who baser?—and while I was anonymously helping you with large sums of money, you forged my name to a legal instrument for ten thousand pounds, to swindle your unknown benefactor, little suspecting who he was."

Longcluse smiled.

"I have heard how you spoke of me. I'm an adventurer, a leg, an assassin, a person whom you were compelled to drop; rather a low person, I fear, if a felon can't afford to sit beside me! You were always too fine a man for me. Your get up was always peculiar; you were famous for that. It will soon be more singular still, when your hair and your clothes are cut after the fashion of the great world you are about to enter. How your friends will laugh!"

Sir Richard heard all this with a helpless stare.

"I have only to stamp on the ground, to call up the men who will accomplish your transformation. I can change your life by a touch, into convict dress, diet, labour, lodging, for the rest of your days. What plea have you to offer to my mercy?"

Sir Richard would have spoken, but his voice failed him. With a second effort, however, he said—"Would it not be more manly if you let me meet my fate, without this."

"And you are such an admirable judge of what is manly, or even gentleman-like!" said Longcluse. "Now, mind, I shall arrest you in five minutes, on your three over-due bills. The men with the writ are in the next room. I sha'n't immediately arrest you for the forgery. That shall hang over you. I mean to make you, for a while, my instrument. Hear, and understand; I mean to marry your sister. She don't like me, but she suits me; I have chosen her, and I'll not be baulked. When that is accomplished, you are safe. No man likes to see his brother a spectacle of British justice, with cropped hair, and a log to his foot. I may hate and despise you, as you deserve, but that would not do. Failing that, however, you shall have justice, I promise you. The course I propose taking is this: you shall be arrested here, for debt. You will be good enough to allow the people who take you, to select your present place of confinement. It is arranged. I will then, by a note, appoint a place of meeting for this evening, where I shall instruct you as to the particulars of that course of conduct I prescribe for you. If you mean to attempt an escape, you had better try it now; I will give you fourteen hours' start, and undertake to catch and bring you back to London as a forger. If you make up your mind to submit to fate, and do precisely as you are ordered, you may emerge. But on the slightest evasion, prevarication, or default, the blow descends. In the meantime we treat each other civilly before these people. Levi is in my hands, and you, I presume, keep your own secret."

"That is all?" inquired Sir Richard, faintly, after a minute's silence.

"All for the present," was the reply; "you will see more clearly, by-and-by, that you are my property, and you will act accordingly."

The two Jewish-looking gentlemen, whom Richard had passed in a conference in their carriage which stood now at the steps of the house, were the sheriff's officers destined to take charge of the fallen gentleman, and convey him, by Levi's direction, to a "sponging house," which, I believe, belonged jointly to him and his partner, Mr. Goldshed.

It was on the principle, perhaps, on which hunters tame wild beasts, by a sojourn at the bottom of a pit-fall, that Mr. Longcluse doomed the young baronet to some ten hours' solitary contemplation of his hopeless immeshment in that castle of Giant Despair, before taking him out and setting him again before him, for the purpose of instructing him in the conditions and duties of the direful life on which he was about to enter.

Mr. Longcluse left the baronet suddenly, and returned to Levi's office no more.

Sir Richard's rôle was cast. He was to figure, at least first, as a captive in the drama for which fate had selected him. He had no wish to retard the progress of the piece. Nothing more odious than his present situation was likely to come.

"You have something to say to me?" said the baronet, making tender, as it were, of himself. The offer was, obligingly, accepted, and the sheriffs, by his lieutenants, made prisoner of Sir Richard Arden, who strode down the stairs between them, and entered the seedy coach, and sitting as far back as he could, drove rapidly toward the City.

Stunned and confused, there was but one image vividly present to his recollection, and that was the baleful face of Walter Longcluse.

CHAPTER LXXI.

NIGHT.

At about eight o'clock that evening, a hurried note reached Alice Arden, at Mortlake. It was from her brother, and said,—

"MY DARLING ALICE,

"I can't get away from town to-night, I am overwhelmed with business; but to-morrow, before dinner, I hope to see you, and stay at Mortlake till next morning.—Your affectionate brother,

"Dick."

The house was quiet earlier than in former times, when Sir Reginald, of rakish memory, was never in his bed till past three o'clock in the morning. Mortlake was an early house now, and all was still by a quarter past eleven. The last candle burning was usually that in Mrs. Tansey's room. She had not yet gone to bed, and was still in "the housekeeper's room," when a tapping came at the window. It reminded her of Mr. Longcluse's visit on the night of the funeral.

She was now the only person up in the house, except Alice, who was at the far side of the building, where, in the next room, her maid was in bed asleep. Alice, who sat at her dressing-table, reading, with her long rich hair dishevelled over her shoulders, was, of course, quite out of hearing.

Martha went to the window with a little frown of uncertainty. Opening a bit of the shutter, she saw Sir Richard's face close to her. Was ever old housekeeper so pestered by nightly tappings at her window-pane?

"La! who'd a thought o' seeing you, Master Richard! why, you told Miss Alice you'd not be here till to-morrow!" she says pettishly, holding the candle high above her head.

He makes a sign of caution to her, and placing his lips near the pane, says,—

"Open the window the least bit in life."

With a dark stare in his face, she obeys. An odd approach, surely, for a master to make to his own house!

"No one up in the house but you?" he whispers, as soon as the window is open.

"Not one!"

"Don't say a word, only listen: come, softly, round to the hall-door, and let me in; and light those candles there, and bring them with you to the hall. Don't let a creature know I have been here, and make no noise for your life!"

The old woman nodded with the same little frown; and he, pointing toward the hall door, walks away silently in that direction.

"What makes you look so white and dowley?" mutters the old woman, as she secures the window, and bars the shutters again.

"Good creature!" whispers Sir Richard, as he enters the hall, and places his hand kindly on her shoulder, and with a very dark look; "you have always been true to me, Martha, and I depend on your good sense; not a word of my having been here to any one—not to Miss Alice! I have to search for papers. I shall be here but an hour or so. Don't lock or bar the door, mind, and get to your bed! Don't come up this way again—good-night!"

"Won't you have some supper?"

"No, thanks."

"A glass of sherry and a bit o' something?"

"Nothing."

And he places his hand on her shoulder gently, and looks toward the corridor that led to her room; then taking up one of the candles she had left alight on the table in the hall, he says,—

"I'll give you a light," and he repeats, with a wondrous heavy sigh, "Good-night, dear old Martha."

"God bless ye, Master Dick. Ye must chirp up a bit, mind," she says very kindly, with an earnest look in her face. "I'm getting to rest—ye needn't fear me walkin' about to trouble ye. But ye must be careful to shut the hall-door close. I agree, as it is a thing to be done; but ye must also knock at my bed-room window when ye've gane out, for I must get up, and lock the door, and make a' safe; and don't ye forget, Master Richard, what I tell ye."

He held the candle at the end of the corridor, down which the wiry old woman went quickly; and when he returned to the hall, and set the candle down again, he felt faint. In his ears are ever the terrible words: "Mind, I take command of the house, I dispose of and appoint the servants; I don't appear, you do all ostensibly—but from garret to cellar, I'm master. I'll look it over, and tell you what is to be done."

Sir Richard roused himself, and having listened at the staircase, he very softly opened the hall-door. The spire of the old church showed hoar in the moonlight. At the left, from under a deep shadow of elms, comes silently a tall figure, and softly ascends the hall-door steps. The door is closed gently.

Alice sitting at her dressing-table, half an hour later, thought she heard steps—lowered her book, and listened. But no sound followed. Again the same light footfalls disturbed her—and again, she was growing nervous. Once more she heard them, very stealthily, and now on the same floor on which her room was. She stands up breathless. There is no noise now. She was thinking of waking her maid, but she remembered that she and Louisa Diaper had in a like alarm, discovered old Martha, only two or three nights before, poking about the china-closet, dusting and counting, at one o'clock in the morning, and had then exacted a promise that she would visit that repository no more, except at seasonable hours. But old Martha was so pig-headed, and would take it for granted that she was fast asleep, and would rather fidget through the house and poke up everything at that hour than at any other.

Quite persuaded of this, Alice takes her candle, determined to scold that troublesome old thing, against whom she is fired with the irritation that attends on a causeless fright. She walks along the gallery quickly, in slippers, flowing dressing-gown and hair, with her candle in her hand, to the head of the stairs, through the great window of which the moonlight streams brightly. Through the keyhole of the door at the opposite side, a ray of candlelight is visible, and from this room opens the china-closet, which is no doubt the point of attraction for the troublesome visitant. Holding the candle high in her left hand, Alice opens the door.

What she sees is this—a pair of candles burning on a small table, on which, with a pencil, Mr. Longcluse is drawing, it seems, with care, a diagram; at the same moment he raises his eyes, and Richard Arden, who is standing with one hand placed on the table over which he is leaning a little, looks quickly round, and rising walks straight to the door, interposing between her and Longcluse.

"Oh, Alice? You didn't expect me: I'm very busy, looking for—looking over papers. Don't mind."

He had placed his hands gently on her shoulders, and she receded as he advanced.

"Oh! it don't matter. I thought—I thought—I did not know."

She was smiling her best. She was horrified. He looked like a ghost. Alice was gazing piteously in his face, and with a little laugh, she began to cry convulsively.

"What is the matter with the little fool! There, there—don't, don't—nonsense!"

With an effort she recovered herself.

"Only a little startled, Dick; I did not think you were there—good-night."

And she hastened back to her chamber, and locked the door; and running into her maid's room, sat down on the side of her bed, and wept hysterically. To the imploring inquiries of her maid, she repeated only the words, "I am frightened," and left her in a startled perplexity.

She knew that Longcluse had seen her, and he, that she had seen him. Their eyes had met. He saw with a bleak rage the contracting look of horror, so nearly hatred, that she fixed on him for a breathless moment. There was a tremor of fury at his heart, as if it could have sprung at her, from his breast, at her throat, and murdered her; and—she looked so beautiful! He gazed with an idolatrous admiration. Tears were welling to his eyes, and yet he would have laughed to see her weltering on the floor. A madman for some tremendous seconds!

CHAPTER LXXII.

MEASURES.

About twelve o'clock next day Richard Arden showed himself at Mortlake. It was a beautiful autumnal day, and the mellow sun fell upon a foliage that was fading into russet and yellow. Alice was looking out from the open window, on the noble old timber whose wide-spread boughs and thinning leaves caught the sunbeams pleasantly. She had heard her brother and his companion go down the stairs, and saw them, from the window, walk quickly down the avenue, till the trees hid them from view. She thought that some of the servants were up, and that the door was secured on their departure; and the effect of the shock she had received gradually subsiding, she looked to her next interview with her brother for an explanation of the occurrence which had so startled her.

That interview was approaching; the cab drove up to the steps, and her brother got out. Anxiously she looked, but no one followed him, and the driver shut the cab-door. Sir Richard kissed his hand to her, as she stood in the window.

From the hall the house opens to the right and left, in two suites of rooms. The room in which Alice stood was called the sage-room, from its being hung in sage-green leather, stamped in gold. It is a small room to the left, and would answer very prettily for a card party or a tête-à-tête. Alice had her work, her books, and her music there; she liked it because the room was small and cheery.

The door opened, and her brother comes in.

"Good Dick, to come so early! welcome, darling," she said, putting her arms about his neck, as he stooped and kissed her, smiling.

He looked very ill, and his smile was painful.

"That was an odd little visit I paid last night," said he, with his dark eyes fixed on her, inquiringly she thought—"very late—quite unexpected. You are quite well to-day?—you look flourishing."

"I wish I could say as much for you, Dick; I'm afraid you are tiring yourself to death."

"I had some one with me last night," said Sir Richard, with his eye still upon her; "I—I don't know whether you perceived that."

Alice looked away, and then said carelessly, but very gravely—

"I did—I saw Mr. Longcluse. I could not believe my eyes, Dick. You must promise me one thing."

"What is that?"

"That he sha'n't come into this house any more—while I am here, I mean."

"That is easily promised," said he.

"And what did he come about, Dick?"

"Oh! he came—he came—I thought I told you; he came about papers. I did not tell you; but he has, after all, turned out very friendly. He is going to do me a very important service."

She looked very much surprised.

The young man glanced through the window, to which he walked; he seemed embarrassed, and then turning to her, he said peevishly—

"You seem to think, Alice, that one can never make a mistake, or change an opinion."

"But I did not say so; only, Dick, I must tell you that I have such a horror of that man—a terror of him—as nothing can ever get over."

"I'm to blame for that."

"No, I can't say you are. I don't mind stories so much as ——"

"As what?"

"As looks."

"Looks! Why, you used to think him a gentlemanly-looking fellow, and so he is."

"Looks and language," said Alice.

"I thought he was a very civil fellow."

"I sha'n't dispute anything. I suppose you have found him a good friend after all, as you say."

"As good a friend as most men," said Sir Richard, growing pale; "they all act from interest: where interests are the same, men are friends. But he has saved me from a great deal, and he may do more; and I believe I was too hasty about those stories, and I think you were right when you refused to believe them without proof."

"I daresay—I don't know—I believe my senses—and all I say is this, if Mr. Longcluse is to come here any more, I must go. He is no gentleman, I think—that is, I can't describe how I dislike him—how I hate him! I'm afraid of him! Dick, you look ill and unhappy: what's the matter?"

"I'm well enough—I'm better; we shall be better—all better by-and-by. I wish the next five weeks were over! We must leave this, we must go to Arden Court; I will send some of the servants there first. I am going to tell them now, they must get the house ready. You shall keep your maid here with you; and when all is ready in Yorkshire, we shall be off—Alice, Alice, don't mind me—I'm miserable—mad!" he says suddenly, and covers his face with his hands, and, for the first time for years, he is crying bitter tears.

Alice was by his side, alarmed, curious, grieved; and with all these emotions mingling in her dark eyes and beautiful features, as she drew his hand gently away, with a rush of affectionate entreaties and inquiries.

"It is all very fine, Alice," he exclaims, with a sudden bitterness; "but I don't believe, to save me from destruction, you would sacrifice one of your least caprices, or reconcile one of your narrowest prejudices."

"What can you mean, dear Richard? only tell me how I can be of any use. You can't mean, of course ——"

She stops with a startled look at him. "You know, dear Dick, that was always out of the question: and surely you have heard that Lord Wynderbroke is to be married to Grace Maubray? It is all settled."

Quite another thought had been in Richard's mind, but he was glad to accept Alice's conjecture.

"Yes, so it is—so, at least, it is said to be—but I am so worried and distracted, I half forget things. Girls are such jolly fools; they throw good men away, and lose themselves. What is to become of you, Alice, if things go wrong with me! I think the old times were best, when the old people settled who was to marry whom, and there was no disputing their decision, and marriages were just as happy, and courtships a great deal simpler; and I am very sure there were fewer secret repinings, and broken hearts, and—threadbare old maids. Don't you be a fool, Alice; mind what I say."

He is leaving the room, but pauses at the door, and returns and places his hand on her arm, looking in her face, and says—

"Yes, mind what I say, for God's sake, and we may all be a great deal happier."

He kisses her, and is gone. Her eyes follow him, as she thinks with a sigh—

"How strange Dick is growing! I'm afraid he has been playing again, and losing. It must have been something very urgent that induced him to make it up again with that low malignant man; and this break-up, and journey to Arden Court! I think I should prefer being there. There is something ominous about this place, picturesque as it is, and much as I like it. But the journey to Yorkshire is only another of the imaginary excursions Dick has been proposing every fortnight; and next year, and the year after, will find us, I suppose, just where we are."

But this conjecture, for once, was mistaken. It was, this time, a veritable break-up and migration; for Martha Tansey came in, with the importance of a person who has a matter of moment to talk over.

"Here's something sudden, Miss Alice; I suppose you've heard. Off to Arden Court in the mornin'. Crozier and me; the footman discharged, and you to follow with Master Richard in a week."

"Oh, then, it is settled. Well, Martha, I am not sorry, and I daresay you and Crozier won't be sorry to see old Yorkshire faces again, and the Court, and the rookery, and the orchard."

"I don't mind; glad enough to see a'ad faces, but I'm a bit o'er a'ad myself for such sudden flittins, and Manx and Darwent, and the rest, is to go by night train to-morrow, and not a housemaid left in Mortlake. But Master Richard says a's provided, and 'twill be but a few days after a's done; and ye'll be down, then, at Arden by the middle o' next week, and I'm no sa sure the change mayn't serve ye; and as your uncle, Master David, and Lady May Penrose, and Miss Maubray—a strackle-brained lass she is, I doubt—and to think o' that a'ad fule, Lord Wynderbroke, takin' sich a young, bonny hizzy to wife! La bless ye, she'll play the hangment wi' that a'ad gowk of a lord, and all his goold guineas won't do. His kist o' money won't hod na time, I warrant ye, when once that lassie gets her pretty fingers under the lid. There'll be gaains on in that house, I warrant, not but he's a gude man, and a fine gentleman as need be," she added, remembering her own strenuous counsel in his favour, when he was supposed to be paying his court to Alice; "and if he was mated wi' a gude lassie, wi' gude blude in her veins, would doubtless keep as honourable a house, and hod his head as high as any lord o' them a'. But as I was saying, Miss Alice, now that Master David, and Lady May, and Miss Maubray, has left Lunnon, there's no one here to pay ye a visit, and ye'd be fairly buried alive here in Mortlake, and ye'll be better, and sa will we a', down at Arden, for a bit; and there's gentle folk down there as gude as ever rode in Lunnon streets, mayhap, and better; and mony a squire, that ony leddy in the land might be proud to marry, and not one but would be glad to match wi' an Arden."

"That is a happy thought," said Alice, laughing.

"And so it is, and no laughing matter," said Martha, a little offended, as she stalked out of the room, and closed the door, grandly, after her.

"And God bless you, dear old Martha," said the young lady, looking towards the door through which she had just passed; "the truest and kindest soul on earth."

Sir Richard did not come back. She saw him no more that evening.

CHAPTER LXXIII.

AT THE BAR OF THE "GUY OF WARWICK."

Next evening there came, not Richard, but a note saying that he would see Alice the moment he could get away from town. As the old servant departed northward, her solitude for the first time began to grow irksome, and as the night approached, worse even than gloomy.

Her extemporised household made her laugh. It was not even a skeleton establishment. The kitchen department had dwindled to a single person, who ordered her luncheon and dinner, only two or three plats, daily, from the "Guy of Warwick." The housemaid's department was undertaken by a single servant, a short, strong woman of some sixty years of age.

This person puzzled Alice a good deal. She came to her, like the others, with a note from her brother, stating her name, and that he had engaged her for the few days they meant to remain roughing it at Mortlake, and that he had received a very good account of her.

This woman has not a bad countenance. There is, indeed, no tenderness in it; but there is a sort of hard good-humour. There are quickness and resolution. She talks fluently of herself and her qualifications, and now and then makes a short curtsey. But she takes no notice of any one of Alice's questions.

A silence sometimes follows, during which Alice repeats her interrogatory perhaps twice, with growing indignation, and then the new comer breaks into a totally independent talk, and leaves the young lady wondering at her disciplined impertinence. It was not till her second visit that she enlightened her.

"I did not send for you. You can go!" said Alice.

"I don't like a house that has children in it, they gives a deal o' trouble," said the woman.

"But I say you may go; you must go, please."

The woman looked round the room.

"When I was with Mrs. Montgomery, she had five, three girls and two boys; la! there never was five such ——"

"Go, this moment, please, I insist on your going; do you hear me, pray?"

But so far from answering, or obeying, this cool intruder continues her harangue before Miss Arden gets half way to the end of her little speech.

"That woman was the greatest fool alive—nothing but spoiling and petting—I could not stand it no longer, so I took Master Tommy by the lug, and pulled him out of the kitchen, the limb, along the passage to the stairs, every inch, and I gave him a slap in the face, the fat young rascal; you could hear all over the house! and didn't he rise the roof! So missus and me, we quarrelled upon it."

"If you don't leave the room, I must; and I shall tell my brother, Sir Richard, how you have behaved yourself; and you may rely upon it ——"

But here again she is overpowered by the strong voice of her visitor.

"It was in my next place, at Mr. Crump's, I took cold in my head, very bad, Miss, indeed, looking out of window to see two fellows fighting, in the lane—in both ears—and so I lost my hearing, and I've been deaf as a post ever since!"

Alice could not resist a laugh at her own indignant eloquence quite thrown away; and she hastily wrote with a pencil on a slip of paper:—

"Please don't come to me except when I send for you."

"La! Ma'am, I forgot!" exclaims the woman, when she had examined it; "my orders was not to read any of your writing."

"Not to read any of my writing!" said Alice, amazed; "then, how am I to tell you what I wish about anything?" she inquires, for the moment forgetting that not one word of her question was heard. The woman makes a curtsey and retires. "What can Richard have meant by giving her such a direction? I'll ask him when he comes."

It was likely enough that the woman had misunderstood him, still she began to wish the little interval destined to be passed at Mortlake before her journey to Yorkshire, ended.

She told her maid, Louisa Diaper, to go down to the kitchen and find out all she could as to what people were in the house, and what duties they had undertaken, and when her brother was likely to arrive.

Louisa Diaper, slim, elegant, and demure, descended among these barbarous animals. She found in the kitchen, unexpectedly, a male stranger, a small, slight man, with great black eyes, a big sullen mouth, a sallow complexion, and a profusion of black ringlets. The deaf woman was conning over some writing of his on a torn-off blank leaf of a letter, and he was twiddling about the pencil, with which he had just traced it, in his fingers, and, in a singing drawl, holding forth to the other woman, who, with a long and high canvas apron on, and the handle of an empty saucepan in her right hand, stood gaping at him, with her arms hanging by her sides.

On the appearance of Miss Diaper, Mr. Levi, for he it was, directs his solemn conversation to that young lady.

"I was just telling them about the robberies in the City and Wesht Hend. La! there'sh bin nothin' like it for twenty year. They don't tell them in the papersh, blesh ye! The 'ome Shecretary takesh precious good care o' that; they don't want to frighten every livin' shoul out of London. But there'll be talk of it in Parliament,

I promish you. I know three opposition membersh myshelf that will move the 'oushe upon it next session."

Mr. Levi wagged his head darkly as he made this political revelation.

"Thish day twel'month the number o' burglariesh in London and the West Hend, including Hizzlington, was no more than fifteen and a half a night; and two robberiesh attended with wiolensh. What wazh it lasht night? I have it in confidensh, from the polishe offish thish morning."

He pulled a pocket-book, rather greasy, from his breast, and from this depositary, it is to be presumed, of statistical secrets, he read the following official memorandum:—

"Number of 'oushes burglarioushly hentered lasht night, including private banksh, charitable hinshtitutions, shops, lodging-'oushes, female hacadamies, and private dwellings, and robbed with more or less wiolench, one thoushand sheven hundred and shixty-sheven. We regret to hadd," he continued, the official return stealing, as it proceeded, gradually into the style of "The Pictorial Calendar of British Crime," a half-penny paper which he took in—"this hinundation of crime seems flowing, or rayther rushing northward, and hazh already enweloped Hizhlington, where a bald-headed clock and watch maker, named Halexander Goggles, wazh murdered with his sheven shmall children, with unigshampled ba-arba-arity."

Mr. Levi eyed the women horribly all round as he ended the sentence, and he added,—

"Hizhlington'sh only down there. It ain't five minutesh walk; only a pleasant shtep; just enough to give a fellow azh has polished off a family there a happetite for another up here. Azh I 'ope to be shaved, I shleep every night with a pair of horshe pishtols, a blunderbush, and a shabre by my bed; and Shir Richard wantsh every door in the 'oushe fasht locked, and the keysh with him, before dark, thish evening, except only such doors as you want open; and he gave me a note to Miss Harden." And he placed the note in Miss Diaper's hand. "He wantsh the 'oushe a bit more schecure," he added, following her towards the hall. "He wishes to make you and she quite shafe, and out of harm's way, if anything should occur. It will be only a few days, you know, till you're both away."

The effect of this little alarm, accompanied by Sir Richard's note, was that Mr. Levi carried out a temporary arrangement, which assigned the suite of apartments in which Alice's room was as those to which she would restrict herself during the few days she was to remain there, the rest of the house, except the kitchen and a servant's room or two down-stairs, being locked up.

By the time Mr. Levi had got the keys together, and all safe in Mortlake, the sun had set, and in the red twilight that followed he set off in his cab towards town. At the "Guy of Warwick"—from the bar of which already was flaring a good broad gas-light—he stopped and got out. There was a full view of the bar from where he stood; and, pretending to rummage his pockets for something, he was looking in to see whether "the coast was clear."

"She's just your sort—not too bad and not too good—not too nashty, and not too nishe; a good-humoured lash, rough and ready, and knowsh a thing or two."

"Ye're there, are ye?" inquired Mr. Levi, playfully, as he crossed the door-stone, and placed his fists on the bar grinning.

"What will you take, Sir, please?" inquired the young woman, at one side of whom was the usual row of taps and pump-handles.

"Now, Miss Phœbe, give me a brandy and shoda, pleashe. When I talked to you in thish 'ere place 'tother night, you wished to engage for a lady's maid. What would you shay to me, if I was to get you a firsht-chop tip-top pla-ashe of the kind? Well, don't you shay a word—that brandy ain't fair measure—and I'll tell you. It'sh a la-ady of ra-ank! where wagesh ish no-o object; and two years' savings, and a good match with a well-to-do 'andsome young fellow, will set you hup in a better place than this 'ere."

"It comes very timely, Sir, for I'm to leave to-morrow, and I was thinking of going home to my uncle in a day or two, in Chester."

"Well it's all settled. Come you down to my offishe, you know where it is, to-morrow, at three, and I'll 'av all partickulars for you, and a note to the lady from her brother, the baronet; and if you be a good girl, and do as you're bid, you'll make a little fortune of it."

She curtsied, with her eyes very round, as he, with a wag of his head drank down what remained of his brandy and soda, and wiping his mouth with his glove, he said, "Three o'clock sha-arp, mind; good-bye, Phœbe, lass, and don't you forget all I said."

He stood ungallantly with his back towards her on the threshold lighting a cigar, and so soon as he had it in his own phrase, "working at high blast," he got into his cab, and jingled towards his office, with all his keys about him.

While Miss Arden remained all unconscious, and even a little amused at the strange shifts to which her brief stay and extemporised household at Mortlake exposed her, a wily and determined strategist was drawing his toils around her.

The process of isolation was nearly completed, without having once excited her suspicions; and, with the same perfidious skill, the house itself was virtually undergoing those modifications which best suited his designs.

Sir Richard appeared at his club as usual. He was compelled to do so. The all-seeing eye of his pale tyrant pursued him everywhere; he lived under terror. A dreadful agony all this time convulsed the man, within whose heart Longcluse suspected nothing but the serenity of death.

"What easier than to tell the story to the police. Meditated duresse. Compulsion. Infernal villain! And then: what then? A pistol to his head, a flash, and—darkness!"

CHAPTER LXXIV.

A LETTER.

Mr. Longcluse knocked at Sir Richard's house in May Fair, and sent up-stairs for the baronet. It was about the same hour at which Mr. Levi was drinking his thirsty potation of brandy and soda at the "Guy of Warwick." The streets were darker than that comparatively open place, and the gas lamp threw its red outline of the sashes upon the dark ceiling, as Mr. Longcluse stood in the drawing-room between the windows, in his great-coat, with his hat on, looking in the dark like an image made of fog.

Sir Richard Arden entered the room.

"You were not at Mortlake to-day," said he.

"No."

"There's a cab at the door that will take you there; your absence for a whole day would excite surmise. Don't stay more than five minutes, and don't mention Louisa Diaper's name, and account for the locking up of all the house, but one suite of rooms, I directed, and come to my house in Bolton Street, direct from Mortlake. That's all."

Without another word, Mr. Longcluse took his departure.

In this cavalier way, and in a cold tone that conveyed all the menace and insult involved in his ruined position, had this conceited young man been ordered about by his betrayer, on his cruel behests, ever since he had come under his dreadful rod. The iron trap that held him fast, locked him in a prison from which, except through the door of death, there seemed no escape.

Outraged pride, the terrors of suspense, the shame and remorse of his own enormous perfidy against his only sister, peopled it with spectres.

As he drove out to Mortlake, pale, frowning, with folded arms, his handsome face thinned and drawn by the cords of pain, he made up his mind. He knocked furiously at Mortlake Hall door. The woman in the canvas apron let him in. The strange face startled him; he had been thinking so intently of one thing. Going up, through the darkened house, with but one candle, and tapping at the door, on the floor above the drawing-room, within which Alice was sitting, with Louisa Diaper for company, and looking at her unsuspicious smile, he felt what a heinous conspirator he was.

He made an excuse for sending the maid to the next room after they had spoken a few words, and then he said,—

"Suppose, Alice, we were to change our plan, would you like to come abroad? Out of this you must come immediately." He was speaking low. "I am in great danger; I must go abroad. For your life, don't seem to suspect anything. Do exactly as I tell you, or else I am utterly ruined, and you, Alice, on your account, very miserable. Don't ask a question, or look a look, that may make Louisa Diaper suspect that you have any doubt as to your going to Arden, or any suspicion of any danger. She is quite true, but not wise, and your left hand must not know what your right hand is doing. Don't be frightened, only be steady and calm. Get together any jewels and money you have, and as little else as you can possibly manage with. Do this yourself; Louisa Diaper must know nothing of it. I will mature our plans, and to-morrow or next day I shall see you again; I can stay but a moment now, and have but time to bid you good-night."

Then he kissed her. How horribly agitated he looked! How cold was the pressure of his hand!

"Hush!" he whispered, and his dark eyes were fixed on the door through which he expected the return of the maid. And as he heard her step, "Not a word, remember!" he said; then bidding her good-night aloud, he quitted the room almost as suddenly as he had appeared, leaving her, for the first time, in the horrors of a growing panic.

Sir Richard leaned back in the cab as he drove into town. He had as yet no plan formed. It was a more complicated exploit than he was at the moment equal to. In Mortlake were two fellows, by way of protectors, placed there for security of the house and people.

These men held possession of the keys of the house, and sat and regaled themselves with their hot punch, or cold brandy and water, and pipes; always one awake, and with ears erect, they kept watch and ward in the room to the right of the hall-door, in which Sir Richard and Uncle David had conversed with the sad Mr. Plumes, on the evening after the old baronet's death. To effect Alice's escape, and reserve for himself a chance of accomplishing his own, was a problem demanding skill, cunning, and audacity.

While he revolved these things an alarm had been sounded in another quarter, which unexpectedly opened a chance of extrication, sudden and startling.

Mr. Longcluse was destined to a surprise to-night. Mr. Longcluse, at his own house, was awaiting the return of Sir Richard. Overlooked in his usually accurate though rapid selection, a particularly shabby and vulgar-looking letter had been thrown aside among circulars, pamphlets, and begging letters, to await his leisure. It was a letter from Paris, and vulgar and unbusiness-like as it looked, there was yet, in its peculiar scrivenery that which, a little more attentively scanned, thrilled him with a terrible misgiving. The post-mark showed it had been delivered four days before. When he saw from whom it came, and had gathered something of its meaning from a few phrases, his dark eyes gleamed and his face grew stern. Was this wretch's hoof to strike to pieces the plans he had so nearly matured? The letter was as follows:—

> "SIR,
>
> "Mr Longcluse, I have been unfortunate With your money which you have Gave me to remove from England, and Keep me in New York. My boxes, and other things, and Ballens of the money in Gold, except about a Hundred pounds, which has kep me from want ever sense, went Down in the Mary Jane, of London, and my cousin went down in her also, which I might as well av Went down myself in her, only for me Stopping in Paris, where I made a trifle of Money, intending to go Out in August. Now, Sir, don't you Seppose I am not in as good Possition as I was when I Harranged with sum difculty With you. The boot with The blood Mark on the Soul is not Lost nor Distroyed, but it is Safe in my Custody; so as Likewise in safe Keeping is The traising, in paper, of the foot Mark in blood on the Floar of the Smoaking Room in question, with the signatures of the witnesses attached; and, Moreover, my Staitment made in the Form of a Information, at the Time, and signed In witness of My signature by two Unekseptinible witnesses. And all Is ready to Produise whenevor his worshop shall Apoynt. i have wrote To mister david Arden on this Supget. i wrote to him just a week ago, he seaming To take a Intrast in this Heer case; and, moreover, the two ieyes that sawd a certain Person about the said smoaking Room, and in the saime, is Boath wide open at This presen Time. mister Longcluse i do not Want to have your Life, but gustice must Taike its coarse unless it is settled of hand Slik. i will harrange the Same as last time, And i must have two hundred And fifty pounds More on this Settlement than i Had last time, for Dellay and loss of Time in this town. I will sign any law paper in reason you may ask of me. My hadress is under cover to Monseer Letexier, air-dresser, and incloses his card, which you Will please send an Anser by return Of post, or else i Must sepose you chose The afare shall take Its coarse; and i am as ever,
>
> "Your obeediant servant to command,
> "PAUL DAVIES."

Never did paper look so dazzlingly white, or letters so intensely black, before Mr. Longcluse's eyes, as those of this ominous letter. He crumpled it up, and thrust it in his trousers pocket, and gave to the position a few seconds of intense thought.

His first thought was, what a fool he was for not having driven Davies to the wall, and settled the matter with the high hand of the law at once. His next, what could bring him to Paris? He was there for something. To see possibly the family of Lebas, and collect and dovetail pieces of evidence, after his detective practice, a process which would be sure to conduct him to the Baron Vanboeren! Was this story of the boot and the tracing of the bloodstained foot-print true? Had this scoundrel reserved the strongest part of his case for this new extortion? Was his trouble to be never ending? If this accursed ferret were once to get into his warren, what power could unearth him, till the mischief was done?

His eye caught again the words, on which, in the expressive phrase which Mr. Davies would have used, his "sight spred" as he held the letter before his eyes—"Mister Loncluse, i do not want to have your life." He ground his teeth, shook his fist in the air, and stamped on the floor with fury, at the thought that a brutal detective, not able to spell two words, and trained for such game as London thieves and burglars, should dare to hold such language to a man of thought and skill, altogether so masterly as he! That he should be outwitted by that clumsy scoundrel!

Well, it was now to begin all over again. It should all go right this time. He thought again for a moment, and then sat down and wrote, commencing with the date and address—

> "PAUL DAVIES,
>
> "I have just received your note, which states that you have succeeded in obtaining some additional information, which you think may lead to the conviction of the murderer of M. Lebas, in the Saloon Tavern. I shall be most happy to pay handsomely any expense of any kind you may be put to in that matter. It is, indeed, no more than I had already undertaken. I am glad to learn that you have also written on the subject to Mr. David Arden, who feels entirely with me. I shall take an early opportunity of seeing him. Persist in your laudable exertions, and I shall not shrink from rewarding you handsomely.
>
> "Yours,
> "WALTER LONGCLUSE."

He addressed the letter carefully, and went himself and put it in the post-office.

By this time Sir Richard Arden was awaiting him at home in his drawing-room, and as he walked homeward, under the lamps, in inward pain, one might have moralised with Peter Pindar—

> "These fleas have other fleas to bite 'em
> And so on ad infinitum."

The secret tyrant had in his turn found a secret tyrant, not less cruel perhaps, but more ignoble.

"You made your visit?" asked Mr. Longcluse.

"Yes."

"Anything to report?"

"Absolutely nothing."

A silence followed.

"Where is Mr. Arden, your uncle?"

"In Scotland."

"How soon does he return?"

"He will not be in town till spring, I believe; he is going abroad, but he passes through Southampton on his way to the Continent, on Friday next."

"And makes some little stay there?"

"I think he stays one night."

"Then I'll go down and see him, and you shall come with me."

Sir Richard stared.

"Yes, and you had better not put your foot in it; and clear your head of all notion of running away," he said, fixing his fiery eyes on Sir Richard, with a sudden ferocity that made him fancy that his secret thoughts had revealed themselves under that piercing gaze. "It is not easy to levant now-a-days, unless one has swifter wings than the wires can carry news with; and if you are false, what more do I need than to blast you? and with your name in the Hue-and-Cry, and a thousand pounds reward for the apprehension of Sir Richard Arden, Baronet, for forgery, I don't see much more that infamy can do for you."

A dark flush crossed Arden's face as he rose.

"Not a word now," cried Longcluse harshly, extending his hand quickly towards him; "I may do that which can't be undone."

CHAPTER LXXV.

BLIGHT AND CHANGE.

Danger to herself, Alice suspected none. But she was full of dreadful conjectures about her brother. There was, she was persuaded, no good any longer in remonstrance or entreaty. She could not upbraid him; but she was sure that the terrible fascination of the gaming-table had caused the sudden ruin he vaguely confessed.

"Oh," she often repeated, "that Uncle David were in town, or that I knew where to find him!"

"But no doubt," she thought, "Richard will hide nothing from him, and perhaps my hinting his disclosures, even to him, would aggravate poor Richard's difficulties and misery."

It was not until the next evening that, about the same hour, she again saw her brother. His good resolutions in the interval had waxed faint. They were not reversed, but only in the spirit of indecision, and something of the apathy of despair, postponed to a more convenient season.

To her he seemed more tranquil. He said vaguely that the reasons for flight were less urgent and that she had better continue her preparations, as before, for her journey to Yorkshire.

Even under these circumstances the journey to Yorkshire was pleasant. There was comfort in the certainty that he would there be beyond the reach of that fatal temptation which had too plainly all but ruined him. From the harrassing distractions, also, which in London had of late beset him, almost without intermission, he might find in the seclusion of Arden a temporary calm. There, with Uncle David's help, there would be time, at least, to ascertain the extent of his losses, and what the old family of Arden might still count upon as their own, and a plan of life might be arranged for the future.

Full of these more cheery thoughts, Alice took leave of her brother.

"I am going," he said, looking at his watch, "direct to Brighton; I have just time to get to the station nicely; business, of course—a meeting to-night with Bexley, who is staying there, and in the morning a long and, I fear, angry discussion with Charrington, who is also at Brighton."

He kissed his sister, sighed deeply, and looking in her eyes for a little, fixedly, he said—

"Alice, darling, you must try to think what sacrifice you can make to save your wretched brother."

Their eyes met as she looked up, her hands about his neck, his on her shoulders; he drew his sister to him quickly, and with another kiss, turned, ran down stairs, got into his cab, and drove down the avenue. She stood looking after him with a heavy heart. How happy they two might have been, if it had not been for the one incorrigible insanity!

About an hour later, as the sun was near its setting, she put on her hat and short grey cloak, and stepped out into its level beams, and looked round smiling. The golden glow and transparent shadows made that beautiful face look more than ever lovely. All around the air was ringing with the farewell songs of the small birds, and, with a heart almost rejoicing in sympathy with that beautiful hour, she walked lightly to the old garden, which in that luminous air, looked, she thought, so sad and pretty.

The well-worn aphorism of the Frenchman, "History repeats itself," was about to assert itself. Sometimes it comes in literal sobriety, sometimes in derisive travesti, sometimes in tragic aggravation.

She is in the garden now. The associations of place recall her strange interview with Mr. Longcluse but a few months before. Since then a blight has fallen on the scenery, and what a change upon the persons! The fruit-leaves are yellow now, and drifts of them lie upon the walks. Mantling ivy, as before, canopies the door, interlaced with climbing roses; but they have long shed their honours. This thick mass of dark green foliage and thorny tendrils forms a deep arched porch, in the shadow of which, suddenly, as on her return she reached it, she sees Mr. Longcluse standing within a step or two of her.

He raises his hand, it might be in entreaty, it might be in menace; she could not, in the few alarmed moments in which she gazed at his dark eyes and pale equivocal face, determine anything.

"Miss Arden, you may hate me; you can't despise me. You must hear me, because you are in my power. I relent, mind you, thus far, that I give you one chance more of reconciliation; don't, for God's sake, throw it from you!" (he was extending his open hand to receive hers). "Why should you prefer an unequal war with me? I tell you frankly you are in my power—don't misunderstand me—in my power to this degree, that you shall voluntarily, as the more tolerable of two alternatives, submit with abject acquiescence to every one of my conditions. Here is my hand; think of the degradation I submit to in asking you to take it. You gave me no chance when I asked forgiveness. I tender you a full forgiveness; here is my hand, beware how you despise it."

Fearful as he appeared in her sight, her fear gave way before her kindling spirit. She had stood before him pale as death—anger now fired her eye and cheek.

"How dare you, Sir, hold such language to me! Do you suppose, if I had told my brother of your cowardice and insolence as I left the abbey the other day, you would have dared to speak to him, much less to me? Let me pass, and never while you live presume to address me more."

Mr. Longcluse, with a slow recoil, smiling fixedly, and bowing, drew back and opened the door for her to pass. He did not any longer look like a villain whose heart had failed him.

Her heart fluttered violently with fear as she saw that he stepped out after her, and walked by her side toward the house. She quickened her pace in great alarm.

"If you had liked me ever so little," said he in that faint and horrible tone she remembered—"one, the smallest particle, of disinterested liking—the grain of mustard-seed—I would have had you fast, and made you happy, made you adore me; such adoration that you could have heard from my own lips the confession of my crimes, and loved me still—loved me more desperately. Now that you hate me, and I hate you, and have you in my power, and while I hate still admire you—still choose you for my wife—you shall hear the same story, and think me all the more dreadful. You sought to degrade me, and I'll humble you in the dust. Suppose I tell you I'm a criminal—the kind of man you have read of in trials, and can't understand, and can scarcely even believe in—the kind of man that seems to you as unaccountable and monstrous as a ghost—your terrors and horror will make my triumph exquisite with an immense delight. I don't want to smooth the way for you; you do nothing for me. I disdain hypocrisy. Terror drives you on; fate coerces you; you can't help yourself, and my delight is to make the plunge terrible. I reveal myself that you may know the sort of person you are yoked to. Your sacrifice shall be the agony of agonies, the death of deaths, and yet you'll find yourself unable to resist. I'll make you submissive as ever patient was to a mad doctor. If it took years to do it, you shall never stir out of this house till it is done. Every spark of insolence in your nature shall be trampled out; I'll break you thoroughly. The sound of my step shall make your heart jump; a look from me shall make you dumb for an hour. You shall not be able to take your eyes off me while I'm in sight, or to forget me for a moment when I am gone. The smallest thing you do, the least word you speak, the very thoughts of your heart, shall all be shaped under one necessity and one fear." (She had reached the hall door). "Up the steps! Yes; you wish to enter? Certainly."

With flashing eyes and head erect, the beautiful girl stepped into the hall, without looking to the right or to the left, or uttering one word, and walked quickly to the foot of the great stair.

If she thought that Mr. Longcluse would respect the barrier of the threshold, she was mistaken. He entered but one step behind her, shut the heavy hall door with a crash, dropped the key into his coat pocket, and signing with his finger to the man in the room to the right, that person stood up briskly, and prepared for action. He closed the door again, saying simply, "I'll call."

The young lady, hearing his step, turned round and stood on the stair, confronting him fiercely.

"You must leave this house this moment," she cried, with a stamp, with gleaming eyes and very pale.

"By-and-by," he replied, standing before her.

Could this be the safe old house in which childish days had passed, in which all around were always friendly and familiar faces? The window stood reflected upon the wall beside her in dim sunset light, and the shadows of the flowers sharp and still that stood there.

"I have friends here who will turn you out, Sir!"

"You have no friends here," he replied, with the same fixed smile.

She hesitated; she stepped down, but stopped in the hall. She remembered instantly that, as she turned, she had seen him take the key from the hall door.

"My brother will protect me."

"Is he here?"

"He'll call you to account to-morrow, when he comes."

"Will he say so?"

"Always—brave, true Richard!" she sobbed, with a strange cry in her words.

"He'll do as I bid him: he's a forger, in my power."

To her wild stare he replied with a low, faint laugh. She clasped her fingers over her temples.

"Oh! no, no, no, no, no, no!" she screamed, and suddenly she rushed into the great room at her right. Her brother—was it a phantom?—stood before her. With one long, shrill scream, she threw herself into his arms, and cried, "It's a lie, darling, it's a lie!" and she had fainted.

He laid her in the great chair by the fire-place. With white lips, and with one fist shaking wildly in the air, he said, with a dreadful shiver in his voice,—

"You villain! you villain! you villain!"

"Don't you be a fool," said Longcluse. "Ring for the maid. There must have been a crisis some time. I'm giving you a fair chance—trying to save you; they all faint—it's a trick with women."

Longcluse looked into her lifeless face, with something of pity and horror mingling in the villany of his countenance.

CHAPTER LXXVI.

PHŒBE CHIFFINCH.

Mr. Longcluse passed into the inner room, as he heard a step approaching from the hall. It was Louisa Diaper, in whose care, with the simple remedy of cold water, the young lady recovered. She was conveyed to her room, and Richard Arden followed, at Longcluse's command, to "keep things quiet."

In an agony of remorse, he remained with his sister's hand in his, sitting by the bed on which she lay. Longcluse had spoken with the resolution that a few sharp and short words should accomplish the crisis, and show her plainly that her brother was, in the most literal and terrible sense, in his power, and thus, indirectly, she also. Perhaps, if she must know the fact, it was as well she should know it now.

Longcluse, I suppose, had reckoned upon Richard's throwing himself upon his sister's mercy. He thought he had done so before, and moved her as he would have wished. Longcluse, no doubt, had spoken to her, expecting to find her in a different mood. Had she yielded, what sort of husband would he have made her? Not cruel, I daresay. Proud of her, he would have been. She should have had the best diamonds in England. Jealous, violent when crossed, but with all his malice and severity, easily by Alice to have been won, had she cared to win him, to tenderness.

Was Sir Richard now seconding his scheme?

Sir Richard had no plan—none for escape, none for a catastrophe, none for acting upon Alice's feelings.

"I am so agitated—in such despair, so stunned! If I had but one clear hour! Oh, God! if I had but one clear hour to think in!"

He was now trying to persuade Alice that Longcluse had, in his rage, used exaggerated language—that it was true he was in his power, but it was for a large sum of money, for which he was his debtor.

"Yes, darling," he whispered, "only be firm. I shall get away, and take you with me—only be secret, and don't mind one word he says when he is angry—he is literally a madman; there is no limit to the violence and absurdity of what he says."

"Is he still in the house?" she whispered.

"Not he."

"Are you certain?"

"Perfectly; with all his rant, he dares not stay: it would be a police-office affair. He's gone long ago."

"Thank God!" she said, with a shudder.

Their agitated talk continued for some time longer. At last, darkly and suddenly, as usual, he took his leave.

When her brother had gone, she touched the bell for Louisa Diaper. A stranger appeared.

The stranger had a great deal of pink ribbon in her cap, she looked shrewd enough, and with a pair of rather good eyes; she looked curiously and steadily on the young lady.

"Who are you?" said Alice, sitting up. "I rang for my maid, Louisa Diaper."

"Please, my lady," she answers, with a short curtsey, "she went into town to fetch some things here from Sir Richard's house."

"How long ago?"

"Just when you was getting better, please, my lady."

"When she returns send her to me. What is your name?"

"Phœbe Chiffinch, please 'm."

"And you are here ——"

"In her place, please my lady."

"Well, when she comes back you can assist. We shall have a great deal to do, and I like your face, Phœbe, and I'm so lonely, I think I'll get you to sit here in the window near me."

And on a sudden the young lady burst into tears, and sobbed and wept bitterly.

The new maid was at her side, pouring all sorts of consolation into her ear, with odd phrases—quite intelligible, I daresay, over the bar of the "Guy of Warwick"—dropping h's in all directions, and bowling down grammatic rules like nine-pins.

She was wonderfully taken by the kind looks and tones of the pretty lady whom she saw in this distress, and with the silk curtains drawn back in the fading flush of evening.

Hard work, hard fare, and harder words had been her portion from her orphaned childhood upward, at the old "Guy of Warwick," with its dubious customers, failing business, and bitter and grumbling old hostess. Shrewd, hard, and not over-nice had Miss Phœbe grown up in that godless school.

But she had taken a fancy, as the phrase is, to the looks of the young lady, and still more to her voice and words, that in her ears sounded so new and strange. There was not an unpleasant sense, too, of the superiority of rank and refinement which inspires an admiring awe in her kind; and so, in a voice that was rather sweet and very cheery, she offered, when the young lady was better, to sit by the bed and tell her a story, or sing her a song.

Everyone knows how his view of his own case may vary within an hour. Alice was now of opinion that there was no reason to reject her brother's version of the terrifying situation. A man who could act like Mr. Longcluse, could, of course, say anything. She had begun to grow more cheerful, and in a little while she accepted the offer of her companion, and heard, first a story, and then a song; and, after all, she talked with her for some time.

"Tell me, now, what servants there are in the house," asked Alice.

"Only two women and myself, please, Miss."

"Is there anyone else in the house, besides ourselves?"

The girl looked down, and up again, in Alice's eyes, and then away to the floor at the other end of the room.

"I was told, Ma'am, not to talk of nothing here, Miss, except my own business, please, my lady."

"My God! This girl mayn't speak truth to me," exclaimed Alice, clasping her hands aghast.

The girl looked up uneasily.

"I should be sent away, Ma'am, if I do."

"Look—listen: in this strait you must be for or against me; you can't be divided. For God's sake be a friend to me now. I may yet be the best friend you ever had. Come, Phœbe, trust me, and I'll never betray you."

She took the girl's hand. Phœbe did not speak. She looked in her face earnestly for some moments, and then down, and up again.

"I don't mind. I'll do what I can for you, Ma'am; I'll tell you what I know. But if you tell them, Ma'am, it will be awful bad for me, my lady."

She looked again, very much frightened, in her face, and was silent.

"No one shall ever know but I. Trust me entirely, and I'll never forget it to you."

"Well, Ma'am, there is two men."

"Who are they?"

"Two men, please 'm. I knows one on 'em—he was keeper on the 'Guy o' Warwick,' please, my lady, when there was a hexecution in the 'ouse. They're both sheriff's men."

"And what are they doing here?"

"A hexecution, my lady."

"That is, to sell the furniture and everything for a debt, isn't that it?" inquired the lady, bewildered.

"Well, that was it below at the 'Guy o' Warwick,' Miss; but Mr. Vargers, he was courting me down there at the 'Guy o' Warwick,' and offered marriage if I would 'av 'ad him, and he tells me heverything, and he says that there's a paper to take you, please, my lady."

"Take me?"

"Yes, my lady; he read it to me in the room by the hall-door. Halice Harden, spinster, and something about the old guv'nor's will, please; and his horder is to take you, please, Miss, if you should offer to go out of the door; and there's two on 'em, and they watches turn about, so you can't leave the 'ouse, please, my lady;

and if you try they'll only lock you up a prisoner in one room a-top o' the 'ouse; and, for your life, my lady, don't tell no one I said a word."

"Oh! Phœbe. What can they mean? What's to become of me? Somehow or other you must get me out of this house. Help me, for God's sake! I'll throw myself from the window—I'll kill myself rather than remain in their power."

"Hush! My lady, please, I may think of something yet. But don't you do nothing 'and hover 'ead. You must have patience. They won't be so sharp, maybe, in a day or two. I'll get you out if I can; and, if I can't, then God's will be done. And I'll make out what I can from Mr. Vargers; and don't you let no one think you likes me, and I'll be sly enough, you may count on me, my lady."

Trembling all over, Alice kissed her.

CHAPTER LXXVII.

MORE NEWS OF PAUL DAVIES.

Louisa Diaper did not appear that night, nor next morning. She had been spirited away like the rest. Sir Richard had told her that his sister desired that she should go into town, and stay till next day, under the care of the housekeeper in town, and that he would bring her a list of commissions which she was to do for her mistress preparatory to starting for Yorkshire. I daresay this young lady liked her excursion to town well enough. It was not till the night after that she started for the North.

Alice Arden, for a time, lost heart altogether. It was no wonder she should.

That her only brother should be an accomplice against her, in a plot so appalling, was enough to overpower her; her horror of Longcluse, the effectual nature of her imprisonment, and the strange and, as she feared, unscrupulous people by whom she had been so artfully surrounded, heightened her terrors to the pitch of distraction.

At times she was almost wild; at others stupefied in despair; at others, again, soothed by the kindly intrepidity of Phœbe, she became more collected. Sometimes she would throw herself on her bed, and sob for an hour in helpless agony; and then, exhausted and overpowered, she would fall for a time into a deep sleep, from which she would start, for several minutes, without the power of collecting her thoughts, and with only the stifled cry, "What is it?—Where am I?" and a terrified look round.

One day, in a calmer mood, as she sat in her room after a long talk with Phœbe, the girl came beside her chair with an oddly made key, with a little strap of white leather to the handle, in her hands.

"Here's a latch-key, Miss; maybe you know what it opens?"

"Where did you find it?"

"In the old china vase over the chimney, please 'm."

"Let me see—oh! dear, yes, this opens the door in the wall of the grounds, in that direction," and she pointed. "Poor papa lent it to my drawing-master. He lived somewhere beyond that, and used to let himself in by it when he came to give me my lessons."

"I remember that door well, Miss," said Phœbe, looking earnestly on the key—"Mr. Crozier let me out that way, one day. Mr. Longcluse has put strangers, you know, in the gatehouse. That's shut against us. I'll tell you what, Miss—wait—well, I'll think. I'll keep this key safe, anyhow; and—the more the merrier," she added with a sudden alacrity, and lifting her finger, by way of signal, for everything now was done with caution here, she left the room, and passed through the suite to the landing, and quietly took out the door-keys, one by one, and returned with her spoil to Alice's room.

"You thought they might lock us up?" whispered Alice.

The girl nodded. "No harm to have 'em, Miss—it won't hurt us." She folded them tightly in a handkerchief, and thrust the parcel as far as her arm could reach between the mattress and the bed. "I'll rip the ticken a bit just now, and stitch them in," whispered the girl.

"Didn't I hear another key clink as you put your hand in?" asked Alice.

The girl smiled, and drew out a large key, and nodded, still smiling as she replaced it.

"What does that open?" whispered Alice eagerly.

"Nothing, Miss," said the girl gravely—"it's the key of the old back-door lock; but there's a new one there now, and this won't open nothing. But I have a use for it. I'll tell you all in time, Miss; and, please, you must keep up your heart, mind."

Sir Richard Arden was not the cold villain you may suppose. He was resolved to make an effort of some kind for the extrication of his sister. He could not bear to open his dreadful situation to his Uncle David, nor to kill himself, nor to defy the vengeance of Longcluse. He would effect her escape and his own simultaneously. In the meantime he must acquiesce, ostensibly at least, in every step determined on by Longcluse.

It was a bright autumnal day as Sir Richard and Mr. Longcluse took the rail to Southampton. Longcluse had his reasons for taking the young baronet with him.

It was near the hour, by the time they got there, when David Arden would arrive from his northern point of departure. Longcluse looked animated—smiling; but a stupendous load lay on his heart. A single clumsy phrase in the letter of that detective scoundrel might be enough to direct the formidable suspicions of that energetic old gentleman upon him. The next hour might throw him altogether upon the defensive, and paralyse his schemes.

Alice Arden, you little dream of the man and the route by which, possibly, deliverance is speeding to you.

Near the steps of the large hotel that looks seaward, Longcluse and Sir Richard lounge, expecting the arrival of David Arden almost momentarily. Up drives a fly, piled with portmanteaus, hat-case, dressing-case, and all the other travelling appurtenances of a comfortable wayfarer. Beside the driver sits a servant. The fly draws up at the door near them.

Mr. Longcluse's seasoned heart throbs once or twice oddly. Out gets Uncle David, looking brown and healthy after his northern excursion. On reaching the top of the steps, he halts, and turns round to look about him. Again Mr. Longcluse feels the same odd sensation.

Uncle David recognises Sir Richard, and smiling greets him. He runs down the steps to meet him. After they have shaken hands, and, a little more coldly, he and Mr. Longcluse, he says,—

"You are not looking yourself, Dick; you ought to have run down to the moors, and got up an appetite. How is Alice?"

"Alice? Oh! Alice is very well, thanks."

"I should like to run up to Mortlake to see her. She has been complaining, eh?"

"No, no—better," says Sir Richard.

"And you forget to tell your uncle what you told me," interposes Mr. Longcluse, "that Miss Arden left Mortlake for Yorkshire yesterday."

"Oh!" said Uncle David, turning to Richard again.

"And the servants went before—two or three days ago," said Sir Richard, looking down for a moment, and hastening, under that clear eye, to speak a little truth.

"Well, I wish she had come with us," said David Arden; "but as she could not be persuaded, I'm glad she is making a little change of air and scene, in any direction. By-the-bye, Mr. Longcluse, you had a letter, had not you, from our friend, Paul Davies?"

"Yes; he seemed to think he had found a clue—from Paris it was—and I wrote to tell him to spare no expense in pushing his inquiries and to draw upon me."

"Well, I have some news to tell you. His exploring voyage will come to nothing; you did not hear?"

"No."

"Why, the poor fellow's dead. I got a letter—it reached me, forwarded from my house in town, yesterday, from the person who hires the lodgings—to say he had died of scarlatina very suddenly, and sending an inventory of the things he left. It is a pity, for he seemed a smart fellow, and sanguine about getting to the bottom of it."

"An awful pity!" exclaimed Longcluse, who felt as if a mountain were lifted from his heart, and the entire firmament had lighted up; "an awful pity! Are you quite sure?"

"There can't be a doubt, I'm sorry to say. Then, as Alice has taken wing, I'll pursue my first plan, and cross by the next mail."

"For Paris?" inquired Mr. Longcluse, carelessly.

"Yes, Sir, for Paris," answered Uncle David deliberately, looking at him; "yes, for Paris."

And then followed a little chat on indifferent subjects. Then Uncle David mentioned that he had an appointment, and must dine with the dull but honest fellow who had asked him to meet him here on a matter of business, which would have done just as well next year, but he wished it now. Uncle David nodded, and waved his hand, as on entering the door he gave them a farewell smile over his shoulder.

CHAPTER LXXVIII.

THE CATACOMBS.

At his disappearance, for Sir Richard the air darkened as when, in the tropics, the sun sets without a twilight, and the silence of an awful night descended.

It seemed that safety had been so near. He had laid his hand upon it, and had let it glide ungrasped between his fingers; and now the sky was black above him, and an unfathomable sea beneath.

Mr. Longcluse was in great spirits. He had grown for a time like the Walter Longcluse of a year before.

They two dined together, and after dinner Mr. Longcluse grew happy, and as he sat with his glass by him, he sang, looking over the waves, a sweet little sentimental song, about ships that pass at sea, and smiles and tears, and "true, boys, true," and "heaven shows a glimpse of its blue." And he walks with Sir Richard to the station, and he says, low, as he leans and looks into the carriage window, of which young Arden was the only occupant—

"Be true to me now, and we may make it up yet."

And so saying, he gives his hand a single pressure as he looks hard in his eyes.

The bell had rung. He was remaining there, he said, for another train. The clapping of the doors had ceased. He stood back. The whistle blew its long piercing yell, and as the train began to glide towards London, the young man saw the white face of Walter Longcluse in deep shadow, as he stood with his back to the lamp, still turned towards him.

The train was now thundering on its course; the solitary lamp glimmered in the roof. He threw himself back, with his foot against the opposite seat.

"Good God! what is one to resolve! All men are cruel when they are exasperated. Might not good yet be made of Longcluse? What creatures women are!—what fools! How easy all might have been made, with the least temper and reflection! What d ——d selfishness!"

Uncle David was now in Paris. The moon was shining over that beautiful city. In a lonely street, in a quarter which fashion had long forsaken—over whose pavement, as yet unconscious of the Revolution, had passed, in the glare of torchlight, the carved and emblazoned carriages of an aristocracy, as shadowy now as the courts of the Cæsars—his footsteps are echoing.

A huge house presents its front. He stops and examines it carefully for a few seconds. It is the house of which he is in search.

At one time the Baron Vanboeren had received patients from the country, to reside in this house. For the last year, during which he had been gathering together his wealth, and detaching himself from business, he had discontinued this, and had gradually got rid of his establishment.

When David Arden rang the bell at the hall-door, which he had to do repeatedly, it was answered at last by an old woman, high-shouldered, skin and bone, with a great nose, and big jaw-bones, and a high-cauled cap. This lean creature looks at him with a vexed and hollow eye. Her bony arm rests on the lock of the hall-door, and she blocks the narrow aperture between its edge and the massive door-case. She inquires in very nasal French what Monsieur desires.

"I wish to see Monsieur the Baron, if he will permit me an interview," answered Mr. Arden in very fair French.

"Monsieur the Baron is not visible; but if Monsieur will, notwithstanding, leave any message he pleases for Monsieur the Baron, I will take care he receives it punctually."

"But Monsieur the Baron appointed me to call to-night at ten o'clock."

"Is Monsieur sure of that?"

"Perfectly."

"Eh, very well; but, if he pleases, I must first learn Monsieur's name."

"My name is Arden."

"I believe Monsieur is right." She took a bit of notepaper from her capacious pocket, and peering at it, spelled aloud, "D-a-v-i-d ——"

"A-r-d-e-n," interrupted and continued the visitor, spelling his name, with a smile.

"A-r-d-e-n," she followed, reading slowly from her paper; "yes, Monsieur is right. You see, this paper says, 'Admit Monsieur David Arden to an interview.' Enter, if you please Monsieur, and follow me."

It was a decayed house of superb proportions, but of a fashion long passed away. The gaunt old woman, with a bunch of large keys clinking at her side, stalked up the broad stairs and into a gallery, and through several rooms opening en suite. The rooms were hung with cobwebs, dusty, empty, and the shutters closed, except here and there where the moonlight gleamed through chinks and seams.

David Arden, before he had seen the Baron Vanboeren in London, had pictured him in imagination a tall old man with classic features, and manners courteous and somewhat stately.

We do not fabricate such images; they rise like exhalations from a few scattered data, and present themselves spontaneously. It is this self-creation that invests them with so much reality in our imaginations, and subjects us to so odd a surprise when the original turns out quite unlike the portrait with which we have been amusing ourselves.

She now pushed open a door, and said, "Monsieur the Baron here is arrived Monsieur David d'Ardennes."

The room in which he now stood was spacious, but very nearly dark. The shutters were closed outside, and the moonlight that entered came through the circular hole cut in each. A large candle on a bracket burned at the further end of the room. There the baron stood. A reflector which interposed between the candle and the door at which David Arden entered directed its light strongly upon something which the baron held, and laid upon the table, in his hand; and now that he turned toward his visitor, it was concentrated upon his large face, revealing, with the force of a Rembrandt, all its furrows and finer wrinkles. He stood out against a background of darkness with remarkable force.

The baron stood before him—a short man in a red waistcoat. He looked more broad-shouldered and short-necked than ever in his shirt-sleeves. He had an instrument in his hand resembling a small bit and brace, and some chips and sawdust on his flannel waistcoat, which he brushed off with two or three sweeps of his short fat fingers. He looked now like a grim old mechanic. There was no vivacity in his putty-coloured features, but there were promptitude and decision in every abrupt gesture. It was his towering, bald forehead, and something of command and savage energy in his lowering face, that redeemed the tout ensemble from an almost brutal vulgarity.

The baron was not in the slightest degree "put out," as the phrase is, at being detected in his present occupation and deshabille.

He bowed twice to David Arden, and said, in English, with a little foreign accent—

"Here is a chair, Monsieur Arden; but you can hardly see it until your eyes have grown a little accustomed to our crépuscula."

This was true enough, for David Arden, though he saw him advance a step or two, could not have known what he held in the hand that was in shadow. The sound, indeed, of the legs of the chair, as he set it down upon the floor, he heard.

"I should make you an apology, Mr. Arden, if I were any longer in my own home, which I am not, although this is still my house; for I have dismissed my servants, sold my furniture, and sent what things I cared to retain over the frontier to my new habitation, whither I shall soon follow; and this house too, I shall sell. I have already two or three gudgeons nibbling, Monsieur."

"This house must have been the hotel of some distinguished family, Baron; it is nobly proportioned," said David Arden.

As his eye became accustomed to the gloom, David Arden saw traces of gilding on the walls. The shattered frames on which the tapestry was stretched in old times remained in the panels, with crops of small, rusty nails visible. The faint candle-light glimmered on a ponderous gilded cornice, which had also sustained violence. The floor was bare, with a great deal of litter, and some scanty furniture. There was a lathe near the spot where David Arden stood, and shavings and splinters under his feet. There was a great block with a vice attached. In a portion of the fire-place was built a furnace. There were pincers and other instruments lying about the room, which had more the appearance of an untidy workshop than of a study, and seemed a suitable enough abode for the uncouth figure that confronted him.

"Ha! Monsieur," growls the baron, "stone walls have ears, you say if only they had tongues; what tales these could tell! This house was one of Madame du Barry's, and was sacked in the great Revolution. The mirrors were let into the plaster in the walls. In some of the rooms there are large fragments still stuck in the wall so fast, you would need a hammer and chisel to dislodge and break them up. This room was an ante-room, and admitted to the lady's bed-room by two doors, this and that. The panels of that other, by which you entered from the stair, were of mirror. They were quite smashed. The furniture, I suppose, flew out of the window; everything was broken up in small bits, and torn to rags, or carried off to the broker after the first fury, and sansculotte families came in and took possession of the wrecked apartments. You will say then, what was left? The bricks, the stones, hardly the plaster on the walls. Yet, Monsieur Arden, I have discovered some of the best treasures the house contained, and they are at present in this room. Are you a collector, Monsieur Arden?"

Uncle David disclaimed the honourable imputation. He was thinking of cutting all this short, and bringing the baron to the point. The old man was at the period when the egotism of age asserts itself, and was garrulous, and being, perhaps, despotic and fierce (he looked both), he might easily take fire and become impracticable. Therefore, on second thoughts, he was cautious.

"You can now see more plainly," said the baron. "Will you approach? Concealed by a double covering of strong paper pasted over it, and painted and gilded, each of these two doors on its six panels contains six distinct masterpieces of Watteau's. I have known that for ten years, and have postponed removing them. Twelve Watteaus, as fine as any in the world! I would not trust their removal to any other hand, and so, the panel comes out without a shake. Come here, Monsieur, if you please. This candle affords a light sufficient to see, at least, some of the beauties of these incomparable works."

"Thanks, Baron, a glance will suffice, for I am nothing of an artist."

He approached. It was true that his sight had grown accustomed to the obscurity, for he could now see the baron's features much more distinctly. His large waxen face was shorn smooth, except on the upper lip, where a short moustache still bristled; short black eyebrows contrasted also with the bald massive forehead, and round the eyes was a complication of mean and cunning wrinkles. Some peculiar lines between these contracted brows gave a character of ferocity to this forbidding and sensual face.

"Now! See there! Those four pictures—I would not sell those four Watteaus for one hundred thousand francs. And the other door is worth the same. Ha!"

"You are lucky, Baron."

"I think so. I do not wish to part with them: I don't think of selling them. See the folds of that brocade! See the ease and grace of the lady in the sacque, who sits on the bank there, under the myrtles, with the guitar on her lap! and see the animation and elegance of that dancing boy with the tambourine! This is a chef-d'œuvre. I ought not to part with that, on any terms—no, never! You no doubt know many collectors, wealthy men, in England. Look at that shot silk, green and purple; and whom do you take that to be a portrait of, that lady with the castanets?"

He was pointing out each object, on which he descanted, with his stumpy finger, his hands being, I am bound to admit, by no means clean.

"If you do happen to know such people, nevertheless, I should not object to your telling them where this treasure may be seen, I've no objection. I should not like to part with them, that is true. No, no, no; but every man may be tempted, it is possible—possible, just possible."

"I shall certainly mention them to some friends."

"Wealthy men, of course," said the baron.

"It is an expensive taste, Baron, and none but wealthy people can indulge it."

"True, and these would be very expensive. They are unique; that lady there is the Du Barry—a portrait worth, alone, six thousand francs. Ha! he! Yes, when I take zese out and place zem, as I mean before I go, to be seen, they will bring all Europe together. Mit speck fangt man mause—with bacon one catches mice!"

"No doubt they will excite attention, Baron. But I feel I am wasting your time and abusing your courtesy in permitting my visit, the immediate object of which was to earnestly beg from you some information which, I think, no one else can give me."

"Information? Oh! ah! Pray resume your chair, Sir. Information? yes, it is quite possible I may have information such as you need, Heaven knows! But knowledge, they say, is power, and if I do you a service I expect as much from you. Eine hand wascht die and're—one hand, Monsieur, washes ze ozer. No man parts wis zat which is valuable, to strangers, wisout a proper honorarium. I receive no more patients here; but you understand, I may be induced to attend a patient: I may be tempted, you understand."

"But this is not a case of attending a patient, Baron," said David Arden, a little haughtily.

"And what ze devil is it, then?" said the baron, turning on him suddenly. "Monsieur will pardon me, but we professional men must turn our time and knowledge to account, do you see? And we don't give eizer wizout being paid, and well paid for them, eh?"

"Of course. I meant nothing else," said David Arden.

"Then, Sir, we understand one another so far, and that saves time. Now, what information can the Baron Vanboeren give to Monsieur David Arden?"

"I think you would prefer my putting my questions quite straight."

"Straight as a sword-thrust, Sir."

"Then, Baron, I want to know whether you were acquainted with two persons, Yelland Mace and Walter Longcluse."

"Yes, I knew zem bos, slightly and yet intimately—intimately and yet but slightly. You wish, perhaps, to learn particulars about those gentlemen?"

"I do."

"Go on: interrogate."

"Do you perfectly recollect the features of these persons?"

"I ought."

"Can you give me an accurate description of Yelland Mace?"

"I can bring you face to face with both."

"By Jove! Sir, are you serious?"

"Mr. Longcluse is in London."

"But you talk of bringing me face to face with them; how soon?"

"In five minutes."

"Oh, you mean a photograph, or a picture?"

"No, in the solid. Here is the key of the catacombs." And he took a key that hung from a nail on the wall.

"Bah, ha, yah!" exploded the baron, in a ferocious sneer, rather than a laugh, and shrugging his great shoulders to his ears, he shook them in barbarous glee, crying—"What clever fellow you are, Monsieur Arden! you see so well srough ze millstone! Ich bin klug und weise—you sing zat song. I am intelligent and wise, eh, he! gra-a, ha, ha!"

He seized the candlestick in one hand, and shaking the key in the other by the side of his huge forehead, he nodded once or twice to David Arden.

"Not much life where we are going; but you shall see zem bose."

"You speak riddles, Baron; but by all means bring me, as you say, face to face with them."

"Very good, Monsieur; you'll follow me," said the baron. And he opened a door that admitted to the gallery, and, with the candle and the keys, he led the way, by this corridor, to an iron door that had a singular appearance, being sunk two feet back in a deep wooden frame, that threw it into shadow. This he unlocked, and with an exertion of his weight and strength, swung slowly open.

CHAPTER LXXIX.

RESURRECTIONS.

David Arden entered this door, and found himself under a vaulted roof of brick. These were the chambers, for there was at least two, which the baron termed his catacombs. Along both walls of the narrow apartment were iron doors, in deep recesses, that looked like the huge ovens of an ogre, sunk deep in the wall, and the baron looked himself not an unworthy proprietor. The baron had the General's faculty of remembering faces and names.

"Monsieur Yelland Mace? Yes, I will show you him; he is among ze dead."

"Dead?"

"Ay, zis right side is dead—all zese."

"Do you mean," says David Arden, "literally that Yelland Mace is no longer living?"

"A, B, C, D, E, F, G," mutters the baron, slowly pointing his finger along the right wall.

"I beg your pardon, Baron, but I don't think you heard me," said David Arden.

"Perfectly, excuse me: H, I, J, K, L, M—M. I will show you now, if you desire it, Yelland Mace; you shall see him now, and never behold him more. Do you wish very much?"

"Intensely—most intensely!" said Uncle David earnestly.

The baron turned full upon him, and leaned his shoulders against the iron door of the recess. He had taken from his pocket a bunch of heavy keys, which he dangled from his clenched fingers, and they made a faint jingle in the silence that followed, for a few seconds.

"Permit me to ask," said the baron, "are your inquiries directed to a legal object?"

"I have no difficulty in saying yes," answered he; "a legal object, strictly."

"A legal object, by which you gain considerably?" he asked slowly.

"By which I gain the satisfaction of seeing justice done upon a villain."

"That is fine, Monsieur. Eternal justice! I have thought and said that very often: Vive la justice eternelle! especially when her sword shears off the head of my enemy, and her scale is laden with napoleons for my purse."

"Monsieur le Baron mistakes, in my case; I have absolutely nothing to gain by the procedure I propose; it is strictly criminal," said David Arden drily.

"Not an estate? not a slice of an estate? Come, come! Thorheit! That is foolish talk."

"I have told you already, nothing," repeated David Arden.

"Then you don't care, in truth, a single napoleon, whether you win or lose. We have been wasting our time, Sir. I have no time to bestow for nothing; my minutes count by the crown, while I remain in Paris. I shall soon depart, and practise no more; and my time will become my own—still my own, by no means yours. I am candid, Sir, and I think you cannot misunderstand me; I must be paid for my time and opportunities."

"I never meant anything else," said Mr. Arden sturdily; "I shall pay you liberally for any service you render me."

"That, Sir, is equally frank; we understand now the principle on which I assist you. You wish to see Yelland Mace, so you shall."

He turned about, and struck the key sharply on the iron door.

"There he waits," said the baron, "and—did you ever see him?"

"No."

"Bah! what a wise man. Then I may show you whom I please, and you know nothing. Have you heard him described?"

"Accurately."

"Well, there is some little sense in it, after all. You shall see."

He unlocked the safe, opened the door, and displayed shelves, laden with rudely-made deal boxes, each of a little more than a foot square. On these were marks and characters in red, some, and some in black, and others in blue.

"Hé! you see," said the baron, pointing with his key, "my mummies are cased in hieroglyphics. Come! Here is the number, the date, and the man."

And lifting them carefully one off the other, he took out a deal box that had stood in the lowest stratum. The cover was loose, except for a string tied about it. He laid it upon the floor, and took out a plaster mask, and brushing and blowing off the saw-dust, held it up.

David Arden saw a face with large eyes closed, a very high and thin nose, a good forehead, a delicately chiselled mouth; the upper lip, though well formed after the Greek model, projected a little, and gave to the chin the effect of receding in proportion. This slight defect showed itself in profile; but the face, looked at full front, was on the whole handsome, and in some degree even interesting.

"You are quite sure of the identity of this?" asked Uncle David earnestly.

There was a square bit of parchment, with two or three short lines, in a character which he did not know, glued to the concave reverse of the mask. The baron took it, and holding the light near, read, "Yelland Mace, suspect for his politics, May 2nd, 1844."

"Yes," said Mr. Arden, having renewed his examination, "it very exactly tallies with the description; the nose aquiline, but very delicately formed. Is that writing in cypher?"

"Yes, in cypher."

"And in what language?"

"German."

David Arden looked at it.

"You will make nothing of it. In these inscriptions, I have employed eight languages—five European, and three Asiatic—I am, you see, something of a linguist—and four distinct cyphers; so having that skill, I gave the benefit of it to my friends; this being secret."

"Secret?—oh!" said Uncle David.

"Yes, secret; and you will please to say nothing of it to any living creature until the twenty-first of October next, when I retire. You understand commerce, Mr. Arden. My practice is confidential, and I should lose perhaps eighty thousand francs in the short space that intervenes, if I were thought to have played a patient such a trick. It is but twenty days of reserve, and then I go and laugh at them, every one. Piff, puff, paff! ha! ha!"

"Yes, I promise that also," said Uncle David dryly, and to himself he thought, "What a consummate old scoundrel!"

"Very good, Sir; we shall want this of Yelland Mace again, just now; his face and coffin, ha! ha! can rest there for the present." He had replaced the mask in its box, and that lay on the floor. The door of the iron press he shut and locked. "Next, I will show you Mr. Longcluse: those are dead."

He waved his short hand toward the row of iron doors which he had just visited.

"Please, Sir, walk with me into this room. Ay, so. Here are the resurrections. Will you be good enough—L, Longcluse, M, one, two, three, four; three, yes, to hold this candlestick for a moment?"

The baron unlocked this door, and, after some rummaging, he took forth a box similar to that he had taken out before.

"Yes, right, Walter Longcluse. I tell you how you will see it best: there is brilliant moonlight, stand there."

Through a circular hole in the wall there streamed a beam of moonlight, that fell upon the plaster-wall opposite with the distinctness of the circle of a magic-lantern.

"You see it—you know it! Ha! ha! His pretty face!"

He held the mask up in the moonlight, and the lineaments, sinister enough, of Mr. Longcluse stood, sharply defined in every line and feature, in intense white and black, against the vacant shadow behind. There was the flat nose, the projecting underjaw, the oblique, sarcastic eyebrow, even the line of the slight but long scar, than ran nearly from his eye to his nostril. The same, but younger.

"There is no doubt about that. But when was it taken? Will you read what is written upon it?"

Uncle David had taken out the candle, and he held it beside the mask. The baron turned it round, and read, "Walter Longcluse, 15th October, 1844."

"The same year in which Mace's was taken?"

"So it is, 1844."

"But there is a great deal more than you have read, written upon the parchment in this one."

"It looks more."

"And is more. Why, count the words, one, two, four, six, eight. There must be thirty, or upwards."

"Well, suppose there are, Sir: I have read, nevertheless, all I mean to read for the present. Suppose we bring these three masks together. We can talk a little then, and I will perhaps tell you more, and disclose to you some secrets of nature and art, of which perhaps you suspect nothing. Come, come, Monsieur! kindly take the candle."

The baron shut the iron door with a clang, and locked it, and, taking up the box, marched into the next room, and placing the boxes one on top of the other, carried them in silence out upon the gallery, accompanied by David Arden.

How desolate seemed the silence of the vast house, in all which, by this time, perhaps, there did not burn another light!

They now re-entered the large and strangely-littered chamber in which he had talked with the baron; they stop among the chips and sawdust with which his work has strewn the floor.

"Set the candle on this table," says he. "I'll light another for a time. See all the trouble and time you cost me!"

He placed the two boxes on the table.

"I am extremely sorry ——"

"Not on my account, you needn't. You'll pay me well for it."

"So I will, Baron."

"Sit you down on that, Monsieur."

He placed a clumsy old chair, with a balloon-back, for his visitor, and, seating himself upon another, he struck his hand on the table, and said, arresting for a moment the restless movement of his eyes, and fixing on him a savage stare—

"You shall see wonders and hear marvels, if only you are willing to pay what they are worth." The baron laughed when he had said this.

CHAPTER LXXX.

ANOTHER.

"You shall sit here, Mr. Arden," said the baron, placing a chair for him. "You shall be comfortable. I grow in confidence with you. I feel inwardly an intuition when I speak wis a man of honour; my demon, as it were, whispers 'Trust him, honour him, make much of him.' Will you take a pipe, or a mug of beer?"

This abrupt invitation Mr. Arden civilly declined.

"Well, I shall have my pipe and beer. See, there is ze barrel—not far to go." He raised the candle, and David Arden saw for the first time the outline of a veritable beer-barrel in the corner, on tressels, such as might have regaled a party of boors in the clear shadow of a Teniers.

"There is the comely beer-cask, not often seen in Paris, in the corner of our boudoir, resting against the only remaining rags of the sky-blue and gold silk—it is rotten now—with which the room was hung, and a gilded cornice—it is black now—over its head; and now, instead of beautiful women and graceful youths, in gold lace and cut velvets and perfumed powder, there are but one rheumatic and crooked old woman, and one old Prussian doctor, in his shirt-sleeves, ha! ha! mutat terra vices! Come, we shall look at these again, and you shall hear more."

He placed the two masks upon the chimney-piece, leaning against the wall.

"And we will illuminate them," says he; and he takes, one after the other, half a dozen pieces of wax candle, and dripping the melting wax on the chimney-piece, he sticks each candle in turn in a little pool of its own wax.

"I spare nothing, you see, to make all plain. Those two faces present a marked contrast. Do you, Mr. Arden, know anything, ever so little, of the fate of Yelland Mace?"

"Nothing. Is he living?"

"Suppose he is dead, what then?"

"In that case, of course, I take my leave of the inquiry, and of you, asking you simply one question, whether there was any correspondence between Yelland Mace and Walter Longcluse?"

"A very intimate correspondence," said the baron.

"Of what nature?"

“Ha! They have been combined in business, in pleasures, in crimes,” said the baron. “Look at them. Can you believe it? So dissimilar! They are opposites in form and character, as if fashioned in expression and in feature each to contradict the other; yet so united!”

“And in crime, you say?”

“Ay, in crime—in all things.”

“Is Yelland Mace still living?” urged David Arden.

“Those features, in life, you will never behold, Sir.”

“He is dead. You said that you took that mask from among the dead. Is he dead?”

“No, Sir; not actually dead, but under a strange condition. Bah; Don't you see I have a secret? Do you prize very highly learning where he is?”

“Very highly, provided he may be secured and brought to trial; and you, Baron, must arrange to give your testimony to prove his identity.”

“Yes; that would be indispensible,” said the baron, whose eyes were sweeping the room from corner to corner, fiercely and swiftly. “Without me you can never lift the veil; without me you can never unearth your stiff and pale Yelland Mace, nor without me identify and hang him.”

“I rely upon your aid, Baron,” said Mr. Arden, who was becoming agitated. “Your trouble shall be recompensed; you may depend upon my honour.”

“I am running a certain risk. I am not a fool, though, like little Lebas. I am not to be made away with like a kitten; and once I move in this matter, I burn my ships behind me, and return to my splendid practice, under no circumstances, ever again.”

The baron's pallid face looked more bloodless, his accent was fiercer, and his countenance more ruffianly as he uttered all this.

“I understood, Baron, that you had quite made up your mind to retire within a very few weeks,” said David Arden.

“Does any man who has lived as long as you or I quite trust his own resolution? No one likes to be nailed to a plan of action an hour before he need be. I find my practice more lucrative every day. I may be tempted to postpone my retirement, and for a while longer to continue to gather the golden harvest that ripens round me. But once I take this step, all is up with that. You see—you understand. Bah! you are no fool; it is plain, all I sacrifice.”

“Of course, Baron, you shall take no trouble, and make no sacrifice, without ample compensation. But are you aware of the nature of the crime committed by that man?”

“I never trouble my head about details; it is enough, the man is a political refugee, and his object concealment.”

“But he was no political refugee; he had nothing to do with politics—he was simply a murderer and a robber.”

“What a little rogue! Will you excuse my smoking a pipe and drinking a little beer? Now, he never hinted that, although I knew him very intimately, for he was my patient for some months; never hinted it, he was so sly.”

"And Mr. Longcluse, was he your patient also?"

"Ha! to be sure he was. You won't drink some beer? No; well, in a moment."

He drew a little jugful from the cask, and placed it, and a pewter goblet, on the table, and then filled, lighted, and smoked his pipe as he proceeded.

"I will tell you something concerning those gentlemen, Mr. Longcluse and Mr. Mace, which may amuse you. Listen."

CHAPTER LXXXI.

BROKEN.

"My hands were very full," said the baron, displaying his stumpy fingers. "I received patients in this house; I had what you call many irons in ze fire. I was making napoleons then, I don't mind telling you, as fast as a man could run bullets. My minutes counted by the crown. It was in the month of May, 1844, late at night, a man called here, wanting to consult me. He called himself Herr von Konigsmark. I went down and saw him in my audience room. He knew I was to be depended upon. Such people tell one another who may be trusted. He told me he was an Austrian proscribed: very good. He proposed to place himself in my hands: very well. I looked him in the face—you have there exactly what I saw."

He extended his hand toward the mask of Yelland Mace.

"'You are an Austrian,' I said, 'a native subject of the empire?'

"'Yes.'

"'Italian?'

"'No.'

"'Hungarian?'

"'No.'

"'Well, you are not German—ha, ha!—I can swear to that.'

"He was speaking to me in German.

"'Your accent is foreign. Come, confidence. You must be no impostor. I must make no mistake, and blunder into a national type of features, all wrong; if I make your mask, it must do us credit. I know many gentlemen's secrets, and as many ladies' secrets. A man of honour! What are you afraid of?'"

"You were not a statuary?" said Uncle David, astonished at his versatility.

"Oh, yes! A statuary, but only in grotesque, you understand. I will show you some of my work by-and-by."

"And I shall perhaps understand."

"You shall, perfectly. With some reluctance, then, he admitted that what I positively asserted was true; for I told him I knew from his accent he was an Englishman. Then, with some little pressure, I invited him to tell his name. He did—it was Yelland Mace. That is Yelland Mace."

He had now finished his pipe: he went over to the chimney-piece, and having knocked out the ashes, and with his pipe pointing to the tip of the long thin plaster nose, he said, "Look well at him. Look till you know all his features by rote. Look till you fix them for the rest of your days well in memory, and then say what in the devil's name you could make of them. Look at that high nose, as thin as a fish-knife. Look at the line of the mouth and chin; see the mild gentlemanlike contour. If you find a fellow with a flat nose, and a pair of upper tusks sticking out an inch, and a squint that turns out one eye like the white of an egg, you pull out the tusks, you raise the skin of the nose, slice a bit out of the cheek, and make a false bridge, as high as you please; heal the cheek with a stitch or two, and operate with the lancet for the squint, and your bust is complete. Bravo! you understand?"

"I confess, Baron, I do not."

"You shall, however. Here is the case—a political refugee, like Monsieur Yelland Mace ——"

"But he was no such thing."

"Well, a criminal—any man in such a situation is, for me, a political refugee zat, for reasons, desires to revisit his country, and yet must be so thoroughly disguised zat by no surprise, and by no process, can he be satisfactorily recognised; he comes to me, tells me his case, and says, 'I desire, Baron, to become your patient,' and so he places himself in my hands, and so—ha, ha! You begin to perceive?"

"Yes, I do! I think I understand you clearly. But, Lord bless me! what a nefarious trade!" exclaimed Uncle David.

The baron was not offended; he laughed.

"Nevertheless," said he, "There's no harm in that. Not that I care much about the question of right or wrong in the matter; but there's none. Bah! who's the worse of his going back? or, if he did not, who's the better?"

Uncle David did not care to discuss this point in ethics, but simply said,—

"And Mr. Longcluse was also a patient of yours?"

"Yes, certainly," said the baron.

"We Londoners know nothing of his history," said Mr. Arden.

"A political refugee, like Mr. Mace," said the baron. "Now, look at Herr Yelland Mace. It was a severe operation, but a beautiful one! I opened the skin with a single straight cut from the lachrymal gland to the nostril, and one underneath meeting it, you see" (he was tracing the line of the scalpel with the stem of his pipe), "along the base of the nose from the point. Then I drew back the skin over the bridge, and then I operated on the bone and cartilage, cutting them and the muscle at the extremity down to a level with the line of the face, and drew the flap of skin back, cutting it to meet the line of the skin of the cheek; there, you see, so much for the nose. Now see the curved eyebrow. Instead of that very well marked arch, I resolved it should slant from the radix of the nose in a straight line obliquely upward; to effect which I removed at the upper edge of each eyebrow, at the corner next the temple, a portion of the skin and muscle, which, being reunited and healed, produced the requisite contraction, and thus drew that end of each brow upward. And now, having disposed of the nose and brows, I come to the mouth. Look at the profile of this mask."

He was holding that of Yelland Mace toward Mr. Arden, and with the bowl of the pipe in his right hand, pointed out the lines and features on which he descanted, with the amber point of the stem.

"Now, if you observe, the chin in this face, by reason of the marked prominence of the nose, has the effect of receding, but it does not. If you continue the perpendicular line of ze forehead, ze chin, you see, meets it. The upper lip, though short and well-formed, projects a good deal. Ze under lip rather retires, and this adds to the receding effect of the chin, you see. My coup-d'œil assured me that it was practicable to give to this feature the character of a projecting under-jaw. The complete depression of the nose more than half accomplished it. The rest is done by cutting away two upper and four under-teeth, and substituting false ones at the desired angle. By that application of dentistry I obtained zis new line." (He indicated the altered outline of the features, as before, with his pipe). "It was a very pretty operation. The effect you could hardly believe. He was two months recovering, confined to his bed, ha! ha! We can't have an immovable mask of living flesh, blood, and bone for nothing. He was threatened with erysipelas, and there was a rather critical inflammation of the left eye. When he could sit up, and bear the light, and looked in the glass, instead of thanking me, he screamed like a girl, and cried and cursed for an hour, ha, ha, ha! He was glad of it afterward: it was so complete. Look at it" (he held up the mask of Yelland Mace): "a face, on the whole, good-looking, but a little of a parrot-face, you know. I took him into my hands with that face, and" (taking up the mask of Mr. Longcluse, and turning it with a slow oscillation so as to present it in every aspect), he added, "these are the features of Yelland Mace as I sent him into the world with the name of Herr Longcluse!"

"You mean to say that Yelland Mace and Walter Longcluse are the same person?" cried David Arden, starting to his feet.

"I swear that here is Yelland Mace before, and here after the operation, call him what you please. When I was in London, two months ago, I saw Monsieur Longcluse. He is Yelland Mace; and these two masks are both masks of the same Yelland Mace."

"Then the evidence is complete," said David Arden, with awe in his face, as he stood for a moment gazing on the masks which the Baron Vanboeren held up side by side before him.

"Ay, the masks and the witness to explain them," said the baron, sturdily.

"It is a perfect identification," murmured Mr. Arden, with his eyes still riveted on the plaster faces. "Good God! how wonderful that proof, so complete in all its parts, should remain!"

"Well, I don't love Longcluse, since so he is named; he disobliged me when I was in London," said the baron. "Let him hang, since so you ordain it. I'm ready to go to London, give my evidence, and produce these plaster casts. But my time and trouble must be considered."

"Certainly."

"Yes," said the baron; "and to avoid tedious arithmetic, and for the sake of convenience, I will agree to visit London, at what time you appoint, to bring with me these two masks, and to give my evidence against Yelland Mace, otherwise Walter Longcluse, my stay in London not to exceed a fortnight, for ten thousand pounds sterling."

"I don't think, Baron, you can be serious," said Mr. Arden, as soon as he had recovered breath.

"Donner-wetter! I will show you that I am!" bawled the baron. "Now or never, Sir. Do as you please. I sha'n't abate a franc. Do you like my offer?"

On the event of this bargain are depending issues of which David Arden knows nothing; the dangers, the agonies, the salvation of those who are nearest to him on earth. The villain Longcluse, and the whole fabric of his machinations, may be dashed in pieces by a word.

How, then, did David Arden, who hated a swindle, answer the old extortioner, who asked him, "Do you like my offer?"

"Certainly not, Sir," said David Arden, sternly.

"Then was scheert's mich! What do I care! No more, no more about it!" yelled the baron in a fury, and dashed the two masks to pieces on the hearth-stone at his feet, and stamped the fragments into dust with his clumsy shoes.

With a cry, old Uncle David rushed forward to arrest the demolition, but too late. The baron, who was liable to such accesses of rage, was grinding his teeth, and rolling his eyes, and stamping in fury.

The masks, those priceless records, were gone, past all hope of restoration. Uncle David felt for a moment so transported with anger, that I think he was on the point of striking him. How it would have fared with him, if he had, I can't tell.

"Now!" howled the baron, "ten times ten thousand pounds would not place you where you were, Sir. You fancied, perhaps, I would stand haggling with you all night, and yield at last to your obstinacy. What is my answer? The floor strewn with the fragments of your calculation. Where will you turn—what will you do now?"

"Suppose I do this," said Uncle David fiercely—"report to the police what I have seen—your masks and all the rest, and accomplish, besides, all I require, by my own evidence as to what I myself saw?"

"And I will confront you, as a witness," said the baron, with a cold sneer, "and deny it all—swear it is a dream, and aid your poor relatives in proving you unfit to manage your own money matters."

Uncle David paused for a moment. The baron had no idea how near he was, at that moment, to a trial of strength with his English visitor. Uncle David thinks better of it, and he contents himself with saying, "I shall have advice, and you shall most certainly hear from me again."

Forth from the room strides David Arden in high wrath. Fearing to lose his way, he bawls over the banister, and through the corridors, "Is any one there?"

and after a time the old woman, who is awaiting him in the hall, replies, and he is once more in the open street.

CHAPTER LXXXII.

DOPPELGANGER.

It was late, he did not know or care how late. He was by no means familiar with this quarter of the city. He was agitated and angry, and did not wish to return to his hotel till he had a little walked off his excitement. Slowly he sauntered along, from street to street. These were old-fashioned, such as were in vogue in the days of the Regency. Tall houses, with gables facing the street; few of them showing any light from their windows, and their dark outlines discernible on high against the midnight sky. Now he heard the voices of people near, emerging from a low theatre in a street at the right. A number of men come along the trottoir, toward Uncle David. They were going to a gaming-house and restaurant at the end of the street, which he had nearly reached. This troop of idlers he accompanies. They turn into an open door, and enter a passage not very brilliantly lighted. At the left was the open door of a restaurant. The greater number of those who enter follow the passage, however, which leads to the roulette-room.

As Uncle David, with a caprice of curiosity, follows slowly in the wake of this accession to the company, a figure passes and goes before him into the room.

With a strange thrill he takes or mistakes this figure for Mr. Longcluse. He pauses, and sees the tall figure enter the roulette-room. He follows it as soon as he recollects himself a little, and goes into the room. The players are, as usual, engrossed by the game. But at the far side beyond these busy people, he sees this person, whom he recognises by a light great-coat, stooping with his lips pretty near the ear of a man who was sitting at the table. He raises himself in a moment more, and stands before Uncle David, and at the first glance he is quite certain that Mr. Longcluse is before him. The tall man stands with folded arms, and looks carelessly round the room, and at Uncle David among the rest.

"Here," he thought, "is the man; and the evidence, clear and conclusive, and so near this very spot, now scattered in dust and fragments, and the witness who might have clenched the case impracticable!"

This tall man, however, he begins to perceive, has points, and strong ones, of dissimilarity, notwithstanding his general resemblance to Mr. Longcluse. His beard and hair are red; his shoulders are broader, and very round; much clumsier and more powerful he looks; and there is an air of vulgarity and swagger and boisterous good spirits about him, certainly in marked contrast with Mr. Longcluse's very quiet demeanour.

Uncle David now finds himself in that uncomfortable state of oscillation between two opposite convictions which, in a matter of supreme importance, amounts very nearly to torture.

This man does not appear at all put out by Mr. Arden's observant presence, nor even conscious of it. A place becomes vacant at the table, and he takes it, and stakes some money, and goes on, and wins and loses, and at last yawns and turns away, and walks slowly round to the door near which David Arden is standing. Is not this the very man whom he saw for a moment on board the steamer, as he crossed? As he passes a jet of gas, the light falls upon his face at an angle that brings out lines that seem familiar to the Englishman, and for the moment determines his doubts. David Arden, with his eyes fixed upon him, says, as he was about to pass him,—

"How d'ye do, Mr. Longcluse?"

The gentleman stops, smiles, and shrugs.

"Pardon, Monsieur," he says in French, "I do not speak English or German."

The quality of the voice that spoke these words was, he thought, different from Mr. Longcluse's—less tone, less depth, and more nasal.

The gentleman pauses and smiles with his head inclined, evidently expecting to be addressed in French.

"I believe I have made a mistake, Sir," hesitates Mr. Arden.

The gentleman inclines his head lower, smiles, and waits patiently for a second or two. Mr. Arden, a little embarrassed, says,—

"I thought, Monsieur, I had met you before in England."

"I have never been in England, Monsieur," says the patient and polite Frenchman, in his own language. "I cannot have had the honour, therefore, of meeting Monsieur there."

He pauses politely.

"Then I have only to make an apology. I beg your—I beg—but surely—I think—by Jove!" he breaks into English, "I can't be mistaken—you are Mr. Longcluse."

The tall gentleman looks so unaffectedly puzzled, and so politely good-natured, as he resumes, in the tones which seem perfectly natural, and yet one note in which David Arden fails to recognise, and says,—

"Monsieur must not trouble himself of having made a mistake: my name is St. Ange."

"I believe I have made a mistake, Monsieur—pray excuse me."

The gentleman bows very ceremoniously, and Monsieur St. Ange walks slowly out, and takes a glass of curaçoa in the outer room. As he is paying the garçon, Mr. Arden again appears, once more in a state of uncertainty, and again leaning to the belief that this person is indeed the Mr. Longcluse who at present entirely possesses his imagination.

The tall stranger with the round shoulders in truth resembled the person who, in a midnight interview on Hampstead Heath, had discussed some momentous questions with Paul Davies, as we remember; but that person spoke in the peculiar accent of the northern border. His beard, too, was exorbitant in length, and flickered wide and red, in the wind. This beard, on the contrary, was short and trim, and hardly so red, I think, as that moss-trooper's. On the whole, the likeness in both cases was somewhat rude and general. Still the resemblance to Longcluse again struck Mr. Arden so powerfully, that he actually followed him into the street and overtook him only a dozen steps away from the door, on the now silent pavement.

Hearing his hurried step behind him, the object of his pursuit turns about and confronts him for the first time with an offended and haughty look.

"Monsieur!" says he a little grimly, drawing himself up as he comes to a sudden halt.

"The impression has forced itself upon me again that you are no other than Mr. Walter Longcluse," says Uncle David.

The tall gentleman recovered his good-humour, and smiled as before, with a shrug.

"I have not the honour of that gentleman's acquaintance, Monsieur, and cannot tell, therefore, whether he in the least resembles me. But as this kind of thing is unusual, and grows wearisome, and may end in putting me out of temper—which is not easy, although quite possible—and as my assurance that I am really myself seems insufficient to convince Monsieur, I shall be happy to offer other evidence of the most unexceptionable kind. My house is only two streets distant. There my wife and daughter await me, and our curé partakes of our little supper at twelve. I am a little late," says he, listening, for the clocks are tolling twelve; "however, it is a little more than two hundred metres, if you will accept my invitation, and I shall be very happy to introduce you to my wife, to my daughter Clotilde, and to our good curé, who is a most agreeable man. Pray come, share our little supper, see what sort of people we are, and in this way—more agreeable, I hope, than any other, and certainly less fallacious—you can ascertain whether I am Monsieur St. Ange, or that other gentleman with whom you are so obliging as to confound me. Pray come; it is not much—a fricasée, a few cutlets, an omelette, and a glass of wine. Madame St. Ange will be charmed to make your acquaintance, my daughter will sing us a song, and you will say that Monsieur le Curé is really a most entertaining companion."

There was something so simple and thoroughly good-natured in this invitation, under all the circumstances, that Mr. Arden felt a little ashamed of his persistent annoyance of so hospitable a fellow, and for the moment he was convinced that he must have been in error.

"Sir," says David Arden, "I am now convinced that I must have been mistaken; but I cannot deny myself the honour of being presented to Madame St. Ange, and I assure you I am quite ashamed of the annoyance I must have caused you, and I offer a thousand apologies."

"Not one, pray," replies the Frenchman, with great good-humour and gaiety. "I felicitate myself on a mistake which promises to result so happily."

So side by side, at a leisurely pace, they pursued their way through these silent streets, and unaccountably the conviction again gradually stole over Uncle David that he was actually walking by the side of Mr. Longcluse.

CHAPTER LXXXIII.

A SHORT PARTING.

The fluctuations of Mr. Arden's conviction continued. His new acquaintance chatted gaily. They passed a transverse street, and he saw him glance quickly right and left, with a shrewd eye that did not quite accord with his careless demeanour.

Here for a moment the moon fell full upon them, and the effect of this new light was, once more, to impair Mr. Arden's confidence in his last conclusions about this person. Again he was at sea as to his identity.

There were the gabble and vociferation of two women quarrelling in the street to the left, and three tipsy fellows, marching home, were singing a trio some way up the street to the right.

They had encountered but one figure—a seedy scrivener, slipshod, shuffling his way to his garret, with a baize bag of law-papers to copy in his left hand, and a sheaf of quills in his right, and a pale, careworn face turned up towards the sky. The streets were growing more silent and deserted as they proceeded.

He was sauntering onward by the side of this urbane and garrulous stranger, when, like a whisper, the thought came, "Take care!"

David Arden stopped short.

"Eh, bien?" said his polite companion, stopping simultaneously, and staring in his face a little grimly.

"On reflection, Monsieur, it is so late, that I fear I should hardly reach my hotel in time if I were to accept your agreeable invitation, and letters probably await me, which I should, at least, read to-night."

"Surely Monsieur will not disappoint me—surely Monsieur is not going to treat me so oddly?" expostulated Monsieur St. Ange.

"Good-night, Sir. Farewell!" said David Arden, raising his hat as he turned to go.

There intervened not two yards between them, and the polite Monsieur St. Ange makes a stride after him, and extends his hand—whether there is a weapon in it, I know not; but he exclaims fiercely,—

"Ha! robber! my purse!"

Fortunately, perhaps, at that moment, from a lane only a few yards away, emerge two gendarmes, and Monsieur St. Ange exclaims, "Ah, Monsieur, mille pardons! Here it is! All safe, Monsieur. Pray excuse my mistake as frankly as I have excused yours. Adieu!"

Monsieur St. Ange raises his hat, shrugs, smiles, and withdrew.

Uncle David thought, on the whole, he was well rid of his ambiguous acquaintance, and strode along beside the gendarmes, who civilly directed him upon his way, which he had lost.

So, then, upon Mr. Longcluse's fortunes the sun shone; his star, it would seem, was in the ascendant. If the evil genius who ruled his destiny was contending, in a chess game, with the good angel of Alice Arden, her game seemed pretty well lost, and the last move near.

When David Arden reached his hotel a note awaited him, in the hand of the Baron Vanboeren. He read it under the gas in the hall. It said:—

> "We must, in this world, forgive and reconsider many things. I therefore pardon you, you me. So soon as you have slept upon our conversation, you will accept an offer which I cannot modify. I always proportion the burden to the back. The rich pay me handsomely; for the poor I have prescribed and operated, sometimes, for nothing! You have the good fortune, like myself, to be childless, wifeless, and rich. When I take a fancy to a thing, nothing stops me; you, no doubt, in like manner. The trouble is something to me; the danger, which you count nothing, to me is much. The compensation I name, estimated without the circumstances, is large; compared with my wealth, trifling; compared with your wealth, nothing; as the condition of a transaction between you and me, therefore, not worth mentioning. The accident of last night I can repair. The original matrix of each mask remains safe in my hands: from this I can multiply casts ad libitum. Both these matrices I will hammer into powder at twelve o'clock to-morrow night, unless my liberal offer shall have been accepted before that hour. I write to a man of honour. We understand each other.

"Emmanuel Vanboeren."

The ruin, then, was not irretrievable; and there was time to take advice, and think it over. In the baron's brutal letter there was a coarse logic, not without its weight.

In better spirits David Arden betook himself to bed. It vexed him to think of submitting to the avarice of that wicked old extortioner; but to that submission, reluctant as he is, it seems probable he will come.

And now his thoughts turn upon the hospitable Monsieur St. Ange, and he begins, I must admit not altogether without reason, to reflect what a fool he has been. He wonders whether that hospitable and polite gentleman had intended to murder him, at the moment when the gendarmes so luckily appeared. And in the midst of his speculations, overpowered by fatigue, he fell asleep, and ate his breakfast next morning very happily.

Uncle David had none of that small diplomatic genius that helps to make a good attorney. That sort of knowledge of human nature would have prompted a careless reception of the baron's note, and an entire absence of that promptitude which seems to imply an anxiety to seize an offer.

Accordingly, it was at about eleven o'clock in the morning that he presented himself at the house of the Baron Vanboeren.

He was not destined to conclude a reconciliation with that German noble, nor to listen to his abrupt loquacity, nor ever more to discuss or negotiate anything whatsoever with him, for the Baron Vanboeren had been found that morning close to his hall door on the floor, shot with no less than three bullets through his body, and his pipe in both hands clenched to his blood-soaked breast like a crucifix. The baron is not actually dead. He has been hours insensible. He cannot live; and the doctor says that neither speech nor recollection can return before he dies.

By whose hands, for what cause, in what manner the world had lost that excellent man, no one could say. A great variety of theories prevail on the subject. He had sent the old servant for Pierre la Roche, whom he employed as a messenger, and he had given him at about a quarter to eleven a note addressed to David Arden, Esquire, which was no doubt that which Mr. Arden had received.

Had Heaven decreed that this investigation should come to naught? This blow seemed irremediable.

David Arden, however, had, as I mentioned, official friends, and it struck him that he might through them obtain access to the rooms in which his interviews with the baron had taken place; and that an ingenious and patient artist in plaster might be found who would search out the matrices, or, at worst, piece the fragments of the mask together, and so, in part, perhaps, restore the demolished evidence. It turned out, however, that the destruction of these relics was too complete for any such experiments; and all that now remained was, upon the baron's letter of the evening before, to move in official quarters for a search for those "matrices" from which it was alleged the masks were taken.

This subject so engrossed his mind, that it was not until after his late dinner that he began once more to think of Monsieur St. Ange, and his resemblance to Mr. Longcluse; and a new suspicion began to envelope those gentlemen in his imagination. A thought struck him, and up got Uncle David, leaving his wine unfinished, and a few minutes more saw him in the telegraph office, writing the following message:—

> "From Monsieur David Arden, etc., to Monsieur Blount, 5 Manchester Buildings, Westminster, London.
>
> "Pray telegraph immediately to say whether Mr. Longcluse is at his house, Bolton Street, Piccadilly."

No answer reached him that night; but in the morning he found a telegram dated 11.30 of the previous night, which said—

> "Mr. Longcluse is ill at his house at Richmond—better to-day."

To this promptly he replied—

> "See him, if possible, immediately at Richmond, and say how he looks. The surrender of the lease in Crown Alley will be an excuse. See him if there. Ascertain with certainty where. Telegraph immediately."

No answer had reached Uncle David at three o'clock P.M.; he had despatched his message at nine. He was impatient, and walked to the telegraph office to make inquiries, and to grumble. He sent another message in querulous and peremptory laconics. But no answer came till near twelve o'clock, when the following was delivered to him:—

> "Yours came while out. Received at 6 P.M. Saw Longcluse at Richmond. Looks seedy. Says he is all right now."

He read this twice or thrice, and lowered the hand whose fingers held it by the corner, and looked up, taking a turn or two about the room; and he thought what a precious fool he must have appeared to Monsieur St. Ange, and then again, with another view of that gentleman's character, what an escape he had possibly had.

So there was no distraction any longer; and he directed his mind now exclusively upon the distinct object of securing possession of the moulds from which the masks were taken; and for many reasons it is not likely that very much will come of his search.

CHAPTER LXXXIV.

AT MORTLAKE.

Events do not stand still at Mortlake. It is now about four o'clock on a fine autumnal afternoon. Since we last saw her, Alice Arden has not once sought to pass the hall-door. It would not have been possible to do so. No one passed that barrier without a scrutiny, and the aid of the key of the man who kept guard at the door, as closely as ever did the office at the hatch of the debtor's prison. The suite of five rooms up-stairs, to which Alice is now strictly confined, is not only comfortable, but luxurious. It had been fitted up for his own use by Sir Reginald years before he exchanged it for those rooms down-stairs which, as he grew older, he preferred.

Levi every day visited the house, and took a report of all that was said and planned up-stairs, in a tête-à-tête with Phœbe Chiffinch, in the great parlour among the portraits. The girl was true to her young and helpless mistress, and was in her confidence, outwitting the rascally Jew, who every time, by Longcluse's order, bribed her handsomely for the information that was misleading him.

From Phœbe the young lady concealed no pang of her agony. Well was it for her that in their craft they had exchanged the comparatively useless Miss Diaper for this poor girl, on whose apprenticeship to strange ways, and a not very fastidious life, they relied for a clever and unscrupulous instrument. Perhaps she had more than the cunning they reckoned upon. "But I 'av' took a liking to ye, Miss, and they'll not make nothing of Phœbe Chiffinch."

Alice was alone in her room, and Phœbe Chiffinch came running up the great staircase singing, and through the intervening suite of rooms, entered that in which her young mistress awaited her return. Her song falters, and dies into a strange ejaculation, as she passes the door.

"The Lord be thanked, that's over and done!" she exclaims, with a face pale from excitement.

"Sit down, Phœbe; you are trembling; you must drink a little water. Are you well?"

"La! quite well, Miss," said Phœbe, more cheerily, and then burst into tears. She gulped down some of the water which the frightened young lady held to her lips, and recovering quickly, she gets on her feet, and says impatiently—"I'm sure, Miss, I don't know what makes me such a fool; but I'm all right now, Ma'am; and you asked me, the other day, about the big key of the old back-door lock that I showed you, and I said, though it could not open no door, I would find a use for it, yet. So I 'av', Miss."

"Go on; I recollect perfectly."

"You remember the bit of parchment I asked you to write the words on yesterday evening, Miss? They was these: 'Passage on the left, from main passage to housekeeper's room,' etc. Well, I was with Mr. Vargers when he locked that passage up, and it leads to a door in the side of the 'ouse, which it opens into the grounds; and in that houter door he left a key, and only took with him the key of the door at the other end, which it opens from the 'ousekeeper's passage. So all seemed sure—sure it is, so long as you can't get into that side passage, which it is locked."

"I understand; go on, Phœbe."

"Well, Miss, the reason I vallied that key I showed you so much, was because it's as like the key of the side passage as one egg is to another, only it won't turn in the lock. So, as that key I must 'av', I tacked the bit of parchment you wrote to the 'andle of the other, which the two matches exactly, and I didn't tell you, Miss, thinking what a taking you'd be in, but I went down to try if I could not take it for the right one."

"It was kind of you not to tell me; go on," said the young lady.

"Well, Miss, I 'ad the key in my pocket, ready to change; and I knew well how 'twould be, if I was found out—I'd get the sack, or be locked up 'ere myself, more likely, and no more chances for you. Mr. Vargers was in the room—the porter's room they calls it now—and in I goes. I did not see no one there, but Vargers and he was lookin' sly, I thought, and him and Mr. Boult has been talking me over, I fancy, and they don't quite trust me. So I began to talk, wheedling him the best I could to let me go into town for an hour; 'twas only for talk, for well I knew I shouldn't get to go; but nothing but chaff did he answer. And then, says I, is Mr. Levice come yet, and he said, he is, but he has a second key of the back door and he may 'av' let himself hout. Well, I says, thinking to make Vargers jealous, he's a werry pleasant gentleman, a bit too pleasant for me, and I'm a-going to the kitchen, and I'd rayther he wastnt there, smoking as he often does, and talking nonsense, when I'm in it. There's others that's nicer, to my fancy, than him—so, jest you go and see, and I'll take care of heverything 'ere till you come back—and don't you be a minute. There was the keys, lying along the chimney-piece, at my left, and the big table in front, and nothing to hinder me from changing mine for his, but Vargers' eye over me. Little I thought he'd 'av' bin so ready to do as I said. But he smiled to himself-like, and he said he'd go and see. So away he went; and I listens at the door till I heard his foot go on the tiles of the passage that goes down by the 'ousekeeper's room, and the billiard-room, to the kitchen; and then on tiptoe, as quick as light, I goes to the chimney-piece, and without a sound, I takes the very key I wanted in my fingers, and drops it into my pocket, but putting down the other in its place, I knocked down the big leaden hink-bottle, and didn't it make a bang on the floor—and a terrible hoarse voice roars out from the tother side of the table—'What the devil are you doing there, huzzy?' Saving your presence, Miss; and up gets Mr. Boult, only half awake, looking as mad as Bedlam, and I thought I would have fainted away! Who'd 'av' fancied he was in the room? He had his 'ead on the table, and the cloak over it, and I think, when they 'eard me a-coming downstairs, they agreed he should 'ide hisself so, to catch me, while Vargers would leave the room, to try if I would meddle with the keys, or the like—and while Mr. Boult was foxing, he fell asleep in right earnest. Warn't it a joke, Miss? So I brazent it hout, Miss, the best I could, and I threatened to complain to Mr. Levi, and said I'd stay no longer, to be talked to, that way, by sich as he. And Boult could not tell Vargers he was asleep, and so I saw him count over the keys, and up I ran, singing."

By this time the girl was on her knees, concealing the key between the beds, with the others.

"Thank God, Phœbe, you have got it! But, oh! all that is before us still!"

"Yes, there's work enough, Miss. I'll not be so frightened no more. Tom Chiffinch, that beat the Finchley pet, after ninety good rounds, was my brother, and I won't show nothing but pluck, Miss, from this out—you'll see."

Alice had proposed writing to summon her friends to her aid. But Phœbe protested against that extremely perilous measure. Her friends were away from London; who could say where? And she believed that the attempt to post the letters would miscarry, and that they were certain to fall into the hands of their jailors. She insisted that Alice should rely on the simple plan of escape from Mortlake.

Martha Tansey, it is true, was anxious. She wondered how it was that she had not once heard from her young mistress since her journey to Yorkshire. And a passage in a letter which had reached her, from the old servant, at David Arden's town house, who had been mystified by Sir Richard, perplexed and alarmed her further, by inquiring how Miss Alice looked, and whether she had been knocked up by the journey to Arden on Wednesday.

So matters stood.

Each evening Mr. Levi was in attendance, and this day, according to rule, she went down to the grand old dining-room.

"How'sh Miss Chiffinch?" said the little Jew, advancing to meet her; "how'sh her grashe the duchess, in the top o' the houshe? Ish my Lady Mount-garret ash proud ash ever?"

"Well, I do think, Mr. Levice, there's a great change; she's bin growing better the last two days, and she's got a letter last night that's seemed to please her."

"Wha'at letter?"

"The letter you gave me last night for her."

"O-oh! Ah! I wonder—eh? Do you happen to know what wa'azh in that ere letter?" he asked, in an insinuating whisper.

"Not I, Mr. Levice. She don't trust me not as far as you'd throw a bull by the tail. You might 'av' managed that better. You must 'a frightened her some way about me. I try to be agreeable all I can, but she won't a-look at me."

"Well, I don't want to know, I'm sure. Did she talk of going out of doors since?"

"No; there's a frost in the hair still, and she says till that's gone she won't stir out."

"That frost will last a bit, I guess. Any more newshe?"

"Nothing."

"Wait a minute 'ere," said Mr. Levi, and he went into the room beyond this, where she knew there were writing materials.

She waited some time, and at length took the liberty of sitting down. She was kept a good while longer. The sun went down; the drowsy crimson that heralds night overspread the sky. She coughed; several fits of coughing she tried at short intervals. Had Mr. Levice, as she called him, forgotten her? He came out at length in the twilight.

"Shtay you 'ere a few minutes more," said that gentleman, as he walked thoughtfully through the room and paused. "You wazh asking yesterday where izh Sir Richard Arden. Well, hezh took hishelf off to Harden in Yorkshire, and he'll not be 'ome again for a week."

Having delivered this piece of intelligence, he nodded, and slowly went to the hall, and closed the door carefully as he left the room. She followed to the door and listened. There was plainly a little fuss going on in the hall. She heard feet in motion, and low talking. She was curious and would have peeped, but the door was secured on the outside. The twilight had deepened, and for the first time she saw that a ray of candle-light came through the key-hole from the inner room. She opened the door softly, and saw a gentleman writing at the table. He was quite alone. He turned, and rose: a tall, slight gentleman, with a singular countenance that startled her.

"You are Phœbe Chiffinch," said a deep, clear voice, sternly, as the gentleman pointed towards her with the plume end of the pen he held in his fingers. "I am Mr. Longcluse. It is I who have sent you two pounds each day by Levi. I hear you have got it all right."

The girl curtseyed, and said "Yes, Sir," at the second effort, for she was startled. He had taken out and opened his pocket-book.

"Here are ten pounds," and he handed her a rustling new note by the corner. "I'll treat you liberally, but you must speak truth, and do exactly as you are ordered by Levi." She curtseyed again. There was something in that gentleman that frightened her awfully.

"If you do so, I mean to give you a hundred pounds when this business is over. I have paid you as my servant, and if you deceive me I'll punish you; and there are two or three little things they complain of at the 'Guy of Warwick,' and" (he swore a hard oath) "you shall hear of them if you do."

She curtseyed, and felt, not angry, as she would if any one else had said it, but frightened, for Mr. Longcluse's was a name of power at Mortlake.

"You gave Miss Arden a letter last night. You know what was in it?"

"Yes, Sir."

"What was it?"

"An offer of marriage from you, Sir."

"Yes: how do you know that?"

"She told me, please, Sir."

"How did she take it? Come, don't be afraid."

"I'd say it pleased her well, Sir."

He looked at her in much surprise, and was silent for a time.

He repeated his question, and receiving a similar answer, reflected on it.

"Yes; it is the best way out of her troubles; she begins to see that," he said, with a strange smile.

He walked to the chimney-piece, and leaned on it; and forgot the presence of Phœbe. She was too much in awe to make any sign. Turning he saw her, suddenly.

"You will receive some directions from Mr. Levi; take care you understand and execute them."

He touched the bell, and Levi opened the door; and she and that person walked together to the foot of the stair, where in a low tone they talked.

CHAPTER LXXXV.

THE CRISIS.

When Phœbe Chiffinch returned to Alice's room, it was about ten o'clock; a brilliant moon was shining on the old trees, and throwing their shadows on the misty grass. The landscape from these upper windows was sad and beautiful, and above the distant trees that were softened by the haze of night rose the silvery spire of the old church, in whose vault her father sleeps with a cold brain, thinking no more of mortgages and writs.

Alice had been wondering what had detained her so long, and by the time she arrived had become very much alarmed.

Relieved when she entered, she was again struck with fear when Phœbe Chiffinch had come near enough to enable her to see her face. She was pale, and with her eyes fixed on her, raised her finger in warning, and then glanced at the door which she had just closed.

Her young mistress got up and approached her, also growing pale, for she perceived that danger was at the door.

"I wish there was bolts to these doors. They've got other keys. Never mind; I know it all now," she whispered, as she walked softly up to the end of the room farthest from the door. "I said I'd stand by you, my lady; don't you lose heart. They're coming here in about a hour."

"For God's sake, what is it?" said Alice faintly, her eyes gazing wider and wider, and her very lips growing white.

"There's work before us, my lady, and there must be no fooling," said the girl, a little sternly. "Mr. Levi, please, has told me a deal, and all they expect from me, the villains. Are you strong enough to take your part in it, Miss? If not, best be quiet; best for both."

"Yes; quite strong, Phœbe. Are we to leave this?"

"I hope, Miss. We can but try."

"There's light, Phœbe," she said, glancing with a shiver from the window. "It's a bright night."

"I wish 'twas darker; but mind you what I say. Longcluse is to be here in a hour. Your brother's coming, God help you! and that little limb o' Satan, that black-eyed, black-nailed, dirty little Jew, Levice! They're not in town, they're out together near this, where a man is to meet them with writings. There's a licence got, Christie Vargers saw Mr. Longcluse showing it to your brother, Sir Richard; and I daren't tell Vargers that I'm for you. He'd never do nothing to vex Mr. Levice, he daren't. There's a parson here, a rum 'un, you may be sure. I think I know something about him; Vargers does. He's in the room now, only one away from this, next the stair head, and Vargers is put to keep the door in the same room. All the doors along, from one room to t'other, is open, from this to the stairs, except the last, which Vargers has the key of it; and all the doors opening from the rooms to the gallery is locked, so you can't get out o' this 'ere without passing through the one where parson is, and Mr. Vargers, please."

"I'll speak to the clergyman," whispered Alice, extending her hands towards the far door; "God be thanked, there's one good man here, and he'll save me!"

"La, bless you child! why that parson had his two pen'orth long ago, and spends half his nights in the lock-up."

"I don't understand, Phœbe."

"He had two years. He's bin in jail, Miss, Vargers says, as often as he has fingers and toes; and he's at his brandy and water as I came through, with his feet on the fender, and his pipe in his mouth. He's here to marry you, please 'm, to Mr. Longcluse, and there's all the good he'll do you; and your brother will give you away, Miss, and Levice and Vargers for witnesses, and me I dessay. It's every bit harranged, and they don't care the rinsing of a tumbler what you say or do; for through with it, slicks, they'll go, and say 'twas all right, in spite of all you can do; and who is there to make a row about it? Not you, after all's done."

"We must get away! I'll lose my life, or I'll escape!"

Phœbe looked at her in silence. I think she was measuring her strength, and her nerve, for the undertaking.

"Well, 'm, it's time it was begun. The time is come. Here's your cloak, Miss, I'll tie a handkerchief over my head, if we get out; and here's the three keys, betwixt the bed and the mattress."

After a moment's search on her knees, she produced them.

"The big one and this I'll keep, and you'll manage this other, please; take it in your right hand—you must use it first. It opens the far door of the room where Vargers is, and if you get through, you'll be at the stair-head then. Don't you come in after me, till you see I have Vargers engaged another way. Go through as light as a bird flies, and take the key out of the door, at the other end, when you unlock it; and close it softly, else he'll see it, and have the house about our ears; and you know the big window at the drawing-room lobby; wait in the hollow of that window till I come. Do you understand, please, Miss?"

Alice did perfectly.

"Hish-sh!" said the maid, with a prolonged caution.

A dead silence followed; for a minute—several minutes neither seemed to breathe.

Phœbe whispered at length—

"Now, Miss, are you ready?"

"Yes," she whispered, and her heart beat for a moment as if it would suffocate her, and then was still; an icy chill stole over her, and as on tip-toe she followed Phœbe, she felt as if she glided without weight or contact, like a spirit.

Through a dark room they passed, very softly, first, a little light under the door showed that there were candles in the next. They halted and listened. Phœbe opened the door and entered.

Standing back in the shadow, Alice saw the room and the people in it, distinctly. The parson was not the sort of contraband clergyman she had fancied, by any means, but a thin hectic man of some four-and-thirty years, only looking a little dazed by brandy and water, and far gone in consumption. Handsome thin features, and a suit of seedy black, and a white choker, indicated that lost gentleman, who was crying silently as he smoked his pipe, I daresay a little bit tipsy, gazing into the fire, with his fatal brandy and water at his elbow.

"Eh! Mr. Vargers, smoking after all I said to you!" murmured Miss Phœbe severely, advancing toward her round-shouldered sweetheart, with her finger raised.

Mr. Vargers replied pleasantly; and as this tender "chaff" flew lightly between the interlocutors, the parson looked still into the fire, hearing nothing of their play and banter, but sunk deep in the hell of his sorrowful memory.

As Phœbe talked on, Vargers grew agreeable and tender, and in about three minutes after her own entrance, she saw with a thrill, imperfectly, just with the "corner of her eye," something pass behind them swiftly toward the outer door. The crisis, then, had come. For a moment there seemed a sudden light before her eyes, and then a dark mist; in another she recovered herself.

Vargers stood up suddenly.

"Hullo! what's gone with the door there?" said he, sternly ending their banter.

If he had been looking on her with an eye of suspicion, he might have seen her colour change. But Phœbe was quick-witted and prompt, and saying, in hushed tones—

"Well, dear, ain't I a fool, leaving the lady's door open? Look ye, now, Mr. Vargers, she's lying fast asleep on her bed; and that's the reason I took courage to come here and ask a favour. But I'd rayther you'd lock her door, for if she waked and missed me she'd be out here, and all the fat in the fire."

"I dessay you're right, Miss," said he, with a more business-like gallantry; and as he shut the door and fumbled in his pocket for the key, she stole a look over her shoulder.

The prisoner had got through, and the door at the other end was closed.

With a secret shudder, she thanked God in her heart, while with a laugh she slapped Mr. Vargers' lusty shoulder, and said wheedlingly, "And now for the favour, Mr. Vargers: you must let me down to the kitchen for five minutes."

A little more banter and sparring followed, which ended in Vargers kissing her, in spite of the usual squall and protest; and on his essaying to let her out, and finding the door unlocked, he swore that it was well she asked, as he'd 'av' got it hot and heavy for forgetting to lock it, when the "swells" came up. The door closed upon her: so far the enterprise was successful.

She stood at the head of the stairs; she went down a few steps, and listened; then cautiously she descended. The moon shone resplendent through the great window at the landing below the drawing-room. It was that at which Uncle David had paused to listen to the minstrelsy of Mr. Longcluse.

Here in that flood of white light stands Alice Arden, like a statue of horror. The girl, without saying a word, takes her by the cold hand, and leads her quickly down to the arch that opens on the hall.

Just as they reached this point, the door of the room, at the right of the hall door, occupied by Mr. Boult, who did duty as porter, opens, and stepping out with a candle in his hand, he calls in a savage tone—

"What's the row?"

Phœbe pushed Alice's hand in the direction of the passage that leads to the housekeeper's room. For a moment the young lady stands irresolute. Her presence of mind returns. She noiselessly takes the hint, and enters the corridor; Phœbe advances to answer his challenge.

"Well, Mr. Boult, and what is the row, pray?" she pertly inquires, walking up to that gentleman, who eyes her sulkily, raising his candle, and displaying as he does so a big patch of red on each cheek-bone, indicative of the brandy, of which he smells potently.

"What's the row?—you're the row! What brings you down here, Miss Chivvige?"

"My legs! There's your answer, you cross boy." She laughed wheedlingly.

"Then walk you up again, and be d—d."

"On! Mr. Boult."

"P! Miss Phibbie."

Mr. Boult was speaking thick, and plainly was in no mood to stand nonsense.

"Now Mr. Boult, where's the good of making yourself disagreeable?"

"Look at this 'ere," he replied, grimly holding a mighty watch, of some white metal, under her eyes—"you know your clock as well as me, Miss Chavvinge. The gentlemen will be in this 'ere awl in twenty minutes."

"All the more need to be quick, Mr. Boult, Sir, and why will you keep me 'ere talking?" she replies.

"You'll go up them 'ere stairs, young 'oman; you'll not put a foot in the kitchen to-night," he says more doggedly.

"Well, we'll see how it will be when they comes and I tells 'em—'Please, gentlemen, the young lady, which you told me most particular to humour her in everything she might call for, wished a cup of tea, which I went down, having locked her door first, which here is the key of it,'" and she held it up for the admiration of Mr. Boult, "'which I consider it the most importantest key in the 'ouse; and though the young lady, she lay on her bed a-gasping, poor thing, for her cup of tea, Mr. Boult stopt me in the awl, and swore she shouldn't have a drop, which

I could not get it, and went hup again, for he smelt all over of brandy, and spoke so wiolent, I daren't do as you desired.'"

"I don't smell of brandy; no, I don't; do I?" he says, appealing to an imaginary audience. "And I don't want to stop you, if so be the case is so. But you'll come to this door and report yourself in five minute's time, or I'll tell 'em there's no good keepin' me 'ere no longer. I don't want no quarrellin' nor disputin', only I'll do my dooty, and I'm not afraid of man, woman, or child!"

With which magnanimous sentiment he turned on his clumsy heel, and entered his apartment again.

In a moment more Phœbe and Alice were at the door which admits to a passage leading literally to the side of the house. This door Phœbe softly unlocks, and when they had entered, locks again on the inside. They stood now on the passage leading to a side door, to which a few paces brought them. She opens it. The cold night air enters, and they step out upon the grass. She locks the door behind them, and throws the key among the nettles that grew in a thick grove at her right.

"Hold my hand, my lady; it's near done now," she whispers almost fiercely; and having listened for a few seconds, and looked up to see if any light appeared in the windows, she ventures, with a beating heart, from under the deep shadow of the gables, into the bright broad moonlight, and with light steps together they speed across the grass, and reach the cover of a long grove of tall trees and underwood. All is silent here.

Soon a distant shouting brings them to a terrible stand-still. Breathlessly Phœbe listens. No; it was not from the house. They resume their flight.

Now under the ivy-laden branches of a tall old tree an owl startles them with its shriek.

As Alice stares around her, when they stop in such momentary alarm, how strange the scene looks! How immense and gloomy the trees about them! How black their limbs stretch across the moon-lit sky! How chill and wild the moonlight spreads over the undulating sward! What a spectral and exaggerated shape all things take in her scared and over-excited gaze!

Now they are approaching the long row of noble beeches that line the boundary of Mortlake. The ivy-bowered wall is near them, and the screen of gigantic hollies that guard the lonely postern through which Phœbe has shrewdly chosen to direct their escape.

Thank God! they are at it. In her hand she holds the key, which shines in the moon-beams.

Hush! what is this? Voices close to the door! Step back behind the holly clump, for your lives, quickly! A key grinds in the lock; the bolt works rustily; the door opens, and tall Mr. Longcluse enters, with every sinister line and shadow of his pale face marked with a death-like sternness, in the moonlight. Mr. Levi enters almost beside him; how white his big eyeballs gleam, as he steps in under the same cold light! Who next?

Her brother! Oh, God! The mad impulse to throw her arms about his neck, and shriek her wild appeal to his manhood, courage, love, and stake all on that momentary frenzy!

As this group halts in silence, while Sir Richard locks the door, the Jew directs his big dark eyes, as she thinks, right upon Phœbe Chiffinch, who stands in the shadow, and is therefore, she faintly hopes, not visible behind the screen of glittering leaves. Her eyes, nevertheless, meet his. He advances his head a little, with more than his usual prying malignity, she thinks. Her heart flutters, and sinks. She is on the point of stepping from her shelter and surrendering. With his cane he strikes at the leaves, aiming, I daresay, at a moth, for nothing is quite below his notice, and he likes smashing even a fly. In this case, having hit or missed it, he turns his fiery eyes, to the infinite relief of the girl, another way.

The three men who have thus stept into the grounds of Mortlake don't utter a word as they stand there. They now recommence their walk toward the house.

Phœbe Chiffinch, breathless, is holding Alice Arden's wrist with a firm grasp. As they brush the holly-leaves, in passing, the very sprays that touch the dresses of the scared girls are stirring. The pale group drifts by in silence. They have each something to meditate on. They are not garrulous. On they walk, like three shadows. The distance widens, the shapes grow fainter.

"They'll soon be at the house, Ma'am, and wild work then. You'll do something for poor Vargers? Well, time enough! You must not lose heart now, my lady. You're all right, if you keep up for ten minutes longer. You don't feel faint-like! Good lawk, Ma'am! rouse up."

"I'm better, Phœbe; I'm quite well again. Come on—come on!"

Carefully, to make as little noise as possible she turned the key in the lock, and they found themselves in a narrow lane running by the wall, and under the trees of Mortlake.

"Which way?"

"Not toward the 'Guy of Warwick.' They'll soon be in chase of us, and that is the way they'll take. 'Twould never do. Come away, my lady; it won't be long till we meet a cab or something to fetch us where you please. Lean on me. I wish we were away from this wall. What way do you mean to go?"

"To my Uncle David's house."

And having exchanged these words, they pursued their way side by side, for a time, in silence.

CHAPTER LXXXVI.

PURSUIT.

Arrived at Mortlake, when Mr. Longcluse had discovered with certainty the flight of Alice Arden, his first thought was that Sir Richard had betrayed him. There was a momentary paroxysm of insane violence, in which, if he could only have discovered that he was the accomplice of Alice's escape, I think he would have killed him.

It subsided. How could Alice Arden have possessed such an influence over this man, who seemed to hate her? He sat down, and placed his hand to his broad, pale forehead, his dark eyes glaring on the floor, in what seemed an intensity of thought and passion. He was seized with a violent trembling fit. It lasted only for a few minutes. I sometimes think he loved that girl desperately, and would have made her an idolatrous husband.

He walked twice or thrice up and down the great parlour in which they sat, and then with cold malignity said to Sir Richard—

"But for you she would have married me; but for you I should have secured her now. Consider, how shall I settle with you?"

"Settle how you will—do what you will. I swear (and he did swear hard enough, if an oath could do it, to satisfy any man) I've had nothing to do with it. I've never had a hint that she meditated leaving this place. I can't conceive how it was done, nor who managed it, and I know no more than you do where she is gone." And he clenched his vehement disclaimer with an imprecation.

Longcluse was silent for a minute.

"She has gone, I assume, to David Arden's house," he said, looking down. "There is no other house to receive her in town, and she does not know that he is away still. She knows that Lady May, and other friends, have gone. She's there. The will makes you, colourably, her guardian. You shall claim the custody of her person. We'll go there, and remove her."

Old Sir Reginald's will, I may remark, had been made years before, when Richard was not twenty-two, and Alice little more than a child, and the baronet and his son good friends.

He stalked out. At the steps was his trap, which was there to take Levi into town. That gentleman, I need not say, he did not treat with much ceremony. He mounted, and Sir Richard Arden beside him; and, leaving the Jew to shift for himself, he drove at a furious pace down the avenue. The porter placed there by Longcluse, of course, opened the gate instantaneously at his call. Outside stood a cab, with a trunk on it. An old woman at the lodge-window, knocking and clamouring, sought admission.

"Let no one in," said Longcluse sternly to the man, who locked the iron gate on their passing out.

"Hallo! What brings her here? That's the old housekeeper!" said Longcluse, pulling up suddenly.

It was quite true. Her growing uneasiness about Alice had recalled the old woman from the North. Martha Tansey, who had heard the clang of the gate and the sound of wheels and hoofs, turned about and came to the side of the tax-cart, over which Longcluse was leaning. In the brilliant moonlight, on the white road, the branches cast a network of black shadow. A patch of light fell clear on the side of the trap, and on Longcluse's ungloved hand as he leaned on it.

"Here am I, Martha Tansey, has lived fifty year wi' the family, and what for am I shut out of Mortlake now?" she demanded, with stern audacity.

A sudden change, however, came over her countenance, which contracted in horror, and her old eyes opened wide and white as she gazed on the back of Longcluse's hand, on which was a peculiar star-shaped scar. She drew back with a low sound, like the growl of a wicked old cat; it rose gradually to such a yell and a cry to God as made Richard's blood run cold, and lifting her hand toward her temple, waveringly, the old woman staggered back, and fell in a faint on the road.

Longcluse jumped down and hammered at the window. "Hallo!" he cried to the man, "send one of your people with this old woman; she's ill. Let her go in that cab to Sir Richard Arden's house in town; you know it." And he cried to the cabman, "Lift her in, will you?"

And having done his devoir thus by the old woman, he springs again into his tax-cart, snatches the reins from Sir Richard, and drives on at a savage pace for town.

Longcluse threw the reins to Sir Richard when they reached David Arden's house, and himself thundered at the door.

They had searched Mortlake House for Alice, and that vain quest had not wasted more than half-an-hour. He rightly conjectured that, if Alice had fled to David Arden's house, some of the servants who received her must be still on the alert. The door is opened promptly by an elderly servant woman.

"Sir Richard Arden is at the door, and he wants to know whether his sister, Miss Arden, has arrived here from Mortlake."

"Yes, Sir; she's up-stairs; but not by no means well, Sir."

Longcluse stepped in, to secure a footing, and beckoning excitedly to Sir Richard, called, "Come in; all right. Don't mind the horse; it will take its chance."

He walked impatiently to the foot of the stairs, and turned again toward the street door.

At this moment, and before Sir Richard had time to come in, there come swarming out of David Arden's study, most unexpectedly, nearly a dozen men, more than half of whom are in the garb of gentlemen, and some three of them police. Uncle David himself, in deep conversation with two gentlemen, one of whom is placing in his breast-pocket a paper which he has just folded, leads the way into the hall.

As they there stand for a minute under the lamp, Mr. Longcluse, gazing at him sternly from the stair, caught his eye. Old David Arden stepped back a little, growing pale, with a sudden frown.

"Oh! Mr. Arden?" says Longcluse, advancing as if he had come in search of him.

"That's enough, Sir," cries Mr. Arden, extending his hand peremptorily toward him; and he adds, with a glance at the constables, "There's the man. That is Walter Longcluse."

Longcluse glances over his shoulder, and then grimly at the group before him, and gathered himself as if for a struggle; the next moment he walks forward frankly, and asks, "What is the meaning of all this?"

"A warrant, Sir," answers the foremost policeman, clutching him by the collar.

"No use, Sir, making a row," expostulates the next, also catching him by the collar and arm.

"Mr. Arden, can you explain this?" says Mr. Longcluse coolly.

"You may as well give in quiet," says the third policeman, producing the warrant. "A warrant for murder. Walter Longcluse, alias Yelland Mace, I arrest you in the Queen's name."

"There's a magistrate here? Oh! yes, I see. How d'ye do, Mr. Harman? My name is Longcluse, as you know. The name Mays, or any other alias, you'll not insult me by applying to me, if you please. Of course this is obvious and utter trumpery. Are there informations, or what the devil is it?"

"They have just been sworn before me, Sir," answered the magistrate, who was a little man, with a wave of his hand, and his head high.

"Well, really! don't you see the absurdity? Upon my soul! It is really too ridiculous! You won't inconvenience me, of course, unnecessarily. My own recognisance, I suppose, will do?"

"Can't entertain your application; quite out of the question," said his worship, with his hands in his pockets, rising slightly on his toes, and descending on his heels, as he delivered this sentence with a stoical shake of his head.

"You'll send for my attorney, of course? I'm not to be humbugged, you know."

"I must tell you, Mr. Longcluse, I can't listen to such language," observes Mr. Harman sublimely.

"If you have informations, they are the dreams of a madman. I don't blame any one here. I say, policeman, you need not hold me quite so hard. I only say, joke or earnest, I can't make head or tail of it; and there's not a man in London who won't be shocked to hear how I've been treated. Once more, Mr. Harman, I tender bail, any amount. It's too ridiculous. You can't really have a difficulty."

"The informations are very strong, Sir, and the offence, you know as well as I do, Mr. Longcluse, is not bailable."

Mr. Longcluse shrugged, and laughed gently.

"I may have a cab or something? My trap's at the door. It's not solemn enough, eh, Mr. Harman? Will you tell one of your fellows to pick up a cab? Perhaps, Mr. Arden, you'll allow me a chair to sit down upon?"

"You can sit in the study, if you please," says David Arden.

And Longcluse enters the room with the police about him, while the servant goes to look for a cab. Sir Richard Arden, you may be sure, was not there. He saw that something was wrong, and he had got away to his own house. On arriving there, he sent to make inquiry, cautiously, at his uncle's, and thus learned the truth.

Standing at the window, he saw his messenger return, let him in himself, and then considered, as well as a man in so critical and terrifying a situation can, the wisest course for him to adopt. The simple one of flight he ultimately resolved on. He knew that Longcluse had still two executions against him, on which, at any moment, he might arrest him. He knew that he might launch at him, at any moment, the thunderbolt which would blast him. He must wait, however, until the morning had confirmed the news; that certain, he dared not act.

With a cold and fearless bearing, Longcluse had by this time entered the dreadful door of a prison. His attorney was with him nearly the entire night.

David Arden, as he promised, had dictated to him in outline the awful case he had massed against his client.

"I don't want any man taken by surprise or at disadvantage; I simply wish for truth," said he.

A copy of the written statement of Paul Davies, whatever it was worth, duly witnessed, was already in his hands; the sworn depositions of the same person, made in his last illness, were also there. There were also the sworn depositions of Vanboeren, who had, after all, recovered speech and recollection; and a deposition, besides, very unexpected, of old Martha Tansey, who swore distinctly to the scar, a very peculiar mark indeed, on the back of his left hand. This the old woman had recognised with horror, at a moment so similar, as the scar, long forgotten, which she had for a terrible moment seen on the hand of Yelland Mace, as he clutched the rail of the gig while engaged in the murder.

The plaster masks, which figured in the affidavits of Vanboeren, and of David Arden, were re-cast from the moulds, and made an effectual identification, corroborated, in a measure, by Mr. Plumes' silhouette of Yelland Mace.

Other surviving witnesses had also turned up, who had deposed when the murder of Harry Arden was a recent event. The whole case was, in the eyes of the attorney, a very awful one. Mr. Longcluse's counsel was called up, like a physician whose patient is in extremis, at dead of night, and had a talk with the attorney, and kept his notes to ponder over.

As early as prison rules would permit, he was with Mr. Longcluse, where the attorney awaited him.

Mr. Blinkinsop looked very gloomy.

"Do you despair?" asked Mr. Longcluse sharply, after a long disquisition.

"Let me ask you one question, Mr. Longcluse. You have, before I ask it, I assume, implicit confidence in us; am I right?"

"Certainly—implicit."

"If you are innocent, we might venture on a line of defence which may possibly break down the case for the Crown. If you are guilty, that line would be fatal." He hesitated, and looked at Mr. Longcluse.

"I know such a question has been asked in like circumstances, and I have no hesitation in telling you that I am not innocent. Assume my guilt."

The attorney, who had been drumming a little tattoo on the table, watches Longcluse earnestly as he speaks, suspending his tune, now lowers his eyes to the table, and resumed his drumming slowly with a very dismal countenance. He had been talking over the chances with this eminent counsel, Mr. Blinkinsop, Q.C., and he knew what his opinion would now be.

"One effect of a judgment in this case is forfeiture?" inquired Mr. Longcluse.

"Yes," answered counsel.

"Everything goes to the Crown, eh?"

"Yes; clearly."

"Well, I have neither wife nor children. I need not care; but suppose I make my will now; that's a good will, ain't it, between this and judgment, if things should go wrong?"

"Certainly," said Mr. Blinkinsop. "No judgment no forfeiture."

"And now, Doctor, don't be afraid; tell me truly, shall I do?" said Mr. Longcluse, leaning back, and looking darkly and steadily in his face.

"It is a nasty case."

"Don't be afraid, I say. I should like to know, are the chances two to one against me?"

"I'm afraid they are."

"Ten to one? Pray say what you think."

"Well, I think so."

Mr. Longcluse grew paler. They were all three silent. After about a minute, he said, in a very low tone,—

"You don't think I have a chance? Don't mislead me."

"It is very gloomy."

Mr. Longcluse pressed his hand to his mouth. There was a silence. Perhaps he wished to hide some nervous movement there. He stood up, walked about a little, and then stood by Mr. Blinkinsop's chair, with his fingers on the back of it.

"We must make a great fight of this," said Mr. Longcluse suddenly. "We'll fight it hard; we must win it. We shall win it, by ——"

And after a short pause, he added gently,—

"That will do. I think I'll rest now; more, perhaps, another time. Good-bye."

As they left the room, he signed to the attorney to stay.
"I have something for you—a word or two."
The attorney turned back, and they remained closeted for a time.

CHAPTER LXXXVII.

CONCLUSION.

Sir Richard Arden had learned how matters were with Mr. Longcluse. He hesitated. Flight might provoke action of the kind for which there seemed no longer a motive.

In an agony of dubitation, as the day wore on, he was interrupted. Mr. Rooke, Mr. Longcluse's attorney, had called. There was no good in shirking a meeting. He was shown in.

"This is for you, Sir Richard," said Mr. Rooke, presenting a large letter. "Mr. Longcluse wrote it about three hours ago, and requested me to place it in your own hand, as I now do."

"It is not any legal paper ——" began Sir Richard.

"I haven't an idea," answered he. "He gave it to me thus. I had some things to do for him afterwards, and a call to make, at his desire, at Mr. David Arden's. When I got home I was sent for again. I suppose you heard the news?"

"No; what is it?"

"Oh, dear, really! They have heard it some time at Mr. Arden's. You didn't hear about Mr. Longcluse?"

"No, nothing, excepting what we all know—his arrest."

The attorney's countenance darkened, and he said, dropping his voice as low as he would have given a message in church—

"Oh, poor gentleman! he died to-day. Some kind of fit, I believe; he's gone!"

Then Mr. Rooke went into particulars, so far as he knew them, and mentioned that the coroner's inquest would be held that afternoon; and so he departed.

Unmixed satisfaction accompanied the hearing of this news in Sir Richard's mind. But with reflection came the terrifying question, "Has Levi got hold of that instrument of torture and ruin—the forged signature?"

In this new horror he saw the envelope which Rooke had handed to him, upon the table. He opened it, and saw the forged deed. Written across it, in Longcluse's hand, were the words—

"Paid by W. Longcluse before due.

"W. Longcluse."

That day's date was added.

So the evidence of his guilt was no longer in the hands of a stranger, and Sir Richard Arden was saved.

David Arden had already received under like circumstances, and by the same hand, two papers of immense importance. The first written in Rooke's hand and duly witnessed, was a very short will, signed by the testator, Walter Longcluse, and leaving his enormous wealth absolutely to David Arden. The second was a letter which attached a trust to this bequest. The letter said—

> "I am the son of Edwin Raikes, your cousin. He had cast me off for my vices, when I committed the crime, not intended to have amounted to murder. It was Harry Arden's determined resistance and my danger that cost him his life. I did kill Lebas. I could not help it. He was a fool, and might have ruined me; and that villain, Vanboeren, has spoken truth for once.
>
> "I meant to set up the Arden family in my person. I should have taken the name. My father relented on his death-bed, and left me his money. I went to New York, and received it. I made a new start in life. On the Bourse in Paris, and in Vienna, I made a fortune by speculation; I improved it in London. You may take it all by my will. Do with half the interest as you please, during your lifetime. The other half pay to Miss Alice Arden, and the entire capital you are to secure to her on your death.
>
> "I had taken assignments of all the mortgages affecting the Arden estates. They must go to Miss Arden, and be secured unalienably to her.
>
> "My life has been arduous and direful. That miserable crime hung over me, and its dangers impeded me at every turn.
>
> "You have played your game well, but with all the odds of the position in your favour. I am tired, beaten. The match is over, and you may rise now and say Checkmate.

"Walter Longcluse."

That Longcluse had committed suicide, of course I can have no doubt. It must have been effected by some unusually subtle poison. The post-mortem examination failed to discover its presence. But there was found in his desk a curious paper, in French, published about five months before, upon certain vegetable poisons, whose presence in the system no chemical test detects, and no external trace records. This paper was noted here and there on the margin, and had been obviously carefully read. Any of these tinctures he could without much trouble have procured from Paris. But no distinct light was ever thrown upon this inquiry.

In a small and lonely house, tenanted by Longcluse, in the then less crowded region of Richmond, were found proofs, no longer needed, of Longcluse's identity, both with the horseman who had met Paul Davies on Hampstead Heath, and the person who crossed the Channel from Southampton with David Arden, and afterwards met him in the streets of Paris, as we have seen. There he had been watching his movements, and traced him, with dreadful suspicion, to the house of Vanboeren. The turn of a die had determined the fate of David Arden that night. Longcluse had afterwards watched and seized an opportunity of entering Vanboeren's house. He knew that the baron expected the return of his messenger, rang the bell, and was admitted. The old servant had gone to her bed, and was far away in that vast house.

Longcluse would have stabbed him, but the baron recognised him, and sprang back with a yell. Instantly Longcluse had used his revolver; but before he could make assurance doubly sure, his quick ear detected a step outside. He then made his exit through a window into a deserted lane at the side of the house, and had not lost a moment in commencing his flight for London.

With respect to the murder of Lebas, the letter of Longcluse pretty nearly explains it. That unlucky Frenchman had attended him through his recovery under the hands of Vanboeren; and Longcluse feared to trust, as it now might turn out, his life, in his giddy keeping. Of course, Lebas had no idea of the nature of his crime, or that in England was the scene of its perpetration. Longcluse had made up his mind promptly on the night of the billiard-match played in the Saloon Tavern. When every eye was fixed upon the balls, he and Lebas met, as they had ultimately agreed, in the smoking-room. A momentary meeting it was to have been. The dagger which he placed in his keeping, Longcluse plunged into his heart. In the stream of blood that instantaneously flowed from the wound Longcluse stepped, and made one distinct impression of his boot-sole on the boards. A tracing of this Paul Davies had made, and had got the signatures of two or three respectable Londoners before the room filled, attesting its accuracy, he affecting, while he did so, to be a member of the detective police, from which body, for a piece of over-cleverness, he had been only a few weeks before dismissed. Having made his tracing, he obscured the blood-mark on the floor.

The opportunity of distinguishing himself at his old craft, to the prejudice of the force, whom he would have liked to mortify, while earning, perhaps, his own restoration, was his first object. The delicacy of the shape of the boot struck him next. He then remembered having seen Longcluse—and his was the only eye that observed him—pass swiftly from the passage leading to the smoking-room at the beginning of the game. His mind had now matter to work upon; and hence his visit to Bolton Street to secure possession of the boot, which he did by an audacious ruse.

His subsequent interview with Mr. Longcluse, in presence of David Arden, was simply a concerted piece of acting, on which Longcluse, when he had made his terms with Davies, insisted, as a security against the re-opening of the extortion.

CONCLUSION.

Nothing will induce Alice to accept one farthing of Longcluse's magnificent legacy. Secretly Uncle David is resolved to make it up to her from his own wealth, which is very great.

Richard Arden's story is not known to any living person but the Jew Levi, and vaguely to his sister, in whose mind it remains as something horrible, but never approached.

Levi keeps the secret for reasons more cogent than charitable. First he kept it to himself as a future instrument of profit. But on his insinuating something that promised such relations to Sir Richard, the young gentleman met it with so bold a front, with fury so unaffected, and with threats so alarming, founded upon a trifling matter of which the Jew had never suspected his knowledge, that Mr. Levi has not ventured either to "utilise" his knowledge, in a profitable way, or afterwards to circulate the story for the solace of his malice. They seem, in Mr. Rooke's phrase, to have turned their backs on one another; and as some years have passed, and lapse of time does not improve the case of a person in Mr. Levi's position, we may safely assume that he will never dare to circulate any definite stories to Sir Richard's prejudice. A sufficient motive, indeed, for doing so exists no longer, for Sir Richard, who had lived an unsettled life travelling on the Continent, and still playing at foreign tables when he could afford it, died suddenly at Florence in the autumn of '69.

Vivian Darnley has been in "the House," now, nearly four years. Uncle David is very proud of him; and more impartial people think that he will, at last, take an honourable place in that assembly. His last speech has been spoken of everywhere with applause. David Arden's immensely increased wealth enables him to entertain very magnificent plans for this young man. He intends that he shall take the name of Arden, and earn the transmission of the title, or the distinction of a greater one.

A year ago Vivian Darnley married Alice Arden, and no two people can be happier.

Lady May, although her girlish ways have not forsaken her, has no present thoughts of making any man happy. She had a great cry all to herself when Sir Richard died, and she now persuades herself that he never meant one word he said of her, and that if the truth were known, although after that day she never spoke to him more, he had never really cared for more than one woman on earth. It was all spite of that odious Lady Wynderbroke!

Alice has never seen Mortlake since the night of her flight from its walls.

The two old servants, Crozier and Martha Tansey, whose acquaintance we made in that suburban seat of the Ardens, are both, I am glad to say, living still, and extremely comfortable.

Phœbe Chiffinch, I am glad to add, was jilted by her uninteresting lover, who little knew what a fortune he was slighting. His desertion does not seem to have broken her heart, or at all affected her spirits. The gratitude of Alice Arden has established her in the prosperous little Yorkshire town, the steep roof, chimneys, and church tower of which are visible, among the trees, from the windows of Arden Court. She is the energetic and popular proprietress of the "Cat and Fiddle," to which thriving inn, at a nominal rent, a valuable farm is attached. A fortune of two thousand pounds from the same grateful friend awaits her marriage, which can't be far off, with the handsome son of rich Farmer Shackleton.

WILLING TO DIE.

TO THE READER.

First, I must tell you how I intend to relate my story. Having never before undertaken to write a long narrative, I have considered and laid down a few rules which I shall observe. Some of these are unquestionably good; others, I daresay, offend against the canons of composition; but I adopt them, because they will enable me to tell my story better than, with my imperfect experience, better rules possibly would. In the first place, I shall represent the people with whom I had to deal quite fairly. I have met some bad people, some indifferent, and some who at this distance of time seem to me like angels in the unchanging light of heaven.

My narrative shall be arranged in the order of the events; I shall not recapitulate or anticipate.

What I have learned from others, and did not witness, that which I narrate, in part, from the hints of living witnesses, and, in part, conjecturally, I shall record in the historic third person; and I shall write it down with as much confidence and particularity as if I had actually seen it; in that respect imitating, I believe, all great historians, modern and ancient. But the scenes in which I have been an actor, that which my eyes have seen, and my ears heard, I will relate accordingly. If I can be clear and true, my clumsiness and irregularity, I hope, will be forgiven me.

My name is Ethel Ware.

I am not an interesting person by any means. You shall judge. I shall be forty-two my next birthday. That anniversary will occur on the first of May, 1873; and I am unmarried.

I don't look quite the old maid I am, they tell me. They say I don't look five-and-thirty, and I am conscious, sitting before the glass, that there is nothing sour or peevish in my features. What does it matter, even to me? I shall, of course, never marry; and, honestly, I don't care to please any one. If I cared twopence how I looked, I should probably look worse than I do.

I wish to be honest. I have looked in the glass since I wrote that sentence. I have just seen the faded picture of what may have been a pretty, at least what is called a piquant face; a forehead broad and well-formed, over which the still dark-brown hair grows low; large and rather good grey eyes and features, with nothing tragic, nothing classic—just fairly good.

I think there was always energy in my face! I think I remember, long ago, something at times comic; at times, also, something sad and tender, and even dreamy, as I fixed flowers in my hair or talked to my image in the glass. All that has been knocked out of me pretty well. What I do see there now is resolution.

There are processes of artificial hatching in use, if I remember rightly, in Egypt, by which you may, at your discretion, make the bird all beak, or all claw, all head, or all drumstick, as you please to develope it, before the shell breaks, by a special application of heat. It is a chick, no doubt, but a monstrous chick; and something like such a chick was I. Circumstances, in my very early days, hatched my character altogether out of equilibrium.

The caloric had been applied quite different in my mother's case, and produced a prodigy of quite another sort.

I loved my mother with a very warm, but, I am now conscious, with a somewhat contemptuous affection. It never was an angry nor an arrogant contempt; a very tender one, on the contrary. She loved me, I am sure, as well as she was capable of loving a child—better than she ever loved my sister—and I would have laid down my life for her; but, with all my love, I looked down upon her, although I did not know it, till I thought my life over in the melancholy honesty of solitude.

I am not romantic. If I ever was it is time I should be cured of all that. I can laugh heartily, but I think I sigh more than most people.

I am not a bit shy, but I like solitude; partly because I regard my kind with not unjust suspicion.

I am speaking very frankly. I enjoy, perhaps you think cynically, this hard-featured self-delineation. I don't spare myself; I need not spare any one else. But I am not a cynic. There is vacillation and timidity in that ironical egotism. It is something deeper with me. I don't delight in that sordid philosophy. I have encountered magnanimity and self-devotion on earth. It is not true that there is neither nobility nor beauty in human nature, that is not also more or less shabby and grotesque.

I have an odd story to tell. On my father's side I am the grand-daughter of a viscount; on my mother's, the grand-daughter of a baronet. I have had my early glimpses of the great world, and a wondrous long stare round the dark world beneath it.

When I lower my hand, and in one of the momentary reveries that tempt a desultory writer tickle my cheek slowly with the feathered end of my pen—for I don't incise my sentences with a point of steel, but, in the old fashion, wing my words with a possibly too appropriate grey-goose plume—I look through a tall window in an old house on the scenery I have loved best and earliest in the world. The noble Welsh mountains are on my right, the purple headlands stooping grandly into the waves; I look upon the sea, the enchanted element, my first love and my last! How often I lean upon my hand and smile back upon the waters that silently smile on me, rejoicing under the summer heavens; and in wintry moonlights, when the north wind drives the awful waves upon the rocks, and I see the foam shooting cloud after cloud into the air, I have found myself, after long hours, still gazing, as if my breath were frozen, on the one peaked black rock, thinking what the storm and foam once gave me up there, until, with a sudden terror, and a gasp, I wake from the spell, and recoil from the white image, as if a spirit had been talking with me all the time.

From this same window, in the fore-ground, I see, in morning light or melancholy sunset, with very perfect and friendly trust, the shadowy old churchyard, where I have arranged my narrow bed shall be. There my mother-earth, at last, shall hold me in her bosom, and I shall find my anodyne and rest. There over me shall hover through the old church windows faintly the sweet hymns and the voices in prayer I heard long ago; there the shadow of tower and tree shall slowly move over the grass above me, from dawn till night, and there, within the fresh and solemn sound of its waves, I shall lie near the ceaseless fall and flow of the sea I loved so well.

I am not sorry, as I sit here, with my vain recollections and my direful knowledge, that my life has been what it was.

A member of the upper ten thousand, I should have known nothing. I have bought my knowledge dear. But truth is a priceless jewel. Would you part with it, fellow-mourner, and return to the simplicities and illusions of early days? Consider the question truly; be honest; and you will answer "No." In the volume of memory, every page of which, like "Cornelius Agrippa's bloody book," has power to evoke a spectre, would you yet erase a line? We can willingly part with nothing that ever was part of mind, or memory, or self. The lamentable past is our own for ever.

Thank Heaven, my childhood was passed in a tranquil nook, where the roar of the world's traffic is not so much as heard; among scenery, where there lurks little capital, and no enterprise; where the good people are asleep; and where, therefore, the irreparable improvements that in other places carry on their pitiless work of obliteration are undreamed of. I am looking out on scenes that remain unchanged as heaven itself. The summer comes and goes; the autumn drifts of leaves, and winter snows; and all things here remain as my round childish eyes beheld them in stupid wonder and delight when first the world was opening upon them. The trees, the tower, the stile, the very gravestones, are my earliest friends; I stretch my arms to the mountains, as if I could fold them to my heart. And in the opening through the ancient trees, the great estuary stretches northward, wider and wider, into the grey horizon of the open sea.

The sinking sun askance,
  Spreads a dull glare,
  Through evening air;
And, in a happy trance,
  Forest and wave, and white cliff stand,
  Like an enchanted sea and land.
The sea-breeze wakens clear and cold,
  Over the azure wide;
Before whose breath, in threads of gold,

The ruddy ripples glide,
And chasing, break and mingle;
While clear as bells,
Each wavelet tells,
O'er the stones on the hollow shingle.
The rising of winds and the fall of the waves!
I love the music of shingle and caves.
And the billows that travel so far to die,
In foam, on the loved shore where they lie.
I lean my cold cheek on my hand;
And as a child, with open eyes,
Listens, in a dim surprise,
To some high story
Of grief and glory,
It cannot understand;
So, like that child,
To meanings of a music wild,
I listen, in a rapture lonely,
Not understanding, listening only,
To a story not for me;
And let my fancies come and go,
And fall and flow,
With the eternal sea.

And so, to leave rhyme, and return to prose, I end my preface, and begin my story here.

CHAPTER I.

AN ARRIVAL.

One of the earliest scenes I can remember with perfect distinctness is this. My sister and I, still denizens of the nursery, had come down to take our tea with good old Rebecca Torkill, the Malory housekeeper, in the room we called the cedar parlour. It is a long and rather sombre room, with two tall windows looking out upon the shadowy court-yard. There are on the wall some dingy portraits, whose pale faces peep out, as it were, through a background of black fog, from the canvas; and there is one, in better order than the others, of a grave man in the stately costume of James the First, which hangs over the mantel-piece. As a child I loved this room; I loved the half-decipherable pictures; it was solemn and even gloomy, but it was with the delightful gloom and solemnity of one of Rebecca Torkill's stories of castles, giants, and goblins.

It was evening now, with a stormy, red sky in the west. Rebecca and we two children were seated round the table, sipping our tea, eating hot cake, and listening to her oft-told tale, entitled the Knight of the Black Castle.

This knight, habited in black, lived in his black castle, in the centre of a dark wood, and being a giant, and an ogre, and something of a magician besides, he used to ride out at nightfall with a couple of great black bags, to stow his prey in, at his saddle-bow, for the purpose of visiting such houses as had their nurseries well-stocked with children. His tall black horse, when he dismounted, waited at the hall-door, which, however mighty its bars and bolts, could not resist certain magical words which he uttered in a sepulchral voice—

"Yoke, yoke,
Iron and oak;
One, two, and three,
Open to me."

At this charmed summons the door turned instantly on its hinges, without warning of creak or rattle, and the black knight mounted the stairs to the nursery, and was drawing the children softly out of their beds, by their feet, before any one knew he was near.

As this story, which with childish love of iteration we were listening to now for the fiftieth time, went on, I, whose chair faced the window, saw a tall man on a tall horse—both looked black enough against the red sky—ride by at a walk.

I thought it was the gaunt old vicar, who used to ride up now and then to visit our gardener's mother, who was sick and weak, and troubling my head no more about him, was instantly as much absorbed as ever in the predatory prowlings of the Knight of the Black Castle.

It was not until I saw Rebecca's face, in which I was staring with the steadiness of an eager interest, undergo a sudden and uncomfortable change, that I discovered my error. She stopped in the middle of a sentence, and her eyes were fixed on the door. Mine followed hers thither. I was more than startled. In the very crisis of a tale of terror, ready to believe any horror, I thought, for a moment, that I actually beheld the Black Knight, and felt that his horse, no doubt, and his saddle-bags, were waiting at the hall-door to receive me and my sister.

What I did see was a man who looked to me gigantic. He seemed to fill the tall door-case. His dress was dark, and he had a pair of leather overalls, I believe they called them, which had very much the effect of jack-boots, and he had a low-crowned hat on. His hair was long and black, his prominent black eyes were fixed on us, his face was long, but handsome, and deadly pale, as it seemed to me, from intense anger. A child's instinctive reading of countenance is seldom at fault. The ideas of power and mystery surround grown persons in the eyes of children. A gloomy or forbidding face upon a person of great stature inspires something like panic; and if that person is a stranger, and evidently transported with anger, his mere appearance in the same room will, I can answer for it, frighten a child half into hysterics. This alarming face, with its black knit brows, and very blue shorn chin, was to me all the more fearful that it was that of a man no longer young. He advanced to the table with two strides, and said, in resonant, deep tones, to which my very heart seemed to vibrate:

"Mr. Ware's not here, but he will be, soon enough; you give him that;" and he hammered down a letter on the table, with a thump of his huge fist. "That's my answer; and tell him, moreover, that I took his letter,"—and he plucked an open letter deliberately from his great-coat pocket—"and tore it, this way and that way, across and across," and he suited the action fiercely to the words, "and left it for him, there!"

So saying, he slapped down the pieces with his big hand, and made our tea-spoons jump and jingle in our cups, and turned and strode again to the door.

"And tell him this," he added, in a tone of calmer hatred, turning his awful face on us again, "that there's a God above us, who judges righteously."

The door shut, and we saw him no more. I and my sister burst into clamorous tears, and roared and cried for a full half hour, from sheer fright—a demonstration which, for a time, gave Rebecca Torkill ample occupation for all her energies and adroitness.

This recollection remains, with all the colouring and exaggeration of a horrible impression received in childhood, fixed in my imagination. I and dear Nelly long remembered the apparition, and in our plays used to call him, after the goblin hero of the romance to which we had been listening when he entered, the Knight of the Black Castle.

The adventure made, indeed, a profound impression upon our nerves, and I have related it, with more detail than it seems to deserve, because it was, in truth, connected with my story; and I afterwards, unexpectedly, saw a good deal more of the awful man in whose presence my heart had quaked, and after whose visit I and my sister seemed for days to have drunk of "the cup of trembling."

I must take up my story now at a point a great many years later.

Let the reader fancy me and my sister Helen; I dark-haired, and a few months past sixteen; she, with flaxen, or rather golden hair and large blue eyes, and only fifteen, standing in the hall at Malory, lighted with two candles; one in the old-fashioned glass bell that swings by three chains from the ceiling, the other carried out hastily from the housekeeper's room, and flaming on the table, in the foggy puffs of the February night air that entered at the wide-open hall-door.

Old Rebecca Torkill stood on the steps, with her broad hand shading her eyes, as if the moon dazzled them.

"There's nothing, dear; no, Miss Helen, it mustn't a' bin the gate. There's no sign o' nothin' comin' up, and no sound nor nothing at all; come in, dear; you shouldn't a' come out to the open door, with your cough in this fog."

So in she stumped, and shut the door; and we saw no more of the dark trunks and boughs of the elms at the other side of the courtyard, with the smoky mist between; and we three trooped together to the housekeeper's room, where we had taken up our temporary quarters.

This was the second false alarm that night, sounded, in Helen's fancy, by the quavering scream of the old iron gate. We had to wait and watch in the fever of expectation for some time longer.

Our old house of Malory was, at the best, in the forlorn condition of a ship of war out of commission. Old Rebecca and two rustic maids, and Thomas Jones, who was boots, gardener, hen-wife, and farmer, were all the hands we could boast; and at least three-fourths of the rooms were locked up, with shutters closed; and many of them, from year to year, never saw the light, and lay in perennial dust.

The truth is, my father and mother seldom visited Malory. They had a house in London, and led a very gay life; were very "good people," immensely in request, and everywhere. Their rural life was not at Malory, but spent in making visits at one country-house after another. Helen and I, their only children, saw very little of them. We sometimes were summoned up to town for a month or two for lessons in dancing, music, and other things, but there we saw little more of them than at home. The being in society, judging by its effects upon them, appeared to me a very harassing and laborious profession. I always felt that we were half in the way and half out of sight in town, and was immensely relieved when we were dismissed again to our holland frocks, and to the beloved solitudes of Malory.

This was a momentous night. We were expecting the arrival of a new governess, or rather companion.

Laura Grey—we knew no more than her name, for in his hurried note we could not read whether she was Miss or Mrs.—my father had told us, was to arrive this night at about nine o'clock. I had asked him, when he paid his last visit of a day here, and announced the coming event, whether she was a married lady; to which he answered, laughing:

"You wise little woman! That's a very pertinent question, though I never thought of it, and I have been addressing her as Miss Grey all this time. She certainly is old enough to be married."

"Is she cross, papa, I wonder?" I further inquired.

"Not cross—perhaps a little severe. 'She whipped two female 'prentices to death, and hid them in the coal-hole,' or something of that kind, but she has a very cool temper;" and so he amused himself with my curiosity.

Now, although we knew that all this, including the quotation, was spoken in jest, it left an uncomfortable suspicion. Was this woman old and ill-tempered? A great deal was in the power of a governess here. An artful woman, who liked power, and did not like us, might make us very miserable.

At length the little party in the housekeeper's room did hear sounds at which we all started up with one consent. They were the trot of a horse's hoofs and the roll of wheels, and before we reached the hall-door the bell was ringing.

Rebecca swung open the door, and we saw in the shadow of the house, with the wheels touching the steps, a one-horse conveyance, with some luggage on top, dimly lighted by the candles in the hall.

A little bonnet was turned towards us from the windows; we could not see what the face was like; a slender hand turned the handle, and a lady, whose figure, though enveloped in a tweed cloak, looked very slight and pretty, came down, and ran up the steps, and hesitated, and being greeted encouragingly by Rebecca Torkill, entered the hall smiling, and showed a very pretty and modest face, rather pale, and very young.

"My name is Grey; I am the new governess," she said, in a pleasant voice, which, with her pretty looks, was very engaging; "and these are the young ladies?" she continued, glancing at Rebecca and back again at us; "you are Ethel, and you Helen Ware?" and a little timidly she offered her hand to each.

I liked her already.

"Shall I go with you to your room," I asked, "while Rebecca is making tea for us in the housekeeper's room? We thought we should be more comfortable there to-night."

"I'm so glad—I shall feel quite at home. It is the very thing I should have liked," she said; and talked on as I led her to her room, which, though very old-fashioned, looked extremely cosy, with a good fire flickering abroad and above on walls and ceiling.

I remember everything about that evening so well. I have reason to remember Miss Laura Grey. Some people would have said that there was not a regular feature in her face, except her eyes, which were very fine; but she had beautiful little teeth, and a skin wonderfully smooth and clear, and there was refinement and energy in her face, which was pale and spiritual, and indescribably engaging. To my mind, whether according to rule or not, she was nothing short of beautiful.

I have reason to remember that pale, pretty young face. The picture is clear and living before me this moment, as it was then in the firelight. Standing there, she smiled on me very kindly—she looked as if she would have kissed me—and then, suddenly thoughtful, she stretched her slender hands to the fire, and, in a momentary reverie, sighed very deeply.

I left her, softly, with her trunks and boxes, which Thomas Jones had already carried up, and ran downstairs.

I remember the pictures of that night with supernatural distinctness; for at that point of time fate changed my life, and with pretty Miss Grey another pale figure entered, draped in black, and calamity was my mate for many a day after.

Our tea-party, however, this night in Mrs. Torkill's room, was very happy. I don't remember what we talked about, but we were in high good-humour with our young lady-superioress, and she seemed to like us.

I am going to tell you very shortly my impressions of this lady. I never met any one in my life who had the same influence over me; and, for a time, it puzzled me. When we were not at French, German, music—our studies, in fact—she was exactly like one of ourselves, always ready to do whatever we liked best, always pleasant, gentle, and, in her way, even merry. When she was alone, or thinking, she was sad. That seemed the habit of her mind; but she was naturally gay and sympathetic, as ready as we for a walk on the strand to pick up shells, for a ride on the donkeys to Penruthyn Priory, to take a sail or a row on the estuary, or a drive in our little pony-carriage anywhere. Sometimes on our rambles we would cross the stile and go into the pretty little churchyard that lies to the left of Malory, near the sea, and if it was a sunny day we would read the old inscriptions and loiter away half an hour among the tombstones.

And when we came home to tea we would sit round the fire and tell stories, of which she had ever so many, German, French, Scotch, Irish, Icelandic, and I know not what; and sometimes we went to the housekeeper's room, and, with Rebecca Torkill's leave, made a hot cake, and baked it on the griddle there, with great delight.

The secret of Laura Grey's power was in her gentle temper, her inflexible conscience, and her angelic firmness in all matters of duty. I never saw her excited, or for a moment impatient; and at idle times, as I said, she was one of ourselves. The only threat she ever used was to tell us that she could not stay at Malory as our governess if we would not do what she thought right. There is in young people an instinctive perception of motive, and no truer spirit than Laura Grey ever lived on earth. I loved her. I had no fear of her. She was our gentle companion and playmate; and yet, in a certain sense, I never stood so much in awe of any human being.

Only a few days after Laura Grey had come home, we were sitting in our accustomed room, which was stately, but not uncomfortably spacious, and, like many at the same side of the house, panelled up to the ceiling. I remember, it was just at the hour of the still early sunset, and the ruddy beams were streaming their last through the trunks of the great elms. We were in high chat over Helen's little sparrow, Dickie, a wonderful bird, whose appetite and spirits we were always discussing, when the door opened, and Rebecca said, "Young ladies, please, here's Mr. Carmel;" and Miss Grey, for the first time, saw a certain person who turns up at intervals and in odd scenes in the course of this autobiography.

The door is at some distance from the window, and through its panes across that space upon the opposite wall the glow of sunset fell mistily, making the clear shadow, in which our visitor stood, deeper. The figure stood out against this background like a pale old portrait, his black dress almost blended with the background; but, indistinct as it was, it was easy to see that the dress he wore was of some ecclesiastical fashion not in use among Church of England men. The coat came down a good deal lower than his knees. His thin slight figure gave him an effect of height far greater than his real stature; his fine forehead showed very white in contrast with his close dark hair, and his thin, delicate features, as he stepped slowly in, with an ascetic smile, and his hand extended, accorded well with ideas of abstinence and penance. Gentle as was his manner, there was something of authority also in it, and in the tones of his voice.

"How do you do, Miss Ethel? How do you do, Miss Helen? I am going to write my weekly note to your mamma, and—oh! Miss Grey, I believe?"—he interrupted himself, and bowed rather low to the young governess, disclosing the small tonsure on the top of his head.

Miss Grey acknowledged his bow, but I could see that she was puzzled and surprised.

"I am to tell your mamma, I hope, that you are both quite well?" he said, addressing himself to me, and taking my hand: "and in good spirits, I suppose, Miss Grey?" he said, apparently recollecting that she was to be recognized; "I may say that?"

He turned to her, still holding my hand.

"Yes, they are quite well, and, I believe, happy," she said, still looking at him, I could see, with curiosity.

It was a remarkable countenance, with large earnest eyes, and a mouth small and melancholy, with those brilliant red lips that people associate with early decay. It was a pale face of suffering and decision, which so vaguely indicated his years that he might be any age you please, from six-and-twenty up to six-and-thirty, as you allowed more or less in the account for the afflictions of a mental and bodily discipline.

He stood there for a little while chatting with us. There was something engaging in this man, cold, severe, and melancholy as his manner was. I was conscious that he was agreeable, and, young as I was, I felt that he was a man of unusual learning and ability.

In a little time he left us. It was now twilight, and we saw him, with his slight stoop, pass our window with slow step and downcast eyes.

CHAPTER II.

OUR CURIOSITY IS PIQUED.

And so that odd vision was gone; and Laura Grey turned to us eagerly for information.

We could not give her much. We were ourselves so familiar with the fact of Mr. Carmel's existence, that it never occurred to us that his appearance could be a surprise to any one.

Mr. Carmel had come about eight months before to reside in the small old house in which the land-steward had once been harboured, and which, built in continuation of the side of the house, forms a sort of retreating wing to it, with a hall-door to itself, but under the same roof.

This Mr. Carmel was, undoubtedly, a Roman Catholic, and an ecclesiastic; of what order I know not. Possibly he was a Jesuit. I never was very learned or very curious upon such points; but some one, I forgot who, told me that he positively was a member of the Society of Jesus.

My poor mother was very High Church, and on very friendly terms with Catholic personages of note. Mr. Carmel had been very ill, and was still in delicate health, and a quiet nook in the country, in the neighbourhood of the sea, had been ordered for him. The vacant house I have described she begged for his use from my father, who did not at all like the idea of lending it, as I could gather from the partly jocular and partly serious discussions which he maintained upon the point, every now and then, at the breakfast-table, when I was last in town.

I remember hearing my father say at last, "You know, my dear Mabel, I'm always ready to do anything you like. I'll be a Catholic myself, if it gives you the least pleasure, only be sure, first, about this thing, that you really do like it. I shouldn't care if the man were hanged—he very likely deserves it—but I'll give him my house if it makes you happy. You must remember, though, the Cardyllion people won't like it, and you'll be talked about, and I daresay he'll make nuns of Ethel and Helen. He won't get a great deal by that, I'm afraid. And I don't see why those pious people—Jesuits, and that sort of persons, who don't know what to do with their money—should not take a house for him if he wants it, or what business they have quartering their friars and rubbish upon poor Protestants like you and me."

The end of it was that about two months later this Mr. Carmel arrived, duly accredited by my father, who told me when he paid us one of his visits of a day, soon after, that he was under promise not to talk to us about religion, and that if he did I was to write to tell him immediately.

When I had told my story to Laura Grey, she was thoughtful for a little time.

"Are his visits only once a week?" she asked.

"Yes," said I.

"And does he stay as short a time always?" she continued.

We both agreed that he usually stayed a little longer.

"And has he never talked on the subject of religion?"

"No, never. He has talked about shells, or flowers, or anything he found us employed about, and always told us something curious or interesting. I had heard papa say that he was engaged upon a work from which great things were expected, and boxes of books were perpetually coming and going between him and his correspondents."

She was not quite satisfied, and in a few days there arrived from London two little books on the great controversy between Luther and the Pope; and out of these, to the best of her poor ability, she drilled us, by way of a prophylactic against Mr. Carmel's possible machinations.

It did not appear, however, to be Mr. Carmel's mission to flutter the little nest of heresy so near him. When he paid his next visit, it so happened that one of these duodecimo disputants lay upon the table. Without thinking, as he talked, he raised it, and read the title on the cover, and smiled gently. Miss Grey blushed. She had not intended disclosing her suspicions.

"In two different regiments, Miss Grey," he said, "but both under the same king;" and he laid the book quietly upon the table again, and talked on of something quite different.

Laura Grey, in a short time, became less suspicious of Mr. Carmel, and rather enjoyed his little visits, and looked forward with pleasure to them.

Could you imagine a quieter or more primitive life than ours, or, on earth, a much happier one?

Malory owns an old-fashioned square pew in the aisle of the pretty church of Cardyllion. In this spacious pew we three sat every Sunday, and on one of these occasions, a few weeks after Miss Grey's arrival, from my corner I thought I saw a stranger in the Verney seat, which is at the opposite side of the aisle, and had not had an occupant for several months. There was certainly a man in it; but the stove that stood nearly between us would not allow me to see more than his elbow, and the corner of an open book, from which I suppose he was reading.

I was not particularly curious about this person. I knew that the Verneys, who were distant cousins of ours, were abroad, and the visitor was not likely to be very interesting.

A long, indistinct sermon interposed, and I did not recollect to look at the Verney pew until the congregation were trooping decorously out, and we had got some way down the aisle. The pew was empty by that time.

"Some one in the Verney's pew," I remarked to our governess, so soon as we were quite out of the shadow of the porch.

"Which is the Verney's pew?" she asked.

I described it.

"Yes, there was. I have got a headache, my dear. Suppose we go home by the Mill Road?"

We agreed.

It is a very pretty, and in places rather a steep road, very narrow, and ascending with a high and wooded bank at its right, and a precipitous and thickly-planted glen to its left. The opposite side is thickly wooded also, and a stream far below splashes and tinkles among the rocks under the darkening foliage.

As we walked up this shadowy road, I saw an old gentleman walking down it, towards us. He was descending at a brisk pace, and wore a chocolate-coloured great-coat, made with a cape, and fitting his figure closely. He wore a hat with a rather wide brim, turned up at the sides. His face was very brown. He had a thin, high nose, with very thin nostrils, rather prominent eyes, and carried his head high. Altogether he struck me as a particularly gentleman-like and ill-tempered looking old man, and his features wore a character of hauteur that was perfectly insolent.

He was pretty near to us by the time I turned to warn our governess, who was beside me, to make way for him to pass. I did not speak; for I was a little startled to see that she was very much flushed, and almost instantly turned deadly pale.

We came nearly to a standstill, and the old gentleman was up to us in a few seconds. As he approached, his prominent eyes were fixed on Laura Grey. He stopped, with the same haughty stare, and, raising his hat, said in a cold, rather high key, "Miss Grey, I think? Miss Laura Grey? You will not object, I dare say, to allow me a very few words?"

The young lady bowed very slightly, and said, in a low tone, "Certainly not."

I saw that she looked pained, and even faint. This old gentleman's manner, and the stern stare of his prominent eyes, embarrassed even me, who did not directly encounter them.

"Perhaps we had better go on, Helen and I, to the seat; we can wait for you there?" I said softly to her.

"Yes, dear, I think it will be as well," she answered gently.

We walked on slowly. The bench was not a hundred steps up the steep. It stands at the side of the road, with its back against the bank. From this seat I could see very well what passed, though, of course, quite out of hearing.

The old gentleman had a black cane in his fingers, which he poked about in the gravel. You would have said from his countenance that at every little stab he punched an enemy's eye out.

First, the gentleman made a little speech, with his head very high, and an air of determination and severity. The young lady seemed to answer, briefly and quietly. Then ensued a colloquy of a minute or more, during which the old gentleman's head nodded often with emphasis, and his gestures became much more decided. The young lady seemed to say little, and very quietly: her eyes were lowered to the ground as she spoke.

She said something, I suppose, which he chose to resent, for he smiled sarcastically, and raised his hat; then, suddenly resuming his gravity, he seemed to speak with a sharp and hectoring air, as if he were laying down the law upon some point once for all.

Laura Grey looked up sharply, with a brilliant colour, and with her head high, replied rapidly for a minute or more, and turning away, without waiting for his answer, walked slowly, with her head still high, towards us.

The gentleman stood looking after her with his sarcastic smile, but that was gone in a moment, and he continued looking, with an angry face, and muttering to himself, until suddenly he turned away, and walked off at a quick pace down the path towards Cardyllion.

A little uneasily, Helen and I stood up to meet our governess. She was still flushed and breathing quickly, as people do from recent agitation.

"No bad news? Nothing unpleasant?" I asked, looking very eagerly into her face.

"No; no bad news, dear."

I took her hand. I felt that she was trembling a little, and she had become again more than usually pale. We walked homeward in silence.

Laura Grey seemed in deep and agitated thought. We did not, of course, disturb her. An unpleasant excitement like that always disposes one to silence. Not a word, I think, was uttered all the way to the steps of Malory. Laura Grey entered the hall, still silent, and when she came down to us, after an hour or two passed in her room, it was plain she had been crying.

CHAPTER III.

THE THIEF IN THE NIGHT.

Of what happened next I have a strangely imperfect recollection. I cannot tell you the intervals, or even the order, in which some of the events occurred. It is not that the mist of time obscures it; what I do recollect is dreadfully vivid; but there are spaces of the picture gone. I see faces of angels, and faces that make my heart sink; fragments of scenes. It is like something reflected in the pieces of a smashed looking-glass.

I have told you very little of Helen, my sister, my one darling on earth. There are things which people, after an interval of half a life, have continually present to their minds, but cannot speak of. The idea of opening them to strangers is insupportable. A sense of profanation shuts the door, and we "wake" our dead alone. I could not have told you what I am going to write. I did not intend inscribing here more than the short, bleak result. But I write it as if to myself, and I will get through it.

To you it may seem that I make too much of this, which is, as Hamlet says, "common." But you have not known what it is to be for all your early life shut out from all but one beloved companion, and never after to have found another.

Helen had a cough, and Laura Grey had written to mamma, who was then in Warwickshire, about it. She was referred to the Cardyllion doctor. He came; he was a skilful man. There were the hushed, dreadful moments, while he listened, through his stethoscope, thoughtfully, to the "still, small voice" of fate, to us inaudible, pronouncing on the dread issues of life or death.

"No sounder lungs in England," said Doctor Mervyn, looking up with a congratulatory smile.

He told her, only, that she must not go in the way of cold, and by-and-by sent her two bottles from his surgery; and so we were happy once more.

But doctors' advices, like the warnings of fate, are seldom obeyed; least of all by the young. Nelly's little pet-sparrow was ailing, or we fancied it was. She and I were up every hour during the night to see after it. Next evening Nelly had a slight pain in her chest. It became worse, and by twelve o'clock was so intense that Laura Grey, in alarm, sent to Cardyllion for the doctor. Thomas Jones came back without him, after a delay of an hour. He had been called away to make a visit somewhere, but the moment he came back he would come to Malory.

It came to be three o'clock; he had not appeared; darling Nelly was in actual torture. Again Doctor Mervyn was sent for; and again, after a delay, the messenger returned with the same dismaying answer. The governess and Rebecca Torkill exhausted in vain their little list of remedies. I was growing terrified. Intuitively I perceived the danger. The doctor was my last earthly hope. Death, I saw, was drawing nearer and nearer every moment, and the doctor might be ten miles away. Think what it was to stand, helpless, by her. Can I ever forget her poor little face, flushed scarlet, and gasping and catching at breath, hands, throat, every sinew quivering in the mortal struggle!

At last a knock and a ring at the hall-door. I rushed to the window; the first chill grey of winter's dawn hung sicklily over the landscape. No one was on the steps, or on the grey gravel of the court. But, yes—I do hear voices and steps upon the stair approaching. Oh! Heaven be thanked, the doctor is come at last!

I ran out upon the lobby, just as I was, in my dressing-gown, with my hair about my shoulders, and slippers on my bare feet. A candlestick, with the candle burnt low, was standing on the broad head of the clumsy old bannister, and Mr. Carmel, in a black riding-coat, with his hat in his hand, and that kind of riding-boots that used to be called clerical, on, was talking in a low, earnest tone to our governess.

The faint grey from the low lobby window was lost at this point, and the delicate features of the pale ecclesiastic, and Miss Grey's pretty and anxious face, were lighted, like a fine portrait of Schalken's, by the candle only.

Throughout this time of agony and tumult, the memory of my retina remains unimpaired, and every picture retains its hold upon my brain. And, oh! had the doctor come? Yes, Mr. Carmel had ridden all the way, fourteen miles, to Llwynan, and brought the doctor back with him. He might not have been here for hours otherwise. He was now downstairs making preparations, and would be in the room in a few minutes.

I looked at that fine, melancholy, energetic face as if he had saved me. I could not thank him. I turned and entered our room again, and told Nelly to be of good courage, that the doctor was come. "And, oh! please God, he'll do you good, my own darling, darling—precious darling!"

In a minute more the doctor was in the room. My eyes were fixed upon his face as he talked to his poor little patient; he did not look at all as he had done on his former visit. I see him before me as I write; his bald head shining in the candle-light, his dissatisfied and gloomy face, and his shrewd light blue eyes, reading her looks askance, as his fingers rested on her pulse.

I remember, as if the sick-room had changed into it, finding myself in the small room opposite, with no one there but the doctor and Miss Grey, we three, in the cold morning light, and his saying, "Well all this comes of violating directions. There is very intense inflammation, and her chest is in a most critical state."

Then Miss Grey said, after a moment's hush, the awful words, "Is there any danger?" and he answered shortly, "I wish I could say there wasn't." I felt my ears sing as if a pistol had been fired. No one spoke for another minute or more.

The doctor stayed, I think, for a long time, and he must have returned after, for he mixed up in almost every scene I can remember during that jumbled day of terror.

There was, I know, but one day, and part of a night. But it seems to me as if whole nights intervened, and suns set and rose, and days uncounted and undistinguished passed, in that miserable period.

The pain subsided, but worse followed; a dreadful cough, that never ceased—a long, agonised struggle against a slow drowning of the lungs. The doctor gave her up. They wanted me to leave the room, but I could not.

The hour had come at last, and she was gone. The wild cry—the terrible farewell—nothing can move inexorable death. All was still.

As the ship lies serene in the caverns of the cold sea, and feels no more the fury of the wind, the strain of cable, and the crash of wave, this forlorn wreck lay quiet now. Oh! little Nelly! I could not believe it.

She lay in her nightdress under the white coverlet. Was this whole scene an awful vision, and was my heart breaking in vain? Oh, poor simple little Nelly, to think that you should have changed into anything so sublime and terrible!

I stood dumb by the bedside, staring at the white face that was never to move again. Such a look I had never seen before. The white glory of an angel was upon it.

Rebecca Torkill spoke to me, I think. I remember her kind, sorrowful old face near me, but I did not hear what she said. I was in a stupor, or a trance. I had not shed a tear; I had not said a word. For a time I was all but mad. In the light of that beautiful transfiguration my heart was bursting with the wildest rebellion against the law of death that had murdered my innocent sister before my eyes; against the fate of which humanity is the sport; against the awful Power who made us! What spirit knows, till the hour of temptation, the height or depth of its own impiety?

Oh, gentle, patient little Nelly! The only good thing I can see in myself in those days is my tender love of you, and my deep inward certainty of my immeasurable inferiority. Gentle, humble little Nelly, who thought me so excelling in cleverness, in wisdom, and countless other perfections, how humble in my secret soul I felt myself beside you, although I was too proud to say so! In your presence my fierce earthy nature stood revealed, and wherever I looked my shadow was cast along the ground by the pure light that shone from you.

I don't know what time passed without a word falling from my lips. I suppose people had other things to mind, and I was left to myself. But Laura Grey stole her hand into mine, she kissed me, and I felt her tears on my cheek.

"Ethel, darling, come with me," she said, crying, very gently. "You can come back again. You'll come with me, won't you? Our darling is happier, Ethel, than ever she could have been on earth, and she will never know change or sorrow again."

I began to sob distractedly. I do really believe I was half out of my mind. I began to talk to her volubly, vehemently, crying passionately all the time. I do not remember now a word I uttered; I know its purport only from the pain, and even horror, I remember in Laura Grey's pale face. It has taken a long and terrible discipline to expel that evil spirit. I know what I was in those days. My pilgrimage since then has been by steep and solitary paths, in great dangers, in darkness, in fear; I have eaten the bread of affliction, and my drink has been of the waters of bitterness; I am tired and footsore yet, though through a glass darkly, I think I can now see why it all was, and I thank God with a contrite heart for the terrors and the mercies he has shown me. I begin to discover through the mist who was the one friend who never forsook me through all those stupendous wanderings, and I long for the time when I shall close my tired eyes, all being over, and lie at the feet of my Saviour.

CHAPTER IV.

MY FATHER.

Forth sped Laura Grey's letter to mamma. She was then at Roydon; papa was with her. The Easter recess had just sent down some distinguished visitors, who were glad to clear their heads for a few days of the hum of the Houses and the smell of the river; and my father, although not in the House, ran down with them. Little Nelly had been his pet, as I was mamma's.

There was an awkwardness in post-office arrangements between the two places then, and letters had to make a considerable circuit. There was a delay of three clear days between the despatch of the letter and the reply.

I must say a word about papa. He was about the most agreeable and careless man on earth. There are men whom no fortune could keep out of debt. A man of that sort seems to me not to have any defined want or enjoyment, but the horizon of his necessities expands in proportion as he rises in fortune, and always exceeds the ring-fence of his estate. What its periphery may be, or his own real wants, signifies very little. His permanent necessity is always to exceed his revenue.

I don't think my father's feelings were very deep. He was a good-natured husband, but, I am afraid, not a good one. I loved him better than I loved mamma. Children are always captivated by gaiety and indulgence. I was not of an age to judge of higher things, and I never missed the article of religion, of which, I believe, he had none. Although he lived so much in society that he might almost be said to have no domestic life whatever, no man could be simpler, less suspicious, or more easily imposed upon.

The answer to Miss Grey's letter was the arrival of my father. He was in passionate grief, and in a state of high excitement. He ran upstairs, without waiting to take off his hat; but at the door of our darling's room he hesitated. I did not know he had arrived till I heard him, some minutes later, walking up and down the room, sobbing. Though he was selfish, he was affectionate. No one liked to go in to disturb him. She lay by this time in her coffin. The tint of clay darkened her pretty features. The angelic beauty that belongs to death is transitory beyond all others. I would not look at her again, to obscure its glory. She lay now in her shroud, a forlorn sunken image of decay.

When he came out he talked wildly and bitterly. His darling had been murdered, he said, by neglect. He upbraided us all round, including Rebecca Torkill, for our cruel carelessness. He blamed the doctor. He had no right, in a country where there was but one physician, to go so far away as fourteen miles, and to stay away so long. He denounced even his treatment. He ought to have bled her. It was, every one knew, the proper way of treating such a case.

Than Laura Grey, no one could have been more scrupulously careful. She could not have prevented, even if she had suspected the possibility of such a thing, her stealing out of bed now and then to look at her sick sparrow. All this injustice was, however, but the raving of his grief.

In poor little Nelly's room my father's affectionate nature was convulsed with sorrow. When he came down I cried with him for a long time. I think this affliction has drawn us nearer. He was more tender to me than I ever remembered him before.

At last the ghastly wait and suspense were ended. I saw no more strange faces in the lobbies; and the strange voices on the stairs and footsteps in the room, and the muffled sounds that made me feel faint, were heard no more. The funeral was over, and pretty Nelly was gone for ever and ever, and I would come in and go out and read my books, and take my walks alone; and the flowers, and the long summer evenings, and the song of birds would come again, and the leaves make their soft shadow in the nooks where we used to sit together in the wood, but gentle little Nelly would never come again.

During these terrible days, Laura Grey was a sister to me, both in affection and in sorrow. Oh, Laura, can I ever forget your tender, patient sympathy? How often my thoughts recall your loved face as I lay my head upon my lonely pillow, and my blessings follow you over the wide sea to your far-off home!

Papa took a long solitary ride that day through the warren, and away by Penruthyn Priory, and did not return till dark.

When he did, he sent for me. I found him in the room which, in the old-fashioned style, was called the oak parlour. A log-fire—we were well supplied from the woods in the rear of the house—lighted the room with a broad pale flicker. My father was looking ill and tired. He was leaning with his elbow on the mantel-piece, and said:

"Ethel, darling, I want to know what you would like best. We are going abroad for a little time; it is the only thing for your mamma. This place would kill her. I shall be leaving this to-morrow afternoon, and you can make up your mind which you would like best—to come with us and travel for some months, or to wait here, with Miss Grey, until our return. You shall do precisely whatever you like best—I don't wish you to hurry yourself, darling. I'd rather you thought it over at your leisure."

Then he sat down and talked about other things; and turned about to the fire with his decanter of sherry by him, and drank a good many glasses, and leaned back in his chair before he had finished it.

My father, I thought, was dozing, but was not sure; and being a good deal in awe of him—a natural consequence of seeing so little of him—I did not venture either to waken him, or to leave the room without his permission.

There are two doors in that room. I was standing irresolutely near that which is next the window, when the other opened, and the long whiskers and good-humoured, sensible face of portly Wynne Williams, the town-clerk and attorney of Cardyllion, entered. My father awoke, with a start, at the sound, and seeing him, smiled and extended his hand.

"How d'ye do, Williams? It's so good of you to come. Sit down. I'm off to-morrow, so I sent you a note. Try that sherry; it is better than I thought. And now I must tell you, that old scoundrel, Rokestone, is going to foreclose the mortgage, and they have served one of the tenants at Darlip with an ejectment; that's more serious; I fancy he means mischief there also. What do you think?"

"I always thought he might give us annoyance there; but Mandrick's opinion was with us. Do you wish me to look after that?"

"Certainly. And he's bothering me about that trust."

"I know," said Mr. Wynne Williams, with rather gloomy rumination.

"That fellow has lost me—I was reckoning it up only a day or two ago—between five and six thousand pounds in mere law costs, beside all the direct mischief he has done me; and he has twice lost me a seat in the House—first by maintaining that petition at King's Firkins, a thing that must have dropped but for his money; he had nothing on earth to do with it, and no motive but his personal, fiendish feelings; and next by getting up the contest against me at Shillingsworth, where, you know, it was ten to one; by Heavens! I should have had a walk over. There is not an injury that man could do me he has not done. I can prove that he swore he would strip me of everything I possessed. It is ever so many years since I saw him—you know all about it—and the miscreant pursues me still relentlessly. He swore to old Dymock, I'm told, and I believe it, that he would never rest till he had brought me to a prison. I could have him before a jury for that. There's some remedy, I suppose, there's some protection? If I had done what I wished ten years ago, I'd have had him out; it's not too late yet to try whether pistols can't settle it. I wish I had not taken advice; in a matter like that, the man who does always does wrong. I daresay, Williams, you think with me, now it's a case for cutting the Gordian knot?"

"I should not advise it, sir; he's an old man, and he's not afraid of what people say, and people know he has fought. He'd have you in the Queen's Bench, and as his feelings are of that nature, I'd not leave him the chance—I wouldn't trust him."

"It's not easy to know what one should do—a miscreant like that. I hope and pray that the curse of——"

My father spoke with a fierce tremble in his voice, and at that moment he saw me. He had forgotten that I was in the room, and said instantly:

"You may as well run away, dear; Mr. Williams and I have some business to talk over—and tiresome business it is. Good night, darling."

So away I went, glad of my escape, and left them talking. My father rang the bell soon, and called for more wine; so I suppose the council sat till late. I joined Laura Grey, to whom I related all that had passed, and my decision on the question, which was, to remain with her at Malory. She kissed me, and said, after a moment's thought:

"But will they think it unkind of you, preferring to remain here?"

"No," I said; "I think I should be rather in the way if I went; and, besides, I know papa is never high with any one, and really means what he says; and I should feel a little strange with them. They are very kind, and love me very much, I know, and so do I love them; but I see them so little, and you are such a friend, and I don't wish to leave this place; I like it better than any other in all the world; and I feel at home with you, more than I could with any one else in the world."

So that point was settled, and next day papa took leave of me very affectionately; and, notwithstanding his excited language, I heard nothing more of pistols and Mr. Rokestone. But many things were to happen before I saw papa again.

I remained, therefore, at Malory, and Laura Grey with me; and the shadow of Mr. Carmel passed the window every evening, but he did not come in to see us, as he used. He made inquiries at the door instead, and talked, sometimes for five minutes together, with Rebecca Torkill. I was a little hurt at this; I did not pretend to Laura to perceive it; but in our walks, or returning in the evening, if by chance I saw his tall, thin, but graceful figure approaching by the same path, I used to make her turn aside and avoid him by a detour. In so lonely a place as Malory the change was marked; and there was pain in that neglect. I would not let him fancy, however, that I wished, any more than he, to renew our old and near acquaintance.

So weeks passed away, and leafy May had come, and Laura Grey and I were sitting in our accustomed room, in the evening, talking in our desultory way.

"Don't you think papa very handsome?" I asked.

"Yes, he is handsome," she answered; "there is something refined as well as clever in his face; and his eyes are fine; and all that goes a great way. But many people might think him not actually handsome, though very good-looking and prepossessing."

"They must be hard to please," I said.

She smiled good-naturedly.

"Mamma fell in love with him at first sight, Rebecca Torkill says," I persisted, "and mamma was not easily pleased. There was a gentleman who was wildly in love with her; a man of very old family, Rebecca says, and good-looking, but she would not look at him when once she had seen papa."

"I think I heard of that. He is a baronet now; but he was a great deal older than Mr. Ware, I believe."

"Yes, he was; but Rebecca says he did not look ten years older than papa, and *he* was very young indeed then," I answered. "It was well for mamma she did not like him, for I once heard Rebecca say that he was a very bad man."

"Did you ever hear of mamma's aunt Lorrimer?" I resumed, after a little pause.

"Not that I recollect."

"She is very rich, Rebecca says. She has a house in London, but she is hardly ever there. She's not very old—not sixty. Rebecca is always wondering whom she will leave her money to; but that don't much matter, for I believe we have more than we want. Papa says, about ten years ago, she lived for nothing but society, and was everywhere; and now she has quite given up all that, and wanders about the Continent."

Our conversation subsided; and there was a short interval in which neither spoke.

"Why is it, Laura," said I, after this little silence, "that you never tell me anything about yourself, and I am always telling you everything I think or remember? Why are you so secret? Why don't you tell me your story?"

"My story; what does it signify? I suppose it is about an average story. Some people are educated to be governesses; and some of us take to it later, or by accident; and we are amateurs, and do our best. The Jewish custom was wise; every one should learn a mechanic's business. Saint Paul was a tent-maker. If fortune upsets the boat, it is well to have anything to lay hold of—anything rather than drowning; an hospital matron, a companion, a governess, there are not many chances, when things go wrong, between a poor woman and the workhouse."

"All this means, you will tell me nothing," I said.

"I am a governess, darling. What does it matter what I was? I am happier with you than ever I thought I could be again. If I had a story that was pleasant to hear, there is no one on earth I would tell it to so readily; but my story—— There is no use in thinking over misfortune," she continued; "there is no greater waste of time than regretting, except wishing. I know, Ethel, you would not pain me. I can't talk about those things; I may another time."

"You shan't speak of them, Laura, unless you wish it. I am ashamed of having bothered you so," I kissed her. "But, will you tell me one thing, for I am really curious about it? I have been thinking about that very peculiar-looking old gentleman, who wore a chocolate-coloured great-coat, and met us in the Mill Walk, and talked to you, you remember, on the Sunday we returned from church that way. Now, I want you to tell me, is that old man's name Rokestone?"

"No, dear, it is not; I don't think he even knows him. But isn't it time for us to have our tea? Will you not make it, while I put our books up in the other room?"

So I undertook this office, and was alone.

The window was raised, the evening was warm, and the sun by this time setting. It was the pensive hour when solitude is pleasant; when grief is mellowed, and even a thoughtless mind, like mine, is tinged with melancholy. I was thinking now of our recluse neighbour. I had seen him pass, as Miss Grey and I were talking. He still despatched those little notes about the inmates of Malory; for mamma always mentioned, when she wrote to me, in her wanderings on the Continent, that she had heard from Mr. Carmel that I was well, and was out every day with my governess, and so on. I wondered why he had quite given up those little weekly visits, and whether I could have unwittingly offended him.

These speculations would recur oftener than perhaps was quite consistent with the disdain I affected on the subject. But people who live in cities have no idea how large a space in one's thoughts, in a solitude like Malory, a neighbour at all agreeable must occupy.

I was ruminating in a great arm-chair, with my hand supporting my head, and my eyes fixed on my foot, which was tapping the carpet, when I heard the cold, clear voice of Mr. Carmel at the window. I looked up, and my eyes met his.

CHAPTER V.

THE LITTLE BLACK BOOK.

Our eyes met, I said; they remained fixed for a moment, and then mine dropped. I had been, as it were, detected, while meditating upon this capricious person. I daresay I even blushed; I certainly was embarrassed. He was repeating his salutation, "How d'ye do, Miss Ware?"

"Oh, I'm very well, thanks, Mr. Carmel," I answered, looking up; "and—and I heard from mamma on Thursday. They are very well; they are at Genoa now. They think of going to Florence in about three weeks."

"I know; yes. And you have no thoughts of joining them?"

"Oh! none. I should not like to leave this. They have not said a word about it lately."

"It is such a time, Miss Ethel, since I had the pleasure of seeing you—I don't mean, of course, at a distance, but near enough to ask you how you are. I dared not ask to see you too soon, and I thought—I fancied—you wished your walks uninterrupted."

I saw that he had observed my strategy; I was not sorry.

"I have often wished to thank you, Mr. Carmel; you were so very kind."

"I had no opportunity, Miss Ethel," he answered, with more feeling than before. "My profession obliges me to be kind—but I had no opportunity—Miss Grey is quite well?"

"She is very well, thanks."

With a softened glory, in level lines, the beams of the setting sun broke, scattered, through the trunks of the old elms, and one touched the head of the pale young man, as he stood at the window, looking in; his delicate and melancholy features were in the shade, and the golden light, through his thick, brown hair, shone softly, like the glory of a saint. As, standing thus, he looked down in a momentary reverie, Laura Grey came in, and paused, in manifest surprise, on seeing Mr. Carmel at the window.

I smiled, in spite of my efforts to look grave, and the governess, advancing, asked the young ecclesiastic how he was? Thus recalled, by a new voice, he smiled and talked with us for a few minutes. I think he saw our tea-equipage, and fancied that he might be, possibly, in the way; for he was taking his leave when I said, "Mr. Carmel, you must take tea before you go."

"Tea!—I find it very hard to resist. Will you allow me to take it, like a beggar-man, at the window? I shall feel less as if I were disturbing you; for you have only to shut the window down, when I grow prosy."

So, laughing, Laura Grey gave him a cup of tea, which he placed on the window-stone, and seating himself a little sideways on the bench that stands outside the window, he leaned in, with his hat off, and sipped his tea and chatted; and sitting as Miss Grey and I did, near the window, we made a very sociable little party of three.

I had quite given up the idea of renewing our speaking acquaintance with Mr. Carmel, and here we were, talking away, on more affable terms than ever! It seemed to me like a dream.

I don't say that Mr. Carmel was chatting with the *insouciance* and gaiety of a French abbé. There was, on the contrary, something very peculiar, both in his countenance and manner, something that suggested the life and sufferings of an ascetic. Something also, not easily defined, of command; I think it was partly in the severe though gentle gravity with which he spoke anything like advice or opinion.

I felt a little awed in his presence, I could not exactly tell why; and yet I was more glad than I would have confessed that we were good friends again. He sipped his cup of tea slowly, as he talked, and was easily persuaded to take another.

"I see, Miss Ethel, you are looking at my book with curious eyes."

It was true; the book was a very thick and short volume, bound in black shagreen, with silver clasps, and lay on the window-stone, beside his cup. He took it up in slender fingers, smiling as he looked at me.

"You wish to know what it is; but you are too ceremonious to ask me. I should be curious myself, if I saw it for the first time. I have often picked out a book from a library, simply for its characteristic binding. Some books look interesting. Now what do you take this to be?"

"Haven't you books called breviaries? I think this is one," said I.

"That is your guess; it is not a bad one—but no, it is not a breviary. What do you say, Miss Grey?"

"Well, I say it is a book of the offices of the Church."

"Not a bad guess, either. But it is no such thing. I think I must tell you—it is what you would call a storybook."

"Really!" I exclaimed, and Miss Grey and I simultaneously conceived a longing to borrow it.

"The book is two hundred and seventy years old, and written in very old French. You would call them stories," he said, smiling on the back of the book; "but you must not laugh at them; for I believe them all implicitly. They are legends."

"Legends?" said I, eagerly—"I should so like to hear one. Do, pray, tell one of them."

"I'll read one, if you command me, into English. They are told here as shortly as it is possible to relate them. Here, for instance, is a legend of John of Parma. I think I can read it in about two minutes."

"I'm sorry it is so short; do, pray, begin," I said.

Accordingly, there being still light enough to read by, he translated the legend as follows:—

"John of Parma, general of the order of Friars Minors, travelling one winter's night, with some brothers of the order, the party went astray in a dense forest, where they wandered about for several hours, unable to find the right path. Wearied with their fruitless efforts, they at length knelt down, and having commended themselves to the protection of the mother of God, and of their patron, Saint Francis, began to recite the first nocturn of the Office of the Blessed Virgin. They had not been long so engaged, when they heard a bell in the distance, and rising at once, and following the direction whence the sound proceeded, soon came to an extensive abbey, at the gate of which they knocked for admittance. The doors were instantly thrown open, and within they beheld a number of monks evidently awaiting their arrival, who, the moment they appeared, led them to a fire, washed their feet, and then seated them at a table, where supper stood ready; and having attended them during their meal, they conducted them to their beds. Wearied with their toilsome journey, the other travellers slept soundly; but John, rising in the night to pray, as was his custom, heard the bell ring for matins, and quitting his cell, followed the monks of the abbey to the chapel, to join with them in reciting the divine office.

"Arrived there, one of the monks began with this verse of the Thirty-fifth Psalm, 'Ibi ceciderunt qui operantur iniquitatem;' to which the choir responded, 'Expulsi sunt nec potuerunt stare.' Startled by the strange despairing tone in which the words were intoned, as well as by the fact that this is not the manner in which matins are usually commenced, John's suspicions were aroused, and addressing the monks, he commanded them, in the name of the Saviour, to tell him who and what they were. Thus adjured, he who appeared an abbot replied, that they were all angels of darkness, who, at the prayer of the Blessed Virgin, and of Saint Francis, had been sent to serve him and his brethren in their need. As he spoke, all disappeared; and the next moment John found himself and his companions in a grotto, where they remained, absorbed in prayer and singing the praises of God, until the return of day enabled them to resume their journey."

"How picturesque that is!" I said, as he closed the little book.

He smiled, and answered:

"So it is. Dryden would have transmuted such a legend into noble verse; painters might find great pictures in it—but, to the faithful, it is more. To me, these legends are sweet and holy readings, telling how the goodness, vigilance, and wisdom of God work by miracles for his children, and how these celestial manifestations have never ceased throughout the history of his Church on earth. To you they are, as I said, but stories; as such you may wish to look into them. I believe, Miss Grey, you may read them without danger." He smiled gently, as he looked at the governess.

"Oh! certainly, Laura," cried I. "I am so much obliged."

"It is very kind of you," said Miss Grey. "They are, I am sure, very interesting; but does this little book contain anything more?"

"Nothing, I am afraid, that could possibly interest you: nothing, in fact, but a few litanies, and what we call elevations—you will see in a moment. There is nothing controversial. I am no proselytiser, Miss Grey,"—he laughed a little—"my duty is quite of a different kind. I am collecting authorities, making extracts and precis, and preparing a work, not of my own, for the press, under a greater than I."

"Recollect, Laura, it is lent to me—isn't it, Mr. Carmel?" I pleaded, as I took the little volume and turned over its pages.

"Very well—certainly," he acquiesced, smiling.

He stood up now. The twilight was deepening; he laid his hand on the window sash, and leaned his forehead upon it, as he looked in, and continued to chat for a few minutes longer; and then, with a slight adieu, he left us.

When he was gone, we talked him over a little.

"I wonder what he is?—a priest only or a Jesuit," said I; "or, perhaps, a member of some other order. I should like so much to know."

"You'd not be a bit wiser if you did," said Laura.

"Oh, you mean because I know nothing of these orders; but I could easily make out. I think he would have told us to-night in the twilight, if we had asked him."

"I don't think he would have told us anything he had not determined beforehand to tell. He has told us nothing about himself we did not know already. We know he is a Roman Catholic, and an ecclesiastic—his tonsure proclaims that; and your mamma told you that he is writing a book, so that is no revelation either. I think he is profoundly reserved, cautious, and resolute; and with a kind of exterior gentleness, he seems to me to be really inflexible and imperious."

"I like that unconscious air of command, but I don't perceive those signs of cunning and reserve. He seemed to grow more communicative the longer he stayed." I answered.

"The darker it grew," she replied. "He is one of those persons who become more confident the more effectually their countenances are concealed. There ceases to be any danger of a conflict between looks and language—a danger that embarrasses some people."

"You are suspicious this evening," I said. "I don't think you like him."

"I don't know him; but I fancy that, talk as he may to us, neither you nor I have for one moment a peep into his real mind. His world may be perfectly celestial and serene, or it may be an ambitious, dark, and bad one; but it is an invisible world for us."

The candles were by this time lighted, and Miss Grey was closing the window, when the glitter of the silver clasp of the little book caught her eye.

"Have you found anything?" said I.

"Only the book—I forgot all about it. I am almost sorry we allowed him to lend it."

"We borrowed it; I don't think he wanted to lend it," said I; "but, however it was, I'm very glad we have got it. One would fancy you had lighted on a scorpion. I'm not afraid of it; I know it can't do any one the least harm, for they are only stories."

"Oh, I think so. I don't see myself that they can do any harm; but I am almost sorry we have got into that sort of relation with him."

"What relation, Laura?"

"Borrowing books and discussing them."

"But we need not discuss them; I won't—and you are so well up in the controversy with your two books of theology, that I think he's in more danger of being converted than you. Give me the book, and I'll find out something to read to you."

CHAPTER VI.

A STRANGER APPEARS.

Next day Miss Grey and I were walking on the lonely road towards Penruthyn Priory. The sea lies beneath it on the right, and on the left is an old grass-grown bank, shaggy with brambles. Round a clump of ancient trees that stand at a bend of this green rampart, about a hundred steps before us, came, on a sudden, Mr. Carmel, and a man dressed also in black, slight, but not so tall as he. They were walking at a brisk pace, and the stranger was talking incessantly to his companion.

That did not prevent his observing us, for I saw him slightly touch Mr. Carmel's arm with his elbow as he looked at us. Mr. Carmel evidently answered a question, and, as he did so, glanced at us; and immediately the stranger resumed his conversation. They were quickly up to us, and stopped. Mr. Carmel raised his hat, and asked leave to introduce his friend. We bowed, so did the stranger; but Mr. Carmel did not repeat his name very distinctly.

This friend was far from prepossessing. He was of middle height, and narrow-shouldered, what they call "putty-faced," and closely shorn, the region of the beard and whisker being defined in smooth dark blue. He looked about fifty. His movements were short and quick, and restless; he rather stooped, and his face and forehead inclined as if he were looking on the ground. But his eyes were not upon the ground; they were very fierce, but seldom rested for more than a moment on any one object. As he made his bow, raising his hat from his massive forehead, first to me, and afterwards to Miss Grey, his eyes, compressed with those wrinkles with which near-sighted people assist their vision, scrutinised us each with a piercing glance under his black eyebrows. It was a face at once intellectual, mean, and intimidating.

"Walking; nothing like walking, in moderation. You have boating here also, and you drive, of course; which do you like best, Miss Ware?" The stranger spoke with a slightly foreign accent, and, though he smiled, with a harsh and rapid utterance.

I forget how I answered this, his first question—rather an odd one. He turned and walked a little way with us.

"Charming country. Heavenly weather. But you must find it rather lonely, living down here. How you must both long for a week in London!"

"For my part, I like this better," I answered. "I don't like London in summer, even in winter I prefer this."

"You have lived here with people you like, I dare say, and for their sakes you love the place?" he mused.

We walked on a little in silence. His words recalled darling Nelly. This was our favourite walk long ago; it led to what we called the blackberry wilderness, rich in its proper fruits in the late autumn, and in May with banks all covered with cowslips and primroses. A sudden thought, that finds simple associations near, is affecting, and my eyes filled with tears. But with an effort I restrained them. The presence of a stranger, the sense of publicity, seals those fountains. How seldom people cry at the funerals of their beloved! They go through the public rite like an execution, pale and collected, and return home to break their hearts alone.

"You have been here some months, Miss Grey. You find Miss Ware a very amenable pupil, I venture to believe. I think I know something of physiognomy, and I may congratulate you on a very sweet and docile pupil, eh?"

Laura Grey, governess as she was, looked a little haughtily at this officious gentleman, who, as he put the question, glanced sharply for a moment at her, and then as rapidly at me, as if to see how it told.

"I think—I hope we are very happy together," said Miss Grey. "I can answer for myself."

"Precisely what I expected," said the stranger, taking a pinch of snuff. "I ought to mention that I am a very particular acquaintance, friend I may say, of Mrs. Ware, and am, therefore, privileged."

Mr. Carmel was walking beside his friend in silence, with his eyes apparently lowered to the ground all this time.

My blood was boiling with indignation at being treated as a mere child by this brusque and impertinent old man. He turned to me.

"I see, by your countenance, young lady, that you respect authority. I think your governess is very fortunate; a dull pupil is a bad bargain, and you are not dull. But a contumacious pupil is utterly intolerable; you are not that, either; you are sweetness and submission itself, eh?"

I felt my cheeks flushing, and I directed on him a glance which, if the fire of ladies' eyes be not altogether a fable, ought at least to have scorched him.

"I have no need of submission, sir. Miss Grey does not think of exercising authority over me. I shall be eighteen my next birthday. I shall be coming out, papa says, in less than a year. I am not treated like a child any longer, sir. I think, Laura, we have walked far enough. Hadn't we better go home? We can take a walk another time—any time would be pleasanter than now."

Without waiting for her answer, I turned, holding my head very high, breathing quickly, and feeling my cheeks in a flame.

The odious stranger, nothing daunted by my dignified resentment, smiled shrewdly, turned about quite unconcernedly, and continued to walk by my side.

On my other side was Laura Grey, who told me afterwards that she greatly enjoyed my spirited treatment of his ill-breeding.

She walked by my side, looking straight before her, as I did. Out of the corners of my eyes I saw the impudent old man marching on as if quite unconscious, or, at least, careless of having given offence. Beyond him I saw, also, in the same oblique way, Mr. Carmel, walking with downcast eyes as before.

He ought to be ashamed, I thought, of having introduced such a person.

I had not time to think a great deal, before the man of the harsh voice and restless eyes suddenly addressed me again.

"You are coming out, you say, Miss Ware, when you are eighteen?"

I made him no answer.

"You are now seventeen, and a year intervenes," he continued, and turning to Mr. Carmel, "Edwyn, run you down to the house, and tell the man to put my horse to."

So Mr. Carmel crossed the stile at the road-side, and disappeared by the path leading to the stables of Malory. And then turning again to me, the stranger said:

"Suppose your father and mother have placed you in my sole charge, with a direction to remove you from Malory, and take you under my immediate care and supervision, to-day; you will hold yourself in readiness to depart immediately, attended by a lady appointed to look after you, with the approbation of your parents—eh?"

"No, sir, I'll not go. I'll remain with Miss Grey. I'll not leave Malory," I replied, stopping short, and turning towards him. I felt myself growing very pale, but I spoke with resolution.

"You'll not? what, my good young lady, not if I show you your father's letter?"

"Certainly not. Nothing but violence shall remove me from Malory, until I see papa himself. He certainly would not do anything so cruel!" I exclaimed, while my heart sank within me.

He studied my face for a moment with his dark and fiery eyes.

"You are a spirited young lady; a will of your own!" he said. "Then you won't obcy your parents?"

"I'll do as I have said," I answered, inwardly quaking.

He addressed Miss Grey now.

"You'll make her do as she's ordered?" said this man, whose looks seemed to me more sinister every moment.

"I really can't. Besides, in a matter of so much importance, I think she is right not to act without seeing her father, or, at least, hearing directly from him."

"Well, I must take my leave," said he. "And I may as well tell you it is a mere mystification; I have no authority, and no wish to disturb your stay at Malory; and we are not particularly likely ever to meet again; and you'll forgive an old fellow his joke, young ladies?"

With these brusque and eccentric sentences, he raised his hat, and with the activity of a younger man, ran up the bank at the side of the road; and, on the summit, looked about him for a moment, as if he had forgotten us altogether; and then, at his leisure, he descended at the other side and was quite lost to view.

Laura Grey and I were both staring in the direction in which he had just disappeared. Each, after a time, looked in her companion's face.

"I almost think he's mad!" said Miss Grey.

"What could have possessed Mr. Carmel to introduce such a person to us?" I exclaimed. "Did you hear his name?" I asked, after we had again looked in the direction in which he had gone, without discovering any sign of his return.

"Droqville, I think," she answered.

"Oh! Laura, I am so frightened! Do you think papa can really intend any such thing? He's too kind. I am sure it is a falsehood."

"It is a joke, he says himself," she answered. "I can't help thinking a very odd joke, and very pointless; and one that did not seem to amuse even himself."

"Then you do not think it is true?" I urged, my panic returning.

"Well, I can't think it is true, because, if it were, why should he say it was a joke? We shall soon know. Perhaps Mr. Carmel will enlighten us."

"I thought he seemed in awe of that man," I said.

"So did I," answered Miss Grey. "Perhaps he is his superior."

"I'll write to-day to papa, and tell him all about it; you shall help me; and I'll implore of him not to think of anything so horrible and cruel."

Laura Grey stopped short, and laid her hand on my wrist for a moment, thinking.

"Perhaps it would be as well if we were to turn about and walk a little further, so as to give him time to get quite away."

"But if he wants to take me away in that carriage, or whatever it is, he'll wait any time for my return."

"So he would; but the more I think over it, the more persuaded I am that there is nothing in it."

"In any case, I'll go back," I said. "Let us go into the house and lock the doors; and if that odious Mr. Droqville attempts to force his way in, Thomas Jones will knock him down; and we'll send Anne Owen to Cardyllion, for Williams, the policeman. I hate suspense. If there is to be anything unpleasant, it is better to have it decided, one way or other, as soon as possible."

Laura Grey smiled, and spoke merrily of our apprehensions; but I don't think she was quite so much at ease as she assumed to be.

Thus we turned about, I, at least, with a heart thumping very fast; and we walked back towards the old house of Malory, where, as you have this moment heard, we had made up our minds to stand a siege.

CHAPTER VII.

TASSO.

I daresay I was a great fool; but if you had seen the peculiar and unpleasant face of Monsieur Droqville, and heard his harsh nasal voice, in which there was something of habitual scorn, you would make excuses. I confess I was in a great fright by the time we had got well into the dark avenue that leads up to the house.

I hesitated a little as we reached that point in the carriage-road, not a long one, which commands a clear view of the hall-door steps. I had heard awful stories of foolish girls spirited away to convents, and never heard of more. I have doubts as to whether, had I seen Monsieur Droqville or his carriage there, I should not have turned about, and ran through the trees. But the courtyard in front of the house was, as usual, empty and still. On its gravel surface reposed the sharp shadows of the pointed gables above, and the tufts of grass on its surface had not been bruised by recent carriage wheels. Instead, therefore, of taking to flight, I hurried forward, accompanied by Laura Grey, to seize the fortress before it was actually threatened.

In we ran, lightly, and locked the hall door, and drew chain and bolt against Monsieur Droqville; and up the great stairs to our room, each infected by the other's panic. Safely in the room, we locked and bolted our door, and stood listening, until we had recovered breath. Then I rang our bell furiously, and up came Anne Owen, or, as her countrymen pronounce it, Anne Wan. There had been, after all, no attack; no human being had attempted to intrude upon our cloistered solitude.

"Where is Mrs. Torkill?" I asked, through the door.

"In the still-room, please, miss."

"Well, you must lock and bolt the back-door, and don't let any one in, either way."

We passed an hour in this state of preparation, and finally ventured downstairs, and saw Rebecca Torkill. From her we learned that the strange gentleman who had been with Mr. Carmel had driven away more than half an hour before; and Laura Grey and I, looking in one another's faces, could not help laughing a little.

Rebecca had overheard a portion of a conversation, which she related to me; but not for years after. At the time she had no idea that it could refer to any one in whom she was interested; and even at this hour I am not myself absolutely certain, but only conjecture, that I was the subject of their talk. I will tell it to you as nearly as I can recollect.

Rebecca Torkill, nearly an hour before, being in the still-room, heard voices near the window, and quietly peeped out.

You must know that immediately in the angle formed by the junction of the old house, known as the steward's house, which Mr. Carmel had been assigned as a residence, and the rear of the great house of Malory, stand two or three great trees, and a screen of yews, behind which, so embossed in ivy as to have the effect of a background of wood, stands the gable of the still-room. This strip of ground, lying immediately in the rear of the steward's house, was a flower-garden; but a part of it is now carpeted with grass, and lies under the shadow of the great trees, and is walled round with the dark evergreens I have mentioned. The rear of the stable-yard of Malory, also mantled with ivy, runs parallel to the back of the steward's house, and forms the other boundary of this little enclosure, which simulates the seclusion of a cloister; and but for the one well-screened window I have mentioned, would really possess it. Standing near this window she saw Mr. Carmel, whom she always regarded with suspicion, and his visitor, that gentleman in black, whose looks nobody seemed to like.

"I told you, sir," said Mr. Carmel, "through my friend Ambrose, I had arranged to have prayers twice a week, at the Church in Paris, for that one soul."

"Yes, yes, yes; that is all very well, very good, of course," answered the hard voice; "but there are things we must do for ourselves—the saints won't shave us, you know."

"I am afraid, sir, I did not quite understand your letter," said Mr. Carmel.

"Yes, you did, pretty well. You see she may be, one day, a very valuable acquisition. It is time you put your shoulder to the wheel—d'ye see? Put your shoulder to the wheel. The man who said all that is able to do it. So mind you put your shoulder to the wheel forthwith."

The younger man bowed.

"You have been sleeping," said the harsh, peremptory voice. "You said there was enthusiasm and imagination. I take that for granted. I find there is spirit, courage, a strong will; obstinacy—impracticability—no milksop—a bit of a virago! Why did not you make out all that for yourself? To discover character you must apply tests. You ought in a single conversation to know everything."

The young man bowed again.

"You shall write to me weekly; but don't post your letters at Cardyllion. I'll write to you through Hickman, in the old way."

She could hear no more, for they moved away. The elder man continued talking, and looked up at the back-windows of Malory, which became visible as they moved away. It was one of his fierce, rapid glances; but he was satisfied, and continued his conversation for two or three minutes more. Then he abruptly turned, and entered the steward's house quickly; and, in two or three minutes more, was driving away from Malory at a rapid pace.

A few days after this adventure—for in our life any occurrence that could be talked over for ten minutes was an adventure—I had a letter in mamma's pretty hand, and in it occurred this passage:

"The other day I wrote to Mr. Carmel, and I asked him to do me a kindness. If he would read a little Italian with you, and Miss Grey I am sure would join, I should be so much pleased. He has passed so much of his life in Rome, and is so accomplished in Italian; simple as people think it, that language is more difficult to pronounce correctly even than French. I forget whether Miss Grey mentioned Italian among the languages she could teach. But however that may be, I think, if Mr. Carmel will take that trouble, it would be very desirable."

Mr. Carmel, however, made no sign. If the injunction to "put his shoulder to the wheel" had been given for my behoof, the promise was but indifferently kept, for I did not see Mr. Carmel again for a fortnight. During the greater part of that interval he was away from Malory, we could not learn where. At the end of that time, one evening, just as unexpectedly as before, he presented himself at the window. Very much the same thing happened. He drank tea with us, and sat on the bench—his bench, he called it—outside the window, and remained, I am sure, two hours, chatting very agreeably. You may be sure we did not lose the opportunity of trying to learn something of the gentleman whom he had introduced to us.

Yes, his name was Droqville.

"We fancied," said Laura, "that he might be an ecclesiastic."

"His being a priest, or not, I am sure you think does not matter much, provided he is a good man, and he is that; and a very clever man, also," answered Mr. Carmel. "He is a great linguist: he has been in almost every country in the world. I don't think Miss Ethel has been a traveller yet, but you have, I dare say." And in that way he led us quietly away from Monsieur Droqville to Antwerp, and I know not where else.

One result, however, did come of this visit. He actually offered his services to read Italian with us. Not, of course, without opening the way for this by directing our talk upon kindred subjects, and thus deviously up to the point. Miss Grey and I, who knew what each expected, were afraid to look at each other; we should certainly have laughed, while he was leading us up so circuitously and adroitly to his "palpable ambuscade."

We settled Monday, Wednesday, and Friday in each week for our little evening readings. Mr. Carmel did not always now sit outside, upon his bench, as at first. He was often at our tea-table, like one of ourselves; and sometimes stayed later than he used to do. I thought him quite delightful. He certainly was clever, and, to me, appeared a miracle of learning; he was agreeable, fluent, and very peculiar.

I could not tell whether he was the coldest man on earth, or the most impassioned. His eyes seemed to me more enthusiastic and extraordinary the oftener and longer I beheld them. Their strange effect, instead of losing, seemed to gain by habit and observation. It seemed to me that the cold and melancholy serenity that held us aloof was artificial, and that underneath it could be detected the play and fire of a nature totally different.

I was always fluctuating in my judgment upon this issue; and the problem occupied me during many an hour of meditation.

How dull the alternate days had become; and how pleasant even the look-forward to our little meetings! Thus, very agreeably, for about a fortnight our readings proceeded, and, one evening on our return, expecting the immediate arrival of our "master," as I called Mr. Carmel, we found, instead, a note addressed to Miss Grey. It began: "Dear Miss Eth," and across these three letters a line was drawn, and "Grey" was supplied. I liked even that evidence that his first thought had been of me. It went on:

> "Duty, I regret, calls me for a time away from Malory, and our Italian readings, I have but a minute to write to tell you not to expect me this evening, and to say I regret I am unable, at this moment, to name the day of my return.
>
> "In great haste, and with many regrets,
>
> Yours very truly,
>
> E. Carmel."

"So he's gone again!" I said, very much vexed. "What shall we do to-night?"

"Whatever you like best; I don't care—I'm sorry he's gone."

"How restless he is! I wonder why he could not stay quietly here; he can't have any real business away. It may be duty; but it looks very like idleness. I dare say he began to think it a bore coming to us so often to read Tasso, and listen to my nonsense; and I think it a very cool note, don't you?"

"Not cool; a little cold; but not colder than he is," said Laura Grey. "He'll come back, when he has done his business; I'm sure he has business; why should he tell an untruth about the matter?"

I was huffed at his going, and more at his note. That pale face, and those large eyes, I thought the handsomest in the world. I took up one of Laura's manuals of The Controversy, which had fallen rather into disuse after the first panic had subsided, and Mr. Carmel had failed to make any, even the slightest, attack upon our faith. I was fiddling with its leaves, and I said:

"If I were an inexperienced young priest, Laura, I should be horribly afraid of those little tea-parties. I dare say he is afraid—afraid of your eyes, and of falling in love with you."

"Certainly not with me," she answered. "Perhaps you mean he is afraid of people talking? I think you and I should be the persons to object to that, if there was a possibility of any such thing. But we are talking folly. These men meet us, and talk to us, and we see them; but there is a wall between, that is simply impassable. Suppose a sheet of plate glass, through which you see as clearly as through air, but as thick as the floor of ice on which a Dutch fair is held. That is what their vow is."

"I wonder whether a girl ever fell in love with a priest. That would be a tragedy!" I said.

"A ridiculous one," answered Laura; "you remember the old spinster who fell in love with the Apollo Belvedere? It could happen only to a madwoman."

I think this was a dull evening to Laura Grey; I know it was for me.

CHAPTER VIII.

THUNDER.

We saw or heard nothing for a week or more of Mr. Carmel. It was possible that he would never return. I was in low spirits. Laura Grey had been shut up by a cold, and on the day of which I am now speaking she had not yet been out. I therefore took my walk alone towards Penruthyn Priory, and, as dejected people not unfrequently do, I was well enough disposed to indulge and even to nurse my melancholy.

A thunder-storm had been for hours moving upwards from the south-east, among the grand ranges of distant mountains that lie, tier beyond tier, at the other side of the estuary, and now it rested on a wide and lurid canopy of cloud upon the summits of the hills and headlands that overlook the water.

It was evening, later than my usual return to tea. I knew that Laura Grey minded half-an-hour here or there as little as I did, and a thunder-storm seen and heard from the neighbourhood of Malory is one of the grandest spectacles in its way on earth. Attracted by the mighty hills on the other side, these awful elemental battles seldom visit our comparatively level shore, and we see the lightning no nearer than about half-way across the water. Vivid against blackening sky and purple mountain, the lightning flies and shivers. From broad hill-side, through rocky gorges, reflected and returned from precipice to precipice, through the hollow windings of the mountains, the thunder rolls and rattles, dies away, explodes again, and at length subsides in the strangest and grandest of all sounds, spreading through all that mountainous region for minutes after, like the roar and tremble of an enormous seething cauldron.

Suppose these aërial sounds reverberating from cliff to cliff, from peak to peak, and crag to crag, from one hill-side to another, like the cannon in the battles of Milton's angels; suppose the light of the setting sun, through a chink in the black curtain of cloud behind me, touching with misty fire the graves and head-stones in the pretty churchyard, where, on the stone bench under the eastern window, I have taken my seat, near the grave of my darling sister; and suppose an uneasy tumult, not a breeze, in the air, sometimes still, and sometimes in moaning gusts, tossing sullenly the boughs of the old trees that darken the churchyard.

For the first time since her death I had now visited this spot without tears. My thoughts of death had ceased to be pathetic, and were, at this moment, simply terrible. "My heart was disquieted within me, and the fear of death had fallen upon me." I sat with my hands clasped together, and my eyes fixed on the thunderous horizon before me, and the grave of my darling under my eyes, and she, in her coffin, but a few feet beneath. The grave, God's prison, as old Rebecca Torkill used to say, and then the Judgment! This new sense of horror and despair was, I dare say, but an unconscious sympathy with the vengeful and melancholy aspect of nature.

I heard a step near me, and turned. It was Mr. Carmel who approached. He was looking more than usually pale, I thought, and ill. I was surprised, and a little confused. I cannot recall our greeting. I said, after that was over, something, I believe, about the thunder-storm.

"And yet," he answered, "you understand these awful phenomena—their causes. You remember our little talk about electricity—here it is! We know all that is but the restoration of an equilibrium. Think what it will be when God restores the moral balance, and settles the equities of eternity! There are moods, times, and situations in which we contemplate justly our tremendous Creator. Fear him who, after he has killed the body, has power to cast into hell. Yea, I say unto you, fear him. Here all suffering is transitory. Weeping may endure for a night, but joy cometh in the morning. This life is the season of time and of mercy; but once in hell, mercy is no more, and eternity opens, and endures, and has no end."

Here he ceased for a time to speak, and looked across the estuary, listening, as it seemed, to the roll and tremble of the thunder. After a little while, he said:

"That you are to die is most certain; nothing more uncertain than the time and manner; by a slow or a sudden death; in a state of grace or sin. Therefore, we are warned to be ready at all hours. Better twenty years too soon than one moment late; for to perish once is to be lost for ever. Your death depends upon your life; such as your life is, such will be your death. How can we dare to live in a state that we dare not die in?"

I sat gazing at this young priest, who, sentence after sentence, was striking the very key-note of the awful thought that seemed to peal and glare in the storm. He stood with his head uncovered, his great earnest eyes sometimes raised, sometimes fixed on me, and the uncertain gusts at fitful intervals tossed his hair this way and that. The light of the setting sun touched his thin hand, and his head, and glimmered on the long grass; the graves lay around us; and the voice of God himself seemed to speak in the air.

Mr. Carmel drew nearer, and in the same earnest vein talked on. There was no particle of which is termed the controversial in what he had said. He had not spoken a word that I could not subscribe. He had quoted, also, from our version of the Bible; but he presented the terrors of revelation with a prominence more tremendous than I was accustomed to, and the tone of his discourse was dismaying.

I will not attempt to recollect and to give you in detail the conversation that followed. He presented, with a savage homeliness of illustration, with the same simplicity and increasing force, the same awful view of Christianity. Beyond the naked strength of the facts, and the terrible brevity with which he stated them in their different aspects, I don't know that there was any special eloquence in his discourse, but in the language of Scripture, his words made "both my ears tingle."

He did not attempt to combat my Protestant tenets directly; that might have alarmed me; he had too much tact for that. Anything he said with that tendency was in the way simply of a discourse of the teaching and practice of his own Church.

"In the little volume of legends you were so good as to say you would like to look into," he said, "you will find the prayer of Saint Louis de Gonzaga; you will also find an anonymous prayer, very pathetic and beautiful. I have drawn a line in red ink down the margin at its side, so it is easily found. These will show you the spirit in which the faithful approach the Blessed Virgin. They may interest you. They will, I am sure, interest your sympathies for those who have suffered, like you, and have found peace and hope in these very prayers."

He then spoke very touchingly of my darling sister, and my tears at last began to flow. It was the strangest half-hour I had ever passed. Religion during that time had appeared in a gigantic and terrible aspect. My grief for my sister was now tinged with terror. Do not we from our Lutheran pulpits too lightly appeal to that potent emotion—fear?

For awhile this tall thin priest in black, whose pale face and earnest eyes seemed to gleam on me with an intense and almost painful enthusiasm, looked like a spirit in the deepening twilight; the thunder rattled and rolled on among the echoing mountains, the gleam of the lightning grew colder and wilder as the darkness increased, and the winds rushed mournfully, and tossed the churchyard grass, and bowed the heads of the great trees about us; and as I walked home, with my head full of awful thoughts, and my heart agitated, I felt as if I had been talking with a messenger from that other world.

CHAPTER IX.

AWAKENED.

We do these proselytising priests great wrong when we fancy them cold-blooded practisers upon our credulity, who seek, for merely selfish ends, to entangle us by sophistries, and inveigle us into those mental and moral catacombs from which there is no escape. We underrate their danger when we deny their sincerity. Mr. Carmel sought to save my soul; nobler or purer motive, I am sure, never animated man. If he acted with caution, and even by stratagem, he believed it was in the direct service of Heaven, and for my eternal weal. I know him better, his strength and his weakness, now—his asceticism, his resolution, his tenderness. That young priest—long dead—stands before me, in the white robe of his purity, king-like. I see him, as I saw him last, his thin, handsome features, the light of patience on his face, the pale smile of suffering and of victory. His tumults and his sorrows are over. Cold and quiet he lies now. My thanks can never reach him; my unavailing blessings and gratitude follow my true and long-lost friend, and tears wrung from a yearning heart.

Laura Grey seemed to have lost her suspicions of this ecclesiastic. We had more of his society than before. Our reading went on, and sometimes he joined us in our walks. I used to see him from an upper window every morning early, busy with spade and trowel, in the tiny flower-garden which belonged to the steward's house. He used to work there for an hour punctually, from before seven till nearly eight. Then he vanished for many hours, and was not seen till nearly evening, and we had, perhaps, our *Gerusalemme Liberata*, or he would walk with us for a mile or more, and talk in his gentle but cold way, pleasantly, on any topic we happened to start. We three grew to be great friends. I liked to see him when he, and, I may add, Laura Grey also, little thought I was looking at his simple garden-work under the shadow of the grey wall from which the old cherry and rose-trees drooped, in picturesque confusion, under overhanging masses of ivy.

He and I talked as opportunity occurred more and more freely upon religion. But these were like lovers' confidences, and, by a sort of tacit consent, never before Laura Grey. Not that I wished to deceive her; but I knew very well what she would think and say of my imprudence. It would have embarrassed me to tell her;

but here remonstrances would not have prevailed; I would not have desisted; we should have quarrelled; and yet I was often on the point of telling her, for any reserve with her pained me.

In this quiet life we had glided from summer into autumn, and suddenly, as before, Mr. Carmel vanished, leaving just such a vague little note as before.

I was more wounded, and a great deal more sorry this time. The solitude I had once loved so well was irksome without him. I could not confess to Laura, scarcely to myself, how much I missed him.

About a week after his disappearance, we had planned to drink tea in the housekeeper's room. I had been sitting at the window in the gable that commanded the view of the steward's garden, which had so often shown me my hermit at his morning's work. The roses were already shedding their honours on the mould, and the sear of autumn was mellowing the leaves of the old fruit-trees. The shadow of the ancient stone house fell across the garden, for by this time the sun was low in the west, and I knew that the next morning would come and go, and the next, and bring no sign of his return, and so on, and on, perhaps for ever.

Never was little garden so sad and silent! The fallen leaves lay undisturbed, and the weeds were already peeping here and there among the flowers.

"Is it part of your religion?" I murmured bitterly to myself, as, with folded hands, I stood a little way back, looking down through the open window, "to leave willing listeners thus half-instructed? Business? What is the business of a good priest? I should have thought the care and culture of human souls was, at least, part of a priest's business. I have no one to answer a question now—no one to talk to. I am, I suppose, forgotten."

I dare say there was some affectation in this. But my dejection was far from affected, and hiding my sorrowful and bitter mood, I left the window and came down the back-stairs to our place of meeting. Rebecca Torkill and Laura Grey were in high chat. Tea being just made, and everything looking so delightfully comfortable, I should have been, at another time, in high spirits.

"Ethel, what do you think? Rebecca has been just telling me that the mystery about Mr. Carmel is quite cleared up. Mr. Prichard, the grocer, in Cardyllion, was visiting his cousin, who has a farm near Plasnwyd, and whom should he see there but our missing friar, in a carriage driving with Mrs. Tredwynyd, of Plasnwyd. She is a beautiful woman still, and one of the richest widows in Wales, Rebecca says; and he has been living there ever since he left this; and his last visit, when we thought he was making a religious sojourn in a monastery, was to the same house and lady! What do you think of that? But it is not near ended yet. Tell the rest of the story, Mrs. Torkill, to Miss Ethel—please do."

"Well, miss, there's nothin' very particular, only they say all round Plasnwyd that she was in love with him, and that he's goin' to turn Protestant, and it's all settled they're to be married. Every one is singin' to the same tune all round Plasnwyd, and what every one says must be true, as I've often heard say."

I laughed, and asked whether our teacake was ready, and looked out of the window. The boughs of the old fruit-trees in the steward's garden hung so near it that the ends of the sprays would tap the glass, if the wind blew. As I leaned against the shutter, drumming a little tune on the window, and looking as careless as any girl could, I felt cold and faint, and my heart was bursting. I don't know what prevented my dropping on the floor in a swoon.

Laura, little dreaming of the effect of this story upon me, was chatting still with Rebecca, and neither perceived that I was moved by the news.

That night I cried for hours in my bed, after Laura Grey was fast asleep. It never occurred to me to canvass the probability of the story. We are so prone to believe what we either greatly desire or greatly fear. The violence of my own emotions startled me. My eyes were opened at last to a part of my danger.

As I whispered, through convulsive sobs, "He's gone, he's gone—I have lost him—he'll never be here any more! Oh! why did you pretend to take an interest in me? Why did I listen to you? Why did I like you?" All this, and as much more girlish lamentation and upbraiding as you please to fancy, dispelled my dream and startled my reason. I had an interval to recover in; happily for me, this wild fancy had not had time to grow into a more impracticable and dangerous feeling. I felt like an awakened somnambulist at the brink of a precipice. Had I become attached to Mr. Carmel, my heart must have broken in silence, and my secret have perished with me.

Some weeks passed, and an advent occurred, which more than my girlish pride and resolutions turned my thoughts into a new channel, and introduced a memorable actor upon the scene of my life.

CHAPTER X.

A SIGHT FROM THE WINDOWS.

We are now in stormy October; a fierce and melancholy month! August and September touch the greenwood leaves with gold and russet, and gently loosen the hold of every little stalk on forest bough; and then, when all is ready, October comes on in storm, with sounds of trump and rushing charge and fury not to be argued or dallied with, and thoroughly executes the sentence of mortality that was recorded in the first faint yellow of the leaf, in the still sun of declining July.

October is all the more melancholy for the still, golden days that intervene, and show the thinned branches in the sunlight, soft, and clear as summer's, and the boughs cast their skeleton shadows across brown drifts of leaves.

On the evening I am going to speak of, there was a wild, threatening sunset, and the boatmen of Cardyllion foretold a coming storm. Their predictions were verified.

The breeze began to sigh and moan through the trees and chimney-stacks of Malory shortly after sunset, and in another hour it came on to blow a gale from the northwest. From that point the wind sweeps right up the estuary from the open sea; and after it has blown for a time, and the waves have gathered their strength, the sea bursts grandly upon the rocks a little in front of Malory.

We were sitting cosily in our accustomed tea-room. The rush and strain of the wind on the windows became momentarily more vehement, till the storm reached its highest and most tremendous pitch.

"Don't you think," said Laura, after an awful gust, "that the windows may burst in? The wind is frightful! Hadn't we better get to the back of the house?"

"Not the least danger," I answered; "these windows have small panes, and immensely strong sashes; and they have stood so many gales that we may trust them for this."

"There again!" she exclaimed. "How awful!"

"No danger to us, though. These walls are thick, and as firm as rock; not like your flimsy brick houses; and the chimneys are as strong as towers. You must come up with me to the window in the tawny-room; there is an open space in the trees opposite, and we can see pretty well. It is worth looking at; you never saw the sea here in a storm."

With very little persuasion, I induced her to run upstairs with me. Along the corridor, we reached the chamber in question, and placing our candle near the door, and running together to the window, we saw the grand spectacle we had come to witness.

Over the sea and land, rock and wood, a dazzling moon was shining. Tattered bits of cloud, the "scud" I believe they call it, were whirling over us, more swiftly than the flight of a bird, as far as your eye could discern: till the sea was lost in the grey mist of the horizon it was streaked and ridged with white. Nearer to the stooping trees that bowed and quivered in the sustained blast, and the little churchyard dormitory that nothing could disturb, the black peaked rock rose above the turmoil, and a dark causeway of the same jagged stone, sometimes defined enough, sometimes submerged, connected it almost with the mainland. A few hundred yards beyond it, I knew, stretched the awful reef on which the Intrinsic, years before I could remember, had been wrecked. Beyond that again, we could see the waves leaping into sheets of foam, that seemed to fall as slowly and softly as clouds of snow. Nearer, on the dark rock, the waves flew up high into the air, like cannon-smoke.

Within these rocks, which make an awful breakwater, full of mortal peril to ships driving before the storm, the estuary, near the shores of Malory, was comparatively quiet.

At the window, looking on this wild scene, we stood, side by side, in the fascination which the sea in its tumultuous mood never fails to exercise. Thus, not once turning our eyes from the never-flagging variety of the spectacle, we gazed for a full half-hour, when, suddenly, there appeared—was it the hull of a vessel shorn of its masts? No, it was a steamer—a large one, with low chimneys. It seemed to be about a mile and a half away, but was driving on very rapidly. Sometimes the hull was quite lost to sight, and then again rose black and sharp on the crest of the sea. We held our breaths. Perhaps the vessel was trying to make the shelter of the pier of Cardyllion; perhaps she was simply driving before the wind.

To me there seemed something uncertain and staggering in the progress of the ship. Before her lay the ominous reef, on which many a good ship and brave life had perished. There was quite room enough, I knew, with good steering, between the head of the reef and the sandbank at the other side, to make the pier of Cardyllion. But was there any one on board who knew the intricate navigation of our dangerous estuary? Could any steering in such a tempest avail? And, above all, had the ship been crippled? In any case, I knew enough to be well aware that she was in danger.

Reader, if you have never witnessed such a spectacle, you cannot conceive the hysterical excitement of that suspense. All those on board are, for the time, your near friends; your heart is among them—their terrors are yours. A ship driving with just the hand and eye of one man for its only chance, under Heaven, against the fury of sea and wind, and a front of deadly rock, is an unequal battle; the strongest heart sickens as the crisis nears, and the moments pass in an unconscious agony of prayer.

Rebecca Torkill joined us at this moment.

"Oh! Rebecca," I said, "there is a ship coming up the estuary—do you think they can escape?"

"The telescope should be on the shelf at the back stair-head," she answered, as soon as she had taken a long look at the steamer. "Lord ha' mercy on them, poor souls!—that's the very way the Intrinsic drove up before the wind the night she was lost; and I think this will be the worse night of the two."

Mrs. Torkill returned with the long sea telescope, in its worn casing of canvas.

I took the first "look out." After wandering hither and thither over a raging sea, and sometimes catching the tossing head of some tree in the foreground, the glass lighted, at length, upon the vessel. It was a large steamer, pitching and yawing frightfully. Even to my inexperienced eye, it appeared nearly unmanageable. I handed the glass to Laura. I felt faint.

Some of the Cardyllion boatmen came running along the road that passes in front of Malory. I saw that two or three of them had already arrived on the rising ground beside the churchyard, and were watching events from that wind-swept point. I knew all the Cardyllion boatmen, for we often employed them, and I said:

"I can't stay here—I must hear what the boatmen say. Come, Laura, come with me."

Laura was willing enough.

"Nonsense! Miss Ethel," exclaimed the housekeeper. "Why, dear Miss Grey, you could not keep hat or bonnet on in a wind like that! You could not keep your feet in it!"

Remonstrance, however, was in vain. I tied a handkerchief tight over my head and under my chin—Laura did the same; and out we both sallied, notwithstanding Rebecca Torkill's protest and entreaty. We had to go by the back door; it would have been impossible to close the hall-door against such a gale.

Now we were out in the bright moonlight under the partial shelter of the trees, which bent and swayed with the roar of a cataract over our heads. Near us was the hillock we tried to gain; it was next to impossible to reach it against the storm. Often we were brought to a standstill, and often forced backward, notwithstanding all our efforts.

At length, in spite of all, we stood on the little platform, from which the view of the rocks and sea beyond was clear. Williams, the boatman, was close to me, at my right hand, holding his low-crowned hat down on his head with his broad, hard hand. Laura was at my other side. Our dresses were slapping and rattling in the storm like the cracking of a thousand whips; and such a roaring was in my ears, although my handkerchief was tied close over them, that I could scarcely hear anything else.

CHAPTER XI.

CATASTROPHE.

The steamer looked very near now and large. It was plain it had no longer any chance of clearing the rocks. The boatmen were bawling to one another, but I could not understand what they said, nor hear more than a word or two at a time.

The steamer mounted very high, and then seemed to dive headlong into the sea, and was lost to sight. Again, in less than a minute, the black mass was toppling at the summit of the sea, and again it seemed swallowed up.

"Her starboard paddle!" shouted a broad-shouldered sailor in a pilot-coat, with his palm to the side of his mouth.

Thomas Jones was among these men, without a hat, and on seeing me he fell back a little. I was only a step or two behind them.

"Thomas Jones," I screamed, and he inclined his ear to my shrill question, "is there no life-boat in Cardyllion?"

"Not one, miss," he roared; "and it could not make head against that if there was."

"Not an inch," bawled Williams.

"Is there any chance?" I cried.

"An anchor from the starn! A bad hold there—she's draggin' of it!" yelled Williams, whose voice, though little more than two feet away, sounded faint and half smothered in the storm.

Just then the steamer reared, or rather swooped, like the enchanted horse, in the air, and high above its black shape shot a huge canopy of foam; and then it staggered over and down, and nothing but raging sea was there.

"O God! are they all lost?" I shrieked.

"Anchor's fast. All right now," roared the man in the pilot-coat.

In some seconds more the vessel emerged, pitching high into the brilliant moonlight, and nearly the same thing was repeated again and again. The seafaring men who were looking on were shouting their opinions to one another, and from the little I was able to hear and understand, I gathered that she might ride it out if she did not drag her anchor, or "part" or "founder." But the sea was very heavy, and the rocks just under her bows now.

In this state of suspense a quarter of an hour or more must have passed. Suddenly the vessel seemed to rise nearer than before. The men crowded forward to the edge of the bank. It was plain something decisive had happened. Nearer it rose again, and then once more plunged forward and disappeared. I waited breathless. I waited longer than before, and longer. Nothing was there but rolling waves and springing foam beyond the rocks. The ship rose no more!

The first agony of suspense was over. Where she had been the waves were sporting in the ghastly moonlight. In my wild horror I screamed—I wrung my hands. I could not turn for a moment from the scene. I was praying all the time the same short prayer over and over again. Minute after minute passed, and still my eyes were fixed on the point where the ship had vanished; my hands were clasped over my forehead, and tears welled down my cheeks.

What's that? Upon the summit of the bare rock, all on a sudden, the figure of a man appeared; behind this mass of black stone, as each wave burst in succession, the foam leaped in clouds. For a moment the figure was seen sharp against the silvery distance; then he stooped, as if to climb down the near side of the rock, and we lost sight of him. The boatmen shouted, and held up each a hand (their others were holding their hats on) in token of succour near, and three or four of them, with Thomas Jones at their head, ran down the slope, at their utmost speed to the jetty, under which, in shelter, lay the Malory boat. Soon it was moving under the bank, four men pulling might and main against the gale; though they rowed in shelter of the reef, on the pinnacle of which we had seen the figure for a moment, still it was a rough sea, and far from safe for an open boat, the spray driving like hail against them, and the boat pitching heavily in the short cross sea.

No other figure crossed the edge of the rock, or for a moment showed upon the bleak reef, all along which clouds of foam were springing high and wild into the air.

The men who had been watching the event from the bank, seemed to have abandoned all further hope, and began to descend the hill to the jetty to await the return of the boat. It did return, bearing the one rescued man.

Laura Grey and I went homeward. We made our way into the back-yard, often forced to run, by the storm, in spite of ourselves. We had hardly reached the house when we saw the boatmen coming up.

We were now in the yard, about to enter the house at the back-door, which stood in shelter of the building. I saw Mrs. Torkill in the steward's house, with one of the maids, evidently in a fuss. I ran in.

"Oh, Miss Ethel, dear, did you see that? Lord a'mercy on us! A whole shipful gone like that! I thought the sight was leaving my eyes."

I answered very little. I felt ill, I was trembling still, and ready to burst again into tears.

"Here's bin Thomas Jones, miss, to ask leave for the drownded man to rest himself for the night, and, as Mr. Carmel's away, I knew your papa and mamma would not refuse; don't you think so, miss? So I said, ay, bring him here. Was I right, miss? And me and Anne Wan is tidyin' a bed for him."

"Quite right, I'm sure," said I, my interest again awakened, and almost at the same moment into the flagged passage came Thomas Jones, followed by several of the Cardyllion boatmen, their great shoes clattering over the flags.

In the front rank of these walked the one mortal who had escaped alive from the ship that was now a wreck on the fatal reef. You may imagine the interest with which I looked at him. I saw a graceful but manly figure, a young man in a short sailor-like coat, his dress drenched and clinging, his hat gone, his forehead and features finely formed, very energetic, and, I thought, stern—browned by the sun; but, allowing for that tint, no drowned face in the sea that night was paler than his, his long black hair, lank with sea-water, thrown back from his face like a mane. There was blood oozing from under its folds near his temple; there was blood also on his hand, which rested on the breast of his coat; on his finger there was a thick gold ring. I had little more than a moment in which to observe all this. He walked in, holding his head high, very faint and fierce, with a slight stagger in his gait, a sullen and defiant countenance, and eyes fixed and gazing straight before him, as I had heard somnambulists described. I saw him in the candle-light for only a moment as he walked by, with boatmen in thick shoes, as I said, clattering beside him. I felt a strange longing to run and clasp him by the hand!

I got into our own back-door, and found Laura Grey in the room in which we usually had our tea. She was as much excited as I.

"Could you have imagined," she almost cried, "anything so frightful? I wish I had not seen it. It will always be before my eyes."

"That is what I feel also; but we could not help it, we could not have borne the suspense. That is the reason why the people who are least able to bear it sometimes see the most dreadful sights."

As we were talking, and wondering where the steamer came from, and what was her name, and how many people were probably on board, in came Rebecca Torkill.

"I sent them boatmen home, miss, that rowed the boat out to the rock for that poor young man, with a pint o' strong ale, every one round, and no doubt he'll give them and Thomas Jones something in hand for taking him off the rock when he comes to himself a bit. He ought to be thanking the Almighty with a contrite heart."

"He did not look as if he was going to pray when I saw him," I said.

"Nor to thank God, nor no one, for anything," she chimed in. "And he sat down sulky and black as you please, at the side o' the bed, and said never a word, but stuck out his foot to Thomas Jones to unbutton his boot. I had a pint o' mulled port ready, and I asked him if I should send for the doctor, and he only shook his head and shrugged his shoulders, as he might turn up his nose at an ugly physic. And he fell a-thinking while Jones was takin' off the other boot, and in place of prayin' or thanks-giving, I heard him muttering to himself and grumbling; and, Lord forgive me if I wrong him, I think I heard him cursing some one. There was a thing for a man just took alive out o' the jaws o' death by the mercy o' God to do! There's them on earth, miss, that no lesson will teach, nor goodness melt, nor judgment frighten, but the last one, and then all's too late."

It was late by this time, and so we all got to our beds. But I lay long awake in the dark, haunted by the ceaseless rocking of that dreadful sea, and the apparition of that one pale, bleeding messenger from the ship of death. How unlike my idea of the rapture of a mortal just rescued from shipwreck! His face was that of one to whom an atrocious secret has been revealed, who was full of resentment and horror; whose lips were sealed.

In my eyes he was the most striking figure that had ever appeared before me. And the situation and my own dreadful excitement had elevated him into a hero.

CHAPTER XII.

OUR GUEST.

The first thing I heard of the stranger in the morning was that he had sent off early to the proprietor of the "Verney Arms" a messenger with a note for two large boxes which he had left there, when the yacht Foam Bell was at Cardyllion about a fortnight before. The note was signed with the letters R. M.

The Foam Bell had lain at anchor off the pier of Cardyllion for only two hours, so no one in the town knew much about her. Two or three of her men, with Foam Bell across the breasts of their blue shirts and on the ribbons of their flat glazed hats, had walked about the quaint town, and drunk their beer at the "George and Garter." But there had not been time to make acquaintance with the townspeople. It was only known that the yacht belonged to Sir Dives Wharton, and that the gentleman who left the boxes in charge of the proprietor of the "Verney Arms," was not that baronet.

The handwriting was the same as that in the memorandum he had left with the hotel-keeper, and which simply told him that the big black boxes were left to be called or written for by Edward Hathaway, and mentioned no person whose initials were R. M. So Mr. Hughes, of the "Verney Arms," drove to Malory to see the gentleman at the steward's house, and having there recognised him as the very gentleman who left the boxes in his charge, he sent them to him as directed.

Shortly after, Doctor Mervyn, our old friend walked up the avenue, and saw me and Laura at the window.

It was a calm, bright morning; the storm had done its awful work, and was at rest, and sea and sky looked glad and gentle in the brilliant sun. Already about fifty drowned persons had been carried up and laid upon the turf in the churchyard in rows, with their faces upward. I was glad it was upon the slope that was hid from us.

How murderous the dancing waves looked in the sunlight! And the black saw-edged reef I beheld with a start and a shudder. The churchyard, too, had a changed expression. What a spectacle lay behind that familiar grassy curve! I did not see the incongruous muster of death. Here a Liverpool dandy; there a white-whiskered City man; sharp bag-men; little children—strange companions in the churchyard—hard-handed sailors; women, too, in silk or serge—no distinction now.

I and Laura could not walk in that direction till all this direful seeking and finding were over.

The doctor, seeing us at the open window, raised his hat. The autumn sun through the thin leaves touched his bald head as he walked over to the window-stool, and placing his knee on the bench on which Mr. Carmel used sometimes to sit, he told us all he knew of the ship and the disaster. It was a Liverpool steamer called the Conway Castle, bound for Bristol. One of her paddles was disabled early in the gale, and thus she drove to leeward, and was wrecked.

"And now," said the doctor, "I'm going to look in upon the luckiest man in the kingdom, the one human being who escaped alive out of that ship. He must have been either the best or the worst man on board—either too good to be drowned or too bad, by Jove! He is the gentleman you were so kind as to afford shelter to last night in the steward's house there, round the corner, and he sent for me an hour ago. I daresay he feels queer this morning; and from what Thomas Jones says, I should not be surprised if he had broken a bone somewhere. Nothing of any great consequence, of course; but he must have got a thund'ring fling on those rocks. When I've seen him—if I find you here—I'll tell you what I think of him."

After this promise, you may be sure we did wait where we were, and he kept his word. We were in a fever of curiosity; my first question was, "Who is he?"

"I guessed you'd ask that the first moment you could," said the doctor, a little pettishly.

"Why?" said I.

"Because it is the very question I can't answer," he replied. "But I'll tell you all I do know," he continued, taking up his old position at the window, and leaning forward with his head in the room.

Every word the oracle spoke we devoured. I won't tell his story in his language, nor with our interruptions. I will give its substance, and in part its details, as I received them. The doctor was at least as curious as we were.

His patient was up, sitting by the fire, in dressing-gown and slippers, which he had taken with other articles of dress from the box which stood open on the floor. The window-curtain was partly drawn, the room rather dark. He saw the young man with his feet on the fender, seated by the wood fire. His features, as they struck the doctor, were handsome and spirited; he looked ill, with pale cheek and lips, speaking low and smiling.

"I'm Doctor Mervyn," said the doctor, making his bow, and eyeing the stranger curiously.

"Oh! Thanks, Doctor Mervyn! I hope it is not a long way from your house, I am here very ridiculously circumstanced. I should not have had any clothes, if it had not been for a very lucky accident, and for a day or two I shall be totally without money—a mere Robinson Crusoe."

"Oh, that don't matter; I shall be very happy to see after you in the meantime, if there should be anything in my way," answered the doctor, bluntly.

"You are very kind, thanks. This place, they tell me, is called Malory. What Mr. Ware is that to whom it belongs?"

"The Honourable Mr. Ware, brother of Lord H——. He is travelling on the Continent at present with his wife, a great beauty some fifteen years since; and his daughter, his only child, is at present here with her governess."

"Oh, I thought some one said he had two?"

The doctor re-asserted the fact, and for some seconds the stranger looked on the floor abstractedly.

"You wished a word or two of advice, I understand?" interrupted the doctor at length. "You have had a narrow escape, sir—a tremendous escape! You must have been awfully shaken. I don't know how you escaped being smashed on those nasty rocks."

"I am pretty well smashed, I fancy," said the young man.

"That's just what I wanted to ascertain."

"From head to foot, I'm covered with bruises," continued the stranger; "I got off with very few cuts. I have one over my temple, and half-a-dozen here and there, and one here on my wrist; but you need not take any trouble about them—a cut, when I get one, heals almost of itself. A bit of court-plaster is all I require for them, and Mrs. Something, the housekeeper here, has given me some; but I'm rather seedy. I must have swallowed a lot of salt water, I fancy. I've got off very well, though, if it's true all the other people were drowned. It was a devil of a fluke; you'd say I was the luckiest fellow alive, ha, ha, ha! I wish I could think so."

He laughed, a little bitterly.

"There are very few men glad to meet death when it comes," said Doctor Mervyn. "Some think they are fit to die, and some know they are not. You know best, sir, what reason you have to be thankful."

"I'm nothing but bruises and aches all over my body. I'm by no means well, and I've lost all my luggage, and papers, and money, since one o'clock yesterday, when I was flourishing. Two or three such reasons for thankfulness would inevitably finish me."

"All except you were drowned, sir," said the doctor, who was known in Cardyllion as a serious-minded man, a little severely.

"Like so many rats in a trap, poor devils," acquiesced the stranger. "They were hatched down. I was the only passenger on deck. I must have been drowned if I had been among them."

"All those poor fellow-passengers of yours," said Doctor Mervyn, in disgust, "had souls, sir, to be saved."

"I suppose so; but I never saw such an assemblage of snobs in my life. I really think that, except poor Haworth—he insisted it would be ever so much pleasanter than the railway; I did not find it so; he's drowned of course—I assure you, except ourselves, there was not a gentleman among them. And Sparks, he's drowned too, and I've lost the best servant I ever had in my life. But I beg your pardon, I'm wasting your time. Do you think I'm ill?"

He extended his wrist, languidly, to enable the doctor to feel his pulse. The physician suppressed his rising answer with an effort, and made his examination.

"Well, sir, you have had a shock."

"By Jove! I should not wonder," acquiesced the young man, with a sneer.

"And you are a good deal upset, and your contusions are more serious than you seem to fancy. I'll make up a liniment here, and I'll send you down something else that will prevent any tendency to fever; and I suppose you would like to be supplied from the 'Verney Arms.' You must not take any wine stronger than claret for the present, and a light dinner, and if you give me a line, or tell me what name——"

"Oh, they know me there, thanks. I got these boxes from there this morning, and they are to send me everything I require."

The doctor wanted his name. The town of Cardyllion, which was in a ferment, wanted it. Of course he must have the name; a medical practitioner who kept a ledger and sent out accounts, it was part of his business to know his patients' names. How could he stand before the wags of the news-room, if he did not know the name of his own patients—of this one, of all others.

"Oh! put me down as R. M. simply," said the young man.

"But wouldn't it be more—more usual, if you had no objections—a little more at length?" insinuated the doctor.

"Well, yes; put it down a little more at length—say R. R. M. Three letters instead of two."

The doctor, with his head inclined, laughed patiently, and the stranger, seeing him about to return to the attack, said a little petulantly: "You see, doctor, I'm not going to give my very insignificant name here to any one. If your book-keeper had it, every one in the town would know it; and Cardyllion is a place at which idle people turn up, and I have no wish to have my stray friends come up to this place to bother me for the two or three days I must stay here. You may suppose me an escaped convict, or anything else you please that will amuse the good people; but I'm hanged if I give my name, thank you!"

After this little interruption, the strictly professional conversation was resumed, and the doctor ended by directing him to stay quiet that day, and not to walk out until he had seen him again next morning.

The doctor then began to mix the ingredients of his liniment. The young man in the silk dressing-gown limped to the window, and leaned his arm upon the sash, looking out, and the doctor observed him, in his ruminations, smiling darkly on the ivy that nodded from the opposite wall, as if he saw a confederate eyeing him from its shadow.

"He didn't think I was looking at him," said the doctor; "but I have great faith in a man's smile when he thinks he is all to himself; and that smile I did not like; it was, in my mind, enough to damn him."

All this, when his interview was over, the doctor came round and told us. He was by no means pleased with his patient, and being a religious man, of a quick temper, would very likely have declined the office of physician in this particular case, if he had not thought, judging by his "properties," which were in a certain style that impressed Doctor Mervyn, and his air, and his refined features, and a sort of indescribable superiority which both irritated and awed the doctor, that he might be a "swell."

He went the length, notwithstanding, of calling him, in his conversation with us, an "inhuman puppy," but he remarked that there were certain duties which no Christian could shirk, among which that of visiting the sick held, of course, in the doctor's mind, due rank.

CHAPTER XIII.

MEETING IN THE GARDEN.

I was a little shy, as country misses are; and, curious as I was, rather relieved when I heard that the shipwrecked stranger had been ordered to keep his quarters strictly, for that day at least. So, by-and-by, as Laura Grey had a letter to write, I put on my hat, and not caring to walk towards the town, and not daring to take the Penruthyn Road, I ran out to the garden. The garden of Malory is one of those monastic enclosures whose fruit-trees have long grown into venerable timber; whose walls are stained by time, and mantled in some places with ivy; where everything has been allowed, time out of mind, to have its own way; where walks are grass-grown, and weeds choke the intervals between old standard pear, and cherry, and apple-trees, and only a little plot of ground is kept in cultivation by a dawdling, desultory man, who carries in his daily basket of vegetables to the cook. There was a really good Ribston-pippin or two in this untidy, but not unpicturesque garden; and these trees were, I need scarcely tell you, a favourite resort of ours.

The gale had nearly stripped the trees of their ruddy honours, and thrifty Thomas Jones had, no doubt, carried the spoil away to store them in the apple-closet. One pippin only dangled still within reach, and I was whacking at this particularly good-looking apple with a long stick, but as yet in vain, when I suddenly perceived that a young man, whom I recognised as the very hero of the shipwreck, was approaching. He walked slowly and a little lame, and was leaning on a stick. He was smiling, and, detected in my undignified and rather greedy exercise—I had been jumping from the ground—I was ready to sink into the earth with shame. Perhaps, if I had been endowed with presence of mind, I should have walked away. But I was not, on that occasion at least; and I stood my ground, stick in hand, affecting not to see his slow advance.

It was a soft sunny day. He had come out without a hat; he had sent to Cardyllion to procure one, and had not yet got it, as he afterwards told me, with an apology for seeming to make himself so very much at home. How he introduced himself I forget; I was embarrassed and disconcerted; I know that he thanked me very much for my "hospitality," called me his "hostess," smiling, and told me that, although he did not know my father, he yet saw him everywhere during the season. Then he talked of the wreck; he described his own adventures very interestingly, and spoke of the whole thing in terms very different from those reported by Doctor Mervyn, and with a great deal of feeling. He asked me if I had seen anything of it from our house; and then it became my turn to speak. I very soon got over my shyness; he was so perfectly well-bred that it was impossible, even for a rustic such as I was, not to feel very soon quite at her ease in his company.

So I talked away, becoming more animated; and he smiled, looking at me, I thought, with a great deal of sympathy, and very much pleased. I thought him very handsome. He had one point of resemblance to Mr. Carmel. His face was pale, but, unlike his, as dark as a gipsy's. Its tint showed the white of his eyes and his teeth with fierce effect. What was the character of the face I saw now? Very different from the death-like phantom that had crossed my sight the night before. It was a face of passion and daring. A broad, low forehead, and resolute mouth, with that pronounced under-jaw which indicates sternness and decision. I contrasted him secretly with Mr. Carmel. But in his finely-cut features, and dark, fierce eyes, the ascetic and noble interest of the sadder face was wanting; but there was, for so young a person as I, a different and a more powerful fascination in the beauty of this young man of the world.

Before we parted I allowed him to knock down the apple I had been trying at, and this rustic service improved our acquaintance.

I began to think, however, that our interview had lasted quite long enough; so I took my leave, and I am certain he would have accompanied me to the house, had I not taken advantage of his lameness, and walked away very quickly.

As I let myself out at the garden-door, in turning I was able, unsuspected, to steal a parting look, and I saw him watching me intently as he leaned against the stem of a gigantic old pear-tree. It was rather pleasant to my vanity to think that I had made a favourable impression upon the interesting stranger.

Next day our guest met me again, near the gate of the avenue, as I was returning to the house.

"I had a call this morning from your clergyman," he said. "He seems a very kind old gentleman, the rector of Cardyllion; and the day is so beautiful, he proposed a sail upon the estuary, and if you were satisfied with him, by way of escort, and my steering—I'm an old sailor—I'm sure you'd find it just the day to enjoy a little boating."

He looked at me, smiling eagerly.

Laura Grey and I had agreed that nothing would tempt us to go upon the water, until all risk of lighting upon one of those horrible discoveries from the wreck, that were now beginning to come to the surface from hour to hour, was quite over. So I made our excuses as best I could, and told him that since the storm we had a horror of sailing. He looked vexed and gloomy. He walked beside me.

"Oh! I understand—Miss Grey? I was not aware—I ought, of course, to have included her. Perhaps your friend would change her mind and induce you to reconsider your decision. It is such a charming day."

I thanked him again, but our going was quite out of the question. He smiled and bowed a little, but looked very much chagrined. I fancied that he thought I meant to snub him, for proposing any such thing on so very slight an acquaintance. I daresay if I had I should have been quite right; but you must remember how young I was, and how unlearned in the world's ways. Nothing, in fact, was further from my intention. To soften matters a little, I said:

"I am very sorry we can't go. We should have liked it, I am sure, so much; but it is quite impossible."

He walked all the way to the hall-door with me; and then he asked if I did not intend continuing my walk a little. I bid him good-bye, however, and went in, very full of the agreeable idea that I had made a conquest.

Laura Grey and I, walking to Cardyllion, met Doctor Mervyn, who stopped to tell us that he had just seen his Malory patient, "R. R. M.," steering Williams's boat, with the old vicar on board.

"By Jove! one would have fancied he had got enough of the water for some time to come," remarked the doctor, in conclusion. "That is the most restless creature I ever encountered in all my professional experience! If he had kept himself quiet yesterday and to-day, he'd have been pretty nearly right by to-morrow; but if he goes on like this I should not wonder if he worked himself into a fever."

CHAPTER XIV.

THE INTRUDER.

Next morning, at about nine o'clock, whom do I see but the restless stranger, to my surprise, again upon the avenue as I return towards the house. I had run down to the gate before breakfast to meet our messenger, and learn whether any letters had come by the post. He, like myself, has come out before his breakfast. He turns on meeting me, and walks towards the house at my side. Never was man more persistent. He had got Williams's boat again, and not only the vicar, but the vicar's wife, was coming for a sail; surely I would venture with her? I was to remember, besides, that they were to sail to the side of the estuary furthest from the wreck; there could be no possible danger there of what I feared—and thus he continued to argue and entreat.

I really wished to go. I said, however, that I must ask Miss Grey, whom, upon some excuse which I now forget, he regretted very much he could not invite to come also. I had given him a conditional promise by the time we parted at the hall-door, and Laura saw no objection to my keeping it, provided old Mrs. Jermyn, the vicar's wife, were there to chaperon me. We were to embark from the Malory jetty, and she was to call for me at about three o'clock.

The shipwrecked stranger left me, evidently very well pleased. When he got into his quarters in the steward's house and found himself all alone, I dare say his dark face gleamed with the smile of which Doctor Mervyn had formed so ill an opinion. I had not yet seen that smile. Heaven help me! I have had reason to remember it.

Laura and I were sitting together, when who should enter the room but Mr. Carmel. I stood up and shook hands. I felt very strangely. I was glad the room was a dark one. I was less observed, and therefore less embarrassed.

It was not till he had been in the room some time that I observed how agitated he looked. He seemed also very much dejected, and from time to time sighed heavily. I saw that something had gone strangely wrong. It was a vague suspense. I was secretly very much frightened.

He would not sit down. He said he had not a moment to stay; and yet he lingered on, I fancied, debating something within himself. He was distrait, and, I thought, irresolute.

After a little talk he said:

"I came just to look in on my old quarters and see my old friends for a few minutes, and then I must disappear again for more than a month, and I find a gentleman in possession."

We hastened to assure him that we had not expected him home for some time, and that the stranger was admitted but for a few days. We told him, each contributing something to the narrative, all about the shipwreck, and the reception of the forlorn survivor in the steward's house.

He listened without a word of comment, almost without breathing, and with his eyes fixed in deep attention on the floor.

"Has he made your acquaintance?" he asked, raising them to me.

"He introduced himself to me," I answered, "but Miss Grey has not seen him."

Something seemed to weigh heavily upon his mind.

"What is your father's present address?" he asked.

I told him, and he made a note of it in his pocket-book. He stood up now, and did at length take his leave.

"I am going to ask you to do a very kind thing. You have heard of sealed orders, not to be opened till a certain point has been reached in a voyage or a march? Will you promise, until I shall have left you fully five minutes, not to open this letter?"

I almost thought he was jesting, but I perceived very quickly that he was perfectly serious. Laura Grey looked at him curiously, and gave him the desired promise as she received the note. His carriage was at the door, and in another minute he was driving rapidly down the avenue. What had led to these odd precautions?—and what had they to do with the shipwrecked stranger?

At about eleven o'clock—that is to say, about ten minutes before Mr. Carmel's visit to us—the stranger had been lying on a sofa in his quarters, with two ancient and battered novels from Austin's Library in Cardyllion, when the door opened unceremoniously, and Mr. Carmel, in travelling costume, stepped into the room. The hall-door was standing open, and Mr. Carmel, on alighting from his conveyance, had walked straight in without encountering any one in the hall. On seeing an intruder in possession he stopped short; the gentleman on the sofa, interrupted, turned towards the door. Thus confronted, each stared at the other.

"Ha! Marston," exclaimed the ecclesiastic, with a startled frown, and an almost incredulous stare.

"Edwyn! by Jove!" responded the stranger, with a rather anxious smile, which faded, however, in a moment.

"What on earth brings you here?" said Mr. Carmel, sternly, after a silence of some seconds.

"What the devil brings you here?" inquired the stranger, almost at the same moment. "Who sent you? What is the meaning of it?"

Mr. Carmel did not approach him. He stood where he had first seen him, and his looks darkened.

"You are the last man living I should have looked for here," said he.

"I suppose we shall find out what we mean by-and-by," said Marston, cynically; "at present I can only tell you that when I saw you I honestly thought a certain old gentleman, I don't mean the devil, had sent you in search of me."

Carmel looked hard at him. "I've grown a very dull man since I last saw you, and I don't understand a joke as well as I once did," said he; "but if you are serious you cannot have learnt that this house has been lent to me by Mr. Ware, its owner, for some months at least; and these, I suppose, are your things? There is not room to put you up here."

"I didn't want to come. I am the famous man you may have read of in the papers—quite unique—the man who escaped alive from the Conway Castle. No Christian refuses shelter to the shipwrecked; and you are a Christian, though an odd one."

Edwyn Carmel looked at him for some seconds in silence.

"I am still puzzled," he said. "I don't know whether you are serious; but, in any case, there's a good hotel in the town—you can go there."

"Thank you—without a shilling," laughed the young man, a little wickedly.

"A word from me will secure you credit there."

"But I'm in the doctor's hands, don't you see?"

"It is nothing very bad," answered Mr. Carmel; "and you will be nearer the doctor there."

The stranger, sitting up straight, replied:

"I suppose I shall; but the doctor likes a walk, and I don't wish him a bit nearer."

"But this is, for the time being, my house, and you must go," replied Edwyn Carmel, coldly and firmly.

"It is also my house, for the time being; for Miss Ware has given me leave to stay here."

The ecclesiastic's lips trembled, and his pale face grew paler, as he stared on the young man for a second or two in silence.

"Marston," he said, "I don't know, of all men, why you should specially desire to pain me."

"Why, hang it! Why should I wish to pain you, Edwyn? I don't. But I have no notion of this sort of hectoring. The idea of your turning me out of the—my house—the house they have lent me! I told you I didn't want to come here; and now I don't want to go away, and I won't."

The churchman looked at him, as if he strove to read his inmost thoughts.

"You know that your going to the hotel could involve no imaginable trouble," urged Edwyn Carmel.

"Go to the hotel yourself, if you think it so desirable a place. I am satisfied with this, and I shall stay here."

"What can be the motive of your obstinacy?"

"Ask that question of yourself, Mr. Carmel, and you may possibly obtain an answer," replied the stranger.

The priest looked again at him, in stern doubt.

"I don't understand your meaning," he said, at last.

"I thought my meaning pretty plain. I mean that I rather think our motives are identical."

"Honestly, Marston, I don't understand you," said Mr. Carmel, after another pause.

"Well, it is simply this: that I think Miss Ware a very interesting young lady, and I like being near her—don't you?"

The ecclesiastic flushed crimson; Marston laughed contemptuously.

"I have been away for more than a month," said the priest, a little paler, looking up angrily; "and I leave this to-day for as long a time again."

"Conscious weakness! Weakness of that sentimental kind sometimes runs in families," said the stranger with a sneer. It was plain that the stranger was very angry; the taunt was wicked, and, whatever it meant, stung Mr. Carmel visibly. He trembled, with a momentary quiver, as if a nerve had been pierced.

There was a silence, during which Mr. Carmel's little French clock over the chimney-piece, punctually wound every week by old Rebecca, might be heard sharply tick, tick, ticking.

"I shall not be deterred by your cruel tongue," said he, very quietly, at length, with something like a sob, "from doing my duty."

"Your duty! Of course, it is always duty; jealousy is quite unknown to a man in holy orders. But there is a difference. You can't tell me the least what I'm thinking of; you always suppose the worst of every one. Your duty! And what, pray, is your duty?"

"To warn Miss Ware and her governess," he answered promptly.

"Warn her of what?" said the stranger, sternly.

"Warn her that a villain has got into this house."

The interesting guest sprang to his feet, with his fists clenched. But he did not strike. He hesitated, and then he said:

"Look here; I'll not treat you as I would a man. You wish me to strike you, you Jesuit, and to get myself into hot water. But I shan't make a fool of myself. I tell you what I'll do with you—if you dare to injure me in the opinion of any living creature, by one word of spoken or hinted slander, I'll make it a police-office affair; and I'll bring out the whole story you found it on; and we'll see which suffers most, you or I, when the world hears it. And now, Mr. Carmel, you're warned. And you know I'm a fellow that means what he says."

Mr. Carmel turned with a pale face, and left the room.

I wonder what the stranger thought. I have often pondered over that scene; and, I believe, he really thought that Mr. Carmel would not, on reflection, venture to carry out his threat.

CHAPTER XV.

A WARNING.

We had heard nothing of Mr. Carmel's arrival. He had not passed our windows, but drove up instead by the back avenue; and now he was gone, and there remained no record of his visit but the letter which Laura held in her fingers, while we both examined it on all sides, and turned it over. It was directed, "To Miss Ware and Miss Grey. Malory." And when we opened it we read these words:

> "DEAR YOUNG LADIES,—I know a great deal of the gentleman who has been permitted to take up his residence in the house adjoining Malory. It is enough for me to assure you that no acquaintance could be much more objectionable and unsafe, especially for young ladies living alone as you do. You cannot, therefore, exercise too much caution in repelling any advances he may make.—
>
> Your true friend, E. CARMEL."

The shock of reading these few words prevented my speaking for some seconds. I had perfect confidence in Mr. Carmel's warning. I was very much frightened. And the vagueness of his language made it the more alarming. The same thoughts struck us both. What fools we were! How is he to be got out of the house? Whom have we to advise with? What is to be done?

In our first panic we fancied that we had got a burglar or an assassin under our roof. Mr. Carmel's letter, however, on consideration, did not bear out quite so violent a conclusion. We resolved, of course, to act upon that letter; and I blamed myself too late for having permitted the stranger to make, even in so slight a way, my acquaintance.

In great trepidation, I despatched a note to Mrs. Jermyn, to say I could not join her boating party. To the stranger I could send neither note nor message. It did not matter. He would, of course, meet that lady at the jetty, and there learn my resolve. Two o'clock arrived. Old Rebecca came in, and told us that the gentleman in the steward's house had asked her whether Mr. Carmel was gone; and on learning that he had actually driven away, hardly waited till she was out of the room "to burst out a-laughing," and talking to himself, and laughing like mad.

"And I don't think, with his laughing and cursing, he's like a man should be that fears God, and is only a day or two out of the jaws of death!"

This description increased our nervousness. Possibly this person was a lunatic, whose keeper had been drowned in the Conway Castle. There was no solution of the riddle which Mr. Carmel had left us to read, however preposterous, that we did not try; none possible, that was not alarming.

About an hour after, passing through the hall, I saw some one, I thought, standing outside, near the window that commands the steps beside the door. This window has a wire-blind, through which, from outside, it is impossible to see. From within, however, looking towards the light, you can see perfectly. I scarcely thought our now distrusted guest would presume to approach our door so nearly; but there he was. He had mounted the steps, I suppose, with the intention of knocking, but he was, instead, looking stealthily from behind the great elm that grows close beside; his hand was leaning upon its trunk, and his whole attention absorbed in watching some object which, judging from the direction of his gaze, must have been moving upon the avenue. I could not take my eyes off him. He was frowning, with compressed lips and eyes dilated; his attitude betokened caution, and as I looked he smiled darkly.

I recovered my self-possession. I took, directly, Doctor Mervyn's view of that very peculiar smile. I was suddenly frightened. There was nothing to prevent the formidable stranger from turning the handle of the door and letting himself into the hall. Two or three light steps brought me to the door, and I instantly bolted it. Then drawing back a little into the hall, I looked again through the window, but the intending visitor was gone.

Who had occupied his gaze the moment before? And what had determined the retreat? It flashed upon me suddenly again that he might be one of those persons who are described as "being known to the police," and that Mr. Carmel had possibly sent constables to arrest him.

I waited breathlessly at the window, to see what would come of it. In a minute more, from the direction in which I had been looking for a party of burly policemen, there arrived only my fragile friend, Laura Grey, who had walked down the road to see whether Mr. and Mrs. Jermyn were coming.

Encouraged by this reinforcement, I instantly opened the hall-door, and looked boldly out. The enemy had completely disappeared.

"Did you see him?" I exclaimed.

"See whom?" she asked.

"Come in quickly," I answered. And when I had shut the hall-door, and again bolted it, I continued. "The man in the steward's house. He was on the steps this moment."

"No, I did not see him; but I was not looking towards the hall-door. I was looking up at the trees, counting the broken boughs—there are thirteen trees injured on the right hand, as you come up."

"Well, I vote we keep the door bolted; he shan't come in here," said I. "This is the second siege you and I have stood together in this house. I do wish Mr. Carmel had been a little more communicative, but I scarcely think he would have been so unfriendly as to leave us quite to ourselves if he had thought him a highwayman, and certainly, if he is one, he is a very gentleman-like robber."

"I think he can merely have meant, as he says, to warn us against making his acquaintance," said Miss Grey; "his letter says only that."

"I wish Mr. Carmel would stay about home," I said, "or else that the steward's house were locked up."

I suppose all went right about the boating party, and that Mrs. Jermyn got my note in good time.

No one called at Malory; the dubious stranger did not invade our steps again. We had constant intelligence of his movements from Rebecca Torkill; and there was nothing eccentric or suspicious about them, so far as we could learn.

Another evening passed, and another morning came; no letter by the post, Rebecca hastened to tell us, for our involuntary guest; a certain sign, she conjectured, that we were to have him for another day. Till money arrived he could not, it was plain, resume his journey.

Doctor Mervyn told us, with his customary accuracy and plenitude of information respecting other people's affairs, when he looked in upon us, after his visit to his patient, that he had posted a letter the morning after his arrival, addressed to Lemuel Blount, Esquire, 5, Brunton Street, Regent's Park; and that on reference to the London Directory, in the news-room, it was duly ascertained by the subscribers that "Blount, Lemuel," was simply entered as "Esquire," without any further clue whatsoever to guide an active-minded and inquiring community to a conclusion. So there, for the present, Doctor Mervyn's story ended.

Our panic by this time was very much allayed. The unobtrusive conduct of the unknown, ever since his momentary approach to our side of the house, had greatly contributed to this. I could not submit to a blockade of any duration; so we took heart of grace, and ventured to drive in the little carriage to Cardyllion, where we had some shopping to do.

CHAPTER XVI.

DOUBTS.

I have been searching all this morning in vain for a sheet of written note paper, almost grown yellow by time when I last saw it. It contains three stanzas of very pretty poetry. At least I once thought so. I was curious to try, after so many years, what I should think of them now. Possibly they were not even original, though there certainly was no lack in the writer of that sort of cleverness which produces pretty verses.

I must tell you how I came by them. I found that afternoon a note, on the window-stool in our tea-room, addressed "Miss Ethel." Laura Grey did not happen to be in the room at the moment. There might have been some debate on the propriety of opening the note if she had been present. I could have no doubt that it came from our guest, and I opened and read it instantly.

In our few interviews I had discovered, once or twice, a scarcely disguised tenderness in the stranger's tones and looks. A very young girl is always pleased, though ever so secretly, with this sort of incense. I know I was. It is a thing hard to give up; and, after all, what was Mr. Carmel likely to know about this young man?—and if he did not know him, what were the canons of criticism he was likely to apply? And whatever the stranger might be, he talked and looked like a gentleman; he was unfortunate, and for the present dependent, I romantically thought, on our kindness. To have received a copy of verses was very pleasant to my girlish self-importance; and the flattery of the lines themselves was charming.

The first shock of Mr. Carmel's warning had evaporated by this time; and I was already beginning to explain away his note. I hid the paper carefully. I loved Laura Grey; but I had, in my inmost soul, a secret awe of her; I knew how peremptory would be her advice, and I said not a word about the verses to her. At the first distant approach of an affair of the heart, how cautious and reserved we grow, and in most girls how suddenly the change from kittens to cats sets in! It was plain he had no notion of shifting his quarters to the hotel. But a little before our early tea-hour, Rebecca Torkill came in and told us what might well account for his not having yet gone to Cardyllion.

"That poor young man," she said, "he's very bad. He's lying on his back, with a handkercher full of eau-de-Cologne on his forehead, and he's sent down to the town for chloroform, and a blister for the back of his neck. He called me in, and indeed, though his talk and his behaviour might well be improved, considering how near he has just bin to death, yet I could not but pity him. Says he, 'Mrs. Torkill, for heaven's sake don't shake the floor, step as light as you can, and close the shutter next the sun,' which I did; and says he, 'I'm in a bad way; I may die before morning. My doctor in town tells me these headaches are very dangerous. They come from the spine.' 'Won't you see Doctor Mervyn, please, sir?' say I. 'Not I,' says he. 'I know all about it better than he'—them were his words—'and if the things that's coming don't set me to rights, I'm a gone man.' And indeed he groaned as he might at parting of soul and body—and here's a nice kettle o' fish, if he should die here, poor, foolish young man, and we not knowing so much as where his people lives, nor even his name. 'Tis a mysterious thing of Providence to do. I can't see how 'twas worth while saving him from drowning, only to bring him here to die of that headache. But all works together, we know. Thomas Jones is away down at the ferry; a nice thing, among a parcel o' women, a strange gentleman dying on a sofa, and not a man in the house! What do you think is best to be done, Miss Grey?"

"If he grows worse, I think you should send for the doctor without asking his leave," she answered. "If it is dangerous, it would not do to have no advice. It is very unlucky."

"Well, it is what I was thinking myself," said the housekeeper; "folks would be talking, as if we let him die without help. I'll keep the boiler full in case he should want a bath. He said his skull was fractured once, where that mark is, near his temple, and that the wound has something to do with it, and, by evil chance, it was just there he got the knock in the wreck of the Conway Castle; the Lord be good to us all!"

So Mrs. Torkill fussed out of the room, leaving us rather uncomfortable; but Laura Grey, at least, was not sorry, although she did not like the cause, that there was no reason to apprehend his venturing out that evening.

Our early tea-things came in. A glowing autumn sunset was declining; the birds were singing their farewell chorus from thick ivy over branch and wall, and Laura and I, each with her own secret, were discussing the chances of the stranger's illness, with exaggerated despondency and alarm. Our talk was interrupted. Through the window, which, the evening being warm, we, secure from intrusion, had left open, we heard a clear manly voice address us as "Miss Ethel and Miss Grey."

Could it be Mr. Carmel come back again? Good Heavens! no; it was the stranger in Mr. Carmel's place, as we had grown to call it. The same window, his hands, it seemed, resting on the very same spot on the window-stone, and his knee, just as Mr. Carmel used to place his, on the stone bench. I had no idea before how stern the stranger's face was; the contrast between the features I had for a moment expected, and those of our guest, revealed the character of his with a force assisted by the misty red beam that glanced on it, with a fierce melancholy, through the trees.

His appearance was as unexpected as if he had been a ghost. It came in the midst of a discussion as to what should be done if, by ill chance, he should die in the steward's house. I can't say how Laura Grey felt; I only know that I stared at his smiling face for some seconds, scarcely knowing whether the apparition was a reality or not.

"I hope you will forgive me; I hope I am not very impertinent; but I have just got up from an astounding headache all right again; and in consequence, in such spirits, that I never thought how audacious I was in venturing this little visit until it was too late."

Miss Grey and I were both too much confounded to say a word. But he rattled on: "I have had a visitor since you were so good as to give me shelter in my shipwrecked state—one quite unexpected. I don't mean my doctor, of course. I had a call to-day much more curious, and wholly unlooked for; an old acquaintance, a fellow named Carmel. I knew him at Oxford, and I certainly never expected to see him again."

"Oh! You know Mr. Carmel?" I said, my curiosity overcoming a kind of reluctance to talk.

"Know him? I rather think I do," he laughed. "Do you know him?"

"Yes," I answered; "that is, not very well; there is, of course, a little formality in our acquaintance—more, I mean, than if he were not a clergyman."

"But do you really know him? I fancied he was boasting when he said so." The gentleman appeared extremely amused.

"Yes; we know him pretty well. But why should it be so unlikely a thing our knowing him?"

"Oh, I did not say that." He still seemed as much amused as a man can quietly be. "But I certainly had not the least idea I should ever see him again, for he owes me a little money. He owes me money, and a grudge besides. There are some men you cannot know anything about without their hating you—that is, without their being afraid of you, which is the same thing. I unluckily heard something about him—quite accidentally, I give you my honour, for I certainly never had the pleasure of knowing him intimately. I don't think he would exactly come to me for a character. I had not an idea that he could be the Mr. Carmel who, they told me, had been permitted by Mr. Ware to reside in his house. I was a good deal surprised when I made the discovery. There can't have been, of course, any inquiry. I should not, I assure you, have spoken to Mr. Carmel had I met him anywhere else; but I could not help telling him how astonished I was at finding him established here. He begged very hard that I would not make a fuss about it, and said that he was going away, and that he would not wait even to take off his hat. So, if that is true, I shan't trouble anyone about him. Mr. Ware would naturally think me very impertinent if I were to interfere."

He now went on to less uncomfortable subjects, and talked very pleasantly. I could see Laura Grey looking at him as opportunity occurred; she was a good deal further in the shade than I and he. I fancied I saw him smile to himself, amused at baffling her curiosity, and he sat back a little further.

"I am quite sorry, Miss Ware," he said, "that I am about to be in funds again. My friends by this time must be weaving my wings—those wings of tissue-paper that come by the post, and take us anywhere. I'm awfully sorry, for I've fallen in love with this place. I shall never forget it." He said these latter words in a tone so low as to reach me only. I was sitting, as I mentioned, very much nearer the window than Laura Grey.

There was in this stranger for me—a country miss, quite inexperienced in the subtle flatteries of voice, manner, looks, which town-bred young ladies accept at their true value—a fascination before which suspicions and alarms melted away. His voice was low and sweet; he was animated, good-humoured, and playful; and his features, though singular, and capable of very grim expression, were handsome.

He talked to me in the same low tone for a few minutes. Happening to look at Laura Grey, I was struck by the anger expressed in her usually serene and gentle face. I fancied that she was vexed at his directing his attentions exclusively to me, and I was rather pleased at my triumph.

"Ethel, dear," she said, "don't you think the air a little cold?"

"Oh, I so very much hope not," he almost whispered to me.

"Cold?" said I. "I think it is so very sultry, on the contrary."

"If you find it too cold, Miss Grey, perhaps you would do wisely, I think, to sit a little further from the window," said Mr. Marston, considerately.

"I am not at all afraid for myself," she answered a little pointedly, "but I am uneasy about Miss Ware. I do think, Ethel, you would do wisely to get a little further from that window."

"But I do assure you I am quite comfortable," I said, in perfect good faith.

I saw Mr. Marston glance for a moment with a malicious smile at Laura Grey. To me the significance of that smile was a little puzzling.

"I see you have got a piano there," he said to me, in his low tones, not meant for her ear. "Miss Grey plays, of course?"

"Yes; very well indeed."

"Well, then, would you mind asking her to play something?"

I had no idea at the time that he wanted simply to find occupation for her, and to fill her ears with her own music, while he talked on with me.

"Laura, will you play that pretty thing of Beethoven's that you tried last night?" I asked.

"Don't ask me, Ethel, dear, to-night; I don't think I could," she answered, I thought a little oddly.

"Perhaps, if Miss Grey knew," he said, smiling, "that she would oblige a shipwrecked stranger extremely, and bind him to do her any service she pleases to impose in return, she might be induced to comply."

"The more you expect from my playing, the less courage I have to play," she said, in reply to his appeal, which was made, I fancied, in a tone of faint irony that seemed to suggest an oblique meaning; and her answer, I also fancied, was spoken as if answering that hidden meaning. It was very quietly done, but I felt the singularity of those tones.

"And why so? Do, I entreat—do play."

"Shouldn't I interrupt your conversation?" she answered.

"I'll not allow you even that excuse," he said; "I'll promise (and won't you, Miss Ware?) to talk whenever we feel inclined. There, now, it's all settled, isn't it? Pray begin."

"No, I am not going to play to-night," she said.

"Who would suppose Miss Grey so resolute; so little a friend to harmony? Well, I suppose we can do nothing; we can't prevail; we can only regret."

I looked curiously at Laura, who had risen, and was approaching the window, close to which she took a chair and sat down.

Mr. Marston was silent. I never saw man look angrier, although he smiled. To his white teeth and vivid eyes his dark skin gave marked effect; and to me, who knew nothing of the situation, the whole affair was most disagreeably perplexing. I was curious to see whether there would be any sign of recognition; but I was sitting at the side that commanded a full view of our guest, and the table so near me that Laura could not have introduced her chair without a very pointed disclosure of her purpose. If Mr. Marston was disposed to snarl and snap at Miss Grey, he very quickly subdued that desire. It would have made a scene, and frightened me, and that would never do.

In his most good-humoured manner, therefore, which speedily succeeded this silent paroxysm, he chatted on, now and then almost whispering a sentence or two to me. What a contrast this gay, reckless, and in a disguised way, almost tender talk, presented to the cold, peculiar, but agreeable conversation of the ascetic enthusiast, in whom this dark-faced, animated man of the world had uncomfortably disturbed my faith!

Laura Grey was restless all this time, angry, frightened. I fancied she was jealous and wounded; and although I was so fond of her, it did not altogether displease me.

The sunlight failed. The reflected glow from the western sky paled into grey, and twilight found our guest still in his place at the window, with his knee on the bench, and his elbows resting on the window-stone, our candles being lighted, chatting, as I thought, quite delightfully, talking sense and nonsense very pleasantly mixed, and hinting a great many very agreeable flatteries.

Laura Grey at length took courage, or panic, which often leads in the same direction, and rising, said quietly, but a little peremptorily: "I am going now, Ethel."

There was, of course, nothing for it but to submit. I confess I was angry. But it would certainly not have been dignified to show my resentment in Mr. Marston's presence. I therefore acquiesced with careless good-humour. The stranger bid us a reluctant good-night, and Laura shut down the window, and drew the little bolt across the window-sash, with, as it seemed to me, a rather inconsistent parade of suspicion. With this ungracious dismissal he went away in high good-humour, notwithstanding.

"Why need we leave the drawing-room so very early?" said I, in a pet.

"We need not go now, as that man is gone," she said, and quickly closed the window-shutters, and drew the curtains.

Laura, when she had made these arrangements, laid her hand on my shoulder, and looked with great affection and anxiety in my face.

"You are vexed, darling, because I got rid of that person."

"No," said I; "but I'm vexed because you got rid of him rudely."

"I should have prevented his staying at the window for a single minute, if I had been quite sure he is the person I suppose. If he is—oh! how I wish he were a thousand miles away!"

"I don't think you would be quite so hard upon him, if he had divided his conversation a little more equally," I said with the bluntness of vexation.

Laura hardly smiled. There was a pained, disappointed look in her face, but the kindest you can imagine.

"No, Ethel, I did not envy your good fortune. There is no one on earth to whom I should not prefer talking."

"But who is he?" I urged.

"I can't tell you."

"Surely you can say the name of the person you take him for?" I insisted.

"I am not certain; if he be the person he resembles, he took care to place himself so that I could not, or, at least, did not, see him well; there are two or three people mixed up in a great misfortune, whom I hate to name, or think of. I thought at one time I recognised him; but afterwards I grew doubtful. I never saw the person I mean more than twice in my life; but I know very well what he is capable of; his name is Marston; but I am not at all certain that this is he."

"You run away with things," I said. "How do you know that Mr. Carmel's account may not be a very unfair one?"

"I don't rely on Mr. Carmel's account of Mr. Marston, if this is he. I knew a great deal about him. You must not ask me how that was, or anything more. He is said to be, and I believe it, a bad, selfish, false man. I am terrified when I think of your having made his acquaintance. If he continues here, we must go up to town. I am half distracted. He dare not give us any trouble there."

"How did he quarrel with Mr. Carmel?" I asked, full of curiosity.

"I never heard; I did not know that he was even acquainted with him; but I think you may be perfectly certain that everything he said about Mr. Carmel is untrue. He knows that Mr. Carmel warned us against making his acquaintance; and his reason for talking as he does, is simply to discredit him. I dare say he'll take an opportunity of injuring him also. There is not time to hear from Mr. Ware. The only course, if he stays here for more than a day or two, is, as I said, to run up to your papa's house in town, and stay there till he is gone."

Again my belief in Mr. Marston was shaken; and I reviewed my hard thoughts of Mr. Carmel with something like compunction. The gloom and pallor of Laura's face haunted me.

CHAPTER XVII.

LEMUEL BLOUNT.

Next morning, at about half-past ten, as Laura and I sat in our breakfast-room, a hired carriage with two horses, which had evidently been driven at a hard pace, passed our window at a walk. The driver, who was leading his beasts, asked a question of Thomas Jones, who was rolling the gravel on the court-yard before the window; and then he led them round the corner toward the steward's house. The carriage was empty; but in another minute it was followed up by the person whom we might presume to have been its occupant. He turned towards our window as he passed, so that we had a full view of this new visitor.

He was a man who looked past sixty, slow-paced, and very solemn; he was dressed in a clumsy black suit; his face was large, square, and sallow; his cheek and chin were smoothly shorn and blue. His hat was low-crowned, and broad in the brim. He had a cotton umbrella in his big gloved hand, and a coloured pocket-handkerchief sticking out of his pocket. A great bunch of seals hung from his watch-chain under his black waistcoat. He was walking so slowly that we had no difficulty in observing these details; and he stopped before the hall-door, as if doubtful whether he should enter there. A word, however, from Thomas Jones set him right, and he in turn disappeared round the corner.

We did not know what to make of this figure, whom we now conjectured to have come in quest of the shipwrecked stranger.

Thomas Jones ran round before him to the door of the steward's house, which he opened; and the new-comer thanked him with a particularly kind smile. He knocked on chance at the door to the right, and the voice of our unknown guest told him to come in.

"Oh, Mr. Blount!" said the young gentleman, rising, hesitating, and then tendering his hand very respectfully, and looking in the sensible, vulgar face of the old man as if he were by no means sure how that tender might be received. "I hope, sir, I have not quite lost your friendship. I hope I retain some, were it ever so little, of the goodwill you once bore me. I hope, at least, that you will allow me to say that I am glad to see you: I feel it."

The old man bowed his head, holding it a little on one side while the stranger spoke; it was the attitude of listening rather than of respect. When the young gentleman had done speaking, his visitor raised his head again. The young man smiled faintly, and still extended his hand, looking very pale. Mr. Blount did not smile in answer; his countenance was very sombre, one might say sad.

"I never yet, sir, refused the hand of any man living when offered to me in sincerity, especially that of one in whom I felt, I may say, at one time a warm interest, although he may have given me reason to alter the opinion I then entertained of him."

Thus speaking, he gravely took the young man's hand, and shook it in a thoughtful, melancholy way, lowering his head again as he had done before.

"I don't ask how my uncle feels towards me," said the young man, half inquiringly.

"You need not," answered the visitor.

"I am at all events very much obliged to you," said the young man, humbly, "for your friendship, Mr. Blount. There is, I know, but one way of interesting your sympathy, and that is by telling you frankly how deep and true my repentance is; how I execrate my ingratitude; how I deplore my weakness and criminality." He paused, looking earnestly at the old man, who, however, simply bowed his head again, and made no comment.

"I can't justify anything I have done; but in my letter I ventured to say a few words in extenuation," he continued. "I don't expect to soften my uncle's just resentment, but I am most anxious, Mr. Blount, my best friend on earth, to recover something, were it ever so little, of the ground I have lost in your opinion."

"Time, sir, tries all things," answered the new-comer, gently; "if you mean to lead a new life, you will have opportunity to prove it."

"Was my uncle softened, ever so little, when he heard that the Conway Castle had gone down?" asked the young man, after a short silence.

"I was with him at breakfast when the morning paper brought the intelligence," said Mr. Blount. "I don't recollect that he expressed any regret."

"I dare say; I can quite suppose it; I ought to have known that he was pleased rather."

"No; I don't think he was pleased. I rather think he exhibited indifference," answered Mr. Blount.

With some grim remarks I believe the young man's uncle had received the sudden news of his death.

"Did my uncle see the letter I wrote to you, Mr. Blount?"

"No."

"And why not?"

"You will not think, I hope, that I would for any consideration use a phrase that could wound you unnecessarily when I tell you?"

"Certainly not."

"Your letter mentioned that you had lost your papers and money in the ship. Now, if it should turn out that you had, in short, misstated anything——"

"Told a lie, you mean," interrupted the young man, his face growing white, and his eyes gleaming.

"It would have been discourteous in me to say so, but such was my meaning," he answered, with a very kind look. "It has been one object with me during my life to reconcile courtesy with truth. I am happy in the belief that I have done so, and I believe during a long life I have never once offended against the laws of politeness. Had you deceived him so soon again it would have sunk you finally and for ever. I thought it advisable, therefore, to give you an opportunity of reconsidering the statements of your letter before committing you by placing them before him as fact."

The young man flushed suddenly. It was his misfortune that he could not resent suspicion, however gross, although he might wince under the insult, all the more that it was just. Rather sulkily he said:

"I can only repeat, sir, that I have not a shilling, nor a cheque; I left every paper and every farthing I possessed in my despatch-box, in my berth. Of course, I can't prove it; I can only repeat that every guinea I had in the world has gone to the bottom."

Mr. Blount raised his head. His square face and massive features confronted the younger man, and his honest brown eyes were fixed upon him with a grave and undisguised inquiry.

"I don't say that you have any certainty of recovering a place in your uncle's esteem, but the slightest prevarication in matters of this kind would be simply suicidal. Now, I ask you, sir, on your honour, did no part of your money, or of your papers, go by rail either to Bristol or to London?"

"Upon my honour, Mr. Blount, not a farthing. I had only about ten pounds in gold, all the rest was in letters of credit and cheques; and, bad as I am, I should scarcely be fool enough to practise a trick, which, from its nature, must be almost instantaneously self-exposed. My uncle could have stopped payment of them; probably he has done so."

"I see you understand something of business, sir."

"I should have understood a great deal more, Mr. Blount, and been a much better man, if I had listened to you long ago. I hope, in future, to be less my own adviser, and more your pupil."

To this flattering speech the old man listened attentively, but made no answer.

"Your letter followed me to Chester," said Mr. Blount, after an interval. "I received it last night. He was in London when I saw him last; and my letter, telling him that you are still living, may not reach him, possibly, for some days. Thus, you see, you would have the start of him, if I may so describe it, without rudeness; and you are aware he has no confidence in you; and, certainly, if you will permit me to say so, he ought not to have any. I have a note of the number of the cheque; you can write a line saying that you have lost it, and requesting that payment may be stopped; and I will enclose it to Messrs. Dignum and Budget."

"There's pen and ink here; I'll do it this moment. I thought you had renounced me also; and I was going to write again to try you once more, before taking to the high road," he said, with dismal jocularity.

It wrung the pride of the young man sorely to write the note. But the bitter pill was swallowed; and he handed it, but with signs of suppressed anger, to Mr. Blount.

"That will answer perfectly," said the man in black.

"It enables you to stop that cheque by this post, without first seeing my uncle; and it relieves you," said the young man, with bitter and pitiless irony, "of the folly of acting in the most trifling matter upon my word of honour. It is certainly making the most of the situation. I have made one great slip—a crime, if you like——"

"Quite so, sir," acquiesced Mr. Blount, with melancholy politeness.

"Under great momentary temptation," continued the young man, "and without an idea of ultimately injuring any human being to the amount of a single farthing. I'm disowned; any one that pleases may safely spit in my face. I'm quite aware how I stand in this infernal pharisaical world."

Mr. Blount looked at him gravely, but made him no answer. The young gentleman did not want to quarrel with Mr. Blount just then. He could not afford it.

"I don't mean you, of course," he said; "you have been always only too much my friend. I am speaking of the world; you know, quite well, if this unlucky thing takes wind, and my uncle's conduct towards me is the very thing to set people talking and inquiring, I may as well take off my hat to you all, drink your healths in a glass of prussic acid, and try how a trip to some other world agrees with me."

"You are speaking, of course, sir, in jest," said Mr. Blount, with some disgust in his grave countenance; "but I may mention that the unfortunate occurrence is known but to your uncle and to me, and to no other person on earth. You bear the name of Marston—you'll excuse me for reminding you, sir—and upon that point he is sensitive and imperious. He considered, sir, that your bearing that name, if I may so say, without being supposed guilty of a rudeness, would slur it; and, therefore, you'll change it, as arranged, on embarking at Southampton. It would be highly inexpedient to annoy your uncle by any inadvertence upon this point. Your contemplating suicide would be—you will pardon the phrase—cowardly and impious. Not, indeed, if I may so say consistently with the rules of politeness," he added, thoughtfully, "that your sudden removal would involve any loss to anybody, except, possibly, some few Jews, and people of that kind."

"Certainly—of course. You need not insist upon that. I feel my degradation, I hope, sufficiently. It is not his fault, at least, if I don't."

"And, from myself, I suggest that he will be incensed, if he learns that you are accepting the hospitality of Mr. Ware's house. I think, sir, that men of the world, especially gentlemen, will regard it, if the phrase be not discourteous, in the light of a shabby act."

"Shabby, sir! what do you mean by shabby?" said Mr. Marston, flaming up.

"I mean, sir—you'll excuse me—paltry; don't you see?—or mean. His feelings would be strongly excited by your partaking of Mr. Ware's hospitality."

"Hospitality! Shelter, you mean; slates, walls—little more than they give a beast in a pound! Why, I don't owe them a crust, or a cup of tea. I get everything from the hotel there, at Cardyllion; and Mr. Ware is a thousand miles away!"

"I speak of it simply as a question of expediency, sir. He will be inflamed against you, if he hears you have, in ever so small a matter, placed yourself under any obligation to Mr. Ware."

"But he need not hear of it; why should you mention it?"

"I cannot practise reserve with a man who treats me with unlimited confidence," he answered, gently. "Why should you not go to the hotel?"

"I have no money."

"But you get everything you want there on credit?"

"Well, yes, that's true; but it would scarcely do to make that move; I have been as ill as ever I was in my life since that awful night on the rocks down there. You can have no idea what it was; and the doctor says I must keep quiet. It isn't worth while moving now; so soon as I have funds, I'll leave this."

"I will lend you what you require, with much pleasure, sir," proffered Mr. Blount.

"Well, thanks, it is not very much, and it's hard to refuse; one feels such a fool without a shilling to give to a messenger, or to the servants; I haven't even a fee for the doctor who has been attending me."

Determined by this pathetic appeal, Mr. Blount took a bank-note of ten pounds from his purse and lent it to Mr. Marston.

"And, I suppose, you'll remove forthwith to the hotel," he said.

"The moment I feel equal to it," he replied. "Why, d—— it, don't you think I'm ready to go, when I'm able? I—I—— Don't mind me, pray. Your looks reprove me. I'm shocked at myself when I use those phrases. I know very well that I have just escaped by a miracle from death. I feel how utterly unfit I was to die; and, I assure you, I'm not ungrateful. You shall see that my whole future life will be the better for it. I'm not the graceless wretch I have been. One such hour as preceded my scaling that rock out there is a lesson for a life. You have often spoken to me on the subjects that ought to interest us all. I mean when I was a boy. Your words have returned upon me. You derive happiness from the good you do to others. I thought you had cast your bread upon the waters to see it no more; but you have found it at last. I am very grateful to you."

Did Mr. Marston believe that good people are open, in the manner of their apostleship, to flattery, as baser mortals are in matters of another sort? It was to be hoped that Mr. Marston felt half what he uttered. His words, however, did produce a favourable and a pleasant impression upon Mr. Blount. His large face beamed for a moment with honest gratification. His eyes looked evil upon him, as if the benevolence of his inmost heart spoke out through them.

"If anything can possibly please him, sir, in connection with you," said Mr. Blount, with all his customary suavity and unconscious bluntness, "it will be to learn that recent events have produced a salutary impression and a total change in you. Not that I suppose he cares very much; but I'm glad to have to represent to him anything favourable in this particular case. I mean to return to London direct, and if your uncle is still there you shall hear in a day or two—at all events very soon; but I wish you were in the hotel."

"Well, I'll go to the hotel, if they can put me up. I'll go at once; address to me to the post-office—Richard Marston, I suppose?"

"Just so, sir, Richard Marston."

Mr. Blount had risen, and stood gravely, prepared to take his leave.

"I have kept you a long time, Mr. Blount; will you take anything?"

Mr. Blount declined refreshments.

"I must leave you now, sir; there is a crisis in every life. What has happened to you is stupendous; the danger and the deliverance. That hour is past. May its remembrance be with you ever—day and night! Do not suppose that it can rest in your mind without positive consequences. It must leave you a great deal better or a great deal worse. Farewell, sir."

So they parted. Mr. Marston seemed to have lost all his spirits and half his energy in that interview. He sat motionless in the chair into which he had thrown himself, and gazed listlessly on the floor in a sulky reverie. At length he said—

"That is a most unpleasant old fellow; I wish he was not so unscrupulously addicted to telling truth."

CHAPTER XVIII.

IDENTIFIED.

It was a gloomy day; I had left Laura Grey in the room we usually occupied, where she was now alone, busy over some of our accounts. I dare say her thoughts now and then wandered into speculations respecting the identity of the visitor who, the night before, evaded her recognition, if indeed he was recognisable by her at all. Her doubts were now resolved. The room door opened, and the tenant of the steward's house entered coolly, and approached the table where she was sitting. Laura Grey did not rise; she did not speak; she sat, pen in hand, staring at him as if she were on the point of fainting. The star-shaped scar on his forehead, fixed there by some old fracture, and his stern and energetic features, were now distinctly before her. He kept his eye fixed upon her, and smiled, dubious of his reception.

"I saw you, Miss Grey, yesterday afternoon, though you did not see me. I avoided your eye then; but it was idle supposing that I could continue even a few days longer in this place without you seeing me. I came last night with my mind made up to reveal myself, but I put it off till we should be to ourselves, as we are now. I saw you half guessed me, but you weren't sure, and I left you in doubt."

He approached till his hands rested upon the table opposite, and said, with a very stern and eager face,

"Miss Grey, upon my honour, upon my soul, if I can give you an assurance which can bind a gentleman, I entreat you to believe me. I shan't offer one syllable contrary to what I now feel to be your wishes. I shan't press you, I shan't ask you to hear me upon the one subject you say you object to. You allege that I have done you a wrong. I will spare no pains to redress it. I will do my utmost in any way you please to dictate. I will do all this, I swear by everything a gentleman holds most sacred, upon one very easy condition."

He paused. He was leaning forward, his dark eyes were fixed upon her with a piercing gaze. She did not, or could not, speak. She was answering his gaze with a stare wilder and darker, but her very lips were white.

"I know I have stood in your way; I admit I have injured you, not by accident; it was with the design and wish to injure you, if the endeavour to detach a fellow like that be an injury. You shall forgive me; the most revengeful woman can forgive a man the extravagances of his jealousy. I am here to renounce all, to retrieve everything. I admit the injury; it shall be repaired."

She spoke now for the first time, and said, hardly above her breath:

"It's irreparable. It can't be undone—quite irreparable."

"When I undertake a thing I do it; I'll do this at any sacrifice—yes, at any, of pride or opinion. Suppose I go to the persons in question, and tell them that they have been deceived, and that I deceived them, and now confess the whole thing a tissue of lies?"

"You'll never do that."

"By Heavens, as I stand here, I'll do it! Do you suppose I care for their opinion in comparison with a real object? I'll do it. I'll write and sign it in your presence; you shall have it to lock up in that desk, and do what you please with it, upon one condition."

A smile of incredulity lighted Laura Grey's face faintly, as she shook her head.

"You don't believe me, but you shall. Tell me what will satisfy you—what practicable proof will convince you. I'll set you right with them. You believe in a Providence. Do you think I was saved from that wreck for nothing?"

Laura Grey looked down upon her desk; his fierce eyes were fixed on her with intense eagerness, for he thought he read in her pale face and her attitude signs of compliance. It needed, he fancied, perhaps but a slight impulse to determine her.

"I'll do it all; but, as I told you, on one condition."

There was a silence for a time. He was still watching her intently.

"Let us both be reasonable," he resumed. "I ought, I now know, to have seen long ago, Miss Grey, that there was no use in my talking to you as I did. I have been mad. There's the whole story; and now I renounce it all. I despair; it's over. I'll give you the very best proof of that. I shall devote myself to another, and you shall aid me. Pray, not a word, till you have heard me out; that's the condition. If you accept it, well. If not, so sure as there is life in me, you may regret it."

"There's nothing more you can do I care for now," she broke out with a look of agony. "Oh, Heaven help me!"

"You'll find there is," he continued, with a quiet laugh. "You can talk as long as you please when your turn comes. Just hear me out. I only want you to have the whole case before you. I say you can help me, and you shall. I'm a very good fellow to work with, and a bitter one to work against. Now, one moment. I have made the acquaintance of a young lady whom I wish to marry. Upon my sacred honour, I have no other intention. She is poor; her father is over head and ears in debt; she can never have a guinea more than two thousand pounds. It can't be sordid, you'll allow. There is a Jesuit fellow hanging about this place. He hates me; he has been in here telling lies of me. I expect you to prevent my being prejudiced by that slanderer. You can influence the young lady in my favour, and enable me to improve our acquaintance. I expect you to do so. These are my conditions. She is Miss Ethel Ware."

The shock of a disclosure so entirely unexpected, and the sting possibly of wounded vanity, made her reply more spirited than it would have been. She stood up, and said, quietly and coldly:

"I have neither right nor power in the matter; and if I had, nothing on earth could induce me to exercise them in your favour. You can write, if you please, to Mr. Ware, for leave to pay your addresses to his daughter. But without his leave you shall not visit here, nor join her in her walks; and if you attempt to do either, I will remove Miss Ware, and place her under the care of some one better able than I to protect her."

The young man looked at her with a very pale face.

"I thought you knew me better, Miss Grey," he said, with an angry sneer. "You refuse your chance of reconciliation."

He paused, as if to allow her time to think better of it.

"Very well; I'm glad I've found you out. Don't you think your situation is rather an odd one—a governess in Mr. Ware's country quarters? We all know pretty well what sort of gentleman Mr. Ware is, a gentleman particularly well qualified by good taste and high spirits to make his house agreeable. He was here, I understand, for about a week a little time ago, but his wife does not trouble your solitude much; and now that he is on his travels, he is succeeded by a young friar. I happen to know what sort of person Carmel was, and is. Was ever young lady so fortunate? One only wonders that Mr. Ware, under these circumstances, is not a little alarmed for the Protestantism of his governess. I should scarcely have believed that you had found so easily so desirable a home; but fate has ordained that I should light upon your retreat, and hear with my own ears the good report of the neighbours, and see with my own eyes how very comfortable and how extremely happy you are."

He smiled and bowed ironically, and drew towards the door.

"There was nothing to prevent our being on the friendliest terms—nothing."

He paused, but she made him no answer.

"No reason on earth why we should not. You could have done me a very trifling kindness. I could have served you vitally."

Another pause here.

"I can ascribe your folly to nothing but the most insensate malice. I shall take care of myself. You ought to know me. Whatever befalls, you have to thank but your own infatuated obstinacy for it."

"I have friends still," she cried, in a sudden burst of agony. "Your cowardice, your threats and insults, your persecution of a creature quite defenceless and heart-broken, and with no one near to help her——"

Her voice faltered.

"Find out your friends, if you have got them; tell them what you please; and, if it is worth while, I will contradict your story. I'll fight your friends. I'll pit my oath against yours."

There was no sneer on his features now, no irony in his tones; he was speaking with the bitter vehemence of undisguised fury.

"I shrink from nothing. Things have happened since to make me more reckless, and by so much the more dangerous. If you knew a little more you would scarcely dare to quarrel with me." He dashed his hand as he spoke upon the table.

"I am afraid—I'm frightened; but nothing on earth shall make me do what you ask."

"That's enough—that closes it," said he. There was a little pause. "And remember, the consequences I promise are a great deal nearer than you probably dream of."

With these words, spoken slowly, with studied meaning, he left the room as suddenly as he had appeared. Laura Grey was trembling. Her thoughts were not very clear. She was shocked, and even terrified.

The sea, which had swallowed all the rest, had sent up that one wicked man alive. How many good, kind, and useful lives were lost to earth, she thought, in those dreadful moments, and that one life, barren of all good, profligate and cruel, singled out alone for mercy!

CHAPTER XIX.

PISTOLS FOR TWO.

I knew nothing of all this. I was not to learn what had passed at that interview till many years later. Laura Grey, on my return, told me nothing. I am sure she was right. There were some things she could not have explained, and the stranger's apparently insane project of marrying penniless me was a secret better in her own keeping than in that of a simple and very self-willed girl.

When I returned there were signs of depression and anxiety in her looks, and her silence and abstraction excited my curiosity. She easily put me off, however. I knew that her spirits sometimes failed her, although she never talked about her troubles; and therefore her dejection was, after all, not very remarkable. We heard nothing more of our guest till next day, when Rebecca Torkill told us that he was again suffering from one of his headaches. The intelligence did not excite all the sympathy she seemed to expect. Shortly after sunset we saw him pass the window of our room, and walk by under the trees.

With an ingrained perversity, the more Laura Grey warned me against this man, the more I became interested in him. She and I were both unusually silent that evening. I think that her thoughts were busy with him; I know that mine were.

"We won't mind opening the window to-night," said Laura.

"I was just thinking how pleasant it would be. Why should we not open it?" I answered.

"Because we should have him here again; and he is not the sort of person your mamma would like you to become acquainted with."

I was a little out of humour, but did not persist. I sat in a sullen silence, my eyes looking dreamily through the window. The early twilight had faded into night by the time the stranger re-appeared. I saw him turn the line of his walk near the window; and seeing it shut, pause for a moment. I dare say he was more vexed than I. He made up his mind, however, against a scene. He looked on the ground and over his shoulder, again at the window.

Mr. Marston walked round the corner to the steward's house. The vague shadows and lights of night were abroad by this time. Candles were in his room; he found Rebecca Torkill there, with a small tankard and a tea-cup on a salver, awaiting his return.

"La! sir, to think of you doing such another wild thing, and you, only this minute, at death's door with your head! And how is it now, please, sir?"

"A thousand thanks. My head is as well as my hat. My headache goes as it comes, in a moment. What is this?"

"Some gruel, please, sir, with sugar, white wine, and nutmeg. I thought you might like it."

"Caudle, by Jove!" smiled the gentleman, "isn't it?"

"Well, it is; and it's none the worse o' that."

"All the better," exclaimed Mr. Marston, who chose to be on friendly terms with the old lady. "How can I thank you?"

"It's just the best thing in the world to make you sleep after a headache. You'll take some while it's hot."

"I can't thank you half enough," he said.

"I'll come back, sir, and see you by-and-by," and the good woman toddled out, leaving him alone with his gruel.

"I must not offend her." He poured some out into his cup, tasted it, and laughed quietly. "Sipping caudle! Well, this is rather a change for Richard Marston, by Jove! A change every day. Let us make a carouse of it," he said, and threw it out of the window.

Mr. Marston threw on his loose wrapper, and folded his muffler about his throat, replaced his hat, and with his cane in his fingers, was about to walk down to the town of Cardyllion. A word or two spoken, quite unsuspiciously, by Doctor Mervyn that morning, had touched a sensitive nerve, and awakened a very acute anxiety in Mr. Marston's mind. The result was his intended visit, at the fall of night, to the High-street of the quaint little town.

He was on the point of setting out, when Rebecca Torkill returned with a sliced lemon on a plate.

"Some likes a squeeze of a lemon in it," she observed, "and I thought I might as well leave it here."

"It is quite delicious, really," he replied, as Mrs. Torkill peeped into the open flagon.

"Why," said she, in unfeigned admiration, "I'm blest if he's left a drop! Ah! ah! Well, it was good; and I'll have some more for you before you go to bed. But you shouldn't drink it off, all at a pull, like that. You might make yourself ill that way."

"We men like good liquor so well—so well—we—we—what was I saying? Oh! yes, we like our liquor so well, we never know when we have had enough. It's a bad excuse; but let it pass. I'm going out for a little walk, it always sets me up after one of those headaches. Good evening, Mrs. Torkill."

He was thinking plainly of other matters than her, or her caudle; and, before she had time to reply, he was out of the door.

It was a sweet, soft night; the moon was up. The walk from Malory to the town is lonely and pretty. He took the narrow road that approaches Cardyllion in an inland line, parallel to the road that runs by the shore of the estuary. His own echoing footsteps among the moon-lit trees was the only sign of life, except the dis-distant barking of a watch-dog, now and then, that was audible. A melancholy wind was piping high in the air, from over the sea; you might fancy it the aërial lamentations of the drowned.

He was passing the churchyard now, and stopped partly to light a cigar, partly to look at the old church, the effect of which, in the moonlight, was singular. Its gable and towers cast a sharp black shadow across the grass and gravestones, like that of a gigantic hand whose finger pointed towards him. He smiled cynically as the fancy struck him.

"Another grave there, I should not wonder if the news is true. What an ass that fellow is! Another grave, I dare say; and in my present luck, I suppose I shall fill it—fill it! That's ambiguous; yes, the more like an oracle. That shadow does look curiously like a finger pointing at me!"

He smoked for a time, leaning on the pier of the iron wicket that from this side admits to the churchyard, and looking in with thoughts very far from edifying.

"This will be the second disagreeable discovery, without reckoning Carmel, I shall have made since my arrival in this queer corner of the world. Who could have anticipated meeting Laura here?—or that whining fool, Carmel? Who would have fancied that Jennings, of all men, would have turned up in this out-of-the-way nook? By Jove! I'm like Saint Paul, hardly out of the shipwreck when a viper fastens on my hand. Old Sprague made us turn all that into elegiacs. I wonder whether I could make elegiacs now."

He loitered slowly on, by the same old road, into Castle Street, the high-street of the quaint little town of steep roofs and many gables. The hall-door of the "Verney Arms" was open, and the light of the lamp glowed softly on the pavement.

Mr. Marston hated suspense. He would rather make a bad bargain, off-hand, than endure the torture of a long negotiation. He would stride out to meet a catastrophe rather than await its slow, sidelong approaches. This intolerance of uncertainty made him often sudden in action. He had come down to the town simply to reconnoitre. He was beginning, by this time, to meditate something more serious. Under the shadow of the houses opposite, he walked slowly up and down the silent flagway, eyeing the door of the "Verney Arms" askance, as he finished his cigar.

It so happened, that exactly as he had thrown away the stump of it, a smoker, who had just commenced his, came slowly down the steps of the "Verney Arms," and stood upon the deserted flagway, and as he puffed indolently, he looked up the street, and down the street, and up at the sky.

The splendid moon shone full on his face, and Mr. Marston knew him. He was tall and slight, and rather good-looking, with a face of great intelligence, heightened with something of enthusiasm, and stood there smoking, in happy unconsciousness that an unfriendly eye was watching him across the street.

Mr. Marston stood exactly opposite. The smoker, who had emerged from the "Verney Arms," stood before the centre of the steps, and Mr. Marston, on a sudden, as if he was bent on walking straight through him into the hotel, walked at a brisk pace across the street, and halted, within a yard, in front of him.

"I understand," said Marston instantly, in a low, stern tone, "that you said at Black's, when I was away yachting, that you had something to say to me."

The smoker had lowered his cigar, and was evidently surprised, as well he might be; he looked at him hard for some time, and at length replied as grimly: "Yes, I said so; yes I do; I mean to speak to you."

"All right; no need to raise our voices here though; I think you had better find some place where we can talk without exciting attention."

"Come this way," said the tall young man, turning suddenly and walking up the street at a leisurely pace. Mr. Marston walked beside him, a yard or two apart. They might be very good friends, for anything that appeared to a passer-by. He turned down a short and narrow by-street, with only room for a house or two, and they found themselves on the little common that is known as the Green of Cardyllion. The sea, at its further side, was breaking in long, tiny waves along the shingle, the wind came over the old castle with a melancholy soughing; the green was solitary; and only here and there, from the windows of the early little town, a light gleamed. The moon shone bright on the green, turning the grass to grey, and silvering the ripples on the dark estuary, and whitening the misty outlines of the noble Welsh mountains across the water. A more tranquillising scene could scarcely be imagined.

When they had got to the further end, they stopped, as if by common consent.

"I'm ready to hear you," said Marston.

"Well, I have only to tell you, and I'm glad of this opportunity, that I have ascertained the utter falsehood of your stories, and that you are a coward and a villain."

"Thanks; that will do, Mr. Jennings," answered Marston, growing white with fury, but speaking with cold and quiet precision. "You have clenched this matter by an insult which I should have answered by cutting you across the face with this,"—and he made his cane whistle in the air,—"but that I reserve you for something more effectual, and shall run no risk of turning the matter into a police-office affair. I have neither pistols nor friend here. We must dispense with formalities; we can do all that is necessary for ourselves, I suppose. I'll call to-morrow, early, at the 'Verney Arms.' A word or two will settle everything."

He raised his hat ever so little, implying that that conference, for the present, was over; but before he could turn, Mr. Jennings, who did not choose to learn more than was unavoidable to his honour, said:

"You will find a note at the bar."

"Address it Richard Wynyard, then."

"Your friend?"

"No; myself."

"Oh! a false name?" sneered Mr. Jennings.

"You may use the true one, of course. My tailor is looking for me a little more zealously, I fancy, than you were; and if you publish it in Cardyllion, it may lead to his arresting me, and saving you all further trouble in this, possibly, agitating affair." The young man accompanied these words with a cold laugh.

"Well, Richard Wynyard be it," said Mr. Jennings, with a slight flush.

And with these words the two young men turned their backs on each other. Mr. Jennings walked along beside the shingle, with the sound of the light waves in his ear, and thinking rather hurriedly, as men will, whom so serious a situation has suddenly overtaken. Marston turned, as I said, the other way, and without entering the town again, approached Malory by the narrow road that passes close under the castle walls, and follows the line of the high banks overlooking the estuary.

If there be courage and mental activity, and no conscience, we have a very dangerous devil. A spoiled child, in which self is supreme, who has no softness of heart, and some cleverness and energy, easily degenerates into that sort of Satan. And yet, in a kind of way, Marston was popular. He could spend money freely—it was not his own—and when he was in spirits he was amusing.

When he stared in Jennings' face this evening, the bruise and burning of an old jealousy were in his heart. The pain of that hellish hate is often lightly inflicted; but what is more cruel than vanity? He had abandoned the pursuit in which that jealousy was born, but the hatred remained. And now he had his revenge in hand. It is a high stake, one's life on a match of pistol-shooting. But his brute courage made nothing of it. It was an effort to him to think himself in danger, and he did not make that effort. He was thinking how to turn the situation to account.

CHAPTER XX.

THE WOOD OF PLAS YLWD.

Next morning, Mr. Marston, we learned, had been down to Cardyllion early. He had returned at about ten o'clock, and he had his luggage packed up, and despatched again to the proprietor of the "Verney Arms." So we might assume that he was gone.

The mountain that had weighed on Laura Grey's spirits was perceptibly lightened. I heard her whisper to herself, "Thank God!" when she heard Rebecca Torkill's report, and the further intelligence that their guest had told her and Thomas Jones that he was going to the town, to return no more to Malory. Laura was now, again, quite like herself. For my part, I was a little glad, and (shall I confess it?) also a little sorry! I had not quite made up my mind respecting this agreeable Mr. Marston, of whom Mr. Carmel and Miss Grey had given each so alarming a character.

About an hour later, I was writing to mamma, and sitting at the window, when, raising my eyes, I saw Laura Grey and Mr. Marston, much to my surprise, walking side by side up the avenue towards the hall-door. They appeared to be in close conversation; Mr. Marston seemed to talk volubly and carelessly, and cut the heads of the weeds with his cane as he sauntered by her side. Laura Grey held her handkerchief to her eyes, except now and then, when she spoke a few words, as it seemed passionately.

When they came to the court-yard, opposite to the hall-door, she broke away from him, hurried across, ran up the steps, and shut the door. He stood where she had left him, looking after her and smiling. I thought he was going to follow; he saw me in the window, and raised his hat, still smiling, and with this farewell salute he turned on his heel and walked slowly away towards the gate. I ran to the hall, and there found Laura Grey. She had been crying, and was agitated.

"Ethel, darling," she said, "let nothing on earth induce you to speak to that man again. I implore of you to give me your solemn promise. If he speaks truth it will not cost you anything, for he says he is going away this moment, not to return."

It certainly looked very like it, for he had actually despatched his two boxes, he had "tipped" the servants handsomely at the steward's house, and having taken a courteous leave of them, and left with Mrs. Torkill a valedictory message of thanks for me, he had got into a "fly" and driven off to the "Verney Arms."

Well, whether for good or ill, he had now unquestionably taken his departure; but not without leaving a sting. The little he had spoken to Miss Grey, at the moment of his flight, had proved, it seemed, a Parthian arrow tipped with poison. She seemed to grow more and more miserable every hour. She had lain down on her bed, and was crying bitterly, and trembling. I began to grow vexed at the cruelty of the man who had deliberately reduced her to that state. I knew not what gave him the power of torturing her. If I was angry, I was also intensely curious. My questions produced no clearer answers than this: "Nothing, dear, that you could possibly understand without first hearing a very long story. I hope the time is coming when I may tell it all to you. But the secret is not mine; it concerns other people; and at present I must keep it."

Mr. Marston had come and gone, then, like a flash of light, leaving my eyes dazzled. The serenity of Malory seemed now too quiet for me; the day was dull. I spent my time sitting in the window, or moping about the place. I must confess that I had, by no means, the horror of this stranger that the warnings of Mr. Carmel and Laura Grey ought, I suppose, to have inspired. On the contrary, his image came before me perpetually, and everything I looked at, the dark trees, the window-sill, the garden, the estuary, and the ribs of rock round which the cruel sea was sporting, recalled the hero of a terrible romance.

I tried in vain to induce Laura to come with me for a walk, late in the afternoon. So I set out alone, turning my back on Cardyllion, in the direction of Penruthyn Priory. The sun was approaching the western horizon as I drew near the picturesque old farm-house of Plas Ylwd.

A little to the south of this stretches a fragment of old forest, covering some nine or ten acres of peaty ground. It is a decaying wood, and in that melancholy and miserable plight, I think, very beautiful. I would commend it as a haunt to artists in search of "studies," who love huge trees with hollow trunks, somc that have "cast" half their boughs as deer do their antlers; some wreathed and laden with ivy, others that stretch withered and barkless branches into the air; ground that is ribbed and unequal, and cramped with great ringed, snake-like roots, that writhe and knot themselves into the earth; here and there over-spread with little jungles of bramble, and broken and burrowed by rabbits.

Into this grand and singular bit of forest, now glorified by the coloured light of evening, I had penetrated some little way. Arrested in my walk by the mellow song of a blackbird, I listened in the sort of ecstasy that every one has, I suppose, experienced under similar circumstances; and I was in the full enjoyment of this sylvan melody, when I was startled, and the bird put to flight, by the near report of fire-arms. Once or twice I had heard boys shooting at the birds in this wood, but they had always accompanied their practice with shouting and loud talking. A dead silence followed this. I had no reason for any misgivings about so natural an interruption in such a place, but I did feel an ominous apprehension. I began to move, and was threading my way through one of these blackberry thickets, when

I heard, close to my side, the branches of some underwood thrust aside, and Mr. Marston, looking pale and wicked, walked quickly by. It was plain he did not see me; I was screened by the stalks and sprays through which I saw him. He had no weapon as he passed me; he was drawing on his glove. The sudden appearance of Mr. Marston whom I believed to be by this time miles away—at the other side of Cardyllion—was a shock that rather confirmed my misgivings.

I waited till he was quite gone, and then passed down the path he had come by. I saw nothing to justify alarm, so I walked a little in the same direction, looking to the right and left. In a little opening among the moss-grown trunks of the trees, I soon saw something that frightened me. It was a man lying on his back, deadly pale, upon the ground; his waistcoat was open, and his shirt-front covered with blood, that seemed to ooze from under his hand, which was pressed on it; his hat was on the ground, some way behind. A pistol lay on the grass beside him, and another not far from his feet.

I was very much frightened, and the sight of blood made me feel faint. The wounded man saw me, I knew, for his eyes were fixed on me; his lips moved, and there was a kind of straining in his throat; he said a word or two, though I could not at first hear what. With a horrible reluctance, I came near and leaned a little over him, and then heard distinctly:

"Pray send help."

I bethought me instantly of the neighbouring farm-house of Plas Ylwd, and knowing this little forest tract well, I ran through it nearly direct to the farm-yard, and quickly succeeded in securing the aid of Farmer Prichard and all his family, except his wife, who stayed at home to get a bed ready for the reception of the wounded stranger. We all trooped back again through the woods, at a trot, I at their head, quite forgetting my dignity in my excitement. The wounded man appeared fainter. But he beckoned to us with his hand, without raising his arm, and with a great effort he said: "The blame is mine—all my fault—remember, if I die. I compelled this meeting."

I got Prichard to send his son, without a moment's delay, to Cardyllion, to bring Dr. Mervyn, and as they got the bleeding man on towards Plas Ylwd, I, in a state of high excitement, walked swiftly homeward, hoping to reach Malory before the declining light failed altogether.

CHAPTER XXI.

THE PATIENT AT PLAS YLWD.

I got home just as the last broad beam of the setting sun was spent, and twilight over-spread churchyard and manor-house, sea and land, with its grey mantle. Lights were gleaming from the drawing-room window as I approached; a very welcome light to me, for it told me that Laura Grey had come down, and I was longing to tell her my story. I found her, as I expected, seated quietly at our tea-table, and saw, in her surprised and eager looks, how much she was struck by the excitement which mine exhibited, as, without waiting to take off my hat or coat, I called on her to listen, and stumbled and hurried through the opening of my strange story.

I had hardly mentioned the sudden appearance of Mr. Marston, when Laura Grey rose with her hands clasped:

"Was any one shot? For God's sake, tell me quickly!"

I described all I had seen. She pressed her hand hard to her heart.

"Oh! he has killed him—the villain! His threats are always true—his promises never. Oh! Ethel, darling, he has been so near me, and I never dreamed it."

"Who? What is it, Laura? Don't, darling, be so frightened; he's not killed—nobody's killed. I daresay it is very trifling, and Doctor Mervyn is with him by this time."

"I am sure he's badly wounded; he has killed him. He has hated him so long, he would never have left him till he had killed him."

She was growing quite distracted; I, all the time, doing my utmost to re-assure her.

"What is his name?" at length I asked.

The question seemed to quiet her. She looked at me, and then down; and then again at me.

Once or twice she had mentioned a brother whom she loved very much, and who was one of her great anxieties. Was this wounded man he? If not, was he a lover? This latter could hardly be; for she had once, after a long, laughing fencing with my close questions, told me suddenly, quite gravely, "I have no lover, and no admirer, except one whom I despise and dislike as much as I can any one on earth." It was very possible that her brother was in debt, or in some other trouble that made her, for the present, object to disclose anything about him. I thought she was going to tell me a great deal now—but I was disappointed. I was again put off; but I knew she spoke truth, for she was the truest person I ever met, when she said that she longed to tell me all her story, and that the time would soon come when she could. But now, poor thing! she was, in spite of all I could say, in a state, very nearly, of distraction. She never was coherent, except when, in answer to her constantly repeated questioning, I again and again described the appearance of the wounded man, which each time seemed to satisfy her on the point of identity, but without preventing her from renewing her inquiries with increasing detail.

That evening passed miserably enough for us both. Doctor Mervyn, on his way to his patient, looked in upon us early next morning, intent on learning all he could from me about the circumstances of the discovery of his patient. I had been too well drilled by prudent Rebecca Torkill, to volunteer any information respecting the unexpected appearance of Mr. Marston so suspiciously near the scene of the occurrence. I described, therefore, simply the spectacle presented by the wounded man, on my lighting upon him in the wood, and his removal to the farmhouse of Plas Ylwd.

"It's all very fine, saying it was a accident," said the doctor, with a knowing nod and a smile. "Accident, indeed! If it was, why should he refuse to say who had a hand in the accident, besides himself? But there's no need to make a secret of the matter, for unless something unexpected should occur, he must, in the ordinary course of things, be well in little more than a week. It's an odd wound. The ball struck the collar bone and broke it, glancing upward. If it had penetrated obliquely downward instead, it might have killed him on the spot."

"Do you know his name?" I inquired.

"No; he's very reserved; fellows in his situation often are; they don't like figuring in the papers, you understand; or being bound over to be of good behaviour; or, possibly, prosecuted. But no trouble will come of this; and he'll be on his legs again in a very few days."

With this re-assuring news the doctor left us. Miss Grey was relieved. One thing seemed pretty certain; and that was that the guilty and victorious duellist would not venture to appear in our part of the world for some time to come.

"Will you come with me to-day, to ask how he gets on?" I said to Laura as soon as the doctor was gone.

"No, I can't do that; but it would be very kind of you: that is, if you have no objection."

"None in the world; we must get Rebecca to make broth, or whatever else the doctor may order, and shall I mention your name to Mrs. Prichard? I mean, do you wish the patient—shall we call him—to know that you are here?"

"Oh! no, pray. He is the last person on earth——"

"You are sure?"

"Perfectly. I entreat, dear Ethel, that you run no risk of my name being mentioned."

"Why, Mr. Marston knows that you are here," I said persistently.

"Bad as that was, this would be intolerable. I know, Ethel, I may rely on you."

"Well, I won't say a word—I won't mention your name, since you so ordain it."

Two or three days passed. As I had been the good Samaritan, in female garb, who aided the wounded man in his distress, I was now the visiting Sister of Mercy, the ministering angel—whatever you are good enough to call me—who every day saw after his wants, and sent, sometimes soup, and sometimes jelly, to favour the recovery of which the doctor spoke so sanguinely.

I did not feel the romantic interest I ought perhaps to have felt in the object of my benevolence. I had no wish to see his face again. I was haunted by a recollection of him that was ghastly. I am not wanting in courage, physical or moral. But I should have made a bad nurse, and a worse soldier; at the sight of blood I immediately grow faint, and a sense of indescribable disgust remains.

I sometimes think we women are perverse creatures. For there is an occult interest about the guilty and audacious, if it be elevated by masculine courage and beauty, and surrounded by ever so little of mystery and romance. Shall I confess it? The image of that wicked Mr. Marston, notwithstanding all Laura's hard epithets, and the startling situation in which I had seen him last, haunted me often, and with something more of fascination than I liked to confess. Let there be energy, cleverness, beauty, and I believe a reckless sort of wickedness will not stand the least in the way of a foolish romance. I think I had energy; I know I was impetuous. Insipid or timid virtue would have had no chance with me.

I was going to the farm-house one day, I forget how long after the occurrence which had established my interesting relations with Plas Ylwd. My mother had a large cheval-glass; it had not often reflected her pretty image; it was the only one in the house, the furniture of which was very much out of date. It had been removed to my room, and before it I now stood, in my hat and jacket, to make a last inspection before I started. What did I see before me? I have courage to speak my real impressions, for there is no one near to laugh at me. A girl of eighteen, above the middle height, slender, with large, dark, grey eyes and long lashes, not much colour, not pink and white, by any means, but a very clear-tinted and marble-smooth skin; lips of carmine-scarlet, and teeth very white; thick, dark brown hair; and a tendency, when talking or smiling, to dimple in cheek and chin. There was something, too, spirited and energetic in the face that I contemplated with so much satisfaction.

I remained this day a little longer before my glass than usual. Half an hour later, I stood at the heavy stone doorway of Plas Ylwd. It is one of the prettiest farm-houses in the world. Round the farm-yard stand very old hawthorn and lime trees, and the farm-house is a composite building in which a wing of the old Tudor manor-house of Plas Ylwd is incorporated, under a common thatch, which has grown brown and discoloured, and sunk and risen into hillocks and hollows by time. The door is protected by a thatched porch, with worn stone pillars; and here I stood, and learned that "the gentleman upstairs" was very well that afternoon, and sitting up; the doctor thought he would be out for a walk in two or three days. Having learned this, and all the rest that it concerned Rebecca Torkill to hear, I took my leave of good Mrs. Prichard, and crossing the stile from the farm-yard, I entered the picturesque old wood in which the inmate of Plas Ylwd had received his wound. Through this sylvan solitude I intended returning to Malory.

CHAPTER XXII.

THE OUTLAW.

As I followed my path over the unequal flooring of the forest, among the crowded trunks of the trees and the thickets of brambles, I saw, on a sudden, Mr. Marston almost beside me. I was a good deal startled, and stood still. There was something in his air and looks, as he stood with his hat raised, so unspeakably deprecatory, that I felt at once re-assured. Without my permission it was plain he would not dream of accompanying me, or even of talking to me. All Laura's warnings and entreaties sounded at that moment in my ears like a far-off and unmeaning tinkle. He had no apologies to make; and yet he looked like a penitent. I was embarrassed, but without the slightest fear of him. I spoke; but I don't recollect what I said.

"I have come here, Miss Ware, as I believe, at some risk; I should have done the same thing had the danger been a hundred times greater. I tried to persuade myself that I came for no other purpose than to learn how that foolish fellow, who would force a quarrel on me, is getting on. But I came, in truth, on no such errand; I came here on the almost desperate chance of meeting you, and in the hope, if I were so fortunate, that you would permit me to say a word in my defence. I am unfortunate in having two or three implacable enemies, and fate has perversely collected them here. Miss Grey stands in very confidential relations with you, Miss Ethel; her prejudices against me are cruel, violent, and in every way monstrous."

He was walking beside me as he said this.

"Mr. Marston," I interposed, "I can't hear you say a word against Miss Grey. I have the highest opinion of her; she is my very dearest friend—she is truth itself."

"One word you say I don't dispute, Miss Ware. She means all she says for truth; but she is cruelly prejudiced, and, without suspecting it, does me the most merciless injustice. Whenever she is at liberty to state her whole case against me—at present I haven't so much as heard it—I undertake to satisfy you of its unfairness. There is no human being to whom I would say all this, or before whom I would stoop to defend myself and sue for an acquittal, where I am blameless, but you, Miss Ware."

I felt myself blushing. I think that sign of emotion fired him.

"I could not tell," he said, extending his hand towards Plas Ylwd, "whether that foolish man was dead or living; and this was the last place on earth I should have come to, in common prudence, while that was in doubt; but I was willing to brave that danger for a chance of seeing you once more—I could not live without seeing you."

He was gazing at me, with eyes glowing with admiration. I thought he looked wonderfully handsome. There was dash and recklessness, I thought, enough for an old-world outlaw, in his talk and looks, and, for all I knew, in his reckless doings; and the scene, the shadow, this solemn decaying forest, accorded well, in my romantic fancy, with the wild character I assigned him. There was something flattering in the devotion of this prompt and passionate man.

"Make me no answer," he continued—"no answer, I entreat. It would be mere madness to ask it now; you know nothing of me but, perhaps, the wildest slanders that prejudice ever believed, or hatred forged. From the moment I saw you, in the old garden at Malory, I loved you! Love at first sight! It was no such infatuation. It was the recalling of some happy dream. I had forgotten it in my waking hours; but I recognised, with a pang and rapture, in you, the spirit that had enthralled me. I loved you long before I knew it. I can't escape, Ethel, I adore you!"

I don't know how I felt. I was pretty sure that I ought to have been very angry. And I was half angry with myself for not being angry. I was, however—which answered just as well, a little alarmed; I felt as a child does when about to enter a dark room, and I drew back at the threshold.

"Pray, Mr. Marston, don't speak so to me any longer. It is quite true, I do not know you; you have no right to talk to me in my walks—pray leave me now."

"I shall obey you, Miss Ware; whatever you command, I shall do. My last entreaty is that you will not condemn me unheard; and pray do not mention to my enemies the infatuation that has led me here, with the courage of despair—no, not quite despair, I won't say that. I shall never forget you. Would to Heaven I could! I shall never forget or escape you; who can disenchant me? I shall never forget, or cease to pursue you, Ethel, I swear by Heaven!"

He looked in my face for a moment, raised my hand gently, but quickly, and pressed it to his lips, before I had recovered from my momentary tumult. I did not turn to look after him. I instinctively avoided that, but I heard his footsteps, in rapid retreat, in the direction of the farm-house which I had just left.

It was not until I had got more than half-way on my return to Malory that I began to think clearly on what had just occurred. What had I been dreaming of? I was shocked to think of it. Here was a total stranger admitted to something like the footing of a declared lover! What was I to do? What would papa or mamma say if my folly were to come to their ears? I did not even know where Mr. Marston was to be found. Some one has compared the Iliad to a frieze, which ceases, but does not end; and precisely of the same kind was this awkward epic of the wood of Plas Ylwd. Who could say when the poet might please to continue his work? Who could say how I could now bring the epic to a peremptory termination?

I must confess, however, although I felt the embarrassment of the situation, this lawless man interested me. Like many whimsical young ladies, I did not quite know my own mind.

On the step of the stile that crosses the churchyard wall, near Malory, I sat down, in rather uncomfortable rumination. I was interrupted by the sound of a step upon the road, approaching from the direction of Malory. I looked up, and, greatly to my surprise, saw Mr. Carmel, quite close to me. I stood up, and walked a few steps to meet him; we shook hands, he smiling, very glad, I knew, to meet me.

"You did not expect to see me so soon again, Miss Ware? And I have ever so much to tell you. I can't say whether it will please or vex you; but if you and Miss Grey will give me my old chair at your tea-table, I will look in for half an hour this evening. I have first to call at old Parry's, and give him a message that reached me from your mamma yesterday."

He smiled again, as he continued his walk, leaving me full of curiosity as to the purport of his news.

CHAPTER XXIII.

A JOURNEY.

Behold us now, about an hour later, at our tea-table. Mr. Carmel, as he had promised, came in and talked, as usual, agreeably; but, if he had any particular news to tell us, he had not yet begun to communicate it.

"You found your old quarters awaiting your return. We have lost our interesting stranger," I said; "I wish you would tell us all you know about him."

Mr. Carmel's head sank; his eyes were fixed, in painful thought, upon the table. "No," he said, looking up sharply, "God knows all, and that's enough. The story could edify no one."

He looked so pained, and even agitated, that I could not think of troubling him more.

"I had grown so attached to this place," said Mr. Carmel, rising and looking from the window, "that I can scarcely make up my mind to say good-bye, and turn my back on it for ever; yet I believe I must in a few days. I don't know. We soldiers, ecclesiastics, I mean, must obey orders, and I scarcely hope that mine will ever call me here again. I have news for you, also, Miss Ethel; I had a letter from your mamma, and a note from Mr. Ware, last night, and there is to be a break-up here, and a movement townward; you are to come out next season, Miss Ethel; your mamma and papa will be in town, for a week or so, in a few days; and, Miss Grey, she hopes you will not leave her on account of the change."

He paused; but she made no answer.

"Oh! darling Laura, you won't leave me?" I exclaimed.

"Certainly not, dear Ethel; and whenever the time for parting comes," she said very kindly, "it will cost me a greater pang than perhaps it will cost you. But though I am neither a soldier nor an ecclesiastic, my movements do not always depend upon myself."

Unrestrained by Mr. Carmel's presence, we kissed each other heartily.

"Here is a note, Miss Grey, enclosed for you," he murmured, and handed it to Laura.

In our eagerness we had got up and stood with Mr. Carmel in the recess of the window. It was twilight, and the table on which the candles burned stood at a considerable distance. To the light Laura Grey took her letter, and as she read it, quite absorbed, Mr. Carmel talked to me in low tones.

As he stood in the dim recess of the window, with trains of withered leaves rustling outside, and the shadow of the sear and half-stript elms upon the court and window, he said, kindly and gently:

"And now, at last, Miss Ethel forsakes her old home, and takes leave of her humble friends, to go into the great world. I don't think she will forget them, and I am sure they won't forget her. We have had a great many pleasant evenings here, and in our conversations in these happy solitudes, the terrors and glories of eternal truth have broken slowly upon your eyes. Beware! If you trifle with Heaven's mercy, the world, or hell, or heaven itself, has no narcotic for the horrors of conscience. In the midst of pleasure and splendour, and the tawdry triumphs of vanity, the words of Saint Paul will startle your ears like thunder. It is impossible for those who were once enlightened, and have tasted of the heavenly gift, and the good word of God, and the powers of the world to come, if they shall fall away, to renew them again unto repentance. The greater the privilege, the greater the liability. The higher the knowledge, the profounder the danger. You have seen the truth afar off; rejoice, therefore, and tremble."

He drew back and joined Miss Grey.

I had been thinking but little, for many weeks, of our many conversations. Incipient convictions had paled in the absence of the sophist or the sage—I knew not which. When he talked on this theme, his voice became cold and stern; his gentleness seemed to me to partake of an awful apathy; he looked like a man who had witnessed a revelation full of horror; my fancy, I am sure, contributed something to the transformation; but it did overawe me. I never was so impressed as by him. The secret was not in his words. It was his peculiar earnestness. He spoke like an eye-witness, and seemed under unutterable fear himself. He had the preacher's master-gift of alarming.

When Mr. Carmel had taken his leave for the night, I told Laura Grey my adventure in the wood of Plas Ylwd. I don't think I told it quite as frankly as I have just described it to you. The story made Miss Grey very grave for a time.

She broke the silence that followed by saying, "I am rather glad, Ethel, that we are leaving this. I think you will be better in town; I know I shall be more comfortable about you. You have no idea, and I earnestly hope you never may have, how much annoyance may arise from an acquaintance with that plausible, wicked man. He won't venture to force his acquaintance upon you in town. Here it is different, of course."

We sat up very late together, chatting this night in my room. I did not quite know how I felt about the impending change. My approaching journey to London was, to me, as great an event as her drive to the ball in her pumpkin-coach was to Cinderella. Of course there was something dazzling and delightful in the prospect. But the excitement and joy were like that of the happy bride who yet weeps because she is looking her last on the old homely life, that will always be dear and dearer as the irrevocable separation goes on. So, though she is sure she is passing into paradise, it is a final farewell to the beloved past. I felt the conflict; I loved Malory better than I could ever love a place again. But youth is the season of enterprise. God has ordained it. We go like the younger son in the parable, selfish, sanguine, adventurous; but the affections revive and turn homeward, and from a changed heart sometimes breaks on the solitude a cry, unheard by living ear, of yearning and grief, that would open the far-off doors, if that were possible, and return.

Next day arrangements took a definite form. All was fuss and preparation. I was to go the day following; Mr. Carmel was to take charge of me on the journey, and place me safely in the hands of Mrs. Beauchamp, our town housekeeper. Laura Grey, having wound up and settled all things at Malory, was to follow to town in less than a week; and, at about the same time, mamma and papa were to arrive.

A drive of ten miles or so brought us to the station; then came a long journey by rail. London was not new to me; but London with my present anticipations was. I was in high spirits, and Mr. Carmel made a very agreeable companion, though I fancied he was a little out of spirits.

I was tired enough that night when I at length took leave of Mr. Carmel at the door of our house in —— Street. The street lamps were already lighted. Mrs. Beauchamp, in a black silk dress, received me with a great deal of quiet respect, and rustled up-stairs before me to show me my room. Her grave and regulated politeness contrasted chillily with the hearty, and sometimes even boisterous welcome of old Rebecca Torkill. Mamma and papa were to be home, she told me, in a few days—she could not say exactly the day. I was, after an hour or so, a great deal lonelier than I had expected to be. I wrote a long letter to Laura, of whom I had taken leave only that morning (what a long time it seemed already!), and told her how much I already wished myself back again in Malory, and urged her to come sooner than she had planned her journey.

CHAPTER XXIV.

ARRIVALS.

Laura had not waited any longer than I for a special justification of a letter. She had nothing to say, and she said it in a letter as long as my own, which reached me at breakfast next morning.

Sitting in a spacious room, looking out into a quiet fashionable street, in a house all of whose decorations and arrangements had an air of cold elegance and newness, the letter, with the friendly Cardyllion postmark on it, seemed to bring with it something of the clear air, and homely comfort, and free life of Malory, and made me yearn all the more for the kind faces, the old house, and beloved scenery I had left behind. It was insufferably dull here, and I soon found myself in that state which is described as not knowing what to do with oneself. For two days no further letter from Laura reached me. On the third, I saw her well-known handwriting on the letter that awaited me on the breakfast-table. As I looked, as people will, at the direction before opening the envelope, I was struck by the postmark "Liverpool," and turning it over and over, I nowhere saw Cardyllion.

I began to grow too uncomfortable to wait longer; I opened the letter with misgivings. At the top of the note there was nothing written but the day of the week. It said—

> "MY DEAREST ETHEL,—A sudden and total change in my unhappy circumstances separates me from you. It is impossible that I should go to London now; and it is possible that I may not see you again for a long time, if ever. I write to say farewell; and in doing so to solemnly repeat my warning against permitting the person who obtained a few days' shelter in the steward's house, after the shipwreck, to maintain even the slightest correspondence or acquaintance with you. Pray, dearest Ethel, trust me in this. I implore of you to follow my advice. You may hear from me again. In the meantime, I am sure you will be glad to know that your poor governess is happy—happier than she ever desired, or ever hoped to be. My fond love is always yours, and my thoughts are hourly with you.—Ever your loving

LAURA GREY."

"May God for ever bless you, darling! Good-bye."

I don't think I could easily exaggerate the effect of this letter. I will not weary you with that most tiresome of all relations, an account of another person's grief.

Mamma and papa arrived that evening. If I had lived less at Malory, and more with mamma, I should not, in some points, have appreciated her so highly. When I saw her, for the first time, after a short absence, I was always struck by her beauty and her elegance, and it seemed to me that she was taller than I recollected her. She was looking very well, and so young! I saw papa but for a moment. He went to his room immediately to dress, and then went off to his club. Mamma took me to her room, where we had tea. She said I had grown, and was very much pleased with my looks. Then she told me all her plans about me. I was to have masters, and I was not to come out till April.

She then got me to relate all the circumstances of Nelly's death, and cried a good deal. Then she had in her maid Lexley, and they held a council together over me on the subject of dress. My Malory wardrobe, from which I had brought up to town with me what I considered an unexceptionable selection, was not laughed at, was not even discussed—it was simply treated as non-extant. It gave me a profound sense of the barbarism in which I had lived.

Laura Grey's letter lay heavy at my heart, but I had not yet mentioned it to mamma. There was no need, however, to screw my courage to that point. Among the letters brought up to her was one from Laura. When she read it she was angry in her querulous way. She threw herself into a chair in a pet. She had confidence in Laura Grey, and foresaw a good deal of trouble to herself in this desertion. "I am so particularly unfortunate!" she began—"everything that can possibly go wrong! everything that never happens to any one else! I could have got her to take you to Monsieur Pontet's, and your drives, and to shop—and—she must be a most unprincipled person. She had no right to go away as she has done. It is too bad! Your papa allows every one of that kind to treat me exactly as they please, and really, when I am at home, my life is one continual misery! What am I to do now? I don't believe any one else was ever so entirely at the mercy of her servants. I don't know, my dear, how I can possibly do all that is to be done for you without assistance—and *there* was a person I thought I could depend upon. A total stranger I should not like, and really, for anything I can see at present, I think you must go back again to Malory, and do the best you can. I am not a strong person. I was not made for all this, and I really feel I could just go to my bed, and cry till morning."

My heart had been very full, and I was relieved by this opportunity of crying.

"I wonder at your crying about so good-for-nothing a person," exclaimed mamma, impatiently. "If she had cared the least about you, she could not have left you as she has done. A satisfactory person, certainly, that young lady has turned out!"

Notwithstanding all this, mamma got over her troubles, and engaged a dull and even-tempered lady, named Anna Maria Pounden, whose manners were quiet and unexceptionable, and whose years were about fifty. She was not much of a companion for me, you may suppose. She answered, however, very well for all purposes intended by mamma. She was lady-like and kind, and seemed made for keeping keys, arranging drawers, packing boxes, and taking care of people when they were ill. She spoke French, besides, fluently, and with a good accent, and mamma insisted that she and I should always talk in that language. All the more persistently for this change, my thoughts were with my beloved friend, Laura Grey.

From Malory, Rebecca Torkill told me, in a rather incoherent letter, the particulars of Laura Grey's departure from Malory. She had gone out for a walk, leaving her things half packed, for she was to go from Malory next day. She did not return; but a note reached Mrs. Torkill, next morning, telling her simply she could not return; and that she would write to mamma and to me in London the same day. Mrs. Torkill's note, like mine, had the Liverpool postmark; and her conjecture was thus expressed: "I don't think, miss, she had no notions to leave that way when she went out. It must have bin something sudding. She went fest, I do sepose to Olyhed, and thens to Liverpule in one of them pakkats. Mr. Williams, the town-clerk, and the vicar and his lady, and Doctor Mervyn, is all certing sure it could be no other wise."

Mamma did not often come down to breakfast, during her short stay at this unseasonable time of year in town. On one of those rare occasions, however, something took place that I must describe.

Mamma was in a pretty morning *negligé* as we used to call such careless dresses then, looking as delicately pretty as the old china tea-cups before her. Papa was looking almost as perplexingly young as she, and I made up the little party to the number of the Graces. Mamma must have been forty, and I really don't think she looked more than two-and-thirty. Papa looked about five-and-thirty; and I think he must have been at least ten years older than he looked. That kind of life that is supposed to wear people out, seemed for them to have had an influence like the elixir vitæ; and I certainly have seen rustics, in the full enjoyment of mountain breezes, simple fare, and early hours, look many a day older than their years. The old rule, so harped upon, that "early to bed and early to rise" is the secret of perpetual youth, I don't dispute; but then, if it be early to go to bed at sunset in winter, say four in the evening, and to rise at four in the morning, is it not still earlier to anticipate that hour, and go to bed at four in the morning, and get up at one in the afternoon? At all events, I know that this mode of life seemed to agree with papa and mamma. I don't think, indeed, that either suffered much from the cares that poison enjoyment, and break down strength. Mamma threw all hers unexamined upon papa; who threw all his with equal nonchalance upon Mr. Norman, a kind of factotum, secretary, comptroller, diplomatist, financier, and every other thing that comes within the words "making oneself generally useful."

I never knew exactly what papa had a year to live upon. Mamma had money also. But they were utterly unfit to manage their own affairs, and I don't think they ever tried. Papa had his worries now and then; but they seldom seemed to last more than a day, or at most a week or two. There were a number of what he thought small sums, varying from two to five thousand pounds, which under old settlements dropped in opportunely, and extricated him. These sums ought to have been treated, not as income, but as capital, as I heard a moneyed man of business say long ago; but papa had not the talent of growing rich, or even of continuing rich, if a good fairy had gifted him with fortune.

Papa was in a reverie, leaning back in his chair; mamma yawned over a letter she was reading; I was drumming some dance music with my fingers on my knee under the table-cloth, when suddenly he said to mamma:

"You don't love your aunt Lorrimer very much?"

"No, I don't love her—I never said I did, did I?"

"No, but I mean, you don't like her, you don't care about her?"

"No," said mamma, languidly, and looking wonderingly at him with her large pretty eyes. "I don't very much—I don't quite know—I have an affection for her."

"You don't love her, and you don't even like her, but you have an affection for her," laughed papa.

"You are so teasing. I did not say that; what I mean is, she has a great many faults and oddities, and I don't like them—but I have an affection for her. Why should it seem so odd to you that one should care for one's relations? I do feel that for her, and there let it rest."

"Well, but it ought not to rest there—as you do like her."

"Why, dear—have you heard anything of her?"

"No; but there is one thing I should not object to hear about her just now."

"One thing? What do you mean, dear?"

"That she had died, and left us her money. I know what a brute I am, and how shocked you are; but I assure you we rather want it at this moment. You write to her, don't you?"

"N-not very often. Once since we saw her at Naples."

"Well, that certainly is not very often," he laughed. "But she writes to you. You thought she seemed rather to like us—I mean you?"

"Yes."

"She has no one else to care about that I know of. I don't pretend to care about her—I think her an old fool."

"She isn't that, dear," said mamma, quietly.

"I wish we knew where she is now. Seriously, you ought to write to her a little oftener, dear; I wish you would."

"I'll write to her, certainly, as soon as I am a little more myself. I could not do it just to-day; I have not been very well, you know."

"Oh! my darling, I did not mean to hurry you. Of course, not till you feel perfectly well; don't suppose I could be such a monster. But—I don't want, of course, to pursue her—but there is a middle course between that and having to drop her. She really has no one else, poor old thing! to care about, or to care about her. Not that *I* care about her, but you're her kinswoman, and I don't see why——"

At this moment the door opened, and there entered, with the air of an assumed intimacy and a certain welcome, a person whom I little expected to see there. I saw him with a shock. It was the man with the fine eyes and great forehead, the energetic gait and narrow shoulders. The grim, mean-looking, intelligent, agreeable man of fifty, Mr. Droqville.

CHAPTER XXV.

THE DOCTOR'S NEWS.

Oh! how do you do, Doctor Droqville?" said mamma, with a very real welcome in looks and accent.

"How d'ye do, Droqville?" said my father, a little dryly, I fancied.

"Have you had your breakfast?" asked mamma.

"Two hours ago."

"We are very late here," said papa.

"I should prefer thinking I am very early, in my primitive quarters," answered Mr. Droqville.

"I had not an idea we should have found you in town, just now."

"In season or out of season, a physician should always be at his post. I'm beginning to learn rather late there's some truth in that old proverb about moss, you know, and rolling stones, and it costs even a bachelor something to keep body and soul together in this mercenary, tailoring, cutlet-eating world." At this moment he saw me, and made me a bow. "Miss Ware?" he said, a little inquiringly to mamma. "Yes, I knew perfectly it was the young lady I had seen at Malory. Some faces are not easily forgotten," he added, gallantly, with a glance at me. "I threatened to run away with her, but she was firm as fate," he smiled and went on; "and I paid a visit to our friend Carmel, you know."

"And how did you think he was?" she asked; and I listened with interest for the answer.

"He's consumptive. He's at this side of the Styx, it is true; but his foot is in the water, and Charon's obolus is always between his finger and thumb. He'll die young. He may live five years, it is true; but he is not likely to live two. And if he happens to take cold and begins to cough, he might not last four months."

"My wife has been complaining," said papa; "I wish you could do something for her. You still believe in Doctor Droqville? I think she half believes you have taken a degree in divinity as well as in medicine; if so, a miracle, now and then, would be quite in your way."

"But I assure you, Doctor Droqville, I never said any such thing. It was you who thought," she said to my father, "that Doctor Droqville was in orders."

Droqville laughed.

"But, Doctor Droqville, I think," said mamma, "you would have made a very good priest."

"There are good priests, madame, of various types; Madame de Genlis, for instance, commends an abbé of her acquaintance; he was a most respectable man, she says, and never ridiculed revealed religion but with moderation."

Papa laughed, but I could see that he did not like Doctor Droqville. There was something dry, and a little suspicious in his manner, so slight that you could hardly define it, but which contrasted strikingly with the decision and *insouciance* of Doctor Droqville's talk.

"But, you know, you never do that, even with moderation; and you can argue so closely when you please."

"There, madame, you do me too much honour. I am the worst logician in the world. I wrote a part of an essay on Christian chivalry, and did pretty well, till I began to reason; the essay ended, and I was swallowed up in this argument—pray listen to it. To sacrifice your life for the lady you adore is a high degree of heroism; but to sacrifice your soul for her is the highest degree of heroism. But the highest degree of heroism is but another name for Christianity; and, therefore, to act thus can't sacrifice your soul, and if it doesn't you don't practise a heroism, and therefore no Christianity, and, therefore, you do sacrifice your soul. But if you do sacrifice your soul, it is the highest heroism—therefore Christianity; and, therefore, you don't sacrifice your soul, and so, *da capo*, it goes on for ever—and I can't extricate myself. When I mean to make a boat, I make a net; and this argument that I invented to carry me some little way on my voyage to truth, not only won't hold water, but has caught me by the foot, entangles, and drowns me. I never went on with my essay."

In this cynical trifling there was a contemptuous jocularity quite apparent to me, although mamma took it all in good faith, and said:

"It is vcry puzzling, but it can't bc truc; and I should think it almost a duty to find out where it is wrong."

Papa laughed, and said:

"My dear, don't you see that Doctor Droqville is mystifying us?"

I was rather glad, for I did not like it. I was vexed for mamma. Doctor Droqville's talk seemed to me an insolence.

"It is quite true, I am no logician; I had better continue as I am. I make a tolerable physician; if I became a preacher, with my defective ratiocination, I should inevitably lose myself and my audience in a labyrinth. You make but a very short stay in town, I suppose?" he broke off suddenly. "It isn't tempting, so many houses sealed—a city of the dead. One does not like, madame, as your Doctor Johnson said to Mrs. Thrale, to come down to vacuity."

"Well, it is only a visit of two or three days. My daughter Ethel is coming out next spring, and she came up to meet us here. I wish her to have a few weeks with masters, and there are more things to be thought of than you would suppose. Do you think there is anything a country miss would do well to read up that we might have forgotten?"

"Read? read? Oh! yes, two things."

"What are they?"

"If she has a sound knowledge of the heathen mythology, and a smattering of the Bible, she'll do very well."

"But she won't talk about the Bible," laughed papa; "people who like it, read it to themselves."

"Very true," said Doctor Droqville, "you never mention it; but, quite unconsciously, you are perpetually alluding to it. Nothing strikes a stranger more, if he understands your language as I do. You had a note from Lady Lorrimer?"

"No," said mamma.

The word "note," I think, struck papa as implying that she was nearer than letter-writing distance, and he glanced quickly at Doctor Droqville.

"And where is Lady Lorrimer now?" asked papa.

"That is what I came to tell you. She is at Mivart's. I told her you were in town, and I fancied you would have had a note from her; but I thought I might as well look in and tell you."

"She's quite well, I hope?" said mamma.

"Now did you ever, Mrs. Ware, in all your life, see her quite well? I never did. She would lose all pleasure in life, if she thought she wasn't leaving it. She arrived last night, and summoned me to her at ten this morning. I felt her pulse. It was horribly regular. She had slept well, and breakfasted well, but that was all. In short, I found her suffering under her usual chronic attack of good health, and, as the case was not to be trifled with, I ordered her instantly some medicine which could not possibly produce any effect whatever; and in that critical state I left her, with a promise to look in again in the afternoon to ascertain that the more robust symptoms were not gaining ground, and in the interval I came to see you and tell you all about it."

"I suppose, then, I should find her in her bed?" said mamma.

"No; I rather think she has postponed dying till after dinner—she ordered a very good one—and means to expire in her sitting-room, where you'll find her. And you have not been very well?"

"Remember the story he has just told you of your aunt Lorrimer, and take care he doesn't tell her the same story of you," said papa, laughing.

"I wish I could," said Doctor Droqville; "few things would please me better. That pain in the nerves of the head is a very real torment."

So he and mamma talked over her head-aches in an undertone for some minutes; and while this was going on there came in a note for mamma. The servant was waiting for an answer in the hall.

"Shall I read it?" said papa, holding it up by the corner. "It is Lady Lorrimer's, I'm sure."

"Do, dear," said mamma, and she continued her confidences in Doctor Droqville's ear.

Papa smiled a little satirically as he read it. He threw it across the table, saying: "You can read it, Ethel; it concerns you rather."

I was very curious. The hand was youthful and pretty, considering Lady Lorrimer's years. It was a whimpering, apathetic, selfish little note. She was miserable, she said, and had quite made up her mind that she could not exist in London smoke. She had sent for the doctor.

She continued: "I shall make an effort to see you, if you can look in about three, for a few minutes. Have you any of your children with you? If they are very quiet I should like to see them. It would amuse me. It is an age since I saw your little people, and I really forget their ages, and even their names. Say if I am to expect you at three. I have told the servant to wait."

People who live in the country fancy themselves of more importance than they really are. I was mortified, and almost shocked at the cool sentences about "the little people," etc.

"Well, you promise to be very quiet, won't you? You won't pull the cat's tail, or light paper in the fire, or roar for plum-cake?" said papa.

"I don't think she wants to see us. I don't think she cares the least about us. Perhaps mamma won't go," I said, resentfully, hoping that she would not pay that homage to the insolent old woman.

Doctor Droqville stood up, having written a prescription.

"Well, I'm off; and I think this will do you a world of good. Can I do any commission for you about town; I shall be in every possible direction in the next three hours?"

No, there was nothing; and this man, whom I somehow liked less than ever, although he rather amused me, vanished, and we saw his cab drive by the window.

"Well, here's her note. You'll go to see her, I suppose?" said papa.

"Certainly; I have a great affection for my aunt. She was very kind to me when there was no one else to care about me."

Mamma spoke with more animation than I believed her capable of—I thought I even saw tears in her eyes. It struck me that she did not like papa's tone in speaking about her. The same thing probably struck him.

"You are quite right, darling, as you always are in a matter of feeling, and you'll take Ethel, won't you?"

"Yes, I should like her to come."

"And you know, if she should ask you, don't tell her I'm a bit better off than I really am. I have had some awful losses lately. I don't like bothering you about business, and it was no fault or negligence of mine; but I really—it is of very great importance she should not do anything less that she intended for you, or anything whimsical or unjust. I give you my honour there isn't a guinea to spare now, it would be a positive cruelty."

Mamma looked at him, but she was by this time so accustomed to alarms of that kind that they did not make a very deep impression upon her.

"I don't think she's likely to talk about such matters, dear," said mamma; "but if she should make any inquiries, I shall certainly tell her the truth."

I remembered Lady Lorrimer long ago at Malory. It was a figure seen in the haze of infancy, and remembered through the distance of many years. I recollect coming down the stairs, the nursery-maid holding me by the hand, and seeing a carriage and servants in the court before the door. I remember, as part of the same dream, sitting in the lap of a strange lady in the drawing-room, who left a vague impression of having been richly dressed, who talked to me in a sweet, gentle voice, and gave me toys, and whom I always knew to have been Lady Lorrimer. How much of this I actually saw, and how much was picked up with the vivid power of reproducing pictures from description that belongs to children, I cannot say; but I always heard of Aunt Lorrimer afterwards with interest, and now at length I was about to see her. Her note had disappointed me, still I was curious.

CHAPTER XXVI.

LADY LORRIMER.

M y curiosity was soon gratified. After luncheon we drove to Mivart's, and there in her sitting-room I saw Lady Lorrimer. I was agreeably surprised. Her figure was still beautiful. She was, I believe, past sixty then; but, like all our family whom I have ever seen, she looked a great deal younger than her years. I thought her very handsome, very like my idea of Mary Queen of Scots in her later years; and her good looks palpably owed nothing to "making up." Her smile was very winning, and her eyes still soft and brilliant. Through so many years, her voice as she greeted us returned with a strange and very sweet recognition upon my ear.

She put her arms about mamma's neck, and kissed her tenderly. In like manner she kissed me. She made me sit beside her on a sofa, and held my hands in hers. Mamma sat opposite in a chair.

Lady Lorrimer might be very selfish—lonely people often are; but she certainly was very affectionate. There were tears in her fine eyes as she looked at me. It was not such a stare as a dealer might bestow on a picture, to which, as a child, I had sometimes been subjected by old friends in search of a likeness. By-and-by she talked of me.

"The flight of my years is so silent," she said, with a sad smile to mamma, "that I forgot, as I wrote to you, how few are left me, and that Ethel is no longer a child. I think her quite lovely; she is like what I remember you, but it is only a likeness—not the same; she does not sacrifice her originality. I'm not afraid, dear, to say all that before you," she said, turning on me for a moment her engaging smile. "I think, Ethel, in this world, where people without a particle of merit are always pushing themselves to the front, young people who have beauty should know it. But, my dear," she said, looking on me again, "good looks don't last very long. Your mamma, there, keeps hers wonderfully; but look at me. I was once a pretty girl, as you are now; and see what I am!

'Le même cours des planètes
  Régle nos jours et nos nuits;
On me vit ce que vous êtes,
  Vous serez ce que je suis.'

"So I qualify my agreeable truths with a little uncomfortable morality. She'll be coming out immediately?"

Mamma told her, hereupon, all her plans about me.

"And so sure as you take her out, her papa will be giving her away; and, remember, I'm to give her her diamonds whenever she marries. You are to write to me whenever anything is settled, or likely to come about. They always know at my house here, when I am on my travels, where a letter will find me. No, you're not to thank me," she interrupted us. "I saw Lady Rimington's, and I intend that your daughter's shall be a great deal better than hers."

Our old Malory housekeeper, Rebecca Torkill, had a saying, "Nothing so grateful as pride." I think I really liked my aunt Lorrimer better for her praises of my good looks than for her munificent intentions about my bridal brilliants. But for either I could only show my pleasure by my looks. I started up to thank her for her promised diamonds. But, as I told you, she would not hear a word, and drew me down gently with a smile again beside her.

Then she talked, and mamma talked. For such a recluse, Lady Lorrimer was a wonderful gossip, and devoured all mamma's news, and told her old stories of all the old people who figured in such oral history. I must do her justice. There seemed to me to be no malice whatever in her stories. The comic was what she enjoyed most. Her lively pictures amused even me, who knew nothing of the originals; and the longer I sat with her, the more confidence did I feel in her good-nature.

A good deal of this conversation was all but whispered, and she had despatched me with her maid to look at some china she had brought home for her cabinets in London, at the other end of the room. When I returned their heads were still very near, and they were talking low with the same animation. I sat down again beside Lady Lorrimer. I had spun out my inspection of the china as long as I could. Lady Lorrimer patted my head gently, as I sat down again, without, I fancy, remembering at the moment that I had been away. She was answering, I think, a remark of mamma's, and upon a subject which had lain rather heavily at my heart since Monsieur Droqville's visit to our breakfast-table that morning.

"I don't know," she said; "Monsieur Droqville is a clever physician, but it seems to me he has always made too much of Mr. Carmel's illness, or delicacy, or whatever it is. I do not think Mr. Carmel is in any real danger—I don't think there is anything seriously wrong with him—more, in fact, than with any other thin young man, and now and then he has a cough. Three years ago, when I first made his acquaintance—and what a charming creature he is!—Monsieur Droqville told me he could not live more than two years; and this morning, when I asked how Mr. Carmel was, he allowed him three years still to live; so if he goes on killing him at that easy rate, he may live as long as Old Parr. And now that I think of it, did you hear a rumour about Sir Harry?"

"There are so many Sir Harrys," said mamma. "Do you mean Sir Harry Rokestone?"

"Of course I mean Sir Harry Rokestone," she answered; "have you heard anything of him?"

"Nothing, but the old story," said mamma.

"And what is that?" asked Lady Lorrimer.

"Only that he hates us with all his heart and soul, and never loses an opportunity of doing us all the mischief he can. He has twice prevented my husband getting into the House—and cost him a great deal more money than he could afford; and he has had opportunities, from those old money dealings that you know of between the two families, of embarrassing my poor husband most cruelly. If you knew what enormous law expenses we have been put to, and all the injuries he has done us, you would say that you never heard of anything so implacable, so malignant, and——"

"So natural," said Lady Lorrimer. "I don't mean to fight Sir Harry Rokestone's battle for him. I dare say he has been stern and vindictive; he was a proud, fierce man; and, my dear Mabel, you treated him very ill; so did Francis Ware. If he treats you as you have treated him, nothing can be much worse. I always liked him better than your husband; he was better, and is better. I use the privilege of an old kinswoman; and I say nothing could have been more foolish than your treatment of him, except your choice of a husband. I think Francis Ware is one of those men who never ought to have married. He is a clever man; but in some respects, and these of very great importance, he has always acted like a fool. Harry Rokestone was worth twenty of him, and would have made a much better husband than ever he did. I always thought he was the handsomer man; he had twice the real ability of Francis Ware; he had all the masculine attributes of mind. I say nothing about his immensely superior wealth; that you chose to regard as a point quite unworthy of consideration. The only thing not in his favour was that he was some years older."

"Twenty years nearly," said mamma.

"Well, my dear, a man with his peculiar kind of good looks, and his commanding character, wears better than a younger man. You recollect the answer of the old French mareschal to the young *petit-maître* who asked him his age. '*Je ne vous le dirai pas precisement; mais soyez sur qu'un âne est plus âgé à vingt ans qu'un homme ne l'est à soixante.*' I don't say that the term would have fairly described Francis Ware. I know very well he was brilliant; but those talents, if there are no more solid gifts to support them, grow less and less suitable as men get into years, until they become frivolous. However, I am sure that Harry Rokestone does hate you both; and he's just the man to make his hatred felt. The time has passed for forgiveness. When the fire of romance has expired, the metal that might have taken another shape cools down and hardens in the mould. He will never forgive or change, I am afraid; and you must both lay your account with his persevering animosity. But, you say, you haven't heard any story about him lately?"

"No, nothing."

"Well, old Mrs. Jennings, of Golden Friars, sometimes writes to me, and she says he is going to marry that rich spinster, Miss Goulding of Wrybiggins. She only says she hears so; and I thought you might know."

"I should not wonder—it is not at all an unlikely thing. I don't see that they could do better; there's nothing to prevent it, so far as I can see."

But although mamma thus applauded the arrangement, I could see that in her inmost heart she did not like it. There is something of desertion in these late marriages of long-cast-off lovers, who have worshipped our shadows in secret, through lonely years; and I could see dimly a sad little mortification in mamma's pretty face.

As we drove home I mused over Lady Lorrimer. The only disagreeable recollection that disturbed my pleasant retrospect was that part of her conversation that referred to papa. She said she "used the privilege of an old kinswoman." I should have said abused it rather. But mamma did not seem to resent it—I suppose they were on terms to discuss him; and they either forgot me, or thought I had no business to be in the way. In every other respect, I was very much pleased with my visit, as I well might be. She was much more clever than I expected, more animated, more fascinating. I was haunted with the thought how lovely she must have been when she was young!

"Don't a great many older women than Lady Lorrimer go out a great deal?" I asked.

"Yes," answered mamma, "but they have young people to take out very often."

"But papa mentioned some this morning, who are everywhere, and never chaperon any one."

"I suppose they enjoy it, as they can't live without it. Pull up that window, dear."

"I wonder very much she doesn't go out; she's so handsome, really beautiful, considering her years, I think; and so very agreeable."

"I suppose she doesn't care," she answered, a little drily.

"But she complained of being lonely," I resumed, "and I thought she sighed when she spoke of my coming out, as if she would like a look at the gay world again."

"My dear, you bore me; I suppose Lady Lorrimer will do, with respect to that, as she does about everything else—precisely what pleases her best."

These words mamma spoke in a way that very plainly expressed: "Now you have heard, once for all, everything I mean to say on this subject; and you will be good enough to talk and think of something quite different."

CHAPTER XXVII.

WHAT CAN SHE MEAN?

We had promised to go and see Lady Lorrimer again next day at the same hour. My head was still full of her. Mamma did not come down to breakfast; so I interrupted papa at his newspaper to sound him, very much as I had sounded her.

"Why doesn't she stay at home, and go out?" he repeated, smiling faintly as he did so. "I suppose she understands her own business; I can't say—but you mustn't say anything of that kind before her. She has done some foolish things, and got herself talked about; and you'll hear it all, I daresay, time enough. She's not a bit worse than other people, but a much greater fool; so don't ask people those questions, it would vex your mamma, and do nobody any good, do you see?"

Shortly after this, Miss Pounden came down to tell me that we were not going to see Lady Lorrimer that day. I was horribly disappointed, and ran up to the drawing-room, where mamma then was, to learn the cause of our visit being put off.

"Here, dear, is my aunt's note," she said, handing it to me, and scarcely interrupting her consultation with her maid about the millinery they were discussing. It was open, and I read these words:

> "MY DEAR MABEL,—I must say good-bye a little earlier than I had intended. My plans are upset. I find my native air insupportable, and fly northward for my life! I am thinking at present of Buxton for a few days; the weather is so genial here, that my doctor tells me I may find it still endurable in that cold region. It grieves me not to see your dear faces before I go. Do not let your pretty daughter forget me. I may, it is just possible, return through London—so we may meet soon again. I shall have left Mivart's and begun my journey before this note reaches you. God bless you, my dear Mabel!—Your affectionate
>
> AUNT."

So she was actually gone! What a dull day it would be! Well, there was no good in railing at fate. But was I ever to see that charming lady more?

In my drive that day with Miss Pounden, thinking it was just possible that Lady Lorrimer, whimsical as she was said to be, might have once more changed her mind, I called at Mivart's to inquire. She was no longer there. She had left with bag and baggage, and all her servants, that morning at nine o'clock. I had called with very little hope of finding that her journey had been delayed, and I drove away with even that small hope extinguished. She was my Mary, Queen of Scots. She had done something too rash and generous for the epicurean, sarcastic, and specious society of London. From the little that papa had said, I conjectured that Lady Lorrimer's secession from society was not quite voluntary; but she interested me all the more. In my dull life the loss of my new acquaintance so soon was a real blow. Mamma was not much of a companion to me. She liked to talk of people she knew, and to people who knew them. Except what concerned my dress and accomplishments, we had as yet no topics in common.

Dear Laura Grey, how I missed you now! The resentment I had felt at first was long since quite lost in my real sorrow, and there remained nothing but affectionate regrets.

I take up the thread of my personal narrative where I dropped it on the day of my ineffectual visit at Lady Lorrimer's hotel. In the afternoon Doctor Droqville came to see mamma. He had been to see Lady Lorrimer that morning, just before she set out on her journey.

"She was going direct to Buxton, as she hinted to you," said Doctor Droqville, "and I advised her to make a week's stay there. When she leaves it, she says she is going on to Westmoreland, and to stay for a fortnight or three weeks at Golden Friars. She's fanciful; there was gout in her family, and she is full of gouty whims and horrors. She is as well as a woman of her years need be, if she would only believe it."

"Have you heard lately from Mr. Carmel?" asked mamma.

I listened with a great deal of interest for the answer.

"Yes, I heard this morning," he replied. "He's in Wales."

"Not at Malory?" said mamma.

"No, not at Malory; a good way from Malory."

I should have liked to ask how long he had been in Wales, for I had been secretly offended at his apparent neglect of me; but I could not muster courage for the question.

Next morning I took it into my head that I should like a walk; and with mamma's leave, Miss Pounden and I set out, of course keeping among the quiet streets in the neighbourhood. While, as we walked, I was in high chat with Miss Pounden, who was chiefly a listener, and sometimes, I must admit, a rather absent one, I raised my eyes and could scarcely believe their report. Not ten yards away, walking up the flagged way towards us, were two figures. One was Lady Lorrimer I was certain. She was dressed in a very full velvet cloak, and had a small book in her hand. At her left, at a distance of more than a yard, walked a woman in a peculiar costume. This woman looked surly, and stumped beside her with a limp, as if one leg were shorter than the other. They approached at a measured pace, looking straight before them, and in total silence.

My eyes were fixed on Lady Lorrimer with a smile, which I every moment expected would be answered by one of recognition from her. But no such thing. She must have seen me; but nearer and nearer they came. They never deviated from their line of march. Lady Lorrimer continued to look straight before her. It was the sternest possible "cut," insomuch that I felt actually incredulous, and began to question my first identification. Her velvet actually brushed my dress as I stood next the railings. She passed me with her head high, and the same stony look.

"Shall we go on, dear?" asked Miss Pounden, who did not understand why we had come to a standstill.

I moved on in silence; but the street being a very quiet one, I turned about for a last look. I saw them ascend the steps of a house, and at the same moment the door opened, and Mr. Carmel came out, with his hat in his hand, and followed the two ladies in. The door was then shut. We resumed our walk homeward. We had a good many streets to go through, and I did not know my way. I was confounded, and walked on in utter silence, looking down in confused rumination on the flags under my feet.

Till we got home I did not say a word; and then I sat down in my room, and meditated on that odd occurrence, as well as my perturbation would let me. It was a strange mixture of surprise, doubt, and intense mortification. It was very stupid of me not to have ascertained at the time the name of the street which was the scene of this incident. Miss Pounden had never seen either Lady Lorrimer or Mr. Carmel; and the occurrence had not made the least impression upon her. She could not therefore help me, ever so little, next day, to recover the name of the street in which I had stood still for a few seconds, looking at she knew not what. There was just a film of doubt, derived from the inexplicable behaviour of the supposed Lady Lorrimer. When I told mamma, she at first insisted it was quite impossible. But, as I persisted, and went into detail, she said it was very odd. She was thoughtful for a little time, and sighed. Then she made me repeat all I had told her, and seemed very uncomfortable, but did not comment upon it. At length she said:

"You must promise me, Ethel, not to say a word about it to your papa. It would only lead to vexation. I have good reasons for thinking so. Speak of it to no one. Let the matter rest. I don't think I shall ever understand some people. But let us talk about it no more."

And with this charge the subject dropped.

CHAPTER XXVIII.

A SEMI-QUARREL.

Mamma did not remain long in town. Bleak as the weather now was, she and papa went to Brighton for a fortnight. They then went, for a few days, to Malory; and from that, northward, to Golden Friars. I dare say papa would have liked to find Lady Lorrimer there. I don't know that he did.

I, meanwhile, was left in the care of Miss Pounden, who made a very staid and careful chaperon. I danced every day, and pounded a piano, and sang a little, and spoke French incessantly to Miss Pounden. My spirits were sustained by the consciousness that I was very soon to come out. I was not entirely abandoned to Miss Pounden's agreeable society. Mr. Carmel re-appeared. Three times a week he came in and read, and spoke Italian with me for an hour, Miss Pounden sitting by—at least, she was supposed to be sitting there on guard—but she really was as often out of the room as in it. One day I said to him:

"You know Lady Lorrimer, my aunt?"

"Yes," he answered, carelessly.

"Did you know she was my aunt?"

"Your great-aunt, yes."

"I wonder, then, why you never mentioned her to me," said I.

"There is nothing to wonder at," he replied, with a smile. "Respecting her, I have no curiosity, and nothing to tell."

"Oh! But you must know something about her—ever so little—and I really know nothing. Why does she lead so melancholy a life?"

"She has sickened of gaiety, I have been told."

"There's something more than that," I insisted.

"She's not young, you know, and society is a laborious calling."

"There's some reason; none of you will tell me," I said. "I used to tell every one everything, until I found that no one told me anything; now I say, 'Ethel, seal your lips, and open your ears; don't you be the only fool in this listening, sly, suspicious world.' But, if you'll tell nothing else, at least you'll tell me this. What were you all about when you opened the door of a house, in some street not far from this, to Lady Lorrimer, and an odd-looking woman who was walking beside her, on the day after she had written to mamma to say she had actually left London. What was the meaning of that deception?"

"I don't know whether Lady Lorrimer out-stayed the time of her intended departure or not," he answered; "she would write what she pleased, and to whom she pleased, without telling me. And now I must tell you, if Lady Lorrimer had confided a harmless secret to me, I should not betray it by answering either 'yes' or 'no' to any questions. Therefore, should you question me upon any such subject, you must not be offended if I am silent."

I was vexed.

"One thing you must tell me," I persisted. "I have been puzzling myself over her very odd looks that day; and also over the odd manner and disagreeable countenance of the woman who was walking at her side. Is Lady Lorrimer, at times, a little out of her mind?"

"Who suggested that question?" he asked, fixing his eyes suddenly on me.

"Who suggested it?" I repeated. "No one. People, I suppose, can ask their own questions."

I was surprised and annoyed, and I suppose looked so. I continued: "That woman looked like a keeper, I fancied, and Lady Lorrimer—I don't know what it was—but there was something so unaccountable about her."

"I don't know a great deal of Lady Lorrimer, but I am grateful to her for, at least, one great kindness, that of having introduced me to your family," he said; "and I can certainly testify that there is no clearer mind anywhere. No suspicion of that kind can approach her; she is said to be one of the cleverest, shrewdest intellects, and the most cultivated, you can imagine. But people say she is an *esprit fort*, and believes in nothing. It does not prevent her doing a kind office for a person such as I. She has more charity than many persons who make loud professions of faith."

I had felt a little angry at this short dialogue. He was practising reserve, and he looked at one time a little stern, and unlike himself.

"But I want to ask you a question—only one more," I said, for I wished to clear up my doubts.

"Certainly," he said, more like himself.

"About my meeting Lady Lorrimer that day, and seeing you, as I told you." I paused, and he simply sat listening. "My question," I continued, "is this—I may as well tell you; the whole thing appeared to me so unaccountable that I have been ever since doubting the reality of what I saw; and I want you simply to tell me whether it did happen as I have described?"

At this renewed attack, Mr. Carmel's countenance underwent no change, even the slightest, that could lead me to an inference; he said, with a smile:

"It might, perhaps, be the easiest thing in the world for me to answer distinctly, 'no;' but I remember that Dean Swift, when asked a certain question, said that Lord Somers had once told him never to give a negative answer, although truth would warrant it, to a question of that kind; because, if he made that his habit, when he could give a denial, whenever he declined to do so, would amount to an admission. I think that a wise rule, and all such questions I omit to answer."

"That is an evasion," I replied, in high indignation.

"Forgive me, it is no evasion—it is simply silence."

"You know it is cowardly, and indirect, and—characteristic," I persisted, in growing wrath.

He was provokingly serene.

"Well, let me give you another reason for silence respecting Lady Lorrimer. Your mamma has specially requested me to keep silence on the subject; and in your case, Miss Ethel, her daughter, can I consider that request otherwise than as a command?"

"Not comprehending casuistry, I don't quite see how your promise to papa, to observe silence respecting the differences of the two Churches, is less binding than your promise to mamma of silence respecting Lady Lorrimer."

"Will you allow me to answer that sarcasm?" he asked, flushing a little.

"How I hate hypocrisy and prevarication!" I repeated, rising even above my old level of scorn.

"I have been perfectly direct," he said, "upon that subject; for the reason I have mentioned, I can't and won't speak."

"Then for the present, I think, we shall talk upon no other," I said, getting up, going out of the room, and treating him at the door to a haughty little bow.

So we parted for that day.

I understood Mr. Carmel, however; I knew that he had acted as he always did when he refused to do what other people wished, from a reason that was not to be overcome; and I don't recollect that I ever renewed my attack. We were on our old terms in a day or two. Between the stanzas of Tasso, often for ten minutes unobserved, he talked upon the old themes—eternity, faith, the Church, the saints, the Blessed Virgin. He supplied me with books; but this borrowing and lending was secret as the stolen correspondence of lovers.

I have thought over that strange period of my life: the little books that wrought such wonders, the spell of whose power is broken now; the tone of mind induced by them, by my solitude, my agitations, the haunting affections of the dead; and all these influences re-acting again upon the cold and supernatural character of Mr. Carmel's talk. My exterior life had been going on, the rural monotony of Malory, its walks, its boating, its little drives; and now the dawning ambitions of a more vulgar scene, the town life, the excitement of a new world were opening. But among these realities, ever recurring, and dominating all, there seemed to be ever present a stupendous vision!

So it seemed to me my life was divided between frivolous realities and a gigantic trance. Into this I receded every now and then, alone and unwatched. The immense perspective of a towering cathedral aisle seemed to rise before me, shafts and ribbed stone, lost in smoke of incense floating high in air; mitres and gorgeous robes, and golden furniture of the altar, and chains of censers and jewelled shrines, glimmering far off in the tapers' starlight, and the inspired painting of the stupendous Sacrifice reared above the altar in dim reality. I fancied I could hear human voices, plaintive and sublime as the aërial choirs heard high over dying saints and martyrs by faithful ears; and the mellow thunder of the organ roll-rolling through unseen arches above. Sometimes, less dimly, I could see the bowed heads of myriads of worshippers, "a great multitude, which no man could number, of all nations, and kindreds, and peoples, and tongues." It was, to my visionary senses, the symbol of the Church. Always the self-same stupendous building, the same sounds and sights, the same high-priest and satellite bishops; but seen in varying lights—now in solemn beams, striking down and crossing the shadow in mighty bars of yellow, crimson, green, and purple through the stained windows, and now in the dull red gleam of the tapers.

Was I more under the influence of religion in this state? I don't believe I was. My imagination was exalted, my anxiety was a little excited, and the subject generally made me more uncomfortable than it did before. Some of the forces were in action which might have pushed me, under other circumstances, into a decided course. One thing, which logically had certainly no bearing upon the question, did affect me, I now know, powerfully. There was a change in Mr. Carmel's manner which wounded me, and piqued my pride. I used to think he took an interest in Ethel Ware. He seemed now to feel none, except in the discharge of his own missionary duties, and I fancied that, if it had not been for his anxiety to acquit himself of a task imposed by others, and exacted by his conscience, I should have seen no more of Mr. Carmel.

I was a great deal too proud to let him perceive my resentment—I was just as usual—I trifled and laughed, read my Italian, and made blunders, and asked questions; and, in those intervals of which I have spoken, I listened to what he had to say, took the books he offered, and thanked him with a smile, but with no great fervour. The temperature of our town drawing-room was perceptibly cooler than that of Malory, and the distance between our two chairs had appreciably increased. Nevertheless, we were apparently, at least, very good friends.

But terms like these are sometimes difficult to maintain. I was vexed at his seeming to acquiesce so easily in my change of manner, which, imperceptible to any one else, I somehow knew could not be hidden from him. I had brought down, and laid on the drawing-room table at which we sat, the only book which I then had belonging to Mr. Carmel. It was rather a dark day. Something in the weather made me a little more cross than usual. Miss Pounden was, according to her wont, flitting to and fro, and not minding in the least what we read or said. I laid down my Tasso, and laughed. Mr. Carmel looked at me a little puzzled.

"That, I think, is the most absurd stanza we have read. I ought, I suppose, to say the most sublime. But it is as impossible to read it without laughing as to read the rest without yawning."

I said this with more scorn than I really felt, but it certainly was one of those passages in which good Homer nods. A hero's head is cut off, I forget his name—a kinsman, I daresay, of Saint Denis; and he is so engrossed with the battle that he forgets his loss, and goes on fighting for some time.

"I hope it is not very wrong, and very stupid, but I am so tired of the *Gerusalemme Liberata*."

He looked at me for a moment or two. I think he did not comprehend the spirit in which I said all this, but perhaps he suspected something of it—he looked a little pained.

"But, I hope, you are not tired of Italian? There are other authors."

"Yes, so there are. I should like Ariosto, I daresay. I like fairy-tales, and that is the reason, I think, I like reading the lives of the saints, and the other books you have been so kind as to lend me."

I said this quite innocently, but there was a great deal of long-husbanded cruelty in it. He dropped his fine eyes to the table, and leaned for a short time on his hand.

"Well, even so, it is something gained to have read them," meditated Mr. Carmel, and looking up at me, he added, "and we never know by what childish instincts and simple paths we may be led to the sublimest elevations."

There was so much gentleness in his tone and looks that my heart smote me. My momentary compunction, however, did not prevent my going on, now that I had got fairly afloat.

"I have brought down the book you were so kind as to lend me last week. I am sure it is very eloquent, but there's so much I cannot understand."

"Can I explain anything?" he began, taking up the book at the same time.

"I did not mean that—no. I was going to return it, with my very best thanks," I said. "I have been reading a great deal that is too high for me—books meant for wiser people and deeper minds than mine."

"The mysteries of faith remain, for all varieties of mind, mysteries still," he answered sadly. "No human vision can pierce the veil. I do not flatter you, but I have met with no brighter intelligence than yours. In death the scales will fall from our eyes. Until then, yea must be yea, and nay, nay, and let us be patient."

"I don't know, Mr. Carmel, that I ought to read these books without papa's consent. I have imperceptibly glided into this kind of reading. 'I will tell you about Swedenborg,' you said; 'we must not talk of Rome or Luther—we can't agree, and they are forbidden subjects,' do you remember? And then you told me what an enemy Swedenborg was of the Catholic Church—you remember that? And then you read me what he said about vastation, as he calls it; and you lent me the book to read; and when you took it back, you explained to me that his account of vastation differs in no respect from purgatory; and in the same way, when I read the legends of the saints, you told me a great deal more of your doctrine; and in the same way, also, you discussed those beautiful old hymns, so that in a little while, although, as you said, Rome and Luther were forbidden subjects, or rather names, I found myself immersed in a controversy, which I did not understand, with a zealous and able priest. You have been artful, Mr. Carmel!"

"Have I been artful in trying to save you?" he answered gently.

"You would not, I think, practise the same arts with other people—you treat me like a fool," I said. "You would not treat that Welsh lady so, whom you visit—I mean—I really forget her name, but you remember all about her."

He rose unconsciously, and looked for a minute from the window.

"A good priest," he said, returning, "is no respecter of persons. Blessed should I be if I could beguile a benighted traveller into safety! Blessed and happy were my lot if I could die in the endeavour thus to save one human soul bent on self-destruction!"

His answer vexed me. The theological level on which he placed all human souls did not please me. After all our friendly evenings at Malory, I did not quite understand his being, as he seemed to boast, no "respecter of persons."

"I am sure that it is quite right," I said, carelessly, "and very prudent, too, because, if you were to lose your life in converting me, or a Hottentot chief, or anyone else, you would, you think, go straight to heaven; so, after all, the wish is not altogether too heroic for this selfish world."

He smiled; but there was doubt, I thought, in the eyes which he turned for a moment upon me.

"Our motives are so mixed," he said, "and death, besides, is to some men less than happier people think; my life has been austere and afflicted; and what remains of it will, I know, be darker. I see sometimes where all is drifting. I never was so happy, and I never shall be, as I have been for a time at Malory. I shall see that place perhaps no more. Happy the people whose annals are dull!" he smiled. "How few believe that well-worn saying in their own case! Yet, Miss Ethel, when you left Malory, you left quiet behind you, perhaps for ever!"

He was silent; I said nothing. The spirit of what he had said echoed, though he knew it not, the forebodings of my own heart. The late evening sun was touching with its slanting beams the houses opposite, and the cold grimy brick in which the dingy taste of our domestic architecture some forty years before delighted; and as I gazed listlessly from my chair, through the window, on the dismal formality of the street, I saw in the same sunlight nothing of those bricks and windows: I saw Malory and the church-tower, the trees, the glimmering blue of the estuary, the misty mountains, all fading in the dreamy quietude of the declining light, and I sighed.

"Well, then," he said, closing the book, "we close Tasso here. If you care to try Ariosto, I shall be only too happy. Shall we commence to-morrow? And as for our other books, those I mean that you were good enough to read——"

"I'm not afraid of them," I said: "we shan't break our old Malory custom yet; and I ought to be very grateful to you, Mr. Carmel."

His countenance brightened, but the unconscious reproach of his wounded look still haunted me. And after he was gone, with a confusion of feelings which I could not have easily analysed, I laid my hands over my eyes, and cried for some time bitterly.

CHAPTER XXIX.

MY BOUQUET.

I remember so vividly the night of my first ball. The excitement of the toilet; mamma's and the maid's consultations and debates; the tremulous anticipations; the "pleasing terror;" the delightful, anxious flutter, and my final look in the tall glass. I hardly knew myself. I gazed at myself with the irrepressible smile of elation. I never had looked so well. There are degrees of that delightful excitement that calls such tints to girlish cheeks, and such fires to the eyes, as visit them no more in our wiser after-life. The enchantment wanes, and the flowers and brilliants fade and we soon cease to see them. I went down to the drawing-room to wait for mamma. The candles were lighted, and whom should I find there but Mr. Carmel?

"I asked your mamma's leave to come and see you dressed for your first ball," he said. "How very pretty it all is!"

He surveyed me, smiling with a melancholy pride, it seemed to me, in my good looks and brilliant dress.

"No longer, and never more, the Miss Ethel of my quiet Malory recollections. Going out at last! If any one can survive the ordeal and come forth scathless, you, I think, will. But to me it seems that this is a farewell, and that my pupil dies tonight, and a new Miss Ethel returns. You cannot help it; all the world cannot prevent it, if so it is to be. As an old friend, I knew I might bring you these."

"Oh, Mr. Carmel, what beautiful flowers!" I exclaimed.

It was certainly an exquisite bouquet; one of those beautiful and costly offerings that perish in an hour, and seems to me like the pearl thrown into the cup of wine.

"I am so grateful. It was so kind of you. It is too splendid a great deal. It is quite impossible that there can be anything like it in the room."

I was really lost in wonder and admiration, and I suppose looked delighted. I was pleased that the flowers should have come from Mr. Carmel's hand.

"If you think that the flowers are worthy of you, you think more highly than I do of them," he answered, with a smile that was at once sad and pleased. "I am such an old friend, you know; a month at quiet Malory counts for a year anywhere else. And as you say of the flowers, I may say more justly of my pupil, there will be no one like her there. It is the compensation of being such as I, that we may speak frankly, like good old women, and no one be offended. And, oh, Miss Ethel, may God grant they be not placed like flowers upon a sacrifice or on the dead. Do not forget your better thoughts. You are entering scenes of illusion, where there is little charity, and almost no sincerity, where cruel feelings are instilled, the love of flattery and dominion awakened, and all the evil and enchantments of the world beset you. Encourage those good thoughts; watch and pray, or a painless and even pleasant death sets in, and no one can arrest it."

How my poor father would have laughed at such an exhortation at the threshold of a ball-room! No doubt it had its comic side, but not for me, and that was all Mr. Carmel cared for.

This was a ball at an official residence, and besides the usual muster, Cabinet and other Ministers would be there, and above all, that judicious rewarder of public virtue, and instructor of the conscience of the hustings, the patronage secretary of the Treasury. Papa had at last discovered a constituency which he thought promised success, he had made it a point, of course, to go to places where he had opportunities for a talk with that important personage. Papa was very sanguine, and now, as usual, whenever he had a project of that kind on hand, was in high spirits.

He came into the drawing-room. He always seemed to me as if he did not quite know whether he liked or disliked Mr. Carmel. Whenever I saw them together, he appeared to me, like Mrs. Malaprop, to begin with a little aversion, and gradually to become more and more genial. He greeted Mr. Carmel a little coldly, and brightened as he looked on me; he was evidently pleased with me, and talked me over with myself very good-humouredly. I took care to show him my flowers. He could not help admiring them.

"These are the best flowers I have seen anywhere. How did you contrive to get them? Really, Mr. Carmel, you are a great deal too kind. I hope Ethel thanked you. Ethel, you ought really to tell Mr. Carmel how very much obliged you are."

"Oh! she has thanked me a great deal too much; she has made me quite ashamed," said he.

And so we talked on, waiting for mamma, and I remember papa said he wondered how Mr. Carmel, who had lived in London and at Oxford, and at other places, where in one kind of life or another one really does live, contrived to exist month after month at Malory, and he drew an amusing and cruel picture of its barbarism and the nakedness of the town of Cardyllion. Mr. Carmel took up the cudgels for both, and I threw in a word wherever I had one to say. I remember this laughing debate, because it led to this little bit of dialogue.

"I fortunately never bought many things there—two brushes, I remember; all their hairs fell out, and they were bald before the combs they sent for to London arrived. If I had been dependent on the town of Cardyllion, I should have been reduced to a state of utter simplicity."

"Oh, but I assure you, papa, they have a great many very nice things at Jones's shop in Castle Street," I remonstrated.

"Certainly not for one's dressing room. There are tubs at the regattas, and sponges at their dinners, I daresay," papa began, in a punning vein.

"But you'll admit that London supplies no such cosmetics as Malory," said Mr. Carmel, with a kind glance at me.

"Well, you have me there, I admit," laughed papa, looking very pleasantly at me, who, no doubt, was at that moment the centre of many wild hopes of his.

Mamma came down now; there was no time to lose. My heart bounded, half with fear. Mr. Carmel came downstairs with us, and saw us into the carriage. He stood at the door-steps smiling, his short cloak wrapped about him, his hat in his hand. Now the horses made their clattering scramble forward; the carriage was in motion. Mr. Carmel's figure, in the attitude of his last look, receded; he was gone; it was like a farewell to Malory, and we were rolling on swiftly towards the ball-room, and a new life for me.

I am not going to describe this particular ball, nor my sensations on entering this new world, so artificial and astonishing. What an arduous life, with its stupendous excitement, fatigues, and publicity! There were in the new world on which I was entering, of course, personal affections and friendships, as among all other societies of human beings. But the canons on which it governs itself are, it seemed to me, inimical to both. The heart gives little, and requires little there. It assumes nothing deeper than relations of acquaintance; and there is no time to bestow on any other. It is the recognised business of every one to enjoy, and if people have pains or misfortunes they had best keep them to themselves, and smile. No one has a right to be ailing or unfortunate, much less to talk as if he were so, in that happy valley. Such people are "tainted wethers of the flock," and are bound to abolish themselves forthwith. No doubt kind things are done, and charitable, by people who live in it. But they are no more intended to see the light of that life than Mr. Snake's good-natured actions were. This dazzling microcosm, therefore, must not be expected to do that which it never undertook. Its exertions in pursuit of pleasure are enormous; its exhaustion prodigious; the necessary restorative cycle must not be interrupted by private agonies, small or great. If that were permitted, who could recruit for his daily task? I am relating, after an interval of very many years, the impressions of a person who, then very young, was a denizen of "the world" only for a short time; but the application of these principles of selfishness seemed to me sometimes ghastly.

One thing that struck me very much in a little time was that society, as it is termed, was so limited in numbers. You might go everywhere, it seemed to me, and see, as nearly as possible, the same people night after night. The same cards always, merely shuffled. This, considering the size and wealth of England and of London, did seem to me unaccountable.

My first season, like that of every girl who is admired and danced with a great deal, was glorified by illusions, chief among which was that the men who danced with me as they could every night did honestly adore me. We learn afterwards how much and how little those triumphs mean; that new faces are liked simply because they are new; and that girls are danced with because they are the fashion and dance well. I am not boasting—I was admired; and papa was in high good-humour and spirits. There is sunshine even in that region; like winter suns, bright but cold. Such as it is, let the birds of that enchanted forest enjoy it while it lasts; flutter their wings and sing in its sheen, for it may not be for long.

CHAPTER XXX.

THE KNIGHT OF THE BLACK CASTLE.

My readings with Mr. Carmel totally ceased; in fact, there was no time for any but that one worship which now absorbed me altogether. Every now and then, however, he was in London, and mamma, in the drawing-room, used at times to converse with him, in so low a tone, so earnestly and so long, that I used to half suspect her of making a shrift, and receiving a whispered absolution. Mamma, indeed, stood as it were with just one foot upon the very topmost point of our "high church," ready to spread her wings, and to float to the still more exalted level of the cross on the dome of St. Peter's. But she always hesitated when the moment for making the aërial ascent arrived, and was still trembling in her old attitude on her old pedestal.

I don't think mamma's theological vagaries troubled papa. Upon all such matters he talked like a good-natured Sadducee; and if religion could have been carried on without priests, I don't think he would have objected to any of its many forms.

Mamma had Mr. Carmel to luncheon often, during his stay in town. Whenever he could find an opportunity, he talked with me. He struggled hard to maintain his hold upon me. Mamma seemed pleased that he should; yet I don't think that she had made up her mind even upon my case. I daresay, had I then declared myself a "Catholic," she would have been in hysterics. Her own religious state, just then, I could not perfectly understand. I don't think she did. She was very uncomfortable about once a fortnight. Her tremors returned when a cold or any other accident had given her a dull day.

When the season was over, I went with papa and mamma to some country houses, and while they completed their circuit of visits Miss Pounden and I were despatched to Malory. The new world which had dazzled me for a time had not changed me. I had acquired a second self; but my old self was still living. It had not touched my heart, nor changed my simple tastes. I enjoyed the quiet of Malory, and its rural ways, and should have been as happy there as ever, if I could only have recovered the beloved companions whom I missed.

My loneliness was very agreeably relieved one day, as I was walking home from Penruthyn Priory, by meeting Mr. Carmel. He joined me, and we sauntered towards home in very friendly talk. He was to make a little stay at the steward's house. We agreed to read *I Promessi Sposi* together. Malory was recovering its old looks. I asked him all the news that he was likely to know and I cared to hear.

"Where was Lady Lorrimer?" I inquired.

Travelling, he told me, on the Continent, he could not say where. "We must not talk of her," he said, with a shrug and a laugh. "I think, Miss Ware, we were never so near quarrelling upon any subject as upon Lady Lorrimer, and I then resolved never again to approach that irritating topic."

So with common consent we talked of other things, among which I asked him:

"Do you remember Mr. Marston?"

"You mean the shipwrecked man who was quartered for some days at the steward's house?" he asked. "Yes—I remember him very well." He seemed to grow rather pale as he looked at me, and added, "Why do you ask?"

"Because," I answered, "you told me that he was in good society, and I have not seen him anywhere—not once."

"He was in society; but he's not in London, nor in England now, I believe. I once knew him pretty well, and I know only too much of him. I know him for a villain; and had he been still in England I should have warned you again, Miss Ethel, and warned your mamma, also, against permitting him to claim your acquaintance. But I don't think he will be seen again in this part of the world—not, at all events, until after the death of a person who is likely to live a long time."

"But what has he done?" I asked.

"I can't tell you—I can't tell you how cruelly he has wounded me," he answered. "I have told you in substance all I know, when I say he is a villain."

"I do believe, Mr. Carmel, your mission on earth is to mortify my curiosity. You won't tell me anything of any one I'm the least curious to hear about."

"He is a person I hate to talk of, or even to think of. He is a villain—he is incorrigible—and, happen what may, a villain, I think, he will be to the end."

I was obliged to be satisfied with this, for I had learned that it was a mere waste of time trying to extract from Mr. Carmel any secret which he chose to keep.

Here, then, in the old scenes, our quiet life began for awhile once more. I did not see more of Mr. Carmel now than formerly, and there continued the slightly altered tone, in talk and manner, which had secretly so sorely vexed me in town, and which at times I almost ascribed to my fancy.

Mr. Carmel's stay at Malory was desultory, too, as before; he was often absent for two or three days together. During one of these short absences, there occurred a very trifling incident, which, however, I must mention.

The castle of Cardyllion is a vast ruin, a military fortress of the feudal times, built on a great scale, and with prodigious strength. Its ponderous walls and towers are covered thick with ivy. It is so vast that the few visitors who are to be found there when the summer is over, hardly disquiet its wide solitudes and its silence. For a time I induced Miss Pounden to come down there nearly every afternoon, and we used to bring our novels, and she, sometimes her work; and we sat in the old castle, feeling, in the quiet autumn, as if we had it all to ourselves. The inner court is nearly two hundred feet square, and, ascending a circular stair in the angle next the great gate, you find yourself at the end of a very dark stone-floored corridor, running the entire length of the building. This long passage is lighted at intervals by narrow loop-holes placed at the left; and in the wall to the right, after having passed several doors, you come, about mid-way, to one admitting to the chapel. It is a small stone-floored chamber, with a lofty groined roof, very gracefully proportioned; a tall stone-shafted window admits a scanty light from the east, over the site of the dismantled altar; deep shadow prevails everywhere else in this pretty chapel, which is so dark in most parts that, in order to read or work, one must get directly under the streak of light that enters through the window, necessarily so narrow as not to compromise the jealous rules of mediæval fortification. A small arch, at each side of the door, opens a view of this chamber from two small rooms, or galleries, reached by steps from this corridor.

We had placed our camp-stools nearly under this window, and were both reading; when I raised my eyes they encountered those of a very remarkable-looking old man, whom I instantly recognised, with a start. It was the man whom we used, long ago, to call the Knight of the Black Castle. His well-formed, bronzed face and features were little changed, except for those lines that time deepens or produces. His dark, fierce eyes were not dimmed by the years that had passed, but his long black hair, which was uncovered, as tall men in those low passages were obliged to remove their hats, was streaked now with grey. This stern old man was gazing fixedly on me, from the arch beside the door, to my left, as I looked at him, and he did not remove his eyes as mine met his. Sullen, gloomy, stern was the face that remained inflexibly fixed in the deep shadow which enhanced its pallor. I turned with an effort to my companion, and said:

"Suppose we come out, and take a turn in the grounds."

To which, as indeed to everything I proposed, Miss Pounden assented.

I walked for a minute or two about the chapel before I stole a glance backward at the place where I had seen the apparition. He was gone. The arch, and the void space behind, were all that remained; there was nothing but deep shadow where that face had loomed. I asked Miss Pounden if she had seen the old man looking in; she had not.

Well, we left the chapel, and retraced our steps through the long corridor, I watching through the successive loop-holes for the figure of the old man pacing the grass beneath; but I did not see him. Down the stairs we came, I peeping into every narrow doorway we passed, and so out upon the grassy level of the inner court. I looked in all directions there, but nowhere could I see him. Under the arched gateway, where the portcullis used to clang, we passed into the outer court, and there I peeped about, also in vain.

I dare say Miss Pounden, if she could wonder at anything, wondered what I could be in pursuit of; but that most convenient of women never troubled me with a question.

Through the outer gate, in turn, we passed, and to Richard Pritchard's lodge, at the side of the gate admitting visitors from Castle Street to the castle grounds. Tall Richard Pritchard, with his thin stoop, his wide-awake hat, brown face, lantern jaws, and perpetual smirk, listened to my questions, and answered that he had let in such a gentleman, about ten minutes before, as I described. This gentleman had given his horse to hold to a donkey-boy outside the gate, and Richard Pritchard went on to say, with his usual volubility, and his curious interpolation of phrases of politeness, without the slightest regard to their connection with the context, but simply to heighten the amiability and polish of his discourse:

"And he asked a deal, miss, about the family down at Malory, I beg your pardon; and when he heard you were there, miss, he asked if you ever came down to the town—yes, indeed. So when I told him you were in the castle now—very well, I thank you, miss—he asked whereabout in the castle you were likely to be—yes, indeed, miss, very true—and he gave me a shilling—he did, indeed—and I showed him the way to the chapel—I beg your pardon, miss—where you very often go—very true indeed, miss; and so I left him at the top of the stairs. Ah, ha! yes, indeed, miss; and he came back just two or three minutes, and took his horse and rode down towards the water gate—very well, I thank you, miss."

This was the substance of Richard Pritchard's information. So, then, he had ridden down Castle Street and out of the town. It was odd his caring to have that look at me. What could he mean by it? His was a countenance ominous of nothing good. After so long an interval, it was not pleasant to see it again, especially associated with inquiries about Malory and its owners, and the sinister attraction which had drawn him to the chapel to gaze upon me, and, as I plainly perceived, by no means with eyes of liking. The years that had immediately followed his last visit, I knew had proved years of great loss and peril to papa. May heaven avert the omen! I silently prayed. I knew that old Rebecca Torkill could not help to identify, him, for I had been curious on the point before. She could not bring to her recollection the particular scene that had so fixed itself upon my memory; for, as she said, in those evil years there was hardly a day that did not bring down some bawling creditor from London to Malory in search of papa.

CHAPTER XXXI.

RUSTICATION.

Malory was not visited that year by either papa or mamma. I had been so accustomed to a lonely life there that my sojourn in that serene and beautiful spot never seemed solitary. Besides, town life would open again for me in the early spring. Had it not been for that near and exciting prospect, without Laura Grey, I might possibly have felt my solitude more; but the sure return to the whirl and music of the world made my rural weeks precious. They were to end earlier even than our return to town. I was written for, to Roydon, where mamma and papa then were making a short visit, and was deposited safely in that splendid but rather dull house by Miss Pounden, who sped forthwith to London, where I suppose she enjoyed her liberty her own quiet way.

I enjoyed very much our flitting from country-house to country-house, and the more familiar society of that kind of life. As these peregrinations and progresses, however, had no essential bearing upon my history, I shall mention them only to say this. At Roydon I met a person whom I very little expected to see there. The same person afterwards turned up at a very much pleasanter house—I mean Lady Mardykes's house at Carsbrook, where a really delightful party were assembled. Who do you think this person was? No titled person—not known to the readers of newspapers, except as a name mentioned now and then as forming a unit in a party at some distinguished house; no brilliant name in the lists of talent; a man apparently not worth propitiating on any score: and yet everywhere, and knowing everybody! Who, I say, do you suppose he was? Simply Doctor Droqville! In London I had seen him very often. He used to drop in at balls or garden-parties for an hour or two, and vanish. There was a certain decision, animation, and audacity in his talk, which seemed, although I did not like it, to please better judges very well. No one appeared to know much more about him than I did. Some people, I suppose, like mamma, did know quite enough; but by far the greater part took him for granted, and seeing that other people had him at their houses, did likewise.

Very agreeably the interval passed; and in due time we found ourselves once more in London.

My second season wanted something of the brilliant delirium of the first; and yet, I think I enjoyed it more. Papa was not in such spirits by any means. I dare say, as my second season drew near its close, he was disappointed that I was not already a peeress. But papa had other grounds for anxiety; and very anxious he began to look. It was quite settled now that at the next election he was to stand for the borough of Shillingsworth, with the support of the Government. Every one said he would do very well in the House; but that we ought to have begun earlier. Papa was full of it; but somehow not quite so sanguine and cheery as he used to be about his projects. I had seen ministers looking so haggard and overworked, and really suffering at times, that I began to think that politics were as fatiguing a pursuit almost as pleasure. The iron seemed to have entered into poor papa's soul already.

Although our breakfast hour was late, mamma was hardly ever down to it, and I not always. But one day when we did happen to be all three at breakfast together, he put down his newspaper with a rustle on his knee, and said to mamma, "I have been intending to ask you this long time, and I haven't had an opportunity—or at least it has gone out of my head when I might have asked; have you been writing lately to Lady Lorrimer?"

"Yes, I—at least, I heard from her, a little more than a week ago—a very kind letter—she wrote from Naples—she has been there for the winter."

"And quite well?"

"Complaining a little, as usual; but I suppose she is really quite well."

"I wish she did not hate me quite so much as she does," said papa. "I'd write to her myself—I dare say you haven't answered her letter?"

"Well, really, you know, just now it is not easy to find time," mamma began.

"Oh! hang it, time! Why, you forget you have really nothing to do," answered papa, more tartly than I had ever heard him speak to mamma before. "You don't answer her letters, I think; at least not for months after you get them! I don't wish you to flatter her—I wish that as little as you do—but I think you might be civil—where's the good of irritating her?"

"I never said I saw any," answered mamma, a little high.

"No; but I see the mischief of it," he continued; "it's utter folly—and it's not right, besides. You'll just lose her, that'll be the end of it—she is the only one of your relations who really cares anything about you—and she intends making Ethel a present—diamonds—it is just, I do believe, that she wishes to show what she intends further. You are the person she would naturally like to succeed her in anything she has to leave; and you take such a time about answering her letters, you seem to wish to vex her. You'll succeed at last—and, I can tell you, you can't afford to throw away friendship just now. I shall want every friend, I mean every real friend, I can count upon. More than you think depends on this affair. If I'm returned for Shillingsworth, I'm quite certain I shall get something very soon—and if I once get it, depend upon it, I shall get on. Some people would say I'm a fool for my pains, but it is money very well spent—it is the only money, I really think, I ever laid out wisely in my life, and it is a very serious matter our succeeding in this. Did not your aunt Lorrimer say that she thought she would be at Golden Friars again this year?"

"Yes, I think so; why?" said mamma, listlessly.

"Because she must have some influence over that beast Rokestone—I often wonder what devil has got hold of my affairs, or how Rokestone happens to meet me at so many points—and if she would talk to him a little, she might prevent his doing me a very serious mischief. She is sure to see him when she goes down there."

"He's not there often, you know; I can always find a time to go to Golden Friars without a chance of seeing him. I shall never see him again, I hope." I thought mamma sighed a little, as she said this. "But I'll write and ask Lady Lorrimer to say whatever you wish to him, when her visit to Golden Friars is quite decided on."

So the conversation ended, and upon that theme was not resumed, at least within my hearing, during the remainder of our stay in town.

My journal, which I kept pretty punctually during that season, lies open on the table before me. I have been aiding my memory with it. It has, however, helped me to nothing that bears upon my story. It is a register, for the most part, of routine. Now we lunched with Lady This—now we went to the Duchess of So-and-so's garden-party—every night either a ball, or a musical party, or the opera. Sometimes I was asked out to dinner, sometimes we went to the play. Ink and leaves are discoloured by time. The score years and more that have passed, have transformed this record of frivolity into a solemn and melancholy Mentor. So many of the names that figure there have since been carved on tombstones! Among those that live still, and hold their heads up, there is change everywhere—some for better, some for worse; and yet riven, shattered, scattered, as this muster-roll is, with perfect continuity and solidity, that smiling Sadduceeic world without a home, the community that lives out of doors, and accepts, as it seems to me, satire and pleasure in lieu of the affections, lives and works on upon its old principles and aliment; diamonds do not fail, nor liveries, nor high-bred horses, nor pretty faces, nor witty men, nor chaperons, nor fools, nor rascals.

I must tell you, however, what does not distinctly appear in this diary. Among the many so-called admirers who asked for dances in the ball-room, were two who appeared to like me with a deeper feeling than the others. One was handsome Colonel Saint-George Dacre, with an estate of thirty thousand a year, as my friends told mamma, who duly conveyed the fact to me. But young ladies, newly come out and very much danced with, are fastidious, and I was hard to please. My heart was not pre-occupied, but even in my lonely life I had seen men who interested me more. I liked my present life and freedom too well, and shrank from the idea of being married. The other was Sir Henry Park, also rich, but older. Papa, I think, looked even higher for me, and fancied that I might possibly marry so as to make political connection for him. He did not, therefore, argue the question with me; but overrating me more than I did myself, thought he was quite safe in leaving me free to do as I pleased.

These gentlemen, therefore, were, with the most polite tenderness for their feelings, dismissed—one at Brighton, in August; the other, a little later, at Carsbrook, where he chose to speak. I have mentioned these little affairs in the order in which they occurred, as I might have to allude to them in the pages that follow.

Every one has, once or twice, in his or her life, I suppose, commenced a diary which was to have been prosecuted as diligently and perseveringly as that of Samuel Pepys. I did, I know, oftener than I could now tell you; I have just mentioned one of mine, and from this fragmentary note-book I give you the following extracts, which happen to help my narrative at this particular point.

"At length, thank Heaven! news of darling Laura Grey. I can hardly believe that I am to see her so soon. I wonder whether I shall be able, a year hence, to recall the delight of this expected moment. It is true, there is a great deal to qualify my happiness, for her language is ominous. Still it will be delightful to meet her, and hear her adventures, and have one of our good long talks together, such as made Malory so happy.

"I was in mamma's room about half-an-hour ago; she was fidgeting about in her dressing-gown and slippers, and had just sat down before her dressing-table, when Wentworth (her maid) came in with letters by the early post. Mamma has as few secrets, I think, as most people, and her correspondence is generally very uninteresting. Whenever I care to read them, she allows me to amuse myself with her letters when she has opened and read them herself. I was in no mood to do so to-day; but I fancied I saw a slight but distinct change in her careless looks as she peeped into one. She read it a second time, and handed it to me. It is, indeed, from Laura Grey! It says that she is in great affliction, and that she will call at our town house 'to-morrow,' that is to-day, 'Thursday,' at one o'clock, to try whether mamma would consent to see her.

"'I think that very cool. I don't object to seeing her, however,' said mamma; 'but she shall know what I think of her.'

"I don't like the idea of such an opening as mamma would make. I must try to see Laura before she meets her. She must have wonders to tell me; it cannot have been a trifling thing that made her use me, apparently, so unkindly.

"Thursday—half-past one. No sign of Laura yet.

"Thursday—six o'clock. She has not appeared! What am I to think?

"Her letter is written, as it seems to me, in the hurry of agitation. I can't understand what all this means.

"Thursday night—eleven o'clock. Before going to bed. Laura has not appeared. No note. Mamma more vexed than I have often seen her. I fancy she had a hope of getting her back again, as I know I had.

"Friday. I waked in the dark, early this morning, thinking of Laura, and fancying every horrible thing that could have befallen her since her note of yesterday morning was written.

"Went to mamma, who had her breakfast in her bed, and told her how miserable I was about Laura Grey. She said, 'There is nothing the matter with Miss Grey, except that she does not know how to behave herself.' I don't agree with mamma, and I am sure that she does not really think any such thing of Laura Grey. I am still very uneasy about her; there is no address to her note.

"I have just been again with mamma, to try whether she can recollect anything by which we could find her out. She says she can remember no circumstance by which we can trace her. Mamma says she had been trying to find a governess at some of the places where lists of ladies seeking such employment are kept, but without finding one who exactly answered; papa had then seen an advertisement in the *Times*, which seemed to promise satisfactorily, and Miss Grey answered mamma's note, and referred to a lady, who immediately called on her; mamma could only recollect that she knew this lady's name, that she had heard of her before, and that she spoke with the greatest affection of Miss Grey, and shed tears while she lamented her determination to seek employment as a governess, instead of living at home with her. The lady had come in a carriage, with servants, and had all the appearance of being rich, and spoke of Laura as her cousin. But neither her name nor address could mamma recollect, and there remained no clue by which to trace her. It was some comfort to think that the lady who claimed her as a kinswoman, and spoke of her with so much affection, was wealthy, and anxious to take her to her own home; but circumstances are always mutable, and life transitory—how can we tell where that lady is now?"

"I have still one hope—Laura may have written one o'clock 'Thursday,' and meant Friday. It is only a chance—still I cling to it.

"Friday—three o'clock. Laura has not appeared. What are we to think? I can't get it out of my head that something very bad has happened. My poor Laura!

"Saturday night—a quarter to eleven. Going to bed. Another day, and no tidings of Laura. I have quite given up the hope of seeing her."

She did not come next day. On the subject on which mamma felt so sharply, she had not an opportunity of giving her a piece of her mind then, or the next day.

So the season being over, behold us again in the country!

After our visit to Carsbrook, mamma and papa were going to Haitly Abbey. For some reason, possibly the very simple one that I had been forgotten in the invitation, I was not to accompany them; I was despatched in charge of old Lady Hester Wigmore, who was going that way, to Chester, where Miss Pounden took me up; and with her, "to my great content," as old Samuel Pepys says, I went to Malory, which I always re-visited with an unutterable affection, as my only true home.

Nothing happened during my stay at Malory, which was unexpectedly interrupted by a note from mamma appointing to meet me at Chester. Papa had been obliged to go to town to consult with some friends, and he was then to go down to Shillingsworth to speak at a public dinner. She and I were going northward. She would tell me all when we met. I need not bring any of my finery with me.

With this scanty information, and some curiosity as to our destination in the North, I arrived at Chester, and there met mamma, from whom I soon learned that our excursion was to lead us into wild and beautiful scenery quite new to me.

CHAPTER XXXII.

AT THE GEORGE AND DRAGON.

We had to wait for a long time at some station, I forget its name. The sun set, and night overtook us before we reached the end of our journey by rail. We had then to drive about twelve miles. The road, for many miles, lay through a desolate black moss. I could not have believed there was anything so savage in England. A thin mist was stretched like a veil over the more distant level of the dark expanse, on which, here and there, a wide pool gleamed faintly under the moonlight. To the right there rose a grand mass of mountain. We were soon driving through a sort of gorge, and found ourselves fenced in by the steep sides of gigantic mountains, as we followed a road that wound and ascended among them. I shall never forget the beautiful effect of the scene suddenly presented, and for the first time, as the road reached its highest elevation, and I saw, with the dark receding sides of the mountain we had been penetrating for a proscenium, my first view of Golden Friars. Oh! how beautiful!

Surrounded by an amphitheatre of Alpine fells, the broad mere of Golden Friars glimmered cold under the moonlight, and the quaint little town of steep gables, built of light grey stone, rose from its grassy margin surrounded by elms, single or in clumps, that looked almost black in contrast with the gleaming lake and the white masonry of the town. It looked like enchanted ground. A silvery hoar-frost seemed to cover the whole scene, giving it a filmy and half-visionary character that enhanced its beauty. I was exclaiming in wonder and delight as every minute some new beauty unfolded itself to view. Mamma was silent, as she looked from the window; I saw that she cried gently, thinking herself unobserved. A beautiful scene, where childish days were passed, awakes so many sweet and bitter fancies! The yearnings for the irrevocable, the heartache of the memory, opened the fountains of her tears; and I was careful not to interrupt her lonely thoughts. I left her to the enjoyment of that melancholy luxury, and gazed on in strange delight.

Here, then, was the dwelling-place of that redoubted enemy of our house whom fate seemed to have ordained as our persecutor. Here lived the old enchanter whose malign spells were woven about us, in busy London and quiet

Malory, or the distant scenes of France and Italy. Even this thought added interest to the romantic scene.

We had now descended to the level of the shore of the lake, along whose margin our road swept in a gentle curve. The fells from this level rose stupendous, all around, striking their silvery peaks into the misty moonlight, and looking so aërial that one might fancy a stone thrown would pass through their sides as if they were vapour. Now we passed under the shadow of the first clump of mighty elms; and now the white fronts and chimneys of the village houses rose in the foreground. There was no sign of life but the barking of the watch-dogs, and the cackling of the vigilant geese, and the light that glanced from the hall of the "George and Dragon," the substantial old inn that, looking across the road, faces the lake and distant fells. At the door of this ancient and comfortable inn drew up our chaise and four horses, no mere ostentation, but a simple necessity, where carriage and luggage were pulled, towards the close of so long a stage, over the steeps where the road pushes its way high among the fells.

So our journey was over; and we stood in the hall. Before we went up to our rooms mamma inquired whether Lady Lorrimer had arrived. Yes, her ladyship had been there since the day before yesterday. Mamma seemed nervous and uncomfortable. She sent down her maid to find out whether Sir Harry Rokestone was in the country; and when the servant returned and told her that he was not expected to arrive at Dorracleugh before a fortnight, she sighed, and I heard her say faintly, "Thank God!"

I confess it was rather a disappointment than a relief to me. I rather wished to see this truculent old wizard. After a sound sleep, which we both needed, I got up and had a little peep at that beautiful place, in the early sunlight, before breakfast. Lady Lorrimer's maid came with inquiries from her mistress, for mamma and me. Her ladyship was not very well, and could not see us till about twelve. She was so vexed at having to put us off, and hoped we were not tired; and also that we would take our dinner with her. To this mamma agreed.

I was curious to see Lady Lorrimer once more. My ideas had grown obscure, and my theory of that kinswoman had been disagreeably disturbed, ever since the evening on which she, or her double, had passed by me so resolutely in the street.

Having heard that she was quite ready to see us, we paid our visit. I wondered how she would receive me, and my suspense amounted almost to excitement as I reached the door. A moment more, and I could not believe that Lady Lorrimer and the woman who so resembled her were the same. Nothing could be more affectionate than Lady Lorrimer. She received us with a very real welcome, and so much pleasure in her looks, tones, and words. She was not, indeed, looking well, but her spirits seemed cheerful. She embraced mamma, and kissed her very fondly; then she kissed me over and over again. I was utterly puzzled, and more than doubted the identity of this warm-hearted, affectionate woman with the person who had chosen to cut me with such offensive and sinister persistence.

"See how this pretty creature looks at me!" she said to mamma, laughing, as she detected my conscious scrutiny.

I blushed and looked down; I did not know what to say.

"I'm very much obliged to you, dear, for looking at me, so few people do now-a-days; and I was just going to steal a good look at you, when I found I was anticipated. I have just been saying to your mamma that I have ordered a boat, and we must all have a sail together on the lake after dinner; what do you say?"

Of course I was delighted; I thought the place perfectly charming.

"I lived the earlier part of my life here," she resumed, "and so did your mamma, you know—when she was a little girl, and until she came to be nineteen or twenty—I forget which you were, dear, when you were married?" she said, turning to mamma.

"Twenty-two," said mamma, smiling.

"Twenty-two? Really! Well, we lived at Mardykes. I'll point out the place on the water when we take our sail; you can't see it from these windows."

"And where does Sir Harry Rokestone live?" I asked.

"You can't see that either from these windows. It is further than Mardykes, at the same side. But we shall see it from the boat."

Then she and mamma began to talk, and I went to the window and looked out.

Lady Lorrimer, with all her airs of conventual seclusion, hungered and thirsted after gossip; and whenever they met, she learned all the stories from mamma, and gave her, in return, old scandal and ridiculous anecdotes about the predecessors of the people with whose sayings, doings, and mishaps mamma amused her.

Two o'clock dinners, instead of luncheons, were the rule in this part of the world. And people turned tea into a very substantial supper, and were all in bed and asleep before the hour arrived at which the London ladies and gentlemen are beginning to dress for a ball.

You are now to suppose us, on a sunny evening, on board the boat that had been moored for some time at the jetty opposite the door of the "George and Dragon." We were standing up the lake, and away from the Golden Friars shore, towards a distant wood, which they told me was the forest of Clusted.

"Look at that forest, Ethel," said Lady Lorrimer. "It is the haunted forest of Clusted—the last resort of the fairies in England. It was there, they say, that Sir Bale Mardykes, long ago, made a compact with the Evil One."

Through the openings of its magnificent trees, as we nearer, from time to time, the ivied ruins of an old manor-house were visible. In this beautiful and, in spite of the monotony of the gigantic fells that surround the lake, ever-varying scenery, my companions gradually grew silent for a time; even I felt the dreamy influence of the scene, and liked the listless silence, in which nothing was heard but the rush of the waters, and the flap of the sail now and then. I was living in a world of fancy: they in a sadder one of memory.

In a little while, in gentle tones, they were exchanging old remembrances; a few words now and then sufficed; the affecting associations of scenes of early life re-visited were crowding up everywhere. As happens to some people when death is near, a change, that seemed to be quite beautiful, came over mamma's mind in the air and lights of this beautiful place! How I wished that she could remain always as she was now!

With the old recollections seemed to return the simple rural spirit of the early life. What is the town life, of which I had tasted, compared with this? How much simpler, tenderer, sublimer, this is! How immensely nearer heaven! The breeze was light, and the signs of the sky assured the boatmen that we need fear none of those gusts and squalls that sometimes burst so furiously down through the cloughs and hollows of the surrounding mountains. I, with the nautical knowledge acquired at Malory, took the tiller, under direction of the boatmen. We had a good deal of tacking to get near enough to the shore at Clusted to command a good view of that fine piece of forest. We then sailed northward, along the margin of the "mere," as they call the lake; and, when we had gone in that direction for a mile or more, turned the boat's head across the water, and ran before the breeze towards the Mardykes side. There is a small island near the other side, with a streak of grey rock and bushes nearly surrounding what looked like a ruined chapel or hermitage, and Lady Lorrimer told me to pass this as nearly as I could.

The glow of evening was by this time in the western sky. The sun was hidden behind the fells that form a noble barrier between Golden Friars and the distant moss of Dardale, where stands Haworth Hall. In deepest purple shadow the mountains here closely overhang the lake. Under these, along the margin, Lady Lorrimer told me to steer.

We were gliding slowly along, so that there was ample leisure to note every tree and rock upon the shore as we passed. As we drifted, rather than sailed, along the shore, there suddenly opened from the margin a narrow valley, reaching about a quarter of a mile. It was a sudden dip in the mountains that here rise nearly from the edge of the lake. Steep-sided and wild was this hollow, and backed by a mountain that, to me, looking up from the level of the lake, appeared stupendous.

The valley lay flat in one unbroken field of short grass. A broad-fronted, feudal tower, with a few more modern buildings about it, stood far back, fronting the river. A rude stone pier afforded shelter to a couple of boats, and a double line of immense lime-trees receded from that point about half-way up to the tower. Whether it was altogether due to the peculiar conformation of the scene, or that it owed its character in large measure to its being enveloped in the deep purple shadow cast by the surrounding mountain, and the strange effect of the glow reflected downward from the evening clouds, which touched the summits of the trees, and the edges of the old tower, like the light of a distant conflagration, I cannot say; but never did I see a spot with so awful a character of solitude and melancholy.

In the gloom we could see a man standing alone on the extremity of the stone pier, looking over the lake. This figure was the only living thing we could discover there.

"Well, dear, now you see it. That's Dorracleugh—that's Harry Rokestone's place," said Lady Lorrimer.

"What a spot! Fit only for a bear or an anchorite. Do you know," she added, turning to mamma, "he is there a great deal more than he used to be, they tell me. I know if I were to live in that place for six months I should never come out of it a sane woman. To do him justice, he does not stay very long here when he does come, and for years he never came at all. He has other places, far away from this; and if a certain event had happened about two-and-twenty years ago," she added, for my behalf, "he intended building quite a regal house a little higher up, on a site that is really enchanting, but your mamma would not allow him; and so, and so——" Lady Lorrimer had turned her glasses during her sentence upon the figure which stood motionless on the end of the pier; and she said, forgetting what she had been telling me, "I really think—I'm nearly certain—that man standing there is Harry Rokestone!"

Mamma started. I looked with all my eyes; little more than a hundred yards interposed, but the shadow was so intense, and the effect of the faint reflected light so odd and puzzling, that I could be certain of nothing, but that the man stood very erect, and was tall and powerfully built. Lady Lorrimer was too much absorbed in her inspection to offer me her glasses, which I was longing to borrow, but for which I could not well ask, and so we sailed slowly by, and the hill that flanked the valley gradually glided between us and the pier, and the figure disappeared from view. Lady Lorrimer, lowering her glasses, said:

"I can't say positively, but I'm very nearly certain it was he."

Mamma said nothing, but was looking pale, and during the rest of our sail seemed absent and uncomfortable, if not unhappy.

CHAPTER XXXIII.

NOTICE TO QUIT.

We drank tea with Lady Lorrimer. Mamma continued very silent, and I think she had been crying in her room.

"They can't tell me here whether Harry has arrived or not," said Lady Lorrimer. "He might have returned by the Dardale Road, and if so, he would not have passed through Golden Friars, so it is doubtful. But I'm pretty sure that was he."

"I wish I were sure of that," said mamma.

"Well, I don't know," said Lady Lorrimer, "what to advise. I was just going to say it might be a wise thing if you were to make up your mind to see him, and to beard the lion in his den."

"No," said mamma; "if you mean to meet him and speak to him, I could not do that. I shall never see him again—nothing but pain could come of it; and he would not see me, and he ought not to see me; and he ought not to forgive me—never!"

"Well, dear, I can't deny it, you did use him very ill. And he is, and always was, a fierce and implacable enemy," answered Lady Lorrimer. "I fancied, perhaps, if he did see you, the old chord might be touched again, and yield something of its old tone on an ear saddened by time. But I daresay you are right. It was a Quixotic inspiration, and might have led to disaster; more probably, indeed, than to victory."

"I am quite sure of that—in fact, I know it," said mamma.

And there followed a silence.

"I sometimes think, Mabel—I was thinking so all this evening," said Lady Lorrimer, "it might have been happier for us if we had never left this lonely place. We might have been happier if we had been born under harder conditions; the power of doing what pleases us best leads us so often into sorrow."

Another silence followed. Mamma was looking over her shoulder, sadly, through the window at the familiar view of lake and mountain, indolently listening.

"I regret it, and I don't regret it," continued Lady Lorrimer. "If I could go back again into my early self—I wish I could—but the artificial life so perverts and enervates one, I hardly know, honestly, what I wish. I only know there is regret enough to make me discontented, and I think I should have been a great deal happier if I had been compelled to stay at Golden Friars, and had never passed beyond the mountains that surround us here. I have not so long as you to live, Mabel, and I'm glad of it. I am not quite so much of a Sadducee as you used to think me, and I hope there may be a happier world for us all. And, now that I have ended my homminy, as they call such long speeches in this country, will you, dear Ethel, give me a cup of tea?"

Lady Lorrimer and I talked. I was curious about some of the places and ruins I had seen, and asked questions, which it seemed to delight her to answer. It is a region abounding in stories strange and marvellous, family traditions, and legends of every kind.

"I think," said mamma, *à propos des bottes*, "if he has returned they are sure to know in the town before ten to-night. Would you mind asking again by-and-by?"

"You mean about Harry Rokestone?"

"Yes."

"I will. I'll make out all about him. We saw his castle to-day," she continued, turning to me. "Our not knowing whether he was there or not made it a very interesting contemplation. You remember the short speech Sheridan wrote to introduce Kelly's song at Drury Lane—'There stands my Matilda's cottage! She must be in it, or else out of it?'"

Again mamma dropped out, and the conversation was maintained by Lady Lorrimer and myself. In a little while mamma took her leave, complaining of a headache; and our kinswoman begged that I would remain for an hour or so, to keep her company. When mamma had bid her good night, and was gone, the door being shut, Lady Lorrimer laughed, and said:

"Now, tell me truly, don't you think if your papa had been with us to-day in the boat, and seen the change that took place in your mamma's looks and spirits from the moment she saw Dorracleugh, and the tall man who stood on the rock, down to the hour of her headache and early good night, he would have been a little jealous?"

I did not quite know whether she was joking or serious, and I fancy there was some puzzle in my face as I answered:

"But it can't be that she liked Sir Harry Rokestone; she is awfully afraid of him—that is the reason, I'm sure, she was so put out. She never liked him."

"Don't be too sure of that, little woman," she answered, gaily.

"Do you really think mamma liked him? Why, she was in love with papa."

"No, it was nothing so deep," said Lady Lorrimer; "she did not love your papa. It was a violent whim, and if she had been left just five weeks to think, she would have returned to Rokestone."

"But there can be no sentiment remaining still," I remarked. "Sir Harry Rokestone is an old man!"

"Yes, he is an old man; he is—let me see—he's fifty-six. And she did choose to marry your papa. But I'm sure she thinks she made a great mistake. I am very sure she thinks that, with all his faults, Rokestone was the more loveable man, the better man, the truer. He would have taken good care of her. I don't know of any one point in which he was your papa's inferior, and there are fifty in which he was immeasurably his superior. He was a handsomer man, if that is worth anything. I think I never saw so handsome a man, in his peculiar style. You think me a very odd old woman to tell you my opinion of your father so frankly; but I am speaking as your mamma's friend and kinswoman, and I say your papa has not used her well. He is good-humoured, and has good spirits, and he has some good-nature, quite subordinated to his selfishness. And those qualities, so far as I know, complete the muster-roll of his virtues. But he has made her, in no respect, a good husband. In some a very bad one. And he employs half-a-dozen attorneys, to whom he commits his business at random; and he is too indolent to look after anything. Of course he's robbed, and everything at sixes and sevens; and he has got your mamma to take legal steps to make away with her money for his own purposes; and the foolish child, the merest simpleton in money matters, does everything he bids her; and I really believe she has left herself without a guinea. I don't like him—no one could who likes *her*. Poor, dear Mabel, she wants energy; I never knew a woman with so little will. She never showed any but once, and that was when she did a foolish thing, and married your father."

"And did Sir Harry Rokestone like mamma very much?" I asked.

"He was madly in love with her, and when she married your papa, he wanted to shoot him. I think he was, without any metaphor, very nearly out of his mind. He has been a sort of anchorite ever since. His money is of no use to him. He is a bitter and eccentric old man."

"And he can injure papa now?"

"So I'm told. Your papa thinks so; and he seldom takes the trouble to be alarmed about danger three or four months distant."

Then, to my disappointment and, also, my relief, that subject dropped. It had interested and pained me; and sometimes I felt that it was scarcely right that I should hear all she was saying, without taking up the cudgels for papa. Now, with great animation, she told me her recollections of her girlish days here at Golden Friars, when the old gentry were such bores and humorists as are no longer to be met with anywhere. And as she made me laugh at these recitals, her maid, whom she had sent down to "the bar" to make an inquiry, returned, and told her something in an undertone. As soon as she was gone, Lady Lorrimer said:

"Yes, it is quite true. Tell your mamma that Harry Rokestone is at Dorracleugh."

She became thoughtful. Perhaps she was rehearsing mentally the mediatory conference she had undertaken.

We had not much more conversation that night; and we soon parted with a very affectionate good-night. My room adjoined mamma's, and finding that she was not yet asleep, I went in and gave her Lady Lorrimer's message. Mamma changed colour, and raised herself suddenly on her elbow, looking in my face.

"Very well, dear," said she, a little flurried. "We must leave this to-morrow morning."

CHAPTER XXXIV.

SIR HARRY'S ANSWER.

A bout eleven o'clock next morning our chaise was at the door of the "George and Dragon." We had been waiting with our bonnets on to say good-bye to Lady Lorrimer. I have seen two or three places in my life to which my affections were drawn at first sight, and this was one of them. I was standing at the window, looking my last at this beautiful scene. Mamma was restless and impatient. I knew she was uneasy lest some accident should bring Sir Harry Rokestone to the door before we had set out upon our journey.

At length Lady Lorrimer's foreign maid came to tell us that milady wished to see us now. Accordingly we followed the maid, who softly announced us.

The room was darkened; only one gleam, through a little opening in the far shutter, touched the curtains of her bed, showing the old-fashioned chintz pattern, like a transparency, through the faded lining. She was no longer the gay Lady Lorrimer of the evening before. She was sitting up among her pillows, nearly in the dark, and the most melancholy, whimpering voice you can imagine came through the gloom from among the curtains.

"Is my sweet Ethel there, also?" she asked when she had kissed mamma. "Oh, that's right; I should not have been happy if I had not bid you good-bye. Give me your hand, darling. And so you are going, Mabel? I'm sorry you go so soon, but perhaps you are right—I think you are. It would not do, perhaps, to meet. I'll do what I can, and write to tell you how I succeed."

Mamma thanked and kissed her again.

"I'm not so well as people think, dear, nor as I wish to think myself. We may not meet for a long time, and I wish to tell you, Mabel—I wish to tell you both—that I won't leave you dependent on that reckless creature, Francis Ware. I want you two to be safe. I have none but you left me to love on earth." Here poor Lady Lorrimer began to cry. "Whenever I write to you, you must come to me; don't let anything prevent you. I am so weak. I want to leave you both very well, and I intend to put it out of my power to change it—who's that at the door? Just open it, Ethel, dear child, and see if any one is there—my maid, I mean—you can say you dropped your handkerchief—hush!"

There was no one in the lobby.

"Shut it quietly, dear; I'll do what I say—don't thank me—don't say a word about it to any one, and if you mention it to Francis Ware, charge him to tell no one else. There, dears, both, don't stay longer. God bless you! Go, go; God bless you!"

And with these words, having kissed us both very fondly, she dismissed us.

Mamma ran down, and out to the carriage very quickly, and sat back as far as she could at the far side. I followed, and all being ready, in a minute more we were driving swiftly from the "George and Dragon," and soon town, lake, forest, and distant fells were hidden from view by the precipitous sides of the savage gorge, through which the road winds its upward way.

Our drive into Golden Friars had been a silent one, and so was our drive from it, though from different causes. I was thinking over our odd interview with poor Lady Lorrimer. In what a low, nervous state she seemed, and how affectionately she spoke! I had no inquisitive tendencies, and I was just at the age when people take the future for granted. No sordid speculations therefore, I can honestly say, were busy with my brain.

We were to have stayed at least ten days at Golden Friars, and here we were flying from it before two days were spent. All our plans were upset by the blight of Sir Harry Rokestone's arrival at least a fortnight before the date of his usual visit, just as Napoleon's Russian calculations were spoilt by the famous early winter of 1812. I was vexed in my way. I should not have been sorry to hear that he had been well ducked in the lake. Mamma was vexed in her own way, also, when, about an hour after, she escaped from the thoughts that agitated her at first, and descended to her ordinary level. A gap of more than a week was made in her series of visits. What was to be done with it?

"Where are you going, mamma?" I asked, innocently enough.

"Nowhere—everywhere. To Chester," she answered, presently.

"And where then?" I asked.

"Why do you ask questions that I can't answer? Why should you like to make me more miserable than I am? Everything is thrown into confusion. I'm sure I don't know the least. I have no plans. I literally don't know where we are to lay our heads to-night. There's no one to take care of us. As usual, whenever I want assistance, there's none to be had, and my maid is so utterly helpless, and your papa in town. I only know that I'm not strong enough for this kind of thing; you can write to your papa when we come to Chester. We shan't see him for Heaven knows how long—he may have left London by this time; and he'll write to Golden Friars—and now that I think of it—oh! how am I to live through all this!—I forgot to tell the people there where to send our letters. Oh! dear, oh! dear, it is such a muddle! And I could not have told them, literally, for I don't know where we are going. We had better just stay at Chester till he comes, whenever that may be; and I really could just lie down and cry."

I was glad we were to ourselves, for mamma's looks and tones were so utterly despairing that in a railway carriage we should have made quite an excitement. In such matters mamma was very easy to persuade by any one who would take the trouble of thinking on himself, and she consented to come to Malory instead; and there, accordingly, we arrived next day, much to the surprise of Rebecca Torkill, who received us with a very glad welcome, solemnized a little by a housekeeper's responsibilities.

Mamma enjoyed her simple life here wonderfully—more, a great deal, than I had ventured to hope. She seemed to me naturally made for a rural life, though fate had consigned her to a town one. She reminded me of the German prince mentioned in Tom Moore's journal, who had a great taste for navigation, but whose principality unfortunately was inland.

Papa did not arrive until the day before that fixed for his and mamma's visit to Dromelton. He was in high spirits, everything was doing well; his canvass was prospering, and now Lady Lorrimer's conversation at parting, as reported by mamma, lighted up the uncertain future with a steady glory, and set his sanguine spirit in a blaze. Attorneys, foreclosures, bills of exchange hovering threateningly in the air, and biding their brief time to pounce upon him, all lost their horrors, for a little, in the exhilarating news.

Mamma had been expecting a letter from Lady Lorrimer—one, at length, arrived this morning. Papa had walked round by the mill-road to visit old Captain Etheridge. Mamma and I were in the drawing-room as she read it. It was a long one. She looked gloomy, and said, when she had come to the end:

"I was right—it was not worth trying. I'm afraid this will vex your papa. You may read it. You heard Aunt Lorrimer talk about it. Yes, I was right. She was a great deal too sanguine."

I read as follows:—

> "My Dearest Mabel,—I have a disagreeable letter to write. You desired me to relate with rigour every savage thing he said—I mean Harry Rokestone, of course—and I must keep my promise, although I think you will hate me for it. I had almost given him up, and thinking that for some reason he was resolved to forget his usual visit to me, and I being equally determined to make him see me, was this morning thinking of writing him a little cousinly note, to say that I was going to see him in his melancholy castle. But to-day, at about one, there came on one of those fine thunder-storms among the fells that you used to admire so much. It grew awfully dark—portentous omen!—and some enormous drops of rain, as big as bullets, came smacking down upon the window-stone. Perhaps these drove him in; for in he came, announced by the waiter, exactly as a very much nearer clap of thunder startled all the echoes of Golden Friars into a hundred reverberations; a finer heralding, and much more characteristic of the scene and man than that flourish of trumpets to which kings always enter in Shakespeare. In he came, my dear Mabel, looking so king-like, and as tall as the Catstean on Dardale Moss, and gloomy as the sky. He is as like Allan Macaulay, in the 'Legend of

Montrose,' as ever. A huge dog, one of that grand sort you remember long ago at Dorracleugh, came striding in beside him. He used to smile long ago. But it is many years, you know, since fortune killed that smile; and he took my poor thin fingers in his colossal hand, with what Clarendon calls a 'glooming' countenance. We talked for some time as well as the thunder and the clatter of the rain, mixed with hail, would let us.

"By the time its violence was a little abated, I, being as you know, not a bad diplomatist, managed, without startling him, to bring him face to face with the subject on which I wished to move him. I may as well tell you at once, my dear Mabel, I might just as well (to return to my old simile) have tried to move the Catstean. When I described the danger in which the proceedings would involve you, as well as your husband, he suddenly smiled; it was his first smile, so far as I remember, for many a day. It was not pleasant sunlight—it was more like the glare of the lightning.

"'We have not very far to travel in life's journey,' I said, 'you and I. We have had our enemies and our quarrels, and fought our battles stoutly enough. It is time we should forget and forgive.'

"'I have forgotten a great deal,' he answered. 'I'll forgive nothing.'

"'You can't mean you have forgotten pretty Mabel?' I exclaimed.

"'Let me bury my dead out of my sight,' was all he said. He did not say it kindly. It was spoken sulkily and peremptorily.

"'Well, Harry,' I said, returning upon his former speech, 'I can't suppose you really intend to forgive nothing.'

"'It is a hypocritical world,' he answered. 'If it were anything else, every one would confess what every one knows, that no one ever forgave any one anything since man was created.'

"'Am I, then, to assume that you will prosecute this matter, to their ruin, through revenge?' I asked, rather harshly.

"'Certainly not,' said he. 'That feud is dead and rotten. It is twenty years and more since I saw them. I'm tired of their names. The man I sometimes remember—I'd like to see him flung over the crags of Darness Heugh—but the girl I never think of—she's clean forgot. To me they are total strangers. I'm a trustee in this matter; why should I swerve from my duty, and incur, perhaps, a danger for those whom I know not?'

"'You are not obliged to do this—you know you are not,' I urged. 'You have the power, that's all, and you choose to exercise it.'

"'Amen, so be it; and now we've said enough,' he replied.

"'No,' I answered, warmly, for it was impossible to be diplomatic with a man like this. 'I must say a word more. I ask you only to treat them as you describe them, that is as strangers. You would not put yourself out of your way to crush a stranger. There was a time when you were kind.'

"'And foolish,' said he.

"'Kind,' I repeated; 'you were a kind man.'

"'The volume of life is full of knowledge,' he answered, 'and I have turned over some pages since then.'

"'A higher knowledge leads us to charity,' I pleaded.

"'The highest to justice,' he said, with a scoff. 'I'm no theologian, but I know that fellow deserves the very worst. He refused to meet me, when a crack or two of a pistol might have blown away our feud, since so you call it—feud with such a mafflin!' Every now and then, when he is excited, out pops one of these strange words. They came very often in this conversation, but I don't remember them. 'The mafflin! the coward!'

"I give you his words; his truculent looks I can't give you. It is plain he has not forgiven him, and never will. Your husband, we all know, did perfectly right in declining that wild challenge. All his friends so advised him. I was very near saying a foolish thing about you, but I saw it in time, and turned my sentence differently; and when I had done, he said:

"'I am going now—the shower is over.' He took my hand, and said 'Good-bye.' But he held it still, and looking me in the face with his gloomy eyes, he added: 'See, I like you well; but if you will talk of those people, or so much as mention their names again, we meet as friends no more.'

"'Think better of it, do, Harry,' I called after him, but he was already clanking over the lobby in his cyclopean shoes. Whether he heard me or not, he walked down the stairs, with his big brute at his heels, without once looking over his shoulder.

"And now, dear Mabel, I have told you everything. You are, of course, to take for granted those Northumbrian words and idioms which drop from him, as I reminded you, as he grows warm in discussion. This is a 'report' rather than a letter, and I have sat up very late to finish it, and I send it to the post-office before I go to bed. Good night, and Heaven bless you, and I hope this gloomy letter may not vex you as much as its purport does me; disappoint you, judging from what you said to me when we talked the matter over, I scarcely think it can."

There is a Latin proverb, almost the only four words of Latin I possess, which says, *Omne ignotum pro magnifico*, for which, and for its translation, I am obliged to Mr. Carmel: "The unknown is taken for the sublime." I did not at the time at all understand the nature of the danger that threatened, and its vagueness magnified it. Papa came in. He read the letter, and the deeper he got in it the paler his face grew, and the more it darkened. He drew a great breath as he laid it down.

"Well, it's not worse than you expected?" said mamma at last. "I hope not. I've had so much to weary, and worry, and break me down; you have no idea what the journey to the Golden Friars was to me. I have not been at all myself. I've been trying to do too much. Ethel there will tell you all I said to my aunt; and really things go so wrong and so unluckily, no matter what one does, that I almost think I'll go to my bed and cry."

"Yes, dear," said papa, thinking, a little bewildered. "It's—it's—it is—it's very perverse. The old scoundrel! I suppose this is something else."

He took up a letter that had followed him by the same post, and nervously broke the seal. I was watching his face intently as he read. It brightened.

"Here—here's a bit of good luck at last! Where's Mabel? Oh, yes! it's from Cloudesly. There are some leases just expired at Ellenston, and we shall get at least two thousand pounds, he thinks, for renewing. That makes it all right for the present. I wish it had been fifteen hundred more; but it's a great deal better than nothing. We'll tide it over, you'll find." And papa kissed her with effusion.

"And you can give three hundred pounds to Le Panier and Tarlton; they have been sending so often lately," said mamma, recovering from her despondency.

CHAPTER XXXV.

LADY MARDYKES'S BALL.

The autumn deepened, and leaves were brown, and summer's leafy honours spread drifting over the short grass and the forest roots. Winter came, and snow was on the ground, and presently spring began to show its buds, and blades, and earliest flowers; and the London season was again upon us.

Lady Lorrimer had gone, soon after our visit to Golden Friars, to Naples for the winter. She was to pass the summer in Switzerland, and the autumn somewhere in the north of Italy, and again she was to winter in her old quarters at Naples. We had little chance, therefore, of seeing her again in England for more than a year. Her letters were written in varying spirits, sometimes cheery, sometimes *de profundis*. Sometimes she seemed to think that she was just going to break up and sink; and then her next letter would unfold plans looking far into the future, and talking of her next visit to England. There was an uneasy and even violent fluctuation in these accounts, which did not exactly suggest the idea of a merely fanciful invalid. She spoke at times, also, of intense and exhausting pain. And she mentioned that in Paris she had been in the surgeons' hands, and that there was still uncertainty as to what good they might have done her. This may have been at the root of her hysterical vacillations. But, in addition to this, there was something very odd in Lady Lorrimer's correspondence. She had told mamma to write to her once a fortnight, and promised to answer punctually; but nothing could be more irregular. At one time, so long an interval as two whole months passed without bringing a line from her. Then, again, she would complain of mamma's want of punctuality. She seemed to have forgotten things that mamma had told her; and sometimes she alluded to things as if she had told them to mamma, which she had never mentioned before. Either the post-office was playing tricks with her letters, or poor Lady Lorrimer was losing her head.

I think, if we had been in a quiet place like Malory, we should have been more uneasy about Lady Lorrimer than, in the whirl of London, we had time to be. There was one odd passage in one of her letters; it was as follows: "Send your letters, not by the post, I move about so much; but, when you have an opportunity, send them by a friend. I wish I were happier. I don't do always as I like. If we were for a time together—but all I do is so uncertain!"

Papa heard more than her letters told of her state of health. A friend of his, who happened to be in Paris at the time, told papa that one of the medical celebrities whom she had consulted there had spoken to him in the most desponding terms of poor Lady Lorrimer's chances of recovery, I do not know whether it was referable to that account of her state of health or simply to the approach of the time when he was to make his *début* in the House; but the fact is that papa gave a great many dinner-parties this season; and mamma took her drives in a new carriage, with a new and very pretty pair of horses; and a great deal of new plate came home; and it was plain that he was making a fresh start in a style suited to his new position, which he assumed to be certain and near. He was playing rather deep upon this throw. It must be allowed, however, that nothing could look more promising.

Sir Luke Pyneweck, a young man, with an estate and an overpowering influence in the town of Shillingsworth, had sat for three years for that borough, not in the House, but in his carriage, or a Bath-chair, in various watering-places at home and abroad—being, in fact, a miserable invalid. This influential young politician had written a confidential letter, with only two or three slips in spelling and grammar, to his friend the Patronage Secretary, telling him to look out for a man to represent Shillingsworth till he had recovered his health, which was not returning quite so quickly as he expected, and promising his strenuous support to the nominee of the minister. Papa's confidence, therefore, was very reasonably justified, and the matter was looked upon by those sages of the lobbies who count the shadowy noses of unborn Houses of Commons as settled. It was known that the dissolution would take place early in the autumn.

Presently there came a letter to the "whip," from his friend Sir Luke Pyneweck, announcing that he was so much better that he had made up his mind to try once more before retiring.

This was a stunning blow to papa. Sir Luke could do without the government better than the government could do without him. And do or say what they might, no one could carry the borough against him. The Patronage Secretary really liked my father; and, I believe, would have wished him, for many reasons, in the House. But what was to be done? Sir Luke was neither to be managed nor bullied; he was cunning and obstinate. He did not want anything for himself, and did not want anything for any other person. With a patriot of that type who could do anything?

It was a pity the "whip" did not know this before every safe constituency was engaged. A pity papa did not know it before he put an organ into Shillingsworth church, and subscribed six hundred pounds towards the building of the meeting-house. I never saw papa so cast down and excited as he was by this disappointment. Looking very ill, however, he contrived to rally his spirits when he was among his friends, and seemed resolved, one way or other, to conquer fortune.

Balls, dinners, concerts, garden-parties, nevertheless, devoured our time, and our drives, and shopping, and visits went on, as if nothing had happened, and nothing was impending.

Two notable engagements for the next week, because they were connected, in the event, with my strange story, I mention now. On Tuesday there was Lady Mardykes's ball, on that day week papa had a political party to dinner, among whom were some very considerable names indeed. Lady Mardykes's balls were always, as you know, among the most brilliant of the season. While dancing one of those quadrilles that give us breathing time between the round dances, I saw a face that riveted my attention, and excited my curiosity. A slight old gentleman, in evening costume, with one of those obsolete under-waistcoats, which seemed to me such a pretty fashion (his was of blue satin), was the person I mean. A forbidding-looking man was this, with a thin face, as brown as a nut, hawk's eyes and beak, thin lips, and a certain character of dignified ill-temper, and even insolence, which, however, did not prevent its being a very gentleman-like face. I instantly recognised him as the old man, in the chocolate-coloured coat, who had talked so sharply, as it seemed to me and poor Nelly, with Laura Grey on the Milk-walk, in the shadow of the steep bank and the overhanging trees.

"Who is that old gentleman standing near the door at the end of the room, with that blue satin about his neck? Now he's speaking to Lady Westerbroke."

"Oh! that's Lord Rillingdon," answered my friend.

"He does not go to many places? I have seen him, I think, but once before," I said.

"No, I fancy he does not care about this sort of thing."

"Doesn't he speak very well? I think I've heard——"

"Yes, he speaks only in Indian debates. He's very well up on India—he was there, you know."

"Don't you think he looks very cross?" I said.

"They say he is very cross," said my informant, laughing: and here the dance was resumed, and I heard no more of him.

Old Lord Rillingdon had his eyes about him. He seemed, as much as possible, to avoid talking to people, and I thought was looking very busily for somebody. As I now and then saw this old man, who, from time to time, changed his point of observation, my thoughts were busy with Laura Grey, and the pain of my uncertainty returned—pain mingled with remorse. My enjoyment of this scene contrasted with her possible lot, upbraided me, and for a time I wished myself at home.

A little later I thought I saw a face that had not been seen in London for more than a year. I was not quite sure, but I thought I saw Monsieur Droqville. In rooms so crowded, one sometimes has so momentary a peep of a distant face that recognition is uncertain. Very soon I saw him again, and this time I had no doubt whatever. He seemed as usual, chatty, and full of energy; but I soon saw, or at least fancied, that he did not choose to see mamma or me. It is just possible I may have been doing him wrong. I did not see him, it is true, so much as once glance towards us; but Doctor or Monsieur Droqville was a man who saw everything, as Rebecca Torkill would say, with half an eye—always noting everything that passed; full of curiosity, suspicion, and conclusion, and with an eye quick and piercing as a falcon's.

This man, I thought, had seen, and was avoiding us, without wishing to appear to do so. It so happened, however, that some time later, in the tea-room, mamma was placed beside him. I was near enough to hear. Mamma recognised him with a smile and a little bow. He replied with just surprise enough in his looks and tones to imply that he had not known, up to that moment, that she was there.

"You are surprised to see me here?" he said; "I can scarcely believe it myself. I've been away thirteen months—a wanderer all over Europe; and I shall be off again in a few days. By-the-bye, you hear from Lady Lorrimer sometimes: I saw her at Naples, in January. She was looking flourishing then, but complaining a good deal. She has not been so well since—but I'll look in upon you to-morrow or the next day. I shall be sure to see her again, immediately. Your friends, the Wiclyffs, were at Baden this summer, so were the D'Acres. Lord Charles is to marry that French lady; it turns out she's rather an heiress; it is very nearly arranged, and they seemed all very well pleased. Have you seen my friend Carmel lately?"

"About three weeks ago; he was going to North Wales," she said.

"He is another of those interesting people who are always dying, and never die," said Monsieur Droqville.

I felt a growing disgust for this unfeeling man. He talked a little longer, and then turned to me and said:

"There's one advantage, Miss Ware, in being an old fellow—one can tell a young lady, in such charming and brilliant looks as yours to-night, what he thinks, just as he might give his opinion upon a picture. But I won't venture mine; I'll content myself with making a petition. I only ask that, when you are a very great lady, you'll remember a threadbare doctor, who would be very glad of an humble post about the court, and who is tired of wandering over the world in search of happiness, and finding a fee only once in fifty miles."

I do not know what was in this man's mind at that moment. If he was a Jesuit, he certainly owed very little to those arts and graces of which rumour allows so large a share to the order. But brusque and almost offensive as I thought him, there was something about him that seemed to command acceptance, and carry him everywhere he chose to go. He went away, and I saw him afterwards talking now to one great lady, and now to another. Lord Rillingdon, who looked like the envious witch whom Madame D'Aulnois introduces sometimes at the feasts of her happy kings and queens, throwing a malign gloom on all about them, had vanished.

That night, however, was to recall, as unexpectedly, another face, a more startling reminder of Malory and Laura Grey.

CHAPTER XXXVI.

NEWS OF LADY LORRIMER.

Old Lord Verney, of all persons in the world, took a fancy to take me down to the tea-room. I think he believed, as other wiser people did, that papa, who was certainly clever, and a very shrewd club-house politician, might come to be somebody in the House, in time.

As usual, he was telling an interminable story, without point or beginning or end, about himself, and all mixed up with the minister, and the opposition leader, and an amendment, and some dismal bill, that I instantly lost my way in. As we entered the tea-room, a large room opening from the landing, he nodded, without interrupting his story, to a gentleman who was going downstairs. My eye followed this recognition, and I saw a tall, rather good-looking young man. I saw him only for a moment. I was so startled that I involuntarily almost stopped Lord Verney as we passed; but I recovered myself instantly. It was tantalising. He always talks as if he were making a speech; one can't, without rudeness, edge in a word; he is so pompous, I dare not interrupt him. He did that office for himself, however, by taking an ice; and I seized the transitory silence, and instantly asked him the name of the gentleman to whom he had bowed; I thought he said, "Mr. Jennings," and as a clever artist of that odd name had lately painted a portrait of Lord Verney, I was satisfied that I had heard him aright.

This was to be a night of odd recognitions. I was engaged to Lord John Roxford, who came up, and saying, "I think this is our dance, Miss Ware?" took me away, to my great relief, from Lord Verney. Well, we danced and talked a little; and I learned nothing that I remember, except that he was to return to Paris the next day. Before he took me to mamma, however, he said:

"A very dear friend has asked me, as the greatest favour I can do him, to introduce him to you, Miss Ware; you will allow me?"

He repeated, I thought—for he was looking for him, and his face at that moment was turned a little away, and the noise considerable—the same name that Lord Verney had mentioned. As Rebecca Torkill used to say, "my heart jumped into my mouth," as I consented. A moment more, and I found myself actually acquainted with the very man! How strange it seemed! Was that smiling young man of fashion the same I had seen stretched on the rugged peat and roots at Plas Ylwd, with white face and leaden lips, and shirt soaked in blood? He was, with his white-gloved hand on the pier-table beside me, inquiring what dance I could give him. I was engaged for this; but I could not risk the chance of forfeiting my talk with my new acquaintance. I gave it to him, and having the next at my disposal, transferred it to the injured man whom I had ousted.

The squabble, the innocent surprise, the regrets, the other hypocrisies, and finally the compromise over, away we went to take our places in the quadrille. I was glad it was not a round dance. I wanted to hear him talk a little. How strange it seemed to me, standing beside him in this artificial atmosphere of wax-light and music! Each affecting the air of an acquaintance made then and there; each perfectly recognising the other, as we stood side by side talking of the new primo tenore, the play, the Aztecs, and I know not what besides!

This young man's manner was different from what I had been accustomed to in ball-rooms. There was none of the trifling, and no sign of the admiration which the conversation and looks of others seemed to imply. His tone, perfectly gentleman-like, was merely friendly, and he seemed to take an interest in me, much as I fancied an unknown relation might. We talked of things of no particular interest, until he happened to ask something of my occasional wanderings in the country. It was my opportunity, and I seized it like a general.

"I like the country," I said. "I enjoy it thoroughly; I've lived nearly all my life in the country, in a place I am so fond of, called Malory. I think all about there so beautiful! It is close to Cardyllion—have you ever seen Cardyllion?"

"Yes, I've been to Cardyllion once—only once, I think. I did not see a great deal of it. But you, now, see a great deal more of the country—you have been to the lakes?"

"Oh! yes; but I want to ask how you liked Cardyllion. How long is it since you were there?"

"About two years, or a little more, perhaps," he answered.

"Oh! that's just about the time the Conway Castle was wrecked—how awful that was! I had a companion then, my dearest friend—Laura Grey was her name; she left us so suddenly, when I was away from Malory, and I have never seen her since. I have been longing so to meet any one who could tell me anything about her. You don't happen to know any one, do you, who knows a young lady of that name? I make it a rule to ask every one I can; and I'm sure I shall make her out at last."

"Nothing like perseverance," said he. "I shall be most happy to be enlisted; and if I should light upon a lady of that name, I may tell her that Miss Ware is very well, and happy?"

"No, not happy—at least, not quite happy, until she writes to tell me where she is, or comes to see me; and tell her I could not have believed she would have been so unkind."

Conversations are as suddenly cut short in ball-rooms as they are in a beleaguered city, where the head of one of the interlocutors is carried off by a round-shot. Our dialogue ended with the sudden arrival of the ill-used man, whom I could no longer postpone, and who carried me off, very much vexed, as you may suppose, and scarcely giving my companion time to make a bow.

Never was "fast dance" so slow as this! At length it was over, and wherever I went my eyes wandered hither and thither in search of the tall young man with whom I had danced. The man who had figured in a scene which had so often returned to my imagination was now gone; I saw him neither in the dancing-rooms nor in any others. By this time there was a constant double current to and from the supper-room, up and down the stairs. As I went down, immediately before me was Monsieur Droqville. He did not follow the stream, but passed into the hall.

Monsieur Droqville put on his loose black wrapper, and wound a shawl about his throat, and glanced, from habit, with his shrewd, hard eyes at the servants as he passed through them in the hall. He jumped into a cab, told the driver where to stop, lighted a cigar, and smoked.

He got out at the corner of a fashionable but rather dingy street not very far away. Then he dismissed his vehicle, walked up the pavement smoking, passed into a still quieter street, also fashionable, that opens from it at an obtuse angle. Here he walked slowly, and, as it were, softly. The faint echo of his own steps was the only sound that met him as he entered it. He crossed, threw his head back, and shrewdly scanned the upper windows, blowing out a thin stream of tobacco-smoke as he looked.

"Not flown yet, *animula, vagula blandula*? Still on the perch," he said, as he crossed the street again.

His cigar was just out, and he threw it away as he reached the steps. He did not need to knock or ring; he admitted himself with a latch-key. A bedroom candlestick in the hall had a candle still burning in it. He took it and walked quietly up. The boards of the stairs and lobbies were bare, and a little dust lay on the wall and bannister, indicating the neglected state of a house abandoned by its tenants for a journey or a very long stay in the country. He opened the back drawing-room door and put his head in. A pair of candles lighted the room. A thin elderly lady, in an odd costume, was the only person there. She wore a white, quilted head-cloth, a black robe, and her beads and cross were at her side. She was reading, with spectacles on, a small book which she held open in both hands, as he peeped in. With a slight start she rose. There was a little crucifix on the table, and a coloured print of the Madonna hung on the wall, on the nail from which a Watteau had been temporarily removed.

"Has your patient been anointed yet?" said Monsieur Droqville, in his short nasal tones.

"Not yet, reverend father," she answered. They were both speaking French.

"Has she been since nearly *in articulo*?"

"At about eleven o'clock, reverend father, her soul seemed at her very lips."

"In this complaint so it will often be. Is Sister Cecilia upstairs?"

"Yes, reverend father."

"Father Edwyn here?"

"Yes, reverend father."

He withdrew his head, closed the door, and walked upstairs. He tapped gently at the door of the front bedroom.

A French nun, in a habit precisely similar to that of the lady downstairs, stood noiselessly at the door. She was comparatively young, wore no spectacles, and had a kind and rather sad countenance. He whispered a word to her, heard her answer softly, and then he entered the room with a soundless step—it was thickly carpeted, and furnished luxuriously—and stood at the side of a huge four-post bed, with stately curtains of silk, within which a miserable shrunken old woman, with a face brown as clay, sunk and flaccid, and staring feebly with wide glassy eyes, with her back coiled into a curve, and laden with shawls, was set up, among pillows, breathing, or rather gasping, with difficulty.

Here she was, bent, we may say, in the grip of two murderers, heart complaint and cancer. The irresistible chemistry of death had set in; the return of "earth to earth" was going on. Who could have recognised, in this breathing effigy of death, poor Lady Lorrimer? But disease now and then makes short work of such transformations.

The good nurse here, like the other downstairs, had her little picture against the wall, and had been curtseying and crossing herself before it, in honest prayer for the dying old lady, to whom Monsieur Droqville whispered something, and then leaned his ear close to her lips. He felt her pulse, and said, "Madame has some time still to meditate and pray."

Again his ear was to her lips. "Doubt it not, madame. Every consolation."

She whispered something more; it lasted longer, and was more earnest this time. Her head was nodding on her shoulders, and her eyes were turned up to his dark energetic face, imploringly.

"You can't do that, madame—it is not yours—you have given it to God."

The woman turned her eyes on him with a piteous look.

"No, madame," he said, sharply; "it is too late to withhold a part. This, madame, is temptation—a weakness of earth; the promises are to her that overcometh."

Her only answer was an hysterical whimper and imperfect sobbing.

"Be calm," he resumed. "It is meritorious. Discharge your mind of it, and the memory of your sacrifice will be sweeter, and its promise more glorious the nearer you draw to your darkest hour on earth."

She had another word to say; her fingers were creeping on the coverlet to his hand.

"No, madame, there won't be any struggle—you will faint, that is all, and waken, we trust among the blest. I'm sorry I can't stay just now. But Father Edwyn is here, and Dr. Garnet."

Again she turned her wavering head towards him, and lifted her eyes, as if to speak.

"No, no, you must not exert yourself—husband your strength—you'll want it, madame."

It was plain, however, she would have one last word more, and a little sourly he stooped his ear again.

"Pardon me, madame, I never said or supposed that after you signed it you were still at liberty to deal with any part; if you have courage to take it back, it is another matter. I won't send you before the Judge Eternal with a sacrilege in your right hand."

He spoke quietly, but very sternly, raising his finger upward, with his eyes fixed upon her, while his dark face looked pale.

She answered only with the same helpless whimper. He beckoned to the nun.

"Let me see that book."

He looked through its pages.

"Read aloud to madame the four first elevations; agony is near."

As he passed from the room, he beckoned the lady in the religious habit again, and whispered in her ear in the lobby:

"Lock this door, and admit none but those you know."

He went down this time to the front drawing-room, and entered it suddenly. Mr. Carmel was seated there, with candles beside him, reading. Down went his book instantly, and he rose.

"Our good friend upstairs won't last beyond three or four hours—possibly five," began Monsieur Droqville. "Garnet will be here in a few minutes; keep the doors bolted! people might come in and disturb the old lady. You need not mind now. I locked the hall-door as I came in. Why don't you make more way with Miss Ware? Her mother is no obstacle—favourable rather. Her father is a mere pagan, and never at home; and the girl likes you."

Mr. Carmel stared.

"Yes, you are blind; but I have my eyes. Why don't you read your Montaigne? '*Les agaceries des femmes sont des declarations d'amour.*' You interest her, and yet you profit nothing by your advantage. There she is, romantic, passionate, Quixotic, and makes, without knowing it, a hero of you. You are not what I thought you."

Mr. Carmel's colour flushed to his very temples; he looked pained and agitated; his eyes were lowered before his superior.

"Why need you look like a fool? Understand me," continued Monsieur Droqville, in his grim, harsh nasals. "The weaknesses of human nature are Heaven's opportunities. The godly man knows how to use them with purity. She is not conscious of the position she gives you; but you should understand its powers. You can illuminate, elevate, save her."

He paused for a moment; Mr. Carmel stood before him with his eyes lowered.

"What account am I to give of you?" he resumed. "Remember, you have no business to be afraid. You must use all influences to save a soul, and serve the Church. A good soldier fights with every weapon he has—sword, pistol, bayonet, fist—in the cause of his king. What shall I say of you? A loyal soldier, but wanting head, wanting action, wanting presence of mind. A theorist, a scholar, a deliberator. But not a man for the field; no *coup d'oeil*, no promptitude, no perception of a great law, where it is opposed by a small quibble, no power of deciding between a trifle and an enormity, between seeing your king robbed or breaking the thief's fingers. Why, can't you see that the power that commands is also the power that absolves? I thought you had tact—I thought you had insinuation. Have I been mistaken? If so, we must cut out other work for you. Have you anything to say?"

He paused only for a second, and in that second Mr. Carmel raised his head to speak; but with a slight downward motion of his hand, and a frown, Droqville silenced him, and proceeded:

"True, I told you not to precipitate matters. But you need not let the fire go out, because I told you not to set the chimney in a blaze. There is Mrs. Ware; her most useful position is where she is, *in equilibrio*. She can serve no one by declaring herself a Catholic; the *eclat* of such a thing would spoil the other mission, that must be conducted with judgment and patience. The old man I told you of is a Puritan, and must see or suspect nothing. While he lives there can be no avowal. But up to that point all must now proceed. Ha! there goes a carriage—that's the third I have heard—Lady Mardykes's party breaking up. The Wares don't return this way. I'll see you again to-morrow. To-night you accomplish your duty here. The old woman upstairs will scarcely last till dawn."

He nodded and left the room as suddenly as he had entered it.

CHAPTER XXXVII.

A LAST LOOK.

A t about eleven o'clock next morning, mamma came to my bedside, having thrown her dressing-gown on, and holding a note in her hand. I was awakened by her calling me by my name; and the extraordinary exertion of getting out of her bed at such an hour, the morning after a ball, even if there had not been consternation in her looks, would have satisfied me that something unusual had happened. I sat up staring at her.

"Oh, dear Ethel, here's a note from Doctor Droqville; I'm so shocked—poor, dear Aunt Lorrimer is dead." And mamma burst into tears, and, sobbing, told me to read the note, which, so soon as I had a little collected myself, I did. It said:

> "DEAR MRS. WARE,—I could not, of course, last night tell you the sad news about Lady Lorrimer. She arrived, it seems, on Tuesday last, to die in England. On leaving Lady Mardykes's last night, I went to her house to make inquiries; she was good enough to wish to see me. I found her in a most alarming state, and quite conscious of her danger. She was sinking rapidly. I was, therefore, by no means surprised, on calling about half an hour ago, to learn that she was no more. I lose no time in communicating the sad intelligence. It will be consolatory to you to learn that the nurses, who were present during her last moments, tell me that she died without any pain or struggle. I shall call tomorrow, as near twelve as I can, to learn whether there is anything in which you think my poor services can be made available.—I remain, dear Mrs. Ware, Ever yours sincerely,
>
> P. DROQVILLE."

I was very sorry. I even shed some tears, a thing oftener written about than done.

Mamma cried for a long time. She had now no near kinswoman left. When we are "pretty well on," and the thinned ranks of one generation only stand between us and death, the disappearance of the old over the verge is a serious matter. Between mamma and Lady Lorrimer, too, there were early recollections and sympathies in common, and the chasm was not so wide.

But for the young, and I was then young, the old seem at best a sort of benevolent ghosts, whose presence, more or less, chills and awes, and whose home is not properly with the younger generation. Their memories are busy with a phantom world that passed away before we were born. They are puckered masks and glassy eyes, peeping from behind the door of the sepulchre that stands ajar, closing little by little to shut them in for ever. I am now but little past forty, yet I feel this isolation stealing upon me. I acquiesce in the law of nature, though it seems a cynical one. I know I am no longer of the young; I grow shy of them; there is a real separation between us.

The world is for the young—it belongs to them, and time makes us ugly, and despised, and solitary, and prepares for our unregretted removal, for nature has ordained that death shall trouble the pleasure and economy of the vigorous, high-spirited world as little as may be.

Mamma was more grieved, a great deal, than I at all expected. I am writing now in solitude, and from my interior convictions, under a sort of obligation to tell, not only nothing but the truth, but the whole truth also; and I confess that mamma was selfish, and, in a degree, exacting. The education of her whole married life had tended to form those habits; but she was also affectionate, and her grief was vehement, and did not subside, as I thought it would, after its first outburst. The only practical result of her grief was a determination to visit the house, and see the remains of the poor lady.

I never could understand the comfort that some people seem to derive from contemplating such a spectacle! To me the sight is simply shocking. Mamma made it a point, however, that I should accompany her. She could not make up her mind to go that day. The next day Doctor Droqville called. Mamma saw him. After they had talked for a little, mamma declared her intention of seeing poor Lady Lorrimer as she lay in her bed.

"Allow me to advise you, as a physician, to do no such thing," said Droqville. "You'll inflict a great deal of pain on yourself, and do nobody any good."

"But unless I see her once more I shall be miserable," pleaded mamma.

"You have not nerve for such scenes," he replied; "you'd not be yourself again for a month after."

I joined my entreaties to Doctor Droqville's representations, and I thought we had finally prevailed over mamma's facile will.

He gave us a brief account of Lady Lorrimer's illness and last moments, and then talked on other subjects; finally he said, "You told me you wished me to return a bracelet that does not answer, to St. Aumand, when I pass again through Paris. I find I shall be there in a few days—can you let me have it now?"

Mamma's maid was out, so she went to get it herself, and, while she was away, Doctor Droqville said to me, with rather a stern look:

"Don't you allow her to go; your mamma has a form of the same affection of the heart. We can't tell her that; but quiet nerves are essential to her. She touches the spring of the mischief, and puts it in action at any moment by agitating herself."

"I think she has given up that intention," I answered; "but for Heaven's sake, Doctor Droqville, tell me, is mamma in any danger?"

"No, if she will only keep quiet. She may live for many years to come; but every woman, of course, who has a weakness of the kind, may kill herself easily and quickly; but—I hear her—don't allow her to go."

Mamma returned, and Doctor Droqville soon took his departure, leaving me very miserable, and very much alarmed. She now talked only of postponing her last look at poor Lady Lorrimer until to-morrow. Her vacillations were truly those of weakness, but they were sometimes violent; and when her emotions overcame her indolence, she was not easily managed.

The dark countenance of Doctor Droqville, as he urged his prohibition, excited vague suspicions. It was by no means benevolent—it was grim, and even angry. It struck me instinctively that he might have some motive, other than the kind one which he professed, in wishing to scare away mamma from the house of death.

Doctor Droqville was, I believe, a very clever physician; but his visits to England, being desultory, he could not, of course, take the position of any but an occasional adviser. He had acquired an influence over mamma, and I think if he had been a resident in London, she would have consulted no other. As matters were, however, Sir Jacob Lake was her "physician in ordinary." To him I wrote the moment I had an opportunity, stating what had occurred, enclosing his fee, and begging of him to look in about two next day, on any pretext he could think of, to determine the question.

Next day came, and with two o'clock, just as we were sitting down to lunch, Sir Jacob arrived. I ran up instantly to the drawing-room, leaving mamma to follow, for sages of his kind have not many minutes to throw away. He relieved my mind a little about mamma, but not quite, and before he had spoken half-a-dozen sentences she came in. He made an excuse of poor Lady Lorrimer's death, and had brought with him two or three letters of hers, describing her case, which he thought might be valuable should any discussion arise respecting the nature of her disease.

The conversation thus directed, I was enabled to put the question on which Doctor Droqville had been so peremptory. Sir Jacob said there was nothing to prevent mamma's going, and that she was a great deal more likely to be agitated by a dogged opposition to a thing she had so set her heart on.

Now that mamma found herself quite at liberty to go, I think she grew a little frightened. She was looking ill; she had eaten nearly nothing for the last two days, seen nobody but Doctor Droqville and the doctor who had just now called, and her head was full of her mourning and mine. Her grief was very real. Through Lady Lorrimer's eyes she had been accustomed to look back into her own early life. They had both seen the same scenes and people that she remembered, and now there was no one left with whom she could talk over old times. Mamma was irresolute till late in the afternoon, and then at last she made up her mind.

We drove through half-a-dozen streets. I did not know in what street my poor aunt Lorrimer's house was. We suddenly pulled up, and the footman came to the door to say that there was a chain across the street at each end. We had nothing for it but to get out and to walk past the paviors who had taken possession of it. The sun was, I suppose, at this time about setting. The sunlight fell faintly on the red brick chimneys above, but all beneath was dark and cold. In its present state it was a melancholy and silent street. It was, I instantly saw, the very same street in which Lady Lorrimer had chosen to pass me by.

"Is that the house, the one with the tan before it?" I asked.

It was. I was now clear upon the point. Into that house I had seen her go. The woman in the odd costume who had walked beside her, Mr. Carmel's thin figure and melancholy ascetic face, and the silence in which they moved, were all remembered, and recalled the sense of curious mystery with which I had observed the parting, more than two years ago, and mingled an unpleasant ingredient in the gloom that deepened about me as I now approached the door.

It was all to be cleared up soon. The door was instantly opened by a man in black placed in the hall. A man also in black, thin, very perpendicular, with a long neck, sallow face, and black eyes, very stern, passed us by in silence with a glance. He turned about before he reached the hall door, and in a low tone, a little grimly, inquired our business. I told him, and also who we were.

We were standing at the foot of the stairs. On hearing our names he took off his hat, and, more courteously, requested us to wait for a moment where we were, till he should procure a person to conduct us to the room. This man was dressed something in the style of our own High-Church divines, except that his black coat was longer, I think. He had hardly left us when there was a ring at the bell, and a poor woman, holding a little girl by the hand, came in, whispered to the man in the hall, and then, passing us by, went up the stairs in silence and disappeared. They were met by a second clergyman coming down, rather corpulent, with a tallowy countenance and spectacles, who looked at us suspiciously, and went out just as a party of three came into the hall, and passed us by like the former.

Almost immediately the clergyman we had first met returned, and conducted us up the stairs as far as the first landing, where we were met by a lady in a strange brown habit, with a rosary, and a hood over her head, whom I instantly knew to be a nun. We followed her up the stairs. There was a strange air of mystery and of publicity in the proceedings; the house seemed pretty well open to all comers; no one who whispered a few words satisfactorily to the porter in the hall failed to obtain immediate access to the upper floor of the house. Everything was carried on in whispers, and there was a perpetual tramping of feet slowly going up and down stairs.

It was much more silent as we reached the level of the drawing-rooms. The nun opened the back drawing-room, and without more ceremony than a quiet movement of her hand, signed to us to go in. I think mamma's heart half failed her; I almost hoped she would change her mind, for she hesitated, and sighed two or three times heavily, with her hand pressed to her heart, and looked very faint.

A LAST LOOK.

The light that escaped through the half-opened door was not that of day, but the light of candles. Mamma took my arm, and in silence hurried me into the room.

Now I will tell you what I saw. The room was hung with black, which probably enhanced the effect of its size, for it appeared very large. The windows were concealed by the hangings of black cloth, which were continued without interruption round all the walls of the room. A great many large wax candles were burning in it, and the black background, reflecting no light, gave to all the objects standing in the room an odd sharpness and relief.

At the far end of the apartment stood a sort of platform, about as wide as a narrow bed, covered with a deep velvet cushion, with a drapery of the same material descending to the floor. On this lay the body of Lady Lorrimer, habited in the robes and hood of the order, I think, of the Carmelites; her hands were placed together on her breast, and her rosary was twined through her fingers. The hood was drawn quite up about the head and cheeks of the corpse. Her dress, the cushion on which she lay, the pillow creased by the pressure of her cold head, were strewn with flowers. I had resolved not to look at it—such sights haunt me afterwards; but an irresistible curiosity overcame me. It was just one momentary glance, but the picture has remained on my inner sight ever since, as if I had gazed for an hour.

There was at the foot of this catafalque an altar, on which was placed a large crucifix; huge candlesticks with tall tapers stood on the floor beside it. Many of the strangers who came in kneeled before the crucifix and prayed, no doubt for the departed spirit. Many smaller crucifixes were hung upon the walls, and before these also others of the visitors from time to time said a prayer. Two nuns stood one at each side of the body, like effigies of contemplation and prayer, telling their beads. It seemed to me that there was a profusion of wax-lights. The transition from the grey evening light, darker in the house, into this illumination of tapers, had a strange influence upon my imagination. The reality of the devotion, and the more awful reality of death, quite overpowered the theatrical character of the effect.

I saw the folly of mamma's irrepressible desire to come here. I thought she was going to faint; I dare say she would have done so, she looked so very ill, but that tears relieved her. They were tears in which grief had but a subordinate share; they were nervous tears, the thunder-shower of the hysteria which had been brewing ever since she had entered the room. I don't know whether she was sorry that she had come. I am sure she would have been better if she had never wished it.

CHAPTER XXXVIII.

STORM.

A few days later, mamma and I were talking in the drawing-room, when the door opened, and papa came in, his umbrella in his hand, and his hat on his head, looking as white as death. He stood for a time without speaking. We were both staring in his face, as dumb as he.

"Droqville's a villain!" he said, suddenly. "They have got that miserable old fool's money—every guinea. I told you how it would be, and now it has all happened!"

"What has happened?" asked mamma, still gazing at him, with a look of terror. I was myself freezing with horror. I never saw despair so near the verge of madness in a human face before as in papa's.

"What? We're ruined! If there's fifty pounds in the bank it's all, and only that between us and nothing."

"My God!" exclaimed mamma, whiter than ever, and almost in a whisper.

"Your God! What are you talking about? It is you that have done it all—filling the house with priests and Jesuits. I knew how it would be, you fool!"

Papa was speaking with the sternness of actual fury.

"I'm not to blame—it is not my doing. Frank, for Heaven's sake, don't speak so—you'll drive me mad! I don't know what they have done—I don't understand it!" cried mamma, and burst into a helpless flood of tears.

"You may as well stop that crying—you can do it in the streets by-and-by. Understand it? By Heaven, you'll understand it well enough before long. I hope you may, as you deserve it!"

With those dreadful looks, and a voice hoarse with passion, poor papa strode out of the room, and we heard him shut the hall-door after him with a crash.

We were left with the vaguest ideas of the nature of our misfortune; his agitation was so great as to assure me that an alarming calamity had really befallen us. Mamma cried on. She was frightened by his evident alarm, and outraged by his violence, so shocking in one usually so gay, gentle, and serene. She went up to her room to cry there, and to declare herself the most miserable of women. Her maid gave her sal-volatile, and I, seeing no good or comfort in my presence, ran down to the drawing-room. I had hardly got into the room, when whom should I see arriving at the door in a cab, with some papers in his hand, but Mr. Forrester, papa's principal attorney. I knew papa was out, and I was so afraid of his attorney's going away without giving us any light on the subject of our alarms that I ran downstairs, and told the servant to show him into the dining-room, and on no account to let him go away. I went into the room myself, and there awaited him. In came Mr. Forrester, and looked surprised at finding me only.

"Oh! Mr. Forrester," I said, going quickly to him, and looking up in his eyes, "what is this about Lady Lorrimer, and—are we quite ruined?"

"Ruined?" he repeated. "Oh, dear, not at all," and he threw a cautionary glance towards the door, and lowered his voice a little. "Why should you be ruined? It's only a disappointment. It has been very artfully done, and I was only this moment at the Temple talking the will over with one of the best men at the Bar, to whom I'm to send a brief, though I can't see, myself, any good that is likely to come of it. Everything has been done, you see, under the best possible advice, and all the statutes steered clear of. Her estates were all turned into money—that is, the reversions sold—two years ago. The whole thing is very nearly a quarter of a million, all in money, and the will declares no trust—a simple bequest. I haven't the slightest hope of any case on the ground of undue influence. I daresay she was, in the meaning of the law, a perfectly free agent; and if she was not, depend upon it we shall never find it out."

"But does it do us any particular injury?" I inquired, not understanding one sentence in three that he spoke.

"Why, no injury, except a disappointment. In the natural course of things, all this, or the bulk of it, might very likely have come to you here. But only that. It now goes elsewhere; and I fear there is not the least chance of disturbing it."

"Then we are not ruined?" I repeated.

He looked at me, as if he were not quite sure of my meaning, and with a smile, answered:

"You are not a bit worse off than you were a year ago. She might have left you money, but she could take nothing from you. You have property at Cardyllion, I think, a place called Malory, and more at Golden Friars, and other things besides. But your country solicitors would know all about those things."

And thus having in some measure reassured me, he took his leave, saying he would go to papa's clubs to look for him.

I ran up to mamma, more cheerful than when I had left her. She, also, was cheered by my report, and being comforted on the immediate subject of her alarm, she began to think that his excitement was due to some fresh disappointment in his electioneering projects, and her resentment at his ill-temper increased.

This was the evening of papa's political dinner-party. A gentleman's party strictly it was to be, and he did not choose to allow poor Aunt Lorrimer's death to prevent it. Perhaps he was sorry now that he had not postponed it; but it was too late to think of that. We were very near the close of the session. The evenings were perceptibly shortening. I remember every particular connected with that evening and night, with a sharp precision.

Papa came in at dusk. He ran upstairs, and before dressing he came into mamma's bedroom, where I was sitting at her bedside. He looked tired and ill, but was comparatively tranquil now.

"Never mind, May," he said; "it will all come right, I daresay. I wish this dinner was not to be till to-morrow. They are talking of putting me up for Dawling. One way or other, we must not despair yet. I'll come up and see you when they go away. We are a small party—only nine, you know—and I don't think there are two among them who won't be of very real use to me. If I get in, I don't despair. I have been very low before, two or three times, and we've got up again. I don't see why we shouldn't now, as we did before."

Judging by his looks, you would have said that papa had just got out of a sick-bed, pale, ill, haggard. He looked at his watch; it was later than he thought, and he went away. We heard him ring for his man, and presently the double knocks began at the hall-door, and his party were arriving. Mamma was not very well, and whenever she was, or fancied herself ill, papa slept in another bed-room, adjoining hers, with a dressing-room off it. Ours was a large house, handsomer than would naturally have fallen to our lot; it had belonged to my grandfather, Lord Chellwood, and when he built the new house in Blank Street settled this upon his younger son.

Mamma and I had some dinner in her room, and some tea there also. She had got over her first alarm. Papa's second visit had been re-assuring, and she took it very nearly for granted that, after some harassing delays, and possibly a good deal of worry, the danger, whatever it was, would subside, as similar dangers had subsided before, and things would run again in their accustomed channel.

It was a very animated party; we could hear the muffled sound of their talking and laughing from the drawing-room, where they were now taking their tea and coffee, and talking, as it seemed, nearly all together. At length, however, the feast was ended, the guests departed, and papa, according to promise, came upstairs, and, with hardly a knock at the door, came in. Had he been drinking more than usual? I don't know. He was in high spirits. He was excited, and looked flushed, and talked incessantly, and laughed ever so much at what seemed to me very indifferent jokes.

I tried to edge in a question or two about the election matters, but he did not seem to mind, or even to hear what I said, but rattled and laughed on in the same breathless spirits.

"I'm going to bed now," he said, suddenly. "I've ever so much to do to-morrow, and I'm tired. I shall be glad when this thing is all ended."

Mamma called after him, "But you did not bid us good-night." The candle, however, vanished through the second bed-room into the dressing-room, and we heard him shut the door.

"He did not hear," said mamma; "his head is so full of his election. He seems very well. I suppose everything will be right, after all."

So mamma and I talked on for a little; but it was high time that she should settle to rest. I kissed her, and away I went to my own room. There my maid, as she brushed my hair, told me all the rumours of the servants' hall and the housekeeper's room about papa's electioneering prospects. All promised great things, and, absurd as these visions were, there was something cheering in listening to them. It was past twelve by the time my maid left me.

Very shortly after I heard a step come to my door, and papa asked, "Can I come in, dear, to say a word?"

"Oh! yes; certainly, papa," I answered, a little curious.

"I won't sit down," he said, looking round the room vaguely. He laid his candle on my table; he had a small box in his hand, in which mamma had told me he kept little lozenges of opium, his use of which had lately given her a great deal of secret uneasiness. "I have found it all out. It was that villain Droqville who did it all. He has brought us very low—broken my heart, my poor child!" He heaved a great sigh. "If that woman had never lived, if we had never heard of her, I should not have been so improvident. But that's all over. You must read your Bible, Ethel; it is a good book; there's something in it—something in it. That governess, Miss Grey, was a good woman. I say you are young; you are not spoiled yet. You must read a little bit every night, or I'll come and scold you. Do you mind? You look very well, Ethel. You must not let your spirits down—your courage. I wish it was morning. All in good time. Get to sleep, darling. Good night—good-bye." He kissed me on the cheek and departed.

I was soon fast asleep. I think the occurrences of the earlier part of the day had made me nervous. I awoke with a start, and a vague consciousness of having been in the midst of an unpleasant dream. I thought I heard mamma call me. I jumped out of bed, threw my dressing-gown about me, and, with bare feet, walked along the lobby, now quite dark, towards mamma's door. When I got almost to it I suddenly recollected that I could not have heard mamma's voice in my room from hers. In total darkness, solitude, and silence, I experienced the sort of chill which accompanies the discovery of such an illusion. I was just turning about, to make a hasty retreat to my own room, when I did hear mamma's voice. I heard her call papa's name, and then there was a silence. I changed my mind. I went on, and tapped at her door. Rather nervously she asked, "Who's there?" and on hearing me answer, told me to come in. There was only the night-light she usually had burning in her room. She was sitting up in her bed, and told me she had been startled by seeing papa looking in at the door (she nodded toward the one that opened to his bedroom). The night-light was placed on a little table close beside it.

"And oh! my dear Ethel, he looked so horribly ill I was frightened; I hardly knew him, and I called to him, but he only said, 'That's enough,' and drew back, and shut the door. He looked so ill, that I should have followed him in, but I found the door locked, and I heard him shut the door of his dressing-room. Do you think he is ill?"

"Oh! no, mamma; if he had been ill he'd have told you so; I'm sure it was the miserable light in this room—everything looks so strange in it." And so with a few words more we bid good-night once again; and, having seen her reclining with her head on her pillow, I made my way back again to my own room.

I felt very uncomfortable; the few words mamma had said presented an image that somehow was mysterious and ill-omened. I held my door open, and listened with my head stretched into the dark. Papa's dressing-room door was nearly opposite. I was re-assured by hearing his step on the floor; then I heard something move; I closed my door once more, and got into bed.

The laws of acoustics are, I believe, well ascertained; and, of course, they never vary. But their action, I confess, has often puzzled me.

In the house where I now write, there are two rooms separated only by a narrow passage, in one of which, under a surgical operation, three dreadful shrieks were uttered, not one of which was, even faintly, heard in the other room, where two near and loving relations awaited the result in the silence and agony of suspense. In the same way, but not so strikingly, because the interposing space is considerably greater, no sound was ever heard in mamma's room, from papa's dressing-room, when the doors were shut. But from my door, when the rest of the house was silent, you could very distinctly hear a heavy step, or any other noise, in that room.

My visit to mamma's room had, as nurses say, "put my sleep astray," and I lay awake until I began to despair of going to sleep again till morning. From my meditations in the dead silence, I was suddenly startled by a sound like the clapping of the dressing-room door with one violent clang. I jumped up again; I thought I should hear papa's step running down the stairs, and all my wild misgivings returned. I put my head out of the door, and listened. I heard no step—nothing stirring. Once more in my dressing-gown I stole out; his candle was still burning, for I saw a ray of light slanting towards the lobby floor from the keyhole of his room, with the motes quivering in it. It pointed like a wand to something white that lay upon the ground. I remembered that this was the open leaf of the old Bible—too much neglected book, alas! in our house—that had fallen from its little shelf on the lobby, and which I had been specially moved to replace as I passed it an hour or two before, seeing, in my superstitious mood, omens in all things. Hurried on, however, by mamma's voice calling me, I had not carried out my intention.

"Dislodged from your place, you may be," I now thought, as I stooped to take the book in my hand; "but never to be trampled on!"

I was interrupted by a voice, a groan, I thought from inside the dressing-room.

I was not quite certain; staring breathlessly at the door, I listened; no sound followed. I stepped to the door and knocked. No answer came. With my lips close to the door, and my hand upon the handle, I called, "Papa, papa, papa!" I was frightened; I pushed open the door, and hesitated. I called again, "Papa—answer, answer! Are you there, papa?" I was calling upon silence. With a little effort I stepped in.

The candle was burning on the table; there was a film of blue smoke hovering in the air—a faint smell of burning. I saw papa lying on the floor; he appeared to have dropped from the arm-chair, and to have fallen over on his back; a pistol lay by his half-open hand; the side of his face looked black and torn, as if a thunderbolt had scorched him, and a stream of blood seemed throbbing from his ear.

The smell of powder, the smoke, the pistol on the ground, told what had happened. Freezing with terror, I screamed the words, "Papa, papa! O God! speak! He's killed!" I was on my knees beside him; he was not quite dead. His eyes were fixed in the earnest stare of the last look, and there was a faint movement of the mouth, as if he were trying to speak. It was only for a few seconds. Then all motion ceased—his jaw fell—he was dead.

I staggered back against the wall, uttering a frightful scream.

Under excitement so tremendous as mine, people, I think, are more than half spiritualized. We seem to find ourselves translated from place to place by thought rather than effort.

It seemed to me only a second after I had left that frightful room, that I stood beside Miss Pounden's bed upstairs. She slept with not only her shutters, but the window open. It was so perfectly silent, the street as well as the house, that through the wall from the nursery next door I could faintly hear a little baby crying. The moonlight shone dazzlingly on the white curtains of Miss Pounden's bed. I shook her by the shoulder, and called her. She started up, and I remember the odd effect of her wide open eyes, lighted by the white reflection, and staring from the shadow at me with a horror that she caught from my looks.

"Merciful Heaven! Miss Ware—my dear child—why are you here?—what is it?"

"Come with me; we must get help. Papa is dreadfully hurt in the dressing-room. Mamma knows nothing of it; don't say a word as you pass her door."

Together we went down, steadily drawing towards the awful room, from which we saw, at the end of the dark passage, the faint flush of the candle fall on the carpet.

When I told Miss Pounden what had happened, nothing would induce her to come with me beyond the lobby. I had to go into the room alone; I had to look in to be sure that he was actually dead. Oh! it was appalling, incredible. I, Ethel Ware, looking at my handsome, gay, good-natured father, killed by his own hands, the smoke of the fatal shot not yet quite cleared away! Why was there no pitying angel near to call me but a minute earlier? My tap at the door would have arrested his hand, and the moment of temptation would have passed harmlessly by. All too late—for time and eternity all is irretrievable now. One glance was sufficient. I could not breathe; I could not, for some dreadful moments, withdraw my eyes. With a faint cry, I stepped backward. I was trembling violently as I asked Miss Pounden to send any one of the servants for Sir Jacob Lake, and to tell whoever was going not to leave his house without him.

I waited in the drawing-room while she went down, and I heard her call to the servants over the stairs. The message was soon arranged, and the messenger gone. I had not cried all this time; I continued walking quickly about the drawing-room, with my hands clenched together, talking wildly to myself and to God. When Miss Pounden returned, I implored of her not to leave me.

"Come up to my room; we'll wait there till Sir Jacob Lake comes. Mamma must not know it, except as he advises. If she learned it too suddenly, she would lose her mind."

CHAPTER XXXIX.

FAREWELL, MISS WARE.

I do not mean to describe the terrible scenes that followed. When death comes attended with a scandal like this, every recollection connected with it is torture. The gross and ghastly publicity, the merciless prying into details, and over all the gloom of the maddest and most mysterious of crimes! You look in vain in the shadow for the consoling image of hope and repose; a medium is spread around that discolours and horrifies, and the Tempter seems to haunt the house.

Then, the outrage of a public tribunal canvassing the agitations and depressions of "the deceased" in the house which within a few days was his own, handling the fatal pistol, discussing the wounds, the silent records of a mental agony that happy men cannot even imagine, and that will for life darken the secret reveries of those who loved the dead!

But as one of our proverbs, old as the days of Glastonbury, says:

"Be the day never so long,
At length cometh the even song."

Mamma is now in her crape and widow's cap; I in my deep mourning also, laden with crape. A great many people have called to inquire, and have left cards. A few notes, which could not be withheld, of embarrassed condolence, have come from the more intimate, who thought themselves obliged to make that sacrifice and exertion. Two or three were very kind indeed. Sore does one feel at the desertions that attend a great and sudden change of fortune. But I do not, on fairly thinking it over, believe that there is more selfishness or less good-nature in the world in which we were living than in that wider world which lies at a lower social level. We are too ready to take the intimacies of pleasure or mere convenience as meaning a great deal more than they ever fairly can mean. They are not contracted to involve the liabilities of friendship. If they did, they would be inconveniently few. You must not expect people to sacrifice themselves for you merely because they think you good company or have similar tastes. When you begin the *facilis deccensus*, people won't walk with you very far on the way. The most you can expect is a graceful, and sometimes a compassionate, farewell.

It was about a fortnight after poor papa's death that some law-papers came, which, understanding as little about such matters as most young ladies do, I sent, with mamma's approval, to Mr. Forrester, who, I mentioned, had been poor papa's man of business in town.

Next day he called. I was with mamma in her room at the time, and the servant came up with a little pencilled note. It said, "The papers are important, and the matter must be looked after immediately, to prevent unpleasantness." Mamma and I were both startled. "Business," which we had never heard of before, now met us sternly face to face, and demanded instant attention. The servant said that Mr. Forrester was waiting in the drawing-room, to know whether mamma wished to see him. She asked me to go down instead, which accordingly I did.

As I entered, he was standing looking from the window with a thoughtful and rather disgusted countenance, as if he had something disagreeable to tell. He came forward and spoke very kindly, and then told me that the papers were notices to the effect that unless certain mortgages were paid off upon a certain early day, which was named, the house and furniture would be sold. He saw how startled I was. He looked very kindly, and as if he pitied me.

"Has your mamma any relation, who understands business, to advise with under her present circumstances?" he asked.

"Chellwood, I think, ought," I began.

"I know. But this will be very troublesome; and they say Lord Chellwood is not a man of business. He'll never undertake it, I'm sure. We can try, if you like; but I think it is merely losing time and a sheet of paper, and he's abroad, I know, at Vichy; for I wrote to him to try to induce him to take an assignment of this very mortgage, and he would not, or said he could not, which means the same thing. I don't think he'll put himself out of his way for anybody. Can you think of no one else?"

"We have very few kinsmen," I answered; "they are too remote, and we know too little about them, to have any chance of their taking any trouble for us."

"But there was a family named Rokestone connected with you at Golden Friars?"

"There is only Sir Harry Rokestone, and he is not friendly. We have reason to know he is very much the reverse," I answered.

"I hope, Miss Ware, you won't think me impertinent, but it is right you should ascertain, without further loss of time, how you stand. There are expenses going on. And all I positively know is that poor Mr. Ware's affairs are left in a very entangled state. Does your mamma know what balance there is in the bank?"

"How much money in the bank?" I repeated. "Papa said there was fifty pounds."

"Fifty pounds! Oh, there must be more than that," he replied, and looked down, with a frown, upon the floor, and, with his hands in his pockets, meditated for a minute or two.

"I don't like acting alone, if it can be helped," he began again; "but if Mrs. Ware, your mamma, wishes it, I'll write to the different professional men, Mr.

Jarlcot at Golden Friars, and Mr. Williams at Cardyllion, and the two solicitors in the south of England, and I'll ascertain for her, as nearly as we can, what is left, and how everything stands, and we must learn at the bank what balance stands to your credit. But I think your mamma should know that she can't possibly afford to live in the way she has been accustomed to, and it would only be prudent and right that she should give all the servants, except two or three whom she can't do without, notice of discharge. Is there a will?"

"I don't know. I think not—mamma thinks not," I said.

"I don't believe there is," he added. "It's not likely, and the law makes as good a will for him as he could have made for himself." He thought for a minute, and then went on. "I felt a great reluctance, Miss Ware, to talk upon these unpleasant subjects: but it would not have been either kind or honest to be silent. You and your mamma will meet your change of circumstances with good sense and good feeling, I am sure. A very great change, I fear, it will be. You are not to consider me as a professional man, tell your mamma. I am acting as a friend. I wish to do all I can to prevent expense, and to put you in possession of the facts as quickly and clearly as I can, and then you will know exactly the case you have to deal with."

He took his leave, with the same air of care, thought, and suppressed fuss which belongs to the overworked man of business.

When these people make a present of their time, they are giving us something more than gold. I was not half grateful enough to him then. Thought and years have enabled me to estimate his good-nature.

I was standing at the window of a back drawing-room, a rather dark room, pondering on the kind but alarming words, at which, as at the sound of a bell, the curtain seemed to rise for a new act in my life. These worldly terrors were mingling a new poison in my grief. The vulgar troubles, which are the hardest to bear, were near us. At this inopportune moment I heard the servant announce some one, and, looking over my shoulder quickly, I saw Mr. Carmel come in. I felt myself grow pale. I saw his eye wander for a moment in search, I fancied, of mamma. I did not speak or move. The mirror reflected my figure back upon myself as I turned towards him. What did he see? Not quite the same Ethel Ware he had been accustomed to. My mourning-dress made me look taller, thinner, and paler than before. I could not have expected to see him; I looked, I suppose, as I felt, excited, proud, pained, resentful.

He came near; his dark eyes looked at me inquiringly. He extended his hand, hesitated, and said:

"I am afraid I did wrong. I ought not to have asked to see you."

"We have not seen anyone—mamma or I—except one old friend, who came a little time ago."

My own voice sounded cold and strange in my ear; I felt angry and contemptuous. Had I not reason? I did not give him my hand, or appear to perceive that he had advanced his. I could see, though I did not look direct at him, that he seemed pained.

"I thought, perhaps, that I had some claim, also, as an old friend," he began, and paused.

"Oh! I quite forgot that," I repeated, in the same tones; "an old friend, to be sure." I felt that I smiled bitterly.

"You look at me as if you hated me, Miss Ware," he said—"why should you? What have I done?"

"Why do you ask me? Ask yourself. Look into your conscience. I think, Mr. Carmel, you are the last person who should have come here."

"I won't affect to misunderstand you; you think I influenced Lady Lorrimer," he said.

"The whole thing is coarse and odious," I said. "I hate to speak or think of it; but, shocking as it is, I must. Lady Lorrimer had no near relations but mamma; and she intended—she told her so in my hearing—leaving money to her by her will. It is, I think, natural and right that people should leave their money to those they love—their own kindred—and not to strangers. I would not complain if Lady Lorrimer had acted of her own thought and will in the matter. But it was far otherwise; a lady, nervous and broken in health, was terrified, as death approached, by people, of whom you were one, and thus constrained to give all she possessed into the hands of strangers, to forward theological intrigues, of which she could understand nothing. I say it was unnatural, cruel, and rapacious. That kind lady, if she had done as she wished, would have saved us from all our misery."

"Will you believe me, Miss Ware?" he said, in the lowest possible tones, grasping the back of the chair, on which his hand rested, very hard, "I never knew, heard, or suspected that Lady Lorrimer had asked or received any advice respecting that will, which I see has been publicly criticised in some of the papers. I never so much as heard that she had made a will. I entreat, Miss Ware, that you will believe me."

"In matters where your Church is concerned, Mr. Carmel, I have heard that prevarication is a merit. With respect to all that concerns poor Lady Lorrimer, I shall never willingly hear another word from you, nor ever speak to you again."

I turned to the window, and looked out for a minute or two, with my fingers on the window-sash. Then I turned again rather suddenly. He was standing on the same spot, in the same attitude, his hands clasped together, his head lowered, his eyes fixed in a reverie on the ground, and I thought I saw the trace of tears on his cheek.

My moving recalled him, and he instantly looked up and said:

"Let me say a word—whatever sacrifice my holy calling may impose, I accept with gratitude to Heaven. We are not pressed into this service—we are volunteers. The bride at the altar never took vow more freely. We have sworn to obey, to suffer, to fight, to die. Forewarned, and with our eyes opened, we have cast all behind us: the vanities, hopes, and affections of mortality—according to the word of God, hating father, mother, sister, brother; we take up the heavy cross, and follow in the blood-stained footsteps of our Master, pressing forward; with blind obedience and desperate stoicism, we smile at hunger, thirst, heat and cold, sickness, perils, bonds, and death. Such soldiers, you are right in thinking, will dare everything but treason. If I had been commanded to withhold information from my dearest friend, to practise any secrecy, or to exert for a given object any influence, I should have done so. All human friendship is subject with me to these inexorable conditions. Is there any prevarication there? But with respect to Lady Lorrimer's will, I suggested nothing, heard nothing, thought nothing."

All this seemed to me very cool. I was angry. I smiled again, and said:

"You must think all that very childish, Mr. Carmel. You tell me you are ready to mislead me upon any subject, and you expect me to believe you upon this."

"Of course that strikes you," he said, "and I have no answer but this: I have no possible motive in deceiving you—all that is past, inexorable, fixed as death itself!"

"I neither know nor care with what purpose you speak. It is clear to me, Mr. Carmel, that with your principles, as I suppose I must call them, you could be no one's friend, and no one but a fool could be yours. It seems to me you are isolated from all human sympathies; toward such a person I could feel nothing but antipathy and fear; you don't stand before me like a fellow-creature, but like a spirit—and not a good one."

"These principles, Miss Ware, of which you speak so severely, Protestants, the most religious, practise with as little scruple as we, in their warfare, in their litigation, in their diplomacy, in their ordinary business, wherever, in fact, hostile action is suspected. If a Laodicean community were as earnest about winning souls as they are about winning battles, or lawsuits, or money, or elections, we should hear very little of such weak exceptions against the inevitable strategy of zeal and faith."

I made him no answer; perhaps I could not do so at the moment. I was excited; his serene temper made me more so.

"I have described my obligations, Miss Ware," he said. "Your lowest view of them can now charge me with no treachery to you. It is true I cannot be a friend in the sense in which the world reads friendship. My first allegiance is to Heaven; and in the greatest, as in the minutest things, all my obedience is due to that organ of its will which Heaven has placed above me. If all men thought more justly, such relations would not require to be disclosed or defended; they would simply be taken for granted—reason deduces them from the facts of our faith; we are the creatures of one God, who has appointed one Church to be the interpreter of his will upon earth."

"Every traitor is a sophist, sir; I have neither skill nor temper for such discussions," I answered, proving my latter position sufficiently. "I had no idea that you could have thought of visiting here, and I hoped I should have been spared the pain of seeing you again. Nor should I like to continue this conversation, because I might be tempted to say even more pointedly what I think than I care to do. Good-bye, Mr. Carmel, good-bye, sir," I repeated, with a quiet emphasis meant to check, as I thought, his evident intention to speak again.

He so understood it. He paused for a moment, undecided, and then said:

"Am I to understand that you command me to come no more?"

"Certainly," I answered, coldly and angrily.

His hand was on the door, and he asked very gently, but I thought with some little agitation:

"And that you now end our acquaintance?"

"Certainly," I repeated, in the same tone.

"Heaven has sent my share of sorrow," he said; "but no soldier of Christ goes to his grave without many scars. I deserve my wounds and submit. It must be long before we meet again under any circumstances; never, perhaps, in this life."

He looked at me. He was very pale, and his large eyes were full of kindness. He held out his hand to me silently, but I did not take it. He sighed deeply, and placed it again on the handle of the door, and said, very low:

"Farewell, Miss Ware—Ethel—my pupil, and may God for ever bless you!" So the door opened, and he went.

I heard the hall door shut. That sullen sound smote my heart like a signal telling me that my last friend was gone.

Few people who have taken an irrevocable step on impulse, even though they have done rightly, think very clearly immediately after. My own act for a while confounded me. I don't think that Mr. Carmel was formed by nature for deception. I think, in my inmost soul, I believed his denial, and was sure that he had neither act nor part in the management of Lady Lorrimer's will. I know I felt a sort of compunction, and I experienced that melancholy doubt as to having been quite in the right, which sometimes follows an angry scene. In this state I returned to mamma to tell her all that had passed.

CHAPTER XL.

A RAINY DAY.

Mamma knew nothing distinctly about the state of our affairs, but she knew something generally of the provision made at her marriage, and she thought we should have about a thousand a year to live upon.

I could hardly recognise the possibility of this, with Mr. Forrester's forbodings. But if that, or even something like it, were secured to us, we could go down to Malory, and live there very comfortably. Mamma's habits of thinking, and the supine routine of her useless life, had sustained a shock, and her mind seemed now to rest with pleasure on the comparative solitude and quiet of a country life.

All our servants, except one or two, were under notice to go. I had also got leave from mamma to get our plate, horses, carriages, and other superfluous things valued, and fifty other trifling measures taken to expedite the winding-up of our old life, and our entrance upon our new one, the moment Mr. Forrester should tell us that our income was ascertained, and available.

I was longing to be gone, so also was mamma. She seemed very easy about our provision for the future, and I, alternating between an overweening confidence and an irrepressible anxiety, awaited the promised disclosures of Mr. Forrester, which were to end our suspense.

Nearly a fortnight passed before he came again. A note reached us the day before, saying that he would call at four, unless we should write in the meantime to put him off. He did come, and I shall never forget the interview that followed. Mamma and I were sitting in the front drawing-room, expecting him. My heart was trembling. I know of no state so intolerable as suspense upon a vital issue. It is the state in which people in money troubles are, without intermission. How it is lived through for years, as often as it is, and without the loss of reason, is in my eyes the greatest physical and psychological wonder of this sorrowful world.

A gloomier day could hardly have heralded the critical exposition that was to disclose our future lot. A dark sky, clouds dark as coal-smoke, and a steady downpour of rain, large-dropped and violent, that keeps up a loud and gusty drumming on the panes, down which the wet is rushing in rivers. Now and then the noise rises to a point that makes conversation difficult. Every minute at this streaming window I was looking into the street, where cabs and umbrellas, few and far between, were scarcely discoverable through the rivulets that coursed over the glass.

At length I saw a cab, like a waving mass of black mist, halt at the door, and a double knock followed. My breath almost left me. In a minute or two the servant, opening the door, said, "Mr. Forrester," and that gentleman stepped into the gloomy room, with a despatch-box in his hand, looking ominously grave and pale. He took mamma's hand, and looked, I thought, with a kind of doubtful inquiry in her face, as if measuring her strength to bear some unpleasant news. I almost forgot to shake hands with him, I was so horribly eager to hear him speak.

Mamma was much more confident than I, and said, as soon as he had placed his box beside him, and sat down:

"I'm so obliged to you, Mr. Forrester; you have been so extremely kind to us. My daughter told me that you intended making inquiries, and letting us know all you heard; I hope you think it satisfactory?"

He looked down, and shook his head in silence. Mamma flushed very much, and stood up, staring at him, and grew deadly pale.

"It is not—it can't be less—I hope it's not—than nine hundred a year. If it is not that, what is to become of us?"

Mamma's voice sounded hard and stern, though she spoke very low. I, too, was staring at the messenger of fate with all my eyes, and my heart was thumping hard.

"Very far from satisfactory. I wish it were anything at all like the sum you have named," said Mr. Forrester, very dejectedly, but gathering courage for his statement as he proceeded. "I'll tell you, Mrs. Ware, the result of my correspondence, and I am really pained and grieved that I should have such a statement to make. I find that you opened your marriage settlement, except the provision for your daughter, which, I regret to say, is little more than a thousand pounds, and she takes nothing during your life, and then we can't put it down at more than forty pounds a year."

"But—but I want to know," broke in poor mamma, with eyes that glared, and her very lips white, "what there is—how much we have got to live on?"

"I hope from my heart there may be something, Mrs. Ware, but I should not be treating you fairly if I did not tell you frankly that it seems to me a case in which relations ought to come forward."

I felt so stunned that I could not speak.

"You mean, ask their assistance?" said mamma. "My good God! I can't—we can't—I could not do that!"

"Mamma," said I, with white lips, "had not we better hear all that Mr. Forrester has to tell us?"

"Allow me," continued mamma, excitedly; "there must be something, Ethel—don't talk folly. We can live at Malory, and, however small our pittance, we must make it do. But I won't consent to beg." Mamma's colour came again as she said this, with a look of haughty resentment at Mr. Forrester. That poor gentleman seemed distressed, and shifted his position a little uneasily.

"Malory," he began, "would be a very suitable place, if an income were arranged. But Malory will be in Sir Harry Rokestone's possession in two or three days, and without his leave you could not get there; and I'm afraid I dare not encourage you to entertain any hopes of a favourable, or even a courteous, hearing in that quarter. Since I had the pleasure of seeing Miss Ware here, about ten days or a fortnight since, I saw Mr. Jarlcot, of Golden Friars; a very intelligent man he evidently is, and does Sir Harry Rokestone's business in that part of the world, and seemed very friendly; but he says that in that quarter"—Mr. Forrester paused, and shook his head gloomily, looking on the carpet—"we have nothing good to look for. He bears your family, it appears an implacable animosity, and does not scruple to express it in very violent language indeed."

"I did not know that Sir Harry Rokestone had any claim upon Malory," said mamma; "I don't know by what right he can prevent our going into my house."

"I'm afraid there can be no doubt as to his right as a trustee; but it was not obligatory on him to enforce it. Some charges ought to have been paid off four years ago; it is a very peculiar deed, and, instead of that, interest has been allowed to accumulate. I took the liberty of writing to Sir Harry Rokestone a very strong letter, the day after my last interview with Miss Ware; but he has taken not the slightest notice of it, and that is very nearly a fortnight ago, and Jarlcot seems to think that, if he lets me off with silence, I'm getting off very easily. They all seem afraid of him down there."

I fancied that Mr. Forrester had been talking partly to postpone a moment of pain. If there was a shock coming, he wanted resolution to precipitate the crisis, and looked again with a perplexed and uneasy countenance on the carpet. He glanced at mamma, once or twice, quickly, as if he had nearly made up his mind to break the short silence that had followed. While he was hesitating, however, I was relieved by mamma's speaking, and very much to the point.

"And how much do you think, Mr. Forrester, we shall have to live upon?"

"That," said he, looking steadfastly on the table, with a very gloomy countenance, "is the point on which, I fear, I have nothing satisfactory—or even hopeful," he added, raising his head, and looking a little stern, and even frightened, "to say. You must only look the misfortune in the face; and a great misfortune it is, accustomed as you have been to everything that makes life happy and easy. It is, as I said before, a case in which relations who are wealthy, and well able to do it, should come forward."

"But do say what it is," said mamma, trembling violently. "I shan't be frightened, only say distinctly. Is it only four hundred?—or only three hundred a year?" She paused, looking imploringly at him.

"I should be doing very wrong if I told you there was anything—anything like that—anything whatever certain, in fact, however small. There's nothing certain, and it would be very wrong to mislead you. I don't think the assets and property will be sufficient to pay the debts."

"Great Heaven! Sir—oh! oh!—is there nothing left?"

He shook his head despondingly. The murder was out now; there was no need of any more questioning—no case could be simpler. We were not worth a shilling!

If in my vain and godless days the doctor at my bedside had suddenly told me that I must die before midnight, I could not have been more bewildered. Without knowing what I did, I turned and walked to the window, on which the rain was thundering, and rolling down in rivers. I heard nothing—my ears were stunned.

CHAPTER XLI.

THE FLITTING.

We were ruined! What must the discovery have been to poor mamma? She saw all the monstrous past—the delirium was dissipated. An abyss was between her and her former life. In the moment of social death, all that she was leaving had become almost grotesque, incredibly ghastly. Here in a moment was something worse than poverty, worse even than death.

During papa's life the possibility of those vague vexations known as "difficulties" and "embarrassments," might have occurred to me, but that I should ever have found myself in the plight in which I now stood had never entered my imagination.

Suppose, on a fine evening, a ship, with a crash like a cannon, tears open her planks on a hidden rock, and the water gushes and whirls above the knees, the waists, the throats of the polite people round the tea-table in the state-cabin, without so much as time interposed to say God bless us! between the warning and the catastrophe, and you have our case!

Young ladies, you live in a vague and pleasant dream. Gaslight in your hall and lobbies, wax lights, fires, decorous servants, flowers, spirited horses, millinery, soups and wines, are products of nature, and come of themselves. There is, nevertheless, such a thing as poverty, as there is such a thing as death. We hold them both as doctrines, and, of course, devoutly believe in them, but when either lays its cold hand on your shoulder, and you look it in the face, you are as much appalled as if you had never heard its name before.

Carelessness, indolence, a pleasurable supineness, without any other grievous fault or enormous mistake, had, little by little, prepared all for the catastrophe. Mamma was very ill that night. In the morning Mr. Forrester came again. Mamma could not see him; but I had a long interview with him. He was very kind. I will tell you, in a few words, the upshot of our conference.

In the first place, the rather startling fact was disclosed that we had, in the world, but nine pounds, eight shillings, which mamma happened still to have in her purse, out of her last money for dress. Nine pounds, eight shillings! That was all that interposed between us and the wide republic of beggary. Then Mr. Forrester told me that mamma must positively leave the house in which we were then residing, to avoid being made, as he said, "administratrix in her own wrong," and put to great annoyance, and seeing any little fund that relations might place at her disposal wasted in expenses and possible litigation.

So it was settled we were to leave the house, but where were we to go? That was provided for. Near High Holborn, in a little street entered between two narrow piers, stood an odd and ancient house, as old as the times of James the First, which was about to be taken down to make way for a model lodging-house. The roof was sound, and the drainage good, that was all he could say for it; and he could get us leave to occupy it, free of rent, until its demolition should be commenced. He had, in fact, already arranged that for mamma.

Poor papa had owed him a considerable sum for law costs. He meant, he said, to remit the greater part of it, and whatever the estate might give him, on account of them, he would hand over to mamma. He feared the sum would be a small one. He thought it would hardly amount to a hundred pounds, but in the meantime she could have fifty pounds on account of it.

She might also remove a very little furniture, but no more than would just suffice, in the scantiest way, for our bed-rooms and one sitting-room, and such things as a servant might take for the kitchen. He would make himself responsible to the creditors for these.

I need not go further into particulars. Of course there were many details to be adjusted, and the conduct of all these arrangements devolved upon me. Mr. Forrester undertook all the dealings with the servants whom it was necessary to dismiss and pay forthwith.

The house was now very deserted. There was no life in it but that feverish fuss like the preparations that condemned people make for their executions. The arrangements for our sorrowful flight went on like the dismal worry of a sick dream. In our changed state we preferred country servants, and I wrote for good old Rebecca Torkill and one of her rustic maids at Malory, who arrived, and entered on their duties the day before our departure. How outlandish these good creatures appeared when transplanted from the primitive life and surroundings of Malory to the artificial scenes of London! But how comfortable and kindly was their clumsiness, compared with the cynical politeness and growing contempt of the cosmopolitan servants of London!

Well, at last we were settled in our strange habitation. It was by no means so uncomfortable as you might have supposed. We found ourselves in a sitting-room of handsome dimensions, panelled with oak up to its ceiling, which, however, from the size of the room, appeared rather low. It was richly moulded, after the style of James the First's reign, but the coarse smear of newly-applied whitewash covered its traceries.

Our scanty furniture was collected at the upper end of the apartment, which was covered with a piece of carpet, and shut off from the lower part of the room by a folding screen. Some kind friend had placed flowers in a glass on the table, and three pretty plants in full blow upon the window-stones. Some books from a circulating library were on the table, and some volumes also of engravings. These little signs of care and refinement took off something of the gaunt and desolate character which would have, otherwise, made this habitation terrifying.

A rich man, with such a house in the country, might have made it curiously beautiful; but where it was, tenanted by paupers, and condemned to early demolition, who was to trouble his head about it?

Mamma had been better in the morning, but was now suffering, again, from a violent palpitation, and was sitting up in her bed; it was her own bed, which had been removed for her use. Rebecca Torkill, who had been for some hours managing everything to receive her, was now in her room. I was in our "drawing-room," I suppose I am to call it, quite alone. My elbows rested on the table, my hands were over my eyes, and I was crying vehemently. These were tears neither of cowardice nor of sorrow. They were tears of rage. I was one of those impracticable and defiant spirits who, standing more in need than any other of the chastisements of Heaven, resent its discipline as an outrage, and upbraid its justice with impious fury. I dried my eyes fiercely. I looked round our strange room with a bitter smile. Black oak floor, black oak panelling up to the ceiling; as evening darkened how melancholy this grew!

I looked out of the window. The ruddy sky of evening was fading into grey. A grass-grown brick wall, as old as the house perhaps, and springing from the two piers, enclosed the space once occupied by the street in which it had stood. Nothing now remained of the other houses but high piles of rubbish, broken bricks, and plaster, through which, now and then, a black spar or plank of worn wood was visible in this dismal enclosure; beyond these hillocks of ruin, and the jagged and worn brick wall, were visible the roofs with slates no bigger than oyster-shells, and the clumsy old chimneys of poverty-stricken dwellings, existing on sufferance, and sure to fall before long beneath the pick and crowbar; beyond these melancholy objects spread the expiring glow of sunset with a veil of smoke before it.

As I looked back upon this sombre room, and then out upon the still more gloomy and ruinous prospcct, with a feeling of disgust and fear, and the intolerable consciousness that we were here under the coercion of actual poverty, you may fancy what my ruminations were. I don't know whether, in my family, there was a vein of that hereditary melancholy called suicidal. I know I felt, just then, its horrible promptings. Like the invitations of the Erl-king in Goethe's ballad, it "whispered low in mine ear." There is nothing so startling as the first real allurement to this tremendous step. There remains a sense of an actual communication at which mind and soul tremble. I felt it once afterwards.

Its insidiousness and power are felt on starting from the dream, and finding oneself, as I did, alone, with silence and darkness and frightful thoughts. I think that, but for mamma, it would have been irresistible. The sudden exertion of my will, and in spite of my impious mood, I am sure, an inward cry to God for help, scared away the brood that had gathered about me with their soft monotonous seduction. Have you ever experienced the same thing? The temptation breaks from you like a murmur changed to a laugh, and leaves you horrified. I hated life; my energies were dead already. Why should I drag on, with broken heart, in solitude and degradation?

Some pitying angel kept me in remembrance of mamma, sick, helpless, so long and entirely in the habit of leaning upon others for counsel and for action. When sickness follows poverty, fate has little left to inflict. One good thing in our present habitation was the fact of its being as completely out of sight as the inmost cavern of the catacombs. That was consolatory. I felt, at first, as if I never should wish to see the light again. But every expression of life is strong in the young; energy, health, spirits, hope.

The dread of this great downfall began to subside, and I could see a little before me; my head grew clearer, and was already full of plans for earning my bread. That, I dare say, would have been easy enough, if I could have made up my mind to leave mamma, or if she could have consented to part with me. But there were many things I could do at home. Mamma was sometimes better, but her spirits never rallied. She cried almost incessantly; I think she was heart-broken. If she could have given me some of her gentleness, and if I could have inspired her with some of my courage, we should have done better.

The day after our arrival, as I looked out of the window listlessly, I saw a van drive between the piers. Two men were on the driver's seat. They stopped before they had got very far. It was difficult navigation among the promontories and islands of rubbish. The driver turned a disgusted look up towards our windows, and made some remark to his companion. They got down and led the horses with circumspection, and with many turns and windings up to the door, and then began to speak to our servant; but, at this interesting moment, I was summoned by Rebecca Torkill to mamma's room, where I forgot all about the van.

But, on returning a few minutes later, I found a piano in our drawing-room. Our rustic maid had not heard or even asked from whom it came; and when a tuner arrived an hour later, I found that nothing could prevail on him to disclose the name of the person or place from which it had come. It had not any indication but the maker's name and that was no guide.

Two, or three days after our flight to this melancholy place, Mr. Forrester called. I saw him in our strange sitting-room. It was pleasant to see a friendly face. He had not many minutes to give me. He listened to my plans, and rather approved of them; told me that he had some clients who might be useful, and that he would make it a point to do what he could with them. Then I thanked him very much for the flowers, and the books, and the piano. But it was not he who had sent them. I began to be rather unpleasantly puzzled about the quarter from which these favours came. Our melancholy habitation must be known to more persons than we supposed. I was thinking uncomfortably on this problem when he went on to say:

"As Mrs. Ware is not well enough to see me, I should like to read to you a draft of the letter I was thinking of sending to-day to Lord Chellwood's house.

He's to be home, I understand, for a day or two before the end of this week; and I want to hit him on the wing, if I can."

He then read the letter for me.

"Pray leave out what you say of me," I said.

"Why, Miss Ware?"

"Because, if I can't live by my own labour, I will die," I answered. "I think it is his duty to do something for mamma, who is ill, and the widow of his brother, and who has lost her provision by poor papa's misfortunes; but I mean to work; and I hope to earn quite enough to support me; and if I can't, as I said, I don't wish to live. I will accept nothing from him."

"And why not from him, Miss Ware? You know he's your uncle. Whom could you more naturally look to in such an emergency?"

"He's not my uncle; papa was his half-brother only, by a later marriage. He never liked papa—nor us."

"Never mind—he'll do something. I've had some experience; and I tell you, he can't avoid contributing in a case like this; it comes too near him," said Mr. Forrester.

"I have seen him—I have heard him talk; I know the kind of person he is. I have heard poor papa say, 'I wish some one would relieve Norman's mind: he seems to fancy we have a design on his pocket, or his will. He is always keeping us at arm's-length. I don't think my wife is ever likely to have to ask him for anything.' I have heard poor papa say, I think, those very words. Bread from his hand would choke me, and I can't eat it."

"Well, Miss Ware, if you object to that passage, I shall strike it out, of course. I wrote a second time to Sir Harry Rokestone, and have not yet had a line in reply, and I don't think it likely I ever shall. I'll try him once more; and if that doesn't bring an answer, I think we may let him alone for some time to come."

And now Mr. Forrester took his leave and was gone. The forlorn old house was silent again.

CHAPTER XLII.

A FORLORN HOPE.

Another week passed; mamma was better—not much better in spirits, but very much apparently in health. She was now a good deal more tranquil, though in great affliction. Poor mamma! No book interested her now but the Bible; the great, wise, gentle friend so seldom listened to when all goes well—always called in to console, when others fail.

Mr. Forrester had got me some work to do—work much more interesting than I had proposed for myself. It was to make a translation of a French work for a publisher. For a few days it was simply experimental, but it was found that I did it well and quickly enough; and I calculated that if I could only obtain constant employment of this kind, I might earn about seventy pounds a year. Here was a resource—something between us and actual want—something between me and the terrible condition of dependence. My ambition was humble enough now.

For about two days this discovery of my power, under favourable circumstances, to make sixty or seventy pounds a year, actually cheered me; but this healthier effect was of short duration. The miseries of our situation were too obvious and formidable to be long kept out of view. Gloom and distraction soon returned—the same rebellious violence inflamed by the fresh alarm of mamma's returning illness.

She was very ill again the night but one after the good news about my translation—breathless, palpitating. I began to grow frightened and desponding about her. I had fancied before that her symptoms were mere indications of her state of mind; but now, when her mind seemed more tranquil, and her nerves quiet, their return was ominous. I was urging her to see Sir Jacob Lake, when Mr. Forrester called, and I went to our drawing-room to see him. He had got a note, cold and petulant, from my uncle, Lord Chellwood, that morning. This letter said that "no person who knew of the number and magnitude of the charges affecting his property could be so unreasonable as to suppose that he could, even if he had the power, which was not quite so clear, think of charging an annuity upon it, however small, for the benefit of any one." That "he deeply commiserated the distressing circumstances in which poor Frank's widow found herself; but surely he, Lord

Chellwood, was not to blame for it. He had never lost an opportunity of pressing upon his brother the obligation he conceived every married man to be under, to make provision for his wife; and had been at the trouble to show him, by some very pertinent figures, how impracticable it was for him to add to the burdens that weighed on the estates, and how totally he, Lord Chellwood, was without the power of mitigating to any extent the consequences of his rashness, if he should leave his wife without a suitable provision." So it went on; and ended by saying that "he might possibly be able, next spring, to make—it could be but a small one—a present to the poor lady, who had certainly much to answer for in the imprudent career in which she had contributed to engage her husband, and during which she had wilfully sacrificed her settlement to the pleasures and vanities of an expensive and unsuitable life." The letter went on in this strain, and hinted that the present he spoke of could not exceed a hundred and fifty pounds, and could not possibly be repeated.

"This looks very black, you see," said the good-natured solicitor. "But I hope it may not be quite so bad as he says. If he could be got to do a little more, a small annuity might be purchased."

I did not like my uncle. It is very hard to get over first impressions, and the repulsion of an entirely uncongenial countenance. There was nothing manly in his face—it was narrow, selfish, conceited. He was pale as wax. He had manners at once dry and languid; and whether it was in his eye or not, I can't say, but there was something in his look, though he smiled as much as was called for, and never said a disagreeable thing, that conveyed very clearly to me, although neither papa nor mamma seemed to perceive it, that he positively disliked us, each and every one, not even excepting poor, gay, good-natured papa. We all knew he was stingy; he had one hobby, and that was the nursing and rehabilitation of the estates which had come to him, with the title, in a very crippled state.

With these feelings, and the pride which is strongest in youth, I fancied that I should have died rather than have submitted to the humiliation of accepting, much less asking, money from his hand.

I must carry you three weeks further on. It was dark; I can't tell you now what o'clock it was; I am sure it was not much earlier than nine. I had my cloak and bonnet on; Rebecca Torkill was at my side, and her thin hand was upon my arm.

"And where are you going, my darling, at this time of night?" she said, looking frightened into my face.

"To see Lord Chellwood; to see papa's unnatural brother; to tell him that mamma must die unless he helps her."

"But, my child, this is no time—you would not go out through them wicked streets at this hour—you shan't go!" she said sturdily, taking a firm hold of my arm.

I snatched it from her grasp angrily, and walked quickly away. I looked over my shoulder, as I reached the two piers, and saw the figure of old Rebecca looking black in the doorway, with a background of misty light from the candle at the foot of the stairs. I think she was wavering between the risk of leaving the house and mamma only half protected, and the urgent necessity of pursuing and bringing me back. I was out of her reach, however, before she could make up her mind.

I was walking as quickly as I could through the streets that led towards Regent Street. I had studied them on the map.

These out-of-the-way streets were quiet now, but not deserted; now and then I passed the blaze of a gin-palace. It was a strange fear and excitement to me to be walking through these poor by-streets by gas-light. No fugitive threading the streets of a town in the throes of revolution had a keener sense of danger, or moved with eye and sinew more ready every moment to start from a walk into a run. I suppose they allow poor people, such as I might well be taken for, walking quickly upon their business, to pass undisturbed. I was not molested.

At length I was in Regent Street. I felt safe now; the broad pavement, the stream of traffic, the long line of gas-lamps, and the still open shops, enabled me, without fear, a little to slacken my pace. I required this relief. I had been ill for two days, and was worse. I felt chilly and aguish; I was suffering from one of those stupendous headaches which possibly give the sufferer some idea of the action of that iron "cap of silence" with which, during the reign of good King Bomba, so many Neapolitan citizens were made acquainted. I can afford to speak lightly of it now; but I was very ill. I ought to have been in my bed. Nothing but my tremor about mamma would have given me nerve and strength for this excursion.

She had that day had a sudden return of the breathlessness and palpitation from which she had suffered so much, and I had succeeded in getting Sir Jacob Lake to come to see her.

It was a hurried visit, as his visits always were. He saw her, gave some general directions, wrote a prescription, spoke cheerfully to her, and his manner seemed to say he apprehended nothing. I came with him to the stairs, which we went down together, and in the drawing-room I heard the astounding words that told me mamma could not live many months, and might be carried off at any moment in one of those attacks. He told me to get her to the country, her native air, if that could be managed, immediately. That might prolong her life a little. It was only a chance, and at best a reprieve. But without it he could not answer for a week. He told me that I must be careful not to let mamma know that he thought her in danger. She was in a critical state, and any agitation might be fatal. He took his leave, and I was alone with his dreadful words in my ears.

Now, how was I to carry out his directions? The journey to Golden Friars, as he planned it, would cost us at least twenty pounds, and he ordered claret, then a very expensive wine, for mamma. He did not know that he was carrying away our last guinea in his pocket. I had but half a sovereign and a few shillings in my purse. Mr. Forrester was out of town; and even if he were within reach, it was scarcely likely that he would lend or bestow anything like the sum required. The work was not sufficiently advanced to justify a hope that he would give me, a stranger, a sum of money on account of a task which I might never complete.

Poverty had come in its direst shape. In the distraction of that dreadful helplessness my pride broke down. This was the reason of my wild excursion.

As I now walked at a more moderate pace, I felt the effect of my unnatural exertion more painfully—every pulse was a throb of torture. It was an effort to keep my mind clear, and to banish perpetually rising confusions, the incipient exhalations of fever. What drowsiness is to the system in health, this tendency to drop into delirium is to the sick.

I found myself, at length, almost exhausted, at my noble kinsman's door. I knocked; I asked to see him. The footman did not recognise me. He simply said, looking across the street over my head, with a careless disdain:

"I say, what's the row, miss?"

Certainly such a visitor as I, and at such an hour, had no very recognisable claim to a ceremonious reception.

"Charles," I said, "don't you know me?—Miss Ware."

The man started a little, looked hard at me, drew himself up formally, as he made his salutation, receding a step, with the hall-door open in his hand.

"Is his lordship at home?" I asked.

"No, miss, he dined out to-day."

"But I must see him, Charles. If he knew it was I he could not refuse. Tell him mamma is dangerously ill, and I have no one to help me."

"He is out, miss; and he sleeps out of town—at Colonel Anson's to-night."

I uttered an exclamation of despair.

"And when is he to return?"

"He will not be in town again for a fortnight, miss; he's going to Harleigh Castle."

I stood on the steps for a minute, stunned by the disappointment, staring helplessly into the man's face.

"Please, shall I call a cab, miss?"

"No—no," I said dreamily. I turned and went away quickly. It troubled me little what the servants might say or think of my strange visit.

This blow was distracting. The doctor had distinctly said that mamma's immediate removal to country air was a necessity.

As people will under excitement, I was walking at the swiftest pace I could. I was pacing under the evergreens of the neighbouring square, back and forward, again and again; I saw young ladies get from a house opposite into a carriage, and drive away, as I once used to do. I hated them—I hated every one who was as fortunate as I once was. I hated the houses on the other side with their well-lighted halls. I hated even the great prosperous shop-keeping class, with their overgrown persons and purses. Why did not fortune take other people, the purse-proud, the scheming, the vicious, the arrogant, the avaricious, instead of us—drag them from their places, and batter and trundle them in the gutter? Here was I, for no fault—none, none!—reduced to a worse plight than a beggar's. The beggar has been brought up to his calling, and can make something of it; while I could not set about it, had not even that form of pluck which people call meanness, and was quite past the age at which the art is to be learned.

All this time I was growing more and more ill. The breathless walking and the angry agitation were precipitating the fever that was already upon me. I had an increasing horror of the dismal abode which was now my home. Distraction like mine demands rapid locomotion as its proper and only anodyne. Despair and quietude quickly subside into madness.

Some public clock not far off struck the hour; I did not count it; but it reminded me suddenly of the risk of exciting alarm at home by delaying my return. So with an effort, and as it were an awakening, I began to direct my steps homewards. But before I reached that melancholy goal, an astounding adventure was fated to befall me.

CHAPTER XLIII.

COLD STEEL.

I am quite certain now that the impious sophistries to which some proud minds in affliction abandon themselves, are the direful suggestions of intelligences immensely superior in power to themselves. When they call to us in the air we listen; when they knock at the door we go down and open to them; we take them in to sup with us, we make them our guests, they become sojourners in the house, and are about our paths, and about our beds, and spying out all our ways; their thoughts become our thoughts, their wickedness our wickedness, their purposes our purposes, till, without perceiving it, we are their slaves. And then when a fit opportunity presents itself, they make, in Doctor Johnson's phrase, "a snatch of us." Something like this was near happening to me. You shall hear.

I grew, on a sudden, faint and cold; a horror of returning home stole over me. I could not go home, and yet I had no other choice but death. I had scarcely thought of death, when a longing seized me. Death grew so beautiful in my eyes! The false smile, the mysterious welcome, the sweep of deep waters, the vague allurement of a profound endless welcome, drew me on and on.

Two men chatting passed me by as one said to the other, "The tide's full in at Waterloo Bridge now; the moon must look quite lovely there." It was spoken in harmony with my thoughts. I had read in my happier days in the papers how poor girls had ended their misery by climbing over the balustrade of Waterloo Bridge, over the black abyss, dotted with the reflected lamps, and stepping off it into the dark air into death. I was going now to that bridge—people would direct me—by the time I reached it the thoroughfare would be still and deserted enough. I can't say I had determined upon this—I can't say I ever thought about it—it was only that the scene and the event had taken possession of me, with the longing of a child for its home.

The streets were quieter now; but some shops were still open. Among these was a jeweller's. The shutters were up, and only the door open. I stepped in, I don't in the least know why. The fever, I suppose, had touched my brain. There were only three men in the shop—one behind the counter, a smiling, ceremonious man, whom I believe to have been the owner—the two others were customers.

One was a young man, sitting on a chair with his elbow on the counter, examining and turning over some jewellery that glittered in a little heap on the counter. The other, older and dressed in black, was leaning over the counter, with his back to me, and discussing, in low, careless tones, the merits of a dagger, which, from their talk, not distinctly heard, I conjectured the young man had been recommending as a specific against garotters. I was in no condition to comprehend or care for the debate. The elder man, as he talked, sometimes laid the little weapon down upon the counter, and sometimes took it up, fitting it in his hand.

The intense light of the gas striking on my eyes made them ache acutely. I don't know why, or how, I entered the shop; I only know that I found myself standing within the door in a blaze of gaslight.

The jeweller, looking at me sharply across the counter, said:

"Well, ma'am?"

I answered:

"Can you give me change for a sovereign?"

I must have been losing my head; for though I spoke in perfect good faith, I had not a shilling about me. It was not forgetfulness, but distinctly an illusion; for I not only had the picture of the imaginary sovereign distinctly before me, but thought I had it actually in my hand.

The jeweller was talking in subdued and urbane accents to his customer, and pointing out, no doubt, the special beauties and workmanship of his *bijouterie.*

"Sorry I can't oblige you; you must try elsewhere," he said, again directing a hard glance at me. I think he was satisfied that I was not a thief; and he continued his talk with the young man who was making his selection, and who was probably a little hard to please. I turned to leave the shop, and the jeweller went into the next room, possibly in search of something more likely to please his fastidious client at the counter.

I had not yet seen the face of either of the visitors to the shop, but I was conscious that the younger of the two had once or twice looked over his shoulder at me. He now said, taking his purse from his pocket—it was but as a parenthesis in his talk with his companion:

"I beg pardon; perhaps I can manage that change for you."

I drew nearer. What occurred next appeared to me like an incident in a dream, in which our motives are often so obscure that our own acts take us by surprise. Whether it was a mad moment or a lucid moment I don't know; for in extreme misery, if our courage does not fail us, our thoughts are always wicked.

I stood there, a slight figure, in crape, cloaked, veiled—in pain, giddy, confused. I cannot tell you what interest the common-place spectacle before me had for me, nor why I stayed there, gazing towards the three gas lamps that seemed each girt with a dazzling halo that made my eyes ache. What sounds and sights smote my sick senses with a jarring recognition? The hard, nasal tones of the elderly man in black, who leaned over the counter, and the pallid, scornful face, with its fine, restless eyes and sinister energy, were those of Monsieur Droqville!

He was talking to his companion, and did not trouble himself to look at me. He little dreamed what an image of death stood at his elbow!

They were not talking any longer about the pretty dagger that lay on the counter, by his open fingers. Monsieur Droqville was now indulging his cynical vein upon another theme. He was finishing a satirical summing up of poor papa's character. I saw the sneer, the shrug; I heard in his hard, bitter talk the name made sacred to me by unutterable calamity; I listened to the outrage from the lips of the man who had done all. Oh, beloved, ruined father! Can I ever forget the pale smile of despair, the cold, piteous voice with which, on that frightful night, he said, "Droqville has done it all—he has broken my heart." And here was the very Droqville, with the scoff, the contempt, the triumph in his pitiless face; and poor papa in his bloody shroud, and mamma dying! What cared I what became of me? An icy chill seemed to stream from my brain through me, to my feet, to my finger tips; as a shadow moves, I had leaned over, and the hand that holds this pen had struck the dagger into Droqville's breast.

In a moment his face darkened, with a horrified, vacant look. His mouth opened, as if to speak or call out, but no sound came; his deep-set eyes, fixed on me, were darkening; he was sinking backward, with a groping motion of his hand, as if to ward off another blow.

Was it real? For a second I stared, freezing with horror; and then, with a gasp, darted through the shop-door.

An accident, as I afterwards learned, had lamed Droqville's companion, and thus favoured my escape. Before many seconds, however, pursuit was on my track. I soon heard its cry and clatter. The street was empty when I ran out. My echoing steps were the only sound there for some seconds. I fled with the speed of the wind. I turned to the left down a narrow street, and from that to the right into a kind of stable lane. I heard shouting and footsteps in pursuit. I ran for some time, but the shouting of sounds and pursuit continued. My strength failed me; I stopped short behind a kind of buttress, beside a coach-house gate; I was hardly a second there. An almost suicidal folly prompted me. I know not why, but I stepped out again from my place of concealment, intending to give myself up to my pursuers. I walked slowly back a few steps towards them. One was now close to me. A man without a hat, crying, "Stop, stop, police!" ran furiously past me. It clearly never entered his mind that I, walking slowly towards him, could possibly be the fugitive.

So this moment, as I expected of perdition, passed innocuously by.

By what instinct, chance, or miracle I made the rest of my way home, I know not. When I reached the door-stone, Rebecca Torkill was standing there watching for me in irrepressible panic.

When she was sure it was I, she ran out, crying, "Oh! God be thanked, miss, it's you, my child!" She caught me in her arms, and kissed me with honest vehemence. I did not return her caress—I was worn out; it all seemed like a frightful dream. Her voice sounded ever so far away. I saw her, as raving people see objects mixed with unrealities. I did not say a word as she conveyed me upstairs with her stalwart arm round my waist.

I heard her say, "Your mamma's better; she's quite easy now." I could not say, "Thank God!" I was conscious that I showed no trace of pleasure, nor even of comprehension, in my looks.

She was looking anxiously in my face as she talked to me, and led me into the drawing-room. I did not utter a word, nor look to the right or left. With a moan I sat down on the sofa. I was shivering uncontrollably.

Another phantom was now before me, talking with Rebecca. It was Mr. Carmel; his large, strange eyes—how dark and haggard they looked—fixed on my face with a gaze almost of agony! Something fell from my hand on the table as my fingers relaxed. I had forgotten that I held anything in them. I saw them both look at it, and then on one another with a glance of alarm, and even horror. It was the dagger, stained with blood, that had dropped upon that homely table.

I was unable to follow their talk. I saw him take it up quickly, and look from it to me, and to Rebecca again, with a horrible uncertainty. It was, indeed, a rather sinister waif to find in the hand of a person evidently so ill as I was, especially with a mark of blood also upon that trembling hand. He looked at it again very carefully; then he put it into Rebecca's hand, and said something very earnestly.

They talked on for a time. I neither understood nor cared what they said; nor cared, indeed, at all what became of me.

"You're not hurt, darling?" she whispered, with her earnest old eyes very near mine.

"I? No. Oh, no!" I answered.

"Not with that knife?"

"No," I repeated.

I was rapidly growing worse.

A little time passed thus, and then I saw Mr. Carmel pray with his hands clasped for a few moments, and I heard him distinctly say to Rebecca, "She's very ill. I'll go for the doctor;" and he added some words to her. He looked ghastly pale: as he gazed in my face, his eyes seemed to burn into my brain. Then another figure was added to the group; our maid glided in, and stood beside Rebecca Torkill, and as it seemed to me, murmured vaguely. I could not understand what she or they said. She looked as frightened as the rest. I had perception enough left to feel that they all thought me dying. So the thought filled my darkened mind that I was indeed passing into the state of the dead. The black curtain that had been suspended over me for so long at last descended, and I remember no more for many days and nights.

The secret was, for the present, mine only. I lay, as the old writers say, "at God's mercy," the sword's point at my throat, in the privation, darkness, and utter helplessness of fever. Safe enough it was with me. My brain could recall nothing; my lips were sealed. But though I was speechless, another person was quickly in possession of the secret.

Some weeks, as I have said, are simply struck out of my existence. When gradually the cold, grey light of returning life stole in upon me, I almost hoped it might be fallacious. I hated to come back to the frightful routine of existence. I was so very weak that even after the fever left me I might easily have died at any moment.

I was promoted at length to the easy-chair, in which, in dressing-gown and slippers, people recover from dangerous illness. There, in the listlessness of exhaustion, I used to sit for hours, without reading, without speaking, without even thinking. Gradually, by little, my spirit revived, and, as life returned, the black cares and fears essential to existence glided in, and gathered round with awful faces.

One day old Rebecca, who, no doubt, had long been anxious, asked:

"How did you come by that knife, Miss Ethel, that you fetched home in your hand the night you took ill?"

"A knife? Did I?" I spoke, quietly suppressing my horror. "What was it like?"

I was almost unconscious until then that I had really taken away the dagger in my hand. This speech of Rebecca's nearly killed me. They were the first words I had heard connecting me distinctly with that ghastly scene.

She described it, and repeated her question.

"Where is it?" I asked.

"Mr. Carmel took it away with him," she replied, "the same night."

"Mr. Carmel?" I repeated, remembering with a new terror his connexion with Monsieur Droqville. "You had no business to allow him to see it, much less—good Heaven!—to take it."

I stood up in my terror, but I was too weak, and stumbled back into the chair.

I would answer no question of hers. She saw that she was agitating me, and desisted.

The whole scene in the jeweller's shop remained emblazoned in vivid tints and lights on my memory. But there was something more, and that perhaps the most terrible ingredient in it.

I had recognised another face besides Droqville's. It started between me and the wounded man as I recoiled from my own blow. One hand was extended towards me, to prevent my repeating the stroke—the other held up the wounded man.

Sometimes I doubted whether the whole of that frightful episode was not an illusion. Sometimes it seemed only that the pale face, so much younger and handsomer than Monsieur Droqville's—the fiery eyes, the frown, the scarred forehead, the suspended smile that had for only that dreadful moment started into light before me so close to my face, were those of a spectre.

The young man who had been turning over the jewels at the counter, and who had offered to give me change for my imaginary sovereign, was the very man I had seen shipwrecked at Malory; the man who had in the wood near Plas Ylwd fought that secret duel; and who had afterwards made, with so reckless an audacity, those mad declarations of love to me; the man who, for a time, had so haunted my imagination, and respecting whom I had received warnings so dark and formidable.

Nothing could be more vivid than this picture, nothing more uncertain than its reality. I did not see recognition in the face; all was so instantaneous. Well, I cared not. I was dying. What was the world to me? I had assigned myself to death; and I was willing to accept that fate rather than re-ascend to my frightful life.

My poor mother, who knew nothing of my strange adventure, had experienced one of those deceitful rallies which sometimes seem to promise a long reprieve, in that form of heart-complaint under which she suffered. She only knew that I had had brain-fever. How near to death I had been she never knew. She was spared, too, the horror of my dreadful adventure. I was now recovering rapidly and surely; but I was so utterly weak and heart-broken that I fancied I must die, and thought that they were either deceived themselves, or trying kindly, but in vain, to deceive me. I was at length convinced by finding myself able, as I have said, to sit up. Mamma was often with me, cheered by my recovery, I dare say she had been more alarmed than Rebecca supposed.

I learned from mamma that the money that had maintained us through my illness had come from Mr. Carmel. Little as it was, it must have cost him exertion to get it; for men in his position cannot, I believe, own money of their own. It was very kind. I said nothing, but I was grateful; his immovable fidelity touched me deeply. I wondered whether Mr. Carmel had often made inquiries during my illness, or had shown an interest in my recovery. But I dared not ask.

CHAPTER XLIV.

AN OMINOUS VISIT.

I have sometimes felt that, even without a revelation, we might have discovered that the human race was born to immortality. Death is an intrusion here. Children can't believe in it. When they see it first, it strikes them with curiosity and wonder. It is a long time before they comprehend its real character, or believe that it is common to all; to the end of our days we are hardly quite sincere when we talk of our own deaths.

Seeing mamma better, I thought no more of her danger than if the angel of death had never been within our doors, and I had never seen the passing shadow of that spectre in her room.

As my strength returned, I grew more and more gloomy and excited. I was haunted by never-slumbering, and very reasonable, fore-castings of danger. In the first place, I was quite in the dark as to whether Monsieur Droqville was dangerously or mortally hurt, and I had no way of learning anything of him. Rebecca, it is true, used to take in, for her special edification, a Sunday paper, in which all the horrors of the week were displayed, and she used to con it over regularly, day after day, till the next number made its appearance. If Monsieur Droqville's name, with which she was familiar, had occurred in this odious register, she had at least had a fair chance of seeing it, and if she had seen it, she would be pretty sure to have mentioned it. Secretly, however, I was in miserable fear. Mr. Carmel had not returned since my recovery had ceased to be doubtful, and he was in possession of the weapon that had fallen from my hand.

In his retention of this damning piece of evidence, and his withdrawing himself so carefully from my presence, coupled with my knowledge of the principles that bound him to treat all private considerations, feelings, and friendships as non-existent, when they stood ever so little in the way of his all-pervading and supreme duty to his order—there was a sinister augury. I lived in secret terror; no wonder I was not recovering quickly.

One day, when we had sat a long time silent, I asked Rebecca how I was dressed the night I had gone to Lord Chellwood's. I was immensely relieved when she told me, among other things, that I had worn a thick black veil. This was all I wanted to be assured of; for I could not implicitly rely upon my recollection through the haze and mirage of fever. It was some comfort to think that neither Monsieur Droqville nor Mr. Marston could have recognised my features.

In this state of suspense I continued for two or three weeks. At the end of that time a little adventure happened. I was sitting in an arm-chair, in our drawing-room, with pillows about me, one afternoon, and had fallen into a doze. Mamma was in the room, and, when I had last seen her, was reading her Bible, which she now did sometimes for hours together—sometimes with tears, always with the trembling interest of one who has lost everything else.

I had fallen asleep. I was waked by tones that terrified me. I thought that I was still dreaming, or that I had lost my reason. I heard the nasal and energetic tones of Monsieur Droqville, talking with his accustomed rapidity in the room—not to mamma, for, as I afterwards found, she had left the room while I was asleep, but to Rebecca.

Happily for me, a screen stood between me and the door, and I suppose he did not know that I was in the room. At every movement of his foot on the floor, at every harsh emphasis in his talk, my heart bounded. I was afraid to move, almost to breathe, lest I should draw his attention to me.

My illness had quite unnerved me. I was afraid that, restless and inquisitive as I knew him to be, he would peep round the screen, and see and talk to me. I did not know the object of his visit; but in terror I surmised it, and I lay among my pillows, motionless, and with my eyes closed, while I heard him examine Rebecca, sharply, as to the date of my illness, and the nature of it.

"When was Miss Ware last out, before her illness?" he asked at length.

"I could not tell you that exactly, sir," answered Rebecca, evasively. "She left the house but seldom, just before she was took ill; for her mamma being very bad, she was but little out of doors then."

He made a pretence of learning the facts of my case simply as a physician, and he offered in that capacity to see me at the moment. He asked the question in an off-hand way. "I can see her, I dare say? I'm a doctor, you know. Where is Miss Ware?"

The moment of silence that intervened before her answer seemed to me to last five minutes. She answered, however, quite firmly:

"No, sir; I thank you. She's attended by a doctor, quite reg'lar, and she's asleep now."

Rebecca had heard me speak with horror of Monsieur Droqville, and did not forget my antipathy.

He hesitated. I heard his fingers drumming, as he mused, upon the other side of the screen.

"Well," he said, dwelling on the word meditatively, "it doesn't matter much. I don't mind; only it might have been as well. However, you can tell Mrs. Ware a note to my old quarters will find me, and I shall be very happy."

And so saying, I heard him walk, at first slowly, from the room, and then run briskly down the stairs. Then the old hall-door shut smartly after him.

The fear that this man inspired, and not without reason, in my mind, was indescribable. I can't be mistaken in my recollection upon that point, for, as soon as he was gone, I fainted.

When I recovered, my fears returned. No one who has not experienced that solitary horror, knows what it is to keep an undivulged secret, full of danger, every hour inspiring some new terror, with no one to consult, and no courage but your own to draw upon. Even mamma's dejected spirits took fire at what she termed the audacity of Monsieur Droqville's visit. My anger, greater than hers, was silenced by fear. Mamma was roused; she ran volubly—though interrupted by many sobs and gushes of tears—over the catalogue of her wrongs and miseries, all of which she laid to Monsieur Droqville's charge.

The storm blew over, however, in an hour or so. But later in the evening mamma was suffering under a return of her illness, brought on by her agitation. It was not violent; still there was suffering; and, to me, gloomier proof that her malady was established, and the grave in a nearer perspective. This turned my alarms into a new channel.

She was very patient and gentle. As I sat by her bedside, looking at her sad face, what unutterable tenderness, what sorrow trembled at my heart! At about six o'clock she had fallen asleep, and with this quietude my thoughts began to wander, and other fears returned. It was for no good, I was sure, that Monsieur Droqville had tracked us to our dismal abode. Whatever he might do in this affair of my crime, or mania, passion would not guide it, nor merely social considerations; it would be directed by a policy the principles of which I could not anticipate. I had no clue to guide me; I was in utter darkness, and surrounded by all the fancies that imagination conjures from the abyss.

I was not destined to wait very long in uncertainty.

CHAPTER XLV.

CONFIDENTIAL.

The sun was setting, when, on tip-toe, scarcely letting my dress rustle, so afraid I was of disturbing mamma's sleep, I stole from her room, intending to give some directions to Rebecca Torkill. As I went down the dusky stairs I passed our Malory maid, who said something, pointing to the drawing-room. I saw her lips move, but, as will happen when one is pre-occupied, I took in nothing of what she said, but, with a mechanical acquiescence, followed the direction of her hand, and entered the sitting-room.

Our house stood upon high ground, and the nearest houses between our front-windows and the west were low, so that the last beams of sunset, red with smoke and mist, passed over their roofs, and shone dimly on the oak panels opposite. The windows were narrow, and the room rather dark. I saw some one standing at the window-frame in the shade. I was startled, and hesitated, close to the door. The figure turned quickly, the sun glancing on his features. It was Mr. Carmel. He came towards me quickly; and he said, as I fancied, very coldly,

"Can you spare me two or three minutes alone, Miss Ware? I have but little to say," he added, as I did not answer. "But it is important, and I will make my words as few as possible."

We were standing close to the door. I assented. He closed it gently, and we walked slowly, side by side, to the window where he had been standing. He turned. The faint sun, like a distant fire, lighted his face. What singular dark eyes he had, so large, so enthusiastic! and had ever human eye such a character of suffering? I knew very well what he was going to speak of. The face, sad, sombre, ascetic, with which I was so familiar, I now, for the first time, understood.

The shadow of the confessional was on it. It was the face of one before whom human nature, in moments of terrible sincerity, had laid bare its direful secrets, and submitted itself to a melancholy anatomisation. To some minds, sympathetic, proud, sensitive the office of the confessor must be full of self-abasement, pain, and horror. We who know our own secrets, and no one else's, know nothing of the astonishment, and melancholy, and disgust that must strike some minds on contemplating the revelations of others, and discovering, for certain, that the standard of human nature is not above such and such a level.

"I have brought you this," he said, scarcely above his breath, holding the knife so that it lay across the hollow of his hand. His haggard eyes were fixed on me, and he said, "I know the whole story of it. Unless you forbid me, I will drop it into the river to-night; it is the evidence of an act for which you are, I thank God, no more accountable than a somnambulist for what she does in her dream. Over Monsieur Droqville I have neither authority nor influence; on the contrary, he can command me. But of this much I am sure—so long as your friends do not attack Lady Lorrimer's will—and I believe they have no idea of taking any such step—you need fear no trouble whatever from him."

I made him no reply, but I think he saw something in my face that made him add, with more emphasis:

"You may be sure of that."

I was immensely and instantly relieved, for I knew that there was not the slightest intention of hazarding any litigation on the subject of the will.

"But," he resumed, in the same cold tones, and with the same anxiety in his dark eyes, "there is a person from whom you may possibly experience annoyance. There are circumstances of which, as yet, you know nothing, that may, not unnaturally, bring you once more into contact with Mr. Marston. If that should happen, you must be on your guard. I understand that he said something that implies his suspicions. It may have been no more than conjecture. It may be that it was impossible he could have recognised you with certainty. If, I repeat, an untoward destiny should bring you together under the same roof, be wise, stand aloof from him, admit nothing; defeat his suspicions and his cunning by impenetrable caution. He has an interest in seeking to disgrace you, and where he has an object to gain he has neither conscience nor mercy. I wish I could inspire you with the horror of that mean and formidable character which so many have acquired by a bitter experience. I can but repeat my warning, and implore of you to act upon it, if the time should come. This thing I retain for the present"—he glanced at the weapon in his hand—"and dispose of it to-night, as I said."

There was no emotion in his manner; no sign of any special interest in me; but his voice and looks were unspeakably earnest, and inspired me with a certain awe.

I had not forgiven Mr. Carmel yet, or rather my pride would not retract; and my parting with him at our former house was fresh in my recollection. So it was, I might suppose, in his; for his manner was cold, and even severe.

"Our old acquaintance ended, Miss Ware, by your command, and, on reflection, with my own willing submission. When last we parted, I thought it unlikely that we should ever meet again, and this interview is not voluntary—necessity compelled it. I have simply done my duty, and, I earnestly hope, not in vain. It must be something very unlooked for, indeed, that shall ever constrain me to trouble you again."

He showed no sign of wishing to bid me a kindlier farewell. The actual, as well as metaphorical, distance between us had widened; he was by this time at the door; he opened it, and took his leave, very coldly. It was very unlike his former parting. I had only said:

"I am very grateful, Mr. Carmel, for your care of me—miserable me!"

He made no answer; he simply repeated his farewell, as gently and coldly as before, and left the room, and I saw him walk away from our door in the fast-fading light. Heavier and heavier was my heart, as I saw him move quickly away. I had yearned, during our cold interview, to put out my hand to him, and ask him, in simple phrase, to make it up with me. I burned to tell him that I had judged him too hardly, and was sorry; but my pride forbade it. His pride too, I thought, had held him aloof, and so I had lost my friend. My eyes filled with tears, that rolled heavily over my cheeks.

I sat at one of our windows, looking, over the distant roofs, towards the discoloured and disappearing tints of evening and the melancholy sky, which even through the smoke of London has its poetry and tenderness, until the light faded, and the moon began to shine through the twilight. Then I went upstairs, and found mamma still sleeping. As I stood by the bed looking at her, Rebecca Torkill at my side whispered:

"She's looking very pale, poor thing, don't you think, miss? Too pale, a deal."

I did think so; but she was sleeping tranquilly. Every change in her looks was now a subject of anxiety, but her hour had not quite come yet. She looked so very pale that I began to fear she had fainted; but she awoke just then, and said she would sit up for a little time. Her colour did not return; she seemed faint, but thought she should be more herself by-and-by.

She came down to the drawing-room, and soon did seem better, and chatted more than she had done, I think, since our awful misfortune had befallen us, and appeared more like her former self; I mean, that simpler and tender self that I had seen far away from artificial London, among the beautiful solitudes of her birthplace.

While we were talking here, Rebecca Torkill, coming in now and then, and lending a word, after the manner of privileged old rustic servants, to keep the conversation going, the business of this story was being transacted in other places.

Something of Mr. Carmel's adventures that night I afterwards learned. He had two or three calls to make before he went to his temporary home. A friend had lent him, during his absence abroad, his rooms in the Temple. Arrived there, he let himself in by a latch-key. It was night, the shutters unclosed, the moon shining outside, and its misty beams, slanting in at the dusky windows, touched objects here and there in the dark room with a cold distinctness.

To a man already dejected, what is more dispiriting than a return to empty and unlighted rooms? Mr. Carmel moved like a shadow through this solitude, and in his melancholy listlessness, stood for a time at the window.

Here and there a light, from a window in the black line of buildings opposite, showed that human thought and eyes were busy; but if these points of light and life made the prospect less dismal, they added by contrast to the gloom that pervaded his own chambers.

As he stood, some dimly-seen movement caught his eye, and, looking over his shoulder, he saw the door through which he himself had come in slowly open, and a man put in his head, and then enter silently, and shut the door. This figure, faintly seen in the imperfect light, resembled but one man of all his acquaintance, and he the last man in the world, as he thought, who would have courted a meeting. Carmel stood for a moment startled and chilled by his presence.

"I say, Carmel, don't you know me?" said a very peculiar voice. "I saw you come in, and intended to knock; but you left your door open."

By this time he had reached the window, and stood beside Mr. Carmel, with the moonlight revealing his features sharply enough. That pale light fell upon the remarkable face of Mr. Marston.

"I'm not a ghost, though I've been pretty near it two or three times. I see what you're thinking—death may have taken better men? I might have been very well spared? and having escaped it, I should have laid the lesson to heart? Well, so I have. I was very nearly killed at the great battle of Fuentas. I fought for the Queen of Spain, and be hanged to her! She owes me fifteen pounds ten and elevenpence, British currency, to this day. It only shows my luck. In that general action there were only four living beings hit so as to draw blood—myself, a venerable orange-woman, a priest's mule, and our surgeon-in-chief, whose thumb and razor were broken off by a spent ball, as he was shaving a grenadier, under an umbrella, while the battle was raging. You see the Spaniard is a discreet warrior, and we very seldom got near enough to hurt each other. I was hit by some blundering beast. He must have shut his eyes, like Gil Blas, for there was not a man in either army who could ever hit anything he aimed at. No matter, he very nearly killed me; half an inch higher, and I must have made up my mind to see you, dear Carmel, no more, and to shut my eyes on this sweet, jesuitical world. It was the first ugly wound of the campaign, and the enemy lived for a long time on the reputation of it. But the truth is, I have suffered a great deal in sickness, wounds, and fifty other ways. I have been as miserable a devil as any righteous man could wish me to be; and I am changed; upon my honour, I'm as different a man from what I was as you are from me. But I can't half see you; do light your candles, I entreat."

"Not while you are here," said Carmel.

"Why, what are you afraid of?" said Marston. "You haven't, I hope, got a little French milliner behind your screen, like Joseph Surface, who, I think, would have made a very pretty Jesuit. Why should you object to light?"

"Your ribaldry is out of place here," said Carmel, who knew very well that Marston had not come to talk nonsense, and recount his adventures in Spain; and that his business, whatever it may be, was likely to be odious. "What right have you to enter my room? What right to speak to me anywhere?"

"Come, Carmel, don't be unreasonable; you know very well I can be of use to you."

"You can be of none," answered Carmel, a little startled; "and if you could, I would not have you. Leave my room, sir."

"You can exorcise some evil spirits, but not me, till I've said my say," answered Marston, with a smile that looked grim and cynical in the moonlight. "I say I can be of use to you."

"It's enough; I won't have it; go," said Carmel, with a sterner emphasis.

Marston smiled again, and looked at him.

"Well, I can be of use," he said, "and I don't want particularly to be of use to you; but you can do me a kindness, and it is better to do it quietly than upon compulsion. Will you be of use to me? I'll show you how?"

"God forbid!" said Carmel, quickly. "It is nothing good, I'm sure."

Marston looked at him with an evil eye; it was a sneer of intense anger.

After some seconds he said, his eyes still fixed askance on Mr. Carmel:

"Forgive us our trespasses, as we forgive, et cætera—eh? I suppose you sometimes pray your paternoster? A pretty time you have kept up that old grudge against me—haven't you—about Ginevra?"

He kept his eyes on Carmel, as if he enjoyed the spectacle of the torture he applied, and liked to see the wince and quiver that accompanied its first thrill.

At the word, Edwyn Carmel's eyes started up from the floor, to which they had been lowered, with a flash to the face of his visitor. His forehead flushed; he remained speechless for some seconds. Marston did not smile; his features were fixed, but there was a secret, cruel smile in his eyes as he watched these evidences of agitation.

"Well, I should not have said the name; I should not have alluded to it; I did wrong," he said, after some seconds; "but I was going, before you riled me, to say how really I blame myself, now, for all that deplorable business. I do, upon my soul! What more can a fellow say, when reparation is impossible, than that he is sorry? Is not repentance all that a man like me can offer? I saw you were thinking of it; you vexed me; I was angry, and I could not help saying what I did. Now do let that miserable subject drop; and hear me, on quite another, without excitement. It is not asking a great deal."

Carmel placed his hand to his head, as if he had not heard what he said, and then groaned.

"Why don't you leave me?" he said, piteously, turning again towards Marston; "don't you see that nothing but pain and reproach can result from your staying here?"

"Let me first say a word," said Marston; "you can assist me in a very harmless and perfectly unobjectionable matter. Every fellow who wants to turn over a new leaf marries. The lady is poor—there is that proof, at least, that it is not sordid; you know her, you can influence her——"

"Perhaps I do know her; perhaps I know who she is—I may as well say, at once, I do. I have no influence; and if I had, I would not use it for you. I think I know your reasons, also; I think I can see them."

"Well, suppose there are reasons, it's not the worse for that," said Marston, growing again angry. "I thought I would just come and try whether you chose to be on friendly terms. I'm willing; but if you won't, I can't help you. I'll make use of you all the same. You had better think again. I'm pleasanter as a friend than an enemy."

"I don't fear you as an enemy, and I do fear you as a friend. I will aid you in nothing; I have long made up my mind," answered Carmel, savagely.

"I think, through Monsieur Droqville, I'll manage that. Oh, yes, you will give me a lift."

"Why should Monsieur Droqville control my conduct?" asked Mr. Carmel sharply.

"It was he who made you a Catholic; and I suspect he has a fast hold on your conscience and obedience. If he chooses to promote the matter, I rather think you must."

"You may think as you please," said Carmel.

"That's a great deal from your Church," sneered Marston; and, changing his tone again, he said: "Look here, Carmel, once more; where's the good in our quarrelling? I won't press that other point, if you don't like; but you must do this, the most trifling thing in the world—you must tell me where Mrs. Ware lives. No one knows since old Ware made a fool of himself, poor devil! But I think you'll allow that, with my feelings, I may, at least, speak to the young lady's mother? Do tell me where they are. You know, of course?"

"If I did know, I should not tell you; so it does not matter," answered Carmel.

Marston looked very angry, and a little silence followed.

"I suppose you have now said everything," resumed Carmel; "and again I desire that you will leave me."

"I mean to do so," said Marston, putting on his hat with a kind of emphasis, "though it's hard to leave such romantic, light, and brilliant company. You might have had peace, and you prefer war. I think there are things you have at heart that I could forward, if all went right with me." He paused, but Carmel made no sign. "Well, you take your own way now, not mine; and, by-and-by, I think you'll have reason to regret it."

Marston left the room, with no other farewell. The clap with which he shut the door, as he went, had hardly ceased to ring round the walls, when Carmel saw him emerge in the court below, and walk away with a careless air, humming a tune in the moonlight.

Why is it that there are men upon earth whose secret thoughts are always such as to justify fear; and nearly all whose plans, if not through malice, from some other secret obliquity, involve evil to others? We have most of us known something of some such man; a man whom we are disposed to watch in silence; who, smile as he may, brings with him a sense of insecurity, and whose departure is a real relief. Such a man seems to me a stranger on earth; his confidences to be with unseen companions; his mental enjoyments not human; and his mission here cruel and mysterious. I look back with wonder and with thankfulness. Fearful is the strait of any one who, in the presence of such an influence, under such a fascination, loses the sense of danger.

CHAPTER XLVI.

AFTER OFFICE HOURS.

Next day our doctor called. He was very kind. He had made mamma many visits, and attended me through my tedious fever, and would never take a fee after the first one. I daresay that other great London physicians, whom the world reputes worldly, often do similar charities by stealth. My own experience is that affliction like ours does not lower the sufferer's estimate of human nature. It is a great discriminator of character, and sifts men like wheat. Those among our friends who are all chaff it blows away altogether; those who have noble attributes, it leaves all noble. There is no more petulance, no more hurry or carelessness; we meet, in after-contact with them, be it much or little, only the finer attributes, gentleness, tenderness, respect, patience.

I do not remember one of those who had known us in better days, among the very few who now knew where to find us, who did not show us even more kindness than they could have had opportunity of showing if we had been in our former position. Who could be kinder than Mr. Forrester? Who more thoughtful than Mr. Carmel, to whom at length we had traced the flowers, and the books, and the piano, that were such a resource to me; and who had, during my illness, come every day to see mamma?

In his necessarily brief visits, Sir Jacob Lake was energetic and cheery; there was in his manner that which inspired confidence; but I fancied this day, as he was taking his leave of mamma, that I observed something like a shadow on his face, a transitory melancholy, that alarmed me. I accompanied him downstairs, and he stopped for a moment in the lobby outside the drawing-room.

"Has there been anything done since about that place—Malory, I think you call it?" he asked.

"No," I answered; "there is not the least chance. Sir Harry Rokestone is going to sell it, Mr. Jarlcot says; just through hatred of us, he thinks. He's an old enemy of ours; he says he hates our very name; and he won't write; he hasn't answered a single letter of Mr. Forrester's."

"I was only going to say that it wouldn't do; she could not bear so long a journey just now. I think she had better make no effort; she must not leave this at present."

"I'm afraid you think her very ill," I said, feeling myself grow pale.

"She is ill; and she will never be much better; but she may be spared to you for a long time yet. This kind of thing, however, is always uncertain; and it may end earlier than we think—I don't say it is likely, only possible. You must send for me whenever you want me; and I'll look in now and then, and see that all goes on satisfactorily."

I began to thank him earnestly, but he stopped me very good-naturedly. He could spare me little more than a minute; I walked with him to the hall-door, and although he said but little, and that little very cautiously, he left me convinced that I might lose my darling mother any day or hour. He had implied this very vaguely, but I was sure of it. People who have suffered great blows like mine, regard the future as an adversary, and believe its threatenings.

In flurry and terror I returned to the drawing-room, and shut the door; then, with the instinct that prevails, I went to mamma's room and sat down beside her.

I suppose every one has felt as I have felt. How magically the society of the patient, if not actually suffering, reassures us! The mere contiguity, the voice, the interest she takes in the common topics of our daily life, the cheerful and easy tone, even the little peevishness about the details of the sick-room, soon throw death again into perspective, and the instinct of life prevails against all facts and logic.

The form of heart-complaint from which my mother suffered had in it nothing revolting. I think I never remember her so pretty. The tint of her lips, and the colour of her cheeks, always lovely, were now more delicately brilliant than ever; and the lustre of her eyes, thus enhanced, was quite beautiful. The white tints a little paler, and her face and figure slightly thinner, but not unbecomingly, brought back a picture so girlish that I wondered while I looked; and when I went away the pretty face haunted me as the saddest and gentlest I had ever seen.

So many people have said that the approach of death induces a change of character, that I almost accept it for a general law of nature. I saw it, I know, in mamma. Not exactly an actual change, perhaps, but, rather, a subsidence of whatever was less lovely in her nature, and a proportionate predominance of all its sweetness and gentleness. There came also a serenity very different from the state of mind in which she had been from papa's death up to the time of my illness. I do not know whether she was conscious of her imminent danger. If she suspected it, she certainly did not speak of it to me or to Rebecca Torkill. But death is a subject on which some people, I believe, practise as many reserves as others do in love.

Next day mamma was much better, and sat in our drawing-room, and I read and talked to her, and amused her with my music. She sat in slippers and dressing-gown in an easy-chair, and we talked over a hundred plans which seemed to interest her. The effort to cheer mamma did me good, and I think we were both happier that day than we had been since ruin had so tragically overtaken us.

While we were thus employed at home, events connected with us and our history were not standing still in other places.

Mr. Forrester's business was very large; he had the assistance of two partners; but all three were hard worked. The offices of the firm occupied two houses in one of the streets which run down from the Strand to the river, at no great distance from Temple Bar. I saw these offices but once in my life; I suppose there was little to distinguish them and their arrangements from those of other well-frequented chambers; but I remember being struck with their air of business and regularity, and by the complicated topography of two houses fused into one.

Mr. Forrester, in his private office, had locked up his desk. He was thinking of taking his leave of business for the day. It was now past four, and he had looked into the office where the collective firm did their business, and where his colleagues were giving audience to a deputation about a complicated winding-up. This momentary delay cost him more time than he intended, for a clerk came in and whispered in his ear:

"A gentleman wants to see you, sir."

"Why, hang it! I've left the office," said Mr. Forrester, tartly—"don't you see? Here's my hat in my hand! Go and look for me in my office, and you'll see I'm not there."

Very deferentially, notwithstanding this explosion, the messenger added:

"I thought, sir, before sending him away, you might like to see him; he seemed to think he was doing us a favour in looking in, and he has been hearing from you, and would not take the trouble to write; and he won't call again."

"What's his name?" asked Mr. Forrester, vacillating a little.

"Sir Harry Rokestone," he said.

"Sir Harry Rokestone? Oh! Well, I suppose I must see him. Yes, I'll see him; bring him up to my private room."

Mr. Forrester had hardly got back, laid aside his hat and umbrella, and placed himself in his chair of state behind his desk, when his aide-de-camp returned and introduced "Sir Harry Rokestone."

Mr. Forrester rose, and received him with a bow. He saw a tall man, with something grand and simple in his gait and erect bearing, with a brown handsome face, and a lofty forehead, noble and stern as if it had caught something of the gloomy character of the mountain scenery among which his home was. He was dressed in the rustic and careless garb of an old-fashioned country gentleman, with gaiters up to his knees, as if he were going to stride out upon the heather with his gun on his shoulder and his dogs at his heel.

Mr. Forrester placed a chair for this gentleman, who, with hardly a nod, and without a word, sat down. The door closed, and they were alone.

CHAPTER XLVII.

SIR HARRY SPEAKS.

You're Mr. Forrester?" said Sir Harry, in a deep, clear voice, quite in character with his appearance, and with a stern eye fixed on the solicitor.

That gentleman made a slight inclination of assent.

"I got all your letters, sir—every one," said the rustic baronet.

Mr. Forrester bowed.

"I did not answer one of them."

Mr. Forrester bowed again.

"Did it strike you, as a man of business, sir, that it was rather an odd omission your not mentioning where the ladies representing the late Mr. Ware's interests—if he had any remaining, which I don't believe—are residing?"

"I had actually written——" answered Mr. Forrester, turning the key in his desk, and slipping his hand under the cover, and making a momentary search. He had hesitated on the question of sending the letter or not; but, having considered whether there could be any possible risk in letting him know, and having come to the conclusion that there was none, he now handed this letter, a little obsolete as it was, to Sir Harry Rokestone.

"What's this?" said Sir Harry, breaking the seal and looking at the contents of the note, and thrusting it, thinking as it seemed all the time of something different, into his coat-pocket.

"The present address of Mrs. and Miss Ware, which I understood you just now to express a wish for," answered Mr. Forrester.

"Express a wish, sir, for their address!" exclaimed Sir Harry, with a scoff. "Dall me if I did, though! What the deaul, man, should I want o' their *address*, as ye call it? They may live where they like for me. And so Ware's dead—died a worse death than the hangman's; and died not worth a plack, as I always knew he would. And what made you write all those foolish letters to me? Why did you go on plaguing me, when you saw I never gave you an answer to one of them? You that should be a man of head, how could ye be such a mafflin?" His northern accent became broader as he became more excited.

The audacity and singularity of this old man disconcerted Mr. Forrester. He did not afterwards understand why he had not turned him out of his room.

"I think, Sir Harry, you will find my reasons for writing very distinctly stated in my letters, if you are good enough to look into them."

"Ay, so I did; and I don't understand them, nor you neither."

It was not clear whether he intended that the reasons or the attorney were beyond his comprehension. Mr. Forrester selected the first interpretation, and, I daresay, rightly, as being the least offensive.

"Pardon me, Sir Harry Rokestone," said he, with a little dry dignity; "I have not leisure to throw away upon writing nonsense; I am one of those men who are weak enough to believe that there are rights besides those defined by statute or common law, and duties, consequently, you'll excuse me for saying, even more obligatory—Christian duties, which, in this particular case, plainly devolve upon you."

"Christian flam! Humbug! and you an attorney!"

"I'm not accustomed, sir, to be talked to in that way," said Mr. Forrester, who felt that his visitor was becoming insupportable.

"Of course you're not; living in this town you never hear a word of honest truth," said Sir Harry; "but I'm not so much in the dark; I understand you pretty well, now; and I think you a precious impudent fellow."

Both gentlemen had risen by this time, and Mr. Forrester, with a flush in his cheeks, replied, raising his head as he stooped over his desk while turning the key in the lock:

"And I beg to say, sir, that I, also, have formed my own very distinct opinion of you!"

Mr. Forrester flushed more decidedly, for he felt, a little too late, that he had perhaps made a rather rash speech, considering that his visitor seemed to have so little control over his temper, and also that he was gigantic.

The herculean baronet, however, who could have lifted him up by the collar, and flung him out of the window, only smiled sardonically, and said:

"Then we part, you and I, wiser men than we met. You write me no more letters, and I'll pay you no more visits."

With another cynical grin, he turned on his heel, and walked slowly down the stairs, leaving Mr. Forrester more ruffled than he had been for many a day.

CHAPTER XLVIII.

THE OLD LOVE.

The hour had now arrived at which our room looked really becoming. It had been a particularly fine autumn; and I have mentioned the effect of a warm sunset streaming through the deep windows upon the oak panelling. This light had begun to fade, and its melancholy serenity had made us silent. I had heard the sound of wheels near our door, but that was nothing unusual, for carts often passed close by, carrying away the rubbish that had accumulated in the old houses now taken down.

Annie Owen, our Malory maid, peeped in at the door—came in, looking frightened and important, and closed it before she spoke. She was turning something about in her fingers.

"What is it, Anne?" I asked.

"Please, miss, there's an old gentleman downstairs; and he wants to know, ma'am," she continued, now addressing mamma, "whether you'll be pleased to see him."

Mamma raised herself, and looked at the girl with anxious, startled eyes.

"What is that you havc got in your hand?" I asked.

"Oh! I beg your pardon, ma'am; he told me to give you this, please." And she handed a card to mamma. She looked at it and grew very pale. She stood up with a flurried air.

"Are you sure?" she said.

"Please, ma'am?" inquired the girl in perplexity.

"No matter. Ethel, dear, it is he. Yes, I'll see him," she said to the girl, in an agitated way; "show him up. Ethel, it's Harry Rokestone—don't go; he is so stern—I know how he'll speak to me—but I ought not to refuse to see him."

I was angry at my mother's precipitation. If it had rested with me, what an answer the savage old man should have had! I was silent. By this time the girl was again at the hall-door. The first moment of indignation over, I was thunderstruck. I could not believe that anything so portentous was on the eve of happening.

The moments of suspense were not many. My eyes were fixed on the door as if an executioner were about to enter by it. It opened, and I saw—need I tell you?—the very same tall, handsome old man I had seen in the chapel of Cardyllion Castle.

"Oh! Mabel," he said, and stopped. It was the most melancholy, broken voice I had ever heard. "My darling!"

My mother stood with her hand stretched vaguely towards him, trembling.

"Oh! Mabel, it is you, and we've met at last!"

He took her hand in one of his, and laid the other suddenly across his eyes and sobbed. There was silence for a good while, and then he spoke again.

"My pretty Mabel! I lost ye; I tried to hate ye, Mabel; but all would not do, for I love ye still. I was mad and broken-hearted—I tried to hate ye, but I couldn't; I'd a' given my life for you all the time, and you shall have Malory—it's your own—I've bought it—ye'll not be too proud to take a gift from the old man, my only darling! The spring and summer are over, it's winter now wi' the old fellow, and he'll soon lie under the grass o' the kirk-garth, and what does it all matter then? And you, bonny Mabel, there's wonderful little change wi' you!"

He was silent again, and tears coursed one another down his rugged cheeks.

"I saw you sometimes a long way off, when you didn't think I was looking, and the sight o' ye wrung my heart, that I didn't hold up my head for a week after. A lonely man I've been for your sake, Mabel; and down to Gouden Friars, and among the fells, and through the lonnins of old Clusted Forest, and sailin' on the mere, where we two often were, thinkin' I saw ye in the shaddas, and your voice in my ear as far away as the call o' the wind—dreams, dreams—and now I've met ye."

He was holding mamma's hand in his, and she was crying bitterly.

"I knew nothing of all this till to-day—I got all Forrester's letters together. I was on the Continent—and you've been complaining, Mabel; but you're looking so young and bonny! It was care, care was the matter, care and trouble; but that's all over, and you shall never know anxiety more—you'll be well again—you shall live at Malory, if you like it, or Gouden Friars—Mardykes is to let. I've a right to help you, Mabel, and you have none to refuse my help, for I'm the only living kinsman you have. I don't count that blackguard lord for anything. You shall never know care again. For twenty years and more an angry man and dow I've been, caring for no one, love or likin, when I had lost yours. But now it is past and over, and the days are sped."

A few melancholy and broken words more, and he was gone, promising to return next day at twelve, having seen Mr. Forrester in the meantime at his house in Piccadilly, and had a talk with him.

He was gone. He had not spoken a word to me—had not even appeared conscious that I was present. I daresay he was not. It was a little mortifying. To me he appeared a mixture, such as I never saw before, of brutality and tenderness. The scene had moved me.

Mamma was now talking excitedly. It had been an agitating meeting, and, till he had disclosed his real feelings, full of uncertainty. To prevent her from exerting herself too much, I took my turn in the conversation, and, looking from the window, still in the direction in which his cab had disappeared, I descanted with immense delight on the likelihood of his forthwith arranging that Malory should become our residence.

As I spoke, I turned about to listen for the answer I expected from mamma. I was shocked to see her look so very ill. I was by her side in a moment. She said a few words scarcely audible, and ceased speaking before she had ended her sentence. Her lips moved, and she made an eager gesture with her hand; but her voice failed. She made an effort, I thought, to rise, but her strength forsook her, and she fainted.

CHAPTER XLIX.

ALONE IN THE WORLD.

Sir Harry did not find Mr. Forrester at home; the solicitor was at a consultation in the Temple. Thither drove the baronet, who was impetuous in most things, and intolerant of delay where an object lay near his heart. Up to the counsel's chambers in the Temple mounted Sir Harry Rokestone. He hammered his double knock at the door as peremptorily as he would have done at his own hall door.

Mr. Forrester afforded him just half a minute; and they parted good friends, having made an appointment for the purpose of talking over poor mamma's affairs, and considering what was best to be done.

Sir Harry strode with the careless step of a mountaineer, along the front of the buildings, till he reached the entrance to which, in answer to a sudden inquiry, Mr. Forrester had directed him. Up the stairs he marched, and stopped at the door of the chambers occupied by Mr. Carmel. There he knocked again as stoutly as before. The door was opened by Edwyn Carmel himself.

"Is Mr. Carmel here?" inquired the old man.

"I am Mr. Carmel," answered he.

"And I am Sir Harry Rokestone," said the baronet. "I found a letter from you this morning; it had been lying at my house unopened for some time," said the baronet.

Mr. Carmel invited him to come in. There were candles lighted, for it was by this time nearly dark; he placed a chair for his visitor: they were alone.

Sir Harry Rokestone seated himself, and began:

"There was no need, sir, of apology for your letter; intervention on behalf of two helpless and suffering ladies was honourable to you; but I had also heard some particulars from their own professional man of business; that, however, you could not have known. I have called to tell you that I quite understand the case. So much for your letter. But, sir, I have been informed that you are a Jesuit."

"I am a Catholic priest, sir."

"Well, sir, I won't press the point; but the ruin of that family has been brought about, so far as I can learn, by gentlemen of that order. They got about that poor foolish creature, Lady Lorrimer; and, by cajoleries and terror, they got hold of every sixpence of her fortune, which, according to all that's right and kind in nature, should have gone to her nearest kindred."

Sir Harry's eyes were fixed on him, as if he expected an answer.

"Lady Lorrimer did, I suppose, what pleased her best in her will," said the young man, coldly; "Mrs. Ware had expectations, I believe, which have been, you say, disappointed."

"And do you mean to tell me that you don't know that fact for certain?" said the old gentleman, growing hot.

"I'm not certain of anything of which I have no proof, Sir Harry," answered Mr. Carmel. "If I were a Jesuit, and your statement were a just one, still I should know no more about the facts than I do now; for it would not be competent for me to inquire into the proceedings of my superiors in the order. It is enough for me to say that I know nothing of any such influence exerted by any human being upon Lady Lorrimer; and I need scarcely add that I have never, by word or act, endeavoured ever so slightly to influence Lady Lorrimer's dealings with her property! Your ear, sir, has been abused by slander."

"By Jea! Here's modesty!" said Sir Harry, exploding in a gruff laugh of scorn, and standing up. "What a pack o' gaumless gannets you must take us for! Look-ye now, young sir. I have my own opinion about all that. And tell your superiors, as you call them, they'll never get a plack of old Harry Rokestone's money, while hand and seal can bind, and law's law; and if I catch a priest in my house, ye may swear he'll get out of it quicker than he came in. I'd thank you more for your letter, sir, if I was a little more sure of the motive; and now I've said my say, and I wish ye good evening."

With a fierce smile, the old man looked at him steadily for a few seconds, and then turning abruptly, left the room and shut the door, with a firm clap, after him.

That was, to me, an anxious night. Mamma continued ill; I had written rather a wild note for our doctor; but he did not come for many hours. He did not say much; he wrote a prescription, and gave some directions; he was serious and reserved, which, in a physician, means alarm. In answer to my flurried inquiries, as I went downstairs by his side, he said:

"I told you, you recollect, that it is a capricious kind of thing; I hope she may be better when I look in in the morning; the nature of it is that it may end at any time, with very little warning; but with caution she may live a year, or possibly two years. I've known cases, as discouraging as hers, where life has been prolonged for three years."

Next morning came, and I thought mamma much better. I told her all that was cheery in the doctor's opinion, and amused her with plans for our future. But the hour was drawing near when doctors' opinions, and friends' hopes and flatteries, and the kindly illusions of plans looking pleasantly into an indefinite future, were to be swallowed in the tremendous event.

About half an hour before our kind doctor's call, mamma's faintness returned. I now began, and not an hour too soon, to despair. The medicine he had ordered the day before, to support her in those paroxysms, had lost its power. Mamma had been for a time in the drawing-room, but having had a long fainting-fit there, I persuaded her, so soon as she was a little recovered, to return to her bed.

I find it difficult, I may say, indeed, impossible, to reduce the occurrences of this day to order. The picture is not, indeed, so chaotic as my recollection of the times and events that attended my darling Nelly's death. The shock, in that case, had affected my mind. But I do not believe that any one retains a perfectly arranged recollection of the flurried and startling scenes that wind up our hopes in the dread catastrophe. I never met a person yet who could have told the story of such a day with perfect accuracy and order.

I don't know what o'clock it was when the doctor came. There is something of the character of sternness in the brief questions, the low tone, and the silent inspection that mark his last visit to the sick-room. What is more terrible than the avowed helplessness that follows, and his evident acquiescence in the inevitable?

"Don't go. Oh, don't go yet; wait till I come back, only a few minutes; there might be a change, and something might be done."

I entreated; I was going up to mamma's room; I had come down with him to the drawing-room.

"Well, my dear, I'll wait." He looked at his watch. "I'll remain with you for ten minutes."

I suppose I looked very miserable, for I saw a great compassion in his face. He was very good-natured, and he added, placing his hand upon my arm, and looking gently in my face, "But, my poor child, you must not flatter yourself with hopes, for I have none—there are none."

But what so headstrong and so persistent as hope? Terrible must be that place where it never comes.

I had scarcely left the drawing-room, when Sir Harry Rokestone, of the kindly change in whom I had spoken to our good doctor, knocked at the hall-door. Our rustic maid, Anne Owen, who was crying, let him in, and told him the sudden news; he laid his hand against the door-post and grew pale. He did not say a word for as long as you might count twenty, then he asked:

"Is the doctor here?"

The girl led the way to the drawing-room.

"Bad news, doctor?" said the tall old man, in an agitated voice, as he entered, with his eyes fixed on Sir Jacob Lake. "My name is Rokestone—Sir Harry Rokestone. Tell me, is it so bad as the servant says? You have not given her up?"

The doctor shook his head; he advanced slowly a step or two to meet Sir Harry, and said, in a low tone:

"Mrs. Ware is dying—sinking very fast."

Sir Harry walked to the mantelpiece, laid his hand on it, and stood there without moving. After a little he turned again, and came to Sir Jacob Lake.

"You London doctors—you're so hurried," he said, a little wildly, "from place to place. I think—I think—look, doctor; save her! save her, man!"—he caught the doctor's wrist in his hand—"and I'll make your fortune. Ye need never do an hour's work more. Man was never so rewarded, not for a queen."

The doctor looked very much offended; but, coarse as the speech was, it was delivered with a pathetic and simple vehemence that disarmed him.

"You mistake me, sir," he said. "I take a very deep interest in this case. I have known Mrs. Ware from the time when she came to live in London. I hope I do my duty in every case, but in this I have been particularly anxious, and I do assure you, if——What's that?"

It was, as Shakespeare says, "a cry of women," the sudden shrilly clamour of female voices heard through distant doors.

The doctor opened the door, and stood at the foot of the stairs.

"Ay, that's it," he said, shaking his head a little. "It's all over."

CHAPTER L.

A PROTECTOR.

I was in mamma's room; I was holding up her head; old Rebecca and Anne Owen were at the bedside. My terrified eyes saw the doctor drawing near softly in the darkened room. I asked him some wild questions, and he answered gently, "No, dear; no, no."

The doctor took his stand at the bedside, and, with his hands behind his back, looked down at her face sadly. Then he leaned over. He laid his hand gently on mamma's, put his fingers to her wrist, felt, also, for the beating of her heart, looked again at her face, and rose from his stooping posture with a little shake of the head and a sigh, looked in the still face once more for a few seconds, and turning to me, said tenderly:

"You had better come away, dear; there's nothing more to be done. You must not distress yourself."

That last look of the physician at his patient, when he stands up, and becomes on a sudden no more than any other spectator, his office over, his command ended, is terrifying.

For two or three minutes I scarcely knew who was going or coming. The doctor, who had just gone downstairs, returned with an earnest request from Sir Harry Rokestone that in an hour or so he might be permitted to come back and take a last look of mamma. He did come back, but his heart failed him. He could not bear to see her now. He went into the drawing-room, and, a few minutes later, Rebecca Torkill came into my room, where, by this time, I was crying alone, and said:

"Ye mustn't take on so, my darling; rouse yourself a bit. That old man, Sir Harry Rokestone, is down in the drawing-room in a bit of a taking, and he says he must see you before he goes."

"I can't see him, Rebecca," I said.

"But what am I to say to him?" said she.

"Simply that. Do tell him I can't go down to see anybody."

"But ain't it as well to go and have it over, miss?—for see you he will, I am sure of that; and I can't manage him."

"Does he seem angry?" I said, "or only in grief? I daresay he is angry. Yesterday, when he was here, he never spoke one word to me—he took no notice of me whatever."

At another time an interview with Sir Harry Rokestone might have inspired many more nervous misgivings; as it was, I had only this: I knew that he had hated papa, and I, as my father's child, might well "stand within his danger," as the old phrase was. And the eccentric and violent old man, I thought, might, in the moment and agony of having lost for ever the object of an affection which my father had crossed, have sent for me, his child, simply to tell me that with my father's blood I had inherited his curse.

"I can't say, miss, indeed. He was talking to himself, and stamping with his thick shoes on the floor a bit as he walked. But ain't it best to have done with him at once, if he ain't friendly, and not keep him here, coming and going?—for see you he will, sooner or later."

"I don't very much care. Perhaps you are right. Yes, I will go down and see him," I said. "Go you down, Rebecca, and tell him that I am coming."

I had been lying on my bed, and required to adjust my hair, and dress a little.

As I came downstairs a few minutes later, I passed poor mamma's door; the key turned in it. Was I walking in a dream? Mamma dead, and Sir Harry Rokestone waiting in the drawing-room to see me! I leaned against the wall, feeling faint for a minute.

As I approached the drawing-room door, which was open, I heard Rebecca's voice talking to him; and then the old man said, in a broken voice:

"Where's the child? Bring her here. I will see the bairn."

I was the "bairn" summoned to his presence. This broad north-country dialect, the language, I suppose, of his early childhood, always returned to him in moments when his feelings were excited. I entered the room, and he strode towards me.

"Ha! the lassie," he cried, gently. There was a little tremor in his deep voice; a pause followed, and he added, vehemently, "By the God above us, I'll never forsake you!"

He held me to his heart for some seconds without speaking.

"Gimma your hand. I love you for her sake," he said, and took my hand firmly and kindly in his, and he looked earnestly in my face for awhile in silence. "You're like her; but, oh! lassie, you'll never be the same. There'll never be another such as Mabel."

Tears, which he did not dry or conceal, trickled down his rugged cheeks.

He had been talking with Rebecca Torkill, and had made her tell him everything she could think of about mamma.

"Sit ye down here, lass," he said to me, having recovered his self-possession. "You are to come home wi' me, to Gouden Friars, or wherever else you like best. You shall have music and flowers, and books and dresses, and you shall have your maid to wait on you, like other young ladies, and you shall bring Rebecca with you. I'll do my best to be kind and helpful; and you'll be a blessing to a very lonely old man; and as I love you now for Mabel's sake, I'll come to love you after for your own."

I did not think his stern old face could look so gentle and sorrowful, and the voice, generally so loud and commanding, speak so tenderly. The light of that look was full of compassion and melancholy, and indicated a finer nature than I had given the uncouth old man credit for. He seemed pleased by what I said; he was doing, he felt, something for mamma in taking care of the child she had left so helpless.

Days were to pass before he could speak to me in a more business-like way upon his plans for my future life, and those were days of agitation and affliction, from which, even in memory, I turn away.

I am going to pass over some little time. An interval of six weeks finds me in a lofty wainscoted room, with two stone-shafted windows, large and tall, in proportion, admitting scarcely light enough however, to make it cheerful. These windows are placed at the end of an oblong apartment, and the view they command is melancholy and imposing. I was looking through the sudden hollow of a mountain gorge, with a level of pasture between its craggy sides, upon a broad lake, nearly three hundred yards away, a barrier of mountains rising bold and purple from its distant margin. A file of gigantic trees stretches from about midway down to the edge of the lake, and partakes of the sombre character of the scene. On the steeps at either side, in groups or singly, stand some dwarf oak and birch-trees, scattered and wild, very picturesque, but I think enhancing the melancholy of the view.

For me this spot, repulsive as it would have been to most young people, had a charm; not, indeed, that of a "happy valley," but the charm of seclusion, which to a wounded soul is above price. Those who have suffered a great reverse will understand my horror of meeting the people whom I had once known, my recoil from recognition, and how welcome are the shadows and silence of the cloister compared with the anguish of a comparative publicity.

Experience had early dissipated the illusions of youth, and taught me to listen to the whisperings of hope with cold suspicion. I had no trust in the future—my ghastly mischances had filled me with disgust and terror. My knowledge haunted me; I could not have learned it from the experience of another, though my instructor had come to me from the dead. I was here, then, under no constraint, not the slightest. It was of my own free choice that I came, and remained here. Sir Harry Rokestone would have taken me anywhere I pleased.

Other people spoke of him differently; I can speak only of my own experience. Nothing could be more considerate and less selfish than his treatment of me, nothing more tender and parental. Kind as he was, however, I always felt a sort of awe in his presence. It was not, indeed, quite the awe that is founded on respect—he was old—in most relations stern—and his uneducated moral nature, impetuous and fierce, seemed capable of tragic things. It was not a playful nature, with which the sympathies and spirits of a young person could at all coalesce.

Thormen Fell, at the north of the lake, that out-topped the rest, and shielded us from the wintry wind, rearing its solemn head in solitude, snowy, rocky, high in air, the first of the fells visible, the first to greet me, far off in the sunshine, with its dim welcome as I returned to Golden Friars. It was friendly, it was kindly, but stood aloof and high, and was always associated in my mind with danger, isolation, and mystery. And I think my liking for Sir Harry Rokestone partook of my affection for Thormen Fell.

So, as you have no doubt surmised, I was harboured in the old baronet's feudal castle of Dorracleugh. A stern, wild, melancholy residence, but one that suited wonderfully my present mood.

He was at home; another old gentleman, whose odd society I liked very well, was also at that time an inmate of the house. I will tell you more about him in my next chapter.

CHAPTER LI.

A WARNING.

The old gentleman I speak of, I had seen once before—it was at Malory. He was that very Mr. Lemuel Blount whom I and Laura Grey had watched with so much interest as he crossed the court-yard before our windows, followed by a chaise.

As Sir Harry and I, at the end of our northward journey from London, arrived before the door of his ancient house of Dorracleugh, Mr. Blount appeared at the threshold in the light, and ran down, before the servant could reach it, to the door of our chaise. There was something kindly and pleasant in the voice of this old man, who was so earnest about our comforts. I afterwards found that he was both wise and simple, a sound adviser, and as merry often as a good-natured boy. He contrasted, in this latter respect, very agreeably for me, with Sir Harry Rokestone, whom solitary life, and a habit of brooding over the irreparable, had made both gloomy and silent.

Mr. Blount was easily amused, and was something of an innocent gossip. He used to go down to the town of Golden Friars every day, and gather all the news, and bring home his budget, and entertain me with it, giving all the information I required with respect to the *dramatis personæ*. He liked boating as well as I did, and although the storms of the equinox prevailed, and the surrounding mountains, with their gorges, made the winds squally and uncertain, and sailing upon the lake in certain states of the weather dangerous, he and I used to venture out I daresay oftener than was strictly prudent. Sir Harry used to attack him for these mad adventures, and once or twice grew as tempestuous almost as the weather. Although I was afraid of Sir Harry, I could not help laughing at Mr. Blount's frightened and penitent countenance, and his stolen glances at Sir Harry, so like what I fancied those of a fat schoolboy might be when called up for judgment before his master.

Sir Harry knew all the signs of the weather, and it ended by his putting us under condition never to go out without his leave, and old Mr. Blount's pleadings and quarrelsome resentment under his prohibition were almost as laughable as his alarms.

In a little time neighbours began to call upon me, and I was obliged, of course, to return these visits; but neighbours do not abound in these wild regions, and my quiet, which I had grown to love, was wonderfully little disturbed.

One morning at breakfast, among the letters laid beside Sir Harry was one, on opening which his face darkened suddenly, and an angry light glowed in his deep-set eyes. He rapped his knuckles on the table, he stood up and muttered, sat down again in a little while, and once more looked into the letter. He read it through this time; and then turning to Lemuel Blount, who had been staring at him in silence, as it seemed to me knowing very well what the subject of the letter must be:

"Look at that," said the Baronet, whisking the letter across the table to Mr. Blount, "I don't understand him—I never did."

Mr. Blount took the letter to the window and read it thoughtfully.

"Come along," said the Baronet, rising, and beckoning him with his finger, "I'll give him an answer."

Sir Harry, with these words, strode out of the room, followed by Mr. Blount; and I was left alone to my vain conjectures. It was a serene and sunny day; the air, as in late autumn it always is, though the sun has not lost its power, was a little sharp. Some hours later, I and my old comrade, Mr. Blount, had taken to the water. A boatman sat in the bow. I held the tiller, abandoned to me by my companion, in right of my admitted superiority in steering, an art which I had learned on the estuary at Cardyllion. Mr. Blount was not so talkative as usual. I said to him at last:

"Do you know, Mr. Blount, I once saw you, before I met you here."

"Did you?" said he. "But I did not see you. Where was that?"

"At Malory, near Cardyllion, after the wreck of the Conway Castle, when Mr. Marston was there."

"Yes, so he was," said the old gentleman; "but I did not know that any of Mr. Ware's family were at home at the time. You may have seen me, but I did not see you—or, if I did, you made no impression upon me."

This was one of my good friend's unconscious compliments which often made me smile.

"And what became of that Mr. Marston?" I asked. "He had a wonderful escape!"

"So he had—he went abroad."

"And is he still abroad?"

"About six weeks ago he left England again; he was here only for a flying visit of two or three months. It would be wise, I think, if he never returned. I think he has definitely settled now, far away from this country, and I don't think we are likely to see his face again. You're not keeping her near enough to the wind."

I was curious to learn more about this Mr. Marston, of whom Mr. Carmel and Laura Grey—each judging him, no doubt, from totally different facts, and from points of view so dissimilar—had expressed such singularly ill opinions.

"You know Mr. Marston pretty well, do you?" I asked.

"Yes, very well; I have been trying to do him a service," answered Mr. Blount. "See, see, there—see—those can't be wild ducks? Blessed are the peace-makers. I wish I could, and I think I may. Now, I think you may put her about, eh?"

I did as he advised.

"I have heard people speak ill of that Mr. Marston," I said; "do you know any reason why he should not be liked?"

"Why, yes—that is by people who sit in judgment upon their neighbours—he has been an ill friend to himself. I know but one bad blot he has made, and that, I happen to be aware, hurt no one on earth but himself; but there is no use in talking about him, it vexes me."

"Only one thing more—where is he now?"

"In America. Put this over your feet, please—the air is cold—allow me to arrange it. Ay, the Atlantic is wide enough—let him rest—out of sight, out of mind, for the present at least, and so best."

Our talk now turned upon other subjects, and returned no more to Mr. Marston during our sail.

In this house, as in most other old country-houses, there is a room that is called the library. It had been assigned to Mr. Blount as his special apartment. He had made me free of it—either to sit there and read, whenever I should take a fancy to do so, or to take away any of the books to the drawing-room. My life was as quiet and humdrum as life could be; but never was mortal in the enjoyment of more absolute liberty. Except in the matter of drowning myself and Mr. Blount in the mere, I could do in all respects exactly as I pleased. Dear old Rebecca Torkill was established as a retainer of the house, to my great comfort—she talked me to sleep every night, and drank a cup of tea every afternoon in my room. The quietude and seclusion of my life recalled my early days, and the peaceful routine of Malory. Of course, a time might come when I should like all this changed a little—for the present, it was the only life I thought endurable.

About a week after my conversation with Mr. Blount during our sail, Sir Harry Rokestone was called away for a short time by business; and I had not been for many days in the enjoyment of my *tête-à-tête* with Mr. Blount, when there occurred an incident which troubled me extremely, and was followed by a state of vague suspense and alarm, such as I never expected to have known in that quiet region.

One morning as I sat at breakfast with Mr. Blount for my *vis-à-vis*, and no one by but the servant who had just handed us our letters, I found before me an envelope addressed with a singularity that struck me as a little ominous. The direction was traced, not in the ordinary handwriting, but in Roman characters, in imitation of printing; and the penmanship was thin and feeble, but quite accurate enough to show that it was not the work of a child.

I was already cudgelling my brains to discover whether I could remember among my friends any waggish person who might play me a trick of this kind; but I could recollect no one; especially at a time when my mourning would have made jesting of that kind so inopportune. Odder still, it bore the Malory post-mark, and unaccountable as this was, its contents were still more so. They were penned in the same Roman character, and to the following effect:

> "MISS WARE,—Within the next ten days, a person will probably visit Golden Friars, who intends you a mischief. So soon as you see, you will recognize your enemy. Yours,—A FRIEND."

My first step would have been to consult Mr. Blount upon this letter; but I could tell him nothing of my apprehensions from Monsieur Droqville, in whom my fears at once recognised the "enemy" pointed at by the letter. It might possibly, indeed, be some one else, but by no means, I thought so probable as the other. Who was my "friend," who subscribed this warning? If it was not Mr. Carmel, who else could he be? And yet, why should not Mr. Carmel write to me as frankly as he had spoken and written before? If it came from him, the warning could not point to Monsieur Droqville. There was more than enough to perplex and alarm one in this enigmatical note.

CHAPTER LII.

MINE ENEMY.

I was afraid to consult even Rebecca Torkill; she was a little given to talking, and my alarms might have become, in a day or two, the property of Sir Harry's housekeeper. There is no use in telling you all the solutions which my fears invented for this riddle.

In my anxiety I wrote to the Rector's wife at Cardyllion, telling her that I had got an anonymous note, bearing the Malory post-mark, affecting so much mystery that I was totally unable to interpret it. I begged of her therefore to take every opportunity of making out, if possible, who was the author, and to tell me whether there was any acquaintance of mine at present there, who might have written such a note by way of a practical joke to mystify me; and I entreated of her to let me know her conjectures. Then I went into the little world of Cardyllion and inquired about all sorts of people, great and small, and finally I asked if Mr. Carmel had been lately there.

In addition to this, I wrote to the post-master, describing the appearance of the letter I had got, and asked whether he could help me to a description of the person who had posted it? Every time a new theory struck me, I read my "friend's" note over again.

At length I began to think that it was most probably the thoughtless production of some real but harmless friend, who intended herself paying me a visit here, on visiting the Golden Friars. A female visitor was very likely, as the note was framed so as to indicate nothing of the sex of the "enemy;" and two or three young lady friends, not very reasonable, had been attacking me in their letters for not answering more punctually.

My mind was perpetually working upon this problem. I was very uncomfortable, and at times frightened, and even agitated. I don't, even now, wonder at the degree to which I suffered.

A note of a dream in one of my fragmentary diaries at that time will show you how nervous I was. It is set down in much greater detail than you or I can afford it here. I will just tell you its "heads," as old sermons say. I thought I had arrived here, at Dorracleugh, after a long journey. Mr. Blount and a servant came in carrying one of my large black travelling boxes, and tugged it along the ground. The servant then went out, and Mr. Blount, who I fancied was very pale, looked at me fixedly, and placing his finger to his lip in token of silence, softly went out, also, and shut the door, leaving me rather awe-struck. My box, I thought, on turning my eyes upon it again, from my gaze at Mr. Blount, seemed much longer, and its shape altered; but such transformations do not trouble us in our dreams, and I began fumbling with the key, which did not easily fit the lock. At length I opened it, and instead of my dresses I saw a long piece of rumpled linen, and perceived that the box was a coffin. With the persistent acquiescence in monstrosities by which dreams are characterized, I experienced the slightest possible bewilderment at this, and drew down the linen covering, and discovered the shrouded face of Mr. Marston. I was absolutely horrified, and more so when the dead man sat up, with his eyes open, in the coffin, and looked at me with an expression so atrocious that I awoke with a scream, and a heart bounding with terror, and lay awake for more than an hour. This dream was the vague embodiment of one of my conjectures, and pointed at one of the persons whom, against all probability, I had canvassed as the "enemy" of my warning.

Solitude and a secret fear go a long way towards making us superstitious. I became more and more nervous as the suspense extended from day to day. I was afraid to go into Golden Friars, lest I should meet my enemy. I made an excuse, and stayed at home from church on Sunday for the same reason. I was afraid even of passing a boat upon the lake. I don't know whether Mr. Blount observed my increased depression; we played our hit of backgammon, nevertheless, as usual, in the evening, and took, when the weather was not boisterous, our little sail on the lake.

I heard from the Rector's wife. She was not able, any more than the Cardyllion postmaster, to throw the least light upon my letter. Mr. Carmel had not been in that part of the world for a long time. I was haunted, nevertheless, by the image of Mr. Marston, whom my dream had fixed in my imagination.

These letters had reached me as usual as we sat at breakfast. Mine absorbed me, and by demolishing all theories, had directed me upon new problems. I sat looking into my tea-cup, as if I could divine from it. I raised my eyes at length and said:

"When did you say—I forget—you last heard from Mr. Marston?"

He looked up. I perceived that he had been just as much engrossed by his letter as I had been with mine. He laid it down, and asked me to repeat my question. I did. Mr. Blount smiled.

"Well, that is very odd. I have just heard from him," said he, raising the letter he had been reading by the corner. "It came by the mail that reached London yesterday evening."

"And where is he?" I asked.

"He's at New York now; but he says he is going in a few days to set out for Canada, or the backwoods—he has not yet made up his mind which. I think, myself, he will choose the back-settlements; he has a passion for adventure."

At these words of Mr. Blount, my theories respecting Mr. Marston fell to the ground, and my fears again gathered about the meaner figure of Monsieur Droqville; and as soon as breakfast was ended, I sat down in the window, and studied my anonymous letter carefully once more.

Business called Mr. Blount that evening to Golden Friars; and after dinner I went into the library, and sat looking out at the noble landscape. A red autumnal sunset illuminated the summits of the steep side of the glen, at my left, leaving all the rest of the cleugh in deep, purple-grey shadow. It opens, as I told you, on the lake, which stretched before me in soft shadow, except where its slow moving ripple caught the light with a fiery glimmer; and far away the noble fells, their peaks and ribs touched with the same misty glow, stood out like majestic shadows, and closed the view sublimely.

I sat here, I can't say reading, although I had an old book open upon my knees. I was too anxious, and my head too busy, to read. Twilight came, and then gradually a dazzling, icy moonlight transformed the landscape. I leaned back in my low chair, my head and shoulders half hidden among the curtains, looking out on the beautiful effect.

This moonlight had prevailed for, I dare say, ten or fifteen minutes, when something occurred to rouse me from my listless reverie. Some object moved upon the window-stone, and caught my eye. It was a human hand suddenly placed there; its fellow instantly followed; an elbow, a hat, a head, a knee; and a man kneeled in the moonlight upon the window-stone, which was there some eight or ten feet from the ground.

Was I awake or in a dream? Gracious Heaven! There were the scarred forehead and the stern face of Mr. Marston with knit brows, and his hand shading his eyes, as he stared close to the glass into the room.

I was in the shadow, and cowered back deeper into the folds of the curtain. He plainly did not see me. He was looking into the further end of the room. I was afraid to cry out; it would have betrayed me. I remained motionless, in the hope that, when he was satisfied that there was no one in the room, he would withdraw from his place of observation, and go elsewhere.

I was watching him with the fascinated terror of a bird, in its ivied nook, when a kite hovers at night within a span of it.

He now seized the window-sash—how I prayed that it had been secured—and with a push or two the window ascended, and he stepped in upon the floor. The cold night air entered with him; he stood for a minute looking into the room, and then very softly he closed the window. He seemed to have made up his mind to establish himself here, for he lazily pushed Mr. Blount's easy-chair into the recess at the window, and sat down very nearly opposite to me. If I had been less shocked and frightened, I might have seen the absurdity of my situation.

He leaned back in Mr. Blount's chair, like a tired man, and extended his heels on the carpet; his hand clutched the arm of the chair. His face was in the bright white light of the moon, his chin was sunk on his chest. His features looked haggard and wicked. Two or three times I thought he saw me, for his eyes were fixed on me for more than a minute; but my perfect stillness, the deep shadow that enveloped me, and the brilliant moonlight in his eyes, protected me.

Suddenly I heard a step—it was Mr. Blount; the door opened, and the step was arrested; to my infinite relief a voice, it was Mr. Blount's, called a little sternly:

"Who's that?"

"The prodigal, the outcast," answered Mr. Marston's deep voice, bitterly. "I have been, and am, too miserable not to make one more trial, and to seek to be reconciled. You, sir, are very kind—you are a staunch friend; but you have never yet done all you could do for me. Why have you not faith? Your influence is unlimited."

"My good gracious!" exclaimed Mr. Blount, not moving an inch from where he stood. "Why, it is only this morning I received your letter from New York. What is all this? I don't understand."

"I came by the same mail that brought my letter. Second thoughts are the best. I changed my mind," said the young man, standing up. "Why should I live the sort of life he seems to have planned for me, if he intends anything better at any time? And if he don't, what do I owe him? It is vindictive and unnatural. I'm worn out; my patience has broken down."

"I could not have believed my eyes," said Mr. Blount. "I did not—dear, dear me! I don't know what to make of it; he'll be very much displeased. Mr. Marston, sir, you seem bent on ruining yourself with him, quite."

"I don't know—what chance have I out there? Out of sight out of mind, you used to say. He'd have forgotten me, you'd have forgotten me; I should not have had a friend soon, who knew or cared whether I was alive or dead. Speak to him; tell him he may as well listen to me. I'm perfectly desperate," and he struck his open hand on the back of the chair, and clenched the sentence with a bitter oath.

"I am not to blame for it," said Mr. Blount.

"I know that; I know it very well, Mr. Blount. You are too good a friend of our family. I know it, and I feel it—I do, indeed; but look here, where's the good of driving a fellow to desperation? I tell you I'll do something that will bring it to a crisis; I can't stand the hell I live in. And let him prosecute me if he likes; it is very easy for me to put a pistol to my head—it's only half a second and it's over—and I'll leave a letter telling the world how he has used me, and then see how he'll like the mess he has made of it."

"Now, pardon me, sir," said Mr. Blount, ceremoniously, "that's all stuff; I mean he won't believe you. When I have an unacceptable truth to communicate, I make it a rule to do so in the most courteous manner; and, happily, I have, hitherto, found the laws of truth and of politeness always reconcilable; he has told me, my dear sir, fifty times, that you are a great deal too selfish ever to hurt yourself. There is no use, then, in trying, if I may be permitted the phrase, to bully him. If you seek, with the smallest chance of success, to make an impression upon Sir Harry Rokestone, you must approach him in a spirit totally unlike that. I'll tell you what you must do. Write me a penitent letter, asking my intercession, and if you can make, with perfect sincerity, fair promises for the future, and carefully avoid the smallest evidence of the spirit you chose to display in your last—and it is very strange if you have learned nothing—I'll try again what I can do."

The young man advanced, and took Mr. Blount's hand and wrung it fervently.

I don't think Mr. Blount returned the demonstration with equal warmth. He was rather passive on the occasion.

"Is he—here?" asked Mr. Marston.

"No, and you must not remain an hour in this house, nor at Golden Friars, nor shall you go to London, but to some perfectly quiet place; write to me, from thence, a letter such as I have described, and I will lay it before him, with such representations of my own as perhaps may weigh with him, and we shall soon know what will come of it. Have the servants seen you?"

"No one."

"So much the better."

"I scaled your window about ten minutes ago. I thought you would soon turn up, and I was right. I know you will forgive me."

"Well, no matter, you had better get away as you came; how was that?"

"By boat, sir; I took it at the Three Oaks."

"It is all the better you were not in the town; I should not like him to know you are in England, until I have got your letter to show him; I hope, sir, you will write in it no more than you sincerely feel. I cannot enter into any but an honest case. Where did your boat wait?"

"At the jetty here."

"Very good; as you came by the window, you may as well go by it, and I will meet you a little way down the path; I may have something more to say."

"Thank you, sir, from my heart," said Marston.

"No, no, don't mind, I want you to get away again; there, get away as quickly as you can." He had opened the window for him. "Ah, you have climbed that many a time when you were a boy; you should know every stone by heart."

"I'll do exactly as you tell me, sir, in all things," said the young man, and dropped lightly from the window-stone to the ground, and I saw his shadowy figure glide swiftly down the grass, towards the great lime-trees that stand in a receding row between the house and the water. Mr. Blount lowered the window quietly, and looked for a moment after him.

"Some men are born to double sorrow—sorrow for others—sorrow for themselves. I don't quite know what to make of him."

The old man sighed heavily, and left the room. I felt very like a spy, and very much ashamed of myself for having overheard a conversation certainly not intended for my ears. I can honestly say it was not curiosity that held me there; that I was beyond measure distressed at my accidental treachery; and that, had there been a door near enough to enable me to escape unseen I should not have overheard a sentence of what had passed. But I had not courage to discover myself; and wanting nerve at the beginning to declare myself, I had, of course, less and less as the conference proceeded, and my situation became more equivocal.

The departure of Mr. Blount, whom I now saw descending the steps in pursuit of his visitor, relieved me, and I got away from the room, haunted by the face that had so lately appeared to me in my ominous dream, and by the voice whose tones excited a strange tremor, and revived stranger recollections.

In the drawing-room, before a quarter of an hour, I was joined by Mr. Blount. Our *tête a tête* was an unusually silent one, and, after tea, we played a rather spiritless hit or two at backgammon.

I was glad when the time came to get to my room, to the genial and garrulous society of Rebecca Torkill; and after my candle was put out, I lay long enough awake, trying to put together the as yet imperfect fragments of a story and a situation which were to form the ground-work of the drama in which I instinctively felt that I was involved.

CHAPTER LIII.

ONE MORE CHANCE.

Sir Harry came home, and met me more affectionately and kindly than ever. I soon perceived that there was something of more than usual gravity under discussion between him and Mr. Blount. I knew, of course, very well what was the question they were debating. I was very uncomfortable while this matter was being discussed; Mr. Blount seemed nervous and uneasy; and it was plain that the decision was not only suspended but uncertain. I don't suppose there was a more perturbed little family in all England at that moment, over whom, at the same time, there hung apparently no cloud of disaster.

At last I could perceive that something was settled; for the discussions between Mr. Blount and Sir Harry seemed to have lost the character of debate and remonstrance, and to have become more like a gloomy confidence and consultation between them. I can only speak of what I may call the external appearance of these conversations, for I was not permitted to hear one word of their substance.

In a little while Sir Harry went away again. This time his journey, I afterwards learned, was to one of the quietest little towns in North Wales, where his chaise drew up at the Bull Inn. The tall northern baronet got out of the chaise, and strode to the bar of that rural hostelry.

"Is there a gentleman named Marston staying here?" he asked of the plump elderly lady who sat within the bow-window of the bar.

"Yes, sir, Mr. Marston, Number Seven, up one pair of stairs."

"Upstairs now?" asked Sir Harry.

"He'll be gone out to take his walk, sir, by this time," answered the lady.

"Can I talk to you for a few minutes, anywhere, madam, in private?" asked Sir Harry.

The old lady looked at him, a little surprised.

"Yes, sir," she said. "Is it anything very particular, please?"

"Yes, ma'am, very particular," answered the baronet.

She called to her handmaid, and installed her quickly in her seat, and so led the baronet to an occupied room on the ground-floor. Sir Harry closed the door, and told her who he was. The landlady recognised his baronetage with a little courtesy.

"I'm a relation of Mr. Marston's, and I've come down here to make an inquiry; I want to know whether he has been leading an orderly, quiet life since he came to your house."

"No one more so, please, sir; a very nice regular gentleman, and goes to church every Sunday he's been here, and that is true. We have no complaint to make of him, please, sir; and he has paid his bill twice since he came here."

The woman looked honest, with frank, round eyes.

"Thank you, ma'am," said Sir Harry; "that will do."

An hour later it was twilight, and Mr. Marston, on entering his sitting-room after his walk, saw the baronet, who got up from his chair before the fire as he came in.

The young man instantly took off his hat, and stood near the door, the very image of humility. Sir Harry did not advance, or offer him his hand; he gave him a nod. Nothing could be colder than this reception.

"So, Richard, you have returned to England, as you have done most other things, without consulting me," said the cold, deep voice of Sir Harry.

"I've acted rashly sir, I fear. I acted on an impulse. I could not resist it. It was only twelve hours before the ship left New York when the thought struck me. I ought to have waited, I ought to have thought it over. It seemed to me my only chance, and I'm afraid it has but sunk me lower in your esteem."

"It is clear you should have asked my leave first, all things considered," said Sir Harry, in the same tone.

The young man bowed his head.

"I see that very clearly now, sir; but I have been so miserable under your displeasure, and I do not always see things as my calmer reason would view them. I thought of nothing but my chance of obtaining your forgiveness, and, at so great a distance, I despaired."

"So it was to please me you set my authority at naught? By Jea! that's logic."

Sir Harry spoke this with a scornful and angry smile.

"I am the only near kinsman you have left, sir, of your blood and name."

"My name, sir!" challenged Sir Harry, fiercely.

"My second name is Rokestone—called after you," pleaded Mr. Marston.

"By my sang, young man, if you and I had borne the same name, I'd have got the Queen's letter, and changed mine to Smith."

To this the young gentleman made no reply. His uncle broke the silence that followed.

"We'll talk at present, if you please, as little as need be; there's nothing pleasant to say between us. But I'll give you a chance; I'll see if you are a changed man, as your letter says. I'll try what work is in you, or what good. You said you'd like farming. Well, we'll see what sort of farmer you'll make. You'll do well to remember 'tis but a trial. In two or three days Mr. Blount will give you particulars by letter. Good evening. Don't come down; stay here. I'll go alone. Say no more;

I'll have no thanks or professions. Your conduct, steadiness, integrity, shall guide me. That's all. Farewell."

Mr. Marston, during this colloquy, had gradually advanced a little, and now stood near the window. Sir Harry accompanied his farewell with a short nod, and stalked down the stairs. Mr. Marston knew he meant what he said, and therefore did not attempt to accompany him downstairs. And so, with a fresh pair of horses, Sir Harry immediately started on his homeward journey.

I, who knew at the time nothing of what I afterwards learned, was still in a suspense which nobody suspected. It was ended one evening by Sir Harry Rokestone, who said:

"To-morrow my nephew, Richard Marston, will be here to stay, I have not yet determined for how long. He is a dull young man. You'll not like him; he has not a word to throw at a dog."

So, whatever his description was worth, his announcement was conclusive, and Richard Marston was to become an inmate of Dorracleugh next day. I find my diary says, under date of the next day:

"I have been looking forward, with a trepidation I can hardly account for, to the arrival which Sir Harry announced yesterday. The event of the day occurred at three o'clock. I was thinking of going out for a walk, and had my hat and jacket on, and was standing in the hall. I wished to postpone, as long as I could, the meeting with Mr. Marston, which I dreaded. At that critical moment his double knock at the hall-door, and the distant peal of our rather deep-mouthed bell, startled me. I guessed it was he, and turned to run up to my room, but met Sir Harry, who said, laying his hand gently on my shoulder:

"'Wait, dear—this is my nephew. I saw him from the window. I want to introduce him.'

"Of course I had to submit. The door was opened. There he was, the veritable Mr. Marston, of Malory, the hero of the Conway Castle, of the duel, and likewise of so many evil stories—the man who had once talked so romantically and so madly to me. I felt myself growing pale, and then blushing. Sir Harry received him coldly enough, and introduced me, simply mentioning my name and his; and then I ran down the steps, with two of the dogs as my companions, while the servants were getting in Mr. Marston's luggage.

"I met him again at dinner. He is very little changed, except that he is much more sun-burnt. He has got a look, too, of command and melancholy. I am sure he has suffered, and suffering, they say, makes people better. He talked very little during dinner, and rather justified Sir Harry's description. Sir Harry talked about the farm he intends for him—they are to look at it to-morrow together. Mr. Blount seems to have got a load off his mind.

"The farm is not so far away as I had imagined—it is only at the other side of the lake, about five hundred acres at Clusted, which came to Sir Harry, Mr. Blount says, through the Mardykes family. I wonder whether there is a house upon it—if so, he will probably live at the other side of the lake, and his arrival will have made very little difference to us. So much the better, perhaps.

"I saw him and Sir Harry, at about eight o'clock this morning, set out together in the big boat, with two men, to cross the lake.

"Farming is, I believe, a very absorbing pursuit. He won't feel his solitude much; and Mr. Blount says he will have to go to fairs and markets. It is altogether a grazing farm."

The reader will perceive that I am still quoting my diary.

"To-day, old Miss Goulding, of Wrybiggins, the old lady whom the gossips of Golden Friars once assigned to Sir Harry as a wife, called with a niece who is with her on a visit, so I suppose they had heard of Mr. Marston's arrival, and came to see what kind of person he is. I'm rather glad they were disappointed. I ordered luncheon for them, and I saw them look toward the door every time it opened, expecting, I am sure, to see Mr. Marston. I maliciously postponed telling them, until the very last moment, that he was at the other side of the mere, as they call the lake, although I suffered for my cruelty, for they dawdled on here almost interminably.

"Sir Harry and Mr. Marston did not return till tea-time, when it was quite dark; they had dined at a farm-house at the other side. Sir Harry seems, I think a little more friendly with him. They talked, it is true, of nothing but farming and live stock; and Mr. Blount joined. I took, therefore, in solitude, to my piano, and, when I was tired of that, to my novel.

"A very dull evening—the dullest, I think, I've passed since we came to Dorracleugh. I daresay Mr. Marston will make a very good farmer. I hope very much there may be a suitable residence found for him at the other side of the lake."

Next my diary contains the following entry:

"Mr. Marston off again at eight o'clock to his farm. Mr. Blount and I took a sail to-day, with Sir Harry's leave, in the small boat. He tells me that there is no necessity for Mr. Marston's going every day to the farm—that Sir Harry has promised him a third of whatever the farm, under his management, makes. He seems very anxious to please Sir Harry. I can't conceive what can have made me so nervous about the arrival of this very humdrum squire, whose sole object appears to be the prosperity of his colony of cows and sheep.

"Sunday.—Of course to-day he has taken a holiday, but he has not given us the benefit of it. He chose to walk all day, instead of going to church with us to Golden Friars. It is not far from Haworth. So he prefers a march of four and twenty miles to the fatigue of our society!"

On the Tuesday following I find, by the same record, Sir Harry went to visit his estate of Tarlton, about forty miles from Golden Friars, to remain away for three or four days. That day I find also Mr. Marston was, as usual, at his farm at Clusted, and did not come home till about nine o'clock.

I went to my room immediately after his arrival, so that he had an uninterrupted *tête-à-tête* with Mr. Blount.

Next day he went away at his usual early hour, and returned not so late. I made an excuse of having some letters to write, and left the two gentlemen to themselves a good deal earlier than the night before.

"Mr. Marston certainly is very little in my way; I have not spoken twenty words to him since his arrival. I begin to think him extremely impertinent."

The foregoing is a very brief note of the day, considering how diffuse and particular I often was when we were more alone. I make up for it on the following day. The text runs thus:

"Mr. Marston has come off his high horse, and broken silence at last. It was blowing furiously in the morning, and I suppose, however melancholy he may be, he has no intention of drowning himself. At all events, there has been no crossing the mere this morning.

"He has appeared, for the first time since his arrival, at breakfast. Sir Harry's absence seems to have removed a great constraint. He talked very agreeably, and seemed totally to have forgotten the subject of farming; he told us a great deal of his semi-military life in Spain, which was very amusing. I know he made me laugh heartily. Old Mr. Blount laughed also. Our breakfast was a very pleasant meal. Mr. Blount was himself in Spain for more than a year when he was young, and got'up and gave us a representation of his host, an eccentric fan-maker, walking with his toes pointed and his chest thrown out, and speaking sonorous Spanish with pompous gesture. I had no idea he had so much fun in him. The good-natured old man seemed quite elated at our applause and very real laughter.

"Mr. Marston suddenly looked across the lake, and recollected his farm.

"'How suddenly that storm went down!' he said. 'I can't say I'm glad of it, for I suppose I must make my usual trip, and visit my four-footed friends over the way.'

"'No,' said Mr. Blount; 'let them shift for themselves to-day; I'll take it on myself. There's no necessity for you going every day as you do.'

"'But how will it be received by the authorities? Will my uncle think it an omission? I should not like him to suppose that, under any temptation, I had forgotten my understanding with him.'

"He glanced at me. Whether he thought me the temptation, or only wished to include me in the question, I don't know.

"'Oh! no,' said Mr. Blount; 'stay at home for this once—I'll explain it all; and we can go out and have a sail, if the day continues as fine as it promises.'

"Mr. Marston hesitated; he looked at me as if for an opinion, but I said nothing.

"'Well,' he said, 'I can't resist. I'll take your advice, Mr. Blount, and make this a holiday.'

"I think Mr. Marston very much improved in some respects. His manners and conversation are not less spirited, but gentler; and he is so very agreeable! I think he has led an unhappy life, and no doubt was often very much in the wrong. But I have remarked that we condemn people not in proportion to their moral guilt, but in proportion to the inconvenience their faults inflict on us. I wonder very much what those stories were which caused Mr. Carmel and Laura Grey to speak of him so bitterly and sternly? They were both so good that things which other people would have thought lightly enough of, would seem to them enormous. I dare say it is all about debt, or very likely play; and people who have possibly lost money by his extravagance have been exaggerating matters, and telling stories their own way. He seems very much sobered now, at all events. One can't help pitying him.

"He went down to the jetty before luncheon. I found afterwards that it was to get cloaks and rugs arranged for me.

"He lunched with us, and we were all very talkative. He certainly will prevent our all falling asleep in this drowsy place. We had such a pleasant sail. I gave him the tiller; but his duties as helmsman did not prevent his talking. We could hear one another very well, in spite of the breeze, which was rather more than Sir Harry would have quite approved of.

"Mr. Marston had many opportunities to-day of talking to me without any risk of being overheard. He did not, however, say a single word in his old vein. I am very glad of this; it would be provoking to lose his conversation, which is amusing, and, I confess, a great resource in this solitude.

"He is always on the watch to find if I want anything, and gets or does it instantly. I wish his farm was at this side of the lake. I dare say when Sir Harry comes back we shall see as little as ever of him. It will end by his being drowned in that dangerous lake. It seems odd that Sir Harry, who is so tender of my life and Mr. Blount's, should have apparently no feeling whatever about his. But it is their affair. I'm not likely to be consulted; so I need not trouble my head about it.

"I write in my room, the day now over, and dear old Rebecca Torkill is fussing about from table to wardrobe, and from wardrobe to drawers, pottering, and fidgeting, and whispering to herself. She has just told me that Mrs. Shackleton, the housekeeper here at Dorracleugh, talked to her a good deal this evening about Mr. Marston. She gives a very good account of him. When he went to school, and to Oxford, she saw him only at intervals, but he was a manly, good-natured boy she said, 'and never, that she knew, any harm in him, only a bit wild, like other young men at such places.' I write, as nearly as I can, Rebecca's words.

"The subject of the quarrel with Sir Harry Rokestone, Mrs. Shackleton says, was simply that Mr. Marston positively refused to marry some one whom his uncle had selected for a niece-in-law. That is exactly the kind of disobedience that old people are sometimes most severe upon. She told Rebecca to be very careful not to say a word of it to the other servants, as it was a great secret.

"After all there may be two sides to this case, as to others, and Mr. Marston's chief mutiny may have been of that kind which writers of romance and tragedy elevate into heroism.

"He certainly is very much improved."

Here my diary for that day left Mr. Marston, and turned to half-a-dozen trifles, treated, I must admit, with much comparative brevity.

CHAPTER LIV.

DANGEROUS GROUND.

Old Mr. Blount was a religious man. Sir Harry, whose ideas upon such subjects I never could exactly divine, went to church every Sunday; but he scoffed at bishops, and neither loved nor trusted clergymen. He had, however, family prayers every morning, at which Mr. Blount officiated, with evident happiness and peace in the light of his simple countenance.

No radiance of this happy light was reflected on the face of Sir Harry Rokestone, who sat by the mantelpiece, in one of the old oak arm chairs, a colossal image of solitude, stern and melancholy, and never, it seemed to me, so much alone as at those moments which seem to draw other mortals nearer. I fancied that some associations connected with such simple gatherings long ago, perhaps, recalled mamma to his thoughts. He seemed to sit in a stern and melancholy reverie, and he would often come over to me, when the prayer was ended, and, looking at me with great affection, ask gently:

"Well, my little lass, do they try to make you happy here? Is there anything you think of that you'd like me to get down from Lunnon? You must think. I'd like to be doing little things for you; think, and tell me this evening." And at such times he would turn on me a look of full-hearted affection, and smoothe my hair caressingly with his old hand.

Sometimes he would say: "You like this place, you tell me; but the winters here, I'm thinking, will be too hard for you."

"But I like a good, cold, frosty winter," I would answer him. "There is nothing I think so pleasant."

"Ay, but maybe ye'll be getting a cough or something."

"No, I assure you I'm one of the few persons on earth who never take cold," I urged, for I really wished to spend the winter at Golden Friars.

"Well, pretty lass, ye shall do as you like best, but you mustn't fall sick; if you do, what's to become o' the auld man?"

You must allow me here to help myself with my diary once more. I am about to quote from what I find there, dated the following Sunday:

"We went to Golden Friars to church as usual; and Mr. Marston, instead of performing his devotions twelve miles away, came with us.

"After the service was ended, Sir Harry, who had a call to make, took leave of us. The day was so fine that we were tempted to walk home instead of driving.

"We chose the path by the lake, and sent the carriage on to Dorracleugh.

"Mr. Blount chooses to talk over the sermon, and I am sure thinks it profane to mention secular subjects on Sunday. I think this a mistake; and I confess I was not sorry when good Mr. Blount stopped and told us he was going into Shenstone's cottage. I felt that a respite of five minutes from the echoes of the good vicar's sermon would be pleasant. But when he went on to say that he was going in to read some of the Bible and talk a little with the consumptive little boy, placing me under Mr. Marston's escort for the rest of the walk, which was about a mile, I experienced a new alarm. I had no wish that Mr. Marston should return to his old heroics.

"I did not well know what to say or do, Mr. Blount's good-bye came so suddenly. My making a difficulty about walking home with Mr. Marston would to him, who knew nothing of what had passed at Malory, have appeared an unaccountable affectation of prudery. I asked Mr. Blount whether he intended staying any time. He answered, 'Half an hour at least; and if the poor boy wishes it, I shall stay an hour,' he added.

"Mr. Marston, who, I am sure, perfectly understood me, did not say a word. I had only to make the best of an uncomfortable situation, and, very nervous, I nodded and smiled my farewell to Mr. Blount, and set out on my homeward march with Mr. Marston.

"I need not have been in such a panic—it was very soon perfectly plain that Mr. Marston did not intend treating me to any heroics.

"'I don't know any one in the world I have a much higher opinion of than Mr. Blount,' he said; 'but I do think it a great mercy to get away from him a little on Sundays; I can't talk to him in his own way, and I turn simply into a Trappist—I become, I mean, perfectly dumb.'

"I agreed, but said that I had such a regard for Mr. Blount that I could not bring myself to vex him.

"'That is my rule also,' he said, 'only I carry it a little further, ever since I received my education,' he smiled, darkly; 'that is, since I begun to suffer, about three years ago, I have learned to practise it with all my friends. You would not believe what constraint I often place upon myself to avoid saying that which is in my heart and next my lips, but which I fear—I fear with too good reason—might not be liked by others. There was a time, I daresay, when Hamlet blurted out everything that came into his mind, before he learned in the school of sorrow to say, "But break my heart, for I must hold my tongue."'

"He looked very expressively, and I thought I knew perfectly what he meant, and that if by any blunder I happened to say a foolish thing, I might find myself, before I knew where I was, in the midst of a conversation as wild as that of the wood of Plas Ylwd.

"In reply to this I said, not very adroitly:

"And what a beautiful play *Hamlet* is! I have been trying to copy Retsch's outline, but I have made such a failure. The faces are so fine and forcible, and the expression of the hands is so wonderful, and my hands are so tame and clumsy; I can do nothing but the ghost, and that is because he is the only absurd figure in the series."

"'Yes,' he acquiesced, 'like a thing in an *opera bouffe*.'

"I could perceive very plainly that my rather precipitate and incoherent excursion into Retsch's outlines, into which he had followed me with the best grace he could, had wounded him. It was equally plain, however, that he was in good faith practising the rule he had just now mentioned, and was by no means the insolent and overbearing suitor he had shown himself in that scene, now removed alike by time and distance, in which I had before seen him.

"No one could be more submissive than he to my distinct decision that there was to be no more such wild talk.

"For the rest of our walk he talked upon totally indifferent subjects. Certainly, of the two, I had been the most put out by his momentary ascent to a more tragic level. I wonder now whether I did not possibly suspect a great deal more than was intended. If so, what a fool I must have appeared! Is there anything so ridiculous as a demonstration of resistance where no attack is meditated? I began to feel so confused and ashamed that I hardly took the trouble to follow what he said. As we approached Dorracleugh, I began to feel more like myself. After a little silence he said what I am going to set down; I have gone over it again and again in my mind; I know I have added nothing, and I really think I write very nearly exactly as he spoke it.

"'When I had that strange escape with my life from the Conway Castle,' he said, 'no man on earth was more willing and less fit to die than I. I don't suppose there was a more miserable man in England. I had disappointed my uncle by doing what seemed a very foolish thing. I could not tell him my motive—no one knew it—the secret was not mine—everything combined to embarrass and crush me. I had the hardest thing on earth to endure—unmerited condemnation was my portion. Some good people, whom, notwithstanding, I have learned to respect, spoke of me to my face as if I had committed a murder. My uncle understands me now, but he has not yet forgiven me. When I was at Malory, I was in a mood to shoot myself through the head; I was desperate, I was bitter, I was furious. Every unlucky thing that could happen did happen there. The very people who had judged me most cruelly turned up; and among them one who forced a quarrel on me, and compelled that miserable duel in which I wished at the time I had been killed.'

"I listened to all this with more interest than I allowed him to see, as we walked on together side by side, I looking down on the path before us, and saying nothing.

"'If it were not for one or two feelings left me, I should not know myself for the shipwrecked man who thanked his young hostess at Malory for her invaluable hospitality,' he said; 'there are some things one never forgets. I often think of Malory—I have thought of it in all kinds of distant, out-of-the-way, savage places; it rises before me as I saw it last. My life has all gone wrong. While hope remains, we can bear anything—but my last hope seems pretty near its setting—and, when it is out, I hope, seeing I cross and return in all weathers, there is drowning enough in that lake to give a poor fool, at least, a cool head and a quiet heart.'

"Then, without any tragic pause, he turned to other things lightly, and never looked towards me to discover what effect his words were producing; but he talked on, and now very pleasantly. We loitered a little at the hall-door. I did not want him to come into the drawing-room, and establish himself there. Here were the open door, the hall, the court-yard, the windows, all manner of possibilities for listeners, and I felt I was protected from any embarrassment that an impetuous companion might please to inflict if favoured by a *tête-à-tête*.

"I must, however, do him justice: he seemed very anxious not to offend—very careful so to mask any disclosure of his feelings as to leave me quite free to 'ignore' it, and, as it seemed to me, on the watch to catch any evidence of my impatience.

"He is certainly very agreeable and odd; and the time passed very pleasantly while we loitered in the court-yard.

"Mr. Blount soon came up, and after a word or two I left them, and ran up to my room."

CHAPTER LV.

MR. CARMEL TAKES HIS LEAVE.

A bout this time there was a sort of fête at Golden Friars. Three very pretty fountains were built by Sir Richard Mardykes and Sir Harry, at the upper end of the town, in which they both have property; and the opening of these was a sort of gala.

I did not care to go. Sir Harry Rokestone and Mr. Blount, were, of course, there; Mr. Marston went, instead, to his farm, at the other side; and I took a whim to go out on the lake, in a row-boat, in the direction of Golden Friars. My boatmen rowed me near enough to hear the music, which was very pretty; but we remained sufficiently far out, to prevent becoming mixed up with the other boats which lay near the shore.

It was a pleasant, clear day, with no wind stirring, and although we were now fairly in winter, the air was not too sharp, and with just a rug about one's feet, the weather was very pleasant. My journal speaks of this evening as follows:

"It was, I think, near four o'clock, when I told the men to row towards Dorracleugh. Before we reached it, the filmy haze of a winter's evening began to steal over the landscape, and a red sunset streamed through the break in the fells above the town with so lovely an effect that I told the men to slacken their speed. So we moved, with only a dip of the oar, now and then; and I looked up the mere, enjoying the magical effect.

"A boat had been coming, a little in our wake, along the shore. I had observed it, but without the slightest curiosity; not even with a conjecture that Sir Harry and Mr. Blount might be returning in it, for I knew that it was arranged that they were to come back together in the carriage.

"Voices from this boat caught my ear; and one suddenly that startled me, just as it neared us. It glided up. I fancy about thirty yards were between the sides of the two boats; and the men, like those in my boat, had been ordered merely to dip their oars, and were now moving abreast of ours; the drips from their oars sparkled like drops of molten metal. What I heard—the only thing I now heard—was the harsh nasal voice of Monsieur Droqville.

"There he was, in his black dress, standing in the stern of the boat, looking round on the landscape, from point to point. The light, as he looked this way and that, touched his energetic bronzed features, the folds of his dress, and the wet planks of the boat, with a fire that contrasted with the grey shadows behind and about.

"I heard him say, pointing with his outstretched arm, 'And is that Dorracleugh?' To which, one of the people in the boat made him an answer.

"I can't think of that question without terror. What has brought that man down here? What interest can he have in seeking out Dorracleugh, except that it happens to be my present place of abode?

"I am sure he did not see me. When he looked in my direction, the sun was in his eyes, and my face in shadow; I don't think he can have seen me. But that matters nothing if he has come down for any purpose connected with me."

A sure instinct told me that Monsieur Droqville would be directed inflexibly by the interests of his order, to consult which, at all times, unawed by consequences to himself or others, was his stern and narrow duty.

Here, in this beautiful and sequestered corner of the world, how far, after all, I had been from quiet. Well might I cry with Campbell's exile—

"Ah! cruel fate, wilt thou never replace me
In a mansion of peace where no perils can chase me?"

My terrors hung upon a secret I dared not disclose. There was no one to help me; for I could consult no one.

The next day I was really ill. I remained in my room. I thought Monsieur Droqville would come to claim an interview; and perhaps would seek, by the power he possessed, to force me to become an instrument in forwarding some of his plans, affecting either the faith or the property of others. I was in an agony of suspense and fear.

Days passed; a week; and no sign of Monsieur Droqville. I began to breathe. He was not a man, I knew, to waste weeks, or even days, in search of the picturesque, in a semi-barbarous region like Golden Friars.

At length I summoned courage to speak to Rebecca Torkill. I told her I had seen Monsieur Droqville, and that I wanted her, without telling the servants at Dorracleugh, to make inquiry at the "George and Dragon," whether a person answering that description had been there. No such person was there. So I might assume he was gone. He had come with Sir Richard Mardykes, I conjectured, from Carsbrook, where he often was. But such a man was not likely to make even a pleasure excursion without an eye to business. He had, I supposed, made inquiries; possibly, he had set a watch upon me. Under the eye of such a master of strategy as Monsieur Droqville I could not feel quite at ease.

Nevertheless, in a little time, such serenity as I had enjoyed at Dorracleugh gradually returned; and I enjoyed a routine life, the dulness of which would have been in another state of my spirits insupportable, with very real pleasure.

We were now deep in winter, and in its snowy shroud how beautiful the landscape looked! Cold, but stimulating and pleasant was the clear, dry air; and our frost-bound world sparkled in the wintry sun.

Old Sir Harry Rokestone, a keen sportsman, proof as granite against cold, was out by moonlight on the grey down with his old-fashioned duck-guns, and, when the lake was not frozen over, with two hardy men manoeuvring his boat for him. Town-bred, Mr. Blount contented himself with his brisk walk, stick in hand, and a couple of the dogs for companions to the town; and Mr. Marston was away upon some mission, on which his uncle had sent him, Mr. Blount said, to try whether he was "capable of business and steady."

One night, at this time, as I sat alone in the drawing-room, I was a little surprised to see old Rebecca Torkill come in with her bonnet and cloak on, looking mysterious and important. Shutting the door, she peeped cautiously round.

"What do you think, miss? Wait—listen," she all but whispered, with her hand raised as she trotted up to my side. "Who do you think I saw, not three minutes ago, at the lime-trees, near the lake?"

I was staring in her face, filled with shapeless alarms.

"I was coming home from Farmer Shenstone's, where I went with some tea for that poor little boy that's ailing, and just as I got over the stile, who should I see, as plain as I see you now, but Mr. Carmel, just that minute got out of his boat, and making as if he was going to walk up to the house. He knew me the minute he saw me—it is a very bright moon—and he asked me how I was; and then how you were, most particular; and he said he was only for a few hours in Golden Friars, and took a boat on the chance of seeing you for a minute, but that he did not know whether you would like it, and he begged of me to find out and bring him word. If you do, he's waiting down there, Miss Ethel, and what shall I say?"

"Come with me," I said, getting up quickly; and, putting on in a moment my seal-skin jacket and my hat, without another thought or word, much to Rebecca's amazement, I sallied out into the still night air. Turning the corner of the old building, at the end of the court-yard, I found myself treading with rapid steps the crisp grass, under a dazzling moon, and before me the view of the distant fells, throwing their snowy speaks high into the air, with the solemn darkness of the lake, and its silvery gleams below, and the shadowy gorge and great lime-trees in the foreground. Down the gentle slope I walked swiftly, leaving Rebecca Torkill a long way behind.

I was now under the towering lime-trees. I paused: with a throbbing heart I held my breath. I heard hollow steps coming up on the other side of the file of gigantic stems. I passed between, and saw Mr. Carmel walking slowly towards me. In a moment he was close to me, and took my hand in his old kindly way.

"This is very kind; how can I thank you, Miss Ware? I had hardly hoped to be allowed to call at the house; I am going a long journey, and have not been quite so well as I used to be, and I thought that if I lost this opportunity, in this uncertain world, I might never see my pupil again. I could hardly bear that, without just saying good-bye."

"And you are going?" I said, wringing his hand.

"Yes, indeed; the ocean will be between us soon, and half the world, and I am not to return."

All his kindness rose up before me—his thoughtful goodness, his fidelity—and I felt for a moment on the point of crying.

He was muffled in furs, and was looking thin and ill, and in the light of the moon the lines of his handsome face were marked as if carved in ivory.

"You and your old tutor have had a great many quarrels, and always made it up again; and now at last we part, I am sure, good friends."

"You are going, and you're ill," was all I could say; but I was conscious there was something of that wild tone that real sorrow gives in my voice.

"How often I have thought of you, Miss Ethel—how often I shall think of you, be my days many or few. How often!"

"I am so sorry, Mr. Carmel—so awfully sorry!" I repeated. I had not unclasped my hand; I was looking in his thin, pale, smiling face with the saddest augury.

"I want you to remember me; it is folly, I know, but it is a harmless folly; all human nature shares in it, and"—there was a little tremble, and a momentary interruption—"and your old tutor, the sage who lectured you so wisely, is, after all, no less a fool than the rest. Will you keep this little cross? It belonged to my mother, and is, by permission of my superiors, my own, so you may accept it with a clear conscience." He smiled. "If you wear it, or even let it lie on your table, it will sometimes"—the same momentary interruption occurred again—"it may perhaps remind you of one who took a deep interest in you."

It was a beautiful little gold cross, with five brilliants in it.

"And oh, Ethel! let me look at you once again."

He led me—it was only a step or two—out of the shadow of the tree into the bright moonlight, and, still holding my hand, looked at me intently for a little time with a smile, to me, the saddest that ever mortal face wore.

"And now, here she stands, my wayward, generous, clever Ethel! How proud I was of my pupil! The heart knoweth its own bitterness," he said gently. "And oh! in the day when our Redeemer makes up his jewels, may you be precious among them! I have seen you; farewell!"

Suddenly he raised my hand, and kissed it gently, twice. Then he turned, and walked rapidly down to the water's edge, and stepped into the boat. The men dipped their oars, and the water rose like diamonds from the touch. I saw his dark figure standing, with arm extended, for a moment, in the stern, in his black cloak, pointing towards Golden Friars. The boat was now three lengths away; twenty—fifty; out on the bosom of the stirless water. The tears that I had restrained burst forth, and sobbing as if my heart would break I ran down to the margin of the lake, and stood upon the broad, flat stone, and waved my hand wildly and unseen towards my friend, whom I knew I was never to see again.

I stood there watching, till the shape of the boat and the sound of the oars were quite lost in the grey distance.

CHAPTER LVI.

"LOVE TOOK UP THE GLASS OF TIME."

Weeks glided by, and still the same clear, bright frost, and low, cold, cheerful suns. The dogs so wild with spirits, the distant sounds travelling so sharp to the ear—ruddy sunsets—early darkness—and the roaring fires at home.

Sir Harry Rokestone's voice, clear and kindly, often heard through the house, calls me from the hall; he wants to know whether "little Ethel" will come out for a ride; or, if she would like a drive with him into the town to see the skaters, for in the shallower parts the mere is frozen.

One day I came into Sir Harry's room, on some errand, I forget what. Mr. Blount was standing, leaning on the mantelpiece, and Sir Harry was withdrawing a large key from the door of an iron safe, which seemed to be built into the wall. Each paused in the attitude in which I had found him, with his eyes fixed on me, in silence. I saw that I was in their way, and said, a little flurried:

"I'll come again; it was nothing of any consequence," and I was drawing back, when Sir Harry said, beckoning to me with his finger:

"Stay, little Ethel—stay a minute—I see no reason, Blount, why we should not tell the lassie."

Mr. Blount nodded acquiescence.

"Come here, my bonny Ethel," said Sir Harry, and turning the key again in the lock, he pulled the door open. "Look in; ye see that shelf? Well, mind that's where I'll leave auld Harry Rokestone's will—ye'll remember where it lies?"

Then he drew me very kindly to him, smoothed my hair gently with his hand, and said:

"God bless you, my bonny lass!" and kissed me on the forehead.

Then locking the door again, he said:

"Ye'll mind, it's this iron box, that's next the picture. That's all, lassie."

And thus dismissed, I took my departure.

In this retreat, time was stealing on with silent steps. Christmas was past. Mr. Marston had returned; he lived, at this season, more at our side of the lake, and the house was more cheerful.

Can I describe Mr. Marston with fidelity? Can I rely even upon my own recollection of him? What had I become? A dreamer of dreams—a dupe of magic. Everything had grown strangely interesting—the lonely place was lonely no more—the old castle of Dorracleugh was radiant with unearthly light. Unconsciously, I had become the captive of a magician. I had passed under a sweet and subtle mania, and was no longer myself. Little by little, hour by hour, it grew, until I was transformed. Well, behold me now, wildly in love with Richard Marston.

Looking back now on that period of my history, I see plainly enough that it was my inevitable fate. So much together, and surrounded by a solitude, we were the only young people in the little group which formed our society. Handsome and fascinating—wayward, and even wicked he might have been, but that I might hope was past—he was energetic, clever, passionate; and of his admiration he never allowed me to be doubtful.

My infatuation had been stealing upon me, but it was not until we had reached the month of May that it culminated in a scene that returns again and again in my solitary reveries, and always with the same tumult of sweet and bitter feelings.

One day before that explanation took place, my diary, from which I have often quoted, says thus:

"May 9th.—There was no letter, I am sure, by the early post from Mr. Marston; Sir Harry or Mr. Blount would have been sure to talk of it at breakfast. It is treating his uncle, I think, a little cavalierly.

"Sailed across the lake to-day, alone, to Clusted, and walked about a quarter of a mile up the forest road. How beautiful everything is looking, but how melancholy! When last I saw this haunted wood, Sir Harry Rokestone and Mr. Marston were with me.

"It seems odd that Mr. Marston stays away so long, and hard to believe that if he tried he might not have returned sooner. He went on the 28th of April, and Mr. Blount thought he would be back again in a week: that would have been on the 5th of this month. I dare say he is glad to get away for a little time—I cannot blame him; I dare say he finds it often very dull, say what he will. I wonder what he meant, the other day, when he said he was 'born to be liked least where he loved most'? He seems very melancholy. I wonder whether there has been some old love and parting? Why, unless he liked some one else, should he have quarrelled with Sir Harry, rather than marry as he wished him? Sir Harry would not have chosen any one for him who was not young and good-looking. I heard him say something one morning that showed his opinion upon that point; and young men, who don't like any one in particular, are easily persuaded to marry. Well, perhaps his constancy will be rewarded; it is not likely that the young lady should have given him up.

"May 10th.—How shall I begin? What have I done? Heaven forgive me if I have done wrong! Oh! kind, true friend, Sir Harry, how have I requited you? It is too late now—the past is past. And yet, in spite of this, how happy I am!

"Let me collect my thoughts, and write down as briefly as I can an outline of the events of this happy, agitating day. No lovelier May day was ever seen. I was enjoying a lonely saunter, about one o'clock, under the boughs of Lynder Wood, here and there catching the gleam of the waters through the trees, and listening from time to time to the call of the cuckoo from the hollows of the forest. In that lonely region there is no more lonely path than this.

"On a sudden, I heard a step approaching fast from behind me on the path, and, looking back, I saw Mr. Marston coming on, with a very glad smile, to overtake me. I stopped; I felt myself blushing. He was speaking as he approached: I was confused, and do not recollect what he said; but hardly a moment passed till he was at my side. He was smiling, but very pale. I suppose he had made up his mind to speak. He did not immediately talk of the point on which hung so much; he spoke of other things—I can recollect nothing of them.

"He began at length to talk upon that other theme that lay so near our hearts; our pace grew slower and slower as he spoke on, until we came to a stand-still under the great beech-tree, on whose bark our initials, now spread by time and touched with lichen, but possibly still legible, are carved.

"Well, he has spoken, and I have answered—I can't remember our words; but we are betrothed in the sight of Heaven by vows that nothing can ever cancel, till those holier vows, plighted at the altar-steps, are made before God himself, or until either shall die.

"Oh! Richard, my love, and is it true? Can it be that you love your poor Ethel with a love so tender, so deep, so desperate? He has loved me, he says, ever since he first saw me, on the day after his escape, in the garden at Malory!

"I liked him from the first. In spite of all their warnings, I could not bring myself to condemn or distrust him long. I never forgot him during the years we have been separated; he has been all over the world since, and often in danger, and I have suffered such great and unexpected changes of fortune—to think of our being brought together at last! Has not Fate ordained it?

"The only thing that darkens the perfect sunshine of to-day is that our attachment and engagement must be a secret. He says so, and I am sure he knows best. He says that Sir Harry has not half forgiven him yet, and that he would peremptorily forbid our engagement. He could unquestionably effect our separation, and make us both inexpressibly miserable. But when I look at Sir Harry's kind, melancholy face, and think of all he has done for me, my heart upbraids me, and to-night I had to turn hastily away, for my eyes filled suddenly with tears."

CHAPTER LVII.

AN AWKWARD PROPOSAL.

I will here make a few extracts more from my diary, because they contain matters traced there merely in outline, and of which it is more convenient to present but a skeleton account.

"May 11th.—Richard went early to his farm to-day. I told him last night that I would come down to see him off this morning. But he would not hear of it; and again enjoined the strictest caution. I must do nothing to induce the least suspicion of our engagement, or even of our caring for each other. I must not tell Rebecca Torkill a word about it, nor hint it to any one of the few friends I correspond with. I am sure he is right; but this secrecy is very painful. I feel so treacherous, and so sad, when I see Sir Harry's kind face.

"Richard was back at three o'clock; we met by appointment, in the same path, in Lynder Wood. He has told ever so much, of which I knew nothing before. Mr. Blount told him, he says, that Sir Harry means to leave me an annuity of two hundred a year. How kind and generous! I feel more than ever the pain and meanness of my reserve. He intends to leave Richard eight hundred a year, and the farm at the other side of the lake. Richard thinks, if he had not displeased him, he would have done more for him. All this, that seems to me very noble, depends, however, upon his continuing to like us, as he does at present. Richard says that he will settle everything he has in the world upon me. It hurts me, his thinking me so mercenary, and talking so soon upon the subject of money and settlements; I let him see this, for the idea of his adding to what my benefactor Sir Harry intended for me had not entered my mind.

"'It is just, my darling, because you are so little calculating for yourself that I must look a little forward for you,' he said, and so tenderly. 'Whose business is it now to think of such things for you, if not mine? And you won't deny me the pleasure of telling you that I can prevent, thank Heaven, some of the dangers you were so willing to encounter for my sake.'

"Then he told me that the bulk of Sir Harry's property is to go to people not very nearly related to him, called Strafford; and he gave me a great charge not to tell a word of all this to a living creature, as it would involve him in a quarrel with Mr. Blount, who had told him Sir Harry's intentions under the seal of secrecy.

"I wish I had not so many secrets to keep; but his goodness to me makes me love Sir Harry better every day. I told him all about Sir Harry's little talk with me about his will. I can have no secrets now from Richard."

For weeks, for months, this kind of life went on, eventless, but full of its own hopes, misgivings, agitations. I loved Golden Friars for many reasons, if things so light as associations and sentiments can so be called—founded they were, however, in imagination and deep affection. One of these was and is that my darling mother is buried there; and the simple and sad inscription on her monument, in the pretty church, is legible on the wall opposite the Rokestone pew.

"That's a kind fellow, the vicar," said Sir Harry; "a bit too simple; but if other sirs were like him, there would be more folk in the church to hear the sermon!"

When Sir Harry made this speech, he and I were sitting in the boat, the light evening air hardly filled the sails, and we were tacking slowly back and forward on the mere, along the shore of Golden Friars. It was a beautiful evening in August, and the little speech and our loitering here were caused by the sweet music that pealed from the organ through the open church windows. The good old vicar was a fine musician; and often in the long summer and autumn evenings, the lonely old man visited the organ-loft and played those sweet and solemn melodies that so well accorded with the dreamlike scene.

It was the music that recalled the vicar to Sir Harry's thoughts—but his liking for him was not all founded upon that, nor even upon his holy life and kindly ways. It was this: that when he read the service at mamma's funeral, the white-haired vicar, who remembered her a beautiful child, wept—and tears rolled down his old cheeks as with upturned eyes he repeated the noble and pathetic farewell.

When it was over, Sir Harry, who had a quarrel with the vicar before, came over and shook him by the hand, heartily and long, speaking never a word—his heart was too full. And from that time he liked him, and did not know how to show it enough.

In these long, lazy tacks, sweeping slowly by the quaint old town in silence, broken only by the ripple of the water along the planks, and the sweet and distant swell of the organ across the water, the time flew by. The sun went down in red and golden vapours, and the curfew from the ivied tower of Golden Friars sounded over the darkened lake—the organ was heard no more—and the boat was making her slow way back again to Dorracleugh.

Sir Harry looked at me very kindly, in silence, for awhile. He arranged a rug about my feet, and looked again in my face.

"Sometimes you look so like bonny Mabel—and when you smile—ye mind her smile? 'Twas very pretty."

Then came a silence.

"I must tell Renwick, when the shooting begins, to send down a brace of birds every day to the vicar," said Sir Harry. "I'll be away myself in a day or two, and I shan't be back again for three weeks. I'll take a house in London, lass—I won't have ye moping here too long—you'd begin to pine for something to look at, and folks to talk to, and sights to see."

I was alarmed, and instantly protested that I could not imagine any life more delightful than this at Golden Friars.

"No, no; it won't do—you're a good lass to say so—but it's not the fact—oh, no—it isn't natural—I can't take you to balls, and all that, for I don't know the people that give them—and all my great lady friends that I knew when I was a younker, are off the hooks by this time—but there's plenty of sights to see besides—there's the waxworks, and the wild beasts, and the players, and the pictures, and all the shows."

"But I assure you, I like Golden Friars, and my quiet life at Dorracleugh, a thousand times better than all the sights and wonders in the world," I protested.

If he had but known half the terror with which I contemplated the possibility of my removal from my then place of abode, he would have given me credit for sincerity in my objections to our proposed migration to the capital.

"No, I say, it won't do; you women can't bring yourselves ever to say right out to us men what you think; you mean well—you're a good little thing—you don't want to put the auld man out of his way—but you'd like Lunnon best, and Lunnon ye shall have. You shall have a house you can see your auld acquaintance in, such, I mean, as showed themselves good-natured when all went wrong wi' ye. You shall show them ye can haud your head as high as ever, and are not a jot down in the world. Never mind, I have said it."

In vain I protested; Sir Harry continued firm. One comfort was that he would not return to put his threat into execution for, at least, three weeks. If anything was wanting to complete my misery, it was Sir Harry's saying after a little silence:

"And see, lass; don't you tell a word of it to Richard Marston; 'twould only make him fancy I'm going to take him; and I'd as lief take the devil—so mind ye, it's a secret."

I smiled as well as I could, and said something that seemed to satisfy him, or he took it for granted, for he went on and talked, being much more communicative this evening than usual; while my mind was busy with the thought of a miserable separation, and all the difficulties of correspondence that accompany a secret engagement.

So great was the anguish of these anticipations that I hazarded one more effort to induce him to abandon his London plans, and to let me continue to enjoy my present life at Dorracleugh.

He was, however, quite immovable; he laughed; he told me, again and again, that it would not "put him out of his way—not a bit;" and he added, "You're falling into a moping, unnatural life, and you've grown to like it, and the more you like it, the less it is fit for you; if you lose your spirits, you can't keep your health long."

And when I still persisted, he looked in my face a little darkly, on a sudden, as if a doubt as to my motive had crossed his mind. That look frightened me. I felt that matters might be worse.

Sir Harry had got it into his head, I found, that my health would break down, unless he provided the sort of change and amusement which he had decided on. I don't know to which of the wiseacres of Golden Friars I was obliged for this crotchet, which promised me such an infinity of suffering, but I had reason to think, afterwards, that old Miss Goulding of Wrybiggins was the friend who originated these misgivings about my health and spirits. She wished, I was told, to marry her niece to Richard Marston, and thought, if I and Sir Harry were out of the way, her plans would act more smoothly.

Richard was at home—it was our tea-time—I had not an opportunity of saying a word to him unobserved. I don't know whether he saw by my looks that I was unhappy.

CHAPTER LVIII.

DANGER.

Sir Harry took his coffee with us, and read to me a little now and then from the papers which had come by the late mails. Mr. Blount had farming news to tell Richard. It was a dreadful tea-party.

I was only able that night to appoint with Richard to meet me, next day, at our accustomed trysting-place.

Three o'clock was our hour of meeting. The stupid, feverish day dragged on, and the time at length arrived. I got on my things quickly, and trembling lest I should be joined by Sir Harry or Mr. Blount, I betook myself through the orchard, and by the wicket in the hedge, to the lonely path through the thick woods where we had, a few months since, plighted our troth.

Richard appeared very soon; he was approaching by the path opposite to that by which I had come.

The foliage was thick and the boughs hang low in that place. You could have fancied him a figure walking in the narrow passage of a monastery, so dark and well-defined is the natural roofing of the pathway there. He raised his open hand, and shook his head as he drew near; he was not smiling; he looked very sombre.

He glanced back over his shoulder, and looked sharply down the path I had come by, and being now very near me, with another gloomy shake of the head, he said, with a tone and look of indescribable reproach and sorrow: "So Ethel has her secrets, and tells me but half her mind."

"What can you mean, Richard?"

"Ah! Ethel, I would not have treated you so," he continued.

"You distract me, Richard; what have I done?"

"I have heard it all by accident, I may say, from old Mr. Blount, who has been simpleton enough to tell me. You have asked my uncle to take you to London, and you are going."

"Asked him! I have all but implored of him to leave me here. I never heard a word of it till last night, as we returned together in the boat. Oh! Richard, how could you think such things? That is the very thing I have been so longing to talk to you about."

"Ethel, darling, are you opening your heart entirely to me now; is there no reserve? No; I am sure there is not; you need not answer."

"It is distracting news; is there nothing I can do to prevent it?" I said.

He looked miserable enough, as walking slowly along the path, and sometimes standing still, we talked it over.

"Yes," he said; "the danger is that you may lead him by resistance to look for some secret motive. If he should suspect our engagement, few worse misfortunes could befall us. Good heavens! shall I ever have a quiet home? Ethel, I know what will happen—you will go to London; I shall be forgotten. It will end in the ruin of all my hopes." So he raved on.

I wept, and upbraided, and vowed my old vows over again.

At length after this tempestuous scene had gone on for some time, we two walking side by side up and down the path, and sometimes stopping short, I crying, if you will, like a fool, he took my hand and looked in my face very sadly, and he said after a little:

"Only I know that he would show more anger, I should have thought that my uncle knew of our engagement, and was acting expressly to frustrate it. He has found work for me at his property near Hull, and from that I am to go to Warwickshire, so that I suppose I can't be here again before the middle of October, and long before then you will be at Brighton, where, Mr. Blount says, he means to take you first, and from that to London."

"But you are not to leave this immediately?" I said.

He smiled bitterly, and answered:

"He takes good care I shall. I am to leave this to-morrow morning."

I could not speak for a moment.

"Oh, Richard, Richard, how am I to live through this separation?" I cried wildly. "You must contrive some way to see me. I shall die unless you do."

"Come, Ethel, let us think it over; it seems to me that we have nothing for it, for the present, but submission. I am perfectly certain that our attachment is not suspected. If it were, far more cruel and effectual measures would be taken. We must, therefore, be cautious. Let us betray nothing of our feelings. You shall see me undergo the ordeal with the appearance of carelessness, and even cheerfulness, although my heart be bursting. You, darling, must do the same; one way or other I will manage to see you sometimes, and to correspond regularly. We are bound each to the other by promises we dare not break, and when I desert you, may God desert me! Ethel, will you say the same?"

"Yes, Richard," I repeated, vehemently, through sobs, "when I forsake you, may God forsake me! You know I could not live without you. Oh! Richard, darling, how shall I see you all this evening, knowing it to be the last? How can I look at you, or hear your voice, and yet no sign, and talk or listen just as usual, as if nothing had gone wrong? Richard, is there no way to escape? Do you think if we told your uncle? Might it not be the best thing after all? Could it possibly make matters worse?"

"Yes, it would, a great deal worse; that is not to be thought of," said Richard, with a thoughtful frown; "I know him better than you do. No; we have nothing for it but patience, and entire trust in one another. As for me, if I am away from you, the more solitary I am, the more bearable my lot. With you it will be different; you will soon be in the stream and whirl of your old life. I shall lose you, Ethel." He stamped on the ground, and struck his forehead with his open hand in sheer distraction. "As for me, I can enjoy nothing without you; I may have been violent, wicked, reckless, what you will; but selfish or fickle, no one ever called me."

I was interrupting him all the time with my passionate vows of fidelity, which he seemed hardly to hear; he was absorbed in his own thoughts. After a silence of a minute or two, he said, suddenly:

"Look here, Ethel; if you don't like your London life, you can't be as well there as here, and you can, if you will, satisfy my uncle that you are better, as well as happier, here at Golden Friars. You can do that, and that is the way to end it—the only way to end it that I see. You can write to me, Ethel, without danger. You will, I know, every day, just a line; and when you tell me how to address mine, you shall have an answer by every post. Don't go out in London, Ethel; you must promise that."

I did, vehemently and reproachfully. I wondered how he could suspect me of wishing to go out. But I could not resent the jealousy that proved his love.

It was, I think, just at this moment that I heard a sound that made my heart bound within me, and then sink with terror. It was the clear, deep voice of Sir Harry, so near that it seemed a step must bring him round the turn in the path, and full in view of us.

"Go, darling, quickly," said Richard, pressing me gently with one hand, and with the other pointing in the direction furthest from the voice that was so near a signal of danger. He himself turned, and walked quickly to meet Sir Harry, who was conferring with his ranger about thinning the timber.

I was out of sight in a moment, and, in agitation indescribable, made my way home.

CHAPTER LIX.

AN INTRUDER.

I t was all true. Richard left Dorracleugh early next morning. Those who have experienced such a separation know its bitterness, and the heartache and apathy that follow.

I was going to be left quite alone, and mistress at Dorracleugh for three weeks at least; perhaps for twice as long. Mr. Blount was to leave next day for France, to pay a visit of a fortnight to Vichy. Sir Harry Rokestone, a few days later, was to leave Dorracleugh for Brighton.

Nothing could be kinder than Sir Harry. It was plain that he suspected nothing of the real situation.

"You'll be missing your hit of backgammon with Lemuel Blount," he said, "and your sail on the mere wi' myself, and our talk round the tea-table of an even-ing. 'Twill be dowly down here, lass; but ye'll be coming soon where you'll see sights and hear noise enough for a dozen. So think o' that, and when we are gone you munnon be glumpin' about the house, but chirp up, and think there are but a few weeks between you and Brighton and Lunnon."

How directly this kind consolation went to the source of my dejection you may suppose.

So the time came, and I was alone. Solitude was a relief. I could sit looking at the lake, watching the track where his boat used to come and go over the water, and thinking of him half the day. I could walk in the pathway, and sit under the old beech-tree, and murmur long talks with him in fancy, without fear of interrup-tion; but oh! the misgivings, the suspense, the dull, endless pain of separation!

Not a line reached me from Richard. He insisted that while I remained at Dorracleugh there should be no correspondence. In Golden Friars, and about the post-office, there were so many acute ears and curious eyes.

Sir Harry had been gone about three weeks, when he sent me a really exquisite little enamelled watch, set in brilliants; it was brought to Dorracleugh by a Golden Friars neighbour whom he had met in his travels. Then, after a silence of a week, another letter came from Sir Harry. He was going up to London, he said, to see after the house, and to be sure that nothing was wanted to "make it smart."

Then some more days of silence followed, interrupted very oddly. I was out, taking my lonely walk in the afternoon, when a chaise with a portmanteau, a hat-box, and some other luggage on top, drove up to the hall-door; the driver knocked and rang, and out jumped Richard Marston, who ran up the steps, and asked the servant, with an accustomed air of command, to take the luggage up to his room.

He had been some minutes in the hall before he inquired whether I was in the house. He sat down on a hall-chair, in his hat and great-coat, just as he had come out of the chaise, lost in deep thought. He seemed for a time undecided where to go; he went to the foot of the stairs, and stopped short, with his hand on the banister, and turned back; then he stood for a little while in the middle of the hall, look-looking down on his dusty boots, again in deep thought; then he walked to the hall-door, stood on the steps in the same undecided state, and sauntered in again, and said to the servant:

"And Miss Ware, you say, is out walking? Well, go you and tell the housekeeper that I have come, and shall be coming and going for a few days, till I hear from London."

The man departed to execute his message. Richard Marston had paid the vicar a visit of about five minutes, as he drove through the town of Golden Friars, and had had a very private and earnest talk with him. He seemed very uncomfortable and fidgety. He took off his hat and laid it down, and put it on again, and looked dark and agitated, like a man in a sudden danger, who expects a struggle for his life. He went again to the foot of the stairs, and listened for a few seconds; and then, without much ado, he walked over and turned the key that was in Sir Harry's study-door, took it out, and went into the room, looking very stern and nervous.

In a little more than five minutes Mrs. Shackleton, the housekeeper, in her thick brown silk, knocked sharply at the door.

"Come in," called Richard Marston's voice.

"I can't, sir."

"Can't? Why? What's the matter?"

"You've bolted it, please, on the inside," she answered, very tartly.

"I? I haven't bolted it," Richard Marston answered, with a quiet laugh. "Try again."

She did, a little fiercely; but the door opened, and disclosed Richard Marston sitting in his uncle's easy chair, with one of the newspapers he had bought in his railway carriage expanded on his knees. He looked up carelessly.

"Well, Mrs. Shackleton, what's the row?"

"No row, sir, please," she answered, sharply rustling into the room, and looking round. She didn't like him. "But the door was bolted, I assure you, sir, only a minute before, when I tried it first; and my master, Sir Harry, told me no one was to be allowed into this room while he's away."

"So I should have thought; his letters lying about—but I found the door open, and the key in the lock—here it is; so I thought it safer to take it out."

The old woman made a short curtsey as she took it, dryly, from his fingers; and she stood, resolutely waiting.

"Oh! I suppose," he said, starting up, and stretching himself, with a smile and a little yawn, "you want me to turn out?"

"Yes, sir, please," said Mrs. Shackleton peremptorily.

The young gentleman cast a careless glance through the far window, looked lazily round, as if to see that he had not forgotten anything, and then said, with a smile:

"Mrs. Shackleton, happy the man who has such a lady to take care of his worldly goods."

"I'm no lady, sir; I'm not above my business," she said, with another hard little curtsey. "I tries to do my dooty accordin' to my conscience. Sorry to have to disturb you, sir."

"Not the least; no disturbance," he said, sauntering out of the room, with another yawn.

He was cudgelling his brains to think what civility he could do the old lady, or how he could please or make her friendly; but Mrs. Shackleton had her northern pride, he knew, which was easily ruffled, and he must approach her very cautiously.

CHAPTER LX.

SIR HARRY'S KEY.

Up to his room he went; his things were all there—he wished to get rid of the dust and smuts of his railway journey.

He made his toilet rapidly; and just as he was about to open his door, a knock came to it.

"What is it?" he asked.

"The vicar has called, sir, and wants to know if you can see him."

"Certainly. Tell him I'll be down in a moment."

Mr. Marston had foreseen this pursuit with a prescience of which he was proud. He went downstairs, and found the white-haired vicar alone in the drawing-room.

"I am so delighted you have come," said Richard Marston, advancing quickly, with an outstretched hand, from the door, without giving him a moment to begin. "I have only had time to dress since I arrived, and I have made up my mind that it is better to replace this key in your hand, without using it—and, in the meantime, it is better in your keeping than in mine. Don't you think so?"

"Well, sir," said the good vicar, "I do. It is odd, but the very same train of thought passed through my mind, and, in fact, induced me to pay you this visit. You see it was placed in my charge, and I think, until it is formally required of me, I should not part with it."

"Just so," acquiesced the young man.

"We both acted, perhaps, a little too precipitately."

"So we did, sir," said Richard Marston, "but I take the entire blame on myself. I'm too apt to be impulsive and foolish. I generally think too late; happily this time, however, I did reflect, and with your concurrence, I am now sure I was right."

The young man paused and thought, with his hand on the vicar's arm.

"One thing," he said, "I would stipulate, however; as we are a good deal in the dark, my reason for declining to take charge of the key would be but half answered, as I must be a great deal in this house, and there may be other keys that open it, and I can't possibly answer for servants, and other people who will be coming and going, unless you will kindly come into the next room with me for a moment."

The vicar consented; and Mr. Marston was eloquent. Mrs. Shackelton was sent for, and with less reluctance opened the door for the vicar, whom she loved. She did not leave it, however—they did not stay long. In a few minutes the party withdrew.

"Won't you have some luncheon?" asked Richard, in the hall.

"No, thank you," said the vicar, "I am very much hurried. I am going to see that poor boy to whom Mr. Blount has been so kind, and who is, I fear, dying."

And with a few words more, and the key again in his keeping, he took his leave.

I was all this time in my favourite haunt, alone, little thinking that the hero of my dreams was near, when suddenly I saw him walking rapidly up the path. With a cry, I ran to meet him. He seemed delighted and radiant with love as he drew me to him, folded me for a moment in his arms, and kissed me passionately. He had ever so much to say; and yet, when I thought it over, there was nothing in it but one delightful promise; and that was that henceforward, he expected to see a great deal more of me than he had hitherto done.

There was a change in his manner, I thought—he spoke with something of the confidence and decision of a lover who had a right to command. He was not more earnest, but more demonstrative. I might have resented his passionate greeting, if I had been myself less surprised and happy at his sudden appearance. He was obliged to go down to the village, but would be back again, he said, very soon. It would not do to make people talk, which they would be sure to do, if he and I were not very cautious.

Therefore I let him go, without entreaty or remonstrance, although it cost me an indescribable pang to lose him, even for an hour, so soon after our long separation. He promised to be back in an hour, and although that was nearly impracticable, I believed him. "Lovers trample upon impossibilities."

By a different route I came home. He had said:

"When I return, I shall come straight to the drawing-room—will you be there?"

So to the drawing-room I went. I was afraid to leave it even for a moment, lest some accident should make him turn back, and he should find the room empty. There was to me a pleasure in obeying him, and I liked him to see it. How I longed for his return! How restless I was! How often I played his favourite airs on the piano; how often I sat at the window, looking down at the trees and the mere, in the direction from which I had so often seen his boat coming, you will easily guess.

All this time I had a secret misgiving. There was a change in Richard's manner, as I have said; there was confidence, security, carelessness—a kind of carelessness—not that he seemed to admire me less—but it was a change. There seemed something ominous about it.

As time wore on I became so restless that I could hardly remain quiet for a minute in any one place. I was perpetually holding the door open, and listening for the sound of horses' hoofs, or wheels, or footsteps. In vain.

An hour beyond the appointed time had passed; two hours. I was beginning to fancy all sorts of horrors. Was he drowned in the mere? Had his horse fallen and killed him? There was no catastrophe too improbable to be canvassed among the wild conjectures of my terror.

The sun was low, and I almost despairing, when the door opened, and Richard came in. I had heard no sound at the door, no step approaching, only he was there.

CHAPTER LXI.

A DISCOVERY.

I started to my feet and was going to meet him, but he raised his hand, as I fancied to warn me that some one was coming. So I stopped short, and he approached.

"I shall be very busy for two or three days, dear Ethel; and," what he added was spoken very slowly, and dropped word by word, "you are such a rogue!"

I was very much astonished. Neither his voice nor look was playful. His face at the moment wore about the most disagreeable expression which human face can wear. That of a smile, not a genuine but a pretended smile, which, at the same time, the person who smiles affects to try to suppress. To me it looks cruel, cynical, mean. I was so amazed, as he looked into my eyes with this cunning, shabby smile, that I could not say a word, and stood stock-still looking in return, in stupid wonder, in his face.

At length I broke out, very pale, for I was shocked, "I can't understand! What is it? Oh, Richard, what can you mean?"

"Now don't be a little fool. I really believe you are going to cry. You are a great deal too clever, you lovely little rogue, to fancy that a girl's tears ever yet did any good. Listen to me; come!"

He walked away, still smiling that insulting smile, and he took my hand in his, and shook his finger at me, with the same cynical affectation of the playful. "What did I mean?"

"Yes, what can you mean?" I stamped the emphasis on the floor, with tears in my eyes. "It is cruel, it is horrible, after our long separation."

"Well, I'll tell you what I mean," he said, and for a moment the smile almost degenerated to a sneer. "Look here; come to the window."

I faltered; I accompanied him to it, looking in his face in an agony of alarm and surprise. It seemed to me like the situation of a horrid dream.

"Do you know how I amused myself during the last twenty miles of my railway journey?" he said. "Well, I'll tell you: I was reading all that time a curious criminal trial, in which a most respectable old gentleman, aged sixty-seven, has just been convicted of having poisoned a poor girl forty years ago, and is to be hanged for it before three weeks!"

"Well?" said I, with an effort—I should not have known my own voice, and I felt a great ball in my throat.

"Well?" he repeated; "don't you see?"

He paused with the same horrid smile; this time, in the silence, he laughed a little; it was no use trying to hide from myself the fact that I dimly suspected what he was driving at. I should have liked to die that moment, before he had time to complete another sentence.

"Now, you see, the misfortune of that sort of thing is that time neither heals nor hides the offence. There is a principle of law which says that no lapse of time bars the Crown. But I see this kind of conversation bores you."

I was near saying something very wild and foolish, but I did not.

"I won't keep you a moment," said he—"just come a little nearer the window; I want you to look at something that may interest you."

I did go a little nearer. I was moving as he commanded, as if I had been mesmerised.

"You lost," he continued, "shortly before your illness, the only photograph you possessed of your sister Helen? But why are you so put out by it? Why should you tremble so violently? It is only I, you know; you need not mind. You dropped that on the floor of a jeweller's shop one night, when I and Droqville happened to be there together, and I picked it up; it represents you both together. I want to restore it; here it is."

I extended my hand to take it. I don't know whether I spoke, but the portrait faded suddenly from my sight, and darkness covered everything. I heard his voice, like that of a person talking in excitement, a long way off, at the other side of a wall in another room—it was no more than a hum, and even that was growing fainter. I forgot everything, in utter unconsciousness, for some seconds. When I opened my eyes, water was trickling down my face and forehead, and the window was open. I sighed deeply. I saw him looking over me with a countenance of gloom and anxiety. In happy forgetfulness of all that had passed, I smiled and said:

"Oh, Richard! Thank God!" and stretched my arms to him.

"That's right—quite right," he said; "you may have every confidence in me."

The dreadful recollection began to return.

"Don't get up yet," he said, earnestly, and even tenderly; "you're not equal to it. Don't think of leaving me—you must have confidence in me. Why didn't you trust me long ago?—trust me altogether? Fear nothing while I am near you."

So he continued speaking, until my recollection had quite returned.

"Why, darling, will you not trust me? Can you be surprised at my being wounded by your reserve? How have I deserved it? Forget the pain of this discovery, and remember only that against all the world, to the last hour of my life, with my last thought, the last drop of my blood, I am your defender."

He kissed my hands passionately; he drew me towards him, and kissed my lips. He murmured caresses and vows of unalterable love—nothing could be more tender and impassioned. I was relieved by a passionate burst of tears.

"It's over now," he said—"it's all over; you'll forgive me, won't you? I have more to forgive, darling, than you—the hardest of all things to forgive in one whom we idolise—a want of confidence in us. You ought to have told me all this before."

I told him, as well as I could between my sobs, that there was no need to tell any one of a madness which had nothing to do with waking thoughts or wishes, and was simply the extravagance of delirium—that I was then actually in fever, had been at the point of death, and that Mr. Carmel knew everything about it.

"Well, darling," he said, "you must trouble your mind no more. Of course you are not accountable for it. If people in brain fever were not carefully watched and restrained, a day would not pass without some tragedy. But what care I, Ethel, if it had been a real crime of passion? Nothing. Do you fancy it would or could, for an instant, have shaken my desperate love for you? Don't you remember Moore's lines:

> 'I ask not, I care not, if guilt's in thy heart;
> I but know that thou lov'st me, whatever thou art.'

"That is my feeling, fixed as adamant; never suspect me. I can't I never can, tell you how I felt your suspicion of my love; how cruel I thought it. What had I done to deserve it? There, darling, take this—it is yours." He kissed the little photograph, he placed it in my hand, he kissed me again fervently. "Look here, Ethel, I came all this way, ever so much out of my way, to see you. I made an excuse of paying the vicar a visit on business—my real business was to see you. I must be this evening at Wrexham, but I shall be here again to-morrow, as early as possible. I am a mere slave at present, and business hurries me from point to point; but cost what it may, I shall be with you some time in the afternoon to-morrow."

"To stay?" I asked.

He smiled, and shook his head.

"I can't say that, darling," he said; he was going towards the door.

"But you'll be here early to-morrow; do you think before two?"

"No, not before two, I am afraid. I may be delayed, and it is a long way; but you may look out for me early in the evening."

Then came a leave-taking. He would not let me come with him to the hall-door—there were servants there, and I looked so ill. I stood at the window and saw him drive away. You may suppose I did feel miserable. I think I was near fainting again when he was gone.

In a little time I was sufficiently recovered to get up to my room, and then I rang for Rebecca Torkill.

I don't know how that long evening went by. The night came, and a miserable nervous night I passed, starting in frightful dreams from the short dozes I was able to snatch.

CHAPTER LXII.

SIR HARRY WITHDRAWS.

Next morning, when the grey light came, I was neither glad nor sorry. The shock of my yesterday's interview with the only man on earth I loved, remained. It was a shock, I think, never to be quite recovered from. I got up and dressed early. How ill and strange I looked out of the glass in my own face!

I did not go down. I remained in my room, loitering over the hours that were to pass before the arrival of Richard. I was haunted by his changed face. I tried to fix in my recollection the earnest look of love on which my eyes had opened from my swoon. But the other would take its place and remain; and I could not get rid of the startled pain of my heart. I was haunted now, as I had been ever since that scene had taken place, with a vague misgiving of something dreadful going to happen.

I think it was between four and five in the evening that Rebecca Torkill came in, looking pale and excited.

"Oh, Miss Ethel, dear, what do you think has happened?" she said, lifting up both hands and eyes as soon as she was in at the door.

"Good Heaven, Rebecca!" I said, starting up; "is it anything bad?"

I was on the point of saying "anything about Mr. Marston?"

"Oh, miss! what do you think? Poor Sir Harry Rokestone is dead."

"Sir Harry dead!" I exclaimed.

"Dead, indeed, miss," said Rebecca. "Thomas Byres is just come up from the vicar's, and he's had a letter from Mr. Blount this morning, and the vicar's bin down at the church with Dick Mattox, the sexton, giving him directions about the vault. Little thought I, when I saw him going away—a fine man he was, six feet two, Adam Bell says, in his boots—little thought I, when I saw him walk down the steps, so tall and hearty, he'd be coming back so soon in his coffin, poor gentleman. But, miss, they say dead folk's past feeling, and what does it all matter now? One man's breath is another man's death. And so the world goes on, and all forgot before long.

> 'To the grave with the dead,
> And the quick to the bread.'

"A rough gentleman he was, but kind—the tenants will be all sorry. They're all talking, the servants, downstairs. He was one that liked to see his tenants and his poor comfortable."

All this and a great deal more Rebecca discoursed. I could hardly believe her news. A letter, I thought, would have been sure to reach Dorracleugh, as soon as the vicar's house, at least.

Possibly this dismaying news would turn out to be mere rumour, I thought, and end in nothing worse than a sharp attack of gout in London. Surely we should have heard of his illness before it came to this catastrophe. Nevertheless I had to tear up my first note to the vicar—I was so flurried, and it was full of blunders—and I was obliged to write another. It was simply to entreat information in this horrible uncertainty, which had for the time superseded all my other troubles.

A mounted messenger was despatched forthwith to the vicar's house. But we soon found that the rumour was everywhere, for people were arriving from all quarters to inquire at the house. It was, it is true, so far as we could learn, mere report; but its being in so many places was worse than ominous.

The messenger had not been gone ten minutes, when Richard Marston arrived. From my room I saw the chaise come to the hall-door, and I ran down at once to the drawing-room. Richard had arrived half an hour before his time. He entered the room from the other door as I came in, and met me eagerly, looking tired and anxious, but very loving. Not a trace of the Richard whose smile had horrified me the day before.

Almost my first question to him was whether he had heard any such rumour. He was holding my hand in his as I asked the question—he laid his other on it, and looked sadly in my eyes as he answered, "It is only too true. I have lost the best friend that man ever had."

I was too much startled to speak for some seconds, then I burst into tears.

"No, no," he said, in answer to something I had said. "It is only too certain—there can be no doubt; look at this."

He took a telegraph paper from his pocket and showed it to me. It was from "Lemuel Blount, London." It announced the news in the usual shocking laconic manner, and said, "I write to you to Dykham."

"I shall get the letter this evening when I reach Dykham, and I'll tell you all that is in it to-morrow. The telegraph message had reached me yesterday, when I saw you, but I could not bear to tell you the dreadful news until I had confirmation, and that has come. The vicar has had a message, about which there can be no mistake. And now, darling, put on your things, and come out for a little walk—I have ever so many things to talk to you about."

Here was a new revolution in my troubled history. More or less of the horror of uncertainty again encompassed my future years. But grief, quite unselfish, predominated in my agitation. I had lost a benefactor. His kind face was before me, and the voice, always subdued to tenderness when he spoke to me, was in my ear. I was grieved to the heart.

I got on my hat and jacket, and with a heavy heart went out with Richard.

For many reasons the most secluded path was that best suited for our walk. Richard Marston had just told the servants the substance of the message he had received that morning from Mr. Blount, so that that they could have no difficulty about answering inquiries at the hall-door.

We soon found ourselves in the path that had witnessed so many of our meetings. I wondered what Richard intended talking about. He had been silent and thoughtful. He hardly uttered a word during our walk, until we had reached what I may call our trysting-tree, the grand old beech-tree, under which a huge log of timber, roughly squared, formed a seat.

Though little disposed myself to speak, his silence alarmed me.

"Ethel, darling," he said, suddenly, "have you formed any plans for the future?"

"Plans!" I echoed. "I don't know—what do you mean, Richard?"

"I mean," he continued, sadly, "have you considered how this misfortune may affect us? Did Sir Harry ever tell you anything about his intentions—I mean what he thought of doing by his will? Don't look so scared, darling," he added, with a melancholy smile; "you will see just now what my reasons are. You can't suppose that a sordid thought ever entered my mind."

I was relieved.

"No; he never said a word to me about his will, except what I told you," I answered.

"Because the people who knew him at Wrexham are talking. Suppose he has cut me off and provided for you, could I any longer in honour hold you to an engagement, to fulfil which I could contribute nothing?"

"Oh, Richard, darling, how can you talk so? Don't you know, whatever I possess on earth is yours."

"Then my little woman refuses to give me up, even if there were difficulties?" he said, pressing my hands, and smiling down upon my face in a kind rapture.

"I could not give you up, Richard—you know I couldn't," I answered.

"My darling!" he exclaimed, softly, looking down upon me still with the same smile.

"Richard, how could you ever have dreamed such a thing? You don't know how you wound me."

"I never thought it, I never believed it, darling. I knew it was impossible; whatever difficulties might come between us, I knew that I could not live without you; and I thought you loved me as well. Nothing then shall part us—nothing. Don't you say so? Say it, Ethel. I swear it, nothing."

I gave him the promise; it was but repeating what I had often said before. Never was vow uttered from a more willing heart. Even now I am sure he reminded me, and, after his manner, loved me with a vehement passion.

"But there are other people, Ethel," he resumed, "who think that I shall be very well off, who think that I shall inherit all my uncle's great fortune. But all may not go smoothly, you see; there may be great difficulties. Promise me, swear it once more, that you will suffer no obstacles to separate us; that we shall be united, be they what they may; that you will never, so help you Heaven, forsake me or marry another."

I did repeat the promise. We walked towards home; I wondering what special difficulty he could be thinking of now; but, restrained by a kind of fear, I did not ask him.

"I'm obliged to go away again, immediately," said he, after another short silence; "but my business will be over to-night, and I shall be here again in the morning, and then I shall be my own master for a time, and have a quiet day or two, and be able to open my heart to you, Ethel."

We walked on again in silence. Suddenly he stopped, laying his hand on my shoulder, and looking sharply into my face, said:

"I'll leave you here—it is time, Ethel, that I should be off." He held my hand in his, and his eyes were fixed steadily upon mine. "Look here," he said, after another pause, "I must make a bitter confession, Ethel; you know me with all my faults—I have no principle of calculation in me—equity and all that sort of thing, would stand a poor chance with me against passion—I am all passion; it has been my undoing, and will yet I hope," and he looked on me with a wild glow in his dark eyes, "be the making of me, Ethel. No obstacle shall separate us, you have sworn; and mind, Ethel, I am a fellow that never forgives, and as Heaven is my judge, if you give me up, I'll not forgive you. But that will never be. God bless you, darling—you shall see me early to-morrow. Go you in that direction—let us keep our secret a day or two longer. You look as if you thought me mad—I'm not that—though I sometimes half think so myself. There has been enough in my life to make a steadier brain than mine crazy. Good-bye, Ethel, darling, till to-morrow. God bless you!"

With these words he left me. His reckless language had plainly a meaning in it. My heart sank as I thought on the misfortune that had reduced me again to uncertainty, and perhaps to a miserable dependence. It was by no means impossible that nothing had been provided for either him or me by Sir Harry Rokestone. Men, prompt and accurate in everything else, so often go on postponing a will until "the door is shut to," and the hour passed for ever. It was horrible allowing such thoughts to intrude; but Richard's conversation was so full of the subject, and my position was so critical and dependent, that it did recur, not with sordid hopes, but in the form of a great and reasonable fear.

When Richard was out of sight, as he quickly was among the trees, I turned back, and sitting down again on the rude bench under our own beech-tree, I had a long and bitter cry, all to myself.

CHAPTER LXIII.

AT THE THREE NUNS.

When Richard Marston left me, his chaise stood at the door, with a team of four horses, quite necessary to pull a four-wheeled carriage over the fells, through whose gorges the road to the nearest railway-station is carried.

The pleasant setting sun flashed over the distant fells, and glimmered on the pebbles of the courtyard, and cast a long shadow of Richard Marston, as he stood upon the steps, looking down upon the yellow, worn flags, in dark thought.

"Here, put this in," he said, handing his only piece of luggage, a black leather travelling-bag, to one of the post-boys. "You know the town of Golden Friars?"

"Yes, sir."

"Well, stop at Mr. Jarlcot's house."

Away went the chaise, with its thin roll of dust, like the smoke of a hedge-fire, all along the road, till they pulled up at Mr. Jarlcot's house.

Out jumped Mr. Marston, and knocked a sharp summons with the brass knocker on the hall-door.

The maid opened the door, and stood on the step with a mysterious look of inquiry in Mr. Marston's face. The rumour that was already slowly spreading in Golden Friars had suddenly been made sure by a telegraphic message from Lemuel Blount to Mr. Jarlcot. His good wife had read it just five minutes before Mr. Marston's arrival.

"When is Mr. Jarlcot to be home again?"

"Day after to-morrow, please, sir."

"Well, when he comes, don't forget to tell him I called. No, this is better," and he wrote in pencil on his card the date and the words, "Called twice—most anxious to see Mr. Jarlcot;" and laid it on the table. "Can I see Mr. Spaight?" he inquired.

Tall, stooping Mr. Spaight, the confidential man, with his bald head, spectacles, and long nose, emerged politely, with a pen behind his ear, at this question, from the door of the front room, which was Mr. Jarlcot's office.

"Oh! Mr. Spaight," said Richard Marston, "have you heard from Mr. Jarlcot to-day?"

"A short letter, Mr. Marston, containing nothing of business—only a few items of news; he's in London till to-morrow—he saw Mr. Blount there."

"Then he has heard, of course, of our misfortune?"

"Yes, sir; and we all sympathise with you, Mr. Marston, deeply, sir, in your affliction. Will you please to step in, sir, and look at the letter?"

Mr. Marston accepted the invitation.

There were two or three sentences that interested him.

"I have had a conversation with Mr. Blount this morning. He fears very much that Sir Harry did not execute the will. I saw Messrs. Hutt and Babbage, who drafted the will; but they can throw no light upon the matter, and say that the result of a search, only, can; which Mr. Blount says won't take five minutes to make."

This was interesting; but the rest was rubbish. Mr. Marston took his leave, got into the chaise again, and drove under the windows of the "George and Dragon," along the already deserted road that ascends the fells from the margin of the lake.

Richard Marston put his head from the window and looked back; there was no living creature in his wake. Before him he saw nothing but the post-boys' stooping backs, and the horses with their four patient heads bobbing before him. The light was failing, still it would have served to read by for a little while; and there was something he was very anxious to read. He was irresolute—there was a risk in it—he could not make up his mind.

He looked at his watch—it would take him nearly three hours to reach the station at the other side of the fells. Unlucky the delay at Dorracleugh!

The light failed. White mists began to crawl across the road, and were spreading and rising fantastically on the hill-sides. The moon came out. He was growing more impatient. In crossing a mountain the eye measures so little distance gained for the time expended. The journey seemed, to him, interminable.

At one of the zig-zag turns of the road, there rises a huge fragment of white stone, bearing a rude resemblance to a horseman; a highwayman, you might fancy him, awaiting the arrival of the travellers. In Richard's eye it took the shape of old Sir Harry Rokestone, as he used to sit, when he had reined in his tall iron-grey hunter, and was waiting to have a word with some one coming up.

He muttered something as he looked sternly ahead at this fantastic reminder. On they drove; the image resolved itself into its rude sides and angles, and was passed; and the pale image of Sir Harry no longer waylaid his nephew.

Slowly the highest point of the road was gained, and then begins the flying descent; and the well-known landmarks, as he consults his watch, from time to time, by the moonlight, assure him that they will reach the station in time to catch the train.

He is there. He pays his post-boys, and with his black travelling-bag in hand, runs out upon the gravelled front, from which the platform extends its length.

"The up-train not come yet?" inquired the young man, looking down the line eagerly.

"Not due for four minutes, Mr. Marston," said the station-master, with officious politeness, "and we shall hardly have it up till some minutes later. They are obliged to slacken speed in the Malwyn cutting at present. Your luggage all right, I hope? Shall I get your ticket for you, Mr. Marston?"

The extraordinary politeness of the official had, perhaps, some connection with the fact that the rumour of Sir Harry's death was there already, and the Rokestone estates extended beyond the railway. Richard Marston was known to be the only nephew of the deceased baronet, and to those who knew nothing of the interior politics of the family, his succession appeared certain.

Mr. Marston thanked him, but would not give him the trouble; he fancied that the station-master, who was perfectly innocent of any treacherous design, wished to play the part of a detective, and find out all he could about his movements and belongings.

Richard Marston got away from him as quickly as he civilly could, without satisfying his curiosity on any point. The train was up, and the doors clapping a few minutes later; and he, with his bag, rug, and umbrella, got into his place with a thin, sour old lady in black, opposite; a nurse at one side, with two children in her charge, who were always jumping down on people's feet, or climbing up again, and running to the window, and bawling questions with incessant clamour; and at his other side, a mummy-coloured old gentleman with an olive-green cloth cap, the flaps of which were tied under his chin, and a cream-coloured muffler.

He had been hoping for a couple of hours' quiet—perhaps a tenantless carriage. This state of things for a man in search of meditation was disappointing.

They were now, at length, at Dykham. A porter in waiting, from the inn called the "Three Nuns," took Marston's bag and rug, and led the way to that house, only fifty yards off, where he took up his quarters for the night.

He found Mr. Blount's promised letter from London there. He did not wait for candles and his sitting-room. In his hat and overcoat, by the gas-light at the bar, he read it breathlessly. It said substantially what Mr. Jarlcot's letter had already told him, and nothing more. It was plain, then, that Sir Harry had left every one in the dark as to whether he had or had not executed the will.

In answer to the waiter's hospitable inquiries about supper, he said he had dined late. It was not true; but it was certain that he had no appetite.

He got a sitting-room to himself; he ordered a fire, for he thought the night chilly. He had bought a couple of books, two or three magazines, and as many newspapers. He had his window-curtains drawn; and their agreeable smell of old tobacco smoke assured him that there would be no objection to his cigar.

"I'll ring when I want anything," he said; "and, in the meantime, let me be quiet."

It was here, when he had been negotiating for Sir Harry the renewal of certain leases to a firm in Dykham, that the telegraph had brought him the startling message, and Mr. Blount said in the same message that he was writing particulars by that day's post.

Mr. Marston had not allowed grass to grow under his feet, as you see; and he was now in the same quarters, about to put the case before himself, with a thorough command of its facts.

CHAPTER LXIV.

THE WILL.

Candles lighted, shutters closed, curtains drawn, and a small but cheerful fire flickering in the grate. The old-fashioned room looked pleasant; Richard Marston was nervous, and not like himself. He looked over the "deaths" in the papers, but Sir Harry's was not among them. He threw the papers one after the other on the table, and read nothing.

He got up and stood with his back to the fire. He looked like a man who had got a chill, whom nothing could warm, who was in for a fever. He was in a state he had not anticipated—he almost wished he had left undone the things he had done.

He bolted the door—he listened at it—he tried it with his hand. He had something in his possession that embarrassed and almost frightened him, as if it had been some damning relic of a murdered man.

He sat down and drew from his breastpocket a tolerably bulky paper, a law-paper with a piece of red tape about it, and a seal affixing the tape to the paper. The paper was endorsed in pencil, in Sir Harry's hand, with the words, "Witnessed by Darby Maync and Hugh Fcnwick," and thc datc followcd.

A sudden thought struck him; he put the paper into his pocket again, and made a quiet search of the room, even opening and looking into the two old cupboards, and peeping behind the curtains to satisfy his nervous fancy that no one was concealed there.

Then again he took out the paper, cut the tape, broke the seal, unfolded the broad document, and holding it extended in both hands, read, "The last will and testament of Sir Harry Rokestone, of Dorracleugh, in the County of——, Baronet."

Here, then, was the great sacrilege. He stood there with the spoils of the dead in his hands. But there was no faltering now in his purpose.

He read on: "I, Harry Rokestone, etc., Baronet, of Dorracleugh, etc., being of sound mind, and in good health, do make this my last will," etc.

And on and on he read, his face darkening.

"Four trustees," he muttered, and read on for awhile, for he could not seize its effect as rapidly and easily as an expert would. "Well, yes, two thousand two hundred pounds sterling by way of annuity—annuity!—to be paid for the term of his natural life, in four equal sums, on the first of May, the first of August—yes, and so on—as a first charge upon all the said estates, and so forth. Well, what else?"

And so he went on humming and humming over the paper, his head slowly turning from side to side as he read.

"And Blount to have two hundred a year! I guessed that old Methodist knew what he was about; and then there's the money. What about the money?" He read on as before. "Five thousand pounds. Five thousand for me. Upon my soul! out of one hundred and twenty thousand pounds in government stock. That's modest, all things considered, and an annuity just of two thousand two hundred a year for my life, the rental of the estates, as I happen to know, being nearly nine thousand." This he said with a sneering, uneasy chuckle. "And that is all!"

And he stood erect, holding the paper by the corner between his finger and thumb, and letting it lie against his knee.

"And everything else," he muttered, "land and money, without exception, goes to Miss Ethel Ware. She the lady of the fee; I a poor annuitant!"

Here he was half stifled with rage and mortification.

"I see now, I see what he means. I see the drift of the whole thing. I see my way. I mustn't make a mistake, though—there can't be any. Nothing can be more distinct."

He folded up the will rapidly, and replaced it in his pocket.

Within the last half hour his forehead had darkened, and his cheeks had hollowed. How strangely these subtle muscular contractions correspond with the dominant moral action of the moment!

He took out another paper, a very old one, worn at the edges, and indorsed "Case on behalf of Richard Rokestone Marston, Esquire." I suppose he had read it at least twenty times that day, during his journey to Dorracleugh. "No, nothing on earth can be clearer or more positive," he thought. "The whole thing is as plain as that two and two make four. It covers everything."

There were two witnesses to this will corresponding with the indorsement, each had signed in presence of the other; all was technically exact.

Mr. Marston had seen and talked with these witnesses on his arrival at Dorracleugh, and learned enough to assure him that nothing was to be apprehended from them. They were persons in Sir Harry's employment, and Sir Harry had called them up on the day that the will was dated, and got them to witness in all about a dozen different documents, which they believed to be leases, but were not sure. Sir Harry had told them nothing about the nature of the papers they were witnessing, and had never mentioned a will to them. Richard Marston had asked Mrs. Shackelton also, and she had never heard Sir Harry speak of a will.

While the news of Sir Harry's death rested only upon a telegraphic message, which might be forged or precipitate, he dared not break the seal and open the will. Mr. Blount's and Mr. Jarlcot's letters, which he had read this evening, took that event out of the possibility of question.

He was safe also in resolving a problem that was now before him. Should he rest content with his annuity and five thousand pounds, or seize the entire property, by simply destroying the will?

If the will were allowed to stand he might count on my fidelity, and secure possession of all it bequeathed by marrying me. He had only to place the will somewhere in Sir Harry's room, where it would be sure to be found, and the affair would proceed in its natural course without more trouble to him.

But Mr. Blount was appointed, with very formidable powers, my guardian, and one of his duties was to see, in the event of my marrying, that suitable settlements were made, and that there was no reasonable objection to the candidate for my hand.

Mr. Blount was a quiet but very resolute man in all points of duty. Knowing what was Sir Harry's opinion of his nephew, would he, within the meaning of the will, accept him as a suitor against whom no reasonable objection lay? And even if this were got over, Mr. Blount would certainly sanction no settlement which did not give me as much as I gave. My preponderance of power, as created by the will, must therefore be maintained by the settlement. I had no voice in the matter; and thus it seems that in most respects, even by marriage, the operation of the will was inexorable. Why, then, should the will exist? and why, with such a fortune and liberty within his grasp, should he submit to conditions that would fetter him?

Even the pleasure of depriving Mr. Blount of his small annuity, ridiculous as such a consideration seemed, had its influence. He was keenly incensed with that officious and interested agent. The vicar, in their first conversation, had opened his eyes as to the action of that pretended friend.

"Mr. Blount told me, just before he left this," said the good vicar, "that he had been urging and even entreating Sir Harry for a long time to execute a will which he had by him, requiring nothing but his signature, but, as yet, without success, and that he feared he would never do it."

Now approached the moment of decision. He had read a trial in the newspapers long before, in which a curious case was proved. A man in the position of a gentleman had gone down to a deserted house that belonged to him, for the express purpose of there destroying a will which would have injuriously affected him.

He had made up his mind to destroy it, but he was haunted with the idea that, do it how he might in the village where he lived, one way or other the crime would be discovered. Accordingly he visited, with many precautions, this old house, which was surrounded closely by a thick wood. From one of the chimneys a boy, in search of jackdaws, saw one little puff of smoke escape, and his curiosity being excited, he climbed to the window of the room to which the chimney corresponded, and peeping in, he saw something flaming on the hob, and near it a man, who started, and hurriedly left the room on observing him.

Fancying pursuit, the detected man took his departure, without venturing to return to the room.

The end of the matter was that his journey to the old house was tracked, and not only did the boy identify him, but the charred pieces of burnt paper found on the hob, having been exposed to chemical action, had revealed the writing, a portion of which contained the signatures of the testator, and the witnesses, and these and other part thus rescued, identified it with the original draft in possession of the dead man's attorney. Thus the crime was proved, and the will set up and supplemented by what, I believe, is termed secondary evidence.

Who could be too cautious, then, in such a matter? It seemed as hard to hide away effectually all traces of a will destroyed as the relics of a murder.

Again he was tempted to spare the will, and rest content with an annuity and safety. It was but a temptation, however, and a passing one.

He unbolted the door softly, and rang the bell. The waiter found him extended on a sofa, apparently deep in his magazine.

He ordered tea—nothing else; he was precise in giving his order—he did not want the servant pottering about his room—he had reasons for choosing to be specially quiet.

The waiter returned with his tea-tray, and found him buried, as before, in his magazine.

"Is everything there?" inquired Richard Marston.

"Everything there? Yes, sir, everything."

"Well, then, you need not come again till I touch the bell."

The waiter withdrew.

Mr. Marston continued absorbed in his magazine for just three minutes. Then he rose softly, stepped lightly to the door, and listened. He bolted it again; tried it, and found it fast.

In a moment the will was in his hand. He gave one dark, searching look round the room, and then he placed the document in the very centre of the embers. He saw it smoke sullenly, and curl and slowly warp, and spring with a faint sound, that made him start more than ever cannon did, into sudden flame. That little flame seemed like a bale-fire to light up the broad sky of night with a vengeful flicker, and throw a pale glare over the wide parks and mosses, the forests, fells, and mere, of dead Sir Harry's great estate; and when the flame leaped up and died, it seemed that there was no light left in the room, and he could see nothing but the myriad little worms of fire wriggling all over the black flakes which he thrust, like struggling enemies, into the hollow of the fire.

Richard Marston was a man of redundant courage, and no scruple. But have all men some central fibre of fear that can be reached, and does the ghost of the conscience they have killed within them sometimes rise and overshadow them with horror? Richard Marston, with his feet on the fender and the tongs in his hands, pressed down the coals upon the ashes of the will, and felt faint and dizzy, as he had done on the night of the shipwreck, when, with bleeding forehead, he had sat down for the first time in the steward's house at Malory.

An event as signal had happened now. After nearly ten minutes had passed, during which he had never taken his eyes off the spot where the ashes were glowing, he got up and took the candle down to see whether a black film of the paper had escaped from the grate. Then stealthily he opened the window to let out any smell of burnt paper.

He lighted his cigar, and smoked; and unbolted the door, rang the bell, and ordered brandy-and-water. The suspense was over, and the crisis past.

He was resolved to sit there till morning, to see that fire burnt out.

CHAPTER LXV.

THE SERPENT'S SMILE.

There came on a sudden a great quiet over Dorracleugh—the quiet of death.

There was no longer any doubt, all the country round, as to the fact that the old baronet was dead. Richard Marston had placed at all the gates notices to the effect that the funeral would not take place for a week, at soonest—that no day had yet been fixed for it, and that early notice should be given.

The slight fuss that had prevailed within doors, for the greater part of a day, had now quite subsided—and, quiet as it always was, Dorracleugh was now more silent and stirless than ever.

I could venture now to extend my walks anywhere about the place, without the risk of meeting any stranger.

If there is a melancholy there is also something sublime and consolatory in the character of the scenery that surrounds it. Every one has felt the influence of lofty mountains near. This region is all beautiful; but the very spirit of solitude and grandeur is over it.

I was just consulting with my maid about some simple provisional mourning, for which I was about to despatch her to the town, when our conference was arrested by the appearance of Richard Marston before the window.

I had my things on, for I thought it not impossible he might arrive earlier than he had the day before.

I told my maid to come again by-and-by; and I went out to meet him.

Well, we were now walking on the wild path, along the steep side of the cleugh, towards the lake. What kind of conversation is this going to be? His voice and manner are very gentle—but he looks pale and stern, like a man going into a battle. The signs are very slight, but dreadful. Oh! that the next half-hour was over! What am I about to hear?

We walked on for a time in silence.

The first thing he said was:

"You are to stay here at Dorracleugh—you must not go—but I'm afraid you will be vexed with me."

Then we advanced about twenty steps; we were walking slowly, and not a word was spoken during that time.

He began again:

"Though, after all, it need not make any real difference. There is no will, Ethel; the vicar can tell you that; he had the key, and has made search—no will; and you are left unprovided for—but that shan't affect you. I am heir-at-law, and nearest-of-kin. You know what that means. Everything he possessed, land or money, comes to me. But—I've put my foot into it; it is too late regretting. I can't marry."

There was an interval of silence—he was looking in my face.

"There! the murder's out. I knew you would be awfully vexed. So am I—miserable—but I can't. That is, perhaps, for many years."

There was another silence. I could no more have spoken than I could, by an effort of my will, have lifted the mountain at the other side of the lake from its foundation.

Perhaps he misinterpreted my silence.

"I ought to have been more frank with you, Ethel—I blame myself very much, I assure you. Can't you guess? Well, I was an awful fool—I'll tell you everything. I feel that I ought to have done so, long ago; but you know, one can't always make up one's mind to be quite frank, and tell a painful story. I am married. In an evil hour, I married a woman in every way unsuited to me—pity me. In a transitory illusion, I sacrificed my life—and, what is dearer, my love. I have not so much as seen her for years, and I am told she is not likely to live long. In the meantime I am yours only—yours entirely and irrevocably, your own. I can offer you safety here, and happiness, my own boundless devotion and adoration, an asylum here, and all the authority and rights of a wife. Ethel—dearest—you won't leave me?"

I looked up in his face, scared—a sudden look, quite unexpected. I saw a cunning, selfish face gloating down on me, with a gross, confident, wicked simper.

That odious smile vanished, his eye shrank; he looked detected or disconcerted for a moment, but he rallied.

"I say, I look on myself, in the sight of heaven, as married to you. You have pledged yourself to me by every vow that can tie woman to man; you have sworn that no obstacle shall keep us apart. That oath was not without a meaning, and you know it wasn't; and, by heaven! you shan't break my heart for nothing! Come, Ethel, be a girl of sense—don't you see we are controlled by fate? Look at the circumstances. Where's the good in quarrelling with me? Don't you see the position I'm placed in, about that miserable evidence? Don't you see that I am able and anxious to do everything for you? Could a girl in your situation do a better or a wiser thing than unite her interests with mine, indissolubly? For God's sake, where's the use of making me desperate? What do you want to drive me to? Why should you insist on making me your enemy? How do you think it's all to end?"

Could I have dreamed that he could ever have looked at me with such a countenance, and spoken to me in such a tone? I felt myself growing colder and colder; I could not move my eyes from him. His image seemed to swim before me; his harsh, frightful tones grow confused. My hands were to my temples, I could not speak; my answer was one piteous scream.

I found myself hurrying along the wild path, towards the house, with hardly a clear recollection, without one clear thought. I don't know whether he tried to detain me, or began to follow me. I remember, at the hall-door, from habit, going up a step or two, in great excitement—we act so nearly mechanically! A kind of horror seized me at sight of the half-open door. I turned and hurried down the avenue.

It was not until I had reached the "George and Dragon"—at the sleepiest hour, luckily, of the tranquil little town of Golden Friars—that I made a first effectual effort to collect my thoughts.

I was simply a fugitive. To return to Dorracleugh, where Richard Marston was now master, was out of the question. I was in a mood to accept all ill news as certain. It never entered my mind that he had intended to deceive me with respect to Sir Harry's will. Neither had he as to my actually unprovided state. Here then I stood a fugitive.

I walked up to Mr. Turnbull, the host of the "George and Dragon," whom I saw at the inn-door, and having heard his brief but genuine condolences, without half knowing what he was saying, I ordered a carriage to bring me to the railway station; and while I was waiting I wrote a note in the quiet little room, with a window looking across the lake, to the good vicar.

Mr. Turnbull was one of those heavy, comfortable persons who are willing to take everybody's business and reasons for granted. He therefore bored me with no surmises as to the reasons of my solitary excursion at so oddly chosen a time.

I think, now, that my wiser course would have been to go to the vicar, and explaining generally my objections to remaining at Dorracleugh, to have asked frankly for permission to place myself under his care until the arrival of Mr. Blount.

There were fifty other things I ought to have thought of, though I only wonder, considering the state in which my mind was at the moment, that I was able to write so coherently as I did to the vicar. I had my purse with me, containing fifty pounds, which poor Sir Harry had given me just before he left Dorracleugh. With no more than this, which I had fortunately brought down with me to the drawing-room, for the purpose of giving my maid a bank-note to take to the town to pay for my intended purchases, I was starting on my journey to London! Without luggage, or servant, or companion, or plan of any kind—inspired by the one instinct, to get as rapidly as possible out of sight and reach of Dorracleugh, and to earn my bread by my own exertions.

CHAPTER LXVI.

LAURA GREY.

You are to suppose my journey safely ended in London. The first thing I did after securing lodgings, and making some few purchases, was to go to the house where my great friend Sir Harry Rokestone, had died. But Mr. Blount, I found, had left London for Golden Friars, only a few hours before my arrival.

Another disappointment awaited me at Mr. Forrester's chambers—he was out of town, taking his holiday.

I began now to experience the consequences of my precipitation. It was too late, however, to reflect; and if the plunge was to be made, perhaps the sooner the better. I wrote to the vicar, to give him my address, also to Mr. Blount, telling him the course on which I had decided. I at once resolved to look for a situation, as governess to very young children. I framed an advertisement with a great deal of care, which I published in the *Times*; but no satisfactory result followed, and two or three days passed in like manner.

After paying for my journey, and my London purchases, there remained to me, of my fifty pounds, about thirty-two. My situation was not so frightful as it might have been. But with the strictest economy a limited time must see my store exhausted; and no one who has not been in such a situation can fancy the ever-recurring panic of counting, day after day, the diminishing chances between you and the chasm to whose edge you are slowly sliding.

A few days brought me a letter from the good vicar. There occurred in it a passage which finally quieted the faint struggle of hope now and then reviving. He said, "I observe by your letter that you are already apprised of the disappointing result of my search for the will of the late Sir Harry Rokestone. He had informed several persons of the spot where, in the event of his executing one, which he always, I am told, treated as very doubtful, it would be found. He had placed the key of the safe along with some other things at his departure, but without alluding to his will. At the request of Mr. Marston I opened the safe, and the result was, I regret to say, that no will was found." I was now, then, in dread earnest to lay my account for a life of agitation and struggle.

At last a promising answer to my advertisement reached me. It said, "The Countess of Rillingdon will be in town till this day week, and will be happy to see L.Y.L.X., whose advertisement appeared in the *Times* of this morning, if possible to-day before two." The house was in Belgrave Square. It was now near twelve. I called immediately with a note, to say I would call at a quarter to two, and at that hour precisely I returned.

It was plain that this was but a flying visit of the patrician owners of the house. Some luggage, still in its shiny black casings, was in the hall; the lamps hung in bags; carpets had disappeared; curtains were pinned up; and servants seemed scanty, and more fussy than in the organized discipline of a household. I told the servant that I had called in consequence of a note from Lady Rillingdon, and he conducted me forthwith up the stairs. We passed on the way a young lady coming down, whom I conjectured to be on the same errand as myself. We exchanged stolen looks as we passed, each, I daresay, conjecturing the other's chances.

"Her ladyship will see you presently," he said, opening a door.

I entered, and whom should I see waiting in the room, in a chair, in her hat, with her parasol in her hand, but Laura Grey.

"Ethel!"

"Laura!"

"Darling!"

And each in a moment was locked in the other's embrace. With tears, with trembling laughter, and more kisses than I can remember, we signalized our meeting.

"How wonderful that I should have met you here, Laura!" said I; though what was the special wonder in meeting her there more than anywhere else, I could not easily have defined. "You must tell me, darling, if you are looking to come to Lady Rillingdon, for, if you are, I would not for the world think of it."

Laura laughed very merrily at this.

"Why, Ethel, what are you dreaming of? I'm Lady Rillingdon!"

Sometimes a mistake seizes upon us with an unaccountable obstinacy. Laura's claiming to be Lady Rillingdon seemed to me simply a jest of that poor kind which relies entirely on incongruity, without so much colour of possibility as to make it humorous.

I laughed, faintly enough, with Laura, from mere politeness, wondering when this poor joke would cease to amuse her; and the more she looked in my face, the more heartily she laughed, and the more melancholy became my endeavour to accompany her.

"What can I do to convince you, darling?" she exclaimed at length, half distracted.

She got up and touched the bell. I began to be a little puzzled. The servant appeared, and she asked:

"Is his lordship at home?"

"I'll inquire, my lady," he answered, and retired.

This indeed was demonstration; I could be incredulous no longer. We kissed again and again, and were once more laughing and gabbling together, when the servant returned with:

"Please, my lady, his lordship went out about half an hour ago."

"I'm so sorry," she said, turning to me, "but he'll be back very soon, I'm sure. I want so much to introduce him; I think you'll like him."

Luncheon soon interrupted us; and when that little interval was over, she took me to the same quiet room, and we talked and mutually questioned, and got out of each the whole history of the other.

There was only one little child of this marriage, which seemed, in every way but that, so happy—a daughter. Their second, a son, had died. This pretty little creature we had with us for a time, and then it went out with its nurse for a drive, and we, over our afternoon tea, resumed our confessions and inquiries. Laura had nearly as much to tell as I. In the midst of our talk Lord Rillingdon came in. I knew whom I was to meet. I was therefore not surprised when the very man whom I had seen faint and bleeding in the wood of Plas Ylwd, whom Richard Marston had shot, and whom I had seen but once since at Lady Mardykse' ball, stood before me. In a moment we were old friends.

He remained with us for about ten minutes, talked kindly and pleasantly, and drank his cup of tea.

These recollections, in my present situation, were agitating. The image of Richard Marston had re-appeared in the sinister shadow in which it had been early presented to me by the friends who had warned me so kindly, but in vain.

In a little time we talked on as before, and everything she told me added to the gloom and horror in which Marston was now shrouded in my sorrowful imagination.

As soon as the first delighted surprise of meeting Laura had a little subsided, my fears returned, and all I had to dread from the active malice of Richard Marston vaguely gathered on my stormy horizon again.

CHAPTER LXVII.

A CHAPTER OF EXPLANATIONS.

Laura's long talk with me resulted in these facts. They cleared up her story.

She was the only daughter of Mr. Grey, of Halston Manor, of whom I had often heard. He had died in possession of a great estate, and of shares in the Great Central Bank worth two hundred thousand pounds. Within a few weeks after his death the bank failed, and the estate was drawn into the ruin. Of her brother there is no need to speak, for he died only a year after, and has no connection with my story.

Laura Grey would have been a suitable, and even a princely match for a man of rank and fortune, had it not been for this sudden and total reverse. Old Lord Rillingdon—Viscount Rillingdon, his son, had won his own position in the peerage by brilliant service—had wished to marry his son to the young lady. No formal overtures had been made; but Lord Rillingdon's house, Northcot Hall, was near, and the young people were permitted to improve their acquaintance into intimacy, and so an unavowed attachment was formed. The crash came, and Lord Rillingdon withdrew his son, Mr. Jennings, from the perilous neighbourhood.

A year elapsed before the exact state of Mr. Grey's affairs was ascertained. During that time Richard Marston, who had seen and admired Laura Grey, whose brother was an intimate friend of his, came to the neighbourhood and endeavoured to insinuate himself into her good graces. He had soon learned her ruined circumstances, and founded the cruellest hopes upon this melancholy knowledge.

To forward his plans he had conveyed scandalous falsehoods to Mr. Jennings, with the object of putting an end to his rivalry. These Mr. Jennings had refused to believe; but there were others no less calculated to excite his jealousy, and to alienate his affection. He had shown the effect of this latter influence by a momentary coldness, which roused Laura Grey's fiery spirit; for gentle as she was, she was proud.

She had written to tell Mr. Jennings that all was over between them, and that she would never see him more. He had replied in a letter which did not reach her till long after, in terms the most passionate and agonising, vowing that he held himself affianced to her while he lived, and would never marry any one but her.

In this state of things Miss Grey had come to us, resolved to support herself by her own exertions.

Lord Rillingdon, having reason to suspect his son's continued attachment to Laura Grey, and having learned accidentally that there was a lady of that name residing at Malory, made a visit to Cardyllion. He was the old gentleman in the chocolate-coloured coat, who had met us as we returned from church, and held a conversation with her, under the trees, on the mill-road.

His object was to exact a promise that she would hold no communication with his son for the future. His tone was insolent, dictatorial, and in the highest degree irritating. She repelled his insinuations with spirit, and peremptorily refused to make any reply whatever to demands urged in a temper so arrogant and insulting.

The result was that he parted from her highly incensed, and without having carried his point, leaving my dear sister and me in a fever of curiosity.

Richard Rokestone Marston was the only near relation of Sir Harry Rokestone. He had fallen under the baronet's just and high displeasure. After a course of wild and wicked extravagance, he had finally ruined himself in the opinion of Sir Harry by committing a fraud, which, indeed, would never have come to light had it not been for a combination of unlucky chances.

In consequence of this his uncle refused to see him; but at Mr. Blount's intercession agreed to allow him a small annual sum, on the strict condition that he was to leave England. It was when actually on his way to London, which, for reason that, except in its result, has no connection with my story, he chose to reach through Bristol, that he had so nearly lost his life in the disaster of the Conway Castle.

Here was the first contact of my story with his.

His short stay at Malory was signalised by his then unaccountable suit to me, and by his collision with Mr. Jennings, who had come down there on some very vague information that Laura Grey was in the neighbourhood. He had succeeded in meeting her, and in renewing their engagement, and at last had persuaded her to consent to a secret marriage, which at first involved the anguish of a long separation, during which a dangerous illness threatened the life of her husband.

I am hurrying through this explanation, but I must relate a few more events and circumstances which throw a light upon some of the passages in the history I have been giving you of my life.

Why did Richard Marston conceive, in perfect good faith, a fixed purpose to marry a girl of whom he knew enough to be aware that she was without that which prudence would have insisted on as a first necessity in his circumstances—money.

Well, it turned out to have been by no means so imprudent a plan. I learned from Mr. Blount the particulars that explained it.

Mr. Blount, who took an interest in him, and had always cherished a belief that he was reclaimable, told him repeatedly that Sir Harry had often said that he would take one of Mabel Ware's daughters for his heiress. This threat he had secretly laughed at, knowing the hostility that subsisted between the families. He was, however, startled at last. Mr. Blount had shown him a letter in which Sir Harry distinctly stated that he had made up his mind to leave everything he possessed to me. This he showed him for the purpose of inducing a patient endeavour to regain his lost place in the old man's regard. It effectually alarmed Richard Marston; and when a chance storm threw him at our door, the idea of averting that urgent danger, and restoring himself to his lost position, by an act of masterly strategy, occurred to him, and instantly bore fruit in action.

After his return, and his admission as an inmate at Dorracleugh, the danger appeared still more urgent, and his opportunities were endless.

He had succeeded, as I have told you, in binding me by an engagement. In that position he was safe, no matter what turned up. He had, however, now made his election; and how cruelly, you already know. Did he, according to his low standard, love me? I believe, so far as was consistent with his nature, he did. He was furious at my having escaped him, and would have pursued, and no doubt discovered me, had he been free at the moment to leave Dorracleugh.

His alleged marriage was, I believe, a fiction. But he could not bear, I think, to lose me; and had he obtained another interview, he would have held very different language. Mr. Blount thought that he had, perhaps, formed some scheme for a marriage of ambition, in favour of which I was to have been put aside. If so, however, I do not think that he would have purchased the enjoyment of such ambition at the price of losing me at once and for ever. I dare say you will laugh at the simplicity of this vanity in a woman who, in a case like this, could suppose such a thing. I do suppose it, notwithstanding. I am sure that, so far as his nature was capable of love, he did love me. With the sad evidences on which this faith was grounded, I will not weary you. Let those vain conclusions rest where they are, deep in my heart.

The important post which Lord Rillingdon had filled, in one of our greatest dependencies, and the skill, courage, and wisdom with which he had directed affairs during a very critical period, had opened a way for him to still higher things. He and Laura were going out in about six months to India, and she and he insisted that I should accompany them as their guest. This would have been too delightful under happier circumstances; but the sense of dependence, however disguised, is dreadful. We are so constructed that for an average mind it is more painful to share in idle dependence the stalled ox of a friend than to work for one's own dinner of herbs.

They were going to Brighton, and I consented to make them a visit there of three or four weeks; after which I was to resume my search for a "situation." Laura entreated me at least to accept the care of her little child; but this, too, I resolutely declined. At first sight you will charge me with folly; but if you, being of my sex, will place yourself for a moment in my situation, you will understand why I refused. I felt that I should have been worse than useless. Laura would never have ordered me about as a good mother would like to order the person in charge of her only child. She would have been embarrassed and unhappy, and I conscious of being in the way.

Two other circumstances need explanation. Laura told me, long after, that she had received a farewell letter from Mr. Carmel, who told her that he had written to warn me, but with much precaution, as Sir Harry had a strong antipathy to persons of his profession, of a danger which he was not then permitted to define. Monsieur Droqville, whom Mr. Marston had courted, and sought to draw into relations with him, had received a letter from that young man, stating that he had made up his mind to leave America by the next ship, and establish himself once more at Dorracleugh. It was Mr. Carmel, then, who had written the note that puzzled me so much, and conveyed it, by another hand, to the post-office of Cardyllion.

Monsieur Droqville had no confidence in Richard Marston. He had been informed, besides, of the exact nature of Sir Harry's will, and of a provision that made his bequest to me void, in case I should embrace the Roman Catholic faith.

It was in consequence of that provision in the draft-will of Sir Harry Rokestone, and from a consideration of the impolicy of any action while Lady Lorrimer's death was so recent, and my indignation so hot, that Droqville had resolved that, for a time, at least, the attempt to gain me to the Church of Rome should not be renewed.

Taking the clear, hard view they do of the office of the Church upon earth, they are right to discriminate. In the sight of Heaven, the souls of Dives and of Lazarus are equally precious. In electing which to convert, then, they discharge but a simple duty in choosing that proselyte who will most strengthen the influence and action of the Church upon earth. In that respect, considering the theories they hold, they do right. Common sense acquits them.

I have now ended my necessary chapter of explanation, and my story goes on its way.

CHAPTER LXVIII.

THE LAST OF THE ROKESTONES.

A solemn low-voiced fuss was going on in the old house at Dorracleugh; preparations and consultations were afoot; a great deal was not being done, but there were the whispering and restlessness of expectation, and the few grisly arrangements for the reception of the coffined guest.

Old Mrs. Shackleton, the housekeeper, crept about the rooms, her handkerchief now and then to her eyes; and the housemaid-in-chief, with her attendant women, was gliding about.

Sir Harry had, years before, left a letter in Mr. Blount's hands, that there might be no delay in searching for a will, directing all that concerned his funeral.

The coffin was to be placed in the great hall of the house, according to ancient custom, on tressels, under the broad span of the chimney. This arrangement is more than once alluded to in Pepys's Diary. He was to be followed to the grave by his tenantry, and such of the gentry, his neighbours, as might please to attend. There was to be ample repast for all comers, consisting of as much "meat and drink of the best as they could consume;" what remained was to be distributed among the poor in the evening.

He was to be laid in the family vault adjoining the church of Golden Friars; a stone with the family arms, and a short inscription, "but no flatteries," was to be set up in the church, on the south wall, next the vault, and near the other family monuments, and it was to mention that he died unmarried, and was the last of the old name of Rokestone, of Dorracleugh.

The funeral was to proceed to Golden Friars, not by the "mere road," but, as in the case of other family funerals, from Dorracleugh to Golden Friars, by the old high-road.

If he should die at home, at Dorracleugh, but not otherwise, he was to be "waked" in the same manner as his father and his grandfather had been.

There were other directions, presents to the sexton and parish-clerk, and details that would weary you.

About twelve o'clock the hearse arrived, and two or three minutes after Mr. Blount drove up in a chaise.

The almost gigantic coffin was carried up the steps, and placed under the broad canopy assigned to it at the upper end of the hall.

Mr. Blount, having given a few directions, inquired for Mr. Marston, and found that gentleman, in a suit of black, in the drawing-room.

He came forward; he did not intend it, but there was something in the gracious and stately melancholy of his reception, which seemed to indicate not only the chief mourner, but the master of the house.

"Altered circumstances—a great change," said Mr. Marston, taking his hand. "Many will feel his death deeply. He was to me—I have said it a thousand times—the best friend that ever man had."

"Yes, yes, sir; he did show wonderful patience and forbearance with you, considering his temper, which was proud and fiery, you know—poor gentleman!—poor Sir Harry!—but grandly generous, sir, grandly generous."

"It is a consolation to me, having lost a friend, and, I may say, a father, who was, in patience, forbearance, and generosity, all you describe, and all you know, that we were lately, thanks, my good friend, mainly to your kind offices, upon the happiest terms. He used to talk to me about that farm; he took such an interest in it—sit down, pray—won't you have some sherry and a biscuit—and such a growing interest in me."

"I think he really was coming gradually not to think quite so ill of you as he did," said good Mr. Blount. "No sherry, no biscuit—no, I shan't mind. I know, sir, that under great and sudden temptation a man may do the thing he ought not to have done, and repent from his heart afterwards, and from very horror of his one great lapse, may walk, all the rest of his life, not only more discreetly, but more safely than a man who has never slipped at all. But Sir Harry was sensitive and fiery. He had thought that you were to represent the old house, and perhaps to bear the name after his death; and that both should be slurred by, if I may be allowed the expression, a shabby crime...."

"Once for all, Mr. Blount, you'll be good enough to remember that such language is offensive and intolerable," interrupted Richard Marston, firmly and sharply. "My uncle had a right to lecture me on the subject—you can havc none."

"Except as a friend," said Mr. Blount. "I shall, however, for the future, observe your wishes upon that subject. You got my letter about the funeral, I see."

"Yes, they are doing everything exactly as you said," said Marston, recovering his affability.

"Here is the letter," said Mr. Blount. "You should run your eye over it."

"Ha! It is dated a long time ago," said Mr. Marston. "It was no sudden presentiment, then. How well he looked when I was leaving this!"

"We are always astonished when death gives no warning," said Mr. Blount; "it hardly ever does to the persons most interested. Doctors, friends, they themselves, are all in a conspiracy to conceal the thief who has got into the bed-room. It matters very little that the survivors have had warning."

Richard Marston shook his head and shrugged his shoulders.

"Some day I must learn prudence," said he.

"Let it be the true prudence," said Mr. Blount. "It is a short foresight that sees no further than the boundary of this life."

Mr. Marston opened the letter, and the old gentleman left him, to see after the preparations.

Some one at Golden Friars—I think it was the vicar—sent me the country paper, with a whole column in mourning, with a deep black edge, giving a full account of the funeral of Sir Harry Rokestone, of Dorracleugh. The ancient family whose name he bore was now extinct. I saw in the list the names of county people who had come in their carriages more than twenty miles to attend the funeral, and people who had come by rail hundreds of miles. It was a great county gathering mostly that followed the last of the Rokestones, of Dorracleugh, to the grave.

CHAPTER LXIX.

SEARCH FOR THE WILL.

The funeral was over; but the old house of Dorracleugh was not quiet again till the night fell, and there was no more to-ing and fro-ing in the stable-yard, and the last tenant had swallowed his last draught of beer, and mounted and ridden away through the mist, over the fells, to his distant farm.

The moon shone peacefully over mere and fell, and on the time-worn church of Golden Friars, and through the window, bright, on the grey flags that lie over Sir Harry Rokestone. Never did she keep serener watch over the first night of a mortal's sleep in his last narrow bed.

Richard Marston saw this pure light, and musing, looked from the window. It shone, he thought, over his wide estate. Beyond the mere, all but Clusted, for many a mile was his own. At this side, away in the direction of distant Haworth, a broad principality of moss and heath, with scattered stretches of thin arable and pasture, ran side by side with the Mardykes estate, magnificent in vastness, if not in rental.

His dreams were not of feudal hospitality and the hearty old-world life. His thoughts were far away from this grand scenery or lonely Dorracleugh. Ambition built his castles in the air; nothing very noble. It was not even the tawdry and tradesman-like ambition of modern times. He had no taste for that particular form of meanness, nor patience for its drudgery. He would subscribe to election funds, place his county influence at the disposal of the minister; spend money on getting and keeping a seat; be found in his place whenever a critical vote was impending; and by force of this, and of his county position, and the old name—for he would take the name of Rokestone, in spite of his uncle's awkward direction about his epitaph, and no one could question his relationship—by dint of all this, with, I daresay, the influence of a high marriage, he hoped to get on, not from place to place, but what would answer him as well, from title to title. First to revive the baronetage, and then, after some fifteen or twenty years more of faithful service, to become Baron Rokestone, of Dorracleugh.

It was not remorse, then, that kept the usurper's eyes wide open, as he lay that night in the dark in his bed, his brain in a fever. His conscience had no more life in it than the window-stone. It troubled him with no compunction. There was at his heart, on the contrary, a vindictive elation at having defeated with so much simplicity the unnatural will of his uncle.

Bright rose the sun next morning over Dorracleugh, a sun of good omen. Richard Marston had appointed three o'clock as the most convenient hour for all members of the conference, for a meeting and a formality. A mere formality, in truth, it was, a search for the will of Sir Harry Rokestone. Mr. Blount had slept at Dorracleugh. Mr. Jarlcot, a short, plump man, of five-and-fifty, with a grave face and a bullet head, covered with short, lank, black hair, accompanied by his confidential man, Mr. Spaight, arrived in his gig, just as the punctual clock of Dorra-Dorracleugh struck three.

Very soon after the old vicar rode up, on his peaceable pony, and came into the drawing-room, where the little party were assembled, with sad, kind face, and gentle, old-fashioned ceremony, with a little powdering of dust in the wrinkles of his clerical costume.

It was with a sense of pleasant satire that Richard Marston had observed old Lemuel Blount ever since he had been assured that the expected will was not forthcoming. These holy men, how they love an annuity! Not that they like money, of course; that's Mammon; but because it lifts them above earthy cares, and gives them the power of relieving the wants of their fellow-Christians. How slyly the old gentleman had managed it! How thoughtful his appointing himself guardian to the young lady! What endless opportunities his powers over the settlements would present of making handsome terms for himself with an intending bridegroom!

On arriving, in full confidence that the will was safe in its iron repository, Christian could not have looked more comfortable when he enjoyed his famous prospect from the delectable mountains. But when it turned out that the will was nowhere, the same Christian, trudging on up the hill of difficulty in his old "burdened fashion," could not have looked more hang-dog and overpowered than he.

His low spirits, his sighs and ejaculations, amused Richard Marston extremely. When he heard him say to himself, when first he learned that the vicar had looked into the safe and found nothing, "How sad! How strange! How very sad!" as he stood at the window, with his head lowered, and his fingers raised, he was tempted to rebuke his audacity with some keen and cautious irony; but those who win may laugh—he could afford to be good-humoured, and a silent sneer contented him.

Mr. Blount, having, as I said, heard that the vicar had searched the "safe," and that Mr. Spaight, accompanied by Mr. Marston, and the housekeeper, had searched all the drawers, desks, boxes, presses, and other lock-up places in the house in vain, for any paper having even a resemblance to a will, said: "It is but a form; but as you propose it, be it so."

And now this form was to be complied with. Mr. Marston told the servant to send Mrs. Shackelton with the keys. Mr. Marston led the way, and four other gentlemen followed, attended by the housekeeper.

There was not much talking; a clatter of feet on uncarpeted floors, the tiny jingle of small keys, the opening of doors, and clapping of lids, and now and then Mrs. Shackelton's hard treble was heard in answer to an interrogatory.

This went on for more than twenty minutes up-stairs, and then the exploring party came down the stairs again, Richard Marston talking to the vicar, Mr. Blount to Mr. Spaight, while Mr. Jarlcot, the attorney, listened to Mrs. Shackleton, the housekeeper.

Richard Marston led the party to Sir Harry's room. The carpet was still on the floor, the curtains hanging still, in gloomy folds, to the ground. Sir Harry's hat and stick lay on the small round table, where he had carelessly thrown them when he came in from his last walk about Dorracleugh, his slippers lay on the hearthrug before his easy-chair, and his pipe was on the mantelpiece.

The party stood in this long and rather gloomy room in straggling disarray, still talking.

"There's Pixie," said old Mr. Spaight, who had been a bit of a sportsman, and loved coursing in his youth, as he stopped before a portrait of a greyhound, poking his long nose and spectacles, with a faint smirk, close into the canvas. "Sir Harry's dog; fine dog, Pixie, won the cup twice on Doppleton Lea thirty-two years ago." But this was a murmured meditation, for he was a staid man of business now, and his liking for dogs and horses was incongruous, and no one in the room heard him. Mr. Jarlcot's voice recalled him.

"Mr. Marston was speaking to you, Mr. Spaight."

"Oh! I was just saying I think nothing could have been more careful," said Mr. Marston, "than the search you made upstairs, in the presence of me and Mrs. Shackleton, on Thursday last?"

"No, sir—certainly nothing—it could not possibly have escaped us," answered Mr. Spaight.

"And that is your opinion also?" asked Mr. Jarlcot of Richard Marston.

"Clearly," he answered.

"I'll make a note of that, if you'll allow me," said Mr. Jarlcot; and he made an entry, with Mr. Marston's concurrence, in his pocket-book.

"And now about this," said Mr. Jarlcot, with a clumsy bow to Mr. Marston, and touching the door of the safe with his open hand.

"You have got the key, sir?" said Marston to the good vicar with silver hair, who stood meekly by, distrait and melancholy, an effigy of saintly contemplation.

"Oh, yes," said the vicar wakening up. "Yes; the key, but—but you know there's nothing there."

He moved the key vaguely about as he looked from one to the other, as if inviting any one who pleased to try.

"I think, sir, perhaps it will be as well if you will kindly open it yourself," said Marston.

"Yes, surely—I suppose so—with all my heart," said the vicar.

The door of the safe opened easily, and displayed the black iron void, into which all looked.

Blessed are they who expect nothing, for they shall not be disappointed. Of course no one was surprised. But Mr. Blount shook his head, lifted up his hands, and groaned audibly, "I am very sorry."

Mr. Marston did not affect to hear him.

CHAPTER LXX.

A DISAPPOINTMENT.

I think," said Mr. Jarlcot, "it will be desirable that I should take a note of any information which Mr. Marston and the vicar may be so good as to supply with respect to the former search in the same place. I think, sir," he continued, addressing the vicar, "you mentioned that the deceased, Sir Harry Rokestone, placed that key in your charge on the evening of his departure from this house for London?"

"So it was, sir," said the vicar.

"Was it out of your possession for any time?"

"For about three quarters of an hour. I handed it to Mr. Marston on his way to this house; but as I was making a sick-call near this, I started not many minutes after he left me, and on the way it struck me that I might as well have back the key. I arrived here, I believe, almost as soon as he, and he quite agreed with me that I had better get the key again into——"

"Into your own custody," interposed Marston. "You may recollect that it was I who suggested it the moment you came."

"And the key was not out of your possession, Mr. Marston, during the interval?" said Mr. Jarlcot.

"Not for one moment," answered Richard Marston, promptly.

"And you did not, I think you mentioned, open that safe?"

"Certainly not. I made no use whatever of that key at any time. I never saw that safe open until the vicar opened it in my presence, and we both saw that it contained nothing; so did Mrs. Shackleton, as intelligent a witness as any. And, I think, we can all—I know I can, for my part—depose, on oath, to the statements we have made."

Mr. Jarlcot raised his eyebrows solemnly, slowly shook his head, and having replaced his note-book in his pocket, drew a long breath in through his rounded lips, with a sound that almost amounted to a whistle.

"Nothing could be more distinct; it amounts to demonstration," he said, raising his head, putting his hands into his trousers-pockets, and looking slowly round the cornice. "Haven't you something to say?" he added, laying his hand gently on Mr. Blount's arm, and then turning a step or two away; while Marston, who could not comprehend what he fancied to be an almost affected disappointment at the failure to discover a will, thought he saw his eyes wander, when he thought no one was looking, curiously to the grate and the hobs; perhaps in search, as he suspected, of paper ashes.

"I am awfully sorry," exclaimed Mr. Blount, throwing himself into a chair in undisguised despondency. "The will, as it was drafted, would have provided splendidly for Miss Ethel Ware, and left you, Mr. Marston, an annuity of two thousand five hundred a year, and a sum of five thousand pounds. For two or three years I had been urging him to execute it; it is evident he never did. He has destroyed the draft, instead of executing it. That hope is quite gone—totally."

Mr. Blount stood up and said, laying his hand upon his forehead, "I am grieved—I am shocked—I am profoundly grieved."

Mr. Marston was strongly tempted to tell Mr. Blount what he thought of him. Jarlcot and he, no doubt, understood one another, and had intended making a nice thing of it.

He could not smile, nor even sneer, just then, but Mr. Marston fixed on Lemuel Blount a sidelong look of the sternest contempt.

"There is, then," said Mr. Blount, collecting himself, "no will."

"That seems pretty clear," said Mr. Marston, with, in spite of himself, a cold scorn in his tone. "I think so; and I rather fancy you think so too."

"Except this," continued Mr. Blount, producing a paper from his pocket, at which he had been fumbling. "Mr. Jarlcot will hand you a copy. I urged him, God knows how earnestly, to revoke it. It was made at the period of his greatest displeasure with you; it leaves everything to Miss Ethel Ware, and gives you, I grieve to say, but an annuity of four hundred a year. It appoints me guardian to the young lady, in the same terms that the latter will would have done, and leaves me, besides, an annuity of five hundred a year, half of which I shall, if you don't object, make over to you."

"Oh! oh! a will! That's all right," said Marston, trying to smile with lips that had grown white; "I, of course, you—we all wish nothing but what is right and fair."

Mr. Jarlcot handed him a new neatly-folded paper, endorsed "Copy of the Will of the late Sir Harry Rokestone, Bart." Richard Marston took it with a hand that trembled, a hand that had not often trembled before.

"Then, I suppose, Mr. Blount, you will look in on me, by-and-by, to arrange about the steps to be taken about proving it," said Mr. Jarlcot.

"It's all right, I dare say," said Mr. Marston, vaguely, looking from man to man uncertainly. "I expected a will, of course: I don't suppose I have a friend among you, gentlemen, why should I? I am sure I have some enemies. I don't know what country attorneys, and nincompoops, and Golden Friars' bumpkins may think of it, but I know what the world will think, that I'm swindled by d—d conspiracy, and that that old man, who's in his grave, has behaved like a villain."

"Oh, Mr. Marston, your dead uncle!" said the good vicar, lifting his hand in deprecation, with gentle horror. "You wouldn't, you can't!"

"What the devil is it to you, sir?" cried Marston, with a look as if he could have struck him. "I say it's all influence, and d—d juggling—I'm not such a simpleton. No one expected, of course, that opportunities like those should not have been improved. The thing's transparent. I wish you joy, Mr. Blount, of your five hundred a year, and you, Mr. Jarlcot, of your approaching management of the estates and the money. If you fancy a will like that, turning his own nephew adrift on the world in favour of methodists and attorneys, and a girl he never saw till the other day, is to pass unchallenged, you're very much mistaken; it's just the thing that always happens when an old man like that dies—there's a will of course—every one understands it. I'll have you all where you won't like."

Mrs. Shackleton, with her mouth pursed, her nose high in the air, and her brows knit over a vivid pair of eyes, was the only one of the group who seemed ready to explode in reply; Mr. Blount looked simply shocked and confounded; the vicar maintained his bewildered and appealing stare; Mr. Spaight's eyebrows were elevated above his spectacles, and his mouth opened, as he leaned forward his long nose; Mr. Jarlcot's brow looked thunderous, and his chops a little flushed; all were staring for some seconds in silence on Mr. Marston, whose concluding sentences had risen almost to a shriek, with a laugh running through it.

"I think, Mr. Marston," said Jarlcot, after a couple of efforts, "you would do well to—to consider, a little, the bearing of your language; I don't think you can quite see its force."

"I wish you could—I mean it; and I'm d—d but you shall feel it too! You shall hear of me sooner than you all think. I'm not a fellow to be pigeoned so simply."

With these words, he walked into the hall, and a few moments after they heard the door shut with a violent clang.

A solemn silence reigned in the room for a little time; these peaceable people seemed stunned by the explosion.

"Evasit, erupit," murmured the vicar, sadly, raising his hands, and shaking his head. "How very painful!"

"I don't wonder—I make great allowances," said Mr. Blount, "I have been very unhappy myself, ever since it was ascertained that he had not executed the new will. I am afraid the young man will never consent to accept a part of my annuity—he is so spirited."

"Don't be uneasy on that point," said Mr. Jarlcot; "if you lodge it, he'll draw it; not—but I think—you might do—better—with your money."

There was something in the tone, undefinable, that prompted a dark curiosity.

Mr. Blount turned on him a quick look of inquiry. Mr. Jarlcot lowered his eyes, and then turned them to the window, with the remark that the summer was making a long stay this year.

Mr. Blount looked down and slowly rubbed his forehead, thinking, and sighing deeply, as he said, "It's a wonderful world, this—may the Lord have mercy on us all!"

CHAPTER LXXI.

A WOMAN'S HEART.

Two or three notices, which, Mr. Jarlcot said, would not cost five pounds, were served on behalf of Mr. Marston, and with these the faint echo of his thunders subsided. There was, in fact, no material for litigation.

"The notices," Mr. Jarlcot said, "came from Marshall and Whitaker, the solicitors who had years before submitted the cases for him, upon his uncle's title, and upon the question of his own position as nearest of kin and heir-at-law. He was very carefully advised as to how exactly he should stand in the event of his uncle's dying intestate."

I was stunned when I heard of my enormous fortune, involving, as it did, his ruin. I would at once have taken measures to deal as generously with him as the other will, of which I then knew no more than that Sir Harry must have contemplated, at one time, the possibility at least of signing it.

When I left Golden Friars I did so with an unalterable resolution never to see Richard Marston again. But this was compatible with the spirit of my intention to provide more suitably for him. I took Mr. Blount into council; but I was disappointed. The will had been made during my father's lifetime, and in evident apprehension of his influence over me, and deprived me of the power of making any charge upon the property, whether land or money. I could do nothing but make him a yearly present of a part of my income, and even that was embarrassed by many ingenious conditions and difficulties.

It was about this time that a letter reached me from Richard Marston, the most extraordinary I had ever read—a mad letter in parts, and wicked—a letter, also, full of penitence and self-upbraiding. "I am a fiend. I have been all cruelty and falsehood, you all mercy and truth," it said. "I have heard of your noble wishes—I know how vain they are. You can do nothing that I would accept. I am well enough. Think no more of the wretch. I have found, too late, I cannot live without you. You shall hear of me no more; only forgive me."

There are parts of this strange letter that I never understood, that may bear many interpretations, no one distinctly.

When Mr. Blount spoke of him he never gave me his conclusions, and it was always in the sad form "Let us hope;" he never said exactly what he suspected. Mr. Jarlcot plainly had but one opinion of him, and that the worst.

I agreed, I think, with neither. I relied on instinct, which no one can analyse or define—the wild inspiration of nature—the saddest, and often the truest guide. Let me not condemn, then, lest I be condemned.

The good here are not without wickedness, nor the wicked without goodness. With death begins the defection. Each character will be sifted as wheat. The eternal Judge will reduce each, by the irresistible chemistry of his power and truth, to its basis, for neither hell nor heaven can receive a mixed character.

I did hear of Richard Marston again once more—it was about five months later, when the news of his death by fever, at Marseilles, reached Mr. Blount.

Since then my life has been a retrospect. Two years I passed in India with my beloved friend, Laura. But my melancholy grew deeper; the shadows lengthened—and an irrepressible yearning to revisit Golden Friars and Malory seized me. I returned to England.

I am possessed of fortune. I thank God for its immunities—I well know how great they are. For its pleasures, I have long ceased to care. To the poor, I try to make it useful—but I am quite conscious that in this there is no merit. I have no pleasure in money. I think I have none in flattery. I need deny myself nothing, and yet be in the eyes of those who measure charity arithmetically a princely Christian benefactress. I wish I were quite sure of having ever given a cup of cold water in the spirit that my Maker commends.

A few weeks after my return, Mr. Blount showed me a letter. The signature startled me. It was from Monsieur Droqville, and a very short one. It was chiefly upon some trifling business, and it said, near the end:

"You sometimes see Miss Ware, I believe; she will be sorry to hear that her old friend, Mr. Carmel, died last summer at his missionary post in South America. A truer soldier of Christ never fell in the field of his labours. Requiescat!"

There was a tremble at my heart, and a swelling. I held the sentence before my eyes till they filled with tears.

My faithful, noble friend! At my side in every trouble. The one of all mortals I have met who strove with his whole heart to win me, according to his lights, to God. May God receive and for ever bless you for it, patient, gentle Edwyn Carmel! His griefs are over. To me there seems an angelic light around him—the pale enthusiast in the robe of his purity stands saint-like before me. I remember all your tender care. I better understand, too, the wide differences that separated us, now, than in my careless girlhood—but these do not dismay me. I know that "in my father's house are many mansions," and I hope that when the clouds that darken this life are passed, we may yet meet and thank and bless you, my noble-hearted friend, where, in one love and light, the redeemed shall walk for evermore.

At Golden Friars I lived again for a short time. But the associations of Dorracleugh were too new and harrowing. I left that place to the care of good Mr.

Blount, who loves it better than any other. He pays me two or three visits every year at Malory, and advises me in all matters of business.

I do not affect the airs of an anchorite. But my life is, most people would think, intolerably monotonous and lonely. To me it is not only endurable, but the sweetest that, in my peculiar state of mind, I could have chosen.

With the flight of my years, and the slow approach of the hour when dust will return to dust, the love of solitude steals on me, and no regrets for the days I have lost, as my friends insist, and no yearnings for a return to an insincere and tawdry world, have ever troubled me. In girlhood I contracted my love of this simple rural solitude, and my premature experience of all that is disappointing and deplorable in life confirms it. But the spell of its power is in its recollections. It is a place, unlike Dorracleugh, sunny and cheerful, as well as beautiful, and this tones the melancholy of its visions, and prevents their sadness from becoming overpowering.

I wonder how many people are living, like me, altogether in the past, and in hourly communion with visionary companions?

Richard Marston, does awaking hour ever pass without, at some moment, recalling your image? I do not mistake you; I have used no measured language in describing you. I know you for the evil, fascinating, reckless man you were. Such a man as, had I never seen you, and only known the sum of his character, I ought to have hated. A man who, being such as he was, meditated against me a measureless wrong. I look into my heart, is there vengeance there against you? Is there judgment? Is there even alienation?

Oh! how is it that reason, justice, virtue, all cannot move you from a secret place in my inmost heart? Can any man who has once been an idol, such as you were, ever perish utterly in that mysterious shrine—a woman's heart? In solitary hours, as I, unseen, look along the sea, my cheeks are wet with tears; in the wide silence of the night my lonely sobs are heard. Is my grief for you mere madness? Why is it that man so differs from man? Why does he often so differ from the noble creature he might have been, and sometimes almost was?

Over an image partly dreamed and partly real, shivered utterly, but still in memory visible, I pour out the vainest of all sorrows.

In the wonderful working that subdues all things to itself—in all the changes of spirit, or the spaces of eternity, is there, shall there never be, from the first failure, evolved the nobler thing that might have been? I care for no other. I can love no other; and were I to live and keep my youth through eternity, I think I never could be interested or won again. Solitude has become dear to me, because he is in it. Am I giving this infinite true love in vain? I comfort myself with one vague hope. I cannot think that nature is so cynical. Does the loved phantom represent nothing? And is the fidelity that nature claims, but an infatuation and a waste?

UNCLE SILAS

A Tale of Bartram-Haugh

TO
THE RIGHT HON.
THE COUNTESS OF GIFFORD,
AS A TOKEN OF
RESPECT, SYMPATHY, AND
ADMIRATION
This Tale
IS INSCRIBED BY
THE AUTHOR

A PRELIMINARY WORD

The writer of this Tale ventures, in his own person, to address a very few words, chiefly of explanation, to his readers. A leading situation in this 'Story of Bartram-Haugh' is repeated, with a slight variation, from a short magazine tale of some fifteen pages written by him, and published long ago in a periodical under the title of 'A Passage in the Secret History of an Irish Countess,' and afterwards, still anonymously, in a small volume under an altered title. It is very unlikely that any of his readers should have encountered, and still more so that they should remember, this trifle. The bare possibility, however, he has ventured to anticipate by this brief explanation, lest he should be charged with plagiarism—always a disrespect to a reader.

May he be permitted a few words also of remonstrance against the promiscuous application of the term 'sensation' to that large school of fiction which transgresses no one of those canons of construction and morality which, in producing the unapproachable 'Waverley Novels,' their great author imposed upon himself? No one, it is assumed, would describe Sir Walter Scott's romances as 'sensation novels;' yet in that marvellous series there is not a single tale in which death, crime, and, in some form, mystery, have not a place.

Passing by those grand romances of 'Ivanhoe,' 'Old Mortality,' and 'Kenilworth,' with their terrible intricacies of crime and bloodshed, constructed with so fine a mastery of the art of exciting suspense and horror, let the reader pick out those two exceptional novels in the series which profess to paint contemporary manners and the scenes of common life; and remembering in the 'Antiquary' the vision in the tapestried chamber, the duel, the horrible secret, and the death of old Elspeth, the drowned fisherman, and above all the tremendous situation of the tide-bound party under the cliffs; and in 'St. Ronan's Well,' the long-drawn mystery, the suspicion of insanity, and the catastrophe of suicide;—determine whether an epithet which it would be a profanation to apply to the structure of any, even the most exciting of Sir Walter Scott's stories, is fairly applicable to tales which, though illimitably inferior in execution, yet observe the same limitations of incident, and the same moral aims.

The author trusts that the Press, to whose masterly criticism and generous encouragement he and other humble labourers in the art owe so much, will insist upon the limitation of that degrading term to the peculiar type of fiction which it was originally intended to indicate, and prevent, as they may, its being made to include the legitimate school of tragic English romance, which has been ennobled, and in great measure founded, by the genius of Sir Walter Scott.

CHAPTER I

AUSTIN RUTHYN, OF KNOWL, AND HIS DAUGHTER

It was winter—that is, about the second week in November—and great gusts were rattling at the windows, and wailing and thundering among our tall trees and ivied chimneys—a very dark night, and a very cheerful fire blazing, a pleasant mixture of good round coal and spluttering dry wood, in a genuine old fireplace, in a sombre old room. Black wainscoting glimmered up to the ceiling, in small ebony panels; a cheerful clump of wax candles on the tea-table; many old portraits, some grim and pale, others pretty, and some very graceful and charming, hanging from the walls. Few pictures, except portraits long and short, were there. On the whole, I think you would have taken the room for our parlour. It was not like our modern notion of a drawing-room. It was a long room too, and every way capacious, but irregularly shaped.

A girl, of a little more than seventeen, looking, I believe, younger still; slight and rather tall, with a great deal of golden hair, dark grey-eyed, and with a countenance rather sensitive and melancholy, was sitting at the tea-table, in a reverie. I was that girl.

The only other person in the room—the only person in the house related to me—was my father. He was Mr. Ruthyn, of Knowl, so called in his county, but he had many other places, was of a very ancient lineage, who had refused a baronetage often, and it was said even a viscounty, being of a proud and defiant spirit, and thinking themselves higher in station and purer of blood than two-thirds of the nobility into whose ranks, it was said, they had been invited to enter. Of all this family lore I knew but little and vaguely; only what is to be gathered from the fireside talk of old retainers in the nursery.

I am sure my father loved me, and I know I loved him. With the sure instinct of childhood I apprehended his tenderness, although it was never expressed in common ways. But my father was an oddity. He had been early disappointed in Parliament, where it was his ambition to succeed. Though a clever man, he failed there, where very inferior men did extremely well. Then he went abroad, and became a connoisseur and a collector; took a part, on his return, in literary and scientific institutions, and also in the foundation and direction of some charities.

But he tired of this mimic government, and gave himself up to a country life, not that of a sportsman, but rather of a student, staying sometimes at one of his places and sometimes at another, and living a secluded life.

Rather late in life he married, and his beautiful young wife died, leaving me, their only child, to his care. This bereavement, I have been told, changed him—made him more odd and taciturn than ever, and his temper also, except to me, more severe. There was also some disgrace about his younger brother—my uncle Silas—which he felt bitterly.

He was now walking up and down this spacious old room, which, extending round an angle at the far end, was very dark in that quarter. It was his wont to walk up and down thus, without speaking—an exercise which used to remind me of Chateaubriand's father in the great chamber of the Château de Combourg. At the far end he nearly disappeared in the gloom, and then returning emerged for a few minutes, like a portrait with a background of shadow, and then again in silence faded nearly out of view.

This monotony and silence would have been terrifying to a person less accustomed to it than I. As it was, it had its effect. I have known my father a whole day without once speaking to me. Though I loved him very much, I was also much in awe of him.

While my father paced the floor, my thoughts were employed about the events of a month before. So few things happened at Knowl out of the accustomed routine, that a very trifling occurrence was enough to set people wondering and conjecturing in that serene household. My father lived in remarkable seclusion; except for a ride, he hardly ever left the grounds of Knowl; and I don't think it happened twice in the year that a visitor sojourned among us.

There was not even that mild religious bustle which sometimes besets the wealthy and moral recluse. My father had left the Church of England for some odd sect, I forget its name, and ultimately became, I was told, a Swedenborgian. But he did not care to trouble me upon the subject. So the old carriage brought my governess, when I had one, the old housekeeper, Mrs. Rusk, and myself to the parish church every Sunday. And my father, in the view of the honest rector who shook his head over him—'a cloud without water, carried about of winds, and a wandering star to whom is reserved the blackness of darkness'—corresponded with the 'minister' of his church, and was provokingly contented with his own fertility and illumination; and Mrs. Rusk, who was a sound and bitter churchwoman, said he fancied he saw visions and talked with angels like the rest of that 'rubbitch.'

I don't know that she had any better foundation than analogy and conjecture for charging my father with supernatural pretensions; and in all points when her orthodoxy was not concerned, she loved her master and was a loyal housekeeper.

I found her one morning superintending preparations for the reception of a visitor, in the hunting-room it was called, from the pieces of tapestry that covered its walls, representing scenes *à la Wouvermans*, of falconry, and the chase, dogs, hawks, ladies, gallants, and pages. In the midst of whom Mrs. Rusk, in black silk, was rummaging drawers, counting linen, and issuing orders.

'Who is coming, Mrs. Rusk?'

Well, she only knew his name. It was a Mr. Bryerly. My papa expected him to dinner, and to stay for some days.

'I guess he's one of those creatures, dear, for I mentioned his name just to Dr. Clay (the rector), and he says there *is* a Doctor Bryerly, a great conjurer among the Swedenborg sect—and that's him, I do suppose.'

In my hazy notions of these sectaries there was mingled a suspicion of necromancy, and a weird freemasonry, that inspired something of awe and antipathy.

Mr. Bryerly arrived time enough to dress at his leisure, before dinner. He entered the drawing-room—a tall, lean man, all in ungainly black, with a white choker, with either a black wig, or black hair dressed in imitation of one, a pair of spectacles, and a dark, sharp, short visage, rubbing his large hands together, and with a short brisk nod to me, whom he plainly regarded merely as a child, he sat down before the fire, crossed his legs, and took up a magazine.

This treatment was mortifying, and I remember very well the resentment of which *he* was quite unconscious.

His stay was not very long; not one of us divined the object of his visit, and he did not prepossess us favourably. He seemed restless, as men of busy habits do in country houses, and took walks, and a drive, and read in the library, and wrote half a dozen letters.

His bed-room and dressing-room were at the side of the gallery, directly opposite to my father's, which had a sort of ante-room *en suite*, in which were some of his theological books.

The day after Mr. Bryerly's arrival, I was about to see whether my father's water caraffe and glass had been duly laid on the table in this ante-room, and in doubt whether he was there, I knocked at the door.

I suppose they were too intent on other matters to hear, but receiving no answer, I entered the room. My father was sitting in his chair, with his coat and waistcoat off, Mr. Bryerly kneeling on a stool beside him, rather facing him, his black scratch wig leaning close to my father's grizzled hair. There was a large tome of their divinity lore, I suppose, open on the table close by. The lank black figure of Mr. Bryerly stood up, and he concealed something quickly in the breast of his coat.

My father stood up also, looking paler, I think, than I ever saw him till then, and he pointed grimly to the door, and said, 'Go.'

Mr. Bryerly pushed me gently back with his hands to my shoulders, and smiled down from his dark features with an expression quite unintelligible to me.

I had recovered myself in a second, and withdrew without a word. The last thing I saw at the door was the tall, slim figure in black, and the dark, significant smile following me: and then the door was shut and locked, and the two Swedenborgians were left to their mysteries.

I remember so well the kind of shock and disgust I felt in the certainty that I had surprised them at some, perhaps, debasing incantation—a suspicion of this Mr. Bryerly, of the ill-fitting black coat, and white choker—and a sort of fear came upon me, and I fancied he was asserting some kind of mastery over my father, which very much alarmed me.

I fancied all sorts of dangers in the enigmatical smile of the lank high-priest. The image of my father, as I had seen him, it might be, confessing to this man in black, who was I knew not what, haunted me with the disagreeable uncertainties of a mind very uninstructed as to the limits of the marvellous.

I mentioned it to no one. But I was immensely relieved when the sinister visitor took his departure the morning after, and it was upon this occurrence that my mind was now employed.

Some one said that Dr. Johnson resembled a ghost, who must be spoken to before it will speak. But my father, in whatever else he may have resembled a ghost, did not in that particular; for no one but I in his household—and I very seldom—dared to address him until first addressed by him. I had no notion how singular this was until I began to go out a little among friends and relations, and found no such rule in force anywhere else.

As I leaned back in my chair thinking, this phantasm of my father came, and turned, and vanished with a solemn regularity. It was a peculiar figure, strongly made, thick-set, with a face large, and very stern; he wore a loose, black velvet coat and waistcoat. It was, however, the figure of an elderly rather than an old man—though he was then past seventy—but firm, and with no sign of feebleness.

I remember the start with which, not suspecting that he was close by me, I lifted my eyes, and saw that large, rugged countenance looking fixedly on me, from less than a yard away.

After I saw him, he continued to regard me for a second or two; and then, taking one of the heavy candlesticks in his gnarled hand, he beckoned me to follow him; which, in silence and wondering, I accordingly did.

He led me across the hall, where there were lights burning, and into a lobby by the foot of the back stairs, and so into his library.

It is a long, narrow room, with two tall, slim windows at the far end, now draped in dark curtains. Dusky it was with but one candle; and he paused near the door, at the left-hand side of which stood, in those days, an old-fashioned press or cabinet of carved oak. In front of this he stopped.

He had odd, absent ways, and talked more to himself, I believe, than to all the rest of the world put together.

'She won't understand,' he whispered, looking at me enquiringly. 'No, she won't. *Will* she?'

Then there was a pause, during which he brought forth from his breast pocket a small bunch of some half-dozen keys, on one of which he looked frowningly, every now and then balancing it a little before his eyes, between his finger and thumb, as he deliberated.

I knew him too well, of course, to interpose a word.

'They are easily frightened—ay, they are. I'd better do it another way.'

And pausing, he looked in my face as he might upon a picture.

'They *are*—yes—I had better do it another way—another way; yes—and she'll not suspect—she'll not suppose.'

Then he looked steadfastly upon the key, and from it to me, suddenly lifting it up, and said abruptly, 'See, child,' and, after a second or two, '*Remember* this key.'

It was oddly shaped, and unlike others.

'Yes, sir.' I always called him 'sir.'

'It opens that,' and he tapped it sharply on the door of the cabinet. 'In the day-time it is always here,' at which word he dropped it into his pocket again. 'You see?—and at night under my pillow—you hear me?'

'Yes, sir.'

'You won't forget this cabinet—oak—next the door—on your left—you won't forget?'

'No, sir.'

'Pity she's a girl, and so young—ay, a girl, and so young—no sense—giddy. You say, you'll *remember*?'

'Yes, sir.'

'It behoves you.'

He turned round and looked full upon me, like a man who has taken a sudden resolution; and I think for a moment he had made up his mind to tell me a great deal more. But if so, he changed it again; and after another pause, he said slowly and sternly—'You will tell nobody what I have said, under pain of my displeasure.'

'Oh! no, sir!'

'Good child!'

'*Except*,' he resumed, 'under one contingency; that is, in case I should be absent, and Dr. Bryerly—you recollect the thin gentleman, in spectacles and a black wig, who spent three days here last month—should come and enquire for the key, you understand, in my absence.'

'Yes, sir.'

So he kissed me on the forehead, and said—

'Let us return.'

Which, accordingly, we did, in silence; the storm outside, like a dirge on a great organ, accompanying our flitting.

CHAPTER II

UNCLE SILAS

When we reached the drawing-room, I resumed my chair, and my father his slow and regular walk to and fro, in the great room. Perhaps it was the uproar of the wind that disturbed the ordinary tenor of his thoughts; but, whatever was the cause, certainly he was unusually talkative that night.

After an interval of nearly half an hour, he drew near again, and sat down in a high-backed arm-chair, beside the fire, and nearly opposite to me, and looked at me steadfastly for some time, as was his wont, before speaking; and said he—

'This won't do—you must have a governess.'

In cases of this kind I merely set down my book or work, as it might be, and adjusted myself to listen without speaking.

'Your French is pretty well, and your Italian; but you have no German. Your music may be pretty good—I'm no judge—but your drawing might be better—yes—yes. I believe there are accomplished ladies—finishing governesses, they call them—who undertake more than any one teacher would have professed in my time, and do very well. She can prepare you, and next winter, then, you shall visit France and Italy, where you may be accomplished as highly as you please.'

'Thank you, sir.'

'You shall. It is nearly six months since Miss Ellerton left you—too long without a teacher.'

Then followed an interval.

'Dr. Bryerly will ask you about that key, and what it opens; you show all that to *him*, and no one else.'

'But,' I said, for I had a great terror of disobeying him in ever so minute a matter, 'you will then be absent, sir—how am I to find the key?'

He smiled on me suddenly—a bright but wintry smile—it seldom came, and was very transitory, and kindly though mysterious.

'True, child; I'm glad you are so wise; *that*, you will find, I have provided for, and you shall know exactly where to look. You have remarked how solitarily I live. You fancy, perhaps, I have not got a friend, and you are nearly right—

nearly, but not altogether. I have a very sure friend—*one*—a friend whom I once misunderstood, but now appreciate.'

I wondered silently whether it could be Uncle Silas.

'He'll make me a call, some day soon; I'm not quite sure when. I won't tell you his name—you'll hear that soon enough, and I don't want it talked of; and I must make a little journey with him. You'll not be afraid of being left alone for a time?'

'And have you promised, sir?' I answered, with another question, my curiosity and anxiety overcoming my awe. He took my questioning very good-humouredly.

'Well—*promise*?—no, child; but I'm under condition; he's not to be denied. I must make the excursion with him the moment he calls. I have no choice; but, on the whole, I rather like it—remember, I say, I rather *like* it.'

And he smiled again, with the same meaning, that was at once stern and sad. The exact purport of these sentences remained fixed in my mind, so that even at this distance of time I am quite sure of them.

A person quite unacquainted with my father's habitually abrupt and odd way of talking, would have fancied that he was possibly a little disordered in his mind. But no such suspicion for a moment troubled me. I was quite sure that he spoke of a real person who was coming, and that his journey was something momentous; and when the visitor of whom he spoke did come, and he departed with him upon that mysterious excursion, I perfectly understood his language and his reasons for saying so much and yet so little.

You are not to suppose that all my hours were passed in the sort of conference and isolation of which I have just given you a specimen; and singular and even awful as were sometimes my *tête-a-têtes* with my father, I had grown so accustomed to his strange ways, and had so unbounded a confidence in his affection, that they never depressed or agitated me in the manner you might have supposed. I had a great deal of quite a different sort of chat with good old Mrs. Rusk, and very pleasant talks with Mary Quince, my somewhat ancient maid; and besides all this, I had now and then a visit of a week or so at the house of some one of our country neighbours, and occasionally a visitor—but this, I must own, very rarely—at Knowl.

There had come now a little pause in my father's revelations, and my fancy wandered away upon a flight of discovery. Who, I again thought, could this intending visitor be, who was to come, armed with the prerogative to make my stay-at-home father forthwith leave his household goods—his books and his child—to whom he clung, and set forth on an unknown knight-errantry? Who but Uncle Silas, I thought—that mysterious relative whom I had never seen—who was, it had in old times been very darkly hinted to me, unspeakably unfortunate or unspeakably vicious—whom I had seldom heard my father mention, and then in a hurried way, and with a pained, thoughtful look. Once only he had said anything from which I could gather my father's opinion of him, and then it was so slight and enigmatical that I might have filled in the character very nearly as I pleased.

It happened thus. One day Mrs. Rusk was in the oak-room, I being then about fourteen. She was removing a stain from a tapestry chair, and I watched the process with a childish interest. She sat down to rest herself—she had been stooping over her work—and threw her head back, for her neck was weary, and in this position she fixed her eyes on a portrait that hung before her.

It was a full-length, and represented a singularly handsome young man, dark, slender, elegant, in a costume then quite obsolete, though I believe it was seen at the beginning of this century—white leather pantaloons and top-boots, a buff waistcoat, and a chocolate-coloured coat, and the hair long and brushed back.

There was a remarkable elegance and a delicacy in the features, but also a character of resolution and ability that quite took the portrait out of the category of mere fops or fine men. When people looked at it for the first time, I have so often heard the exclamation—'What a wonderfully handsome man!' and then, 'What a clever face!' An Italian greyhound stood by him, and some slender columns and a rich drapery in the background. But though the accessories were of the luxurious sort, and the beauty, as I have said, refined, there was a masculine force in that slender oval face, and a fire in the large, shadowy eyes, which were very peculiar, and quite redeemed it from the suspicion of effeminacy.

'Is not that Uncle Silas?' said I.

'Yes, dear,' answered Mrs. Rusk, looking, with her resolute little face, quietly on the portrait.

'He must be a very handsome man, Mrs. Rusk. Don't you think so?' I continued.

'He *was*, my dear—yes; but it is forty years since that was painted—the date is there in the corner, in the shadow that comes from his foot, and forty years, I can tell you, makes a change in most of us;' and Mrs. Rusk laughed, in cynical good-humour.

There was a little pause, both still looking on the handsome man in top-boots, and I said—

'And why, Mrs. Rusk, is papa always so sad about Uncle Silas?'

'What's that, child?' said my father's voice, very near. I looked round, with a start, and flushed and faltered, receding a step from him.

'No harm, dear. You have said nothing wrong,' he said gently, observing my alarm. 'You said I was always sad, I think, about Uncle Silas. Well, I don't know how you gather that; but if I were, I will now tell you, it would not be unnatural. Your uncle is a man of great talents, great faults, and great wrongs. His talents have not availed him; his faults are long ago repented of; and his wrongs I believe he feels less than I do, but they are deep. Did she say any more, madam?' he demanded abruptly of Mrs. Rusk.

'Nothing, sir,' with a stiff little courtesy, answered Mrs. Rusk, who stood in awe of him.

'And there is no need, child,' he continued, addressing himself to me, 'that you should think more of him at present. Clear your head of Uncle Silas. One day, perhaps, you will know him—yes, very well—and understand how villains have injured him.

Then my father retired, and at the door he said—

'Mrs. Rusk, a word, if you please,' beckoning to that lady, who trotted after him to the library.

I think he then laid some injunction upon the housekeeper, which was transmitted by her to Mary Quince, for from that time forth I could never lead either to talk with me about Uncle Silas. They let me talk on, but were reserved and silent themselves, and seemed embarrassed, and Mrs. Rusk sometimes pettish and angry, when I pressed for information.

Thus curiosity was piqued; and round the slender portrait in the leather pantaloons and top-boots gathered many-coloured circles of mystery, and the handsome features seemed to smile down upon my baffled curiosity with a provoking significance.

Why is it that this form of ambition—curiosity—which entered into the temptation of our first parent, is so specially hard to resist? Knowledge is power—and power of one sort or another is the secret lust of human souls; and here is, beside the sense of exploration, the undefinable interest of a story, and above all, something forbidden, to stimulate the contumacious appetite.

CHAPTER III

A NEW FACE

I think it was about a fortnight after that conversation in which my father had expressed his opinion, and given me the mysterious charge about the old oak cabinet in his library, as already detailed, that I was one night sitting at the great drawing-room window, lost in the melancholy reveries of night, and in admiration of the moonlighted scene. I was the only occupant of the room; and the lights near the fire, at its farther end, hardly reached to the window at which I sat.

The shorn grass sloped gently downward from the windows till it met the broad level on which stood, in clumps, or solitarily scattered, some of the noblest timber in England. Hoar in the moonbeams stood those graceful trees casting their moveless shadows upon the grass, and in the background crowning the undulations of the distance, in masses, were piled those woods among which lay the solitary tomb where the remains of my beloved mother rested.

The air was still. The silvery vapour hung serenely on the far horizon, and the frosty stars blinked brightly. Everyone knows the effect of such a scene on a mind already saddened. Fancies and regrets float mistily in the dream, and the scene affects us with a strange mixture of memory and anticipation, like some sweet old air heard in the distance. As my eyes rested on those, to me, funereal but glorious woods, which formed the background of the picture, my thoughts recurred to my father's mysterious intimations and the image of the approaching visitor; and the thought of the unknown journey saddened me.

In all that concerned his religion, from very early association, there was to me something of the unearthly and spectral.

When my dear mamma died I was not nine years old; and I remember, two days before the funeral, there came to Knowl, where she died, a thin little man, with large black eyes, and a very grave, dark face.

He was shut up a good deal with my dear father, who was in deep affliction; and Mrs. Rusk used to say, 'It is rather odd to see him praying with that little scarecrow from London, and good Mr. Clay ready at call, in the village; much good that little black whipper-snapper will do him!'

With that little black man, on the day after the funeral, I was sent out, for some reason, for a walk; my governess was ill, I know, and there was confusion in the house, and I dare say the maids made as much of a holiday as they could.

I remember feeling a sort of awe of this little dark man; but I was not afraid of him, for he was gentle, though sad—and seemed kind. He led me into the garden—the Dutch garden, we used to call it—with a balustrade, and statues at the farther front, laid out in a carpet-pattern of brilliantly-coloured flowers. We came down the broad flight of Caen stone steps into this, and we walked in silence to the balustrade. The base was too high at the spot where we reached it for me to see over; but holding my hand, he said, 'Look through that, my child. Well, you can't; but *I* can see beyond it—shall I tell you what? I see ever so much. I see a cottage with a steep roof, that looks like gold in the sunlight; there are tall trees throwing soft shadows round it, and flowering shrubs, I can't say what, only the colours are beautiful, growing by the walls and windows, and two little children are playing among the stems of the trees, and we are on our way there, and in a few minutes shall be under those trees ourselves, and talking to those little children. Yet now to me it is but a picture in my brain, and to you but a story told by me, which you believe. Come, dear; let us be going.'

So we descended the steps at the right, and side by side walked along the grass lane between tall trim walls of evergreens. The way was in deep shadow, for the sun was near the horizon; but suddenly we turned to the left, and there we stood in rich sunlight, among the many objects he had described.

'Is this your house, my little men?' he asked of the children—pretty little rosy boys—who assented; and he leaned with his open hand against the stem of one of the trees, and with a grave smile he nodded down to me, saying—

'You see now, and hear, and *feel* for yourself that both the vision and the story were quite true; but come on, my dear, we have further to go.'

And relapsing into silence we had a long ramble through the wood, the same on which I was now looking in the distance. Every now and then he made me sit down to rest, and he in a musing solemn sort of way would relate some little story, reflecting, even to my childish mind, a strange suspicion of a spiritual meaning, but different from what honest Mrs. Rusk used to expound to me from the Parables, and, somehow, startling in its very vagueness.

Thus entertained, though a little awfully, I accompanied the dark mysterious little 'whipper-snapper' through the woodland glades. We came, to me quite unexpectedly, in the deep sylvan shadows, upon the grey, pillared temple, four-fronted, with a slanting pedestal of lichen-stained steps, the lonely sepulchre in which I had the morning before seen poor mamma laid. At the sight the fountains of my grief reopened, and I cried bitterly, repeating, 'Oh! mamma, mamma, little mamma!' and so went on weeping and calling wildly on the deaf and the silent. There was a stone bench some ten steps away from the tomb.

'Sit down beside me, my child,' said the grave man with the black eyes, very kindly and gently. 'Now, what do you see there?' he asked, pointing horizontally with his stick towards the centre of the opposite structure.

'Oh, *that*—that place where poor mamma is?'

'Yes, a stone wall with pillars, too high for either you or me to see over. But——'

Here he mentioned a name which I think must have been Swedenborg, from what I afterwards learnt of his tenets and revelations; I only know that it sounded to me like the name of a magician in a fairy tale; I fancied he lived in the wood which surrounded us, and I began to grow frightened as he proceeded.

'But Swedenborg sees beyond it, over, and *through* it, and has told me all that concerns us to know. He says your mamma is not there.'

'She is taken away!' I cried, starting up, and with streaming eyes, gazing on the building which, though I stamped my feet in my distraction, I was afraid to approach. 'Oh, *is* mamma taken away? Where is she? Where have they brought her to?'

I was uttering unconsciously very nearly the question with which Mary, in the grey of that wondrous morning on which she stood by the empty sepulchre, accosted the figure standing near.

'Your mamma is alive but too far away to see or hear us. Swedenborg, standing here, can see and hear her, and tells me all he sees, just as I told you in the garden about the little boys and the cottage, and the trees and flowers which you could not see. You believed in when *I* told you. So I can tell you now as I did then; and as we are both, I hope, walking on to the same place just as we did to the trees and cottage. You will surely see with your own eyes how true the description is which I give you.'

I was very frightened, for I feared that when he had done his narrative we were to walk on through the wood into that place of wonders and of shadows where the dead were visible.

He leaned his elbow on his knee, and his forehead on his hand, which shaded his downcast eyes. In that attitude he described to me a beautiful landscape, radiant with a wondrous light, in which, rejoicing, my mother moved along an airy path, ascending among mountains of fantastic height, and peaks, melting in celestial colouring into the air, and peopled with human beings translated into the same image, beauty, and splendour. And when he had ended his relation, he rose, took my hand, and smiling gently down on my pale, wondering face, he said the same words he had spoken before—

'Come, dear, let us go.'

'Oh! no, no, *no*—not now,' I said, resisting, and very much frightened.

'Home, I mean, dear. We cannot walk to the place I have described. We can only reach it through the gate of death, to which we are all tending, young and old, with sure steps.'

'And where is the gate of death?' I asked in a sort of whisper, as we walked together, holding his hand, and looking stealthily. He smiled sadly and said—

'When, sooner or later, the time comes, as Hagar's eyes were opened in the wilderness, and she beheld the fountain of water, so shall each of us see the door open before us, and enter in and be refreshed.'

For a long time following this walk I was very nervous; more so for the awful manner in which Mrs. Rusk received my statement—with stern lips and upturned hands and eyes, and an angry expostulation: 'I do wonder at you, Mary Quince, letting the child walk into the wood with that limb of darkness. It is a mercy he did not show her the devil, or frighten her out of her senses, in that lonely place!'

Of these Swedenborgians, indeed, I know no more than I might learn from good Mrs. Rusk's very inaccurate talk. Two or three of them crossed in the course of my early life, like magic-lantern figures, the disk of my very circumscribed observation. All outside was and is darkness. I once tried to read one of their books upon the future state—heaven and hell; but I grew after a day or two so nervous that I laid it aside. It is enough for me to know that their founder either saw or fancied he saw amazing visions, which, so far from superseding, confirmed and interpreted the language of the Bible; and as dear papa accepted their ideas, I am happy in thinking that they did not conflict with the supreme authority of holy writ.

Leaning on my hand, I was now looking upon that solemn wood, white and shadowy in the moonlight, where, for a long time after that ramble with the visionary, I fancied the gate of death, hidden only by a strange glamour, and the dazzling land of ghosts, were situate; and I suppose these earlier associations gave to my reverie about my father's coming visitor a wilder and a sadder tinge.

CHAPTER IV

MADAME DE LA ROUGIERRE

On a sudden, on the grass before me, stood an odd figure—a very tall woman in grey draperies, nearly white under the moon, courtesying extraordinarily low, and rather fantastically.

I stared in something like a horror upon the large and rather hollow features which I did not know, smiling very unpleasantly on me; and the moment it was plain that I saw her, the grey woman began gobbling and cackling shrilly—I could not distinctly hear *what* through the window—and gesticulating oddly with her long hands and arms.

As she drew near the window, I flew to the fireplace, and rang the bell frantically, and seeing her still there, and fearing that she might break into the room, I flew out of the door, very much frightened, and met Branston the butler in the lobby.

'There's a woman at the window!' I gasped; 'turn her away, please.'

If I had said a man, I suppose fat Branston would have summoned and sent forward a detachment of footmen. As it was, he bowed gravely, with a—

'Yes,'m—shall,'m.'

And with an air of authority approached the window.

I don't think that he was pleasantly impressed himself by the first sight of our visitor, for he stopped short some steps of the window, and demanded rather sternly—

'What ye doin' there, woman?'

To this summons, her answer, which occupied a little time, was inaudible to me. But Branston replied—

'I wasn't aware, ma'am; I heerd nothin'; if you'll go round *that* way, you'll see the hall-door steps, and I'll speak to the master, and do as he shall order.'

The figure said something and pointed.

'Yes, that's it, and ye can't miss the door.'

And Mr. Branston returned slowly down the long room, and halted with outturned pumps and a grave inclination before me, and the faintest amount of interrogation in the announcement—

'Please,'m, she says she's the governess.'

'The governess! *What* governess?'

Branston was too well-bred to smile, and he said thoughtfully—

'P'raps,'m, I'd best ask the master?'

To which I assented, and away strode the flat pumps of the butler to the library.

I stood breathless in the hall. Every girl at my age knows how much is involved in such an advent. I also heard Mrs. Rusk, in a minute or two more, emerge I suppose from the study. She walked quickly, and muttered sharply to herself—an evil trick, in which she indulged when much 'put about.' I should have been glad of a word with her; but I fancied she was vexed, and would not have talked satisfactorily. She did not, however, come my way; merely crossing the hall with her quick, energetic step.

Was it really the arrival of a governess? Was that apparition which had impressed me so unpleasantly to take the command of me—to sit alone with me, and haunt me perpetually with her sinister looks and shrilly gabble?

I was just making up my mind to go to Mary Quince, and learn something definite, when I heard my father's step approaching from the library: so I quietly re-entered the drawingroom, but with an anxious and throbbing heart.

When he came in, as usual, he patted me on the head gently, with a kind of smile, and then began his silent walk up and down the room. I was yearning to question him on the point that just then engrossed me so disagreeably; but the awe in which I stood of him forbade.

After a time he stopped at the window, the curtain of which I had drawn, and the shutter partly opened, and he looked out, perhaps with associations of his own, on the scene I had been contemplating.

It was not for nearly an hour after, that my father suddenly, after his wont, in a few words, apprised me of the arrival of Madame de la Rougierre to be my governess, highly recommended and perfectly qualified. My heart sank with a sure presage of ill. I already disliked, distrusted, and feared her.

I had more than an apprehension of her temper and fear of possibly abused authority. The large-featured, smirking phantom, saluting me so oddly in the moonlight, retained ever after its peculiar and unpleasant hold upon my nerves.

'Well, Miss Maud, dear, I hope you'll like your new governess—for it's more than *I* do, just at present at least,' said Mrs. Rusk, sharply—she was awaiting me in my room. 'I hate them French-women; they're not natural, I think. I gave her her supper in my room. She eats like a wolf, she does, the great raw-boned hannimal. I wish you saw her in bed as I did. I put her next the clock-room—she'll hear the hours betimes, I'm thinking. You never saw such a sight. The great long nose and hollow cheeks of her, and oogh! such a mouth! I felt a'most like little Red Riding-Hood—I did, Miss.'

Here honest Mary Quince, who enjoyed Mrs. Rusk's satire, a weapon in which she was not herself strong, laughed outright.

'Turn down the bed, Mary. She's very agreeable—she is, just now—all newcomers is; but she did not get many compliments from me, Miss—no, I rayther think not. I wonder why honest English girls won't answer the gentry for governesses, instead of them gaping, scheming, wicked furriners? Lord forgi' me, I think they're all alike.'

Next morning I made acquaintance with Madame de la Rougierre. She was tall, masculine, a little ghastly perhaps, and draped in purple silk, with a lace cap, and great bands of black hair, too thick and black, perhaps, to correspond quite naturally with her bleached and sallow skin, her hollow jaws, and the fine but grim wrinkles traced about her brows and eyelids. She smiled, she nodded, and then for a good while she scanned me in silence with a steady cunning eye, and a stern smile.

'And how is she named—what is Mademoiselle's name?' said the tall stranger.

'*Maud*, Madame.'

'Maud!—what pretty name! Eh bien! I am very sure my dear Maud she will be very good little girl—is not so?—and I am sure I shall love you vary moche. And what 'av you been learning, Maud, my dear cheaile—music, French, German, eh?'

'Yes, a little; and I had just begun the use of the globes when my governess went away.'

I nodded towards the globes, which stood near her, as I said this.

'Oh! yes—the globes;' and she spun one of them with her great hand. 'Je vous expliquerai tout cela à fond.'

Madame de la Rougierre, I found, was always quite ready to explain everything 'à fond;' but somehow her 'explications,' as she termed them, were not very intelligible, and when pressed her temper woke up; so that I preferred, after a while, accepting the expositions just as they came.

Madame was on an unusually large scale, a circumstance which made some of her traits more startling, and altogether rendered her, in her strange way, more awful in the eyes of a nervous *child,* I may say, such as I was. She used to look at me for a long time sometimes, with the peculiar smile I have mentioned, and a great finger upon her lip, like the Eleusinian priestess on the vase.

She would sit, too, sometimes for an hour together, looking into the fire or out of the window, plainly seeing nothing, and with an odd, fixed look of something like triumph—very nearly a smile—on her cunning face.

She was by no means a pleasant *gouvernante* for a nervous girl of my years. Sometimes she had accesses of a sort of hilarity which frightened me still more than her graver moods, and I will describe these by-and-by.

CHAPTER V

SIGHTS AND NOISES

There is not an old house in England of which the servants and young people who live in it do not cherish some traditions of the ghostly. Knowl has its shadows, noises, and marvellous records. Rachel Ruthyn, the beauty of Queen Anne's time, who died of grief for the handsome Colonel Norbrooke, who was killed in the Low Countries, walks the house by night, in crisp and sounding silks. She is not seen, only heard. The tapping of her high-heeled shoes, the sweep and rustle of her brocades, her sighs as she pauses in the galleries, near the bed-room doors; and sometimes, on stormy nights, her sobs.

There is, beside, the 'link-man', a lank, dark-faced, black-haired man, in a sable suit, with a link or torch in his hand. It usually only smoulders, with a deep red glow, as he visits his beat. The library is one of the rooms he sees to. Unlike 'Lady Rachel,' as the maids called her, he is seen only, never heard. His steps fall noiseless as shadows on floor and carpet. The lurid glow of his smouldering torch imperfectly lights his figure and face, and, except when much perturbed, his link never blazes. On those occasions, however, as he goes his rounds, he ever and anon whirls it around his head, and it bursts into a dismal flame. This is a fearful omen, and always portends some direful crisis or calamity. It occurs, only once or twice in a century.

I don't know whether Madame had heard anything of these phenomena; but she did report which very much frightened me and Mary Quince. She asked us who walked in the gallery on which her bed-room opened, making a rustling with her dress, and going down the stairs, and breathing long breaths here and there. Twice, she said, she had stood at her door in the dark, listening to these sounds, and once she called to know who it was. There was no answer, but the person plainly turned back, and hurried towards her with an unnatural speed, which made her jump within her door and shut it.

When first such tales are told, they excite the nerves of the young and the ignorant intensely. But the special effect, I have found, soon wears out The tale simply takes it's place with the rest. It was with Madame's narrative.

About a week after its relation, I had my experience of a similar sort. Mary Quince went down-stairs for a night-light, leaving me in bed, a candle burning in the room, and being tired. I fell asleep before her return. When I awoke the candle had been extinguished. But I heard a step softly approaching. I jumped up—quite forgetting the ghost, and thinking only of Mary Quince—and opened the door, expecting to see the light of her candle. Instead, all was dark, and near me I heard the fall of a bare foot on the oak floor. It was as if some one had stumbled. I said, 'Mary,' but no answer came, only a rustling of clothes and a breathing at the other side of the gallery, which passed off towards the upper staircase. I turned into my room, freezing with horror, and clapt my door. The noise wakened Mary Quince, who had returned and gone to her bed half an hour before.

About a fortnight after this, Mary Quince, a very veracious spinster, reported to me, that having got up to fix the window, which was rattling, at about four o'clock in the morning, she saw a light shining from the library window. She could swear to its being a strong light, streaming through the chinks of the shutter, and moving. No doubt the link was waved about his head by the angry 'link-man.'

These strange occurrences helped, I think, just then to make me nervous, and prepared the way for the odd sort of ascendency which, through my sense of the mysterious and super-natural, that repulsive Frenchwoman was gradually, and it seemed without effort, establishing over me.

Some dark points of her character speedily emerged from the prismatic mist with which she had enveloped it.

Mrs. Rusk's observation about the agreeability of new-comers I found to be true; for as Madame began to lose that character, her good-humour abated very perceptibly, and she began to show gleams of another sort of temper, that was lurid and dangerous.

Notwithstanding this, she was in the habit of always having her Bible open by her, and was austerely attentive at morning and evening services, and asked my father, with great humility, to lend her some translations of Swedenborg's books, which she laid much to heart.

When we went out for our walk, if the weather were bad we generally made our promenade up and down the broad terrace in front of the windows. Sullen and malign at times she used to look, and as suddenly she would pat me on the shoulder caressingly, and smile with a grotesque benignity, asking tenderly, 'Are you fatigue, ma chère?' or 'Are you cold-a, dear Maud?'

At first these abrupt transitions puzzled me, sometimes half frightened me, savouring, I fancied, of insanity. The key, however, was accidentally supplied, and I found that these accesses of demonstrative affection were sure to supervene whenever my father's face was visible through the library windows.

I did not know well what to make of this woman, whom I feared with a vein of superstitious dread. I hated being alone with her after dusk in the school-room. She would sometimes sit for half an hour at a time, with her wide mouth drawn down at the corners, and a scowl, looking into the fire. If she saw me looking at her, she would change all this on the instant, affect a sort of languor, and lean her head upon her hand, and ultimately have recourse to her Bible. But I fancied she did not read, but pursued her own dark ruminations, for I observed that the open book might often lie for half an hour or more under her eyes and yet the leaf never turned.

I should have been glad to be assured that she prayed when on her knees, or read when that book was before her; I should have felt that she was more canny and human. As it was, those external pieties made a suspicion of a hollow contrast with realities that helped to scare me; yet it was but a suspicion—I could not be certain.

Our rector and the curate, with whom she was very gracious, and anxious about my collects and catechism, had an exalted opinion of her. In public places her affection for me was always demonstrative.

In like manner she contrived conferences with my father. She was always making excuses to consult him about my reading, and to confide in him her sufferings, as I learned, from my contumacy and temper. The fact is, I was altogether quiet and submissive. But I think she had a wish to reduce me to a state of the most abject bondage. She had designs of domination and subversion regarding the entire household, I now believe, worthy of the evil spirit I sometimes fancied her.

My father beckoned me into the study one day, and said he—

'You ought not to give poor Madame so much pain. She is one of the few persons who take an interest in you; why should she have so often to complain of your ill-temper and disobedience?—why should she be compelled to ask my permission to punish you? Don't be afraid, I won't concede that. But in so kind a person it argues much. Affection I can't command—respect and obedience I may—and I insist on your rendering *both* to Madame.'

'But sir,' I said, roused into courage by the gross injustice of the charge, 'I have always done exactly as she bid me, and never said one disrespectful word to Madame.'

'I don't think, child, *you* are the best judge of that. Go, and *amend*.' And with a displeased look he pointed to the door. My heart swelled with the sense of wrong, and as I reached the door I turned to say another word, but I could not, and only burst into tears.

'There—don't cry, little Maud—only let us do better for the future. There—there—there has been enough.'

And he kissed my forehead, and gently put me out and closed the door.

In the school-room I took courage, and with some warmth upbraided Madame.

'Wat wicked cheaile!' moaned Madame, demurely. 'Read aloud those three—yes, *those* three chapters of the Bible, my dear Maud.'

There was no special fitness in those particular chapters, and when they were ended she said in a sad tone—

'Now, dear, you must commit to memory this pretty priaire for umility of art.'

It was a long one, and in a state of profound irritation I got through the task.

Mrs. Rusk hated her. She said she stole wine and brandy whenever the opportunity offered—that she was always asking her for such stimulants and pretending pains in her stomach. Here, perhaps, there was exaggeration; but I knew it was true that I had been at different times despatched on that errand and pretext for brandy to Mrs. Rusk, who at last came to her bedside with pills and a mustard blister only, and was hated irrevocably ever after.

I felt all this was done to torture me. But a day is a long time to a child, and they forgive quickly. It was always with a sense of danger that I heard Madame say she must go and see Monsieur Ruthyn in the library, and I think a jealousy of her growing influence was an ingredient in the detestation in which honest Mrs. Rusk held her.

CHAPTER VI

A WALK IN THE WOOD

Two little pieces of by-play in which I detected her confirmed my unpleasant suspicion. From the corner of the gallery I one day saw her, when she thought I was out and all quiet, with her ear at the keyhole of papa's study, as we used to call the sitting-room next his bed-room. Her eyes were turned in the direction of the stairs, from which only she apprehended surprise. Her great mouth was open, and her eyes absolutely goggled with eagerness. She was devouring all that was passing there. I drew back into the shadow with a kind of disgust and horror. She was transformed into a great gaping reptile. I felt that I could have thrown something at her; but a kind of fear made me recede again toward my room. Indignation, however, quickly returned, and I came back, treading briskly as I did so. When I reached the angle of the gallery again. Madame, I suppose, had heard me, for she was half-way down the stairs.

'Ah, my dear Cheaile, I am so glad to find you, and you are dress to come out. We shall have so pleasant walk.'

At that moment the door of my father's study opened, and Mrs. Rusk, with her dark energetic face very much flushed, stepped out in high excitement.

'The Master says you may have the brandy-bottle, Madame and I'm glad to be rid of it—*I* am.'

Madame courtesied with a great smirk, that was full of intangible hate and insult.

'Better your own brandy, if drink you must!' exclaimed Mrs. Rusk. 'You may come to the store-room now, or the butler can take it.'

And off whisked Mrs. Rusk for the back staircase.

There had been no common skirmish on this occasion, but a pitched battle.

Madame had made a sort of pet of Anne Wixted, an underchambermaid, and attached her to her interest economically by persuading me to make her presents of some old dresses and other things. Anne was such an angel!

But Mrs. Rusk, whose eyes were about her, detected Anne, with a brandy-bottle under her apron, stealing up-stairs. Anne, in a panic, declared the truth. Madame had commissioned her to buy it in the town, and convey it to her bed-room. Upon this, Mrs. Rusk impounded the flask; and, with Anne beside her, rather precipitately appeared before 'the Master.' He heard and summoned Madame. Madame was cool, frank, and fluent. The brandy was purely medicinal. She produced a document in the form of a note. Doctor Somebody presented his compliments to Madame de la Rougierre, and ordered her a table-spoonful of brandy and some drops of laudanum whenever the pain of stomach returned. The flask would last a whole year, perhaps two. She claimed her medicine.

Man's estimate of woman is higher than woman's own. Perhaps in their relations to men they are generally more trustworthy—perhaps woman's is the juster, and the other an appointed illusion. I don't know; but so it is ordained.

Mrs. Rusk was recalled, and I saw, as you are aware, Madame's procedure during the interview.

It was a great battle—a great victory. Madame was in high spirits. The air was sweet—the landscape charming—I, so good—everything so beautiful! Where should we go? *this* way?

I had made a resolution to speak as little as possible to Madame, I was so incensed at the treachery I had witnessed; but such resolutions do not last long with very young people, and by the time we had reached the skirts of the wood we were talking pretty much as usual.

'I don't wish to go into the wood, Madame.

'And for what?'

'Poor mamma is buried there.'

'Is *there* the vault?' demanded Madame eagerly.

I assented.

'My faith, curious reason; you say because poor mamma is buried there you will not approach! Why, cheaile, what would good Monsieur Ruthyn say if he heard such thing? You are surely not so unkain', and I am with you. *Allons*. Let us come—even a little part of the way.'

And so I yielded, though still reluctant.

There was a grass-grown road, which we easily reached, leading to the sombre building, and we soon arrived before it.

Madame de la Rougierre seemed rather curious. She sat down on the little bank opposite, in her most languid pose—her head leaned upon the tips of her fingers.

'How very sad—how solemn!' murmured Madame. 'What noble tomb! How triste, my dear cheaile, your visit 'ere must it be, remembering a so sweet maman. There is new inscription—is it not new?' And so, indeed, it seemed.

'I am fatigue—maybe you will read it aloud to me slowly and solemnly, my dearest Maud?'

As I approached, I happened to look, I can't tell why, suddenly, over my shoulder; I was startled, for Madame was grimacing after me with a vile derisive distortion. She pretended to be seized with a fit of coughing. But it would not do: she saw that I had detected her, and she laughed aloud.

'Come here, dear cheaile. I was just reflecting how foolish is all this thing—the tomb—the epitaph. I think I would 'av none—no, no epitaph. We regard them first for the oracle of the dead, and find them after only the folly of the living. So I despise. Do you think your house of Knowl down there is what you call haunt, my dear?'

'Why?' said I, flushing and growing pale again. I felt quite afraid of Madame, and confounded at the suddenness of all this.

'Because Anne Wixted she says there is ghost. How dark is this place! and so many of the Ruthyn family they are buried here—is not so? How high and thick are the trees all round! and nobody comes near.'

And Madame rolled her eyes awfully, as if she expected to see something unearthly, and, indeed, looked very like it herself.

'Come away, Madame,' I said, growing frightened, and feeling that if I were once, by any accident, to give way to the panic that was gathering round me, I should instantaneously lose all control of myself. 'Oh, come away! do, Madame—I'm frightened.'

'No, on the contrary, sit here by me. It is very odd, you will think, ma chêre—un goût bizarre, vraiment!—but I love very much to be near to the dead people—in solitary place like this. I am not afraid of the dead people, nor of the ghosts. 'Av you ever see a ghost, my dear?'

'Do, Madame, *pray* speak of something else.'

'Wat little fool! But no, you are not afraid. I 'av seen the ghosts myself. I saw one, for example, last night, shape like a monkey, sitting in the corner, with his arms round his knees; very wicked, old, old man his face was like, and white eyes so large.'

'Come away, Madame! you are trying to frighten me,' I said, in the childish anger which accompanies fear. Madame laughed an ugly laugh, and said—

'Eh bien! little fool!—I will not tell the rest if you are really frightened; let us change to something else.'

'Yes, yes! oh, do—pray do.'

'Wat good man is your father!'

'Very—the kindest darling. I don't know why it is, Madame, I am so afraid of him, and never could tell him how much I love him.'

This confidential talking with Madame, strange to say, implied no confidence; it resulted from fear—it was deprecatory. I treated her as if she had human sympathies, in the hope that they might be generated somehow.

'Was there not a doctor from London with him a few months ago? Dr. Bryerly, I think they call him.'

'Yes, a Doctor Bryerly, who remained a few days. Shall we begin to walk towards home, Madame? Do, pray.'

'Immediately, cheaile; and does your father suffer much?'

'No—I think not.'

'And what then is his disease?'

'Disease! he has *no* disease. Have you heard anything about his health, Madame?' I said, anxiously.

'Oh no, ma foi—I have heard nothing; but if the doctor came, it was not because he was quite well.'

'But that doctor is a doctor in theology, I fancy. I know he is a Swedenborgian; and papa is so well, he *could* not have come as a physician.'

'I am very glad, ma chère, to hear; but still you know your father is old man to have so young cheaile as you. Oh, yes—he is old man, and so uncertain life is. 'As he made his will, my dear? Every man so rich as he, especially so old, aught to 'av made his will.'

'There is no need of haste, Madame; it is quite time enough when his health begins to fail.'

'But has he really compose no will?'

'I really don't know, Madame.'

'Ah, little rogue! you will not tell—but you are not such fool as you feign yourself. No, no; you know everything. Come, tell me all about—it is for your advantage, you know. What is in his will, and when he wrote?'

'But, Madame, I really know nothing of it. I can't say whether there is a will or not. Let us talk of something else.'

'But, cheaile, it will not kill Monsieur Ruthyn to make his will; he will not come to lie here a day sooner by cause of that; but if he make no will, you may lose a great deal of the property. Would not that be pity?'

'I really don't know anything of his will. If papa has made one, he has never spoken of it to me. I know he loves me—that is enough.'

'Ah! you are not such little goose—you do know everything, of course. Come tell me, little obstinate, otherwise I will break your little finger. Tell me everything.'

'I know nothing of papa's will. You don't know, Madame, how you hurt me. Let us speak of something else.'

'You do know, and you must tell, petite dure-tête, or I will break a your little finger.'

With which words she seized that joint, and laughing spitefully, she twisted it suddenly back. I screamed while she continued to laugh.

'Will you tell?'

'Yes, yes! let me go,' I shrieked.

She did not release it immediately however, but continued her torture and discordant laughter. At last she finally released my finger.

'So she is going to be good cheaile, and tell everything to her affectionate gouvernante. What do you cry for, little fool?'

'You've hurt me very much—you have broken my finger,' I sobbed.

'Rub it and blow it and give it a kiss, little fool! What cross girl! I will never play with you again—never. Let us go home.'

Madame was silent and morose all the way home. She would not answer my questions, and affected to be very lofty and offended.

This did not last very long, however, and she soon resumed her wonted ways. And she returned to the question of the will, but not so directly, and with more art.

Why should this dreadful woman's thoughts be running so continually upon my father's will? How could it concern her?

CHAPTER VII

CHURCH SCARSDALE

I think all the females of our household, except Mrs. Rusk, who was at open feud with her and had only room for the fiercer emotions, were more or less afraid of this inauspicious foreigner.

Mrs. Rusk would say in her confidences in my room—

'Where does she come from?—is she a French or a Swiss one, or is she a Canada woman? I remember one of *them* when I was a girl, and a nice limb *she* was, too! And who did she live with? Where was her last family? Not one of us knows nothing about her, no more than a child; except, of course, the Master—I do suppose he made enquiry. She's always at hugger-mugger with Anne Wixted. I'll pack that *one* about her business, if she doesn't mind. Tattling and whispering eternally. It's not about her own business she's a-talking. Madame de la Rougepot, I call her. She *does* know how to paint up to the ninety-nines—she does, the old cat. I beg your pardon, Miss, but *that* she is—a devil, and no mistake. I found her out first by her thieving the Master's gin, that the doctor ordered him, and filling the decanter up with water—the old villain; but she'll be found out yet, she will; and all the maids is afraid on her. She's not right, they think—a witch or a ghost—I should not wonder. Catherine Jones found her in her bed asleep in the morning after she sulked with you, you know, Miss, with all her clothes on, what-ever was the meaning; and I think she has frightened *you,* Miss and has you as nervous as anythink—I do,' and so forth.

It was true. I *was* nervous, and growing rather more so; and I think this cynical woman perceived and intended it, and was pleased. I was always afraid of her concealing herself in my room, and emerging at night to scare me. She began sometimes to mingle in my dreams, too—always awfully; and this nourished, of course, the kind of ambiguous fear in which, in waking hours, I held her.

I dreamed one night that she led me, all the time whispering something so very fast that I could not understand her, into the library, holding a candle in her other hand above her head. We walked on tiptoe, like criminals at the dead of night, and stopped before that old oak cabinet which my father had indicated in so odd a way to me. I felt that we were about some contraband practice. There was a key in the door, which I experienced a guilty horror at turning, she whispering in the same unintelligible way, all the time, at my ear. I *did* turn it; the door opened quite softly, and within stood my father, his face white and malignant, and glaring close in mine. He cried in a terrible voice, 'Death!' Out went Madame's candle, and at the same moment, with a scream, I waked in the dark—still fancying myself in the library; and for an hour after I continued in a hysterical state.

Every little incident about Madame furnished a topic of eager discussion among the maids. More or less covertly, they nearly all hated and feared her. They fancied that she was making good her footing with 'the Master;' and that she would then oust Mrs. Rusk—perhaps usurp her place—and so make a clean sweep of them all. I fancy the honest little housekeeper did not discourage that suspicion.

About this time I recollect a pedlar—an odd, gipsified-looking man—called in at Knowl. I and Catherine Jones were in the court when he came, and set down his pack on the low balustrade beside the door.

All sorts of commodities he had—ribbons, cottons, silks, stockings, lace, and even some bad jewellry; and just as he began his display—an interesting matter in a quiet country house—Madame came upon the ground. He grinned a recognition, and hoped 'Madamasel' was well, and 'did not look to see *her* here.'

'Madamasel' thanked him. 'Yes, vary well,' and looked for the first time decidedly 'put out.'

'Wat a pretty things!' she said. 'Catherine, run and tell Mrs. Rusk. She wants scissars, and lace too—I heard her say.'

So Catherine, with a lingering look, departed; and Madame said—

'Will you, dear cheaile, be so kind to bring here my purse, I forgot on the table in my room; also, I advise you, bring *your*.'

Catherine returned with Mrs. Rusk. Here was a man who could tell them something of the old Frenchwoman, at last! Slyly they dawdled over his wares, until Madame had made her market and departed with me. But when the coveted opportunity came, the pedlar was quite impenetrable. 'He forgot everything; he did not believe as he ever saw the lady before. He called a Frenchwoman, all the world over, Madamasel—that wor the name on 'em all. He never seed her in partiklar afore, as he could bring to mind. He liked to see 'em always, 'cause they makes the young uns buy.'

This reserve and oblivion were very provoking, and neither Mrs. Rusk nor Catherine Jones spent sixpence with him;—he was a stupid fellow, or worse.

Of course Madame had tampered with him. But truth, like murder, will out some day. Tom Williams, the groom, had seen her, when alone with him, and pretending to look at his stock, with her face almost buried in his silks and Welsh linseys, talking as fast as she could all the time, and slipping *money*, he did suppose, under a piece of stuff in his box.

In the mean time, I and Madame were walking over the wide, peaty sheep-walks that lie between Knowl and Church Scarsdale. Since our visit to the mausoleum in the wood, she had not worried me so much as before. She had been, indeed, more than usually thoughtful, very little talkative, and troubled me hardly at all about French and other accomplishments. A walk was a part of our daily routine. I now carried a tiny basket in my hand, with a few sandwiches, which were to furnish our luncheon when we reached the pretty scene, about two miles away, whither we were tending.

We had started a little too late; Madame grew unwontedly fatigued and sat down to rest on a stile before we had got half-way; and there she intoned, with a dismal nasal cadence, a quaint old Bretagne ballad, about a lady with a pig's head:—

'This lady was neither pig nor maid,
And so she was not of human mould;
Not of the living nor the dead.
Her left hand and foot were warm to touch;
Her right as cold as a corpse's flesh!
And she would sing like a funeral bell, with a ding-dong tune.
The pigs were afraid, and viewed her aloof;
And women feared her and stood afar.
She could do without sleep for a year and a day;
She could sleep like a corpse, for a month and more.
No one knew how this lady fed—
On acorns or on flesh.
Some say that she's one of the swine-possessed,
That swam over the sea of Gennesaret.
A mongrel body and demon soul.
Some say she's the wife of the Wandering Jew,
And broke the law for the sake of pork;
And a swinish face for a token doth bear,
That her shame is now, and her punishment coming.'

And so it went on, in a gingling rigmarole. The more anxious I seemed to go on our way, the more likely was she to loiter. I therefore showed no signs of impatience, and I saw her consult her watch in the course of her ugly minstrelsy, and slyly glance, as if expecting something, in the direction of our destination.

When she had sung to her heart's content, up rose Madame, and began to walk onward silently. I saw her glance once or twice, as before, toward the village of Trillsworth, which lay in front, a little to our left, and the smoke of which hung in a film over the brow of the hill. I think she observed me, for she enquired—

'Wat is that a smoke there?'

'That is Trillsworth, Madame; there is a railway station there.'

'Oh, le chemin de fer, so near! I did not think. Where it goes?'

I told her, and silence returned.

Church Scarsdale is a very pretty and odd scene. The slightly undulating sheep-walk dips suddenly into a wide glen, in the lap of which, by a bright, winding rill, rise from the sward the ruins of a small abbey, with a few solemn trees scattered round. The crows' nests hung untenanted in the trees; the birds were foraging far away from their roosts. The very cattle had forsaken the place. It was solitude itself.

Madame drew a long breath and smiled.

'Come down, come down, cheaile—come down to the churchyard.'

As we descended the slope which shut out the surrounding world, and the scene grew more sad and lonely. Madame's spirits seemed to rise.

'See 'ow many grave-stones—one, *two* hundred. Don't you love the dead, cheaile? I will teach you to love them. You shall see me die here to-day, for half an hour, and be among them. That is what I love.'

We were by this time at the little brook's side, and the low churchyard wall with a stile, reached by a couple of stepping-stones, across the stream, immediately at the other side.

'Come, now!' cried Madame, raising her face, as if to sniff the air; 'we are close to them. You will like them soon as I. You shall see five of them. Ah, ça ira, ça ira, ça ira! Come cross quickily! I am Madame la Morgue—Mrs. Deadhouse! I will present you my friends, Monsieur Cadavre and Monsieur Squelette. Come, come, leetle mortal, let us play. Ouaah!' And she uttered a horrid yell from her enormous mouth, and pushing her wig and bonnet back, so as to show her great, bald head. She was laughing, and really looked quite mad.

'No, Madame, I will not go with you,' I said, disengaging my hand with a violent effort, receding two or three steps.

'Not enter the churchyard! Ma foi—wat mauvais goût! But see, we are already in shade. The sun he is setting soon—where well you remain, cheaile? I will not stay long.'

'I'll stay here,' I said, a little angrily—for I *was* angry as well as nervous; and through my fear was that indignation at her extravagances which mimicked lunacy so unpleasantly, and were, I knew, designed to frighten me.

Over the stepping-stones, pulling up her dress, she skipped with her long, lank legs, like a witch joining a Walpurgis. Over the stile she strode, and I saw her head wagging, and heard her sing some of her ill-omened rhymes, as she capered solemnly, with many a grin and courtesy, among the graves and headstones, towards the ruin.

CHAPTER VIII

THE SMOKER

Three years later I learned—in a way she probably little expected, and then did not much care about—what really occurred there. I learned even phrases and looks—for the story was related by one who had heard it told—and therefore I venture to narrate what at the moment I neither saw nor suspected. While I sat, flushed and nervous, upon a flat stone by the bank of the little stream, Madame looked over her shoulder, and perceiving that I was out of sight, she abated her pace, and turned sharply towards the ruin which lay at her left. It was her first visit, and she was merely exploring; but now, with a perfectly shrewd and businesslike air, turning the corner of the building, she saw, seated upon the edge of a grave-stone, a rather fat and flashily-equipped young man, with large, light whiskers, a jerry hat, green cutaway coat with gilt buttons, and waistcoat and trousers rather striking than elegant in pattern. He was smoking a short pipe, and made a nod to Madame, without either removing it from his lips or rising, but with his brown and rather good-looking face turned up, he eyed her with something of the impudent and sulky expression that was habitual to it.

'Ha, Deedle, you are there! an' look so well. I am here, too, quite *a*lon; but my friend, she wait outside the churchyard, by-side the leetle river, for she must not think I know you—so I am come *a*lon.'

'You're a quarter late, and I lost a fight by you, old girl, this morning,' said the gay man, and spat on the ground; 'and I wish you would not call me Diddle. I'll call you Granny if you do.'

'Eh bien! *Dud,* then. She is vary nice—wat you like. Slim waist, wite teeth, vary nice eyes—dark—wat you say is best—and nice leetle foot and ankle.'

Madame smiled leeringly. Dud smoked on.

'Go on,' said Dud, with a nod of command.

'I am teach her to sing and play—she has such sweet voice!

There was another interval here.

'Well, that isn't much good. I hate women's screechin' about fairies and flowers. Hang her! there's a scarecrow as sings at Curl's Divan. Such a caterwauling upon a stage! I'd like to put my two barrels into her.'

By this time Dud's pipe was out, and he could afford to converse.

'You shall see her and decide. You will walk down the river, and pass her by.'

'That's as may be; howsoever, it would not do, nohow, to buy a pig in a poke, you know. And s'pose I shouldn't like her, arter all?'

Madame sneered, with a patois ejaculation of derision.

'Vary good! Then some one else will not be so 'ard to please—as you will soon find.'

'Some one's bin a-lookin' arter her, you mean?' said the young man, with a shrewd uneasy glance on the cunning face of the French lady.

'I mean precisely—that which I mean,' replied the lady, with a teazing pause at the break I have marked.

'Come, old 'un, none of your d—— old chaff, if you want me to stay here listening to you. Speak out, can't you? There's any chap as has bin a-lookin' arter her—is there?'

'Eh bien! I suppose some.'

'Well, you *suppose,* and *I* suppose—we may *all* suppose, I guess; but that does not make a thing be, as wasn't before; and you tell me as how the lass is kep' private up there, and will be till you're done educating her—a precious good 'un that is!' And he laughed a little lazily, with the ivory handle of his cane on his lip, and eyeing Madame with indolent derision.

Madame laughed, but looked rather dangerous.

'I'm only chaffin', you know, old girl. *You*'ve bin chaffin'—w'y shouldn't *I*? But I don't see why she can't wait a bit; and what's all the d——d hurry for? *I*'m in no hurry. I don't want a wife on my back for a while. There's no fellow marries till he's took his bit o' fun, and seen life—is there! And why should I be driving with her to fairs, or to church, or to meeting, by jingo!—for they say she's a Quaker—with a babby on each knee, only to please them as will be dead and rotten when *I*'m only beginning?'

'Ah, you are such charming fellow; always the same—always sensible. So I and my friend we will walk home again, and you go see Maggie Hawkes. Good-a-by, Dud—good-a-by.'

'Quiet, you fool!—can't ye?' said the young gentleman, with the sort of grin that made his face vicious when a horse vexed him. 'Who ever said I wouldn't go look at the girl? Why, you know that's just what I come here for—don't you? Only when I think a bit, and a notion comes across me, why shouldn't I speak out? I'm not one o' them shilly-shallies. If I like the girl, I'll not be mug in and mug out about it. Only mind ye, I'll judge for myself. Is that her a-coming?'

'No; it was a distant sound.'

Madame peeped round the corner. No one was approaching.

'Well, you go round that a-way, and you only look at her, you know, for she is such fool—so nairvous.'

'Oh, is that the way with her?' said Dud, knocking out the ashes of his pipe on a tombstone, and replacing the Turkish utensil in his pocket. 'Well, then, old lass, good-bye,' and he shook her hand. 'And, do ye see, don't ye come up till I pass, for

I'm no hand at play-acting; an' if you called me "sir," or was coming it dignified and distant, you know, I'd be sure to laugh, a'most, and let all out. So good-bye, d'ye see, and if you want me again be sharp to time, mind.

From habit he looked about for his dogs, but he had not brought one. He had come unostentatiously by rail, travelling in a third-class carriage, for the advantage of Jack Briderly's company, and getting a world of useful wrinkles about the steeplechase that was coming off next week.

So he strode away, cutting off the heads of the nettles with his cane as he went; and Madame walked forth into the open space among the graves, where I might have seen her, had I stood up, looking with the absorbed gaze of an artist on the ruin.

In a little while, along the path, I heard the clank of a step, and the gentleman in the green cutaway coat, sucking his cane, and eyeing me with an offensive familiar sort of stare the while, passed me by, rather hesitating as he did so.

I was glad when he turned the corner in the little hollow close by, and disappeared. I stood up at once, and was reassured by a sight of Madame, not very many yards away, looking at the ruin, and apparently restored to her right mind. The last beams of the sun were by this time touching the uplands, and I was longing to recommence our walk home. I was hesitating about calling to Madame, because that lady had a certain spirit of opposition within her, and to disclose a small wish of any sort was generally, if it lay in her power, to prevent its accomplishment.

At this moment the gentleman in the green coat returned, approaching me with a slow sort of swagger.

'I say, Miss, I dropped a glove close by here. May you have seen it?'

'No, sir,' I said, drawing back a little, and looking, I dare say, both frightened and offended.

'I do think I must 'a dropped it close by your foot, Miss.'

'No, sir,' I repeated.

'No offence, Miss, but you're sure you didn't hide it?'

I was beginning to grow seriously uncomfortable.

'Don't be frightened, Miss; it's only a bit o' chaff. I'm not going to search.'

I called aloud, 'Madame, Madame!' and he whistled through his fingers, and shouted, 'Madame, Madame,' and added, 'She's as deaf as a tombstone, or she'll hear that. Gi'e her my compliments, and say I said you're a beauty, Miss;' and with a laugh and a leer he strode off.

Altogether this had not been a very pleasant excursion. Madame gobbled up our sandwiches, commending them every now and then to me. But I had been too much excited to have any appetite left, and very tired I was when we reached home.

'So, there is lady coming to-morrow?' said Madame, who knew everything. 'Wat is her name? I forget.'

'Lady Knollys,' I answered.

'Lady Knollys—wat odd name! She is very young—is she not?'

'Past fifty, I think.'

'Hélas! She's vary old, then. Is she rich?'

'I don't know. She has a place in Derbyshire.'

'Derbyshire—that is one of your English counties, is it not?'

'Oh yes, Madame,' I answered, laughing. 'I have said it to you twice since you came;' and I gabbled through the chief towns and rivers as catalogued in my geography.

'Bah! to be sure—of course, cheaile. And is she your relation?'

'Papa's first cousin.'

'Won't you present-a me, pray?—I would so like!'

Madame had fallen into the English way of liking people with titles, as perhaps foreigners would if titles implied the sort of power they do generally with us.

'Certainly, Madame.'

'You will not forget?'

'Oh no.'

Madame reminded me twice, in the course of the evening, of my promise. She was very eager on this point. But it is a world of disappointment, influenza, and rheumatics; and next morning Madame was prostrate in her bed, and careless of all things but flannel and James's powder.

Madame was *désolée*; but she could not raise her head. She only murmured a question.

'For 'ow long time, dear, will Lady Knollys remain?'

'A very few days, I believe.'

'Hélas! 'ow onlucky! maybe to-morrow I shall be better Ouah! my ear. The laudanum, dear cheaile!'

And so our conversation for that time ended, and Madame buried her head in her old red cashmere shawl.

CHAPTER IX

MONICA KNOLLYS

Punctually Lady Knollys arrived. She was accompanied by her nephew, Captain Oakley.

They arrived a little before dinner; just in time to get to their rooms and dress. But Mary Quince enlivened my toilet with eloquent descriptions of the youthful Captain whom she had met in the gallery, on his way to his room, with the servant, and told me how he stopped to let her pass, and how 'he smiled so 'ansom.'

I was very young then, you know, and more childish even than my years; but this talk of Mary Quince's interested me, I must confess, considerably. I was painting all sort of portraits of this heroic soldier, while affecting, I am afraid, a hypocritical indifference to her narration, and I know I was very nervous and painstaking about my toilet that evening. When I went down to the drawing-room, Lady Knollys was there, talking volubly to my father as I entered—a woman not really old, but such as very young people fancy aged—energetic, bright, saucy, dressed handsomely in purple satin, with a good deal of lace, and a rich point—I know not how to call it—not a cap, a sort of head-dress—light and simple, but grand withal, over her greyish, silken hair.

Rather tall, by no means stout, on the whole a good firm figure, with something kindly in her look. She got up, quite like a young person, and coming quickly to meet me with a smile—

'My young cousin!' she cried, and kissed me on both cheeks. 'You know who I am? Your cousin Monica—Monica Knollys—and very glad, dear, to see you, though she has not set eyes on you since you were no longer than that paper-knife. Now come here to the lamp, for I must look at you. Who is she like? Let me see. Like your poor mother, I think, my dear; but you've the Aylmer nose—yes—not a bad nose either, and, come I very good eyes, upon my life—yes, certainly something of her poor mother—not a bit like you, Austin.'

My father gave her a look as near a smile as I had seen there for a long time, shrewd, cynical, but kindly too, and said he—

'So much the better, Monica, eh?'

'It was not for me to say—but you know, Austin, you always were an ugly creature. How shocked and indignant the little girl looks! You must not be vexed, you loyal little woman, with Cousin Monica for telling the truth. Papa was and will be ugly all his days. Come, Austin, dear, tell her—is not it so?'

'What! depose against myself! That's not English law, Monica.'

'Well, maybe not; but if the child won't believe her own eyes, how is she to believe me? She has long, pretty hands—you have—and very nice feet too. How old is she?'

'How old, child?' said my father to me, transferring the question.

She recurred again to my eyes.

'That is the true grey—large, deep, soft—very peculiar. Yes, dear, very pretty—long lashes, and such bright tints! You'll be in the Book of Beauty, my dear, when you come out, and have all the poet people writing verses to the tip of your nose—and a very pretty little nose it is!'

I must mention here how striking was the change in my father's spirit while talking and listening to his odd and voluble old Cousin Monica. Reflected from bygone associations, there had come a glimmer of something, not gaiety, indeed, but like an appreciation of gaiety. The gloom and inflexibility were gone, and there was an evident encouragement and enjoyment of the incessant sallies of his bustling visitor.

How morbid must have been the tendencies of his habitual solitude, I think, appeared from the evident thawing and brightening that accompanied even this transient gleam of human society. I was not a companion—more childish than most girls of my age, and trained in all his whimsical ways, never to interrupt a silence, or force his thoughts by unexpected question or remark out of their monotonous or painful channel.

I was as much surprised at the good-humour with which he submitted to his cousin's saucy talk; and, indeed, just then those black-panelled and pictured walls, and that quaint, misshapen room, seemed to have exchanged their stern and awful character for something wonderfully pleasanter to me, notwithstanding the unpleasantness of the personal criticism to which the plain-spoken lady chose to subject me.

Just at that moment Captain Oakley joined us. He was my first actual vision of that awful and distant world of fashion, of whose splendours I had already read something in the three-volumed gospel of the circulating library.

Handsome, elegant, with features almost feminine, and soft, wavy, black hair, whiskers and moustache, he was altogether such a knight as I had never beheld, or even fancied, at Knowl—a hero of another species, and from the region of the demigods. I did not then perceive that coldness of the eye, and cruel curl of the voluptuous lip—only a suspicion, yet enough to indicate the profligate man, and savouring of death unto death.

But I was young, and had not yet the direful knowledge of good and evil that comes with years; and he was so very handsome, and talked in a way that was so new to me, and was so much more charming than the well-bred converse of the humdrum county families with whom I had occasionally sojourned for a week at a time.

It came out incidentally that his leave of absence was to expire the day after to-morrow. A Lilliputian pang of disappointment followed this announcement. Already I was sorry to lose him. So soon we begin to make a property of what pleases us.

I was shy, but not awkward. I was flattered by the attention of this amusing, perhaps rather fascinating, young man of the world; and he plainly addressed himself with diligence to amuse and please me. I dare say there was more effort than I fancied in bringing his talk down to my humble level, and interesting me and making me laugh about people whom I had never heard of before, than I then suspected.

Cousin Knollys meanwhile was talking to papa. It was just the conversation that suited a man so silent as habit had made him, for her frolic fluency left him little to supply. It was totally impossible, indeed, even in our taciturn household, that conversation should ever flag while she was among us.

Cousin Knollys and I went into the drawing-room together, leaving the gentlemen—rather ill-assorted, I fear—to entertain one another for a time.

'Come here, my dear, and sit near me,' said Lady Knollys, dropping into an easy chair with an energetic little plump, 'and tell me how you and your papa get on. I can remember him quite a cheerful man once, and rather amusing—yes, indeed—and now you see what a bore he is—all by shutting himself up and nursing his whims and fancies. Are those your drawings, dear?'

'Yes, very bad, I'm afraid; but there are a few, *better*, I think in the portfolio in the cabinet in the hall.'

'They are by *no* means bad, my dear; and you play, of course?'

'Yes—that is, a little—pretty well, I hope.'

'I dare say. I must hear you by-and-by. And how does your papa amuse you? You look bewildered, dear. Well, I dare say, amusement is not a frequent word in this house. But you must not turn into a nun, or worse, into a puritan. What is he? A Fifth-Monarchy-man, or something—I forget; tell me the name, my dear.'

'Papa is a Swedenborgian, I believe.'

'Yes, yes—I forgot the horrid name—a Swedenborgian, that is it. I don't know exactly what they think, but everyone knows they are a sort of pagans, my dear. He's not making one of *you*, dear—is he?'

'I go to church every Sunday.'

'Well, that's a mercy; Swedenborgian is such an ugly name, and besides, they are all likely to be damned, my dear, and that's a serious consideration. I really wish poor Austin had hit on something else; I'd much rather have no religion, and enjoy life while I'm in it, than choose one to worry me here and bedevil me hereafter. But some people, my dear, have a taste for being miserable, and provide, like poor Austin, for its gratification in the next world as well as here. Ha, ha, ha! how grave the little woman looks! Don't you think me very wicked? You know you do; and very likely you are right. Who makes your dresses, my dear? You *are* such a figure of fun!'

'Mrs. Rusk, I think, ordered *this* dress. I and Mary Quince planned it. I thought it very nice. We all like it very well.'

There was something, I dare say, very whimsical about it, probably very absurd, judged at least by the canons of fashion, and old Cousin Monica Knollys, in whose eye the London fashions were always fresh, was palpably struck by it as if it had been some enormity against anatomy, for she certainly laughed very heartily; indeed, there were tears on her cheeks when she had done, and I am sure my aspect of wonder and dignity, as her hilarity proceeded, helped to revive her merriment again and again as it was subsiding.

'There, you mustn't be vexed with old Cousin Monica,' she cried, jumping up, and giving me a little hug, and bestowing a hearty kiss on my forehead, and a jolly little slap on my cheek. 'Always remember your cousin Monica is an outspoken, wicked old fool, who likes you, and never be offended by her nonsense. A council of three—you all sat upon it—Mrs. Rusk, you said, and Mary Quince, and your wise self, the weird sisters; and Austin stepped in, as Macbeth, and said, 'What is't ye do?' you all made answer together, 'A something or other without a name!' Now, seriously, my dear, it is quite unpardonable in Austin—your papa, I mean—to hand you over to be robed and bedizened according to the whimsies of these wild old women—aren't they old? If they know better, it's positively *fiendish.* I'll blow him up—I will indeed, my dear. You know you're an heiress, and ought not to appear like a jack-pudding.'

'Papa intends sending me to London with Madame and Mary Quince, and going with me himself, if Doctor Bryerly says he may make the journey, and then I am to have dresses and everything.'

'Well, that is better. And who is Doctor Bryerly—is your papa ill?'

'Ill; oh no; he always seems just the same. You don't think him ill-*looking* ill, I mean?' I asked eagerly and frightened.

'No, my dear, he looks very well for his time of life; but why is Doctor What's-his-name here? Is he a physician, or a divine, or a horse-doctor? and why is his leave asked?'

'I—I really don't understand.'

'Is he a what d'ye call'em—a Swedenborgian?'

'I believe so.'

'Oh, I see; ha, ha, ha! And so poor Austin must ask leave to go up to town. Well, go he shall, whether his doctor likes it or not, for it would not do to send you there in charge of your Frenchwoman, my dear. What's her name?'

'Madame de la Rougierre.'

CHAPTER X

LADY KNOLLYS REMOVES A COVERLET

Lady Knollys pursued her enquiries.

'And why does not Madame make your dresses, my dear? I wager a guinea the woman's a milliner. Did not she engage to make your dresses?'

'I—I really don't know; I rather think not. She is my governess—a finishing governess, Mrs. Rusk says.'

'Finishing fiddle! Hoity-toity! and my lady's too grand to cut out your dresses and help to sew them? And what *does* she do? I venture to say she's fit to teach nothing but devilment—not that she has taught *you* much, my dear—*yet* at least. I'll see her, my dear; where is she? Come, let us visit Madame. I should so like to talk to her a little.'

'But she is ill,' I answered, and all this time I was ready to cry for vexation, thinking of my dress, which must be very absurd to elicit so much unaffected laughter from my experienced relative, and I was only longing to get away and hide myself before that handsome Captain returned.

'Ill! is she? what's the matter?'

'A cold—feverish and rheumatic, she says.'

'Oh, a cold; is she up, or in bed?'

'In her room, but not in bed.'

'I should so like to see her, my dear. It is not mere curiosity, I assure you. In fact, curiosity has nothing on earth to do with it. A governess may be a very useful or a very useless person; but she may also be about the most pernicious inmate imaginable. She may teach you a bad accent, and worse manners, and heaven knows what beside. Send the housekeeper, my dear, to tell her that I am going to see her.'

'I had better go myself, perhaps,' I said, fearing a collision between Mrs. Rusk and the bitter Frenchwoman.

'Very well, dear.'

And away I ran, not sorry somehow to escape before Captain Oakley returned.

As I went along the passage, I was thinking whether my dress could be so very ridiculous as my old cousin thought it, and trying in vain to recollect any evidence of a similar contemptuous estimate on the part of that beautiful and garrulous dandy. I could not—quite the reverse, indeed. Still I was uncomfortable and feverish—girls of my then age will easily conceive how miserable, under similar circumstances, such a misgiving would make them.

It was a long way to Madame's room. I met Mrs. Rusk bustling along the passage with a housemaid.

'How is Madame?' I asked.

'Quite well, I believe,' answered the housekeeper, drily. 'Nothing the matter that *I* know of. She eat enough for two to-day. I wish *I* could sit in my room doing nothing.'

Madame was sitting, or rather reclining, in a low arm-chair, when I entered the room, close to the fire, as was her wont, her feet extended near to the bars, and a little coffee equipage beside her. She stuffed a book hastily between her dress and the chair, and received me in a state of langour which, had it not been for Mrs. Rusk's comfortable assurances, would have frightened me.

'I hope you are better, Madame,' I said, approaching.

'Better than I deserve, my dear cheaile, sufficiently well. The people are all so good, trying me with every little thing, like a bird; here is café—Mrs. Rusk-a, poor woman, I try to swallow a little to please her.'

'And your cold, is it better?'

She shook her head languidly, her elbow resting on the chair, and three finger-tips supporting her forehead, and then she made a little sigh, looking down from the corners of her eyes, in an interesting dejection.

'Je sens des lassitudes in all the members—but I am quaite 'appy, and though I suffer I am console and oblige des bontés, ma chère, que vous avez tous pour moi;' and with these words she turned a languid glance of gratitude on me which dropped on the ground.

'Lady Knollys wishes very much to see you, only for a few minutes, if you could admit her.'

'Vous savez les malades see *never* visitors,' she replied with a startled sort of tartness, and a momentary energy. 'Besides, I cannot converse; je sens de temps en temps des douleurs de tête—of head, and of the ear, the right ear, it is parfois agony absolutely, and now it is here.'

And she winced and moaned, with her eyes closed and her hand pressed to the organ affected.

Simple as I was, I felt instinctively that Madame was shamming. She was over-acting; her transitions were too violent, and beside she forgot that I knew how well she could speak English, and must perceive that she was heightening the interest of her helplessness by that pretty tessellation of foreign idiom. I there-fore said with a kind of courage which sometimes helped me suddenly—

'Oh, Madame, don't you really think you might, without much inconvenience, see Lady Knollys for a very few minutes?'

'Cruel cheaile! you know I have a pain of the ear which makes me 'orribly suffer at this moment, and you demand me whether I will not converse with strangers. I did not think you would be so unkain, Maud; but it is impossible, you must see—quite impossible. I never, you *know*, refuse to take trouble when I am able—never—*never*.'

And Madame shed some tears, which always came at call, and with her hand pressed to her ear, said very faintly,

'Be so good to tell your friend how you see me, and how I suffer, and leave me, Maud, for I wish to lie down for a little, since the pain will not allow me to remain longer.'

So with a few words of comfort which could not well be refused, but I dare say betraying my suspicion that more was made of her sufferings than need be, I returned to the drawing-room.

'Captain Oakley has been here, my dear, and fancying, I suppose, that you had left us for the evening, has gone to the billiard-room, I think,' said Lady Knollys, as I entered.

That, then, accounted for the rumble and smack of balls which I had heard as I passed the door.

'I have been telling Maud how detestably she is got up.'

'Very thoughtful of you, Monica!' said my father.

'Yes, and really, Austin, it is quite clear you ought to marry; you want some one to take this girl out, and look after her, and who's to do it? She's a dowdy—don't you see? Such a dust! And it *is* really such a pity; for she's a very pretty creature, and a clever woman could make her quite charming.'

My father took Cousin Monica's sallies with the most wonderful good-humour. She had always, I fancy, been a privileged person, and my father, whom we all feared, received her jolly attacks, as I fancy the grim Front-de-Boeufs of old accepted the humours and personalities of their jesters.

'Am I to accept this as an overture?' said my father to his voluble cousin.

'Yes, you may, but not for myself, Austin—I'm not worthy. Do you remember little Kitty Weadon that I wanted you to marry eight-and-twenty years ago, or more, with a hundred and twenty thousand pounds? Well, you know, she has got ever so much now, and she is really a most amiable old thing, and though *you* would not have her then, she has had her second husband since, I can tell you.'

'I'm glad I was not the first,' said my father.

'Well, they really say her wealth is absolutely immense. Her last husband, the Russian merchant, left her everything. She has not a human relation, and she is in the best set.'

'You were always a match-maker, Monica,' said my father, stopping, and putting his hand kindly on hers. 'But it won't do. No, no, Monica; we must take care of little Maud some other way.'

I was relieved. We women have all an instinctive dread of second marriages, and think that no widower is quite above or below that danger; and I remember, whenever my father, which indeed was but seldom, made a visit to town or anywhere else, it was a saying of Mrs. Rusk—

'I shan't wonder, neither need you, my dear, if he brings home a young wife with him.'

So my father, with a kind look at her, and a very tender one on me, went silently to the library, as he often did about that hour.

I could not help resenting my Cousin Knollys' officious recommendation of matrimony. Nothing I dreaded more than a step-mother. Good Mrs. Rusk and Mary Quince, in their several ways, used to enhance, by occasional anecdotes and frequent reflections, the terrors of such an intrusion. I suppose they did not wish a revolution and all its consequences at Knowl, and thought it no harm to excite my vigilance.

But it was impossible long to be vexed with Cousin Monica.

'You know, my dear, your father is an oddity,' she said. 'I don't mind him—I never did. You must not. Cracky, my dear, cracky—decidedly cracky!'

And she tapped the corner of her forehead, with a look so sly and comical, that I think I should have laughed, if the sentiment had not been so awfully irreverent.

'Well, dear, how is our friend the milliner?'

'Madame is suffering so much from pain in her ear, that she says it would be quite impossible to have the honour—'

'Honour—fiddle! I want to see what the woman's like. Pain in her ear, you say? Poor thing! Well, dear, I think I can cure that in five minutes. I have it myself, now and then. Come to my room, and we'll get the bottles.

So she lighted her candle in the lobby, and with a light and agile step she scaled the stairs, I following; and having found the remedies, we approached Madame's room together.

I think, while we were still at the end of the gallery, Madame heard and divined our approach, for her door suddenly shut, and there was a fumbling at the handle. But the bolt was out of order.

Lady Knollys tapped at the door, saying—'we'll come in, please, and see you. I've some remedies, which I'm sure will do you good.'

There was no answer; so she opened the door, and we both entered. Madame had rolled herself in the blue coverlet, and was lying on the bed, with her face buried in the pillow, and enveloped in the covering.

'Perhaps she's asleep?' said Lady Knollys, getting round to the side of the bed, and stooping over her.

Madame lay still as a mouse. Cousin Monica set down her two little vials on the table, and, stooping again over the bed, began very gently with her fingers to lift the coverlet that covered her face. Madame uttered a slumbering moan, and turned more upon her face, clasping the coverlet faster about her.

'Madame, it is Maud and Lady Knollys. We have come to relieve your ear. Pray let me see it. She can't be asleep, she's holding the clothes so fast. Do, pray, allow me to see it.'

CHAPTER XI

LADY KNOLLYS SEES THE FEATURES

Perhaps, if Madame had murmured, 'It is quite well—pray permit me to sleep,' she would have escaped an awkwardness. But having adopted the rôle of the exhausted slumberer, she could not consistently speak at the moment; neither would it do by main force, to hold the coverlet about her face, and so her presence of mind forsook her. Cousin Monica drew it back and hardly beheld the profile of the sufferer, when her good-humoured face was lined and shadowed with a dark curiosity and a surprise by no means pleasant. She stood erect beside the bed, with her mouth firmly shut and drawn down at the corners, in a sort of recoil and perturbation, looking down upon the patient.

'So that's Madame de la Rougierre?' at length exclaimed Lady Knollys, with a very stately disdain. I think I never saw anyone look more shocked.

Madame sat up, very flushed. No wonder, for she had been wrapped so close in the coverlet. She did not look quite at Lady Knollys, but straight before her, rather downward, and very luridly.

I was very much frightened and amazed, and felt on the point of bursting into tears.

'So, Mademoiselle, you have married, it seems, since I had last the honour of seeing you? I did not recognise Mademoiselle under her new name.'

'Yes—I *am* married, Lady Knollys; I thought everyone who knew me had heard of that. Very respectably married, for a person of my rank. I shall not need long the life of a governess. There is no harm, I hope?'

'I hope not,' said Lady Knollys, drily, a little pale, and still looking with a dark sort of wonder upon the flushed face and forehead of the governess, who was looking downward, straight before her, very sulkily and disconcerted.

'I suppose you have explained everything satisfactorily to Mr. Ruthyn, in whose house I find you?' said Cousin Monica.

'Yes, certainly, everything he requires—in effect there is *nothing* to explain. I am ready to answer to any question. Let *him* demand me.'

'Very good, Mademoiselle.'

'*Madame*, if you please.'

'I forgot—*Madame*—yes, I shall apprise him of everything.'

Madame turned upon her a peaked and malign look, smiling askance with a stealthy scorn.

'For myself, I have nothing to conceal. I have always done my duty. What fine scene about nothing absolutely—what charming remedies for a sick person! Ma foi! how much oblige I am for these so amiable attentions!'

'So far as I can see, Mademoiselle—Madame, I mean—you don't stand very much in need of remedies. Your ear and head don't seem to trouble you just now. I fancy these pains may now be dismissed.'

Lady Knollys was now speaking French.

'Mi ladi has diverted my attention for a moment, but that does not prevent that I suffer frightfully. I am, of course, only poor governess, and such people perhaps ought not to have pain—at least to show when they suffer. It is permitted us to die, but not to be sick.'

'Come, Maud, my dear, let us leave the invalid to her repose and to nature. I don't think she needs my chloroform and opium at present.'

'Mi ladi is herself a physic which chases many things, and powerfully affects the ear. I would wish to sleep, notwithstanding, and can but gain that in silence, if it pleases mi ladi.'

'Come, my dear,' said Lady Knollys, without again glancing at the scowling, smiling, swarthy face in the bed; 'let us leave your instructress to her *concforto*.'

'The room smells all over of brandy, my dear—does she drink?' said Lady Knollys, as she closed the door, a little sharply.

I am sure I looked as much amazed as I felt, at an imputation which then seemed to me so entirely incredible.

'Good little simpleton!' said Cousin Monica, smiling in my face, and bestowing a little kiss on my cheek; 'such a thing as a tipsy lady has never been dreamt of in your philosophy. Well, we live and learn. Let us have our tea in my room—the gentlemen, I dare say, have retired.'

I assented, of course, and we had tea very cosily by her bedroom fire.

'How long have you had that woman?' she asked suddenly, after, for her, a very long rumination.

'She came in the beginning of February—nearly ten months ago—is not it?'

'And who sent her?'

'I really don't know; papa tells me so little—he arranged it all himself, I think.'

Cousin Monica made a sound of acquiescence—her lips closed and a nod, frowning hard at the bars.

'It *is* very odd!' she said; 'how people *can* be such fools!' Here there came a little pause. 'And what sort of person is she—do you like her?'

'Very well—that is, *pretty* well. You won't tell?—but she rather frightens me. I'm sure she does not intend it, but somehow I am very much afraid of her.'

'She does not beat you?' said Cousin Monica, with an incipient frenzy in her face that made me love her.

'Oh no!'

'Nor ill-use you in any way?'

'No.'

'Upon your honour and word, Maud?'

'No, upon my honour.'

'You know I won't tell her anything you say to me; and I only want to know, that I may put an end to it, my poor little cousin.'

'Thank you, Cousin Monica very much; but really and truly she does not ill-use me.'

'Nor threaten you, child?'

'Well, *no*—no, she does not threaten.'

'And how the plague *does* she frighten you, child?'

'Well, I really—I'm half ashamed to tell you—you'll laugh at me—and I don't know that she wishes to frighten me. But there is something, is not there, ghosty, you know, about her?'

'*Ghosty*—is there? well, I'm sure I don't know, but I suspect there's something devilish—I mean, she seems roguish—does not she? And I really think she has had neither cold nor pain, but has just been shamming sickness, to keep out of my way.'

I perceived plainly enough that Cousin Monica's damnatory epithet referred to some retrospective knowledge, which she was not going to disclose to me.

'You knew Madame before,' I said. 'Who is she?'

'She assures me she is Madame de la Rougierre, and, I suppose, in French phrase she so calls herself,' answered Lady Knollys, with a laugh, but uncomfortably, I thought.

'Oh, dear Cousin Monica, do tell me—is she—is she very wicked? I am so afraid of her!'

'How should I know, dear Maud? But I do remember her face, and I don't very much like her, and you may depend on it. I will speak to your father in the morning about her, and don't, darling, ask me any more about her, for I really have not very much to tell that you would care to hear, and the fact is I *won't* say any more about her—there!'

And Cousin Monica laughed, and gave me a little slap on the cheek, and then a kiss.

'Well, just tell me this——'

'Well, I *won't* tell you this, nor anything—not a word, curious little woman. The fact is, I have little to tell, and I mean to speak to your father, and he, I am sure, will do what is right; so don't ask me any more, and let us talk of something pleasanter.'

There was something indescribably winning, it seemed to me, in Cousin Monica. Old as she was, she seemed to me so girlish, compared with those slow, unexceptionable young ladies whom I had met in my few visits at the county houses. By this time my shyness was quite gone, and I was on the most intimate terms with her.

'You know a great deal about her, Cousin Monica, but you won't tell me.'

'Nothing I should like better, if I were at liberty, little rogue; but you know, after all, I don't really say whether I *do* know anything about her or not, or what sort of knowledge it is. But tell me what you mean by ghosty, and all about it.'

So I recounted my experiences, to which, so far from laughing at me, she listened with very special gravity.

'Does she write and receive many letters?'

I had seen her write letters, and supposed, though I could only recollect one or two, that she received in proportion.

'Are *you* Mary Quince?' asked my lady cousin.

Mary was arranging the window-curtains, and turned, dropping a courtesy affirmatively toward her.

'You wait on my little cousin, Miss Ruthyn, don't you?'

'Yes,'m,' said Mary, in her genteelest way.

'Does anyone sleep in her room?'

'Yes,'m, *I*—please, my lady.'

'And no one else?'

'No,'m—please, my lady.'

'Not even the *governess*, sometimes?

'No, please, my lady.'

'Never, you are quite sure, my dear?' said Lady Knollys, transferring the question to me.

'Oh, no, never,' I answered.

Cousin Monica mused gravely, I fancied even anxiously, into the grate; then stirred her tea and sipped it, still looking into the same point of our cheery fire.

'I like your face, Mary Quince; I'm sure you are a good creature,' she said, suddenly turning toward her with a pleasant countenance. 'I'm very glad you have got her, dear. I wonder whether Austin has gone to his bed yet!'

'I think not. I am certain he is either in the library or in his private room—papa often reads or prays alone at night, and—and he does not like to be interrupted.'

'No, no; of course not—it will do very well in the morning.'

Lady Knollys was thinking deeply, as it seemed to me.

'And so you are afraid of goblins, my dear,' she said at last, with a faded sort of smile, turning toward me; 'well, if *I* were, I know what *I* should do—so soon as I, and good Mary Quince here, had got into my bed-chamber for the night, I should stir the fire into a good blaze, and bolt the door—do you see, Mary Quince?—bolt the door and keep a candle lighted all night. You'll be very attentive to her, Mary Quince, for I—I don't think she is very strong, and she must not grow nervous: so get to bed early, and don't leave her alone—do you see?—and—and remember to bolt the door, Mary Quince, and I shall be sending a little Christmas-box to my cousin, and I shan't forget you. Good-night.'

And with a pleasant courtesy Mary fluttered out of the room.

CHAPTER XII

A CURIOUS CONVERSATION

We each had another cup of tea, and were silent for awhile.

'We must not talk of ghosts now. You are a superstitious little woman, you know, and you shan't be frightened.'

And now Cousin Monica grew silent again, and looking briskly around the room, like a lady in search of a subject, her eye rested on a small oval portrait, graceful, brightly tinted, in the French style, representing a pretty little boy, with rich golden hair, large soft eyes, delicate features, and a shy, peculiar expression.

'It is odd; I think I remember that pretty little sketch, very long ago. I think I was then myself a child, but that is a much older style of dress, and of wearing the hair, too, than I ever saw. I am just forty-nine now. Oh dear, yes; that is a good while before I was *born*. What a strange, pretty little boy! a mysterious little fellow. Is he quite sincere, I wonder? What rich golden hair! It is very clever—a French artist, I dare say—and who *is* that little boy?'

'I never heard. Some one a hundred years ago, I dare say. But there is a picture down-stairs I am so anxious to ask you about!'

'Oh!' murmured Lady Knollys, still gazing dreamily on the crayon.

'It is the full-length picture of Uncle Silas—I want to ask you about him.'

At mention of his name, my cousin gave me a look so sudden and odd as to amount almost to a start.

'Your uncle Silas, dear? It is very odd, I was just thinking of him;' and she laughed a little.

'Wondering whether that little boy could be he.'

And up jumped active Cousin Monica, with a candle in her hand, upon a chair, and scrutinised the border of the sketch for a name or a date.

'Maybe on the back?' said she.

And so she unhung it, and there, true enough, not on the back of the drawing, but of the frame, which was just as good, in pen-and-ink round Italian letters, hardly distinguishable now from the discoloured wood, we traced—

'*Silas Aylmer Ruthyn, Ætate* viii. 15 *May*, 1779.'

'It is very odd I should not have been told or remembered who it was. I think if I had *ever* been told I *should* have remembered it. I do recollect this picture, though, I am nearly certain. What a singular child's face!'

And my cousin leaned over it with a candle on each side, and her hand shading her eyes, as if seeking by aid of these fair and half-formed lineaments to read an enigma.

The childish features defied her, I suppose; their secret was unfathomable, for after a good while she raised her head, still looking at the portrait, and sighed.

'A very singular face,' she said, softly, as a person might who was looking into a coffin. 'Had not we better replace it?'

So the pretty oval, containing the fair golden hair and large eyes, the pale, unfathomable sphinx, remounted to its nail, and the *funeste* and beautiful child seemed to smile down oracularly on our conjectures.

'So is the face in the large portrait—*very* singular—more, I think, than that—handsomer too. This is a sickly child, I think; but the full-length is so manly, though so slender, and so handsome too. I always think him a hero and a mystery, and they won't tell me about him, and I can only dream and wonder.'

'He has made more people than you dream and wonder, my dear Maud. I don't know what to make of him. He is a sort of idol, you know, of your father's, and yet I don't think he helps him much. His abilities were singular; so has been his misfortune; for the rest, my dear, he is neither a hero nor a wonder. So far as I know, there are very few sublime men going about the world.'

'You really must tell me all you know about him, Cousin Monica. Now don't refuse.'

'But why should you care to hear? There is really nothing pleasant to tell.'

'That is just the reason I wish it. If it were at all pleasant, it would be quite commonplace. I like to hear of adventures, dangers, and misfortunes; and above all, I love a mystery. You know, papa will never tell me, and I dare not ask him; not that he is ever unkind, but, somehow, I am afraid; and neither Mrs. Rusk nor Mary Quince will tell me anything, although I suspect they know a good deal.'

'I don't see any good in telling you, dear, nor, to say the truth, any great harm either.'

'No—now that's *quite* true—no harm. There *can't* be, for I *must* know it all some day, you know, and better now, and from *you*, than perhaps from a stranger, and in a less favourable way.'

'Upon my word, it is a wise little woman; and really, that's not such bad sense after all.'

So we poured out another cup of tea each, and sipped it very comfortably by the fire, while Lady Knollys talked on, and her animated face helped the strange story.

'It is not very much, after all. Your uncle Silas, you know, is living?'

'Oh yes, in Derbyshire.'

'So I see you do know something of him, sly girl! but no matter. You know how very rich your father is; but Silas was the younger brother, and had little more than a thousand a year. If he had not played, and did not care to marry, it would have been quite enough—ever so much more than younger sons of dukes often have; but he was—well, a *mauvais sujet*—you know what that is. I don't want to say any ill of him—more than I really know—but he was fond of his pleasures, I suppose, like other young men, and he played, and was always losing, and your father for a long time paid great sums for him. I believe he was really a most expensive and vicious young man; and I fancy he does not deny that now, for they say he would change the past if he could.

I was looking at the pensive little boy in the oval frame—aged eight years—who was, a few springs later, 'a most expensive and vicious young man,' and was now a suffering and outcast old one, and wondering from what a small seed the hemlock or the wallflower grows, and how microscopic are the beginnings of the kingdom of God or of the mystery of iniquity in a human being's heart.

'Austin—your papa—was very kind to him—*very*; but then, you know, he's an oddity, dear—he *is* an oddity, though no one may have told you before—and he never forgave him for his marriage. Your father, I suppose, knew more about the lady than I did—I was young then—but there were various reports, none of them pleasant, and she was not visited, and for some time there was a complete estrangement between your father and your uncle Silas; and it was made up, rather oddly, on the very occasion which some people said ought to have totally separated them. Did you ever hear anything—anything *very* remarkable—about your uncle?'

'No, never, they would not tell me, though I am sure they know. Pray go on.'

'Well, Maud, as I have begun, I'll complete the story, though perhaps it might have been better untold. It was something rather shocking—indeed, *very* shocking; in fact, they insisted on suspecting him of having committed a murder.'

I stared at my cousin for some time, and then at the little boy, so refined, so beautiful, so *funeste*, in the oval frame.

'Yes, dear,' said she, her eyes following mine; 'who'd have supposed he could ever have—have fallen under so horrible a suspicion?'

'The wretches! Of course, Uncle Silas—of course, he's innocent?' I said at last.

'Of course, my dear,' said Cousin Monica, with an odd look; 'but you know there are some things as bad almost to be suspected of as to have done, and the country gentlemen chose to suspect him. They did not like him, you see. His politics vexed them; and he resented their treatment of his wife—though I really think, poor Silas, he did not care a pin about her—and he annoyed them whenever he could. Your papa, you know, is very proud of his family—*he* never had the slightest suspicion of your uncle.'

'Oh no!' I cried vehemently.

'That's right, Maud Ruthyn,' said Cousin Monica, with a sad little smile and a nod. 'And your papa was, you may suppose, very angry.'

'Of course he was,' I exclaimed.

'You have no idea, my dear, *how* angry. He directed his attorney to prosecute, by wholesale, all who had said a word affecting your uncle's character. But the lawyers were against it, and then your uncle tried to fight his way through it, but the men would not meet him. He was quite slurred. Your father went up and saw the Minister. He wanted to have him a Deputy-Lieutenant, or something, in his county. Your papa, you know, had a very great influence with the Government. Beside his county influence, he had two boroughs then. But the Minister was afraid, the feeling was so very strong. They offered him something in the Colonies, but your father would not hear of it—that would have been a banishment, you know. They would have given your father a peerage to make it up, but he would not accept it, and broke with the party. Except in that way—which, you know, was connected with the reputation of the family—I don't think, considering his great wealth, he has done very much for Silas. To say truth, however, he was very liberal before his marriage. Old Mrs. Aylmer says he made a vow *then* that Silas should never have more than five hundred a year, which he still allows him, I believe, and he permits him to live in the place. But they say it is in a very wild, neglected state.'

'You live in the same county—have you seen it lately, Cousin Monica?'

'No, not very lately,' said Cousin Monica, and began to hum an air abstractedly.

CHAPTER XIII

BEFORE AND AFTER BREAKFAST

Next morning early I visited my favourite full-length portrait in the chocolate coat and top-boots. Scanty as had been my cousin Monica's notes upon this dark and eccentric biography, they were everything to me. A soul had entered that enchanted form. Truth had passed by with her torch, and a sad light shone for a moment on that enigmatic face.

There stood the *roué*—the duellist—and, with all his faults, the hero too! In that dark large eye lurked the profound and fiery enthusiasm of his ill-starred passion. In the thin but exquisite lip I read the courage of the paladin, who would have 'fought his way,' though single-handed, against all the magnates of his county, and by ordeal of battle have purged the honour of the Ruthyns. There in that delicate half-sarcastic tracery of the nostril I detected the intellectual defiance which had politically isolated Silas Ruthyn and opposed him to the landed oligarchy of his county, whose retaliation had been a hideous slander. There, too, and on his brows and lip, I traced the patience of a cold disdain. I could now see him as he was—the prodigal, the hero, and the martyr. I stood gazing on him with a girlish interest and admiration. There was indignation, there was pity, there was hope. Some day it might come to pass that I, girl as I was, might contribute by word or deed towards the vindication of that long-suffering, gallant, and romantic prodigal. It was a flicker of the Joan of Arc inspiration, common, I fancy, to many girls. I little then imagined how profoundly and strangely involved my uncle's fate would one day become with mine.

I was interrupted by Captain Oakley's voice at the window. He was leaning on the window-sill, and looking in with a smile—the window being open, the morning sunny, and his cap lifted in his hand.

'Good-morning, Miss Ruthyn. What a charming old place! quite the setting for a romance; such timber, and this really *beautiful* house. I *do* so like these white and black houses—wonderful old things. By-the-by, you treated us very badly last night—you did, indeed; upon my word, now, it really was too bad—running away, and drinking tea with Lady Knollys—so she says. I really—I should not like to tell you how very savage I felt, particularly considering how very short my time is.'

I was a shy, but not a giggling country miss. I knew I was an heiress; I knew I was somebody. I was not the least bit in the world conceited, but I think this knowledge helped to give me a certain sense of security and self-possession, which might have been mistaken for dignity or simplicity. I am sure I looked at him with a fearless enquiry, for he answered my thoughts.

'I do really assure you, Miss Ruthyn, I am quite serious; you have no idea how very much we have missed you.'

There was a little pause, and, like a fool, I lowered my eyes, and blushed.

'I—I was thinking of leaving to-day; I am so unfortunate—my leave is just out—it is so unlucky; but I don't quite know whether my aunt Knollys will allow me to go.'

'*I*?—certainly, my dear Charlie, *I* don't want you at all,' exclaimed a voice—Lady Knollys's—briskly, from an open window close by; 'what could put that in your head, dear?'

And in went my cousin's head, and the window shut down.

'She is *such* an oddity, poor dear Aunt Knollys,' murmured the young man, ever so little put out, and he laughed. 'I never know quite what she wishes, or how to please her; but she's *so* good-natured; and when she goes to town for the season—she does not always, you know—her house is really very gay—you can't think——'

Here again he was interrupted, for the door opened, and Lady Knollys entered. 'And you know, Charles,' she continued, 'it would not do to forget your visit to Snodhurst; you wrote, you know, and you have only to-night and to-morrow. You are thinking of nothing but that moor; I heard you talking to the gamekeeper; I know he is—is not he, Maud, the brown man with great whiskers, and leggings? I'm very sorry, you know, but I really must spoil your shooting, for they do expect you at Snodhurst, Charlie; and do not you think this window a little too much for Miss Ruthyn? Maud, my dear, the air is very sharp; shut it down, Charles, and you'd better tell them to get a fly for you from the town after luncheon. Come, dear,' she said to me. 'Was not that the breakfast bell? Why does not your papa get a gong?—it is so hard to know one bell from another.'

I saw that Captain Oakley lingered for a last look, but I did not give it, and went out smiling with Cousin Knollys, and wondering why old ladies are so uniformly disagreeable.

In the lobby she said, with an odd, good-natured look—

'Don't allow any of his love-making, my dear. Charles Oakley has not a guinea, and an heiress would be very convenient. Of course he has his eyes about him. Charles is not by any means foolish; and I should not be at all sorry to see him well married, for I don't think he will do much good any other way; but there are degrees, and his ideas are sometimes very impertinent.'

I was an admiring reader of the *Albums*, the *Souvenirs*, the *Keepsakes*, and all that flood of Christmas-present lore which yearly irrigated England, with pretty covers and engravings; and floods of elegant twaddle—the milk, not destitute of water, on which the babes of literature were then fed. On this, my genius throve. I had a little album, enriched with many gems of original thought and observation, which I jotted down in suitable language. Lately, turning over these faded leaves of rhyme and prose, I lighted, under this day's date, upon the following sage reflection, with my name appended:—

'Is there not in the female heart an ineradicable jealousy, which, if it sways the passions of the young, rules also the *advice* of the *aged*? Do they not grudge to youth the sentiments (though Heaven knows how *shadowed* with sorrow) which they can *no longer inspire*, perhaps even *experience*; and does not youth, in turn, sigh over the envy which has *power to blight*?

MAUD AYLMER RUTHYN.'

'He has not been making love to me,' I said rather tartly, 'and he does not seem to me at all impertinent, and I really don't care the least whether he goes or stays.'

Cousin Monica looked in my face with her old waggish smile, and laughed.

'You'll understand those London dandies better some day, dear Maud; they are very well, but they like money—not to keep, of course—but still they like it and know its value.'

At breakfast my father told Captain Oakley where he might have shooting, or if he preferred going to Dilsford, only half an hour's ride, he might have his choice of hunters, and find the dogs there that morning.

The Captain smiled archly at me, and looked at his aunt. There was a suspense. I hope I did not show how much I was interested—but it would not do. Cousin Monica was inexorable.

'Hunting, hawking, fishing, fiddle-de-dee! You know, Charlie, my dear, it is quite out of the question. He is going to Snodhurst this afternoon, and without quite a rudeness, in which I should be involved too, he really can't—you know you can't, Charles! and—and he *must* go and keep his engagement.'

So papa acquiesced with a polite regret, and hoped another time.

'Oh, leave all that to me. When you want him, only write me a note, and I'll send him or bring him if you let me. I always know where to find him—don't I, Charlie?—and we shall be only too happy.'

Aunt Monica's influence with her nephew was special, for she 'tipped' him handsomely every now and then, and he had formed for himself agreeable expectations, besides, respecting her will. I felt rather angry at his submitting to this sort of tutelage, knowing nothing of its motive; I was also disgusted by Cousin Monica's tyranny.

So soon as he had left the room, Lady Knollys, not minding me, said briskly to papa, 'Never let that young man into your house again. I found him making speeches, this morning, to little Maud here; and he really has not two pence in the world—it is amazing impudence—and you know such absurd things do happen.'

'Come, Maud, what compliments did he pay you?' asked my father.

I was vexed, and therefore spoke courageously. 'His compliments were not to me; they were all to the house,' I said, drily.

'Quite as it should be—the house, of course; it is that he's in love with,' said Cousin Knollys.

'Twas on a widow's jointure land,
The archer, Cupid, took his stand.'

'Hey! I don't quite understand,' said my father, slily.

'Tut! Austin; you forget Charlie is my nephew.'

'So I did,' said my father.

'Therefore the literal widow in this case *can* have no interest in view but one, and that is yours and Maud's. I wish him well, but he shan't put my little cousin and her expectations into his empty pocket—*not* a bit of it. And *there's* another reason, Austin, why you should marry—you have no eye for these things, whereas a clever *woman* would see at a glance and prevent mischief.'

'So she would,' acquiesced my father, in his gloomy, amused way. 'Maud, you must try to be a clever woman.'

'So she will in her time, but that is not come yet; and I tell you, Austin Ruthyn, if you won't look about and marry somebody, somebody may possibly marry you.'

'You were always an oracle, Monica; but *here* I am lost in total perplexity,' said my father.

'Yes; sharks sailing round you, with keen eyes and large throats; and you have come to the age precisely when men *are* swallowed up alive like Jonah.'

'Thank you for the parallel, but you know that was not a happy union, even for the fish, and there was a separation in a few days; not that I mean to trust to that; but there's no one to throw me into the jaws of the monster, and I've no notion of jumping there; and the fact is, Monica, there's no monster at all.'

'I'm not so sure.'

'But I'm quite sure,' said my father, a little drily. 'You forget how old I am, and how long I've lived alone—I and little Maud;' and he smiled and smoothed my hair, and, I thought, sighed.

'No one is ever too old to do a foolish thing,' began Lady Knollys.

'Nor to say a foolish thing, Monica. This has gone on too long. Don't you see that little Maud here is silly enough to be frightened at your fun.'

So I was, but I could not divine how he guessed it.

'And well or ill, wisely or madly, I'll *never* marry; so put that out of your head.'

This was addressed rather to me, I think, than to Lady Knollys, who smiled a little waggishly on me, and said—

'To be sure, Maud; maybe you are right; a stepdame is a risk, and I ought to have asked you first what you thought of it; and upon my honour,' she continued merrily but kindly, observing that my eyes, I know not exactly from what feeling, filled with tears, 'I'll never again advise your papa to marry, unless you first tell me you wish it.'

This was a great deal from Lady Knollys, who had a taste for advising her friends and managing their affairs.

'I've a great respect for instinct. I believe, Austin, it is truer than reason, and yours and Maud's are both against me, though I know I have reason on my side.'

My father's brief wintry smile answered, and Cousin Monica kissed me, and said—

'I've been so long my own mistress that I sometimes forget there are such things as fear and jealousy; and are you going to your governess, Maud?'

CHAPTER XIV

ANGRY WORDS

I was going to my governess, as Lady Knollys said; and so I went. The undefinable sense of danger that smote me whenever I beheld that woman had deepened since last night's occurrence, and was taken out of the region of instinct or prepossession by the strange though slight indications of recognition and abhorrence which I had witnessed in Lady Knollys on that occasion.

The tone in which Cousin Monica had asked, 'are you going to your governess?' and the curious, grave, and anxious look that accompanied the question, disturbed me; and there was something odd and cold in the tone as if a remembrance had suddenly chilled her. The accent remained in my ear, and the sharp brooding look was fixed before me as I glided up the broad dark stairs to Madame de la Rougierre's chamber.

She had not come down to the school-room, as the scene of my studies was called. She had decided on having a relapse, and accordingly had not made her appearance down-stairs that morning. The gallery leading to her room was dark and lonely, and I grew more nervous as I approached; I paused at the door, making up my mind to knock.

But the door opened suddenly, and, like a magic-lantern figure, presented with a snap, appeared close before my eyes the great muffled face, with the forbidding smirk, of Madame de la Rougierre.

'Wat you mean, my dear cheaile?' she inquired with a malevolent shrewdness in her eyes, and her hollow smile all the time disconcerting me more even than the suddenness of her appearance; 'wat for you approach so softly? I do not sleep, you see, but you feared, perhaps, to have the misfortune of wakening me, and so you came—is it not so?—to leesten, and looke in very gentily; you want to know how I was. Vous êtes bien aimable d'avoir pensé à moi. Bah!' she cried, suddenly bursting through her irony. 'Wy could not Lady Knollys come herself and leesten to the keyhole to make her report? Fi donc! wat is there to conceal? Nothing. Enter, if you please. Every one they are welcome!' and she flung the door wide, turned her back upon me, and, with an ejaculation which I did not understand, strode into the room.

'I did not come with any intention, Madame, to pry or to intrude—you don't think so—you *can't* think so—you can't possibly mean to insinuate anything so insulting!'

I was very angry, and my tremors had all vanished now.

'No, not for *you*, dear cheaile; I was thinking to miladi Knollys, who, without cause, is my enemy. Every one has enemy; you will learn all that so soon as you are little older, and without cause she is mine. Come, Maud, speak a the truth—was it not miladi Knollys who sent you here doucement, doucement, so quaite to my door—is it not so, little rogue?'

Madame had confronted me again, and we were now standing in the middle of her floor.

I indignantly repelled the charge, and searching me for a moment with her oddly-shaped, cunning eyes, she said—

'That is good cheaile, you speak a so direct—I like that, and am glad to hear; but, my dear Maud, that woman——'

'Lady Knollys is papa's cousin,' I interposed a little gravely.

'She does hate a me so, you av no idea. She as tryed to injure me several times, and would employ the most innocent person, unconsciously you know, my dear, to assist her malice.'

Here Madame wept a little. I had already discovered that she could shed tears whenever she pleased. I have heard of such persons, but I never met another before or since.

Madame was unusually frank—no one ever knew better when to be candid. At present I suppose she concluded that Lady Knollys would certainly relate whatever she knew concerning her before she left Knowl; and so Madame's reserves, whatever they might be, were dissolving, and she growing childlike and confiding.

'Et comment va monsieur votre père aujourd'hui?'

'Very well,' I thanked her.

'And how long miladi Knollys her visit is likely to be?'

'I could not say exactly, but for some days.'

'Eh bien, my dear cheaile, I find myself better this morning, and we must return to our lessons. Je veux m'habiller, ma chère Maud; you will wait me in the school-room.'

By this time Madame, who, though lazy, could make an effort, and was capable of getting into a sudden hurry, had placed herself before her dressing-table, and was ogling her discoloured and bony countenance in the glass.

'Wat horror! I am so pale. Quel ennui! wat bore! Ow weak av I grow in two three days!'

And she practised some plaintive, invalid glances into the mirror. But on a sudden there came a little sharp inquisitive frown as she looked over the frame of the glass, upon the terrace beneath. It was only a glance, and she sat down languidly in her arm-chair to prepare, I suppose, for the fatigues of the toilet.

My curiosity was sufficiently aroused to induce me to ask—

'But why, Madame, do you fancy that Lady Knollys dislikes you?'

''Tis not fancy, my dear Maud. Ah ha, no! Mais c'est toute une histoire—too tedious to tell now—some time maybe—and you will learn when you are little older, the most violent hatreds often they are the most without cause. But, my dear cheaile, the hours they are running from us, and I must dress. Vite, vite! so you run away to the school-room, and I will come after.'

Madame had her dressing-case and her mysteries, and palpably stood in need of repairs; so away I went to my studies. The room which we called the school-room was partly beneath the floor of Madame's bed-chamber, and commanded the same view; so, remembering my governess's peering glance from her windows, I looked out, and saw Cousin Monica making a brisk promenade up and down the terrace-walk. Well, that was quite enough to account for it. I had grown very curious, and I resolved when our lessons were over to join her and make another attempt to discover the mystery.

As I sat over my books, I fancied I heard a movement outside the door. I suspected that Madame was listening. I waited for a time, expecting to see the door open, but she did not come; so I opened it suddenly myself, but Madame was not on the threshold nor on the lobby. I heard a rustling, however, and on the staircase over the banister I saw the folds of her silk dress as she descended.

She is going, I thought, to seek an interview with Lady Knollys. She intends to propitiate that dangerous lady; so I amused some eight or ten minutes in watching Cousin Monica's quick march and right-about face upon the parade-ground of the terrace. But no one joined her.

'She is certainly talking to papa,' was my next and more probable conjecture. Having the profoundest distrust of Madame, I was naturally extremely jealous of the confidential interviews in which deceit and malice might make their representations plausibly and without answer.

'Yes, I'll run down and see—see *papa*; she shan't tell lies behind my back, horrid woman!'

At the study-door I knocked, and forthwith entered. My father was sitting near the window, his open book before him, Madame standing at the other side of the table, her cunning eyes bathed in tears, and her pocket-handkerchief pressed to her mouth. Her eyes glittered stealthily on me for an instant: she was sobbing—*désolée*, in fact—that grim grenadier lady, and her attitude was exquisitely dejected and timid. But she was, notwithstanding, reading closely and craftily my father's face. He was not looking at her, but rather upward toward the ceiling, reflectively leaning on his hand, with an expression, not angry, but rather surly and annoyed.

'I ought to have heard of this before, Madame,' my father was saying as I came in; 'not that it would have made any difference—not the least; mind that. But it was the kind of thing that I ought to have heard, and the omission was not strictly right.'

Madame, in a shrill and lamentable key, opened her voluble reply, but was arrested by a nod from my father, who asked me if I wanted anything.

'Only—only that I was waiting in the school-room for Madame, and did not know where she was.'

'Well, she is here, you see, and will join you up-stairs in a few minutes.'

So back I went again, huffed, angry, and curious, and sat back in my chair with a clouded countenance, thinking very little about lessons.

When Madame entered, I did not lift my head or eyes.

'Good cheaile! reading,' said she, as she approached briskly and reassured.

'No,' I answered tartly; 'not good, nor a child either; I'm not reading, I've been thinking.'

'Très-bien!' she said, with an insufferable smile, 'thinking is very good also; but you look unhappy—very, poor cheaile. Take care you are not grow jealous for poor Madame talking sometime to your papa; you must not, little fool. It is only for a your good, my dear Maud, and I had no objection you should stay.'

'*You*! Madame!' I said loftily. I was very angry, and showed it through my dignity, to Madame's evident satisfaction.

'No—it was your papa, Mr. Ruthyn, who weesh to speak alone; for me I do not care; there was something I weesh to tell him. I don't care who know, but Mr. Ruthyn he is deeferent.'

I made no remark.

'Come, leetle Maud, you are not to be so cross; it will be much better you and I to be good friends together. Why should a we quarrel?—wat nonsense! Do you imagine I would anywhere undertake a the education of a young person unless I could speak with her parent?—wat folly! I would like to be your friend, however, my poor Maud, if you would allow—you and I together—wat you say?'

'People grow to be friends by liking, Madame, and liking comes of itself, not by bargain; I like every one who is kind to me.'

'And so I. You are like me in so many things, my dear Maud! Are you quaite well to-day? I think you look fateague; so I feel, too, vary tire. I think we weel put off the lessons to to-morrow. Eh? and we will come to play la grace in the garden.'

Madame was plainly in a high state of exultation. Her audience had evidently been satisfactory, and, like other people, when things went well, her soul lighted up into a sulphureous good-humour, not very genuine nor pleasant, but still it was better than other moods.

I was glad when our calisthenics were ended, and Madame had returned to her apartment, so that I had a pleasant little walk with Cousin Monica.

We women are persevering when once our curiosity is roused, but she gaily foiled mine, and, I think, had a mischievous pleasure in doing so. As we were going in to dress for dinner, however, she said, quite gravely—

'I am sorry, Maud, I allowed you to see that I have any unpleasant impressions about that governess lady. I shall be at liberty some day to explain all about it, and, indeed, it will be enough to tell your father, whom I have not been able to find all day; but really we are, perhaps, making too much of the matter, and I cannot say that I know anything against Madame that is conclusive, or—or, indeed, at all; but that there are reasons, and—you must not ask any more—no, you must not.'

That evening, while I was playing the overture to Cenerentola, for the entertainment of my cousin, there arose from the tea-table, where she and my father were sitting, a spirited and rather angry harangue from Lady Knollys' lips; I turned my eyes from the music towards the speakers; the overture swooned away with a little hesitating babble into silence, and I listened.

Their conversation had begun under cover of the music which I was making, and now they were too much engrossed to perceive its discontinuance. The first sentence I heard seized my attention; my father had closed the book he was reading, upon his finger, and was leaning back in his chair, as he used to do when at all angry; his face was a little flushed, and I knew the fierce and glassy stare which expressed pride, surprise, and wrath.

'Yes, Lady Knollys, there's an animus; I know the spirit you speak in—it does you no honour,' said my father.

'And I know the spirit *you* speak in, the spirit of *madness*,' retorted Cousin Monica, just as much in earnest. 'I can't conceive how you *can* be so *demented*, Austin. What has perverted you? are you *blind*?'

'*You* are, Monica; your own unnatural prejudice—*unnatural* prejudice, blinds you. What is it all?—*nothing*. Were I to act as you say, I should be a *coward* and a traitor. I see, I *do* see, all that's real. I'm no Quixote, to draw my sword on illusions.'

'There should be no halting here. How *can* you—do you ever *think*? I wonder if you can breathe. I feel as if the evil one were in the house.'

A stern, momentary frown was my father's only answer, as he looked fixedly at her.

'People need not nail up horseshoes and mark their door-stones with charms to keep the evil spirit out,' ran on Lady Knollys, who looked pale and angry, in her way, 'but you open your door in the dark and invoke unknown danger. How can you look at that child that's—she's *not* playing,' said Knollys, abruptly stopping.

My father rose, muttering to himself, and cast a lurid glance at me, as he went in high displeasure to the door. Cousin Monica, now flushed a little, glanced also silently at me, biting the tip of her slender gold cross, and doubtful how much I had heard.

My father opened the door suddenly, which he had just closed, and looking in, said, in a calmer tone—

'Perhaps, Monica, you would come for a moment to the study; I'm sure you have none but kindly feelings towards me and little Maud, there; and I thank you for your good-will; but you must see other things more reasonably, and I think you will.'

Cousin Monica got up silently and followed him, only throwing up her eyes and hands as she did so, and I was left alone, wondering and curious more than ever.

CHAPTER XV

A WARNING

I sat still, listening and wondering, and wondering and listening; but I ought to have known that no sound could reach me where I was from my father's study. Five minutes passed and they did not return. Ten, fifteen. I drew near the fire and made myself comfortable in a great arm-chair, looking on the embers, but not seeing all the scenery and *dramatis personae* of my past life or future fortunes, in their shifting glow, as people in romances usually do; but fanciful castles and caverns in blood-red and golden glare, suggestive of dreamy fairy-land, salamanders, sunsets, and palaces of fire-kings, and all this partly shaping and partly shaped by my fancy, and leading my closing eyes and drowsy senses off into dream-land. So I nodded and dozed, and sank into a deep slumber, from which I was roused by the voice of my cousin Monica. On opening my eyes, I saw nothing but Lady Knollys' face looking steadily into mine, and expanding into a good-natured laugh as she watched the vacant and lack-lustre stare with which I returned her gaze.

'Come, dear Maud, it is late; you ought to have been in your bed an hour ago.'

Up I stood, and so soon as I had begun to hear and see aright, it struck me that Cousin Monica was more grave and subdued than I had seen her.

'Come, let us light our candles and go together.'

Holding hands, we ascended, I sleepy, she silent; and not a word was spoken until we reached my room. Mary Quince was in waiting, and tea made.

'Tell her to come back in a few minutes; I wish to say a word to you,' said Lady Knollys.

The maid accordingly withdrew.

Lady Knollys' eyes followed her till she closed the door behind her.

'I'm going in the morning.'

'So soon!'

'Yes, dear; I could not stay; in fact, I should have gone tonight, but it was too late, and I leave instead in the morning.'

'I am so sorry—so *very* sorry,' I exclaimed, in honest disappointment, and the walls seemed to darken round me, and the monotony of the old routine loomed more terrible in prospect.

'So am I, dear Maud.'

'But can't you stay a little longer; *won't* you?'

'No, Maud; I'm vexed with Austin—very much vexed with your father; in short, I can't conceive anything so entirely preposterous, and dangerous, and insane as his conduct, now that his eyes are quite opened, and I must say a word to you before I go, and it is just this:—you must cease to be a mere child, you must try and be a woman, Maud: now don't be frightened or foolish, but hear me out. That woman—what does she call herself—Rougierre? I have reason to believe is—in fact, from circumstances, *must* be your enemy; you will find her very deep, daring, and unscrupulous, I venture to say, and you can't be too much on your guard. Do you quite understand me, Maud?'

'I do,' said I, with a gasp, and my eyes fixed on her with a terrified interest, as if on a warning ghost.

'You must bridle your tongue, mind, and govern your conduct, and command even your features. It is hard to practise reserve; but you must—you must be secret and vigilant. Try and be in appearance just as usual; don't quarrel; tell her nothing, if you do happen to know anything, of your father's business; be always on your guard when with her, and keep your eye upon her everywhere. Observe everything, disclose nothing—do you see?'

'Yes,' again I whispered.

'You have good, honest servants about you, and, thank God, they don't like her. But you must not repeat to them one word I am now saying to you. Servants are fond of dropping hints, and letting things ooze out in that way, and in their quarrels with her would compromise you—you understand me?'

'I do,' I sighed, with a wild stare.

'And—and, Maud, don't let her meddle with your food.'

Cousin Monica gave me a pale little nod, and looked away.

I could only stare at her; and under my breath I uttered an ejaculation of terror.

'Don't be so frightened; you must not be foolish; I only wish you to be upon your guard. I have my suspicions, but I may be quite wrong; your father thinks I am a fool; perhaps I am—perhaps not; maybe he may come to think as I do. But you must not speak to him on the subject; he's an odd man, and never did and never will act wisely, when his passions and prejudices are engaged.'

'Has she ever committed any great crime?' I asked, feeling as if I were on the point of fainting.

'No, dear Maud, I never said anything of the kind; don't be so frightened: I only said I have formed, from something I know, an ill opinion of her; and an unprincipled person, under temptation, is capable of a great deal. But no matter how wicked she may be, you may defy her, simply by assuming her to be so, and acting with caution; she is cunning and selfish, and she'll do nothing desperate. But I would give her no opportunity.'

'Oh, dear! Oh, Cousin Monica, don't leave me.'

'My dear, I *can't* stay; your papa and I—we've had a quarrel. I know I'm right, and he's wrong, and he'll come to see it soon, if he's left to himself, and then all will be right. But just now he misunderstands me, and we've not been civil to one another. I could not think of staying, and he would not allow you to come away with me for a short visit, which I wished. It won't last, though; and I do assure you, my dear Maud, I am quite happy about you now that you are quite on your guard. Just act respecting that person as if she were capable of any treachery, without showing distrust or dislike in your manner, and nothing will remain in her power; and write to me whenever you wish to hear from me, and if I can be of any real use, I don't care, I'll come: so there's a wise little woman; do as I've said, and depend upon it everything will go well, and I'll contrive before long to get that nasty creature away.'

Except a kiss and a few hurried words in the morning when she was leaving, and a pencilled farewell for papa, there was nothing more from Cousin Monica for some time.

Knowl was dark again—darker than ever. My father, gentle always to me, was now—perhaps it was contrast with his fitful return to something like the world's ways, during Lady Knollys' stay—more silent, sad, and isolated than before. Of Madame de la Rougierre I had nothing at first particular to remark. Only, reader, if you happen to be a rather nervous and very young girl, I ask you to conceive my fears and imaginings, and the kind of misery which I was suffering. Its intensity I cannot now even myself recall. But it overshadowed me perpetually—a care, an alarm. It lay down with me at night and got up with me in the morning, tinting and disturbing my dreams, and making my daily life terrible. I wonder now that I lived through the ordeal. The torment was secret and incessant, and kept my mind in unintermitting activity.

Externally things went on at Knowl for some weeks in the usual routine. Madame was, so far as her unpleasant ways were concerned, less tormenting than before, and constantly reminded me of 'our leetle vow of friendship, you remember, dearest Maud!' and she would stand beside me, and looked from the window with her bony arm round my waist, and my reluctant hand drawn round in hers; and thus she would smile, and talk affectionately and even playfully; for at times she would grow quite girlish, and smile with her great carious teeth, and begin to quiz and babble about the young 'faylows,' and tell bragging tales of her lovers, all of which were dreadful to me.

She was perpetually recurring, too, to the charming walk we had had together to Church Scarsdale, and proposing a repetition of that delightful excursion, which, you may be sure, I evaded, having by no means so agreeable a recollection of our visit.

One day, as I was dressing to go out for a walk, in came good Mrs. Rusk, the housekeeper, to my room.

'Miss Maud, dear, is not that too far for you? It is a long walk to Church Scarsdale, and you are not looking very well.'

'To Church Scarsdale?' I repeated; 'I'm not going to Church Scarsdale; who said I was going to Church Scarsdale? There is nothing I should so much dislike.'

'Well, I never!' exclaimed she. 'Why, there's old Madame's been down-stairs with me for fruit and sandwiches, telling me you were longing to go to Church Scarsdale——'

'It's quite untrue,' I interrupted. 'She knows I hate it.'

'She does?' said Mrs. Rusk, quietly; 'and you did not tell her nothing about the basket? Well—if there isn't a story! Now what may she be after—what is it—what *is* she driving at?'

'I can't tell, but I won't go.'

'No, of course, dear, you won't go. But you may be sure there's some scheme in her old head. Tom Fowkes says she's bin two or three times to drink tea at Farmer Gray's—now, could it be she's thinking to marry him?' And Mrs. Rusk sat down and laughed heartily, ending with a crow of derision.

'To think of a young fellow like that, and his wife, poor thing, not dead a year—maybe she's got money?'

'I don't know—I don't care—perhaps, Mrs. Rusk, you mistook Madame. I will go down; I am going out.'

Madame had a basket in her hand. She held it quietly by her capacious skirt, at the far side, and made no allusion to the preparation, neither to the direction in which she proposed walking, and prattling artlessly and affectionately she marched by my side.

Thus we reached the stile at the sheep-walk, and then I paused.

'Now, Madame, have not we gone far enough in this direction?—suppose we visit the pigeon-house in the park?'

'Wat folly! my dear a Maud—you cannot walk so far.'

'Well, towards home, then.'

'And wy not a this way? We ave not walk enough, and Mr. Ruthyn he will not be pleased if you do not take proper exercise. Let us walk on by the path, and stop when you like.'

'Where do you wish to go, Madamc?'

'Nowhere particular—come along; don't be fool, Maud.'

'This leads to Church Scarsdale.'

'A yes indeed! wat sweet place! bote we need not a walk all the way to there.'

'I'd rather not walk outside the grounds to-day, Madame.'

'Come, Maud, you shall not be fool—wat you mean, Mademoiselle?' said the stalworth lady, growing yellow and greenish with an angry mottling, and accosting me very gruffly.

'I don't care to cross the stile, thank you, Madame. I shall remain at this side.'

'You shall do wat I tell you!' exclaimed she.

'Let go my arm, Madame, you hurt me,' I cried.

She had griped my arm very firmly in her great bony hand, and seemed preparing to drag me over by main force.

'Let me go,' I repeated shrilly, for the pain increased.

'La!' she cried with a smile of rage and a laugh, letting me go and shoving me backward at the same time, so that I had a rather dangerous tumble.

I stood up, a good deal hurt, and very angry, notwithstanding my fear of her.

'I'll ask papa if I am to be so ill-used.'

'Wat av I done?' cried Madame, laughing grimly from her hollow jaws; I did all I could to help you over—'ow could I prevent you to pull back and tumble if you would do so? That is the way wen you petites Mademoiselles are naughty and hurt yourself they always try to make blame other people. Tell a wat you like—you think I care?'

'Very well, Madame.'

'Are a you coming?'

'No.'

She looked steadily in my face and very wickedly. I gazed at her as with dazzled eyes—I suppose as the feathered prey do at the owl that glares on them by night. I neither moved back nor forward, but stared at her quite helplessly.

'You are nice pupil—charming young person! So polite, so obedient, so amiable! I will walk towards Church Scarsdale,' she continued, suddenly breaking through the conventionalism of her irony, and accosting me in savage accents. 'You weel stay behind if you dare. I tell you to accompany—do you hear?'

More than ever resolved against following her, I remained where I was, watching her as she marched fiercely away, swinging her basket as though in imagination knocking my head off with it.

She soon cooled, however, and looking over her shoulder, and seeing me still at the other side of the stile, she paused, and beckoned me grimly to follow her. Seeing me resolutely maintain my position, she faced about, tossed her head, like an angry beast, and seemed uncertain for a while what course to take with me.

She stamped and beckoned furiously again. I stood firm. I was very much frightened, and could not tell to what violence she might resort in her exasperation. She walked towards me with an inflamed countenance, and a slight angry wagging of the head; my heart fluttered, and I awaited the crisis in extreme trepidation. She came close, the stile only separating us, and stopped short, glaring and grinning at me like a French grenadier who has crossed bayonets, but hesitates to close.

CHAPTER XVI

DOCTOR BRYERLY LOOKS IN

What had I done to excite this ungovernable fury? We had often before had such small differences, and she had contented herself with being sarcastic, teasing, and impertinent.

'So, for future you are gouvernante and I the cheaile for you to command—is not so?—and you must direct where we shall walk. Très-bien! we shall see; Monsieur Ruthyn he shall know everything. For me I do not care—not at all—I shall be rather pleased, on the contrary. Let him decide. If I shall be responsible for the conduct and the health of Mademoiselle his daughter, it must be that I shall have authority to direct her wat she must do—it must be that she or I shall obey. I ask only witch shall command for the future—voilà tout!'

I was frightened, but resolute—I dare say I looked sullen and uncomfortable. At all events, she seemed to think she might possibly succeed by wheedling; so she tried coaxing and cajoling, and patted my cheek, and predicted that I would be 'a good cheaile,' and not 'vex poor Madame,' but do for the future 'wat she tell a me.'

She smiled her wide wet grin, smoothed my hand, and patted my cheek, and would in the excess of her conciliatory paroxysm have kissed me; but I withdrew, and she commented only with a little laugh, and a 'Foolish little thing! but you will be quite amiable just now.'

'Why, Madame,' I asked, suddenly raising my head and looking her straight in the face, 'do you wish me to walk to Church Scarsdale so particularly to-day?'

She answered my steady look with a contracted gaze and an unpleasant frown.

'Wy do I?—I do not understand a you; there is *no* particular day—wat folly! Wy I like Church Scarsdale? Well, it is such pretty place. There is all! Wat leetle fool! I suppose you think I want to keel a you and bury you in the churchyard?'

And she laughed, and it would not have been a bad laugh for a ghoul.

'Come, my dearest Maud, you are not a such fool to say, if *you* tell me me go thees a way, I weel go that; and if you say, go that a way, I weel go thees—you are rasonable leetle girl—come along—*alons donc*—we shall av soche agreeable walk—weel a you?'

But I was immovable. It was neither obstinacy nor caprice, but a profound fear that governed me. I was then afraid—yes, *afraid*. Afraid of *what*? Well, of going with Madame de la Rougierre to Church Scarsdale that day. That was all. And I believe that instinct was true.

She turned a bitter glance toward Church Scarsdale, and bit her lip. She saw that she must give it up. A shadow hung upon her drab features. A little scowl—a little sneer—wide lips compressed with a false smile, and a leaden shadow mottling all. Such was the countenance of the lady who only a minute or two before had been smiling and murmuring over the stile so amiably with her idiomatic 'blarney,' as the Irish call that kind of blandishment.

There was no mistaking the malignant disappointment that hooked and warped her features—my heart sank—a tremendous fear overpowered me. Had she intended poisoning me? What was in that basket? I looked in her dreadful face. I felt for a minute quite frantic. A feeling of rage with my father, with my Cousin Monica, for abandoning me to this dreadful rogue, took possession of me, and I cried, helplessly wringing my hands—

'Oh! it is a shame—it is a shame—it is a shame!'

The countenance of the gouvernante relaxed. I think she in turn was frightened at my extreme agitation. It might have worked unfavourably with my father.

'Come, Maud, it is time you should try to control your temper. You shall not walk to Church Scarsdale if you do not like—I only invite. *There*! It is quite as you please, where we shall walk then? Here to the peegeon-house? I think you say. Tout bien! Remember I concede you everything. Let us go.'

We went, therefore, towards the pigeon-house, through the forest trees; I not speaking as the children in the wood did with their sinister conductor, but utterly silent and scared; she silent also, meditating, and sometimes with a sharp side-glance gauging my progress towards equanimity. Her own was rapid; for Madame was a philosopher, and speedily accommodated herself to circumstances. We had not walked a quarter of an hour when every trace of gloom had left her face, which had assumed its customary brightness, and she began to sing with a spiteful hilarity as we walked forward, and indeed seemed to be approaching one of her waggish, frolicsome moods. But her fun in these moods was solitary. The joke, whatever it was, remained in her own keeping. When we approached the ruined brick tower—in old times a pigeon-house—she grew quite frisky, and twirled her basket in the air, and capered to her own singing.

Under the shadow of the broken wall, and its ivy, she sat down with a frolicsome *plump*, and opened her basket, inviting me to partake, which I declined. I must do her justice, however, upon the suspicion of poison, which she quite disposed of by gobbling up, to her own share, everything which the basket contained.

The reader is not to suppose that Madame's cheerful demeanour indicated that I was forgiven. Nothing of the kind. One syllable more, on our walk home, she addressed not to me. And when we reached the terrace, she said—

'You will please, Maud, remain for two—three minutes in the Dutch garden, while I speak with Mr. Ruthyn in the study.'

This was spoken with a high head and an insufferable smile; and I more haughtily, but quite gravely, turned without disputing, and descended the steps to the quaint little garden she had indicated.

I was surprised and very glad to see my father there. I ran to him, and began, 'Oh! papa!' and then stopped short, adding only, 'may I speak to you now?'

He smiled kindly and gravely on me.

'Well, Maud, say your say.'

'Oh, sir, it is only this: I entreat that our walks, mine and Madame's may be confined to the grounds.'

'And why?'

'I—I'm afraid to go with her.'

'*Afraid!*' he repeated, looking hard at me. 'Have you lately had a letter from Lady Knollys?'

'No, papa, not for two months or more.'

There was a pause.

'And why *afraid*, Maud?'

'She brought me one day to Church Scarsdale; you know what a solitary place it is, sir; and she frightened me so that I was afraid to go with her into the church-yard. But she went and left me alone at the other side of the stream, and an impudent man passing by stopped and spoke to me, and seemed inclined to laugh at me, and altogether frightened me very much, and he did not go till Madame happened to return.'

'What kind of man—young or old?'

'A young man; he looked like a farmer's son, but very impudent, and stood there talking to me whether I would or not; and Madame did not care at all, and laughed at me for being frightened; and, indeed, I am very uncomfortable with her.'

He gave me another shrewd look, and then looked down cloudily and thought.

'You say you are uncomfortable and frightened. How is this—what causes these feelings?'

'I don't know, sir; she likes frightening me; I am afraid of her—we are all afraid of her, I think. The servants, I mean, as well as I.'

My father nodded his head contemptuously, twice or thrice, and muttered, 'A pack of fools!'

'And she was so very angry to-day with me, because I would not walk again with her to Church Scarsdale. I am very much afraid of her. I—' and quite unpremeditatedly I burst into tears.

'There, there, little Maud, you must not cry. She is here only for your good. If you are afraid—even *foolishly* afraid—it is enough. Be it as you say; your walks are henceforward confined to the grounds; I'll tell her so.'

I thanked him through my tears very earnestly.

'But, Maud, beware of prejudice; women are unjust and violent in their judgments. Your family has suffered in some of its members by such injustice. It behoves us to be careful not to practise it.'

That evening in the drawing-room my father said, in his usual abrupt way—

'About my departure, Maud: I've had a letter from London this morning, and I think I shall be called away sooner than I at first supposed, and for a little time we must manage apart from one another. Do not be alarmed. You shall not be in Madame de la Rougierre's charge, but under the care of a relation; but even so, little Maud will miss her old father, I think.'

His tone was very tender, so were his looks; he was looking down on me with a smile, and tears were in his eyes. This softening was new to me. I felt a strange thrill of surprise, delight, and love, and springing up, I threw my arms about his neck and wept in silence. He, I think, shed tears also.

'You said a visitor was coming; some one, you mean, to go away with. Ah, yes, you love him better than me.'

'No, dear, no; but I *fear* him; and I am sorry to leave you, little Maud.'

'It won't be very long,' I pleaded.

'No, dear,' he answered with a sigh.

I was tempted almost to question him more closely on the subject, but he seemed to divine what was in my mind, for he said—

'Let us speak no more of it, but only bear in mind, Maud, what I told you about the oak cabinet, the key of which is here,' and he held it up as formerly: 'you remember what you are to do in case Doctor Bryerly should come while I am away?'

'Yes, sir.'

His manner had changed, and I had returned to my accustomed formalities.

It was only a few days later that Dr. Bryerly actually did arrive at Knowl, quite unexpectedly, except, I suppose, by my father. He was to stay only one night.

He was twice closeted in the little study up-stairs with my father, who seemed to me, even for him, unusually dejected, and Mrs. Rusk inveighing against 'them rubbitch,' as she always termed the Swedenborgians, told me 'they were making him quite shaky-like, and he would not last no time, if that lanky, lean ghost of a fellow in black was to keep prowling in and out of his room like a tame cat.'

I lay awake that night, wondering what the mystery might be that connected my father and Dr. Bryerly. There was something more than the convictions of their strange religion could account for. There was something that profoundly agitated my father. It may not be reasonable, but so it is. The person whose presence, though we know nothing of the cause of that effect, is palpably attended with pain to anyone who is dear to us, grows odious, and I began to detest Doctor Bryerly.

It was a grey, dark morning, and in a dark pass in the gallery, near the staircase, I came full upon the ungainly Doctor, in his glossy black suit.

I think, if my mind had been less anxiously excited on the subject of his visit, or if I had not disliked him so much, I should not have found courage to accost him as I did. There was something sly, I thought, in his dark, lean face; and he looked so low, so like a Scotch artisan in his Sunday clothes, that I felt a sudden pang of indignation, at the thought that a great gentleman, like my father, should have suffered under his influence, and I stopped suddenly, instead of passing him by with a mere salutation, as he expected, 'May I ask a question, Doctor Bryerly?'

'Certainly'

'Are you the friend whom my father expects?'

'I don't quite see.'

'The friend, I mean, with whom he is to make an expedition to some distance, I think, and for some little time?'

'No,' said the Doctor, with a shake of his head.

'And who is he?'

'I really have not a notion, Miss.'

'Why, he said that *you knew*,' I replied.

The Doctor looked honestly puzzled.

'Will he stay long away? pray tell me.'

The Doctor looked into my troubled face with inquiring and darkened eyes, like one who half reads another's meaning; and then he said a little briskly, but not sharply—

'Well, *I* don't know, I'm sure, Miss; no, indeed, you must have mistaken; there's nothing that *I* know.'

There was a little pause, and he added—

'No. He never mentioned any friend to me.' I fancied that he was made uncomfortable by my question, and wanted to hide the truth. Perhaps I was partly right.

'Oh! Doctor Bryerly, pray, *pray* who is the friend, and where is he going?'

'I do *assure* you,' he said, with a strange sort of impatience, 'I don't know; it is all nonsense.'

And he turned to go, looking, I think, annoyed and disconcerted.

A terrific suspicion crossed my brain like lightning.

'Doctor, one word,' I said, I believe, quite wildly. 'Do you—do you think his mind is at all affected?'

'Insane?' he said, looking at me with a sudden, sharp inquisitiveness, that brightened into a smile. 'Pooh, pooh! Heaven forbid! not a saner man in England.'

Then with a little nod he walked on, carrying, as I believed, notwithstanding his disclaimer, the secret with him. In the afternoon Doctor Bryerly went away.

CHAPTER XVII

AN ADVENTURE

For many days after our quarrel, Madame hardly spoke to me. As for lessons, I was not much troubled with them. It was plain, too, that my father had spoken to her, for she never after that day proposed our extending our walks beyond the precincts of Knowl.

Knowl, however, was a very considerable territory, and it was possible for a much better pedestrian than I to tire herself effectually, without passing its limits. So we took occasionally long walks.

After some weeks of sullenness, during which for days at a time she hardly spoke to me, and seemed lost in dark and evil abstraction, she once more, and somewhat suddenly, recovered her spirits, and grew quite friendly. Her gaieties and friendliness were not reassuring, and in my mind presaged approaching mischief and treachery. The days were shortening to the wintry span. The edge of the red sun had already touched the horizon as Madame and I, overtaken at the warren by his last beams, were hastening homeward.

A narrow carriage-road traverses this wild region of the park, to which a distant gate gives entrance. On descending into this unfrequented road, I was surprised to see a carriage standing there. A thin, sly postilion, with that pert, turned-up nose which the old caricaturist Woodward used to attribute to the gentlemen of Tewkesbury, was leaning on his horses, and looked hard at me as I passed. A lady who sat within looked out, with an extra-fashionable bonnet on, and also treated us to a stare. Very pink and white cheeks she had, very black glossy hair and bright eyes—fat, bold, and rather cross, she looked—and in her bold way she examined us curiously as we passed.

I mistook the situation. It had once happened before that an intending visitor at Knowl had entered the place by that park-road, and lost several hours in a vain search for the house.

'Ask him, Madame, whether they want to go to the house; I dare say they have missed their way,' whispered I.

'*Eh bien,* they will find again. I do not choose to talk to post-boys; *allons*!'

But I asked the man as we passed, 'Do you want to reach the house?'

By this time he was at the horses' heads, buckling the harness.

'Noa,' he said in a surly tone, smiling oddly on the winkers, but, recollecting his politeness, he added, 'Noa, thankee, misses, it's what they calls a picnic; we'll be takin' the road now.'

He was smiling now on a little buckle with which he was engaged.

'Come—nonsense!' whispered Madame sharply in my ear, and she whisked me by the arm, so we crossed the little stile at the other side.

Our path lay across the warren, which undulates in little hillocks. The sun was down by this time, blue shadows were stretching round us, colder in the splendid contrast of the burnished sunset sky.

Descending over these hillocks we saw three figures a little in advance of us, not far from the path we were tracing. Two were standing smoking and chatting at intervals: one tall and slim, with a high chimney-pot, worn a little on one side, and a white great-coat buttoned up to the chin; the other shorter and stouter, with a dark-coloured wrapper. These gentlemen were facing rather our way as we came over the edge of the eminence, but turned their backs on perceiving our approach. As they did so, I remember so well each lowered his cigar suddenly with the simultaneousness of a drill. The third figure sustained the picnic character of the group, for he was repacking a hamper. He stood suddenly erect as we drew near, and a very ill-looking person he was, low-browed, square-chinned, and with a broad, broken nose. He wore gaiters, and was a little bandy, very broad, and had a closely-cropped bullet head, and deep-set little eyes. The moment I saw him, I beheld the living type of the burglars and bruisers whom I had so often beheld with a kind of scepticism in *Punch*. He stood over his hamper and scowled sharply at us for a moment; then with the point of his foot he jerked a little fur cap that lay on the ground into his hand, drew it tight over his lowering brows, and called to his companions, just as we passed him—'Hallo! mister. How's this?'

'All right,' said the tall person in the white great-coat, who, as he answered, shook his shorter companion by the arm, I thought angrily.

This shorter companion turned about. He had a muffler loose about his neck and chin. I thought he seemed shy and irresolute, and the tall man gave him a great jolt with his elbow, which made him stagger, and I fancied a little angry, for he said, as it seemed, a sulky word or two.

The gentleman in the white surtout, however, standing direct in our way, raised his hat with a mock salutation, placing his hand on his breast, and forthwith began to advance with an insolent grin and an air of tipsy frolic.

'Jist in time, ladies; five minutes more and we'd a bin off. Thankee, Mrs. Mouser, ma'am, for the honour of the meetin', and more particular for the pleasure of making your young lady's acquaintance—niece, ma'am? daughter, ma'am? granddaughter, by Jove, is it? Hallo! there, mild 'n, I say, stop packin'.' This was to the ill-favoured person with the broken nose. 'Bring us a couple o' glasses and a bottle o' curaçoa; what are you fear'd on, my dear? this is Lord Lollipop, here, a reg'lar charmer, wouldn't hurt a fly, hey Lolly? Isn't he pretty, Miss? and I'm Sir Simon Sugarstick—so called after old Sir Simon, ma'am; and I'm so tall and straight, Miss, and slim—ain't I? and ever so sweet, my honey, when you come to know me, just like a sugarstick; ain't I, Lolly, boy?'

'I'm Miss Ruthyn, tell them, Madame,' I said, stamping on the ground, and very much frightened.

'Be quaite, Maud. If you are angry, they will hurt us; leave me to speak,' whispered the gouvernante.

All this time they were approaching from separate points. I glanced back, and saw the ruffianly-looking man within a yard or two, with his arm raised and one finger up, telegraphing, as it seemed, to the gentlemen in front.

'Be quaite, Maud,' whispered Madame, with an awful adjuration, which I do not care to set down. 'They are teepsy; don't seem 'fraid.'

I *was* afraid—terrified. The circle had now so narrowed that they might have placed their hands on my shoulders.

'Pray, gentlemen, wat you want? *weel* a you 'av the goodness to permit us to go on?'

I now observed for the first time, with a kind of shock, that the shorter of the two men, who prevented our advance, was the person who had accosted me so offensively at Church Scarsdale. I pulled Madame by the arm, whispering, 'Let us run.'

'Be quaite, my dear Maud,' was her only reply.

'I tell you what,' said the tall man, who had replaced his high hat more jauntily than before on the side of his head, 'We've caught you now, fair game, and we'll let you off on conditions. You must not be frightened, Miss. Upon my honour and soul, I mean no mischief; do I, Lollipop? I call him Lord Lollipop; it's only chaff, though; his name's Smith. Now, Lolly, I vote we let the prisoners go, when we just introduce them to Mrs. Smith; she's sitting in the carriage, and keeps Mr. S. here in precious good order, I promise you. There's easy terms for you, eh, and we'll have a glass o' curaçoa round, and so part friends. Is it a bargain? Come!'

'Yes, Maud, we must go—wat matter?' whispered Madame vehemently.

'You shan't,' I said, instinctively terrified.

'You'll go with Ma'am, young 'un, won't you?' said Mr. Smith, as his companion called him.

Madame was holding my arm, but I snatched it from her, and would have run; the tall man, however, placed his arms round me and held me fast with an affectation of playfulness, but his grip was hard enough to hurt me a good deal. Being now thoroughly frightened, after an ineffectual struggle, during which I heard Madame say, 'You fool, Maud, weel you come with me? see wat you are doing,' I began to scream, shriek after shriek, which the man attempted to drown with loud hooting, peals of laughter, forcing his handkerchief against my mouth, while Madame continued to bawl her exhortations to 'be quaite' in my ear.

'I'll lift her, I say!' said a gruff voice behind me.

But at this instant, wild with terror, I distinctly heard other voices shouting. The men who surrounded me were instantly silent, and all looked in the direction of the sound, now very near, and I screamed with redoubled energy. The ruffian behind me thrust his great hand over my mouth.

'It is the gamekeeper,' cried Madame. '*Two* gamekeepers—we are safe—thank Heaven!' and she began to call on Dykes by name.

I only remember, feeling myself at liberty—running a few steps—seeing Dykes' white furious face—clinging to his arm, with which he was bringing his gun to a level, and saying, 'Don't fire—they'll murder us if you do.'

Madame, screaming lustily, ran up at the same moment.

'Run on to the gate and lock it—I'll be wi' ye in a minute,' cried he to the other gamekeeper; who started instantly on this mission, for the three ruffians were already in full retreat for the carriage.

Giddy—wild—fainting—still terror carried me on.

'Now, Madame Rogers—s'pose you take young Misses on—I must run and len' Bill a hand.'

'No, no; you moste not,' cried Madame. 'I am fainting myself, and more villains they may be near to us.'

But at this moment we heard a shot, and, muttering to himself and grasping his gun, Dykes ran at his utmost speed in the direction of the sound.

With many exhortations to speed, and ejaculations of alarm, Madame hurried me on toward the house, which at length we reached without further adventure.

As it happened, my father met us in the hall. He was perfectly transported with fury on hearing from Madame what had happened, and set out at once, with some of the servants, in the hope of intercepting the party at the park-gate.

Here was a new agitation; for my father did not return for nearly three hours, and I could not conjecture what might be occurring during the period of his absence. My alarm was greatly increased by the arrival in the interval of poor Bill, the under-gamekeeper, very much injured.

Seeing that he was determined to intercept their retreat, the three men had set upon him, wrested his gun, which exploded in the struggle, from him, and beat him savagely. I mention these particulars, because they convinced everybody that there was something specially determined and ferocious in the spirit of the party, and that the fracas was no mere frolic, but the result of a predetermined plan.

My father had not succeeded in overtaking them. He traced them to the Lugton Station, where they had taken the railway, and no one could tell him in what direction the carriage and posthorses had driven.

Madame was, or affected to be, very much shattered by what had occurred. Her recollection and mine, when my father questioned us closely, differed very materially respecting many details of the *personnel* of the villanous party. She was obstinate and clear; and although the gamekeeper corroborated my description of them, still my father was puzzled. Perhaps he was not sorry that some hesitation was forced upon him, because although at first he would have gone almost any length to detect the persons, on reflection he was pleased that there was not evidence to bring them into a court of justice, the publicity and annoyance of which would have been inconceivably distressing to me.

Madame was in a strange state—tempestuous in temper, talking incessantly—every now and then in floods of tears, and perpetually on her knees pouring forth torrents of thanksgiving to Heaven for our joint deliverance from the hands of those villains. Notwithstanding our community of danger and her thankfulness on my behalf, however, she broke forth into wrath and railing whenever we were alone together.

'Wat fool you were! so disobedient and obstinate; if you 'ad done wat *I* say, then we should av been quaite safe; those persons they were tipsy, and there is nothing so dangerous as to quarrel with tipsy persons; I would 'av brought you quaite safe—the lady she seem so nice and quaite, and we should 'av been safe with her—there would 'av been nothing absolutely; but instead you would scream and pooshe, and so they grow quite wild, and all the impertinence and violence follow of course; and that a poor Bill—all his beating and danger to his life it is cause entairely by you.'

And she spoke with more real virulence than that kind of upbraiding generally exhibits.

'The beast!' exclaimed Mrs. Rusk, when she, I, and Mary Quince were in my room together, 'with all her crying and praying, I'd like to know as much as she does, maybe, about them rascals. There never was sich like about the place, long as I remember it, till she came to Knowl, old witch! with them unmerciful big bones of hers, and her great bald head, grinning here, and crying there, and her nose everywhere. The old French hypocrite!'

Mary Quince threw in an observation, and I believe Mrs. Rusk rejoined, but I heard neither. For whether the housekeeper spoke with reflection or not, what she said affected me strangely. Through the smallest aperture, for a moment, I had had a peep into Pandemonium. Were not peculiarities of Madame's demeanour and advice during the adventure partly accounted for by the suggestion? Could the proposed excursion to Church Scarsdale have had any purpose of the same sort? What was proposed? How was Madame interested in it? Were such immeasurable treason and hypocrisy possible? I could not explain nor quite believe in the shapeless suspicion that with these light and bitter words of the old housekeeper had stolen so horribly into my mind.

After Mrs. Rusk was gone I awoke from my dismal abstraction with something like a moan and a shudder, with a dreadful sense of danger.

'Oh! Mary Quince,' I cried, 'do you think she really knew?'

'*Who*, Miss Maud?'

'Do you think Madame knew of those dreadful people? Oh, no—say you don't—you don't believe it—tell me she did not. I'm distracted, Mary Quince, I'm frightened out of my life.'

'There now, Miss Maud, dear—there now, don't take on so—why should she?—no sich a thing. Mrs. Rusk, law bless you, she's no more meaning in what she says than the child unborn.'

But I was really frightened. I was in a horrible state of uncertainty as to Madame de la Rougierre's complicity with the party who had beset us at the warren, and afterwards so murderously beat our poor gamekeeper. How was I ever to get rid of that horrible woman? How long was she to enjoy her continual opportunities of affrighting and injuring me?

'She hates me—she hates me, Mary Quince; and she will never stop until she has done me some dreadful injury. Oh! will no one relieve me—will no one take her away? Oh, papa, papa, papa! you will be sorry when it is too late.'

I was crying and wringing my hands, and turning from side to side, at my wits' ends, and honest Mary Quince in vain endevoured to quiet and comfort me.

CHAPTER XVIII

A MIDNIGHT VISITOR

The frightful warnings of Lady Knollys haunted me too. Was there no escape from the dreadful companion whom fate had assigned me? I made up my mind again and again to speak to my father and urge her removal. In other things he indulged me; here, however, he met me drily and sternly, and it was plain that he fancied I was under my cousin Monica's influence, and also that he had secret reasons for persisting in an opposite course. Just then I had a gay, odd letter from Lady Knollys, from some country house in Shropshire. Not a word about Captain Oakley. My eye skimmed its pages in search of that charmed name. With a peevish feeling I tossed the sheet upon the table. Inwardly I thought how ill-natured and unwomanly it was.

After a time, however, I read it, and found the letter very good-natured. She had received a note from papa. He had 'had the impudence to forgive *her* for *his* impertinence.' But for my sake she meant, notwithstanding this aggravation, really to pardon him; and whenever she had a disengaged week, to accept his invitation to Knowl, from whence she was resolved to whisk me off to London, where, though I was too young to be presented at Court and come out, I might yet—besides having the best masters and a good excuse for getting rid of Medusa—see a great deal that would amuse and surprise me.

'Great news, I suppose, from Lady Knollys?' said Madame, who always knew who in the house received letters by the post, and by an intuition from whom they came.

'Two letters—you and your papa. She is quite well, I hope?'

'Quite well, thank you, Madame.'

Some fishing questions, dropped from time to time, fared no better. And as usual, when she was foiled even in a trifle, she became sullen and malignant.

That night, when my father and I were alone, he suddenly closed the book he had been reading, and said—

'I heard from Monica Knollys to-day. I always liked poor Monnie; and though she's no witch, and very wrong-headed at times, yet now and then she does say a thing that's worth weighing. Did she ever talk to you of a time, Maud, when you are to be your own mistress?'

'No,' I answered, a little puzzled, and looking straight in his rugged, kindly face.

'Well, I thought she might—she's a rattle, you know—always *was* a rattle, and that sort of people say whatever comes uppermost. But that's a subject for me, and more than once, Maud, it has puzzled me.'

He sighed.

'Come with me to the study, little Maud.'

So, he carrying a candle, we crossed the lobby, and marched together through the passage, which at night always seemed a little awesome, darkly wainscoted, uncheered by the cross-light from the hall, which was lost at the turn, leading us away from the frequented parts of the house to that misshapen and lonely room about which the traditions of the nursery and the servants' hall had had so many fearful stories to recount.

I think my father had intended making some disclosure to me on reaching this room. If so, he changed his mind, or at least postponed his intention.

He had paused before the cabinet, respecting the key of which he had given me so strict a charge, and I think he was going to explain himself more fully than he had done. But he went on, instead, to the table where his desk, always jealously locked, was placed, and having lighted the candles which stood by it, he glanced at me, and said—

'You must wait a little, Maud; I shall have something to say to you. Take this candle and amuse yourself with a book meanwhile.'

I was accustomed to obey in silence. I chose a volume of engravings, and ensconced myself in a favourite nook in which I had often passed a half-hour similarly. This was a deep recess by the fireplace, fenced on the other side by a great old escritoir. Into this I drew a stool, and, with candle and book, I placed myself snugly in the narrow chamber. Every now and then I raised my eyes and saw my father either writing or ruminating, as it seemed to me, very anxiously at his desk.

Time wore on—a longer time than he had intended, and still he continued absorbed at his desk. Gradually I grew sleepy, and as I nodded, the book and room faded away, and pleasant little dreams began to gather round me, and so I went off into a deep slumber.

It must have lasted long, for when I wakened my candle had burnt out; my father, having quite forgotten me, was gone, and the room was dark and deserted. I felt cold and a little stiff, and for some seconds did not know where I was.

I had been wakened, I suppose, by a sound which I now distinctly heard, to my great terror, approaching. There was a rustling; there was a breathing. I heard a creaking upon the plank that always creaked when walked upon in the passage. I held my breath and listened, and coiled myself up in the innermost recess of my little chamber.

Sudden and sharp, a light shone in from the nearly-closed study door. It shone angularly on the ceiling like a letter L reversed. There was a pause. Then some one knocked softly at the door, which after another pause was slowly pushed open. I expected, I think, to see the dreaded figure of the linkman. I was scarcely less frightened to see that of Madame de la Rougierre. She was dressed in a sort of grey silk, which she called her Chinese silk—precisely as she had been in the daytime. In fact, I do not think she had undressed. She had no shoes on. Otherwise her toilet was deficient in nothing. Her wide mouth was grimly closed, and she stood scowling into the room with a searching and pallid scrutiny, the candle held high above her head at the full stretch of her arm.

Placed as I was in a deep recess, and in a seat hardly raised above the level of the floor, I escaped her, although it seemed to me for some seconds, as I gazed on this spectre, that our eyes actually met.

I sat without breathing or winking, staring upon the formidable image which with upstretched arm, and the sharp lights and hard shadows thrown upon her corrugated features, looked like a sorceress watching for the effect of a spell.

She was plainly listening intensely. Unconsciously she had drawn her lower lip altogether between her teeth, and I well remember what a deathlike and idiotic look the contortion gave her. My terror lest she should discover me amounted to positive agony. She rolled her eyes stealthily from corner to corner of the room, and listened with her neck awry at the door.

Then to my father's desk she went. To my great relief, her back was towards me. She stooped over it, with the candle close by; I saw her try a key—it could be nothing else—and I heard her blow through the wards to clear them.

Then, again, she listened at the door, candle in hand, and then with long tiptoe steps came back, and papa's desk in another moment was open, and Madame cautiously turning over the papers it contained.

Twice or thrice she paused, glided to the door, and listened again intently with her head near the ground, and then returned and continued her search, peeping into papers one after another, tolerably methodically, and reading some quite through.

While this felonious business was going on, I was freezing with fear lest she should accidentally look round and her eyes light on me; for I could not say what she might not do rather than have her crime discovered.

Sometimes she would read a paper twice over; sometimes a whisper no louder than the ticking of a watch, sometimes a brief chuckle under her breath, bespoke the interest with which here and there a letter or a memorandum was read.

For about half an hour, I think, this went on; but at the time it seemed to me all but interminable. On a sudden she raised her head and listened for a moment, replaced the papers deftly, closed the desk without noise, except for the tiny click of the lock, extinguished the candle, and rustled stealthily out of the room, leaving in the darkness the malign and hag-like face on which the candle had just shone still floating filmy in the dark.

Why did I remain silent and motionless while such an outrage was being committed? If, instead of being a very nervous girl, preoccupied with an undefinable terror of that wicked woman, I had possessed courage and presence of mind, I dare say I might have given an alarm, and escaped from the room without the slightest risk. But so it was; I could no more stir than the bird who, cowering under its ivy, sees the white owl sailing back and forward under its predatory cruise.

Not only during her presence, but for more than an hour after, I remained cowering in my hiding-place, and afraid to stir, lest she might either be lurking in the neighborhood, or return and surprise me.

You will not be astonished, that after a night so passed I was ill and feverish in the morning. To my horror, Madame de la Rougierre came to visit me at my bedside. Not a trace of guilty consciousness of what had passed during the night was legible in her face. She had no sign of late watching, and her toilet was exemplary.

As she sat smiling by me, full of anxious and affectionate enquiry, and smoothed the coverlet with her great felonious hand, I could quite comprehend the dreadful feeling with which the deceived husband in the 'Arabian Nights' met his ghoul wife, after his nocturnal discovery.

Ill as I was, I got up and found my father in that room which adjoined his bedchamber. He perceived, I am sure, by my looks, that something unusual had happened. I shut the door, and came close beside his chair.

'Oh, papa, I have such a thing to tell you!' I forgot to call him 'Sir.' 'A secret; and you won't say who told you? Will you come down to the study?'

He looked hard at me, got up, and kissing my forehead, said—'Don't be frightened, Maud; I venture to say it is a mare's nest; at all events, my child, we will take care that no danger reaches you; come, child.'

And by the hand he led me to the study. When the door was shut, and we had reached the far end of the room next the window, I said, but in a low tone, and holding his arm fast—

'Oh, sir, you don't know what a dreadful person we have living with us—Madame de la Rougierre, I mean. Don't let her in if she comes; she would guess what I am telling you, and one way or another I am sure she would kill me.'

'Tut, tut, child. You *must* know that's nonsense,' he said, looking pale and stern.

'Oh no, papa. I am horribly frightened, and Lady Knollys thinks so too.'

'Ha! I dare say; one fool makes many. We all know what Monica thinks.'

'But I *saw* it, papa. She stole your key last night, and opened your desk, and read all your papers.'

'Stole my key!' said my father, staring at me perplexed, but at the same instant producing it. 'Stole it! Why here it is!'

'She unlocked your desk; she read your papers for ever so long. Open it now, and see whether they have not been stirred.'

He looked at me this time in silence, with a puzzled air; but he did unlock the desk, and lifted the papers curiously and suspiciously. As he did so he uttered a few of those inarticulate interjections which are made with closed lips, and not always intelligible; but he made no remark.

Then he placed me on a chair beside him, and sitting down himself, told me to recollect myself, and tell him distinctly all I had seen. This accordingly I did, he listening with deep attention.

'Did she remove any paper?' asked my father, at the same time making a little search, I suppose, for that which he fancied might have been stolen.

'No; I did not see her take anything.'

'Well, you are a good girl, Maud. Act discreetly. Say nothing to anyone—not even to your cousin Monica.'

Directions which, coming from another person would have had no great weight, were spoken by my father with an earnest look and a weight of emphasis that made them irresistibly impressive, and I went away with the seal of silence upon my lips.

'Sit down, Maud, *there*. You have not been very happy with Madame de la Rougierre. It is time you were relieved. This occurrence decides it.'

He rang the bell.

'Tell Madame de la Rougierre that I request the honour of seeing her for a few minutes here.'

My father's communications to her were always equally ceremonious. In a few minutes there was a knock at the door, and the same figure, smiling, courtesying, that had scared me on the threshold last night, like the spirit of evil, presented itself.

My father rose, and Madame having at his request taken a chair opposite, looking, as usual in his presence, all amiability, he proceeded at once to the point.

'Madame de la Rougierre, I have to request you that you will give me the key now in your possession, which unlocks this desk of mine.'

With which termination he tapped his gold pencil-case suddenly on it.

Madame, who had expected something very different, became instantly so pale, with a dull purplish hue upon her forehead, that, especially when she had twice essayed with her white lips, in vain, to answer, I expected to see her fall in a fit.

She was not looking in his face; her eyes were fixed lower, and her mouth and cheek sucked in, with a strange distortion at one side.

She stood up suddenly, and staring straight in his face, she succeeded in saying, after twice clearing her throat—

'I cannot comprehend, Monsieur Ruthyn, unless you intend to insult me.'

'It won't do, Madame; I must have that false key. I give you the opportunity of surrendering it quietly here and now.'

'But who dares to say I possess such thing?' demanded Madame, who, having rallied from her momentary paralysis, was now fierce and voluble as I had often seen her before.

'You know, Madame, that you can rely on what I say, and I tell you that you were seen last night visiting this room, and with a key in your possession, opening this desk, and reading my letters and papers contained in it. Unless you forthwith give me that key, and any other false keys in your possession—in which case I shall rest content with dismissing you summarily—I will take a different course. You know I am a magistrate;—and I shall have you, your boxes, and places upstairs, searched forthwith, and I will prosecute you criminally. The thing is clear; you aggravate by denying; you must give me that key, if you please, instantly, otherwise I ring this bell, and you shall see that I mean what I say.'

There was a little pause. He rose and extended his hand towards the bell-rope. Madame glided round the table, extended her hand to arrest his.

'I will do everything, Monsieur Ruthyn—whatever you wish.'

And with these words Madame de la Rougierre broke down altogether. She sobbed, she wept, she gabbled piteously, all manner of incomprehensible roulades of lamentation and entreaty; coyly, penitently, in a most interesting agitation, she produced the very key from her breast, with a string tied to it. My father was little moved by this piteous tempest. He coolly took the key and tried it in the desk, which it locked and unlocked quite freely, though the wards were complicated. He shook his head and looked her in the face.

'Pray, who made this key? It is a new one, and made expressly to pick this lock.'

But Madame was not going to tell any more than she had expressly bargained for; so she only fell once more into her old paroxysm of sorrow, self-reproach, extenuation, and entreaty.

'Well,' said my father,' I promised that on surrendering the key you should go. It is enough. I keep my word. You shall have an hour and a half to prepare in. You must then be ready to depart. I will send your money to you by Mrs. Rusk; and if you look for another situation, you had better not refer to me. Now be so good as to leave me.'

Madame seemed to be in a strange perplexity. She bridled up, dried her eyes fiercely, and dropped a great courtesy, and then sailed away towards the door. Before reaching it she stopped on the way, turning half round, with a peaked, pallid glance at my father, and she bit her lip viciously as she eyed him. At the door the same repulsive pantomime was repeated, as she stood for a moment with her hand upon the handle. But she changed her bearing again with a sniff, and with a look of scorn, almost heightened to a sneer, she made another very low courtesy and a disdainful toss of her head, and so disappeared, shutting the door rather sharply behind her.

CHAPTER XIX

AU REVOIR

Mrs. Rusk was fond of assuring me that Madame 'did not like a bone in my skin.' Instinctively I knew that she bore me no good-will, although I really believe it was her wish to make me think quite the reverse. At all events I had no desire to see Madame again before her departure, especially as she had thrown upon me one momentary glance in the study, which seemed to me charged with very peculiar feelings.

You may be very sure, therefore, that I had no desire for a formal leave-taking at her departure. I took my hat and cloak, therefore, and stole out quietly.

My ramble was a sequestered one, and well screened, even at this late season, with foliage; the pathway devious among the stems of old trees, and its flooring interlaced and groined with their knotted roots. Though near the house, it was a sylvan solitude; a little brook ran darkling and glimmering through it, wild strawberries and other woodland plants strewed the ground, and the sweet notes and flutter of small birds made the shadow of the boughs cheery.

I had been fully an hour in this picturesque solitude when I heard in the distance the ring of carriage-wheels, announcing to me that Madame de la Rougierre had fairly set out upon her travels. I thanked heaven; I could have danced and sung with delight; I heaved a great sigh and looked up through the branches to the clear blue sky.

But things are oddly timed. Just at this moment I heard Madame's voice close at my ear, and her large bony hand was laid on my shoulder. We were instantly face to face—I recoiling, and for a moment speechless with fright.

In very early youth we do not appreciate the restraints which act upon malignity, or know how effectually fear protects us where conscience is wanting. Quite alone, in this solitary spot, detected and overtaken with an awful instinct by my enemy, what might not be about to happen to me at that moment?

'Frightened as usual, Maud,' she said quietly, and eyeing me with a sinister smile, 'and with cause you think, no doubt. Wat 'av you done to injure poor Madame? Well, I think I know, little girl, and have quite discover the cleverness of my sweet little Maud. Eh—is not so? Petite carogne—ah, ha, ha!'

I was too much confounded to answer.

'You see, my dear cheaile,' she said, shaking her uplifted finger with a hideous archness at me, 'you could not hide what you 'av done from poor Madame. You cannot look so innocent but I can see your pretty little villany quite plain—you dear little diablesse.

'Wat I 'av done I 'av no reproach of myself for it. If I could explain, your papa would say I 'av done right, and you should thank me on your knees; but I cannot explain yet.'

She was speaking, as it were, in little paragraphs, with a momentary pause between each, to allow its meaning to impress itself.

'If I were to choose to explain, your papa he would implore me to remain. But no—I would not—notwithstanding your so cheerful house, your charming servants, your papa's amusing society, and your affectionate and sincere heart, my sweet little maraude.

'I am to go to London first, where I 'av, oh, so good friends! next I will go abroad for some time; but be sure, my sweetest Maud, wherever I may 'appen to be, I will remember you—ah, ha! Yes; *most certainly*, I will remember you.

'And although I shall not be always near, yet I shall know everything about my charming little Maud; you will not know how, but I shall indeed, *everything*. And be sure, my dearest cheaile, I will some time be able to give you the sensible proofs of my gratitude and affection—you understand.

'The carriage is waiting at the yew-tree stile, and I must go on. You did not expect to see me—here; I will appear, perhaps, as suddenly another time. It is great pleasure to us both—this opportunity to make our adieux. Farewell! my dearest little Maud. I will never cease to think of you, and of some way to recompense the kindness you 'av shown for poor Madame.'

My hand hung by my side, and she took, not it, but my thumb, and shook it, folded in her broad palm, and looking on me as she held it, as if meditating mischief. Then suddenly she said—

'You will always remember Madame, I *think*, and I will remind you of me beside; and for the present farewell, and I hope you may be as 'appy as you deserve.'

The large sinister face looked on me for a second with its latent sneer, and then, with a sharp nod and a spasmodic shake of my imprisoned thumb, she turned, and holding her dress together, and showing her great bony ankles, she strode rapidly away over the gnarled roots into the perspective of the trees, and I did not awake, as it were, until she had quite disappeared in the distance.

Events of this kind made no difference with my father; but every other face in Knowl was gladdened by the removal. My energies had returned, my spirits were come again. The sunlight was happy, the flowers innocent, the songs and flutter of the birds once more gay, and all nature delightful and rejoicing.

After the first elation of relief, now and then a filmy shadow of Madame de la Rougierre would glide across the sunlight, and the remembrance of her menace return with an unexpected pang of fear.

'Well, if *there* isn't impittens!' cried Mrs. Rusk. 'But never you trouble your head about it, Miss. Them sort's all alike—you never saw a rogue yet that was found out and didn't threaten the honest folk as he was leaving behind with all sorts; there was Martin the gamekeeper, and Jervis the footman, I mind well how hard they swore all they would not do when they was a-going, and who ever heard of them since? They always threatens that way—them sort always does, and none ever the worse—not but she would if she could, mind ye, but there it is; she can't do nothing but bite her nails and cuss us—not she—ha, ha, ha!'

So I was comforted. But Madame's evil smile, nevertheless, from time to time, would sail across my vision with a silent menace, and my spirits sank, and a Fate, draped in black, whose face I could not see, took me by the hand, and led me away, in the spirit, silently, on an awful exploration from which I would rouse myself with a start, and Madame was gone for a while.

She had, however, judged her little parting well. She contrived to leave her glamour over me, and in my dreams she troubled me.

I was, however, indescribably relieved. I wrote in high spirits to Cousin Monica; and wondered what plans my father might have formed about me, and whether we were to stay at home, or go to London, or go abroad. Of the last—the pleasantest arrangement, in some respects—I had nevertheless an occult horror. A secret conviction haunted me that were we to go abroad, we should there meet Madame, which to me was like meeting my evil genius.

I have said more than once that my father was an odd man; and the reader will, by this time, have seen that there was much about him not easily understood. I often wonder whether, if he had been franker, I should have found him less odd than I supposed, or more odd still. Things that moved me profoundly did not apparently affect him at all. The departure of Madame, under the circumstances which attended it, appeared to my childish mind an event of the vastest importance. No one was indifferent to the occurrence in the house but its master. He never alluded again to Madame de la Rougierre. But whether connected with her exposure and dismissal, I could not say, there did appear to be some new care or trouble now at work in my father's mind.

'I have been thinking a great deal about you, Maud. I am anxious. I have not been so troubled for years. Why has not Monica Knollys a little more sense?'

This oracular sentence he spoke, having stopped me in the hall; and then saying, 'We shall see,' he left me as abruptly as he appeared.

Did he apprehend any danger to me from the vindictiveness of Madame?

A day or two afterwards, as I was in the Dutch garden, I saw him on the terrace steps. He beckoned to me, and came to meet me as I approached.

'You must be very solitary, little Maud; it is not good. I have written to Monica: in a matter of detail she is competent to advise; perhaps she will come here for a short visit.'

I was very glad to hear this.

'*You* are more interested than for my time *I* can be, in vindicating his character.'

'Whose character, sir?' I ventured to enquire during the pause that followed.

One trick which my father had acquired from his habits of solitude and silence was this of assuming that the context of his thoughts was legible to others, forgetting that they had not been spoken.

'Whose?—your uncle Silas's. In the course of nature he must survive me. He will then represent the family name. Would you make some sacrifice to clear that name, Maud?'

I answered briefly; but my face, I believe, showed my enthusiasm.

He turned on me such an approving smile as you might fancy lighting up the rugged features of a pale old Rembrandt.

'I can tell you, Maud; if my life could have done it, it should not have been undone—*ubi lapsus, quid feci*. But I had almost made up my mind to change my plan, and leave all to time—*edax rerum*—to illuminate or to *consume*. But I think little Maud would like to contribute to the restitution of her family name. It may cost you something—are you willing to buy it at a sacrifice? Is there—I don't speak of fortune, that is not involved—but is there any other honourable sacrifice you would shrink from to dispel the disgrace under which our most ancient and honourable name must otherwise continue to languish?'

'Oh, none—none indeed, sir—I am delighted!'

Again I saw the Rembrandt smile.

'Well, Maud, I am sure there is *no* risk; but you are to suppose there is. Are you still willing to accept it?'

Again I assented.

'You are worthy of your blood, Maud Ruthyn. It will come soon, and it won't last long. But you must not let people like Monica Knollys frighten you.'

I was lost in wonder.

'If you allow them to possess you with their follies, you had better recede in time—they may make the ordeal as terrible as hell itself. You have zeal—have you nerve?'

I thought in such a cause I had nerve for anything.

'Well, Maud, in the course of a few months—and it may be sooner—there must be a change. I have had a letter from London this morning that assures me of that. I must then leave you for a time; in my absence be faithful to the duties that will arise. To whom much is committed, of him will much be required. You shall promise me not to mention this conversation to Monica Knollys. If you are a talking girl, and cannot trust yourself, say so, and we will not ask her to come. Also, don't invite her to talk about your uncle Silas—I have reasons. Do you quite understand my conditions?'

'Yes, sir.'

'Your uncle Silas,' he said, speaking suddenly in loud and fierce tones that sounded from so old a man almost terrible, 'lies under an intolerable slander. I don't correspond with him; I don't sympathise with him; I never quite did. He has grown religious, and that's well; but there are things in which even religion should not bring a man to acquiesce; and from what I can learn, he, the person primarily affected—the cause, though the innocent cause—of this great calamity—bears it with an easy apathy which is mistaken, and liable easily to be mistaken, and such as no Ruthyn, under the circumstances, ought to exhibit. I told him what he ought to do, and offered to open my purse for the purpose; but he would not, or *did* not; indeed, he *never* took my advice; he followed his own, and a foul and dismal shoal he has drifted on. It is not for his sake—why should I?-that I have longed and laboured to remove the disgraceful slur under which his ill-fortune has thrown us. He troubles himself little about it, I believe—he's meek, meeker than I. He cares less about his children than I about you, Maud; he is selfishly sunk in futurity—a feeble visionary. I am not so. I believe it to be a duty to take care of others beside myself. The character and influence of an ancient family is a peculiar heritage—sacred but destructible; and woe to him who either destroys or suffers it to perish!'

This was the longest speech I ever heard my father speak before or after. He abruptly resumed—

'Yes, we will, Maud—you and I—we'll leave one proof on record, which, fairly read, will go far to convince the world.'

He looked round, but we were alone. The garden was nearly always solitary, and few visitors ever approached the house from that side.

'I have talked too long, I believe; we are children to the last. Leave me, Maud. I think I know you better than I did, and I am pleased with you. Go, child—I'll sit here.'

If he had acquired new ideas of me, so had I of him from that interview. I had no idea till then how much passion still burned in that aged frame, nor how full of energy and fire that face, generally so stern and ashen, could appear. As I left him seated on the rustic chair, by the steps, the traces of that storm were still discernible on his features. His gathered brows, glowing eyes, and strangely hectic face, and the grim compression of his mouth, still showed the agitation which, somehow, in grey old age, shocks and alarms the young.

CHAPTER XX

AUSTIN RUTHYN SETS OUT ON HIS JOURNEY

The Rev. William Fairfield, Doctor Clay's somewhat bald curate, a mild, thin man, with a high and thin nose, who was preparing me for confirmation, came next day; and when our catechetical conference was ended, and before lunch was announced, my father sent for him to the study, where he remained until the bell rang out its summons.

'We have had some interesting—I may say *very* interesting—conversation, your papa and I, Miss Ruthyn,' said my reverend *vis-à-vis*, so soon as nature was refreshed, smiling and shining, as he leaned back in his chair, his hand upon the table, and his finger curled gently upon the stem of his wine-glass. 'It never was your privilege, I believe, to see your uncle, Mr. Silas Ruthyn, of Bartram-Haugh?'

'No—never; he leads so retired—so *very* retired a life.'

'Oh, no,—of course, no; but I was going to remark a likeness—I mean, of course, a *family* likeness—only *that* sort of thing—you understand—between him and the profile of Lady Margaret in the drawing-room—is not it Lady Margaret?—which you were so good as to show me on Wednesday last. There certainly *is* a likeness. I *think* you would agree with me, if you had the pleasure of seeing your uncle.'

'You know him, then? I have never seen him.'

'Oh dear, yes—I am happy to say, I know him very well. I have that privilege. I was for three years curate of Feltram, and I had the honour of being a pretty constant visitor at Bartram-Haugh during that, I may say, protracted period; and I think it really never has been my privilege and happiness, I may say, to enjoy the acquaintance and society of so very experienced a Christian, as my admirable friend, I may call him, Mr. Ruthyn, of Bartram-Haugh. I look upon him, I do assure you, quite in the light of a saint; not, of course, in the Popish sense, but in the very highest, you will understand me, which *our* Church allows,—a man built up in faith—full of faith—faith and grace—altogether exemplary; and I often ventured to regret, Miss Ruthyn, that Providence in its mysterious dispensations should have placed him so far apart from his brother, your respected father. His influence and opportunities would, no doubt, we may venture to hope, at least have been blessed; and, perhaps, we—my valued rector and I—might possibly have seen more of him at church, than, I deeply regret, we *have* done.' He shook his head a little, as he smiled with a sad complacency on me through his blue steel spectacles, and then sipped a little meditative sherry.

'And you saw a good deal of my uncle?'

'Well, a *good* deal, Miss Ruthyn—I may say a *good* deal—principally at his own house. His health is wretched—miserable health—a sadly afflicted man he has been, as, no doubt, you are aware. But afflictions, my dear Miss Ruthyn, as you remember Doctor Clay so well remarked on Sunday last, though birds of ill omen, yet spiritually resemble the ravens who supplied the prophet; and when they visit the faithful, come charged with nourishment for the soul.

'He is a good deal embarrassed pecuniarily, I should say,' continued the curate, who was rather a good man than a very well-bred one. 'He found a difficulty—in fact it was not in his power—to subscribe generally to our little funds, and—and objects, and I used to say to him, and I really felt it, that it was more gratifying, such were his feeling and his power of expression, to be refused by him than assisted by others.'

'Did papa wish you to speak to me about my uncle?' I enquired, as a sudden thought struck me; and then I felt half ashamed of my question.

He looked surprised.

'No, Miss Ruthyn, certainly not. Oh dear, no. It was merely a conversation between Mr. Ruthyn and me. He never suggested my opening that, or indeed any other point in my interview with you, Miss Ruthyn—not the least.'

'I was not aware before that Uncle Silas was so religious.'

He smiled tranquilly, not quite up to the ceiling, but gently upward, and shook his head in pity for my previous ignorance, as he lowered his eyes—

'I don't say that there may not be some little matters in a few points of doctrine which we could, perhaps, wish otherwise. But these, you know, are speculative, and in all essentials he is Church—not in the perverted modern sense; far from it—unexceptionably Church, strictly so. Would there were more among us of the same mind that is in him! Ay, Miss Ruthyn, even in the highest places of the Church herself.'

The Rev. William Fairfield, while fighting against the Dissenters with his right hand, was, with his left, hotly engaged with the Tractarians. A good man I am sure he was, and I dare say sound in doctrine, though naturally, I think, not very wise. This conversation with him gave me new ideas about my uncle Silas. It quite agreed with what my father had said. These principles and his increasing years would necessarily quiet the turbulence of his resistance to injustice, and teach him to acquiesce in his fate.

You would have fancied that one so young as I, born to wealth so vast, and living a life of such entire seclusion, would have been exempt from care. But you have seen how troubled my life was with fear and anxiety during the residence of Madame de la Rougierre, and now there rested upon my mind a vague and awful anticipation of the trial which my father had announced, without defining it.

An 'ordeal' he called it, requiring not only zeal but nerve, which might possibly, were my courage to fail, become frightful, and even intolerable. What, and of what nature, could it be? Not designed to vindicate the fair fame of the meek and submissive old man—who, it seemed, had ceased to care for his bygone wrongs, and was looking to futurity—but the reputation of our ancient family.

Sometimes I repented my temerity in having undertaken it. I distrusted my courage. Had I not better retreat, while it was yet time? But there was shame and even difficulty in the thought. How should I appear before my father? Was it not important—had I not deliberately undertaken it—and was I not bound in conscience? Perhaps he had already taken steps in the matter which committed *him*. Besides, was I sure that, even were I free again, I would not once more devote myself to the trial, be it what it might? You perceive I had more spirit than courage. I think I had the mental attributes of courage; but then I was but a hysterical girl, and in so far neither more nor less than a coward.

No wonder I distrusted myself; no wonder also my will stood out against my timidity. It was a struggle, then; a proud, wild resolve against constitutional cowardice.

Those who have ever had cast upon them more than their strength seemed framed to bear—the weak, the aspiring, the adventurous and self-sacrificing in will, and the faltering in nerve—will understand the kind of agony which I sometimes endured.

But, again, consolation would come, and it seemed to me that I must be exaggerating my risk in the coming crisis; and certain at least, if my father believed it attended with real peril, he would never have wished to see me involved in it. But the silence under which I was bound was terrifying—double so when the danger was so shapeless and undivulged.

I was soon to understand it all—soon, too, to know all about my father's impending journey, whither, with what visitor, and why guarded from me with so awful a mystery.

That day there came a lively and goodnatured letter from Lady Knollys. She was to arrive at Knowl in two or three days' time. I thought my father would have been pleased, but he seemed apathetic and dejected.

'One does not always feel quite equal to Monica. But for you—yes, thank God. I wish she could only stay, Maud, for a month or two; I may be going then, and would be glad—provided she talks about suitable things—very glad, Maud, to leave her with you for a week or so.'

There was something, I thought, agitating my father secretly that day. He had the strange hectic flush I had observed when he grew excited in our interview in the garden about Uncle Silas. There was something painful, perhaps even terrible, in the circumstances of the journey he was about to make, and from my heart I wished the suspense were over, the annoyance past, and he returned.

That night my father bid me good-night early and went up-stairs. After I had been in bed some little time, I heard his hand-bell ring. This was not usual. Shortly after I heard his man, Ridley, talking with Mrs. Rusk in the gallery. I could not be mistaken in their voices. I knew not why I was startled and excited, and had raised myself to listen on my elbow. But they were talking quietly, like persons giving or taking an ordinary direction, and not in the haste of an unusual emergency.

Then I heard the man bid Mrs. Rusk good-night and walk down the gallery to the stairs, so that I concluded he was wanted no more, and all must therefore be well. So I laid myself down again, though with a throbbing at my heart, and an ominous feeling of expectation, listening and fancying footsteps.

I was going to sleep when I heard the bell ring again; and, in a few minutes, Mrs. Rusk's energetic step passed along the gallery; and, listening intently, I heard, or fancied, my father's voice and hers in dialogue. All this was very unusual, and again I was, with a beating heart, leaning with my elbow on my pillow.

Mrs. Rusk came along the gallery in a minute or so after, and stopping at my door, began to open it gently. I was startled, and challenged my visitor with—

'Who's there?'

'It's only Rusk, Miss. Dearie me! and are you awake still?'

'Is papa ill?'

'Ill! not a bit ill, thank God. Only there's a little black book as I took for your prayer-book, and brought in here; ay, here it is, sure enough, and he wants it. And then I must go down to the study, and look out this one, "C, 15;" but I can't read the name, noways; and I was afraid to ask him again; if you be so kind to read it, Miss—I suspeck my eyes is a-going.'

I read the name; and Mrs. Rusk was tolerably expert at finding out books, as she had often been employed in that way before. So she departed.

I suppose that this particular volume was hard to find, for she must have been a long time away, and I had actually fallen into a doze when I was roused in an instant by a dreadful crash and a piercing scream from Mrs. Rusk. Scream followed scream, wilder and more terror-stricken. I shrieked to Mary Quince, who was sleeping in the room with me:—'Mary, do you hear? what is it? It is something dreadful.'

The crash was so tremendous that the solid flooring even of my room trembled under it, and to me it seemed as if some heavy man had burst through the top of the window, and shook the whole house with his descent. I found myself standing at my own door, crying, 'Help, help! murder! murder!' and Mary Quince, frightened half out of her wits, by my side.

I could not think what was going on. It was plainly something most horrible, for Mrs. Rusk's screams pealed one after the other unabated, though with a muffled sound, as if the door was shut upon her; and by this time the bells of my father's room were ringing madly.

'They are trying to murder him!' I cried, and I ran along the gallery to his door, followed by Mary Quince, whose white face I shall never forget, though her entreaties only sounded like unmeaning noises in my ears.

'Here! help, help, help!' I cried, trying to force open the door.

'Shove it, shove it, for God's sake! he's across it,' cried Mrs. Rusk's voice from within; 'drive it in. I can't move him.'

I strained all I could at the door, but ineffectually. We heard steps approaching. The men were running to the spot, and shouting as they did so—

'Never mind; hold on a bit; here we are; all right;' and the like.

We drew back, as they came up. We were in no condition to be seen. We listened, however, at my open door.

Then came the straining and bumping at the door. Mrs. Rusk's voice subsided to a sort of wailing; the men were talking all together, and I suppose the door opened, for I heard some of the voices, on a sudden, as if in the room; and then came a strange lull, and talking in very low tones, and not much even of that.

'What is it, Mary? what *can* it be?' I ejaculated, not knowing what horror to suppose. And now, with a counterpane about my shoulders, I called loudly and imploringly, in my horror, to know what had happened.

But I heard only the subdued and eager talk of men engaged in some absorbing task, and the dull sounds of some heavy body being moved.

Mrs. Rusk came towards us looking half wild, and pale as a spectre, and putting her thin hands to my shoulders, she said—'Now, Miss Maud, darling, you must go back again; 'tisn't no place for you; you'll see all, my darling, time enough—you will. There now, there, like a dear, do get into your room.'

What was that dreadful sound? Who had entered my father's chamber? It was the visitor whom we had so long expected, with whom he was to make the unknown journey, leaving me alone. The intruder was Death!

CHAPTER XXI

ARRIVALS

My father was dead—as suddenly as if he had been murdered. One of those fearful aneurisms that lie close to the heart, showing no outward sign of giving way in a moment, had been detected a good time since by Dr. Bryerly. My father knew what must happen, and that it could not be long deferred. He feared to tell me that he was soon to die. He hinted it only in the allegory of his journey, and left in that sad enigma some words of true consolation that remained with me ever after. Under his rugged ways was hidden a wonderful tenderness. I could not believe that he was actually dead. Most people for a minute or two, in the wild tumult of such a shock, have experienced the same skepticism. I insisted that the doctor should be instantly sent for from the village.

'Well, Miss Maud, dear, I *will* send to please you, but it is all to no use. If only you saw him yourself you'd know that. Mary Quince, run you down and tell Thomas, Miss Maud desires he'll go down this minute to the village for Dr. Elweys.'

Every minute of the interval seemed to me like an hour. I don't know what I said, but I fancied that if he were not already dead, he would lose his life by the delay. I suppose I was speaking very wildly, for Mrs. Rusk said—

'My dear child, you ought to come in and see him; indeed but you should, Miss Maud. He's quite dead an hour ago. You'd wonder all the blood that's come from him—you would indeed; it's soaked through the bed already.'

'Oh, don't, don't, *don't*, Mrs. Rusk.'

'Will you come in and see him, just?

'Oh, no, no, no, no!'

'Well, then, my dear, don't of course, if you don't like; there's no need. Would not you like to lie down, Miss Maud? Mary Quince, attend to her. I must go into the room for a minute or two.'

I was walking up and down the room in distraction. It was a cool night; but I did not feel it. I could only cry:—'Oh, Mary, Mary! what shall I do? Oh, Mary Quince! what shall I do?'

It seemed to me it must be near daylight by the time the Doctor arrived. I had dressed myself. I dared not go into the room where my beloved father lay.

I had gone out of my room to the gallery, where I awaited Dr. Elweys, when I saw him walking briskly after the servant, his coat buttoned up to his chin, his hat in his hand, and his bald head shining. I felt myself grow cold as ice, and colder and colder, and with a sudden sten my heart seemed to stand still.

I heard him ask the maid who stood at the door, in that low, decisive, mysterious tone which doctors cultivate—

'In *here*?'

And then, with a nod, I saw him enter.

'Would not you like to see the Doctor, Miss Maud?' asked Mary Quince.

The question roused me a little.

'Thank you, Mary; yes, I must see him.'

And so, in a few minutes, I did. He was very respectful, very sad, semi-undertakerlike, in air and countenance, but quite explicit. I heard that my dear father 'had died palpably from the rupture of some great vessel near the heart.' The disease had, no doubt, been 'long established, and is in its nature incurable.' It is 'consolatory in these cases that in the act of dissolution, which is instantaneous, there can be no suffering.' These, and a few more remarks, were all he had to offer; and having had his fee from Mrs. Rusk, he, with a respectful melancholy, vanished.

I returned to my room, and broke into paroxysms of grief, and after an hour or more grew more tranquil.

From Mrs. Rusk I learned that he had seemed very well—better than usual, indeed—that night, and that on her return from the study with the book he required, he was noting down, after his wont, some passages which illustrated the text on which he was employing himself. He took the book, detaining her in the room, and then mounting on a chair to take down another book from a shelf, he had fallen, with the dreadful crash I had heard, dead upon the floor. He fell across the door, which caused the difficulty in opening it. Mrs. Rusk found she had not strength to force it open. No wonder she had given way to terror. I think I should have almost lost my reason.

Everyone knows the reserved aspect and the taciturn mood of the house, one of whose rooms is tenanted by that mysterious guest.

I do not know how those awful days, and more awful nights, passed over. The remembrance is repulsive. I hate to think of them. I was soon draped in the conventional black, with its heavy folds of crape. Lady Knollys came, and was very kind. She undertook the direction of all those details which were to me so inexpressibly dreadful. She wrote letters for me beside, and was really most kind and useful, and her society supported me indescribably. She was odd, but her eccentricity was leavened with strong common sense; and I have often thought since with admiration and gratitude of the tact with which she managed my grief.

There is no dealing with great sorrow as if it were under the control of our wills. It is a terrible phenomenon, whose laws we must study, and to whose conditions we must submit, if we would mitigate it. Cousin Monica talked a great deal of my father. This was easy to her, for her early recollections were full of him.

One of the terrible dislocations of our habits of mind respecting the dead is that our earthly future is robbed of them, and we thrown exclusively upon retrospect. From the long look forward they are removed, and every plan, imagination, and hope henceforth a silent and empty perspective. But in the past they are all they ever were. Now let me advise all who would comfort people in a new bereavement to talk to them, very freely, all they can, in this way of the dead. They will engage in it with interest, they will talk of their own recollections of the dead, and listen to yours, though they become sometimes pleasant, sometimes even laughable. I found it so. It robbed the calamity of something of its supernatural and horrible abruptness; it prevented that monotony of object which is to the mind what it is to the eye, and prepared the faculty for those mesmeric illusions that derange its sense.

Cousin Monica, I am sure, cheered me wonderfully. I grow to love her more and more, as I think of all her trouble, care, and kindness.

I had not forgotten my promise to dear papa about the key, concerning which he had evinced so great an anxiety. It was found in the pocket where he had desired me to remember he always kept it, except when it was placed, while he slept, under his pillow.

'And so, my dear, that wicked woman was actually found picking the lock of your poor papa's desk. I *wonder* he did not punish her—you know that is *burglary*.'

'Well, Lady Knollys, you know she is gone, and so I care no more about her—that is, I mean, I need not fear her.'

'No, my dear, but you must call me Monica—do you mind—I'm your cousin, and you call me Monica, unless you wish to vex me. No, of course, you need not be afraid of her. And she's gone. But I'm an old thing, you know, and not so tender-hearted as you; and I confess I should have been very glad to hear that the wicked old witch had been sent to prison and hard labour—I should. And what do you suppose she was looking for—what did she want to steal? I think I can guess—what do *you* think?'

'To read the papers; maybe to take bank-notes—I'm not sure,' I answered.

'Well, I think most likely she wanted to get at your poor papa's *will*—that's *my* idea.

'There is nothing surprising in the supposition, dear,' she resumed. 'Did not you read the curious trial at York, the other day? There is nothing so valuable to steal as a will, when a great deal of property is to be disposed of by it. Why, you would have given her ever so much money to get it back again. Suppose you go down, dear—I'll go with you, and open the cabinet in the study.'

'I don't think I can, for I promised to give the key to Dr. Bryerly, and the meaning was that *he* only should open it.'

Cousin Monica uttered an inarticulate 'H'm!' of surprise or disapprobation.

'Has he been written to?'

'No, I do not know his address.'

'Not know his address! come, that is curious,' said Knollys, a little testily.

I could not—no one now living in the house could furnish even a conjecture. There was even a dispute as to which train he had gone by—north or south—they crossed the station at an interval of five minutes. If Dr. Bryerly had been an evil spirit, evoked by a secret incantation, there could not have been more complete darkness as to the immediate process of his approach.

'And how long do you mean to wait, my dear? No matter; at all events you may open the *desk*; you may find papers to direct you—you may find Dr. Bryerly's address—you may find, heaven knows what.'

So down we went—I assenting—and we opened the desk. How dreadful the desecration seems—all privacy abrogated—the shocking compensation for the silence of death!

Henceforward all is circumstantial evidence—all conjectural—except the *litera scripta*, and to this evidence every note-book, and every scrap of paper and private letter, must contribute—ransacked, bare in the light of day—what it can.

At the top of the desk lay two notes sealed, one to Cousin Monica, the other to me. Mine was a gentle and loving little farewell—nothing more—which opened afresh the fountains of my sorrow, and I cried and sobbed over it bitterly and long.

The other was for 'Lady Knollys.' I did not see how she received it, for I was already absorbed in mine. But in awhile she came and kissed me in her girlish, goodnatured way. Her eyes used to fill with tears at sight of my paroxysms of grief. Then she would begin, 'I remember it was a saying of his,' and so she would repeat it—something maybe wise, maybe playful, at all events consolatory—and the circumstances in which she had heard him say it, and then would follow the recollections suggested by these; and so I was stolen away half by him, and half by Cousin Monica, from my despair and lamentation.

Along with these lay a large envelope, inscribed with the words 'Directions to be complied with immediately on my death.' One of which was, 'Let the event be *forthwith* published in the *county* and principal *London* papers.' This step had been already taken. We found no record of Dr. Bryerly's address.

We made search everywhere, except in the cabinet, which I would on no account permit to be opened except, according to his direction, by Dr. Bryerly's hand. But nowhere was a will, or any document resembling one, to be found. I had now, therefore, no doubt that his will was placed in the cabinet.

In the search among my dear father's papers we found two sheafs of letters, neatly tied up and labelled—these were from my uncle Silas.

My cousin Monica looked down upon these papers with a strange smile; was it satire—was it that indescribable smile with which a mystery which covers a long reach of years is sometimes approached?

These were odd letters. If here and there occurred passages that were querulous and even abject, there were also long passages of manly and altogether noble sentiment, and the strangest rodomontade and maunderings about religion. Here and there a letter would gradually transform itself into a prayer, and end with a doxology and no signature; and some of them expressed such wild and disordered views respecting religion, as I imagine he can never have disclosed to good Mr. Fairfield, and which approached more nearly to the Swedenborg visions than to anything in the Church of England.

I read these with a solemn interest, but my cousin Monica was not similarly moved. She read them with the same smile—faint, serenely contemptuous, I thought—with which she had first looked down upon them. It was the countenance of a person who amusedly traces the working of a character that is well understood.

'Uncle Silas is very religious?' I said, not quite liking Lady Knollys' looks.

'Very,' she said, without raising her eyes or abating her old bitter smile, as she glanced over a passage in one of his letters.

'You don't think he *is*, Cousin Monica?' said I. She raised her head and looked straight at me.

'Why do you say that, Maud?'

'Because you smile incredulously, I think, over his letters.'

'Do I?' said she; 'I was not thinking—it was quite an accident. The fact is, Maud, your poor papa quite mistook me. I had no prejudice respecting him—no theory. I never knew what to think about him. I do not think Silas a product of nature, but a child of the Sphinx, and I never could understand him—that's all.'

'I always felt so too; but that was because I was left to speculation, and to glean conjectures as I might from his portrait, or anywhere. Except what you told me, I never heard more than a few sentences; poor papa did not like me to ask questions about him, and I think he ordered the servants to be silent.'

'And much the same injunction this little note lays upon me—not quite, but something like it; and I don't know the meaning of it.'

And she looked enquiringly at me.

'You are not to be *alarmed* about your uncle Silas, because your being afraid would unfit you for an *important service* which you have undertaken for your family, the nature of which I shall soon understand, and which, although it is quite *passive*, would be made very sad if *illusory fears* were allowed to *steal into your mind*.'

She was looking into the letter in poor papa's handwriting, which she had found addressed to her in his desk, and emphasised the words, I suppose, which she quoted from it.

'Have you any idea, Maud, darling, what this *service* may be?' she enquired, with a grave and anxious curiosity in her countenance.

'None, Cousin Monica; but I have thought long over my undertaking to do it, or submit to it, be it what it may; and I will keep the promise I voluntarily made, although I know what a coward I am, and often distrust my courage.'

'Well, I am not to frighten you.'

'How could you? Why should I be afraid? *Is* there anything frightful to be disclosed? Do tell me—you *must* tell me.'

'No, darling, I did not mean *that*—I don't mean that;—I could, if I would; I—I don't know exactly what I meant. But your poor papa knew him better than I—in fact, I did not know him at all—that is, ever quite understood him—which your poor papa, I see, had ample opportunities of doing.' And after a little pause, she added—'So you do not know what you are expected to do or to undergo.'

'Oh! Cousin Monica, I know you think he committed that murder,' I cried, starting up, I don't know why, and I felt that I grew deadly pale.

'I don't believe any such thing, you little fool; you must not say such horrible things, Maud,' she said, rising also, and looking both pale and angry. 'Shall we go out for a little walk? Come, lock up these papers, dear, and get your things on; and if that Dr. Bryerly does not turn up to-morrow, you must send for the Rector, good Doctor Clay, and let him make search for the will—there may be directions about many things, you know; and, my dear Maud, you are to remember that Silas is *my* cousin as well as your uncle. Come, dear, put on your hat.'

So we went out together for a little cloistered walk.

CHAPTER XXII

SOMEBODY IN THE ROOM WITH THE COFFIN

When we returned, a 'young' gentleman had arrived. We saw him in the parlour as we passed the window. It was simply a glance, but such a one as suffices to make a photograph, which we can study afterwards, at our leisure. I remember him at this moment—a man of six-and-thirty—dressed in a grey travelling suit, not over-well made; light-haired, fat-faced, and clumsy; and he looked both dull and cunning, and not at all like a gentleman.

Branston met us, announced the arrival, and handed me the stranger's credentials. My cousin and I stopped in the passage to read them.

'*That's* your uncle Silas's,' said Lady Knollys, touching one of the two letters with the tip of her finger.

'Shall we have lunch, Miss?'

'Certainly.' So Branston departed.

'Read it with me, Cousin Monica,' I said. And a very curious letter it was. It spoke as follows:—

'How can I thank my beloved niece for remembering her aged and forlorn kinsman at such a moment of anguish?'

I had written a note of a few, I dare say, incoherent words by the next post after my dear father's death.

'It is, however, in the hour of bereavement that we most value the ties that are broken, and yearn for the sympathy of kindred.'

Here came a little distich of French verse, of which I could only read *ciel* and *l'amour*.

'Our quiet household here is clouded with a new sorrow. How inscrutable are the ways of Providence! I—though a few years younger—how much the more infirm—how shattered in energy and in mind—how mere a burden—how entirely *de trop*—am spared to my sad place in a world where I can be no longer useful, where I have but one business—prayer, but one hope—the tomb; and he—apparently so robust—the centre of so much good—so necessary to you—so necessary, alas! to me—is taken! He is gone to his rest—for us, what remains but to bow our heads, and murmur, "His will be done"? I trace these lines with a trembling hand, while tears dim my old eyes. I did not think that any earthly event could have moved me so profoundly. From the world I have long stood aloof. I once led a life of pleasure—alas! of wickedness—as I now do one of austerity; but as I never was rich, so my worst enemy will allow I never was avaricious. My sins, I thank my Maker, have been of a more reducible kind, and have succumbed to the discipline which Heaven has provided. To earth and its interests, as well as to its pleasures, I have long been dead. For the few remaining years of my life I ask but quiet—an exemption from the agitations and distractions of struggle and care, and I trust to the Giver of all Good for my deliverance—well knowing, at the same time, that whatever befalls will, under His direction, prove best. Happy shall I be, my dearest niece, if in your most interesting and, in some respects, forlorn situation, I can be of any use to you. My present religious adviser—of whom I ventured to ask counsel on your behalf—states that I ought to send some one to represent me at the melancholy ceremony of reading the will which my beloved and now happy brother has, no doubt, left behind; and the idea that the experience and professional knowledge possessed by the gentleman whom I have selected may possibly be of use to you, my dearest niece, determines me to place him at your disposal. He is the junior partner in the firm of Archer and Sleigh, who conduct any little business which I may have from time to time; may I entreat your hospitality for him during a brief stay at Knowl? I write, even for a moment, upon these small matters of business with an effort—a painful one, but necessary. Alas! my brother! The cup of bitterness is now full. Few and evil must the remainder of my old days be. Yet, while they last, I remain always for my beloved niece, that which all her wealth and splendour cannot purchase—a loving and faithful kinsman and friend,

SILAS RUTHYN.'

'Is not it a kind letter?' I said, while tears stood in my eyes.

'Yes,' answered Lady Knollys, drily.

'But don't you think it so, really?'

'Oh! kind, very kind,' she answered in the same tone, 'and perhaps a little cunning.'

'Cunning!—how?'

'Well, you know I'm a peevish old Tabby, and of course I scratch now and then, and see in the dark. I dare say Silas is sorry, but I don't think he is in sackcloth and ashes. He has reason to be sorry and anxious, and I say I think he is both; and you know he pities you very much, and also himself a good deal; and he wants money, and you—his beloved niece—have a great deal—and altogether it is an affectionate and prudent letter: and he has sent his attorney here to make a note of the will; and you are to give the gentleman his meals and lodging; and Silas, very thoughtfully, invites you to confide your difficulties and troubles to *his* solicitor. It is very kind, but not imprudent.'

'Oh, Cousin Monica, don't you think at such a moment it is hardly natural that he should form such petty schemes, even were he capable at other times of practising so low? Is it not judging him hardly? and you, you know, so little acquainted with him.'

'I told you, dear, I'm a cross old thing—and there's an end; and I really don't care two pence about him; and of the two I'd much rather he were no relation of ours.'

Now, was not this prejudice? I dare say in part it was. So, too, was my vehement predisposition in his favour. I am afraid we women are factionists; we always take a side, and nature has formed us for advocates rather than judges; and I think the function, if less dignified, is more amiable.

I sat alone at the drawing-room window, at nightfall, awaiting my cousin Monica's entrance.

Feverish and frightened I felt that night. It was a sympathy, I fancy, with the weather. The sun had set stormily. Though the air was still, the sky looked wild and storm-swept. The crowding clouds, slanting in the attitude of flight, reflected their own sacred aspect upon my spirits. My grief darkened with a wild presaging of danger, and a sense of the supernatural fell upon me. It was the saddest and most awful evening that had come since my beloved father's death.

All kinds of shapeless fears environed me in silence. For the first time, dire misgivings about the form of faith affrighted me. Who were these Swedenborgians who had got about him—no one could tell how—and held him so fast to the close of his life? Who was this bilious, bewigged, black-eyed Doctor Bryerly, whom none of us quite liked and all a little feared; who seemed to rise out of the ground, and came and went, no one knew whence or whither, exercising, as I imagined, a mysterious authority over him? Was it all good and true, or a heresy and a witchcraft? Oh, my beloved father! was it all well with you?

When Lady Knollys entered, she found me in floods of tears, walking distractedly up and down the room. She kissed me in silence; she walked back and forward with me, and did her best to console me.

'I think, Cousin Monica, I would wish to see him once more. Shall we go up?'

'Unless you really wish it very much, I think, darling, you had better not mind it. It is happier to recollect them as they were; there's a change, you know, darling, and there is seldom any comfort in the sight.'

'But I do wish it *very* much. Oh! won't you come with me?'

And so I persuaded her, and up we went hand in hand, in the deepening twilight; and we halted at the end of the dark gallery, and I called Mrs. Rusk, growing frightened.

'Tell her to let us in, Cousin Monica,' I whispered.

'She wishes to see him, my lady—does she?' enquired Mrs. Rusk, in an undertone, and with a mysterious glance at me, as she softly fitted the key to the lock.

'Are you quite sure, Maud, dear?'

'Yes, yes.'

But when Mrs. Rusk entered bearing the candle, whose beam mixed dismally with the expiring twilight, disclosing a great black coffin standing upon trestles, near the foot of which she took her stand, gazing sternly into it, I lost heart again altogether and drew back.

'No, Mrs. Rusk, she won't; and I am very glad, dear,' she added to me. 'Come, Mrs. Rusk, come away. Yes, darling,' she continued to me, 'it is much better for you;' and she hurried me away, and down-stairs again. But the awful outlines of that large black coffin remained upon my imagination with a new and terrible sense of death.

I had no more any wish to see him. I felt a horror even of the room, and for more than an hour after a kind of despair and terror, such as I have never experienced before or since at the idea of death.

Cousin Monica had had her bed placed in my room, and Mary Quince's moved to the dressing-room adjoining it. For the first time the superstitious awe that follows death, but not immediately, visited me. The idea of seeing my father enter the room, or open the door and look in, haunted me. After Lady Knollys and I were in bed, I could not sleep. The wind sounded mournfully outside, and the small sounds, the rattlings, and strainings that responded from within, constantly startled me, and simulated the sounds of steps, of doors opening, of knockings, and so forth, rousing me with a palpitating heart as often as I fell into a doze.

At length the wind subsided, and these ambiguous noises abated, and I, fatigued, dropped into a quiet sleep. I was awakened by a sound in the gallery—which I could not define. A considerable time had passed, for the wind was now quite lulled. I sat up in my bed a good deal scared, listening breathlessly for I knew not what.

I heard a step moving stealthily along the gallery. I called my cousin Monica softly; and we both heard the door of the room in which my father's body lay unlocked, some one furtively enter, and the door shut.

'What can it be? Good Heavens, Cousin Monica, do you hear it?'

'Yes, dear; and it is two o'clock.'

Everyone at Knowl was in bed at eleven. We knew very well that Mrs. Rusk was rather nervous, and would not, for worlds, go alone, and at such an hour, to the room. We called Mary Quince. We all three listened, but we heard no other sound. I set these things down here because they made so terrible an impression upon me at the time.

It ended by our peeping out, all three in a body, upon the gallery. Through each window in the perspective came its blue sheet of moonshine; but the door on which our attention was fixed was in the shade, and we thought we could discern the glare of a candle through the key-hole. While in whispers we were debating this point together, the door opened, the dusky light of a candle emerged, the shadow of a figure crossed it within, and in another moment the mysterious Doctor Bryerly—angular, ungainly, in the black cloth coat that fitted little better than a coffin—issued from the chamber, candle in hand; murmuring, I suppose, a prayer—it sounded like a farewell—as much frightened as if I had just seen a sorcerer stealing stepped cautiously upon the gallery floor, shutting and locking the door upon the dead; and then having listened for a second, the saturnine figure, casting a gigantic and distorted shadow upon the ceiling and side-wall from the lowered candle, strode lightly down the long dark passage, away from us.

I can only speak for myself, and I can honestly say that I felt as much frightened as if I had just seen a sorcerer stealing from his unhallowed business. I think Cousin Monica was also affected in the same way, for she turned the key on the inside of the door when we entered. I do not think one of us believed at the moment that what we had seen was a Doctor Bryerly of flesh and blood, and yet the first thing we spoke of in the morning was Doctor Bryerly's arrival. The mind is a different organ by night and by day.

CHAPTER XXIII

I TALK WITH DOCTOR BRYERLY

Doctor Bryerly had, indeed, arrived at half-past twelve o'clock at night. His summons at the hall-door was little heard at our remote side of the old house of Knowl; and when the sleepy, half-dressed servant opened the door, the lank Doctor, in glossy black clothing, was standing alone, his portmanteau on its end upon the steps, and his vehicle disappearing in the shadows of the old trees.

In he came, sterner and sharper of aspect than usual.

'I've been expected? I'm Doctor Bryerly. Haven't I? So, let whoever is in charge of the body be called. I must visit it forthwith.'

So the Doctor sat in the back drawing-room, with a solitary candle; and Mrs. Rusk was called up, and, grumbling much and very peevish, dressed and went down, her ill-temper subsiding in a sort of fear as she approached the visitor.

'How do you do, Madam? A sad visit this. Is anyone watching in the room where the remains of your late master are laid?'

'No.'

'So much the better; it is a foolish custom. Will you please conduct me to the room? I must pray where he lies—no longer *he*! And be good enough to show me my bedroom, and so no one need wait up, and I shall find my way.'

Accompanied by the man who carried his valise, Mrs. Rusk showed him to his apartment; but he only looked in, and then glanced rapidly about to take 'the bearings' of the door.

'Thank you—yes. Now we'll proceed, here, along here? Let me see. A turn to the right and another to the left—yes. He has been dead some days. Is he yet in his coffin?'

'Yes, sir; since yesterday afternoon.'

Mrs. Rusk was growing more and more afraid of this lean figure sheathed in shining black cloth, whose eyes glittered with a horrible sort of cunning, and whose long brown fingers groped before him, as if indicating the way by guess.

'But, of course, the lid's not on; you've not screwed him down, hey?'

'No, sir.'

'That's well. I must look on the face as I pray. He is in his place; I here on earth. He in the spirit; I in the flesh. The neutral ground lies there. So are carried the vibrations, and so the light of earth and heaven reflected back and forward—apaugasma, a wonderful though helpless engine, the ladder of Jacob, and behold the angels of God ascending and descending on it. Thanks, I'll take the key. Mysteries to those who *will* live altogether in houses of clay, no mystery to such as will use their eyes and read what is revealed. *This* candle, it is the longer, please; no—no need of a pair, thanks; just this, to hold in my hand. And remember, all depends upon the willing mind. Why do you look frightened? Where is your faith? Don't you know that spirits are about us at all times? Why should you fear to be near the body? The spirit is everything; the flesh profiteth nothing.'

'Yes, sir,' said Mrs. Rusk, making him a great courtesy in the threshold.

She was frightened by his eerie talk, which grew, she fancied, more voluble and energetic as they approached the corpse.

'Remember, then, that when you fancy yourself alone and wrapt in darkness, you stand, in fact, in the centre of a theatre, as wide as the starry floor of heaven, with an audience, whom no man can number, beholding you under a flood of light. Therefore, though your body be in solitude and your mortal sense in darkness, remember to walk as being in the light, surrounded with a cloud of witnesses. Thus walk; and when the hour comes, and you pass forth unprisoned from the tabernacle of the flesh, although it still has its relations and its rights'—and saying this, as he held the solitary candle aloft in the doorway, he nodded towards the coffin, whose large black form was faintly traceable against the shadows beyond—'you will rejoice; and being clothed upon with your house from on high, you will not be found naked. On the other hand, he that loveth corruption shall have enough thereof. Think upon these things. Good-night.'

And the Swedenborgian Doctor stepped into the room, taking the candle with him, and closed the door upon the shadowy still-life there, and on his own sharp and swarthy visage, leaving Mrs. Rusk in a sort of panic in the dark alone, to find her way to her room the best way she could.

Early in the morning Mrs. Rusk came to my room to tell me that Doctor Bryerly was in the parlour, and begged to know whether I had not a message for him. I was already dressed, so, though it was dreadful seeing a stranger in my then mood, taking the key of the cabinet in my hand, I followed Mrs. Rusk downstairs.

Opening the parlour door, she stepped in, and with a little courtesy said,—

'Please, sir, the young mistress—Miss Ruthyn.'

Draped in black and very pale, tall and slight, 'the young mistress' was; and as I entered I heard a newspaper rustle, and the sound of steps approaching to meet me.

Face to face we met, near the door; and, without speaking, I made him a deep courtesy.

He took my hand, without the least indication on my part, in his hard lean grasp, and shook it kindly, but familiarly, peering with a stern sort of curiosity into my face as he continued to hold it. His ill-fitting, glossy black cloth, ungainly presence, and sharp, dark, vulpine features had in them, as I said before, the vulgarity of a Glasgow artisan in his Sabbath suit. I made an instantaneous motion to withdraw my hand, but he held it firmly.

Though there was a grim sort of familiarity, there was also decision, shrewdness, and, above all, kindness, in his dark face—a gleam on the whole of the masterly and the honest—that along with a certain paleness, betraying, I thought, restrained emotion, indicated sympathy and invited confidence.

'I hope, Miss, you are pretty well?' He pronounced 'pretty' as it is spelt. 'I have come in consequence of a solemn promise exacted more than a year since by your deceased father, the late Mr. Austin Ruthyn of Knowl, for whom I cherished a warm esteem, being knit besides with him in spiritual bonds. It has been a shock to you, Miss?'

'It has, indeed, sir.'

'I've a doctor's degree, I have—Doctor of Medicine, Miss. Like St. Luke, preacher and doctor. I was in business once, but this is better. As one footing fails, the Lord provides another. The stream of life is black and angry; how so many of us get across without drowning, I often wonder. The best way is not to look too far before—just from one stepping-stone to another; and though you may wet your feet, He won't let you drown—He has not allowed me.'

And Doctor Bryerly held up his head, and wagged it resolutely.

'You are born to this world's wealth; in its way a great blessing, though a great trial, Miss, and a great trust; but don't suppose you are destined to exemption from trouble on that account, any more than poor Emmanuel Bryerly. As the sparks fly upwards, Miss Ruthyn! Your cushioned carriage may overturn on the highroad, as I may stumble and fall upon the footpath. There are other troubles than debt and privation. Who can tell how long health may last, or when an accident may happen the brain; what mortifications may await you in your own high sphere; what unknown enemies may rise up in your path; or what slanders may asperse your name—ha, ha! It is a wonderful equilibrium—a marvellous dispensation—ha, ha!' and he laughed with a shake of his head, I thought a little sarcastically, as if he was not sorry my money could not avail to buy immunity from the general curse.

'But what money can't do, *prayer* can—bear that in mind, Miss Ruthyn. We can all pray; and though thorns and snares, and stones of fire lie strewn in our way, we need not fear them. He will give His angels charge over us, and in their hands they will bear us up, for He hears and sees everywhere, and His angels are innumerable.'

He was now speaking gently and solemnly, and paused. But another vein of thought he had unconsciously opened in my mind, and I said—

'And had my dear papa no other medical adviser?'

He looked at me sharply, and flushed a little under his dark tint. His medical skill was, perhaps, the point on which his human vanity vaunted itself, and I dare say there was something very disparaging in my tone.

'And if he *had* no other, he might have done worse. I've had many critical cases in my hands, Miss Ruthyn. I can't charge myself with any miscarriage through ignorance. My diagnosis in Mr. Ruthyn's case has been verified by the result. But I was *not* alone; Sir Clayton Barrow saw him, and took my view; a note will reach him in London. But this, excuse me, is not to the present purpose. The late Mr. Ruthyn told me I was to receive a key from you, which would open a cabinet where he had placed his will—ha! thanks,—in his study. And, I think, as there may be directions about the funeral, it had better be read forthwith. Is there any gentleman—a relative or man of business—near here, whom you would wish sent for?'

'No, none, thank you; I have confidence in you, sir.'

I think I spoke and looked frankly, for he smiled very kindly, though with closed lips.

'And you may be sure, Miss Ruthyn, your confidence shall not be disappointed.' Here was a long pause. 'But you are very young, and you must have some one by in your interest, who has some experience in business. Let me see. Is not the Rector, Dr. Clay, at hand? In the town?—very good; and Mr. Danvers, who manages the estate, *he* must come. And get Grimston—you see I know all the names—Grimston, the attorney; for though he was not employed about this will, he has been Mr. Ruthyn's solicitor a great many years: we must have Grimston; for, as I suppose you know, though it is a short will, it is a very strange one. I expostulated, but you know he was very decided when he took a view. He read it to you, eh?'

'No, sir.'

'Oh, but he told you so much as relates to you and your uncle, Mr. Silas Ruthyn, of Bartram-Haugh?'

'No, indeed, sir.'

'Ha! I wish he had.'

And with these words Doctor Bryerly's countenance darkened.

'Mr. Silas Ruthyn is a religious man?'

'Oh, *very*!' said I.

'You've seen a good deal of him?'

'No, I never saw him,' I answered.

'H'm? Odder and odder! But he's a good man, isn't he?'

'Very good, indeed, sir—a very religious man.'

Doctor Bryerly was watching my countenance as I spoke, with a sharp and anxious eye; and then he looked down, and read the pattern of the carpet like bad news, for a while, and looking again in my face, askance, he said—

'He was very near joining *us*—on the point. He got into correspondence with Henry Voerst, one of our best men. They call us Swedenborgians, you know; but I dare say that won't go much further, now. I suppose, Miss Ruthyn, one o'clock would be a good hour, and I am sure, under the circumstances, the gentlemen will make a point of attending.'

'Yes, Dr. Bryerly, the notes shall be sent, and my cousin, Lady Knollys, would I am sure attend with me while the will is being read—there would be no objection to her presence?'

'None in the world. I can't be quite sure who are joined with me as executors. I'm almost sorry I did not decline; but it is too late regretting. One thing you must believe Miss Ruthyn: in framing the provisions of the will I was never consulted—although I expostulated against the only very unusual one it contains when I heard it. I did so strenuously, but in vain. There was one other against which I protested—having a right to do so—with better effect. In no other way does the will in any respect owe anything to my advice or dissuasion. You will please believe this; also that I am your friend. Yes, indeed, it is my duty.'

The latter words he spoke looking down again, as it were in soliloquy; and thanking him, I withdrew.

When I reached the hall, I regretted that I had not asked him to state distinctly what arrangements the will made so nearly affecting, as it seemed, my relations with my uncle Silas, and for a moment I thought of returning and requesting an explanation. But then, I bethought me, it was not very long to wait till one o'clock—so *he*, at least, would think. I went up-stairs, therefore, to the 'schoolroom,' which we used at present as a sitting-room, and there I found Cousin Monica awaiting me.

'Are you quite well, dear?' asked Lady Knollys, as she came to meet and kiss me.

'Quite well, Cousin Monica.'

'No nonsense, Maud! you're as white as that handkerchief—what's the matter? Are you ill—are you frightened? Yes, you're trembling—you're terrified, child.'

'I believe I *am* afraid. There *is* something in poor papa's will about Uncle Silas—about *me*. I don't know—Doctor Bryerly says, and he seems so uncomfortable and frightened himself, I am sure it is something very bad. I am *very* much frightened—I am—I *am*. Oh, Cousin Monica! you won't leave me?'

So I threw my arms about her neck, clasping her very close, and we kissed one another, I crying like a frightened child—and indeed in experience of the world I was no more.

CHAPTER XXIV

THE OPENING OF THE WILL

Perhaps the terror with which I anticipated the hour of one, and the disclosure of the unknown undertaking to which I had bound myself, was irrational and morbid. But, honestly, I doubt it; my tendency has always been that of many other weak characters, to act impetuously, and afterwards to reproach myself for consequences which I have, perhaps, in reality, had little or no share in producing.

It was Doctor Bryerly's countenance and manner in alluding to a particular provision in my father's will that instinctively awed me. I have seen faces in a nightmare that haunted me with an indescribable horror, and yet I could not say wherein lay the fascination. And so it was with his—an omen, a menace, lurked in its sallow and dismal glance.

'You must not be so frightened, darling,' said Cousin Monica. 'It is foolish; it *is, really*; they can't cut off your head, you know: they can't really harm you in any essential way. If it involved a risk of a little money, you would not mind it; but men are such odd creatures—they measure all sacrifices by money. Doctor Bryerly would look just as you describe, if you were doomed to lose 500*l*., and yet it would not kill you.'

A companion like Lady Knollys is reassuring; but I could not take her comfort altogether to heart, for I felt that she had no great confidence in it herself.

There was a little French clock over the mantelpiece in the school-room, which I consulted nearly every minute. It wanted now but ten minutes of one.

'Shall we go down to the drawing-room, dear?' said Cousin Knollys, who was growing restless like me.

So down-stairs we went, pausing by mutual consent at the great window at the stair-head, which looks out on the avenue. Mr. Danvers was riding his tall, grey horse at a walk, under the wide branches toward the house, and we waited to see him get off at the door. In his turn he loitered there, for the good Rector's gig, driven by the Curate, was approaching at a smart ecclesiastical trot.

Doctor Clay got down, and shook hands with Mr. Danvers; and after a word or two, away drove the Curate with that upward glance at the windows from which so few can refrain.

I watched the Rector and Mr. Danvers loitering on the steps as a patient might the gathering of surgeons who are to perform some unknown operation. They, too, glanced up at the window as they turned to enter the house, and I drew back. Cousin Monica looked at her watch.

'Four minutes only. Shall we go to the drawing-room?'

Waiting for a moment to let the gentlemen get by on the way to the study, we, accordingly, went down, and I heard the Rector talk of the dangerous state of Grindleston bridge, and wondered how he could think of such things at a time of sorrow. Everything about those few minutes of suspense remains fresh in my recollection. I remember how they loitered and came to a halt at the corner of the oak passage leading to the study, and how the Rector patted the marble head and smoothed the inflexible tresses of William Pitt, as he listened to Mr. Danvers' details about the presentment; and then, as they went on, I recollect the boisterous nose-blowing that suddenly resounded from the passage, and which I then referred, and still refer, intuitively to the Rector.

We had not been five minutes in the drawing-room when Branston entered, to say that the gentlemen I had mentioned were all assembled in the study.

'Come, dear,' said Cousin Monica; and leaning on her arm I reached the study door. I entered, followed by her. The gentlemen arrested their talk and stood up, those who were sitting, and the Rector came forward very gravely, and in low tones, and very kindly, greeted me. There was nothing emotional in this salutation, for though my father never quarrelled, yet an immense distance separated him from all his neighbours, and I do not think there lived a human being who knew him at more than perhaps a point or two of his character.

Considering how entirely he secluded himself, my father was, as many people living remember, wonderfully popular in his county. He was neighbourly in everything except in seeing company and mixing in society. He had magnificent shooting, of which he was extremely liberal. He kept a pack of hounds at Dollerton, with which all his side of the county hunted through the season. He never refused any claim upon his purse which had the slightest show of reason. He subscribed to every fund, social, charitable, sporting, agricultural, no matter what, provided the honest people of his county took an interest in it, and always with a princely hand; and although he shut himself up, no one could say that he was inaccessible, for he devoted hours daily to answering letters, and his checque-book contributed largely in those replies. He had taken his turn long ago as High Sheriff; so there was an end of that claim before his oddity and shyness had quite secluded him. He refused the Lord-Lieutenancy of his county; he declined every post of personal distinction connected with it. He could write an able as well as a genial letter when he pleased; and his appearances at public meetings, dinners, and so forth were made in this epistolary fashion, and, when occasion presented, by magnificent contributions from his purse.

If my father had been less goodnatured in the sporting relations of his vast estates, or less magnificent in dealing with his fortune, or even if he had failed to exhibit the intellectual force which always characterised his letters on public matters, I dare say that his oddities would have condemned him to ridicule, and possibly to dislike. But every one of the principal gentlemen of his county, whose judgment was valuable, has told me that he was a remarkably able man, and that his failure in public life was due to his eccentricities, and in no respect to deficiency in those peculiar mental qualities which make men feared and useful in Parliament.

I could not forbear placing on record this testimony to the high mental and the kindly qualities of my beloved father, who might have passed for a misanthrope or a fool. He was a man of generous nature and powerful intellect, but given up to the oddities of a shyness which grew with years and indulgence, and became inflexible with his disappointments and affliction.

There was something even in the Rector's kind and ceremonious greeting which oddly enough reflected the mixed feelings in which awe was not without a place, with which his neighbours had regarded my dear father.

Having done the honours—I am sure looking woefully pale—I had time to glance quietly at the only figure there with which I was not tolerably familiar. This was the junior partner in the firm of Archer and Sleigh who represented my uncle Silas—a fat and pallid man of six-and-thirty, with a sly and evil countenance, and it has always seemed to me, that ill dispositions show more repulsively in a pale fat face than in any other.

Doctor Bryerly, standing near the window, was talking in a low tone to Mr. Grimston, our attorney.

I heard good Dr. Clay whisper to Mr. Danvers—

'Is not that Doctor Bryerly—the person with the black—the black—it's a wig, I think—in the window, talking to Abel Grimston?'

'Yes; that's he.'

'Odd-looking person—one of the Swedenborg people, is not he?' continued the Rector.

'So I am told.'

'Yes,' said the Rector, quietly; and he crossed one gaitered leg over the other, and, with fingers interlaced, twiddled his thumbs, as he eyed the monstrous sectary under his orthodox old brows with a stern inquisitiveness. I thought he was meditating theologic battle.

But Dr. Bryerly and Mr. Grimston, still talking together, began to walk slowly from the window, and the former said in his peculiar grim tones—

'I beg pardon, Miss Ruthyn; perhaps you would be so good as to show us which of the cabinets in this room your late lamented father pointed out as that to which this key belongs.'

I indicated the oak cabinet.

'Very good, ma'am—very good,' said Doctor Bryerly, as he fumbled the key into the lock.

Cousin Monica could not forbear murmuring—

'Dear! what a brute!'

The junior partner, with his dumpy hands in his pocket, poked his fat face over Mr. Grimston's shoulder, and peered into the cabinet as the door opened.

The search was not long. A handsome white paper enclosure, neatly tied up in pink tape, and sealed with large red seals, was inscribed in my dear father's hand:—'Will of Austin R. Ruthyn, of Knowl.' Then, in smaller characters, the date, and in the corner a note—'This will was drawn from my instructions by Gaunt, Hogg, and Hatchett, Solicitors, Great Woburn Street, London, A.R.R.'

'Let *me* have a squint at that indorsement, please, gentlemen,' half whispered the unpleasant person who represented my uncle Silas.

"*Tisn't* an indorsement. There, look—a memorandum on an envelope,' said Abel Grimston, gruffly.

'Thanks—all right—that will do,' he responded, himself making a pencil-note of it, in a long clasp-book which he drew from his coat-pocket.

The tape was carefully cut, and the envelope removed without tearing the writing, and forth came the will, at sight of which my heart swelled and fluttered up to my lips, and then dropped down dead as it seemed into its place.

'Mr. Grimston, you will please to read it,' said Doctor Bryerly, who took the direction of the process. 'I will sit beside you, and as we go along you will be good enough to help us to understand technicalities, and give us a lift where we want it.'

'It's a short will,' said Mr. Grimston, turning over the sheets '*very*—considering. Here's a codicil.'

'I did not see that,' said Doctor Bryerly.

'Dated only a month ago.'

'Oh!' said Doctor Bryerly, putting on his spectacles. Uncle Silas's ambassador, sitting close behind, had insinuated his face between Doctor Bryerly's and the reader's of the will.

'On behalf of the surviving brother of the testator,' interposed the delegate, just as Abel Grimston had cleared his voice to begin, 'I take leave to apply for a copy of this instrument. It will save a deal of trouble, if the young lady as represents the testator here has no objection.'

'You can have as many copies as you like when the will is proved,' said Mr. Grimston.

'I know that; but supposing as all's right, where's the objection?'

'Just the objection there always is to acting irregular,' replied Mr. Grimston.

'You don't object to act disobliging, it seems.'

'You can do as I told you,' replied Mr. Grimston.

'Thank you for nothing,' murmured Mr. Sleigh.

And the reading of the will proceeded, while he made elaborate notes of its contents in his capacious pocket-book.

'I, Austin Alymer Ruthyn Ruthyn, being, I thank God, of sound mind and perfect recollection,' &c, &c.; and then came a bequest of all his estates real, chattels real, copyrights, leases, chattels, money, rights, interests, reversions, powers, plate, pictures, and estates and possessions whatsoever, to four persons—Lord

Ilbury, Mr. Penrose Creswell of Creswell, Sir William Aylmer, Bart., and Hans Emmanuel Bryerly, Doctor of Medicine, 'to have and to hold,' &c. &c. Whereupon my Cousin Monica ejaculated 'Eh?' and Doctor Bryerly interposed—

'Four trustees, ma'am. We take little but trouble—you'll see; go on.'

Then it came out that all this multifarious splendour was bequeathed in trust for me, subject to a bequest of 15,000*l.* to his only brother, Silas Aylmer Ruthyn, and 3,500*l.* each to the two children of his said brother; and lest any doubt should arise by reason of his, the testator's decease as to the continuance of the arrangement by way of lease under which he enjoyed his present habitation and farm, he left him the use of the mansion-house and lands of Bartram-Haugh, in the county of Derbyshire, and of the lands of so-and-so and so-and-so, adjoining thereto, in the said county, for the term of his natural life, on payment of a rent of 5*s.* per annum, and subject to the like conditions as to waste, &c., as are expressed in the said lease.

'By your leave, may I ask is them dispositions all the devises to my client, which is his only brother, as it seems to me you've seen the will before?' enquired Mr. Sleigh.

'Nothing more, unless there is something in the codicil,' answered Dr. Bryerly.

But there was no mention of him in the codicil.

Mr. Sleigh threw himself back in his chair, and sneered, with the end of his pencil between his teeth. I hope his disappointment was altogether for his client. Mr. Danvers fancied, he afterwards said, that he had probably expected legacies which might have involved litigation, or, at all events, law costs, and perhaps a stewardship; but this was very barren; and Mr. Danvers also remarked, that the man was a very low practitioner, and wondered how my uncle Silas could have commissioned such a person to represent him.

So far the will contained nothing of which my most partial friend could have complained. The codicil, too, devised only legacies to servants, and a sum of 1,000*l.*, with a few kind words, to Monica, Lady Knollys, and a further sum of 3,000*l.* to Dr. Bryerly, stating that the legatee had prevailed upon him to erase from the draft of his will a bequest to him to that amount, but that, in consideration of all the trouble devolving upon him as trustee, he made that bequest by his codicil; and with these arrangements the permanent disposition of his property was completed.

But that direction to which he and Doctor Bryerly had darkly alluded, was now to come, and certainly it was a strange one. It appointed my uncle Silas my sole guardian, with full parental authority over me until I should have reached the age of twenty-one, up to which time I was to reside under his care at Bartram-Haugh, and it directed the trustees to pay over to him yearly a sum of 2,000*l.* during the continuance of the guardianship for my suitable maintenance, education, and expenses.

You have now a sufficient outline of my father's will. The only thing I painfully felt in this arrangement was, the break-up—the dismay that accompanies the disappearance of home. Otherwise, there was something rather pleasurable in the idea. As long as I could remember, I had always cherished the same mysterious curiosity about my uncle, and the same longing to behold him. This was about to be gratified. Then there was my cousin Milicent, about my own age. My life had been so lonely, that I had acquired none of those artificial habits that induce the fine-lady nature—a second, and not always a very amiable one. She had lived a solitary life, like me. What rambles and readings we should have together! what confidences and castle-buildings! and then there was a new country and a fine old place, and the sense of interest and adventure that always accompanies change in our early youth.

There were four letters all alike with large, red seals, addressed respectively to each of the trustees named in the will. There was also one addressed to Silas Alymer Ruthyn, Esq., Bartram-Haugh Manor, &c. &c., which Mr. Sleigh offered to deliver. But Doctor Bryerly thought the post-office was the more regular channel. Uncle Silas's representative was questioning Doctor Bryerly in an under-tone.

I turned my eyes on my cousin Monica—I felt so inexpressibly relieved—expecting to see a corresponding expression in her countenance. But I was startled. She looked ghastly and angry. I stared in her face, not knowing what to think. Could the will have personally disappointed her? Such doubts, though we fancy in after-life they belong to maturity and experience only, do sometimes cross our minds in youth. But the suggestion wronged Lady Knollys, who neither expected nor wanted anything, being rich, childless, generous, and frank. It was the unexpected character of her countenance that scared me, and for a moment the shock called up corresponding moral images.

Lady Knollys, starting up, raised her head, so as to see over Mr. Sleigh's shoulder, and biting her pale lip, she cleared her voice and demanded—

'Doctor Bryerly, pray, sir, is the reading concluded?'

'Concluded? Quite. Yes, nothing more,' he answered with a nod, and continued his talk with Mr. Danvers and Abel Grimston.

'And to whom,' said Lady Knollys, with an effort, 'will the property belong, in case—in case my little cousin here should die before she comes of age?'

'Eh? Well—wouldn't it go to the heir-at-law and next of kin?' said Doctor Bryerly, turning to Abel Grimston.

'Ay—to be sure,' said the attorney, thoughtfully.

'And who is that?' pursued my cousin.

'Well, her uncle, Mr. Silas Ruthyn. He's both heir-at-law and next of kin,' pursued Abel Grimston.

'Thank you,' said Lady Knollys.

Doctor Clay came forward, bowing very low, in his standing collar and single-breasted coat, and graciously folded my hand in his soft wrinkled grasp—

'Allow me, my dear Miss Ruthyn, while expressing my regret that we are to lose you from among our little flock—though I trust but for a short, a very short time—to say how I rejoice at the particular arrangement indicated by the will we have just heard read. My curate, William Fairfield, resided for some years in the same spiritual capacity in the neighbourhood of your, I will say, admirable uncle, with occasional intercourse with whom he was favoured—may I not say blessed?—a true Christian Churchman—a Christian gentleman. Can I say more? A most happy, happy choice.' A very low bow here, with eyes nearly closed, and a shake of the head. 'Mrs. Clay will do herself the honour of waiting upon you, to pay her respects, before you leave Knowl for your temporary sojourn in another sphere.'

So, with another deep bow—for I had become a great personage all at once—he let go my hand cautiously and delicately, as if he were setting down a curious china tea-cup. And I courtesied low to him, not knowing what to say, and then to the assembly generally, who all bowed. And Cousin Monica whispered, briskly, 'Come away,' and took my hand with a very cold and rather damp one, and led me from the room.

CHAPTER XXV

I HEAR FROM UNCLE SILAS

Without saying a word, Cousin Monica accompanied me to the school-room, and on entering she shut the door, not with a spirited clang, but quietly and determinedly.

'Well, dear,' she said, with the same pale, excited countenance, 'that certainly is a sensible and charitable arrangement. I could not have believed it possible, had I not heard it with my ears.'

'About my going to Bartram-Haugh?'

'Yes, exactly so, under Silas Ruthyn's guardianship, to spend two—*three*—of the most important years of your education and your life under that roof. Is *that*, my dear, what was in your mind when you were so alarmed about what you were to be called upon to do, or undergo?'

'No, no, indeed. I had no notion what it might be. I was afraid of something serious,' I answered.

'And, my dear Maud, did not your poor father speak to you as if it *was* something serious?' said she. 'And so it *is*, I can tell you, something serious, and *very* serious; and I think it ought to be prevented, and I certainly *will* prevent it if I possibly can.'

I was puzzled utterly by the intensity of Lady Knollys' protest. I looked at her, expecting an explanation of her meaning; but she was silent, looking steadfastly on the jewels on her right-hand fingers, with which she was drumming a staccato march on the table, very pale, with gleaming eyes, evidently thinking deeply. I began to think she *had* a prejudice against my uncle Silas.

'He is not very rich,' I commenced.

'Who?' said Lady Knollys.

'Uncle Silas,' I replied.

'No, certainly; he's in debt,' she answered.

'But then, how very highly Doctor Clay spoke of him!' I pursued.

'Don't talk of Doctor Clay. I do think that man is the greatest goose I ever heard talk. I have no patience with such men,' she replied.

I tried to remember what particular nonsense Doctor Clay had uttered, and I could recollect nothing, unless his eulogy upon my uncle were to be classed with that sort of declamation.

'Danvers is a very proper man and a good accountant, I dare say; but he is either a very deep person, or a fool—*I* believe a fool. As for your attorney, I suppose he knows his business, and also his interest, and I have no doubt he will consult it. I begin to think he best man among them, the shrewdest and the most reliable, is that vulgar visionary in the black wig. I saw him look at you, Maud, and I liked his face, though it is abominably ugly and vulgar, and cunning, too; but I think he's a just man, and I dare say with right feelings—I'm *sure* he has.'

I was quite at a loss to divine the gist of my cousin's criticism.

'I'll have some talk with Dr. Bryerly; I feel convinced he takes my view, and we must really think what had best be done.'

'Is there anything in the will, Cousin Monica, that does not appear?' I asked, for I was growing very uneasy. 'I wish you would tell me. What view do you mean?'

'No view in particular; the view that a desolate old park, and the house of a *neglected* old man, who is very poor, and has been desperately foolish, is not the right place for you, particularly at your years. It is quite shocking, and I *will* speak to Doctor Bryerly. May I ring the bell, dear?'

'Certainly;' and I rang it.

'When does he leave Knowl?'

I could not tell. Mrs. Rusk, however, was sent for, and she could tell us that he had announced his intention of taking the night train from Drackleton, and was to leave Knowl for that station at half-past six o'clock.

'May Rusk give or send him a message from me, dear?' asked Lady Knollys.

Of course she might.

'Then please let him know that I request he will be so good as to allow me a very few minutes, just to say a word before he goes.'

'You kind cousin!' I said, placing my two hands on her shoulders, and looking earnestly in her face; 'you are anxious about me, more than you say. Won't you tell me why? I am much more unhappy, really, in ignorance, than if I understood the cause.'

'Well, dear, haven't I told you? The two or three years of your life which are to form you are destined to be passed in utter loneliness, and, I am sure, neglect. You can't estimate the disadvantage of such an arrangement. It is full of disadvantages. How it could have entered the head of poor Austin—although I should not say that, for I am sure I do understand it,—but how he could for any purpose have directed such a measure is quite inconceivable. I never heard of anything so foolish and abominable, and I will prevent it if I can.'

At that moment Mrs. Rusk announced that Doctor Bryerly would see Lady Knollys at any time she pleased before his departure.

'It shall be this moment, then,' said the energetic lady, and up she stood, and made that hasty general adjustment before the glass, which, no matter under what circumstances, and before what sort of creature one's appearance is to be made, is a duty that every woman owes to herself. And I heard her a moment after, at the stair-head, directing Branston to let Dr. Bryerly know that she awaited him in the drawing-room.

And now she was gone, and I began to wonder and speculate. Why should my cousin Monica make all this fuss about, after all, a very natural arrangement? My uncle, whatever he might have been, was now a good man—a religious man—perhaps a little severe; and with this thought a dark streak fell across my sky.

A cruel disciplinarian! had I not read of such characters?—lock and key, bread and water, and solitude! To sit locked up all night in a dark out-of-the-way room, in a great, ghosty, old-fashioned house, with no one nearer than the other wing. What years of horror in one such night! Would not this explain my poor father's hesitation, and my cousin Monica's apparently disproportioned opposition? When an idea of terror presents itself to a young person's mind, it transfixes and fills the vision, without respect of probabilities or reason.

My uncle was now a terrible old martinet, with long Bible lessons, lectures, pages of catechism, sermons to be conned by rote, and an awful catalogue of punishments for idleness, and what would seem to him impiety. I was going, then, to a frightful isolated reformatory, where for the first time in my life I should be subjected to a rigorous and perhaps barbarous discipline.

All this was an exhalation of fancy, but it quite overcame me. I threw myself, in my solitude, on the floor, upon my knees, and prayed for deliverance—prayed that Cousin Monica might prevail with Doctor Bryerly, and both on my behalf with the Lord Chancellor, or the High Sheriff, or whoever else my proper deliverer might be; and when my cousin returned, she found me quite in an agony.

'Why, you little fool! what fancy has taken possession of you now?' she cried.

And when my new terror came to light, she actually laughed a little to reassure me, and she said—

'My dear child, your uncle Silas will never put you through your duty to your neighbour; all the time you are under his roof you'll have idleness and liberty enough, and too much, I fear. It is neglect, my dear, not discipline, that I'm afraid of.'

'I think, dear Cousin Monica, you are afraid of something more than neglect,' I said, relieved, however.

'I *am* afraid of more than neglect,' she replied promptly; 'but I hope my fears may turn out illusory, and that possibly they may be avoided. And now, for a few hours at least, let us think of something else. I rather like that Doctor Bryerly. I could not get him to say what I wanted. I don't think he's Scotch, but he is very cautious, and I am sure, though he would not say so, that he thinks of the matter exactly as I do. He says that those fine people, who are named as his co-trustees, won't take any trouble, and will leave everything to him, and I am sure he is right. So we must not quarrel with him, Maud, nor call him hard names, although he certainly is intolerably vulgar and ugly, and at times very nearly impertinent—I suppose without knowing, or indeed very much caring.'

We had a good deal to think of, and talked incessantly. There were bursts and interruptions of grief, and my kind cousin's consolations. I have often since been so lectured for giving way to grief, that I wonder at the patience exercised by her during this irksome visit. Then there was some reading of that book whose claims are always felt in the terrible days of affliction. After that we had a walk in the yew garden, that quaint little cloistered quadrangle—the most solemn, sad, and antiquated of gardens.

'And now, my dear, I must really leave you for two or three hours. I have ever so many letters to write, and my people must think I'm dead by this time.'

So till tea-time I had poor Mary Quince, with her gushes of simple prattle and her long fits of vacant silence, for my companion. And such a one, who can con over by rote the old friendly gossip about the dead, talk about their ways, and looks, and likings, without much psychologic refinement, but with a simple admiration and liking that never measured them critically, but always with faith and love, is in general about as comfortable a companion as one can find for the common moods of grief.

It is not easy to recall in calm and happy hours the sensations of an acute sorrow that is past. Nothing, by the merciful ordinance of God, is more difficult to remember than pain. One or two great agonies of that time I do remember, and they remain to testify of the rest, and convince me, though I can see it no more, how terrible all that period was.

Next day was the funeral, that appalling necessity; smuggled away in whispers, by black familiars, unresisting, the beloved one leaves home, without a farewell, to darken those doors no more; henceforward to lie outside, far away, and forsaken, through the drowsy heats of summer, through days of snow and nights of tempest, without light or warmth, without a voice near. Oh, Death, king of terrors! The body quakes and the spirit faints before thee. It is vain, with hands clasped over our eyes, to scream our reclamation; the horrible image will not be excluded. We have just the word spoken eighteen hundred years ago, and our trembling faith. And through the broken vault the gleam of the Star of Bethlehem.

I was glad in a sort of agony when it was over. So long as it remained to be done, something of the catastrophe was still suspended. Now it was all over.

The house so strangely empty. No owner—no master! I with my strange momentary liberty, bereft of that irreplaceable love, never quite prized until it is lost. Most people have experienced the dismay that underlies sorrow under such circumstances.

The apartment of the poor outcast from life is now dismantled. Beds and curtains taken down, and furniture displaced; carpets removed, windows open and doors locked; the bedroom and anteroom were henceforward, for many a day, uninhabited. Every shocking change smote my heart like a reproach.

I saw that day that Cousin Monica had been crying for the first time, I think, since her arrival at Knowl; and I loved her more for it, and felt consoled. My tears have often been arrested by the sight of another person weeping, and I never could explain why. But I believe that many persons experience the same odd reaction.

The funeral was conducted, in obedience to his brief but peremptory direction, very privately and with little expense. But of course there was an attendance, and the tenants of the Knowl estate also followed the hearse to the mausoleum, as it is called, in the park, where he was laid beside my dear mother. And so the repulsive ceremonial of that dreadful day was over. The grief remained, but there was rest from the fatigue of agitation, and a comparative calm supervened.

It was now the stormy equinoctial weather that sounds the wild dirge of autumn, and marches the winter in. I love, and always did, that grand undefinable music, threatening and bewailing, with its strange soul of liberty and desolation.

By this night's mail, as we sat listening to the storm, in the drawing-room at Knowl, there reached me a large letter with a great black seal, and a wonderfully deep-black border, like a widow's crape. I did not recognise the handwriting; but on opening the funereal missive, it proved to be from my uncle Silas, and was thus expressed:—

'MY DEAREST NIECE,—This letter will reach you, probably, on the day which consigns the mortal remains of my beloved brother, Austin, your dear father, to the earth. Sad ceremony, from taking my mournful part in which I am excluded by years, distance, and broken health. It will, I trust, at this season of desolation, be not unwelcome to remember that a substitute, imperfect—unworthy—but most affectionately zealous, for the honoured parent whom you have just lost, has been appointed, in me, your uncle, by his will. I am aware that you were present during the reading of it, but I think it will be for our mutual satisfaction that our new and more affectionate relations should be forthwith entered upon. My conscience and your safety, and I trust convenience, will thereby be consulted. You will, my dear niece, remain at Knowl, until a few simple arrangements shall have been completed for your reception at this place. I will then settle the details of your little journey to us, which shall be performed as comfortably and easily as possible. I humbly pray that this affliction may be sanctified to us all, and that in our new duties we may be supported, comforted, and directed. I need not remind you that I now stand to you *in loco parentis*, which means in the relation of father, and you will not forget that you are to remain at Knowl until you hear further from me.

'I remain, my dear niece, your most affectionate uncle and guardian,

SILAS RUTHYN.'

'P.S.—Pray present my respects to Lady Knollys, who, I understand, is sojourning at Knowl. I would observe that a lady who cherishes, I have reason to fear, unfriendly feelings against your uncle, is not the most desirable companion for his ward. But upon the express condition that I am not made the subject of your discussions—a distinction which could not conduce to your forming a just and respectful estimate of me—I do not interpose my authority to bring your intercourse to an immediate close.'

As I read this postscript, my cheek tingled as if I had received a box on the ear. Uncle Silas was as yet a stranger. The menace of authority was new and sudden, and I felt with a pang of mortification the full force of the position in which my dear father's will had placed me.

I was silent, and handed the letter to my cousin, who read it with a kind of smile until she came, as I supposed, to the postscript, when her countenance, on which my eyes were fixed, changed, and with flushed cheeks she knocked the hand that held the letter on the table before her, and exclaimed—

'Did I ever hear! Well, if this isn't impertinence! *What* an old man that is!'

There was a pause, during which Lady Knollys held her head high with a frown, and sniffed a little.

'I did not intend to talk about him, but now I *will*. I'll talk away just whatever I like; and I'll stay here just as long as you let me, Maud, and you need not be one atom afraid of him. Our intercourse to an "immediate close," indeed! I only wish he were here. He should hear something!'

And Cousin Monica drank off her entire cup of tea at one draught, and then she said, more in her own way—

'I'm better!' and drew a long breath, and then she laughed a little in a waggish defiance. 'I wish we had him here, Maud, and *would* not we give him a bit of our minds! And this before the poor will is so much as proved!'

'I am almost glad he wrote that postscript; for although I don't think he has any authority in that matter while I am under my own roof,' I said, extemporising a legal opinion, 'and, therefore, shan't obey him, it has somehow opened my eyes to my real situation.'

I sighed, I believe, very desolately, for Lady Knollys came over and kissed me very gently and affectionately.

'It really seems, Maud, as if he had a supernatural sense, and heard things through the air over fifty miles of heath and hill. You remember how, just as he was probably writing that very postscript yesterday, I was urging you to come and stay with me, and planning to move Dr. Bryerly in our favour. And so I will, Maud, and to me you *shall* come—my guest, mind—I should be so delighted; and really if Silas is under a cloud, it has been his own doing, and I don't see that it is your business to fight his battle. He can't live very long. The suspicion, whatever it is dies with him, and what could poor dear Austin prove by his will but what everybody knew quite well before—his own strong belief in Silas's innocence? What an awful storm! The room trembles. Don't you like the sound? What they used to call 'wolving' in the old organ at Dorminster!'

CHAPTER XXVI

THE STORY OF UNCLE SILAS

And so it was like the yelling of phantom hounds and hunters, and the thunder of their coursers in the air—a furious, grand and supernatural music, which in my fancy made a suitable accompaniment to the discussion of that enigmatical person—martyr—angel—demon—Uncle Silas—with whom my fate was now so strangely linked, and whom I had begun to fear.

'The storm blows from that point,' I said, indicating it with my hand and eye, although the window shutters and curtains were closed. 'I saw all the trees bend that way this evening. That way stands the great lonely wood, where my darling father and mother lie. Oh, how dreadful on nights like this, to think of them—a vault!—damp, and dark, and solitary—under the storm.'

Cousin Monica looked wistfully in the same direction, and with a short sigh she said—

'We think too much of the poor remains, and too little of the spirit which lives for ever. I am sure they are happy.' And she sighed again. 'I wish I dare hope as confidently for myself. Yes, Maud, it is sad. We are such materialists, we can't help feeling so. We forget how well it is for us that our present bodies are not to last always. They are constructed for a time and place of trouble—plainly mere temporary machines that wear out, constantly exhibiting failure and decay, and with such tremendous capacity for pain. The body lies alone, and so it ought, for it is plainly its good Creator's will; it is only the tabernacle, not the person, who is clothed upon after death, Saint Paul says, "with a house which is from heaven." So Maud, darling, although the thought will trouble us again and again, there is nothing in it; and the poor mortal body is only the cold ruin of a habitation which *they* have forsaken before we do. So this great wind, you say, is blowing toward us from the wood there. If so, Maud, it is blowing from Bartram-Haugh, too, over the trees and chimneys of that old place, and the mysterious old man, who is quite right in thinking I don't like him; and I can fancy him an old enchanter in his castle, waving his familiar spirits on the wind to fetch and carry tidings of our occupations here.'

I lifted my head and listened to the storm, dying away in the distance sometimes—sometimes swelling and pealing around and above us—and through the dark and solitude my thoughts sped away to Bartram-Haugh and Uncle Silas.

'This letter,' I said at last, 'makes me feel differently. I think he is a stern old man—is he?'

'It is twenty years, now, since I saw him,' answered Lady Knollys. 'I did not choose to visit at his house.'

'Was that before the dreadful occurrence at Bartram-Haugh?'

'Yes—before, dear. He was not a reformed rake, but only a ruined one then. Austin was very good to him. Mr. Danvers says it is quite unaccountable how Silas can have made away with the immense sums he got from his brother from time to time without benefiting himself in the least. But, my dear, he played; and trying to help a man who plays, and is unlucky—and some men are, I believe, habitually unlucky—is like trying to fill a vessel that has no bottom. I think, by-the-by, my hopeful nephew, Charles Oakley, plays. Then Silas went most unjustifiably into all manner of speculations, and your poor father had to pay everything. He lost something quite astounding in that bank that ruined so many country gentlemen—poor Sir Harry Shackleton, in Yorkshire, had to sell half his estate. But your kind father went on helping him, up to his marriage—I mean in that extravagant way which was really totally useless.'

'Has my aunt been long dead?'

'Twelve or fifteen years—more, indeed—she died before your poor mamma. She was very unhappy, and I am sure would have given her right hand she had never married Silas.'

'Did you like her?'

'No, dear; she was a coarse, vulgar woman.'

'Coarse and vulgar, and Uncle Silas's wife!' I echoed in extreme surprise, for Uncle Silas was a man of fashion—a beau in his day—and might have married women of good birth and fortune, I had no doubt, and so I expressed myself.

'Yes, dear; so he might, and poor dear Austin was very anxious he should, and would have helped him with a handsome settlement, I dare say, but he chose to marry the daughter of a Denbigh innkeeper.'

'How utterly incredible!' I exclaimed.

'Not the least incredible, dear—a kind of thing not at all so uncommon as you fancy.'

'What!—a gentleman of fashion and refinement marry a person—'

'A barmaid!—just so,' said Lady Knollys. 'I think I could count half a dozen men of fashion who, to my knowledge, have ruined themselves just in a similar way.'

'Well, at all events, it must be allowed that in this he proved himself altogether unworldly.'

'Not a bit unworldly, but very vicious,' replied Cousin Monica, with a careless little laugh. 'She was very beautiful, curiously beautiful, for a person in her station. She was very like that Lady Hamilton who was Nelson's sorceress—

elegantly beautiful, but perfectly low and stupid. I believe, to do him justice, he only intended to ruin her; but she was cunning enough to insist upon marriage. Men who have never in all their lives denied themselves the indulgence of a single fancy, cost what it may, will not be baulked even by that condition if the *penchant* be only violent enough.'

I did not half understand this piece of worldly psychology, at which Lady Knollys seemed to laugh.

'Poor Silas, certainly he struggled honestly against the consequences, for he tried after the honeymoon to prove the marriage bad. But the Welsh parson and the innkeeper papa were too strong for him, and the young lady was able to hold her struggling swain fast in that respectable noose—and a pretty prize he proved!'

'And she died, poor thing, broken-hearted, I heard.'

'She died, at all events, about ten years after her marriage; but I really can't say about her heart. She certainly had enough ill-usage, I believe, to kill her; but I don't know that she had feeling enough to die of it, if it had not been that she drank: I am told that Welsh women often do. There was jealousy, of course, and brutal quarrelling, and all sorts of horrid stories. I visited at Bartram-Haugh for a year or two, though no one else would. But when that sort of thing began, of course I gave it up; it was out of the question. I don't think poor Austin ever knew how bad it was. And then came that odious business about wretched Mr. Charke. You know he—he committed suicide at Bartram.'

'I never heard about that,' I said; and we both paused, and she looked sternly at the fire, and the storm roared and ha-ha-ed till the old house shook again.

'But Uncle Silas could not help that,' I said at last.

'No, he could not help it,' she acquiesced unpleasantly.

'And Uncle Silas was'—I paused in a sort of fear.

'He was suspected by some people of having killed him'—she completed the sentence.

There was another long pause here, during which the storm outside bellowed and hooted like an angry mob roaring at the windows for a victim. An intolerable and sickening sensation overpowered me.

'But *you* did not suspect him, Cousin Knollys?' I said, trembling very much.

'No,' she answered very sharply. 'I told you so before. Of course I did not.'

There was another silence.

'I wish, Cousin Monica,' I said, drawing close to her, 'you had not said *that* about Uncle Silas being like a wizard, and sending his spirits on the wind to listen. But I'm very glad you never suspected him.' I insinuated my cold hand into hers, and looked into her face I know not with what expression. She looked down into mine with a hard, haughty stare, I thought.

'Of *course* I never suspected him; and *never* ask me *that* question again, Maud Ruthyn.'

Was it family pride, or what was it, that gleamed so fiercely from her eyes as she said this? I was frightened—I was wounded—I burst into tears.

'What is my darling crying for? I did not mean to be cross. *Was* I cross?' said this momentary phantom of a grim Lady Knollys, in an instant translated again into kind, pleasant Cousin Monica, with her arms about my neck.

'No, no, indeed—only I thought I had vexed you; and, I believe, thinking of Uncle Silas makes me nervous, and I can't help thinking of him nearly always.'

'Nor can I, although we might both easily find something better to think of. Suppose we try?' said Lady Knollys.

'But, first, I must know a little more about that Mr. Charke, and what circumstances enabled Uncle Silas's enemies to found on his death that wicked slander, which has done no one any good, and caused some persons so much misery. There is Uncle Silas, I may say, ruined by it; and we all know how it darkened the life of my dear father.'

'People will talk, my dear. Your uncle Silas had injured himself before that in the opinion of the people of his county. He was a black sheep, in fact. Very bad stories were told and believed of him. His marriage certainly was a disadvantage, you know, and the miserable scenes that went on in his disreputable house—all that predisposed people to believe ill of him.'

'How long is it since it happened?'

'Oh, a long time; I think before you were born,' answered she.

'And the injustice still lives—they have not forgotten it yet?' said I, for such a period appeared to me long enough to have consigned anything in its nature perishable to oblivion.

Lady Knollys smiled.

'Tell me, like a darling cousin, the whole story as well as you can recollect it. Who was Mr. Charke?'

'Mr. Charke, my dear, was a gentleman on the turf—that is the phrase, I think—one of those London men, without birth or breeding, who merely in right of their vices and their money are admitted to associate with young dandies who like hounds and horses, and all that sort of thing. That set knew him very well, but of course no one else. He was at the Matlock races, and your uncle asked him to Bartram-Haugh; and the creature, Jew or Gentile, whatever he was, fancied there was more honour than, perhaps, there really was in a visit to Bartram-Haugh.'

'For the kind of person you describe, it *was*, I think, a rather unusual honour to be invited to stay in the house of a man of Uncle Ruthyn's birth.'

'Well, so it was perhaps; for though they knew him very well on the course, and would ask him to their tavern dinners, they would not, of course, admit him to the houses where ladies were. But Silas's wife was not much regarded at Bartram-Haugh. Indeed, she was very little seen, for she was every evening tipsy in her bedroom, poor woman!'

'How miserable!' I exclaimed.

'I don't think it troubled Silas very much, for she drank gin, they said, poor thing, and the expense was not much; and, on the whole, I really think he was glad she drank, for it kept her out of his way, and was likely to kill her. At this time your poor father, who was thoroughly disgusted at his marriage, had stopped the supplies, you know, and Silas was very poor, and as hungry as a hawk, and they said he pounced upon this rich London gamester, intending to win his money. I am telling you now all that was said afterwards. The races lasted I forget how many days, and Mr. Charke stayed at Bartram-Haugh all this time and for some days after. It was thought that poor Austin would pay all Silas's gambling debts, and so this wretched Mr. Charke made heavy wagers with him on the races, and they played very deep, besides, at Bartram. He and Silas used to sit up at night at cards. All these particulars, as I told you, came out afterwards, for there was an inquest, you know, and then Silas published what he called his "statement," and there was a great deal of most distressing correspondence in the newspapers.'

'And why did Mr. Charke kill himself?' I asked.

'Well, I will tell you first what all are agreed about. The second night after the races, your uncle and Mr. Charke sat up till between two and three o'clock in the morning, quite by themselves, in the parlour. Mr. Charke's servant was at the Stag's Head Inn at Feltram, and therefore could throw no light upon what occurred at night at Bartram-Haugh; but he was there at six o'clock in the morning, and very early at his master's door by his direction. He had locked it, as was his habit, upon the inside, and the key was in the lock, which turned out afterwards a very important point. On knocking he found that he could not awaken his master, because, as it appeared when the door was forced open, his master was lying dead at his bedside, not in a pool, but a perfect pond of blood, as they described it, with his throat cut.'

'How horrible!' cried I.

'So it was. Your uncle Silas was called up, and greatly shocked of course, and he did what I believe was best. He had everything left as nearly as possible in the exact state in which it had been found, and he sent his own servant forthwith for the coroner, and, being himself a justice of the peace, he took the depositions of Mr. Charke's servant while all the incidents were still fresh in his memory.'

'Could anything be more straightforward, more right and wise?' I said.

'Oh, nothing of course,' answered Lady Knollys, I thought a little drily.

CHAPTER XXVII

MORE ABOUT TOM CHARKE'S SUICIDE

So the inquest was held, and Mr. Manwaring, of Wail Forest, was the only juryman who seemed to entertain the idea during the inquiry that Mr. Charke had died by any hand but his own.

'And how *could* he fancy such a thing?' I exclaimed indignantly.

'Well, you will see the result was quite enough to justify them in saying as they did, that he died by his own hand. The window was found fastened with a screw on the inside, as it had been when the chambermaid had arranged it at nine o'-clock; no one could have entered through it. Besides, it was on the third story, and the rooms are lofty, so it stood at a great height from the ground, and there was no ladder long enough to reach it. The house is built in the form of a hollow square, and Mr. Charke's room looked into the narrow court-yard within. There is but one door leading into this, and it did not show any sign of having been open for years. The door was locked upon the inside, and the key in the lock, so that nobody could have made an entrance that way either, for it was impossible, you see, to unlock the door from the outside.'

'And how could they affect to question anything so clear?' I asked.

'There did come, nevertheless, a kind of mist over the subject, which gave those who chose to talk unpleasantly an opportunity of insinuating suspicions, though they could not themselves find the clue of the mystery. In the first place, it appeared that he had gone to bed very tipsy, and that he was heard sing ing and noisy in his room while getting to bed—not the mood in which men make away with themselves. Then, although his own razor was found in that dreadful blood (it is shocking to have to hear all this) near his right hand, the fingers of his left were cut to the bone. Then the memorandum book in which his bets were noted was nowhere to be found. That, you know, was very odd. His keys were there attached to a chain. He wore a great deal of gold and trinkets. I saw him, wretched man, on the course. They had got off their horses. He and your uncle were walking on the course.'

'Did he look like a gentleman?' I inquired, as I dare say, other young ladies would.

'He looked like a Jew, my dear. He had a horrid brown coat with a velvet cape, curling black hair over his collar, and great whiskers, very high shoulders, and he was puffing a cigar straight up into the air. I was shocked to see Silas in such company.'

'And did his keys discover anything?' I asked.

'On opening his travelling desk and a small japanned box within it a vast deal less money was found than was expected—in fact, very little. Your uncle said that he had won some of it the night before at play, and that Charke complained to him when tipsy of having had severe losses to counterbalance his gains on the races. Besides, he had been paid but a small part of those gains. About his book it appeared that there were little notes of bets on the backs of letters, and it was said that he sometimes made no other memorandum of his wagers—but this was disputed—and among those notes there was not one referring to Silas. But, then, there was an omission of all allusion to his transactions with two other well-known gentlemen. So that was not singular.'

'No, certainly; that was quite accounted for,' said I.

'And then came the question,' continued she, 'what motive could Mr. Charke possibly have had for making away with himself.'

'But is not that very difficult to make out in many cases?' I interposed.

'It was said that he had some mysterious troubles in London, at which he used to hint. Some people said that he really was in a scrape, but others that there was no such thing, and that when he talked so he was only jesting. There was no suspicion during the inquest that your uncle Silas was involved, except those questions of Mr. Manwaring's.'

'What were they?' I asked.

'I really forget; but they greatly offended your uncle, and there was a little scene in the room. Mr. Manwaring seemed to think that some one had somehow got into the room. Through the door it could not be, nor down the chimney, for they found an iron bar across the flue, near the top in the masonry. The window looked into a court-yard no bigger than a ball-room. They went down and examined it, but, though the ground beneath was moist, they could not discover the slightest trace of a footprint. So far as they could make out, Mr. Charke had hermetically sealed himself into his room, and then cut his throat with his own razor.'

'Yes,' said I, 'for it was all secured—that is, the window and the door—upon the inside, and no sign of any attempt to get in.'

'Just so; and when the walls were searched, and, as your uncle Silas directed, the wainscoting removed, some months afterwards, when the scandal grew loudest, then it was evident that there was no concealed access to the room.'

'So the answer to all those calumnies was simply that the crime was impossible,' said I. 'How dreadful that such a slander should have required an answer at all!'

'It was an unpleasant affair even then, although I cannot say that anyone supposed Silas guilty; but you know the whole thing was disreputable, that Mr. Charke was a discreditable inmate, the occurrence was horrible, and there was a glare of publicity which brought into relief the scandals of Bartram-Haugh. But in a little time it became, all on a sudden, a great deal worse.'

My cousin paused to recollect exactly.

'There were very disagreeable whispers among the sporting people in London. This person, Charke, had written two letters, Yes—two. They were published about two months after, by the villain to whom they were written; he wanted to extort money. They were first talked of a great deal among that set in town; but the moment they were published they produced a sensation in the country, and a storm of newspaper commentary. The first of these was of no great consequence, but the second was very startling, embarrassing, and even alarming.'

'What was it, Cousin Monica?' I whispered.

'I can only tell you in a general way, it is so very long since I read it; but both were written in the same kind of slang, and parts as hard to understand as a prize fight. I hope you never read those things.'

I satisfied this sudden educational alarm, and Lady Knollys proceeded.

'I am afraid you hardly hear me, the wind makes such an uproar. Well, listen. The letter said distinctly, that he, Mr. Charke, had made a very profitable visit to Bartram-Haugh, and mentioned in exact figures for how much he held your uncle Silas's I.O.U.'s, for he could not pay him. I can't say what the sum was. I only remember that it was quite frightful. It took away my breath when I read it.'

'Uncle Silas had lost it?' I asked.

'Yes, and owed it; and had given him those papers called I.O.U.'s promising to pay, which, of course, Mr. Charke had locked up with his money; and the insinuation was that Silas had made away with him, to get rid of this debt, and that he had also taken a great deal of his money.

'I just recollect these points which were exactly what made the impression,' continued Lady Knollys, after a short pause; 'the letter was written in the evening of the last day of the wretched man's life, so that there had not been much time for your uncle Silas to win back his money; and he stoutly alleged that he did not owe Mr. Charke a guinea. It mentioned an enormous sum as being actually owed by Silas; and it cautioned the man, an agent, to whom he wrote, not to mention the circumstance, as Silas could only pay by getting the money from his wealthy brother, who would have the management; and he distinctly said that he had kept the matter very close at Silas's request. That, you know, was a very awkward letter, and all the worse that it was written in brutally high spirits, and not at all like a man meditating an exit from the world. You can't imagine what a sensation the publication of these letters produced. In a moment the storm was up, and certainly Silas did meet it bravely—yes, with great courage and ability. What a pity he did not early enter upon some career of ambition! Well, well, it is idle regretting. He suggested that the letters were forgeries. He alleged that Charke was in the habit of boasting, and telling enormous falsehoods about his gambling transactions, especially in his letters. He reminded the world how often men affect high animal spirits at the very moment of meditating suicide. He alluded, in a manly and graceful way, to his family and their character. He took a high and menacing tone with his adversaries, and he insisted that what they dared to insinuate against him was physically impossible.'

I asked in what form this vindication appeared.

'It was a letter, printed as a pamphlet; everybody admired its ability, ingenuity, and force, and it was written with immense rapidity.'

'Was it at all in the style of his letters?' I innocently asked.

My cousin laughed.

'Oh, dear, no! Ever since he avowed himself a religious character, he had written nothing but the most vapid and nerveless twaddle. Your poor dear father used to send his letters to me to read, and I sometimes really thought that Silas was losing his faculties; but I believe he was only trying to write in character.'

'I suppose the general feeling was in his favour?' I said.

'I don't think it was, anywhere; but in his own county it was certainly unanimously against him. There is no use in asking why; but so it was, and I think it would have been easier for him with his unaided strength to uproot the Peak than to change the convictions of the Derbyshire gentlemen. They were all against him. Of course there were predisposing causes. Your uncle published a very bitter attack upon them, describing himself as the victim of a political conspiracy: and I recollect he mentioned that from the hour of the shocking catastrophe in his house, he had forsworn the turf and all pursuits and amusements connected with it. People sneered, and said he might as well go as wait to be kicked out.'

'Were there law-suits about all this?' I asked.

'Everybody expected that there would, for there were very savage things printed on both sides, and I think, too, that the persons who thought worst of him expected that evidence would yet turn up to convict Silas of the crime they chose to impute; and so years have glided away, and many of the people who remembered the tragedy of Bartram-Haugh, and took the strongest part in the denunciation, and ostracism that followed, are dead, and no new light had been thrown upon the occurrence, and your uncle Silas remains an outcast. At first he was quite wild with rage, and would have fought the whole county, man by man, if they would have met him. But he had since changed his habits and, as he says, his aspirations altogether.'

'He has become religious.'

'The only occupation remaining to him. He owes money; he is poor; he is isolated; and he says, sick and religious. Your poor father, who was very decided and inflexible, never helped him beyond the limit he had prescribed, after Silas's *mésalliance*. He wanted to get him into Parliament, and would have paid his expenses, and made him an allowance; but either Silas had grown lazy, or he understood his position better than poor Austin, or he distrusted his powers, or possibly he really is in ill-health; but he objected his religious scruples. Your poor papa thought self-assertion possible, where an injured man has right to rely upon, but he had been very long out of the world, and the theory won't do. Nothing is harder than to get a person who has once been effectually slurred, received again. Silas, I think, was right. I don't think it was practicable.

'Dear child, how late it is!' exclaimed Lady Knollys suddenly, looking at the Louis Quatorze clock, that crowned the mantelpiece.

It was near one o'clock. The storm had a little subsided, and I took a less agitated and more confident view of Uncle Silas than I had at an earlier hour of that evening.

'And what do you think of him?' I asked.

Lady Knollys drummed on the table with her finger points as she looked into the fire.

'I don't understand metaphysics, my dear, nor witchcraft. I sometimes believe in the supernatural, and sometimes I don't. Silas Ruthyn is himself alone, and I can't define him, because I don't understand him. Perhaps other souls than human are sometimes born into the world, and clothed in flesh. It is not only about that dreadful occurrence, but nearly always throughout his life; early and late he has puzzled me. I have tried in vain to understand him. But at one time of his life I am sure he was awfully wicked—eccentric indeed in his wickedness—gay, frivolous, secret, and dangerous. At one time I think he could have made poor Austin do almost anything; but his influence vanished with his marriage, never to return again. No; I don't understand him. He always bewildered me, like a shifting face, sometimes smiling, but always sinister, in an unpleasant dream.'

CHAPTER XXVIII

I AM PERSUADED

So now at last I had heard the story of Uncle Silas's mysterious disgrace. We sat silent for a while, and I, gazing into vacancy, sent him in a chariot of triumph, chapletted, ringed, and robed through the city of imagination, crying after him, 'Innocent! innocent! martyr and crowned!' All the virtues and honesties, reason and conscience, in myriad shapes—tier above tier of human faces—from the crowded pavement, crowded windows, crowded roofs, joined in the jubilant acclamation, and trumpeters trumpeted, and drums rolled, and great organs and choirs through open cathedral gates, rolled anthems of praise and thanksgiving, and the bells rang out, and cannons sounded, and the air trembled with the roaring harmony; and Silas Ruthyn, the full-length portrait, stood in the burnished chariot, with a proud, sad, clouded face, that rejoiced not with the rejoicers, and behind him the slave, thin as a ghost, white-faced, and sneering something in his ear: while I and all the city went on crying 'Innocent! innocent! martyr and crowned!' And now the reverie was ended; and there were only Lady Knollys' stern, thoughtful face, with the pale light of sarcasm on it, and the storm outside thundering and lamenting desolately.

It was very good of Cousin Monica to stay with me so long. It must have been unspeakably tiresome. And now she began to talk of business at home, and plainly to prepare for immediate flight, and my heart sank.

I know that I could not then have defined my feelings and agitations. I am not sure that I even now could. Any misgiving about Uncle Silas was, in my mind, a questioning the foundations of my faith, and in itself an impiety. And yet I am not sure that some such misgiving, faint, perhaps, and intermittent, may not have been at the bottom of my tribulation.

I was not very well. Lady Knollys had gone out for a walk. She was not easily tired, and sometimes made a long excursion. The sun was setting now, when Mary Quince brought me a letter which had just arrived by the post. My heart throbbed violently. I was afraid to break the broad black seal. It was from Uncle Silas. I ran over in my mind all the unpleasant mandates which it might contain, to try and prepare myself for a shock. At last I opened the letter. It directed me to hold myself in readiness for the journey to Bartram-Haugh. It stated that I might bring two maids with me if I wished so many, and that his next letter would give me the details of my route, and the day of my departure for Derbyshire; and he said that I ought to make arrangements about Knowl during my absence, but that he was hardly the person properly to be consulted on that matter. Then came a prayer that he might be enabled to acquit himself of his trust to the full satisfaction of his conscience, and that I might enter upon my new relations in a spirit of prayer.

I looked round my room, so long familiar, and now so endeared by the idea of parting and change. The old house—dear, dear Knowl, how could I leave you and all your affectionate associations, and kind looks and voices, for a strange land!

With a great sigh I took Uncle Silas's letter, and went down stairs to the drawing-room. From the lobby window, where I loitered for a few moments, I looked out upon the well-known forest-trees. The sun was down. It was already twilight, and the white vapours of coming night were already filming their thinned and yellow foliage. Everything looked melancholy. How little did those who envied the young inheritrex of a princely fortune suspect the load that lay at her heart, or, bating the fear of death, how gladly at that moment she would have parted with her life!

Lady Knollys had not yet returned, and it was darkening rapidly; a mass of black clouds stood piled in the west, through the chasms of which was still reflected a pale metallic lustre.

The drawing-room was already very dark; but some streaks of this cold light fell upon a black figure, which would otherwise have been unseen, leaning beside the curtains against the window frame.

It advanced abruptly, with creaking shoes; it was Doctor Bryerly.

I was startled and surprised, not knowing how he had got there. I stood staring at him in the dusk rather awkwardly, I am afraid.

'How do you do, Miss Ruthyn?' said he, extending his hand, long, hard, and brown as a mummy's, and stooping a little so as to approach more nearly, for it was not easy to see in the imperfect light. 'You're surprised, I dare say, to see me here so soon again?'

'I did not know you had arrived. I am glad to see you, Doctor Bryerly. Nothing unpleasant, I hope, has happened?'

'No, nothing unpleasant, Miss. The will has been lodged, and we shall have probate in due course; but there has been something on my mind, and I'm come to ask you two or three questions which you had better answer very considerately. Is Miss Knollys still here?'

'Yes, but she is not returned from her walk.'

'I am glad she is here. I think she takes a sound view, and women understand one another better. As for me, it is plainly my duty to put it before you as it strikes me, and to offer all I can do in accomplishing, should you wish it, a different arrangement. You don't know your uncle, you said the other day?'

'No, I've never seen him.'

'You understand your late father's intention in making you his ward?'

'I suppose he wished to show his high opinion of my uncle's fitness for such a trust.'

'That's quite true; but the nature of the trust in this instance is extraordinary.'

'I don't understand.'

'Why, if you die before you come to the age of twenty-one, the entire of the property will go to him—do you see?—and he has the custody of your person in the meantime; you are to live in his house, under his care and authority. You see now, I think, how it is; and I did not like it when your father read the will to me, and I said so. Do *you*?'

I hesitated to speak, not sure that I quite comprehended him.

'And the more I think of it, the less I like it, Miss,' said Doctor Bryerly, in a calm, stern tone.

'Merciful Heaven! Doctor Bryerly, you can't suppose that I should not be as safe in my uncle's house as in the Lord Chancellor's?' I ejaculated, looking full in his face.

'But don't you see, Miss, it is not a fair position to put your uncle in,' replied he, after a little hesitation.

'But suppose *he* does not think so. You know, if he does, he may decline it.'

'Well that's true—but he won't. Here is his letter'—and he produced it—'announcing officially that he means to accept the office; but I think he ought to be told it is not *delicate*, under all circumstances. You know, Miss, that your uncle, Mr. Silas Ruthyn, was talked about unpleasantly once.'

'You mean'—I began.

'I mean about the death of Mr. Charke, at Bartram-Haugh.'

'Yes, I have heard that,' I said; he was speaking with a shocking *aplomb*.

'We assume, of course, *unjustly*; but there are many who think quite differently.'

'And possibly, Doctor Bryerly, it was for that very reason that my dear papa made him my guardian.'

'There can be no doubt of that, Miss; it was to purge him of that scandal.'

'And when he has acquitted himself honourably of that trust, don't you think such a proof of confidence so honourably fulfilled must go far to silence his traducers?'

'Why, if all goes well, it may do a little; but a great deal less than you fancy. But take it that you happen to *die*, Miss, during your minority. We are all mortal, and there are three years and some months to go; how will it be then? Don't you see? Just fancy how people will talk.'

'I think you know that my uncle is a religious man?' said I.

'Well, Miss, what of that?' he asked again.

'He is—he has suffered intensely,' I continued. 'He has long retired from the world; he is very religious. Ask our curate, Mr. Fairfield, if you doubt it.'

'But I am not disputing it, Miss; I'm only supposing what may happen—an accident, we'll call it small-pox, diphtheria, *that's* going very much. Three years and three months, you know, is a long time. You proceed to Bartram-Haugh, thinking you have much goods laid up for many years; but your Creator, you know, may say, "Thou fool, this day is thy soul required of thee." You go—and what pray is thought of your uncle, Mr. Silas Ruthyn, who walks in for the entire inheritance, and who has long been abused like a pickpocket, or worse, in his own county, I'm told?'

'You are a religious man, Doctor Bryerly, according to your lights?' I said.

The Swedenborgian smiled.

'Well, knowing that he is so too, and having yourself experienced the power of religion, do not you think him deserving of every confidence? Don't you think it well that he should have this opportunity of exhibiting both his own character and the reliance which my dear papa reposed on it, and that we should leave all consequences and contingencies in the hands of Heaven?'

'It appears to have been the will of Heaven hitherto,' said Doctor Bryerly—I could not see with what expression of face, but he was looking down, and drawing little diagrams with his stick on the dark carpet, and spoke in a very low tone—'that your uncle should suffer under this ill report. In countervailing the appointment of Providence, we must employ our reason, with conscientious diligence, as to the means, and if we find that they are as likely to do mischief as good, we have no right to expect a special interposition to turn our experiment into an ordeal. I think you ought to weigh it well—I am sure there are reasons against it. If you make up your mind that you would rather be placed under the care, say of Lady Knollys, I will endeavour all I can to effect it.'

'That could not be done without his consent, could it?' said I.

'No, but I don't despair of getting that—on terms, of course,' remarked he.

'I don't quite understand,' I said.

'I mean, for instance, if he were allowed to keep the allowance for your maintenance—eh?'

'I mistake my uncle Silas very much,' I said, 'if that allowance is any object whatever to him compared with the moral value of the position. If he were deprived of that, I am sure he would decline the other.'

'We might try him at all events,' said Doctor Bryerly, on whose dark sinewy features, even in this imperfect light, I thought I detected a smile.

'Perhaps,' said I, 'I appear very foolish in supposing him actuated by any but sordid motives; but he is my near relation, and I can't help it, sir.'

'That is a very serious thing, Miss Ruthyn,' he replied. 'You are very young, and cannot see it at present, as you will hereafter. He is very religious, you say, and all that, but his house is not a proper place for you. It is a solitude—its master an outcast, and it has been the repeated scene of all sorts of scandals, and of one great crime; and Lady Knollys thinks your having been domesticated there will be an injury to you all the days of your life.'

'So I do, Maud,' said Lady Knollys, who had just entered the room unperceived,—'How do you do, Doctor Bryerly?—a serious injury. You have no idea how entirely that house is condemned and avoided, and the very name of its inmates tabooed.'

'How monstrous—how cruel!' I exclaimed.

'Very unpleasant, my dear, but perfectly natural. You are to recollect that quite independently of the story of Mr. Charke, the house was talked about, and the county people had cut your uncle Silas long before that adventure was dreamed of; and as to the circumstance of your being placed in his charge by his brother, who took, from strong family feeling, a totally one-sided view of the affair from the first, having the slightest effect in restoring his position in the county, you must quite give that up. Except me, if he will allow me, and the clergyman, not a soul in the country will visit at Bartram-Haugh. They may pity you, and think the whole thing the climax of folly and cruelty; but they won't visit at Bartram, or know Silas, or have anything to do with his household.'

'They will see, at all events, what my dear papa's opinion was.'

'They know that already,' answered she, 'and it has not, and ought not to have, the slightest weight with them. There are people there who think themselves just as great as the Ruthyns, or greater; and your poor father's idea of carrying it by a demonstration was simply the dream of a man who had forgotten the world, and learned to exaggerate himself in his long seclusion. I know he was beginning himself to hesitate; and I think if he had been spared another year that provision of his will would have been struck out.'

Doctor Bryerly nodded, and he said—

'And if he had the power to dictate *now*, would he insist on that direction? It is a mistake every way, injurious to you, his child; and should you happen to die during your sojourn under your uncle's care, it would woefully defeat the testator's object, and raise such a storm of surmise and inquiry as would awaken all England, and send the old scandal on the wing through the world again.'

'Doctor Bryerly will, I have no doubt, arrange it all. In fact, I do not think it would be very difficult to bring Silas to terms; and if you do not consent to his trying, Maud, mark my words, you will live to repent it.'

Here were two persons viewing the question from totally different points; both perfectly disinterested; both in their different ways, I believe, shrewd and even wise; and both honourable, urging me against it, and in a way that undefinably alarmed my imagination, as well as moved my reason. I looked from one to the other—there was a silence. By this time the candles had come, and we could see one another.

'I only wait your decision, Miss Ruthyn,' said the trustee, 'to see your uncle. If his advantage was the chief object contemplated in this arrangement, he will be the best judge whether his interest is really best consulted by it or no; and I think he will clearly see that it is *not* so, and will answer accordingly.'

'I cannot answer now—you must allow me to think it over—I will do my best. I am very much obliged, my dear Cousin Monica, you are so very good, and you too, Doctor Bryerly.'

Doctor Bryerly by this time was looking into his pocket-book, and did not acknowledge my thanks even by a nod.

'I must be in London the day after to-morrow. Bartram-Haugh is nearly sixty miles from here, and only twenty of that by rail, I find. Forty miles of posting over those Derbyshire mountains is slow work; but if you say *try*, I'll see him to-morrow morning.'

'You must say try—you *must*, my dear Maud.'

'But how can I decide in a moment? Oh, dear Cousin Monica, I am so distracted!'

'But *you* need not decide at all; the decision rests with *him*. Come; he is more competent than you. You *must* say yes.'

Again I looked from her to Doctor Bryerly, and from him to her again. I threw my arms about her neck, and hugging her closely to me, I cried—

'Oh, Cousin Monica, dear Cousin Monica, advise me. I am a wretched creature. You must advise me.'

I did not know till now how irresolute a character was mine.

I knew somehow by the tone of her voice that she was smiling as she answered—

'Why, dear, I have advised you; I *do* advise you;' and then she added, impetuously, 'I entreat and implore, if you really think I love you, that you will *follow* my advice. It is your duty to leave your uncle Silas, whom you believe to be more competent than you are, to decide, after full conference with Doctor Bryerly, who knows more of your poor father's views and intentions in making that appointment than either you or I.'

'Shall I say, yes?' I cried, drawing her close, and kissing her helplessly.' Oh, tell me—tell me to say, yes.'

'Yes, of course, *yes*. She agrees, Doctor Bryerly, to your kind proposal.'

'I am to understand so?' he asked.

'Very well—yes, Doctor Bryerly,' I replied.

'You have resolved wisely and well,' said he, briskly, like a man who has got a care off his mind.

'I forgot to say, Doctor Bryerly—it was very rude—that you must stay here to-night.'

'He *can't*, my dear,' interposed Lady Knolly's; 'it is a long way.'

'He will dine. Won't you, Doctor Bryerly?'

'No; he can't. You know you can't, sir,' said my cousin, peremptorily. 'You must not worry him, my dear, with civilities he can't accept. He'll bid us good-bye this moment. Good-bye, Doctor Bryerly. You'll write immediately; don't wait till you reach town. Bid him good-bye, Maud. I'll say a word to you in the hall.'

And thus she literally hurried him out of the room, leaving me in a state of amazement and confusion, not able to review my decision—unsatisfied, but still unable to recall it.

I stood where they had left me, looking after them, I suppose, like a fool.

Lady Knollys returned in a few minutes. If I had been a little cooler I was shrewd enough to perceive that she had sent poor Doctor Bryerly away upon his travels, to find board and lodging half-way to Bartram, to remove him forthwith from my presence, and thus to make my decision—if mine it was—irrevocable.

'I applaud you, my dear,' said Cousin Knollys, in her turn embracing me heartily. 'You are a sensible little darling, and have done exactly what you ought to have done.'

'I hope I have,' I faltered.

'Hope? fiddle! stuff! the thing's as plain as a pikestaff.'

And in came Branston to say that dinner was served.

CHAPTER XXIX

HOW THE AMBASSADOR FARED

Lady Knollys, I could plainly see, when we got into the brighter lights at the dinner table, was herself a good deal excited; she was relieved and glad, and was garrulous during our meal, and told me all her early recollections of dear papa. Most of them I had heard before; but they could not be told too often.

Notwithstanding my mind sometimes wandered, *often* indeed, to the conference so unexpected, so suddenly decisive, possibly so momentous; and with a dismayed uncertainly, the question—had I done right?—was always before me.

I dare say my cousin understood my character better, perhaps, after all my honest self-study, then I do even now. Irresolute, suddenly reversing my own decisions, impetuous in action as she knew me, she feared, I am sure, a revocation of my commission to Doctor Bryerly, and thought of the countermand I might send galloping after him.

So, kind creature, she laboured to occupy my thoughts, and when one theme was exhausted found another, and had always her parry prepared as often as I directed a reflection or an enquiry to the re-opening of the question which she had taken so much pains to close.

That night I was troubled. I was already upbraiding myself. I could not sleep, and at last sat up in bed, and cried. I lamented my weakness in having assented to Doctor Bryerly's and my cousin's advice. Was I not departing from my engagement to my dear papa? Was I not consenting that my Uncle Silas should be induced to second my breach of faith by a corresponding perfidy?

Lady Knollys had done wisely in despatching Doctor Bryerly so promptly; for, most assuredly, had he been at Knowl next morning when I came down I should have recalled my commission.

That day in the study I found four papers which increased my perturbation. They were in dear papa's handwriting, and had an indorsement in these words—'Copy of my letter addressed to ——, one of the trustees named in my will.' Here, then, were the contents of those four sealed letters which had excited mine and Lady Knollys' curiosity on the agitating day on which the will was read.

It contained these words:—

'I name my oppressed and unhappy brother, Silas Ruthyn, residing at my house of Bartram-Haugh, as guardian of the person of my beloved child, to convince the world if possible, and failing that, to satisfy at least all future generations of our family, that his brother, who knew him best, had implicit confidence in him, and that he deserved it. A cowardly and preposterous slander, originating in political malice, and which never have been whispered had he not been poor and imprudent, is best silenced by this ordeal of purification. All I possess goes to him if my child dies under age; and the custody of her person I commit meanwhile to him alone, knowing that she is as safe in his as she could have been under my own care. I rely upon your remembrance of our early friendship to make this known wherever an opportunity occurs, and also to say what your sense of justice may warrant.'

The other letters were in the same spirit. My heart sank like lead as I read them. I quaked with fear. What had I done? My father's wise and noble vindication of our dishonoured name I had presumed to frustrate. I had, like a coward, receded from my easy share in the task; and, merciful Heaven, I had broken my faith with the dead!

With these letters in my hand, white with fear, I flew like a shadow to the drawing-room where Cousin Monica was, and told her to read them. I saw by her countenance how much alarmed she was by my looks, but she said nothing, only read the letters hurriedly, and then exclaimed—

'Is this all, my dear child? I really fancied you had found a second will, and had lost everything. Why, my dearest Maud, we knew all this before. We quite understood poor dear Austin's motive. Why are you so easily disturbed?'

'Oh, Cousin Monica, I think he was right; it all seems quite reasonable now; and I—oh, what a crime!—it must be stopped.'

'My dear Maud, listen to reason. Doctor Bryerly has seen your uncle at Bartram at least two hours ago. You *can't* stop it, and why on earth should you if you could? Don't you think your uncle should be consulted?' said she.

'But he has *decided.* I have his letter speaking of it as settled; and Doctor Bryerly—oh, Cousin Monica, he's gone *to tempt him*.'

'Nonsense, girl! Doctor Bryerly is a good and just man, I do believe, and has, beside, no imaginable motive to pervert either his conscience or his judgment. He's not gone to tempt him—stuff!—but to unfold the facts and invite his consideration; and I say, considering how thoughtlessly such duties are often undertaken, and how long Silas has been living in lazy solitude, shut out from the world, and unused to discuss anything, I do think it only conscientious and honourable that he should have a fair and distinct view of the matter in all its bearings submitted to him before he indolently incurs what may prove the worst danger he was ever involved in.'

So Lady Knollys argued, with feminine energy, and I must confess, with a good deal of the repetition which I have sometimes observed in logicians of my own sex, and she puzzled without satisfying me.

'I don't know why I went to that room,' I said, quite frightened; 'or why I went to that press; how it happened that these papers, which we never saw there before, were the first things to strike my eye to-day.'

'What do you mean, dear?' said Lady Knollys.

'I mean this—I think I was *brought* there, and that *there* is poor papa's appeal to me, as plain as if his hand came and wrote it upon the wall.' I nearly screamed the conclusion of this wild confession.

'You are nervous, my darling; your bad nights have worn you out. Let us go out; the air will do you good; and I do assure you that you will very soon see that we are quite right, and rejoice conscientiously that you have acted as you did.'

But I was not to be satisfied, although my first vehemence was quieted. In my prayers that night my conscience upbraided me. When I lay down in bed my nervousness returned fourfold. Everybody at all nervously excitable has suffered some time or another by the appearance of ghastly features presenting themselves in every variety of contortion, one after another, the moment the eyes are closed. This night my dear father's face troubled me—sometimes white and sharp as ivory, sometimes strangely transparent like glass, sometimes all hanging in cadaverous folds, always with the same unnatural expression of diabolical fury.

From this dreadful vision I could only escape by sitting up and staring at the light. At length, worn out, I dropped asleep, and in a dream I distinctly heard papa's voice say sharply outside the bed-curtain:—'Maud, we shall be late at Bartram-Haugh.'

And I awoke in a horror, the wall, as it seemed, still ringing with the summons, and the speaker, I fancied, standing at the other side of the curtain.

A miserable night I passed. In the morning, looking myself like a ghost, I stood in my night-dress by Lady Knollys' bed.

'I have had my warning,' I said. 'Oh, Cousin Monica, papa has been with me, and ordered me to Bartram-Haugh; and go I will.'

She stared in my face uncomfortably, and then tried to laugh the matter off; but I know she was troubled at the strange state to which agitation and suspense had reduced me.

'You're taking too much for granted, Maud,' said she; 'Silas Ruthyn, most likely, will refuse his consent, and insist on your going to Bartram-Haugh.'

'Heaven grant!' I exclaimed; 'but if he doesn't, it is all the same to me, go I will. He may turn me out, but I'll go, and try to expiate the breach of faith that I fear is so horribly wicked.'

We had several hours still to wait for the arrival of the post. For both of us the delay was a suspense; for me an almost agonising one. At length, at an unlooked-for moment, Branston did enter the room with the post-bag. There was a large letter, with the Feltram post-mark, addressed to Lady Knollys—it was Doctor Bryerly's despatch; we read it together. It was dated on the day before, and its purport was thus:—

'RESPECTED MADAM,—I this day saw Mr. Silas Ruthyn at Bartram-Haugh, and he peremptorily refuses, on any terms, to vacate the guardianship, or to consent to Miss Ruthyn's residing anywhere but under his own immediate care. As he bases his refusal, first upon a conscientious difficulty, declaring that he has no right, through fear of personal contingencies, to abdicate an office imposed in so solemn a way, and so naturally devolving on him as only brother to the deceased; and secondly upon the effect such a withdrawal, at the instance of the acting trustee, would have upon his own character, amounting to a public self-condemnation; and as he refused to discuss these positions with me, I could make no way whatsoever with him. Finding, therefore, that his mind was quite made up, after a short time I took my leave. He mentioned that preparations for his niece's reception are being completed, and that he will send for her in a few days; so that I think it will be advisable that I should go down to Knowl, to assist Miss Ruthyn with any advice she may require before her departure, to discharge servants, get inventories made, and provide for the care of the place and grounds during her minority.

'I am, respected Madam, yours truly,
HANS E. BRYERLY.'

I can't describe to you how chapfallen and angry my cousin looked. She sniffed once or twice, and then said, rather bitterly, in a subdued tone:—

'Well, *now*; I hope you are pleased?'

'No, no, no; you *know* I'm not—grieved to the heart, my only friend, my dear Cousin Monica; but my conscience is at rest; you don't know what a sacrifice it is; I am a most unhappy creature. I feel an indescribable foreboding. I am frightened; but you won't forsake me, Cousin Monica.'

'No, darling, never,' she said, sadly.

'And you'll come and see me, won't you, as often as you can?'

'Yes, dear; that is if Silas allows me; and I'm sure he will,' she added hastily, seeing, I suppose, my terror in my face. 'All I can do, you may be sure I will, and perhaps he will allow you to come to me, now and then, for a short visit. You know I am only six miles away—little more than half an hour's drive, and though I hate Bartram, and detest Silas—Yes, I *detest Silas*,' she repeated in reply to my surprised gaze—'I *will* call at Bartram—that is, I say, if he allows me; for, you know, I haven't been there for a quarter of a century; and though I never understood Silas, I fancy he forgives no sins, whether of omission or commission.'

I wondered what old grudge could make my cousin judge Uncle Silas always so hardly—I could not suppose it was justice. I had seen my hero indeed lately so disrespectfully handled before my eyes, that he had, as idols will, lost something of his sacredness. But as an article of faith, I still cultivated my trust in his divinity, and dismissed every intruding doubt with an exorcism, as a suggestion of the evil one. But I wronged Lady Knollys in suspecting her of pique, or malice, or anything more than that tendency to take strong views which some persons attribute to my sex.

So, then, the little project of Cousin Monica's guardianship, which, had it been poor papa's wish, would have made me so very happy, was quite knocked on the head, to revive no more. I comforted myself, however, with her promise to re-open communications with Bartram-Haugh, and we grew resigned.

I remember, next morning, as we sat at a very late breakfast, Lady Knollys, reading a letter, suddenly made an exclamation and a little laugh, and read on with increased interest for a few minutes, and then, with another little laugh, she looked up, placing her hand, with the open letter in it, beside her tea-cup.

'You'll not guess whom I've been reading about,' said she, with her head the least thing on one side, and an arch smile.

I felt myself blushing—cheeks, forehead, even down to the tips of my fingers. I anticipated the name I was to hear. She looked very much amused. Was it possible that Captain Oakley was married?

'I really have not the least idea,' I replied, with that kind of overdone carelessness which betrays us.

'No, I see quite plainly you have not; but you can't think how prettily you blush,' answered she, very much diverted.

'I really don't care,' I replied, with some little dignity, and blushing deeper and deeper.

'Will you make a guess?' she asked.

'I *can't* guess.'

'Well, shall I tell you?'

'Just as you please.'

'Well, I will—that is, I'll read a page of my letter, which tells it all. Do you know Georgina Fanshawe?' she asked.

'Lady Georgina? No.'

'Well, no matter; she's in Paris now, and this letter is from her, and she says—let me see the place—"Yesterday, what do you think?—quite an apparition!—you shall hear. My brother Craven yesterday insisted on my accompanying him to Le Bas' shop in that odd little antique street near the Grève; it is a wonderful old curiosity shop. I forget what they call them here. When we went into this place it was very nearly deserted, and there were so many curious things to look at all about, that for a minute or two I did not observe a tall woman, in a grey silk and a black velvet mantle, and quite a nice new Parisian bonnet. You will be *charmed*, by-the-by, with the new shape—it is only out three weeks, and is quite *indescribably* elegant, *I* think, at least. They have them, I am sure, by this time at Molnitz's, so I need say no more. And now that I am on this subject of dress, I have got your lace; and I think you will be very ungrateful if you are not *charmed* with it." Well, I need not read all that—here is the rest;' and she read—

'"But you'll ask about my mysterious *dame* in the new bonnet and velvet mantle; she was sitting on a stool at the counter, not buying, but evidently selling a quantity of stones and trinkets which she had in a card-box, and the man was picking them up one by one, and, I suppose, valuing them. I was near enough to see such a darling little pearl cross, with at least half a dozen really good pearls in it, and had begun to covet them for my set, when the lady glanced over my shoulder, and she knew me—in fact, we knew one another—and who do you think she was? Well—you'll not guess in a week, and I can't wait so long; so I may as well tell you at once—she was that horrid old Mademoiselle Blassemare whom you pointed out to me at Elverston; and I never forgot her face since—nor she, it seems, mine, for she turned away very quickly, and when I next saw her, her veil was down."'

'Did not you tell me, Maud, that you had lost your pearl cross while that dreadful Madame de la Rougierre was here?'

'Yes; but—'

'I know; but what has she to do with Mademoiselle de Blassemare, you were going to say—they are one and the same person.'

'Oh, I perceive,' answered I, with that dim sense of danger and dismay with which one hears suddenly of an enemy of whom one has lost sight for a time.

'I'll write and tell Georgie to buy that cross. I wager my life it is yours,' said Lady Knollys, firmly.

The servants, indeed, made no secret of their opinion of Madame de la Rougierre, and frankly charged her with a long list of larcenies. Even Anne Wixted, who had enjoyed her barren favour while the gouvernante was here, hinted privately that she had bartered a missing piece of lace belonging to me with a gipsy pedlar, for French gloves and an Irish poplin.

'And so surely as I find it is yours, I'll set the police in pursuit.'

'But you must not bring me into court,' said I, half amused and half alarmed.

'No occasion, my dear; Mary Quince and Mrs. Rusk can prove it perfectly.'

'And why do you dislike her so very much?' I asked.

Cousin Monica leaned back in her chair, and searched the cornice from corner to corner with upturned eyes for the reason, and at last laughed a little, amused at herself.

'Well, really, it is not easy to define, and, perhaps, it is not quite charitable; but I know I hate her, and I know, you little hypocrite, you hate her as much as I;' and we both laughed a little.

'But you must tell me all you know of her history.'

'Her history?' echoed she. 'I really know next to nothing about it; only that I used to see her sometimes about the place that Georgina mentions, and there were some unpleasant things said about her; but you know they may be all lies. The worst I *know* of her is her treatment of you, and her robbing the desk'—(Cousin Monica always called it her *robbery*)—'and I think that's enough to hang her. Suppose we go out for a walk?'

So together we went, and I resumed about Madame; but no more could I extract—perhaps there was not much more to hear.

CHAPTER XXX

ON THE ROAD

All at Knowl was indicative of the break-up that was so near at hand. Doctor Bryerly arrived according to promise. He was in a whirl of business all the time. He and Mr. Danvers conferred about the management of the estate. It was agreed that the grounds and gardens should be let, but not the house, of which Mrs. Rusk was to take the care. The gamekeeper remained in office, and some out-door servants. But the rest were to go, except Mary Quince, who was to accompany me to Bartram-Haugh as my maid.

'Don't part with Quince,' said Lady Knollys, peremptorily 'they'll want you, but *don't*.'

She kept harping on this point, and recurred to it half a dozen times every day.

'They'll say, you know, that she is not fit for a lady's maid, as she certainly is *not*, if it in the least signified in such a wilderness as Bartram-Haugh; but she is attached, trustworthy, and honest; and those are qualities valuable everywhere, especially in a solitude. Don't allow them to get you a wicked young French milliner in her stead.'

Sometimes she said things that jarred unpleasantly on my nerves, and left an undefined sense of danger. Such as:—

'I know she's true to you, and a good creature; but is she shrewd enough?'

Or, with an anxious look:—

'I hope Mary Quince is not easily frightened.'

Or, suddenly:—

'Can Mary Quince write, in case you were ill?'

Or,

'Can she take a message exactly?'

Or,

'Is she a person of any enterprise and resource, and cool in an emergency?'

Now, these questions did not come all in a string, as I write them down here, but at long intervals, and were followed quickly by ordinary talk; but they generally escaped from my companion after silence and gloomy thought; and though I could extract nothing more defined than these questions, yet they seemed to me to point at some possible danger contemplated in my good cousin's dismal ruminations.

Another topic that occupied my cousin's mind a good deal was obviously the larceny of my pearl cross. She made a note of the description furnished by the recollection, respectively, of Mary Quince, Mrs. Rusk, and myself. I had fancied her little vision of the police was no more than the result of a momentary impulse; but really, to judge by her methodical examinations of us, I should have fancied that she had taken it up in downright earnest.

Having learned that my departure from Knowl was to be so very soon, she resolved not to leave me before the day of my journey to Bartram-Haugh; and as day after day passed by, and the hour of our leave-taking approached, she became more and more kind and affectionate. A feverish and sorrowful interval it was to me.

Of Doctor Bryerly, though staying in the house, we saw almost nothing, except for an hour or so at tea-time. He breakfasted very early, and dined solitarily, and at uncertain hours, as business permitted.

The second evening of his visit, Cousin Monica took occasion to introduce the subject of his visit to Bartram-Haugh.

'You saw him, of course?' said Lady Knollys.

'Yes, he saw me; he was not well. On hearing who I was, he asked me to go to his room, where he sat in a silk dressing-gown and slippers.'

'About business principally,' said Cousin Monica, laconically.

'That was despatched in very few words; for he was quite resolved, and placed his refusal upon grounds which it was difficult to dispute. But difficult or no, mind you, he intimated that he would hear nothing more on the subject—so that was closed.'

'Well; and what is his religion now?' inquired she, irreverently.

'We had some interesting conversation on the subject. He leans much to what we call the doctrine of correspondents. He is read rather deeply in the writings of Swedenborg, and seemed anxious to discuss some points with one who professes to be his follower. To say truth, I did not expect to find him either so well read or so deeply interested in the subject.'

'Was he angry when it was proposed that he should vacate the guardianship?'

'Not at all. Contrariwise, he said he had at first been so minded himself. His years, his habits, and something of the unfitness of the situation, the remoteness of Bartram-Haugh from good teachers, and all that, had struck him, and nearly determined him against accepting the office. But then came the views which I stated in my letter, and they governed him; and nothing could shake them, he said, or induce him to re-open the question in his own mind.'

All the time Doctor Bryerly was relating his conference with the head of the family at Bartram-Haugh my cousin commented on the narrative with a variety of little 'pishes' and sneers, which I thought showed more of vexation than contempt.

I was glad to hear all that Doctor Bryerly related. It gave me a kind of confidence; and I experienced a momentary reaction. After all, could Bartram-Haugh be more lonely than I had found Knowl? Was I not sure of the society of my Cousin Millicent, who was about my own age? Was it not quite possible that my sojourn in Derbyshire might turn out a happy though very quiet remembrance through all my after-life? Why should it not? What time or place would be happy if we gave ourselves over to dismal imaginations?

So the summons reached me from Uncle Silas. The hours at Knowl were numbered.

The evening before I departed I visited the full-length portrait of Uncle Silas, and studied it for the last time carefully, with deep interest, for many minutes; but with results vaguer than ever.

With a brother so generous and so wealthy, always ready to help him forward; with his talents; with his lithe and gorgeous beauty, the shadow of which hung on that canvas—what might he not have accomplished? whom might he not have captivated? And yet where and what was he? A poor and shunned old man, occupying a lonely house and place that did not belong to him, married to degradation, with a few years of suspected and solitary life before him, and then swift oblivion his best portion.

I gazed on the picture, to fix it well and vividly in my remembrance. I might still trace some of its outlines and tints in its living original, whom I was next day to see for the first time in my life.

So the morning came—my last for many a day at Knowl—a day of partings, a day of novelty and regrets. The travelling carriage and post horses were at the door. Cousin Monica's carriage had just carried her away to the railway. We had embraced with tears; and her kind face was still before me, and her words of comfort and promise in my ears. The early sharpness of morning was still in the air; the frosty dew still glistened on the window-panes. We had made a hasty breakfast, my share of which was a single cup of tea. The aspect of the house how strange! Uncarpeted, uninhabited, doors for the most part locked, all the servants but Mrs. Rusk and Branston departed. The drawing-room door stood open, and a charwoman was washing the bare floor. I was looking my last—for who could say how long?—on the old house, and lingered. The luggage was all up. I made Mary Quince get in first, for every delay was precious; and now the moment was come. I hugged and kissed Mrs. Rusk in the hall.

'God bless you, Miss Maud, darling. You must not fret; mind, the time won't be long going over—*no* time at all; and you'll be bringing back a fine young gentleman—who knows? as great as the Duke of Wellington, for your husband; and I'll take the best of care of everything, and the birds and the dogs, till you come back; and I'll go and see you and Mary, if you'll allow, in Derbyshire;' and so forth.

I got into the carriage, and bid Branston, who shut the door, good-bye, and kissed hands to Mrs. Rusk, who was smiling and drying her eyes and courtesying on the hall-door steps. The dogs, who had started gleefully with the carriage, were called back by Branston, and driven home, wondering and wistful, looking back with ears oddly cocked and tails dejected. My heart thanked them for their kindness, and I felt like a stranger, and very desolate.

It was a bright, clear morning. It had been settled that it was not worth the trouble changing from the carriage to the railway for sake of five-and-twenty miles, and so the entire journey of sixty miles was to be made by the post road—the pleasantest travelling, if the mind were free. The grander and more distant features of the landscape we may see well enough from the window of the railway-carriage; but it is the foreground that interests and instructs us, like a pleasant gossiping history; and *that* we had, in old days, from the post-chaise window. It was more than travelling picquet. Something of all conditions of life—luxury and misery—high spirits and low;—all sorts of costume, livery, rags, millinery; faces buxom, faces wrinkled, faces kind, faces wicked;—no end of interest and suggestion, passing in a procession silent and vivid, and all in their proper scenery. The golden corn-sheafs—the old dark-alleyed orchards, and the high streets of antique towns. There were few dreams brighter, few books so pleasant.

We drove by the dark wood—it always looked dark to me—where the 'mausoleum' stands—where my dear parents both lay now. I gazed on its sombre masses not with a softened feeling, but a peculiar sense of pain, and was glad when it was quite past.

All the morning I had not shed a tear. Good Mary Quince cried at leaving Knowl; Lady Knollys' eyes were not dry as she kissed and blessed me, and promised an early visit; and the dark, lean, energetic face of the housekeeper was quivering, and her cheeks wet, as I drove away. But I, whose grief was sorest, never shed a tear. I only looked about from one familiar object to another, pale, excited, not quite apprehending my departure, and wondering at my own composure.

But when we reached the old bridge, with the tall osiers standing by the buttress, and looked back at poor Knowl—the places we love and are leaving look so fairy-like and so sad in the clear distance, and this is the finest view of the gabled old housc, with its slanting mcadow-lands and noble timber reposing in solemn groups—I gazed at the receding vision, and the tears came at last, and I wept in silence long after the fair picture was hidden from view by the intervening uplands.

I was relieved, and when we had made our next change of horses, and got into a country that was unknown to me, the new scenery and the sense of progress worked their accustomed effects on a young traveller who had lived a particularly secluded life, and I began to experience, on the whole, a not unpleasurable excitement.

Mary Quince and I, with the hopefulness of inexperienced travellers, began already to speculate about our proximity to Bartram-Haugh, and were sorely disappointed when we heard from the nondescript courier—more like a ostler than a servant, who sat behind in charge of us and the luggage, and represented my guardian's special care—at nearly one o'clock, that we had still forty miles to go, a considerable portion of which was across the high Derbyshire mountains, before we reached Bartram-Haugh.

The fact was, we had driven at a pace accommodated rather to the convenience of the horses than to our impatience; and finding, at the quaint little inn where we now halted, that we must wait for a nail or two in a loose shoe of one of our relay, we consulted, and being both hungry, agreed to beguile the time with an early dinner, which we enjoyed very sociably in a queer little parlour with a bow window, and commanding, with a litle garden for foreground, a very pretty landscape.

Good Mary Quince, like myself, had quite dried her tears by this time, and we were both highly interested, and I a little nervous, too, about our arrival and reception at Bartram. Some time, of course, was lost in this pleasant little parlour, before we found ourselves once more pursuing our way.

The slowest part of our journey was the pull up the long mountain road, ascending zig-zag, as sailors make way against a head-wind, by tacking. I forget the name of the pretty little group of houses—it did not amount to a village—buried in trees, where we got our *four* horses and two postilions, for the work was severe. I can only designate it as the place where Mary Quince and I had our tea, very comfortably, and bought some gingerbread, very curious to look upon, but quite uneatable.

The greater portion of the ascent, when we were fairly upon the mountain, was accomplished at a walk, and at some particularly steep points we had to get out and go on foot. But this to me was quite delightful. I had never scaled a mountain before, and the ferns and heath, the pure boisterous air, and above all the magnificent view of the rich country we were leaving behind, now gorgeous and misty in sunset tints, stretching in gentle undulations far beneath us, quite enchanted me.

We had just reached the summit when the sun went down. The low grounds at the other side were already lying in cold grey shadow, and I got the man who sat behind to point out as well as he could the site of Bartram-Haugh. But mist was gathering over all by this time. The filmy disk of the moon which was to light us on, so soon as twilight faded into night, hung high in air. I tried to see the sable mass of wood which he described. But it was vain, and to acquire a clear idea of the place, as of its master, I must only wait that nearer view which an hour or two more would afford me.

And now we rapidly descended the mountain side. The scenery was wilder and bolder than I was accustomed to. Our road skirted the edge of a great heathy moor. The silvery light of the moon began to glimmer, and we passed a gipsy bivouac with fires alight and caldrons hanging over them. It was the first I had seen. Two or three low tents; a couple of dark, withered crones, veritable witches; a graceful girl standing behind, gazing after us; and men in odd-shaped hats, with gaudy waistcoats and bright-coloured neck-handkerchiefs and gaitered legs, stood lazily in front. They had all a wild tawdry display of colour; and a group of alders in the rear made a background of shade for tents, fires, and figures.

I opened a front window of the chariot, and called to the postboys to stop. The groom from behind came to the window.

'Are not those gipsies?' I enquired.

'Yes, please'm, them's gipsies, sure, Miss,' he answered, glancing with that odd smile, half contemptuous, half superstitious, with which I have since often observed the peasants of Derbyshire eyeing those thievish and uncanny neighbours.

CHAPTER XXXI

BARTRAM-HAUGH

In a moment a tall, lithe girl, black-haired, black-eyed, and, as I thought, inexpressibly handsome, was smiling, with such beautiful rings of pearly teeth, at the window; and in her peculiar accent, with a suspicion of something foreign in it, proposing with many courtesies to tell the lady her fortune.

I had never seen this wild tribe of the human race before—children of mystery and liberty. Such vagabondism and beauty in the figure before me! I looked at their hovels and thought of the night, and wondered at their independence, and felt my inferiority. I could not resist. She held up her slim oriental hand.

'Yes, I'll hear my fortune,' I said, returning the sibyl's smile instinctively.

'Give me some money, Mary Quince. No, *not* that,' I said, rejecting the thrifty sixpence she tendered, for I had heard that the revelations of this weird sisterhood were bright in proportion to the kindness of their clients, and was resolved to approach Bartram with cheerful auguries. 'That five-shilling piece,' I insisted; and honest Mary reluctantly surrendered the coin.

So the feline beauty took it, with courtesies and 'thankees,' smiling still, and hid it away as if she stole it, and looked on my open palm still smiling; and told me, to my surprise, that there was *somebody* I liked very much, and I was almost afraid she would name Captain Oakley; that he would grow very rich, and that I should marry him; that I should move about from place to place a great deal for a good while to come. That I had some enemies, who should be sometimes so near as to be in the same room with me, and yet they should not be able to hurt me. That I should see blood spilt and yet not my own, and finally be very happy and splendid, like the heroine of a fairy tale.

Did this strange, girlish charlatan see in my face some signs of shrinking when she spoke of enemies, and set me down for a coward whose weakness might be profitable? Very likely. At all events she plucked a long brass pin, with a round bead for a head, from some part of her dress, and holding the point in her fingers, and exhibiting the treasure before my eyes, she told me that I must get a charmed pin like that, which her grandmother had given to her, and she ran glibly through a story of all the magic expended on it, and told me she could not part with it; but its virtue was that you were to stick it through the blanket, and while it was there neither rat, nor cat, nor snake—and then came two more terms in the catalogue, which I suppose belonged to the gipsy dialect, and which she explained to mean, as well as I could understand, the first a malevolent spirit, and the second 'a cove to cut your throat,' could approach or hurt you.

A charm like that, she gave me to understand, I must by hook or by crook obtain. She had not a second. None of her people in the camp over there possessed one. I am ashamed to confess that I actually paid her a pound for this brass pin! The purchase was partly an indication of my temperament, which could never let an opportunity pass away irrevocably without a struggle, and always apprehended 'Some day or other I'll reproach myself tor having neglected it!' and partly a record of the trepidations of that period of my life. At all events I had her pin, and she my pound, and I venture to say I was the gladder of the two.

She stood on the road-side bank courtseying and smiling, the first enchantress I had encountered, and I watched the receding picture, with its patches of fire-light, its dusky groups and donkey carts, white as skeletons in the moonlight, as we drove rapidly away.

They, I suppose, had a wild sneer and a merry laugh over my purchase, as they sat and ate their supper of stolen poultry, about their fire, and were duly proud of belonging to the superior race.

Mary Quince, shocked at my prodigality, hinted a remonstrance.

'It went to my heart, Miss, it did. They're such a lot, young and old, all alike thieves and vagabonds, and many a poor body wanting.'

'Tut, Mary, never mind. Everyone has her fortune told some time in her life, and you can't have a good one without paying. I think, Mary, we must be near Bartram now.'

The road now traversed the side of a steep hill, parallel to which, along the opposite side of a winding river, rose the dark steeps of a corresponding upland, covered with forest that looked awful and dim in the deep shadow, while the moonlight rippled fitfully upon the stream beneath.

'It seems to be a beautiful country,' I said to Mary Quince, who was munching a sandwich in the corner, and thus appealed to, adjusted her bonnet, and made an inspection from *her* window, which, however, commanded nothing but the heathy slope of the hill whose side we were traversing.

'Well, Miss, I suppose it is; but there's a deal o' mountains—is not there?'

And so saying, honest Mary leaned back again, and went on with her sandwich.

We were now descending at a great pace. I knew we were coming near. I stood up as well as I could in the carriage, to see over the postilions' heads. I was eager, but frightened too; agitated as the crisis of the arrival and meeting approached. At last, a long stretch of comparatively level country below us, with masses of wood as well as I could see irregularly overspreading it, became visible as the narrow valley through which we were speeding made a sudden bend.

Down we drove, and now I did perceive a change. A great grass-grown park-wall, overtopped with mighty trees; but still on and on we came at a canter that seemed almost a gallop. The old grey park-wall flanking us at one side, and a pretty pastoral hedgerow of ash-trees, irregularly on the other.

At last the postilions began to draw bridle, and at a slight angle, the moon shining full upon them, we wheeled into a wide semicircle formed by the receding park-walls, and halted before a great fantastic iron gate, and a pair of tall fluted piers, of white stone, all grass-grown and ivy-bound, with great cornices, surmounted with shields and supporters, the Ruthyn bearings washed by the rains of Derbyshire for many a generation of Ruthyns, almost smooth by this time, and looking bleached and phantasmal, like giant sentinels, with each a hand clasped in his comrade's, to bar our passage to the enchanted castle—the florid tracery of the iron gate showing like the draperies of white robes hanging from their extended arms to the earth.

Our courier got down and shoved the great gate open, and we entered, between sombre files of magnificent forest trees, one of those very broad straight avenues whose width measures the front of the house. This was all built of white stone, resembling that of Caen, which parts of Derbyshire produce in such abundance.

So this was Bartram, and here was Uncle Silas. I was almost breathless as I approached. The bright moon shining full on the white front of the old house revealed not only its highly decorated style, its fluted pillars and doorway, rich and florid carving, and balustraded summit, but also its stained and moss-grown front. Two giant trees, overthrown at last by the recent storm, lay with their upturned roots, and their yellow foliage still flickering on the sprays that were to bloom no more, where they had fallen, at the right side of the court-yard, which, like the avenue, was studded with tufted weeds and grass.

All this gave to the aspect of Bartram a forlorn character of desertion and decay, contrasting almost awfully with the grandeur of its proportions and richness of its architecture.

There was a ruddy glow from a broad window in the second row, and I thought I saw some one peep from it and disappear; at the same moment there was a furious barking of dogs, some of whom ran scampering into the court-yard from a half-closed side door; and amid their uproar, the bawling of the man in the back seat, who jumped down to drive them off, and the crack of the postilions' whips, who struck at them, we drew up before the lordly door-steps of this melancholy mansion.

Just as our attendant had his hand on the knocker the door opened, and we saw, by a not very brilliant candle-light, three figures—a shabby little old man, thin, and very much stooped, with a white cravat, and looking as if his black clothes were too large, and made for some one else, stood with his hand upon the door; a young, plump, but very pretty female figure, in unusually short petticoats, with fattish legs, and nice ankles, in boots, stood in the centre; and a dowdy maid, like an old charwoman, behind her.

The household paraded for welcome was not certainly very brilliant. Amid the riot the trunks were deliberately put down by our attendant, who kept shouting to the old man at the door, and to the dogs in turn; and the old man was talking and pointing stiffly and tremulously, but I could not hear what he said.

'Was it possible—could that mean-looking old man be Uncle Silas?'

The idea stunned me; but I almost instantly perceived that he was much too small, and I was relieved, and even grateful. It was certainly an odd mode of procedure to devote primary attention to the trunks and boxes, leaving the travellers still shut up in the carriage, of which they were by this time pretty well tired. I was not sorry for the reprieve, however: being nervous about first impressions, and willing to defer mine, I sat shyly back, peeping at the candle and moonlight picture before me, myself unseen.

'Will you tell—yes or no—is my cousin in the coach?' screamed the plump young lady, stamping her stout black boot, in a momentary lull.

Yes, I was there, sure.

'And why the puck don't you let her out, you stupe, you?'

'Run down, Giblets, you never do nout without driving, and let Cousin Maud out. You're very welcome to Bartram.' This greeting was screamed at an amazing pitch, and repeated before I had time to drop the window, and say 'thank you.' 'I'd a let you out myself—there's a good dog, you would na' bite Cousin' (the parenthesis was to a huge mastiff, who thrust himself beside her, by this time quite pacified)—'only I daren't go down the steps, for the governor said I shouldn't.'

The venerable person who went by the name of Giblets had by this time opened the carriage door, and our courier, or 'boots'—he looked more like the latter functionary—had lowered the steps, and in greater trepidation than I experienced when in after-days I was presented to my sovereign, I glided down, to offer myself to the greeting and inspection of the plain-spoken young lady who stood at the top of the steps to receive me.

She welcomed me with a hug and a hearty buss, as she called that salutation, on each cheek, and pulled me into the hall, and was evidently glad to see me.

'And you're tired a bit, I warrant; and who's the old 'un, who?' she asked eagerly, in a stage whisper, which made my ear numb for five minutes after. 'Oh, oh, the maid! and a precious old 'un—ha, ha, ha! But lawk! how grand she is, with her black silk, cloak and crape, and I only in twilled cotton, and rotten old Coburg for Sundays. Odds! it's a shame; but you'll be tired, you will. It's a smartish pull, they do say, from Knowl. I know a spell of it, only so far as the "Cat and Fiddle," near the Lunnon-road. Come up, will you? Would you like to come in first and talk a bit wi' the governor? Father, you know, he's a bit silly, he is, this while.' I found that the phrase meant only *bodily* infirmity. 'He took a pain o' Friday, newralgie—something or other he calls it—rheumatics it is when it takes old "Giblets" there; and he's sitting in his own room; or maybe you'd like better to come to your bedroom first, for it is dirty work travelling, they do say.'

Yes; I preferred the preliminary adjustment. Mary Quince was standing behind me; and as my voluble kinswoman talked on, we had each ample time and opportunity to observe the personnel of the other; and she made no scruple of letting me perceive that she was improving it, for she stared me full in the face, taking in evidently feature after feature; and she felt the material of my mantle pretty carefully between her finger and thumb, and manually examined my chain and trinkets, and picked up my hand as she might a glove, to con over my rings.

I can't say, of course, exactly what impression I may have produced on her. But in my cousin Milly I saw a girl who looked younger than her years, plump, but with a slender waist, with light hair, lighter than mine, and very blue eyes, rather round; on the whole very good-looking. She had an odd swaggering walk, a toss of her head, and a saucy and imperious, but rather good-natured and honest countenance. She talked rather loud, with a good ringing voice, and a boisterous laugh when it came.

If *I* was behind the fashion, what would Cousin Monica have thought of her? She was arrayed, as she had stated, in black twilled cotton expressive of her affliction; but it was made almost as short in the skirt as that of the prints of the Bavarian broom girls. She had white cotton stockings, and a pair of black leather boots, with leather buttons, and, for a lady, prodigiously thick soles, which reminded me of the navvy boots I had so often admired in *Punch.* I must add that the hands with which she assisted her scrutiny of my dress, though pretty, were very much sunburnt indeed.

'And what's *her* name?' she demanded, nodding to Mary Quince, who was gazing on her awfully, with round eyes, as an inland spinster might upon a whale beheld for the first time.

Mary courtesied, and I answered.

'Mary Quince,' she repeated. 'You're welcome, Quince. What shall I call her? I've a name for all o' them. Old Giles there, is Giblets. He did not like it first, but he answers quick enough now; and Old Lucy Wyat there,' nodding toward the old woman, 'is Lucia de l'Amour.' A slightly erroneous reading of Lammermoor, for my cousin sometimes made mistakes, and was not much versed in the Italian opera. 'You know it's a play, and I call her L'Amour for shortness;' and she laughed hilariously, and I could not forbear joining; and, winking at me, she called aloud, 'L'Amour.'

To which the crone, with a high-cauled cap, resembling Mother Hubbard, responded with a courtesy and 'Yes,'m.'

'Are all the trunks and boxes took up?'

They were.

'Well, we'll come now; and what shall I call you, Quince? Let me see.'

'According to your pleasure, Miss,' answered Mary, with dignity, and a dry courtesy.

'Why, you're as hoarse as a frog, Quince. We'll call you Quinzy for the present. That'll do. Come along, Quinzy.'

So my Cousin Milly took me under the arm, and pulled me forward; but as we ascended, she let me go, leaning back to make inspection of my attire from a new point of view.

'Hallo, cousin,' she cried, giving my dress a smack with her open hand. 'What a plague do you want of all that bustle; you'll leave it behind, lass, the first bush you jump over.'

I was a good deal astounded. I was also very near laughing, for there was a sort of importance in her plump countenance, and an indescribable grotesqueness in the fashion of her garments, which heightened the outlandishness of her talk, in a way which I cannot at all describe.

What palatial wide stairs those were which we ascended, with their prodigious carved banisters of oak, and each huge pillar on the landing-place crowned with a shield and carved heraldic supporters; florid oak panelling covered the walls. But of the house I could form no estimate, for Uncle Silas's housekeeping did not provide light for hall and passages, and we were dependent on the glimmer of a single candle; but there would be quite enough of this kind of exploration in the daylight.

So along dark oak flooring we advanced to my room, and I had now an opportunity of admiring, at my leisure, the lordly proportions of the building. Two great windows, with dark and tarnished curtains, rose half as high again as the windows of Knowl; and yet Knowl, in its own style, is a fine house. The door-frames, like the window-frames, were richly carved; the fireplace was in the same massive style, and the mantelpiece projected with a mass of very rich carving. On the whole I was surprised. I had never slept in so noble a room before.

The furniture, I must confess, was by no means on a par with the architectural pretensions of the apartment. A French bed, a piece of carpet about three yards square, a small table, two chairs, a toilet table—no wardrobe—no chest of drawers. The furniture painted white, and of the light and diminutive kind, was particularly ill adapted to the scale and style of the apartment, one end only of which it occupied, and that but sparsely, leaving the rest of the chamber in the nakedness of a stately desolation. My cousin Milly ran away to report progress to 'the Governor,' as she termed Uncle Silas.

'Well, Miss Maud, I never did expect to see the like o' that!' exclaimed honest Mary Quince, 'Did you ever see such a young lady? She's no more like one o' the family than I am. Law bless us! and what's she dressed like? Well, well, well!' And Mary, with a rueful shake of her head, clicked her tongue pathetically to the back of her teeth, while I could not forbear laughing.

'And such a scrap o' furniture! Well, well, well!' and the same ticking of the tongue followed.

But, in a few minutes, back came Cousin Milly, and, with a barbarous sort of curiosity, assisted in unpacking my trunks, and stowing away the treasures, on which she ventured a variety of admiring criticisms, in the presses which, like cupboards, filled recesses in the walls, with great oak doors, the keys of which were in them.

As I was making my hurried toilet, she entertained me now and then with more strictly personal criticisms.

'Your hair's a shade darker than mine—it's none the better o' that though—is it? Mine's said to be the right shade. I don't know—what do you say?'

I conceded the point with a good grace.

'I wish my hands was as white though—you do lick me there; but it's all gloves, and I never could abide 'em. I think I'll try though—they *are* very white, sure.'

'I wonder which is the prettiest, you or me? *I* don't know, *I*'m sure—which do *you* think?'

I laughed outright at this challenge, and she blushed a little, and for the first time seemed for a moment a little shy.

'Well, you *are* a half an inch longer than me, I think—don't you?'

I was fully an inch taller, so I had no difficulty in making the proposed admission.

'Well, you do look handsome! doesn't she, Quinzy, lass? but your frock comes down almost to your heels—it does.'

And she glanced from mine to hers, and made a little kick up with the heel of the navvy boot to assist her in measuring the comparative distance.

'Maybe mine's a thought too short?' she suggested. 'Who's there? Oh! it's you, is it?' she cried as Mother Hubbard appeared at the door. 'Come in, L'Amour—don't you know, lass, you're always welcome?'

She had come to let us know that Uncle Silas would be happy to see me whenever I was ready; and that my cousin Millicent would conduct me to the room where he awaited me.

In an instant all the comic sensations awakened by my singular cousin's eccentricities vanished, and I was thrilled with awe. I was about to see in the flesh—faded, broken, aged, but still identical—that being who had been the vision and the problem of so many years of my short life.

CHAPTER XXXII

UNCLE SILAS

I thought my odd cousin was also impressed with a kind of awe, though different in degree from mine, for a shade overcast her face, and she was silent as we walked side by side along the gallery, accompanied by the crone who carried the candle which lighted us to the door of that apartment which I may call Uncle Silas's presence chamber.

Milly whispered to me as we approached—

'Mind how you make a noise; the governor's as sharp as a weasel, and nothing vexes him like that.'

She was herself toppling along on tiptoe. We paused at a door near the head of the great staircase, and L'Amour knocked timidly with her rheumatic knuckles.

A voice, clear and penetrating, from within summoned us to enter. The old woman opened the door, and the next moment I was in the presence of Uncle Silas.

At the far end of a handsome wainscoted room, near the hearth in which a low fire was burning, beside a small table on which stood four waxlights, in tall silver candlesticks, sat a singular-looking old man.

The dark wainscoting behind him, and the vastness of the room, in the remoter parts of which the light which fell strongly upon his face and figure expended itself with hardly any effect, exhibited him with the forcible and strange relief of a finely painted Dutch portrait. For some time I saw nothing but him.

A face like marble, with a fearful monumental look, and, for an old man, singularly vivid strange eyes, the singularity of which rather grew upon me as I looked; for his eyebrows were still black, though his hair descended from his temples in long locks of the purest silver and fine as silk, nearly to his shoulders.

He rose, tall and slight, a little stooped, all in black, with an ample black velvet tunic, which was rather a gown than a coat, with loose sleeves, showing his snowy shirt some way up the arm, and a pair of wrist buttons, then quite out of fashion, which glimmered aristocratically with diamonds.

I know I can't convey in words an idea of this apparition, drawn as it seemed in black and white, venerable, bloodless, fiery-eyed, with its singular look of power, and an expression so bewildering—was it derision, or anguish, or cruelty, or patience?

The wild eyes of this strange old man were fixed upon me as he rose; an habitual contraction, which in certain lights took the character of a scowl, did not relax as he advanced toward me with his thin-lipped smile. He said something in his clear, gentle, but cold voice, the import of which I was too much agitated to catch, and he took both my hands in his, welcomed me with a courtly grace which belonged to another age, and led me affectionately, with many inquiries which I only half comprehended, to a chair near his own.

'I need not introduce my daughter; she has saved me that mortification. You'll find her, I believe, good-natured and affectionate; *au reste*, I fear a very rustic Miranda, and fitted rather for the society of Caliban than of a sick old Prospero. Is it not so, Millicent?'

The old man paused sarcastically for an answer, with his eyes fixed severely on my odd cousin, who blushed and looked uneasily to me for a hint.

'I don't know who they be—neither one nor t'other.'

'Very good, my dear,' he replied, with a little mocking bow. 'You see, my dear Maud, what a Shakespearean you have got for a cousin. It's plain, however, she has made acquaintance with some of our dramatists: she has studied the rôle of *Miss Hoyden* so perfectly.'

It was not a reasonable peculiarity of my uncle that he resented, with a good deal of playful acrimony, my poor cousin's want of education, for which, if he were not to blame, certainly neither was she.

'You see her, poor thing, a result of all the combined disadvantages of want of refined education, refined companionship, and, I fear, naturally, of refined tastes; but a sojourn at a good French conventual school will do wonders, and I hope to manage by-and-by. In the meantime we jest at our misfortunes, and love one another, I hope, cordially.'

He extended his thin, white hand with a chilly smile towards Milly, who bounced up, and took it with a frightened look; and he repeated, holding her hand rather slightly I thought, 'Yes, I hope, very cordially,' and then turning again to me, he put it over the arm of his chair, and let it go, as a man might drop something he did not want from a carriage window.

Having made this apology for poor Milly, who was plainly bewildered, he passed on, to her and my relief, to other topics, every now and then expressing his fears that I was fatigued, and his anxiety that I should partake of some supper or tea; but these solicitudes somehow seemed to escape his remembrance almost as soon as uttered; and he maintained the conversation, which soon degenerated into a close, and to me a painful examination, respecting my dear father's illness and its symptoms, upon which I could give no information, and his habits, upon which I could.

Perhaps he fancied that there might be some family predisposition to the organic disease of which his brother died, and that his questions were directed rather to the prolonging of his own life than to the better understanding of my dear father's death.

How little was there left to this old man to make life desirable, and yet how keenly, I afterwards found, he clung to it. Have we not all of us seen those to whom life was not only *undesirable*, but positively painful—a mere series of bodily torments, yet hold to it with a desperate and pitiable tenacity—old children or young, it is all the same.

See how a sleepy child will put off the inevitable departure for bed. The little creature's eyes blink and stare, and it needs constant jogging to prevent his nodding off into the slumber which nature craves. His waking is a pain; he is quite worn out, and peevish, and stupid, and yet he implores a respite, and deprecates repose, and vows he is not sleepy, even to the moment when his mother takes him in her arms, and carries him, in a sweet slumber, to the nursery. So it is with us old children of earth and the great sleep of death, and nature our kind mother. Just so reluctantly we part with consciousness, the picture is, even to the last, so interesting; the bird in the hand, though sick and moulting, so inestimably better than all the brilliant tenants of the bush. We sit up, yawning, and blinking, and stupid, the whole scene swimming before us, and the stories and music humming off into the sound of distant winds and waters. It is not time yet; we are not fatigued; we are good for another hour still, and so protesting against bed, we falter and drop into the dreamless sleep which nature assigns to fatigue and satiety.

He then spoke a little eulogy of his brother, very polished, and, indeed, in a kind of way, eloquent. He possessed in a high degree that accomplishment, too little cultivated, I think, by the present generation, of expressing himself with perfect precision and fluency. There was, too, a good deal of slight illustrative quotation, and a sprinkling of French flowers, over his conversation, which gave to it a character at once elegant and artificial. It was all easy, light, and pointed, and being quite new to me, had a wonderful fascination.

He then told me that Bartram was the temple of liberty, that the health of a whole life was founded in a few years of youth, air, and exercise, and that accomplishments, at least, if not education, should wait upon health. Therefore, while at Bartram, I should dispose of my time quite as I pleased, and the more I plundered the garden and gipsied in the woodlands, the better.

Then he told me what a miserable invalid he was, and how the doctors interfered with his frugal tastes. A glass of beer and a mutton chop—his ideal of a dinner—he dared not touch. They made him drink light wines, which he detested, and live upon those artificial abominations all liking for which vanishes with youth.

There stood on a side-table, in its silver coaster, a long-necked Rhenish bottle, and beside it a thin pink glass, and he quivered his fingers in a peevish way toward them.

But unless he found himself better very soon, he would take his case into his own hands, and try the dietary to which nature pointed.

He waved his fingers toward his bookcases, and told me his books were altogether at my service during my stay; but this promise ended, I must confess, disappointingly. At last, remarking that I must be fatigued, he rose, and kissed me with a solemn tenderness, placed his hand upon what I now perceived to be a large Bible, with two broad silk markers, red and gold, folded in it—the one, I might conjecture, indicating the place in the Old, the other in the New Testament. It stood on the small table that supported the waxlights, with a handsome cut bottle of eau-de-cologne, his gold and jewelled pencil-case, and his chased repeater, chain, and seals, beside it. There certainly were no indications of poverty in Uncle Silas's room; and he said impressively—

'Remember that book; in it your father placed his trust, in it he found his reward, in it lives my only hope; consult it, my beloved niece, day and night, as the oracle of life.'

Then he laid his thin hand on my head, and blessed me, and then kissed my forehead.

'No—a!' exclaimed Cousin Milly's lusty voice. I had quite forgotten her presence, and looked at her with a little start. She was seated on a very high old-fashioned chair; she had palpably been asleep; her round eyes were blinking and staring glassily at us; and her white legs and navvy boots were dangling in the air.

'Have you anything to remark about Noah?' enquired her father, with a polite inclination and an ironical interest.

'No—a,' she repeated in the same blunt accents; 'I didn't snore; did I? No—a.'

The old man smiled and shrugged a little at me—it was the smile of disgust.

'Good night, my dear Maud;' and turning to her, he said, with a peculiar gentle sharpness, 'Had not you better wake, my dear, and try whether your cousin would like some supper?'

So he accompanied us to the door, outside which we found L'Amour's candle awaiting us.

'I'm awful afraid of the Governor, I am. Did I snore that time?'

'No, dear; at least, I did not hear it,' I said, unable to repress a smile.

'Well, if I didn't, I was awful near it,' she said, reflectively.

We found poor Mary Quince dozing over the fire; but we soon had tea and other good things, of which Milly partook with a wonderful appetite.

'I *was* in a qualm about it,' said Milly, who by this time was quite herself again. 'When he spies me a-napping, maybe he don't fetch me a prod with his pencil-case over the head. Odd! girl, it *is* sore.'

When I contrasted the refined and fluent old gentleman whom I had just left, with this amazing specimen of young ladyhood, I grew sceptical almost as to the possibility of her being his child.

I was to learn, however, how little she had, I won't say of his society, but even of his presence—that she had no domestic companion of the least pretensions to education—that she ran wild about the place—never, except in church, so much as saw a person of that rank to which she was born—and that the little she knew of reading and writing had been picked up, in desultory half-hours, from a person who did not care a pin about her manners or decorum, and perhaps rather enjoyed her grotesqueness—and that no one who was willing to take the least trouble about her was competent to make her a particle more refined than I saw her—the wonder ceased. We don't know how little is heritable, and how much simply training, until we encounter some-such spectacle as that of my poor cousin Milly.

When I lay down in my bed and reviewed the day, it seemed like a month of wonders. Uncle Silas was always before me; the voice so silvery for an old man—so preternaturally soft; the manners so sweet, so gentle; the aspect, smiling, suffering, spectral. It was no longer a shadow; I had now seen him in the flesh. But, after all, was he more than a shadow to me? When I closed my eyes I saw him before me still, in necromantic black, ashy with a pallor on which I looked with fear and pain, a face so dazzlingly pale, and those hollow, fiery, awful eyes! It sometimes seemed as if the curtain opened, and I had seen a ghost.

I had seen him; but he was still an enigma and a marvel. The living face did not expound the past, any more than the portrait portended the future. He was still a mystery and a vision; and thinking of these things I fell asleep.

Mary Quince, who slept in the dressing-room, the door of which was close to my bed, and lay open to secure me against ghosts, called me up; and the moment I knew where I was I jumped up, and peeped eagerly from the window. It commanded the avenue and court-yard; but we were many windows removed from that over the hall-door, and immediately beneath ours lay the two giant lime trees, prostrate and uprooted, which I had observed as we drove up the night before.

I saw more clearly in the bright light of morning the signs of neglect and almost of dilapidation which had struck me as I approached. The court-yard was tufted over with grass, seldom from year to year crushed by the carriage-wheels, or trodden by the feet of visitors. This melancholy verdure thickened where the area was more remote from the centre; and under the windows, and skirting the walls to the left, was reinforced by a thick grove of nettles. The avenue was all grass-grown, except in the very centre, where a narrow track still showed the roadway The handsome carved balustrade of the court-yard was discoloured with lichens, and in two places gapped and broken; and the air of decay was heightened by the fallen trees, among whose sprays and yellow leaves the small birds were hopping.

Before my toilet was completed, in marched my cousin Milly. We were to breakfast alone that morning, 'and so much the better,' she told me. Sometimes the Governor ordered her to breakfast with him, and 'never left off chaffing her' till his newspaper came, and 'sometimes he said such things he made her cry,' and then he only 'boshed her more,' and packed her away to her room; but she was by chalks nicer than him, talk as he might. '*Was* not she nicer? was not she? was not she?' Upon this point she was so strong and urgent that I was obliged to reply by a protest against awarding the palm of elegance between parent and child, and declaring I liked her very much, which I attested by a kiss.

'I know right well which of us you do think's the nicest, and no mistake, only you're afraid of him; and he had no business boshing me last night before you. I knew he was at it, though I couldn't twig him altogether; but wasn't he a sneak, now, wasn't he?'

This was a still more awkward question; so I kissed her again, and said she must never ask me to say of my uncle in his absence anything I could not say to his face.

At which speech she stared at me for a while, and then treated me to one of her hearty laughs, after which she seemed happier, and gradually grew into better humour with her father.

'Sometimes, when the curate calls, he has me up—for he's as religious as six, he is—and they read Bible and prays, ho—don't they? You'll have that, lass, like me, to go through; and maybe I don't hate it; oh, no!'

We breakfasted in a small room, almost a closet, off the great parlour, which was evidently quite disused. Nothing could be homelier than our equipage, or more shabby than the furniture of the little apartment. Still, somehow, I liked it. It was a total change; but one likes 'roughing it' a little at first.

CHAPTER XXXIII

THE WINDMILL WOOD

I had not time to explore this noble old house as my curiosity prompted; for Milly was in such a fuss to set out for the 'blackberry dell' that I saw little more than just so much as I necessarily traversed in making my way to and from my room.

The actual decay of the house had been prevented by my dear father; and the roof, windows, masonry, and carpentry had all been kept in repair. But short of indications of actual ruin, there are many manifestations of poverty and neglect which impress with a feeling of desolation. It was plain that not nearly a tithe of this great house was inhabited; long corridors and galleries stretched away in dust and silence, and were crossed by others, whose dark arches inspired me in the distance with an awful sort of sadness. It was plainly one of those great structures in which you might easily lose yourself, and with a pleasing terror it reminded me of that delightful old abbey in Mrs. Radcliffe's romance, among whose silent staircases, dim passages, and long suites of lordly, but forsaken chambers, begirt without by the sombre forest, the family of La Mote secured a gloomy asylum.

My cousin Milly and I, however, were bent upon an open-air ramble, and traversing several passages, she conducted me to a door which led us out upon a terrace overgrown with weeds, and by a broad flight of steps we descended to the level of the grounds beneath. Then on, over the short grass, under the noble trees, we walked; Milly in high good-humour, and talking away volubly, in her short garment, navvy boots, and a weather-beaten hat. She carried a stick in her gloveless hand. Her conversation was quite new to me, and resembled very much what I would have fancied the holiday recollections of a schoolboy; and the language in which it was sustained was sometimes so outlandish, that I was forced to laugh outright—a demonstration which she plainly did not like.

Her talk was about the great jumps she had made—how she snow-balled the chaps' in winter—how she could slide twice the length of her stick beyond 'Briddles, the cow-boy.'

With this and similar conversation she entertained me.

The grounds were delightfully wild and neglected. But we had now passed into a vast park beautifully varied with hollows and uplands, and such glorious old timber massed and scattered over its slopes and levels. Among these, we got at last into a picturesque dingle; the grey rocks peeped from among the ferns and wild flowers, and the steps of soft sward along its sides were dark in the shadows of silver-stemmed birch, and russet thorn, and oak, under which, in the vaporous night, the Erl-king and his daughter might glide on their aërial horses.

In the lap of this pleasant dell were the finest blackberry bushes, I think, I ever saw, bearing fruit quite fabulous; and plucking these, and chatting, we rambled on very pleasantly.

I had first thought of Milly's absurdities, to which, in description, I cannot do justice, simply because so many details have, by distance of time, escaped my recollection. But her ways and her talk were so indescribably grotesque that she made me again and again quiver with suppressed laughter.

But there was a pitiable and even a melancholy meaning underlying the burlesque.

This creature, with no more education than a dairy-maid, I gradually discovered had fine natural aptitudes for accomplishment—a very sweet voice, and wonderfully delicate ear, and a talent for drawing which quite threw mine into the shade. It was really astonishing.

Poor Milly, in all her life, had never read three books, and hated to think of them. One, over which she was wont to yawn and sigh, and stare fatiguedly for an hour every Sunday, by command of the Governor, was a stout volume of sermons of the earlier school of George III., and a drier collection you can't fancy. I don't think she read anything else. But she had, notwithstanding, ten times the cleverness of half the circulating library misses one meets with. Besides all this, I had a long sojourn before me at Bartram-Haugh, and I had learned from Milly, as I had heard before, what a perennial solitude it was, with a ludicrous fear of learning Milly's preposterous dialect, and turning at last into something like her. So I resolved to do all I could for her—teach her whatever I knew, if she would allow me—and gradually, if possible, effect some civilising changes in her language, and, as they term it in boarding-schools, her demeanour.

But I must pursue at present our first day's ramble in what was called Bartram Chase. People can't go on eating blackberries always; so after a while we resumed our walk along this pretty dell, which gradually expanded into a wooded valley—level beneath and enclosed by irregular uplands, receding, as it were, in mimic bays and harbours at some points, and running out at others into broken promontories, ending in clumps of forest trees.

Just where the glen which we had been traversing expanded into this broad, but wooded valley, it was traversed by a high and close paling, which, although it looked decayed, was still very strong.

In this there was a wooden gate, rudely but strongly constructed, and at the side we were approaching stood a girl, who was leaning against the post, with one arm resting on the top of the gate.

This girl was neither tall nor short—taller than she looked at a distance; she had not a slight waist; sooty black was her hair, with a broad forehead, perpendicular but low; she had a pair of very fine, dark, lustrous eyes, and no other good feature—unless I may so call her teeth, which were very white and even. Her face was rather short, and swarthy as a gipsy's; observant and sullen too; and she did not move, only eyed us negligently from under her dark lashes as we drew near. Altogether a not unpicturesque figure, with a dusky, red petticoat of drugget, and tattered jacket of bottle-green stuff, with short sleeves, which showed her brown arms from the elbow.

'That's Pegtop's daughter,' said Milly.

'Who is Pegtop?' I asked.

'He's the miller—see, yonder it is,' and she pointed to a very pretty feature in the landscape, a windmill, crowning the summit of a hillock which rose suddenly above the level of the treetops, like an island in the centre of the valley.

'The mill not going to-day, Beauty?' bawled Milly.

'No—a, Beauty; it baint,' replied the girl, loweringly, and without stirring.

'And what's gone with the stile?' demanded Milly, aghast. 'It's tore away from the paling!'

'Well, so it be,' replied the wood nymph in the red petticoat, showing her fine teeth with a lazy grin.

'Who's a bin and done all that?' demanded Milly.

'Not you nor me, lass,' said the girl.

''Twas old Pegtop, your father, did it,' cried Milly, in rising wrath.

''Appen it wor,' she replied.

'And the gate locked.'

'That's it—the gate locked,' she repeated, sulkily, with a defiant side-glance at Milly.

'And where's Pegtop?'

'At t'other side, somewhere; how should I know where he be?' she replied.

'Who's got the key?'

'Here it be, lass,' she answered, striking her hand on her pocket.

'And how durst you stay us here? Unlock it, huzzy, this minute!' cried Milly, with a stamp.

Her answer was a sullen smile.

'Open the gate this instant!' bawled Milly.

'Well, I *won't.*'

I expected that Milly would have flown into a frenzy at this direct defiance, but she looked instead puzzled and curious—the girl's unexpected audacity bewildered her.

'Why, you fool, I could get over the paling as soon as look at you, but I won't. What's come over you? Open the gate, I say, or I'll make you.'

'Do let her alone, dear,' I entreated, fearing a mutual assault. 'She has been ordered, may be, not to open it. Is it so, my good girl?'

'Well, thou'rt not the biggest fool o' the two,' she observed, commendatively, 'thou'st hit it, lass.'

'And who ordered you?' exclaimed Milly.

'Fayther.'

'Old Pegtop. Well, *that's* summat to laugh at, it is—our servant a-shutting us out of our own grounds.'

'No servant o' yourn!'

'Come, lass, what do you mean?'

'He be old Silas's miller, and what's that to thee?'

With these words the girl made a spring on the hasp of the padlock, and then got easily over the gate.

'Can't you do that, cousin?' whispered Milly to me, with an impatient nudge. 'I *wish* you'd try.'

'No, dear—come away, Milly,' and I began to withdraw.

'Lookee, lass, 'twill be an ill day's work for thee when I tell the Governor,' said Milly, addressing the girl, who stood on a log of timber at the other side, regarding us with a sullen composure.

'We'll be over in spite o' you,' cried Milly.

'You lie!' answered she.

'And why not, huzzy?' demanded my cousin, who was less incensed at the affront than I expected. All this time I was urging Milly in vain to come away.

'Yon lass is no wild cat, like thee—that's why,' said the sturdy portress.

'If I cross, I'll give you a knock,' said Milly.

'And I'll gi' thee another,' she answered, with a vicious wag of the head.

'Come, Milly, *I'll* go if *you* don't,' I said.

'But we must not be beat,' whispered she, vehemently, catching my arm; 'and ye *shall* get over, and *see* what I will gi' her!'

'I'll *not* get over.'

'Then I'll break the door, for ye *shall* come through,' exclaimed Milly, kicking the stout paling with her ponderous boot.

'Purr it, purr it, purr it!' cried the lass in the red petticoat with a grin.

'Do you know who this lady is?' cried Milly, suddenly.

'She is a prettier lass than thou,' answered Beauty.

'She's *my* cousin Maud—Miss Ruthyn of Knowl—and she's a deal richer than the Queen; and the Governor's taking care of her; and he'll make old Pegtop bring you to reason.'

The girl eyed me with a sulky listlessness, a little inquisitively, I thought.

'See if he don't,' threatened Milly.

'You positively *must* come,' I said, drawing her away with me.

'Well, shall we come in?' cried Milly, trying a last summons.

'You'll not come in that much,' she answered, surlily, measuring an infinitesimal distance on her finger with her thumb, which she pinched against it, the gesture ending with a snap of defiance, and a smile that showed her fine teeth.

'I've a mind to shy a stone at you,' shouted Milly.

'Faire away; I'll shy wi' ye as long as ye like, lass; take heed o' yerself;' and Beauty picked up a round stone as large as a cricket ball.

With difficulty I got Milly away without an exchange of missiles, and much disgusted at my want of zeal and agility.

'Well, come along, cousin, I know an easy way by the river, when it's low,' answered Milly. 'She's a brute—is not she?'

As we receded, we saw the girl slowly wending her way towards the old thatched cottage, which showed its gable from the side of a little rugged eminence embowered in spreading trees, and dangling and twirling from its string on the end of her finger the key for which a battle had so nearly been fought.

The stream was low enough to make our flank movement round the end of the paling next it quite easy, and so we pursued our way, and Milly's equanimity returned, and our ramble grew very pleasant again.

Our path lay by the river bank, and as we proceeded, the dwarf timber was succeeded by grander trees, which crowded closer and taller, and, at last, the scenery deepened into solemn forest, and a sudden sweep in the river revealed the beautiful ruin of a steep old bridge, with the fragments of a gate-house on the farther side.

'Oh, Milly darling!' I exclaimed, 'what a beautiful drawing this would make! I should so like to make a sketch of it.'

'So it would. *Make* a picture—*do*!—here's a stone that's pure and flat to sit upon, and you look very tired. Do make it, and I'll sit by you.'

'Yes, Milly, I *am* tired, a little, and I *will* sit down; but we must wait for another day to make the picture, for we have neither pencil nor paper. But it is much too pretty to be lost; so let us come again to-morrow.'

'To-morrow be hanged! you'll do it to-day, bury-me-wick, but you *shall*; I'm wearying to see you make a picture, and I'll fetch your conundrums out o' your drawer, for do't you shall.'

CHAPTER XXXIV

ZAMIEL

It was all vain my remonstrating. She vowed that by crossing the stepping-stones close by she could, by a short cut, reach the house, and return with my pencils and block-book in a quarter of an hour. Away then, with many a jump and fling, scampered Milly's queer white stockings and navvy boots across the irregular and precarious stepping-stones, over which I dared not follow her; so I was fain to return to the stone so 'pure and flat,' on which I sat, enjoying the grand sylvan solitude, the dark background and the grey bridge mid-way, so tall and slim, across whose ruins a sunbeam glimmered, and the gigantic forest trees that slumbered round, opening here and there in dusky vistas, and breaking in front into detached and solemn groups. It was the setting of a dream of romance.

It would have been the very spot in which to read a volume of German folk-lore, and the darkening colonnades and silent nooks of the forest seemed already haunted with the voices and shadows of those charming elves and goblins.

As I sat here enjoying the solitude and my fancies among the low branches of the wood, at my right I heard a crashing, and saw a squat broad figure in a stained and tattered military coat, and loose short trousers, one limb of which flapped about a wooden leg. He was forcing himself through. His face was rugged and wrinkled, and tanned to the tint of old oak; his eyes black, beadlike, and fierce, and a shock of sooty hair escaped from under his battered wide-awake nearly to his shoulders. This forbidding-looking person came stumping and jerking along toward me, whisking his stick now and then viciously in the air, and giving his fell of hair a short shake, like a wild bull preparing to attack.

I stood up involuntarily with a sense of fear and surprise, almost fancying I saw in that wooden-legged old soldier, the forest demon who haunted Der Freischütz.

So he approached shouting—

'Hollo! you—how came you here? Dost 'eer?'

And he drew near panting, and sometimes tugging angrily in his haste at his wooden leg, which sunk now and then deeper than was convenient in the sod. This exertion helped to anger him, and when he halted before me, his dark face smirched with smoke and dust, and the nostrils of his flat drooping nose expanded and quivered as he panted, like the gills of a fish; an angrier or uglier face it would not be easy to fancy.

'Ye'll all come when ye like, will ye? and do nout but what pleases yourselves, won't you? And who'rt thou? Dost 'eer—who *are* ye, I say; and what the deil seek ye in the woods here? Come, bestir thee!'

If his wide mouth and great tobacco-stained teeth, his scowl, and loud discordant tones were intimidating, they were also extremely irritating. The moment my spirit was roused, my courage came.

'I am Miss Ruthyn of Knowl, and Mr. Silas Ruthyn, your master, is my uncle.'

'Hoo!' he exclaimed more gently, 'an' if Silas be thy uncle thou'lt be come to live wi' him, and thou'rt she as come overnight—eh?'

I made no answer, but I believe I looked both angrily and disdainfully.

'And what make ye alone here? and how was I to know't, an' Milly not wi' ye, nor no one? But Maud or no Maud, I wouldn't let the Dooke hisself set foot inside the palin' without Silas said let him. And you may tell Silas them's the words o' Dickon Hawkes, and I'll stick to'm—and what's more I'll tell him *myself*—I will; I'll tell him there be no use o' my striving and straining hee, day an' night and night and day, watchin' again poachers, and thieves, and gipsies, and they robbing lads, if rules won't be kep, and folk do jist as they pleases. Dang it, lass, thou'rt in luck I didn't heave a brick at thee when I saw thee first.'

'I'll complain of you to my uncle,' I replied.

'So do, and and 'appen thou'lt find thyself in the wrong box, lass; thou canst na' say I set the dogs arter thee, nor cau'd thee so much as a wry name, nor heave a stone at thee—did I? Well? and where's the complaint then?'

I simply answered, rather fiercely,

'Be good enough to leave me.'

'Well, I make no objections, mind. I'm takin' thy word—thou'rt Maud Ruthyn—'appen thou be'st and 'appen thou baint. I'm not aweer on't, but I takes thy word, and all I want to know's just this, did Meg open the gate to thee?'

I made him no answer, and to my great relief I saw Milly striding and skipping across the unequal stepping-stones.

'Hallo, Pegtop! what are you after now?' she cried, as she drew near.

'This man has been extremely impertinent. You know him, Milly?' I said.

'Why that's Pegtop Dickon. Dirty old Hawkes that never was washed. I tell you, lad, ye'll see what the Governor thinks o't—a-ha! He'll talk to you.'

'I done or said nout—not but I *should*, and there's the fack—she can't deny't; she hadn't a hard word from I; and I don't care the top o' that thistle what no one says—not I. But I tell thee, Milly, I stopped *some* o' thy pranks, and I'll stop more. Ye'll be shying no more stones at the cattle.'

'Tell your tales, and welcome, cried Milly. 'I wish I was here when you jawed cousin. If Winny was here she'd catch you by the timber toe and put you on your back.'

'Ay, she'll be a good un yet if she takes arter thee,' retorted the old man with a fierce sneer.

'Drop it, and get away wi' ye,' cried she, 'or maybe I'd call Winny to smash your timber leg for you.'

'A-ha! there's more on't. She's a sweet un. Isn't she?' he replied sardonically.

'You did not like it last Easter, when Winny broke it with a kick.'

''Twas a kick o' a horse,' he growled with a glance at me.

''Twas no such thing—'twas Winny did it—and he laid on his back for a week while carpenter made him a new one.' And Milly laughed hilariously.

'I'll fool no more wi' ye, losing my time; I won't; but mind ye, I'll speak wi' Silas.' And going away he put his hand to his crumpled wide-awake, and said to me with a surly difference—

'Good evening, Miss Ruthyn—good evening, ma'am—and ye'll please remember, I did not mean nout to vex thee.'

And so he swaggered away, jerking and waddling over the sward, and was soon lost in the wood.

'It's well he's a little bit frightened—I never saw him so angry, I think; he is awful mad.'

'Perhaps he really is not aware how very rude he is,' I suggested.

'I hate him. We were twice as pleasant with poor Tom Driver—he never meddled with any one, and was always in liquor; Old Gin was the name he went by. But this brute—I do hate him—he comes from Wigan, I think, and he's always spoiling sport—and he whops Meg—that's Beauty, you know, and I don't think she'd be half as bad only for him. Listen to him whistlin'.'

'I did hear whistling at some distance among the trees.'

'I declare if he isn't callin' the dogs! Climb up here, I tell ye,' and we climbed up the slanting trunk of a great walnut tree, and strained our eyes in the direction from which we expected the onset of Pegtop's vicious pack.

But it was a false alarm.

'Well, I don't think he *would* do that, after all—*hardly*; but he is a brute, sure!'

'And that dark girl who would not let us through, is his daughter, is she?'

'Yes, that's Meg—Beauty, I christened her, when I called him Beast; but I call him Pegtop now, and she's Beauty still, and that's the way o't.'

'Come, sit down now, an' make your picture,' she resumed so soon as we had dismounted from our position of security.

'I'm afraid I'm hardly in the vein. I don't think I could draw a straight line. My hand trembles.'

'I wish you could, Maud,' said Milly, with a look so wistful and entreating, that considering the excursion she had made for the pencils, I could not bear to disappoint her.

'Well, Milly, we must only try; and if we fail we can't help it. Sit you down beside me and I'll tell you why I begin with one part and not another, and you'll see how I make trees and the river, and—yes, *that* pencil, it is hard and answers for the fine light lines; but we must begin at the beginning, and learn to copy drawings before we attempt real views like this. And if you wish it, Milly, I'm resolved to teach you everything I know, which, after all, is not a great deal, and we shall have such fun making sketches of the same landscapes, and then comparing.'

And so on, Milly, quite delighted, and longing to begin her course of instruction, sat down beside me in a rapture, and hugged and kissed me so heartily that we were very near rolling together off the stone on which we were seated. Her boisterous delight and good-nature helped to restore me, and both laughing heartily together, I commenced my task.

'Dear me! who's that?' I exclaimed suddenly, as looking up from my block-book I saw the figure of a slight man in the careless morning-dress of a gentleman, crossing the ruinous bridge in our direction, with considerable caution, upon the precarious footing of the battlement, which alone offered an unbroken passage.

This was a day of apparitions! Milly recognised him instantly. The gentleman was Mr. Carysbroke. He had taken The Grange only for a year. He lived quite to himself, and was very good to the poor, and was the only gentleman, for ever so long, who had visited at Bartram, and oddly enough nowhere else. But he wanted leave to cross through the grounds, and having obtained it, had repeated his visit, partly induced, no doubt, by the fact that Bartram boasted no hospitalities, and that there was no risk of meeting the county folk there.

With a stout walking-stick in his hand, and a short shooting-coat, and a wide-awake hat in much better trim than Zamiel's, he emerged from the copse that covered the bridge, walking at a quick but easy pace.

'He'll be goin' to see old Snoddles, I guess,' said Milly, looking a little frightened and curious; for Milly, I need not say, was a bumpkin, and stood in awe of this gentleman's good-breeding, though she was as brave as a lion, and would have fought the Philistines at any odds, with the jawbone of an ass.

''Appen he won't see us,' whispered Milly, hopefully.

But he did, and raising his hat, with a cheerful smile, that showed very white teeth, he paused.

'Charming day, Miss Ruthyn.'

I raised my head suddenly as he spoke, from habit appropriating the address; it was so marked that he raised his hat respectfully to me, and then continued to Milly—

'Mr. Ruthyn, I hope, quite well? but I need hardly ask, you seem so happy. Will you kindly tell him, that I expect the book I mentioned in a day or two, and when it comes I'll either send or bring it to him immediately?'

Milly and I were standing, by this time, but she only stared at him, tongue-tied, her cheeks rather flushed, and her eyes very round, and to facilitate the dialogue, as I suppose, he said again—

'He's quite well, I hope?'

Still no response from Milly, and I, provoked, though myself a little shy, made answer—

'My uncle, Mr. Ruthyn, is very well, thank you,' and I felt that I blushed as I spoke.

'Ah, pray excuse me, may I take a great liberty? you are Miss Ruthyn, of Knowl? Will you think me very impertinent—I'm afraid you will—if I venture to introduce myself? My name is Carysbroke, and I had the honour of knowing poor Mr. Ruthyn when I was quite a little boy, and he has shown a kindness for me since, and I hope you will pardon the liberty I fear I've taken. I think my friend, Lady Knollys, too, is a relation of yours; what a charming person she is!'

'Oh, is not she? such a darling!' I said, and then blushed at my outspoken affection.

But he smiled kindly, as if he liked me for it; and he said—

'You know whatever I think, I dare not quite say that; but frankly I can quite understand it. She preserves her youth so wonderfully, and her fun and her good-nature are so entirely girlish. What a sweet view you have selected,' he continued, changing all at once. 'I've stood just at this point so often to look back at that exquisite old bridge. Do you observe—you're an artist, I see—something very peculiar in that tint of the grey, with those odd cross stains of faded red and yellow?'

'I do, indeed; I was just remarking the peculiar beauty of the colouring—was not I, Milly?'

Milly stared at me, and uttered an alarmed 'Yes,' and looked as if she had been caught in a robbery.

'Yes, and you have so very peculiar a background,' he resumed. 'It was better before the storm though; but it is very good still.'

Then a little pause, and 'Do you know this country at all?' rather suddenly.

'No, not in the least—that is, I've only had the drive to this place; but what I did see interested me very much.'

'You will be charmed with it when you know it better—the very place for an artist. I'm a wretched scribbler myself, and I carry this little book in my pocket,' and he laughed deprecatingly while he drew forth a thin fishing-book, as it looked. 'They are mere memoranda, you see. I walk so much and come unexpectedly on such pretty nooks and studies, I just try to make a note of them, but it is really more writing than sketching; my sister says it is a cipher which nobody but myself understands. However, I'll try and explain just two—because you really ought to go and see the places. Oh, no; not that,' he laughed, as accidentally the page blew over, 'that's the Cat and Fiddle, a curious little pot-house, where they gave me some very good ale one day.'

Milly at this exhibited some uneasy tokens of being about to speak, but not knowing what might be coming, I hastened to observe on the spirited little sketches to which he meant to draw my attention.

'I want to show you only the places within easy reach—a short ride or drive.'

So he proceeded to turn over two or three, in addition to the two he had at first proposed, and then another; then a little sketch just tinted, and really quite a charming little gem, of Cousin Monica's pretty gabled old house; and every subject had its little criticism, or its narrative, or adventure.

As he was about returning this little sketch-book to his pocket, still chatting to me, he suddenly recollected poor Milly, who was looking rather lowering; but she brightened a good deal as he presented it to her, with a little speech which she palpably misunderstood, for she made one of her odd courtesies, and was about, I thought, to put it into her large pocket, and accept it as a present.

'Look at the drawings, Milly, and then return it,' I whispered.

At his request I allowed him to look at my unfinished sketch of the bridge, and while he was measuring distances and proportions with his eye, Milly whispered rather angrily to me.

'And why should I?'

'Because he wants it back, and only meant to lend it to you,' whispered I.

'*Lend* it to me—and after you! Bury-me-wick if I look at a leaf of it,' she retorted in high dudgeon. 'Take it, lass; give it him yourself—I'll not,' and she popped it into my hand, and made a sulky step back.

'My cousin is very much obliged,' I said, returning the book, and smiling for her, and he took it smiling also and said—

'I think if I had known how very well you draw, Miss Ruthyn, I should have hesitated about showing you my poor scrawls. But these are not my best, you know; Lady Knollys will tell you that I can really do better—a great deal better, I think.'

And then with more apologies for what he called his impertinence, he took his leave, and I felt altogether very much pleased and flattered.

He could not be more than twenty-nine or thirty, I thought, and he was decidedly handsome—that is, his eyes and teeth, and clear brown complexion were—and there was something distinguished and graceful in his figure and gesture; and altogether there was the indescribable attraction of intelligence; and I fancied—though this, of course, was a secret—that from the moment he spoke to us he felt an interest in me. I am not going to be vain. It was a *grave* interest, but still an interest, for I could see him studying my features while I was turning over his sketches, and he thought I saw nothing else. It was flattering, too, his anxiety that I should think well of his drawing, and referring me to Lady Knollys. Carysbroke—had I ever heard my dear father mention that name? I could not recollect it. But then he was habitually so silent, that his not doing so argued nothing.

CHAPTER XXXV

WE VISIT A ROOM IN THE SECOND STOREY

Mr. Carysbroke amused my fancy sufficiently to prevent my observing Milly's silence, till we had begun our return homeward.

'The Grange must be a pretty house, if that little sketch be true; is it far from this?'

''Twill be two mile.'

'Are you vexed, Milly?' I asked, for both her tone and looks were angry.

'Yes, I am vexed; and why not lass?'

'What has happened?'

'Well, now, that is rich! Why, look at that fellow, Carysbroke: he took no more notice to me than a dog, and kep' talking to you all the time of his pictures, and his walks, and his people. Why, a pig's better manners than that.'

'But, Milly dear, you forget, he tried to talk to you, and you would not answer him,' I expostulated.

'And is not that just what I say—I can't talk like other folk—ladies, I mean. Every one laughs at me; an' I'm dressed like a show, I am. It's a shame! I saw Polly Shives—what a lady she is, my eyes!—laughing at me in church last Sunday. I was minded to give her a bit of my mind. An' I know I'm queer. It's a shame, it is. Why should *I* be so rum? it is a shame! I don't want to be so, nor it isn't my fault.'

And poor Milly broke into a flood of tears, and stamped on the ground, and buried her face in her short frock, which she whisked up to her eyes; and an odder figure of grief I never beheld.

'And I could not make head or tail of what he was saying,' cried poor Milly through her buff cotton, with a stamp; 'and you twigged every word o't. An' why am I so? It's a shame—a shame! Oh, ho, ho! it's a shame!'

'But, my dear Milly, we were talking of *drawing*, and you have not learned yet, but you shall—I'll teach you; and then you'll understand all about it.'

'An' every one laughs at me—even you; though you try, Maud, you can scarce keep from laughing sometimes. I don't blame you, for I know I'm queer; but I can't help it; and it's a shame.'

'Well, my dear Milly, listen to me: if you allow me, I assure you, I'll teach you all the music and drawing I know. You have lived very much alone; and, as you say, ladies have a way of speaking of their own that is different from the talk of other people.'

'Yes, that they have, an' gentlemen too—like the Governor, and that Carysbroke; and a precious lingo it is—dang it—why, the devil himself could not understand it; an' I'm like a fool among you. I could 'most drown myself. It's a shame! It is—you know it is.—It's a shame!'

'But I'll teach you that lingo too, if you wish it, Milly; and you shall know everything that I know; and I'll manage to have your dresses better made.'

By this time she was looking very ruefully, but attentively, in my face, her round eyes and nose swelled, and her cheeks all wet.

'I think if they were a little longer—yours is longer, you know;' and the sentence was interrupted by a sob.

'Now, Milly, you must not be crying; if you choose you may be just as the same as any other lady—and you shall; and you will be very much admired, I can tell you, if only you will take the trouble to quite unlearn all your odd words and ways, and dress yourself like other people; and I will take care of that if you let me; and I think you are very clever, Milly; and I know you are very pretty.'

Poor Milly's blubbered face expanded into a smile in spite of herself; but she shook her head, looking down.

'Noa, noa, Maud, I fear 'twon't be.' And indeed it seemed I had proposed to myself a labour of Hercules.

But Milly was really a clever creature, could see quickly, and when her ungainly dialect was mastered, describe very pleasantly; and if only she would endure the restraint and possessed the industry requisite, I did not despair, and was resolved at least to do my part.

Poor Milly! she was really very grateful, and entered into the project of her education with great zeal, and with a strange mixture of humility and insubordination.

Milly was in favour of again attacking 'Beauty's' position on her return, and forcing a passage from this side; but I insisted on following the route by which we had arrived, and so we got round the paling by the river, and were treated to a provoking grin of defiance by 'Beauty,' who was talking across the gate to a slim young man, arrayed in fustian, and with an odd-looking cap of rabbit-skin on his head, which, on seeing us, he pulled sheepishly to the side of his face next to us, as he lounged, with his arm under his chin, on the top bar of the gate.

After our encounter of to-day, indeed, it was Miss 'Beauty's' wont to exhibit a kind of jeering disdain in her countenance whenever we passed.

I think Milly would have engaged her again, had I not reminded her of her undertaking, and exerted my new authority.

'Look at that sneak, Pegtop, there, going up the path to the mill. He makes belief now he does not see us; but he does, though, only he's afraid we'll tell the

Governor, and he thinks Governor won't give him his way with you. I hate that Pegtop: he stopped me o' riding the cows a year ago, he did.'

I thought Pegtop might have done worse. Indeed it was plain that a total reformation was needed here; and I was glad to find that poor Milly seemed herself conscious of it; and that her resolution to become more like other people of her station was not a mere spasm of mortification and jealousy, but a genuine and very zealous resolve.

I had not half seen this old house of Bartram-Haugh yet. At first, indeed, I had but an imperfect idea of its extent. There was a range of rooms along one side of the great gallery, with closed window-shutters, and the doors generally locked. Old L'Amour grew cross when we went into them, although we could see nothing; and Milly was afraid to open the windows—not that any Bluebeard revelations were apprehended, but simply because she knew that Uncle Silas's order was that things should be left undisturbed; and this boisterous spirit stood in awe of him to a degree which his gentle manners and apparent quietude rendered quite surprising.

There were in this house, what certainly did not exist at Knowl, and what I have never observed, thought they may possibly be found in other old houses—I mean, here and there, very high hatches, which we could only peep over by jumping in the air. They crossed the long corridors and great galleries; and several of them were turned across and locked, so as to intercept the passage, and interrupt our explorations.

Milly, however, knew a queer little, very steep and dark back stair, which reached the upper floor; so she and I mounted, and made a long ramble through rooms much lower and ruder in finish than the lordly chambers we had left below. These commanded various views of the beautiful though neglected grounds; but on crossing a gallery we entered suddenly a chamber, which looked into a small and dismal quadrangle, formed by the inner walls of this great house, and of course designed only by the architect to afford the needful light and air to portions of the structure.

I rubbed the window-pane with my handkerchief and looked out. The surrounding roof was steep and high. The walls looked soiled and dark. The windows lined with dust and dirt, and the window-stones were in places tufted with moss, and grass, and groundsel. An arched doorway had opened from the house into this darkened square, but it was soiled and dusty; and the damp weeds that overgrew the quadrangle drooped undisturbed against it. It was plain that human footsteps tracked it little, and I gazed into that blind and sinister area with a strange thrill and sinking.

'This is the second floor—there is the enclosed court-yard'—I, as it were, soliloquised.

'What are you afraid of, Maud? you look as ye'd seen a ghost,' exclaimed Milly, who came to the window and peeped over my shoulder.

'It reminded me suddenly, Milly, of that frightful business.'

'What business, Maud?—what a plague are ye thinking on?' demanded Milly, rather amused.

'It was in one of these rooms—maybe this—yes, it certainly *was* this—for see, the panelling has been pulled off the wall—that Mr. Charke killed himself.'

I was staring ruefully round the dim chamber, in whose corners the shadows of night were already gathering.

'Charke!—what about him?—who's Charke?' asked Milly.

'Why, you must have heard of him,' said I.

'Not as I'm aware on,' answered she. 'And he killed himself, did he, hanged himself, eh, or blowed his brains out?'

'He cut his throat in one of these rooms—*this* one, I'm sure—for your papa had the wainscoting stripped from the wall to ascertain whether there was any second door through which a murderer could have come; and you see these walls are stripped, and bear the marks of the woodwork that has been removed,' I answered.

'Well, that *was* awful! I don't know how they have pluck to cut their throats; if I was doing it, I'd like best to put a pistol to my head and fire, like the young gentleman did, they say, in Deadman's Hollow. But the fellows that cut their throats, they must be awful game lads, I'm thinkin', for it's a long slice, you know.'

'Don't, don't, Milly dear. Suppose we come away,' I said, for the evening was deepening rapidly into night.

'Hey and bury-me-wick, but here's the blood; don't you see a big black cloud all spread over the floor hereabout, don't ye see?' Milly was stooping over the spot, and tracing the outline of this, perhaps, imaginary mapping, in the air with her finger.

'No, Milly, you could not see it: the floor is too dark, and it's all in shadow. It must be fancy; and perhaps, after all, this is not the room.'

'Well—I think, I'm *sure* it *is*. Stand—just look.'

'We'll come in the morning, and if you are right we can see it better then. Come away,' I said, growing frightened.

And just as we stood up to depart, the white high-cauled cap and large sallow features of old L'Amour peeped in at the door.

'Lawk! what brings you here?' cried Milly, nearly as much startled as I at the intrusion.

'What brings *you* here, miss?' whistled L'Amour through her gums.

'We're looking where Charke cut his throat,' replied Milly.

'Charke the devil!' said the old woman, with an odd mixture of scorn and fury. "Tisn't his room; and come ye out of it, please. Master won't like when he hears how you keep pulling Miss Maud from one room to another, all through the house, up and down.'

She was gabbling sternly enough, but dropped a low courtesy as I passed her, and with a peaked and nodding stare round the room, the old woman clapped the door sharply, and locked it.

'And who has been a talking about Charke—a pack o lies, I warrant. I s'pose you want to frighten Miss Maud here' (another crippled courtesy) 'wi' ghosts and like nonsense.'

'You're out there: 'twas she told me; and much about it. Ghosts, indeed! I don't vally them, not I; if I did, I know who'd frighten me,' and Milly laughed.

The old woman stuffed the key in her pocket, and her wrinkled mouth pouted and receded with a grim uneasiness.

'A harmless brat, and kind she is; but wild—wild—she will be wild.'

So whispered L'Amour in my ear, during the silence that followed, nodding shakily toward Milly over the banister, and she courtesied again as we departed, and shuffled off toward Uncle Silas's room.

The Governor is queerish this evening,' said Milly, when we were seated at our tea. 'You never saw him queerish, did you?'

'You must say what you mean, more plainly, Milly. You don't mean ill, I hope?'

'Well! I don't know what it is; but he does grow very queer sometimes—you'd think he was dead a'most, maybe two or three days and nights together. He sits all the time like an old woman in a swound. Well, well, it is awful!'

'Is he insensible when in that state?' I asked, a good deal alarmed.

'I don't know; but it never signifies anything. It won't kill him, I do believe; but old L'Amour knows all about it. I hardly ever go into the room when he's so, only when I'm sent for; and he sometimes wakes up and takes a fancy to call for this one or that. One day he sent for Pegtop all the way to the mill; and when he came, he only stared at him for a minute or two, and ordered him out o' the room. He's like a child a'most, when he's in one o' them dazes.'

I always knew when Uncle Silas was 'queerish,' by the injunctions of old L'Amour, whistled and spluttered over the banister as we came up-stairs, to mind how we made a noise passing master's door; and by the sound of mysterious to-ings and fro-ings about his room.

I saw very little of him. He sometimes took a whim to have us breakfast with him, which lasted perhaps for a week; and then the order of our living would relapse into its old routine.

I must not forget two kind letters from Lady Knollys, who was detained away, and delighted to hear that I enjoyed my quiet life; and promised to apply, in person, to Uncle Silas, for permission to visit me.

She was to be for the Christmas at Elverston, and that was only six miles away from Bartram-Haugh, so I had the excitement of a pleasant look forward.

She also said that she would include poor Milly in her invitation; and a vision of Captain Oakley rose before me, with his handsome gaze turned in wonder on poor Milly, for whom I had begun to feel myself responsible.

CHAPTER XXXVI

AN ARRIVAL AT DEAD OF NIGHT

I have sometimes been asked why I wear an odd little turquois ring—which to the uninstructed eye appears quite valueless and altogether an unworthy companion of those jewels which flash insultingly beside it. It is a little keepsake, of which I became possessed about this time.

'Come, lass, what name shall I give you?' cried Milly, one morning, bursting into my room in a state of alarming hilarity.

'My own, Milly.'

'No, but you must have a nickname, like every one else.'

'Don't mind it, Milly.'

'Yes, but I will. Shall I call you Mrs. Bustle?'

'You shall do no such thing.'

'But you must have a name.'

'I refuse a name.'

'But I'll give you one, lass.'

'And *I* won't have it.'

'But you can't help me christening you.'

'I can decline answering.'

'But I'll make you,' said Milly, growing very red.

Perhaps there was something provoking in my tone, for I certainly was very much disgusted at Milly's relapse into barbarism.

'You can't,' I retorted quietly.

'See if I don't, and I'll give ye one twice as ugly.'

I smiled, I fear, disdainfully.

'And I think you're a minx, and a slut, and a fool,' she broke out, flushing scarlet.

I smiled in the same unchristian way.

'And I'd give ye a smack o' the cheek as soon as look at you.'

And she gave her dress a great slap, and drew near me, in her wrath. I really thought she was about tendering the ordeal of single combat.

I made her, however, a paralysing courtesy, and, with immense dignity, sailed out of the room, and into Uncle Silas's study, where it happened we were to breakfast that morning, and for several subsequent ones.

During the meal we maintained the most dignified reserve; and I don't think either so much as looked at the other.

We had no walk together that day.

I was sitting in the evening, quite alone, when Milly entered the room. Her eyes were red, and she looked very sullen.

'I want your hand, cousin,' she said, at the same time taking it by the wrist, and administering with it a sudden slap on her plump cheek, which made the room ring, and my fingers tingle; and before I had recovered from my surprise, she had vanished.

I called after her, but no answer; I pursued, but she was running too; and I quite lost her at the cross galleries.

I did not see her at tea, nor before going to bed; but after I had fallen asleep I was awakened by Milly, in floods of tears.

'Cousin Maud, will ye forgi' me—you'll never like me again, will ye? No—I know ye won't—I'm such a brute—I hate it—it's a shame. And here's a Banbury cake for you—I sent to the town for it, and some taffy—won't ye eat it? and here's a little ring—'tisn't as pretty as your own rings; and ye'll wear it, maybe, for my sake—poor Milly's sake, before I was so bad to ye—if ye forgi' me; and I'll look at breakfast, and if it's on your finger I'll know you're friends wi' me again; and if ye don't, I won't trouble you no more; and I think I'll just drown myself out o' the way, and you'll never see wicked Milly no more.'

And without waiting a moment, leaving me only half awake, and with the sensations of dreaming, she scampered from the room, in her bare feet, with a petticoat about her shoulders.

She had left her candle by my bed, and her little offerings on the coverlet by me. If I had stood an atom less in terror of goblins than I did, I should have followed her, but I was afraid. I stood in my bare feet at my bedside, and kissed the poor little ring and put it on my finger, where it has remained ever since and always shall. And when I lay down, longing for morning, the image of her pale, imploring, penitential face was before me for hours; and I repented bitterly of my cool provoking ways, and thought myself, I dare say justly, a thousand times more to blame than Milly.

I searched in vain for her before breakfast. At that meal, however, we met, but in the presence of Uncle Silas, who, though silent and apathetic, was formidable; and we, sitting at a table disproportionably large, under the cold, strange gaze of my guardian, talked only what was inevitable, and that in low tones; for whenever Milly for a moment raised her voice, Uncle Silas would wince, place his thin white fingers quickly over his ear, and look as if a pain had pierced his brain, and then shrug and smile piteously into vacancy. When Uncle Silas, therefore, was not in the talking vein himself—and that was not often—you may suppose there was very little spoken in his presence.

When Milly, across the table, saw the ring upon my finger, she, drawing in her breath, said, 'Oh!' and, with round eyes and mouth, she looked so delighted; and she made a little motion, as if she was on the point of jumping up; and then her poor face quivered, and she bit her lip; and staring imploringly at me, her eyes filled fast with tears, which rolled down her round penitential cheeks.

I am sure I felt more penitent than she. I know I was crying and smiling, and longing to kiss her. I suppose we were very absurd; but it is well that small matters can stir the affections so profoundly at a time of life when great troubles seldom approach us.

When at length the opportunity did come, never was such a hug out of the wrestling ring as poor Milly bestowed on me, swaying me this way and that, and burying her face in my dress, and blubbering—

'I was so lonely before you came, and you so good to me, and I such a devil; and I'll never call you a name, but Maud—my darling Maud.'

'You must, Milly—Mrs. Bustle. I'll be Mrs. Bustle, or anything you like. You must.' I was blubbering like Milly, and hugging my best; and, indeed, I wonder how we kept our feet.

So Milly and I were better friends than ever.

Meanwhile, the winter deepened, and we had short days and long nights, and long fireside gossipings at Bartram-Haugh. I was frightened at the frequency of the strange collapses to which Uncle Silas was subject. I did not at first mind them much, for I naturally fell into Milly's way of talking about them.

But one day, while in one of his 'queerish' states, he called for me, and I saw him, and was unspeakably scared.

In a white wrapper, he lay coiled in a great easy chair. I should have thought him dead, had I not been accompanied by old L'Amour, who knew every gradation and symptom of these strange affections.

She winked and nodded to me with a ghastly significance, and whispered—

'Don't make no noise, miss, till he talks; he'll come to for a bit, anon.'

Except that there was no sign of convulsions, the countenance was like that of an epileptic arrested in one of his contortions.

There was a frown and smirk like that of idiotcy, and a strip of white eyeball was also disclosed.

Suddenly, with a kind of chilly shudder, he opened his eyes wide, and screwed his lips together, and blinked and stared on me with a fatuised uncertainty, that gradually broke into a feeble smile.

'Ah! the girl—Austin's child. Well, dear, I'm hardly able—I'll speak to-morrow—next day—it is tic—neuralgia, or something—*torture*—tell her.'

So, huddling himself together, he lay again in his great chair, with the same inexpressible helplessness in his attitude, and gradually his face resumed its dreadful cast.

'Come away, miss: he's changed his mind; he'll not be fit to talk to you noways all day, maybe,' said the old woman, again in a whisper.

So forth we stole from the room, I unspeakably shocked. In fact, he looked as if he were dying, and so, in my agitation, I told the crone, who, forgetting the ceremony with which she usually treated me, chuckled out derisively,

'A-dying is he? Well, he be like Saint Paul—he's bin a-dying daily this many a day.'

I looked at her with a chill of horror. She did not care, I suppose, what sort of feelings she might excite, for she went on mumbling sarcastically to herself. I had paused, and overcame my reluctance to speak to her again, for I was really very much frightened.

'Do you think he is in danger? Shall we send for a doctor?' I whispered.

'Law bless ye, the doctor knows all about it, miss.' The old woman's face had a gleam of that derision which is so shocking in the features of feebleness and age.

'But it is a *fit*, it is paralytic, or something horrible—it can't be *safe* to leave him to chance or nature to get through these terrible attacks.'

'There's no fear of him, 'tisn't no fits at all, he's nout the worse o't. Jest silly a bit now and again. It's been the same a dozen year and more; and the doctor knows all about it,' answered the old woman sturdily. 'And ye'll find he'll be as mad as bedlam if ye make any stir about it.'

That night I talked the matter over with Mary Quince.

'They're very dark, miss; but I think he takes a deal too much laudlum,' said Mary.

To this hour I cannot say what was the nature of those periodical seizures. I have often spoken to medical men about them, since, but never could learn that excessive use of opium could altogether account for them. It was, I believe, certain, however, that he did use that drug in startling quantities. It was, indeed, sometimes a topic of complaint with him that his neuralgia imposed this sad necessity upon him.

The image of Uncle Silas, as I had seen him that day, troubled and affrighted my imagination, as I lay in my bed; I had slept very well since my arrival at Bartram. So much of the day was passed in the open air, and in active exercise, that this was but natural. But that night I was nervous and wakeful, and it was past two o'clock when I fancied I heard the sound of horses and carriage-wheels on the avenue.

Mary Quince was close by, and therefore I was not afraid to get up and peep from the window. My heart beat fast as I saw a post-chaise approach the courtyard. A front window was let down, and the postilion pulled up for a few seconds.

In consequence of some directions received by him, I fancied he resumed his route at a walk, and so drew up at the hall-door, on the steps of which a figure awaited his arrival. I think it was old L'Amour, but I could not be quite certain. There was a lantern on the top of the balustrade, close by the door. The chaise-lamps were lighted, for the night was rather dark.

A bag and valise, as well as I could see, were pulled from the interior by the post-boy, and a box from the top of the vehicle, and these were carried into the hall.

I was obliged to keep my cheek against the window-pane to command a view of the point of debarkation, and my breath upon the glass, which dimmed it again almost as fast as I wiped it away, helped to obscure my vision. But I saw a tall figure, in a cloak, get down and swiftly enter the house, but whether male or female I could not discern.

My heart beat fast. I jumped at once to a conclusion. My uncle was worse—was, in fact, dying; and this was the physician, too late summoned to his bedside.

I listened for the ascent of the doctor, and his entrance at my uncle's door, which, in the stillness of the night, I thought I might easily hear, but no sound reached me. I listened so for fully five minutes, but without result. I returned to the window, but the carriage and horses had disappeared.

I was strongly tempted to wake Mary Quince, and take counsel with her, and persuade her to undertake a reconnoissance. The fact is, I was persuaded that my uncle was in extremity, and I was quite wild to know the doctor's opinion. But, after all, it would be cruel to summon the good soul from her refreshing nap. So, as I began to feel very cold, I returned to my bed, where I continued to listen and conjecture until I fell asleep.

In the morning, as was usual, before I was dressed, in came Milly.

'How is Uncle Silas?' I eagerly enquired.

'Old L'Amour says he's queerish still; but he's not so dull as yesterday,' answered she.

'Was not the doctor sent for?' I asked.

'Was he? Well, that's odd; and she said never a word o't to me,' answered she.

'I'm asking only,' said I.

'I don't know whether he came or no,' she replied; 'but what makes you take that in your head?'

'A chaise arrived here between two and three o'clock last night.'

'Hey! and who told you?' Milly seemed all on a sudden highly interested.

'I saw it, Milly; and some one, I fancy the doctor, came from it into the house.'

'Fudge, lass! who'd send for the doctor? 'Twasn't he, I tell you. What was he like?' said Milly.

'I could only see clearly that he, or *she*, was tall, and wore a cloak,' I replied.

'Then 'twasn't him nor t'other I was thinking on, neither; and I'll be hanged but I think it will be Cormoran,' cried Milly, with a thoughtful rap with her knuckle on the table.

Precisely at this juncture a tapping came to the door.

'Come in,' said I.

And old L'Amour entered the room, with a courtesy.

'I came to tell Miss Quince her breakfast's ready,' said the old lady.

'Who came in the chaise, L'Amour?' demanded Milly.

'What chaise?' spluttered the beldame tartly.

'The chaise that came last night, past two o'clock,' said Milly.

'That's a lie, and a damn lie!' cried the beldame. 'There worn't no chaise at the door since Miss Maud there come from Knowl.'

I stared at the audacious old menial who could utter such language.

'Yes, there was a chaise, and Cormoran, as I think, be come in it,' said Milly, who seemed accustomed to L'Amour's daring address.

'And there's another damn lie, as big as the t'other,' said the crone, her haggard and withered face flushing orange all over.

'I beg you will not use such language in my room,' I replied, very angrily. 'I saw the chaise at the door; your untruth signifies very little, but your impertinence here I will not permit. Should it be repeated, I will assuredly complain to my uncle.'

The old woman flushed more fiercely as I spoke, and fixed her bleared glare on me, with a compression of her mouth that amounted to a wicked grimace. She resisted her angry impulse, however, and only chuckled a little spitefully, saying,

'No offence, miss: it be a way we has in Derbyshire o' speaking our minds. No offence, miss, were meant, and none took, as I hopes,' and she made me another courtesy.

'And I forgot to tell you, Miss Milly, the master wants you this minute.'

So Milly, in mute haste, withdrew, followed closely by L'Amour.

CHAPTER XXXVII

DOCTOR BRYERLY EMERGES

When Milly joined me at breakfast, her eyes were red and swollen. She was still sniffing with that little sobbing hiccough, which betrays, even were there no other signs, recent violent weeping. She sat down quite silent.

'Is he worse, Milly?' I enquired, anxiously.

'No, nothing's wrong wi' him; he's right well,' said Milly, fiercely.

'What's the matter then, Milly dear?'

'The poisonous old witch! 'Twas just to tell the Gov'nor how I'd said 'twas Cormoran that came by the po'shay last night.'

'And who is Cormoran?' I enquired.

'Ay, there it is; I'd like to tell, and you want to hear—and I just daren't, for he'll send me off right to a French school—hang it—hang them all!—if I do.'

'And why should Uncle Silas care?' said I, a good deal surprised.

'They're a-tellin' lies.'

'Who?' said I.

'L'Amour—that's who. So soon as she made her complaint of me, the Gov'nor asked her, sharp enough, did anyone come last night, or a po'shay; and she was ready to swear there was no one. Are ye quite sure, Maud, you really did see aught, or 'appen 'twas all a dream?'

'It was no dream, Milly; so sure as you are there, I saw exactly what I told you,' I replied.

'Gov'nor won't believe it anyhow; and he's right mad wi' me; and he threatens me he'll have me off to France; I wish 'twas under the sea. I hate France—I do—like the devil. Don't you? They're always a-threatening me wi' France, if I dare say a word more about the po'shay, or—or anyone.'

I really was curious about Cormoran; but Cormoran was not to be defined to me by Milly; nor did she, in reality, know more than I respecting the arrival of the night before.

One day I was surprised to see Doctor Bryerly on the stairs. I was standing in a dark gallery as he walked across the floor of the lobby to my uncle's door, his hat on, and some papers in his hand.

He did not see me; and when he had entered Uncle Silas's door, I went down and found Milly awaiting me in the hall.

'So Doctor Bryerly is here,' I said.

'That's the thin fellow, wi' the sharp look, and the shiny black coat, that went up just now?' asked Milly.

'Yes, he's gone into your papa's room,' said I.

"Appen 'twas he come 'tother night. He may be staying here, though we see him seldom, for it's a barrack of a house—it is.'

The same thought had struck me for a moment, but was dismissed immediately. It certainly was *not* Doctor Bryerly's figure which I had seen.

So, without any new light gathered from this apparition, we went on our way, and made our little sketch of the ruined bridge. We found the gate locked as before; and, as Milly could not persuade me to climb it, we got round the paling by the river's bank.

While at our drawing, we saw the swarthy face, sooty locks, and old weather-stained red coat of Zamiel, who was glowering malignly at us from among the trunks of the forest trees, and standing motionless as a monumental figure in the side aisle of a cathedral. When we looked again he was gone.

Although it was a fine mild day for the wintry season, we yet, cloaked as we were, could not pursue so still an occupation as sketching for more than ten or fifteen minutes. As we returned, in passing a clump of trees, we heard a sudden outbreak of voices, angry and expostulatory; and saw, under the trees, the savage old Zamiel strike his daughter with his stick two great blows, one of which was across the head. 'Beauty' ran only a short distance away, while the swart old wood-demon stumped lustily after her, cursing and brandishing his cudgel.

My blood boiled. I was so shocked that for a moment I could not speak; but in a moment more I screamed—

'You brute! How dare you strike the poor girl?'

She had only run a few steps, and turned about confronting him and us, her eyes gleaming fire, her features pale and quivering to suppress a burst of weeping. Two little rivulets of blood were trickling over her temple.

'I say, faything, look at that,' she said, with a strange tremulous smile, lifting her hand, which was smeared with blood.

Perhaps he was ashamed, and the more enraged on that account, for he growled another curse, and started afresh to reach her, whirling his stick in the air. Our voices, however, arrested him.

'My uncle shall hear of your brutality. The poor girl!'

'Strike him, Meg, if he does it again; and pitch his leg into the river to-night, when he's asleep.'

'I'd serve *you* the same;' and out came an oath. 'You'd have her lick her fayther, would ye? Look out!'

And he wagged his head with a scowl at Milly, and a flourish of his cudgel.

'Be quiet, Milly,' I whispered, for Milly was preparing for battle; and I again addressed him with the assurance that, on reaching home, I would tell my uncle how he had treated the poor girl.

''Tis you she may thank for't, a wheedling o' her to open that gate,' he snarled.

'That's a lie; we went round by the brook,' cried Milly.

I did not think proper to discuss the matter with him; and looking very angry, and, I thought, a little put out, he jerked and swayed himself out of sight. I merely repeated my promise of informing my uncle as he went, to which, over his shoulder, he bawled—

'Silas won't mind ye *that*;' snapping his horny finger and thumb.

The girl remained where she had stood, wiping the blood off roughly with the palm of her hand, and looking at it before she rubbed it on her apron.

'My poor girl,' I said, 'you must not cry. I'll speak to my uncle about you.'

But she was not crying. She raised her head, and looked at us a little askance, with a sullen contempt, I thought.

'And you must have these apples—won't you?' We had brought in our basket two or three of those splendid apples for which Bartram was famous.

I hesitated to go near her, these Hawkeses, Beauty and Pegtop, were such savages. So I rolled the apples gently along the ground to her feet.

She continued to look doggedly at us with the same expression, and kicked away the apples sullenly that approached her feet. Then, wiping her temple and forehead in her apron, without a word, she turned and walked slowly away.

'Poor thing! I'm afraid she leads a hard life. What strange, repulsive people they are!'

When we reached home, at the head of the great staircase old L'Amour was awaiting me; and with a courtesy, and very respectfully, she informed me that the Master would be happy to see me.

Could it be about my evidence as to the arrival of the mysterious chaise that he summoned me to this interview? Gentle as were his ways, there was something undefinable about Uncle Silas which inspired fear; and I should have liked few things less than meeting his gaze in the character of a culprit.

There was an uncertainty, too, as to the state in which I might find him, and a positive horror of beholding him again in the condition in which I had last seen him.

I entered the room, then, in some trepidation, but was instantly relieved. Uncle Silas was in the same health apparently, and, as nearly as I could recollect it, in precisely the same rather handsome though negligent garb in which I had first seen him.

Doctor Bryerly—what a marked and vulgar contrast, and yet, somehow, how reassuring!—sat at the table near him, and was tying up papers. His eyes watched me, I thought, with an anxious scrutiny as I approached; and I think it was not until I had saluted him that he recollected suddenly that he had not seen me before at Bartram, and stood up and greeted me in his usual abrupt and somewhat familiar way. It was vulgar and not cordial, and yet it was honest and indefinably kind.

Up rose my uncle, that strangely venerable, pale portrait, in his loose Rembrandt black velvet. How gentle, how benignant, how unearthly, and inscrutable!

'I need not say how she is. Those lilies and roses, Doctor Bryerly, speak their own beautiful praises of the air of Bartram. I almost regret that her carriage will be home so soon. I only hope it may not abridge her rambles. It positively does me good to look at her. It is the glow of flowers in winter, and the fragrance of a field which the Lord hath blessed.'

'Country air, Miss Ruthyn, is a right good kitchen to country fare. I like to see young women eat heartily. You have had some pounds of beef and mutton since I saw you last,' said Dr. Bryerly.

And this sly speech made, he scrutinised my countenance in silence rather embarrassingly.

'My system, Doctor Bryerly, as a disciple of Aesculapius you will approve—health first, accomplishment afterwards. The Continent is the best field for elegant instruction, and we must see the world a little, by-and-by, Maud; and to me, if my health be spared, there would be an unspeakable though a melancholy charm in the scenes where so many happy, though so many wayward and foolish, young days were passed; and I think I should return to these picturesque solitudes with, perhaps, an increased relish. You remember old Chaulieu's sweet lines—

Désert, aimable solitude,
Séjour du calme et de la paix,
Asile où n'entrèrent jamais
Le tumulte et l'inquiétude.

I can't say that care and sorrow have not sometimes penetrated these sylvan fastnesses; but the tumults of the world, thank Heaven!—never.'

There was a sly scepticism, I thought, in Doctor Bryerly's sharp face; and hardly waiting for the impressive 'never,' he said—

'I forgot to ask, who is your banker?'

'Oh! Bartlet and Hall, Lombard Street,' answered Uncle Silas, dryly and shortly.

Dr. Bryerly made a note of it, with an expression of face which seemed, with a sly resolution, to say, 'You shan't come the anchorite over me.'

I saw Uncle Silas's wild and piercing eye rest suspiciously on me for a moment, as if to ascertain whether I felt the spirit of Doctor Bryerly's almost interruption; and, nearly at the same moment, stuffing his papers into his capacious coat pockets, Doctor Bryerly rose and took his leave.

When he was gone, I bethought me that now was a good opportunity of making my complaint of Dickon Hawkes. Uncle Silas having risen, I hesitated, and began,

'Uncle, may I mention an occurrence—which I witnessed?'

'Certainly, child,' he answered, fixing his eye sharply on me. I really think he fancied that the conversation was about to turn upon the phantom chaise.

So I described the scene which had shocked Milly and me, an hour or so ago, in the Windmill Wood.

'You see, my dear child, they are rough persons; their ideas are not ours; their young people must be chastised, and in a way and to a degree that we would look upon in a serious light. I've found it a bad plan interfering in strictly domestic misunderstandings, and should rather not.'

'But he struck her violently on the head, uncle, with a heavy cudgel, and she was bleeding very fast.'

'Ah?' said my uncle, dryly.

'And only that Milly and I deterred him by saying that we would certainly tell you, he would have struck her again; and I really think if he goes on treating her with so much violence and cruelty he may injure her seriously, or perhaps kill her.'

'Why, you romantic little child, people in that rank of life think absolutely nothing of a broken head,' answered Uncle Silas, in the same way.

'But is it not horrible brutality, uncle?'

'To be sure it is brutality; but then you must remember they are brutes, and it suits them,' said he.

I was disappointed. I had fancied that Uncle Silas's gentle nature would have recoiled from such an outrage with horror and indignation; and instead, here he was, the apologist of that savage ruffian, Dickon Hawkes.

'And he is always so rude and impertinent to Milly and to me,' I continued.

'Oh! impertinent to you—that's another matter. I must see to that. Nothing more, my dear child?'

'Well, there *was* nothing more.'

'He's a useful servant, Hawkes; and though his looks are not prepossessing, and his ways and language rough, yet he is a very kind father, and a most honest man—a thoroughly moral man, though severe—a very rough diamond though, and has no idea of the refinements of polite society. I venture to say he honestly believes that he has been always unexceptionably polite to you, so we must make allowances.'

And Uncle Silas smoothed my hair with his thin aged hand, and kissed my forehead.

'Yes, we must make allowances; we must be kind. What says the Book?—"Judge not, that ye be not judged." Your dear father acted upon that maxim—so noble and so awful—and I strive to do so. Alas! dear Austin, *longo intervalle*, far behind! and you are removed—my example and my help; you are gone to your rest, and I remain beneath my burden, still marching on by bleak and alpine paths, under the awful night.

O nuit, nuit douloureuse! O toi, tardive aurore!
Viens-tu? vas-tu venir? es-tu bien loin encore?

And repeating these lines of Chenier, with upturned eyes, and one hand lifted, and an indescribable expression of grief and fatigue, he sank stiffly into his chair, and remained mute, with eyes closed for some time. Then applying his scented handkerchief to them hastily, and looking very kindly at me, he said—

'Anything more, dear child?'

'Nothing, uncle, thank you, very much, only about that man, Hawkes; I dare say that he does not mean to be so uncivil as he is, but I am really afraid of him, and he makes our walks in that direction quite unpleasant.'

'I understand quite, my dear. I will see to it; and you must remember that nothing is to be allowed to vex my beloved niece and ward during her stay at Bartram—nothing that her old kinsman, Silas Ruthyn, can remedy.'

So with a tender smile, and a charge to shut the door 'perfectly, but without clapping it,' he dismissed me.

Doctor Bryerly had not slept at Bartram, but at the little inn in Feltram, and he was going direct to London, as I afterwards learned.

'Your ugly doctor's gone away in a fly,' said Milly, as we met on the stairs, she running up, I down.

On reaching the little apartment which was our sitting-room, however, I found that she was mistaken; for Doctor Bryerly, with his hat and a great pair of woollen gloves on, and an old Oxford grey surtout that showed his lank length to advantage, buttoned all the way up to his chin, had set down his black leather bag on the table, and was reading at the window a little volume which I had borrowed from my uncle's library.

It was Swedenborg's account of the other worlds, Heaven and Hell.

He closed it on his finger as I entered, and without recollecting to remove his hat, he made a step or two towards me with his splay, creaking boots. With a quick glance at the door, he said—

'Glad to see you alone for a minute—very glad.'

But his countenance, on the contrary, looked very anxious.

CHAPTER XXXVIII

A MIDNIGHT DEPARTURE

'I'm going this minute—I—I want to know'—another glance at the door—'are you really quite comfortable here?'

'Quite,' I answered promptly.

'You have only your cousin's company?' he continued, glancing at the table, which was laid for two.

'Yes; but Milly and I are very happy together.'

'That's very nice; but I think there are no teachers, you see—painters, and singers, and that sort of thing that is usual with young ladies. No teachers of that kind—of *any* kind—are there?' 'No; my uncle thinks it better I should lay in a store of health, he says.'

'I know; and the carriage and horses have not come; how soon are they expected?'

'I really can't say, and I assure you I don't much care. I think running about great fun.'

'You walk to church?'

'Yes; Uncle Silas's carriage wants a new wheel, he told me.'

'Ay, but a young woman of your rank, you know, it is not usual she should be without the use of a carriage. Have you horses to ride?'

I shook my head.

'Your uncle, you know, has a very liberal allowance for your maintenance and education.'

I remembered something in the will about it, and Mary Quince was constantly grumbling that 'he did not spend a pound a week on our board.'

I answered nothing, but looked down.

Another glance at the door from Doctor Bryerly's sharp black eyes.

'Is he kind to you?'

'Very kind—most gentle and affectionate.'

'Why doesn't he keep company with you? Does he ever dine with you, or drink tea, or talk to you? Do you see much of him?'

'He is a miserable invalid—his hours and regimen are peculiar. Indeed I wish very much you would consider his case; he is, I believe, often insensible for a long time, and his mind in a strange feeble state sometimes.'

'I dare say—worn out in his young days; and I saw that preparation of opium in his bottle—he takes too much.'

'Why do you think so, Doctor Bryerly?'

'It's made on water: the spirit interferes with the use of it beyond a certain limit. You have no idea what those fellows can swallow. Read the "Opium Eater." I knew two cases in which the quantity exceeded De Quincy's. Aha! it's new to you?' and he laughed quietly at my simplicity.

'And what do you think his complaint is?' I asked.

'Pooh! I haven't a notion; but, probably, one way or another, he has been all his days working on his nerves and his brain. These men of pleasure, who have no other pursuit, use themselves up mostly, and pay a smart price for their sins. And so he's kind and affectionate, but hands you over to your cousin and the servants. Are his people civil and obliging?'

'Well, I can't say much for them; there is a man named Hawkes, and his daughter, who are very rude, and even abusive sometimes, and say they have orders from my uncle to shut us out from a portion of the grounds; but I don't believe that, for Uncle Silas never alluded to it when I was making my complaint of them to-day.'

'From what part of the grounds is that?' asked Doctor Bryerly, sharply.

I described the situation as well as I could.

'Can we see it from this?' he asked, peeping from the window.

'Oh, no.'

Doctor Bryerly made a note in his pocket-book here, and I said—

'But I am really quite sure it was a story of Dickon's, he is such a surly, disobliging man.'

'And what sort is that old servant that came in and out of his room?'

'Oh, that is old L'Amour,' I answered, rather indirectly, and forgetting that I was using Milly's nickname.

'And is *she* civil?' he asked.

No, she certainly was not; a most disagreeable old woman, with a vein of wickedness. I thought I had heard her swearing.

'They don't seem to be a very engaging lot,' said Doctor Bryerly;' but where there's one, there will be more. See here, I was just reading a passage,' and he opened the little volume at the place where his finger marked it, and read for me a few sentences, the purport of which I well remember, although, of course, the words have escaped me.

It was in that awful portion of the book which assumes to describe the condition of the condemned; and it said that, independently of the physical causes in that state operating to enforce community of habitation, and an isolation from superior spirits, there exist sympathies, aptitudes, and necessities which would, of themselves, induce that depraved gregariousness, and isolation too.

'And what of the rest of the servants, are they better?' he resumed.

We saw little or nothing of the others, except of old 'Giblets,' the butler, who went about like a little automaton of dry bones, poking here and there, and whispering and smiling to himself as he laid the cloth; and seeming otherwise quite unconscious of an external world.

'This room is not got up like Mr. Ruthyn's: does he talk of furnishings and making things a little smart? No! Well, I must say, I think he might.'

Here there was a little silence, and Doctor Bryerly, with his accustomed simultaneous glance at the door, said in low, cautious tones, very distinctly—

'Have you been thinking at all over that matter again, I mean about getting your uncle to forego his guardianship? I would not mind his first refusal. You could make it worth his while, unless he—that is—unless he's very unreasonable indeed; and I think you would consult your interest, Miss Ruthyn, by doing so and, if possible, getting out of this place.'

'But I have not thought of it at all; I am much happier here than I had at all expected, and I am very fond of my cousin Milly.'

'How long have you been here exactly?'

I told him. It was some two or three months.

'Have you seen your other cousin yet—the young gentleman?'

'No.'

'H'm! Aren't you very lonely?' he enquired.

'We see no visitors here; but that, you know, I was prepared for.'

Doctor Bryerly read the wrinkles on his splay boot intently and peevishly, and tapped the sole lightly on the ground.

'Yes, it is very lonely, and the people a bad lot. You'd be pleasanter somewhere else—with Lady Knollys, for instance, eh?'

'Well, *there* certainly. But I am very well here: really the time passes very pleasantly; and my uncle is so kind. I have only to mention anything that annoys me, and he will see that it is remedied: he is always impressing that on me.'

'Yes, it is not a fit place for you,' said Doctor Bryerly. 'Of course, about your uncle,' he resumed, observing my surprised look, 'it is all right: but he's quite helpless, you know. At all events, *think* about it. Here's my address—Hans Emmanuel Bryerly, M.D., 17 King Street, Covent Garden, London—don't lose it, mind,' and he tore the leaf out of his note-book.

'Here's my fly at the door, and you must—you must' (he was looking at his watch)—'mind you *must* think of it seriously; and so, you see, don't let anyone see that. You'll be sure to leave it throwing about. The best way will be just to scratch it on the door of your press, inside, you know; and don't put my name—you'll remember that—only the rest of the address; and burn this. Quince is with you?'

'Yes,' I answered, glad to have a satisfactory word to say.

'Well, don't let her go; it's a bad sign if they wish it. Don't consent, mind; but just tip me a hint and you'll have me down. And any letters you get from Lady Knollys, you know, for she's very plain-spoken, you'd better burn them off-hand. And I've stayed too long, though; mind what I say, scratch it with a pin, and burn that, and not a word to a mortal about it. Good-bye; oh, I was taking away your book.'

And so, in a fuss, with a slight shake of the hand, getting up his umbrella, his bag, and tin box, he hurried from the room; and in a minute more, I heard the sound of his vehicle as it drove away.

I looked after it with a sigh; the uneasy sensations which I had experienced respecting my sojourn at Bartram-Haugh were re-awakened.

My ugly, vulgar, true friend was disappearing beyond those gigantic lime trees which hid Bartram from the eyes of the outer world. The fly, with the doctor's valise on top, vanished, and I sighed an anxious sigh. The shadow of the overarching trees contracted, and I felt helpless and forsaken; and glancing down the torn leaf, Doctor Bryerly's address met my eye, between my fingers.

I slipt it into my breast, and ran up-stairs stealthily, trembling lest the old woman should summon me again, at the head of the stairs, into Uncle Silas's room, where under his gaze, I fancied, I should be sure to betray myself.

But I glided unseen and safely by, entered my room, and shut my door. So listening and working, I, with my scissors' point, scratched the address where Doctor Bryerly had advised. Then, in positive terror, lest some one should even knock during the operation, I, with a match, consumed to ashes the tell-tale bit of paper.

Now, for the first time, I experienced the unpleasant sensations of having a secret to keep. I fancy the pain of this solitary liability was disproportionately acute in my case, for I was naturally very open and very nervous. I was always on the point of betraying it *apropos des bottes*—always reproaching myself for my duplicity; and in constant terror when honest Mary Quince approached the press, or good-natured Milly made her occasional survey of the wonders of my wardrobe. I would have given anything to go and point to the tiny inscription, and say:—'This is Doctor Bryerly's address in London. I scratched it with my scissors' point, taking every precaution lest anyone—you, my good friends, included—should surprise me. I have ever since kept this secret to myself, and trembled whenever your frank kind faces looked into the press. There—you at last know all about it. Can you ever forgive my deceit?'

But I could not make up my mind to reveal it; nor yet to erase the inscription, which was my alternative thought. Indeed I am a wavering, irresolute creature as ever lived, in my ordinary mood. High excitement or passion only can inspire me with decision. Under the inspiration of either, however, I am transformed, and often both prompt and brave.

'Some one left here last night, I think, Miss,' said Mary Quince, with a mysterious nod, one morning. "Twas two o'clock, and I was bad with the toothache, and went down to get a pinch o' red pepper—leaving the candle a-light here lest you should awake. When I was coming up—as I was crossing the lobby, at the far end of the long gallery—what should I hear, but a horse snorting, and some people a-talking, short and quiet like. So I looks out o' the window; and there surely I did see two horses yoked to a shay, and a fellah a-pullin' a box up o' top; and out comes a walise and a bag; and I think it was old Wyat, please'm, that Miss Milly calls L'Amour, that stood in the doorway a-talking to the driver.'

'And who got into the chaise, Mary?' I asked.

'Well, Miss, I waited as long as I could; but the pain was bad, and me so awful cold; I gave it up at last, and came back to bed, for I could not say how much longer they might wait. And you'll find, Miss,'twill be kep' a secret, like the shay as you saw'd, Miss, last week. I hate them dark ways, and secrets; and old Wyat—she does tell stories, don't she?—and she as ought to be partickler, seein' her time be short now, and she so old. It is awful, an old un like that telling such crams as she do.'

Milly was as curious as I, but could throw no light on this. We both agreed, however, that the departure was probably that of the person whose arrival I had accidentally witnessed. This time the chaise had drawn up at the side door, round the corner of the left side of the house; and, no doubt, driven away by the back road.

Another accident had revealed this nocturnal move. It was very provoking, however, that Mary Quince had not had resolution to wait for the appearance of the traveller. We all agreed, however, that we were to observe a strict silence, and that even to Wyat—L'Amour I had better continue to call her—Mary Quince was not to hint what she had seen. I suspect, however, that injured curiosity asserted itself, and that Mary hardly adhered to this self-denying resolve.

But cheerful wintry suns and frosty skies, long nights, and brilliant starlight, with good homely fires in our snuggery—gossipings, stories, short readings now and then, and brisk walks through the always beautiful scenery of Bartram-Haugh, and, above all, the unbroken tenor of our life, which had fallen into a serene routine, foreign to the idea of danger or misadventure, gradually quieted the qualms and misgivings which my interview with Doctor Bryerly had so powerfully resuscitated.

My cousin Monica, to my inexpressible joy, had returned to her country-house; and an active diplomacy, through the post-office, was negotiating the re-opening of friendly relations between the courts of Elverston and of Bartram.

At length, one fine day, Cousin Monica, smiling pleasantly, with her cloak and bonnet on, and her colour fresh from the shrewd air of the Derbyshire hills, stood suddenly before me in our sitting-room. Our meeting was that of two school-companions long separated. Cousin Monica was always a girl in my eyes.

What a hug it was; what a shower of kisses and ejaculations, enquiries and caresses! At last I pressed her down into a chair, and, laughing, she said—

'You have no idea what self-denial I have exercised to bring this visit about. I, who detest writing, have actually written five letters to Silas; and I don't think I said a single impertinent thing in one of them! What a wonderful little old thing your butler is! I did not know what to make of him on the steps. Is he a struldbrug, or a fairy, or only a ghost? Where on earth did your uncle pick him up? I'm sure he came in on All Hallows E'en, to answer an incantation—not your future husband, I hope—and he'll vanish some night into gray smoke, and whisk sadly up the chimney. He's the most venerable little thing I ever beheld in my life. I leaned back in the carriage and thought I should absolutely die of laughing. He's gone up to prepare your uncle for my visit; and I really am very glad, for I'm sure I shall look as young as Hebe after *him*. But who is this? Who are you, my dear?'

This was addressed to poor Milly, who stood at the corner of the chimney-piece, staring with her round eyes and plump cheeks in fear and wonder upon the strange lady.

'How stupid of me,' I exclaimed. 'Milly, dear, this is your cousin, Lady Knollys.'

'And so *you* are Millicent. Well, dear, I am very glad to see you.' And Cousin Monica was on her feet again in an instant, with Milly's hand very cordially in hers; and she gave her a kiss upon each cheek, and patted her head.

Milly, I must mention, was a much more presentable figure than when I first encountered her. Her dresses were at least a quarter of a yard longer. Though very rustic, therefore, she was not so barbarously grotesque, by any means.

CHAPTER XXXIX

COUSIN MONICA AND UNCLE SILAS MEET

Cousin Monica, with her hands upon Milly's shoulders, looked amusedly and kindly in her face. 'And,' said she, 'we must be very good friends—you funny creature, you and I. I'm allowed to be the most saucy old woman in Derbyshire—quite incorrigibly privileged; and nobody is ever affronted with me, so I say the most shocking things constantly.'

'I'm a bit that way, myself; and I think,' said poor Milly, making an effort, and growing very red; she quite lost her head at that point, and was incompetent to finish the sentiment she had prefaced.

'You think? Now, take my advice, and never wait to think my dear; talk first, and think afterwards, that is my way; though, indeed, I can't say I ever think at all. It is a very cowardly habit. Our cold-blooded cousin Maud, there, thinks sometimes; but it is always such a failure that I forgive her. I wonder when your little pre-Adamite butler will return. He speaks the language of the Picts and Ancient Britons, I dare say, and your father requires a little time to translate him. And, Milly dear, I am very hungry, so I won't wait for your butler, who would give me, I suppose, one of the cakes baked by King Alfred, and some Danish beer in a skull; but I'll ask you for a little of that nice bread and butter.'

With which accordingly Lady Knollys was quickly supplied; but it did not at all impede her utterance.

'Do you think, girls, you could be ready to come away with me, if Silas gives leave, in an hour or two? I should so like to take you both home with me to Elverston.'

'How delightful! you darling,' cried I, embracing and kissing her; 'for my part, I should be ready in five minutes; what do you say, Milly?'

Poor Milly's wardrobe, I am afraid, was more portable than handsome; and she looked horribly affrighted, and whispered in my ear—

'My best petticoat is away at the laundress; say in a week, Maud.'

'What does she say?' asked Lady Knollys.

'She fears she can't be ready,' I answered, dejectedly.

'There's a deal of my slops in the wash,' blurted out poor Milly, staring straight at Lady Knollys.

'In the name of wonder, what does my cousin mean?' asked Lady Knollys.

'Her things have not come home yet from the laundress,' I replied; and at this moment our wondrous old butler entered to announce to Lady Knollys that his master was ready to receive her, whenever she was disposed to favour him; and also to make polite apologies for his being compelled, by his state of health, to give her the trouble of ascending to his room.

So Cousin Monica was at the door in a moment, over her shoulder calling to us, 'Come, girls.'

'Please, not yet, my lady—you alone; and he requests the young ladies will be in the way, as he will send for them presently.'

I began to admire poor 'Giblets' as the wreck of a tolerably respectable servant.

'Very good; perhaps it is better we should kiss and be friends in private first,' said Cousin Knollys, laughing; and away she went under the guidance of the mummy.

I had an account of this *tête-à-tête* afterwards from Lady Knollys.

'When I saw him, my dear,' she said, 'I could hardly believe my eyes; such white hair—such a white face—such mad eyes—such a death-like smile. When I saw him last, his hair was dark; he dressed himself like a modern Englishman; and he really preserved a likeness to the full-length portrait at Knowl, that you fell in love with, you know; but, angels and ministers of grace! such a spectre! I asked myself, is it necromancy, or is it delirium tremens that has reduced him to this? And said he, with that odious smile, that made me fancy myself half insane—

'"You see a change, Monica."

'What a sweet, gentle, insufferable voice he has! Somebody once told me about the tone of a glass flute that made some people hysterical to listen to, and I was thinking of it all the time. There was always a peculiar quality in his voice.

'"I do see a change, Silas," I said at last; "and, no doubt, so do you in me—a great change."

'"There has been time enough to work a greater than I observe in you since you last honoured me with a visit," said he.

'I think he was at his old sarcasms, and meant that I was the same impertinent minx he remembered long ago, uncorrected by time; and so I am, and he must not expect compliments from old Monica Knollys.

'"It is a long time, Silas; but that, you know, is not my fault," said I.

'"Not your fault, my dear—your instinct. We are all imitative creatures: the great people ostracised me, and the small ones followed. We are very like turkeys, we have so much good sense and so much generosity. Fortune, in a freak, wounded my head, and the whole brood were upon me, pecking and gobbling, gobbling and pecking, and you among them, dear Monica. It wasn't your fault, only your instinct, so I quite forgive you; but no wonder the peckers wear better than the pecked. You are robust; and I, what I am."

'"Now, Silas, I have not come here to quarrel. If we quarrel now, mind, we can never make it up—we are too old, so let us forget all we can, and try to forgive something; and if we can do neither, at all events let there be truce between us while I am here."

'"My personal wrongs I can quite forgive, and I do, Heaven knows, from my heart; but there are things which ought not to be forgiven. My children have been ruined by it. I may, by the mercy of Providence, be yet set right in the world, and so soon as that time comes, I will remember, and I will act; but my children—you will see that wretched girl, my daughter—education, society, all would come too late—my children have been ruined by it."

'"I have not done it; but I know what you mean," I said. "You menace litigation whenever you have the means; but you forget that Austin placed you under promise, when he gave you the use of this house and place, never to disturb my title to Elverston. So there is my answer, if you mean that."

'"I mean what I mean," he replied, with his old smile.

'"You mean then," said I, "that for the pleasure of vexing me with litigation, you are willing to forfeit your tenure of this house and place."

'"Suppose I *did* mean precisely that, why should I forfeit anything? My beloved brother, by his will, has given me a right to the use of Bartram-Haugh for my life, and attached no absurd condition of the kind you fancy to his gift."

'Silas was in one of his vicious old moods, and liked to menace me. His vindictiveness got the better of his craft; but he knows as well as I do that he never could succeed in disturbing the title of my poor dear Harry Knollys; and I was not at all alarmed by his threats; and I told him so, as coolly as I speak to you now.

'"Well, Monica," he said, "I have weighed you in the balance, and you are not found wanting. For a moment the old man possessed me: the thought of my children, of past unkindness, and present affliction and disgrace, exasperated me, and I was mad. It was but for a moment—the galvanic spasm of a corpse. Never was breast more dead than mine to the passions and ambitions of the world. They are not for white locks like these, nor for a man who, for a week in every month, lies in the gate of death. Will you shake hands? *Here*—I *do* strike a truce; and I *do* forget and forgive *everything*."

'I don't know what he meant by this scene. I have no idea whether he was acting, or lost his head, or, in fact, why or how it occurred; but I am glad, darling, that, unlike myself, I was calm, and that a quarrel has not been forced upon me.'

When our turn came and we were summoned to the presence, Uncle Silas was quite as usual; but Cousin Monica's heightened colour, and the flash of her eyes, showed plainly that something exciting and angry had occurred.

Uncle Silas commented in his own vein upon the effect of Bartram air and liberty, all he had to offer; and called on me to say how I liked them. And then he called Milly to him, kissed her tenderly, smiled sadly upon her, and turning to Cousin Monica, said—

'This is my daughter Milly—oh! she has been presented to you down-stairs, has she? You have, no doubt, been interested by her. As I told her cousin Maud, though I am not yet quite a Sir Tunbelly Clumsy, she is a very finished Miss Hoyden. Are not you, my poor Milly? You owe your distinction, my dear, to that line of circumvallation which has, ever since your birth, intercepted all civilisation on its way to Bartram. You are much obliged, Milly, to everybody who, whether naturally or *un*-naturally, turned a sod in that invisible, but impenetrable, work. For your accomplishments—rather singular than fashionable—you are indebted, in part, to your cousin, Lady Knollys. Is not she, Monica? *Thank* her, Milly.'

'This is your *truce*, Silas,' said Lady Knollys, with a quiet sharpness. 'I think, Silas Ruthyn, you want to provoke me to speak in a way before these young creatures which we should all regret.'

'So my badinage excites your temper, Monnie. Think how you *would* feel, then, if I had found you by the highway side, mangled by robbers, and set my foot upon your throat, and spat in your face. But—stop this. Why have I said this? simply to emphasize my forgiveness. See, girls, Lady Knollys and I, cousins long estranged, forget and forgive the past, and join hands over its buried injuries.'

'Well, *be* it so; only let us have done with ironies and covert taunts.'

And with these words their hands were joined; and Uncle Silas, after he had released hers, patted and fondled it with his, laughing icily and very low all the time.

'I wish so much, dear Monica,' he said, when this piece of silent by-play was over, 'that I could ask you to stay to-night; but absolutely I have not a bed to offer, and even if I had, I fear my suit would hardly prevail.'

Then came Lady Knollys' invitation for Milly and me. He was very much obliged; he smiled over it a great deal, meditating. I thought he was puzzled; and amid his smiles, his wild eyes scanned Cousin Monica's frank face once or twice suspiciously.

There was a difficulty—an *undefined* difficulty—about letting us go that day; but on a future one—soon—*very* soon—he would be most happy.

Well, there was an end of that little project, for to-day at least; and Cousin Monica was too well-bred to urge it beyond a certain point.

'Milly, my dear, will you put on your hat and show me the grounds about the house? May she, Silas? I should like to renew my acquaintance.'

'You'll see them sadly neglected, Monnie. A poor man's pleasure grounds must rely on Nature, and trust to her for effects. Where there is fine timber, however, and abundance of slope, and rock, and hollow, we sometimes gain in picturesqueness what we lose by neglect in luxury.'

Then, as Cousin Monica said she would cross the grounds by a path, and meet her carriage at a point to which we would accompany her, and so make her way home, she took leave of Uncle Silas; a ceremony whereat—without, I thought, much zeal at either side—a kiss took place.

'Now, girls!' said Cousin Knollys, when we were fairly in motion over the grass, 'what do you say—will he let you come—yes or no? I can't say, but I think, dear,'—this to Milly—' he ought to let you see a little more of the world than appears among the glens and bushes of Bartram. Very pretty they are, like yourself; but very wild, and very little seen. Where is your brother, Milly; is not he older than you?'

'I don't know where; and he is older by six years and a bit.'

By-and-by, when Milly was gesticulating to frighten some herons by the river's brink into the air, Cousin Monica said confidentially to me—

'He has run away, I'm told—I wish I could believe it—and enlisted in a regiment going to India, perhaps the best thing for him. Did you see him here before his judicious self-banishment?'

'No.'

'Well, I suppose you have had no loss. Doctor Bryerly says from all he can learn he is a very bad young man. And now tell me, dear, *is* Silas kind to you?'

'Yes, always gentle, just as you saw him to-day; but we don't see a great deal of him—very little, in fact.'

'And how do you like your life and the people?' she asked.

'My life, very well; and the people, *pretty* well. There's an old women we don't like, old Wyat, she is cross and mysterious and tells untruths; but I don't think she is dishonest—so Mary Quince says—and that, you know, is a point; and there is a family, father and daughter, called Hawkes, who live in the Windmill Wood, who are perfect savages, though my uncle says they don't mean it; but they are very disagreeable, rude people; and except them we see very little of the servants or other people. But there has been a mysterious visit; some one came late at night, and remained for some days, though Milly and I never saw them, and Mary Quince saw a chaise at the side-door at two o'clock at night.'

Cousin Monica was so highly interested at this that she arrested her walk and stood facing me, with her hand on my arm, questioning and listening, and lost, as it seemed, in dismal conjecture.

'It is not pleasant, you know,' I said.

'No, it is not pleasant,' said Lady Knollys, very gloomily.

And just then Milly joined us, shouting to us to look at the herons flying; so Cousin Monica did, and smiled and nodded in thanks to Milly, and was again silent and thoughtful as we walked on.

'You are to come to me, mind, both of you girls,' she said, abruptly;' you *shall*. I'll manage it.'

When silence returned, and Milly ran away once more to try whether the old gray trout was visible in the still water under the bridge, Cousin Monica said to me in a low tone, looking hard at me—

'You've not seen anything to frighten you, Maud? Don't look so alarmed, dear,' she added with a little laugh, which was not very merry, however. 'I don't mean frighten in any awful sense—in fact, I did not mean frighten at all. I meant—I can't exactly express it—anything to vex, or make you uncomfortable; have you?'

'No, I can't say I have, except that room in which Mr. Charke was found dead.'

'Oh! you saw that, did you?—I should like to see it so much. Your bedroom is not near it?'

'Oh, no; on the floor beneath, and looking to the front. And Doctor Bryerly talked a little to me, and there seemed to be something on his mind more than he chose to tell me; so that for some time after I saw him I really was, as you say, frightened; but, except that, I really have had no cause. And what was in your mind when you asked me?'

'Well, you know, Maud, you are afraid of ghosts, banditti, and *every*thing; and I wished to know whether you were uncomfortable, and what your particular bogle was just now—that, I assure you, was all; and I know,' she continued, suddenly changing her light tone and manner for one of pointed entreaty, 'what Doctor Bryerly said; and I *implore* of you, Maud, to think of it seriously; and when you come to me, you shall do so with the intention of remaining at Elverston.'

'Now, Cousin Monica, is this fair? You and Doctor Bryerly both talk in the same awful way to me; and I assure you, you don't know how nervous I am sometimes, and yet you won't, either of you, say what you mean. Now, Monica, dear cousin, won't you tell me?'

'You see, dear, it is so lonely; it's a strange place, and he so odd. I don't like the place, and I don't like him. I've tried, but I can't, and I think I never shall. He may be a very—what was it that good little silly curate at Knowl used to call him?—a very advanced Christian—that is it, and I hope he is; but if he is only what he used to be, his utter seclusion from society removes the only check, except personal fear—and he never had much of that—upon a very bad man. And you must know, my dear Maud, what a prize you are, and what an immense trust it is.'

Suddenly Cousin Monica stopped short, and looked at me as if she had gone too far.

'But, you know, Silas may be very good *now*, although he was wild and selfish in his young days. Indeed I don't know what to make of him; but I am sure when you have thought it over, you will agree with me and Doctor Bryerly, that you must not stay here.'

It was vain trying to induce my cousin to be more explicit.

'I hope to see you at Elverston in a very few days. I will *shame* Silas into letting you come. I don't like his reluctance.'

'But don't you think he must know that Milly would require some little outfit before her visit?'

'Well, I can't say. I hope that is all; but be it what it may, I'll *make* him let you come, and *immediately*, too.'

After she had gone, I experienced a repetition of those undefined doubts which had tortured me for some time after my conversation with Dr. Bryerly. I had truly said, however, I was well enough contented with my mode of life here, for I had been trained at Knowl to a solitude very nearly as profound.

CHAPTER XL

IN WHICH I MAKE ANOTHER COUSIN'S ACQUAINTANCE

My correspondence about this time was not very extensive. About once a fortnight a letter from honest Mrs. Rusk conveyed to me how the dogs and ponies were, in queer English, oddly spelt; some village gossip, a critique upon Doctor Clay's or the Curate's last sermon, and some severities generally upon the Dissenters' doings, with loves to Mary Quince, and all good wishes to me. Sometimes a welcome letter from cheerful Cousin Monica; and now, to vary the series, a copy of complimentary verses, without a signature, very adoring—very like Byron, I then fancied, and now, I must confess, rather vapid. Could I doubt from whom they came?

I had received, about a month after my arrival, a copy of verses in the same hand, in a plaintive ballad style, of the soldierly sort, in which the writer said, that as living his sole object was to please me, so dying I should be his latest thought; and some more poetic impieties, asking only in return that when the storm of battle had swept over, I should 'shed a tear' on seeing 'the *oak lie*, where it fell.' Of course, about this lugubrious pun, there could be no misconception. The Captain was unmistakably indicated; and I was so moved that I could no longer retain my secret; but walking with Milly that day, confided the little romance to that unsophisticated listener, under the chestnut trees. The lines were so amorously dejected, and yet so heroically redolent of blood and gunpowder, that Milly and I agreed that the writer must be on the verge of a sanguinary campaign.

It was not easy to get at Uncle Silas's 'Times' or 'Morning Post,' which we fancied would explain these horrible allusions; but Milly bethought her of a sergeant in the militia, resident in Feltram, who knew the destination and quarters of every regiment in the service; and circuitously, from this authority, we learned, to my infinite relief, that Captain Oakley's regiment had still two years to sojourn in England.

I was summoned one evening by old L'Amour, to my uncle's room. I remember his appearance that evening so well, as he lay back in his chair; the pillow; the white glare of his strange eye; his feeble, painful smile.

'You'll excuse my not rising, dear Maud, I am so miserably ill this evening.'

I expressed my respectful condolence.

'Yes; I *am* to be pitied; but pity is of no use, dear,' he murmured, peevishly. 'I sent for you to make you acquainted with your cousin, my son. Where are you Dudley?'

A figure seated in a low lounging chair, at the other side of the fire, and which till then I had not observed, at these words rose up a little slowly, like a man stiff after a day's hunting; and I beheld with a shock that held my breath, and fixed my eyes upon him in a stare, the young man whom I had encountered at Church Scarsdale, on the day of my unpleasant excursion there with Madame, and who, to the best of my belief, was also one of that ruffianly party who had so unspeakably terrified me in the warren at Knowl.

I suppose I looked very much affrighted. If I had been looking at a ghost I could not have felt much more scared and incredulous.

When I was able to turn my eyes upon my uncle he was not looking at me; but with a glimmer of that smile with which a father looks on a son whose youth and comeliness he admires, his white face was turned towards the young man, in whom I beheld nothing but the image of odious and dreadful associations.

'Come, sir,' said my uncle, we must not be too modest. Here's your cousin Maud—what do you say?'

'How are ye, Miss?' he said, with a sheepish grin.

'Miss! Come, come. Miss us, no Misses,' said my uncle; 'she is Maud, and you Dudley, or I mistake; or we shall have you calling Milly, madame. She'll not refuse you her hand, I venture to think. Come, young gentleman, speak for yourself.'

'How are ye, Maud?' he said, doing his best, and drawing near, he extended his hand.' You're welcome to Bartram-Haugh, Miss.'

'Kiss your cousin, sir. Where's your gallantry? On my honour, I disown you,' exclaimed my uncle, with more energy than he had shown before.

With a clumsy effort, and a grin that was both sheepish and impudent, he grasped my hand and advanced his face. The imminent salute gave me strength to spring back a step or two, and he hesitated.

My uncle laughed peevishly.

'Well, well, that will do, I suppose. In my time first-cousins did not meet like strangers; but perhaps we were wrong; we are learning modesty from the Americans, and old English ways are too gross for us.'

'I have—I've seen him before—that is;' and at this point I stopped.

My uncle turned his strange glare, in a sort of scowl of enquiry, upon me.

'Oh!—hey! why this is news. You never told me. Where have you met—eh, Dudley?'

'Never saw her in my days, so far as I'm aweer on,' said the young man.

'No! Well, then, Maud, will *you* enlighten us?' said Uncle Silas, coldly.

'I *did* see that young gentleman before,' I faltered.

'Meaning *me*, ma'am?' he asked, coolly.

'Yes—certainly *you*. I *did*, uncle,' answered I.

'And where was it, my dear? Not at Knowl, I fancy. Poor dear Austin did not trouble me or mine much with his hospitalities.'

This was not a pleasant tone to take in speaking of his dead brother and benefactor; but at the moment I was too much engaged upon the one point to observe it.

'I met'—I could not say my cousin—'I met him, uncle—your son—that young gentleman—I *saw* him, I should say, at Church Scarsdale, and afterwards with some other persons in the warren at Knowl. It was the night our gamekeeper was beaten.'

'Well, Dudley, what do you say to that?' asked Uncle Silas.

'I never *was* at them places, so help me. I don't know where they be; and I never set eyes on the young lady before, as I hope to be saved, in all my days,' said he, with a countenance so unchanged and an air so confident that I began to think I must be the dupe of one of those strange resemblances which have been known to lead to positive identification in the witness-box, afterwards proved to be utterly mistaken.

'You look so—so *uncomfortable*, Maud, at the idea of having seen him before, that I hardly wonder at the vehemence of his denial. There was plainly something disagreeable; but you see as respects him it is a total mistake. My boy was always a truth-telling fellow—you may rely implicitly on what he says. You were *not* at those places?'

'I wish I may——,' began the ingenuous youth, with increased vehemence.

'There, there—that will do; your honour and word as a gentleman—and *that* you are, though a poor one—will quite satisfy your cousin Maud. Am I right, my dear? I do assure you, as a gentleman, I never knew him to say the thing that was not.'

So Mr. Dudley Ruthyn began, not to curse, but to swear, in the prescribed form, that he had never seen me before, or the places I had named, 'since I was weaned, by——'

'That's enough now shake hands, if you won't kiss, like cousins,' interrupted my uncle.

And very uncomfortably I did lend him my hand to shake.

'You'll want some supper, Dudley, so Maud and I will excuse your going. Good-night, my dear boy,' and he smiled and waved him from the room.

'That's as fine a young fellow, I think, as any English father can boast for his son—true, brave, and kind, and quite an Apollo. Did you observe how finely proportioned he is, and what exquisite features the fellow has? He's rustic and rough, as you see; but a year or two in the militia—I've a promise of a commission for him—he's too old for the line—will form and polish him. He wants nothing but manner; and I protest when he has had a little drilling of that kind, I do believe he'll be as pretty a fellow as you'd find in England.'

I listened with amazement. I could discover nothing but what was disagreeable in the horrid bumpkin, and thought such an instance of the blindness of parental partiality was hardly credible.

I looked down, dreading another direct appeal to my judgment; and Uncle Silas, I suppose, referred those downcast looks to maiden modesty, for he forbore to task mine by any new interrogatory.

Dudley Ruthyn's cool and resolute denial of ever having seen me or the places I had named, and the inflexible serenity of his countenance while doing so, did very much shake my confidence in my own identification of him. I could not be *quite* certain that the person I had seen at Church Scarsdale was the very same whom I afterwards saw at Knowl. And now, in this particular instance, after the lapse of a still longer period, could I be perfectly certain that my memory, deceived by some accidental points of resemblance, had not duped me, and wronged my cousin, Dudley Ruthyn?

I suppose my uncle had expected from me some signs of acquiesence in his splendid estimate of his cub, and was nettled at my silence. After a short interval he said—

'I've seen something of the world in my day, and I can say without a misgiving of partiality, that Dudley is the material of a perfect English gentleman. I am not blind, of course—the training must be supplied; a year or two of good models, active self-criticism, and good society. I simply say that the *material* is there.'

Here was another interval of silence.

'And now tell me, child, what these recollections of Church—Church—*what*?'

'Church Scarsdale,' I replied.

'Yes, thank you—Church Scarsdale and Knowl—are?'

So I related my stories as well as I could.

'Well, dear Maud, the adventure of Church Scarsdale is hardly so terrific as I expected,' said Uncle Silas with a cold little laugh; 'and I don't see, if he had really been the hero of it, why he should shrink from avowing it. I know I should not. And I really can't say that your pic-nic party in the grounds of Knowl has frightened me much more. A lady waiting in the carriage, and two or three tipsy young men. Her presence seems to me a guarantee that no mischief was meant; but champagne is the soul of frolic, and a row with the gamekeepers a natural consequence. It happened to me once—forty years ago, when I was a wild young buck—one of the worst rows I ever was in.'

And Uncle Silas poured some eau-de-cologne over the corner of his handkerchief, and touched his temples with it.

'If my boy had been there, I do assure you—and I know him—he would say so at once. I fancy he would rather *boast* of it. I never knew him utter an untruth. When you know him a little you'll say so.'

With these words Uncle Silas leaned back exhausted, and languidly poured some of his favourite eau-de-cologne over the palms of his hands, nodded a farewell, and, in a whisper, wished me good-night.

'Dudley's come,' whispered Milly, taking me under the arm as I entered the lobby. 'But I don't care: he never gives me nout; and he gets money from Governor, as much as he likes, and I never a sixpence. It's a shame!'

So there was no great love between the only son and only daughter of the younger line of the Ruthyns.

I was curious to learn all that Milly could tell me of this new inmate of Bartram-Haugh; and Milly was communicative without having a great deal to relate, and what I heard from her tended to confirm my own disagreeable impressions about him. She was afraid of him. He was a 'woundy ugly customer in a wax, she could tell me.' He was the only one 'she ever knowed as had pluck to jaw the Governor.' But he was 'afeard on the Governor, too.'

His visits to Bartram-Haugh, I heard, were desultory; and this, to my relief, would probably not outlast a week or a fortnight. 'He *was* such a fashionable cove:' he was always 'a gadding about, mostly to Liverpool and Birmingham, and sometimes to Lunnun, itself.' He was 'keeping company one time with Beauty, Governor thought, and he was awfully afraid he'd a married her; but that was all bosh and nonsense; and Beauty would have none of his chaff and wheedling, for she liked Tom Brice;' and Milly thought that Dudley never 'cared a crack of a whip for her.' He used to go to the Windmill to have 'a smoke with Pegtop;' and he was a member of the Feltram Club, that met at the 'Plume o' Feathers.' He was 'a rare good shot,' she heard; and 'he was before the justices for poaching, but they could make nothing of it.' And the Governor said 'it was all through spite of him—for they hate us for being better blood than they.' And 'all but the squires and those upstart folk loves Dudley, he is so handsome and gay—though he be a bit cross at home.' And, 'Governor says, he'll be a Parliament man yet, spite o' them all.'

Next morning, when our breakfast was nearly ended, Dudley tapped at the window with the end of his clay pipe—a 'churchwarden' Milly called it—just such a long curved pipe as Joe Willet is made to hold between his lips in those charming illustrations of 'Barnaby Rudge'—which we all know so well—and lifting his 'wide-awake' with a burlesque salutation, which, I suppose, would have charmed the 'Plume of Feathers,' he dropped, kicked and caught his 'wide-awake,' with an agility and gravity, as he replaced it, so inexpressibly humorous, that Milly went off in a loud fit of laughter, with the ejaculation—

'Did you ever?'

It was odd how repulsively my confidence in my original identification always revived on unexpectedly seeing Dudley after an interval.

I could perceive that this piece of comic by-play was meant to make a suitable impression on me. I received it, however, with a killing gravity; and after a word or two to Milly, he lounged away, having first broken his pipe, bit by bit, into pieces, which he balanced in turn on his nose and on his chin, from which features he jerked them into his mouth, with a precision which, along with his excellent pantomime of eating them, highly excited Milly's mirth and admiration.

CHAPTER XLI

MY COUSIN DUDLEY

Greatly to my satisfaction, this engaging person did not appear again that day. But next day Milly told me that my uncle had taken him to task for the neglect with which he was treating us.

'He did pitch into him, sharp and short, and not a word from him, only sulky like; and I so frightened, I durst not look up almost; and they said a lot I could not make head or tail of; and Governor ordered me out o' the room, and glad I was to go; and so they had it out between them.'

Milly could throw no light whatsoever upon the adventures at Church Scarsdale and Knowl; and I was left still in doubt, which sometimes oscillated one way and sometimes another. But, on the whole, I could not shake off the misgivings which constantly recurred and pointed very obstinately to Dudley as the hero of those odious scenes.

Oddly enough, though, I now felt far less confident upon the point than I did at first sight. I had begun to distrust my memory, and to suspect my fancy; but of this there could be no question, that between the person so unpleasantly linked in my remembrance with those scenes, and Dudley Ruthyn, a striking, though possibly only a general resemblance did exist.

Milly was certainly right as to the gist of Uncle Silas's injunction, for we saw more of Dudley henceforward.

He was shy; he was impudent; he was awkward; he was conceited;—altogether a most intolerable bumpkin. Though he sometimes flushed and stammered, and never for a moment was at his ease in my presence, yet, to my inexpressible disgust, there was a self-complacency in his manner, and a kind of triumph in his leer, which very plainly told me how satisfied he was as to the nature of the impression he was making upon me.

I would have given worlds to tell him how odious I thought him. Probably, however, he would not have believed me. Perhaps he fancied that 'ladies' affected airs of indifference and repulsion to cover their real feelings. I never looked at or spoke to him when I could avoid either, and then it was as briefly as I could. To do him justice, however, he seemed to have no liking for our society, and certainly never seemed altogether comfortable in it.

I find it hard to write quite impartially even of Dudley Ruthyn's personal appearance; but, with an effort, I confess that his features were good, and his figure not amiss, though a little fattish. He had light whiskers, light hair, and a pink complexion, and very good blue eyes. So far my uncle was right; and if he had been perfectly gentlemanlike, he really might have passed for a handsome man in the judgment of some critics.

But there was that odious mixture of *mauvaise honte* and impudence, a clumsiness, a slyness, and a consciousness in his bearing and countenance, not distinctly boorish, but *low*, which turned his good looks into an ugliness more intolerable than that of feature; and a corresponding vulgarity pervading his dress, his demeanour, and his very walk, marred whatever good points his figure possessed. If you take all this into account, with the ominous and startling misgivings constantly recurring, you will understand the mixed feelings of anger and disgust with which I received the admiration he favoured me with.

Gradually he grew less constrained in my presence, and certainly his manners were not improved by his growing ease and confidence.

He came in while Milly and I were at luncheon, jumped up, with a 'right-about face' performed in the air, sitting on the sideboard, whence grinning slyly and kicking his heels, he leered at us.

'Will you have something, Dudley?' asked Milly.

'No, lass; but I'll look at ye, and maybe drink a drop for company.'

And with these words, he took a sportsman's flask from his pocket; and helping himself to a large glass and a decanter, he compounded a glass of strong brandy-and-water, as he talked, and refreshed himself with it from time to time.

'Curate's up wi' the Governor,' he said, with a grin. 'I wanted a word wi' him; but I s'pose I'll hardly git in this hour or more; they're a praying and disputing, and a Bible-chopping, as usual. Ha, ha! But 'twon't hold much longer, old Wyat says, now that Uncle Austin's dead; there's nout to be made o' praying and that work no longer, and it don't pay of itself.'

'O fie! For shame, you sinner!' laughed Milly. 'He wasn't in a church these five years, he says, and then only to meet a young lady. Now, isn't he a sinner, Maud—isn't he?'

Dudley, grinning, looked with a languishing slyness at me, biting the edge of his wide-awake, which he held over his breast.

Dudley Ruthyn probably thought there was a manly and desperate sort of fascination in the impiety he professed.

'I wonder, Milly,' said I, 'at your laughing. How *can* you laugh?'

'You'd have me cry, would ye?' answered Milly.

'I certainly would not have you laugh,' I replied.

'I know I wish *some* one 'ud cry for me, and I know who,' said Dudley, in what he meant for a very engaging way, and he looked at me as if he thought I must feel flattered by his caring to have my tears.

Instead of crying, however, I leaned back in my chair, and began quietly to turn over the pages of Walter Scott's poems, which I and Milly were then reading in the evenings.

The tone in which this odious young man spoke of his father, his coarse mention of mine, and his low boasting of his irreligion, disgusted me more than ever with him.

'They parsons be slow coaches—awful slow. I'll have a good bit to wait, I s'pose. I should be three miles away and more by this time—drat it!' He was eyeing the legging of the foot which he held up while he spoke, as if calculating how far away that limb should have carried him by this time. 'Why can't folk do their Bible and prayers o' Sundays, and get it off their stomachs? I say, Milly lass, will ye see if Governor be done wi' the Curate? Do. I'm a losing the whole day along o' him.'

Milly jumped up, accustomed to obey her brother, and as she passed me, whispered, with a wink—

'*Money.*'

And away she went. Dudley whistled a tune, and swung his foot like a pendulum, as he followed her with his side-glance.

'I say, it is a hard case, Miss, a lad o' spirit should be kept so tight. I haven't a shilling but what comes through his fingers; an' drat the tizzy he'll gi' me till he knows the reason why.'

'Perhaps,' I said, 'my uncle thinks you should earn some for yourself.'

'I'd like to know how a fella's to earn money now-a-days. You wouldn't have a gentleman to keep a shop, I fancy. But I'll ha' a fistful jist now, and no thanks to he. Them executors, you know, owes me a deal o' money. Very honest chaps, of course; but they're cursed slow about paying, I know.'

I made no remark upon this elegant allusion to the executors of my dear father's will.

'An' I tell ye, Maud, when I git the tin, I know who I'll buy a farin' for. I do, lass.'

The odious creature drawled this with a sidelong leer, which, I suppose, he fancied quite irresistible.

I am one of those unfortunate persons who always blushed when I most wished to look indifferent; and now, to my inexpressible chagrin, with its accustomed perversity, I felt the blush mount to my cheeks, and glow even on my forehead.

I saw that he perceived this most disconcerting indication of a sentiment the very idea of which was so detestable, that, equally enraged with myself and with him, I did not know how to exhibit my contempt and indignation.

Mistaking the cause of my discomposure, Mr. Dudley Ruthyn laughed softly, with an insufferable suavity.

'And there's some'at, lass, I must have in return. Honour thy father, you know; you would not ha' me disobey the Governor? No, you wouldn't—would ye?'

I darted at him a look which I hoped would have quelled his impertinence; but I blushed most provokingly—more violently than ever.

'I'd back them eyes again' the county, I would,' he exclaimed, with a condescending enthusiasm. 'You're awful pretty, you are, Maud. I don't know what came over me t'other night when Governor told me to buss ye; but dang it, ye shan't deny me now, and I'll have a kiss, lass, in spite o' thy blushes.'

He jumped from his elevated seat on the sideboard, and came swaggering toward me, with an odious grin, and his arms extended. I started to my feet, absolutely transported with fury.

'Drat me, if she baint a-going to fight me!' he chuckled humorously.

'Come, Maud, you would not be ill-natured, sure? Arter all, it's only our duty. Governor bid us kiss, didn't he?'

'Don't—*don't*, sir. Stand back, or I'll call the servants.'

And as it was I began to scream for Milly.

'There's how it is wi' all they cattle! You never knows your own mind—ye don't,' he said, surlily. 'You make such a row about a bit o' play. Drop it, will you? There's no one a-harming you—is there? *I*'m not, for sartain.'

And, with an angry chuckle, he turned on his heel, and left the room.

I think I was perfectly right to resist, with all the vehemence of which I was capable, this attempt to assume an intimacy which, notwithstanding my uncle's opinion to the contrary, seemed to me like an outrage.

Milly found me alone—not frightened, but very angry. I had quite made up my mind to complain to my uncle, but the Curate was still with him; and, by the time he had gone, I was cooler. My awe of my uncle had returned. I fancied that he would treat the whole affair as a mere playful piece of gallantry. So, with the comfortable conviction that he had had a lesson, and would think twice before repeating his impertinence, I resolved, with Milly's approbation, to leave matters as they were.

Dudley, greatly to my comfort, was huffed with me, and hardly appeared, and was sulky and silent when he did. I lived then in the pleasant anticipation of his departure, which, Milly thought, would be very soon.

My uncle had his Bible and his consolations; but it cannot have been pleasant to this old *roué*, converted though he was—this refined man of fashion—to see his son grow up an outcast, and a Tony Lumpkin; for whatever he may have thought of his natural gifts, he must have known how mere a boor he was.

I try to recall my then impressions of my uncle's character. Grizzly and chaotic the image rises—silver head, feet of clay. I as yet knew little of him.

I began to perceive that he was what Mary Quince used to call 'dreadful particular'—I suppose a little selfish and impatient. He used to get cases of turtle from Liverpool. He drank claret and hock for his health, and ate woodcock and other light and salutary dainties for the same reason; and was petulant and vicious about the cooking of these, and the flavour and clearness of his coffee.

His conversation was easy, polished, and, with a sentimental glazing, cold; but across this artificial talk, with its French rhymes, racy phrases, and fluent eloquence, like a streak of angry light, would, at intervals, suddenly gleam some dismal thought of religion. I never could quite satisfy myself whether they were affectations or genuine, like intermittent thrills of pain.

The light of his large eyes was very peculiar. I can liken it to nothing but the sheen of intense moonlight on burnished metal. But that cannot express it. It glared white and suddenly—almost fatuous. I thought of Moore's lines whenever I looked on it:—

> Oh, ye dead! oh, ye dead! whom we know by the light you give
> From your cold gleaming eyes, though you move like men who live.

I never saw in any other eye the least glimmer of the same baleful effulgence. His fits, too—his hoverings between life and death—between intellect and insanity—a dubious, marsh-fire existence, horrible to look on!

I was puzzled even to comprehend his feelings toward his children. Sometimes it seemed to me that he was ready to lay down his soul for them; at others, he looked and spoke almost as if he hated them. He talked as if the image of death was always before him, yet he took a terrible interest in life, while seemingly dozing away the dregs of his days in sight of his coffin.

Oh! Uncle Silas, tremendous figure in the past, burning always in memory in the same awful lights; the fixed white face of scorn and anguish! It seems as if the Woman of Endor had led me to that chamber and showed me a spectre.

Dudley had not left Bartram-Haugh when a little note reached me from Lady Knollys. It said—

'DEAREST MAUD,—I have written by this post to Silas, beseeching a loan of you and my Cousin Milly. I see no reason your uncle can possibly have for refusing me; and, therefore, I count confidently on seeing you both at Elverston tomorrow, to stay for at least a week. I have hardly a creature to meet you. I have been disappointed in several visitors; but another time we shall have a gayer house. Tell Milly—with my love—that I will not forgive her if she fails to accompany you.

'Believe me ever your affectionate cousin,

'MONICA KNOLLYS.'

Milly and I were both afraid that Uncle Silas would refuse his consent, although we could not divine any sound reason for his doing so, and there were many in favour of his improving the opportunity of allowing poor Milly to see some persons of her own sex above the rank of menials.

At about twelve o'clock my uncle sent for us, and, to our great delight, announced his consent, and wished us a very happy excursion.

CHAPTER XLII

ELVERSTON AND ITS PEOPLE

So Milly and I drove through the gabled high street of Feltram next day. We saw my gracious cousin smoking with a man like a groom, at the door of the 'Plume of Feathers.' I drew myself back as we passed, and Milly popped her head out of the window.

'I'm blessed,' said she, laughing, 'if he hadn't his thumb to his nose, and winding up his little finger, the way he does with old Wyat—L'Amour, ye know; and you may be sure he said something funny, for Jim Jolliter was laughin', with his pipe in his hand.'

'I wish I had not seen him, Milly. I feel as if it were an ill omen. He always looks so cross; and I dare say he wished us some ill,' I said.

'No, no, you don't know Dudley: if he were angry, he'd say nothing that's funny; no, he's not vexed, only shamming vexed.'

The scenery through which we passed was very pretty. The road brought us through a narrow and wooded glen. Such studies of ivied rocks and twisted roots! A little stream tinkled lonely through the hollow. Poor Milly! In her odd way she made herself companionable. I have sometimes fancied an enjoyment of natural scenery not so much a faculty as an acquirement. It is so exquisite in the instructed, so strangely absent in uneducated humanity. But certainly with Milly it was inborn and hearty; and so she could enter into my raptures, and requite them.

Then over one of those beautiful Derbyshire moors we drove, and so into a wide wooded hollow, where was our first view of Cousin Monica's pretty gabled house, beautified with that indescribable air of shelter and comfort which belongs to an old English residence, with old timber grouped round it, and something in its aspect of the quaint old times and bygone merrymakings, saying sadly, but genially, 'Come in: I bid you welcome. For two hundred years, or more, have I been the home of this beloved old family, whose generations I have seen in the cradle and in the coffin, and whose mirth and sorrows and hospitalities I remember. All their friends, like you, were welcome; and you, like them, will here enjoy the warm illusions that cheat the sad conditions of mortality; and like them you will go your way, and others succeed you, till at last I, too, shall yield to the general law of decay, and disappear.'

By this time poor Milly had grown very nervous; a state which she described in such very odd phraseology as threw me, in spite of myself—for I affected an impressive gravity in lecturing her upon her language—into a hearty fit of laughter.

I must mention, however, that in certain important points Milly was very essentially reformed. Her dress, though not very fashionable, was no longer absurd. And I had drilled her into speaking and laughing quietly; and for the rest I trusted to the indulgence which is always, I think, more honestly and easily obtained from well-bred than from under-bred people.

Cousin Monica was out when we arrived; but we found that she had arranged a double-bedded room for me and Milly, greatly to our content; and good Mary Quince was placed in the dressing-room beside us.

We had only just commenced our toilet when our hostess entered, as usual in high spirits, welcomed and kissed us both again and again. She was, indeed, in extraordinary delight, for she had anticipated some stratagem or evasion to prevent our visit; and in her usual way she spoke her mind as frankly about Uncle Silas to poor Milly as she used to do of my dear father to me.

'I did not think he would let you come without a battle; and you know if he chose to be obstinate it would not have been easy to get you out of the enchanted ground, for so it seems to be with that awful old wizard in the midst of it. I mean, Silas, your papa, my dear. Honestly, is not he very like Michael Scott?'

'I never saw him,' answered poor Milly. 'At least, that I'm aware of,' she added, perceiving us smile. 'But I do think he's a thought like old Michael Dobbs, that sells the ferrets, maybe you mean him?'

'Why, you told me, Maud, that you and Milly were reading Walter Scott's poems. Well, no matter. Michael Scott, my dear, was a dead wizard, with ever so much silvery hair, lying in his grave for ever so many years, with just life enough to scowl when they took his book; and you'll find him in the "Lay of the Last Minstrel," exactly like your papa, my dear. And my people tell me that your brother Dudley has been seen drinking and smoking about Feltram this week. How long does he remain at home? Not very long, eh? And, Maud, dear, he has not been making love to you? Well, I see; of course he has. And *apropos* of lovemaking, I hope that impudent creature, Charles Oakley, has not been teasing you with notes or verses.'

'Indeed but he has though,' interposed Miss Milly; a good deal to my chagrin, for I saw no particular reason for placing his verses in Cousin Monica's hands. So I confessed the two little copies of verses, with the qualification, however, that I did not know from whom they came.

'Well now, dear Maud, have not I told you fifty times over to have nothing to say to him? I've found out, my dear, he plays, and he is very much in debt. I've made a vow to pay no more for him. I've been such a fool, you have no notion; and I'm speaking, you know, against myself; it would be such a relief if he were to find a wife to support him; and he has been, I'm told, very sweet upon a rich old maid—a button-maker's sister, in Manchester.'

This arrow was well shot.

'But don't be frightened: you are richer as well as younger; and, no doubt, will have your chance first, my dear; and in the meantime, I dare say, those verses, like Falstaff's *billet-doux,* you know, are doing double duty.'

I laughed, but the button-maker was a secret trouble to me; and I would have given I know not what that Captain Oakley were one of the company, that I might treat him with the refined contempt which his deserts and my dignity demanded.

Cousin Monica busied herself about Milly's toilet, and was a very useful lady's maid, chatting in her own way all the time; and, at last, tapping Milly under the chin with her finger, she said, very complacently—

'I think I have succeeded, Miss Milly; look in the glass. She really is a very pretty creature.'

And Milly blushed, and looked with a shy gratification, which made her still prettier, on the mirror.

Milly indeed was very pretty. She looked much taller now that her dresses were made of the usual length. A little plump she was, beautifully fair, with such azure eyes, and rich hair.

'The more you laugh the better, Milly, for you've got very pretty teeth—very pretty; and if you were my daughter, or if your father would become president of a college of magicians, and give you up to me, I venture to say I would place you very well; and even as it is we must try, my dear.'

So down to the drawing-room we went; and Cousin Monica entered, leading us both by the hands.

By this time the curtains were closed, and the drawing-room dependent on the pleasant glow of the fire, and the slight provisional illumination usual before dinner.

'Here are my two cousins,' began Lady Knollys: 'this is Miss Ruthyn, of Knowl, whom I take the liberty of calling Maud; and this is Miss Millicent Ruthyn, Silas's daughter, you know, whom I venture to call Milly; and they are very pretty, as you will see, when we get a little more light, and they know it very well themselves.'

And as she spoke, a frank-eyed, gentle, prettyish lady, not so tall as I, but with a very kind face, rose up from a book of prints, and, smiling, took our hands.

She was by no means young, as I then counted youth—past thirty, I suppose—and with an air that was very quiet, and friendly, and engaging. She had never been a mere fashionable woman plainly; but she had the ease and polish of the best society, and seemed to take a kindly interest both in Milly and me; and Cousin Monica called her Mary, and sometimes Polly. That was all I knew of her for the present.

So very pleasantly the time passed by till the dressing-bell rang, and we ran away to our room.

'Did I say anything very bad?' asked poor Milly, standing exactly before me, so soon as our door was shut.

'Nothing, Milly; you are doing admirably.'

'And I do look a great fool, don't I?' she demanded.

'You look extremely pretty, Milly; and not a bit like a fool.'

'I watch everything. I think I'll learn it at last; but it comes a little troublesome at first; and they do talk different from what I used—you were quite right there.'

When we returned to the drawing-room, we found the party already assembled, and chatting, evidently with spirit.

The village doctor, whose name I forget, a small man, grey, with shrewd grey eyes, sharp and mulberry nose, whose conflagration extended to his rugged cheeks, and touched his chin and forehead, was conversing, no doubt agreeably, with Mary, as Cousin Monica called her guest.

Over my shoulder, Milly whispered—

'Mr. Carysbroke.'

And Milly was quite right: that gentleman chatting with Lady Knollys, his elbow resting on the chimney-piece, was, indeed, our acquaintance of the Windmill Wood. He instantly recognised us, and met us with his pleased and intelligent smile.

'I was just trying to describe to Lady Knollys the charming scenery of the Windmill Wood, among which I was so fortunate as to make your acquaintance, Miss Ruthyn. Even in this beautiful county I know of nothing prettier.'

Then he sketched it, as it were, with a few light but glowing words.

'What a sweet scene!' said Cousin Monica: 'only think of her never bringing me through it. She reserves it, I fancy, for her romantic adventures; and you, I know, are very benevolent, Ilbury, and all that kind of thing; but I am not quite certain that you would have walked along that narrow parapet, over a river, to visit a sick old woman, if you had not happened to see two very pretty demoiselles on the other side.'

'What an ill-natured speech! I must either forfeit my character for disinterested benevolence, so justly admired, or disavow a motive that does such infinite credit to my taste,' exclaimed Mr. Carysbroke. 'I think a charitable person would have said that a philanthropist, in prosecuting his virtuous, but perilous vocation, was unexpectedly *rewarded* by a vision of angels.'

'And with these angels loitered away the time which ought to have been devoted to good Mother Hubbard, in her fit of lumbago, and returned without having set eyes on that afflicted Christian, to amaze his worthy sister with poetic bablings about wood-nymphs and such pagan impieties,' rejoined Lady Knollys.

'Well, be just,' he replied, laughing; 'did not I go next day and see the patient?'

'Yes; next day you went by the same route—in quest of the dryads, I am afraid—and were rewarded by the spectacle of Mother Hubbard.'

'Will nobody help a humane man in difficulties?' Mr. Carysbroke appealed.

'I do believe,' said the lady whom as yet I knew only as Mary, 'that every word that Monica says is perfectly true.'

'And if it be so, am I not all the more in need of help? Truth is simply the most dangerous kind of defamation, and I really think I'm most cruelly persecuted.'

At this moment dinner was announced, and a meek and dapper little clergyman, with smooth pink cheeks, and tresses parted down the middle, whom I had not seen before, emerged from shadow.

This little man was assigned to Milly, Mr. Carysbroke to me, and I know not how the remaining ladies divided the doctor between them.

That dinner, the first at Elverston, I remember as a very pleasant repast. Everyone talked—it was impossible that conversation should flag where Lady Knollys was; and Mr. Carysbroke was very agreeable and amusing. At the other side of the table, the little pink curate, I was happy to see, was prattling away, with a modest fluency, in an under-tone to Milly, who was following my instructions most conscientiously, and speaking in so low a key that I could hardly hear at the opposite side one word she was saying.

That night Cousin Monica paid us a visit, as we sat chatting by the fire in our room; and I told her—

'I have just been telling Milly what an impression she has made. The pretty little clergyman—*il en est épris*—he has evidently quite lost his heart to her. I dare say he'll preach next Sunday on some of King Solomon's wise sayings about the irresistible strength of women.'

'Yes,' said Lady Knollys,' or maybe on the sensible text, "Whoso findeth a wife findeth a good thing, and obtaineth favour," and so forth. At all events, I may say, Milly, whoso findeth a husband such as he, findeth a tolerably good thing. He is an exemplary little creature, second son of Sir Harry Biddlepen, with a little independent income of his own, beside his church revenues of ninety pounds a year; and I don't think a more harmless and docile little husband could be found anywhere; and I think, Miss Maud, *you* seemed a good deal interested, too.'

I laughed and blushed, I suppose; and Cousin Monica, skipping after her wont to quite another matter, said in her odd frank way—

'And how has Silas been?—not cross, I hope, or very odd. There was a rumour that your brother, Dudley, had gone a soldiering to India, Milly, or somewhere; but that was all a story, for he has turned up, just as usual. And what does he mean to do with himself? He has got some money now—your poor father's will, Maud. Surely he doesn't mean to go on lounging and smoking away his life among poachers, and prize-fighters, and worse people. He ought to go to Australia, like Thomas Swain, who, they say, is making a fortune—a great fortune—and coming home again. That's what your brother Dudley should do, if he has either sense or spirit; but I suppose he won't—too long abandoned to idleness and low company—and he'll not have a shilling left in a year or two. Does he know, I wonder, that his father has served a notice or something on Dr. Bryerly, telling him to pay sixteen hundred pounds of poor Austin's legacy to *him*, and saying that he has paid debts of the young man, and holds his acknowledgments to that amount? He won't have a guinea in a year if he stays here. I'd give fifty pounds he was in Van Diemen's Land—not that I care for the cub, Milly, any more than you do; but I really don't see any honest business he has in England.'

Milly gaped in a total puzzle as Lady Knollys rattled on.

'You know, Milly, you must not be talking about this when you go home to Bartram, because Silas would prevent your coming to me any more if he thought I spoke so freely; but I can't help it: so you must promise to be more discreet than I. And I am told that all kinds of claims are about to be pressed against him, now that he is thought to have got some money; and he has been cutting down oak and selling the bark, Doctor Bryerly has been told, in that Windmill Wood; and he has kilns there for burning charcoal, and got a man from Lancashire who understands it—Hawk, or something like that.'

'Ay, Hawkes—Dickon Hawkes; that's Pegtop, you know, Maud,' said Milly.

'Well, I dare say; but a man of very bad character, Dr. Bryerly says; and he has written to Mr. Danvers about it—for that is what they call waste, cutting down and selling the timber, and the oakbark, and burning the willows, and other trees that are turned into charcoal. It is all *waste*, and Dr. Bryerly is about to put a stop to it.'

'Has he got your carriage for you, Maud, and your horses?' asked Cousin Monica, suddenly.

'They have not come yet, but in a few weeks, Dudley says, positively—'

Cousin Monica laughed a little and shook her head.

'Yes, Maud, the carriage and horses will always be coming in a few weeks, till the time is over; and meanwhile the old travelling chariot and post-horses will do very well;' and she laughed a little again.

'That's why the stile's pulled away at the paling, I suppose; and Beauty—Meg Hawkes, that is—is put there to stop us going through; for I often spied the smoke beyond the windmill,' observed Milly.

Cousin Monica listened with interest, and nodded silently.

I was very much shocked. It seemed to me quite incredible. I think Lady Knollys read my amazement and my exalted estimate of the heinousness of the procedure in my face, for she said—

'You know we can't quite condemn Silas till we have heard what he has to say. He may have done it in ignorance; or, it is just possible, he may have the right.'

'Quite true. He may have the right to cut down trees at Bartram-Haugh. At all events, I am sure he thinks he has,' I echoed.

The fact was, that I would not avow to myself a suspicion of Uncle Silas. Any falsehood there opened an abyss beneath my feet into which I dared not look.

'And now, dear girls, good-night. You must be tired. We breakfast at a quarter past nine—not too early for you, I know.'

And so saying, she kissed us, smiling, and was gone.

I was so unpleasantly occupied, for some time after her departure, with the knaveries said to be practised among the dense cover of the Windmill Wood, that I did not immediately recollect that we had omitted to ask her any particulars about her guests.

'Who can Mary be?' asked Milly.

'Cousin Monica says she's engaged to be married, and I think I heard the Doctor call her *Lady* Mary, and I intended asking her ever so much about her; but what she told us about cutting down the trees, and all that, quite put it out of my head. We shall have time enough to-morrow, however, to ask questions. I like her very much, I know.'

'And I think,' said Milly, 'it is to Mr. Carysbroke she's to be married.'

'Do you?' said I, remembering that he had sat beside her for more than a quarter of an hour after tea in very close and low-toned conversation; 'and have you any particular reason?' I asked.

'Well, I heard her once or twice call him "dear," and she called him his Christian name, just like Lady Knollys did—Ilbury, I think—and I saw him gi' her a sly kiss as she was going up-stairs.'

I laughed.

'Well, Milly,' I said, 'I remarked something myself, I thought, like confidential relations; but if you really saw them kiss on the staircase, the question is pretty well settled.'

'Ay, lass.'

'You're not to say *lass*.'

'Well, *Maud, then*. I did see them with the corner of my eye, and my back turned, when they did not think I could spy anything, as plain as I see you now.'

I laughed again; but I felt an odd pang—something of mortification—something of regret; but I smiled very gaily, as I stood before the glass, unmaking my toilet preparatory to bed.

'Maud—Maud—fickle Maud!—What, Captain Oakley already superseded! and Mr. Carysbroke—oh! humiliation—engaged.' So I smiled on, very much vexed; and being afraid lest I had listened with too apparent an interest to this impostor, I sang a verse of a gay little chanson, and tried to think of Captain Oakley, who somehow had become rather silly.

CHAPTER XLIII

NEWS AT BARTRAM GATE

Milly and I, thanks to our early Bartram hours, were first down next morning; and so soon as Cousin Monica appeared we attacked her.

'So Lady Mary is the *fiancée* of Mr. Carysbroke,' said I, very cleverly; 'and I think it was very wicked of you to try and involve me in a flirtation with him yesterday.'

'And who told you that, pray?' asked Lady Knollys, with a pleasant little laugh.

'Milly and I discovered it, simple as we stand here,' I answered.

'But you did not flirt with Mr. Carysbroke, Maud, did you?' she asked.

'No, certainly not; but that was not your doing, wicked woman, but my discretion. And now that we know your secret, you must tell us all about her, and all about him; and in the first place, what is her name—Lady Mary what?' I demanded.

'Who would have thought you so cunning? Two country misses—two little nuns from the cloisters of Bartram! Well, I suppose I must answer. It is vain trying to hide anything from you; but how on earth did you find it out?'

'We'll tell you that presently, but you shall first tell us who she is,' I persisted.

'Well, that I will, of course, without compulsion. She is Lady Mary Carysbroke,' said Lady Knollys.

'A relation of Mr. Carysbroke's,' I asserted.

'Yes, a relation; but who told you he was Mr. Carysbroke?' asked Cousin Monica.

'Milly told me, when we saw him in the Windmill Wood.'

'And who told you, Milly?'

'It was L'Amour,' answered Milly, with her blue eyes very wide open.

'What does the child mean? L'Amour! You don't mean *love*?' exclaimed Lady Knollys, puzzled in her turn.

'I mean old Wyat; *she* told me and the Governor.'

'You're *not* to say that,' I interposed.

'You mean your father?' suggested Lady Knollys.

'Well, yes; father told her, and so I knew him.'

'What could he mean?' exclaimed Lady Knollys, laughing, as it were, in soliloquy; 'and I did not mention his name, I recollect now. He recognised you, and you him, when you came into the room yesterday; and now you must tell me how you discovered that he and Lady Mary were to be married.'

So Milly restated her evidence, and Lady Knollys laughed unaccountably heartily; and she said—

'They *will* be *so* confounded! but they deserve it; and, remember, *I* did not say so.'

'Oh! we acquit you.'

'All I say is, such a deceitful, dangerous pair of girls—all things considered—I never heard of before,' exclaimed Lady Knollys. 'There's no such thing as conspiring in your presence.'

'Good morning. I hope you slept well.' She was addressing the lady and gentleman who were just entering the room from the conservatory. 'You'll hardly sleep so well to-night, when you have learned what eyes are upon you. Here are two very pretty detectives who have found out your secret, and entirely by your imprudence and their own cleverness have discovered that you are a pair of betrothed lovers, about to ratify your vows at the hymeneal altar. I assure you I did not tell of you; you betrayed yourselves. If you will talk in that confidential way on sofas, and call one another stealthily by your Christian names, and actually kiss at the foot of the stairs, while a clever detective is scaling them, apparently with her back toward you, you must only take the consequences, and be known prematurely as the hero and heroine of the forthcoming paragraph in the "Morning Post."'

Milly and I were horribly confounded, but Cousin Monica was resolved to place us all upon the least formal terms possible, and I believe she had set about it in the right way.

'And now, girls, I am going to make a counter-discovery, which, I fear, a little conflicts with yours. This Mr. Carysbroke is Lord Ilbury, brother of this Lady Mary; and it is all my fault for not having done my honours better; but you see what clever match-making little creatures they are.'

'You can't think how flattered I am at being made the subject of a theory, even a mistaken one, by Miss Ruthyn.'

And so, after our modest fit was over, Milly and I were very merry, like the rest, and we all grew a great deal more intimate that morning.

I think altogether those were the pleasantest and happiest days of my life: gay, intelligent, and kindly society at home; charming excursions—sometimes riding—sometimes by carriage—to distant points of beauty in the county. Evenings varied with music, reading, and spirited conversation. Now and then a visitor for a day or two, and constantly some neighbour from the town, or its dependencies, dropt in. Of these I but remember tall old Miss Wintletop, most entertaining of rustic old maids, with her nice lace and thick satin, and her small, kindly round face—pretty, I dare say, in other days, and now frosty, but kindly—who told us such delightful old stories of the county in her father's and grandfather's time;

who knew the lineage of every family in it, and could recount all its duels and elopements; give us illustrative snatches from old election squibs, and lines from epitaphs, and tell exactly where all the old-world highway robberies had been committed: how it fared with the chief delinquents after the assizes; and, above all, where, and of what sort, the goblins and elves of the county had made themselves seen, from the phantom post-boy, who every third night crossed Windale Moor, by the old coach-road, to the fat old ghost, in mulberry velvet, who showed his great face, crutch, and ruffles, by moonlight, at the bow window of the old court-house that was taken down in 1803.

You cannot imagine what agreeable evenings we passed in this society, or how rapidly my good Cousin Milly improved in it. I remember well the intense suspense in which she and I awaited the answer from Bartram-Haugh to kind Cousin Monica's application for an extension of our leave of absence.

It came, and with it a note from Uncle Silas, which was curious, and, therefore, is printed here:—

'MY DEAR LADY KNOLLYS,—To your kind letter I say yes (that is, for another week, not a fortnight), with all my heart. I am glad to hear that my starlings chatter so pleasantly; at all events the refrain is not that of Sterne's. They can get out; and do get out; and shall get out as much as they please. I am no gaoler, and shut up nobody but myself. I have always thought that young people have too little liberty. My principle has been to make little free men and women of them from the first. In morals, altogether—in intellect, more than we allow—*self*-education is that which abides; and *it* only begins where constraint ends. Such is my theory. My practice is consistent. Let them remain for a week longer, as you say. The horses shall be at Elverston on Tuesday, the 7th. I shall be more than usually sad and solitary till their return; so pray, I selfishly entreat, do not extend their absence. You will smile, remembering how little my health will allow me to see of them, even when at home; but as Chaulieu so prettily says—I stupidly forget the words, but the sentiment is this—"although concealed by a sylvan wall of leaves, impenetrable—(he is pursuing his favourite nymphs through the alleys and intricacies of a rustic labyrinth)—yet, your songs, your prattle, and your laughter, faint and far away, inspire my fancy; and, through my ears, I see your unseen smiles, your blushes, your floating tresses, and your ivory feet; and so, though sad, am happy; though alone, in company;"—and such is my case.

'One only request, and I have done. Pray remind them of a promise made to me. The Book of Life—the fountain of life—it must be drunk of, night and morning, or their spiritual life expires.

'And now, Heaven bless and keep you, my dear cousin; and with all assurances of affection to my beloved niece and my child, believe me ever yours affectionately.

'SILAS RUTHYN.'

Said Cousin Monica, with a waggish smile—

'And so, girls, you have Chaulieu and the evangelists; the French rhymester in his alley, and Silas in the valley of the shadow of death; perfect liberty, and a peremptory order to return in a week;—all illustrating one another. Poor Silas! old as he is, I don't think his religion fits him.'

I really rather liked his letter. I was struggling hard to think well of him, and Cousin Monica knew it; and I really think if I had not been by, she would often have been less severe on him.

As we were all sitting pleasantly about the breakfast table a day or two after, the sun shining on the pleasant wintry landscape, Cousin Monica suddenly exclaimed—

'I quite forgot to tell you that Charles Oakley has written to say he is coming on Wednesday. I really don't want him. Poor Charlie! I wonder how they manage those doctors' certificates. I know nothing ails him, and he'd be much better with his regiment.'

Wednesday!—how odd. Exactly the day after my departure. I tried to look perfectly unconcerned. Lady Knollys had addressed herself more to Lady Mary and Milly than to me, and nobody in particular was looking at me. Notwithstanding, with my usual perversity, I felt myself blushing with a brilliancy that may have been very becoming, but which was so intolerably provoking that I would have risen and left the room but that matters would have been so infinitely worse. I could have boxed my odious ears. I could almost have jumped from the window.

I felt that Lord Ilbury saw it. I saw Lady Mary's eyes for a moment resting gravely on my tell-tale—my lying cheeks—for I really had begun to think much less celestially of Captain Oakley. I was angry with Cousin Monica, who, knowing my blushing infirmity, had mentioned her nephew so suddenly while I was strapped by etiquette in my chair, with my face to the window, and two pair of most disconcerting eyes, at least, opposite. I was angry with myself—generally angry—refused more tea rather dryly, and was laconic to Lord Ilbury, all which, of course, was very cross and foolish; and afterwards, from my bed-room window, I saw Cousin Monica and Lady Mary among the flowers, under the drawing-room window, talking, as I instinctively knew, of that little incident. I was standing at the glass.

'My odious, stupid, *perjured* face' I whispered, furiously, at the same time stamping on the floor, and giving myself quite a smart slap on the cheek. 'I *can't* go down—I'm ready to cry—I've a mind to return to Bartram to-day; I am *always* blushing; and I wish that impudent Captain Oakley was at the bottom of the sea.'

I was, perhaps, thinking more of Lord Ilbury than I was aware; and I am sure if Captain Oakley had arrived that day, I should have treated him with most unjustifiable rudeness.

Notwithstanding this unfortunate blush, the remainder of our visit passed very happily for me. No one who has not experienced it can have an idea how intimate a small party, such as ours, will grow in a short time in a country house.

Of course, a young lady of a well-regulated mind cannot possibly care a pin about any one of the opposite sex until she is well assured that he is beginning, at least, to like her better than all the world beside; but I could not deny to myself that I was rather anxious to know more about Lord Ilbury than I actually did know.

There was a 'Peerage,' in its bright scarlet and gold uniform, corpulent and tempting, upon the little marble table in the drawing-room. I had many opportunities of consulting it, but I never could find courage to do so.

For an inexperienced person it would have been a matter of several minutes, and during those minutes what awful risk of surprise and detection. One day, all being quiet, I did venture, and actually, with a beating heart, got so far as to find out the letter 'Il,' when I heard a step outside the door, which opened a little bit, and I heard Lady Knollys, luckily arrested at the entrance, talk some sentences outside, her hand still upon the door-handle. I shut the book, as Mrs. Bluebeard might the door of the chamber of horrors at the sound of her husband's step, and skipped to a remote part of the room, where Cousin Knollys found me in a mysterious state of agitation.

On any other subject I would have questioned Cousin Monica unhesitatingly; upon this, somehow, I was dumb. I distrusted myself, and dreaded my odious habit of blushing, and knew that I should look so horribly guilty, and become so agitated and odd, that she would have reasonably concluded that I had quite lost my heart to him.

After the lesson I had received, and my narrow escape of detection in the very act, you may be sure I never trusted myself in the vicinity of that fat and cruel 'Peerage,' which possessed the secret, but would not disclose without compromising me.

In this state of tantalizing darkness and conjecture I should have departed, had not Cousin Monica quite spontaneously relieved me.

The night before our departure she sat with us in our room, chatting a little farewell gossip.

'And what do you think of Ilbury?' she asked.

'I think him clever and accomplished, and amusing; but he sometimes appears to me very melancholy—that is, for a few minutes together—and then, I fancy, with an effort, re-engages in our conversation.'

'Yes, poor Ilbury! He lost his brother only about five months since, and is only beginning to recover his spirits a little. They were very much attached, and people thought that he would have succeeded to the title, had he lived, because Ilbury is *difficile*—or a philosopher—or a *Saint Kevin*; and, in fact, has begun to be treated as a premature old bachelor.'

'What a charming person his sister, Lady Mary, is. She has made me promise to write to her,' I said, I suppose—such hypocrites are we—to prove to Cousin Knollys that I did not care particularly to hear anything more about him.

'Yes, and so devoted to him. He came down here, and took The Grange, for change of scene and solitude—of all things the worst for a man in grief—a morbid whim, as he is beginning to find out; for he is very glad to stay here, and confesses that he is much better since he came. His letters are still addressed to him as Mr. Carysbroke; for he fancied if his rank were known, that the county people would have been calling upon him, and so he would have found himself soon involved in a tiresome round of dinners, and must have gone somewhere else. You saw him, Milly, at Bartram, before Maud came?'

Yes, she had, when he called there to see her father.

'He thought, as he had accepted the trusteeship, that he could hardly, residing so near, omit to visit Silas. He was very much struck and interested by him, and he has a better opinion of him—you are not angry, Milly—than some ill-natured people I could name; and he says that the cutting down of the trees will turn out to have been a mere slip. But these slips don't occur with clever men in other things; and some persons have a way of always making them in their own favour. And, to talk of other things, I suspect that you and Milly will probably see Ilbury at Bartram; for I think he likes you very much.'

You; did she mean *both*, or only me?

So our pleasant visit was over. Milly's good little curate had been much thrown in her way by our deep and dangerous cousin Monica. He was most laudably steady; and his flirtation advanced upon the field of theology, where, happily, Milly's little reading had been concentrated. A mild and earnest interest in poor, pretty Milly's orthodoxy was the leading feature of his case; and I was highly amused at her references to me, when we had retired at night, upon the points which she had disputed with him, and her anxious reports of their low-toned conferences, carried on upon a sequestered ottoman, where he patted and stroked his crossed leg, as he smiled tenderly and shook his head at her questionable doctrine. Milly's reverence for her instructor, and his admiration, grew daily; and he was known among us as Milly's confessor.

He took luncheon with us on the day of our departure, and with an adroit privacy, which in a layman would have been sly, presented her, in right of his holy calling, with a little book, the binding of which was mediaeval and costly, and whose letter-press dealt in a way which he commended, with some points on which she was not satisfactory; and she found on the fly-leaf this little inscription:—'Presented to Miss Millicent Ruthyn by an earnest well-wisher, 1st December 1844.' A text, very neatly penned, followed this; and the 'presentation' was made unctiously indeed, but with a blush, as well as the accustomed smile, and with eyes that were lowered.

The early crimson sun of December had gone down behind the hills before we took our seats in the carriage.

Lord Ilbury leaned with his elbow on the carriage window, looking in, and he said to me—

'I really don't know what we shall do, Miss Ruthyn; we shall all feel so lonely. For myself, I think I shall run away to Grange.'

This appeared to me as nearly perfect eloquence as human lips could utter.

His hand still rested on the window, and the Rev. Sprigge Biddlepen was standing with a saddened smirk on the door steps, when the whip smacked, the horses scrambled into motion, and away we rolled down the avenue, leaving behind us the pleasantest house and hostess in the world, and trotting fleetly into darkness towards Bartram-Haugh.

We were both rather silent. Milly had her book in her lap, and I saw her every now and then try to read her 'earnest well-wisher's' little inscription, but there was not light to read by.

When we reached the great gate of Bartram-Haugh it was dark. Old Crowl, who kept the gate, I heard enjoining the postilion to make no avoidable noise at the hall-door, for the odd but startling reason that he believed my uncle 'would be dead by this time.'

Very much shocked and frightened, we stopped the carriage, and questioned the tremulous old porter.

Uncle Silas, it seemed, had been 'silly-ish' all yesterday, and 'could not be woke this morning,' and 'the doctor had been here twice, being now in the house.'

'Is he better?' I asked, tremblingly.

'Not as I'm aweer on, Miss; he lay at God's mercy two hours agone; 'appen he's in heaven be this time.'

'Drive on—drive fast,' I said to the driver. 'Don't be frightened, Milly; please Heaven we shall find all going well.'

After some delay, during which my heart sank, and I quite gave up Uncle Silas, the aged little servant-man opened the door, and trotted shakily down the steps to the carriage side.

Uncle Silas had been at death's door for hours; the question of life had trembled in the scale; but now the doctor said 'he might do.'

'Where was the doctor?'

'In master's room; he blooded him three hours agone.'

I don't think that Milly was so frightened as I. My heart beat, and I was trembling so that I could hardly get up-stairs.

CHAPTER XLIV

A FRIEND ARISES

At the top of the great staircase I was glad to see the friendly face of Mary Quince, who stood, candle in hand, greeting us with many little courtesies, and a very haggard and pallid smile.

'Very welcome, Miss, hoping you are very well.'

'All well, and you are well, Mary? and oh! tell us quickly how is Uncle Silas?'

'We thought he was gone, Miss, this morning, but doing fairly now; doctor says in a trance like. I was helping old Wyat most of the day, and was there when doctor blooded him, an' he spoke at last; but he must be awful weak, he took a deal o' blood from his arm, Miss; I held the basin.'

'And he's better—decidedly better?' I asked.

'Well, he's better, doctor says; he talked some, and doctor says if he goes off asleep again, and begins a-snoring like he did before, we're to loose the bandage, and let him bleed till he comes to his self again; which, it seems to me and Wyat, is the same thing a'most as saying he's to be killed off-hand, for I don't believe he has a drop to spare, as you'll say likewise, Miss, if you'll please look in the basin.'

This was not an invitation with which I cared to comply. I thought I was going to faint. I sat on the stairs and sipped a little water, and Quince sprinkled a little in my face, and my strength returned.

Milly must have felt her father's danger more than I, for she was affectionate, and loved him from habit and relation, although he was not kind to her. But I was more nervous and more impetuous, and my feelings both stimulated and overpowered me more easily. The moment I was able to stand I said—thinking of nothing but the one idea—

'We must see him—*come*, Milly.'

I entered his sitting-room; a common 'dip' candle hanging like the tower of Pisa all to one side, with a dim, long wick, in a greasy candlestick, profaned the table of the fastidious invalid. The light was little better than darkness, and I crossed the room swiftly, still transfixed by the one idea of seeing my uncle.

His bed-room door beside the fireplace stood partly open, and I looked in.

Old Wyat, a white, high-cauled ghost, was pottering in her slippers in the shadow at the far side of the bed. The doctor, a stout little bald man, with a paunch and a big bunch of seals, stood with his back to the fireplace, which corresponded with that in the next room, eyeing his patient through the curtains of the bed with a listless sort of importance.

The head of the large four-poster rested against the opposite wall. Its foot was presented toward the fireplace; but the curtains at the side, which alone I could see from my position, were closed.

The little doctor knew me, and thinking me, I suppose, a person of consequence, removed his hands from behind him, suffering the skirts of his coat to fall forward, and with great celerity and gravity made me a low but important bow; then choosing more particularly to make my acquaintance he further advanced, and with another reverence he introduced himself as Doctor Jolks, in a murmured diapason. He bowed me back again into my uncle's study, and the light of old Wyat's dreadful candle.

Doctor Jolks was suave and pompous. I longed for a fussy practitioner who would have got over the ground in half the time.

Coma, madam; coma. Miss Ruthyn, your uncle, I may tell you, has been in a very critical state; highly so. Coma of the most obstinate type. He would have sunk—he must have gone, in fact, had I not resorted to a very extreme remedy, and bled him freely, which happily told precisely as we could have wished. A wonderful constitution—a marvellous constitution—prodigious nervous fibre; the greatest pity in the world he won't give himself fair play. His habits, you know, are quite, I may say, destructive. We do our best—we do all we can, but if the patient won't cooperate it can't possibly end satisfactorily.'

And Jolks accompanied this with an awful shrug. 'Is there *anything*? Do you think change of air? What an awful complaint it is,' I exclaimed.

He smiled, mysteriously looking down, and shook his head undertaker-like.

'Why, we can hardly call it a *complaint*, Miss Ruthyn. I look upon it he has been poisoned—he has had, you understand me,' he pursued, observing my startled look, 'an overdose of opium; you know he takes opium habitually; he takes it in laudanum, he takes it in water, and, most dangerous of all, he takes it solid, in lozenges. I've known people take it moderately. I've known people take it to excess, *but* they all were particular as to *measure,* and *that* is exactly the point I've tried to impress upon him. The habit, of course, you understand is formed, there's no uprooting that; but he won't *measure*—he goes by the eye and by sensation, which I need not tell you, Miss Ruthyn, is going by *chance;* and opium, as no doubt you are aware, is strictly a poison; a poison, no doubt, which habit will enable you to partake of, I may say, in considerable quantities, without fatal consequences, but still a poison; and to exhibit a poison *so*, is, I need scarcely tell you, to trifle with death. He has been so threatened, and for a time he changes his haphazard mode of dealing with it, and then returns; he may escape—of course, that is possible—but he may any day overdo the thing. I don't think the present crisis will result seriously. I am very glad, independently of the honour of making your acquaintance, Miss Ruthyn, that you and your cousin have returned; for, however zealous, I fear the servants are deficient in intelligence; and as in the event of a recurrence of the symptoms—which, however, is not probable—I would beg to inform you of their nature, and how exactly best to deal with them.'

So upon these points he delivered us a pompous little lecture, and begged that either Milly or I would remain in the room with the patient until his return at two or three o'clock in the morning; a reappearance of the coma 'might be very bad indeed.'

Of course Milly and I did as we were directed. We sat by the fire, scarcely daring to whisper. Uncle Silas, about whom a new and dreadful suspicion began to haunt me, lay still and motionless as if he were actually dead.

'Had he attempted to poison himself?'

If he believed his position to be as desperate as Lady Knollys had described it, was this, after all, improbable? There were strange wild theories, I had been told, mixed up in his religion.

Sometimes, at an hour's interval, a sign of life would come—a moan from that tall sheeted figure in the bed—a moan and a pattering of the lips. Was it prayer—*what* was it? who could guess what thoughts were passing behind that white-fillited forehead?

I had peeped at him: a white cloth steeped in vinegar and water was folded round his head; his great eyes were closed, so were his marble lips; his figure straight, thin, and long, dressed in a white dressing-gown, looked like a corpse 'laid out' in the bed; his gaunt bandaged arm lay outside the sheet that covered his body.

With this awful image of death we kept our vigil, until poor Milly grew so sleepy that old Wyat proposed that she should take her place and watch with me.

Little as I liked the crone with the high-cauled cap, she would, at all events, keep awake, which Milly could not. And so at one o'clock this new arrangement began.

'Mr. Dudley Ruthyn is not at home?' I whispered to old Wyat.

'He went away wi' himself yesternight, to Cloperton, Miss, to see the wrestling; it was to come off this morning.'

'Was he sent for?'

'Not he.'

'And why not?'

'He would na' leave the sport for this, I'm thinking,' and the old woman grinned uglily.

'When is he to return?'

'When he wants money.'

So we grew silent, and again I thought of suicide, and of the unhappy old man, who just then whispered a sentence or two to himself with a sigh.

For the next hour he had been quite silent, and old Wyat informed me that she must go down for candles. Ours were already burnt down to the sockets.

'There's a candle in the next room,' I suggested, hating the idea of being left alone with the patient.

'Hoot! Miss. I *dare* na' set a candle but wax in his presence,' whispered the old woman, scornfully.

'I think if we were to stir the fire, and put on a little more coal, we should have a great deal of light.'

'He'll ha' the candles,' said Dame Wyat, doggedly; and she tottered from the chamber, muttering to herself; and I heard her take her candle from the next room and depart, shutting the outer door after her.

Here was I then alone, but for this unearthly companion, whom I feared inexpressibly, at two o'clock, in the vast old house of Bartram.

I stirred the fire. It was low, and would not blaze. I stood up, and, with my hand on the mantelpiece, endeavoured to think of cheerful things. But it was a struggle against wind and tide—vain; and so I drifted away into haunted regions.

Uncle Silas was perfectly still. I would not suffer myself to think of the number of dark rooms and passages which now separated me from the other living tenants of the house. I awaited with a false composure the return of old Wyat.

Over the mantelpiece was a looking-glass. At another time this might have helped to entertain my solitary moments, but now I did not like to venture a peep. A small thick Bible lay on the chimneypiece, and leaning its back against the mirror, I began to read in it with a mind as attentively directed as I could. While so engaged in turning over the leaves, I lighted upon two or three odd-looking papers, which had been folded into it. One was a broad printed thing, with names and dates written into blank spaces, and was about the size of a quarter of a yard of very broad ribbon. The others were mere scraps, with 'Dudley Ruthyn' penned in my cousin's vulgar round-hand at the foot. While I folded and replaced these, I really don't know what caused me to fancy that something was moving behind me, as I stood with my back toward the bed. I do not recollect any sound whatever; but instinctively I glanced into the mirror, and my eyes were instantly fixed by what I saw.

The figure of Uncle Silas rose up, and dressed in a long white morning gown, slid over the end of the bed, and with two or three swift noiseless steps, stood behind me, with a death-like scowl and a simper. Preternaturally tall and thin, he stood for a moment almost touching me, with the white bandage pinned across his forehead, his bandaged arm stiffly by his side, and diving over my shoulder, with his long thin hand he snatched the Bible, and whispered over my head—'The serpent beguiled her and she did eat;' and after a momentary pause, he glided to the farthest window, and appeared to look out upon the midnight prospect.

It was cold, but he did not seem to feel it. With the same inflexible scowl and smile, he continued to look out for several minutes, and then with a great sigh, he sat down on the side of his bed, his face immovably turned towards me, with the same painful look.

It seemed to me an hour before old Wyat came back; and never was lover made happier at sight of his mistress than I to behold that withered crone.

You may be sure I did not prolong my watch. There was now plainly no risk of my uncle's relapsing into lethargy. I had a long hysterical fit of weeping when I got into my room, with honest Mary Quince by my side.

Whenever I closed my eyes, the face of Uncle Silas was before me, as I had seen it reflected in the glass. The sorceries of Bartram were enveloping me once more.

Next morning the doctor said he was quite out of danger, but very weak. Milly and I saw him; and again in our afternoon walk we saw the doctor marching under the trees in the direction of the Windmill Wood.

'Going down to see that poor girl there?' he said, when he had made his salutation, prodding with his levelled stick in the direction. 'Hawke, or Hawkes, I think.'

'Beauty's sick, Maud,' exclaimed Milly.

'*Hawkes*. She's upon my dispensary list. Yes,' said the doctor, looking into his little note-book—'Hawkes.'

'And what is her complaint?'

'Rheumatic fever.'

'Not infectious?'

'Not the least—no more, as we say, Miss Ruthyn, than a broken leg,' and he laughed obligingly.

So soon as the doctor had departed, Milly and I agreed to follow to Hawkes' cottage and enquire more particularly how she was. To say truth, I am afraid it was rather for the sake of giving our walk a purpose and a point of termination, than for any very charitable interest we might have felt in the patient.

Over the inequalities of the upland slope, clumped with trees, we reached the gabled cottage, with its neglected little farm-yard. A rheumatic old woman was the only attendant; and, having turned her ear in an attitude of attention, which induced us in gradually exalted keys to enquire how Meg was, she informed us in very loud tones that she had long lost her hearing and was perfectly deaf. And added considerately—

'When the man comes in, 'appen he'll tell ye what ye want.'

Through the door of a small room at the further end of that in which we were, we could see a portion of the narrow apartment of the patient, and hear her moans and the doctor's voice.

'We'll see him, Milly, when he comes out. Let us wait here.'

So we stood upon the door-stone awaiting him. The sounds of suffering had moved my compassion and interested us for the sick girl.

'Blest if here isn't Pegtop,' said Milly.

And the weather-stained red coat, the swarthy forbidding face and sooty locks of old Hawkes loomed in sight, as he stumped, steadying himself with his stick, over the uneven pavement of the yard. He touched his hat gruffly to me, but did not seem half to like our being where we were, for he looked surlily, and scratched his head under his wide-awake.

'Your daughter is very ill, I'm afraid,' said I.

'Ay—she'll be costin' me a handful, like her mother did,' said Pegtop.

'I hope her room is comfortable, poor thing.'

'Ay, that's it; she be comfortable enough, I warrant—more nor I. It be all Meg, and nout o' Dickon.'

'When did her illness commence?' I asked.

'Day the mare wor shod—*Saturday*. I talked a bit wi' the workus folk, but they won't gi'e nout—dang 'em—an' how be *I* to do't? It be all'ays hard bread wi' Silas, an' a deal harder now she' ta'en them pains. I won't stan' it much longer. Gammon! If she keeps on that way I'll just cut. See how the workus fellahs 'ill like *that*!'

'The Doctor gives his services for nothing,' I said.

'An' *does* nothin', bless him! ha, ha. No more nor that old deaf gammon there that costs me three tizzies a week, and haint worth a h'porth—no more nor Meg there, that's making all she can o' them pains. They be all a foolin' o' me, an' thinks I don't know't. Hey? *we*'ll see.'

All this time he was cutting a bit of tobacco into shreds on the window-stone.

'A workin' man be same as a hoss; if he baint cared, he can't work—'tisn't in him:' and with these words, having by this time stuffed his pipe with tobacco, he poked the deaf lady, who was pattering about with her back toward him, rather viciously with the point of his stick, and signed for a light.

'It baint in him, you can't get it out o' 'im, no more nor ye'll draw smoke out o' this,' and he raised his pipe an inch or two, with his thumb on the bowl, 'without backy and fire. 'Tisn't in it.'

'Maybe I can be of some use?' I said, thinking.

'Maybe,' he rejoined.

By this time he received from the old deaf abigail a flaming roll of brown paper, and, touching his hat to me, he withdrew, lighting his pipe and sending up little white puffs, like the salute of a departing ship.

So he did not care to hear how his daughter was, and had only come here to light his pipe!

Just then the Doctor emerged.

'We have been waiting to hear how your poor patient is to-day?' I said.

'Very ill, indeed, and utterly neglected, I fear. If she were equal to it—but she's not—I think she ought to be removed to the hospital immediately.'

'That poor old woman is quite deaf, and the man is so surly and selfish! Could you recommend a nurse who would stay here till she's better? I will pay her with pleasure, and anything you think might be good for the poor girl.'

So this was settled on the spot. Doctor Jolks was kind, like most men of his calling, and undertook to send the nurse from Feltram with a few comforts for the patient; and he called Dickon to the yard-gate, and I suppose told him of the arrangement; and Milly and I went to the poor girl's door and asked, 'May we come in?'

There was no answer. So, with the conventional construction of silence, we entered. Her looks showed how ill she was. We adjusted her bed-clothes, and darkened the room, and did what we could for her—noting, beside, what her comfort chiefly required. She did not answer any questions. She did not thank us. I should almost have fancied that she had not perceived our presence, had I not observed her dark, sunken eyes once or twice turned up towards my face, with a dismal look of wonder and enquiry.

The girl was very ill, and we went every day to see her. Sometimes she would answer our questions—sometimes not. Thoughtful, observant, surly, she seemed; and as people like to be thanked, I sometimes wonder that we continued to throw our bread upon these ungrateful waters. Milly was specially impatient under this treatment, and protested against it, and finally refused to accompany me into poor Beauty's bed-room.

'I think, my good Meg,' said I one day, as I stood by her bed—she was now recovering with the sure reascent of youth—'that you ought to thank Miss Milly.'

'I'll *not* thank her,' said Beauty, doggedly.

'Very well, Meg; I only thought I'd ask you, for I think you ought.'

As I spoke, she very gently took just the tip of my finger, which hung close to her coverlet, in her fingers, and drew it beneath, and before I was aware, burying her head in the clothes, she suddenly clasped my hand in both hers to her lips, and kissed it passionately, again and again, sobbing. I felt her tears.

I tried to withdraw my hand, but she held it with an angry pull, continuing to weep and kiss it.

'Do you wish to say anything, my poor Meg?' I asked.

'Nout, Miss,' she sobbed gently; and she continued to kiss my hand and weep. But suddenly she said, 'I won't thank Milly, for it's a' *you*; it baint her, she hadn't the thought—no, no, it's a' you, Miss. I cried hearty in the dark last night, thinkin' o' the apples, and the way I knocked them awa' wi' a pur o' my foot, the day father rapped me ower the head wi' his stick; it was kind o' you and very bad o' me. I wish you'd beat me, Miss; ye're better to me than father or mother—better to me than a'; an' I wish I could die for you, Miss, for I'm not fit to look at you.'

I was surprised. I began to cry. I could have hugged poor Meg.

I did not know her history. I have never learned it since. She used to talk with the most utter self-abasement before me. It was no religious feeling—it was a kind of expression of her love and worship of me—all the more strange that she was naturally very proud. There was nothing she would not have borne from me except the slightest suspicion of her entire devotion, or that she could in the most trifling way wrong or deceive me.

I am not young now. I have had my sorrows, and with them all that wealth, virtually unlimited, can command; and through the retrospect a few bright and pure lights quiver along my life's dark stream—dark, but for them; and these are shed, not by the splendour of a splendid fortune, but by two or three of the simplest and kindest remembrances, such as the poorest and homeliest life may count up, and beside which, in the quiet hours of memory, all artificial triumphs pale, and disappear, for they are never quenched by time or distance, being founded on the affections, and so far heavenly.

CHAPTER XLV

A CHAPTER-FULL OF LOVERS

We had about this time a pleasant and quite unexpected visit from Lord Ilbury. He had come to pay his respects, understanding that my uncle Silas was sufficiently recovered to see visitors. 'And I think I'll run up-stairs first, and see him, if he admits me, and then I have ever so long a message from my sister, Mary, for you and Miss Millicent; but I had better dispose of my business first—don't you think so?—and I shall return in a few minutes.'

And as he spoke our tremulous old butler returned to say that Uncle Silas would be happy to see him. So he departed; and you can't think how pleasant our homely sitting-room looked with his coat and stick in it—guarantees of his return.

'Do you think, Milly, he is going to speak about the timber, you know, that Cousin Knollys spoke of? I do hope not.'

'So do I,' said Milly. 'I wish he'd stayed a bit longer with us first, for if he does, father will sure to turn him out of doors, and we'll see no more of him.'

'Exactly, my dear Milly; and he's so pleasant and good-natured.'

'And he likes you awful well, he does.'

'I'm sure he likes us both equally, Milly; he talked a great deal to you at Elverston, and used to ask you so often to sing those two pretty Lancashire ballads,' I said; 'but you know when you were at your controversies and religious exercises in the window, with that pillar of the church, the Rev. Spriggs Biddlepen—'

'Get awa' wi' your nonsense, Maud; how could I help answering when he dodged me up and down my Testament and catechism?—an I 'most hate him, I tell you, and Cousin Knollys, you're such fools, I do. And whatever you say, the lord likes you uncommon, and well you know it, ye hussy.'

'I know no such thing; and you don't think it, *you* hussy, and I really don't care who likes me or who doesn't, except my relations; and I make the lord a present to you, if you'll have him.'

In this strain were we talking when he re-entered the room, a little sooner than we had expected to see him.

Milly, who, you are to recollect, was only in process of reformation, and still retained something of the Derbyshire dairymaid, gave me a little clandestine pinch on the arm just as he made his appearance.

'I just refused a present from her,' said odious Milly, in answer to his enquiring look, 'because I knew she could not spare it.'

The effect of all this was that I blushed one of my overpowering blushes. People told me they became me very much; I hope so, for the misfortune was frequent; and I think nature owed me that compensation.

'It places you both in a most becoming light,' said Lord Ilbury, quite innocently. 'I really don't know which most to admire—the generosity of the offer or of the refusal.'

'Well, it *was* kind, if you but knew. I'm 'most tempted to tell him,' said Milly.

I checked her with a really angry look, and said, 'Perhaps you have not observed it; but I really think, for a sensible person, my cousin Milly here talks more nonsense than any twenty other girls.'

'A twenty-girl power! That's an immense compliment. I've the greatest respect for nonsense, I owe it so much; and I really think if nonsense were banished, the earth would grow insupportable.'

'Thank you, Lord Ilbury,' said Milly, who had grown quite easy in his company during our long visit at Elverston; 'and I tell you, Miss Maud, if you grow saucy, I'll accept your present, and what will you say then?'

'I really don't know; but just now I want to ask Lord Ilbury how he thinks my uncle looks; neither I nor Milly have seen him since his illness.'

'Very much weaker, I think; but he may be gaining strength. Still, as my business was not quite pleasant, I thought it better to postpone it, and if you think it would be right, I'll write to Doctor Bryerly to ask him to postpone the discussion for a little time.'

I at once assented, and thanked him; indeed, if I had had my way, the subject should never have been mentioned, I felt so hardhearted and rapacious; but Lord Ilbury explained that the trustees were constrained by the provisions of the will, and that I really had no power to release them; and I hoped that Uncle Silas also understood all this.

'And now,' said he, 'we've returned to Grange, my sister and I, and it is nearer than Elverston, so that we are really neighbours; and Mary wants Lady Knollys to fix a time she owes us a visit, you know—and you really must come at the same time; it will be so very pleasant, the same party exactly meeting in a new scene; and we have not half explored our neighbourhood; and I've got down all those Spanish engravings I told you of, and the Venetian missals, and all the rest. I think I remember very accurately the things you were most interested by, and they're all there; and really you must promise, you and Miss Millicent Ruthyn. And I forgot to mention—you know you complained that you were ill supplied with books, so Mary thought you would allow her to share her supply—they are the new books, you know—and when you have read yours, you and she can exchange.'

What girl was ever quite frank about her likings? I don't think I was more of a cheat than others; but I never could tell of myself. It is quite true that this duplicity and reserve seldom deceives. Our hypocrisies are forced upon some of our sex by the acuteness and vigilance of all in this field of enquiry; but if we are sly, we are also lynx-eyed, capital detectives, most ingenious in fitting together the bits and dovetails of a cumulative case; and in those affairs of love and liking, have a terrible exploratory instinct, and so, for the most part, when detected we are found out not only to be in love, but to be rogues moreover.

Lady Mary was very kind; but had Lady Mary of her own mere motion taken all this trouble? Was there no more energetic influence at the bottom of that welcome chest of books, which arrived only half an hour later? The circulating library of those days was not the epidemic and ubiquitous influence to which it has grown; and there were many places where it could not find you out.

Altogether that evening Bartram had acquired a peculiar beauty—a bright and mellow glow, in which even its gate-posts and wheelbarrow were interesting, and next day came a little cloud—Dudley appeared.

'You may be sure he wants money,' said Milly. 'He and father had words this morning.'

He took a chair at our luncheon, found fault with everything in his own laconic dialect, ate a good deal notwithstanding, and was sulky, and with Milly snappish. To me, on the contrary, when Milly went into the hall, he was mild and whimpering, and disposed to be confidential.

'There's the Governor says he hasn't a bob! Danged if I know how an old fellah in his bed-room muddles away money at that rate. I don't suppose he thinks I can git along without tin, and he knows them trustees won't gi'e me a tizzy till they get what they calls an opinion—dang 'em! Bryerly says he doubts it must all go under settlement. They'll settle me nicely if they do; and Governor knows all about it, and won't gi'e me a danged brass farthin', an' me wi' bills to pay, an' lawyers—dang 'em—writing letters. He knows summat o' that hisself, does Governor; and he might ha' consideration a bit for his own flesh and blood, *I* say. But he never does nout for none but hisself. I'll sell his books and his jewels next fit he takes—that's how I'll fit him.'

This amiable young man, glowering, with his elbows on the table and his fingers in his great whiskers, followed his homily, where clergymen append the blessing, with a muttered variety of very different matter.

'Now, Maud,' said he, pathetically, leaning back suddenly in his chair, with all his conscious beauty and misfortunes in his face, 'is not it hard lines?'

I thought the appeal was going to shape itself into an application for money; but it did not.

'I never know'd a reel beauty—first-chop, of course, I mean—that wasn't kind along of it, and I'm a fellah as can't git along without sympathy—that's why I say it—an' isn't it hard lines? Now, *say* it's hard lines—*haint* it, Maud?'

I did not know exactly what hard lines meant, but I said—

'I suppose it is very disagreeable.'

And with this concession, not caring to hear any more in the same vein, I rose, intending to take my departure.

'No, that's jest it. I knew ye'd say it, Maud. Ye're a kind lass—ye be—'tis in yer pretty face. I like ye awful, I do—there's not a handsomer lass in Liverpool nor Lunnon itself—*no* where.'

He had seized my hand, and trying to place his arm about my waist, essayed that salute which I had so narrowly escaped on my first introduction.

'*Don't*, sir,' I exclaimed in high indignation, escaping at the same moment from his grasp.

'No offence, lass; no harm, Maud; you must not be so shy—we're cousins, you know—an' I wouldn't hurt ye, Maud, no more nor I'd knock my head off. I wouldn't.'

I did not wait to hear the rest of his tender protestations, but, without showing how nervous I was, I glided out of the room quietly, making an orderly retreat, the more meritorious as I heard him call after me persuasively—'Come back, Maud. What are ye afeard on, lass? Come back, I say—do now; there's a good wench.'

As Milly and I were taking our walk that day, in the direction of the Windmill Wood, to which, in consequence perhaps of some secret order, we had now free access, we saw Beauty, for the first time since her illness, in the little yard, throwing grain to the poultry.

'How do you find yourself to-day, Meg? I am *very* glad to see you able to be about again; but I hope it is not too soon.'

We were standing at the barred gate of the little enclosure, and quite close to Meg, who, however, did not choose to raise her head, but, continuing to shower her grain and potato-skins among her hens and chickens, said in a low tone—

'Father baint in sight? Look jist round a bit and say if ye see him.'

But Dickon's dusky red costume was nowhere visible.

So Meg looked up, pale and thin, and with her old grave, observant eyes, and she said quietly—

"Tisn't that I'm not glad to see ye; but if father was to spy me talking friendly wi' ye, now that I'm hearty, and you havin' no more call to me, he'd be all'ays a watching and thinkin' I was tellin' o' tales, and 'appen he'd want me to worrit ye for money, Miss Maud; an' 'tisn't here he'd spend it, but in the Feltram pottusses, he would, and we want for nothin' that's good for us. But that's how 'twould be, an' he'd all'ays be a jawing and a lickin' of I; so don't mind me, Miss Maud, and 'appen I might do ye a good turn some day.'

A few days after this little interview with Meg, as Milly and I were walking briskly—for it was a clear frosty day—along the pleasant slopes of the sheep-walk, we were overtaken by Dudley Ruthyn. It was not a pleasant surprise. There was this mitigation, however: we were on foot, and he driving in a dog-cart along the track leading to the moor, with his dogs and gun. He brought his horse for a moment to a walk, and with a careless nod to me, removing his short pipe from his mouth, he said—

'Governor's callin' for ye, Milly; and he told me to send you slick home to him if I saw you, and I think he'll gi'e ye some money; but ye better take him while he's in the humour, lass, or mayhap ye'll go long without.'

And with those words, apparently intent on his game, he nodded again, and, pipe in mouth, drove at a quick trot over the slope of the hill, and disappeared.

So I agreed to await Milly's return while she ran home, and rejoined me where I was. Away she ran, in high spirits, and I wandered listlessly about in search of some convenient spot to sit down upon, for I was a little tired.

She had not been gone five minutes, when I heard a step approaching, and looking round, saw the dog-cart close by, the horse browsing on the short grass, and Dudley Ruthyn within a few paces of me.

'Ye see, Maud, I've bin thinkin' why you're so vexed wi' me, an' I thought I'd jest come back an' ask ye what I may a' done to anger ye so; there's no sin in that, I think—is there?'

'I'm not angry. I did not say so. I hope that's enough,' I said, startled; and, notwithstanding my speech, *very* angry, for I felt instinctively that Milly's despatch homeward was a mere trick, and I the dupe of this coarse stratagem.

'Well then, if ye baint angry, so much the better, Maud. I only want to know why you're afeard o' me. I never struck a man foul, much less hurt a girl, in my days; besides, Maud, I likes ye too well to hurt ye. Dang it, lass, you're my cousin, ye know, and cousins is all'ays together and lovin' like, an' none says again' it.'

'I've nothing to explain—there *is* nothing to explain. I've been quite friendly,' I said, hurriedly.

'*Friendly!* Well, if there baint a cram! How can ye think it friendly, Maud, when ye won't a'most shake hands wi' me? It's enough to make a fellah sware, or cry a'most. Why d'ye like aggravatin' a poor devil? Now baint ye an ill-natured little puss, Maud, an' I likin' ye so well? You're the prettiest lass in Derbyshire; there's nothin' I wouldn't do for ye.'

And he backed his declaration with an oath.

'Be so good, then, as to re-enter your dog-cart and drive away,' I replied, very much incensed.

'Now, there it is again! Ye can't speak me civil. Another fellah'd fly out, an' maybe kiss ye for spite; but I baint that sort, I'm all for coaxin' and kindness, an' ye won't let me. What *be* you drivin' at, Maud?'

'I think I've said very plainly, sir, that I wish to be alone. You've *nothing* to say, except utter nonsense, and I've heard quite enough. Once for all, I beg, sir, that you will be so good as to leave me.'

'Well, now, look here, Maud; I'll do anything you like—burn me if I don't—if you'll only jest be kind to me, like cousins should. What did I ever do to vex you? If you think I like any lass better than you—some fellah at Elverston's bin talkin', maybe—it's nout but lies an' nonsense. Not but there's lots o' wenches likes me well enough, though I be a plain lad, and speaks my mind straight out.'

'I can't see that you are so frank, sir, as you describe; you have just played a shabby trick to bring about this absurd and most disagreeable interview.'

'And supposin' I did send that fool, Milly, out o' the way, to talk a bit wi' you here, where's the harm? Dang it, lass, ye mustn't be too hard. Didn't I say I'd do whatever ye wished?'

'And you *won't*,' said I.

'Ye mean to get along out o' this? Well, now, I *will*. There! No use, of course, askin' you to kiss and be friends, before I go, as cousins should. Well, don't be riled, lass, I'm not askin' it; only mind, I do like you awful, and 'appen I'll find ye in better humour another time. Good-bye, Maud; I'll make ye like me at last.'

And with these words, to my comfort, he addressed himself to his horse and pipe, and was soon honestly on his way to the moor.

CHAPTER XLVI

THE RIVALS

All the time that Dudley chose to persecute me with his odious society, I continued to walk at a brisk pace toward home, so that I had nearly reached the house when Milly met me, with a note which had arrived for me by the post, in her hand.

'Here, Milly, are more verses. He is a very persevering poet, whoever he is.' So I broke the seal; but this time it was prose. And the first words were 'Captain Oakley!'

I confess to an odd sensation as these remarkable words met my eye. It might possibly be a proposal. I did not wait to speculate, however, but read these sentences traced in the identical handwriting which had copied the lines with which I had been twice favoured.

'Captain Oakley presents his compliments to Miss Ruthyn, and trusts she will excuse his venturing to ask whether, during his short stay in Feltram, he might be permitted to pay his respects at Bartram-Haugh. He has been making a short visit to his aunt, and could not find himself so near without at least attempting to renew an acquaintance which he has never ceased to cherish in memory. If Miss Ruthyn would be so very good as to favour him with ever so short a reply to the question he ventures most respectfully to ask, her decision would reach him at the Hall Hotel, Feltram.'

'Well, he's a roundabout fellah, anyhow. Couldn't he come up and see you if he wanted to? They poeters, they do love writing long yarns—don't they?' And with this reflection, Milly took the note and read it through again.

'It's jolly polite anyhow, isn't it Maud?' said Milly, who had conned it over, and accepted it as a model composition.

I must have been, I think, naturally a rather shrewd girl; and considering how very little I had seen of the world—nothing in fact—I often wonder now at the sage conclusions at which I arrived.

Were I to answer this handsome and cunning fool according to his folly, in what position should I find myself? No doubt my reply would induce a rejoinder, and that compel another note from me, and that invite yet another from him; and however his might improve in warmth, they were sure not to abate. Was it his impertinent plan, with this show of respect and ceremony, to drag me into a clandestine correspondence? Inexperienced girl as I was, I fired at the idea of becoming his dupe, and fancying, perhaps, that there was more in merely answering his note than it would have amounted to, I said—

'That kind of thing may answer very well with button-makers, but ladies don't like it. What would your papa think of it if he found that I had been writing to him, and seeing him without his permission? If he wanted to see me he could have'—(I really did not know exactly what he could have done)—'he could have timed his visit to Lady Knollys differently; at all events, he has no right to place me in an embarrassing situation, and I am certain Cousin Knollys would say so; and I think his note both shabby and impertinent.'

Decision was not with me an intellectual process. When quite cool I was the most undecided of mortals, but once my feelings were excited I was prompt and bold.

'I'll give the note to Uncle Silas,' I said, quickening my pace toward home; 'he'll know what to do.'

But Milly, who, I fancy, had no objection to the little romance which the young officer proposed, told me that she could not see her father, that he was ill, and not speaking to anyone.

'And arn't ye making a plaguy row about nothin'? I lay a guinea if ye had never set eyes on Lord Ilbury you'd a told him to come, and see ye, an' welcome.'

'Don't talk like a fool, Milly. You never knew me do anything deceitful. Lord Ilbury has no more to do with it, you know very well, than the man in the moon.'

I was altogether very indignant. I did not speak another word to Milly. The proportions of the house are so great, that it is a much longer walk than you would suppose from the hall-door to Uncle Silas's room. But I did not cool all that way; and it was not till I had just reached the lobby, and saw the sour, jealous face, and high caul of old Wyat, and felt the influence of that neighbourhood, that I paused to reconsider. I fancied there was a cool consciousness of success behind all the deferential phraseology of Captain Oakley, which nettled me extremely. No; there could be no doubt. I tapped softly at the door.

'What is it *now*, Miss?' snarled the querulous old woman, with her shrivelled fingers on the door-handle.

'Can I see my uncle for a moment?'

'He's tired, and not a word from him all day long.'

'Not ill, though?'

'Awful bad in the night,' said the old crone, with a sudden savage glare in my face, as if *I* had brought it about.

'Oh! I'm very sorry. I had not heard a word of it.'

'No one does but old Wyat. There's Milly there never asks neither—his own child!'

'Weakness, or what?'

'One o' them fits. He'll slide awa' in one o' them some day, and no one but old Wyat to know nor ask word about it; that's how 'twill be.'

'Will you please hand him this note, if he is well enough to look at it, and say I am at the door?'

She took it with a peevish nod and a grunt, closing the door in my face, and in a few minutes returned—

'Come in wi' ye,' said Dame Wyat, and I appeared.

Uncle Silas, who, after his nightly horror or vision, lay extended on a sofa, with his faded yellow silk dressing-gown about him, his long white hair hanging toward the ground, and that wild and feeble smile lighting his face—a glimmer I feared to look upon—his long thin arms lay by his sides, with hands and fingers that stirred not, except when now and then, with a feeble motion, he wet his temples and forehead with eau de Cologne from a glass saucer placed beside him.

'Excellent girl! dutiful ward and niece!' murmured the oracle; 'heaven reward you—your frank dealing is your own safety and my peace. Sit you down, and say who is this Captain Oakley, when you made his acquaintance, what his age, fortune, and expectations, and who the aunt he mentions.'

Upon all these points I satisfied him as fully as I was able.

'Wyat—the white drops,' he called, in a thin, stern tone. 'I'll write a line presently. I can't see visitors, and, of course, you can't receive young captains before you've come out. Farewell! God bless you, dear.'

Wyat was dropping the 'white' restorative into a wine-glass and the room was redolent of ether. I was glad to escape. The figures and whole *mise en scène* were unearthly.

'Well, Milly,' I said, as I met her in the hall, 'your papa is going to write to him.'

I sometimes wonder whether Milly was right, and how I should have acted a few months earlier.

Next day whom should we meet in the Windmill Wood but Captain Oakley. The spot where this interesting *rencontre* occurred was near that ruinous bridge on my sketch of which I had received so many compliments. It was so great a surprise that I had not time to recollect my indignation, and, having received him very affably, I found it impossible, during our brief interview, to recover my lost altitude.

After our greetings were over, and some compliments neatly made, he said—

'I had such a curious note from Mr. Silas Ruthyn. I am sure he thinks me a very impertinent fellow, for it was really anything but inviting—extremely rude, in fact. But I could not quite see that because he does not want me to invade his bed-room—an incursion I never dreamed of—I was not to present myself to you, who had already honoured me with your acquaintance, with the sanction of those who were most interested in your welfare, and who were just as well qualified as he, I fancy, to say who were qualified for such an honour.'

'My uncle, Mr. Silas Ruthyn, you are aware, is my guardian; and this is my cousin, his daughter.'

This was an opportunity of becoming a little lofty, and I improved it. He raised his hat and bowed to Milly.

'I'm afraid I've been very rude and stupid. Mr. Ruthyn, of course, has a perfect right to—to—in fact, I was not the least aware that I had the honour of so near a relation's—a—a—and what exquisite scenery you have! I think this country round Feltram particularly fine; and this Bartram-Haugh is, I venture to say, about the very most beautiful spot in this beautiful region. I do assure you I am tempted beyond measure to make Feltram and the Hall Hotel my head-quarters for at least a week. I only regret the foliage; but your trees show wonderfully, even in winter, so many of them have got that ivy about them. They say it spoils trees, but it certainly beautifies them. I have just ten days' leave unexpired; I wish I could induce you to advise me how to apply them. What shall I do, Miss Ruthyn?'

'I am the worst person in the world to make plans, even for myself, I find it so troublesome. What do you say? Suppose you try Wales or Scotland, and climb up some of those fine mountains that look so well in winter?'

'I should much prefer Feltram. I so wish you would recommend *it*. What is this pretty plant?'

'We call that Maud's myrtle. She planted it, and it's very pretty when it's full in blow,' said Milly.

Our visit to Elverston had been of immense use to us both.

'Oh! planted by *you?*' he said, very softly, with a momentary corresponding glance. 'May I—ever so little—just a leaf?'

And without waiting for permission, he held a sprig of it next his waistcoat.

'Yes, it goes very prettily with those buttons. They are *very* pretty buttons; are not they, Milly? A present, a souvenir, I dare say?'

This was a terrible hit at the button-maker, and I thought he looked a little oddly at me, but my countenance was so 'bewitchingly simple' that I suppose his suspicions were allayed.

Now, it was very odd of me, I must confess, to talk in this way, and to receive all those tender allusions from a gentleman about whom I had spoken and felt so sharply only the evening before. But Bartram was abominably lonely. A civilised person was a valuable waif or stray in that region of the picturesque and the brutal; and to my lady reader especially, because she will probably be hardest upon me, I put it—can you not recollect any such folly in your own past life? Can you not in as many minutes call to mind at least six similar inconsistencies of your own practising? For my part, I really can't see the advantage of being the weaker sex if we are always to be as strong as our masculine neighbours.

There was, indeed, no revival of the little sentiment which I had once experienced. When these things once expire, I do believe they are as hard to revive as our dead lap-dogs, guinea-pigs, and parrots. It was my perfect coolness which enabled me to chat, I flatter myself, so agreeably with the refined Captain, who plainly thought me his captive, and was probably now and then thinking what was to be done to utilise that little bit of Bartram, or to beautify some other, when he should see fit to become its master, as we rambled over these wild but beautiful grounds.

It was just about then that Milly nudged me rather vehemently, and whispered 'Look there!'

I followed with mine the direction of her eyes, and saw my odious cousin, Dudley, in a flagrant pair of cross-barred peg-tops, and what Milly before her reformation used to call other 'slops' of corresponding atrocity, approaching our refined little party with great strides. I really think that Milly was very nearly ashamed of him. I certainly was. I had no apprehension, however, of the scene which was imminent.

The charming Captain mistook him probably for some rustic servant of the place, for he continued his agreeable remarks up to the very moment when Dudley, whose face was pale with anger, and whose rapid advance had not served to cool him, without recollecting to salute either Milly or me, accosted our elegant companion as follows:—

'By your leave, master, baint you summat in the wrong box here, don't you think?'

He had planted himself directly in his front, and looked unmistakably menacing.

'May I speak to him? Will you excuse me?' said the Captain blandly.

'Ow—ay, they'll excuse ye ready enough, I dessay; you're to deal wi' me though. Baint ye in the wrong box now?'

'I'm not conscious, sir, of being in a box at all,' replied the Captain, with severe disdain. 'It strikes me you are disposed to get up a row. Let us, if you please, get a little apart from the ladies if that is your purpose.'

'I mean to turn you out o' this the way ye came. If you make a row, so much the wuss for you, for I'll lick ye to fits.'

'Tell him not to fight,' whispered Milly; 'he'll a no chance wi' Dudley.'

I saw Dickon Hawkes grinning over the paling on which he leaned.

'Mr. Hawkes,' I said, drawing Milly with me toward that unpromising mediator, 'pray prevent unpleasantness and go between them.'

'An' git licked o' both sides? Rather not, Miss, thank ye,' grinned Dickon, tranquilly.

'Who are you, sir?' demanded our romantic acquaintance, with military sternness.

'I'll tell you who you are—you're Oakley, as stops at the Hall, that Governor wrote, over-night, not to dare show your nose inside the grounds. You're a half-starved cappen, come down here to look for a wife, and——'

Before Dudley could finish his sentence, Captain Oakley, than whose face no regimentals could possibly have been more scarlet, at that moment, struck with his switch at Dudley's handsome features.

I don't know how it was done—by some 'devilish cantrip slight.' A smack was heard, and the Captain lay on his back on the ground, with his mouth full of blood.

'How do ye like the taste o' that?' roared Dickon, from his post of observation.

In an instant Captain Oakley was on his feet again, hatless, looking quite frantic, and striking out at Dudley, who was ducking and dipping quite coolly, and again the same horrid sound, only this time it was double, like a quick postman's knock, and Captain Oakley was on the grass again.

'Tapped his smeller, by—!' thundered Dickon, with a roar of laughter.

'Come away, Milly—I'm growing ill,' said I.

'Drop it, Dudley, I tell ye; you'll kill him,' screamed Milly.

But the devoted Captain, whose nose, and mouth, and shirt-front formed now but one great patch of blood, and who was bleeding beside over one eye, dashed at him again.

I turned away. I felt quite faint, and on the point of crying, with mere horror.

'Hammer away at his knocker,' bellowed Dickon, in a frenzy of delight.

'He'll break it now, if it ain't already,' cried Milly, alluding, as I afterwards understood, to the Captain's Grecian nose.

'Brayvo, little un!' The Captain was considerably the taller.

Another smack, and, I suppose, Captain Oakley fell once more.

'Hooray! the dinner-service again, by ——,' roared Dickon. 'Stick to that. Over the same ground—subsoil, I say. He han't enough yet.'

In a perfect tremor of disgust, I was making as quick a retreat as I could, and as I did, I heard Captain Oakley shriek hoarsely—

'You're a d—— prizefighter; I can't box you.'

'I told ye I'd lick ye to fits,' hooted Dudley.

'But you're the son of a gentleman, and by —— you shall fight me *as* a gentleman.'

A yell of hooting laughter from Dudley and Dickon followed this sally.

'Gi'e my love to the Colonel, and think o' me when ye look in the glass—won't ye? An' so you're goin' arter all; well, follow what's left o' yer nose. Ye forgot some o' yer ivories, didn't ye, on th' grass?'

These and many similar jibes followed the mangled Captain in his retreat.

CHAPTER XLVII

DOCTOR BRYERLY REAPPEARS

No one who has not experienced it can imagine the nervous disgust and horror which such a spectacle as we had been forced in part to witness leaves upon the mind of a young person of my peculiar temperament.

It affected ever after my involuntary estimate of the principal actors in it. An exhibition of such thorough inferiority, accompanied by such a shock to the feminine sense of elegance, is not forgotten by any woman. Captain Oakley had been severely beaten by a smaller man. It was pitiable, but also undignified; and Milly's anxieties about his teeth and nose, though in a certain sense horrible, had also a painful suspicion of the absurd.

People say, on the other hand, that superior prowess, even in such barbarous contests, inspires in our sex an interest akin to admiration. I can positively say in my case it was quite the reverse. Dudley Ruthyn stood lower than ever in my estimation; for though I feared him more, it was by reason of these brutal and cold-blooded associations.

After this I lived in constant apprehension of being summoned to my uncle's room, and being called on for an explanation of my meeting with Captain Oakley, which, notwithstanding my perfect innocence, looked suspicious, but no such inquisition resulted. Perhaps he did not suspect me; or, perhaps, he thought, not in his haste, all women are liars, and did not care to hear what I might say. I rather lean to the latter interpretation.

The exchequer just now, I suppose, by some means, was replenished, for next morning Dudley set off upon one of his fashionable excursions, as poor Milly thought them, to Wolverhampton. And the same day Dr. Bryerly arrived.

Milly and I, from my room window, saw him step from his vehicle to the court-yard.

A lean man, with sandy hair and whiskers, was in the chaise with him. Dr. Bryerly descended in the unchangeable black suit that always looked new and never fitted him.

The Doctor looked careworn, and older, I thought, by several years, than when I last saw him. He was not shown up to my uncle's room; on the contrary, Milly, who was more actively curious than I, ascertained that our tremulous butler informed him that my uncle was not sufficiently well for an interview. Whereupon Dr. Bryerly had pencilled a note, the reply to which was a message from Uncle Silas, saying that he would be happy to see him in five minutes.

As Milly and I were conjecturing what it might mean, and before the five minutes had expired, Mary Quince entered.

'Wyat bid me tell you, Miss, your uncle wants you *this minute*.'

When I entered his room, Uncle Silas was seated at the table, with his desk before him. He looked up. Could anything be more dignified, suffering, and venerable?

'I sent for you, dear,' he said very gently, extending his thin, white hand, and taking mine, which he held affectionately while he spoke, 'because I desire to have no secrets, and wish you thoroughly to know all that concerns your own interests while subject to my guardianship; and I am happy to think, my beloved niece, that you requite my candour. Oh, here is the gentleman. Sit down, dear.'

Doctor Bryerly was advancing, as it seemed, to shake hands with Uncle Silas, who, however, rose with a severe and haughty air, not the least over-acted, and made him a slow, ceremonious bow. I wondered how the homely Doctor could confront so tranquilly that astounding statue of hauteur.

A faint and weary smile, rather sad than comtemptuous, was the only sign he showed of feeling his repulse.

'How do *you* do, Miss?' he said, extending his hand, and greeting me after his ungallant fashion, as if it were an afterthought.

'I think I may as well take a chair, sir,' said Doctor Bryerly, sitting down serenely, near the table, and crossing his ungainly legs.

My uncle bowed.

'You understand the nature of the business, sir. Do you wish Miss Ruthyn to remain?' asked Doctor Bryerly.

'I *sent* for her, sir,' replied my uncle, in a very gentle and sarcastic tone, a smile on his thin lips, and his strangely-contorted eyebrows raised for a moment contemptuously. 'This gentleman, my dear Maud, thinks proper to insinuate that I am robbing you. It surprises me a little, and, no doubt, you—I've nothing to conceal, and wished you to be present while he favours me more particularly with his views. I'm right, I think, in describing it as *robbery*, sir?'

'Why,' said Doctor Bryerly thoughtfully, for he was treating the matter as one of right, and not of feeling, 'it would be, certainly, taking that which does not belong to you, and converting it to your own use; but, at the worst, it would more resemble *thieving*, I think, than robbery.'

I saw Uncle Silas's lip, eyelid, and thin cheek quiver and shrink, as if with a thrill of tic-douloureux, as Doctor Bryerly spoke this unconsciously insulting answer. My uncle had, however, the self-command which is learned at the gaming-table. He shrugged, with a chilly, sarcastic, little laugh, and a glance at me.

'Your note says *waste*, I think, sir?'

'Yes, waste—the felling and sale of timber in the Windmill Wood, the selling of oak bark and burning of charcoal, as I'm informed,' said Bryerly, as sadly and quietly as a man might relate a piece of intelligence from the newspaper.

'Detectives? or private spies of your own—or, perhaps, my servants, bribed with my poor brother's money? A very high-minded procedure.'

'Nothing of the kind, sir.'

My uncle sneered.

'I mean, sir, there has been no undue canvass for evidence, and the question is simply one of right; and it is our duty to see that this inexperienced young lady is not defrauded.'

'By her own uncle?'

'By anyone,' said Doctor Bryerly, with a natural impenetrability that excited my admiration.

'Of course you come armed with an opinion?' said my smiling uncle, insinuatingly.

'The case is before Mr. Serjeant Grinders. These bigwigs don't return their cases sometimes so quickly as we could wish.'

'Then you have *no* opinion?' smiled my uncle.

'My solicitor is quite clear upon it; and it seems to me there can be no question raised, but for form's sake.'

'Yes, for form's sake you take one, and in the meantime, upon a nice question of law, the surmises of a thick-headed attorney and of an ingenious apoth—I beg pardon, physician—are sufficient warrant for telling my niece and ward, in my presence, that I am defrauding her!'

My uncle leaned back in his chair, and smiled with a contemptuous patience over Doctor Bryerly's head, as he spoke.

'I don't know whether I used that expression, sir, but I am speaking merely in a technical sense. I mean to say, that, whether by mistake or otherwise, you are exercising a power which you don't lawfully possess, and that the effect of that is to impoverish the estate, and, by so much as it benefits you, to wrong this young lady.'

'I'm a technical defrauder, I see, and your manner conveys the rest. I thank my God, sir, I am a *very* different man from what I once was.' Uncle Silas was speaking in a low tone, and with extraordinary deliberation. 'I remember when I should have certainly knocked you down, sir, or *tried* it, at least, for a great deal less.'

'But seriously, sir, what *do* you propose?' asked Doctor Bryerly, sternly and a little flushed, for I think the old man was stirred within him; and though he did not raise his voice, his manner was excited.

'I propose to defend my rights, sir,' murmured Uncle Silas, very grim. 'I'm not without an opinion, though you are.'

You seem to think, sir, that I have a pleasure in annoying you; you are quite wrong. I hate annoying anyone—constitutionally—I *hate* it; but don't you see, sir, the position I'm placed in? I wish I could please everyone, and do my duty.'

Uncle Silas bowed and smiled.

'I've brought with me the Scotch steward from Tolkingden, *your* estate, Miss, and if you let us we will visit the spot and make a note of what we observe, that is, assuming that you admit waste, and merely question our law.'

'If you please, sir, you and your Scotchman shall do *no such thing*; and, bearing in mind that I neither deny nor admit anything, you will please further never more to present yourself, under any pretext whatsoever, either in this house or on the grounds of Bartram-Haugh, during my lifetime.'

Uncle Silas rose up with the same glassy smile and scowl, in token that the interview was ended.

'Good-bye, sir,' said Doctor Bryerly, with a sad and thoughtful air, and hesitating for a moment, he said to me, 'Do you think, Miss, you could afford me a word in the hall?'

'Not a word, sir,' snarled Uncle Silas, with a white flash from his eyes.

There was a pause.

'Sit where you are, Maud.'

Another pause.

'If you have anything to say to my ward, sir, you will please to say it *here*.'

Doctor Bryerly's dark and homely face was turned on me with an expression of unspeakable compassion.

'I was going to say, that if you think of any way in which I can be of the least service, Miss, I'm ready to act, that's all; mind, *any* way.'

He hesitated, looking at me with the same expression as if he had something more to say; but he only repeated—

'That's all, Miss.'

'Won't you shake hands, Doctor Bryerly, before you go?' I said, eagerly approaching him.

Without a smile, with the same sad anxiety in his face, with his mind, as it seemed to me, on something else, and irresolute whether to speak it or be silent, he took my fingers in a very cold hand, and holding it so, and slowly shaking it, his grave and troubled glance unconsciously rested on Uncle Silas's face, while in a sad tone and absent way he said—

'Good-bye, Miss.'

From before that sad gaze my uncle averted his strange eyes quickly, and looked, oddly, to the window.

In a moment more Doctor Bryerly let my hand go with a sigh, and with an abrupt little nod to me, he left the room; and I heard that dismallest of sounds, the retreating footsteps of a true friend, *lost*.

'Lead us not into temptation; if we pray so, we must not mock the eternal Majesty of Heaven by walking into temptation of our own accord.'

This oracular sentence was not uttered by my uncle until Doctor Bryerly had been gone at least five minutes.

'I've forbid him my house, Maud—first, because his perfectly unconscious insolence tries my patience nearly beyond endurance; and again, because I have heard unfavourable reports of him. On the question of right which he disputes, I am perfectly informed. I am your tenant, my dear niece; when I am gone you will learn how *scrupulous* I have been; you will see how, under the pressure of the most agonising pecuniary difficulties, the terrific penalty of a misspent youth, I have been careful never by a hair's breadth to transgress the strict line of my legal privileges; alike, as your tenant, Maud, and as your guardian; how, amid frightful agitations, I have kept myself, by the miraculous strength and grace vouchsafed me—*pure*.

'The world,' he resumed after a short pause, 'has no faith in any man's conversion; it never forgets what he was, it never believes him anything better, it is an inexorable and stupid judge. What I was I will describe in blacker terms, and with more heartfelt detestation, than my traducers—a reckless prodigal, a godless profligate. Such I was; what I am, I am. If I had no hope beyond this world, of all men most miserable; but with that hope, a sinner saved.'

Then he waxed eloquent and mystical. I think his Swedenborgian studies had crossed his notions of religion with strange lights. I never could follow him quite in these excursions into the region of symbolism. I only recollect that he talked of the deluge and the waters of Mara, and said, 'I am washed—I am sprinkled,' and then, pausing, bathed his thin temples and forehead with eau de Cologne; a process which was, perhaps, suggested by his imagery of sprinkling and so forth.

Thus refreshed, he sighed and smiled, and passed to the subject of Doctor Bryerly.

'Of Doctor Bryerly, I know that he is sly, that he loves money, was born poor, and makes nothing by his profession. But he possesses many thousand pounds, under my poor brother's will, of *your money*; and he has glided with, of course a modest "nolo episcopari," into the acting trusteeship, with all its multitudinous opportunities, of your immense property. That is not doing so badly for a visionary Swedenborgian. Such a man *must* prosper. But if he expected to make money of me, he is disappointed. Money, however, he will make of his trusteeship, as you will see. It is a dangerous resolution. But if he will seek the life of Dives, the worst I wish him is to find the death of Lazarus. But whether, like Lazarus, he be borne of angels into Abraham's bosom, or, like the rich man, only dies and is buried, and *the rest*, neither living nor dying do I desire his company.'

Uncle Silas here seemed suddenly overtaken by exhaustion. He leaned back with a ghastly look, and his lean features glistened with the dew of faintness. I screamed for Wyat. But he soon recovered sufficiently to smile his odd smile, and with it and his frown, nodded and waved me away.

CHAPTER XLVIII

QUESTION AND ANSWER

My uncle, after all, was not ill that day, after the strange fashion of his malady, be it what it might. Old Wyat repeated in her sour laconic way that there was 'nothing to speak of amiss with him.' But there remained with me a sense of pain and fear. Doctor Bryerly, notwithstanding my uncle's sarcastic reflections, remained, in my estimation, a true and wise friend. I had all my life been accustomed to rely upon others, and here, haunted by many unavowed and ill-defined alarms and doubts, the disappearance of an active and able friend caused my heart to sink.

Still there remained my dear Cousin Monica, and my pleasant and trusted friend, Lord Ilbury; and in less than a week arrived an invitation from Lady Mary to the Grange, for me and Milly, to meet Lady Knollys. It was accompanied, she told me, by a note from Lord Ilbury to my uncle, supporting her request; and in the afternoon I received a message to attend my uncle in his room.

'An invitation from Lady Mary Carysbroke for you and Milly to meet Monica Knollys; have you received it?' asked my uncle, so soon as I was seated. Answered in the affirmative, he continued—

'Now, Maud Ruthyn, I expect the truth from you; I have been frank, so shall you. Have you ever heard me spoken ill of by Lady Knollys?'

I was quite taken aback.

I felt my cheeks flushing. I was returning his fierce cold gaze with a stupid stare, and remained dumb.

'Yes, Maud, you *have*.'

I looked down in silence.

'I *know* it; but it is right you should answer; have you or have you not?'

I had to clear my voice twice or thrice. There was a kind of spasm in my throat.

'I am trying to recollect,' I said at last.

'*Do* recollect,' he replied imperiously.

There was a little interval of silence. I would have given the world to be, on any conditions, anywhere else in the world.

'Surely, Maud, you don't wish to deceive your guardian? Come, the question is a plain one, and I know the truth already. I ask you again—have you ever heard me spoken ill of by Lady Knollys?'

'Lady Knollys,' I said, half articulately,' speaks very freely, and often half in jest; but,' I continued, observing something menacing in his face, 'I have heard her express disapprobation of some things you have done.'

'Come, Maud,' he continued, in a stern, though still a low key, 'did she not insinuate that charge—then, I suppose, in a state of incubation, the other day presented here full-fledged, with beak and claws, by that scheming apothecary—the statement that I was defrauding you by cutting down timber upon the grounds?'

'She certainly did mention the circumstance; but she also argued that it might have been through ignorance of the extent of your rights.'

'Come, come, Maud, you must not prevaricate, girl. I *will* have it. Does she not habitually speak disparagingly of me, in your presence, and *to* you? *Answer*.'

I hung my head.

'Yes or no?'

'Well, perhaps so—yes,' I faltered, and burst into tears.

'There, don't cry; it may well shock you. Did she not, to your knowledge, say the same things in presence of my child Millicent? I know it, I repeat—there is no use in hesitating; and I command you to answer.'

Sobbing, I told the truth.

'Now sit still, while I write my reply.'

He wrote, with the scowl and smile so painful to witness, as he looked down upon the paper, and then he placed the note before me—

'Read that, my dear.'

It began—

'MY DEAR LADY KNOLLYS.—You have favoured me with a note, adding your request to that of Lord Ilbury, that I should permit my ward and my daughter to avail themselves of Lady Mary's invitation. Being perfectly cognisant of the ill-feeling you have always and unaccountably cherished toward me, and also of the terms in which you have had the delicacy and the conscience to speak of me before and to my child and my ward, I can only express my amazement at the modesty of your request, while peremptorily refusing it. And I shall conscientiously adopt effectual measures to prevent your ever again having an opportunity of endeavouring to destroy my influence and authority over my ward and my child, by direct or insinuated slander.

'Your defamed and injured kinsman,
SILAS RUTHYN.'

I was stunned; yet what could I plead against the blow that was to isolate me? I wept aloud, with my hands clasped, looking on the marble face of the old man.

Without seeming to hear, he folded and sealed his note, and then proceeded to answer Lord Ilbury.

When that note was written, he placed it likewise before me, and I read it also through. It simply referred him to Lady Knollys 'for an explanation of the unhappy circumstances which compelled him to decline an invitation which it would have made his niece and his daughter so happy to accept.'

'You see, my dear Maud, how frank I am with you,' he said, waving the open note, which I had just read, slightly before he folded it. 'I think I may ask you to reciprocate my candour.'

Dismissed from this interview, I ran to Milly, who burst into tears from sheer disappointment, so we wept and wailed together. But in my grief I think there was more reason.

I sat down to the dismal task of writing to my dear Lady Knollys. I implored her to make her peace with my uncle. I told her how frank he had been with me, and how he had shown me his sad reply to her letter. I told her of the interview to which he had himself invited me with Dr. Bryerly; how little disturbed he was by the accusation—no sign of guilt; quite the contrary, perfect confidence. I implored of her to think the best, and remembering my isolation, to accomplish a reconciliation with Uncle Silas. 'Only think,' I wrote, 'I only nineteen, and two years of solitude before me. What a separation!' No broken merchant ever signed the schedule of his bankruptcy with a heavier heart than did I this letter.

The griefs of youth are like the wounds of the gods—there is an ichor which heals the scars from which it flows: and thus Milly and I consoled ourselves, and next day enjoyed our ramble, our talk and readings, with a wonderful resignation to the inevitable.

Milly and I stood in the relation of *Lord Duberly* to *Doctor Pangloss*. I was to mend her 'cackleology,' and the occupation amused us both. I think at the bottom of our submission to destiny lurked a hope that Uncle Silas, the inexorable, would relent, or that Cousin Monica, that siren, would win and melt him to her purpose.

Whatever comfort, however, I derived from the absence of Dudley was not to be of very long duration; for one morning, as I was amusing myself alone, with a piece of worsted work, thinking, and just at that moment not unpleasantly, of many things, my cousin Dudley entered the room.

'Back again, like a bad halfpenny, ye see. And how a' ye bin ever since, lass? Purely, I warrant, be your looks. I'm jolly glad to see ye, I am; no cattle going like ye, Maud.'

'I think I must ask you to let go my hand, as I can't continue my work,' I said, very stiffly, hoping to chill his enthusiasm a little.

'Anything to pleasure ye, Maud, 'tain't in my heart to refuse ye nout. I a'bin to Wolverhampton, lass—jolly row there—and run over to Leamington; a'most broke my neck, faith, wi' a borrowed horse arter the dogs; ye would na care, Maud, if I broke my neck, would ye? Well, 'appen, jest a little,' he good-naturedly supplied, as I was silent.

'Little over a week since I left here, by George; and to me it's half the almanac like; can ye guess the reason, Maud?'

'Have you seen your sister, Milly, or your father, since your return?' I asked coldly.

'*They'll* keep, Maud, never mind 'em; it be you I want to see—it be you I wor thinkin' on a' the time. I tell ye, lass, I'm all'ays a thinkin' on ye.'

'I think you ought to go and see your father; you have been away, you say, some time. I don't think it is respectful,' I said, a little sharply.

'If ye bid me go I'd a'most go, but I could na quite; there's nout on earth I would na do for you, Maud, excep' leaving you.'

'And that,' I said, with a petulant flush, 'is the only thing on earth I would ask you to do.'

'Blessed if you baint a blushin', Maud,' he drawled, with an odious grin.

His stupidity was proof against everything.

'It is *too* bad!' I muttered, with an indignant little pat of my foot and mimic stamp.

'Well, you lasses be queer cattle; ye're angry wi' me now, cos ye think I got into mischief—ye do, Maud; ye know't, ye buxsom little fool, down there at Wolverhampton; and jest for that ye're ready to turn me off again the minute I come back; 'tisn't fair.'

'I don't *understand* you, sir; and I *beg* that you'll leave me.'

'Now, didn't I tell ye about leavin' ye, Maud? 'tis the only thing I can't compass for yer sake. I'm jest a child in yere hands, I am, ye know. I can lick a big fellah to pot as limp as a rag, by George!'—(his oaths were not really so mild)—'ye see summat o' that t'other day. Well, don't be vexed, Maud; 'twas all along o' you; ye know, I wor a bit jealous, 'appen; but anyhow I can do it; and look at me here, jest a child, I say, in yer hands.'

'I wish you'd go away. Have you nothing to do, and no one to see? Why *can't* you leave me alone, sir?'

''Cos I can't, Maud, that's jest why; and I wonder, Maud, how can you be so ill-natured, when you see me like this; how can ye?'

'I wish Milly would come,' said I peevishly, looking toward the door.

'Well, I'll tell you how it is, Maud. I may as well have it out. I like you better than any lass that ever I saw, a deal; you're nicer by chalks; there's none like ye—there isn't; and I wish you'd have me. I ha'n't much tin—father's run through a deal, he's pretty well up a tree, ye know; but though I baint so rich as some folk, I'm a better man, 'appen; and if ye'd take a tidy lad, that likes ye awful, and 'id die for your sake, why here he is.'

'What can you mean, sir?' I exclaimed, rising in indignant bewilderment.

'I mean, Maud, if ye'll marry me, you'll never ha' cause to complain; I'll never let ye want for nout, nor gi'e ye a wry word.'

'Actually a proposal!' I ejaculated, like a person speaking in a dream.

I stood with my hand on the back of a chair, staring at Dudley; and looking, I dare say, as stupefied as I felt.

'There's a good lass, ye would na deny me,' said the odious creature, with one knee on the seat of the chair behind which I was standing, and attempting to place his arm lovingly round my neck.

This effectually roused me, and starting back, I stamped upon the ground with actual fury.

'What has there ever been, sir, in my conduct, words, or looks, to warrant this unparalleled audacity? But that you are as stupid as you are impertinent, brutal, and ugly, you must, long ago, sir, have seen how I dislike you. How dare you, sir? Don't presume to obstruct me; I'm going to my uncle.'

I had never spoken so violently to mortal before.

He in turn looked a little confounded; and I passed his extended but motionless arm with a quick and angry step.

He followed me a pace or two, however, before I reached the door, looking horridly angry, but stopped, and only swore after me some of those 'wry words' which I was never to have heard. I was myself, however, too much incensed, and moving at too rapid a pace, to catch their import; and I had knocked at my uncle's door before I began to collect my thoughts.

'Come in,' replied my uncle's voice, clear, thin, and peevish.

I entered and confronted him.

'Your son, sir, has insulted me.'

He looked at me with a cold curiosity steadly for a few seconds, as I stood panting before him with flaming cheeks.

'Insulted you?' repeated he. 'Egad, you surprise me!'

The ejaculation savoured of 'the old man,' to borrow his scriptural phrase, more than anything I had heard from him before.

'*How?*' he continued; 'how has Dudley *insulted* you, my dear child? Come, you're excited; sit down; take time, and tell me all about it. I did not know that Dudley was here.'

'I—he—it *is* an insult. He knew very well—he *must* know I dislike him; and he presumed to make a proposal of marriage to me.'

'O—o—oh!' exclaimed my uncle, with a prolonged intonation which plainly said, Is that the mighty matter?

He looked at me as he leaned back with the same steady curiosity, this time smiling, which somehow frightened me, and his countenance looked to me wicked, like the face of a witch, with a guilt I could not understand.

'And that is the amount of your complaint. He made you a formal proposal of marriage!'

'Yes; he proposed for me.'

As I cooled, I began to feel just a very little disconcerted, and a suspicion was troubling me that possibly an indifferent person might think that, having no more to complain of, my language was perhaps a little exaggerated, and my demeanour a little too tempestuous.

My uncle, I dare say, saw some symptoms of this misgiving, for, smiling still, he said—

'My dear Maud, however just, you appear to me a little cruel; you don't seem to remember how much you are yourself to blame; you have one faithful friend at least, whom I advise your consulting—I mean your looking-glass. The foolish fellow is young, quite ignorant in the world's ways. He is in love—desperately enamoured.

Aimer c'est craindre, et craindre c'est souffrir.

And suffering prompts to desperate remedies. We must not be too hard on a rough but romantic young fool, who talks according to his folly and his pain.'

CHAPTER XLIX

AN APPARITION

'But, after all,' he suddenly resumed, as if a new thought had struck him, 'is it quite such folly, after all? It really strikes me, dear Maud, that the subject may be worth a second thought. No, no, you won't refuse to hear me,' he said, observing me on the point of protesting. 'I am, of course, assuming that you are fancy free. I am assuming, too, that you don't care twopence about Dudley, and even that you fancy you dislike him. You know in that pleasant play, poor Sheridan—delightful fellow!—all our fine spirits are dead—he makes Mrs. Malaprop say there is nothing like beginning with a little aversion. Now, though in matrimony, of course, that is only a joke, yet in love, believe me, it is no such thing. His own marriage with Miss Ogle, I *know*, was a case in point. She expressed a positive horror of him at their first acquaintance; and yet, I believe, she would, a few months later, have died rather than not have married him.'

I was again about to speak, but with a smile he beckoned me into silence.

'There are two or three points you must bear in mind. One of the happiest privileges of your fortune is that you may, without imprudence, marry simply for love. There are few men in England who could offer you an estate comparable with that you already possess; or, in fact, appreciably increase the splendour of your fortune. If, therefore, he were in all other respects eligible, I can't see that his poverty would be an objection to weigh for one moment. He is quite a rough diamond. He has been, like many young men of the highest rank, too much given up to athletic sports—to that society which constitutes the aristocracy of the ring and the turf, and all that kind of thing. You see, I am putting all the worst points first. But I have known so many young men in my day, after a madcap career of a few years among prizefighters, wrestlers, and jockeys—learning their slang and affecting their manners—take up and cultivate the graces and the decencies. There was poor dear Newgate, many degrees lower in that kind of frolic, who, when he grew tired of it, became one of the most elegant and accomplished men in the House of Peers. Poor Newgate, he's gone, too! I could reckon up fifty of my early friends who all began like Dudley, and all turned out, more or less, like Newgate.'

At this moment came a knock at the door, and Dudley put in his head most inopportunely for the vision of his future graces and accomplishments.

'My good fellow,' said his father, with a sharp sort of playfulness, 'I happen to be talking about my son, and should rather not be overheard; you will, therefore, choose another time for your visit.'

Dudley hesitated gruffly at the door, but another look from his father dismissed him.

'And now, my dear, you are to remember that Dudley has fine qualities—the most affectionate son in his rough way that ever father was blessed with; most admirable qualities—indomitable courage, and a high sense of honour; and lastly, that he has the Ruthyn blood—the purest blood, I maintain it, in England.'

My uncle, as he said this, drew himself up a little, unconsciously, his thin hand laid lightly over his heart with a little patting motion, and his countenance looked so strangely dignified and melancholy, that in admiring contemplation of it I lost some sentences which followed next.

'Therefore, dear, naturally anxious that my boy should not be dismissed from home—as he must be, should you persevere in rejecting his suit—I beg that you will reserve your decision to this day fortnight, when I will with much pleasure hear what you may have to say on the subject. But till then, observe me, not a word.'

That evening he and Dudley were closeted for a long time. I suspect that he lectured him on the psychology of ladies; for a bouquet was laid beside my plate every morning at breakfast, which it must have been troublesome to get, for the conservatory at Bartram was a desert. In a few days more an anonymous green parrot arrived, in a gilt cage, with a little note in a clerk's hand, addressed to 'Miss Ruthyn (of Knowl), Bartram-Haugh,' &c. It contained only 'Directions for caring green parrot,' at the close of which, *underlined*, the words appeared—'The bird's name is Maud.'

The bouquets I invariably left on the table-cloth, where I found them—the bird I insisted on Milly's keeping as her property. During the intervening fortnight Dudley never appeared, as he used sometimes to do before, at luncheon, nor looked in at the window as we were at breakfast. He contented himself with one day placing himself in my way in the hall in his shooting accoutrements, and, with a clumsy, shuffling kind of respect, and hat in hand, he said—

'I think, Miss, I must a spoke uncivil t'other day. I was so awful put about, and didn't know no more nor a child what I was saying; and I wanted to tell ye I'm sorry for it, and I beg your pardon—very humble, I do.'

I did not know what to say. I therefore said nothing, but made a grave inclination, and passed on.

Two or three times Milly and I saw him at a little distance in our walks. He never attempted to join us. Once only he passed so near that some recognition was inevitable, and he stopped and in silence lifted his hat with an awkward respect. But although he did not approach us, he was ostentatious with a kind of telegraphic civility in the distance. He opened gates, he whistled his dogs to 'heel,' he drove away cattle, and then himself withdrew. I really think he watched us occasionally to render these services, for in this distant way we encountered him decidedly oftener than we used to do before his flattering proposal of marriage.

You may be sure that we discussed, Milly and I, that occurrence pretty constantly in all sorts of moods. Limited as had been her experience of human society, she very clearly saw *now* how far below its presentable level was her hopeful brother.

The fortnight sped swiftly, as time always does when something we dislike and shrink from awaits us at its close. I never saw Uncle Silas during that period. It may seem odd to those who merely read the report of our last interview, in which his manner had been more playful and his talk more trifling than in any other, that from it I had carried away a profounder sense of fear and insecurity than from any other. It was with a foreboding of evil and an awful dejection that on a very dark day, in Milly's room, I awaited the summons which I was sure would reach me from my punctual guardian.

As I looked from the window upon the slanting rain and leaden sky, and thought of the hated interview that awaited me, I pressed my hand to my troubled heart, and murmured, 'O that I had wings like a dove! then would I flee away, and be at rest.'

Just then the prattle of the parrot struck my ear. I looked round on the wire cage, and remembered the words, 'The bird's name is Maud.'

'Poor bird!' I said. 'I dare say, Milly, it longs to get out. If it were a native of this country, would not you like to open the window, and then the door of that cruel cage, and let the poor thing fly away?'

'Master wants Miss Maud,' said Wyat's disagreeable tones, at the half-open door.

I followed in silence, with the pressure of a near alarm at my heart, like a person going to an operation.

When I entered the room, my heart beat so fast that I could hardly speak. The tall form of Uncle Silas rose before me, and I made him a faltering reverence.

He darted from under his brows a wild, fierce glance at old Wyat, and pointed to the door imperiously with his skeleton finger. The door shut, and we were alone.

'A chair?' he said, pointing to a seat.

'Thank you, uncle, I prefer standing,' I faltered.

He also stood—his white head bowed forward, the phosphoric glare of his strange eyes shone upon me from under his brows—his finger-nails just rested on the table.

'You saw the luggage corded and addressed, as it stands ready for removal in the hall?' he asked.

I had. Milly and I had read the cards which dangled from the trunk-handles and gun-case. The address was—'Mr. Dudley R. Ruthyn, Paris, *viâ* Dover.'

'I am old—agitated—on the eve of a decision on which much depends. Pray relieve my suspense. Is my son to leave Bartram to-day in sorrow, or to remain in joy? Pray answer quickly.'

I stammered I know not what. I was incoherent—wild, perhaps; but somehow I expressed my meaning—my unalterable decision. I thought his lips grew whiter and his eyes shone brighter as I spoke.

When I had quite made an end, he heaved a great sigh, and turning his eyes slowly to the right and the left, like a man in a helpless distraction, he whispered—

'God's will be done.'

I thought he was upon the point of fainting—a clay tint darkened the white of his face; and, seeming to forget my presence, he sat down, looking with a despairing scowl on his ashy old hand, as it lay upon the table.

I stood gazing at him, feeling almost as if I had murdered the old man—he still gazing askance, with an imbecile scowl, upon his hand.

'Shall I go, sir?' I at length found courage to whisper.

'*Go?*' he said, looking up suddenly; and it seemed to me as if a stream of cold sheet-lightning had crossed and enveloped me for a moment.

'Go?—oh!—a—yes—*yes*, Maud—go. I must see poor Dudley before his departure,' he added, as it were, in soliloquy.

Trembling lest he should revoke his permission to depart, I glided quickly and noiselessly from the room.

Old Wyat was prowling outside, with a cloth in her hand, pretending to dust the carved door-case. She frowned a stare of enquiry over her shrunken arm on me, as I passed. Milly, who had been on the watch, ran and met me. We heard my uncle's voice, as I shut the door, calling Dudley. He had been waiting, probably, in the adjoining room. I hurried into my chamber, with Milly at my side, and there my agitation found relief in tears, as that of girlhood naturally does.

A little while after we saw from the window Dudley, looking, I thought, very pale, get into a vehicle, on the top of which his luggage lay, and drive away from Bartram.

I began to take comfort. His departure was an inexpressible relief. His final departure! a distant journey!

We had tea in Milly's room that night. Firelight and candles are inspiring. In that red glow I always felt and feel more safe, as well as more comfortable, than in the daylight—quite irrationally, for we know the night is the appointed day of such as love the darkness better than light, and evil walks thereby. But so it is. Perhaps the very consciousness of external danger enhances the enjoyment of the well-lighted interior, just as the storm does that roars and hurtles over the roof.

While Milly and I were talking, very cosily, a knock came to the room-door, and, without waiting for an invitation to enter, old Wyat came in, and glowering at us, with her brown claw upon the door-handle, she said to Milly—

'Ye must leave your funnin', Miss Milly, and take your turn in your father's room.'

'Is he ill?' I asked.

She answered, addressing not me, but Milly—

'A wrought two hours in a fit arter Master Dudley went. 'Twill be the death o' him, I'm thinkin', poor old fellah. I wor sorry myself when I saw Master Dudley a going off in the moist to-day, poor fellah. There's trouble enough in the family without a' that; but 'twon't be a family long, I'm thinkin'. Nout but trouble, nout but trouble, since late changes came.'

Judging by the sour glance she threw on me as she said this, I concluded that I represented those 'late changes' to which all the sorrows of the house were referred.

I felt unhappy under the ill-will even of this odious old woman, being one of those unhappily constructed mortals who cannot be indifferent when they reasonably ought, and always yearn after kindness, even that of the worthless.

'I must go. I wish you'd come wi' me, Maud, I'm so afraid all alone,' said Milly, imploringly.

'Certainly, Milly,' I answered, not liking it, you may be sure; 'you shan't sit there alone.'

So together we went, old Wyat cautioning us for our lives to make no noise.

We passed through the old man's sitting-room, where that day had occurred his brief but momentous interview with me, and his parting with his only son, and entered the bed-room at the farther end.

A low fire burned in the grate. The room was in a sort of twilight. A dim lamp near the foot of the bed at the farther side was the only light burning there. Old Wyat whispered an injunction not to speak above our breaths, nor to leave the fireside unless the sick man called or showed signs of weariness. These were the directions of the doctor, who had been there.

So Milly and I sat ourselves down near the hearth, and old Wyat left us to our resources. We could hear the patient breathe; but he was quite still. In whispers we talked; but our conversation flagged. I was, after my wont, upbraiding myself for the suffering I had inflicted. After about half an hour's desultory whispering, and intervals, growing longer and longer, of silence, it was plain that Milly was falling asleep.

She strove against it, and I tried hard to keep her talking; but it would not do—sleep overcame her; and I was the only person in that ghastly room in a state of perfect consciousness.

There were associations connected with my last vigil there to make my situation very nervous and disagreeable. Had I not had so much to occupy my mind of a distinctly practical kind—Dudley's audacious suit, my uncle's questionable toleration of it, and my own conduct throughout that most disagreeable period of my existence,—I should have felt my present situation a great deal more.

As it was, I thought of my real troubles, and something of Cousin Knollys, and, I confess, a good deal of Lord Ilbury. When looking towards the door, I thought I saw a human face, about the most terrible my fancy could have called up, looking fixedly into the room. It was only a 'three-quarter,' and not the whole figure—the door hid that in a great measure, and I fancied I saw, too, a portion of the fingers. The face gazed toward the bed, and in the imperfect light looked like a livid mask, with chalky eyes.

I had so often been startled by similar apparitions formed by accidental lights and shadows disguising homely objects, that I stooped forward, expecting, though tremulously, to see this tremendous one in like manner dissolve itself into its harmless elements; and now, to my unspeakable terror, I became perfectly certain that I saw the countenance of Madame de la Rougierre.

With a cry, I started back, and shook Milly furiously from her trance.

'Look! look!' I cried. But the apparition or illusion was gone.

I clung so fast to Milly's arm, cowering behind her, that she could not rise.

'Milly! Milly! Milly! Milly!' I went on crying, like one struck with idiotcy, and unable to say anything else.

In a panic, Milly, who had seen nothing, and could conjecture nothing of the cause of my terror, jumped up, and clinging to one another, we huddled together into the corner of the room, I still crying wildly, 'Milly! Milly! *Milly*!' and nothing else.

'What is it—where is it—what do you see?' cried Milly, clinging to me as I did to her.

'It will come again; it will come; oh, heaven!'

'What—what is it, Maud?'

'The face! the face!' I cried. 'Oh, Milly! Milly! Milly!'

We heard a step softly approaching the open door, and, in a horrible *sauve qui peut*, we rushed and stumbled together toward the light by Uncle Silas's bed. But old Wyat's voice and figure reassured us.

'Milly,' I said, so soon as, pale and very faint, I reached my apartment, 'no power on earth shall ever tempt me to enter that room again after dark.'

'Why, Maud dear, what, in Heaven's name, did you see?' said Milly, scarcely less terrified.

'Oh, I can't; I can't; I can't, Milly. Never ask me. It is haunted. The room is haunted *horribly*.'

'Was it Charke?' whispered Milly, looking over her shoulder, all aghast.

'No, no—don't ask me; a fiend in a worse shape.' I was relieved at last by a long fit of weeping; and all night good Mary Quince sat by me, and Milly slept by my side. Starting and screaming, and drugged with sal-volatile, I got through that night of supernatural terror, and saw the blessed light of heaven again.

Doctor Jolks, when he came to see my uncle in the morning, visited me also. He pronounced me very hysterical, made minute enquiries respecting my hours and diet, asked what I had had for dinner yesterday. There was something a little comforting in his cool and confident pooh-poohing of the ghost theory. The result was, a regimen which excluded tea, and imposed chocolate and porter, earlier hours, and I forget all beside; and he undertook to promise that, if I would but observe his directions, I should never see a ghost again.

CHAPTER L

MILLY'S FAREWELL

A few days' time saw me much better. Doctor Jolks was so contemptuously sturdy and positive on the point, that I began to have comfortable doubts about the reality of my ghost; and having still a horror indescribable of the illusion, if such it were, the room in which it appeared, and everything concerning it, I would neither speak, nor, so far as I could, think of it.

So, though Bartram-Haugh was gloomy as well as beautiful, and some of its associations awful, and the solitude that reigned there sometimes almost terrible, yet early hours, bracing exercise, and the fine air that predominates that region, soon restored my nerves to a healthier tone.

But it seemed to me that Bartram-Haugh was to be to me a vale of tears; or rather, in my sad pilgrimage, that valley of the shadow of death through which poor Christian fared alone and in the dark.

One day Milly ran into the parlour, pale, with wet cheeks, and, without saying a word, threw her arms about my neck, and burst into a paroxysm of weeping.

'What is it, Milly—what's the matter, dear—what is it?' I cried aghast, but returning her close embrace heartily.

'Oh! Maud—Maud darling, he's going to send me away.'

'Away, dear! *where* away? And leave me alone in this dreadful solitude, where he knows I shall die of fear and grief without you? Oh! no—no, it *must* be a mistake.'

'I'm going to France, Maud—I'm going away. Mrs. Jolks is going to London, day ar'ter to-morrow, and I'm to go wi' her; and an old French lady, he says, from the school will meet me there, and bring me the rest o' the way.'

'Oh—ho—ho—ho—ho—o—o—o!' cried poor Milly, hugging me closer still, with her head buried in my shoulder, and swaying me about like a wrestler, in her agony.

'I never wor away from home afore, except that little bit wi' you over there at Elverston; and you wor wi' me then, Maud; an' I love ye—better than Bartram—better than a'; an' I think I'll die, Maud, if they take me away.'

I was just as wild in my woe as poor Milly; and it was not until we had wept together for a full hour—sometimes standing—sometimes walking up and down the room—sometimes sitting and getting up in turns to fall on one another's necks,—that Milly, plucking her handkerchief from her pocket, drew a note from it at the same time, which, as it fell upon the floor, she at once recollected to be one from Uncle Silas to me.

It was to this effect:—

'I wish to apprise my dear niece and ward of my plans. Milly proceeds to an admirable French school, as a pensionnaire, and leaves this on Thursday next. If after three months' trial she finds it in any way objectionable, she returns to us. If, on the contrary, she finds it in all respects the charming residence it has been presented to me, you, on the expiration of that period, join her there, until the temporary complication of my affairs shall have been so far adjusted as to enable me to receive you once more at Bartram. Hoping for happier days, and wishing to assure you that three months is the extreme limit of your separation from my poor Milly, I have written this, feeling alas! unequal to seeing you at present.

'Bartram, Tuesday.

'P.S.—I can have no objection to your apprising Monica Knollys of these arrangements. You will understand, of course, not a copy of this letter, but its substance.'

Over this document, scanning it as lawyers do a new Act of Parliament, we took comfort. After all, it was limited; a separation not to exceed three months, possibly much shorter. On the whole, too, I pleased myself with thinking Uncle Silas's note, though peremptory, was kind.

Our paroxysms subsided into sadness; a close correspondence was arranged. Something of the bustle and excitement of change supervened. If it turned out to be, in truth, a 'charming residence,' how very delightful our meeting in France, with the interest of foreign scenery, ways, and faces, would be!

So Thursday arrived—a new gush of sorrow—a new brightening up—and, amid regrets and anticipations, we parted at the gate at the farther end of the Windmill Wood. Then, of course, were more good-byes, more embraces, and tearful smiles. Good Mrs. Jolks, who met us there, was in a huge fuss; I believe it was her first visit to the metropolis, and she was in proportion heated and important, and terrified about the train, so we had not many last words.

I watched poor Milly, whose head was stretched from the window, her hand waving many adieux, until the curve of the road, and the clump of old ash-trees, thick with ivy, hid Milly, carriage and all, from view. My eyes filled again with tears. I turned towards Bartram. At my side stood honest Mary Quince.

'Don't take on so, Miss; 'twon't be no time passing; three months is nothing at all,' she said, smiling kindly.

I smiled through my tears and kissed the good creature, and so side by side we re-entered the gate.

The lithe young man in fustian, whom I had seen talking with Beauty on the morning of our first encounter with that youthful Amazon, was awaiting our re-entrance with the key in his hand. He stood half behind the open wicket. One lean brown cheek, one shy eye, and his sharp upturned nose, I saw as we passed. He was treating me to a stealthy scrutiny, and seemed to shun my glance, for he shut the door quickly, and busied himself locking it, and then began stubbing up some thistles which grew close by, with the toe of his thick shoe, his back to us all the time.

It struck me that I recognised his features, and I asked Mary Quince.

'Have you seen that young man before, Quince?'

'He brings up game for your uncle, sometimes, Miss, and lends a hand in the garden, I believe.'

'Do you know his name, Mary?'

'They call him Tom, I don't know what more, Miss.'

'Tom,' I called; 'please, Tom, come here for a moment.'

Tom turned about, and approached slowly. He was more civil than the Bartram people usually were, for he plucked off his shapeless cap of rabbit-skin with a clownish respect.

'Tom, what is your other name,—Tom *what*, my good man?' I asked.

'Tom Brice, ma'am.'

'Haven't I seen you before, Tom Brice?' I pursued, for my curiosity was excited, and with it much graver feelings; for there certainly *was* a resemblance in Tom's features to those of the postilion who had looked so hard at me as I passed the carriage in the warren at Knowl, on the evening of the outrage which had scared that quiet place.

''Appen you may have, ma'am,' he answered, quite coolly, looking down the buttons of his gaiters.

'Are you a good whip—do you drive well?'

'I'll drive a plough wi' most lads hereabout,' answered Tom.

'Have you ever been to Knowl, Tom?'

Tom gaped very innocently.

'Anan,' he said.

'Here, Tom, is half-a-crown.'

He took it readily enough.

'That be very good,' said Tom, with a nod, having glanced sharply at the coin.

I can't say whether he applied that term to the coin, or to his luck, or to my generous self.

'Now, Tom, you'll tell me, have you ever been to Knowl?'

'Maught a' bin, ma'am, but I don't mind no sich place—no.'

As Tom spoke this with great deliberation, like a man who loves truth, putting a strain upon his memory for its sake, he spun the silver coin two or three times into the air and caught it, staring at it the while, with all his might.

'Now, Tom, recollect yourself, and tell me the truth, and I'll be a friend to you. Did you ride postilion to a carriage having a lady in it, and, I think, several gentlemen, which came to the grounds of Knowl, when the party had their luncheon on the grass, and there was a—a quarrel with the gamekeepers? Try, Tom, to recollect; you shall, upon my honour, have no trouble about it, and I'll try to serve you.'

Tom was silent, while with a vacant gape he watched the spin of his half-crown twice, and then catching it with a smack in his hand, which he thrust into his pocket, he said, still looking in the same direction—

'I never rid postilion in my days, ma'am. I know nout o' sich a place, though 'appen I maught a' bin there; Knowl, ye ca't. I was ne'er out o' Derbyshire but thrice to Warwick fair wi' horses be rail, an' twice to York.'

'You're certain, Tom?'

'Sartin sure, ma'am.'

And Tom made another loutish salute, and cut the conference short by turning off the path and beginning to hollo after some trespassing cattle.

I had not felt anything like so nearly sure in this essay at identification as I had in that of Dudley. Even of Dudley's identity with the Church Scarsdale man, I had daily grown less confident; and, indeed, had it been proposed to bring it to the test of a wager, I do not think I should, in the language of sporting gentlemen, have cared to 'back' my original opinion. There was, however, a sufficient uncertainty to make me uncomfortable; and there was another uncertainty to enhance the unpleasant sense of ambiguity.

On our way back we passed the bleaching trunks and limbs of several ranks of barkless oaks lying side by side, some squared by the hatchet, perhaps sold, for there were large letters and Roman numerals traced upon them in red chalk. I sighed as I passed them by, not because it was wrongfully done, for I really rather leaned to the belief that Uncle Silas was well advised in point of law. But, alas! here lay low the grand old family decorations of Bartram-Haugh, not to be replaced for centuries to come, under whose spreading boughs the Ruthyns of three hundred years ago had hawked and hunted!

On the trunk of one of these I sat down to rest, Mary Quince meanwhile pattering about in unmeaning explorations. While thus listlessly seated, the girl Meg Hawkes, walked by, carrying a basket.

'Hish!' she said quickly, as she passed, without altering a pace or raising her eyes; 'don't ye speak nor look—fayther spies us; I'll tell ye next turn.'

'Next turn'—when was that? Well, she might be returning; and as she could not then say more than she had said, in merely passing without a pause, I concluded to wait for a short time and see what would come of it.

After a short time I looked about me a little, and I saw Dickon Hawkes—Pegtop, as poor Milly used to call him—with an axe in his hand, prowling luridly among the timber.

Observing that I saw him, he touched his hat sulkily, and by-and-by passed me, muttering to himself. He plainly could not understand what business I could have in that particular part of the Windmill Wood, and let me see it in his countenance.

His daughter did pass me again; but this time he was near, and she was silent. Her next transit occurred as he was questioning Mary Quince at some little distance; and as she passed precisely in the same way, she said—

'Don't you be alone wi' Master Dudley nowhere for the world's worth.'

The injunction was so startling that I was on the point of questioning the girl. But I recollected myself, and waited in the hope that in her future transits she might be more explicit. But one word more she did not utter, and the jealous eye of old Pegtop was so constantly upon us that I refrained.

There was vagueness and suggestion enough in the oracle to supply work for many an hour of anxious conjecture, and many a horrible vigil by night. Was I never to know peace at Bartram-Haugh?

Ten days of poor Milly's absence, and of my solitude, had already passed, when my uncle sent for me to his room.

When old Wyat stood at the door, mumbling and snarling her message, my heart died within me.

It was late—just that hour when dejected people feel their anxieties most—when the cold grey of twilight has deepened to its darkest shade, and before the cheerful candles are lighted, and the safe quiet of the night sets in.

When I entered my uncle's sitting-room—though his window-shutters were open and the wan streaks of sunset visible through them, like narrow lakes in the chasms of the dark western clouds—a pair of candles were burning; one stood upon the table by his desk, the other on the chimneypiece, before which his tall, thin figure stooped. His hand leaned on the mantelpiece, and the light from the candle just above his bowed head touched his silvery hair. He was looking, as it seemed, into the subsiding embers of the fire, and was a very statue of forsaken dejection and decay.

'Uncle!' I ventured to say, having stood for some time unperceived near his table.

'Ah, yes, Maud, my dear child—my *dear* child.'

He turned, and with the candle in his hand, smiling his silvery smile of suffering on me. He walked more feebly and stiffly, I thought, than I had ever seen him move before.

'Sit down, Maud—pray sit there.'

I took the chair he indicated.

'In my misery and my solitude, Maud, I have invoked you like a spirit, and you appear.'

With his two hands leaning on the table, he looked across at me, in a stooping attitude; he had not seated himself. I continued silent until it should be his pleasure to question or address me.

At last he said, raising himself and looking upward, with a wild adoration—his finger-tips elevated and glimmering in the faint mixed light—

'No, I thank my Creator, I am not quite forsaken.'

Another silence, during which he looked steadfastly at me, and muttered, as if thinking aloud—

'My guardian angel!—my guardian angel! Maud, *you* have a heart.' He addressed me suddenly—'Listen, for a few moments, to the appeal of an old and broken-hearted man—your guardian—your uncle—your *suppliant*. I had resolved never to speak to you more on this subject. But I was wrong. It was pride that inspired me—mere pride.'

I felt myself growing pale and flushed by turns during the pause that followed.

'I'm very miserable—very nearly desperate. What remains for me—what remains? Fortune has done her worst—thrown in the dust, her wheels rolled over me; and the servile world, who follow her chariot like a mob, stamp upon the mangled wretch. All this had passed over me, and left me scarred and bloodless in this solitude. It was not my fault, Maud—I say it was no fault of mine; I have no remorse, though more regrets than I can count, and all scored with fire. As people passed by Bartram, and looked upon its neglected grounds and smokeless chimneys, they thought my plight, I dare say, about the worst a proud man could be reduced to. They could not imagine one half its misery. But this old hectic—this old epileptic—this old spectre of wrongs, calamities, and follies, had still one hope—my manly though untutored son—the last male scion of the Ruthyns. Maud, have I lost him? His fate—my fate—I may say *Milly's fate*;—we all await your sentence. He loves you, as none but the very young can love, and that once only in a life. He loves you desperately—a most affectionate nature—a Ruthyn, the best blood in England—the last man of the race; and I—if I lose him I lose all; and you will see me in my coffin, Maud, before many months. I stand before you in the attitude of a suppliant—shall I kneel?'

His eyes were fixed on me with the light of despair, his knotted hands clasped, his whole figure bowed toward me. I was inexpressibly shocked and pained.

'Oh, uncle! uncle!' I cried, and from very excitement I burst into tears.

I saw that his eyes were fixed on me with a dismal scrutiny. I think he divined the nature of my agitation; but he determined, notwithstanding, to press me while my helpless agitation continued.

'You see my suspense—you see my miserable and frightful suspense. You are kind, Maud; you love your father's memory; your pity your father's brother; you would not say no, and place a pistol at his head?'

'Oh! I must—I must—I *must* say no. Oh! spare me, uncle, for Heaven's sake. Don't question me—don't press me. I could not—I *could* not do what you ask.'

'I yield, Maud—I yield, my dear. I will *not* press you; you shall have time, your *own* time, to think. I will accept no answer now—no, *none*, Maud.'

He said this, raising his thin hand to silence me.

'There, Maud, enough. I have spoken, as I always do to you, frankly, perhaps too frankly; but agony and despair will speak out, and plead, even with the most obdurate and cruel.'

With these words Uncle Silas entered his bed-chamber, and shut the door, not violently, but with a resolute hand, and I thought I heard a cry.

I hastened to my own room. I threw myself on my knees, and thanked Heaven for the firmness vouchsafed me; I could not believe it to have been my own.

I was more miserable in consequence of this renewed suit on behalf of my odious cousin than I can describe. My uncle had taken such a line of importunity that it became a sort of agony to resist. I thought of the possibility of my hearing of his having made away with himself, and was every morning relieved when I heard that he was still as usual. I have often wondered since at my own firmness. In that dreadful interview with my uncle I had felt, in the whirl and horror of my mind, on the very point of submitting, just as nervous people are said to throw themselves over precipices through sheer dread of falling.

CHAPTER LI

SARAH MATILDA COMES TO LIGHT

Some time after this interview, one day as I sat, sad enough, in my room, looking listlessly from the window, with good Mary Quince, whom, whether in the house or in my melancholy rambles, I always had by my side, I was startled by the sound of a loud and shrill female voice, in violent hysterical action, gabbling with great rapidity, sobbing, and very nearly screaming in a sort of fury.

I started up, staring at the door.

'Lord bless us!' cried honest Mary Quince, with round eyes and mouth agape, staring in the same direction.

'Mary—Mary, what can it be?'

'Are they beating some one down yonder? I don't know where it comes from,' gasped Quince.

'I will—I will—I'll see her. It's her I want. Oo—hoo—hoo—hoo—oo—o—Miss Maud Ruthyn of Knowl. Miss Ruthyn of Knowl. Hoo—hoo—hoo—hoo—oo!'

'What on earth can it be?' I exclaimed, in great bewilderment and terror.

It was now plainly very near indeed, and I heard the voice of our mild and shaky butler evidently remonstrating with the distressed damsel.

'I'll see her,' she continued, pouring a torrent of vile abuse upon me, which stung me with a sudden sense of anger. What had I done to be afraid of anyone? How dared anyone in my uncle's house—in *my* house—mix my name up with her detestable scurrilities?

'For Heaven's sake, Miss, don't ye go out,' cried poor Quince; 'it's some drunken creature.'

But I was very angry, and, like a fool as I was, I threw open the door, exclaiming in a loud and haughty key—

'Here is Miss Ruthyn of Knowl. Who wants to see her?'

A pink and white young lady, with black tresses, violent, weeping, shrill, voluble, was flouncing up the last stair, and shook her dress out on the lobby; and poor old Giblets, as Milly used to call him, was following in her wake, with many small remonstrances and entreaties, perfectly unheeded.

The moment I looked at this person, it struck me that she was the identical lady whom I had seen in the carriage at Knowl Warren. The next moment I was in doubt; the next, still more so. She was decidedly thinner, and dressed by no means in such lady-like taste. Perhaps she was hardly like her at all. I began to distrust all these resemblances, and to fancy, with a shudder, that they originated, perhaps, only in my own sick brain.

On seeing me, this young lady—as it seemed to me, a good deal of the barmaid or lady's-maid species—dried her eyes fiercely, and, with a flaming countenance, called upon me peremptorily to produce her 'lawful husband.' Her loud, insolent, outrageous attack had the effect of enhancing my indignation, and I quite forget what I said to her, but I well remember that her manner became a good deal more decent. She was plainly under the impression that I wanted to appropriate her husband, or, at least, that he wanted to marry me; and she ran on at such a pace, and her harangue was so passionate, incoherent, and unintelligible, that I thought her out of her mind: she was far from it, however. I think if she had allowed me even a second for reflection, I should have hit upon her meaning. As it was, nothing could exceed my perplexity, until, plucking a soiled newspaper from her pocket, she indicated a particular paragraph, already sufficiently emphasised by double lines of red ink at its sides. It was a Lancashire paper, of about six weeks since, and very much worn and soiled for its age. I remember in particular a circular stain from the bottom of a vessel, either of coffee or brown stout. The paragraph was as follows, recording an event a year or more anterior to the date of the paper:—

'MARRIAGE.—On Tuesday, August 7, 18—, at Leatherwig Church, by the Rev. Arthur Hughes, Dudley R. Ruthyn, Esq., only son and heir of Silas Ruthyn, Esq., of Bartram-Haugh, Derbyshire, to Sarah Matilda, second daughter of John Mangles, Esq., of Wiggan, in this county.'

At first I read nothing but amazement in this announcement, but in another moment I felt how completely I was relieved; and showing, I believe, my intense satisfaction in my countenance—for the young lady eyed me with considerable surprise and curiosity—I said

'This is extremely important. You must see Mr. Silas Ruthyn this moment. I am certain he knows nothing of it. I will conduct you to him.'

'No more he does—I know that myself,' she replied, following me with a self-asserting swagger, and a great rustling of cheap silk.

As we entered, Uncle Silas looked up from his sofa, and closed his *Revue des Deux Mondes*.

'What is all this?' he enquired, drily.

'This lady has brought with her a newspaper containing an extraordinary statement which affects our family,' I answered.

Uncle Silas raised himself, and looked with a hard, narrow scrutiny at the unknown young lady.

'A libel, I suppose, in the paper?' he said, extending his hand for it.

'No, uncle—no; only a marriage,' I answered.

'Not Monica?' he said, as he took it. 'Pah, it smells all over of tobacco and beer,' he added, throwing a little eau de Cologne over it.

He raised it with a mixture of curiosity and disgust, saying again 'pah,' as he did so.

He read the paragraph, and as he did his face changed from white, all over, to lead colour. He raised his eyes, and looked steadily for some seconds at the young lady, who seemed a little awed by his strange presence.

'And you are, I suppose, the young lady, Sarah Matilda *née* Mangles, mentioned in this little paragraph?' he said, in a tone you would have called a sneer, were it not that it trembled.

Sarah Matilda assented.

'My son is, I dare say, within reach. It so happens that I wrote to arrest his journey, and summon him here, some days since—some days since—some days since,' he repeated slowly, like a person whose mind has wandered far away from the theme on which he is speaking.

He had rung his bell, and old Wyat, always hovering about his rooms, entered.

'I want my son, immediately. If not in the house, send Harry to the stables; if not there, let him be followed, instantly. Brice is an active fellow, and will know where to find him. If he is in Feltram, or at a distance, let Brice take a horse, and Master Dudley can ride it back. He must be here without the loss of one moment.'

There intervened nearly a quarter of an hour, during which whenever he recollected her, Uncle Silas treated the young lady with a hyper-refined and ceremonious politeness, which appeared to make her uneasy, and even a little shy, and certainly prevented a renewal of those lamentations and invectives which he had heard faintly from the stair-head.

But for the most part Uncle Silas seemed to forget us and his book, and all that surrounded him, lying back in the corner of his sofa, his chin upon his breast, and such a fearful shade and carving on his features as made me prefer looking in any direction but his.

At length we heard the tread of Dudley's thick boots on the oak boards, and faint and muffled the sound of his voice as he cross-examined old Wyat before entering the chamber of audience.

I think he suspected quite another visitor, and had no expectation of seeing the particular young lady, who rose from her chair as he entered, in an opportune flood of tears, crying—

'Oh, Dudley, Dudley!—oh, Dudley, could you? Oh, Dudley, your own poor Sal! You could not—you would not—your lawful wife!'

This and a good deal more, with cheeks that streamed like a window-pane in a thunder-shower, spoke Sarah Matilda with all her oratory, working his arm, which she clung to, up and down all the time, like the handle of a pump. But Dudley was, manifestly, confounded and dumbfoundered. He stood for a long time gaping at his father, and stole just one sheepish glance at me; and, with red face and forehead, looked down at his boots, and then again at his father, who remained just in the attitude I have described, and with the same forbidding and dreary intensity in his strange face.

Like a quarrelsome man worried in his sleep by a noise, Dudley suddenly woke up, as it were, with a start, in a half-suppressed exasperation, and shook her off with a jerk and a muttered curse, as she whisked involuntarily into a chair, with more violence than could have been pleasant.

'Judging by your looks and demeanour, sir, I can almost anticipate your answers,' said my uncle, addressing him suddenly. 'Will you be good enough—pray, madame (parenthetically to our visitor), command yourself for a few moments. Is this young person the daughter of a Mr. Mangles, and is her name Sarah Matilda?'

'I dessay,' answered Dudley, hurriedly.

'Is she your wife?'

'Is she my wife?' repeated Dudley, ill at ease.

'Yes, sir; it is a plain question.'

All this time Sarah Matilda was perpetually breaking into talk, and with difficulty silenced by my uncle.

'Well, 'appen she says I am—does she?' replied Dudley.

'Is she your wife, sir?'

'Mayhap she so considers it, after a fashion,' he replied, with an impudent swagger, seating himself as he did so.

'What do *you* think, sir?' persisted Uncle Silas.

'I don't think nout about it,' replied Dudley, surlily.

'Is that account true?' said my uncle, handing him the paper.

'They wishes us to believe so, at any rate.'

'Answer directly, sir. We have our thoughts upon it. If it be true, it is capable of *every* proof. For expedition's sake I ask you. There is no use in prevaricating.'

'Who wants to deny it? It *is* true—there!'

'*There!* I knew he would,' screamed the young woman, hysterically, with a laugh of strange joy.

'Shut up, will ye?' growled Dudley, savagely.

'Oh, Dudley, Dudley, darling! what have I done?'

'Bin and ruined me, jest—that's all.'

'Oh! no, no, no, Dudley. Ye know I wouldn't. I could not—*could* not hurt ye, Dudley. No, no, no!'

He grinned at her, and, with a sharp side-nod, said—

'Wait a bit.'

'Oh, Dudley, don't be vexed, dear. I did not mean it. I would not hurt ye for all the world. Never.'

'Well, never mind. You and yours tricked me finely; and now you've got me—that's all.'

My uncle laughed a very odd laugh.

'I knew it, of course; and upon my word, madame, you and he make a very pretty couple,' sneered Uncle Silas.

Dudley made no answer, looking, however, very savage.

And with this poor young wife, so recently wedded, the low villain had actually solicited me to marry him!

I am quite certain that my uncle was as entirely ignorant as I of Dudley's connection, and had, therefore, no participation in this appalling wickedness.

'And I have to congratulate you, my good fellow, on having secured the affections of a very suitable and vulgar young woman.'

'I baint the first o' the family as a' done the same,' retorted Dudley.

At this taunt the old man's fury for a moment overpowered him. In an instant he was on his feet, quivering from head to foot. I never saw such a countenance—like one of those demon-grotesques we see in the Gothic side-aisles and groinings—a dreadful grimace, monkey-like and insane—and his thin hand caught up his ebony stick, and shook it paralytically in the air.

'If ye touch me wi' that, I'll smash ye, by ——!' shouted Dudley, furious, raising his hands and hitching his shoulder, just as I had seen him when he fought Captain Oakley.

For a moment this picture was suspended before me, and I screamed, I know not what, in my terror. But the old man, the veteran of many a scene of excitement, where men disguise their ferocity in calm tones, and varnish their fury with smiles, had not quite lost his self-command. He turned toward me and said—

'Does he know what he's saying?'

And with an icy laugh of contempt, his high, thin forehead still flushed, he sat down trembling.

'If you want to say aught, I'll hear ye. Ye may jaw me all ye like, and I'll stan' it.'

'Oh, I may speak? Thank you,' sneered Uncle Silas, glancing slowly round at me, and breaking into a cold laugh.

'Ay, I don't mind cheek, not I; but you must not go for to do that, ye know. Gammon. I won't stand a blow—I won't fro *no* one.

'Well, sir, availing myself of your permission to speak, I may remark, without offence to the young lady, that I don't happen to recollect the name Mangles among the old families of England. I presume you have chosen her chiefly for her virtues and her graces.'

Mrs. Sarah Matilda, not apprehending this compliment quite as Uncle Silas meant it, dropped a courtesy, notwithstanding her agitation, and, wiping her eyes, said, with a blubbered smile—

'You're very kind, sure.'

'I hope, for both your sakes, she has got a little money. I don't see how you are to live else. You're too lazy for a game-keeper; and I don't think you could keep a pot-house, you are so addicted to drinking and quarrelling. The only thing I am quite clear upon is, that you and your wife must find some other abode than this. You shall depart this evening: and now, Mr. and Mrs. Dudley Ruthyn, you may quit this room, if you please.'

Uncle Silas had risen, and made them one of his old courtly bows, smiling a death-like sneer, and pointing to the door with his trembling fingers.

'Come, will ye?' said Dudley, grinding his teeth. 'You're pretty well done here.'

Not half understanding the situation, but looking woefully bewildered, she dropped a farewell courtesy at the door.

'Will ye *cut*?' barked Dudley, in a tone that made her jump; and suddenly, without looking about, he strode after her from the room.

'Maud, how shall I recover this? The vulgar *villain*—the *fool*! What an abyss were we approaching! and for me the last hope gone—and for me utter, utter, irretrievable ruin.'

He was passing his fingers tremulously back and forward along the top of the mantelpiece, like a man in search of something, and continued so, looking along it, feebly and vacantly, although there was nothing there.

'I wish, uncle—you do not know how much I wish—I could be of any use to you. Maybe I can?'

He turned, and looked at me sharply.

'Maybe you can,' he echoed slowly. 'Yes, maybe you can,' he repeated more briskly.' Let us—let us see—let us think—that d—— fellow!—my head!'

'You're not well, uncle?'

'Oh! yes, very well. We'll talk in the evening—I'll send for you.'

I found Wyat in the next room, and told her to hasten, as I thought he was ill. I hope it was not very selfish, but such had grown to be my horror of seeing him in one of his strange seizures, that I hastened from the room precipitately—partly to escape the risk of being asked to remain.

The walls of Bartram House are thick, and the recess at the doorway deep. As I closed my uncle's door, I heard Dudley's voice on the stairs. I did not wish to be seen by him or by his 'lady', as his poor wife called herself, who was engaged in vehement dialogue with him as I emerged, and not caring either to re-enter my uncle's room, I remained quietly ensconced within the heavy door-case, in which position I overheard Dudley say with a savage snarl—

'You'll jest go back the way ye came. I'm not goin' wi' ye, if that's what ye be drivin' at—dang your impitins!'

'Oh! Dudley, dear, what have I done what *have* I done—ye hate me so?'

'What a' ye done? Ye vicious little beast, ye! You've got us turned out an' disinherited wi' yer d——d bosh, that's all; don't ye think it's enough?'

I could only hear her sobs and shrill tones in reply, for they were descending the stairs; and Mary Quince reported to me, in a horrified sort of way, that she saw him bundle her into the fly at the door, like a truss of hay into a hay-loft. And he stood with his head in at the window, scolding her, till it drove away.

'I knew he wor jawing her, poor thing! By the way he kep' waggin' his head—an' he had his fist inside, a shakin' in her face I'm sure he looked wicked enough for anything; an' she a crying like a babby, an' lookin' back, an' wavin' her wet hankicher to him—poor thing!—and she so young! 'Tis a pity. Dear me! I often think, Miss, 'tis well for me I never was married. And see how we all would like to get husbands for all that, though so few is happy together. 'Tis a queer world, and them that's single is maybe the best off after all.'

CHAPTER LII

THE PICTURE OF A WOLF

I went down that evening to the sitting-room which had been assigned to Milly and me, in search of a book—my good Mary Quince always attending me. The door was a little open, and I was startled by the light of a candle proceeding from the fireside, together with a considerable aroma of tobacco and brandy.

On my little work-table, which he had drawn beside the hearth, lay Dudley's pipe, his brandy-flask, and an empty tumbler; and he was sitting with one foot on the fender, his elbow on his knee, and his head resting in his hand, weeping. His back being a little toward the door, he did not perceive us; and we saw him rub his knuckles in his eyes, and heard the sounds of his selfish lamentation.

Mary and I stole away quietly, leaving him in possession, wondering when he was to leave the house, according to the sentence which I had heard pronounced upon him.

I was delighted to see old 'Giblets' quietly strapping his luggage in the hall, and heard from him in a whisper that he was to leave that evening by rail—he did not know whither.

About half an hour afterwards, Mary Quince, going out to reconnoitre, heard from old Wyat in the lobby that he had just started to meet the train.

Blessed be heaven for that deliverance! An evil spirit had been cast out, and the house looked lighter and happier. It was not until I sat down in the quiet of my room that the scenes and images of that agitating day began to move before my memory in orderly procession, and for the first time I appreciated, with a stunning sense of horror and a perfect rapture of thanksgiving, the value of my escape and the immensity of the danger which had threatened me. It may have been miserable weakness—I think it was. But I was young, nervous, and afflicted with a troublesome sort of conscience, which occasionally went mad, and insisted, in small things as well as great, upon sacrifices which my reason now assures me were absurd. Of Dudley I had a perfect horror; and yet had that system of solicitation, that dreadful and direct appeal to my compassion, that placing of my feeble girlhood in the seat of the arbiter of my aged uncle's hope or despair, been long persisted in, my resistance might have been worn out—who can tell?—and I self-sacrificed! Just as criminals in Germany are teased, and watched, and cross-examined, year after year, incessantly, into a sort of madness; and worn out with the suspense, the iteration, the self-restraint, and insupportable fatigue, they at last cut all short, accuse themselves, and go infinitely relieved to the scaffold—you may guess, then, for me, nervous, self-diffident, and alone, how intense was the comfort of knowing that Dudley was actually married, and the harrowing importunity which had just commenced for ever silenced.

That night I saw my uncle. I pitied him, though I feared him. I was longing to tell him how anxious I was to help him, if only he could point out the way. It was in substance what I had already said, but now strongly urged. He brightened; he sat up perpendicularly in his chair with a countenance, not weak or fatuous now, but resolute and searching, and which contracted into dark thought or calculation as I talked.

I dare say I spoke confusedly enough. I was always nervous in his presence; there was, I fancy, something mesmeric in the odd sort of influence which, without effort, he exercised over my imagination.

Sometimes this grew into a dismal panic, and Uncle Silas—polished, mild—seemed unaccountably horrible to me. Then it was no longer an accidental fascination of electro-biology. It was something more. His nature was incomprehensible by me. He was without the nobleness, without the freshness, without the softness, without the frivolities of such human nature as I had experienced, either within myself or in other persons. I instinctively felt that appeals to sympathies or feelings could no more affect him than a marble monument. He seemed to accommodate his conversation to the moral structure of others, just as spirits are said to assume the shape of mortals. There were the sensualities of the gourmet for his body, and there ended his human nature, as it seemed to me. Through that semi-transparent structure I thought I could now and then discern the light or the glare of his inner life. But I understood it not.

He never scoffed at what was good or noble—his hardest critic could not nail him to one such sentence; and yet, it seemed somehow to me that his unknown nature was a systematic blasphemy against it all. If fiend he was, he was yet something higher than the garrulous, and withal feeble, demon of Goethe. He assumed the limbs and features of our mortal nature. He shrouded his own, and was a profoundly reticent Mephistopheles. Gentle he had been to me—kindly he had nearly always spoken; but it seemed like the mild talk of one of those goblins of the desert, whom Asiatic superstition tells of, who appear in friendly shapes to stragglers from the caravan, beckon to them from afar, call them by their names, and lead them where they are found no more. Was, then, all his kindness but a phosphoric radiance covering something colder and more awful than the grave?

'It is very noble of you, Maud—it is angelic; your sympathy with a ruined and despairing old man. But I fear you will recoil. I tell you frankly that less than twenty thousand pounds will not extricate me from the quag of ruin in which I am entangled—lost!'

'Recoil! Far from it. I'll do it. There must be some way.'

'Enough, my fair young protectress—celestial enthusiast, enough. Though you do not, yet I recoil. I could not bring myself to accept this sacrifice. What signifies, even to me, my extrication? I lie a mangled wretch, with fifty mortal wounds on my crown; what avails the healing of one wound, when there are so many beyond all cure? Better to let me perish where I fall; and reserve your money for the worthier objects whom, perhaps, hereafter may avail to save.'

'But I *will* do this. I must. I cannot see you suffer with the power in my hands unemployed to help you,' I exclaimed.

'Enough, dear Maud; the will is here—enough: there is balm in your compassion and good-will. Leave me, ministering angel; for the present I cannot. If you *will*, we can talk of it again. Good-night.'

And so we parted.

The attorney from Feltram, I afterwards heard, was with him nearly all that night, trying in vain to devise by their joint ingenuity any means by which I might tie myself up. But there were none. I could not bind myself.

I was myself full of the hope of helping him. What was this sum to me, great as it seemed? Truly nothing. I could have spared it, and never felt the loss.

I took up a large quarto with coloured prints, one of the few books I had brought with me from dear old Knowl. Too much excited to hope for sleep in bed, I opened it, and turned over the leaves, my mind still full of Uncle Silas and the sum I hoped to help him with.

Unaccountably one of those coloured engravings arrested my attention. It represented the solemn solitude of a lofty forest; a girl, in Swiss costume, was flying in terror, and as she fled flinging a piece of meat behind her which she had taken from a little market-basket hanging upon her arm. Through the glade a pack of wolves were pursuing her.

The narrative told, that on her return homeward with her marketing, she had been chased by wolves, and barely escaped by flying at her utmost speed, from time to time retarding, as she did so, the pursuit, by throwing, piece by piece, the contents of her basket, in her wake, to be devoured and fought for by the famished beasts of prey.

This print had seized my imagination. I looked with a curious interest on the print: something in the disposition of the trees, their great height, and rude boughs, interlacing, and the awful shadow beneath, reminded me of a portion of the Windmill Wood where Milly and I had often rambled. Then I looked at the figure of the poor girl, flying for her life, and glancing terrified over her shoulder. Then I gazed on the gaping, murderous pack, and the hoary brute that led the van; and then I leaned back in my chair, and I thought—perhaps some latent association suggested what seemed a thing so unlikely—of a fine print in my portfolio from Vandyke's noble picture of Belisarius. Idly I traced with my pencil, as I leaned back, on an envelope that lay upon the table, this little inscription. It was mere fiddling; and, absurd as it looked, there was nothing but an honest meaning in it:—'20,000*l*. Date Obolum Belisario!' My dear father had translated the little Latin inscription for me, and I had written it down as a sort of exercise of memory; and also, perhaps, as expressive of that sort of compassion which my uncle's fall and miserable fate excited invariably in me. So I threw this queer little memorandum upon the open leaf of the book, and again the flight, the pursuit, and the bait to stay it, engaged my eye. And I heard a voice near the hearthstone, as I thought, say, in a stern whisper, 'Fly the fangs of Belisarius!'

'What's that?' said I, turning sharply to Mary Quince.

Mary rose from her work at the fireside, staring at me with that odd sort of frown that accompanies fear and curiosity.

'You spoke? Did you speak?' I said, catching her by the arm, very much frightened myself.

'No, Miss; no, dear!' answered she, plainly thinking that I was a little wrong in my head.

There could be no doubt it was a trick of the imagination, and yet to this hour I could recognise that clear stern voice among a thousand, were it to speak again.

Jaded after a night of broken sleep and much agitation, I was summoned next morning to my uncle's room.

He received me *oddly*, I thought. His manner had changed, and made an uncomfortable impression upon me. He was gentle, kind, smiling, submissive, as usual; but it seemed to me that he experienced henceforth toward me the same half-superstitous repulsion which I had always felt from him. Dream, or voice, or vision—which had done it? There seemed to be an unconscious antipathy and fear. When he thought I was not looking, his eyes were sometimes grimly fixed for a moment upon me. When I looked at him, his eyes were upon the book before him; and when he spoke, a person not heeding what he uttered would have fancied that he was reading aloud from it.

There was nothing tangible but this shrinking from the encounter of our eyes. I said he was kind as usual. He was even more so. But there was this new sign of our silently repellant natures. Dislike it could not be. He knew I longed to serve him. Was it shame? Was there not a shade of horror in it?

'I have not slept,' said he. 'For me the night has passed in thought, and the fruit of it is this—I *cannot*, Maud, accept your noble offer.'

'I am *very* sorry,' exclaimed I, in all honesty.

'I know it, my dear niece, and appreciate your goodness; but there are many reasons—none of them, I trust, ignoble—and which together render it impossible. No. It would be misunderstood—my honour shall not be impugned.'

'But, sir, that could not be; you have never proposed it. It would be all, from first to last, *my* doing.'

'True, dear Maud, but I know, alas! more of this evil and slanderous world than your happy inexperience can do. Who will receive our testimony? None—no, not one. The difficulty—the insuperable moral difficulty is this—that I should expose myself to the plausible imputation of having worked upon you, unduly, for this end; and more, that I could not hold myself quite free from blame. It is your voluntary goodness, Maud. But you are young, inexperienced; and it is, I hold it, my duty to stand between you and any dealing with your property at so unripe an age. Some people may call this Quixotic. In my mind it is an imperious mandate of conscience; and I peremptorily refuse to disobey it, although within three weeks an execution will be in this house!'

I did not quite know what an execution meant; but from two harrowing novels, with whose distresses I was familiar, I knew that it indicated some direful process of legal torture and spoliation.

'Oh, uncle I—oh, sir!—you cannot allow this to happen. What will people say of me? And—and there is poor Milly—and *everything*! Think what it will be.'

'It cannot be helped—*you* cannot help it, Maud. Listen to me. There will be an execution here, I cannot say exactly how soon, but, I think, in a little more than a fortnight. I must provide for your comfort. You must leave. I have arranged that you shall join Milly, for the present, in France, till I have time to look about me. You had better, I think, write to your cousin, Lady Knollys. She, with all her oddities, has a heart. Can you say, Maud, that I have been kind?'

'You have never been anything but kind,' I exclaimed.

'That I've been self-denying when you made me a generous offer?' he continued. 'That I now act to spare you pain? You may tell her, not as a message from me, but as a fact, that I am seriously thinking of vacating my guardianship—that I feel I have done her an injustice, and that, so soon as my mind is a little less tortured, I shall endeavour to effect a reconciliation with her, and would wish ultimately to transfer the care of your person and education to *her*. You may say I have no longer an interest even in vindicating my name. My son has wrecked himself by a marriage. I forgot to tell you he stopped at Feltram, and this morning wrote to pray a parting interview. If I grant it, it shall be the last. I shall never see him or correspond with him more.'

The old man seemed much overcome, and held his hankerchief to his eyes.

'He and his wife are, I understand, about to emigrate; the sooner the better,' he resumed, bitterly. 'Deeply, Maud, I regret having tolerated his suit to you, even for a moment. Had I thought it over, as I did the whole case last night, nothing could have induced me to permit it. But I have lived for so long like a monk in his cell, my wants and observation limited to the narrow compass of this chamber, that my knowledge of the world has died out with my youth and my hopes: and I did not, as I ought to have done, consider many objections. Therefore, dear Maud, on this one subject, I entreat, be silent; its discussion can effect nothing now. I was wrong, and frankly ask you to forget my mistake.'

I had been on the point of writing to Lady Knollys on this odious subject, when, happily, it was set at rest by the disclosure of yesterday; and being so, I could have no difficulty in acceding to my uncle's request. He was conceding so much that I could not withhold so trifling a concession in return.

'I hope Monica will continue to be kind to poor Milly after I am gone.'

Here there were a few seconds of meditation.

'Maud, you will not, I think, refuse to convey the substance of what I have just said in a letter to Lady Knollys, and perhaps you would have no objection to let me see it when it is written. It will prevent the possibility of its containing any misconception of what I have just spoken: and, Maud, you won't forget to say whether I have been kind. It would be a satisfaction to me to know that Monica was assured that I never either teased or bullied my young ward.'

With these words he dismissed me; and forthwith I completed such a letter as would quite embody what he had said; and in my own glowing terms, being in high good-humour with Uncle Silas, recorded my estimate of his gentleness and good-nature; and when I submitted it to him, he expressed his admiration of what he was pleased to call my cleverness in so exactly conveying what he wished, and his gratitude for the handsome terms in which I had spoken of my old guardian.

CHAPTER LIII

AN ODD PROPOSAL

As I and Mary Quince returned from our walk that day, and had entered the hall, I was surprised most disagreeably by Dudley's emerging from the vestibule at the foot of the great staircase. He was, I suppose, in his travelling costume—a rather soiled white surtout, a great coloured muffler in folds about his throat, his 'chimney-pot' on, and his fur cap sticking out from his pocket. He had just descended, I suppose, from my uncle's room. On seeing me he stepped back, and stood with his shoulders to the wall, like a mummy in a museum.

I pretended to have a few words to say to Mary before leaving the hall, in the hope that, as he seemed to wish to escape me, he would take the opportunity of getting quickly off the scene.

But he had changed his mind, it would seem, in the interval; for when I glanced in that direction again he had moved toward us, and stood in the hall with his hat in his hand. I must do him the justice to say he looked horribly dismal, sulky, and frightened.

'Ye'll gi'e me a word, Miss—only a thing I ought to say—for your good; by ——, mind, it's for *your* good, Miss.'

Dudley stood a little way off, viewing me, with his hat in both hands and a 'glooming' countenance.

I detested the idea of either hearing or speaking to him; but I had no resolution to refuse, and only saying 'I can't imagine what you can wish to speak to me about,' I approached him. 'Wait there at the banister, Quince.'

There was a fragrance of alcohol about the flushed face and gaudy muffler of this odious cousin, which heightened the effect of his horribly dismal features. He was speaking, besides, a little thickly; but his manner was dejected, and he was treating me with an elaborate and discomfited respect which reassured me.

'I'm a bit up a tree, Miss,' he said shuffling his feet on the oak floor. 'I behaved a d—— fool; but I baint one o' they sort. I'm a fellah as 'ill fight his man, an' stan' up to 'm fair, don't ye see? An' *baint* one o' they sort—no, *dang* it, I baint.'

Dudley delivered his puzzling harangue with a good deal of undertoned vehemence, and was strangely agitated. He, too, had got an unpleasant way of avoiding my eye, and glancing along the floor from corner to corner as he spoke, which gave him a very hang-dog air.

He was twisting his fingers in his great sandy whisker, and pulling it roughly enough to drag his cheek about by that savage purchase; and with his other hand he was crushing and rubbing his hat against his knee.

'The old boy above there be half crazed, I think; he don't mean half as he says thof, not he. But I'm in a bad fix anyhow—a regular sell it's been, and I can't get a tizzy out of him. So, ye see, I'm up a tree, Miss; and he sich a one, he'll make it a wuss mull if I let him. He's as sharp wi' me as one o' them lawyer chaps, dang 'em, and he's a lot of I O's and rubbitch o' mine; and Bryerly writes to me he can't gi'e me my legacy, 'cause he's got a notice from Archer and Sleigh a warnin' him not to gi'e me as much as a bob; for I signed it away to governor, he says—which I believe's a lie. I may a' signed some writing—'appen I did—when I was a bit cut one night. But that's no way to catch a gentleman, and 'twon't stand. There's justice to be had, and 'twon't *stand*, I say; and I'm not in 'is hands that way. Thof I may be a bit up the spout, too, I don't deny; only I baint agoin' the whole hog all at once. I'm none o' they sort. He'll find I baint.'

Here Mary Quince coughed demurely from the foot of the stair, to remind me that the conversation was protracted.

'I don't very well understand,' I said gravely; 'and I am now going up-stairs.'

'Don't jest a minute, Miss; it's only a word, ye see. We'll be goin' t' Australia, Sary Mangles, an' me, aboard the *Seamew*, on the 5th. I'm for Liverpool to-night, and she'll meet me there, an'—an', please God Almighty, ye'll never see me more; an I'd rather gi'e ye a lift, Maud, before I go: an' I tell ye what, if ye'll just gi'e me your written promise ye'll gi'e me that twenty thousand ye were offering to gi'e the Governor, I'll take ye cleverly out o' Bartram, and put ye wi' your cousin Knollys, or anywhere ye like best.'

'Take me from Bartram—for twenty thousand pounds! Take me away from my guardian! You seem to forget, sir,' my indignation rising as I spoke, 'that I can visit my cousin, Lady Knollys, whenever I please.'

'Well, that is as it may be,' he said, with a sulky deliberation, scraping about a little bit of paper that lay on the floor with the toe of his boot.

'It *is* as it may be, and that is as I say, sir; and considering how you have treated me—your mean, treacherous, and infamous suit, and your cruel treason to your poor wife, I am amazed at your effrontery.'

I turned to leave him, being, in truth, in one of my passions.

'Don't ye be a flying' out,' he said peremptorily, and catching me roughly by the wrist,' I baint a-going to vex ye. What a mouth you be, as can't see your way! Can't ye speak wi' common sense, like a woman—dang it—for once, and not keep brawling like a brat—can't ye see what I'm saying? I'll take ye out o' all this, and put ye wi' your cousin, or wheresoever you list, if ye'll gi'e me what I say.'

He was, for the first time, looking me in the face, but with contracted eyes, and a countenance very much agitated.

'Money?' said I, with a prompt disdain.

'Ay, money—twenty thousand pounds—*there*. On or off?' he replied, with an unpleasant sort of effort.

'You ask my promise for twenty thousand pounds, and you shan't have it.'

My cheeks were flaming, and I stamped on the ground as I spoke.

If he had known how to appeal to my better feelings, I am sure I should have done, perhaps not quite that, all at once at least, but something handsome, to assist him. But this application was so shabby and insolent! What could he take me for? That I should suppose his placing me with Cousin Monica constituted her my guardian? Why, he must fancy me the merest baby. There was a kind of stupid cunning in this that disgusted my good-nature and outraged my self-importance.

'You won't gi'e me that, then?' he said, looking down again, with a frown, and working his mouth and cheeks about as I could fancy a man rolling a piece of tobacco in his jaw.

'Certainly *not*, sir,' I replied.

'*Take* it, then,' he replied, still looking down, very black and discontented.

I joined Mary Quince, extremely angry. As I passed under the carved oak arch of the vestibule, I saw his figure in the deepening twilight. The picture remains in its murky halo fixed in memory. Standing where he last spoke in the centre of the hall, not looking after me, but downward, and, as well as I could see, with the countenance of a man who has lost a game, and a ruinous wager too—that is black and desperate. I did not utter a syllable on the way up. When I reached my room, I began to reconsider the interview more at my leisure. I was, such were my ruminations, to have agreed at once to his preposterous offer, and to have been driven, while he smirked and grimaced behind my back at his acquaintances, through Feltram in his dog-cart to Elverston; and then, to the just indignation of my uncle, to have been delivered up to Lady Knolly's guardianship, and to have handed my driver, as I alighted, the handsome fare of 20.000*l*. It required the impudence of Tony Lumpkin, without either his fun or his shrewdness, to have conceived such a prodigious practical joke.

'Maybe you'd like a little tea, Miss?' insinuated Mary Quince.

'What impertinence!' I exclaimed, with one of my angry stamps on the floor. 'Not you, dear old Quince,' I added. 'No—no tea just now.'

And I resumed my ruminations, which soon led me to this train of thought—'Stupid and insulting as Dudley's proposition was, it yet involved a great treason against my uncle. Should I be weak enough to be silent, may he not, wishing to forestall me, misrepresent all that has passed, so as to throw the blame altogether upon me?'

This idea seized upon me with a force which I could not withstand; and on the impulse of the moment I obtained admission to my uncle, and related exactly what had passed. When I had finished my narrative, which he listened to without once raising his eyes, my uncle cleared his throat once or twice, as if to speak. He was smiling—I thought with an effort, and with elevated brows. When I concluded, he hummed one of those sliding notes, which a less refined man might have expressed by a whistle of surprise and contempt, and again he essayed to speak, but continued silent. The fact is, he seemed to me very much disconcerted. He rose from his seat, and shuffled about the room in his slippers, I believe affecting only to be in search of something, opening and shutting two or three drawers, and turning over some books and papers; and at length, taking up some loose sheets of manuscript, he appeared to have found what he was looking for, and began to read them carelessly, with his back towards me, and with another effort to clear his voice, he said at last—

'And pray, what could the fool mean by all that?'

'I think he must have taken me for an idiot, sir,' I answered.

'Not unlikely. He has lived in a stable, among horses and ostlers; he has always seemed to me something like a centaur—that is a centaur composed not of man and horse, but of an ape and an ass.'

And upon this jibe he laughed, not coldly and sarcastically, as was his wont, but, I thought, flurriedly. And, continuing to look into his papers, he said, his back still toward me as he read—

'And he did not favour you with an exposition of his meaning, which, except in so far as it estimated his deserts at the modest sum you have named, appears to me too oracular to be interpreted without a kindred inspiration?'

And again he laughed. He was growing more like himself.

'As to your visiting your cousin, Lady Knollys, the stupid rogue had only five minutes before heard me express my wish that you should do so before leaving this. I am quite resolved you shall—that is, unless, dear Maud, you should yourself object; but, of course, we must wait for an invitation, which, I conjecture, will not be long in coming. In fact, your letter will naturally bring it about, and, I trust, open the way to a permanent residence with her. The more I think it over, the more am I convinced, dear niece, that as things are likely to turn out, my roof would be no desirable shelter for you; and that, under all circumstances, hers would. Such were my motives, Maud, in opening, through your letter, a door of reconciliation between us.'

I felt that I ought to have kissed his hand—that he had indicated precisely the future that I most desired; and yet there was within me a vague feeling, akin to suspicion—akin to dismay which chilled and overcast my soul.

'But, Maud,' he said, 'I am disquieted to think of that stupid jackanapes presuming to make you such an offer! A creditable situation truly—arriving in the dark at Elverston, under the solitary escort of that wild young man, with whom you would have fled from my guardianship; and, Maud, I tremble as I ask myself the question, would he have conducted you to Elverston at all? When you have lived as long in the world as I, you will appreciate its wickedness more justly.' Here there was a little pause.

'I know, my dear, that were he convinced of his legal marriage with that young woman,' he resumed, perceiving how startled I looked, 'such an idea, of course, would not have entered his head; but he does not believe any such thing. Contrary to fact and logic, he does honestly think that his hand is still at his disposal; and I certainly do suspect that he would have employed that excursion in endeavouring to persuade you to think as he does. Be that how it may, however, it is satisfactory to me to know that you shall never more be troubled by one word from that ill-regulated young man. I made him my adieux, such as they were, this evening; and never more shall he enter the walls of Bartram-Haugh while we two live.'

Uncle Silas replaced the papers which had ostensibly interested him so much, and returned. There was a vein which was visible near the angle of his lofty temple, and in moments of agitation stood out against the surrounding pallor in a knotted blue cord; and as he came back smiling askance, I saw this sign of inward tumult.

'We can, however, afford to despise the follies and knaveries of the world, Maud, as long as we act, as we have hitherto done, with perfect confidence in each other. Heaven bless you, dear Maud! Your report troubled me, I believe, more than it need—troubled me a good deal; but reflection assures me it is nothing. He is gone. In a few days' time he will be on the sea. I will issue my orders to-morrow morning, and he will never more, during his brief stay in England, gain admission to Bartram-Haugh. Good-night, my good niece; I thank you.'

And so I returned to Mary Quince, on the whole happier than I had left her, but still with the confused and jarring vision I could not interpret perpetually rising before me; and as, from time to time, shapeless anxieties agitated me, relieving them by appeals to Him who alone is wise and strong.

Next day brought me a goodnatured gossiping letter from dear Milly, written in compulsory French, which was, in some places, very difficult to interpret. She gave me a very pleasant account of the place, and her opinion of the girls who were inmates, and mentioned some of the nuns with high commendation. The language plainly cramped poor Milly's genius; but although there was by no means so much fun as an honest English letter would have brought me, there could be no mistake about her liking the place, and she expressed her honest longing to see me in the most affectionate terms.

This letter came enclosed in one to my uncle, from the proper authority in the convent; and as there was neither address within, nor post-mark without, I was as much in the dark as ever as to poor Milly's whereabouts.

Pencilled across the envelope of this letter, in my uncle's hand, were the words, 'Let me have your answer when sealed, and I will transmit it.—S.R.'

When, accordingly, some days later, I did place my letter to Milly in my uncle's hands, he told me the reason of his reserves on the subject.

'I thought it best, dear Maud, not to plague you with a secret, and Milly's present address is one. It will in a few weeks become the rallying-point of our diverse routes, when you shall meet her, and I join you both. Nobody, until the storm shall have blown over, must know where I am to be found, except my lawyer; and I think you would prefer ignorance to the trouble of keeping a secret on which so much may depend.'

This being reasonable, and even considerate, I acquiesced.

In that interval there reached me such a charming, gay, and affectionate letter—a very *long* letter, too—though the writer was scarcely seven miles away, from dear Cousin Monica, full of pleasant gossip, and rose-coloured and golden castles in the air, and the kindest interest in poor Milly, and the warmest affection for me.

One other incident varied that interval, if possible more pleasantly than those. It was the announcement, in a Liverpool paper, of the departure of the *Seamew*, bound for Melbourne; and among the passengers were reported 'Dudley Ruthyn, Esquire, of Bartram-H., and Mrs. D. Ruthyn.'

And now I began to breathe freely, I plainly saw the end of my probation approaching: a short excursion to France, a happy meeting with Milly, and then a delightful residence with Cousin Monica for the remainder of my nonage.

You will say then that my spirits and my serenity were quite restored. Not quite. How marvellously lie our anxieties, in filmy layers, one over the other! Take away that which has lain on the upper surface for so long—the care of cares—the only one, as it seemed to you, between your soul and the radiance of Heaven—and straight you find a new stratum there. As physical science tells us no fluid is without its skin, so does it seem with this fine medium of the soul, and these successive films of care that form upon its surface on mere contact with the upper air and light.

What was my new trouble? A very fantastic one, you will say—the illusion of a self-tormentor. It was the face of Uncle Silas which haunted me. Notwithstanding the old pale smile, there was a shrinking grimness, and the always-averted look.

Sometimes I fancied his mind was disordered. I could not account for the eerie lights and shadows that flickered on his face, except so. There was a look of shame and fear of me, amazing as that seems, in the sheen of his peaked smile.

I thought, 'Perhaps he blames himself for having tolerated Dudley's suit—for having urged it on grounds of personal distress—for having altogether lowered, though under sore temptation, both himself and his office; and he thinks that he has forfeited my respect.'

Such was my analysis; but in the *coup-d'oeil* of that white face that dazzled me in darkness, and haunted my daily reveries with a faded light, there was an intangible character of the insidious and the terrible.

CHAPTER LIV

IN SEARCH OF MR. CHARKE'S SKELETON

On the whole, however, I was unspeakably relieved. Dudley Ruthyn, Esq., and Mrs. D. Ruthyn, were now skimming the blue waves on the wings of the *Seamew*, and every morning widened the distance between us, which was to go on increasing until it measured a point on the antipodes. The Liverpool paper containing this golden line was carefully preserved in my room; and like the gentleman who, when much tried by the shrewish heiress whom he had married, used to retire to his closet and read over his marriage settlement, I used, when blue devils haunted me, to unfold my newspaper and read the paragraph concerning the *Seamew*.

The day I now speak of was a dismal one of sleety snow. My own room seemed to me cheerier than the lonely parlour, where I could not have had good Mary Quince so decorously.

A good fire, that kind and trusty face, the peep I had just indulged in at my favourite paragraph, and the certainty of soon seeing my dear cousin Monica, and afterwards affectionate Milly, raised my spirits.

'So,' said I, 'as old Wyat, you say, is laid up with rheumatism, and can't turn up to scold me, I think I'll run up stairs and make an exploration, and find poor Mr. Charke's skeleton in a closet.'

'Oh, law, Miss Maud, how can you say such things!' exclaimed good old Quince, lifting up her honest grey head and round eyes from her knitting.

I had grown so familiar with the frightful tradition of Mr. Charke and his suicide, that I could now afford to frighten old Quince with him.

'I am quite serious. I am going to have a ramble up-stairs and down-stairs, like goosey-goosey-gander; and if I do light upon his chamber, it is all the more interesting. I feel so like Adelaide, in the "Romance of the Forest," the book I was reading to you last night, when she commenced her delightful rambles through the interminable ruined abbey in the forest.'

'Shall I go with you, Miss?'

'No, Quince; stay there; keep a good fire, and make some tea. I suspect I shall lose heart and return very soon;' and with a shawl about me, cowl fashion, over my head, I stole up-stairs.

I shall not recount with the particularity of the conscientious heroine of Mrs. Ann Radcliffe, all the suites of apartments, corridors, and lobbies, which I threaded in my ramble. It will be enough to mention that I lighted upon a door at the end of a long gallery, which, I think, ran parallel with the front of the house; it interested me because it had the air of having been very long undisturbed. There were two rusty bolts, which did not evidently belong to its original securities, and had been, though very long ago, somewhat clumsily superadded. Dusty and rusty they were, but I had no difficulty in drawing them back. There was a rusty key, I remember it well, with a crooked handle in the lock; I tried to turn it, but could not. My curiosity was piqued. I was thinking of going back and getting Mary Quince's assistance. It struck me, however, that possibly it was not locked, so I pulled the door and it opened quite easily. I did not find myself in a strangely-furnished suite of apartments, but at the entrance of a gallery, which diverged at right angles from that through which I had just passed; it was very imperfectly lighted, and ended in total darkness.

I began to think how far I had already come, and to consider whether I could retrace my steps with accuracy in case of a panic, and I had serious thoughts of returning.

The idea of Mr. Charke was growing unpleasantly sharp and menacing; and as I looked down the long space before me, losing itself among ambiguous shadows, lulled in a sinister silence, and as it were inviting my entrance like a trap, I was very near yielding to the cowardly impulse.

But I took heart of grace and determined to see a little more. I opened a side-door, and entered a large room, where were, in a corner, some rusty and cobwebbed bird-cages, but nothing more. It was a wainscoted room, but a white mildew stained the panels. I looked from the window: it commanded that dismal, weed-choked quadrangle into which I had once looked from another window. I opened a door at its farther end, and entered another chamber, not quite so large, but equally dismal, with the same prison-like look-out, not very easily discerned through the grimy panes and the sleet that was falling thickly outside. The door through which I had entered made a little accidental creak, and, with my heart at my lips, I gazed at it, expecting to see Charke, or the skeleton of which I had talked so lightly, stalk in at the half-open aperture. But I had an odd sort of courage which was always fighting against my cowardly nerves, and I walked to the door, and looking up and down the dismal passage, was reassured.

Well, one room more—just that whose deep-set door fronted me, with a melancholy frown, at the opposite end of the chamber. So to it I glided, shoved it open, advancing one step, and the great bony figure of Madame de la Rougierre was before me.

I could see nothing else.

The drowsy traveller who opens his sheets to slip into bed, and sees a scorpion coiled between them, may have experienced a shock the same in kind, but immeasurably less in degree.

She sat in a clumsy old arm-chair, with an ancient shawl about her, and her bare feet in a delft tub. She looked a thought more withered. Her wig shoved back disclosed her bald wrinkled forehead, and enhanced the ugly effect of her exaggerated features and the gaunt hollows of her face. With a sense of incredulity and terror I gazed, freezing, at this evil phantom, who returned my stare for a few seconds with a shrinking scowl, dismal and grim, as of an evil spirit detected.

The meeting, at least then and there, was as complete a surprise for her as for me. She could not tell how I might take it; but she quickly rallied, burst into a loud screeching laugh, and, with her old Walpurgis gaiety, danced some fantastic steps in her bare wet feet, tracking the floor with water, and holding out with finger and thumb, in dainty caricature, her slammakin old skirt, while she sang some of her nasal patois with an abominable hilarity and emphasis.

With a gasp, I too recovered from the fascination of the surprise. I could not speak though for some seconds, and Madame was first.

'Ah, dear Maud, what surprise! Are we not overjoy, dearest, and cannot speak? I am full of joy—quite charmed—*ravie*—of seeing you. So are you of me, your face betray. Ah! yes, thou dear little baboon! here is poor Madame once more! Who could have imagine?'

'I thought you were in France, Madame,' I said, with a dismal effort.

'And so I was, dear Maud; I 'av just arrive. Your uncle Silas he wrote to the superioress for gouvernante to accompany a young lady—that is you, Maud—on her journey, and she send me; and so, ma chère, here is poor Madame arrive to charge herself of that affair.'

'How soon do we leave for France, Madame?' I asked.

'I do not know, but the old women—wat is her name?'

'Wyat,' I suggested.

'Oh! oui, Waiatt;—she says two, three week. And who conduct you to poor Madame's apartment, my dear Maud?' She inquired insinuatingly.

'No one, I answered promptly: 'I reached it quite accidentally, and I can't imagine why you should conceal yourself.' Something like indignation kindled in my mind as I began to wonder at the sly strategy which had been practised upon me.

'I 'av not conceal myself, Mademoiselle,' retorted the governness. 'I 'av act precisally as I 'av been ordered. Your uncle, Mr. Silas Ruthyn, he is afraid, Waiatt says, to be interrupted by his creditors, and everything must be done very quaitly. I have been commanded to avoid *me faire voir*, you know, and I must obey my employer—voilà tout!'

'And for how long have you been residing here?' I persisted, in the same resentful vein.

"Bout a week. It is soche triste place! I am so glad to see you, Maud! I've been so isolée, you dear leetle fool!'

'You are *not* glad, Madame; you don't love me—you never did,' I exclaimed with sudden vehemence.

'Yes, I am *very* glad; you know not, chère petite *niaise*, how I 'av desire to educate you a leetle more. Let us understand one another. You think I do not love you, Mademoiselle, because you have mentioned to your poor papa that little *dérèglement* in his library. I have repent very often that so great indiscretion of my life. I thought to find some letters of Dr. Braierly. I think that man was trying to get your property, my dear Maud, and if I had found something I would tell you all about. But it was very great *sottise*, and you were very right to denounce me to Monsieur. Je n'ai point de rancune contre vous. No, no, none at all. On the contrary, I shall be your *gardienne tutelaire*—wat you call?—guardian angel—ah, yes, that is it. You think I speak *par dérision*; not at all. No, my dear cheaile, I do not speak *par moquerie*, unless perhaps the very least degree in the world.'

And with these words Madame laughed unpleasantly, showing the black caverns at the side of her mouth, and with a cold, steady malignity in her gaze.

'Yes,' I said; 'I know what you mean, Madame—you *hate* me.'

'Oh! wat great ogly word! I am shock! *vous me faites honte*. Poor Madame, she never hate any one; she loves all her friends, and her enemies she leaves to Heaven; while I am, as you see, more gay, more *joyeuse* than ever, they have not been 'appy—no, they have not been fortunate these others. Wen I return, I find always some of my enemy they 'av die, and some they have put themselves into embarrassment, or there has arrived to them some misfortune;' and Madame shrugged and laughed a little scornfully.

A kind of horror chilled my rising anger, and I was silent.

'You see, my dear Maud, it is very natural you should think I hate you. When I was with Mr. Austin Ruthyn, at Knowl, you know you did not like a me—never. But in consequence of our intimacy I confide you that which I 'av of most dear in the world, my reputation. It is always so. The pupil can *calomniate*, without been discover, the gouvernante. 'Av I not been always kind to you, Maud? Which 'av I use of violence or of sweetness the most? I am, like other persons, *jalouse de ma réputation*; and it was difficult to suffer with patience the banishment which was invoked by you, because chiefly for your good, and for an indiscretion to which I was excited by motives the most pure and laudable. It was you who spied so cleverly—eh! and denounce me to Monsieur Ruthyn? Helas! wat bad world it is!'

'I do not mean to speak at all about that occurrence, Madame; I will not discuss it. I dare say what you tell me of the cause of your engagement here is true, and I suppose we must travel, as you say, in company; but you must know that the less we see of each other while in this house the better.'

'I am not so sure of that, my sweet little *béte*; your education has been neglected, or rather entirely abandoned, since you 'av arrive at this place, I am told. You must not be a *bestiole*. We must do, you and I, as we are ordered. Mr. Silas Ruthyn he will tell us.'

All this time Madame was pulling on her stockings, getting her boots on, and otherwise proceeding with her dowdy toilet. I do not know why I stood there talking to her. We often act very differently from what we would have done upon reflection. I had involved myself in a dialogue, as wiser generals than I have entangled themselves in a general action when they meant only an affair of outposts.

I had grown a little angry, and would not betray the least symptom of fear, although I felt that sensation profoundly.

'My beloved father thought you so unfit a companion for me that he dismissed you at an hour's notice, and I am very sure that my uncle will think as he did; you are *not* a fit companion for me, and had my uncle known what had passed he would never have admitted you to this house—never!'

'Helas! *Quelle disgrace*! And you really think so, my dear Maud,' exclaimed Madame, adjusting her wig before her glass, in the corner of which I could see half of her sly, grinning face, as she ogled herself in it.

'I do, and so do you, Madame,' I replied, growing more frightened.

'It may be—we shall see; but everyone is not so cruel as you, *ma chère petite calomniatrice*.'

'You shan't call me those names,' I said, in an angry tremor.

'What name, dearest cheaile?'

'*Calomniatrice*—that is an insult.'

'Why, my most foolish little Maud, we may say rogue, and a thousand other little words in play which we do not say seriously.

'You are not playing—you never play—you are angry, and you hate me,' I exclaimed, vehemently.

'Oh, fie!—wat shame! Do you not perceive, dearest cheaile, how much education you still need? You are proud, little demoiselle; you must become, on the contrary, quaite humble. Je ferai baiser le babouin à vous—ha, ha, ha! I weel make a you to kees the monkey. You are too proud, my dear cheaile.'

'I am not such a fool as I was at Knowl,' I said; 'you shall not terrify me here. I will tell my uncle the whole truth,' I said.

'Well, it may be that is the best,' she replied, with provoking coolness.

'You think I don't mean it?'

'Of course you *do*,' she replied.

'And we shall see what my uncle thinks of it.'

'We shall see, my dear,' she replied, with an air of mock contrition.

'Adieu, Madame!'

'You are going to Monsieur Ruthyn?—very good!'

I made her no answer, but more agitated than I cared to show her, I left the room. I hurried along the twilight passage, and turned into the long gallery that opened from it at right angles. I had not gone half-a-dozen steps on my return when I heard a heavy tread and a rustling behind me.

'I am ready, my dear; I weel accompany you,' said the smirking phantom, hurrying after me.

'Very well,' was my reply; and threading our way, with a few hesitations and mistakes, we reached and descended the stairs, and in a minute more stood at my uncle's door.

My uncle looked hard and strangely at us as we entered. He looked, indeed, as if his temper was violently excited, and glared and muttered to himself for a few seconds; and treating Madame to a stare of disgust, he asked peevishly—

'Why am I disturbed, pray?'

'Miss Maud a Ruthyn, she weel explain,' replied Madame, with a great courtesy, like a boat going down in a ground swell.

'*Will* you explain, my dear?' he asked, in his coldest and most sarcastic tone.

I was agitated, and I am sure my statement was confused. I succeeded, however, in saying what I wanted.

'Why, Madame, this is a grave charge! Do you admit it, pray?'

Madame, with the coolest possible effrontery, denied it all; with the most solemn asseverations, and with streaming eyes and clasped hands, conjured me melodramatically to withdraw that intolerable story, and to do her justice. I stared at her for a while astounded, and turning suddenly to my uncle, as vehemently asserted the truth of every syllable I had related.

'You hear, my dear child, you hear her deny everything; what am I to think? You must excuse the bewilderment of my old head. Madame de la—that lady has arrived excellently recommended by the superioress of the place where dear Milly awaits you, and such persons are particular. It strikes me, my dear niece, that you must have made a mistake.'

I protested here. But he went on without seeming to hear the parenthesis—

'I know, my dear Maud, that you are quite incapable of wilfully deceiving anyone; but you are liable to be deceived like other young people. You were, no doubt, very nervous, and but half awake when you fancied you saw the occurrence you describe; and Madame de—de—'

'De la Rougierre,' I supplied.

'Yes, thank you—Madame de la Rougierre, who has arrived with excellent testimonials, strenuously denies the whole thing. Here is a conflict, my dear—in my mind a presumption of mistake. I confess I should prefer that theory to a peremptory assumption of guilt.'

I felt incredulous and amazed; it seemed as if a dream were being enacted before me. A transaction of the most serious import, which I had witnessed with my own eyes, and described with unexceptionable minuteness and consistency, is discredited by that strange and suspicious old man with an imbecile coolness. It was quite in vain my reiterating my statement, backing it with the most earnest asseverations. I was beating the air. It did not seem to reach his mind. It was all received with a simper of feeble incredulity.

He patted and smoothed my head—he laughed gently, and shook his while I insisted; and Madame protested her purity in now tranquil floods of innocent tears, and murmured mild and melancholy prayers for my enlightenment and reformation. I felt as if I should lose my reason.

'There now, dear Maud, we have heard enough; it is, I do believe, a delusion. Madame de la Rougierre will be your companion, at the utmost, for three or four weeks. Do exercise a little of your self-command and good sense—you know how I am tortured. Do not, I entreat, add to my perplexities. You may make yourself very happy with Madame if you will, I have no doubt.'

'I propose to Mademoiselle,' said Madame, drying her eyes with a gentle alacrity, 'to profit of my visit for her education. But she does not seem to weesh wat I think is so useful.'

'She threatened me with some horrid French vulgarism—*de faire baiser le babouin à moi*, whatever that means; and I know she hates me,' I replied, impetuously.

'Doucement—doucement!' said my uncle, with a smile at once amused and compassionate. 'Doucement! ma chère.'

With great hands and cunning eyes uplifted, Madame tearfully—for her tears came on short notice—again protested her absolute innocence. She had never in all her life so much as heard one so villain phrase.

'You see, my dear, you have misheard; young people never attend. You will do well to take advantage of Madame's short residence to get up your French a little, and the more you are with her the better.'

'I understand then, Mr. Ruthyn, you weesh I should resume my instructions?' asked Madame.

'Certainly; and converse all you can in French with Mademoiselle Maud. You will be glad, my dear, that I've insisted on it,' he said, turning to me, 'when you have reached France, where you will find they speak nothing else. And now, dear Maud—no, not a word more—you must leave me. Farewell, Madame!'

And he waved us out a little impatiently; and I, without one look toward Madame de la Rougierre, stunned and incensed, walked into my room and shut the door.

CHAPTER LV

THE FOOT OF HERCULES

I stood at the window—still the same leaden sky and feathery sleet before me—trying to estimate the magnitude of the discovery I had just made. Gradually a kind of despair seized me, and I threw myself passionately on my bed, weeping aloud.

Good Mary Quince was, of course, beside me in a moment, with her pale, concerned face.

'Oh, Mary, Mary, she's come—that dreadful woman, Madame de la Rougierre, has come to be my governess again; and Uncle Silas won't hear or believe anything about her. It is vain talking; he is prepossessed. Was ever so unfortunate a creature as I? Who could have fancied or feared such a thing? Oh, Mary, Mary, what am I to do? what is to become of me? Am I never to shake off that vindictive, terrible woman?'

Mary said all she could to console me. I was making too much of her. What was she, after all, more than a governess?—she could not hurt me. I was not a child no longer—she could not bully me now; and my uncle, though he might be deceived for a while, would not be long finding her out.

Thus and soforth did good Mary Quince declaim, and at last she did impress me a little, and I began to think that I had, perhaps, been making too much of Madame's visit. But still imagination, that instrument and mirror of prophecy, showed her formidable image always on its surface, with a terrible moving background of shadows.

In a few minutes there was a knock at my door, and Madame herself entered. She was in walking costume. There had been a brief clearing of the weather, and she proposed our making a promenade together.

On seeing Mary Quince she broke into a rapture of compliment and greeting, and took what Mr. Richardson would have called her passive hand, and pressed it with wonderful tenderness.

Honest Mary suffered all this somewhat reluctantly, never smiling, and, on the contrary, looking rather ruefully at her feet.

'Weel you make a some tea? When I come back, dear Mary Quince, I 'av so much to tell you and dear Miss Maud of all my adventures while I 'av been away; it will make a you laugh ever so much. I was—what you theenk?—near, ever so near to be married!' And upon this she broke into a screeching laugh, and shook Mary Quince merrily by the shoulder.

I sullenly declined going out, or rising; and when she had gone away, I told Mary that I should confine myself to my room while Madame stayed.

But self-denying ordinances self-imposed are not always long observed by youth. Madame de la Rougierre laid herself out to be agreeable; she had no end of stories—more than half, no doubt, pure fictions—to tell, but all, in that triste place, amusing. Mary Quince began to entertain a better opinion of her. She actually helped to make beds, and tried to be in every way of use, and seemed to have quite turned over a new leaf; and so gradually she moved me, first to listen, and at last to talk.

On the whole, these terms were better than a perpetual skirmish; but, notwithstanding all her gossip and friendliness, I continued to have a profound distrust and even terror of her.

She seemed curious about the Bartram-Haugh family, and all their ways, and listened darkly when I spoke. I told her, bit by bit, the whole story of Dudley, and she used, whenever there was news of the Seamew, to read the paragraph for my benefit; and in poor Milly's battered little Atlas she used to trace the ship's course with a pencil, writing in, from point to point, the date at which the vessel was 'spoken' at sea. She seemed amused at the irrepressible satisfaction with which I received these minutes of his progress; and she used to calculate the distance;—on such a day he was two hundred and sixty miles, on such another five hundred; the last point was more than eight hundred—good, better, best—best of all would be those 'deleecious antipode, w'ere he would so soon promener on his head twelve thousand mile away;' and at the conceit she would fall into screams of laughter.

Laugh as she might, however, there was substantial comfort in thinking of the boundless stretch of blue wave that rolled between me and that villainous cousin.

I was now on very odd terms with Madame. She had not relapsed into her favourite vein of oracular sarcasm and menace; she had, on the contrary, affected her good-humoured and genial vein. But I was not to be deceived by this. I carried in my heart that deep-seated fear of her which her unpleasant goodhumour and gaiety never disturbed for a moment. I was very glad, therefore, when she went to Todcaster by rail, to make some purchases for the journey which we were daily expecting to commence; and happy in the opportunity of a walk, good old Mary Quince and I set forth for a little ramble.

As I wished to make some purchases in Feltram, I set out, with Mary Quince for my companion. On reaching the great gate we found it locked. The key, however, was in it, and as it required more than the strength of my hand to turn, Mary tried it. At the same moment old Crowle came out of the sombre lodge by its side, swallowing down a mouthful of his dinner in haste. No one, I believe, liked the long suspicious face of the old man, seldom shorn or washed, and furrowed with great, grimy perpendicular wrinkles. Leering fiercely at Mary, not pretending to see me, he wiped his mouth hurriedly with the back of his hand, and growled—

'Drop it.'

'Open it, please, Mr. Crowle,' said Mary, renouncing the task.

Crowle wiped his mouth as before, looking inauspicious; shuffling to the spot, and muttering to himself, he first satisfied himself that the lock was fast, and then lodged the key in his coat-pocket, and still muttering, retraced his steps.

'We want the gate open, please,' said Mary.

No answer.

'Miss Maud wants to go into the town,' she insisted.

'We wants many a thing we can't get,' he growled, stepping into his habitation.

'Please open the gate,' I said, advancing.

He half turned on his threshold, and made a dumb show of touching his hat, although he had none on.

'Can't, ma'am; without an order from master, no one goes out here.'

'You won't allow me and my maid to pass the gate?' I said.

''Tisn't *me*, ma'am,' said he; 'but I can't break orders, and no one goes out without the master allows.'

And without awaiting further parley, he entered, shutting his hatch behind him.

So Mary and I stood, looking very foolish at one another. This was the first restraint I had experienced since Milly and I had been refused a passage through the Windmill paling. The rule, however, on which Crowle insisted I felt confident could not have been intended to apply to me. A word to Uncle Silas would set all right; and in the meantime I proposed to Mary that we should take a walk—my favourite ramble—into the Windmill Wood.

I looked toward Dickon's farmstead as we passed, thinking that Beauty might have been there. I did see the girl, who was plainly watching us. She stood in the doorway of the cottage, withdrawn into the shade, and, I fancied, anxious to escape observation. When we had passed on a little, I was confirmed in that belief by seeing her run down the footpath which led from the rear of the farmyard in the direction contrary to that in which we were moving.

'So,' I thought, 'poor Meg falls from me!'

Mary Quince and I rambled on through the wood, till we reached the windmill itself, and seeing its low arched door open, we entered the chiaro-oscuro of its circular basement. As we did so I heard a rush and the creak of a plank, and looking up, I saw just a foot—no more—disappearing through the trap-door.

In the case of one we love or fear intensely, what feats of comparative anatomy will not the mind unconsciously perform? Constructing the whole living animal from the turn of an elbow, the curl of a whisker, a segment of a hand. How instantaneous and unerring is the instinct!

'Oh, Mary, what have I seen!' I whispered, recovering from the fascination that held my gaze fast to the topmost rounds of the ladder, that disappeared in the darkness above the open door in the loft. 'Come, Mary—come away.'

At the same instant appeared the swarthy, sullen face of Dickon Hawkes in the shadow of the aperture. Having but one serviceable leg, his descent was slow and awkward, and having got his head to the level of the loft he stopped to touch his hat to me, and to hasp and lock the trap-door.

When this was done, the man again touched his hat, and looked steadily and searchingly at me for a second or so, while he got the key into his pocket.

'These fellahs stores their flour too long 'ere, ma'am. There's a deal o' trouble a-looking arter it. I'll talk wi' Silas, and settle that.'

By this time he had got upon the worn-tiled floor, and touching his hat again, he said—

'I'm a-goin' to lock the door, ma'am!'

So with a start, and again whispering—

'Come, Mary—come away'—

With my arm fast in hers, we made a swift departure.

'I feel very faint, Mary,' said I. 'Come quickly. There's nobody following us?'

'No, Miss, dear. That man with the wooden leg is putting a padlock on the door.'

'Come *very* fast,' I said; and when we had got a little farther, I said, 'Look again, and see whether anyone is following.'

'No one, Miss,' answered Mary, plainly surprised. 'He's putting the key in his pocket, and standin' there a-lookin' after us.'

'Oh, Mary, did not you see it?'

'What, Miss?' asked Mary, almost stopping.

'Come on, Mary. Don't pause. They will observe us,' I whispered, hurrying her forward.

'What did you see, Miss?' repeated Mary.

'*Mr. Dudley*,' I whispered, with a terrified emphasis, not daring to turn my head as I spoke.

'Lawk, Miss!' remonstrated honest Quince, with a protracted intonation of wonder and incredulity, which plainly implied a suspicion that I was dreaming.

'Yes, Mary. When we went into that dreadful room—that dark, round place—I saw his foot on the ladder. *His* foot, Mary I can't be mistaken. *I won't be questioned*. You'll *find* I'm right. He's *here*. He never went in that ship at all. A fraud has been practised on me—it is infamous—it is terrible. I'm frightened out of my life. For heaven's sake, look back again, and tell me what you see.'

'*Nothing*, Miss,' answered Mary, in contagious whispers, 'but that wooden-legged chap, standin' hard by the door.'

'And no one with him?'

'No one, Miss.'

We got without pursuit through the gate in the paling. I drew breath so soon as we had reached the cover of the thicket near the chestnut hollow, and I began to reflect that whoever the owner of the foot might be—and I was still instinctively certain that it was no other than Dudley—concealment was plainly his object. I need not, then, be at all uneasy lest he should pursue us.

As we walked slowly and in silence along the grassy footpath, I heard a voice calling my name from behind. Mary Quince had not heard it at all, but I was quite certain.

It was repeated twice or thrice, and, looking in considerable doubt and trepidation under the hanging boughs, I saw Beauty, not ten yards away, standing among the underwood.

I remember how white the eyes and teeth of the swarthy girl looked, as with hand uplifted toward her ear, she watched us while, as it seemed, listening for more distant sounds.

Beauty beckoned eagerly to me, advancing, with looks of great fear and anxiety, two or three short steps toward me.

'*She* baint to come,' said Beauty, under her breath, so soon as I had nearly reached her, pointing without raising her hand at Mary Quince.

'Tell her to sit on the ash-tree stump down yonder, and call ye as loud as she can if she sees any fellah a-comin' this way, an' rin ye back to me;' and she impatiently beckoned me away on her errand.

When I returned, having made this dispositions, I perceived how pale the girl was.

'Are you ill, Meg?' I asked.

'Never ye mind. Well enough. Listen, Miss; I must tell it all in a crack, an' if she calls, rin awa' to her, and le' me to myself, for if fayther or t'other un wor to kotch me here, I think they'd kill me a'most. Hish!'

She paused a second, looking askance, in the direction where she fancied Mary Quince was. Then she resumed in a whisper—

'Now, lass, mind ye, ye'll keep what I say to yourself. You're not to tell that un nor any other for your life, mind, a word o' what I'm goin' to tell ye.'

'I'll not say a word. Go on.'

'Did ye see Dudley?'

'I think I saw him getting up the ladder.'

'In the mill? Ha! that's him. He never went beyond Todcaster. He staid in Feltram after.'

It was my turn to look pale now. My worst conjecture was established.

CHAPTER LVI

I CONSPIRE

'That's a bad un, he is—oh, Miss, Miss Maud! It's nout that's good as keeps him an' fayther—(mind, lass, ye promised you would not tell no one)—as keeps them two a-talkin' and a-smokin' secret-like together in the mill. An' fayther don't know I found him out. They don't let me into the town, but Brice tells me, and he knows it's Dudley; and it's nout that's good, but summat very bad. An' I reckon, Miss, it's all about you. Be ye frightened, Miss Maud?'

I felt on the point of fainting, but I rallied.

'Not much, Meg. Go on, for Heaven's sake. Does Uncle Silas know he is here?'

'Well, Miss, they were with him, Brice told me, from eleven o'clock to nigh one o' Tuesday night, an' went in and come out like thieves, 'feard ye'd see 'em.'

'And how does Brice know anything bad?' I asked, with a strange freezing sensation creeping from my heels to my head and down again—I am sure deadly pale, but speaking very collectedly.

'Brice said, Miss, he saw Dudley a-cryin' and lookin' awful black, and says he to fayther, "'Tisn't in my line nohow, an' I can't;" and says fayther to he, "No one likes they soart o' things, but how can ye help it? The old boy's behind ye wi' his pitchfork, and ye canna stop." An' wi' that he bethought him o' Brice, and says he, "What be ye a-doin' there? Get ye down wi' the nags to blacksmith, do ye." An' oop gits Dudley, pullin' his hat ower his brows, an' says he, "I wish I was in the *Seamew*. I'm good for nout wi' this thing a-hangin' ower me." An' that's all as Brice heard. An' he's afeard o' fayther and Dudley awful. Dudley could lick him to pot if he crossed him, and he and fayther 'ud think nout o' havin' him afore the justices for poachin', and swearin' him into gaol.'

'But why does he think it's about *me*?'

'Hish!' said Meg, who fancied she heard a sound, but all was quiet. 'I can't say—we're in danger, lass. I don't know why—but *he* does, an' so do I, an', for that matter, so do *ye*.'

'Meg, I'll leave Bartram.'

'Ye can't.'

'Can't. What do you mean, girl?'

'They won't let ye oot. The gates is all locked. They've dogs—they've bloodhounds, Brice says. Ye *can't* git oot, mind; put that oot o' your head.

'I tell ye what ye'll do. Write a bit o' a note to the lady yonder at Elverston; an' though Brice be a wild fellah, and 'appen not ower good sometimes, he likes me, an' I'll make him take it. Fayther will be grindin' at mill to-morrow. Coom ye here about one o'clock—that's if ye see the mill-sails a-turnin'—and me and Brice will meet ye here. Bring that old lass wi' ye. There's an old French un, though, that talks wi' Dudley. Mind ye, that un knows nout o' the matter. Brice be a kind lad to me, whatsoe'er he be wi' others, and I think he won't split. Now, lass, I must go. God help ye; God bless ye; an', for the world's wealth, don't ye let one o' them see ye've got ought in your head, not even that un.'

Before I could say another word, the girl had glided from me, with a wild gesture of silence, and a shake of her head.

I can't at all account for the state in which I was. There are resources both of energy and endurance in human nature which we never suspect until the tremendous voice of necessity summons them into play. Petrified with a totally new horror, but with something of the coldness and impassiveness of the transformation, I stood, spoke, and acted—a wonder, almost a terror, to myself.

I met Madame on my return as if nothing had happened. I heard her ugly gabble, and looked at the fruits of her hour's shopping, as I might hear, and see, and talk, and smile, in a dream.

But the night was dreadful. When Mary Quince and I were alone, I locked the door. I continued walking up and down the room, with my hands clasped, looking at the inexorable floor, the walls, the ceiling, with a sort of imploring despair. I was afraid to tell my dear old Mary. The least indiscretion would be failure, and failure destruction.

I answered her perplexed solicitudes by telling her that I was not very well—that I was uneasy; but I did not fail to extract from her a promise that she would not hint to mortal, either my suspicions about Dudley, or our rencontre with Meg Hawkes.

I remember how, when, after we had got, late at night, into bed, I sat up, shivering with horror, in mine, while honest Mary's tranquil breathing told how soundly she slept. I got up, and looked from the window, expecting to see some of those wolfish dogs which they had brought to the place prowling about the courtyard. Sometimes I prayed, and felt tranquillised, and fancied that I was perhaps to have a short interval of sleep. But the serenity was delusive, and all the time my nerves were strung hysterically. Sometimes I felt quite wild, and on the point of screaming. At length that dreadful night passed away. Morning came, and a less morbid, though hardly a less terrible state of mind. Madame paid me an early visit. A thought struck me. I knew that she loved shopping, and I said, quite carelessly—

'Your yesterday's shopping tempts me, Madame, and I must get a few things before we leave for France. Suppose we go into Feltram to-day, and make my purchases, you and I?'

She looked from the corner of her cunning eye in my face without answering. I did not blench, and she said—

'Vary good. I would be vary 'appy,' and again she looked oddly at me.

'Wat hour, my dear Maud? One o'clock? I think that weel de very well, eh?'

I assented, and she grew silent.

I wonder whether I did look as careless as I tried. I do not know. Through the whole of this awful period I was, I think, supernatural; and I even now look back with wonder upon my strange self-command.

Madame, I hoped, had heard nothing of the order which prohibited my exit from the place. She would herself conduct me to Feltram, and secure, by accompanying me, my free egress.

Once in Feltram, I would assert my freedom, and manage to reach my dear cousin Knollys. Back to Bartram no power should convey me. My heart swelled and fluttered in the awful suspense of that hour.

Oh, Bartram-Haugh! how came you by those lofty walls? Which of my ancestors had begirt me with an impassable barrier in this horrible strait?

Suddenly I remembered my letter to Lady Knollys. If I were disappointed in effecting my escape through Feltram, all would depend upon it.

Having locked my door, I wrote as follows:—

'Oh, my beloved cousin, as you hope for comfort in *your* hour of fear, aid me now. Dudley has returned, and is secreted somewhere about the grounds. It is a *fraud.* They all pretend to me that he is gone away in the *Seamew*; and he or they had his name published as one of the passengers. Madame de la Rougierre has appeared! She is here, and my uncle insists on making her my close companion. I am at my wits' ends. I cannot escape—the walls are a prison; and I believe the eyes of my gaolers are always upon me. Dogs are kept for pursuit—yes, *dogs*! and the gates are locked against my escape. God help me! I don't know where to look, or whom to trust. I fear my uncle more than all. I think I could bear this better if I knew what their plans are, even the worst. If ever you loved or pitied me, dear cousin, I conjure you, help me in this extremity. Take me away from this. Oh, darling, for God's sake take me away!

'Your distracted and terrified cousin,
MAUD'

'BARTRAM-HAUGH.'

I sealed this letter jealously, as if the inanimate missive would burst its cerements, and proclaim my desperate appeal through all the chambers and passages of silent Bartram.

Old Quince, greatly to cousin Monica's amusement, persisted in furnishing me with those capacious pockets which belonged to a former generation. I was glad of this old-world eccentricity now, and placed my guilty letter, that, amidst all my hypocrisies, spoke out with terrible frankness, deep in this receptacle, and having hid away the pen and ink, my accomplices, I opened the door, and resumed my careless looks, awaiting Madame's return.

'I was to demand to Mr. Ruthyn the permission to go to Feltram, and I think he will allow. He want to speak to you.'

With Madame I entered my uncle's room. He was reclining on a sofa, his back towards us, and his long white hair, as fine as spun glass, hung over the back of the couch.

'I was going to ask you, dear Maud, to execute two or three little commissions for me in Feltram.'

My dreadful letter felt lighter in my pocket, and my heart beat violently.

'But I have just recollected that this is a market-day, and Feltram will be full of doubtful characters and tipsy persons, so we must wait till to-morrow; and Madame says, very kindly, that she will, as she does not so much mind, make any little purchases to-day which cannot conveniently wait.'

Madame assented with a courtesy to Uncle Silas, and a great hollow smile to me.

By this time Uncle Silas had raised himself from his reclining posture, and was sitting, gaunt and white, upon the sofa.

'News of my prodigal to-day,' he said, with a peevish smile, drawing the newspaper towards him. 'The vessel has been spoken again. How many miles away, do you suppose?'

He spoke in a plaintive key, looking at me, with hungry eyes, and a horribly smiling countenance.

'How far do you suppose Dudley is to-day?' and he laid the palm of his hand on the paragraph as he spoke. *Guess*!'

For a moment I fancied this was a theatric preparation to give point to the disclosure of Dudley's real whereabouts.

'It was a very long way. Guess!' he repeated.

So, stammering a little and pale, I performed the required hypocrisy, after which my uncle read aloud for my benefit the line or two in which were recorded the event, and the latitude and longitude of the vessel at the time, of which Madame made a note in her memory, for the purpose of making her usual tracing in poor Milly's Atlas.

I cannot say how it really was, but I fancied that Uncle Silas was all the time reading my countenance, with a grim and practised scrutiny; but nothing came of it, and we were dismissed.

Madame loved shopping, even for its own sake, but shopping with opportunities of peculation still more. She she had had her luncheon, and was dressed for the excursion, she did precisely what I now most desired—she proposed to take charge of my commissions and my money; and thus entrusted, left me at liberty to keep tryst at the Chestnut Hollow.

So soon as I had seen Madame fairly off, I hurried Mary Quince, and got my things on quickly. We left the house by the side entrance, which I knew my uncle's windows did not command. Glad was I to feel a slight breeze, enough to make the mill-sails revolve; and as we got further into the grounds, and obtained a distant view of the picturesque old windmill, I felt inexpressibly relieved on seeing that it was actually working.

We were now in the Chestnut Hollow, and I sent Mary Quince to her old point of observation, which commanded a view of the path in the direction of the Windmill Wood, with her former order to call 'I've found it,' as loudly as she could, in case she should see anyone approaching.

I stopped at the point of our yesterday's meeting. I peered under the branches, and my heart beat fast as I saw Meg Hawkes awaiting me.

CHAPTER LVII

THE LETTER

'Come away, lass,' whispered Beauty, very pale; 'he's here—Tom Brice.'

And she led the way, shoving aside the leafless underwood, and we reached Tom. The slender youth, groom or poacher—he might answer for either—with his short coat and gaitered legs, was sitting on a low horizontal bough, with his shoulder against the trunk.

'*Don't* ye mind; sit ye still, lad,' said Meg, observing that he was preparing to rise, and had entangled his hat in the boughs. 'Sit ye still, and hark to the lady. He'll take it, Miss Maud, if he can; wi' na ye, lad?'

'E'es, I'll take it,' he replied, holding out his hand.

'Tom Brice, you won't deceive me?'

'Noa, sure,' said Tom and Meg nearly in the same breath.

'You are an honest English lad, Tom—you would not betray me?' I was speaking imploringly.

'Noa, sure,' repeated Tom.

There was something a little unsatisfactory in the countenance of this light-haired youth, with the sharpish upturned nose. Throughout our interview he said next to nothing, and smiled lazily to himself, like a man listening to a child's solemn nonsense, and leading it on, with an amused irony, from one wise sally to another.

Thus it seemed to me that this young clown, without in the least intending to be offensive, was listening to me with a profound and lazy mockery.

I could not choose, however; and, such as he was, I must employ him or none.

'Now, Tom Brice, a great deal depends on this.'

'That's true for her, Tom Brice,' said Meg, who now and then confirmed my asseverations.

'I'll give you a pound *now*, Tom,' and I placed the coin and the letter together in his hand. 'And you are to give this letter to Lady Knollys, at Elverston; you know Elverston, don't you?'

'He does, Miss. Don't ye, lad?'

'E'es.'

'Well, do so, Tom, and I'll be good to you so long as I live.'

'D'ye hear, lad?'

'E'es,' said Tom; 'it's very good.'

'You'll take the letter, Tom? 'I said, in much greater trepidation as to his answer than I showed.

'E'es, I'll take the letter,' said he, rising, and turning it about in his fingers under his eye, like a curiosity.

'Tom Brice,' I said, 'If you can't be true to me, say so; but don't take the letter except to give it to Lady Knollys, at Elverston. If you won't promise that, let me have the note back. Keep the pound; but tell me that you won't mention my having asked you to carry a letter to Elverston to anyone.'

For the first time Tom looked perfectly serious. He twiddled the corner of my letter between his finger and thumb, and wore very much the countenance of a poacher about to be committed.

'I don't want to chouce ye, Miss; but I must take care o' myself, ye see. The letters goes all through Silas's fingers to the post, and he'd know damn well this worn't among 'em. They do say he opens 'em, and reads 'em before they go; an' that's his diversion. I don't know; but I do believe that's how it be; an' if this one turned up, they'd all know it went be hand, and I'd be spotted for't.'

'But you know who I am, Tom, and I'd save you,' said I, eagerly.

'Ye'd want savin' yerself, I'm thinkin', if that feel oot,' said Tom, cynically. 'I don't say, though, I'll not take it—only this—I won't run my head again a wall for no one.'

'Tom,' I said, with a sudden inspiration, 'give me back the letter, and take me out of Bartram; take me to Elverston; it will be the best thing—for *you*, Tom, I mean—it will indeed—that ever befell you.'

With this clown I was pleading, as for my life; my hand was on his sleeve. I was gazing imploringly in his face.

But it would not do; Tom Brice looked amused again, swung his head a little on one side, grinning sheepishly over his shoulder on the roots of the trees beside him, as if he were striving to keep himself from an uncivil fit of laughter.

'I'll do what a wise lad may, Miss; but ye don't know they lads; they bain't that easy come over; and I won't get knocked on the head, nor sent to gaol 'appen, for no good to thee nor me. There's Meg there, she knows well enough I could na' manage that; so I won't try it, Miss, by no chance; no offence, Miss; but I'd rayther not, an' I'll just try what I can make o'this; that's all I can do for ye.'

Tom Brice, with these words, stood up, and looked uneasily in the direction of the Windmill Wood.

'Mind ye, Miss, coom what will, ye'll not tell o' me?'

'Whar 'ill ye go now, Tom?' inquired Meg, uneasily.

'Never ye mind, lass,' answered he, breaking his way through the thicket, and soon disappearing.

'E'es that 'ill be it—he'll git into the sheepwalk behind the mound. They're all down yonder; git ye back, Miss, to the hoose—be the side-door; mind ye, don't go round the corner; and I'll jest sit awhile among the bushes, and wait a good time for a start. And good-bye, Miss; and don't ye show like as if there was aught out o' common on your mind. Hish!'

There was a distant hallooing.

'That be fayther!' she whispered, with a very blank countenance, and listened with her sunburnt hand to her ear.

'Tisn't me, only Davy he'll be callin',' she said, with a great sigh, and a joyless smile. 'Now git ye away i' God's name.'

So running lightly along the path, under cover of this thick wood, I recalled Mary Quince, and together we hastened back again to the house, and entered, as directed, by the side-door, which did not expose us to be seen from the Windmill Wood, and, like two criminals, we stole up by the backstairs, and so through the side-gallery to my room; and there sat down to collect my wits, and try to estimate the exact effect of what had just occurred.

Madame had not returned. That was well; she always visited my room first, and everything was precisely as I had left it—a certain sign that her prying eyes and busy fingers had not been at work during my absence.

When she did appear, strange to say, it was to bring me unexpected comfort. She had in her hand a letter from my dear Lady Knollys—a gleam of sunlight from the free and happy outer world entered with it. The moment Madame left me to myself, I opened it and read as follows:—

'I am so happy, my dearest Maud, in the immediate prospect of seeing you. I have had a really kind letter from poor Silas—*poor* I say, for I really compassionate his situation, about which he has been, I do believe, quite frank—at least Ilbury says so, and somehow he happens to know. I have had quite an affecting, changed letter. I will tell you all when I see you. He wants me ultimately to undertake that which would afford me the most unmixed happiness—I mean the care of you, my dear girl. I only fear lest my too eager acceptance of the trust should excite that vein of opposition which is in most human beings, and induce him to think over his offer less favourably again. He says I must come to Bartram, and stay a night, and promises to lodge me comfortably; about which last I honestly do not care a pin, when the chance of a comfortable evening's gossip with you is in view. Silas explains his sad situation, and must hold himself in readiness for early flight, if he would avoid the risk of losing his personal liberty. It is a sad thing that he should have so irretrievably ruined himself, that poor Austin's liberality seems to have positively precipitated his extremity. His great anxiety is that I should see you before you leave for your short stay in France. He thinks you must leave before a fortnight. I am thinking of asking you to come over here; I know you would be just as well at Elverston as in France; but perhaps, as he seems disposed to do what we all wish, it may be safer to let him set about it in his own way. The truth is, I have so set my heart upon it that I fear to risk it by crossing him even in a trifle. He says I must fix an early day next week, and talks as if he meant to urge me to make a longer visit than he defined. I shall be only too happy. I begin, my dear Maud, to think that there is no use in trying to control events, and that things often turn out best, and most exactly to our wishes, by being left quite to themselves. I think it was Talleyrand who praised the talent of *waiting* so much. In high spirits, and with my head brimful of plans, I remain, dearest Maud, ever your affectionate cousin,

MONICA.'

Here was an inexplicable puzzle! A faint radiance of hope, however, began to overspread a landscape only a few minutes before darkened by total eclipse; but construct what theory I might, all were inconsistent with many well-established and awful incongruities, and their wrecks lay strown over the troubled waters of the gulf into which I gazed.

Why was Madame here? Why was Dudley concealed about the place? Why was I a prisoner within the walls? What were those dangers which Meg Hawkes seemed to think so great and so imminent as to induce her to risk her lover's safety for my deliverance? All these menacing facts stood grouped together against the dark certainty that never were men more deeply interested in making away with one human being, than were Uncle Silas and Dudley in removing me.

Sometimes to these dreadful evidences I abandoned my soul. Sometimes, reading Cousin Monica's sunny letter, the sky would clear, and my terrors melt away like nightmares in the morning. I never repented, however, that I had sent my letter by Tom Brice. Escape from Bartram-Haugh was my hourly longing.

That evening Madame invited herself to tea with me. I did not object. It was better just then to be on friendly relations with everybody, if possible, even on their own terms. She was in one of her boisterous and hilarious moods, and there was a perfume of brandy.

She narrated some compliments paid her that morning in Feltram by that 'good crayature' Mrs. Litheways, the silk-mercer, and what "ansom faylow' was her new foreman—(she intended plainly that I should 'queez' her)—and how 'he follow' her with his eyes wherever she went. I thought, perhaps, he fancied she might pocket some of his lace or gloves. And all the time her great wicked eyes were rolling and glancing according to her ideas of fascination, and her bony face grinning and flaming with the 'strong drink' in which she delighted. She sang twaddling chansons, and being, as was her wont under such exhilarating influences, in a vapouring mood, she vowed that I should have my carriage and horses immediately.

'I weel try what I can do weeth your Uncle Silas. We are very good old friends, Mr. Ruthyn and I,' she said with a leer which I did not understand, and which yet frightened me.

I never could quite understand why these Jezebels like to insinuate the dreadful truth against themselves; but they do. Is it the spirit of feminine triumph overcoming feminine shame, and making them vaunt their fall as an evidence of bygone fascination and existing power? Need we wonder? Have not women preferred hatred to indifference, and the reputation of witchcraft, with all its penalties, to absolute insignificance? Thus, as they enjoyed the fear inspired among simple neighbours by their imagined traffic with the father of ill, did Madame, I think, relish with a cynical vainglory the suspicion of her satanic superiority.

Next morning Uncle Silas sent for me. He was seated at his table, and spoke his little French greeting, smiling as usual, pointing to a chair opposite.

'How far, I forget,' he said, carelessly laying his newspaper on the table, 'did you yesterday guess Dudley to be?'

'Eleven hundred miles I thought it was.'

'Oh yes, so it was;' and then there was an abstracted pause. 'I have been writing to Lord Ilbury, your trustee,' he resumed. I ventured to say, my dear Maud—(for having thoughts of a different arrangement for you, more suitable under my distressing circumstances, I do not wish to vacate without some expression of your estimate of my treatment of you while under my roof)—I ventured to say that you thought me kind, considerate, indulgent,—may I say so?'

I assented. What could I say?

'I said you had enjoyed our poor way of living here—our rough ways and liberty. Was I right?'

Again I assented.

'And, in fact, that you had nothing to object against your poor old uncle, except indeed his poverty, which you forgave. I think I said truth. Did I, dear Maud?'

Again I acquiesced.

All this time he was fumbling among the papers in his coatpocket.

'That is satisfactory. So I expected you to say,' he murmured. 'I expected no less.'

On a sudden a frightful change spread across his face. He rose like a spectre with a white scowl.

'Then how do you account for that?' he shrieked in a voice of thunder, and smiting my open letter to Lady Knollys, face upward, upon the table.

I stared at my uncle, unable to speak, until I seemed to lose sight of him; but his voice, like a bell, still yelled in my ears.

'There! young hypocrite and liar! explain that farrago of slander which you bribed my servant to place in the hands of my kinswoman, Lady Knollys.'

And so on and on it went, I gazing into darkness, until the voice itself became indistinct, grew into a buzz, and hummed away into silence.

I think I must have had a fit.

When I came to myself I was drenched with water, my hair, face, neck, and dress. I did not in the least know where I was. I thought my father was ill, and spoke to him. Uncle Silas was standing near the window, looking unspeakably grim. Madame was seated beside me, and an open bottle of ether, one of Uncle Silas's restoratives, on the table before me.

'Who's that—who's ill—is anyone dead?' I cried.

At last I was relieved by long paroxysms of weeping. When I was sufficiently recovered, I was conveyed into my own room.

CHAPTER LVIII

LADY KNOLLYS' CARRIAGE

Next morning—it was Sunday—I lay on my bed in my dressing-gown, dull, apathetic, with all my limbs sore, and, as I thought, rheumatic, and feeling so ill that I did not care to speak or lift my head. My recollection of what had passed in Uncle Silas's room was utterly confused, and it seemed to me as if my poor father had been there and taken a share—I could not remember how—in the conference.

I was too exhausted and stupid to clear up this horrible muddle, and merely lay with my face toward the wall, motionless and silent, except for a great sigh every now and then.

Good Mary Quince was in the room—there was some comfort in that; but I felt quite worn out, and had rather she did not speak to me; and indeed for the time I felt absolutely indifferent as to whether I lived or died.

Cousin Monica this morning, at pleasant Elverston, all-unconscious of my sad plight, proposed to Lady Mary Carysbroke and Lord Ilbury, her guests, to drive over to church at Feltram, and then pay us a visit at Bartram-Haugh, to which they readily agreed.

Accordingly, at about two o'clock, this pleasant party of three arrived at Bartram. They walked, having left the carriage to follow when the horses were fed; and Madame de la Rougierre, who was in my uncle's room when little Giblets arrived to say that the party were in the parlour, whispered for a little with my uncle, who then said—

'Miss Maud Ruthyn has gone out to drive, but I shall be happy to see Lady Knollys here, if she will do me the favour to come up-stairs and see me for a few moments; and you can mention that I am very far from well.'

Madame followed him out upon the lobby, and added, holding him by the collar, and whispering earnestly in his ear—

'Bring hair ladysheep up by the backstairs—mind, the *back*stairs.'

And the next moment Madame entered my room, with long tiptoe steps, and looking, Mary Quince said, as if she were going to be hanged.

On entering she looked sharply round, and being satisfied of Mary Quince's presence, she turned the key in the door, and made some affectionate enquiries about me in a whisper; and then she stole to the window and peeped out, standing back some way; after which she came to my bedside, murmured some tender sentences, drew the curtain a little, and making some little fidgety adjustments about the room; among the rest she took the key from the lock, quietly, and put it into her pocket.

This was so odd a procedure that honest Mary Quince rose stoutly from her chair, pointing to the lock, with her frank little blue eyes fixed on Madame, and she whispered—'Won't you put the key in the lock, please?'

'Oh, certainly, Mary Queence; but it is better it shall be locked, for I think her uncle he is coming to see her, and I am sure she would be very much frightened, for he is very much displease, don't you see? and we can tell him she is not well enough, or asleep, and so he weel go away again, without any trouble.'

I heard nothing of this, which was conducted in close whispers; and Mary, although she did not give Madame credit for caring whether I was frightened or not, and suspected her motives in everything, acquiesced grudgingly, fearing lest her alleged reason might possibly be the true one.

So Madame hovered about the door, uneasily; and of what went on elsewhere during that period Lady Knollys afterwards gave me the following account:—

'We were very much disappointed; but of course I was glad to see Silas, and your little hobgoblin butler led me up-stairs to his room a different way, I think, from that I came before; but I don't know the house of Bartram well enough to speak positively. I only know that I was conducted quite across his bedroom, which I had not seen on my former visit, and so into his sitting-room, where I found him.

'He seemed very glad to see me, came forward smiling—I disliked his smile always—with both hands out, and shook mine with more warmth than I ever remembered in his greeting before, and said—

'"My dear, *dear* Monica, how *very* good of you—the very person I longed to see! I have been miserably ill, the sad consequence of still more miserable anxiety. Sit down, pray, for a moment."

'And he paid me some nice little French compliment in verse.

'"And where is Maud?" said I.

'"I think Maud is by this time about halfway to Elverston," said the old gentleman. "I persuaded her to take a drive, and advised a call there, which seemed to please her, so I conjecture she obeyed."

'"How *very* provoking!" cried I.

'"My poor Maud will be sadly disappointed, but you will console her by a visit—you have promised to come, and I shall try to make you comfortable. I shall be happier, Monica, with this proof of our perfect reconciliation. You won't deny me?"

'"Certainly not. I am only too glad to come," said I; "and I want to thank you, Silas."

'"For what?" said he.

'"For wishing to place Maud in my care. I am very much obliged to you."

'"I did not suggest it, I must say, Monica, with the least intention of obliging *you*," said Silas.

'I thought he was going to break into one of his ungracious moods.

'"But I *am* obliged to you—very much obliged to you, Silas; and you sha'n't refuse my thanks."

'"I am happy, at all events, Monica, in having won your good-will; we learn at last that in the affections only are our capacities for happiness; and how true is St. Paul's preference of love—the principle that abideth! The affections, dear Monica, are eternal; and being so, celestial, divine, and consequently happy, deriving happiness, and bestowing it."

'I was always impatient of his or anybody else's metaphysics; but I controlled myself, and only said, with my customary impudence—

'"Well, dear Silas, and when do you wish me to come?"

'"The earlier the better," said he.

'"Lady Mary and Ilbury will be leaving me on Tuesday morning. I can come to you in the afternoon, if you think Tuesday a good day."

'"Thank you, dear Monica. I shall be, I trust, enlightened by that day as to my enemies' plans. It is a humiliating confession, Monica, but I am past feeling that. It is quite possible that an execution may be sent into this house to-morrow, and an end of all my schemes. It is not likely, however—hardly possible—before three weeks, my attorney tells me. I shall hear from him to-morrow morning, and then I shall ask you to name a very early day. If we are to have an unmolested fortnight certain, you shall hear, and name your own day."

'Then he asked me who had accompanied me, and lamented ever so much his not being able to go down to receive them; and he offered luncheon, with a sort of Ravenswood smile, and a shrug, and I declined, telling him that we had but a few minutes, and that my companions were walking in the grounds near the house.

'I asked whether Maud was likely to return soon?

'"Certainly not before five o'clock." He thought we should probably meet her on our way back to Elverston; but could not be certain, as she might have changed her plans.

'So then came—no more remaining to be said—a very affectionate parting. I believe all about his legal dangers was strictly true. How he could, unless that horrid woman had deceived him, with so serene a countenance tell me all those gross untruths about Maud, I can only admire.'

In the meantime, as I lay in my bed, Madame, gliding hither and thither, whispering sometimes, listening at others, I suddenly startled them both by saying—

'Whose carriage?'

'What carriage, dear?' inquired Quince, whose ears were not so sharp as mine.

Madame peeped from the window.

''Tis the physician, Doctor Jolks. He is come to see your uncle, my dear,' said Madame.

'But I hear a female voice,' I said, sitting up.

'No, my dear; there is only the doctor,' said Madame. 'He is come to your uncle. I tell you he is getting out of his carriage,' and she affected to watch the doctor's descent.

'The carriage is driving away!' I cried.

'Yes, it is draiving away,' she echoed.

But I had sprung from my bed, and was looking over her shoulder, before she perceived me.

'It is Lady Knollys!' I screamed, seizing the window-frame to force it up, and, vainly struggling to open it, I cried—

'I'm here, Cousin Monica. For God's sake, Cousin Monica—Cousin Monica!'

'You are mad, Meess—go back,' screamed Madame, exerting her superior strength to force me back.

But I saw deliverance and escape gliding away from my reach, and, strung to unnatural force by desperation, I pushed past her, and beat the window wildly with my hands, screaming—

'Save me—save me! Here, here, Monica, here! Cousin, cousin, oh! save me!'

Madame had seized my wrists, and a wild struggle was going on. A window-pane was broken, and I was shrieking to stop the carriage. The Frenchwoman looked black and haggard as a fury, as if she could have murdered me.

Nothing daunted—frantic—I screamed in my despair, seeing the carriage drive swiftly away—seeing Cousin Monica's bonnet, as she sat chatting with her *vis-à-vis*.

'Oh, oh, oh!' I shrieked, in vain and prolonged agony, as Madame, exerting her strength and matching her fury against my despair, forced me back in spite of my wild struggles, and pushed me sitting on the bed, where she held me fast, glaring in my face, and chuckling and panting over me.

I think I felt something of the despair of a lost spirit.

I remember the face of poor Mary Quince—its horror, its wonder—as she stood gaping into my face, over Madame's shoulder, and crying—

'What is it, Miss Maud? What is it, dear?' And turning fiercely on Madame, and striving to force her grasp from my wrists, 'Are you hurting the child? Let her go—let her go.'

'I *weel* let her go. Wat old fool are you, Mary Queence! She is mad, I think. She 'as lost hair head.'

'Oh, Mary, cry from the window. Stop the carriage!' I cried.

Mary looked out, but there was by this time, of course, nothing in sight.

'Why don't a you stop the carriage?' sneered Madame. 'Call a the coachman and the postilion. W'ere is the footman? Bah! *elle a le cerveau mal timbré*.'

'Oh, Mary, Mary, is it gone—is it gone? Is there nothing there?' cried I, rushing to the window; and turning to Madame, after a vain straining of my eyes, my face against the glass—

'Oh, cruel, cruel, wicked woman! why have you done this? What was it to you? Why do you persecute me? What good *can* you gain by my ruin?'

'Rueen! Par bleu! ma chère, you talk too fast. Did not a you see it, Mary Queence? It was the doctor's carriage, and Mrs. Jolks, and that eempudent faylow, young Jolks, staring up to the window, and Mademoiselle she come in soche shocking déshabille to show herself knocking at the window. 'Twould be very nice thing, Mary Queence, don't you think?'

I was sitting now on the bedside, crying in mere despair. I did not care to dispute or to resist. Oh! why had rescue come so near, only to prove that it could not reach me? So I went on crying, with a clasping of my hands and turning up of my eyes, in incoherent prayer. I was not thinking of Madame, or of Mary Quince, or any other person, only babbling my anguish and despair helplessly in the ear of heaven.

'I did not think there was soche fool. Wat *enfant gaté*! My dear cheaile, wat a can you *mean* by soche strange language and conduct? Wat for should a you weesh to display yourself in the window in soche 'orrible déshabille to the people in the doctor's coach?'

'It was *Cousin Knollys*—Cousin Knollys. Oh, Cousin Knollys! You're gone—you're gone—you're *gone*!'

'And if it was Lady Knollys' coach, there was certainly a coachman and a footman; and whoever has the coach there was young gentlemen in it. If it was Lady Knollys' carriage it would 'av been *worse* than the doctor.'

'It is no matter—it is all over. Oh, Cousin Monica, your poor Maud—where is she to turn? Is there no help?'

That evening Madame visited me again, in one of her sedate and moral moods. She found me dejected and passive, as she had left me.

'I think, Maud, there is news; but I am not certain.'

I raised my head and looked at her wistfully.

'I think there is letter of *bad* news from the attorney in London.'

'Oh!' I said, in a tone which I am sure implied the absolute indifference of dejection.

'But, my dear Maud, if't be so, we shall go at once, you and me, to join Meess Millicent in France. La belle France! You weel like so moche! We shall be so gay. You cannot imagine there are such naice girl there. They all love a me so moche, you will be delight.'

'How soon do we go?' I asked.

'I do not know. Bote I was to bring in a case of eau de cologne that came this evening, and he laid down a letter and say:—"The blow has descended, Madame! My niece must hold herself in readiness." I said, "For what, Monsieur?" *twice*; bote he did not answer. I am sure it is *un procès*. They 'av ruin him. Eh bien, my dear. I suppose we shall leave this triste place immediately. I am so rejoice. It appears to me *un cimetière*!'

'Yes, I should like to leave it,' I said, sitting up, with a great sigh and sunken eyes. It seemed to me that I had quite lost all sense of resentment towards Madame. A debility of feeling had supervened—the fatigue, I suppose, and prostration of the passions.

'I weel make excuse to go into his room again,' said Madame; 'and I weel endeavor to learn something more from him, and I weel come back again to you in half an hour.'

She departed. But in half an hour did not return. I had a dull longing to leave Bartram-Haugh. For me, since the departure of poor Milly, it had grown like the haunt of evil spirits, and to escape on any terms from it was a blessing unspeakable.

Another half-hour passed, and another, and I grew insufferably feverish. I sent Mary Quince to the lobby to try and see Madame, who, I feared, was probably to-ing and fro-ing in and out of Uncle Silas's room.

Mary returned to tell me that she had seen old Wyat, who told her that she thought Madame had gone to her bed half an hour before.

CHAPTER LIX

A SUDDEN DEPARTURE

'Mary,' said I, 'I am miserably anxious to hear what Madame may have to tell; she knows the state I am in, and she would not like so much trouble as to look in at my door to say a word. Did you hear what she told me?'

'No, Miss Maud,' she answered, rising and drawing near.

'She thinks we are going to France immediately, and to leave this place perhaps for ever.'

'Heaven be praised for that, if it be so, Miss!' said Mary, with more energy than was common with her, 'for there is no luck about it, and I don't expect to see you ever well or happy in it.'

'You must take your candle, Mary, and make out her room, up-stairs; I found it accidentally myself one evening.'

'But Wyat won't let us up-stairs.'

'Don't mind her, Mary; I tell you to go. You must try. I can't sleep till we hear.'

'What direction is her room in, Miss?' asked Mary.

'Somewhere in *that* direction, Mary,' I answered, pointing. 'I cannot describe the turns; but I think you will find it if you go along the great passage to your left, on getting to the top of the stairs, till you come to the cross-galleries, and then turn to your left; and when you have passed four or perhaps five doors, you must be very near it, and I am sure she will hear if you call.'

'But will she tell me—she *is* such a rum un, Miss?' suggested Mary.

'Tell her exactly what I have said to you, and when she learns that you already know as much as I do, she may—unless, indeed, she wishes to torture me. If she won't, perhaps at least you can persuade her to come to me for a moment. Try, dear Mary; we can but fail.'

'Will you be very lonely, Miss, while I am away?' asked Mary, uneasily, as she lighted her candle.

'I can't help it, Mary. Go. I think if I heard we were going, I could almost get up and dance and sing. I can't bear this dreadful uncertainty any longer.'

'If old Wyat is outside, I'll come back and wait here a bit, till she's out o' the way,' said Mary; 'and, anyhow, I'll make all the haste I can. The drops and the sal-volatile is here, Miss, by your hand.'

And with an anxious look at me, she made her exit, softly, and did not immediately return, by which I concluded that she had found the way clear, and had gained the upper story without interruption.

This little anxiety ended, its subsidence was followed by a sense of loneliness, and with it, of vague insecurity, which increased at last to such a pitch, that I wondered at my own madness in sending my companion away; and at last my terrors so grew, that I drew back into the farthest corner of the bed, with my shoulders to the wall, and my bed-clothes huddled about me, with only a point open to peep at.

At last the door opened gently.

'Who's there?' I cried, in extremity of horror, expecting I knew not whom.

'Me, Miss,' whispered Mary Quince, to my unutterable relief; and with her candle flared, and a wild and pallid face, Mary Quince glided into the room, locking the door as she entered.

I do not know how it was, but I found myself holding Mary fast with both my hands as we stood side by side on the floor.

'Mary, you are terrified; for God's sake, what is the matter?' I cried.

'No, Miss,' said Mary, faintly, 'not much.'

'I see it in your face. What is it?'

'Let me sit down, Miss. I'll tell you what I saw; only I'm just a bit queerish.'

Mary sat down by my bed.

'Get in, Miss; you'll take cold. Get into bed, and I'll tell you. It is not much.'

I did get into bed, and gazing on Mary's frightened face, I felt a corresponding horror.

'For mercy's sake, Mary, say what it is?'

So again assuring me 'it was not much,' she gave me in a somewhat diffuse and tangled narrative the following facts:—

On closing my door, she raised her candle above her head and surveyed the lobby, and seeing no one there she ascended the stairs swiftly. She passed along the great gallery to the left, and paused a moment at the cross gallery, and then recollected my directions clearly, and followed the passage to the right.

There are doors at each side, and she had forgotten to ask me at which Madame's was. She opened several. In one room she was frightened by a bat, which had very nearly put her candle out. She went on a little, paused, and began to lose heart in the dismal solitude, when on a sudden, a few doors farther on, she thought she heard Madame's voice.

She said that she knocked at the door, but receiving no answer, and hearing Madame still talking within, she opened it.

There was a candle on the chimneypiece, and another in a stable lantern near the window. Madame was conversing volubly on the hearth, with her face toward the window, the entire frame of which had been taken from its place: Dickon

Hawkes, the Zamiel of the wooden leg, was supporting it with one hand, as it leaned imperfectly against the angle of the recess. There was a third figure standing, buttoned up in a surtout, with a bundle of tools under his arm, like a glazier, and, with a silent thrill of fear, she distinctly recognised the features as those of Dudley Ruthyn.

"Twas him, Miss, so sure as I sit here! Well, like that, they were as mute as mice; three pairs of eyes were on me. I don't know what made me so study like, but som'at told me I should not make as though I knew any but Madame; and so I made a courtesy, as well as I could, and I said, "Might I speak a word wi' ye, please, on the lobby?"

'Mr. Dudley was making belief be this time to look out at window, wi' his back to me, and I kept looking straight on Madame, and she said, "They're mendin' my broken glass, Mary," walking between them and me, and coming close up to me very quick; and so she marched me backward out o' the door, prating all the time.

'When we were on the lobby, she took my candle from my hand, shutting the door behind her, and she held the light a bit behind her ear; so'twas full on my face, as she looked sharp into it; and, after a bit, she said again, in her queer lingo—there was two panes broke in her room, and men sent for to mend it.

'I was awful frightened when I saw Mr. Dudley, for I could not believe any such thing before, and I don't know how I could look her in the face as I did and not show it. I was as smooth and cool as yonder chimneypiece, and she has an awful evil eye to stan' against; but I never flinched, and I think she's puzzled, for as cunning as she is, whether I believe all she said, or knowed 'twas a pack o' stories. So I told her your message, and she said she had not heard another word since; but she did believe we had not many more days here, and would tell you if she heard to-night, when she brought his soup to your uncle, in half an hour's time.'

I asked her, as soon as I could speak, whether she was perfectly certain as to the fact that the man in the surtout was Dudley, and she made answer—

'I'd swear to him on that Bible, Miss.'

So far from any longer wishing Madame's return that night, I trembled at the idea of it. Who could tell who might enter the room with her when the door opened to admit her?

Dudley, so soon as he recovered the surprise, had turned about, evidently anxious to prevent recognition; Dickon Hawkes stood glowering at her. Both might have hope of escaping recognition in the imperfect light, for the candle on the chimneypiece was flaring in the air, and the light from the lantern fell in spots, and was confusing.

What could that ruffian, Hawkes, be doing in the house? Why was Dudley there? Could a more ominous combination be imagined? I puzzled my distracted head over all Mary Quince's details, but could make nothing of their occupation. I know of nothing so terrifying as this kind of perpetual puzzling over ominous problems.

You may imagine how the long hours of that night passed, and how my heart beat at every fancied sound outside my door.

But morning came, and with its light some reassurance. Early, Madame de la Rougierre made her appearance; she searched my eyes darkly and shrewdly, but made no allusion to Mary Quince's visit. Perhaps she expected some question from me, and, hearing none, thought it as well to leave the subject at rest.

She had merely come in to say that she had heard nothing since, but was now going to make my uncle's chocolate; and that so soon as her interview was ended she would see me again, and let me hear anything she should have gleaned.

In a little while a knock came to my door, and Mary Quince was ordered by old Wyat into my uncle's room. She returned flushed, in a huge fuss, to say that I was to be up and dressed for a journey in half an hour, and to go straight, when dressed, to my uncle's room.

It was good news; at the same time it was a shock. I was glad. I was stunned. I jumped out of bed, and set about my toilet with an energy quite new to me. Good Mary Quince was busily packing my boxes, and consulting as to what I should take with me, and what not.

Was Mary Quince to accompany me? He had not said a word on that point; and I feared from his silence she was to remain. There was comfort, however, in this—that the separation would not be for long; I felt confident of that; and I was about to join Milly, whom I loved better than I could have believed before our separation; but whatsoever the conditions might be, it was an indescribable relief to have done with Bartram-Haugh, and leave behind me its sinister lines of circumvallation, its haunted recesses, and the awful spectres that had lately appeared within its walls.

I stood too much in awe of my uncle to fail in presenting myself punctually at the close of the half-hour. I entered his sitting-room under the shadow of sour old Wyat's high-cauled cap; she closed the door behind me, and the conference commenced.

Madame de la Rougierre sat there, dressed and draped for a journey, and with a thick black lace veil on. My uncle rose, gaunt and venerable, and with a harsh and severe countenance. He did not offer his hand; he made me a kind of bow, more of repulsion than of respect. He remained in a standing position, supporting his crooked frame by his hand, which he leaned on a despatch-box; he glared on me steadily with his wild phosphoric eyes, from under the dark brows I have described to you, now corrugated in lines indescribably stern.

'You shall join my daughter at the Pension, in France; Madame de la Rougierre shall accompany you,' said my uncle, delivering his directions with the stern monotony and the measured pauses of a person dictating an important despatch to a secretary.' Old Mrs. Quince shall follow with me, or, if alone, in a week. You shall pass to-night in London; to-morrow night you proceed thence to Dover, and cross by the mail-packet. You shall now sit down and write a letter to your cousin Monica Knollys, which I will first read and then despatch. Tomorrow you shall write a note to Lady Knollys, from *London*, telling her how you have got over so much of your journey, and that you cannot write from Dover, as you must instantly start by the packet on reaching it; and that until my affairs are a little settled, you cannot write to her from France, as it is of high importance to my safety that no clue should exist as to our address. Intelligence, however, shall reach her through my attorneys, Archer and Sleigh, and I trust we shall soon return. You will, please, submit that latter note to Madame de la Rougierre, who has my directions to see that it contains no *libels* upon my character. Now, sit down.'

So, with those unpleasant words tingling in my ears, I obeyed.

'*Write*,' said he, when I was duly placed. 'You shall convey the substance of what I say in your own language. The immiment danger this morning announced of an execution—rememher the word,' and he spelled it for me—'being put into this house either this afternoon or to-morrow, compels me to anticipate my plans, and despatch you for France this day. That you are starting with an attendant.' Here an uneasy movement from Madame, whose dignity was perhaps excited. 'An *attendant*,' he repeated, with a discordant emphasis; 'and you can, if you please—but I don't *solicit* that justice—say that you have been as kindly treated here as my unfortunate circumstances would permit. That is all. You have just fifteen minutes to write. Begin.'

I wrote accordingly. My hysterical state had made me far less combative than I might have proved some months since, for there was much that was insulting as well as formidable in his manner. I completed my letter, however, to his satisfaction in the prescribed time; and he said, as he laid it and its envelope on the table—

'Please to remember that this lady is not your attendant only, but that she has authority to direct every detail respecting your journey, and will make all the necessary payments on the way. You will please, then, implicitly to comply with her directions. The carriage awaits you at the hall-door.'

Having thus spoken, with another grim bow, and 'I wish you a safe and pleasant journey,' he receded a step or two, and I, with an undefinable kind of melancholy, though also with a sense of relief, withdrew.

My letter, I afterwards found, reached Lady Knollys, accompanied by one from Uncle Silas, who said—'Dear Maud apprises me that she has written to tell you something of our movements. A sudden crisis in my miserable affairs compels a break-up as sudden here. Maud joins my daughter at the Pension, in France. I purposely omit the address, because I mean to reside in its vicinity until this storm shall have blown over; and as the consequences of some of my unhappy entanglements might pursue me even there, I must only for the present spare you the pain and trouble of keeping a secret. I am sure that for some little time you will excuse the girl's silence; in the meantime you shall hear of them, and perhaps circuitously, from me. Our dear Maud started this morning *en route* for her destination, very sorry, as am I, that she could not enjoy first a flying visit to Elverston, but in high spirits, notwithstanding, at the new life and sights before her.'

At the door my beloved old friend, Mary Quince, awaited me.

'Am I going with you, Miss Maud?'

I burst into tears and clasped her in my arms.

'I'm not,' said Mary, very sorrowfully; 'and I never was from you yet, Miss, since you wasn't the length of my arm.'

And kind old Mary began to cry with me.

'Bote you are coming in a few days, Mary Quince,' expostulated Madame. 'I wonder you are soche fool. What is two, three days? Bah! nonsense, girl.'

Another farewell to poor Mary Quince, quite bewildered at the suddenness of her bereavement. A serious and tremulous bow from our little old butler on the steps. Madame bawling through the open window to the driver to make good speed, and remember that we had but nineteen minutes to reach the station. Away we went. Old Crowle's iron *grille* rolled back before us. I looked on the receding landscape, the giant trees—the palatial, time-stained mansion. A strange conflict of feelings, sweet and bitter, rose and mingled in the reverie. Had I been too hard and suspicious with the inhabitants of that old house of my family? Was my uncle *justly* indignant? Was I ever again to know such pleasant rambles as some of those I had enjoyed with dear Millicent through the wild and beautiful woodlands I was leaving behind me? And there, with my latest glimpse of the front of Bartram-Haugh, I beheld dear old Mary Quince gazing after us. Again my tears flowed. I waved my handkerchief from the window; and now the park-wall hid all from view, and at a great pace, throught the steep wooded glen, with the rocky and precipitous character of a ravine, we glided; and when the road next emerged, Bartram-Haugh was a misty mass of forest and chimneys, slope and hollow, and we within a few minutes of the station.

CHAPTER LX

THE JOURNEY

Waiting for the train, as we stood upon the platform, I looked back again toward the wooded uplands of Bartram; and far behind, the fine range of mountains, azure and soft in the distance, beyond which lay beloved old Knowl, and my lost father and mother, and the scenes of my childhood, never embittered except by the sibyl who sat beside me.

Under happier circumstances I should have been, at my then early age, quite wild with pleasurable excitement on entering London for the first time. But black Care sat by me, with her pale hand in mine: a voice of fear and warning, whose words I could not catch, was always in my ear. We drove through London, amid the glare of lamps, toward the West-end, and for a little while the sense of novelty and curiosity overcame my despondency, and I peeped eagerly from the window; while Madame, who was in high good-humour, spite of the fatigues of our long railway flight, screeched scraps of topographic information in my ear; for London was a picture-book in which she was well read.

'That is Euston Square, my dear—Russell Square. Here is Oxford Street—Haymarket. See, there is the Opera House—Hair Majesty's Theatre. See all the carriages waiting;' and so on, till we reached at length a little narrow street, which she told me was off Piccadilly, where we drew up before a private house, as it seemed to me—a family hotel—and I was glad to be at rest for the night.

Fatigued with the peculiar fatigue of railway travelling, dusty, a little chilly, with eyes aching and wearied, I ascended the stairs silently, our garrulous and bustling landlady leading the way, and telling her oft-told story of the house, its noble owner in old time, and how those fine drawing-rooms were taken every year during the Session by the Bishop of Rochet-on-Copeley, and at last into our double-bedded room.

I would fain have been alone, but I was too tired and dejected to care very much for anything.

At tea, Madame expanded in spirit, like a giant refreshed, and chattered and sang; and at last, seeing that I was nodding, advised my going to bed, while she ran across the street to see 'her dear old friend, Mademoiselle St. Eloi, who was sure to be up, and would be offended if she failed to make her ever so short a call.'

I cared little what she said, and was glad to be rid of her even for a short time, and was soon fast asleep.

I saw her, I know not how much later, poking about the room, like a figure in a dream, and taking off her things.

She had her breakfast in bed next morning, and I was, to my comfort, left to take mine in solitary possession of our sitting-room; where I began to wonder how little annoyance I had as yet suffered from her company, and began to speculate upon the chances of my making the journey with tolerable comfort.

Our hostess gave me five minutes of her valuable time. Her talk ran chiefly upon nuns and convents, and her old acquaintance with Madame; and it seemed to me that she had at one time driven a kind of trade, no doubt profitable enough, in escorting young ladies to establishments on the Continent; and although I did not then quite understand the tone in which she spoke to me, I often thought afterwards that Madame had represented me as a young person destined for the holy vocation of the veil.

When she was gone, I sat listlessly looking out of the window, and saw some chance equipages drive by, and now and then a fashionable pedestrian; and wondered if this quiet thoroughfare could really be one of the arteries so near the heart of the tumultuous capital.

I think my nervous vitality must have burnt very low just then, for I felt perfectly indifferent about all the novelty and world of wonders beyond, and should have hated to leave the dull tranquillity of my window for an excursion through the splendours of the unseen streets and palaces that surrounded me.

It was one o'clock before Madame joined me; and finding me in this dull mood, she did not press me to accompany her in her drive, no doubt well pleased to be rid of me.

After tea that evening, as we sat alone in our room, she entertained me with some very odd conversation—at the time unintelligible—but which acquired a tolerably distinct meaning from the events that followed.

Two or three times that day Madame appeared to me on the point of saying something of grave import, as she scanned me with her bleak wicked stare.

It was a peculiarity of hers, that whenever she was pressed upon by an anxiety that really troubled her, her countenance did not look sad or solicitous, as other people's would, but simply wicked. Her great gaunt mouth was compressed and drawn down firmly at the corners, and her eyes glared with a dismal scowl.

At last she said suddenly—

'Are you ever grateful, Maud?'

'I hope so, Madame,' I answered.

'And how do you show your gratitude? For instance, would a you do great deal for a person who would run *risque* for your sake?'

It struck me all at once that she was sounding me about poor Meg Hawkes, whose fidelity, notwithstanding the treason or cowardice of her lover, Tom Brice, I never doubted; and I grew at once wary and reserved.

'I know of no opportunity, thank Heaven, for any such service, Madame. How can anyone serve me at present, by themselves incurring danger? What do you mean?'

'Do you like, for example, to go to that French Pension? Would you not like better some other arrangement?'

'Of course there are other arrangements I should like better; but I see no use in talking of them; they are not to be,' I answered.

'What other arrangements do you mean, my dear cheaile?' enquired Madame. 'You mean, I suppose, you would like better to go to Lady Knollys?'

'My uncle does not choose it at present; and except with his consent nothing can be done!'

'He weel never consent, dear cheaile.'

'But he *has* consented—not immediately indeed, but in a short time, when his affairs are settled.'

'*Lanternes*! They will never be settle,' said Madame.

'At all events, for the present I am to go to France. Milly seems very happy, and I dare say I shall like it too. I am very glad to leave Bartram-Haugh, at all events.'

'But your uncle weel bring you back there,' said Madame, drily.

'It is doubtful whether he will ever return to Bartram himself,' I said.

'Ah!' said Madame, with a long-drawn nasal intonation, 'you theenk I hate you. You are quaite wrong, my dear Maud. I am, on the contrary, very much interested for you—I am, I assure you, dear a cheaile.'

And she laid her great hand, with joints misshapen by old chilblains, upon the back of mine. I looked up in her face. She was not smiling. On the contrary, her wide mouth was drawn down at the corners ruefully, as before, and she gazed on my face with a scowl from her abysmal eyes.

I used to think the flare of that irony which lighted her face so often immeasurably worse than any other expression she could assume; but this lack-lustre stare and dismal collapse of feature was more wicked still.

'Suppose I should bring you to Lady Knollys, and place you in her charge, what would a you do then for poor Madame?' said this dark spectre.

I was inwardly startled at these words. I looked into her unsearchable face, but could draw thence nothing but fear. Had she made the same overture only two days since, I think I would have offered her half my fortune. But circumstances were altered. I was no longer in the panic of despair. The lesson I had received from Tom Brice was fresh in my mind, and my profound distrust of her was uppermost. I saw before me only a tempter and betrayer, and said—

'Do you mean to imply, Madame, that my guardian is not to be trusted, and that I ought to make my escape from him, and that you are really willing to aid me in doing so?'

This, you see, was turning the tables upon her. I looked her steadily in the face as I spoke. She returned my gaze with a strange stare and a gape, which haunted me long after; and it seemed as we sat in utter silence that each was rather horribly fascinated by the other's gaze.

At last she shut her mouth sternly, and eyes me with a more determined and meaning scowl, and then said in a low tone—

'I believe, Maud, that you are a cunning and wicked little thing.'

'Wisdom is not cunning, Madame; nor is it wicked to ask your meaning in explicit language,' I replied.

'And so, you clever cheaile, we two sit here, playing at a game of chess, over this little table, to decide which shall destroy the other—is it not so?'

'I will not allow you to destroy me,' I retorted, with a sudden flash.

Madame stood up, and rubbed her mouth with her open hand. She looked to me like some evil being seen in a dream. I was frightened.

'You are going to hurt me!' I ejaculated, scarce knowing what I said.

'If I were, you deserve it. You are very *malicious*, ma chère: or, it may be, only very stupid.'

A knock came to the door.

'Come in,' I cried, with a glad sense of relief.

A maid entered.

'A letter, please, 'm,' she said, handing it to me.

'For *me*,' snarled Madame, snatching it.

I had seen my uncle's hand, and the Feltram post-mark.

Madame broke the seal, and read. It seemed but a word, for she turned it about after the first momentary glance, and examined the interior of the envelope, and then returned to the line she had already read.

She folded the letter again, drawing her nails in a sharp pinch along the creases, as she stared in a blank, hesitating way at me.

'You arc stupid little ingrate, I am employ by Monsieur Ruthyn, and of course I am faithful to my employer. I do not want to talk to you. *There*, you may read that.'

She jerked the letter before me on the table. It contained but these words:—

Bartram-Haugh:
'30th January, 1845.

'MY DEAR MADAME,

'Be so good as to take the half-past eight o'clock train to <u>*Dover*</u> to-night. Beds are prepared.—Yours very truly,

SILAS RUTHYN.'

I cannot say what it was in this short advice that struck me with fear. Was it the thick line beneath the word 'Dover,' that was so uncalled for, and gave me a faint but terrible sense of something preconcerted?

I said to Madame—

'Why is "Dover" underlined?'

'I do not know, little fool, no more than you. How can I tell what is passing in your oncle's head when he make that a mark?'

'Has it not a meaning, Madame?'

'How can you talk like that?' she answered, more in her old way. 'You are either mocking of me, or you are becoming truly a fool!'

She rang the bell, called for our bill, saw our hostess; while I made a few hasty prepartions in my room.

'You need not look after the trunks—they will follow us all right. Let us go, cheaile—we 'av half an hour only to reach the train.'

No one ever fussed like Madame when occasion offered. There was a cab at the door, into which she hurried me. I assumed that she would give all needful directions, and leaned back, very weary and sleepy already, though it was so early, listening to her farewell screamed from the cab-step, and seeing her black cloak flitting and flapping this way and that, like the wings of a raven disturbed over its prey.

In she got, and away we drove through a glare of lamps, and shop-windows, still open; gas everywhere, and cabs, busses, and carriages, still thundering through the streets. I was too tired and too depressed to look at those things. Madame, on the contrary, had her head out of the window till we reached the station.

'Where are the rest of the boxes?' I asked, as Madame placed me in charge of her box and my bag in the office of the terminus.

'They will follow with Boots in another cab, and will come safe with us in this train. Mind those two, we weel bring in the carriage with us.'

So into a carriage we got; in came Madame's box and my bag; Madame stood at the door, and, I think, frightened away intending passengers, by her size and shrillness.

At last the bell rang her into her place, the door clapt, the whistle sounded, and we were off.

CHAPTER LXI

OUR BED-CHAMBER

I had passed a miserable night, and, indeed, for many nights had not had my due proportion of sleep. Still I sometimes fancy that I may have swallowed something in my tea that helped to make me so irresistibly drowsy. It was a very dark night—no moon, and the stars soon hid by the gathering clouds. Madame sat silent, and ruminating in her place, with her rugs about her. I, in my corner similarly enveloped, tried to keep awake. Madame plainly thought I was asleep already, for she stole a leather flask from her pocket, and applied it to her lips, causing an aroma of brandy.

But it was vain struggling against the influence that was stealing over me, and I was soon in a profound and dreamless slumber.

Madame awoke me at last, in a huge fuss. She had got out all our things and hurried them away to a close carriage which was awaiting us. It was still dark and starless. We got along the platform, I half asleep, the porter carrying our rugs, by the glare of a pair of gas-jets in the wall, and out by a small door at the end.

I remember that Madame, contrary to her wont, gave the man some money. By the puzzling light of the carriage-lamps we got in and took our seats.

'Go on,' screamed Madame, and drew up the window with a great chuck; and we were enclosed in darkness and silence, the most favourable conditions for thought.

My sleep had not restored me as it might; I felt feverish, fatigued, and still very drowsy, though unable to sleep as I had done.

I dozed by fits and starts, and lay awake, or half-awake, sometimes, not thinking but in a way imagining what kind of a place Dover would be; but too tired and listless to ask Madame any questions, and merely seeing the hedges, grey in the lamplight, glide backward into darkness, as I leaned back.

We turned off the main road, at right angles, and drew up.

'Get down and poosh it, it is open,' screamed Madame from the window.

A gate, I suppose, was thus passed; for when we resumed our brisk trot, Madame bawled across the carriage—

'We are now in the 'otel grounds.'

And so all again was darkness and silence, and I fell into another doze, from which, on waking, I found that we had come to a standstill, and Madame was standing on the low step of an open door, paying the driver. She, herself, pulled her box and the bag in. I was too tired to care what had become of the rest of our luggage.

I descended, glancing to the right and left, but there was nothing visible but a patch of light from the lamps on a paved ground and on the wall.

We stepped into the hall or vestibule, and Madame shut the door, and I thought I heard the key turn in it. We were in total darkness.

'Where are the lights, Madame—where are the people?' I asked, more awake than I had been.

''Tis pass three o'clock, cheaile, bote there is always light here.' She was groping at the side; and in a moment more lighted a lucifer match, and so a bedroom candle.

We were in a flagged lobby, under an archway at the right, and at the left of which opened long flagged passages, lost in darkness; a winding stair, barely wide enough to admit Madame, dragging her box, led upward under a doorway, in a corner at the right.

'Come, dear cheaile, take your bag; don't mind the rugs, they are safe enough.'

'But where are we to go? There is no one!' I said, looking round in wonder. It certainly was a strange reception at an hotel.

'Never mind, my dear cheaile. They know me here, and I have always the same room ready when I write for it. Follow me quaitely.'

So she mounted, carrying the candle. The stair was steep, and the march long. We halted at the second landing, and entered a gaunt, grimy passage. All the way up we had not heard a single sound of life, nor seen a human being, nor so much as passed a gaslight.

'Viola! here 'tis, my dear old room. Enter, dearest Maud.'

And so I did. The room was large and lofty, but shabby and dismal. There was a tall four-post bed, with its foot beside the window, hung with dark-green curtains, of some plush or velvet texture, that looked like a dusty pall. The remaining furniture was scant and old, and a ravelled square of threadbare carpet covered a patch of floor at the bedside. The room was grim and large, and had a cold, vault-like atmosphere, as if long uninhabited; but there were cinders in the grate and under it. The imperfect light of our mutton-fat candle made all this look still more comfortless.

Madame placed the candle on the chimneypiece, locked the door, and put the key in her pocket.

'I always do so in '*otel*' said she, with a wink at me.

And, then with a long 'ha!' expressive of fatigue and relief, she threw herself into a chair.

'So 'ere we are at last!' said she; 'I'm glad. *There's* your bed, Maud. *Mine* is in the dressing-room.'

She took the candle, and I went in with her. A shabby press bed, a chair, and table were all its furniture; it was rather a closet than a dressing-room, and had no door except that through which we had entered. So we returned, and very tired, wondering, I sat down on the side of my bed and yawned.

'I hope they will call us in time for the packet,' I said.

'Oh yes, they never fail,' she answered, looking steadfastly on her box, which she was diligently uncording.

Uninviting as was my bed, I was longing to lie down in it; and having made those ablutions which our journey rendered necessary, I at length lay down, having first religiously stuck my talismanic pin, with the head of sealing-wax, into the bolster.

Nothing escaped the restless eye of Madame.

'Wat is that, dear cheaile?' she enquired, drawing near and scrutinising the head of the gipsy charm, which showed like a little ladybird newly lighted on the sheet.

'Nothing—a charm—folly. Pray, Madame, allow me to go to sleep.'

So, with another look and a little twiddle between her finger and thumb, she seemed satisfied; but, unhappily for me, she did not seem at all sleepy. She busied herself in unpacking and displaying over the back of the chair a whole series of London purchases—silk dresses, a shawl, a sort of lace demi-coiffure then in vogue, and a variety of other articles.

The vainest and most slammakin of women—the merest slut at home, a milliner's lay figure out of doors—she had one square foot of looking-glass upon the chimneypiece, and therein tried effects, and conjured up grotesque simpers upon her sinister and weary face.

I knew that the sure way to prolong this worry was to express my uneasiness under it, so I bore it as quietly as I could; and at last fell fast asleep with the gaunt image of Madame, with a festoon of grey silk with a cerise stripe, pinched up in her finger and thumb, and smiling over her shoulder across it into the little shaving-glass that stood on the chimney.

I awoke suddenly in the morning, and sat up in my bed, having for a moment forgotten all about our travelling. A moment more, however, brought all back again.

'Are we in time, Madame?'

'For the packet?' she enquired, with one of her charming smiles, and cutting a caper on the floor. 'To be sure; you don't suppose they would forget. We have two hours yet to wait.'

'Can we see the sea from the window?'

'No, dearest cheaile; you will see't time enough.

'I'd like to get up,' I said.

'Time enough, my dear Maud; you are fatigued; are you sure you feel quite well?'

'Well enough to get up; I should be better, I think, out of bed.'

'There is no hurry, you know; you need not even go by the next packet. Your uncle, he tell me, I may use my discretion.'

'Is there any water?'

'They will bring some.'

'Please, Madame, ring the bell.'

She pulled it with alacrity. I afterwards learnt that it did not ring.

'What has become of my gipsy pin?' I demanded, with an unaccountable sinking of the heart.

'Oh! the little pin with the red top? maybe it 'as fall on the ground; we weel find when you get up.'

I suspected that she had taken it merely to spite me. It would have been quite the thing she would have liked. I cannot describe to you how the loss of this little 'charm' depressed and excited me. I searched the bed; I turned over all the bedclothes; I searched in and outside; at last I gave up.

'How odious!' I cried; 'somebody has stolen it merely to vex me.'

And, like a fool as I was, I threw myself on my face on the bed and wept, partly in anger, partly in dismay.

After a time, however, this blew over. I had a hope of recovering it. If Madame had stolen it, it would turn up yet. But in the meantime its disappearance troubled me like an omen.

'I am afraid, my dear cheaile, you are not very well. It is really very odd you should make such fuss about a pin! Nobody would believe! Do you not theenk it would be a good plan to take a your breakfast in your bed?

She continued to urge this point for some time. At last, however, having by this time quite recovered my self-command, and resolved to preserve ostensibly fair terms with Madame, who could contribute so essentially to make me wretched during the rest of my journey, and possibly to prejudice me very seriously on my arrival, I said quietly—

'Well, Madame, I know it is very silly; but I had kept that foolish little pin so long and so carefully, that I had grown quite fond of it; but I suppose it is lost, and I must content myself, though I cannot laugh as you do. So I will get up now, and dress.'

'I think you will do well to get all the repose you can,' answered Madame; 'but as you please,' she added, observing that I was getting up.

So soon as I had got some of my things on, I said—

'Is there a pretty view from the window?'

'No,' said Madame.

I looked out and saw a dreary quadrangle of cut stone, in one side of which my window was placed. As I looked a dream rose up before me.

'This hotel,' I said, in a puzzled way. '*Is* it a hotel? Why this is just like—it *is* the inner court of Bartram-Haugh!'

Madame clapped her large hands together, made a fantastic *chassé* on the floor, burst into a great nasal laugh like the scream of a parrot, and then said—

'Well, dearest Maud, is not clever trick?'

I was so utterly confounded that I could only stare about me in stupid silence, a spectacle which renewed Madame's peals of laughter.

'We are at Bartram-Haugh!' I repeated, in utter consternation. 'How was this done?'

I had no reply but shrieks of laughter, and one of those Walpurgis dances in which she excelled.

'It is a mistake—is it? *What* is it?'

'All a mistake, of course. Bartram-Haugh, it is so like Dover, as all philosophers know.'

I sat down in total silence, looking out into the deep and dark enclosure, and trying to comprehend the reality and the meaning of all this.

'Well, Madame, I suppose you will be able to satisfy my uncle of your fidelity and intelligence. But to me it seems that his money has been ill-spent, and his directions anything but well observed.'

'Ah, ha! Never mind; I think he will forgive me,' laughed Madame.

Her tone frightened me. I began to think, with a vague but overpowering sense of danger, that she had acted under the Machiavellian directions of her superior.

'You have brought me back, then, by my uncle's orders?'

'Did I say so?'

'No; but what you have said can have no other meaning, though I can't believe it. And why have I been brought here? What is the object of all this duplicity and trick. I *will* know. It is not possible that my uncle, a gentleman and a kinsman, can be privy to so disreputable a manouvre.'

'First you will eat your breakfast, dear Maud; next you can tell your story to your uncle, Monsieur Ruthyn; and then you shall hear what he thinks of my so terrible misconduct. What nonsense, cheaile! Can you not think how many things may 'appen to change a your uncle's plans? Is he not in danger to be arrest? Bah! You are cheaile still; you cannot have intelligence more than a cheaile. Dress yourself, and I will order breakfast.'

I could not comprehend the strategy which had been practised on me. Why had I been so shamelessly deceived? If it were decided that I should remain here, for what imaginable reason had I been sent so far on my journey to France? Why had I been conveyed back with such mystery? Why was I removed to this uncomfortable and desolate room, on the same floor with the apartment in which Charke had met his death, and with no window commanding the front of the house, and no view but the deep and weed-choked court, that looked like a deserted churchyard in a city?

'I suppose I may go to my own room?' I said.

'Not to-day, my dear cheaile, for it was all disarrange when we go 'way; 'twill be ready again in two three days.'

'Where is Mary Quince?' I asked.

'Mary Quince!—she has follow us to France,' said Madame, making what in Ireland they call a bull.

'They are not sure where they will go or what will do for day or two more. I will go and get breakfast. Adieu for a moment.'

Madame was out of the door as she said this, and I thought I heard the key turn in the lock.

CHAPTER LXII

A WELL-KNOWN FACE LOOKS IN

You who have never experienced it can have no idea how angry and frightened you become under the sinister insult of being locked into a room, as on trying the door I found I was.

The key was in the lock; I could see it through the hole. I called after Madame, I shook at the solid oak-door, beat upon it with my hands, kicked it—but all to no purpose.

I rushed into the next room, forgetting—if indeed I had observed it, that there was no door from it upon the gallery. I turned round in an angry and dismayed perplexity, and, like prisoners in romances, examined the windows.

I was shocked and affrighted on discovering in reality what they occasionally find—a series of iron bars crossing the window! They were firmly secured in the oak woodwork of the window-frame, and each window was, besides, so compactly screwed down that it could not open. This bedroom was converted into a prison. A momentary hope flashed on me—perhaps all the windows were secured alike! But it was no such thing: these gaol-like precautions were confined to the windows to which I had access.

For a few minutes I felt quite distracted; but I bethought me that I must now, if ever, control my terrors and exert whatever faculties I possessed.

I stood upon a chair and examined the oak-work. I thought I detected marks of new chiselling here and there. The screws, too, looked new; and they and the scars on the woodwork were freshly smeared over with some coloured stuff by way of disguise.

While I was making these observations, I heard the key stealthily stirred. I suspect that Madame wished to surprise me. Her approaching step, indeed, was seldom audible; she had the soft tread of the feline tribe.

I was standing in the centre of the room confronting her when she entered.

'Why did you lock the door, Madame?' I demanded.

She slipped in suddenly with an insidious smirk, and locked the door hastily.

'Hish!' whispered Madame, raising her broad palm; and then screwing in her cheeks, she made an ogle over her shoulder in the direction of the passage.

'Hish! be quiate, cheaile, weel you, and I weel tale you everything presently.'

She paused, with her ear laid to the door.

'Now I can speak, ma chère; I weel tale a you there is bailiff in the house, two, three, four soche impertinent fallows! They have another as bad as themselve to make a leest of the furniture: we most keep them out of these rooms, dear Maud.'

'You left the key in the door on the outside,' I retorted; 'that was not to keep them out, but me in, Madame.'

'*Deed* I leave the key in the door?' ejaculated Madame, with both hands raised, and such a genuine look of consternation as for a moment shook me.

It was the nature of this woman's deceptions that they often puzzled though they seldom convinced me.

'I re-ally think, Maud, all those so frequent changes and excite-ments they weel overturn my poor head.'

'And the windows are secured with iron bars—what are they for?' I whispered sternly, pointing with my finger at these grim securities.

'That is for more a than forty years, when Sir Phileep Aylmer was to reside here, and had this room for his children's nursery, and was afraid they should fall out.'

'But if you look you will find these bars have been put here very recently: the screws and marks are quite new.'

'*Eendeed!*' ejaculated Madame, with prolonged emphasis, in precisely the same consternation. 'Why, my dear, they told a me down stair what I have tell a you, when I ask the reason! Late a me see.'

And Madame mounted on a chair, and made her scrutiny with much curiosity, but could not agree with me as to the very recent date of the carpentry.

There is nothing, I think, so exasperating as that sort of falsehood which affects not to see what is quite palpable.

'Do you mean to say, Madame, that you really think those chisellings and screws are forty years old?'

'How can I tell, cheaile? What does signify whether it is forty or only fourteen years? Bah! we av other theeng to theenk about. Those villain men! I am glad to see bar and bolt, and lock and key, at least, to our room, to keep soche faylows out!'

At that moment a knock came to the door, and Madame's nasal 'in moment' answered promptly, and she opened the door, stealthily popping out her head.

'Oh, that is all right; go you long, no ting more, go way.'

'Who's there?' I cried.

'Hold a your tongue,' said Madame imperiously to the visitor, whose voice I fancied I recognised—'*go* way.'

Out slipped Madame again, locking the door; but this time she returned immediately, bearing a tray with breakfast.

I think she fancied that I would perhaps attempt to break away and escape; but I had no such thought at that moment. She hastily set down the tray on the floor at the threshold, locking the door as before.

My share of breakfast was a little tea; but Madame's digestion was seldom disturbed by her sympathies, and she ate voraciously. During this process there was a silence unusual in her company; but when her meal was ended she proposed a reconnaissance, professing much uncertainty as to whether my Uncle had been arrested or not.

'And in case the poor old gentleman be poot in what you call stone jug, where are *we* to go my dear Maud—to Knowl or to Elverston? You must direct.'

And so she disappeared, turning the key in the door as before. It was an old custom of hers, locking herself in her room, and leaving the key in the lock; and the habit prevailed, for she left it there again.

With a heavy heart I completed my simple toilet, wondering all the while how much of Madame's story might be false and how much, if any, true. Then I looked out upon the dingy courtyard below, in its deep damp shadow, and thought, 'How could an assassin have scaled that height in safety, and entered so noiselessly as not to awaken the slumbering gamester?' Then there were the iron bars across my window. What a fool had I been to object to that security!

I was labouring hard to reassure myself, and keep all ghastly suspicions at arm's length. But I wished that my room had been to the front of the house, with some view less dismal.

Lost in these ruminations of fear, as I stood at the window I was startled by the sound of a sharp tread on the lobby, and by the key turning in the lock of my door.

In a panic I sprang back into the corner, and stood with my eyes fixed upon the door. It opened a little, and the black head of Meg Hawkes was introduced.

'Oh, Meg!' I cried; 'thank God!'

'I guessed'twas you, Miss Maud. I am feared, Miss.'

The miller's daughter was pale, and her eyes, I thought, were red and swollen.

'Oh, Meg! for God's sake, what is it all?'

'I darn't come in. The old un's gone down, and locked the cross-door, and left me to watch. They think I care nout about ye, no more nor themselves. I donna know all, but summat more nor her. They tell her nout, she's so gi'n to drink; they say she's not safe, an' awful quarrelsome. I hear a deal when fayther and Master Dudley be a-talkin' in the mill. They think, comin' in an' out, I don't mind; but I put one think an' t'other together. An' don't ye eat nor drink nout here, Miss; hide away this; it's black enough, but wholesome anyhow!' and she slipt a piece of a coarse loaf from under her apron. '*Hide* it mind. Drink nout but the water in the jug there—it's clean spring.'

'Oh, Meg! Oh, Meg! I know what you mean,' said I, faintly.

'Ay, Miss, I'm feared they'll try it; they'll try to make away wi' ye somehow. I'm goin' to your friends arter dark; I darn't try it no sooner. I'll git awa to Ellerston, to your lady-cousin, and I'll bring 'em back wi' me in a rin; so keep a good hairt, lass. Meg Hawkes will stan' to ye. Ye were better to me than fayther and mother, and a';' and she clasped me round the waist, and buried her head in my dress; 'an I'll gie my life for ye, darling, and if they hurt ye I'll kill myself.'

She recovered her sterner mood quickly—

'Not a word, lass,' she said, in her old tone. 'Don't ye try to git away—they'll *kill* ye—ye *can't* do't. Leave a' to me. It won't be, whatever it is, till two or three o'clock in the morning. I'll ha'e them a' here long afore; so keep a brave heart—there's a darling.'

I suppose she heard, or fancied she heard, a step approaching, for she said—

'Hish!'

Her pale wild face vanished, the door shut quickly and softly, and the key turned again in the lock.

Meg, in her rude way, had spoken softly—almost under her breath; but no prophecy shrieked by the Pythoness ever thundered so madly in the ears of the hearer. I dare say that Meg fancied I was marvellously little moved by her words. I felt my gaze grow intense, and my flesh and bones literally freeze. She did not know that every word she spoke seemed to burst like a blaze in my brain. She had delivered her frightful warning, and told her story coarsely and bluntly, which, in effect, means distinctly and concisely; and, I dare say, the announcement so made, like a quick bold incision in surgery, was more tolerable than the slow imperfect mangling, which falters and recedes and equivocates with torture. Madame was long away. I sat down at the window, and tried to appreciate my dreadful situation. I was stupid—the imagery was all frightful; but I beheld it as we sometimes see horrors—heads cut off and houses burnt—in a dream, and without the corresponding emotions. It did not seem as if all this were really happening to me. I remember sitting at the window, and looking and blinking at the opposite side of the building, like a person unable but striving to see an object distinctly, and every minute pressing my hand to the side of my head and saying—

'Oh, it won't be—it won't be—Oh no!—never!—it could not be!' And in this stunned state Madame found me on her return.

But the valley of the shadow of death has its varieties of dread. The 'horror of great darkness' is disturbed by voices and illumed by sights. There are periods of incapacity and collapse, followed by paroxysms of active terror. Thus in my journey during those long hours I found it—agonies subsiding into lethargies, and these breaking again into frenzy. I sometimes wonder how I carried my reason safely through the ordeal.

Madame locked the door, and amused herself with her own business, without minding me, humming little nasal snatches of French airs, as she smirked on her silken purchases displayed in the daylight. Suddenly it struck me that it was very dark, considering how early it was. I looked at my watch; it seemed to me a great effort of concentration to understand it. Four o'clock, it said. Four o'clock! It would be dark at five—*night* in one hour!

'Madame, what o'clock is it? Is it evening?' I cried with my hand to my forehead, like a person puzzled.

'Two three minutes past four. It had five minutes to four when I came upstairs,' answered she, without interrupting her examination of a piece of darned lace which she was holding close to her eyes at the window.

'Oh, Madame! *Madame!* I'm frightened,' cried I, with a wild and piteous voice, grasping her arm, and looking up, as shipwrecked people may their last to heaven, into her inexorable eyes. Madame looked frightened too, I thought, as she stared into my face. At last she said, rather angrily, and shaking her arm loose—

'What you mean, cheaile?'

'Oh save me, Madame!—oh save me!—oh save me, Madame!' I pleaded, with the wild monotony of perfect terror, grasping and clinging to her dress, and looking up, with an agonised face, into the eyes of that shadowy Atropos.

'Save a you, indeed! Save! What *niaiserie*!'

'Oh, Madame! Oh, *dear* Madame! for God's sake, only get me away—get me from this, and I'll do everything you ask me all my life—I will—*indeed*, Madame, I will! Oh save me! save me! *save* me!'

I was clinging to Madame as to my guardian angel in my agony.

'And who told you, cheaile, you are in any danger?' demanded Madame, looking down on me with a black and witchlike stare.

'I am, Madame—I am—in great danger! Oh, Madame, think of me—take pity on me! I have none to help me—there is no one but God and you!'

Madame all this time viewed me with the same dismal stare, like a sorceress reading futurity in my face.

'Well, maybe you are—how can I tell? Maybe your uncle is mad—maybe you are mad. You have been my enemy always—why should I care?'

Again I burst into wild entreaty, and, clasping her fast, poured forth my supplications with the bitterness of death.

'I have no confidence in you, little Maud; you are little rogue—petite traîtresse! Reflect, if you can, how you 'av always treat Madame. You 'av attempt to ruin me—you conspire with the bad domestics at Knowl to destroy me—and you expect me here to take a your part! You would never listen to me—you 'ad no mercy for me—you join to hunt me away from your house like wolf. Well, what you expect to find me now? *Bah*!'

This terrific 'Bah!' with a long nasal yell of scorn, rang in my ears like a clap of thunder.

'I say you are mad, petite insolente, to suppose I should care for you more than the poor hare it will care for the hound—more than the bird who has escape will love the oiseleur. I do not care—I ought not care. It is your turn to suffer. Lie down on your bed there, and suffer quaitely.'

CHAPTER LXIII

SPICED CLARET

I did not lie down; but I despaired. I walked round and round the room, wringing my hands in utter distraction. I threw myself at the bedside on my knees. I could not pray; I could only shiver and moan, with hands clasped, and eyes of horror turned up to heaven. I think Madame was, in her malignant way, perplexed. That some evil was intended me I am sure she was persuaded; but I dare say Meg Hawkes had said rightly in telling me that she was not fully in their secrets.

The first paroxysm of despair subsided into another state. All at once my mind was filled with the idea of Meg Hawkes, her enterprise, and my chances of escape. There is one point at which the road to Elverston makes a short ascent: there is a sudden curve there, two great ash-trees, with a roadside stile between, at the right side, covered with ivy. Driving back and forward, I did not recollect having particularly remarked this point in the highway; but now it was before me, in the thin light of the thinnest segment of moon, and the figure of Meg Hawkes, her back toward me, always ascending towards Elverston. It was constantly the same picture—the same motion without progress—the same dreadful suspense and impatience.

I was now sitting on the side of the bed, looking wistfully across the room. When I did not see Meg Hawkes, I beheld Madame darkly eyeing first one then another point of the chamber, evidently puzzling over some problem, and in one of her most savage moods—sometimes muttering to herself, sometimes protruding, and sometimes screwing up her great mouth.

She went into her own room, where she remained, I think, nearly ten minutes, and on her return there was that in the flash of her eyes, the glow of her face, and the peculiar fragrance that surrounded her, that showed she had been partaking of her favourite restorative.

I had not moved since she left my room.

She paused about the middle of the floor, and looked at me with what I can only describe as her wild-beast stare.

'You are a very secrete family, you Ruthyns—you are so coning. I hate the coning people. By my faith, I weel see Mr. Silas Ruthyn, and ask wat he mean. I heard him tell old Wyat that Mr. Dudley is gone away to-night. He shall tell me everything, or else I weel make echec et mat aussi vrai que je vis.'

Madame's words had hardly ceased, when I was again watching Meg Hawkes on the steep road, mounting, but never reaching, the top of the acclivity, on the way to Elverston, and mentally praying that she might be brought safely there. Vain prayer of an agonised heart! Meg's journey was already frustrated: she was not to reach Elverston in time.

Madame revisited her apartment, and returned, not, I think, improved in temper. She walked about the room, hustling the scanty furniture hither and thither as she encountered it. She kicked her empty box out of her way, with a horrid crash, and a curse in French. She strode and swaggered round the room, muttering all the way, and turning the corners of her course with a furious whisk. At last, out of the door she went. I think she fancied she had not been sufficiently taken into confidence as to what was intended for me.

It was now growing late, and yet no succour! I was seized, I remember, with a dreadful icy shivering.

I was listening for signals of deliverance. At ever distant sound, half stifled with a palpitation, these sounds piercing my ear with a horrible and exaggerated distinctness—'Oh Meg!—Oh cousin Monica!—Oh come! Oh Heaven, have mercy!—Lord, have mercy!' I thought I heard a roaring and jangle of voices. Perhaps it came from Uncle Silas's room. It might be the tipsy violence of Madame. It might—merciful Heaven!—be the arrival of friends. I started to my feet; I listened, quivering with attention. Was it in my brain?—was it real? I was at the door, and it seemed to open of itself. Madame had forgotten to lock it; she was losing her head a little by this time. The key stood in the gallery door beyond; it too, was open. I fled wildly. There was a subsiding sound of voices in my uncle's room. I was, I know not how, on the lobby at the great stair-head outside my uncle's apartment. My hand was on the banisters, my foot on the first step, when below me and against the faint light that glimmered through the great window on the landing I saw a bulky human form ascending, and a voice said 'Hush!' I staggered back, and at that instant fancied, with a thrill of conviction, I heard Lady Knollys's voice in Uncle Silas' room.

I don't know how I entered the room; I was there like a ghost. I was frightened at my own state.

Lady Knollys was not there—no one but Madame and my guardian.

I can never forget the look that Uncle Silas fixed on me as he cowered, seemingly as appalled as I.

I think I must have looked like a phantom newly risen from the grave.

'What's that?—where do you come from?' whispered he.

'Death! death!' was my whispered answer, as I froze with terror where I stood.

'What does she mean?—what does all this mean?' said Uncle Silas, recovering wonderfully, and turning with a withering sneer on Madame. 'Do you think it

right to disobey my plain directions, and let her run about the house at this hour?'
'Death! death! Oh, pray to God for you and me!' I whispered in the same dreadful tones.

My uncle stared strangely at me again; and after several horrible seconds, in which he seemed to have recovered himself, he said, sternly and coolly—

'You give too much place to your imagination, niece. Your spirits are in an odd state—you ought to have advice.'

'Oh, uncle, pity me! Oh, uncle, you are good! you're kind; you're kind when you think. You could not—you could not—could not! Oh, think of your brother that was always so good to you! He sees me here. He sees us both. Oh, save me, uncle—save me!—and I'll give up everything to you. I'll pray to God to bless you—I'll never forget your goodness and mercy. But don't keep me in doubt. If I'm to go, oh, for God's sake, shoot me now!'

'You were always odd, niece; I begin to fear you are insane,' he replied, in the same stern icy tone.

'Oh, uncle—oh!—am I? Am I *mad*?'

'I hope not; but you'll conduct yourself like a sane person if you wish to enjoy the privileges of one.'

Then, with his finger pointing at me, he turned to Madame, and said, in a tone of suppressed ferocity—

'What's the meaning of this?—why is she here?'

Madame was gabbling volubly, but to me it was only a shrilly noise. My whole soul was concentrated in my uncle, the arbiter of my life, before whom I stood in the wildest agony of supplication.

That night was dreadful. The people I saw dizzily, made of smoke or shining vapour, smiling or frowning, I could have passed my hand through them. They were evil spirits.

'There's no ill intended you; by —— there's none,' said my uncle, for the first time violently agitated. 'Madame told you why we've changed your room. You told her about the bailiffs, did not you? 'with a stamp of fury he demanded of Madame, whose nasal roullades of talk were running on like a accompaniment all the time. She had told me indeed only a few hours since, and now it sounded to me like the echo of something heard a month ago or more.

'You can't go about the house, d—n it, with bailiffs in occupation. There now—there's the whole thing. Get to your room, Maud, and don't vex me. There's a good girl.'

He was trying to smile as he spoke these last words, and, with quavering soft tones, to quiet me; but the old scowl was there, the smile was corpse-like and contorted, and the softness of his tones was more dreadful than another man's ferocity.

'There, Madame, she'll go quite gently, and you can call if you want help. Don't let it happen again.'

'Come, Maud,' said Madame, encircling but not hurting my arm with her grip; 'let us go, my friend.'

I did go, you will wonder, as well you may—as you may wonder at the docility with which strong men walk through the press-room to the drop, and thank the people of the prison for their civility when they bid them good-bye, and facilitate the fixing of the rope and adjusting of the cap. Have you never wondered that they don't make a last battle for life with the unscrupulous energy of terror, instead of surrendering it so gently in cold blood, on a silent calculation, the arithmetic of despair?

I went up-stairs with Madame like a somnambulist. I rather quickened my step as I drew near my room. I went in, and stood a phantom at the window, looking into the dark quadrange. A thin glimmering crescent hung in the frosty sky, and all heaven was strewn with stars. Over the steep roof at the other side spread on the dark azure of the night this glorious blazonry of the unfathomable Creator. To me a dreadful scroll—inexorable eyes—the cloud of cruel witnesses looking down in freezing brightness on my prayers and agonies.

I turned about and sat down, leaning my head upon my arms. Then suddenly I sat up, as for the first time the picture of Uncle Silas's littered room, and the travelling bags and black boxes plied on the floor by his table—the desk, hat-case, umbrella, coats, rugs, and mufflers, all ready for a journey—reached my brain and suggested thought. The *mise en scène* had remained in every detail fixed upon my retina; and how I wondered—'When is he going—how soon? Is he going to carry me away and place me in a madhouse?'

'Am I—am I mad?' I began to think. 'Is this all a dream, or is it real?'

I remembered how a thin polite gentleman, with a tall grizzled head and a black velvet waistcoat, came into the carriage on our journey, and said a few words to me; how Madame whispered him something, and he murmured 'Oh!' very gently, with raised eyebrows, and a glance at me, and thenceforward spoke no more to me, only to Madame, and at the next station carried his hat and other travelling chattels into another carriage. Had she told him I was mad?

These horrid bars! Madame always with me! The direful hints that dropt from my uncle! My own terrific sensations!—All these evidences revolved in my brain, and presented themselves in turn like writings on a wheel of fire.

There came a knock to the door—

Oh, Meg! Was it she? No; old Wyat whispered Madame something about her room.

So Madame re-entered, with a little silver tray and flagon in her hands, and a glass. Nothing came from Uncle Silas in ungentlemanlike fashion.

'Drink, Maud,' said Madame, raising the cover, and evidently enjoying the fragrant steam.

I could not. I might have done so had I been able to swallow anything—for I was too distracted to think of Meg's warning.

Madame suddenly recollected her mistake of that evening, and tried the door; but it was duly locked. She took the key from her pocket and placed it in her breast.

'You weel 'av these rooms to yourself, ma chère. I shall sleep downstairs to-night.'

She poured out some of the hot claret into the glass abstractedly, and drank it off.

"Tis very good—I drank without theenk. Bote 'tis very good. Why don't you drink some?'

'I could not', I repeated. And Madame boldly helped herself.

'Vary polite, certally, to Madame was it to send nothing at all for *hair*' (so she pronounced 'her'); 'bote is all same thing.' And so she ran on in her tipsy vein, which was loud and sarcastic, with a fierce laugh now and then.

Afterwards I heard that they were afraid of Madame, who was given to cross purposes, and violent in her cups. She had been noisy and quarrelsome downstairs. She was under the delusion that I was to be conveyed away that night to a remote and safe place, and she was to be handsomely compensated for services and evidence to be afterwards given. She was not to be trusted, however, with the truth. That was to be known but to three people on earth.

I never knew, but I believe that the spiced claret which Madame drank was drugged. She was a person who could, I have been told. Drink a great deal without exhibiting any change from it but an inflamed colour and furious temper. I can only state for certain what I saw, and that was, that shortly after she had finished the claret she laid down upon my bed, and, I now know, fell asleep. I then thought she was *feigning* sleep only, and that she was really watching me.

About an hour after this I suddenly heard a little *clink* in the yard beneath. I peeped out, but saw nothing. The sound was repeated, however—sometimes more frequently, sometimes at long intervals. At last, in the deep shadow next the farther wall, I thought I could discover a figure, sometimes erect, sometimes stooping and bowing toward the earth. I could see this figure only in the rudest outline mingling with the dark.

Like a thunderbolt it smote my brain. 'They are making my grave!'

After the first dreadful stun I grew quite wild, and ran up and down the room wringing my hands and gasping prayers to heaven. Then a calm stole over me—such a dreadful calm as I could fancy glide over one who floated in a boat under the shadow of the 'Traitor's Gate,' leaving life and hope and trouble behind.

Shortly after there came a very low tap at my door; then another, like a tiny post-knock. I could never understand why it was I made no answer. Had I done so, and thus shown that I was awake, it might have sealed my fate. I was standing in the middle of the floor staring at the door, which I expected to see open, and admit I knew not what troop of spectres.

CHAPTER LXIV

THE HOUR OF DEATH

It was a very still night and frosty. My candle had long burnt out. There was still a faint moonlight, which fell in a square of yellow on the floor near the window, leaving the rest of the room in what to an eye less accustomed than mine had become to that faint light would have been total darkness. Now, I am sure, I heard a soft whispering outside my door. I knew that I was in a state of siege! The crisis was come, and strange to say, I felt myself grow all at once resolute and self-possessed. It was not a subsidence, however, of the dreadful excitement, but a sudden screwing-up of my nerves to a pitch such as I cannot describe.

I suppose the people outside moved with great caution; and the perfect solidity of the floor, which had not anywhere a creaking board in it, favoured their noiseless movements. It was well for me that there were in the house three persons whom it was part of their plan to mystify respecting my fate. This alone compelled the extreme caution of their proceedings. They suspected that I had placed furniture against the door, and were afraid to force it, lest a crash, a scream, perhaps a long and shrilly struggle, might follow.

I remained for a space which I cannot pretend to estimate in the same posture, afraid to stir—afraid to move my eye from the door.

A very peculiar grating sound above my head startled me from my watch—something of the character of sawing, only more crunching, and with a faint continued rumble in it—utterly inexplicable. It sounded over that portion of the roof which was farthest from the door, toward which I now glided; and as I took my stand under cover of the projecting angle of a clumsy old press that stood close by it, I perceived the room a little darkened, and I saw a man descend and take his stand upon the window-stone. He let go a rope, which, however, was still fast round his body, and employed both his hands, with apparently some exertion, about something at the side of the window, which in a moment more, in one mass, bars and all, swung noiselessly open, admitting the frosty night-air; and the man, whom I now distinctly saw to be Dudley Ruthyn, kneeled on the sill, and stept, after a moment's listening, into the room. His foot made no sound upon the floor; his head was bare, and he wore his usual short shooting-jacket.

I cowered to the ground in my post of observation. He stood, as it seemed to me irresolutely for a moment, and then drew from his pocket an instrument which I distinctly saw against the faint moonlight. Imagine a hammer, one end of which had been beaten out into a longish tapering spike, with a handle something longer than usual. He drew stealthily to the window, and seemed to examine this hurriedly, and tested its strength with a twist or two of his hand. And then he adjusted it very carefully in his grasp, and made two or three little experimental picks with it in the air.

I remained perfectly still, with a terrible composure, crouched in my hiding-place, my teeth clenched, and prepared to struggle like a tigress for my life when discovered. I thought his next measure would be to light a match. I saw a lantern, I fancied, on the window-sill. But this was not his plan. He stole, in a groping way, which seemed strange to me, who could distinguish objects in this light, to the side of my bed, the exact position of which he evidently knew; he stooped over it. Madame was breathing in the deep respiration of heavy sleep. Suddenly but softly he laid, as it seemed to me, his left hand over her face, and nearly at the same instant there came a scrunching blow; an unnatural shriek, beginning small and swelling for two or three seconds into a yell such as are imagined in haunted houses, accompanied by a convulsive sound, as of the motion of running, and the arms drumming on the bed; and then another blow—and with a horrid gasp he recoiled a step or two, and stood perfectly still. I heard a horrible tremor quivering through the joints and curtains of the bedstead—the convulsions of the murdered woman. It was a dreadful sound, like the shaking of a tree and rustling of leaves. Then once more he steps to the side of the bed, and I heard another of those horrid blows—and silence—and another—and more silence—and the diabolical surgery was ended. For a few seconds, I think, I was on the point of fainting; but a gentle stir outside the door, close to my ear, startled me, and proved that there had been a watcher posted outside. There was a little tapping at the door.

'Who's that?' whispered Dudley, hoarsely.

'A friend,' answered a sweet voice.

And a key was introduced, the door quickly unlocked, and Uncle Silas entered. I saw that frail, tall, white figure, the venerable silver locks that resembled those upon the honoured head of John Wesley, and his thin white hand, the back of which hung so close to my face that I feared to breathe. I could see his fingers twitching nervously. The smell of perfumes and of ether entered the room with him.

Dudley was trembling now like a man in an ague-fit.

'Look what you made me do!' he said, maniacally.

'Steady, sir!' said the old man, close beside me.

'Yes, you damned old murderer! I've a mind to do for you.'

'There, Dudley, like a dear boy, don't give way; it's done. Right or wrong, we can't help it. You must be quiet,' said the old man, with a stern gentleness.

Dudley groaned.

'Whoever advised it, you're a gainer, Dudley,' said Uncle Silas.

Then there was a pause.

'I hope that was not heard,' said Uncle Silas.

Dudley walked to the window and stood there.

'Come, Dudley, you and Hawkes must use expedition. You know you must get that out of the way.'

'I've done too much. I won't do nout; I'll not touch it. I wish my hand was off first; I wish I was a soger. Do as ye like, you an' Hawkes. I won't go nigh it; damn ye both—and *that*!' and he hurled the hammer with all his force upon the floor.

'Come, come, be reasonable, Dudley, dear boy. There's nothing to fear but your own folly. You won't make a noise?'

'Oh, oh, my God!' said Dudley, hoarsely, and wiped his forehead with his open hand.

'There now, you'll be all well in a minute,' continued the old man.

'You said 'twouldn't hurt her. If I'd a known she'd a screeched like that I'd never a done it. 'Twas a damn lie. You're the damndest villain on earth.'

'Come, Dudley!' said the old man under his breath, but very sternly, 'make up your mind. If you don't choose to go on, it can't be helped; only it's a pity you began. For *you* it is a good deal—it does not much matter for *me*.'

'Ay, for *you*!' echoed Dudley, through his set teeth. 'The old talk!'

'Well, sir,' snarled the old man, in the same low tones, 'you should have thought of all this before. It's only taking leave of the world a year or two sooner, but a year or two's something. I'll leave you to do as you please.'

'Stop, will you? Stop here. I know it's a fixt thing now. If a fella does a thing he's damned for, you might let him talk a bit anyhow. I don't care much if I was shot.'

'There now—*there*—just stick to that, and don't run off again. There's a box and a bag here; we must change the direction, and take them away. The box has some jewels. Can you see them? I wish we had a light.'

'No, I'd rayther not; I can see well enough. I wish we were out o' this. *Here's* the box.'

'Pull it to the window,' said the old man, to my inexpressible relief advancing at last a few steps.

Coolness was given me in that dreadful moment, and I knew that all depended on my being prompt and resolute. I stood up swiftly. I often thought if I had happened to wear silk instead of the cachmere I had on that night, its rustle would have betrayed me.

I distinctly saw the tall stooping figure of my uncle, and the outline of his venerable tresses, as he stood between me and the dull light of the window, like a shape cut in card.

He was saying 'just to *there*,' and pointing with his long arm at that contracting patch of moonlight which lay squared upon the floor. The door was about a quarter open, and just as Dudley began to drag Madame's heavy box, with my jewel-case in it, across the floor from her room, inhaling a great breath—with a mental prayer for help—I glided on tiptoe from the room and found myself on the gallery floor.

I turned to my right, simply by chance, and followed a long gallery in the dark, not running—I was too fearful of making the least noise—but walking with the tiptoe-swiftness of terror. At the termination of this was a cross-gallery, one end of which—that to my left—terminated in a great window, through which the dusky night-view was visible. With the instinct of terror I chose the darker, and turned again to my right; hurrying through this long and nearly dark passage, I was terrified by a light, about thirty feet before me, emerging from the ceiling. In spotted patches this light fell through the door and sides of a stable lantern, and showed me a ladder, down which, from an open skylight I suppose for the cool night-air floated in my face, came Dickon Hawkes notwithstanding his maimed condition, with so much celerity as to leave me hardly a moment for consideration.

He sat on the last round of the ladder, and tightened the strap of his wooden leg.

At my left was a door-case open, but no door. I entered; it was a short passage about six feet long, leading perhaps to a backstair, but the door at the end was locked.

I was forced to stand in this recess, then, which afforded no shelter, while Pegtop stumped by with his lantern in his hand. I fancy he had some idea of listening to his master unperceived, for he stopped close to my hiding-place, blew out the candle, and pinched the long snuff with his horny finger and thumb.

Having listened for a few seconds, he stumped stealthily along the gallery which I had just traversed, and turned the corner in the direction of the chamber where the crime had just been committed, and the discovery was impending. I could see him against the broad window which in the daytime lighted this long passage, and the moment he had passed the corner I resumed my flight.

I descended a stair corresponding with that backstair, as I am told, up which Madame had led me only the night before. I tried the outer door. To my wild surprise it was open. In a moment I was upon the step, in the free air, and as instantaneously was seized by the arm in the gripe of a man.

It was Tom Brice, who had already betrayed me, and who was now, in surtout and hat, waiting to drive the carriage with the guilty father and son from the scene of their abhorred outrage.

CHAPTER LXV

IN THE OAK PARLOUR

So it was vain: I was trapped, and all was over.

I stood before him on the step, the white moon shining on my face. I was trembling so that I wonder I could stand, my helpless hands raised towards him, and I looked up in his face. A long shuddering moan—'Oh—oh—oh!' was all I uttered.

The man, still holding my arm, looked, I thought frightened, into my white dumb face.

Suddenly he said, in a wild, fierce whisper—

'Never say another word' (I had not uttered one). 'They shan't hurt ye, Miss; git ye in; I don't care a damn!'

It was an uncouth speech. To me it was the voice of an angel. With a burst of gratitude that sounded in my own ears like a laugh, I thanked God for those blessed words.

In a moment more he had placed me in the carriage, and almost instantly we were in motion—very cautiously while crossing the court, until he had got the wheels upon the grass, and then at a rapid pace, improving his speed as the distance increased. He drove along the side of the back-approach to the house, keeping on the grass; so that our progress, though swaying like that of a ship in a swell, was very nearly as noiseless.

The gate had been left unlocked—he swung it open, and remounted the box. And we were now beyond the spell of Bartram-Haugh, thundering—Heaven be praised!—along the Queen's highway, right in the route to Elverston. It was literally a gallop. Through the chariot windows I saw Tom stand as he drove, and every now and then throw an awful glance over his shoulder. Were we pursued? Never was agony of prayer like mine, as with clasped hands and wild stare I gazed through the windows on the road, whose trees and hedges and gabled cottages were chasing one another backward at so giddy a speed.

We were now ascending that identical steep, with the giant ash-trees at the right and the stile between, which my vision of Meg Hawkes had presented all that night, when my excited eye detected a running figure within the hedge. I saw the head of some one crossing the stile in pursuit, and I heard Brice's name shrieked.

'Drive on—on—on!' I screamed.

But Brice pulled up. I was on my knees on the floor of the carriage, with clasped hands, expecting capture, when the door opened, and Meg Hawkes, pale as death, her cloak drawn over her black tresses, looked in.

'Oh!—ho!—ho!—thank God!' she screamed. 'Shake hands, lass. Tom, yer a good un! He's a good lad, Tom.'

'Come in, Meg—you must sit by me,' I said, recovering all at once.

Meg made no demur. 'Take my hand,' I said offering mine to her disengaged one.

'I can't, Miss—my arm's broke.'

And so it was, poor thing! She had been espied and overtaken in her errand of mercy for me, and her ruffian father had felled her with his cudgel, and then locked her into the cottage, whence, however, she had contrived to escape, and was now flying to Elverston, having tried in vain to get a hearing in Feltram, whose people had been for hours in bed.

The door being shut upon Meg, the steaming horses were instantly at a gallop again.

Tom was still watching as before, with many an anxious glance to rearward, for pursuit. Again he pulled up, and came to the window.

'Oh, what is it?' cried I.

''Bout that letter, Miss; I couldn't help. 'Twas Dickon, he found it in my pocket. That's a'.'

'Oh yes!—no matter—thank you—thank Heaven! Are we near Elverston?'

''Twill be a mile, Miss: and please'm to mind I had no finger in't.'

'Thanks—thank you—you're very good—I shall *always* thank you, Tom, as long as I live!'

At length we entered Elverston. I think I was half wild. I don't know how I got into the hall. I was in the oak-parlour, I believe, when I saw cousin Monica. I was standing, my arms extended. I could not speak; but I ran with a loud long scream into her arms. I forget a great deal after that.

CONCLUSION

Oh, my beloved cousin Monica! Thank Heaven, you are living still, and younger, I think, than I in all things but in years.

And Milly, my dear companion, she is now the happy wife of that good little clergyman, Sprigge Biddlepen. It has been in my power to be of use to them, and he shall have the next presentation to Dawling.

Meg Hawkes, proud and wayward, and the most affectionate creature on earth, was married to Tom Brice a few months after these events; and, as both wished to emigrate, I furnished them with the capital, and I am told they are likely to be rich. I hear from my kind Meg often, and she seems very happy.

CONCLUSION

My dear old friends, Mary Quince and Mrs. Rusk, are, alas! growing old, but living with me, and very happy. And after long solicitation, I persuaded Doctor Bryerly, the best and truest of ministers, with my dearest friend's concurrence, to undertake the management of the Derbyshire estates. In this I have been most fortunate. He is the very person for such a charge—so punctual, so laborious, so kind, and so shrewd.

In compliance with medical advice, cousin Monica hurried me away to the Continent, where she would never permit me to allude to the terrific scenes which remain branded so awfully on my brain. It needed no constraint. It is a sort of agony to me even now to think of them.

The plan was craftily devised. Neither old Wyat nor Giles, the butler, had a suspicion that I had returned to Bartram. Had I been put to death, the secret of my fate would have been deposited in the keeping of four persons only—the two Ruthyns, Hawkes, and ultimately Madame. My dear cousin Monica had been artfully led to believe in my departure for France, and prepared for my silence. Suspicion might not have been excited for a year after my death, and then would never, in all probability, have pointed to Bartram as the scene of the crime. The weeds would have grown over me, and I should have lain in that deep grave where the corpse of Madame de la Rougierre was unearthed in the darksome quadrangle of Bartram-Haugh.

It was more than two years after that I heard what had befallen at Bartram after my flight. Old Wyat, who went early to Uncle Silas's room, to her surprise—for he had told her that he was that night to accompany his son, who had to meet the mailtrain to Derby at five o'clock in the morning—saw her old master lying on the sofa, much in his usual position.

'There was nout much strange about him,' old Wyat said, 'but that his scent-bottle was spilt on its side over on the table, and he dead.'

She thought he was not quite cold when she found him, and she sent the old butler for Doctor Jolks, who said he died of too much 'loddlum.'

Of my wretched uncle's religion what am I to say? Was it utter hypocrisy, or had it at any time a vein of sincerity in it? I cannot say. I don't believe that he had any heart left for religion, which is the highest form of affection, to take hold of. Perhaps he was a sceptic with misgivings about the future, but past the time for finding anything reliable in it. The devil approached the citadel of his heart by stealth, with many zigzags and parallels. The idea of marrying me to his son by fair means, then by foul, and, when that wicked chance was gone, then the design of seizing all by murder, supervened. I dare say that Uncle Silas thought for a while that he was a righteous man. He wished to have heaven and to escape hell, if there were such places. But there were other things whose existence was not speculative, of which some he coveted, and some he dreaded more, and temptation came. 'Now if any man build upon this foundation, gold, silver, precious stones, wood, hay, stubble, every man's work shall be made manifest; for the day shall declare it, because it shall be revealed by fire; and the fire shall try every man's work of what sort it is.' There comes with old age a time when the heart is no longer fusible or malleable, and must retain the form in which it has cooled down. 'He that is unjust, let him be unjust still; he which is filthy, let him be filthy still.'

Dudley had disappeared; but in one of her letters, Meg, writing from her Australian farm, says: 'There's a fella in toon as calls hisself Colbroke, wi' a good hoose o' wood, 15 foot length, and as by 'bout as silling o' the pearler o' Bartram—only lots o' rats, they do say, my lady—a bying and sellin' of goold back and forred wi' the diggin foke and the marchants. His chick and mouth be wry wi' scar o' burns or vitterel, an' no wiskers, bless you; but my Tom ee toll him he knowed him for Master Doodley. I ant seed him; but he sade ad shute Tom soon is look at 'im, an' denide it, wi' mouthful o' curses and oaf. Tom baint right shure; if I seed un wons i'd no for sartin; but 'appen,'twil best be let be.' This was all.

Old Hawkes stood his ground, relying on the profound cunning with which their actual proceedings had been concealed, even from the suspicions of the two inmates of the house, and on the mystery that habitually shrouded Bartram-Haugh and all its belongings from the eyes of the outer world.

Strangely enough, he fancied that I had made my escape long before the room was entered; and, even if he were arrested, there was no evidence, he was certain, to connect *him* with the murder, all knowledge of which he would stoutly deny.

There was an inquest on the body of my uncle, and Dr. Jolks was the chief witness. They found that his death was caused by 'an excessive dose of laudanum, accidentally administered by himself.'

It was not until nearly a year after the dreadful occurrences at Bartram that Dickon Hawkes was arrested on a very awful charge, and placed in gaol. It was an old crime, committed in Lancashire, that had found him out. After his conviction, as a last chance, he tried a disclosure of all the circumstances of the unsuspected death of the Frenchwoman. Her body was discovered buried where he indicated, in the inner court of Bartram-Haugh, and, after due legal enquiry, was interred in the churchyard of Feltram.

Thus I escaped the horrors of the witness-box, or the far worse torture of a dreadful secret.

Doctor Bryerly, shortly after Lady Knollys had described to him the manner in which Dudley entered my room, visited the house of Bartram-Haugh, and minutely examined the windows of the room in which Mr. Charke had slept on the night of his murder. One of these he found provided with powerful steel hinges, very craftily sunk and concealed in the timber of the window-frame, which was secured by an iron pin outside, and swung open on its removal. This was the room in which they had placed me, and this the contrivance by means of which the room had been entered. The problem of Mr. Charke's murder was solved.

I have penned it. I sit for a moment breathless. My hands are cold and damp. I rise with a great sigh, and look out on the sweet green landscape and pastoral hills, and see the flowers and birds and the waving boughs of glorious trees—all images of liberty and safety; and as the tremendous nightmare of my youth melts into air, I lift my eyes in boundless gratitude to the God of all comfort, whose mighty hand and outstretched arm delivered me. When I lower my eyes and unclasp my hands, my cheeks are wet with tears. A tiny voice is calling me 'Mamma!' and a beloved smiling face, with his dear father's silken brown tresses, peeps in.

'Yes, darling, our walk. Come away!'

I am Lady Ilbury, happy in the affection of a beloved and noblehearted husband. The shy useless girl you have known is now a mother—trying to be a good one; and this, the last pledge, has lived.

I am not going to tell of sorrows—how brief has been my pride of early maternity, or how beloved were those whom the Lord gave and the Lord has taken away. But sometimes as, smiling on my little boy, the tears gather in my eyes, and he wonders, I can see, why they come, I am thinking—and trembling while I smile—to think, how strong is love, how frail is life; and rejoicing while I tremble that, in the deathless love of those who mourn, the Lord of Life, who never gave a pang in vain, conveys the sweet and ennobling promise of a compensation by eternal reunion. So, through my sorrows, I have heard a voice from heaven say, 'Write, from hencefore blessed are the dead that die in the Lord!'

This world is a parable—the habitation of symbols—the phantoms of spiritual things immortal shown in material shape. May the blessed second-sight be mine—to recognise under these beautiful forms of earth the ANGELS who wear them; for I am sure we may walk with them if we will, and hear them speak!

Wilkie Collins Collection (complete and unabridged):The Woman in White, The Moonstone, No Name, Armadale
Wilkie Collins
Benediction Classics, 2012
1136 pages
ISBN: 978-1-78139-328-4

Available from www.amazon.com, www.amazon.co.uk

Wilkie Collins (1824-1889) is best known as the innovator of the detective novel. He was a prolific writer, with 30 novels, more than 60 short stories, 14 plays, and more than 100 non-fiction pieces to his name. He was a close friend of Charles Dickens and one of the best known and loved Victorian Fiction writers. After his death, his popularity diminished as Dickens's grew. Now, Collins is once again becoming popular with most of his books in print and film, television and radio adaptations being made. There is much still to be discovered about this great author and this volume contains his four most popular novels.

Henry James - Notable Works, including (complete and unabridged): The American, The Turn of the Screw, The Portrait of a Lady, The Wings of the Dove, Daisy Miller and The Ambassadors
Henry James
Benediction Classics, 2013
1128 pages
ISBN: 978-1-78139-371-0

Available from www.amazon.com, www.amazon.co.uk

Henry James (1843 - 1916) was born in American but eventually settled in England. He is considered to be a key figure of 19th-century literary realism. His writing explores the perceptions of a character, and his works have been compared with impressionist paintings. His novels brought new life and interest into narrative fiction.

This omnibus edition includes his notable works:

The American,
The Turn of the Screw,
The Portrait of a Lady,
The Wings of the Dove,
Daisy Miller,
The Ambassadors

Flaxman Low, Occult Psychologist - Collected Stories
E. and H. Heron
Benediction Classics, 2012
96 pages
ISBN: 978-1-78139-219-5

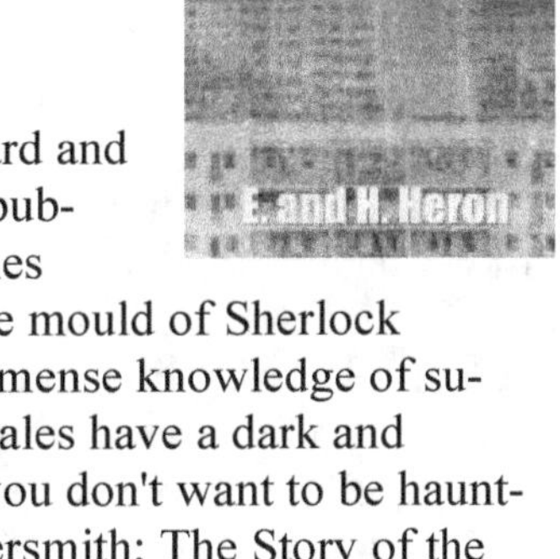

Available from www.amazon.com, www.amazon.co.uk

E. and H. Heron were the pen names of Hesketh Pritchard and his mother Kate. Their Flaxman Low stories were first published in 1899, and have been reprinted a number of times since. Flaxman Low himself is a psychic detective in the mould of Sherlock Holmes. He investigates psychic mysteries using his immense knowledge of supernatural phenomena and powers of observation. The tales have a dark and macabre mood. Do not read these stories before bed if you don't want to be haunted during the night. The Story of the Spaniards, Hammersmith; The Story of the Moor Road; The Story of Baelbrow; The Story of Yand Manor House; The Story of Sevens Hall; The Story of Saddler's Croft; The Story of Konnor Old House.

The Complete Raffles (complete and unabridged) includes: The Amateur Cracksman, The Black Mask (aka Raffles: Further Adventures of the Amateur Cracksman), A Thief in the Night and Mr. Justice Raffles (novel)
E. W. Hornung
Benediction Classics, 2013
480 pages
ISBN: 978-1-78139-360-4

Available from www.amazon.com, www.amazon.co.uk

Arthur J. Raffles is a character by E. W. Hornung. He is a gentleman thief, living in a salubrious part of London, playing Cricket and supporting himself through his ingenious burglaries. He has a sidekick called Harry "Bunny" Manders who is brave and loyal, frequently saving the day. Raffles is a master of disguise imitating accents flawlessly. This book contain all the Raffles stories, enjoy Hornung's unique crime stories, where, in stealing as in sport, played by a devilishly handsome and charming master. The Amateur Cracksman (the early period, in which Raffles really is an amateur thief) The Black Mask (after Raffles's and Bunny's exposure) (U.S. title: Raffles: Further Adventures of the Amateur Cracksman), A Thief in the Night, Mr. Justice Raffles (novel).

Also from Benediction Books ...

Wandering Between Two Worlds: Essays on Faith and Art
Anita Mathias
Benediction Books, 2007
152 pages
ISBN: 0955373700

Available from www.amazon.com, www.amazon.co.uk

In these wide-ranging lyrical essays, Anita Mathias writes, in lush, lovely prose, of her naughty Catholic childhood in Jamshedpur, India; her large, eccentric family in Mangalore, a sea-coast town converted by the Portuguese in the sixteenth century; her rebellion and atheism as a teenager in her Himalayan boarding school, run by German missionary nuns, St. Mary's Convent, Nainital; and her abrupt religious conversion after which she entered Mother Teresa's convent in Calcutta as a novice. Later rich, elegant essays explore the dualities of her life as a writer, mother, and Christian in the United States-- Domesticity and Art, Writing and Prayer, and the experience of being "an alien and stranger" as an immigrant in America, sensing the need for roots.

About the Author

Anita Mathias is the author of *Wandering Between Two Worlds: Essays on Faith and Art*. She has a B.A. and M.A. in English from Somerville College, Oxford University, and an M.A. in Creative Writing from the Ohio State University, USA. Anita won a National Endowment of the Arts fellowship in Creative Non-fiction in 1997. She lives in Oxford, England with her husband, Roy, and her daughters, Zoe and Irene.

Anita's website:
http://www.anitamathias.com, and
Anita's blog Dreaming Beneath the Spires:
http://dreamingbeneaththespires.blogspot.com

The Church That Had Too Much
Anita Mathias
Benediction Books, 2010
52 pages
ISBN: 9781849026567

Available from www.amazon.com, www.amazon.co.uk

The Church That Had Too Much was very well-intentioned. She wanted to love God, she wanted to love people, but she was both hampered by her muchness and the abundance of her possessions, and beset by ambition, power struggles and snobbery. Read about the surprising way The Church That Had Too Much began to resolve her problems in this deceptively simple and enchanting fable.

About the Author

Anita Mathias is the author of *Wandering Between Two Worlds: Essays on Faith and Art*. She has a B.A. and M.A. in English from Somerville College, Oxford University, and an M.A. in Creative Writing from the Ohio State University, USA. Anita won a National Endowment of the Arts fellowship in Creative Non-fiction in 1997. She lives in Oxford, England with her husband, Roy, and her daughters, Zoe and Irene.

Anita's website:
http://www.anitamathias.com, and
Anita's blog Dreaming Beneath the Spires:
http://dreamingbeneaththespires.blogspot.com

www.ingramcontent.com/pod-product-compliance
Lightning Source LLC
Chambersburg PA
CBHW080811020826
48982CB00017B/899
9781781394946